THE BRADY FAMILY

A COMPLETE ROM-COM SERIES

LAINEY DAVIS

CONTENT NOTE

I hope it's not too much of a spoiler to tell you this book features pregnancy.

℔

At the time I wrote this book, Americans like these characters had a choice whether to continue their pregnancy. Effective June 24, 2022, Americans no longer have that choice. If I were writing this book today, the plot and emotions expressed would be different. The stakes would be different. These characters would have had a different journey, and I think this trope carries new weight. Because our right to bodily autonomy has been revoked, I know reading this story might be difficult for some. Please know that I am fighting for reproductive justice.

FOUNDATION
A GROUCHY GEEK ROMANCE

CHAPTER ONE
NICOLE

MY ASSISTANT, MARK, STANDS OUTSIDE MY OFFICE DOOR, TIMIDLY FIDGETING WITH a crisp piece of paper. "I'm supposed to give you a message from the boss."

"I thought *I* was the boss, Mark." I don't look up from my spreadsheet. Of course I know he's referring to the company owner, Tim Stag, but I suspect Tim and his wife, Alice, are going to ask me to babysit again while they go out with my best friend and her husband. Who happens to be Tim's brother.

I can hear Mark breathing rapidly, and I glance up. He's holding a cream colored hand-written note. The fancy letterhead means Alice helped write it, and that usually signifies a big ask. If Tim wanted a profit and loss report, he'd just send a text.

Or shout from his office.

Mark rubs his fingers along the paper and shifts his weight, trying to melt into the door frame. I sigh. "I'm not going to watch his baby again if that's what he's asking. I told you to tell him no to that shit."

"It's something different this time," Mark says, and walks into my office. He presents the paper to me.

"Aw hell no. Definitely not. Tell him no."

Mark flushes. "Donna said I was to tell you this is not negotiable."

Donna is Tim's executive assistant and is generally the final say in all matters of actual importance.

"Hm." I read it again.

Nicole—you will join the Stag Law marathon relay team, to compete in the Pittsburgh Marathon on Sunday, May 2. We will produce a faster collective time than Beltane Engineering. Alice will be adjusting meals accordingly. Participation is not optional.
—TS

ℬ

"WELL, SHIT," I mutter. "Where do I even start with this?" I say that last bit louder, hoping for an answer, but Mark has already backed out of the office.

Tim is an avid runner and, thanks to his perky wife yanking him out of a funk, he's an avid joiner. If there's a golf outing or boat rowing or softball opportunity to schmooze with other businesses here in Pittsburgh, Tim is on it.

He just usually knows better than to include me in this nonsense.

Tim never tires of bitching to his family that Beltane has an unfair advantage in the corporate relay challenge. All the big firms bet money on the outcome, which they donate to charities. So of course the charities get in on it until the pressure is pretty high for corporate fitness bragging rights.

It drives Tim bananas that his staff at a sports law firm is not fitter and faster than a squad of gangly math nerds. While the Stag Law senior staffers are out perfecting their golf game to woo clients, the engi-nerds all seem to be distance runners.

I give zero shits about any of this, but my boss repeatedly reminds me that our law firm represents a lot of athletes. It's good for our image to appear competitively athletic. Then he reminds me that, as his director of strategy, I'm the one who said that last bit about our image.

Both of Tim's brothers are huge runners, too, so Tim keeps trying to sneak them on the payroll so they count for our corporate teams. I point out that there's no way to cook the books to include a retired pro hockey player or a world renowned glass artist on a law firm's roster.

I look down at my legs. Thick and solid, they will absolutely catch my cell phone if I drop it while I'm sitting on the toilet. But running?

Do I have a treadmill desk in my office? Sure. But that's mostly so I can angry-pace while I'm on the phone. I am not what you might call a runner. I am also not what you might call a person who exercises.

I think back to all the times my mother insisted I go to the gym or go running to "slim down," and how violently I had refused to do anything of the kind. There's a war inside me, where one side is raging against my mother's body shaming, and the other side is recoiling from anyone—including my sub-conscience—telling me I can't do something.

I bite my lip. I consider the options. I remind myself that Tim is not my mother, and that his request here is fully related to his own dumb pride and has nothing to do with him wanting me to fit into any sort of mold of what anyone says a woman should look like.

I sigh and weigh my options, deciding I need to call my best friend to figure out why in the hell Tim thought I'd do this.

I look at the time and figure it's late enough in the morning that I can call my best friend without pulling her out of some sort of baby nap. Emma is married to Tim's brother Thatcher, and the whole damn herd of Stags is about as fertile as a pack of rabbits. She and Thatcher just had their second bunny in as many years.

Since my family are a bunch of assholes and I'm not giving up any of my precious time with Emma, I've become an honorary Stag family member. Tim is still my boss, though. We do work to keep each other at a bit of a distance—him because he has control issues and me because he reminds me of my hyper-controlling parents.

It's different with Emma, though. I pretend to be a grouch about her babies, but I know how many health struggles she overcame to get them here. Hell, I helped her find the right doctors for her epilepsy when we lived together in college.

Emma's phone rings and rings. I'm about to hang up in frustration when she picks up on the tenth ring. "Nik," she whisper yells. "I got them both to sleep! At the same time!"

"If I pretend to be excited for you, can we skip ahead to my drama?" I *am* excited for Emma. I know how important sleep is for her, and how rarely her kids succumb to this state. She knows I'm just fucking with her. I have an image to maintain, after all.

"Spill," she says, louder now, and I can hear her walking down the hall of her house. I fill her in on Tim's memo, and she laughs loudly. "He was just over here complaining about the marathon again yesterday. You know how he gets about not-winning."

"I do, but how did he determine that *I* am the great, curvaceous hope for Stag Law? I mean, isn't his wife the next logical step?"

Each of the corporate teams is supposed to include at least one person who identifies as female. We don't exactly have a ton of women working here at Stag Law, something I've been working on ever since I arrived a year ago. Tim's wife is the corporate chef here and I know she at least exercises occasionally. I've seen her in actual running clothes in the past.

"Well," Emma says with her mouth full of something. She must be trying to cram in a meal before her fawns wake up. "If I tell you, you can't tell them you know."

"Fuck a duck, is she pregnant *again?* What's that—four for them? Five?"

Emma laughs. "Three, Nicole. Tim and Alice will have 3 kids. She's angling for 4 and he wants to stop at 3, if you care about the family debates." I do not care about this debate. Like I said—I'm keeping *some* distance.

"Is there anyone else at work who can do this," I mutter, as if Emma would know the answer. I mentally scroll through the other female employees, and can see why Tim sent me this invite. The rest are all knocking on retirement's door or pregnant. I sigh.

"Will you come with me to buy some workout clothes? That seems like the sort of thing I have to try on in person."

"Ooh, a trip to the mall is a great idea. I need bath fizzies for once I'm allowed to submerge again. Pick me up at 6?"

I make plans to go shopping with Emma, promising that I'll be nice to the baby when I pick them up. I'm not actually a monster—I am glad my friend found her perfect life partner and have admitted that the two of them owe it to humanity to reproduce their sexy genes. I just don't know anything about kids and they make me nervous, like I might break them or fuck them up as much as my parents did me.

I look up the details of the race online. I'll have to run five miles. In a row. I don't know if I can do that. That's more than three times the distance from my house to my office, and I don't even walk that far each day. *Can people really run that far without stopping?*

"Mark!" I shout for him to come back. He pops his head around the doorframe again. "Can you get me a coach or something? What's it even called when someone shows you how to run?"

Mark's face breaks into a relieved grin. "That's the good news," he gleams. "Mr. Stag also forwarded me a schedule for training events. He has a whole series of memos about team building and workplace morale and cardiovascu—"

"Yeah, yeah. I get it. Shit, Mark. Do you know how my ass is going to look at a team jog? Don't answer that." He backs out of the office again.

Mark emails me the schedule and training information for the relay team. Is Tim serious with this bullshit? The training program starts this month. In January. It's not like we have an empire to run or anything—we all have plenty of time for speed work and zone dieting, whatever the hell that is. The good news about all of this is that the city finally finished work on that recreation path along the river.

My townhouse in Lawrenceville is at least walking distance from the running path so I don't have to run along the sidewalk while all the hipsters stand in line for ramen and barbecue.

Still, though. Running in the snow translates to Tim Stag giving me another raise. I pull up the company calendar app and pencil myself in for a meeting with the CEO.

CHAPTER TWO
ZACK

 crowds. My brother Liam leans a sneakered foot up on the tailgate of my truck, stretching his hamstring in the parking lot while the sky figures out if it's going to snow or just look foreboding all day. "Tell me again why we're doing this?"

Liam just growls, and I join him in the stretch.

Our father jogs up in an electric blue track suit he probably bought in Cuba when it wasn't legal for Americans to travel there. "Hope you drank your protein shakes, boys," he says, slapping Liam on the ass. "Corporate team training starts right here, right now. Gotta maintain that Beltane legacy."

I roll my eyes, not bothering to point out that I have no intention of competing for the company relay team in this year's marathon. We have this discussion every year, and every year I am bullied into running with my extended family. Meanwhile, I've never even gotten to run the full marathon in my hometown. The relay takes place at the same time, with the long distance runners blending in with relayers who switch out every five miles or so.

I always feel like an asshole on the fourth or fifth section, starting on fresh legs while the runners around me have been pounding the pavement for 20 miles.

I feel like I want to explain to all of them that I'm actually a full marathoner. I just have to drive to other cities and run their marathons to feel their masochistic, amazing pain.

Dad catches my scowl, and he says, "To sweeten the pot, I'll cover the New York marathon registration fee, since a relay leg isn't nearly challenging enough for my Brady boys."

My cousin Orla coughs and glares at my dad. "Right. Brady *FAMILY*," he says, clapping her on the shoulder. "Well it hardly counts as a challenge for you, dear. It's not like I can kick you off the relay team for dragging ass."

"Just what I always wanted," she says, rolling her eyes. "To be the token female in a herd of men performing feats of strength." My brothers and cousin start in on each other, slinging foul comebacks, when the event organizer jumps up on a boulder with a megaphone.

"Good morning, titans of industry!" he shouts, grinning. I groan. "Who's excited to be here for our kickoff run?" I tune out his chipper voice and look around, seeing the regular crew. There's the corporate bankers, the out of shape CPA firm, the doctors, and the academics. And then I do a double take, fixated on a mop of chestnut hair swirling in the gray light.

I cannot stop staring at the woman shivering off to the side with a group of scrawny lawyers from Stag Law. I see their boss stretching his quads, wearing headphones, ready to gallop down the path as soon as the whistle blows. I feel one of my brothers punch my shoulder. "Ouch!" I glare at him. "What was that for?"

"Were you even listening? Seasoned runners are supposed to pair up with someone new, to help them pace and work their breath and all that shit."

"What's your point? I'm not doing that." It's one thing to be here. They can't make me be coach to an amateur.

The guy with the megaphone jumps down from the boulder and picks up two orange buckets from the ground. Climbing back onto his perch, he shouts, "Your group leaders have taken the liberty of identifying team members who are beginners, and those with a bit more experience and wisdom to share today." He starts reaching into the buckets and calling out names, pairing people at random. "This is what it's all about!" he says.

I feel my blood pounding in my ears. I watch as people awkwardly team up and start off jogging or stretching. A small voice inside wants me to get stuck with the woman over there, with all the hair. That voice is coming straight from my dick, who keeps reminding me how nice it would be to run right behind her, staring at that round ass moving down the path.

"Shut up," I mutter to my junk, as if it had actually said those things out loud.

Some of the pairs are doing secret handshake moves and laughing. This is like a nightmare for me. But then I hear the organizer say, "Zack Brady, you're going to be helping to coach your new best friend...Nicole Kennedy!"

ℬ

NICOLE KENNEDY DOES INDEED TURN out to be the woman with out of control hair and ice green eyes. She's short and curvy and looks like she's never run a day in her life. My family members all flip me the bird as they tear off down the trail—apparently there were way more experts than beginners needing a coach.

Dad gives me a grin, and then Nicole and I are in a standoff, waiting to see who will approach whom first. She stands with her legs spread wide, arms crossed, eyes seeming to say *I do not make the first move in these situations.*

I roll my eyes and approach her. "Isaac Brady," I say. "Zack." I offer her my hand, and she raises an eyebrow, keeping both hands on her rounded hips. God, I love when women wear tight leggings to go running. Jesus, the ass on this woman. *What the fuck am I doing here?* "So...we're doing this I guess," I say. "What's your typical pace?"

She cocks a brow at me. "If I knew what typical pace meant, I wouldn't be in the beginner group, would I?" So that's how this is going to go, I guess.

"Ok," I say, gesturing down the trail. "Today's run is 2 miles, and the plan is to do a steady pace. So why don't you start running at a pace where you feel comfortable talking."

"Talking? How will I know if it's a comfortable talking pace?"

This is going to be harder than I thought. "You're going to have to talk to me to test it out." This gets, if not exactly a smile, at least an amused expression. I get a definite no-nonsense, don't-fuck-with-me vibe from Ms. Nicole Kennedy. I like it. I don't want to be fucked with, either.

We start running, faster than I thought we'd go. Everything she's wearing looks brand new, like she went out shopping for this experience. Certain she's going to burn out, I test the waters and talk to her. "Tell me how you wound up here today."

She falls into step beside me and snaps that her boss is making her be here. "What are the consequences if you refuse?"

She keeps her eyes straight ahead when she tells me, "He'd be a miserable asshole and a bear to work with. Which I'm now re-evaluating, since my alternative is apparently training with you."

She's sparring with me, and I am shocked to discover I like it. A lot. I don't spend a lot of time with women, apart from my cousin. There aren't a ton of women in geotechnical engineering, and I spend all my free time trail running.

The women I do encounter aren't like this one. She...sizzles.

I'm not sure what comes over me, but I nudge her with my elbow. I'm never playful with women. I'm not even interested in being playful with *this* woman. Am I? But then she turns and smiles, a real smile. I feel my heart change course, which makes me feel ridiculous. Is it possible to have a stroke in response to a beautiful woman smiling? I speed up a bit to course correct, just to see if she can keep up. "Still able to talk?"

"Fuck. This. Shit," she huffs, her breath coming out in white puffs of condensation. "Happy?"

I grin. I am happy. She might be complaining about a January run—who wouldn't? But she's not quitting. She's not slowing. She's just grouchy about it.

I hear her breath coming a little faster, but we're a mile in at this point. "We're almost at the turn around," I say, and sure enough, we start to see runners headed back from their training loop. "Oh shit," I mutter, noticing my brothers.

"Hey now!" Cal says, stopping on the path and causing Liam to crash into him.

Orla runs on ahead like she doesn't know any of us, my dad hot on her tail. "Don't fall behind, Cal. You know better than this," Dad says.

"Who's your new training buddy?" Cal pivots on the path and starts running next to Nicole, who is starting to sweat. I try not to stare at the sheen on her upper lip, despite the frigid air outside. She is probably wearing too many layers. Shit, now I'm thinking about peeling her out of her layers. I can't stop picturing her round ass and thick thighs melting out of those leggings. I start wondering how heavy her breasts would feel in my hands when I zipped her out of her fleece.

"Nicole Kennedy," she says, offering a hand to Cal. It's good to hear she can still talk. "Reluctant relay runner in training."

"Well we've got that in common," Cal says, falling into step beside her. I can see him turning up the charm and while the logical response would be for me to embrace this, take the attention from myself, I can feel rage simmering in my stomach at the thought of Cal putting the moves on Nicole.

"You don't seem too reluctant, considering you're running extra along with us," Nicole says. Interesting how her voice is softer with him. Friendly. I don't like that, either.

"My brothers would rather be training for the full marathon, but our father makes us do the relay corporate challenge." I shove him when he tries to swerve in closer to Nicole.

"Don't act like you wouldn't rather do the full, too, man." He shoves me back and I stumble. I reach a hand for Nicole to steady myself before I face plant on the trail, and I gasp at the electric current I feel when my skin connects with her waist.

I feel a seismic tremor roll through my body as she turns around to look at me. I'm in serious trouble.

CHAPTER THREE
NICOLE

I'M DYING. I FEEL LIKE MY LUNGS ARE BURNING. I'LL BE DAMNED IF I LET THE BRADY brothers notice, though. Of course my broody, sexy-as-sin new running partner would have a huge family. Of course they're all lithe and interested in running. They probably go jogging with my boss Tim and his brothers.

I noticed Isaac speed up a half mile ago and I'm working my ovaries off trying to keep the new pace and pretend like I'm actually able to talk. Really, I am desperate to wheeze, to gasp in gulps of air. But Isaac said I should be comfortable enough to talk at this pace, and I'll be damned if I let myself seem like a weak link. Who decided people should converse while they're running? This feels like torture. Of course these two Brady boys are able to chitchat.

My mind drifts and I start thinking about Isaac's thighs in those tapered running pants. I fantasize about poking his long muscles. Just jabbing one of my cold fingers into the side of his leg. God, I bet they're firm as marble. *Halfway done with this run,* I think as we turn around and head back the way we came. This won't be terrible. Will it? *Just focus on the thighs,* I tell myself.

"Whoah," I feel a hand on my hip and I look down to see the sweaty paw of Isaac Brady clutching at my fleece as he stumbles on the gravel.

"Sorry," he mutters quickly, regaining his footing. "My dickhead brother shoved me into you."

"My bad, Nicky." Cal runs ahead of us and turns around, jogging backwards and giving a high five to the passing group leader with the megaphone.

"Do not call me Nicky," I tell Cal, gritting my teeth so I don't wheeze. I can't wait to at least cough so I can draw enough wind to keep going.

"My bad again," Cal says, and then he looks between me and Isaac, and back again. He seems confused for a second and he says, "Well, I'm going to hurry ahead before all the free bagels are gone," and he dashes down the path.

"What was all that about?" I have to focus all my oxygen to make the sentence sound normal. I cannot let him know I'm struggling. I refuse.

"All what?"

I turn my head to stare at Isaac, incredulous. "Your brother just scurried away when I yelled at him about calling me Nicky."

Isaac actually laughs at this, and I feel my insides respond to the low rumble of sound he makes as he runs. "Maybe he doesn't like to be yelled at."

I snort. "He'd better not spend time with me, then. I yell at everyone."

"Noted," Isaac says, and he grins again. I like that I made him grin. It seems like something difficult to do, and I like being good at things. Which is partly why this running situation is making me act like such an asshole. I'm way out of my element here. Hell, I can't even breathe.

We run in silence for a bit after that. The bagels at the parking lot are sounding better and better. Isaac's shoe crunches over some litter on the trail, and I brave a proper wheeze and puff of wind as the sound of him kicking the plastic away masks the noises of me dying. But it doesn't work.

"Is this pace too fast?"

"I'm fine." It takes all my control again to keep my voice even, natural sounding. Maybe the flames I feel inside aren't related to my attraction to him at all. More likely, I'm dying of asphyxiation. Oxygen deprivation. I'll have to ask Emma to look up whether that's a real thing.

"Hey, why don't you unzip your pullover a little, or even lose a layer." His voice sounds a little far off, even though I can see that he's right by my side. Isn't he?

"You're not getting me out of my clothes that easy," I spit out. And then, to my horror, I get dizzy and I think I black out for a second, because the next thing I know I'm tumbling into the hedge along the path.

When I open my eyes, I realize my body is being cradled by something warm and firm. I'm disoriented, but comfortable.

Mmm, maybe it's one of those massage chairs I've been telling Mark to install in my office. This is fantastic. So warm, gently moving.

Fuck. I open my eyes all the way and stare into the concerned face of Isaac Brady. "What happened," I ask, struggling to sit up.

"Hey, easy," he says, setting a hand on my shoulder. "You just passed out."

I wriggle away from his touch before his heat burns through to my bones. My heart is pounding in my ears and my chest is heaving. I guess the jig is up, and I feel myself recoiling at the idea that he's seen me in a weak spot. What the hell is he doing to me? I should know better than to let someone else take up rent-free space in my head. There is no reason I should care about this guy at all. "It's fine," I tell him. "I am just not used to running like this, like I said."

"You were pushing yourself too hard. It's too cold to be doing that—"

I cut him off by wheezing and hacking like my lungs are on fire. Seriously, it feels like knives are slicing through my chest. "It's called kilo cough," Isaac says, resting a hand on my back. "You pushed yourself too hard, *like I said.*" I don't have enough air to yell at him for spitting my words back at me.

"My lungs hurt worse than my legs," I wail in between bouts of painful coughs.

He just nods and helps me to my feet. "You put in what? Two miles of max effort just to prove to me that you didn't need to breathe hard or slow down?" He raises an eyebrow and looks smug.

Who the fuck is this guy? I want to punch him in the dick, but thinking that causes me to look down at said body part and seeing the bulge inside his track pants makes me lick my lips in between coughs.

"Don't flatter yourself," I tell him. "I'm only pushing myself because my boss is expecting our team to beat your fucking firm in the marathon."

This gets a laugh out of him. "Stag Law wants to beat Beltane? That'll be the day." He hooks a hand under my upper arm and guides me down the path. We're close enough to the parking lot now that I can see one of his siblings running along toward us. Is it the same one as before? I can't tell them apart when I'm hacking up a lung. Meanwhile, Isaac starts to list the different endurance events he and his family participate in as a group. All the -thons, apparently.

"You all right there, Ms. Kennedy?" The same brother as before holds out a cup of water and I snatch it from him greedily. As I slurp down the icy liquid he laughs and says, "See? I learn from my mistakes and I come bearing peace offerings. What happened?"

I open my mouth to tell him I'm dying from this ridiculous training exercise, but Isaac growls, "She's fine. We're good here, Cal."

I look at Issac. This is interesting. Isaac clearly doesn't want his brother hanging around us.

However, "Don't speak for me, Isaac. Don't ever speak *for* me." I turn to face Cal again. "I'm great. Never been better. You said there were bagels?"

CHAPTER FOUR
ZACK

I CHECK THE TEXT FROM MY BROTHER LIAM BEFORE MY FINGERS FREEZE AND I CAN'T use my phone anymore. I'm in the right place at the right time. My jagoff brothers are just fucking late. I should have known they'd do this. It's not even light out yet and I feel like an asshole with my headlamp on for our morning run.

I'm about to get back in my truck and head home when I hear them rolling up. My shoulders relax a bit when I see the two men crammed inside Cal's ancient vehicle. We're all here, I guess. I work to stuff down the twinge of jealousy I always feel when I'm reminded how close they are. We have different mothers, but Cal and Liam would never suggest I was any less their brother.

It's all my own head that twists my thoughts.

"Let's go, before my balls snap off." Liam springs from the car and takes off down the trailhead without waiting for the rest of us. He's dreaming if he thinks we won't catch him. This isn't like yesterday—that was equal parts full family activity and work requirement.

We all work for my dad and my uncle—two brothers who started an engineering firm over 30 years ago when nobody else was really doing that.

None of us particularly liked running at first, but just like studying engineering in college, we weren't given a choice about it. In our father's house, we run five miles a day at minimum, and we bleed, sweat, and dream engineering principles. It's just part of our DNA. Not sure where Orla puts her miles in. She never comes running with us, but she clocks decent times in the races we run, whether she likes it or not.

Uncle Kellen doesn't compete. He says his leisurely run into work each morning is enough for him. I wish I had the nerve to buck against the family expectations like that. Maybe someday if I've lived through what Uncle Kellen has, I'll let go of all my fucks, too.

Liam's pace is too slow, even given the steep trail as we descend down into Frick Park. When I shoulder past him and he growls, I grin. At least we can keep it interesting if we're going to push each other.

Soon the three of us are jostling for the lead on the narrow path, laughing and shoving each other as we run through the park. It's hard not to feel like a little kid, running with my brothers in the woods. Damn, I'm glad we did this after all, even if I did have to get up before dawn.

It's not yet 7 by the time we finish, so we end up waiting a few minutes outside for the Frick Cafe to open. Another tradition, we always grab breakfast here after our park runs.

Like some sort of unspoken competition, none of us wants to be the first to complain about the cold, so we alternate grunts. I see the wait staff through the painted windows and raise my eyebrows at one of our favorite servers. She takes pity on us and opens the door a few minutes early, nodding her head toward our typical booth in the back.

"Bring on the protein special, Em. You know the drill," Cal says, sending a wink, earning himself an elbow to the ribs from Liam. "Eventually she'll come home with me for a shower," Cal says, sliding into his seat and spreading across the entire bench.

I kick his thigh to make room and slide next to him. Crossing my arms, I take a minute to appreciate the warmth in the cafe. Liam's voice pulls me out of my daze.

"Did Uncle Kellen decide about the dam project yet?" The server brings out steaming plates of turkey sausage and eggs and protein pancakes, but Liam holds my gaze until I answer him.

"He didn't. Wants to think about it another week." Beltane Engineering is bidding on a major dam restoration project, and the sudden retirement of our geotechnical team leader has left me scrambling to prove myself ready to fill his shoes.

When Kenny Hudson collapsed on the job from a heart attack, my dad responded typically: he visited Kenny at the hospital, insisted he retire and enjoy his dotage, and then called each of his sons to lecture us about our health. Again, not sure if Orla got a lecture. She keeps to herself.

You'd think being the boss's son with an engineering degree from MIT would give me an edge for a promotion, but if you thought that, you never spent much time with Mick and Kellen Brady. Two brothers—the yin to the other's yang—they never seem to agree on anything except that nothing their kids do is ever quite good enough.

My uncle won't say so, but he's pitting me against the new guy from Texas and waiting to see which of us can solve another client's sinkhole problem first before assigning us the lead role on the dam.

"No pressure, right Zack?" Cal talks with his mouth full and nudges Liam, waiting for him to laugh. "Get it? Pressure? Geotechnical? Nobody?"

I roll my eyes. "Yes, I get it."

"Want to run the sinkhole plan by us, see if anything sticks?" Liam always wants to collaborate, even though as a structural engineer he doesn't have much overlap in my work. I start to map out my idea to him, talking about back filling the space under our client's access road, maybe utilizing a plastic bubble technique to displace some of the shifting that's been causing sinkholes at a manufacturing site outside the city. "We'd replace some of the dirt fill with these plastic bubbles. The sphere shape makes them very structurally sound," I tell him, and he nods.

"We use those in concrete flooring sometimes for less weight at the same strength," he says.

By the time we leave breakfast, I'm actually feeling ready to present at our meeting later today. "Hey, thanks, brother." Liam nods. "See you all at the office?" The two of them live in an industrial loft space our dad picked up on a whim. It's like a college dorm at their place, complete with nosy landlord, but what I lack in companionship at my house, I make up for in calling all my own shots. Cal flips me off as they pile back in his SUV and head home, most likely to wrestle for who gets first shower.

I'm the first Brady to arrive at the office, and I take advantage of the quiet to organize my plans. By the time my uncle rolls in with Texas Ted at his side, I'm feeling confident. I even allow myself a slight smile when our office admin announces it's time for all the civil engineers to gather for the weekly planning meeting. As soon as we settle this sinkhole issue, our top priority at Beltane Engineering will be to make headway on winning this dam project.

I can smell the opportunity when I see that someone from the sales team is joining us this morning. Uncle Kellen wouldn't call them in if it weren't time to coordinate our pitch. I'm grateful I got an opportunity to talk through the pitch with Liam this morning. Everything feels fresh. From here on out, I plan to be neck deep in soil calculations and talus slopes.

I grit my teeth when my dad sticks his head into the meeting. "Zack, good. You're here."

"I've been here for an hour, Dad."

He ignores my snide comment. "Kellen, I need to borrow my kid for a minute." My uncle nods and gestures for me to hand him my notes on the sinkholes. I feel my guts collapsing in on themselves like the soil beneath our client's dump trucks. My blood runs cold as I realize my father is pulling me away from my opportunity to advance at this company, in this career he insisted I pursue. White hot rage nearly blinds me as I follow him into the elevator.

"Can you push 6 for me, kiddo? We're going up into my office." I don't say a word, don't tell him to push his own fucking elevator button instead of clutching his Yerba mate with two hands. Slowly, deliberately, I extend a finger and jab as the doors slide shut, along with everything I've planned for the past year.

CHAPTER FIVE
NICOLE

MORNINGS ARE MY FAVORITE TIME OF DAY. I DON'T SPEND MUCH TIME AT MY HOUSE these days, but when I am there, I like to be out on my sun porch with a cup of hot coffee. I chose this house because the gently sloping backyard looks out on the Allegheny River. I'm close enough to walk to work downtown-- not that I ever would do such a thing in heels--and I live close to anything I would want to buy, if I were the sort of person who regularly went shopping in real life.

My sunroom is divine, no matter who's asking. And the fact that I rebuilt it myself makes it even better. Everything I see around me is mine, down to the studs. I remodeled this place one inch at a time over the years since I bought it.

I sink into the papasan chair on my porch, just enjoying my house. I had an early night after hanging out with Emma. Her younger baby got really fussy and I could tell she wanted to be alone with him, so I just went home and got a normal night's sleep for once.

Not before tossing and turning for a long while, thinking about my reluctant running coach and how he had scooped me into his arms when my lungs stubbornly refused to breathe properly on our training run. The experience really showed me how much I'm going to need to work to get ready for this thing.

Fucking Tim. He's probably sitting at home smugly telling Alice how he'll make an athlete out of me yet. Gag.

Rather than take a practice run this morning, I slid into my "workout" leggings and curled up in my sunroom, waiting for dawn to strike the barges slowly floating past on the river.

As the sun comes up, I squint into my back yard and notice a long line of mud that definitely was not there the day before. Staring, I stand and walk to the glass wall of my sun room. The line is too big to have been dug by some asshole's dog in search of a bone. I notice that it extends into my neighbor's yard. A ridge in the grass.

I frown at it. My neighbor, Valerie, is a crotchety old busybody who thinks I stole her hedge. We've been in a fight about it since I bought this place. It was planted on my fucking side of the property line, and it was ugly as fuck, so I had it removed and now I can enjoy my view of the river. She's still not over it, though, and I imagine this new trench is her doing.

She's probably planning some new landscaping nightmare, I decide, and make a mental note to call and fight with her later.

I finish my coffee, and get ready for work. We're launching some major new strategic initiatives this year, partnering with other industry experts to help our athlete clients create charitable foundations. I spend the entire day pulling together comparison plans about competitor firms in other cities, ignoring everyone except Mark, and I only talk to him when he brings Pad Thai for lunch. I'm still pissed off about the coerced marathon gang.

I practically died this weekend training for that nonsense...is what I told Tim in a series of angry text messages. He knows I'm pouting. He probably also knows me well enough to understand that I hate doing things I'm not awesome at. I'd much prefer to be coerced into this next year when I've had time to get good at it first.

ℬ

I GET HOME from work and reach for my mail, where I notice a neon pink note card sticking out among my bills and Bust magazine. When I get inside, I drop my stuff on the little table I selected for just this purpose, and I read the note.

Scratched in hurried handwriting, it reads "we need to discuss your latest work in the backyard." It's from Valerie, which makes me frown, because I assumed that ridge was her doing.

Unless it still is and she wants to fill me in on whatever nonsense she's scheming. I reach for my phone to pull up a copy of our property survey for her perusal, when she starts banging on my front door.

"Nicole, I know you're there. Open up."

"Um, hi, Valerie." I step back a foot and she bursts into my house, stomping her feet on my mat and shivering like she just walked here from Ohio instead of next door. "What's going on?"

Valerie pulls a packet of rolled up paper from her back pocket. "The yard is basically sliding into the river," she says, gesturing toward the sun room. "That ridge of dirt is just unsightly today, but mark my words. In a week we're going to have a crater back there."

I raise an eyebrow at her. I have no idea what she did for a living before she retired, but I doubt it's related to yard slides. "And how do you know this exactly?"

I gesture for the papers Valerie offers and begin reading skeptically. "Rotational landslide," I say. "This looks like a page from a high school textbook."

"Precisely," Valerie says, tapping the pages. When I don't respond, she says, "As you know, I retired after a long career teaching high school science."

I glance at the diagrams. "I actually didn't know that, Valerie. We only ever talk about landscaping." We don't chat about her career path, but I do sometimes hand her a glass of wine to drink while we bicker from our back patios.

As two single, female homeowners, we mostly communicate about the shared wall of our townhouses and the shared yards suffering from our opposite aesthetics.

Her papers all seem to relate more to giant hillsides than urban back-yards. Valerie believes, because she's been walking her cat back there apparently, that the yard has been slowly shifting and basically making its way into the river.

I walk away from Valerie and open a bottle of wine. She follows and, when I raise a brow at her, she sidles up to my counter. I guess she thinks we're going to sit down and talk about this together.

I sigh.

"Look. I've had a really long day at work. My boss is making me run a marathon. I just don't have the energy left for a landslide tonight."

Valerie laughs maniacally, like I'm the one who's being ridiculous here, and explains that this will all unfold over the course of the next few weeks. I maintain the right to stare at her like she's an idiot and I start to tune her out, thinking instead of the new branding plan I want Tim to greenlight at work. Valerie coughs eventually, and I realize I'm supposed to respond.

"Can you say that again?" I ask. "This is all just a lot to digest." *Nice recovery, Nik. You're such an asshole.* Valerie suggests we each tap into our respective networks for advice and regroup in a few days to make a plan to save the yard.

By the time I shoo her out of my house, I have almost forgotten about the entire thing. I have filed the yard ridge away as a nuisance to deal with later. After work settles down.

I definitely push it into the back of my mind as I lie in my tub with a joint, searching the Internet for all the ways I could die training for a marathon relay. Seems like there are actually a lot of ways I could drop over dead, if I'm to trust all these horror stories online.

This is doing nothing to help me calm down. Taking another puff of my doobie, I decide there's only one thing to be done if I'm going to salvage this day.

I need to get off.

I reach for my shelf of tub toys, selecting my most trustworthy vibrator, and close my eyes. But my clit doesn't seem to be working. "What the hell?" I shout into the cavernous bathroom, my words echoing off the tile.

I try another toy, but I can't even get so much as a tingle. I twist over the edge of my tub and grab my phone, pulling up some of my favorite tasteful porn. I crank the vibrator into high gear. Nothing.

Enraged, I decide this inability to orgasm is also related to being strong-armed into marathon participation. I throw the vibrator across the room and stare at my ceiling. Something is definitely off in my life.

IN THE MORNING, I wake up still angry, still convinced this marathon business is the root cause of my stress and my pussy problem. I decide that the only way through is through. And when Nicole Kennedy goes through something, she does it to kick ass and take names.

My to-do list today includes, apart from my work for work, hunting down a proper sports bra. This morning, I tried another little running attempt and my unrestrained knockers almost hit me in the teeth.

"Mark!" I lean over his office and then wince when I see his eyes widen in fear. I take my tone down a notch. "Do you work out?"

He nearly spits out his coffee. "Um, I'm gay and I'm single and I don't have kids. Yes. The answer is yes."

"Do you know where I can get a good sports bra?"

Mark looks at me, squints, turns his head to the side. "Did you hear the part where I said I'm gay? I mean, I can look it up for you on the internet..."

I scoff. "Forget it. Hold my calls. I'm going to find Alice."

Alice Stag is puttering around the office kitchen space. She cooks from scratch and serves breakfast and a sit-down lunch here every day. It's been a great opportunity to get staff members talking to each other. We've seen a lot of really interesting collaborations grow out of these mealtime conversations.

Today, I'm hoping I can ask her about her rack without insulting her. "Hey, Alice," I say, leaning in to get a muffin from the stainless steel counter.

She breaks into a smile. "Nicole! You never join us for breakfast. To what do I owe the pleasure?"

I feel a twinge of guilt at always sending Mark to fetch me a smoothie rather than come in here and say hello to her. She's so perky, and she has hair with the same texture as mine, so she always has good advice about products. I sigh. "I, um, need your advice about bras."

Alice's face lights up. "Oh, I have a place for you! Yes. This is great." She rattles on and on about how her boobs change size and shape so much since she started having babies. "They're, like, a J cup one day and back down to a D the next. I swear! But this woman is a bra whisperer."

Alice tells me about a fancy store north of the city, where all the big chested women go to find supportive bras that are actually pretty.

"I don't need pretty. I need something that will strap down these boulders."

Alice nods. "You'll be in good hands."

I'm skeptical. "There had better not be anything beige," I tell her.

"Trust me! You'll leave there with like ten bras. I mean, I don't actually know what color the sports bras are...but probably not beige."

I text Emma to see if she can go with me after work, and she immediately video chats me back. "Holy shit, Nik. Alice has been bugging me to go there since I got pregnant with Ricky! Yes."

"I had no idea bras were such a big thing."

She makes a face. "Um, yes you did. You're always bitching about your back hurting." She has a point. This all feels like more support for why I shouldn't be a runner. Emma continues feeding me my dose of reality. "You keep avoiding dealing with this because of your mom," she says, hitting me where it hurts. My mother finds everything about my body to be distasteful, and I swear she used to only buy me beige old-lady bras as an incentive to diet and slim down into a more acceptable size for her country club crowd.

"They sell the prettiest pink lace at the department store, Nicole," she'd say with a fake smile. *"Your sister has the loveliest B cups."*

I groan. "So anyway!" Emma's face lights up. "I'm looking and they have wine night tonight. Let's make it a whole thing. Can you give a ride to my friend Maddie, too?"

"Maddie from college?" Emma nods. "Yeah, sure. I haven't seen her in ages."

After work, I open my trunk and grab the carseat I bought to make things easier when I go places with Emma. She can't drive because of her epilepsy, and I'm not going to just stand around while her husband wrestles with car seat straps each time Emma and I want to go out.

Tim personally taught me how to install the thing, and he's as fastidious about safety as he is about, well, everything. I place one knee in the seat and tug on the belt, securing it, before I drive to grab my friend and her baby.

Once Emma and Maddie and baby Ricky pile in, we head to the boob store while I listen to the two of them talk shop about work. Emma eventually looks at me and tilts her head to the side. "You're awfully quiet. It's weird."

I shrug. "Things are weird," I say, nodding. Emma squints and Maddie leans forward, studying me. I hear the baby fart in the back seat. I sigh. "I couldn't come last night. My pussy is broken," I tell them, blurting it out in the open.

"Ok, this is important," Emma says. "Tell us everything."

I talk about the race I'm being coerced into, the feelings it dregs up about my mom, how it necessitates me buying this new bra "and now I'm hauling all your asses to some boob-tique. The timing is just a lot with our new foundation initiative. Oh, and there's a trench forming in my back yard and my neighbor is being super annoying about it."

Maddie whistles. "That's a whole lot. I actually remember your mom visiting one time in college," she says. "She was an ice cold snob about our dorm, remember?"

I nod. "Indeed. Can we not talk about her?"

Maddie moves to talking about her new fling, adjusting her bust and saying she hopes to find something lacy to wear for him. Emma actually pulls out her boob to show me how the clasp of a nursing bra works and I almost have to pull over.

"Why does your nipple look like that?" I hiss.

She shrugs. "It's been in someone's mouth nonstop for a few months. He stretched it out." Emma laughs and I shake my head.

When we finally get to the shop, laid out elegantly in shades of purple with cushioned benches all over for people to sit and chat, Emma and Maddie shove me forward and explain to the store owner that I need sports bras *and* sexy bras.

Judy The Boob Whisperer beams and hustles me into a fitting room, where she somehow finds 13 things that are comfortable, beautiful, and hold my tits in place all at once. "Jesus, Emma, you weren't kidding," I shout over the curtain.

"Told you," she sings, clinking her wine glass with Maddie while they wait their turn for the magic bra lady.

The whole experience reminds me how glad I am that I adopted Emma as my family. She and Maddie and Boobie-Judy all gush about how sexy I look in the bras, and they're right, damn it. I've worked hard for decades to silence the voices inside telling me what my body is supposed to look like, and what it means that it does not meet that standard.

Sometimes, I guess, I just need this outside reinforcement. I buy a dozen different bras and drink a glass of wine while Emma takes her turn in the fitting room. I try not to gag when Judy hands her a sexy nursing bra, explaining that it comes with a risk. "You might wind up pregnant again if you get that one," she says, grinning.

CHAPTER SIX
NICOLE

The next morning, I'm fully decked out in my new boulder-holder and enough layers that I feel confident I can run two miles on my own before the public humiliation of the next group run this weekend. I remember that Isaac Brady will be there again—I refuse to call him Zack, because that's just not the right nickname for Isaac and he's a smug jerk who hasn't earned a nickname from me yet.

This entire week at work, Tim hasn't shut the hell up about the relay team. He's "Tim Stag Excited," which involves micromanagement and 100 texts per day about stretching and lactic acid. I will never, ever reveal to him that I did wind up doing some of his leg stretches and they did actually feel really good.

I only tried them because I was curious, damn it.

The only slightly redeeming factor is that the other guys from work are all also receiving these hyper-detailed info dumps. At least Tim's not assuming I'm clueless because I'm female.

I lace up my new sneakers, pull on a knitted hat with a puff ball on top, and walk out back through my sun room door. I decide I'm going to stretch while the sun rises, because that feels poetic or something. Only as I make my way through the frosty grass out back, I notice the ridge isn't so much a ridge as a trench.

"Mother fucker," I screech as I walk closer. Valerie was absolutely right about this thing. The bottom half of our back yard is a foot lower than the part where I sit to drink beer in the summer evenings. So much for my test run. I consider banging on my neighbor's door, but I remember it's six in the morning.

"Emma," I mutter. "Emma will be awake." I dial my girl, who picks up almost as soon as it starts ringing.

"Nik! You're up early. Well, you don't sleep, do you?"

"I sleep *and* I'm up early. Ems--there's a fucking trench in my back yard."

"What do you mean?" I hear rustling on her end, like she's sitting up in bed.

"I don't know. My stupid neighbor says we're having a landslide. What the fuck do I even do with a landslide?"

"Hmm." I can hear Emma shifting around and something makes a gurgling sound.

"Are you holding a baby right now?"

"I am! Ricky is going to keep on nursing while Mama does some phone research. Aren't you? Aren't you, precious? Yes!" I tune her out while I walk back inside and start making coffee. Emma used to be a reporter. I know she's probably simultaneously searching her special databases while she coos all that nonsense to her kid.

I hear Thatcher start murmuring to her in the background and I nearly gag. He's so freaking smitten with her. He even makes glass sculptures of her and the kids to display in his gallery along with his other glass art. I shouldn't be so bitchy about that. Emma's in a good place. But I also don't need to hear her husband waking up in the morning. It feels too intimate, and reminds me that I'll never have anything like that.

"You want me to give you a call in a bit?"

"No! Nik, stay on the phone. If we end the call I will get too deep in baby work and forget all this has ever happened. I'm pulling something up about urban landslides. You need to call a...geotechnical engineer."

"A what now?" She repeats herself. "Huh. I had absolutely no idea there was a specific person you could call about this."

"Well," she says, chewing. Thatcher must have brought her some food. I approve of this. "I don't think they just work with landslides. Like, they are the people to call about fracking and earthquakes and stuff."

"Fracking?"

"I mean, and other stuff, too..."

I sigh. "Thanks, Emma. I appreciate your help."

"I'm glad we connected! I miss your angry voice!"

"We just hung out."

"Well, and I had to end it early because Ricky was a mess..."

"I love you and I'm hanging up now because I have to go to work and get Mark to make me an appointment with one of these fracking guys."

"Are you wearing the new bras?"

I smile at this. "As a matter of fact I am." We hang up and I change for work, sliding into a navy blue lacy bra that lifts my boobs so high and cinches them in so tight in front that I look like the prow of a ship. I swear, my clothes fit differently when I wear this thing.

Even without the run, I feel much more centered as I head for the office in my killer outfit. I decide stressing about the yard trench must be as much of a workout as actually running. Or maybe having a good friend to lean on builds as many endorphins as a workout. Either way, I feel great.

At work, I stop in the kitchen to get my breakfast from Alice in person.

She smiles at me and wolf whistles. "I see you met with Judy," she says.

"Is it that obvious?" I grab a muffin, skeptically.

Alice nods. "Oh yeah. You're walking differently today. You look amazing."

"Well I will accept the compliment, Mrs. Stag. Thank you." I grin. She waves and gives me a thumbs up as I head out.

By the time I sit down at my desk, I actually ask Mark for help in a nice voice, which leads him to burst into my office and place the back of his hand on my forehead.

"What the hell are you doing?" I crumple a muffin wrapper and throw it at him.

"Oh thank god," he says, brushing crumbs off his shoulder. "When you used the word 'please' I worried you were dying."

I roll my eyes. "Well, whenever you get a chance, I need to call one of those engineer bobbies."

"Oh, please, god, let his name be Bobby. In tight jeans...maybe a hard hat."

"Mark, we have a ton to do for the foundation meeting." I tap my pen on the edge of my desk, trying not to let my thoughts drift to Isaac Brady in a hard hat and faded jeans. I am absolutely not picturing him in a tool belt. Nope. My running coach is nowhere near my thoughts at all as I busy myself to launch a new arm of the company.

I cross and uncross my legs, eventually deciding I need the treadmill desk. I pace out my nervous energy until Mark sends a text confirming an appointment with a geotechnical engineer.

CHAPTER SEVEN
ZACK

"Have a seat, son," my father gestures toward the mismatched "furniture" in his office. I've got my pick between an Argentinian saddle and a low stool from Ethiopia. He always brings this stuff back from his travels, which is fine I guess, but then he expects his clients to sit on it. And he's still got a Rolodex full of Fortune-ranked contacts.

I opt for the saddle, wishing I could ride my ass on out of here instead. He starts slurping his mate and for the thousandth time offers me a sip of the foul green brew.

"I don't want any MATE, Dad." I pronounce it wrong because I'm irritated with him.

"Zack, you know it's mah-tay," he chides, shaking his head.

"Dad, I was going to present about the sink hole to Uncle Kellen...can we speed this up?"

"You and your brothers are always in such a damn hurry," he says, setting down his gourd cup.

"Yeah, because you always force us to go running and be efficient."

"Don't be a smart ass. We're building rapport here. But don't think for a second I won't smoke your ass on the running trail."

I hold my hands up in surrender. Dad can still blaze. I do hope I inherited his longevity. He takes a sip of his drink and tells me, "You know, this mate is from Paraguay. I went there about a year ago. Met with their Presidente, even."

Dad tells these stories that journey around and around the subject at hand. He's not an engineer--just wanted to work with his brother and thought he could help Kellen sell engineering services in an era when nobody else was doing that, but industrial facilities were starting to wear out. Dad ropes in the clients, telling them stories about hair dye mishaps or broken shoes or, apparently, gourds and tea. Uncle Kellen swoops in and points out the rust spots on their bridges and the cracks in their dams.

Dad tells me how he sat down for tea with the president of Paraguay after they ran into one another at a shop near the airport.

Dad asked El Presidente for advice and has been chugging Yerba every day since. "The Presidente told me they've been having unusually wet weather, and I've been keeping my eye on the news." Dad continues, telling me how there have been floods in Peru, mudslides in Ecuador, and widespread landslides in Paraguay. "Those mountains are the home of that Yerba plant," he says, chugging the last of his bitter tea.

He leans back in his chair and stares out the window at the city coming to life. "I got a call from a friend today. Someone from Stag Law needs a geotechnical engineer at her house. I'd like you to handle this for me."

"You want me to handle a residential project??" I'm so fucking insulted I can barely spit the words out. It barely registers that he's talking about Stag Law, the competition in the damn corporate marathon relay. I can't get past the idea that I would ever go consult on a residential project.

I've been clawing my way up toward major industrial projects for years. I'm not about to go talk about swimming pools or some shit with some golf buddy of my dad's. "I thought you only pursue repeat business. What the hell is the point of a residential one-off?"

"Tim Stag is a valuable person to know," Dad says. "He and I sit on the board of the hospital together and *his* clients have very, very deep pockets if they can manage not to blow it all on hookers and booze. When his executive assistant calls me personally, I tell her I will have my own son investigate the situation, because Beltane Engineering values our relationship with Stag Law."

I swallow. My dad always makes me feel like an asshole. He could have just led off by telling me someone important needed something done. He could have offered some fucking context about why he's sending me out on a landscaping project. I don't even know Tim Stag apart from seeing him at runs. I'm the guy with his hands in the dirt, not some schmoozer. I sigh. "Tell me what I need to know."

ℬ

I'm in my office gathering up my field supplies when my brothers stick their head in the door. Liam folds his arms and leans against the door frame. "Heard Texas Ted talking about sink hole detail."

"I'm sure you did," I grunt, shoving my hard hat in my bag. I still have no real idea what to expect on this job site. "Dad's sending me out to inspect a mysterious trench because he wants to make nice with Tim Stag."

Cal perks up at this. "Tim Stag? Like Tyrion Stag's brother?" I shrug.

"Zack. Come on, dude, the hockey player? His brother's firm represents like, every pro athlete in PA. You're going to get bowl game tickets out of this."

Liam strokes his chin. "That chick from the running group works at Stag Law. Isn't that what she said?"

I grunt again and hoist up my bag. "I'll be in Lawrenceville," I tell them. "Uncertain if I'll be back after."

Cal nods. "We can all go for ramen after work. You know, if you make it back alive."

"Very funny, Callum. You're buying."

ℬ

Dad gives me an address to a remodeled townhouse in a gentrified area of Lawrenceville. Of course, the hot shot client lives here. These houses are flipped with no character. Faux marble counters. All the internal walls are ripped out and it's all meant to look like old factory floors. I shudder, thinking about going inside--I should have my brother Liam look up the plans to make sure nothing load bearing has been dismantled before I sit whoever it is down to discuss whatever the fuck is going on with her back yard.

I circle the block looking for parking, imagining this homeowner as a prissy, high maintenance sorority girl. I finally find a spot down the road and parallel park my truck, muttering under my breath with annoyance that this woman I haven't met is ruining basically everything about my month.

Of course, I know that rationally, I'm actually angry about the assignment I didn't get. I'm angry that Ted's presentation was chosen for the sink holes. I'm angry that I don't even know if my uncle showed my ideas to the team. I imagine them all talking about me while I wasn't in there.

Poor old Zack. Sent off on a grunt project for his dad.

I sigh. I need to nip these thoughts, get them under control. I crunch through the frozen turf around back of her house, and then I whistle through my teeth.

This is not good.

What I see before me is the beginning of the end of a major landslide. The two townhouses unfortunate enough to be on the property look like they're the last bastions of the old neighborhood before the house flippers and condo developers moved in.

There's a tidy back yard with two patios and the one that matches the address Dad gave me has a killer sun room, with views of the river. I inhale, telling myself this is at least a tastefully renovated property. The mystery owner has built back a small amount of credibility, despite having a yard that's about the crumble into the Allegheny River. I take some time carefully navigating the fissure, testing the ground to see if the landslide will hold my weight before I crouch to take measurements. I'm not sure how long I spend studying the situation when I hear a voice say, "Are you the fracking guy?"

I look up over my shoulder and see a woman silhouetted by the sun. She is short and curvy and not dressed appropriately to be walking around a landslide in the freezing cold. "Get back," I shout, gruffly.

I stand up and approach her, and then halt in my tracks because *fuck me sideways*. It's Nicole. Standing in the crisp air, cheeks pink, this woman is as beautiful as she is angry.

"Excuse me?" she puts her hands on her hips and plants her heel-clad feet. "Nobody tells me what to do on my own property."

I stalk up close to her, closer than I intend, but I'm shaken by my response to her pale skin and seemingly endless supply of hair, that blows around in the frigid breeze off the river. "You've got a rotational landslide here, and this entire area is unsafe. Especially dressed like that."

She huffs and a piece of chestnut brown hair sticks to her cheek. I have to fight off every urge to reach out and brush it aside so I can see her green eyes flash at me. "Listen, Isaac, I'm about to pay you thousands of dollars to fix whatever's going on back here. This shit was a lump in the grass yesterday. Are you going to fix it or should I call someone who knows what they're doing?"

"Let's make one thing very clear here," I tell her, urging her back toward solid ground. "There is nobody--NOBODY--in this city or any other in the tri-state area who knows this soil better than I do. So when I tell you to get back, that means haul your fancy shoes and your pretty skirt back to the curb where it's safe." My nostrils flare. She had to go and suggest I am an inferior engineer on the same day as this bullshit with my dad at work.

"You're being ridiculous," she says. "This is basically a sink hole. We get those around here all the time because the sewer system is collapsing, or some such nonsense."

Sink hole. I shake my head and gesture along the line in her yard. "You see this--what did you call it? A trench? Tomorrow this is going to shift six feet further down toward the river. The day after that, you'll be able to repel here, it'll be so far gone. I'm probably going to have to have the city condemn your house."

She gasps. That got her attention I guess. I wasn't totally serious about that, but if the fault line moves like I predict it will, it's going to be a close call as to whether she can stay here. Plus she pissed me off.

"You've got to be kidding me," she says.

"Do I look like I'm kidding?" I shove my calculator into my back pocket and start walking around front of her property. "Look, I'm freezing my balls off out here and I'm sick of arguing with you while your hair's blowing in my mouth. I'll have my office send you the information at your office."

She snorts. "Are you being huffy because of our lack of rapport as running partners?"

I glare at her. "I'm being 'huffy' because I'm supposed to be addressing an impactful industrial project, not a domestic landscaping issue."

"So it's not that big a deal then?" Her voice cracks a little and I ease up. I did just tell her she might lose her home.

When I look up at her, I see her pink tongue running along those red fucking lips and I have to grit my teeth to stop a moan escaping my mouth. *Client,* I mutter. *She's a client. Dad sent you here. Think of Dad. Think of Dad.*

"I'll run some numbers, ok? I'll get you the information." I spin on my heel and start walking down the street back toward my truck, hoping I can catch my breath out of sight of her piercing green eyes. I reach my truck and climb inside, not turning around to look as she starts to shout something down the street after me. Her people know how to reach my people.

Shit. I didn't want this fucking job when I thought it was about mulch and landscaping. Now it's a fucking landslide inside city limits with a high-maintenance, high-heeled, she-devil for a client.

All the work of a major industrial project, ten times the bureaucratic hassle, and I still won't get the promotion I've fucking earned over the past five years. And I have to fucking teach her how to go running on Sunday.

I need to think. My head is swimming with how rapidly my day changed from a nice run with my brothers before work...into a hellscape. A literal landslide of silt is pouring into my career right now. I storm back into my office and slam the door. Our offices are tiny—the ancient building has long hallways with door after door. Dad renovated a bit to make a space for cubicles, but at nearly 30, I had at least managed to work my way up to my own office.

The heavy door bounces back open again a minute later and my cousin Orla bursts into the room.

She pulls the door shut and leans against it, raising her eyebrows at me, waiting for me to speak.

Orla and my Uncle Kellen lived with us after her mother died. Where my father cycled through women like laundry, Uncle Kel was deeply devoted to my departed aunt. I'm not sure he'll ever get over losing her. Since Dad was between wives when Aunt Helen died, Kellen and Orla just moved in to the big house for the few years left until Orla left for college.

Uncle Kellen has, for a long time, been the keeper of the feelings in our big Brady family. He's always the one who can tell when something's wrong, and he's the one to come and figure out how to make things right again.

I'm sure he told Orla, hence her visit here now.

I sigh. "Dad sent me on a pet project."

"So I heard. And?"

I explain about the landslide. "Honestly? I'm not even sure how we go about fixing that in city limits. Right on the bank of the river like that. It's going to be a god damned disaster. And for what? Because Dad wants to make nice with this broad's boss? I don't get it."

Orla strides across the room and looks at my desk, where I've still got the sticky note from my dad with Nicole Kennedy's address scribbled on it. She pulls out her phone and taps around for awhile. She whistles. "She's not too bad to look at," Orla says. "Even if she can't run for shit." I snort. "Says she's the strategy director for Stag Law. They specialize in representing athletes, but *she* specializes in optimizing staff performance and..." she pauses to read. "Fostering relationships with stakeholders, developing solutions, et cetera, et cetera. Sounds like exactly the kind of shit your dad does here."

I scowl at her. "What's your point?"

"You think Uncle Mick's trying to poach her? I mean why else would he give a fuck about a residential project."

"This is why I don't like you, Orla. Because you say shit like that and it makes total fucking sense, and now I'm panicking about the big picture instead of just being angry that I lost a project to Texas Ted."

She punches me in the shoulder. "Come," she says. "Let's have an off-site meeting and I'll buy you a drink."

CHAPTER EIGHT
NICOLE

I'M SEETHING WHEN I STOMP BACK INTO THE STAG LAW OFFICES. I CAN'T TELL IF I'M more annoyed that Valerie was right or that I have to deal with my running coach and his hot, broody face. That I saw looming above me when I passed the fuck out on my first run.

I cannot have him coming to my house. I just cannot.

"Donna," I let myself into her office and rap my fingers on the door frame. She looks up at me, questioningly. "I hear you're the one who found me the geotechnical engineer to fix the trench?"

She blushes. *What the hell?* "Did Mick Brady come to look at your yard personally? Don't be insulted by him, dear. He's just like that."

"No." This reaction is so unexpected I slump against her door frame. "He sent his son Isaac." I think back to the lanky guy in the tight-but-worn jeans, hard hat, tool belt. I make a mental note to focus on that image later. Alone in my shower. The fucking tool belt ought to be enough to break through the strike my clit has been on lately.

Donna smiles. "Mick has three nice young sons. Just like our Mr. Stag is one of three boys! I only had the one son—"

"Donna, I'm sorry. I'm freaking out here. He says I have a rotational landslide, and I looked that shit up on the drive back here and it's going to cost a quarter million dollars to repair my fucking back yard."

She pales. "Oh, I'm sure the Bradys won't charge you the regular rate! Goodness. Nobody could afford that."

No shit, I think. Her phone rings, and her face lights up again. "This is Beltane Engineering," she says to me. "Should I just transfer to you directly?"

"Is it Isaac??" Oh, god, I cannot be just talking to him on the phone right now. I need to work out a strategy for coming back from passing out.

Donna shakes her head. She mouths "admin."

I nod and walk back toward my office. As promised, Isaac had "his people" call with information. Some teenager on the phone is prattling on about something called a "headscarp" and confirms my worst fears: a conservative estimate for the repair is a quarter million dollars for the concrete, soil and heavy machinery. Not even including the labor.

I try my best to thank him politely and retreat into my office couch to regroup. Even if I split the cost with Valerie, I don't have that kind of money just lying around. Even though I got my townhouse for a few thousand bucks, I took out a home equity loan when I restored it.

And let's be honest. I'm doing ok in the salary department, but not too many people have a quarter million dollars liquid just lying around.

I pull up an internet search for Isaac Brady and learn that he's apparently some genius when it comes to soil and weight loads. He's won awards from the environmental protection people for repairing dams and coal mines. I sigh. If this guy, moody fucker though he may be, tells me this headscarf thing is going on in my yard, it's unlikely that he's wrong.

I try not to fixate on his suggestion that the city was going to condemn my house. My fucking house! The minute I signed that deed, I felt like I was finally free from my parents' expectations and all the ways I failed to meet them. I didn't even know how to use a lawn mower when I got that house, let alone how to refinish floors and hang sheetrock.

Every online tutorial I watched, every contractor I brought in just as a consultant, I felt like I was coming into my self. It paid off at work, too. If I could use a belt sander by myself, I sure as shit could present my ideas to a room full of men set on overlooking me.

I really feel like I'm going to cry, and this is very, very unusual for me. I call Emma, crossing my fingers that she can answer the phone. If one or more of her kids is asleep, she can only ever text. "Hey," she whispers.

"Ems," I start, and then I burst into tears. Actual boo-hoo sobs out loud.

"Woah, Nicole, what's wrong, love?"

I tell her about the landslide, that it's so expensive to fix it might as well cost ten million dollars. "I might lose my house," I sob.

"Ok. So do you want solutions or comfort?"

I consider this. I grew up in a house without comfort. My mother has had too much botox to emote. My sister is her protege. Refined girls do not cry, they do not smear their makeup, and they most certainly do not grow curves and curls like I sprouted and refused to rein in. "Solutions," I tell Emma, and take a deep breath.

I hear Emma walking down a hallway, presumably where she can talk louder. "Ok, so first you need to call your homeowners insurance and see if this is covered, although I doubt it will be or Zack would have mentioned that."

"Isaac," I correct her.

"I thought you said he goes by Zack?"

"Exactly. And that's a stupid fucking nickname for Isaac," I snap at my friend. "I'm sorry," I say immediately.

"Ok, so we're going to calm down and do some comfort before we keep going with the solutions."

I take a deep breath. She's right. I'm spiraling. "You're resourceful," I hear Emma say. "You're a bad ass bitch who takes no shit. Not from wolves on Wall Street and certainly not from a damn crack in the ground. Right?"

I nod. Which she can't see, because she keeps prodding. "Right?"

"Yes," I tell her. "I'm going to defeat this. Just like all the other challenges."

"Exactly!" She shouts. "So step one, call the insurance. Step two, you need to talk to my sister-in-law."

"Which one?" Since I work for Stag Law, I realize she must be talking about Juniper Jones, Tyrion Stag's wife. Juniper was a lawyer here for a long time, but is now a judge of...something.

Emma's going on about how Juniper is constantly settling property dispute cases and knows all the jargon. "Juniper can help you figure out who to sue," Emma says.

"Sue?" Jesus, I do not have time for a lawsuit. I don't have time for a landslide. I'm supposed to be training for this damn marathon and, oh I don't know, directing the strategy for a major law firm looking to expand operations.

"Nik, my love, there's got to be a reason the earth opened up and swallowed your yard. You need to find the reason, and sue to make the culprit pay for the restoration."

It had not occurred to me that there might be a culprit here. "I literally thought I had just pissed off the gods," I tell her. She's one thousand per cent right, of course. It all just sounds like so much work. I flop over my desk and rest my cheek on the wood and close my eyes as Emma continues. "Does Zack really think the city will condemn your house?"

"I think he was just saying that to be a smart-ass." But I'm not sure. I hear Emma telling me I can come stay with her and Thatcher any time and I thank her, hang up the phone, and head back home.

I'm useless to anyone where work is concerned. I draw a bath and slide into the tub, trying to forget my stress about the house. I'm not sure what is happening this week, but my entire world has been turned upside-down.

I'm desperate to relax. It feels like there's a geyser waiting to erupt in my guts. I wonder if masturbating will help, even though it hasn't been going very well the past few times I've tried. I close my eyes and pull up my handyman fantasy images of Isaac in his jeans, squatting in my yard, and my fingers go to town on my clit.

But nothing happens. I growl in frustration and turn the water back on, adjusting myself so the flow runs over my crotch. Nothing. "What in the fucking hell is this?"

I start to wonder if running has broken my clit or something. I kick at the faucet in a rage and head downstairs. I pull the cork out of yesterday's wine bottle with my teeth and start drinking straight from the bottle.

As I chug the wine, I try porn. I try online pictures I find of Isaac and his brothers running different races. I try everything I can think of short of zapping my clit with my taser, but nothing works. Eventually, I'm too drunk to care about my inability to come and I pass out on my couch.

CHAPTER NINE
ZACK

When I get to work in the morning, my dad's secretary tells me to reassign all projects and only prioritize the Kennedy Landslide. "Seriously?" She nods. This is an unprecedented, inefficient use of my time.

I blow out a breath and get to work on the notes I took yesterday. I have an email from Nicole's homeowner's insurance, and I grimace, knowing I have to explain to them exactly what I found.

This earth movement is a textbook case of a slump landslide, I type. I send them some numbers, estimate that the headscarp will shift rapidly and that the foundation of the house will likely be at risk. I'm fairly certain the insurance will refuse to cover Nicole's property, and I'm also pretty sure the city is going to need to condemn the house.

I make notes about the names of the property owners nearby whose land might be affected. I take some time looking up nearby construction projects and making lists of the different utilities that might be impacted. The last thing I want is a backhoe to blow through a gas line in Nicole's back yard.

And then I sit and stare at the plans for the lot, noting how close her house is to the river. There's basically no way I'm going to be able to do anything without rigging a barge on the water. I rake a hand through my hair and decide to drive over there.

I find a parking spot right next to Nicole's house and strap on my tool belt, grab my tablet and head out to survey the ground. It looks like there's been even more of a shift since I was last here, and I squat down to take some more measurements.

I'm bent over with my tape measure in the fissure when I feel something nudge me in the ass. "Hey," a voice growls at me. "Hey!"

I whip my head around to find an old woman staring at me, hands on her hips. "Did you just kick me?"

"I did. You want to tell me what you're doing back here? This is still private property last I checked." I glance around, not sure what I'm looking for. People usually don't question why I'm at a job site, especially when I'm wearing a hard hat, but then again, this is my first domestic project.

I clear my throat. "I'm Zack Brady with Beltane Engineering. Ms. Kennedy has hired me to assess your landslide situation."

Her face lights up. "Aha! So she admits I was right!" She crosses her arms. "What sort of engineer are you?"

She proceeds to question my alma mater, to ask me about my advanced geotechnical licensure, to ask what the hell I'm doing handling a private property landslide if I'm really as experienced as all that. I sigh. "You got me, ma'am," I tell her. "But I'm here. And you should step back and be careful. Try not to come into the back yard."

She pulls out a lawn chair and sits on her patio with her arms crossed, watching as I measure and take notes. I study the yard and am halfway through creating a 3-d model on my tablet when Nicole appears out of her back door, her hair whipping in the winter wind. She's so fucking sexy, even frowning at me in constant disapproval.

I give a small wave in acknowledgement that I saw her and return to my model as the wind from the river picks up. I hear the old lady yelling over to Nicole. "So I see you decided to take me seriously?"

"Yes, Valerie," Nicole spits back. "The growing crater in the yard was a good clue." Then, her voice softer, Nicole asks, "Did your homeowners refuse to cover?" They shout back and forth for a bit about the cost of the repair. I try to study the plans of the condo complex a few properties down, but the wind is freezing and making it hard for me to open any of my folders of paper printouts.

"Hey," I shout as Nicole is starting a string of curse words about bureaucracy. "Mind if I look at these in your house? Out of the wind?"

Nicole raises a brow at me but shrugs and gestures toward the house. When Valerie moves to follow, Nicole shakes her head. "Not today, Val. I can't handle you today." I hear the woman scoff as Nicole slams the glass door shut behind me. "She drives me fucking insane," Nicole says as she hangs up her coat and slips out of her heels.

I look down at my dirty boots and swallow. I'm used to trailers on work sites. I'll have to remember to get some shoe covers or something if I'm going to spend any significant time here. I sigh and bend over to loosen my laces and when I look up, Nicole is staring at me.

I wiggle my toes in my socks and take in my surroundings. I see immediately that I was very, very wrong in my initial assumption of this place as a quick flip for a trendy hipster. That might be the trend in the neighborhood, but this is a fucking historic restoration of artisan proportions.

"You own this place," I ask, looking at the original oak floors that gleam under an oil finish. Nicole has exposed brick in the kitchen off the sun porch. Marble counters gleam around stainless appliances, and it looks like she consulted an actual lighting engineer when she chose the fixtures. The entire space is bathed in warm light, with no dim patches or dark corners.

"Yes, Isaac. I own my house." She starts banging around the kitchen. "Do you need water?"

I nod. "I'm sorry. I just was expecting it to look...less nice in here. I've been inside some of the remodels in this neighborhood..." My voice drifts off and I study her face. When she rolls her eyes, I know that she, too, is familiar with the rapid gentrification happening in her part of the city. Ten years ago, you almost had to pay people to buy houses here. Now, this place would go for over a million. Well, before the back yard fell apart. I clear my throat. "Who was your contractor?"

She sneers and slides the water across the counter. "Listen, Brady," she says, rapping her nails against the counter. "I rebuilt this fucking place myself, fueled by the power of my rage at society. Otherwise I wouldn't give a shit about the yard falling off. So make yourself comfortable at the counter I polished and get to fixing my land."

She storms out of the room before I can respond, and I feel my dick twitch in my pants. I look around again at the meticulously tiled back splash with perfectly matched grout. I sip the water she gave me and remind myself the curvaceous woman who passed out after running two miles is a client. Moreover, she's someone my dad is interested in for the business, which makes her twenty levels of off limits.

I spread my work out on her counter and lose myself in construction blueprints and court hearing notices. Inspection reports for nearby construction. Eventually, I hear the doorbell ring. I ignore it, because this isn't my house and I'm trying to concentrate, but Nicole doesn't come downstairs. It rings again and whoever it is starts knocking.

I sigh and head toward the front of the house, glancing up the carpeted stairs to see if she will emerge, but there's nothing. When I open the turquoise door a delivery guy thrusts a box into my arms. "Can you sign?" He holds out his digital signature pad and my brows shoot up.

"Um, I don't live here."

"Look, pal, can you just sign? I got a quota to meet and I'm double parked." I look over his shoulder and see there's already a line of cars sitting behind the delivery van, frustrated, on Nicole's street. I scribble my name and he scurries away.

When I look down at the box, I almost drop it when I see the label under the EXPEDITED DELIVERY sticker. "Babe Rocket," I mutter, as I look at the picture. Nicole Kennedy overnighted herself a huge purple vibrator with rotating parts and, according to the package, a satisfaction guarantee.

The thought of Nicole being satisfied turns me on so fast, so overwhelmingly that I rush to the kitchen and gather my things. I have to get the hell out of here and jerk off. There's no question of me doing anything else. My blood pounds in my temples as I set the box on the counter and storm out of the house without letting her know that I'm leaving.

The delivery confirms that this wild woman, who apparently gets dirty with construction projects, spends her nights making herself come and I know that I will actually explode if I don't do something about how much that turns me on.

I barely breathe until I'm at home, where I rip open my pants like a teenager. I squeeze my eyes shut in my kitchen, leaning against the sink, and imagine Nicole in those running leggings, biting her lip while her frizzy hair swirls around her body. I angrily pound at my cock, my knuckles grinding against the teeth of my zipper.

As I stroke myself faster and faster, I imagine her face transformed by pleasure. Only it's not the purple vibrator I picture as she screams her release. In my fantasy she moans for my cock, my name on her plump lips as she rolls those thick hips, and I come into my sink. My dick throbs in my hand and the salty semen stings the abrasions on my knuckles. I slump over, my breath ragged, as I try to regain my composure.

"Fuck," I mutter. This is going to be a problem.

CHAPTER TEN
NICOLE

"He took his shoes off when he came inside," I explain to Tim during our meeting the next day. "Is that weird?"

Tim shrugs. "It seems polite. What's he doing today while you're not home?"

It's actually snowing out today, even though it's supposed to go back up to 40 by the end of the week. I hadn't considered that Isaac would be standing around outside all day in the snow at my house. "Hm. Doesn't he go into his office to do...math or whatever?"

Tim scowls, thinking. "I don't know. Want me to call my contact at Beltane and ask what's typical?" I open my mouth to protest, but Tim already has his phone out. "Mick! Yeah, hey. Tim Stag. Yes, I know you know. I'm fine. Yep, kids are fine. Having a third soon!" I tune him out while they get through the small talk portion of their conversation.

I called this meeting to map out our strategy in advance of our first in-house foundation project. Our client Augusto Cruz, a baseball player, is coming in with his publicity team to listen to our pitch about the foundation he wants to set up to benefit his home country of Paraguay.

We still haven't decided the direction he should go. Tim thinks he should start youth baseball programs. Augusto wants to just "help the country," but hasn't provided more direction than that. It's my job to think about the big picture—Augusto setting up a successful foundation means more of our clients will look to us for guidance when they do the same.

With several pro sports organizations holding their drafts in the coming months, we're about to have a bunch of first-year star athletes looking for ways to spend their millions.

I pore over the background files about Augusto's upbringing and I hear Tim mention the man to Mick Brady. "I know," Tim shouts, jovially. "I've never been to Paraguay before. I have no idea what we're stepping into down there." Tim is quiet for a bit, then he grins. "You know," he says, "I would love it if you joined us. Yeah, I'm serious, too."

My eyes bulge at Tim. *Did he just invite Mick Brady on our company trip?* Tim's not supposed to make these kinds of decisions for the company without consulting me, his director of strategy. The last thing I need is some smarmy golf buddy of Tim's joining us on a fact-finding trip just as our firm decides how we're going to branch out into philanthropic legal support for our clients.

"Hey, Mick, thanks for all the info. Have your admin get in touch with Donna so we can find a time for us to grab lunch." Tim hangs up and rocks back in his chair. "Mick says Zack is fine in the snow. But! It also turns out Mick's met the president of Paraguay. I invited him to come with us when we go there. Mick Brady. Not the president of Paraguay. He'll already be there. Anyway, it never hurts to know someone who can grease wheels."

I want to punch my boss in the face right now, so I try to focus on Isaac doing math out in the snow in my back yard. I wince. But back to the matter of strategy. "I heard you invite him," I tell Tim. "Want to tell me what we're supposed to do with an engineer on our information gathering trip for Augusto Cruz's foundation?"

Tim laughs. "Oh, Mick's not an engineer. His brother handles all the engineering in their company. Mick's a sociologist." Tim flips open his folder, signaling that he's getting ready to start our meeting in earnest. "He studies people and lands them clients. Pretty sure he just met the prez while playing golf."

Tim pivots to our upcoming meeting, noting a few different ideas from the publicity people at the baseball team HQ. Most people seem to want Augusto to focus his charitable giving on building baseball opportunities in a country where there really isn't much baseball. I am leaning that direction, too. I sort of tune Tim out worrying about Isaac freezing his fingers in the snow while he measures my yard.

Yesterday, he looked really fucking hot squatting in those jeans and peering into the trench. I squirm a bit in my seat, remembering how I'd come downstairs to find him gone, the package for the vibrator I ordered sitting on the counter. He must have signed for the delivery, and I've already called the company to ream them out for their indiscrete packaging. At least I didn't have the thing shipped to me at work!

Isaac knows I ordered a vibrator, I think as Tim talks about legal mumbo jumbo. *Isaac doesn't know I think about him while I use it. Or that it doesn't help.*

When we wrap up our meeting, I head into my office and look up Isaac's phone number, wondering if his business card number will ring his cell or his desk phone. His deep voice answers, "Zack Brady," and I get so irritated again by his nickname that I forget I'm calling to be nice to him.

"Why in the hell do you go by Zack when your name is Isaac?"

I hear him exhale. "I assume this is my favorite client calling?"

"Yes!" I shriek, and then I have to get control of myself. I fire up the treadmill under my desk and start pacing, feeling instantly better as I start moving my legs. "But really. Your nickname is ridiculous."

"If you must know, my oldest brother couldn't say my full name when I was a baby and I've gone by Zack ever since."

"You're saying a baby could pronounce ZACK but somehow not EYE-ZACK?" I start walking faster. I have no idea why I'm so focused on his nickname. It's just that he's such an Isaac. Dark and sexy and grouchy. Zacks are outgoing and perky.

He sighs. "Did you have questions related to your rotational landslide or did you just call to criticize me?"

Smug little shit, I think. But secretly I love that he's not intimidated by my smart mouth. "I was calling about your work environment," I tell him. "I'm going to set up a contractor lock on my house so you can get in to get warm and, I don't know, pee. And stuff."

"You want me to pee in your house?"

"Well I don't want you to whip it out and piss in the river!" And now I'm thinking about Isaac Brady whipping out his dick and I have to turn up the speed on my treadmill so I can calm down by walking even faster. I hear him rustling some papers around.

He clears his throat. "I have been going back and forth with your home-owners insurance—"

"Yes," I interrupt him. "I know those fuckers are refusing to pay anything. My friend Emma says I need to figure out who to sue for your fee."

"Well, yes, that's what I wanted to talk with you about—"

"I have an appointment with Juniper Jones," I tell him, starting to huff a bit. I kick off my heels and feel my calf muscles relax while the treadmill keeps cranking under my desk. My mother would be absolutely horrified to learn I have a treadmill under my desk so I can pace when I get irritated, but everything I do horrifies my mother. The fact that I get irritated. The fact that I work in a non-secretarial career. I shake my head and concentrate on what Isaac is saying.

"Juniper is a magisterial judge," he says. "I've testified in cases before her in the past."

"You have?"

"Well of course I have," he says. "I told you. I usually handle industrial or large corporate projects. So when a coal mine is forced to meet government regulations, I need to testify—"

"Ok, ok, I get it. You're very smart and important. I just thought Juniper could recommend a lawyer."

"Well," I can hear him rapping on his desk in the background. He sighs. "Beltane has several attorneys on retainer. I can get someone on the case to help out."

Wow. This is so unexpected that I hop off the treadmill and stand on the carpet in my tights. "You can do that?"

"It's literally what you're paying me for." He pauses and laughs. "Or, it will be once I make sure someone can actually pay my fee."

"Very funny."

"That's why I laughed."

Who is this guy? "Ok, well, I'll text you the code for the contractor lock and you can let yourself in and out whenever you need." We hang up and I close my eyes, maybe wishing he wasn't the son of the man evidently trying to infiltrate my new strategic initiative at work. In other circumstances, I might tackle Isaac Brady to the ground and jump his bones. I sigh, reminding myself that I can't get involved with this guy, even if his banter is hot as fuck.

CHAPTER ELEVEN
ZACK

I ration my visits into Nicole's house. I let myself go in there to use her bathroom and only pause in the kitchen to get warm for five minutes. Anything past that, and I start fantasizing about her. The sight of her running shoes by the back door gets me hard.

Her briefcase propped against the end table by the front door gets me hard.

Every single thing in this house either reminds me of her smart-ass mouth or her incredible competence at everything apart from running. The other day, I was inside and overheard her completely dismantle a reporter over the phone. There I was, mid-piss, watching my dick spring to life at the thought of her yelling.

Today I'm meeting our property lawyer, Justin, at the house. I stop by the hardware store to buy a few sets of shoe covers. Ordinarily, we'd just be hanging out in a portable trailer to discuss this stuff, but I want to make sure we don't trash Nicole's floors.

And there I go again, thinking of her refinishing them herself. I close my eyes, trying to chase away the image of her in cutoffs, kneeling as she uses the drum sander, her tits shaking with the vibration of the power tools. My dick is pretty chapped from the daily, frantic masturbation sessions I'm scheduling each morning when I wake up. "Fuck," I mutter.

I sit in my truck and pull out some of the zoning notes I got for nearby construction projects. Something seems off about the condo project a few properties down, but I can't figure out what just yet. I'm deep in thought about it when Justin raps on my window. I jump.

"You ok in there, big guy?" Justin calls my brothers and me "big guy" when he's in a good mood, as if we aren't all lanky. I hop out of the truck and gesture toward Nicole's front door.

"Good to see you," I say as I type in the code on the lock box. His brows shoot up as I hand him the shoe covers. I shrug. "It's a residential gig," I tell him. "Don't want to wreck the client's floors."

"The client," he says, and then whistles as he looks around Nicole's house.

"She did all this herself," I tell him, not sure why I'm bragging about Nicole's obvious artisinal skill at hands-on remodeling. He runs his hand along the mantle that has to be original to the house, the intricate carvings in the wood gleaming under the soft glow of the recessed overhead lights. I again admire the finish on the hardwood floors, thinking about her squatting over them spreading the oil. *Is it normal that this turns me on so much?*

Justin and I spread out at Nicole's dining room table—an amazing piece, made of reclaimed wood, that suits the room absolutely perfectly. It actually has me reconsidering the dumpster-dive furniture I've had in my place since I first bought it after grad school.

Justin shows me all the research he's done on previous urban landslides. "It's always due to water," he says, like I don't know this already. But Pittsburgh hasn't had any torrential rains recently and the previous summer wasn't even all that wet, considering.

"There's no natural reason this particular piece of property should be sliding into the Allegheny River," I tell him, gesturing at Nicole and her neighbor's back yard.

Justin's eyes gleam. "I know. No natural reason. So we need to figure out which of these developers didn't do their diligence with their rainwater management," he jabs his thumb at the neighborhood plans showing new construction projects.

"Oh, no big deal," I tell him. "We just need to inspect the plumbing and sewer systems for tens of thousands of square feet of multi-unit residential housing."

Justin rocks back in his chair, and I kick him with my blue-booty-covered foot. I might murder him if he scuffs Nicole's floors. He rolls his eyes. "One of these guys has got to be draining their roof water into the soil. That was what happened with that Glaston landslide, remember?"

A few years ago, a new manufacturing plant was just pumping their rainwater into the hill behind their facility, and the hill slid down onto the highway. That was the first project my dad and uncle let me take the lead on mitigating. When I discovered the rainwater situation and partnered with Justin so the state could sue the Glaston company, my dad gave me a bonus check that paid for my truck.

Justin and I study the plans for a bit and make notes. I decide I'll head out to take readings tomorrow at first light so I can see what's happening with nearby buildings. If I'm honest, I'm pretty excited to test some of the new equipment we got to check stability and soil composition. I'm midway through explaining our new pneumatic shear machine when I see Justin perk up and stare at something behind my head.

Turning around, I see Nicole, and the first thing to fall out of my mouth is, "Oh. It's you."

"Yes, shocking for me to be in my own home, I know," she throws her stuff down on the table. She's dressed impeccably again, as she always seems to be for work. This woman is so complex. The contrast of her refined businesswear with my image of her mudding drywall is almost too much for my dick to handle in my jeans. "Will you all be staying for dinner since you've made yourselves so comfortable?"

Justin laughs and stands, introducing himself. I catch him scanning her body and resist the urge to growl out loud. His eyes dart over to me and he coughs. "I'm going to head out, Brady," he says. "Call me as soon as you've tracked those numbers."

He makes his way out the door while Nicole leans into her fridge so that all I can see is her ass in the pencil skirt she wore to work today. I breathe slowly through my nose, trying like hell to not walk over there and smack it.

When Nicole emerges from the fridge with a cheese stick, she seems confused to see me still sitting at her table in my shoe covers. "I wasn't actually inviting you to dinner," she says.

"Don't you want to hear about what we did today?"

"Have you located the person who will pay to fix my fucking yard?" She raises an eyebrow at me, but I can barely tell because her curly hair covers half her face from when she was bent over in the fridge. My eyes dip to the tailored blouse that nips in at her waist below her stunning cleavage.

I shake my head, biting my tongue, and stare up at her ceiling. As I'm admiring the lighting, a thought occurs to me. "Did you do all the electrical work yourself, too?" My body clenches as I wait for her response. There's "good at renovations," and then there's fucking around with electrical stuff.

She bites her cheese stick and frowns at me. "I pulled out all the knob and tube wiring myself and hired someone to rewire once I had all the fixtures mapped out," she says.

I relax. "My cousin will be relieved to hear it."

"Not sure why you'd tell her." Nicole reaches for a banana and leans against the counter, just staring at me and chewing. I feel my heart racing and I need to say something to her, but I also feel a strange urge to bust her balls the way she does mine.

"Want to go for a run?" As soon as I say the words, I'm shaking my head. First of all, I already put in six miles today and my legs are feeling it. Second, what kind of idiot question is that?

Nicole tilts her head to the side and blows a puff of air at the hair falling over her face. "Don't you usually trot around with your brothers?"

"They're with their mom tonight," I say, and clench my body again. I have no idea why I said that. Why I invited personal discussion, especially after she made it clear I shouldn't be talking about her house with Orla.

She bites the banana, a move so phallic I have to believe she's doing it on purpose. "You have a different mom than your brothers?" She stares at me as she chews.

I just nod. "My dad collects wives." I'm definitely not interested in going into more specifics, and I'm both relieved and terrified when Nicole sighs, shrugs, and says, "Ok, but is it safe to run at night? It's pitch black dark outside."

I grin. "I'll protect you."

That gets a laugh. "You gonna run in those bootie things?" She points at my shoe covers. I grin.

"I've got my running stuff in my truck," I tell her. "Give me five minutes."

CHAPTER TWELVE
NICOLE

I can't begin to understand why I agreed to go for a run with Isaac Brady. I mean, an additional run. We're supposed to meet again for a group run this weekend, but this feels unnecessary. Except...this skinny bastard looked so fucking cute in those blue shoe covers and my cold, dead heart melted a little when he explained that he didn't want to mess up my floors.

He comes out of my bathroom wearing black running pants that aren't skin tight exactly, but definitely show me which side his junk hangs toward. I nod, approvingly. I also had gone upstairs to change while he ran out for his stuff.

"So what all do we take with us for a night run?" I look around, as if I've got fancy flashlights or something.

Isaac gestures outside. "This is a city, Nicole. There are street lights."

"We're just going to run on Butler Street?" I'm horrified. I hadn't considered that we'd run on the main road, where people are out eating at trendy, cute restaurants or waiting in line to get tattoos or some shit.

I pick up my keys and thread them between my fingers to stab potential abductors, wondering if I've lost my mind.

Isaac takes my keys from me and clunks the massive network of keychains on the counter. "We can use the contractor code to get back in," he says gently. I slide my cell into the pocket on my leggings as he watches.

We head outside and I draw in a shaky breath. It's cold out here.

"We'll go slow," he says. "You'll warm up soon, I promise." He lets me set the pace and we run for a few blocks up to the main road, where he's right. It's bright as day out here between the neon lights from the shops and the street lights.

I've been practicing and I can already tell I'm getting fitter. Or maybe less bad at running. Either way, I'm going faster than last time.

"Remember, talking pace," he says. His deep voice sounds patronizing, and I fucking hate that I passed out the last time we exercised together because I was too damn stubborn to let him see me struggling to catch my breath.

"Don't tell me what to do," I spit at him.

"See? You're talking just fine." I can tell by the way he moves that he's holding back, and I hate him for being fitter than me. "Now what are you going to talk about?"

We come to a red light and Isaac pulls to a stop. I realize we'll probably be doing this a lot, given how short the blocks are. "This is nice—getting breaks," I tell him, and I mean it. By the time the light changes, I'm ready to start running again, and I actually smile, enjoying myself as we weave in between some people coming out of a bar.

"You doing ok," he asks, swerving a bit around some construction tape where they've got half the sidewalk torn up.

I nod and when we get to the next red light, I put my hands on my hips, drawing in deep breaths, letting him see how hard I've been working even at this snail pace, but oddly not caring so much. He points toward the river and says, "My brothers and I run on that trail sometimes. Cal always manages to find rail ties. He makes them into shit. Bottle openers and stuff."

I'm pretty sure that's the most words I've ever heard him string together. "It must be nice to get along with your siblings," I respond, puffing along. The next light is green when we get there. "My sister and my mother don't really approve of me. At all."

"Hm," he says. "Guess we have that in common."

"You don't go take your mom out to dinner?"

He makes a sound that's halfway between a laugh and a cry. He looks over at me and I brush my hair back from my face to meet his eye. He frowns. "She walked out on my dad and me when I was a baby," he says. "Haven't heard from her since."

"Shit," I say. The next light is green again, so we keep going. This has to have been at least a mile. "Well," I spit out, feeling like I need to have some sort of comeback to that, but not sure this is the time for black humor. "I can't say I'd prefer that to weekly lectures about my fat ass and my 'alternative lifestyle.'" I make air quotes as I realize I'm not struggling to breathe or make jokes.

Huh, I think. *I'm really getting better at this.*

I can see The Abbey ahead. I love that place. It used to be a funeral home, and they totally redid it to make a kick-ass bar-restaurant-coffee shop combo. It's sort of ridiculous, and the food is amazing, and I love to sit there and work sometimes, alternating a glass of wine with an iced coffee just because I can.

Isaac sees where my eyes land and he raises a brow at me. "Want to stop to hydrate?"

"Holy shit, yes," I say. I grab his arm and run faster until I'm tugging open the door to the bar. I'm not even out of breath. The hostess looks at us and makes a face, and only then do I remember that we're wearing running clothes and, frankly, Isaac smells like his were worn already.

He doesn't seem phased that we're in a trendy place looking like we just finished jazzercise. "We're just here for drinks," he says, placing his hand on my back and guiding me over toward the bar. I stare at his arm, stunned by how good it feels on my back. I don't typically go out with men who take charge like this. I definitely don't go out with guys who wear workout gear to a trendy bar. Not that I'm "out" with Isaac. We just happen to be getting a drink after a training run for some corporate nonsense our bosses are forcing us into.

There's only one stool open at the bar and Isaac gestures toward it. "What," I say. "You think I'm so feeble after the run that I need to sit? Like I'm going to collapse? Maybe *you* need to sit so you don't pass out from the stink fumes from those skanky running clothes."

"Fair enough," he says, giving his shirt a sniff and smiling. "I did already run this morning. Don't mind if I do sit."

He makes a big show of sinking into the stool and stretching out his long legs. He puts his arms up on the bar, grinning. "Maybe you can give me laundry advice. That setup you've got on the first floor is pretty sweet."

I lean against the bar next to him, regretting giving up the stool. My lower back starts to hurt as my heart rate slows down. I shiver, realizing I worked up a sweat getting here and it must be evaporating and making me cold. *Oh god, do I stink as much as Isaac?*

I try to catch a whiff of myself and the smug fucker catches me. He leans toward me, smiling, and takes an exaggerated sniff. "Don't worry," he says. "You don't smell any worse than me."

CHAPTER THIRTEEN
ZACK

"This is probably going to come out wrong," I start, "but how did you get interested in home renovations? You're a refined businesswoman…" She snorts. "I mean by appearances. Nobody would call your personality refined."

She nods, tapping her fingers on the bar and looking impatient. "I bought a shit hole house in a shit hole neighborhood to spite my parents and I made it nice to prove that I could."

I nod. "I, too, bought a shit hole house. But I haven't put in the time to fix it up much."

She looks at me, considering. "I did most of the work when I was right out of college," she says. "I was lower on the ladder at work and had more time."

I finally manage to flag down the bartender and order us each a light beer. There's no way I'll make it back to Nicole's house on foot if I drink anything heavier.

"What's with Beltane," she asks, chewing on a plastic drink stirrer.

"Beltane?"

"Yeah," she says. "The name of your family's company? It's a sun festival right? Like a Celtic pagan sort of thing?"

I shrug. "My grandma emigrated here from Ireland. My family's kind of into all that stuff. Dad believes in a *Lion King* sort of approach to business."

She starts twirling a stray lock of hair around one finger, and I have to

57

exercise all my self-control not to lean over and join in, entwining my fingers with hers in those messy locks. "Lion King approach?"

I crack a smile. "Yeah. You know. 'Everything the light touches is our kingdom.'" I do my best James Earl Jones impression and Nicole bursts out laughing. I decide I'll give up all my independence and my entire reputation as a hard-ass if I can hear her make that sound again.

We talk about her first job as a project manager at a tech company, and it turns out she knows my college roommate, Rayland. "You lived with Ray-Ray?" Her eyes go wide. "No, actually that makes sense. He's some brooding genius." The bartender comes back with our beers and she continues. "He was actually a dream to work with because I never had to hound him for anything. He always met deadlines and entered everything on our project spreadsheets. When he left for grad school, the idiot who replaced him was a nightmare."

I laugh. "You'd love working with engineers," I tell her. "Brooding cyborg describes just about all of us except maybe my brother Cal."

I reach for my wallet to pay and Nicole actually growls at me. "You're not buying my damn drink," she says.

"You're about to be a quarter million dollars in the red, Ms. Kennedy," I remind her. "You should accept the beer."

"How many times do I have to tell you to stop telling me what to do?" Her face turns red. I love driving her wild like this. I make a mental note to tell her what to do every time I see her, and another mental note to *imagine* telling her what to do while naked…later when I'm home alone, that is. I already beat off once today thinking about Nicole, but after this I'm going to have to go again when I get home.

I'm not proud of it, but looking at her now, all sweaty in her tight running stuff, I'm not sorry about it either. The bartender takes my card and looks between me and Nicole. "Both beers on the one card," I tell him, not taking my eyes off Nicole.

She glares at me, picks up her drink, and chugs it down in about three seconds. She just opens her throat and pours the liquid down like it's water, and slams the glass down on the bar before I even can get mine raise to my lips.

"There," she says. "We hydrated. I'm heading back."

"Shit," I mutter as she makes her way through the crowd toward the door. *She's actually serious.* I knock back a few swigs of my drink and quickly sign the credit card receipt and take off after her. The second she gets outside, she starts running, but I know she can't hold that pace for long, so I go slow and steady. She runs along in good form, lasting much longer than I expect.

I decide right there in the cold, chasing her, that I don't give a shit anymore that she's a client. That line I didn't want to cross has slid right into the river with her yard. I have to catch her, and I have to touch her. When she steps aside to bend over, hands on her thighs, breathing heavy, I come up behind her and place my hand on her back, the heat of her body radiating through the cold and into my palms.

Christ, she feels good. As she breathes heavily, I lean down so my mouth is right near her ear. "I had no idea you could open your throat like that," I whisper. "You should show me again."

She whips her head over at me and growls as she stands up straight. I watch her decide to let go of her restraint. She shoves me toward the alley, planting two hands right on my chest and pressing hard. My back hits the bricks and I grin at her, heaving and glaring.

I press off the wall and box her in against the opposite wall, her face in the shadows of the alley, her breath puffing out in a cold white cloud in the night air. "Why'd you run out of there?"

She shrugs. "You pissed me off."

I lean in closer, rocking my hips into her and her eyes drop to my crotch when she feels how hard I am. "Maybe I like when you're pissed off." My voice is low, mouth right by her ear.

"What are you doing," she says, but her eyes tell me she knows exactly what I'm doing.

"Waiting for you to tell me to stop," I say, leaning in closer, closer as my heart pounds in my ears. I can see her own pulse ticking in her neck. She doesn't tell me to stop, and I don't, crushing my mouth against hers.

Her plump lips are cold against mine, and she tastes like light beer. She moans into my mouth and I thrust my hips against hers, pinning her against the wall. My dick is so hard I can feel it straining against the seams of my running pants. I don't dare take my hands off the brick wall beside her head, though. Once I lay my hands on her again, I'm not going to be able to stop, and I'm not quite so far gone that I'm going to fuck her in an alley.

Unless she asks for that.

She digs her hands into my shoulders as she tries to pull my head closer into hers, her tongue sliding into my mouth and tangling with mine. And then she pulls back just as suddenly. "Well what the fuck do we do now," she spits out, looking around, as if a warm bed will suddenly appear in the winter night.

I laugh, half at her and half at the ridiculous predicament. "Now we run back to your house so I can fuck you," I say, knowing it's a bad idea and utterly powerless to stop.

She takes a deep breath and ducks out from under my arm. She starts running, faster than before. "Easy," I tell her, falling into stride beside her. "If you pass out, I won't be able to bend you over that counter of yours."

"You wish," she says, puffing but not sounding winded. "When we do this, I'm on top." She puffs again, but speeds up. We get to a red light and I laugh as she looks both ways for cars and runs through the intersection without stopping to catch her breath.

I admit, I'm pretty pleased with the thought of her riding me, those tits bobbing near my face as she finds her rhythm. But I can't bring myself to just let her get her way. Everything about tonight feels like a challenge, and after the time I've had at work lately, I'm in the mood to win.

I dismiss the thought that fucking her is not going to make anything at work any easier.

I lean down toward her ear again as we weave through a crowd of people. "No," I say. "I'm going to strip you out of those tights and bend you over so your ass is in the air. I'm going to smack it until your cold skin turns pink while I shove my cock into you from behind, and you're going to come so hard your screams will shake a little more of your back yard into the river."

She stops abruptly and I almost trip over her. She turns to look at me. "Do not joke about my landslide, Isaac," she says. There's something about the sound of my full name on her lips that has my cock jolting in my pants again. Nobody calls me that except her.

"Don't tell me what to do, Ms. Kennedy," I say, starting to run again. We pick up the pace until we're sprinting toward her townhouse. The old lady next door sticks her head out and tries to talk to Nicole but she mutters something to her and punches at the numbers on the key pad.

The door opens and she grabs me by the shirt, hauling me inside. She actually tries to shove me to the floor and climb on top of me, but I reach for her arm and pull her in toward my chest. We stay like this for a few beats, both of us catching our breath from the run, from the adrenaline. She licks her lip and her eyes flash, and I lose control.

"Turn around," I tell her, spinning her in my arms and frog walking her through to the kitchen. When we get to the counter, I take each of her hands in mine and place them against the dark marble. "Hold on," I growl.

CHAPTER FOURTEEN
NICOLE

Nobody talks to me this way, I think, as Isaac Brady does exactly what he said he would and yanks down my pants. Nobody has ever talked to me this way, and nobody has made me feel this fucking excited before, either.

I love sex, and I love it on my terms, which means me on top grinding just so against my date's pubic bone until I detonate my lady rocket. I don't do relationships. I don't really even do second dates. I have no room in my life for that. Sex is for release, animalistic and sweaty. Then I go home and sleep in my own damn bed by myself as God intended.

So when I feel the crack of Isaac's palm on the cold skin of my ass, I shriek. In that instant, I realize I've been going about this very, very wrong. He rubs his hand on my ass cheek a few times and then brings his hand down on the other cheek. I gasp as his cold finger tips massage their way between my legs, finding me wet and hot and wanting.

He slides one long finger inside me. It's cold and smooth, the contrast to my own sizzling heat making me pant. "Fuck, Isaac," I mutter, biting my lip and looking over my shoulder. I see him standing there, wild eyed, with one hand palming his dick above the waistband of his pulled-down pants while the other hand thrusts in and out of my pussy.

He looks dark and fierce and very, very sexy. "What are you waiting for," I say.

He pulls his hand out of me and wraps it in my hair, giving it a tug and bending my head back. "I'm clean," he growls, "and I don't have a condom. I want to fuck you bare."

"Oh shit," I pant as he tugs again on my hair, the tingles on my scalp in contrast to the slow, aching pulse of my core. "Yes," I breathe. This isn't a thing I do, not with the men who are happy enough to let me take charge of our carefully choreographed encounters. Isaac Brady isn't satisfied and his long arms feel powerful. At home on my body.

"Please," I beg. I actually fucking beg him to take me raw. He grunts as he slides inside me, spearing me on his cock in one swift thrust that makes both of us groan.

The angle of my hips somehow makes his cock feel like it's brushing against every nerve ending in my body. As he thrusts inside me, harder and faster, I feel my orgasm building on its own. Like he's scraping it out of me. I refuse to tell him it feels good, and I have just enough brain capacity to realize that's ridiculous.

"Come for me, Nicole," he grunts, giving my hair another tug.

"Don't tell me what to do," I spit back at him, thrusting my hips back to meet his as we crash together. He's got one hand on my hip for leverage and I hear the sound of our bodies slapping together. Both of us have our pants around our ankles, fully dressed on top as his bare cock slides in and out. I'm so wet, I can feel my slick arousal coating my upper thighs the harder he fucks me. Jesus, I had no idea it feels so good to get totally pounded like this.

"You feel so fucking good," he says, growling. I can feel his sack bumping against my crotch, and I like that, too.

"I love feeling your balls," I groan, leaning forward more, my hands sliding across the counter as my palms start to sweat.

Isaac redoubles his efforts, thrusting impossibly fast. I close my eyes. *Can I really come this way,* I wonder, and I pick up one hand to reach between my legs, desperate for the friction. He roars and pulls my hand away, pinning it down on the counter with the hand that had been in my hair, which is now flying all over the place as my body jolts with his thrusts.

He smacks my ass again, and I just...let go. I stop thinking and my body takes over until I'm coming. I come so long and so hard that my forehead drops against the counter. I cry with relief that my clit isn't broken, and then I come some more. I feel my moans practically shaking the windows in their panes and I know I'm screaming his name, screaming for him to keep going. "Fill me up, Isaac," I shriek. "Jesus, fuck, this feels so good. I want your come."

And he gives it to me. With two more slamming thrusts that bounce my hip bones off the cabinets, I feel his balls slap against me again and then I feel him swell inside me, thrusting and spurting as he bites my shoulder and breathes against my ear.

"Nicole," he moans, still spasming. Finally, he stills, and he leans against my back. I slump over the counter, my chest heaving.

Soon, my legs start cramping, whether from running or being fucked in this position I'm not sure. I grimace and try to move out from under him, but this makes him slide out from my body and I feel...empty once his cock leaves me, even though I can still feel it right there, wet and sticky against my ass cheek.

I wriggle out of his long arms and grab for a water glass in the sink, not caring if it's dirty. I start chugging water and I realize he's staring at me. And no wonder. I've got my pants around my ankles, my ass is probably red from being slapped, and I'm downing water like I'm in a boat race at kegger.

I finish the water and groan in gratitude. And then my baggage starts taking over my thought patterns. I just fucked my engineer in my kitchen, and I really fucking liked it, and I can't handle that right now.

"You can head on out now," I tell him, flipping my hair back out of my eyes. "We've both got work tomorrow and I'm sure you're hungry."

"What?"

I gesture toward the door. "You don't have to stay. You don't have to cuddle me or anything like that."

Isaac stands staring at me, his mouth working up and down. I've stunned him, and that surprises me. I thought we were on the same page here. I like that I can see so much of myself in him. No nonsense. Nothing emotional. We just had a fucking great time, and now we can each go on home to bed and get on with our evening.

"You're serious right now?" Isaac's eyebrows are so far up his forehead I almost can't see them behind his messed up sex hair.

"Yes, Isaac. I'm kicking you the hell out so I can go wash your spunk from my vag and go to bed."

He laughs as he squats down to pull up his pants, shaking his head. Then he keeps laughing. "What?" I stand with my hands on my hips, refusing to give him the satisfaction of seeing me bend over to pull up the pants he probably ripped pulling them down over my birthing hips.

That's what my mother calls my wide ass. Birthing hips.

"Tell me something," he says, reaching for his keys where he left them on my counter with his gym bag.

"What?" I repeat, my voice getting shrill and high. I start tapping my nails against the counter.

"Was I better than the purple Babe Rocket?"

I feel the flush start at my knees and rise to the top of my ears. I thought we were both going to silently agree not to discuss that he'd signed for delivery of the vibrator I drunk-ordered last week. I haven't even managed to get off with the thing yet, and am probably going to send it back for a refund. Although something tells me I can conjure up memories of this kitchen tryst and it'll work just fine. "Get out, Isaac," I finally spit out at him. "Just go home."

And then he does something truly surprising. He laughs, slings his gym bag over his shoulder, and leans in to kiss my cheek, pausing to rest his forehead against mine. "I'll see you tomorrow," he says.

Then he's gone.

CHAPTER FIFTEEN
NICOLE

I wriggle uncomfortably on the stoop at Emma's house on Saturday after ringing the bell to their loft. Stag family dinner is usually at Tim and Alice's house, and it's usually on Sunday, but Emma and Thatcher are hosting a birthday party for their oldest kid, Wesley.

I can never decide if I'm supposed to just go up or wait to be greeted. If this were a normal day at Emma and Thatcher's house, I'd let myself in and help myself to her cheese drawer. But her parents are probably up there, and my boss. Years of growing up in Madeline Kennedy's household, with her cold, rigid manners, are hard to shake.

Sometimes I think I'm extra crass on purpose just as an added 'fuck you' to my prim mother. I shake my shoulders and shove the door open, adjusting my grip on the gift bag I'm carrying, and wincing a little as I climb the steps. I'm not sure if it was the run or the rough sex that's left me tender, but I'm not looking forward to the group run tomorrow if this keeps up.

At least I know my clit's not broken.

I hear the Stag family before I even slide open the door to the remodeled loft space. Emma's husband designed this place and did most of the work with his brothers. Which of course means that I helped with a lot of the work, too, because I knew how to do all this stuff. I smile, remembering those late nights with the Brothers Stag and Emma, giving each other shit and working together toward a common goal. As far as I'm concerned, those are my family memories. The ones that make me feel good.

I met Emma in college, at the very beginning of my quest to shed my family. She was also working to overcome her family's restrictive treatment of her epilepsy, and I really feel like the two of us grew up together, becoming confident women who make our own decisions. My mom used to complain when her friends achieved something, would hiss about how they probably cheated some system. When Emma got her book published and started winning awards, I was the first person in line with a paperback copy for an autograph.

When she got pregnant unexpectedly and wasn't sure what she wanted to do, I helped her make a fucking spreadsheet so she could come to her own conclusions.

I catch myself smiling at the sight inside. Emma's husband and their two kids, his brothers and all their zillion kids are building a tower from magnetic blocks. Tim's oldest kid, Petey, keeps kicking the tower over. "Little jerk," I mutter, adding my gift bag to the heap.

Emma catches sight of me and runs over, pulling me in for a hug like it's been months since we've seen each other. She's the only person who ever embraces me like this, really folds into the hug. *Ladies don't squeeze, darling,* my mother used to say when I'd try to hug her if I was upset.

"I'm so glad you're here," Emma says. "I know these big family dinners aren't your favorite."

I shrug. "They're growing on me," I tell her, honestly. Emma still has hold of my hands and cocks her head to the side, pondering something.

"Were you limping just now? Walking?"

"Ugh." I roll my eyes. "I've been training for that marathon thing Tim is making me run." At the sound of his name, my boss extracts himself from the heap of children and heads toward me.

"Nicole! Did I hear you mention the marathon?" Tim and his brothers have probably run ten miles this morning before the party. That thought leads me to think about Isaac running with his brothers, and then my mind wanders back to my kitchen last night and I realize I shouldn't be at a kids' party with my filthy brain.

"I'm working up to the four mile training run tomorrow," I tell him, gratefully accepting the cocktail Emma hands me. One reason I tolerate the Stags so well is they offer cocktails, even at baby parties. Tim frowns at the drink.

"It's very important that we beat Beltane," he says, gesturing at my drink. "I can have Tyrion send you the meal plan he made for us when my brothers and I were training for the full marathon."

I glare daggers at Tim and gulp down the drink. "Look, boss, I know your brother is a professional athlete and his wife is an olympian, but that's not me." I reach for one of the pastries sitting on the counter and bite into it. "I'm going to give this my best, but I'm not eating kale."

"Well then, you're not giving it your best, are you?" He crosses his arms. I can tell Tim and I are about to launch into a scold-a-thon, but we're interrupted by Emma's parents floating over to us.

Her parents and mine have gotten along swimmingly since Emma and I met in the dorms, which shows what I think of her parents. To be fair, Emma and her mom have been really working on their relationship since she got with Thatcher. I clench my entire body as her mom leans in for cheek kisses. "Nicole, you look radiant," she says.

"Thank you, Mrs. Cheswick. You look like the very definition of a glamorous grandma." She pinches her lips as Senator Cheswick chuckles.

He reaches out for a handshake and then frowns. "Say," he says, "what's this I hear about trouble with your property?"

"I'm not sure this is the place for—" Emma's mom starts to interrupt. But given the choice between talking about running with my boss, talking about babies with my best friend, or bitching about my yard with her dad...

"Ugh, Mr. Cheswick, I'm going to need another drink if I'm going to talk about the landslide." He laughs again, like I'm not serious, and I remember that Emma also comes from a house where real emotions were discouraged. "I've been stressed as fuck about my yard, frankly," I say, watching Mrs. Cheswick's eyes bulge out of her head.

Running with Isaac and banging Isaac were the two moments in over a week where I wasn't on the brink of hyperventilating that my yard was going to slide into the river and cost me two lifetimes worth of savings to get back.

I raise my eyebrows and take a sip of my drink, and give him the bare details of my situation. He scratches his chin. "You got an engineer on the job? I probably know a guy..."

"Let me guess," I tell him, sucking on an ice cube. "You know the folks from Beltane Engineering?"

He nods, grinning. "Mick and I go way back," he says. I remember what Isaac told me about his father collecting wives and I frown.

"Well, Mick's youngest son, Isaac, is handling the repair for me and I guess for my neighbor, even though I can't stand the old bat."

Emma's dad frowns and fiddles with his tie. "Landslides…gosh, Nicole, that's going to be expensive to repair."

I crunch down on the ice and nod. "Can I be really honest right now," I tell him, knowing I'm only going to be half honest because the real me would give his wife a heart attack. "I don't want to talk about money at my best friend's son's birthday party."

I excuse myself, and they look relieved, as I make my way back to the living room to watch a sticky toddler open his birthday presents. I nod toward Maddie, who mouths *nice rack* to me, and I laugh. I try to tamp down the feelings of fear that Isaac and his lawyer won't be able to find someone responsible for the landslide costs, that the city will condemn my house and I'll be tossed out on the street.

Maddie's right about my rack. I try to focus on how good I feel in another one of the fancy bras while I watch the little Stag open his gifts.

Wesley makes his way to my bag, and I allow myself a smug moment of happiness when he squeals about the plain red playground ball I brought him. "Wish we could roll it around in my back yard, kid," I mutter.

CHAPTER SIXTEEN
ZACK

Cal and Liam meet me by the running trail early on Sunday morning. The two of them aren't saddled with a beginner for the group run, but all of us are used to running way more than the four miles scheduled for today's group run. We can get in at least six miles before the crowds arrive, if we hurry.

I park next to Cal and interrupt him and Liam arguing about their living arrangements.

"I don't get why you don't want to move in with Granny," Cal says, smacking Liam's ass when he bends to stretch his hamstrings. "She'll feed us and she won't hear you coming in with your special company."

Liam kicks Cal in the ankle, making him hop on one foot in pain. "First of all, she won't feed us because she doesn't cook anymore, which you'd know if you visited more often." They're talking about our dad's Irish mother, who lives alone in Dad's childhood home that he refuses to sell. Granny is almost 90, grouchy as Liam, and neither dad nor Uncle Kellen can convince her to downgrade to a senior living arrangement.

Callum has been pushing Liam to end the lease on their bachelor pad so they can move in with our grandmother and maybe get some contractors in there to at least keep the squirrels out of the chimney.

Liam continues, saying, "and you're nuts if you think I'd be bringing special company into that drafty old house with my grandmother home."

I grunt my agreement with Liam. Cal is the ladies' man among us. I sniff and adjust my shirt, hoping my mannerisms don't give away the fact that I've had my own special company this week. Normally, I view my runs with my brothers as a time to escape the frustrations of work, but all of us view engineering as part of us. Our brains are just wired to think methodically and find solutions to problems. So I break code a bit to talk about the landslide project with them.

"I could use your advice if the two of you are done fighting over Granny." They look at me, eyes wide.

Liam snorts. "Yeah, because we're such model citizens. We're great at advice, Zack." We start running west on the path, toward the old prison by the Ohio River.

"I meant engineering advice. We all know Uncle Kellen is the only Brady worth giving out life advice." This gets a few grunts of approval and we run three abreast up the path, hopping around small patches of black ice. Nobody else is out this way, and the group runs will head the opposite direction on the recreational trail.

I tell my brothers about the landslide and my conversation with Jared. "I've combed through blueprints for the major construction projects nearby," I say, "but nothing seems off."

"Yeah, because the plans are made by engineers," Liam spits out. "Who did the actual construction on each of the sites?"

Liam is a structural engineer. While he works mostly on bridge projects throughout the city and with industrial clients in the region, he knows a lot about the local construction firms and the ones who cross their t's and dot their i's.

I try to picture the list of projects near Nicole's house. "I think Kellinger did a few. Rothermel definitely did one. I'd have to look."

"If any of them are Meyer, you should send one of my inspectors out to look at the work," he says, explaining that he recently found a number of potentially deadly errors on a bridge repair work that the Meyer company had completed. "Without my guys checking, we could have had a 20-ton crane collapse, spilling god knows what chemicals. God. I hate sloppy work." He spits off to the side of the path in frustration, then unzips his top layer.

As the sun comes out from behind a cloud, I can tell it's going to be warm by the time our group run finishes. I wish I had layered up like Liam. "I'll take a look. Thanks, brother."

They return to bickering about what to do about our grandmother, wondering why she won't just go move in with Uncle Kellen, since he lives alone in a much smaller house in a nearby neighborhood.

By the time we reach the prison, turn around, and run back to where we started, the corporate teams for the group run have begun to gather. Orla flips me the bird when she sees us.

"Thanks a lot, assholes," she says, gesturing toward our dad. "I've had to listen to at least six of his long stories so far. Why didn't you tell me you were pre-gaming?"

I'm about to apologize for leaving her out, when my dad catches my eye and gestures for me to come over to him. "Zack, great. I want you to come meet someone."

He starts pulling me over toward the Stag Law crew. Nicole is pouting by her boss and some other guys I assume work with them at the law firm. Her eyes widen as she sees me coming toward them with my dad. "Tim, Ms. Kennedy, I want you to meet my youngest son. Zack's going to come with us when we head to Paraguay."

Nicole and I both whip our heads toward Dad. "What?" We say at once. Dad laughs. "Trust me," he says. "This is a good idea. I want to tell you some of the ideas I had about our meeting with El Presidente."

Tim looks like he's not quite sure what to say to this new information and he frowns, considering. I don't blame him. From what I understand, this trip is a big opportunity for his firm to help establish a charitable foundation with one of their baseball player clients. Dad doesn't miss a beat, though. He claps Tim on the back.

"Why don't the four of us grab some brunch after this run and we can talk it over."

Nicole crosses her arms over her chest as the run leader picks up the bullhorn and starts his cheery welcome speech. "Tim, don't you have family dinner on Sunday afternoons? With your pregnant wife?"

He considers this as we start following the crowd toward the starting place for the run. "Hm," Tim says. "It's true, Mick. I've got some family obligations today. But you know what, I trust Nicole to run point on this. Plus she knows Zack already! You three go talk it out and brief me later." Tim claps Nicole on the back. "For now, though," he says, grinning, "I've got to pound out some miles to make sure Old Man Brady eats my dust in the relay."

Dad and Tim laugh and take off at a quick pace, talking about who knows what. Nicole looks at me like this is somehow my fault. "You're absolutely not coming along on my business trip," she says. "For one thing, you've got to fix my damn yard."

"Now who's telling who what to do," I tease. The fact that she doesn't want me to come along makes me decide I'm going to Paraguay now no matter what.

"It's whom," she says, not looking at me as she takes off toward the 16th Street Bridge. I guess we're not going to talk about Friday night.

CHAPTER SEVENTEEN
NICOLE

I RUN THE ENTIRE FOUR MILES WITHOUT STOPPING, AND I WANT TO CELEBRATE THAT fact with Isaac, but I'm too pissed off about him and his father sabotaging my trip to Paraguay. Tim Stag hired me to strategize the future of his law firm, and I can't do that when he's looping in golf buddies behind my back and having them bring their damn kids along on my information gathering trips for our clients.

Throughout the entirety of the run, my thoughts alternated between remembering Friday night and the way I feel strangled by Tim lately. He's not listening to me at work and, worse, he's making decisions without consulting me at all. I realize my miles were achieved in part thanks to my anger, and marvel that my head is feeling a bit clearer by the time we reach the turn-around point.

Isaac seemed as surprised by his father's antics as me, so at least there's that. I can hear him keeping pace right behind me throughout our run, and it drives me bananas that he doesn't say anything to me. I want him to pick a fight, say something annoying, drag me by the ponytail off into the bushes and fuck me again.

Ok, where did that last part come from? My thighs are burning as I speed up for the final stretch of our run, trying and failing to forget how it felt to spend time with him on Friday, to wrestle with his long, firm body in my kitchen until he had me screaming and panting for more.

Isaac's dad stands in the parking lot clapping his hands and cracking gum as we run up to him. "Is my son talking to you about your stride, Nicole? I know you're the competition and all, but he's also supposed to be coaching you here on these group runs."

"My stride?" I look over at Zack, confused.

He stares daggers at his father. "We just got past breath work, Dad. I'm not going to dump everything on her at once."

"What the hell is wrong with my stride?" Does he mean the way I'm moving my legs? God, are there things to change about that? Who are these people that they think they can stand there and watch me run and talk about my legs moving?

Mick Brady squints at his son, thinks for a minute, and shakes his head. "Zack's right, honey. I'm sure you'll get to talking about footwork eventually."

"I'm not your honey," I huff at him. And then I remember that he's a friend of my boss and I suck a breath in through my teeth. I ought to be using that 'in through the nose and out through the mouth' breathing method Isaac talks about when we're working hard. "I prefer Nicole or Ms. Kennedy."

Mick nods. "My bad, my bad. Let's head over to Mulligan's. We can walk. They've got great eggs." He starts off toward a dingy looking diner near the 16th Street bridge, and I'm surprised. He seems like the kind of man who'd hire a driver to take us to the William Penn or something more glamorous. Something serving alcohol at least.

When we get inside, Mick greets the hostess familiarly and Isaac stews, silently. We sit, the two of them opposite me at a small booth, and Mick orders rounds of orange juice for the table. "We all need the sugar after a long run," he says. "You get your miles in before the group run, son?"

My eyes widen as Isaac nods. They chat, apparently having all run about 10 miles today altogether. Here I was feeling so proud to run four without stopping to rest. And here I was feeling proud that I didn't pass out this time. Apparently I'm in over my head in both athletics and business lately.

We order our breakfasts, and Mick chastises his son for getting extra sausage, facing toward me and saying, "My boys never listen to me about healthy foods. The older two at least have their mother to influence them a bit. This one thinks I'm full of shit."

Isaac points a fork at his father and retorts, "First of all, you are full of shit, and second, I can eat sausage once a week. I'm not going to clog my arteries."

I frown, focusing back on what Mick said about Cal and Liam's mom. I remember what Zack said, about not seeing his mom since he was a baby. My own mother would have fainted if she saw me order an omelet with the yolks in it, let alone a side of bacon. In front of men, no less.

Mick leans back and presses his lips together. "Hmm," he says. "Guess he probably didn't tell you about his mother when he was surveying your rotational landslide." I open my mouth to correct him, but Mick charges on ahead. "Thing is, Ms. Kennedy, I make better decisions about engineering than I do about my personal life."

"Dad, we don't need to talk about this."

Mick waves a hand at his son and tries to bat away the toast Isaac is buttering. "It's white bread, son. This stuff will kill you! Look at your grand-father." Mick turns toward me. "Zack's mother thought having a baby would help our relationship. She...she wasn't cut out to be anyone's parent." Zack looks like he's going to snap his butter knife in half, slathering the butter and smashing the bread to pieces in the process. "She skipped town not too long after Zack was born. He grew up coming to work with me most of the time. That's what gave him such an edge as an engineer, I think."

Mick talks about Isaac's early aptitude for math, describing earth dams he'd build in the puddles on work sites and the ways he'd put on a tiny hard hat to join his uncle inspecting mine shafts. "I think my boy here can feel the earth move beneath his hands," Mick says. "That's why I want him to come with us to Paraguay."

The food arrives and I dig in to my omelet, catching Isaac's eye as he just looks at me, smoldering and sweaty. When I lick my lip, I taste salt on my skin, reminding me of how he tasted the other night in my kitchen. Mick keeps talking. "You know, we're going in late February, right at the tail end of their rainy season. Did you know that?"

I shake my head. "I haven't read much about the country..." I pretty much only read up on Augusto Cruz and his immediate family.

Mick nods and winks. "That entire region has terrible landslides. Just devastating. They don't have a lot of infrastructure to start with, I mean compared to here. And what they do have gets washed away in these monsoons. Your Mr. Cruz would know all about it, especially if he managed to make a name for himself as a ball player despite all this."

"Hm." I start to feel a bit foolish that I don't already know more about the region we're visiting, and make a note to start skimming the news sections and reading up on Paraguay and surrounding nations.

"I ask you," Mick continues, pausing to eat some fruit. "What do you think is important to this flashy baseball player? These other guys, they start foundations, it buys what? Shoes and gloves for kids in Puerto Rico? Batting helmets? Those things aren't going to do a sniff of good to kids who can't walk to school because the road washed out."

"Dad, I don't think Nicole wants to hear about landslides while she's eating."

"Of course she does," Mick counters. "Her client is creating a foundation. That foundation could service the foundation of his homeland. Reinforce the roads so they don't wash into the sea." This is starting to sound more and more interesting, and I can see why Tim likes spending time with this guy. I would never have thought to care about how the rainy season somewhere might impact how its celebrity athletes share their wealth. But I'm also not convinced it's relevant to a foundation that Augusto Cruz will create.

"This is really fascinating," I say, and I swear I can see Isaac's neck muscles spasm. I pull out my phone and tap in a few notes to remind myself what Mick is saying. "Flood relief," I say. "That could have appeal to donors. And people in Pittsburgh can relate to that, especially fans who live along the Mon River."

I'm not fully convinced what I'm saying is true.

Mick nods. "Now, do you know what flood relief means?"

"Oh, Jesus. Here we go." Isaac throws down his napkin, crosses his arms, and leans back. I shake my head.

"We're not talking about boxes of Red Cross rations or sand bags to hold back the river. Flood relief, real relief, means someone with geotechnical knowledge proposing sustainable, affordable solutions. To repair roads, restore power. Secure the foundations of the homes built on the hillsides before they slide into the roads that just got repaired. Getting the nation functioning again at full capacity. That's flood relief."

"I have never thought about that at all," I tell him, truthfully. I chase my orange juice with a glass of water and try to process everything Mick is saying. "So where do you and Isaac come in to all of that?"

Mick grins. Isaac shakes his head. "Well, Augusto Cruz's foundation could help the government of Paraguay finance these infrastructure improvements. Pay the right experts to develop plans, supervise and execute the repair work for the nation." He claps Isaac on the back and rubs his shoulder. "Imagine if my son leads off his small talk with the president of Paraguay, talking about how he saved your house from falling into the Allegheny River?"

Now it's my turn to squint and cross my arms. I'm feeling really manipulated here, and I don't like it at all. Mick points a long finger at me. "This could be a very mutually beneficial trip for our companies, Ms. Kennedy. If we play our cards right."

CHAPTER EIGHTEEN
ZACK

I SPEND THE NEXT FEW DAYS IN A BLACK MOOD. MY DAD ALWAYS DOES SHIT LIKE this, steam rolling everyone in his path. Sure, his idea is sound. Probably even good. But he should have tipped me off to this plan from the beginning. He wants me to be all grateful to him that he saw this long term vision when he sent me to Nicole's back yard initially, rather than give me the promotion I've been working toward for years.

And I hate how Nicole looked steamrolled about the whole plan. I could tell that's not what she was going for at all, but also that she was in a hard spot between my dad and her boss leaping at Dad's ideas.

He wants me to be thankful that he's bothering to bring me by his side on this grand humanitarian mission. "Pah." I growl at the dirt in Nicole's yard. Blowing out a long breath, I note that the ground has sunk at least another foot since I was here last. It doesn't seem to be moving more horizontally, but I know I'm going to have to involve the city inspector soon if the slide doesn't settle. Nicole is going to murder me if her house gets condemned.

"But I'm going to tell her this is happening so she's well informed. Because I fucking respect her and nobody likes this sort of surprise," I mutter to myself, letting my tape measure snap back in with an angry snick.

I hate how I'm a sidekick for my father. All that shit about him fostering my love of the earth, as if his twisted version of childcare, dragging me to construction sites, was a positive thing.

"Yoo hoo!" I look over to see Nicole's neighbor waving her arms at me from her patio. "Can I talk to you?"

I start muttering under my breath while I extract myself from the trench in Nicole's half of the yard. It's deep enough that I had to toss a ladder down there today. I sigh, brushing the mud off my knees as I make my way toward Valerie. "What can I do for you, ma'am?"

"Have you read about the alligators? In the river?"

I squint my eyes at her and sniff to see if she's been drinking. "Alligators?"

She starts waving a newspaper in my face. "We've got alligators in the damn rivers! Some crack pot was keeping them at home and let them loose. Now they're mating or coming after us or I don't even know."

"Ma'am, I'm wondering if maybe you have me confused for someone else. I'm just an engineer—"

"What I want to know is whether my yard will become a ramp for these reptiles. Are they going to bite my ass while I'm pruning my hedge?"

I look out at her half of the yard, severed in half by the jagged trench formed by the landslide. On the far side of her property, her small raised garden beds sit untouched by the trauma. The trench running perpendicular to the shared property line is filled with the remains of what was surely once a fine hedge. "I don't think you need to be pruning your hedge any time soon."

"Don't be a smart ass. I see why she likes you," Valerie says, bonking me with the rolled up newspaper. "Are the gators going to climb onto my porch?"

I sigh. "I really don't think your yard is at any additional or different risk for alligators than any of your neighbors," I tell her. "But you'd have to call animal control to be certain."

I hear the patio door open on Nicole's half of the property and she sticks her head out. "Valerie, leave him alone. I hired him first," she says, but I can tell she's only half trying to sound mean.

"Have to pay me to hire me," I mutter, but neither of them hears me. Valerie crosses her arms over her chest and stares.

"You know, I'm on a fixed income," she says, softer now. I nod.

Nicole's face softens. "Val, I told you, I'm on top of this, ok? We'll rise or fall together on this. Isaac has a lawyer looking into it for us, ok?"

The three of us stand there for a few beats until Valerie nods and spins around, heading back into her house. "You wanna come in," Nicole asks, squinting at me as I make my way back to her trench to grab my ladder.

I want to. I want to take out all my frustrations and smack her ass again until the skin turns pink. I want to bite her neck and have her bite me back. But it's a bad idea. "Can't today," I say, not looking up at her. I walk out of her yard carrying the ladder before I have a chance to let my dick change my mind.

I don't go home after work, though. I drive over to my uncle's house, and smile when I see my cousin Orla's car in the driveway. That means there will be homemade dinner today.

I knock on the door. Orla throws it open and points at my feet. "Boots off," she says, pointing next at the black plastic tray inside the door. My uncle hasn't visited a job site in a decade, but his door is always open to Orla and me and my brothers...which means he's always ready to intercept our filth before we bombard his tidy home.

"Like I was gonna drag mud through the house," I mutter. Orla heads back into the kitchen and starts pouring me a glass of wine. My uncle stands at the stove, stirring something that smells amazing.

Kellen is as tall and slender as my father, and the pair of them are fit and fast, despite being in their 50's. But where my father always has an angle, Kellen is pure kindness. And so I frequently drive over to his place and pour my heart out to him, most often when I'm pissed at my dad. Like right now.

I scowl at the white wine Orla poured and when my uncle catches sight of my face, he gestures at me to sit, and reaches for his bottle of Irish whiskey that he keeps by the stove. Pouring me a few fingers, he wags a wooden spoon at me and says, "Spill, kid."

Orla makes herself scarce, mumbling something about her laundry.

Grateful, I sputter out the whole story from the diner, backtrack to the day I didn't get to present about the big dam project. "If he had this long-term vision, why didn't he tip me off? He made me look like an asshole in front of Nicole."

"Nicole, is it?" Kellen's brows shoot up as he leans on the counter. "That the woman with the rotational landslide in her back yard?"

I nod and sip my drink, swirling the liquid in the glass and smelling it like I'd been taught, letting it slide into my mouth and down my throat. My father and uncle both agree that it's a sin to slam back the holy water of our motherland.

We used to go to Ireland together once a year to see Granny and

Grandad's cousins. There's no real drinking age over there, and the Brady kids came of age drinking whiskey on the banks of the Duff River. Even as a teen, tipsy, I was interested in the land around the river, how the soil changed as the river charged closer to the ocean.

A timer beeps, and Kellen stoops to pull a pan from the oven. "Lucky for you, I always make extra if Orla's coming over," he says. "Unlucky for her, she won't have leftovers for her lunch tomorrow." We share a laugh at that.

"Need help setting the table?" The question is a courtesy. When we eat here, we fix our plates by the stove and generally stand or sit around the counter on tall stools. By the time Uncle Kellen felt ready to move out on his own with Orla, we were all teenagers, off to track meets and math olympics and robotics clubs.

Engineers to our souls, we made the most of efficient conversations over hearty food at this counter. Tonight would be no different. "Orla," Kellen shouts down the hall. "Chicken's out." He looks at me and sighs. "Your father should have given you some preparation before he sprung all that on the client. He gets so wrapped up in his long-term visions, he can't ever figure out the details of the moment."

I roll my eyes. "Yeah, yeah, that's where you've always come in. I know it. But you didn't have to stand there while Tim Stag and Nicole Kennedy looked like they weren't sure who to trust anymore."

"I'll talk to my brother about his plans for the Paraguay project," Kellen says, turning off the burners under the sauce and the vegetables. Orla saunters back into the room with a basket of clean, folded clothes, which she drops on the floor by the back door.

"Meanwhile," he says, scooping out a plate of food and handing it to me, "want to tell me about your progress with *Nicole.*"

Orla snorts, and I know neither of them is thinking about the project in her back yard. That just sends my mood back further into the dark side. I wanted Nicole to be my private business, a delicious secret just for me.

In a world with two older brothers, no mother, and a distracted father obsessed with work, I never had very many indulgences. Giving in to my lust for that woman was decadent and intoxicating, and it can never happen again.

She's too much. Too wild, too smart, too capable. The kind of woman I could let myself relax around. And, evidently, part of my dad's business schemes. That makes her off limits for my own emotional safety. Keeping my guard up around people was always the one thing keeping me afloat. It was too easy for people I cared about to walk out of my life otherwise.

My cousin and my uncle stare at me and I realize they're expecting an answer. "Project is coming along," I say. "I've got the plans drawn up to secure the yard. Gonna have to build a retaining wall. I'm going there tomorrow to walk the property line again with the plans for the nearby residential construction."

The two of them share a glance and a smile, and I know I haven't done a good job at all of hiding my extracurricular feelings for this particular client. Kellen chews a bit, thinking. "I wasn't asking about the work, kiddo."

I swallow and shake my head. "There can't be anything other than the work," I tell him. "Not with her wrapped up in Dad's business interests." Kellen frowns, makes eyes with Orla, and nods. I don't add the part where there can't be anything more because I can already tell that Nicole Kennedy has the power to eviscerate me. If I let her in, it'll crush me when she decides to hit the road. It's better that she kicked me out with my pants around my ankles. Just sex. Just that once.

We finish our meal in silence.

CHAPTER NINETEEN
NICOLE

Maddie picks up Emma, who says she has two hours to chill before she has to go home and feed Ricky, so the two of them come to my house to ogle the trench in the yard. We stand in the sun room drinking wine and staring at it.

Maddie taps on the glass and frowns. "If only there were a bra for your yard," she says, adjusting her own fine rack. We nod, sighing.

Emma squints. "So any movement with getting the insurance to pay? Or finding someone to sue?" I shake my head.

"And what about your orgasm situation," Maddie asks.

I pound my forehead against the glass, muttering, "at least that's been partially solved."

"Partially?" Emma and Maddie raise their brows in unison while I nod.

"I might have boned the nerdy engineer."

Maddie claps her hands. "Ooh, this is excellent information. Where's the rest of the wine?"

They pester me until I explain that I came for him, hard, and Emma starts jumping up and down. She knows my whole deal with sex, that I only like it specific ways and under specific terms. But somehow it feels inappropriate to elaborate on the religious experience I had with him in my kitchen. I decide to pivot and tell them how I'm feeling sabotaged at work.

"Want me to have Thatcher talk to Tim?" Emma starts patting my back.

"Absolutely fucking not, Emma Stag. This is my career and I'm going to solve it. I just wanted to vent about it."

Maddie nods furiously. "Yes. I'm here for you. Vent away, because that's some bullshit." She starts to explain how things aren't going so hot for her at work, either. There are some layoffs coming up at the newspaper and she's feeling concerned. Emma actually hasn't been replaced since she left to be a full time author, and Maddie and the other writers were already pulling double duty before the layoffs.

"Work is shitty," I say. "Just all around."

"Yeah," they say, nodding.

"But also I love what I do," I tell them. I open a box of crackers and we pass that around, still staring at the trench. "I really love my fucking job."

We all sigh and munch our snacks a bit longer in silence before Emma says she has to go before her boobs burst. I'm actually sort of curious to see what that looks like, but I trust her to know her body. I walk the girls out to Maddie's car with hugs and promises to call with updates about the work situation.

"And the orgasms. Keep us posted about those," Emma says, looking serious enough that I laugh. I haven't been able to coax any more from my body manually yet, but the day is young. The sky looks slightly ominous as Maddie pulls out of her parking spot.

I head inside and decide I could map out some plans for work or I could try out the Babe Rocket one more time. Babe Rocket wins out, and I rummage under my bed trying to find it from where it rolled around on the floor the last time I threw it across the room.

I'm just about to settle back on my sheets and crank it up when I'm startled by the onset of a sudden rainstorm. Squinting out the window, I see a man standing in the back yard. *Isaac.*

What the hell is he doing standing out there in the rain?

CHAPTER TWENTY
ZACK

I spend the morning drawing up the plan of attack for Nicole's yard. Nobody has contacted me with any more details about traveling to Paraguay, so I do nothing else regarding the research for that project. We haven't figured out funding for Nicole's project yet—I know she doesn't have a quarter million dollars. She can't even put her house up for a loan at this point.

So until I find a culprit for her insurance to sue, we're stuck spinning our wheels planning a restoration, rather than executing.

The sun peeks out around three in the afternoon, so I decide to head over to her place. I've got the plans in my truck for the apartment complexes nearby, and after studying them a bit, I stand in her yard, just staring. These are new, trendy construction projects, with roof gardens and shit.

One of the condo buildings even has a damn labyrinth in the back courtyard. I scoff, imagining people walking laps back there, trying to find inner peace. Hell, my dad will probably crash their labyrinth party and walk out of there with six new contracts to engineer meditation chambers in everyone's office.

I kick a beer can that's rolling along the sidewalk, wondering why I can't see what it is that led to Nicole's yard just falling off the back of her property. Yes, this is Pittsburgh and these things happen. But it's always after an unseasonal torrential rain.

And then, as if I conjured the weather by thinking it, the sky rips open and it begins to pour. "Fuck," I shout, but I don't head for my truck.

I stand with my hands on my hips staring at the neighboring building, with its rain garden and its rain barrels. I stand there, getting soaked to the skin, hoping above hope that a solution presents itself to me, that I can find something. But all I'm feeling is wet.

"Isaac! Isaac Brady!" Nobody calls me Isaac, except Nicole, and I love the sound of my full name on her lips. I turn to find her standing on her patio, waving her arms at me to come toward her. And of course I do. "What in the hell are you doing out here in this weather?" She looks at me like I've lost my mind.

I shrug. "Engineers frequently work outside in all sorts of weather," I tell her, trying to sound nonchalant, but my teeth start chattering and the jig is up.

"Well, come inside and get warm at least," she says, heading in through the sliding door.

"You finally gonna give me that laundry tutorial?" I stop right inside the door, not really sure what to do. I can't very well walk through her house and streak mud everywhere, drip streams of water on her oil finished hardwood floors. I take off my hard hat and set my phone on the little table inside the door.

She just stares at me, considering.

I'm considering, too. What am I doing inside her house? Can I handle it if I'm inside her again and then she tosses me out? Nicole bites the side of her lip and crosses her arms over her chest, and I realize that not fucking her is impossible right now.

She sighs, pretending to be exasperated. "Well I can't very well give you a tutorial if you're still wearing the wet, muddy clothes." She raises a brow at me and I'm done.

I unzip and peel off my sopping wet fleece jacket and toss that down on the mat inside the door and, not taking my eyes off hers, I start to slowly unbutton my shirt. It's a terrible idea being in here with her. It's terrible for me to give in to my feelings for this woman, because I don't just lust after her.

I crave her smart mouth and the way she cares about her elderly neighbor, even if she acts like Valerie is a pain in the ass. I crave her attention to detail, the way she's carefully set up her home so that everything has a place.

I know I will come to regret this, because I can't let myself get attached to anyone who might leave me. My own mother didn't want me. I've got my siblings and my cousin, and that's enough for me. Women have always just been a diversion for me. I end relationships before they get serious.

But I don't care about any of that as Nicole stands in the hall, beckoning for me. I brush my hair out of my eyes and walk toward her, ignoring the gnawing fear that Nicole will become one more woman in my life who walks out on me just as I succumb to needing her.

I finish unbuttoning my shirt. I want those detail-oriented fingers on my skin.

Nicole stands, considering me, watching as I strip in her kitchen. I pull the belt from my jeans and toss it next to my fleece and I unfasten my pants, letting them pool at my ankles. Wearing just my boxers, I bend over to untie my work boots. I hear Nicole's breath increase in speed as she watches me.

And then my teeth start chattering again and she approaches me. "Come with me," she says, stooping to pick up my stuff. I follow her down the hall, close enough that I know my breath tickles her neck as she shoves my clothes in her washer. "Do you have anything else in your pockets that shouldn't get wet?" She sets my wallet and keys on the counter in her laundry room.

I shake my head and press myself against her back, craving her heat and her nearness in equal degrees. Cranking the dial to start the machine, Nicole sighs and turns around. Her green eyes meet mine and we stare at each other, our breath matching pace.

"You going to stare at me all night while I shiver in your laundry room?" I feel like giving her shit because I want to see how she responds. Her mouth curls up in a grin.

"I considered it," she says. She reaches out a hand and traces my dick through my boxers, and even though I'm chilled through, it springs to life at her touch. "As you saw, I've got some pretty good hardware to service my own needs."

"I shouldn't have signed for it," I say, snaking a hand through her messy curls. "I should have turned them away and walked directly upstairs and shown you what a real cock can—" Her mouth crashes into mine, cutting off my comeback.

I back her up against the washer as her tongue probes my mouth. Her teeth close on my lip and we moan together. As she drags her short nails along my shoulders, I shudder again and she pulls her head back. "Bed," she says. "It's warmer there."

Grabbing my hand, she starts striding through the narrow house and up the stairs. I notice that the hardwood doesn't even creak beneath our feet, and my mind starts drifting to the work she must have done installing a sub-floor, before I shake my head and focus on the woman in front of me.

CHAPTER TWENTY-ONE
NICOLE

I wasn't going to invite him inside. I really wasn't. But when I saw him standing there in the rain, just staring at the apartment building a few doors down, the water streaking off his coat, rolling off his hard hat...well, it made me want him to bend me over the counter again.

Now that I've got him inside and mostly naked, he's not bending me over the counter, so much as trailing behind me, drooling and shivering. I shove him into my bed and pull the covers up from the foot of the bed, where they're still bunched from when I climbed out this morning.

My bedroom is the only messy place in my house. In my universe, really. I keep everything else strategically, painstakingly organized. But this room? Nobody is ever in here. My housekeeper doesn't even come in here. This king-sized bed is mine to thrash around in, and I've got mismatched blankets chosen not for looks, but for comfort.

The flannel sheets I've got on there right now? They feel like...well they feel like really nice flannel fucking sheets, and I shove Isaac onto them with a grunt, shirking out of my clothes as I climb in on top of him.

He props himself half up on his elbows, a move that shows off the ridges of his stomach muscles. I guess that's what ten miles a day will do for a body. "Damn, Brady," I say, straddling him and shoving him all the way back down to the sheets. "I didn't even get to see you naked last time."

The smug fucker laces his fingers together behind his head and grins at me. "You can stare at me naked all you want, Ms. Kennedy." I like the way he says my name like that, deep and slow, teasing but still holding a hint of danger that reminds me of the feral way he plowed into me the last time we tried this.

"This is a terrible idea," I mutter, reaching behind my back to unclasp my bra. I hadn't planned on seeing him today, on him seeing me, but I'm grateful for the deep red, satiny bra that hoists my breasts inward and upward. I can see his dick twitch in his boxers as I peel away the bra.

"Just awful," he mutters, his rough palms reaching up to my breasts. He cups the sensitive skin there, weighing my tits in his hands before rolling the nipples between his thumbs and forefingers. "You're so fucking beautiful," he says, and there's a serious look in his eyes that I don't like.

It's a look that says this is more than just chemistry, more than just two people whose pheromones attract. I ease out of his grasp and kneel on the bed, sliding his boxers down his legs as he lifts his hips to help.

"Oh shit. Oh god. Nicole," he starts muttering as I lick my way down his firm legs and squeeze his cock, jutting out of the dark tangle of pubic hair that stands out in stark contrast to his pale, muscled skin.

I take my time studying this unfamiliar terrain with the tip of my tongue and one careful fingertip. "Is this ok?" When I look up to his eyes again, they're screwed tight and I see he's biting his lip.

"Fuck, yes, Nicole. Do not stop. Please. Oh god." One of his hands twists into my hair while the other smacks the headboard as I start to circle his cock head with my tongue.

My hand slides down his shaft, his foreskin bunching in my hand and making a sort of cushion while I stroke him. No wonder this felt so good inside me. His dick is magnificent, long and hard and smooth. A perfect cock. I slide my mouth over him, bobbing my head up and down a few times before releasing him with a pop. "You ready to talk about laundry now? Feeling warmer?"

When his eyes meet mine this time, I swear he growls at me as he sits up and lifts me from under my armpits. He rolls us around so he's on top of me then, and his mouth drops to my nipple. He laves his tongue along the hard nub and, pushing my tits together with his hands, switches over to the other side as he rocks his cock along my wet underwear.

"The only laundry I care about right now are these dirty panties," he says, and he moves to start sliding them down my legs. And then he brings them to his face and fucking sniffs my panties, moaning before dipping a hand right to my center.

Jesus, he's filthy and crass and I fucking love it. "Obscene," I murmur, rocking my hips to encourage his hand closer to my pulsing core. I gasp as he slides a thick finger inside of me. Apparently Isaac Brady is fantastic at fucking me frantically in the kitchen, and leisurely in my bed.

"You're as wet as my clothes," he murmurs, sliding his finger deeper, deeper still, before crooking it toward him in a move that sends waves of pleasure right through me.

This is where I should explain to him that I have to be on top in order to come, that guys have been trying for years to get me off in various other layouts and it just doesn't work unless I'm the one controlling the friction, controlling the pace. The last time was a fluke, and my clit has been broken. But before I can tell him, he pulls his hand out from inside me and smacks my clit sharply.

"Eyes up here, Nicole," he says, and my mouth drops open. He pinches my clit, then rubs it, then slides his finger back inside me and I splinter to pieces as my eyes lock on his. I swear I can feel the lightning bolt travel between us. He urges me on with just the fire of his gaze, and he sends me the orgasm through his flaming pupils.

Staring into his face, I come undone. "Isaac," I wail, a guttural noise seeping from my body as I moan and thrash around on the covers. "Isaac!"

I come so long, so hard, I swear I'm going to come out of my skin, but his hand is on my shoulder, holding me flat and grounding me. "You look so fucking sexy when you come," he says. He withdraws his hand from my throbbing channel and strokes my upper thigh, staring at me like I'm the most amazing thing he's ever seen.

And then he actually says, "You're the most beautiful woman I've ever seen," and I gasp.

"I need you inside me," I tell him, my fingers fumbling on the slick skin of his shoulders, trying to pull him closer. I could drown in his eyes in this moment, the way he's looking at me like I'm everything to him.

"Hm," he says, not moving. He stares at my bedside table like he's looking for a condom, but we already discussed this last time.

"Ugh, it's fine. I've got a shot in my arm. I won't get pregnant." I don't make a habit of fucking men without protection. In fact, I never do that. But I was so carried away and he felt so god damned good, the way he took charge of me like that, made me come. Literally MADE me come. I shudder.

I press a finger against his swollen lips. "Now fuck me."

He bites the tip of my finger as he thrusts inside. My eyes roll up in my head at the pleasure of feeling stretched by him. His cock is everywhere as he grinds and thrusts. He's pounding into me until my tits shake, and he stares down at them from his position propped up on his elbows.

"Fuck yeah," he says, grinning. He thrusts a few more times and then abruptly pulls out and rolls me on my stomach. "On your knees, Nicole."

I'm too overcome to consider not following his instructions. I rest my weight on my forearms and lift my ass, and he slams into me as his palms press down on my shoulders. I love it. "Jesus, Isaac. This is amazing," I grunt out as he presses me down while filling me up.

The angle of this sends pleasure rippling through my entire body. I can feel him stroking every nerve inside my pussy. "Where do you come from?" I roar and moan and just succumb to him pounding through me, bare and so hard compared to my swollen softness.

He growls again and stiffens and I feel him swell inside me. And then, abruptly, he pulls out and I feel the hot splatter of his release spray across my back. I look over my shoulder to see him holding his dick, staring as it spurts.

It's the dirtiest thing anyone has ever done to me, and I love it so intensely I'm not sure what to do. While Isaac's dick twitches, he reaches between my legs and rubs slow circles above my cleft until I come again, shuddering and writhing beneath him and both of us heave, out of breath and exhausted.

CHAPTER TWENTY-TWO
NICOLE

"You going to kick me out again?" Isaac mops at my back with a tissue until he cleans up most of his hot mess. He rolls up on his side and brushes the matted curls off my sweaty forehead, then flicks my nose.

I frown at him. "Not just yet. You hungry?" He nods. I climb out of bed and reach for my pajamas—I've got a ratty college t-shirt and mesh shorts stationed near my bed—when I remember that all his clothes are in my washer.

"I don't think I have anything that'll fit you," I say, frowning. He climbs out of bed naked and presses up behind me. I can feel his half-hard cock against my ass in the mesh shorts.

"Why should I get dressed? Aren't you going to strip me again soon enough?"

I turn toward him as I start to gather my hair into a loose ponytail. "What makes you think you'll get lucky again?"

When he smiles, I think it's the first time I've seen him truly do that. His whole face lights up. The glow of it warms my heart a little, which makes me nervous. "I've got plans for you and that exposed brick downstairs," he says, stooping to grab his damp boxers and sliding them up his legs.

I stare at his long quads, so firm and defined. I really should go running with him more often. We walk downstairs and he starts going on and on, admiring the mortar I repointed inside, rubbing his hand along the drywall and complimenting the smooth finish.

When we pass the laundry room, I shove him right up against the washer and peel out of my pajamas. "You're just using me for my home renovation skills," I tease, loving every one of his keen observations about the work I've done on my house. I watch as he quickly gets hard and my eyes water as he pulls out his dick. He lifts me and sits me on the edge of the washer, then spears into me as if we didn't finish fucking ten minutes before.

We fuck, frantically this time, as I mutter that I'm so happy I can't even see straight. I've been so fucked in the head between work and my fear that I might lose my house. I can feel the stress shaking loose from my bones as I give in to the pleasure I'm drawing from Isaac.

After, I pull a pizza from my freezer and we eat naked in my kitchen, not giving a shit who sees us through my glass patio doors. He reaches out to wipe a dab of sauce from my lip and sucks it off his finger, and I decide I'm in trouble, because I want to fuck him again.

"I don't really do relationships," I tell him, reaching to take a sip from the beer we're sharing, since I only had one in my fridge. I have to defuse the energy between us before I get used to the way I feel around him.

His eyebrows shoot up. "Is that what this is? I don't do relationships, either," he says. Then he grins. "I thought I was just here to learn about laundry."

He takes the beer back and downs a big swig of it. He wipes his mouth with his wrist, which should be gross, but neither of us has plates or napkins as we eat from the tray, leaning on my counter. "Seriously, though," he says. "You heard about me and my mom. That pretty much fucked me up for relationships." I don't say anything, just look at him. What's to say?

"My parents didn't exactly foster attachment," I tell him with a sigh.

"Well don't hold back on me, Nicole. Seems fair I should know about your shit since you know why I'll be holding you at a distance emotionally."

I snort out a laugh. "Did you ever watch the Gilmore Girls?" He shakes his head. "It's this show about mothers and daughters...the grandma character is a filthy rich country club lady with pearls and sensible pumps, and no real tolerance for behavior outside the expected." I sigh, reaching for my hair.

"This was never refined enough for my mother. And she resented my smart mouth and the way I always insisted on being given credit for being right—I'm always right, Isaac Brady. Let's just clear that up right now."

"We'll see," he says, finishing off the beer.

I nod my head toward a framed picture of Emma and me on our college campus in the Oakland neighborhood of the city. In the picture, we're beaming, arms around each other in our caps and gowns, standing beneath one of the pink cherry trees on campus on graduation day. Both of us have wild hair—hers red, mine brown—and both of us have mothers who never quite understood us. "My parents refused to help me pay for college because I chose a partial scholarship at a state school instead of a posh, all-female college they felt was more appropriate."

Isaac squints. "I take it withholding the tuition wasn't due to hardship?"

I shake my head. "They thought they could punish or shame me into my role as an obedient daughter en route to being an obedient wife to one of the sons of their club buddies." I don't like remembering these rejections, and I sigh.

"They wouldn't even co-sign my loans," I tell him, explaining how I attended part-time that first year until I could work things out to stop being on their tax forms and qualify for financial aide on my own.

He just stares at me for a bit and swallows.

Then, he reaches for a piece of pizza crust on the tray and snaps it in half, handing me one. "To shitty parents," he says, clinking his crust against mine and then throwing it in the sink. "Let's dispose of their shitty example." He turns on my garbage disposal and I smile.

"What comes next with my trench?"

Isaac frowns toward the back door. "I need to figure out who fucked up their drainage," he tells me. "The storm today gave me an idea." He tells me he's going to come over the next time it rains, bring some equipment and really study the storm runoff from the big buildings around my condo. We talk for awhile about the process, but when I yawn, he raps his knuckles on the counter.

Isaac tells me he will see me at the group run this weekend and gets his clothes from my dryer. I stand by awkwardly as he gets dressed and ties his boots. I want to tell him to come inside when he's done for the day tomorrow. I want to see what else he will come up with to surprise me in the bedroom. But that feels too much like a commitment and I already feel weird having shared personal shit with him about my fucked up family.

When he leaves, I pull up the files Mark prepared for me about Paraguay and South America. For the first time in ages, I'm not distracted by my anxiety about financing the trench in my yard. I'm not panicked about it all sliding into the river. I trust that Isaac will make sure my house is ok.

It was true what I told him—that I paid for school with loans and created paid internship opportunities for myself before such things were popular. My summer salaries with tech startups paid my rent and because Emma and I always lived in shithole apartments, I saved enough to buy this place in cash after graduation.

A sense of unease nags at me as I look out into the black night. In many ways, I'm relying on Isaac's word that things are going to be ok. Being beholden to people sets my teeth on edge. Takes me right back to those long fights with my parents about my education. The things they screamed at me about money and responsibility and decorum are forever burned in my brain as a betrayal.

I vowed then never again to depend on anyone. For anything. I look at the files from Mark. He had sent them to Tim as well, and I see Tim's comments in the shared online documents. I remind myself that Tim is family with my best friend, Tim is someone I trust, and Tim trusts the Brady family when it comes to engineering.

That meeting with Mick at the diner was weird, but the man's ideas had merit. I bury myself in my research, and try to silence the doubting voice inside my head.

CHAPTER TWENTY-THREE
ZACK

"You're in a good mood for once." Liam nudges my shoulder in the kitchen at work and holds up his coffee mug toward me. I pour the steaming liquid into his cup and clink glasses with him. We both take it black, like our father.

Sometimes I hate having anything in common with the batty old asshole, but it's hard to begrudge someone their coffee preference.

"Missed you on the run this morning," he says as we sip our drinks, leaning against the wall.

I shrug. I was too sore this morning to even think about the additional chaffing involved in my daily run. Tomorrow, I'll regret skipping the work-out, but this morning I actually slept until seven.

"Hey," I say to my brother. He raises his eyebrows, and I am about to ask him if he thinks we will ever have a chance at being normal in a relation-ship. If he thinks a woman will ever stick with us for the long haul.

But asking him that will of course lead to questions, and I'm not ready to think about the questions I know he's going to ask about Nicole. I blow on my coffee and stall, trying to think of how I can change the subject to something safer.

Something work related.

"You remember my roommate from MIT? Ray?"

Liam nods. "Good dude. Heard he moved to Pittsburgh awhile back."

"Yeah," I say. "He was at a tech startup for awhile but he's in grad school now for machine learning." The two of us talk about what we think that means, whether Ray builds robots or autonomous vehicles or something totally different.

"What makes you bring him up?" Liam asks the question casually, and of course he'd wonder. And of course I can't tell him Nicole used to work with Ray, and the reason I know that is because I'm fucking her brains out every opportunity I get. I'm not sure how to talk to my brother about Nicole.

I scowl until I think of a response. "I think I'm going to call him to see if he has any ideas about Nicole's landslide. Maybe a robot can help figure out where the water's coming from or something."

Liam shakes his head and chuckles. "Or," he says, rinsing his empty mug in the sink, "you could go stand out there in the rain and see for yourself."

He starts to walk out of the kitchen and I shout after him that I did just that yesterday, but he's already gone.

I look up Ray and dial the number for his lab on campus, figuring he's probably in there. He answers with a grunt on the second ring. "Hey, man," I say. "It's Zack Brady."

"Zack? Holy shit! I keep meaning to call you."

ℬ

WE MEET for lunch near campus, since it's easier for me to get around the city than it is for him to leave his robots unattended. I watch in fascination as he orders the same bland food he's always survived on, while I coat my sandwich with several different types of hot sauce. Ray tells me that machine learning basically means he writes computer programs that help computers make predictions, put pieces of information together and "learn" what to expect next.

He talks with his mouth full of buttered noodles. "You still doing stuff with geotechnical engineering?"

I nod, and tell him a little bit about some of the dam restorations I've done. His eyes glaze over until I say, "I actually am working right now on a landslide project for someone you know. Nicole Kennedy?"

Ray's eyes bulge out of his head. "The medusa?"

"What's that mean?"

He gestures toward his head and mimics a spiral motion with his finger. "Curly hair looks like snakes, eyes will turn you to stone if you piss her off? I never met anyone else who could make a bunch of programmers fall in line and keep to a schedule." He reminds me that programmers usually work late into the night and sleep all day, and apparently, Nicole managed to get them to flip their schedules to regular business hours so they could actually meet with developers and investors when she was at the tech company with Ray.

"So she's got a landslide problem? Where?"

An hour and two bowls of buttered noodles later, Ray has explained to me that his thesis project is actually related to landslides. And he asks me to consult with him on his research. He's building special cameras and a computer program that will analyze the images to predict where the earth might slide away.

He's using some of the hillier streets in Pittsburgh to start this project, but aims to branch out to bigger applications. "There's more money in industry," he tells me, shrugging like I don't already know that industry is the bread and butter of engineering companies like Beltane. "If I can help prevent one coal mine from collapsing, it'll fund program development to aid foreign governments and shit whose entire road systems are washing away every spring."

Our conversation is such a contrast to the way things happen at work, where I'm always feeling blindsided or like my reports aren't being read.

I leave the meeting with Ray feeling electrified, energized about my work for the first time since before I got sent to Nicole's yard. I squeeze in a few hours of measurements and studying blue prints for her problem, but then I hole up in my office and really dive into the work Ray asked me to look over.

He rides his bike to my office and pulls up an external hard drive with hours of video footage of different hillsides around the region. "It would take a human hours to watch all this film, right?" I nod, rolling my eyes. Ray clicks around and explains that his program is teaching the computer to watch the footage and pull out anything forbidding.

"That's where you come in," he says, looking around. "Hey, Nicole's not here is she? She's not going to come in here and yell at me?"

"No, man, I told you this landslide thing is in her back yard. She's at her house."

He seems relieved. "Ok, well I need you to help me tell the program what to look for."

And just like I'd done with Nicole, just like I was doing for my own documentation, I explain to Ray some of the signs of an impending landslide. But this time, I'm using formulas and quantifying soil disruption. I'm in full geek mode, talking numbers with my former roommate, who's lapping it all up excitedly, typing furiously while I talk.

"This is so great, Zack," he says, leaning back in a relaxed posture I'm not used to seeing him in. We break for the evening and I toss his bike in the back of my truck, giving him a ride back to his apartment.

"I thought Nicole said she didn't yell at you too much," I say at a red light. "She mentioned that you always had your shit together."

I can see his eyes bulge wide in the dark. "She is the most intimidating woman I've ever met," he says slowly, swallowing.

"Hm, can't argue with that," I tell him. Except I don't find Nicole intimidating. I find her exhilarating. I admire how she is in charge in every environment, and how she tries to intimidate me in the bedroom, but then seems to love it when I take back control.

I can't tell any of this to Ray, so I drop him off and promise to call him soon with my input.

I should probably clear this side hustle consulting gig with my dad or my uncle, but I decide not to say anything about that, either. It feels important to me to keep these things to myself. Delicious secrets that are just for my enjoyment, nothing I have to share with my family and nothing any of them can yank away from me.

Dad has finally filled Uncle Kellen in on his Paraguay scheme, so in the morning, we have a team meeting about it first thing. And by team, I mean me, my dad, and my uncle, all trying to make sense of what my dad *isn't* saying in between his observations and stories.

My dad, as usual, is not paying attention and is instead cracking open pistachios. I know he's listening, and that this is just the way his mind works. I know that he has raging ADHD and came of age long before there was any medication for that. I know all this, and still I take it personally when he doesn't pause to acknowledge my part in this arm of our business.

This is just the same as always. Dad will be way past thinking about Paraguay before we even get there, and we haven't even really planned out what is going to happen on that trip...which isn't our company's trip.

I tug at my hair and scrub a hand along my chin. My uncle wants me to put together some bullet points about the landslide-related projects Beltane has completed, and I fight my urge to point out that this seems more appropriate for the head of the department to prepare. In fact, the head of the department should be the one going on the trip with my dad.

Kellen moves on to talk about my brothers' work and ends the meeting to move on to the electrical department.

I smile as he leaves, thinking about how Orla will be giving a presentation during the meeting and will probably get promoted soon. It won't be because her dad is in charge. She really knows her shit. I realize that Nicole actually reminds me a lot of Orla. Neither of them take an ounce of crap from anyone, and both of them are the smartest person in a lot of rooms.

Suddenly, I get angry at myself for having these feelings about Nicole, and angry that I'm not standing up to my dad. Nicole's stirring up a sense of yearning I work so hard to keep buried. I know my mom has fucked me up when it comes to relationships and yes, I fucking know I have issues with my dad and constantly seeking his approval.

I can't even bring myself to press the issue of my promotion with my father or tell him about my consulting gig, but I also can't bring myself to quit Beltane and go work somewhere I'm not just going to be known as Mick Brady's kid.

This is why I don't do relationships with women.

I'm too fucked up. I can't let myself yearn for anything resembling intimacy with a woman, because I have nothing like that to give in return. I leave the conference room and know that I need to get out of here. I need something to distract me, to help me stuff my problems back down where I can manage them. I need to avoid the swirling feelings I have about work, about Nicole.

I drive toward her house anyway, hoping I can drown myself in numbers and data.

CHAPTER TWENTY-FOUR
NICOLE

I've decided we need to do some focus groups. It feels inappropriate for me to go into any more meetings with Augusto or to travel to Paraguay without polling donors and potential donors. We need to find out where and how people are likely to spend their philanthropic dollars.

When I bring this up to Tim during our one on one meeting, he tunes me out and latches on to discussing infrastructure projects in South America.

"Tim," I interrupt. He looks up at me, surprised. "You're not listening to me." He squints and frowns. "What do you even care about infrastructure? You're a lawyer. You work with rich, athletic clients about their contracts."

I blow out a breath and sink back into my chair. He just stares at me, but starts nodding. "Ok, wow." There's a long pause.

"I'm sorry I interrupted you and I'm sorry I shouted, but I'm feeling a little steam rolled with this initiative, Tim. I feel like you're not letting me do what you hired me for, which is to direct our company strategy."

"I can see how you feel that way," he says, speaking slowly. "But I also feel like you're being close minded about this approach. It's a sound idea."

We glare at each other and I close my eyes. I rub my temples and try to refrain from pounding on the table. I'm not sure if part of me wants to see him crash and burn spectacularly at this or what exactly is happening. I just know I'm off my game. "You know what, Tim, you're right."

I stand up and gather my things. "I'm going to work from home and get you some numbers and Mark will write something up about our approach for the meetings in Paraguay."

I storm out of the office before he can say anything else that might cause me to yell something I'll later regret.

I tell Mark I'm going to work from home for the rest of the day and that I'll call him later, but I know I need to calm down before I can even think of doing anything else work related.

I change into my running things and I fully intend to bang out a really respectable three miles and get back to my game plan for work, until I see Isaac in the trench in my back yard.

He's staring at neighboring buildings again, frowning, seated at the edge of the crack with his legs dangling down into the abyss where I sort of dreamed of once building a fire ring.

I approach him cautiously, fighting the urge to nudge him with my sneaker because I don't want him to fall in the pit. "Isaac?"

He looks up and puts a hand over his eyes against the glare. "Nicole. I didn't think you'd be home so early. I was just..." He waves his hands around vaguely.

"Come for a run with me?" I try to keep my tone light, but the truth is I'm excited to go for a run with Isaac. I'm glad to see his dark hair and think about his ass with that tool belt slung around his hips. He's the first person today who hasn't irritated me.

Isaac grins. "Let me go grab my stuff."

I follow him out to the truck and he reaches into his passenger seat for his duffel bag. "Is it already-used sweaty running stuff?" Another grin.

"You know it." He takes off his muddy boots and tosses them into the truck, walking to my front door in his socks, and I follow him again, not sure what's driving me to do it.

I could just wait for him outside, but I want to be around him in case I think of something I want to tell him. He cocks a brow at me when I stand in front of the bathroom. "You're going to watch me change? Into sweaty tights?"

I purse my lips, trying to decide. "No," I say. "I guess not. But I think I'm going to peel them off you after."

"We'd better get going, then." He growls and grabs my hand, tossing his phone on my counter and pulling the door shut behind us as we take off toward the trail. Only a few other runners are out in the middle of this wintery day. February in Pittsburgh is mostly gray. The temperature can fluctuate between zero and sixty degrees, depending on the day, and today is one of the cold, damp-air yucky ones.

I don't mind it when I'm running with Isaac, though. I actually feel my head clearing and am beginning to see why it could be valuable to expand my friend circle beyond just Emma and her relatives.

Isaac and I chat about the unpredictability of the weather as we run, both of us noticing that unpredictability is upsetting to us. He tells me that his friend Ray calls me Medusa, and I snort with laughter, remembering the startled expressions on all those guys' faces when I led meetings.

"I had to be rough with them," I explain to Isaac. "Nobody there would listen to me if I was anything other than intimidating. I had to choose between being liked and being effective."

Isaac looks over at me, his expression unreadable, and after awhile he says, "I think you're effective *and* I like you."

I stumble over a crack in the pathway when he says that, caught off guard by his earnest admission. "Well, I like you, I guess," I retort.

I'm filled with lust for him, and the chemistry between us is great, but as I run by his side, setting the pace and venting to him about my frustrations at work, I realize that I really am coming to enjoy Isaac Brady as a..." what are we exactly?" I blurt.

"What are we?" He stops running and stares at me, hands on his hips.

I nod. "Yes, I mean I know I'm your client and you're my running coach and your dad is strangely entwined with my boss. But what are *we?*" He doesn't answer, his eyes wide. "Are we fuck buddies? Are we dating?"

Isaac scratches at his chin, considering. "Do we have to decide?" he asks. "I've been enjoying the spontaneity of...whatever this is."

I start running again, thinking about what he asked. "I think I might feel better about it all if there was a time limit or parameters." I pick up the pace a tiny bit and find I'm still able to talk as I run. I'm getting pretty good at this. "How fast are we running right now?"

He checks his watch. "About ten minute miles. That's a massive improvement from a month ago, Nicole!"

He gives me a high five and then says, "Hmmm. Parameters."

I'm about to tell him we should wrap up our adventures by the time he breaks ground on my yard, or something, so we can both avoid catching feelings and getting ensnared in each other's bullshit. But then, the heavens open and it starts pouring buckets.

I curse, but the change in the weather seems to delight Isaac for some reason. "Are you insane?" He turns for my house and starts sprinting to get back. I'm able to almost keep up with him for a bit, until he turns to face me and slows. I'm breathing heavy in front of him and not even embarrassed, and that just starts to worry me as well.

"I've been waiting for it to rain again," he shouts above the crashing water sounds. "I want to go and stare at the apartment complexes and see about their stormwater runoff." He starts explaining technical terms to me about the dirt and the water and I don't understand a word of it.

I focus instead on the way his shirt clings to him in the rain and the way it looks when he brushes the curtain of dark hair back from his eyes with his forearm. *Sexy as sin.*

When we get near my house, he runs around back and makes a beeline for the building next door, and stares. He squints. And then he picks me up and starts to spin me around in the rain, kissing me. It takes my breath away, the cold, salty feel of his lips against mine in the downpour.

I gasp when he sets me down and points at the hip condo building that's only partially inhabited. "Look at the downspouts," he says. "Do you have your phone on you? Can I make a video?"

Wide eyed, I pull my phone from my leggings and hand it to him. He struggles to pull up the camera icon with the wet screen, but gets it to work and narrates while he records. "Despite trendy stormwater mitigation systems written into the building plans, the downspouts are overrun," he says. I watch over his shoulder to see what he's filming, to see from his perspective. Storm water is gushing from the eaves of the building, pouring from the roof.

"It's all flowing directly into the soil of your and Valerie's yard," he says, turning and recording the water. "Son of a bitch," he mutters. "This is it!"

CHAPTER TWENTY-FIVE
ZACK

JUST AS MY BROTHER PREDICTED, THE WORK DONE BY THE MEYER CONSTRUCTION crew is subpar. Who even knows how many thousand gallons of rainwater are dislodging the soil in Nicole's yard? Jesus, she's lucky her whole house didn't slide into the river.

I hand her back her phone and grab her hand, sprinting toward her house. My clothes are soaked and heavy, and I'm fucking elated.

Nicole's fingers shake as she tries to type the code on the keypad at her house, and I kiss her neck, guiding her fingers with my hand. As soon as we get inside, I start stripping her, peeling off the wet layers. I was going to fuck her after our run anyway, and now I find I can't wait to get her naked.

"I want to celebrate this," I say, nipping at the sensitive skin below her ear. I love that I know she gets goosebumps when I do that.

"The torrent?" She asks, moaning softly as I pull the wet bra up and over her cold rack. Her nipples stand painfully erect, so tight and perky as she shivers.

"Yes. The torrent of water. It's so bad for them." I move on to stripping off my own clothes, but I notice that she's really shivering. "Hot shower?"

"God, yes, please," she shouts, and then squeals when I toss her over one shoulder and bound up her stairs.

I head into the bathroom and turn on her shower full blast while she digs some towels out from the linen closet. The white tile gleams under the heat lamp in the ceiling. "This room is amazing," I mutter, as always imagining her on her hands and knees doing the work of restoring it. "Did you do the tile?"

I turn to see her answer, but she's already stepped into the spray. I stare as she rubs the hot water along her skin, trying to chase out the cold. "Isaac," she says, pinching her nipples in the steam. "I don't want to talk about tile or torrents right now."

B

AFTER, in her bed, limbs tangled with mine around the damp mess of her sheets, she says, "Explain it now. About the water and my trench."

"It's a headscarp," I correct, tracing my finger along the curve of her hip. I love how soft she is, how warm and present. "And anyway, that condo building has been slowly eroding your soil foundation since that roof went up."

She chews her lip and twirls a finger through my chest hair. "Sooo this means..."

I smack her butt and cup the flesh in my palm, squeezing. "We're going to sue the fuck out of them and you won't have to pay me out of pocket."

I feel her limbs relax, melt into mine a little more. "What comes next?" She breathes.

I grin again. "Next comes my favorite part. I let Jason do his thing to get the funds in line and I start engineering the solution to your problem. You're not going to see much of me for awhile because I'll be in my happy place."

"Where's that? Buried in a bunch of computer monitors?" She squints at me in the fading light. I shake my head.

"Nah. I'll be standing in the mud in your yard using my favorite tools to do calculations." She smiles, content. I like this. I like that I've made her happy. I like that I've solved a geotechnical mystery. Most of all, I like that the rain bought me more time with her.

She stretches and stares at me, considering something. "I have shit to do, Isaac."

"Oh." I can't mask my disappointment. I know by now that she's not a cuddler, and neither am I normally. But I wasn't expecting her to kick me out of her bed again so soon.

I feel her fingers curl around my arm and I look down at her hand. "You can stay," she says, "and do your math here. But I've got to do some work. Is what I'm saying."

This seems like a pretty big deal, especially considering we hadn't gotten around to talking about her parameters before the rain storm. But I'm not going to argue with her and I'm sure as shit not going to leave if she's letting me stay.

She tosses on a ratty old bathrobe and I cram myself into an old pair of her mesh shorts to go downstairs and grab my bag and change. When I come out of the bathroom, I find her curled up on her couch with her laptop open, biting her lip as she types furiously and mutters to herself.

I set myself up at the kitchen counter where I don't think I'll disturb her, and call up my brother Liam on video chat. He answers with a confused look. "Aren't you down the hall from me in your office right now?"

"Nope." I spin around, showing him my surroundings, before stopping to consider the questions this might inspire. "I made headway in Nicole Kennedy's landslide situation," I tell Liam once I realize he's staring at me and waiting.

"Oh yeah?"

I nod. "Meyer," I tell him. His eyes go wide. "They were the contractor on the condo building next to Nicole and Valerie's property—Valerie is the old lady who owns the other half of Nicole's duplex."

Liam gives me a 'yeah, yeah,' gesture, and I tell him about the video. "I was out there taking some calculations, looking over the building design compared with the construction sketches, when it started to rain."

He snorts. "I was caught out in that, too, on my way to lunch with Granny."

I email him the video. "Take a look at the fine craftsmanship on their roof garden." Liam's eyes bulge as he watches the streams of water pouring off the roof, running along the ground toward Nicole's property.

"Holy shit!" He says, leaning in to stare. "I guess you got them. Hell, even I know that amount of water runoff can't be good for the soil integrity."

I grin and thank my brother again for his insight that led me to this discovery. "I need to call Jared so he can work his lawyer magic."

"Not so fast," Liam starts to protest. "We need to talk about why you're not wearing a shirt and whose house you're sitting in right now."

"What's that?" I stall. "Bad connection, bro. Sorry. Talk to you later."

I hang up abruptly and get together an email for Jared. Lawyers have a special gift for taking something cut and dry and making it take an entire day to document and spin into paperwork for an insurance claim and lawsuit.

I keep thinking about Nicole, how she'd smiled when I told her the news. I keep thinking about lying in her bedroom, where the original beams are exposed in her ceiling and I know she stripped off generations of paint to salvage the trim and repair the transoms above the windows.

I look over at her, still working away happily. I don't want to interrupt her, so I send her a text from where I sit.

> Jared the lawyer is going to send you enough paperwork to fill in your yard.

When her phone bings she looks over at it, and then over at me. I wave. She laughs, but picks her computer back up. "You gonna leave me hanging?" I wad up a napkin from the holder on the counter and toss it toward her, but it doesn't quite make it.

Like a loon, I grin at her until she picks up her phone and starts tapping. After what seems like forever, she writes

> Just make sure you clear that with Valerie first or else she'll accuse me of burning her plant roots. Again.

The rest of the day is all calculations and paperwork, seething phone calls from the crew at Meyer Construction, vowing to never work with Beltane ever again. Good riddance, I say. I know I have nothing to do with that aspect of the business, but my uncle does.

My stomach rumbles, and I decide I've had enough work for one day. I start opening cabinets noisily, looking for something I can slap together and call it a meal, but Nicole basically has no food here.

"What are you doing out there?" She shouts from the living room, where she doesn't look up from her laptop.

"Well I was going to make you dinner, but you don't have any food in this house."

"Accurate," she says, finally closing the lid and looking at me. "We can't go out with you looking like that."

I run my hands over my chest, dancing, "what, like this? You can't handle all this?" I feel light and facetious. Is this, maybe, happiness creeping in on me? I run over to where she's sitting and dive onto her on the couch, making her squeal. "Don't worry," I murmur into her ear, tickling her and loving when she laughs. "It can be a private show."

We place an order for delivery and miss the doorbell when the food arrives, but I'm too wrapped up in her to care.

CHAPTER TWENTY-SIX
NICOLE

A few days later, I come in to work to discover Mark looking smug. He's smirking at me when I reach for the coffee he's pretending to hold out of my reach. "What in the hell do you know?" I chide him. "Spill."

"Two things," he says, settling in to the chair opposite my desk and crossing his ankle up onto the opposite knee so I can see his brightly colored socks.

"Mark, we're not in tech anymore. You can wear normal socks to work," I tell him, dying to know what he knows.

"I like the fun ones," he says, spreading out his papers and pulling out his fancy gel pen. "So, first, your mother called to remind you that her birthday party is coming soon. Don't roll your eyes at me. I also talked to Alice in the kitchen, and she mentioned how Emma has been practicing saying no to everyone and everything. Something about being swamped with revisions for her new novel and also having to take care of the babies."

I groan. Emma is always my date to my mother's fancy birthday brunch. This year, the entire thing has more gravitas because Mom is turning 50. In reality, she's turning 52, but she's been lying about her age for decades and would rather people think she had me as a teenager than admit she's getting older.

"So why does that make you smirk like a smug asshole?"

Mark grins. "Because now you have to find an actual date or else tell

Mama she should change the headcount because you don't have a plus one."

"It's really cruel that you revel so much in my mother's nonsense." I chug the coffee. Mark knows exactly what color I like it—just a splash of milk to cut the bitterness. He also knows I'm mostly full of shit, because his own parents treat him like garbage, too. I was glad to bring him with me when Tim recruited me to Stag Law, and glad to give him enough of a raise that Mark doesn't have to worry about asking his parents for money ever again.

"So, thing two is that we had a call from Beltane Engineering this morning."

I arch a brow. I haven't seen Isaac in a few days, but I see traces of him in the yard. Marks from him placing a ladder. Spray painted lines on the ground. Sometimes I go out there before work, hoping I'll catch him, but I always have to leave before he gets there and he's gone by the time I get home.

Mark looks over his notes. "Seems like the asshole contractor is going to settle. It's possible Zack Brady mentioned that you work with high profile professional athletes with lots of media connections. I guess that building has been struggling to sell condo units? Anyway! Everything is coming up roses for you in the back yard department."

"Hm." I tap my nails on the desk. This feels too easy. Like the threat was too great for the amount of work involved in the solution. Something isn't right, but I can't place what it might be. "Was it Isaac who called?"

I try very hard to keep the anticipation out of my voice and control my facial features. I don't think Mark is buying it, though, because he grins. "It was indeed. Which reminded me how much time you two are spending together training for the run. I might have suggested you'd be stopping by Beltane in person to thank him."

"Jesus, Mark. You're impossible."

"No, honey, *you're* impossible to work with when you're not getting laid. And it's been a long ass time since you've had me block off any evenings or arrange for any dry cleaning that wasn't work appropriate." He looks me up and down, frowning.

I'm not about to let him know I've been getting plenty of penis. "Can we transition from personal updates to actual work yet?"

Mark snorts. "He's going along to Paraguay, right? This is work. So you're going over there with this briefing after you and I hash out the itinerary and strategy for your meetings with Augusto's contacts."

And so, two hours later, I find myself calling a car service to drive me to the Beltane Engineering building, with a thick file of meeting strategies I feel uncomfortable about. Despite the focus groups and the information I pulled together about other foundations, Tim is fully convinced we need to create a charity dedicated to landslide mitigation...for a pro baseball player who can't even say the word mitigation.

Tim has fully drunk Mick Brady's kool-aid and is dead set on us diving into the infrastructure approach to Augusto's foundation.

I'm so conflicted, because helping to improve roads and access to school buildings feels like a cause that's fascinating and obviously meaningful to Augusto personally, but all of our numbers and market research indicates that donors just aren't enthused about their tax write-off going toward construction projects...unless it's constructing sports facilities.

The whole situation makes me wish I hadn't pushed Tim to delve into foundation work at all.

I enter the lobby of Beltane, admiring the original woodwork and exquisite tile patterns on the floors. Someone had taken great care to restore this space, honoring its original splendor. "Hey, I know you!" Mick Brady himself emerges from a side door before I can approach the receptionist. "Not honey, right?" My nostrils flare at him, but he smiles. "Ms. Kennedy, what brings you down here?"

"Just coming by to finalize some things with my landslide situation," I tell him with a shrug. I don't really feel like delving into trip details with him and trust that Isaac will pass along the pertinent information. I also suspect Mick won't read it anyway.

Mick smiles and leans on the reception desk. "Emily," he says. "Ms. Kennedy here is a very important person. Can you make sure she gets the good coffee? I'm going to walk her up to Zack myself."

"Oh, you don't have to do that," Emily and I both say at once, causing us both to smile. But Mick waves us off and gestures toward another door. I'm surprised that we're taking the stairs, but then I remember that the Bradys are a family who run ten miles a day. Mick doesn't even hesitate as he hops up two flights. Something tells me he doesn't mask his age like my mother does, but then again, Isaac said he dates women closer to my age than his own.

"Here you are, dear," Mick says, pointing down a poorly lit hallway flanked by rows of cubicles. The door at the end of the hall says Zack Brady, and an entire army of young engineers looks up at me as I make my way down the aisle with the company CEO.

"Zack!" Mick hollers, startling the few employees who hadn't yet looked up to gaze at us. I hear rustling sounds and the door cracks open. "Your girlfriend is here."

CHAPTER TWENTY-SEVEN
ZACK

MY FATHER JUST REFERRED TO NICOLE KENNEDY AS MY GIRLFRIEND. IN FRONT OF AN entire room of my colleagues. If I could just control the muscles of my face, this would be fine, because my dad makes these kinds of inappropriate jokes about most women.

But she doesn't know this, and we never bring clients up to the offices, so the whole thing just throws me so hard, I just stand there with my mouth hanging open while Nicole glares at my father.

"Mr. Brady," she says. "Mick, let's not get ahead of ourselves."

He winks at her. "I know how it is," he says. "You're saving yourself for my brother."

"Jesus Christ, Dad." I feel myself blushing. I vow to leave the company and go work somewhere else, somewhere the management controls their impulses and gives employees promotions without sending them jumping through deranged hoops.

"Aw, come on, son. You're always so damn serious! I ran into Nicole in the lobby. She says she's here to talk about the hole in her yard." Dad winks again and takes off, stopping to greet some of the people in cubicles as he goes.

I stand frozen in shock and horror until Nicole clears her throat and raises her brows. "Can we talk?"

Shaking myself back to consciousness, I nod and gesture into my office. It's kind of a mess and I don't really have space in here for visitors. I try to clear some tools off the folding chair so she can sit, but she makes a face at the dirt that crumples off the measurement devices I'd used at her property yesterday.

"Sorry," I mumble. "I would have met you in the conference room if…" I drift off. "I don't want you to think I said anything to my father about us," I say, my eyes no doubt conveying the panic I feel about her reaction to all of this. "I know we didn't talk about parameters yet."

"He seems like the wrong person to confide a secret to," she says. Then she leans toward me. "Is that what I am, Isaac? Your dirty secret?"

Fuck. Me. That mouth on her…I exhale slowly, letting my cheeks puff out as I adjust my flannel shirt. "You're not a secret," I tell her. *Liar.* "Unless you want to be?"

"I haven't figured out what to do with you, to be honest," she says. She tosses a folder on my desk. "So ostensibly, I came to thank you for your work on my yard. Is what Mark said true? Is it really just…handled?"

I scratch at the stubble on my chin. "Yeah, seems like it," I tell her. "My brother Liam has worked with that company before. They're always taking shortcuts, and then the developers have to call us in to fix shit after the inspections fail." I shrug. "Jared mentioned that you work closely with half the pro athletes in the city, and that just happens to be the target market they're trying to sell condos to."

Another professional link in the chain between our companies. Another reason it's a bad idea for me to be involved with her. Yet here I am, half hard and longing to kiss her.

I reach for a folder of my own and slide it toward her. "These are the plans to fix your yard," I tell her. "If you're comfortable with all of this, I can break ground next week."

"Next week?" Her eyes are wide as she thumbs through the 3D renderings I printed for her to see what I think we can do to restore the yard. "I guess I have to consult with Valerie. Who knows what she wants for her half."

I nod. "I mean, the landscaping and patio work is obviously decorative. My work pretty much ends when we've got the dirt level. That was just to help you visualize what it will look like." Nicole and Valerie will lose about two feet of yard, and their property will end with a tiered retaining wall, rather than dropping straight off like a sheer cliff by the river bank.

She looks dazed. I want to reach for her, rub her shoulder, tell her to take her time. Instead I sit down and pull open the file she brought. "Am I really coming along to all these meetings in Paraguay?"

She rolls her eyes. "Well, we can't very well leave you sitting in the car," she says. "Tim is totally stoked to have your father coming along with us. You don't have to talk at the meetings. Ideally, you'll say nothing," she says, pointedly.

And of course I have no business speaking up at strategy meetings for a professional baseball star to start his charity foundation, and I would never dream of opening my mouth at those meetings, but the way she tells me what to do...it ignites something primal in me as much as her vulnerability a minute before awoke some unfamiliar urge to offer comfort. "You telling me what to do, Kennedy?"

I stand back up from my chair and she draws in her breath. I can see the pulse tick at her throat above the prim blouse she's wearing today along with loose trousers that hide the luscious curves I've been dreaming of touching again. She swallows. "I'm not the one who has trouble keeping quiet, if I recall." I run a thumb along her jaw, restraining myself from grabbing her hair and pulling her in for a claiming kiss.

"About that," she says, and closes her eyes. "Would you consider being my date for a party this weekend? We'd have to miss the group run."

"Your date?" She nods. "In public? Should I wear sweaty workout gear again?"

"Oh, god no." She shudders. "It's for my mother's birthday party, and you have to wear a suit. A nice suit." She looks me up and down.

"You're making this sound so appealing. Missing a run, wearing an uncomfortable suit...tell me more."

She blushes. "Well, I've told you about my mother...and I usually take Emma to Mom's birthday brunches, but Emma is unavailable."

"Aha. So I'm a consolation date. Excellent." I'm loving messing with her, watching her fidget with the papers and squirm. Obviously I can't wait to go out with her, and I'm relieved she even still wants to be around me after my dad called her my girlfriend and set off her fight or flight response.

"I'll make it worth your while," she says, standing and coming closer, chewing that bottom lip of hers. I'm practically sweating, I want her so badly right now.

"Tell me more about that," I say, sliding my hands in my jeans pockets so I don't reach out and cup her ass or pull her against my hard-on.

She grins. "I'll buy us *each* our own beer to share in my kitchen. Naked." She places her hands on my chest, just resting them there, transferring her heat into me. I'm sure she can feel me trembling, aching for her. She stretches up on her tip-toes and slowly brings her mouth to mine, kissing me softly, briefly, before pulling back and looking up at me. Her brown eyes are huge, searching, hoping I'll say yes. This feels dangerous, but it's useless to refuse her.

"Deal," I whisper, and I lean in and kiss her back. I work her mouth gently, slipping my tongue inside to caress hers briefly before I pull back with great difficulty, clear my throat again, and open my office door. "Text me the details?"

She nods and, gathering her things, retreats from my office, leaving behind a cloud of desire so thick I have to unbutton my collar so I can breathe.

CHAPTER TWENTY-EIGHT
NICOLE

Isaac picks me up Sunday morning ten minutes early, carrying coffee. I'm so impressed by the sight of him in his suit that I can't even think of something snarky to say to him, so I stand in my doorway staring at his dark, mussed hair, his dark scruff, and the fitted suit that makes him look like sex on legs.

I pretend I'm blowing off the coffee while I regain control of my mouth, making a mental note of how he looks leaning against my door frame, sipping coffee. I fully intend to recall this image while I use my purple toy. Ever since he assured me my finances are in order, it's like the floodgates reopened between my legs. I suppose it doesn't hurt that I'm also recalling his handiwork down there when I try to rub one out.

"You gonna stare at me all day or should we go celebrate your beloved mother?" Isaac casually sips his coffee, but I see a smile pull at the corner of his eyes.

"I might stare a bit longer," I tell him, but I back up from the door to grab my bag and my heels. It doesn't matter what I wear—my mother will have something terrible to say about it, so I went with what I like. My spike heels are at least two inches taller than Mom would consider decent, but I've got a tea-length wrap dress and pearls. It just so happens that the dress has a deep vee neck and the long pearls nestle in between my pushed up breasts.

For the millionth time, I feel grateful Emma and Maddie made me buy so many of the amazing bras at that shop. I can barely handle how good my tits look in this dress, and I'm glad, considering who I'll have on my arm today. Man. Candy.

"I really owe you for this," I tell Isaac as I hop on one foot, fastening the buckle on my right shoe. Suddenly I feel his firm grip on my arm, steadying me so I can put on my shoe. "I guess I could have sat down to do this."

"But then I'd miss an opportunity to look down your top," he says, doing just that. He's seen me naked multiple times before, but something about his words makes me blush. I feel the heat circulating between us, and I know we have to leave now or we're going to be late because I'm going to destroy his sharply pressed suit.

"You got your running stuff for later?" Isaac looked up a trail near the country club south of the city so we can still get in our training run, even if we're missing the group run with our colleagues. I nod, hoisting up the bag I've stuffed with layers and multiple choices for workout wear. The weather today could pull one of its most volatile mood swings, and I'd be set.

I settle into his truck, trying not to spontaneously orgasm as he drops an arm over the back of my seat when he puts the truck in reverse to back out of his parking spot. I want to nestle into his armpit and inhale his after-shave. I let myself enjoy a deep sniff before he brings his arm back to the gear shift and gets us going toward the bridge.

I watch his phone buzz repeatedly in the console as he drives and stare at him, puzzled. I'd have been checking my messages at red lights and impatiently yelling at whoever kept messaging me. But then I realize Isaac needs both hands to drive a stick shift. "Hm," I say. "Want me to see who's trying to get ahold of you?"

He shakes his head, shifting gears and driving south toward the Fort Pitt Tunnel. "It's my brothers. They don't believe me that I'm with you— they think I'm just skipping out on a family run."

I pick up his phone, raising my brow in question. He doesn't respond, so I read his screen. Cal and Liam have sent a series of profanity and emojis, and Orla wrote in all caps

PICS OR IT DIDN'T HAPPEN!

I bite my lip and look at him again as he merges. The entrance to the tunnel involves multiple lane changes over a short period of time, so I know Isaac is deep in concentration. I click the camera icon on his lock screen and snap a selfie of us in the cab of his truck. His phone doesn't seem to be password protected, and it lets me send the pic to his family group text thread that he's labeled Meddling Assholes.

Once we're safely in the tunnel, Isaac looks over at me. "What did you just do?"

"I sent them proof that you're not home in bed." I shrug. "Your dad already thinks I'm your girlfriend..."

I have no idea what I'm doing here. It feels like I'm playing with fire, but everything is so comfortable with Isaac. The phone starts buzzing again as his family alternately sends exploding head emojis, curse words, and GIFs of crackling flames. "I'll just assume the hot references are for me," I tell him.

He laughs. We spend the rest of the drive talking about how we love to hate the people who hound us. His siblings and cousin, my best friend and her vast extended family of Stags. Emma added me to the Stag family group chat a few years ago when she eloped with Thatcher at my boss's house on Christmas Eve. I feel a hell of a lot more comfortable with Stag banter than I do headed into this morning's stiff world of gin and frown lines.

Isaac tosses his keys to the valet and drapes an arm over my shoulders as we walk through the doors. "Am I a 'make out with you during a toast' date today or just 'insinuate that I've seen you naked' when we're talking to your dad?"

I'm sorry, I'm drunk on the scent of you and can't concentrate right now. "Um, maybe neither of those?" We really need to set the parameters of whatever it is we're doing. We just keep getting interrupted.

Isaac snorts and I can see him rearing up for a comeback, but my sister comes rushing over to me. "Nicky, what on *earth* are you wearing? Who in the holy hell is this?" Naomi, two years older than me, is pregnant with her third child.

The first two are sitting primly at a table with their hands on their laps, causing me to wonder if my sister has given them drugs. When I go to Stag family functions, the children run around like electrocuted insects. I believe Emma when she tells me that children just come out that way. Kennedy children, by contrast, have the joy wrung out of them via stern looks and shaming threats.

I plaster on a fake smile for my sister.

"Good to see you, Naomi. This is my..." I hesitate before I say the words, the lie feeling strange in my mouth. "This is my boyfriend, Isaac Brady."

"Glad to meet you," he says, offering his hand for a shake. My sister presents him with a limp wrist, and Isaac seems unsure what to do. He makes a face at me before placing a kiss on my sister's knuckles, which makes me laugh into my fist.

Naomi pulls her hand back, making a face. "Mother is by the bar, greeting guests with mimosas," she says, gesturing vaguely. "I'm sure you two need to clean up after driving so far and from such a...difficult neighborhood."

This time Isaac can't even hide the shock on his face, but pulls his arm tightly around my waist. "We don't want to keep your mother waiting, babe." He steers me toward her and I grit my teeth, desperate to dismantle every one of my sister's layered insults. But before I can catch my breath, I hear my mother hissing similar sentiments about my appearance.

"I thought you were dieting, dear," she says, her face immobile and prim. Isaac's eyes fly wide and he opens his mouth.

I pinch his leg and grin at my mother. "I said I'd started running, Mom. Isaac is helping me train for the marathon relay."

"Hmm," she says. "And this is your trainer?"

I clench all my muscles. "Isaac is my boyfriend. As I said in my email."

"A boyfriend would come around to dinner and meet your father." Mom doesn't offer him a hand, so he keeps his arm around me and leans in to grab two flutes of mimosas with the other hand. His long fingers handle the glass stems delicately and he hands one to me with a smile.

"A pleasure to meet you, Mrs. Kennedy. Should we drink to timeless beauty?" She looks medium flattered and starts smoothing her skirt. "I'm sorry I haven't come around to meet you and Nicole's father. I'll have to correct that as soon as possible."

His thumb starts stroking my arm as he keeps a firm-yet-relaxed grip around my shoulder. I like how it feels, having him with me while I talk to her. Emma usually just hides behind a giant glass of alcohol and steels herself to listen to me vent later.

"And what do you *do*, Isaac?" Mom purses her lips and stares him up and down. I take a smug satisfaction that I know she's searching for something to disapprove of about how he looks, and is coming up short. He's a god damned fox and I can't wait to fuck him later.

I bite my cheek, realizing how much I'm enjoying my time with him, how much he seems to be enjoying his time with me here in the lion's den. It feels unsafe, this comfort I feel around him. I can't make sense of it. I realize Isaac is talking about work, about my yard.

"Did I hear someone say Brady?" My dad wanders over and snags a mimosa of his own. "Travis Kennedy," he says, holding out a hand toward Isaac.

"Zack Brady," he says, removing his arm from around me to shake hands with my father. "I'm pleased to meet you finally. Nicole has said so much about you."

"Zack? I thought you just said his name was Isaac?" My mother clutches at her necklace again, looking confused, but Dad barrels on with questions for my arm candy.

"You Mick Brady's son or Kellen's? No, wait. Kellen just has the one daughter. Your dad and I go way back." Of course my father knows Isaac's father. They probably grease palms together and smoke cigars in places where their female colleagues are still not invited.

I smile while Isaac talks about working with his father and uncle and feel relieved when he puts his arm back around my shoulders. He's actually anchoring me to the earth, and realizing that sets me on edge again.

"Well it's good you have this man to depend on, sweetie," my father says, jolting me back to the conversation.

"What?"

"Saving your house. Teaching you how to run." Dad winks. "Seems like this is a good one to keep around longer than a week."

My mother scoffs. "Honestly, Travis. Do not encourage her abominable behavior. It's indecent."

"Isaac isn't some casual fling," I spit out, realizing that it's already true. "We've been together for nearly two months."

Dad smiles. "Two months and you already can't live without him. You and your dad should give me a call, son," Dad says. I don't hear him as he invites Isaac golfing, can't pay attention as we take our seats for toasts and plated brunch.

My parents keep emphasizing how dependent I am on Isaac. And they're right. My life has been falling to shit the past few months. I'm not asserting myself at work. The strategy of our project with Augusto isn't mine so much as it's Isaac's father's.

I'm fully dependent on Isaac to save my home and keep me from bankruptcy. I'm not even in charge of my own weekends anymore since my boss strong-armed me into an athletic activity I hate. And my dad isn't even aware of the strange entanglement between Isaac's family and my career trajectory right now.

Somehow, when I was too distracted by getting fucked in my kitchen, I let go of everything that makes me *me*. Everything I've become, I did to escape this life I'm surrounded by at the country club. I took my own direction with school, took charge of my career, and took charge of my own living environment.

And now what is happening to me? I'm becoming a woman who swoons over a man, someone who depends on his problem solving skills and hell, I'm even depending on his dick to bring back my lost orgasms. The second my mother sets down her fork, signaling that she's finished eating, I turn to Isaac. "We need to go," I tell him, my breath coming fast and shallow. "Now."

CHAPTER TWENTY-NINE
ZACK

I REALLY THOUGHT NICOLE AND I WOULD SPEND THE AFTERNOON DEFILING HER parents' country club under the guise of going running, but something shifted in her mood after talking with her mother. I can tell she is upset because she doesn't say a word as I drive back to the city.

Not concentrating, driving on instinct, I realize I drove toward my house. I am almost ready to turn onto my street when I notice, and I pull over abruptly. "Hey, I wasn't paying attention. This is my neighborhood." I run a hand through my hair and look at her, expecting her to lash out and call me an idiot.

"That's fine," she says, looking out the window. "We can run in the park, right?"

"Sure," I tell her, pulling out again as she stares at my hand on the gear shift. "You can change at my place."

I had gradually loosened my tie and unbuttoned my shirt along the route home, and it's a small hit to my pride when she doesn't even stare at me. I chose this outfit carefully, wanting her to like how I look when I'm dressed up. Now, she's so affected by whatever happened at the country club, she's not yelling or even talking. "Can I do anything," I say, feeling an urge to make things right somehow.

She sighs. "Take me running and don't baby me about our pace."

Well that I can do. I take mental stock of the condition of my house—I wasn't expecting anyone. But things are generally pretty tidy in there unless I've had my family over. It's been awhile since the four of us Brady kids hung out.

"The bathroom is at the top of the stairs," I tell her, gesturing for her to enter the front door ahead of me. Nicole sort of mopes her way up there, and I follow to go change in my bedroom.

I shed my suit quickly and toss on running shorts with a tech shirt. It's probably 45 degrees but I know I'll be sweating between staring at Nicole's ass and running a few miles. Stepping into the hall, I gasp, realizing that Nicole hasn't shut the bathroom door all the way.

My house is one of the old ones, built around 1920, and half my doors don't shut at all in the humid summers and none of them latch the rest of the year. So the bathroom door is cracked a full inch, just enough for me to see the swell of her breasts as she wrestles into her sports bra. She's already wearing her running tights.

If this were another day, I'd kick the door open and tackle her into my shower.

I close my eyes and remind myself this woman is upset. Not wanting me to invade her space and bend her over my bathroom counter. But fuck, do I want to. It's worse that she's upset. Sex, I can deliver. Emotional comfort? I have no idea what that even looks like.

I head downstairs to check my phone, noticing about ten thousand texts from my family.

CAL:

Can I bring a date to the wedding?

LIAM:

Cal, don't be an asshole. Of course Zack's family gets a plus-one.

ORLA:

I want to know what she did to get you into your best suit. You usually only dress that nice for court.

And on and on.

I hate all of you.

Call responds immediately.

Ooh, he's done with brunch. Probably sat with Nicole's Mom and Dad in a super comfortable conversation.

ℬ

BEFORE I CAN DECIDE on a witty retort, I hear Nicole making her way downstairs. "Can you show me the route we'll take?" She gestures outside toward the park. I had been planning to just play it by ear and weave through Frick Park, but Nicole seems interested in something more structured.

Parameters for everything, I think.

I flip over my tablet on the counter and pull up one of my running apps. "You feeling like hills or flat course?" I raise a brow at her. I know she's had a hard morning, but I still don't know if that makes her more likely to pound out a challenge or if she feels so mentally drained she can only go for a flat run on street level.

"Show me the hills," she says, and I feel myself fall for her a little bit more. *Careful,* my inner voice warns. I go over the map of the Tranquil Trail, a stretch of park I run with my brothers. It's kind of a brutal path, despite the name. It changes elevation, winds along Fern Hollow Creek and eventually spits you out in Homewood Cemetery, intersecting with other trails whose names reference the ravines and hollows that contribute to Pittsburgh's reputation for hilly terrain.

"I can't believe all this is right in the city," she says, staring.

"You don't ever wander around Frick Park?"

She shakes her head. "I'm not really an outdoorsy person." She shrugs. "Let's get out there."

We head out from my house and down the wooden stairs into the woods. I let her set the pace, and it feels faster than her usual. "Don't blow your wad on the downhill," I try to warn her.

"I asked you to push me," she snips back at me. "I've been practicing."

It has been over a month since we started this, but that's not really enough time for her to build enough endurance to go from passing out to what I estimate is an 8-minute mile pace on steep hills. But, I figure, she's feeling salty and she'll probably just stop if it gets too hard. "You asked for it," I tell her.

We make it a mile and a half before she spies a picnic table just off the path, makes a beeline for it, and collapses on top. She lies on her back, her chest heaving, arms spread wide beside her. I follow and lean over her. Once I make sure she's ok, I nudge her with my sneaker. "Come on, Hoss. Want to be out here till dark?"

She raises a brow. "Did you call me Hoss? Like from Bonanza?"

"Your dad watch that show, too?"

She starts laughing, and I can feel some of her stress melt away. Her whole demeanor changes, and I'm glad I made the joke about the old western.

"Are you implying that I have ample girth?" Nicole sits up on the table, hugging her knees into her chest and compressing her tits. I stare and I don't try to hide it.

"I'm implying that you're falling behind." I decide not to mention that I like her girth, and that she's thick in all the best places. Maybe later when she's in a better mood.

As we meander through the woods, Nicole comments on the way a lot of the land seems washed out, how some of the paths seem likely to crumble down into the ravines. "A lot of it is similar to what we'll be talking about in Paraguay," I tell her. "There's actually some interesting research at the university about the landslides in the Pittsburgh region." We run along while I tell her about the machine learning algorithms working to predict which hillsides will fail.

"You working on all that stuff with Ray-Ray?"

I nod. "He and his team are hooking cameras up to commuter buses to track hillside conditions. I've actually been consulting with them a little bit, to help analyze their images, from a soil composition standpoint. That was going to be something I focused on if my dad had given me the promotion."

Shit. I hadn't intended to air all this deep shit to Nicole. Hand't wanted to whine to her about being passed over for the department head.

"I didn't know you were up for a promotion." She slows down some more and this pace seems sustainable. I can tell by her breathing that she can keep this up for a long time. I try to keep her talking.

"Yeah. I had big plans for some industrial projects. When the guy in charge of the geotechnical engineers retired, I really thought I was a shoe-in. Not even because my dad owns the company."

"Well what happened?"

I kick a stick out of the path and weigh my words. "My dad got a bug up his ass about Paraguay and sent me to your house. I still have no idea what his end goal is with all that."

"Well I sure don't know either, but my boss has a hard-on for that project, too." She looks at me, her eyes serious. "I'm glad you're on my side, about that whole thing feeling like an overreach."

"Everything with my dad is an overreach," I tell her. But I'm not able to articulate what feels off now that she's said it. Was that a threat? Is she threatened by my family? I mean, probably. My dad is really fucking weird and bombarded her with personal drama basically as soon as he met her. I shake it off. "Except his claims about our running speed," I say. "Team Brady is going to kick Team Stag's ass in that race."

I laugh and we finish out our run without any further incidents.

Back at my house, her mood is definitely lighter, but I'm not catching a sex vibe from her. I feel awkward again, wondering if I'm supposed to ask her again if she's ok. I opt to make her a sandwich instead, and I love how her face transforms when she watches me squirt an N shape with the mustard on hers, and a Z on mine.

"Zack is still a stupid nickname for Isaac," she says, softly. She turns my plate so it looks like the mustard is an N. "I'm going to eat both of these."

She starts to, her eyes sparkling as she takes a bite out of each sandwich, but eventually she hands mine to me and we eat standing in my kitchen, the way my family does. It feels so natural and so right to have her here, that I want to detain her when she says she needs to get going.

I try to drive Nicole home and, if I'm honest, try to convince her to let me come inside her house, but she insists on calling her friend Emma for a ride. "They're all at family dinner on the east end anyway. It's on their way to take me home after."

Eventually, I figure she needs a chance to unload on her friend, work through whatever made her so upset at her mother's birthday party. So I try to be a gentleman and kiss her cheek before she leaves. "Thank you for letting me be your date today," I whisper, and I lean toward her. But Nicole stiffens and closes her eyes. My lips barely brush her cheek as she rushes toward Emma and Thatcher's Audi SUV.

She climbs in the back and wedges herself between the two carseats and I furrow my brow, waving as they drive off, wondering if I fucked everything up before I even decided whether I was able to move forward.

CHAPTER THIRTY
NICOLE

I have no idea what to pack for a trip to Paraguay. All that talk with Mick about landslides left me thinking the country is covered in mud, but the internet shows me that the capital city is...well, a city. I sigh. I start filling my bag with things for both an expedition into a rainforest and a boardroom. I spy the purple Babe Rocket on the floor of my closet where I threw it the last time it didn't help me get off.

I bite my lip. I could tell Isaac wanted me yesterday. I sure as hell wanted him. My god, the way he looked in that suit. And then he made me a fucking sandwich and that was somehow even hotter than him in the suspenders and dress shirt with his tie loosened on the drive back.

I don't know why I had to get all weird. Isaac did absolutely nothing to indicate he even wanted anything more with me than casual fucking. We both have talked about how we're not cut out for long term relationships. He was mostly putting on an act for my parents because I'd asked him to.

Because I didn't want my mother to *think* I wasn't capable of hanging onto a man longterm, of getting married like my perfect sister. I sigh.

I pick up the vibrator, thinking I should at least rinse it off and find someplace to stash it. If I'm going to blow Isaac off, I'm going to need this until I find someone else to meet my needs. Hm, I don't love the idea of that. First of all, none of the other men can get me off the way he can.

The man is a magician. Like, how does he know exactly how to create friction on my clit when nobody else seems to be able to figure it out? It's not like I haven't tried with enough men. I scowl at the vibrator, then toss it in my suitcase.

My phone pings with a new text message and I feel my heart race. *Stop it,* I chide myself, angry that I'm hoping to hear from Isaac when I have no reason to hope he'd reach out. I didn't even let him drive me home from our date yesterday.

The message is from Emma.

> So excited for your trip! Bring me back something interesting? Don't forget to pack chapstick.

I roll my eyes, but smile. It's going to be humid and 90 degrees in Paraguay.

The next day, on the flight, I sit next to Tim but glower at him the entire time. Augusto is of course flying down on a chartered flight that better suits his schedule. I can't put a finger on what specifically has been bugging me so much about this entire ordeal, so I chew on it along with the ice from my drink until we roll up to the hotel.

Tim checks in ahead of me and heads straight up to his room. With nobody else around, feeling a bit of a buzz from the jet lag and long hours, combined with the bloody Marys I gulped on the plane, I lean in to ask the clerk, "Has Isaac Brady checked in yet?"

He squints at his monitor and nods. "Yes, ma'am. But unfortunately I am not at liberty to tell you which room he is in." When I pout and sigh, starting to gather my bags, the clerk asks, "Can I deliver a message to Mr. Brady for you, perhaps?" His eyebrows shoot up.

I don't know what I'm thinking. I have no earthly reason to reach out to Isaac...except that I enjoy spending time with him and looking at his abs. Ok, and I like the way he takes me apart from the inside and puts me back together again with orgasms as glue. The clerk slides me a pad and pen, and I write, "Call Nicole, room 687."

Two minutes after I toss my purse on my hotel bed, the little phone on the nightstand starts buzzing. Suddenly I'm blushing like it's middle school or something, and I chalk that up to the jet lag, too, before I stride over to the phone and clear my throat. "Hello?"

"You summoned me, madam?" I can hear the smile in his voice. Snarky prick. Whatever.

"Yes. Do you want to go for a run?"

We meet in the lobby and head out along the river trail. The hotel is nestled along the Paraguay River, with views of the mountains of Argentina in the distance. The humidity has burned off a bit by mid afternoon and the air starts to feel crisp.

Isaac runs in just a pair of shorts, with his t-shirt stuffed in one of the loose pockets. It's all I can do not to drool as I keep pace beside him. "You've got that Monica Gellar hair," he jokes, referencing my favorite episode of *Friends* when the gang goes to the Caribbean and the humidity makes Monica's hair go haywire.

He's not wrong—my curls are unruly on the best of days, and as I run, they fly into my mouth, stick to my shoulders, flap in the breeze. I don't mind it, though. It feels so good to be out here, pushing myself. I've come a long way since January, damn it. I'm not pounding out ten miles a day like Isaac, but according to him we are doing a 5k in about a half hour.

"We should do a half marathon together this summer," he says, and I stop in my tracks to stare at him.

"A half marathon? Are you kidding?"

His eyebrows shoot up into his head. "Would I ever joke with you?" When I smack his arm, he pretends to collapse in pain, and we wrestle around for a little, eventually coming to sit on a bench by a fountain. "Seriously, Nicole. You're becoming a bonafide runner." He nudges me with his shoulder. "You could hang with the Brady clan."

"A half marathon? Come on." I clutch at my elbows and lean back on the bench.

"Nicole, you're doing four miles regularly without much distress. If you can do four, you can do eight. If you can do eight, you can do 13. I'll help you."

I look at him, his face totally serious. Like he's suggesting I do this thing he enjoys, this difficult and inconceivable thing, just for fun. "You're nuts, Isaac Brady," I say, quietly. But I like that he thinks it's possible for me to run a half marathon. That he isn't suggesting it to help me burn calories or as a way to get glory for his business. He seems to genuinely enjoy running and wants to share that with me for some reason.

He stands and offers me his hand, pulling me up from the bench, and then blowing a raspberry against my forearm before running off ahead. So of course I chase him, smiling when I'm able to keep up with him without much effort.

We finish our loop and walk back into the hotel, the air conditioning feeling especially grand after running in the heat. Isaac leans over the water fountain in the lobby, and I stare at him openly, my tongue sweeping along my lips at the sight of him.

I drink my fill after he's done, closing my eyes in relief. Then I feel his hand on my back. The heat of his palm practically melts the shirt off my back. I forget why I was ever upset with him, why I felt off kilter earlier.

Fuck it, I think, straightening up from the water fountain. "Want to help me stretch my muscles? In my room?"

His brows fly up and he nods his head toward the elevator. He presses the button with his knuckle and when we get inside, he says, "Just to be clear, you were using a euphemism?"

I shake my head, laughing. "No. I need your help stretching my hamstrings." He starts to frown a bit and I dig my key card out from the snug pocket of my leggings. "I always feel so loose after you bend me over and ram that big dick into me."

He's on me like a man starving, licking and sucking at my neck as we wrestle-walk down the hall to my room. I can feel his hard-on pressed against my back as I fiddle with the lock on the room door, and as soon as we're inside, I'm in the air.

Isaac tosses me onto the bed and is on top of me an instant later, kicking my suitcase off the bed and sending the contents flying. As he starts peeling off my sneakers and workout clothes, something catches his eye and he pauses.

"Is that the package I signed for," he asks, pointing with my shoe at the purple vibrator rolling across the tile floor of the hotel room.

I crawl up the bed and spread my legs, nodding, letting my hand dip down to roll my nipples between my fingers. I'm horny as fuck and he's already mostly undressed. I start using my feet to pull down his shorts.

"I'm going to make you forget you even own that thing," he growls, grabbing at my ankles. He tosses my legs up over his shoulders and I squeal as he slides his fingers along my damp seam.

"I brought it because I couldn't stop thinking about you," I confess, the last sentence I can eke out before he drives me insane plunging his tongue inside my pussy. "Fuck, Isaac."

He growls again, the deep tenor vibrating against my lower lips, sending gentle waves through my clit. "I want to ruin you," he grunts, sliding two fingers inside me now.

"Oh god," I pant, feeling the orgasm build. "I'm so close already." How does he do this? How does he— "Fuck! Yes! Yes! Isaac, yes, holy shit. Right there!"

I come so hard I see stars and my body jerks violently in his grasp, my heels kicking into his back, my thighs smashing against his ears until I fear I might suffocate him. I feel so much wetness. So much warmth. When I open my eyes, I see Isaac kneeling between my legs, gently lowering my limbs to meet the mattress.

"That. Was. Hot," he says, punctuating each word with a stroke of his index finger along the tops of my thighs, where my wetness is seeping, yearning for him. I just fucking squirted for Isaac Brady and I'm too stunned to move or do anything about it.

But then he's sliding inside me, and I'm wrapping my legs around his waist as best I can. "Fuck me, Nicole, you feel so good. I've never felt anything so wet before. This pussy is so fucking perfect. Are you this wet for me?"

His dark eyes meet mine as he thrusts slowly, deep and long, pulling almost the entire way out each time before crashing back in. I sigh and I nod, but he puts a hand on my chin. "Say it."

"I'm sopping wet for you, Isaac. I'm wet each time I think about you."

And with those words, I unleash the wild demons inside him. He sets a brutal pace, and I pull him against me with all four limbs, thrusting my hips up against his, meeting his every thrust until I feel him swell even larger.

Then he's coming, spurting inside me while he drops one hand to the apex of my thighs, gently rubbing my clit until I come a second time, right along with him.

He collapses on top of me and I feel like he's uncorked something inside me.

My thoughts are clear for the first time since he told me I wasn't losing my house. "I can see it now," I murmur into his neck.

"Ungh?" He slides off me to the side, but makes no effort to move or wipe up.

"I know why I'm mad at Tim," I tell him, and I wriggle a bit out beneath him to stretch and reach for the tissues.

"Wait," he says, grabbing my wrist before I dab between my legs. He props himself on one elbow and peers between my legs, staring.

"What are you doing?"

"Watching my seed drip out of you."

"Your fucking *seed*, Isaac? Gross."

He shrugs and I move my arm again to wipe myself up, but he holds my wrist. "Just let me look at it for a minute. Tell me why you're so pissed off."

"I'm not going to talk to you while you're staring at a pool of jizz seeping out of my twat."

He sighs and takes the tissue from me, dabbing reverently at the mess between my legs. "Better?"

I nod. "So anyway!" I toss a pillow at his head and he ducks, shooting the wadded up tissue for the small trashcan in the corner. "Tim's been telling me what to do since he made me sign up for that damn race."

"Isn't he your boss?"

I roll my eyes. "I mean, that's only sort of a technicality. He hired me to tell *him* what to do with his company. I'm the strategic mind behind Stag Law. At least I was." Isaac flops back down on the bed and starts playing with my hair. It feels really fucking good and I try to remember if I've ever had anyone do this.

Emma used to braid my hair for me every now and then if I needed it to be tight and stay back for awhile. But this is meditative twirling and stroking. It's putting me in a trance. "And then Tim has been obsessed with us beating you guys in the race, and listening to Mick's ideas about this fucking foundation."

I sit up. Isaac follows, asking, "What's wrong?"

"I feel like a shitty person, but Augusto isn't going to find the support he wants if his foundation mission is mitigating landslides in South America. It's just..."

I drift off. Isaac lies back down on the bed, clasping his hands together behind his dark hair. "I ran focus groups. I pulled data from other foundations. I just never asserted myself about it." I nestle into his armpit, noticing that he smells of sweat and soap and sunscreen. And...me. I smell myself on him; I smell our sex session. I like it, and I can sort of see what appealed to him just now about staring between my legs. "People watch sports to escape," I whisper. "Our American audience isn't going to be ready to fund this project."

He nods. "I hear you."

I sigh, relieved he's not pissed off or rushing to defend his dad. Isaac swallows, and I stare at his Adam's apple moving along his throat. I reach out a finger to trace the path of his neck, feeling content.

"So, we still have those meetings with the President tomorrow," I tell him, tapping my fingers against the firm skin of his neck. "But I'm going to assert a new direction for the meeting. A more appropriate direction."

Isaac nods, his eyes closed like he's going to drift off. I'm not really ready to move on to sleepovers. How the hell do I get him out of here? Am I an asshole—stealing orgasms from him, making him listen to all my problems, and then tossing him out?

Probably.

He seems to notice my discomfort eventually, though, because he rolls onto his stomach and props his chin on my bicep. "You're putting up walls, Nicole." When I don't say anything, he nips at the side of my boob with his teeth. "I can tell because I do it, too."

He stands up, and I feel the chill immediately once his heat leave my side. "Where you going?"

He bends and slips into his briefs and shorts, pulling the shirt from his pocket and sliding it over his head. He's still got his ankle socks on from our run. I reach for the sheet and pull it over my nakedness, feeling goosebumps spring up all over my skin. "I have to prepare for our presentation," he says, slipping into his sneakers.

"Right, but, like I said, I'm redirecting the meeting." My voice drifts off. Why in the hell had I agreed to have him come to the meetings in the first place? There's no earthly reason he should be here with us. It's ridiculous, how off my game I've been. Ever since that damn crack in my yard. It's like the earth opened up and swallowed all my good sense.

"Be that as it may," he says, his voice growing cold and distant, "I'm also here with *my* boss, and I have to be ready to convince the president of Paraguay that nothing is more urgent than hiring Beltane to help mitigate the nation's landslide problems."

"Excuse me?"

"Excuse you what?" His eyes look sharp. "You think this..." he gestures around the room, "means that I'm not still looking to advance in my career? I'm sorry that you aren't happy with what's going on at work, but I still need to bring my A game."

"This is some grade A bullshit, Isaac. What the fuck are you even talking about right now?" I feel like throwing pillows at his head. No, I feel like bashing his head off the walls of the hotel room or maybe smashing a mirror over his head to show him how ridiculous he sounds. "I thought we both agreed that it's inappropriate that your father brought you here. This isn't a Beltane project."

"And just what do you know about Beltane projects? You just said yourself you deal with entertainment superstars. Our company does life changing work, Nicole." His nostrils flare. I'm not even sure where this is coming from, but all I know is that he needs to get the hell out of here or I'm going to slice his aorta.

"Get out," I spit. "Get out and lose my number."

"Already forgotten, Medusa."

After he spits that out, he turns to walk out of the room. The vibrator is on the floor near the door, having stopped its roll. Isaac looks at it and kicks it toward the bed. He opens the door, steps into the hall, and closes it without another word.

CHAPTER THIRTY-ONE
ZACK

I don't sleep. Between my shame at acting like such a petulant child with Nicole, and wanting to wring my dad's neck, I'm not sure what to do with my emotions. I recognize that it's a good thing that I ripped the bandage off with her before things got too serious.

I also don't shower because I can't bear to wash away the last lingering remnants of her scent on my hands, on my skin. Yes. I marinated in my own post-run, post-sex funk. So that's about the level of functioning I've reached.

My father asks to meet me for breakfast to prepare for our meeting, and I only agree because I feel the need to tear into him about how badly he has ruined my life so far this spring. I know he wants to go for a run, so I still don't shower, because what's another layer of salt when I'm already wounded and sweaty?

I know damn well my father won't sit down to eat until we run ten miles together.

"There's my boy," he says, jovially, not showing the slightest sign of jet lag or weariness. I can keep up on our run, but just barely. He's decades older and waves a chipper hello to every person we pass out along the riverbank. I often wonder if there's an actual fuse lit inside him.

When we do sit down, Dad orders a Yerba mate and pulls out his own gourd cup from his fanny pack, to the delight of our server. "You should really get your own gourd while you're here," Dad says, ordering a cup of the foul brew for me, too.

I listen while he and the server talk about the magic properties of the tea, and then I wish I could melt into the floor when they pivot to discussing its effects on bowel health. "Jesus, dad," I growl as the server pops off to the back to get us bread and cheese. "You always do this shit."

He sips his drink and frowns at me. "And what is it that I do?"

I scoff. "Please. You know damn well that you're always buttering everyone up—everyone but your kids—and using everything to your own gain." He leans back in his chair and crosses his arms, letting me rant. So I do. "You're using me as a fucking puppet here to get Beltane some damn government contract we aren't equipped to service, and it's not even the direction Stag Law wants to be going with their foundation work."

"Anything else?" He keeps sipping from his damn gourd. I rub my hands along my thighs, shaking my head back and forth.

"Jesus." I pull at my hair by the roots. "I earned that fucking promotion, Dad. And you pulled me out of the meeting like some child to come to your office and run off for a domestic project."

"That domestic project brought us to this opportunity today, son. We've been over this."

"No, *you've* been over this. You have this whole twisted vision swirling around in your gourd head and you only let us peons in on your ideas at the last second so we look like idiots with no time to prepare."

I read half the night, fighting jet lag and trying to make sense of all the notes, all the papers Kellen put together. I still couldn't make heads or tails of what we are even supposed to be saying later, what my role is in this circus.

I exhale and chug down my water. I am sure the mate drink is probably amazing for my insides, but I'm too angry at my dad to consider tasting it. His face reveals nothing when he asks, "So you're angry that you're not leading the division at work?"

"Fuck. Yes. That's what I'm saying. Instead I'm following you around sipping tea on the off chance one of your random connections pays off."

The server comes back with our food and my dad thanks her, asks after her family in fluent Spanish. She beams and hands him the sugar bowl, saying something back to him that I can't understand. When she's gone, he looks at me for a long while without speaking, which is unusual for him because he doesn't often shut the fuck up.

"Son, I don't want you to lead a damned division in the office." I throw my napkin down on the table and stand up, sick of this shit and ready to bail. "Sit down," he snaps, and I don't. But I stand, staring at him. "I want you to run the entire company," he says. "You and your brothers—you're going to run the company someday. I'm not going to be around forever, you know."

I roll my eyes and sit back down. "Dad, you're in your fifties and healthier than most people my age." He waves a hand. "Even if it were true that you wanted me to take a leadership role, don't you think leading a division is the next logical step in that trajectory?"

I don't tell him that I have no desire to run the organization, to worry about profit and loss sheets and board members. If my father can't see that I need my hands in the dirt, that my mind needs to be crunching actual calculations...

"What do you dream about at night, son?"

Nicole, screaming my name, naked. I shrug, not sure where he's going with this.

"Your uncle and I dreamed very different things when we were young, but all the roads led us together at Beltane. He lives and breathes engineering and numbers and order. I see how all the wheels turn at the other organizations who need engineers." Dad picks the cheese off the bread and takes small bites, washing it down with his tea. "Your brothers are like Kellen." He points a fork at me. "But you've got ideas."

"First of all, my brothers have amazing ideas." Dad rolls his own eyes at me, and I shove a wad of cheese in my mouth. He challenges me again to tell him what I dream about at night, and I sigh. "You know, my buddy from MIT is at the university back in Pittsburgh working on machine learning."

"Robots?"

I shrug. "I guess. Anyway I know they're working on landslide prediction stuff, and they've got contacts with the state, and they're looking to form a startup when he's done with his Ph.D."

Dad's brows raise. "See, son, this is what I'm talking about. You've got ideas. This is really relevant for today's meeting. Why didn't you bring this up sooner?"

The mention of today's meetings sours my stomach. "Dad, you didn't fucking brief me on this trip or these meetings. You pulled me along like an idiot after sending me to work on someone's yard."

He waves a hand at me. "You thinking of leaving your family to go work for this robot guy?"

I shrug. I've thought about it. A lot more recently, since Ray has started having conversations with investors. But I've also heard the line my dad gives to engineers when they get better offers. *I might not be able to pay you as well as them, but my work is steady. Beltane builds long-term, repeat business. Our competitors shoot the moon and dry up every few years.* He's not wrong.

Dad leans back in his seat. "You really don't want to come along today and meet the president of Paraguay?"

I shake my head. "I do not want to do that, no."

"Tell me more about landslide prediction. What's that got to do with engineering?"

I explain how Ray's software films hills over time and computer programs analyze any changes, shooting out alerts when things seem unstable. In a city like Pittsburgh, where the rivers slowly carved the land from the hills over the eons, our major roadways snake through rocky ledges and shaky valleys. The earth is slippery when it rains, which is almost all the time.

"Increasingly, the state is having to spend millions repairing rail lines and state highways buried after a brutal storm." Dad nods. I know he knows this, because Beltane inspects a lot of the factories cranking out the concrete and asphalt for the repair work. "Ray had the idea to put his special cameras on city buses."

Dad scratches his chin at that. "They're doing the same routes every day, passing the same hills and whatnot." I nod. "Bring Ray in for a meeting. Let's poach him from those tech assholes."

I crack a gin at that. "What tech assholes do you know?"

He waves a hand. "All those assholes Cal spends time with." Dad pulls a pen out of his shirt pocket and starts writing things down on his napkin. We talk about how machine learning can be useful in a lot of areas at Beltane. I tell him what's been nagging at me. "A guy like that Ray...he can help our inspection program, probably. Figure out what elements need to be replaced in the dams and power plants, really help us help our clients improve their efficiency."

Dad squints off into the distance and drinks the last of his tea. "This could be a really bold new direction for us, Zacky. Really make an impact."

I resist the urge to remind him we could have had this conversation a month ago if he'd open a door for such things, or, you know, ask me questions before mapping out a grand design. He pats my hand. "You're more like your uncle in some ways. You need to open your mouth more if you see people burning the wrong fire."

"You want me to call you out on your bullshit?"

"Well sure! What am I paying you for?" He laughs. "Seriously, kid. I've always been like this."

"I'm well aware." I spent a lot of time trailing after his whims, especially when my brothers were at their mom's house. I always begged to go along with them, until I was old enough to understand why that couldn't be.

Dad lets his hand linger on mine. "You and this company...you're the things I've fought for, son."

I don't respond, because I have no idea what he's talking about. I wouldn't describe his absentee style of parenting "fighting" so much as "too busy or too unskilled to realize his preschooler soiled his pants on a job site he shouldn't have been visiting."

"I'm a lousy husband," Dad says. "I know that. I've given up marrying them, son. You probably noticed. But your mother, she wasn't ready for you." He swallows. "I know she got pregnant to try and keep me...try to get me to be faithful to her." He shrugs. "Not sure why she thought I'd be true to her after I left Liam and Cal's mother for her."

"Come on, Dad."

"I've never been any good at being a husband, and I'm probably a crap father, but damn it, I fought for you. Once you were born, your mother wanted alimony. She wanted full custody, but I wasn't going to let you go. God, Isaac, it killed me when your brothers went to their mother's house. I know I had no idea what to do with the three of you when you were home destroying our house, but it was too quiet without you there. I wasn't letting you go."

"So what are you saying? You stripped mom of all custody with some shark lawyer?"

He eyes flash at me. "Absolutely not. No. Son, she saw she wasn't getting the money from me she wanted, and she wasn't winning me back and she...well, she left. She left both of us. You know that."

I sit for a few minutes and absorb the idea that my mother had at one point claimed to want me, even if it was for the child support payments she thought she'd get from my father. I'm not sure how to feel about that, whether it makes me feel better or worse or, I don't know. Just more complete in the knowledge that I was thoroughly unloved.

Dad leans back in his chair and closes his eyes. "It probably didn't seem like it, Zack, but I treasured those one on one days we had together. You were what got me through the long weeks your brothers were gone. They didn't get to come to work with me like you did." He shrugs. "I don't know.

I guess I wanted you to see me where I was most comfortable. In the one environment where I never seem to lose interest." He sighs, shrugs again. "I wanted you to love what I love."

We stare at each other until I reach for the plate and start gnawing off pieces of the bread. Dad says, "Look, if you don't want to come to the meeting, why don't you go back to Pittsburgh and reach out to Ray. Get him in the office for a meeting, and get me a briefing."

"If I do this, you're not going to go off on some unexpected tangent? This is my friend and I've been consulting with him as he builds his software. I'm already invested in this, Dad."

"I'm not going to—"

"If I prepare a briefing for you, we're going to have a meeting about it *before* the meeting and you and I are going to talk about the strategy of the meeting and the ask from Ray *together*."

"Sure, son. Of course."

"Don't say 'of course' like this is normal for you. If you want me to really take over for you, to love this thing that you love, then you're going to have to start include me in whatever is going on in that head of yours."

"Point taken."

As I walk away from him, I hear him muttering that I sound like his brother, and it's probably the greatest compliment my father has ever handed out.

I THROW my things together in my bag and head for the airport, feeling guilty that I'm not saying goodbye to Nicole, until I remember how we ended things yesterday. Or, rather, how I ended things between us. For good. I sink into my business class seat on the flight, and play back everything my father had said over breakfast this morning.

He didn't say anything surprising or new, really. Except for the part about having to fight for custody of me. That was new information. But it was just the cavalier way he said he's no good with women. A terrible partner. Like he's just accepted that his brother and his business are enough for him.

I can't stop seeing myself in his words. Because who am I? A grouchy fucker who defines himself by what's going well at work, who channels college relationships into work...hell, my dad even said I'm like him. I know he meant somehow that I'm the ideas guy in the operation, but it's there.

"Lone wolf," I mutter, thinking back to Nicole tossing me out of bed each time I've been in there with her. She must be able to see it, too.

I pull out my tablet and have to close out of all the apps I have open for calculations on her property. I try typing up some notes about the briefing for my father, about all the work I've been doing with Ray related to teaching the computer to predict landslides. It blows my mind, how someone like me can teach a computer to know about the pressures and properties of soil. But here we are.

There's no way I'm going to be able to oversee Nicole's yard work and get my shit together to meet with Ray.

I sigh. It's probably best if I don't go back over there, anyway. I can't concentrate around her, and she hates me. Because I was a shit to her. But of course, now I'm thinking about being with her. I think constantly about her hair blowing into my mouth, or listening to her on the phone with clients calming them down, or stirring them up as the case may be.

She doesn't need me, and she sure as shit doesn't need me distracted while I'm making critical plans to repair the yard behind the house she renovated with her bare hands.

I start an email to one of the junior engineers in the geotechnical division at Beltane. I can have Lisa take over the work and I can supervise, make sure everything seems kosher before we get the heavy machinery in there. It's probably best this way. Clean break. Outsource the interactions to Lisa, focus on the meeting with Ray.

"Eye on the prize, Zack," I mutter to myself on the plane. Only problem is, I keep losing track of what the real prize might be.

CHAPTER THIRTY-TWO
NICOLE

The room falls silent as I click the slide presentation forward on the screen. Almost as soon as we filed in, Tim had dropped an arm around Augusto's shoulders and started in on a speech about how this young man would help restore the nation of Paraguay to splendor.

There was a lot of cross talk, with Mick Brady trying to use the weather as a transition to talking about landslides, and Augusto's agent frowning in response to the president tapping his pen, looking frustrated. I don't know where the fuck Isaac is, but he hasn't been present for any of the tours or meetings this morning and he's not here now.

Amidst the din, I stood, cleared my throat, and dimmed the lights, a trick I learned when I was trying to get dude bro coders to shut up and listen to my words.

I pull up some images I put together after our focus group data, of smiling kids running around, of a smiling young Augusto sitting on a ledge, his feet dangling off the edge in threadbare shoes. "Mr. Cruz is so proud of his heritage and would like to craft his charitable foundation in such a way that it supports the people of his homeland."

Augusto smiles. The president's frown lessens slightly.

I flick ahead through a series of press photos of Augusto from training camp, the rookie draft, and some random footage of him walking to and from the baseball field. "Augusto has come a long way from the skinny guy who loved American baseball so much he formed a park league with his friends from school." I click again.

The screen flashes a shot of him sitting on the roof of the dugout, smiling, legs dangling over the edge in a pose that echoes the childhood picture from earlier. He grins and sits a little higher in his seat. I continue. "Turns out, the one thing Augusto loves almost as much as Paraguay is sneakers."

Tim frowns and shoots me a glare. Mick Brady has a fake smile plastered on his face and his knee shakes nervously.

I pull up some numbers and a bar graph. "I've surveyed known philanthropic foundations and high profile donors. I've done focus group studies with likely donors. As you can see here, we asked them about their propensity to contribute toward various types of causes."

I listed infrastructure projects, clean water, improved education, and sports facilities. And, of course, I asked them how they felt about supporting a company that gets necessities like shoes and athletic clothing to young kids who can't afford such things.

"Based on some similar models from other companies, and considering the high likability of Mr. Cruz as a famous role model, these are the predictions for the first year of Cruzwear—a line of fashion sneakers, athletic shorts, and baseball gloves."

I advance to a slide with a lot of zeroes on it and I wink at Augusto's manager. A number of late night calls and last-minute cramming in my hotel room led to this pitch. This is the strategy that's going to work, and it might be shitty that I left Tim out of the planning loop for it, but I'm not sorry about it.

"We're going to do a buy-one, give-one model," I explain. "Regular customers who purchase a pair of Augusto's high end fashion sneakers will be providing a pair for a school child in Paraguay who doesn't have access to athletic footwear. These aren't just sub-par shoes, but high performance athletic apparel that's built to last. Cruzwear will let kids run and play on rough terrain, in mud, in the rain."

Augusto looks like he's going to cry with happiness. Even Mick Brady has an enthralled expression by this point. "The foundation arm of the business will establish the production factory here, in Paraguay, and train and hire local people to manufacture the line. The foundation will thus support the local economy, while providing young children with the tools they need to chase after their own athletic dreams."

ℬ

An hour later, I'm seated at the bar with Augusto's agent, Dennis. We're knocking back South American wine and feeling damn excited about what is sure to be an insanely busy year ahead. The paperwork and logistics in establishing all of this are going to drive somebody bananas. It won't be me. I'll either be fired, or hard at work mapping out a strategy for the next Stag Law client who wants support with their charitable giving.

Augusto comes up to us, grinning. "Hey, Ms. Kennedy," he says, eyes sparkling. "You know I love this! I was starting to get a little worried about all that monsoon talk earlier in the day."

"Worried?"

He shakes his head. "You know...fixing roads here? Construction? Sometimes it's not so above ground..."

I frown, not sure what he means. Dennis coughs into his fist, saying, "corruption," and I understand. Augusto is worried about getting involved at the government level.

"In fact," he continues. "I do not even know if it's such a good idea to build a factory here."

"Oh," I say, chewing the inside of my cheek. "Well we can work all those details out. The important part is the shoes, right?"

Augusto beams and holds up his foot, clad in a vibrant orange high-top shoe that brightly contrasts his slick dark suit.

Tim, Mick, and the president's chief of staff emerge from a cigar room just then, and I stiffen. Augusto and Dennis take off to celebrate with Augusto's home town crowd, but I remain seated, raising a brow at Tim and waiting for him to come over.

When he sits next to me, he leans his forearms on the bar and inhales and slowly exhales through his nose. "I hate the smell of cigar smoke," he says, frowning and signaling for the bartender.

Once he orders a water, he drinks it slowly before turning to look at me, where I continue to sip my wine. "That meeting was very different from what we discussed back in Pittsburgh," he says slowly.

"Indeed it was." I don't shy away from his gaze and I'm not afraid of his anger. I know my friendship with Emma will survive even if my time with Stag Law has come to an end. I'd rather go out having stood up for myself and my ideas, having stood my ground about the parameters of my role as strategy director.

Tim inhales again and sets the water glass down on the bar. "Augusto is thrilled with your idea," he says, and I nod. *Duh,* I think, but I know better than to say so out loud. He clears his throat. "I wasn't aware the focus group numbers were so striking," he says, gesturing a hand. "I admit I got caught up in the idea of a humanitarian infrastructure project."

"Well maybe you should go work for the peace corps," I snap, before I can catch myself. Tim chuckles.

"Maybe in a former life." He raps his knuckles on the bar. "I owe you an apology for the way I've behaved leading up to this trip."

My mouth drops open in a wide O. I really thought he was coming over here to yell at me. He runs a hand through his hair. "I've been really stressed out since Alice got pregnant this third time," he says. "And you know, things with my father are...strained. Anyway, he's not someone I go to for advice." Tim sighs. "Can I be really honest?" I nod. "Sometimes I get... Mick always seems like everyone's dad, you know? I think I got wrapped up in Mick Brady's enthusiasm."

I roll my eyes. "I'm sure Mick really thought his idea was mutually beneficial," I tell him. "It's not the worst idea in the world. It's just...it's not Augusto and it's not the right model for a business for a star athlete."

Tim nods. "You've learned a lot about the industry since I brought you on board," he says, the side of his mouth turning up in a grin.

"Maybe you should pay me more," I tell him, nudging him with my shoulder. But I rest my hand on his. "You're a great dad, Tim. I know Thatcher looks to you as role model and all that shit."

He chuckles, and the sides of his mouth turn up into a small smile. He holds his glass toward me in a toast. "Things are about to get really intense for you at work, Nicole Kennedy. I hope this doesn't impact your marathon training."

CHAPTER THIRTY-THREE
NICOLE

Isaac doesn't call. *Forget my number*, I'd told him. And he chose then to start doing what I tell him. I feel like some sort of psychopath, thinking about him all the fucking time. But it's hard not to when so much about my life centers around him. The trench in my yard. The group training runs he's apparently skipping now. The orgasms that have gone missing again since I threw him out of my hotel room.

Maddie and Emma are on their way over to my house to see the work in the back yard. I got an emailed set of finalized plans from someone at Beltane Engineering and signed them digitally from the plane on the way back. I would have loved to see the look on my own face when I realized I was being passed off to an underling.

Now, this Lisa person is at my house every day with a clipboard, every bit as serious and earnest as Isaac as she measures shit and bosses around a set of contractors.

Lisa says the money has come in for the remediation, and she's got a barge sailing up the Allegheny River with digging equipment.

I hear a whistle behind me and turn to see my friends standing in my yard. Maddie carries a six pack of beer and Emma hands me a bag of chips. "This is…" Maddie shakes her head and gestures at the boat sailing up laden with dirt. They're bringing it in by water, which I guess is good so the dump trucks don't have to trash the grass on my front yard to get it back here.

The three of us set up some chairs on the patio and watch the chaos for awhile, the roar of the machinery robbing them of any opportunity to ask me uncomfortable questions. When the crew takes a break, the quiet feels loud and Emma clears her throat. "So," she says. "I don't see Zack over there..."

Hearing the name Zack, Lisa looks over and shouts. "Mr. Brady has put me in charge of the project," she says. "Once again, I assure you I've passed all my exams and am highly qualified to supervise the remediation."

"No worries, Lisa," I say. "We're just not interested in staring at your ass when you bend over."

She flushes. "Oh." She looks back at her clipboard and tries to hide a laugh.

Emma shakes her head at me. "Thatcher and his brothers went for a run yesterday," she says. The three of them often do that, and more often than not they wind up having a fist fight as they "help" each other figure out solutions to their emotional drama.

"Who has a black eye," I ask before I shove a handful of chips into my mouth, glad we're pivoting to work talk already. Maddie snorts.

Emma just laughs. "Thatcher came home stunned into silence because Tim was talking about how he was wrong and should have trusted you more."

I just continue eating chips and shrug. "Show me the lie," I say. Emma swats at my shoulder.

"He's lucky to have you," she says. "You know trusting people is Tim's major weakness."

"Yeah, well, mine, too. Apart from you, obviously," I say. But I had forgotten that Tim and I have that in common—our sense that we are the only ones we can rely on in the world. Tim's been pretty actively working on it. I've just been leaning in to my role as a control freak.

Just then, Valerie walks over toward us with a lawn chair. "Not in the mood, Valerie," I say, but Maddie hands her a beer, twisting off the top of the bottle before she hands it to my neighbor.

"Got your note about the lawsuit," Valerie says, gesturing at the barge. "I notice you didn't seek my approval before the work began."

"Well, that's true."

"Good thing that Lisa person came over for a signature," Valerie huffs as she settles into her chair. She points a knuckle at a shaggy-haired guy in a flannel with the sleeves cut off. "You gals all staring at the looker over there operating the excavator?"

"Duh," Maddie says with a snort. We all share a laugh.

"Just don't get used to sitting over here with us," I tell Val. "I'll put up a fence, I swear to god, and block all the sun from your hedges."

"Oh, like I enjoy putting up with your snappy bullshit," Val retorts with a grin. She reaches for the bag of chips and I hand it to her, glad we seem to be speaking the same language for once.

"Now," she says, staring at me. "Why don't you tell me why that gal is running the show now instead of the broody drink of water you've been canoodling?"

I whip my head around and glare at Valerie. "Because Isaac Brady is an arrogant piece of toilet paper and I'm done wiping my ass with him."

The women around me swallow, wide-eyed. It's a good thing the excavator fires its engine back up, because that's about all I can handle saying about him. My insides churn. I'm feeling something I recognize as emotional pain, and I practice deep breathing to shove it all back down inside, where I store all my responses to the things my parents have said to me over the years.

Emma stands up and wraps her arms around me. "What are you doing," I shout over the machinery. Maddie stands up and smashes me into a hug from the other side. Thankfully, Valerie stays where she is, but the second she leans forward and begins patting my leg, I lose control.

I look down at my shirt and see wet splotches, realizing my eyes are crying.

"Just let it out, babe," Emma says. And I do. I let it all out. All the years of rejection from the people who were supposed to love me. All my stress at the prospect of losing a home I had literally crafted for myself with my bare hands. All my rage that my boss had reneged on our arrangement until I stood up and yanked back control over the meetings I was supposed to be orchestrating.

And finally, I cry—yes, ok, it's me crying. Not just my eyes—I cry for Isaac, who seemed like he was worthy of peeling back my fortress walls. Just a little. Not a lot. But as soon as I did, he stomped all over everything. I cry on my friends until I'm all dried up inside.

Emma sits back down and smiles at me. "Don't you feel better?" She asks. "Like, you think you'd feel totally empty after gushing out all the heavy shit, but I find, after a big cry, I feel renewed. Remember when Thatcher and I were on the outs and you helped me cry?"

I nod. She's right. She's always right. That's why I love her. She's both right *and* good, has her priorities in the right place. And she listens to me when I call her out on her bullshit. Which is the only reason I consider listening to her when she says, "Now, I think you should call Isaac tomorrow."

CHAPTER THIRTY-FOUR
ZACK

ORLA, LIAM AND CAL STAND ON MY FRONT PORCH POUNDING SO HARD ON MY FRONT window, I worry they'll shatter the glass. I crack one eye open to make sure I'm not imagining them out there, and then try to go back to sleep on my couch, where I've fallen asleep with my laptop on my chest.

Eventually, one of them locates the key they each have to get in my house and soon, all of them are standing above me, smelling like sweat and Brady rage.

"Dude. You stink." Cal waves at the air, pulling his t-shirt up over his nose and mouth. I groan. It's been three days since I got home from South America, and I've only slept a handful of hours. I've been here in my living room the entire time, working with Ray on his research and typing up plans to bring him in to speak with my dad and Uncle Kellen.

"Like you guys smell so good," I mutter, trying to hide my head under a throw pillow, but Liam yanks it away and tosses it across the room. He stands above me with his hands on his hips, glowering.

"You've missed several family runs, and at least two group runs for the corporate relay," he says, disapproving. He pauses, and adds, "Your girlfriend wasn't there today, either, so we came to make sure you were—"

"Jesus, Liam, that's not why we're here." Orla cuts him off and I struggle to sit up at the mention of Nicole. Thoughts of her sting my breastbone, like when I run too fast on a frigid day, even though I'm working really hard on ghosting her until she forgets my name.

"We're actually worried about Zack's health and safety," Orla continues. "Uncle Mick didn't seem worried when you didn't come back to work after Paraguay, but—and I'm not trying to imply anything negative here—but that really isn't super informative. If Mick's not worried, I mean."

"It's not like your dad was worried," Cal interjects, helping himself to the bag of corn chips I have by my feet on the couch. "Uncle Kellen just sort of mumbled and grunted when we asked him if he'd heard anything."

The room falls silent as they all find someplace to sit, and then I become aware that they're waiting for me to say something. "Dude," Cal says, bouncing a chip off my forehead. "You have to tell us what's going on."

I sigh and drape a forearm over my face. "Well the big thing is that I finally had it out with Dad."

"Had it out how? Like...you told him to fuck off about the relay team?"

I shake my head and struggle to sit up. Liam hands me his water bottle and I squirt a bunch into my mouth. "I mean, we were talking about when my mom left."

Liam nods. "That's a significant conversation. Did he have his gourd tea?"

"Oh man," Cal makes a fart sound with his mouth. "Dad and that fucking tea. Am I right?" He looks around and Orla glares daggers at him. "Sorry, sorry. Zack, please. Continue."

I sigh and tell them about my fight with Dad. "It wasn't a fight in the end, I guess. But anyway, he heard what I had to say about my friend Ray and his machine learning research and...well, I'm pitching him and Kellen later this week."

I tell them about the landslide work, how I'm imagining we can apply Ray's machine learning interests to a bunch of aspects of our work at Beltane. By the time I'm done talking through it all, I'm actually feeling really good because I realize I've internalized a lot of the material I've been writing out for the past few days. I grin and rub my hands through my hair, trying to smooth it out.

"It's good you don't work from home much," Orla says, frowning. "You look like shit."

I grin at her. "Thanks, cuz. Seriously, I like it that you always tell it to me straight."

She sniffs, and seems to regret it, between the post-run funk of my brothers and my unshowered odor. "I thought that's what you like about Nicole."

God, please don't make me talk about Nicole, I think. But I'm not lucky enough to avoid that land mine. "One minute you're suited up taking her on a date and the next...you're grunting like a cave man when I say her name." Orla is giving me her very best bossy face, like she's gearing up to twist my earlobe until I talk to her.

I clench my thighs together in case she gets any ideas about punching me in the junk like she used to do when we were much younger. "Look," I tell them. "Things were getting intense with Nicole. Neither of us can handle that right now. We've got work shit."

Liam says, "hmmm" like he knows something. "I overheard Lisa talking about the project at her house. Since when do you outsource a job midway through?"

Since I'm terrified to see her and face the reality that I'm catching feelings for her. Since my dad told me she totally dismantled that meeting in Paraguay and somehow Beltane still got a consulting contract. Since I made her think I doubted her ability to bad ass her way out of that situation so that everyone wins.

I shrug. "Like I said, when I fought with Dad I told him how I felt about being passed over for that department head position. This presentation with Ray is top priority for me and in my opinion, a top priority for the future of the company. Lisa is more than capable of taking the lead at this stage."

My siblings and Orla share a silent conversation with each other and then grunt at me a few times before standing. "Ok," Cal says.

But Orla coughs into her hand, saying "bullshit." And I roll my eyes at her.

"Well," Cal continues, "we're all going to the cafe because we've earned some greasy diner food. You're not invited unless you promise to shower and come to work tomorrow."

I throw a couch cushion at them as they file out of my house.

CHAPTER THIRTY-FIVE
ZACK

"WELCOME ABOARD, RAYLAND," UNCLE KELLEN SAYS, SHAKING HANDS WITH MY friend the following week. Beltane wasn't able to offer Ray a dazzling salary for when he finishes his PhD, but we can offer him total creative control over his machine learning projects, absolute freedom over the types of projects he selects and, of course, the responsibility to lead his division and begin creating software to help all the different divisions of Beltane serve their clients more efficiently.

It's been a few decades since we added a new division to the Beltane Engineering portfolio. This is the most exciting thing to happen since Cal talked Dad into getting some drones. Already, Cal and Ray are deep in conversation about who will manage the drone projects meant to make our inspection safer. I hear Ray say something about programming unmanned robots to scope through pipes, and soon my entire family is calling for whiskey and walking toward a nearby bar.

"This is a fine day for Beltane Engineering," my father says, pulling me in for a side hug. He means it, too. He didn't have to fake enthusiasm for any of my or Ray's ideas, and he actually suggested a sweet bonus for me as a finder's fee for getting Ray on board.

Professionally, my life is a dream. I've got everything I set out to achieve, really. Autonomy over the projects I'm working on. The opportunity to put my hands in the dirt. Ray and I are actually working with three neighboring counties to monitor landslides all around Pittsburgh and every day I spend helping the programmers with their data points is like the Olympics for a guy obsessed with math and pressure and soil composition.

The only problem is, despite my own insistence that I need to be a lone wolf, that the love and acceptance of my family is enough to fulfill me personally, I can't shake the ache in my chest when I think about Nicole.

I keep reminding myself we weren't actually together. We never set parameters, let alone made declarations of monogamy or said anything about feelings. I just...need her. And as I stare at the drink in my hand, I know that the reason she's not here is because I shoved her away.

She would have left anyway, I think, swirling the whiskey in my glass. *It would've fizzled out and she'd leave.*

If all these things are true, why does it feel like such shit when Lisa tugs on my sleeve and asks me to sign off on some new permits for the project with Nicole's yard?

"Give us a minute, Lisa," my uncle says, tugging on my sleeve and pulling me over to a table where he and Orla are sitting with some snacks. I say nothing, but reach for a soft pretzel bite and dip it into the warm cheese. Kellen looks at me and rests a hand on my shoulder. "Can't help but notice you're a bit glum, kiddo," he says.

"Only you would say a word like 'glum,'" I mutter.

Kellen sighs. "My Orla tells me you're skipping family runs lately." He waits for me to crack and start talking to him, but he might as well not hold his breath. I eat another pretzel. It might be the first food I've had today, which explains a lot about how my guts are churning.

Eventually, I look over at him and Orla, blinking at me like two Irish owls, and say, "I'm a lone wolf." As I say it, I recognize that I'm probably drunk.

"Hmm," Kellen says, sizing me up. "Lone wolf? Tell me what you mean by that." I can tell he doesn't actually want me to respond, so I don't. He continues. "Were you alone when your brother Liam helped you figure out who should be financially responsible for your client's rotational landslide? Were you perhaps alone when your college roommate brought a new direction and energy into the family business?" He leans forward, his voice dropping. "Were you alone at the country club with Bitchy Bitsy Kennedy denigrating her daughter where everyone could hear? Don't look at me like that. I talk to people."

Kellen yanks the bowl of soft pretzel bites away from me and sets his hand on mine. "We're engineers, son. Precision is important to us, so let me explain to you why you are not a lone wolf. The etymology of that expression refers to a female wolf, one who has been driven out of the pack. If anyone is a lone wolf in this scenario, it's your mother."

I open my mouth to interject something, but nothing comes to mind, so I close it and he continues. "Nobody is saying she needed to put up with your father's philandering. But anyone who's going to use a tiny baby as a pawn for financial gain is going to get the cold shoulder from this family." He snorts. "You are not a lone wolf. You are very much an integral part of the pack here, Isaac. You and I both know that large ungulates are easier to bring down when you've got help."

With that, he stands, kisses Orla on the cheek, and glides away from the table before I have a chance to work out who is the ungulate and who is my helper-wolf in his metaphor. Sensing my distress, Orla says, "He means you need to call Nicole and eat crow for whatever asshole things you said and did to her."

"What do you know about it," I scoff, trying to reach for the soft pretzels again.

"I know your head hasn't been in the game since your trip, and your split times are suffering." She shrugs. "Your run tracker posts are still set to public, by the way. You need to adjust the notifications in your app."

CHAPTER THIRTY-SIX
NICOLE

I haven't taken Emma's advice about calling Isaac, and the longer he doesn't call me, either, the angrier I get at both of them. Why would she suggest I grovel to him when he was the one who was rude? I don't have time for rude.

I also miss him like crazy. I miss his beard scruff on my thighs and his snarky text messages. I miss sitting at my house and working next to him, yet not feeling suffocated by him.

Ever since we set our course with Augusto, work has been like a high-speed boat race, and I'm loving getting splashed with the sea foam. Everything is thrilling, from deciding which designers to hire to mapping out production schedules. It might be possible I'm fast tracking everything so that I'm working around the clock and not taking time to dwell on my confusing feelings.

Augusto has already approved a shoe design, in fact, and some local university students have somehow stitched up a few pairs in the maker space, whatever that entails. So yeah. Work is amazing. Lisa says I'm about a week away from being able to plant grass in my back yard, and I'm feeling beyond ready for the relay run.

I haven't told Tim anything about my budding enjoyment of running as stress relief. He doesn't need to know he had a good idea, and he doesn't need to know I've started actually using my treadmill desk for sprint drills in the middle of the day. I looked up a speed program online.

I'm determined to finish my portion of the relay in under 45 minutes. Emma and Maddie said my calves are starting to look cut, and I'll go ahead and accept the compliment in time for tea-length dresses and pedal pusher pants.

Mark interrupts me as I'm flexing my calves, staring at the subtle way my body has changed. That feels too passive—my body hasn't changed. I fucking chiseled myself a new shape. I'm going to phrase it that way.

"Nicole? Nicole!" He taps his loafered foot impatiently when I don't answer.

I sigh. "What am I late for now?"

He sits down and spreads out a stack of papers. "We're finalizing guest lists for Augusto's launch party. You've already approved media outlets and foundation heads, athletes, the fabulously wealthy…"

"I trust your judgement, Mark," I tell him, patting his hand. "That's why I promoted you to run point on this event."

He rolls his eyes. "Ok, well, like I said I'm getting Alice to vet the caterers and suggest drink pairings for the signature cocktails, oh! And I'm choosing the band. Augusto said 'anything South American sounding,' so I've got a drum corps coming and—"

"Mark, babe, I'm working on the notes for the investor meeting that happens prior to the party."

He practically snorts at me before leaning forward. "Are you bringing a date?"

I snort out a puff of laughter at that. "Mark, I will have absolutely zero time to entertain a stupid date. Besides, I don't need to network or look good for the boss. I'm already basically related to the boss."

"Nicole." His voice is firm and there's something new behind his tone. "You work on a team, you know."

"Yes, Mark, I'm well aware of all the valuable contributions of my coll—"

"Babe. You're working us all to the bone and we're tired. The team has sent me to tell you we need a night off. So if you can please approve all these invoices, expenses, and seating charts, I can deliver a little relaxation." His nostrils flare a bit as he stands, glowering at me.

"Oh," I tell him. I sink lower into my chair, feeling defeated. I've been selfish. "I wish you'd told me this a week ago, Mark. Shit."

He sighs. "It's ok. Now. Sign these papers so I can go the fuck home and swing some kettlebells and maybe get laid this weekend."

I snort. "What must that be like." I start signing the papers and reading over everything he's prepared. It's all in order. The vendors, the venue, the presentation plans for the event. Mark even has someone writing prepared remarks for Tim and me to deliver.

Eventually I realize Mark is staring at me, and I look up at him, confused. "What?"

"Don't 'what' me! You know exactly what it feels like to get predictably laid and you're being too damn stubborn to make it happen for yourself."

"Oh, christ, not you, too."

"Yeah, yeah, he was an asshole in Paraguay. Jet lagged, tired from running, under pressure from his family. The man said some fucked up shit. Nicole, you also said he encouraged you and seemed to actually care about the things that interest you. Namely spackle."

I bite my lip. It's true, Isaac seemed worth my time for awhile. But I'm not sure if I can deal with someone who cracks like that under pressure.

Seeming to read my mind, Mark raises a brow at me. "He stood out in the rain in your yard in February. In Pittsburgh. Trying to make sure you could save your house."

"He was trying to make sure he could get paid for the work," I counter, shoving the pile of completed paperwork toward Mark.

He gathers them up and shakes his head. "I don't believe that, and neither do you." But then he smiles and gives me a salute. "Don't call me this weekend. I'm busy. But I'll see you Monday."

And with that, he bustles away and I realize there's no more work for the weekend, nothing pressing to attend to. In freeing up the staff, I've also sentenced myself to two entire days of myself.

When I get home, I change and go for a run. I concentrate on the rhythm of my feet on the pavement, on timing my breath with my steps. I run along the trail that I never use, realizing when I get close to my office that I've got a lot of steam left.

I manage to tune out all the nagging thoughts of my parents and my job and Isaac Brady. I'm just running, feeling my lungs open up. Sweating. I start laughing, because it feels so damn good. By the time I get home, I've gone six entire miles. *If you can run four, you can run eight.*

It feels strange to realize that such a thing is entirely possible. I never stopped to consider that I might be able to run at all, but then I suppose I never thought I could take a sledge hammer to a wall to expose the original brick fireplace. "And look at me now," I mutter aloud.

I wander around back to find Valerie sitting outside, staring at the yard. The landscape folks are coming next week to level everything off and plant grass. She and I are supposed to discuss whether we're doing sod or seeds or…whatever.

The fervor with which I want to avoid being alone with my thoughts is so intense that I feel my arm waving at Valerie. "Hey," I shout, cringing on the inside. "You have a second to talk about the landscape stuff?"

She looks at me in shock, which is fair because I always am super crabby when I talk to her. It's not that she's completely annoying. It just bothers me to think that maybe I'm on the same life path as her. No spouse. No kids. Living alone, retired, with nobody but a bitchy neighbor to yell at as our neighborhood gentrifies around us.

She pats the chair next to her on her patio and I sink into it. "You thinking of the sod?"

Valerie shakes her head. "Hard pass. We should do perennial ryegrass now, and after the heat of summer, have them come back and lay Kentucky bluegrass."

"Wow," I say, impressed. "You've really put some thought into this."

"What the hell else have I got to do," she says, and then laughs. "I'm just messing with you. My friend teaches at that Penn State extension program. Do you know they have an entire major in turf grass there?"

"I did not know this, Valerie."

She nods. "Yes! Kids can go to college and study grass. A few of my students have done that, over the years."

"I had no idea." And it's true, and it's also true that I'm interested in the idea of this, the way she talks about how it's important to study biology and even meteorology.

"I bet Zack knows turf grass specialists," she says. "His line of work, especially if he's helping rejuvenate the land after strip mining…yes, I bet he knows plenty about turf management."

"I don't really want to talk about Zack, Val, if that's ok."

She sighs. "Welp," she says, pointing at the yard. "Perennial ryegrass, then. You let me handle this part, huh? Seeing as you got everything going with the foundation beneath us."

I smile. "Just no ugly hedges."

"For the last god damn time, Nicole, I was going to trim it and shape it. You just never let me over on your side!"

CHAPTER THIRTY-SEVEN
ZACK

It's been a month. A month in which I have hardly slept, have ingested more than I think I need to know about machine learning, and have thought of Nicole Kennedy no less than seven thousand times per minute.

The longer I don't call her to apologize, the more I feel like I shouldn't bother. *She's probably moved on by now,* I think, and the image of her with another man turns my blood to ice.

Orla says I need to grovel, do something epic. I have no idea what that means. I'm not an epic guy, and she seems to really dislike having attention brought to her in crowds anyway. There are literally zero examples from my life of people using good communication skills to navigate a problem in a healthy way.

I'm pulled from my thoughts when Em, the admin for our building, raps on my office door. "You got a minute, Zack?"

"Sure," I tell her, tossing my pen across the desk. "What's up?"

Em pushes the door open wider to reveal Valerie, the woman who lives next to Nicole, standing in the hall. "She says she's here to talk turf..."

I chuckle. "Come on in, Val. What can I do for you?" Em smiles and backs out, closing the door behind her as Val sinks into the folding chair. I really have to do more with the furniture in here.

"I'm not actually here to talk about landscaping," she says, scowling at me a bit.

"Well, is there a problem with the project? Should I call Lisa to join us?" I reach for my phone but she swats at my arm.

"No! I'm here to talk about what an idiot you are."

Stunned, I widen my eyes. "Okaaaay. Care to elaborate?"

She crosses her arms over her chest and huffs. "Do you know that tonight, Nicole Kennedy is going to a fancy sneaker party with no date?"

"I did not, but I really don't see—"

"And, further, did you know that she cries in her sun room? And stomps around the back yard kicking dirt and muttering about what an idiot you are? I hear her out there, on the phone with her friend, and then they hang up and Nicole *cries*. She didn't even cry when her yard crumpled into the sea."

I open my mouth to explain that while the Allegheny River eventually reaches the Chesapeake Bay, her yard actually was sliding into the river. But Valerie presses on. "She's rude and abrasive on the outside, but I think we both know that she's very vulnerable beneath that shell. She's like... tectonic plates sliding around over liquid magma."

"Tectonic plates?"

She waves a hand. "Don't tell me you've got a masters degree in geotechnical engineering and you don't know about plate tectonics."

"Well, of course I know how earthquakes happen. But what does this have to do with Nicole?"

Valerie plants both hands on the desk. "I called that assistant of hers and told him I want you to be her sneaker date at the fancy party." She reaches into her bag and pulls out an index card with neat handwriting. "He says to wear dark jeans and sneakers, obviously."

"Valerie, I can't just show up at her work function. It would make her upset."

"She's upset all the damn time! Haven't you been listening?"

My heart lurched when Valerie said Nicole has been crying. She can't have been crying about me, can she? Surely it was related to work pressure or something else with the house. Something she loves and cares about. "Boy," Valerie says, continuing to shake her head. "It's no wonder I never got into a relationship myself. Men are completely clueless."

I'm not about to disagree with her. She taps at the note card on the desk and says, "Tonight. Don't mess this up." And she flounces out of the office without another word.

Sneaker party. Famous athletes. Nicole giving speech. Dark jeans and rolled up sleeves—makes her hot and bothered.

I have to laugh at the thought of Valerie taking notes from Nicole's assistant about what turns her on. This all feels a bit ridiculous. Showing up at her work event into a room where half the people probably think I'm a dick for ruining whatever we had simmering together.

The Nicole I know wouldn't have told a lot of them, though. She keeps everything so tight to the vest. *I wonder if she likes vests,* I think, watching as my subconscious plans my outfit for tonight even as my conscious, rational mind rejects the idea of swooping in to catch her off guard.

I sigh and look around the office. I gather my things and head home, wondering if I even have any sneakers apart from my running shoes. I look at the note card again, consider the past month and how even though things have been going exactly as I'd hoped professionally, I still feel like shit most of the time because my personal life is, frankly, ruined. And that's my own damn fault.

Lots of people have now told me to do something about this. The only thing standing in my way here is me being an idiot. I go up one flight of stairs to my brother Cal's office. "Hey," I say. "I need you to help me pick out something to wear."

THE PARTY IS BEING HELD in a new gallery space on the north shore of the river, near the sports stadiums. I hand my keys to the valet out front and smooth my hands over my outfit. Cal lent me a pair of dark rinse jeans that feel entirely too tight, but he says they look perfect with the bright orange high-tops and blue dress shirt he had me wear untucked, sleeves rolled as per instructions from Mark.

I feel like I swallowed a Lego brick, knowing she's in there and is likely to reject me and kick me out of her life forever for showing up here like this after what I said in the hotel and then just not calling her for so long.

"Name?" There's a girl in overalls at the door, a beanie slouched over her head and very expensive diamond earrings glinting in the light shining behind her.

"Um, Zack Brady. I'm not sure if I'm on the list…"

She smiles. "You are. Welcome. Enjoy a peach crostini as you enter."

A peach crostini. A server appears and hands me a square little plate made from bamboo. I pop the appetizer into my mouth while I scan the room, and then I see her. My mouth dries out and my blood surges when I look at her, laughing and talking with her boss and Augusto Cruz.

She seems so comfortable, so confident. Her wild curls are down and just springing everywhere. Her green eyes flash above a black sheath dress with a boxy sort of neckline that shows the swell of her cleavage. I feel an uncontrollable urge to run across the room and tackle her to the ground, massaging her ass and kissing her, trying to make up for the past month where I've just wallowed in my own stupidity.

I stare as a staff member in a headset pulls her aside and waves her up on stage. Nicole kicks off the speaking portion of the program, introducing herself as the director of strategy for Stag Law. The room erupts into cheers as she smiles a 1,000 watt smile, talking about this new foundation that Augusto wanted to create.

She is electric on stage, talking without notes, smoothly and confidently. She introduces her boss, and makes to exit the stage, ceding the limelight to the guy with his name on the business. Someone hands me a drink and I clutch it, swallowing as I watch Tim Stag ask Nicole to stick around for additional recognition for her vision and leadership.

"You know," Tim says, draping an arm around her shoulders. "My big idea was to bring you all here to talk about landslides. Obviously I'm not the visionary around here. Let's put our hands together for Cruz Wear. Are these shoes comfortable or what?" Tim holds up a foot and Nicole laughs. The staff are all wearing black and gold high tops with a C across the toe. Cruz, I guess.

Augusto takes the mic and starts introducing the board of directors for the foundation and I take a deep breath. This is my moment. Either I swoop in and win back Nicole, or I should leave now and never darken her door again.

The decision is made for me, though, because I watch her notice me standing there. Her head snaps my direction and her eyes flare. She stalks toward me, and I have the hugest grin on my face because I'm so happy to see her, even if she looks mad as hell.

"What the hell are you doing here," she hiss-whispers.

"I missed you," I tell her, truthfully. "I came to grovel."

"Yes, but how in the fuck did you get in? This is an invitation-only event for wealthy people." She crosses her arms and taps the toe of one sneaker-clad foot. I notice that her calf muscles are looking tight. I smile wider, proud of her for working so hard on her running.

Realizing she expects and answer, I cough. "Mark basically sent me," I say. "He and Valerie conspired."

She rolls her eyes so hard I worry she will get vertigo. "Those fucking assholes," she mutters, tossing her curls over one shoulder so she can see me better to glare at me. "Well." And I'm worried she's going to call security. Get them to toss me out. But she raises a brow. "You said there'd be groveling?"

I look over my shoulders. "Can we maybe go somewhere? To talk?"

"Nope." She puts her hands on her hips. "Grovel."

"You were so incredible up there," I tell her. I reach for her hand, wanting to touch her. Needing to feel connected to her. She shakes her head. I sigh. "I loved watching you in your element, watching your boss acknowledge how brilliant you are," I tell her. She tilts her head, expectantly. I sigh again. "I'm so fucking sorry, Nicole. I know I don't deserve for you to hear me groveling. I push people away," I tell her. "But you do, too. Because we've both been shit on by people who are supposed to love us and, well, I lost my temper in Paraguay."

I watch her demeanor shift a little. Just the slightest hint that she's on board with what I'm saying, so I push on. "That entire trip was the culmination of a lifetime of me not standing up to my father, of me not standing up for my ideas, whether that's at work or in my personal life." I reach for her hand again, drawn to her, and this time she lets me. When my fingers touch the soft, smooth skin of her wrist, I feel strength radiating through me. Just being near her, I feel more whole. I plow ahead.

"I had a huge fight with my dad that next day, Nicole, and I came out of it in a totally new direction at work, in a totally new place. And as hard as it was to have that discussion with him, it feels one thousand times harder to open up to you and let you know how I feel."

"And how exactly do you feel, Isaac?" Her voice is softer now, though. Less irate.

"Well, I'm crazy about you. I think about you as I'm falling asleep at night. I find myself thinking of annoying things to text you and imagining what your face would look like if I did. And then I remember that I fucked everything up with you and I just have to add the witty texts to my note file."

"You have a note file? Of jokes?" She's trying not to smile, biting her bottom lip, leaving delicious indentations in the plump skin and driving me mad with want.

"I have a file of jokes I want to share with *you*," I clarify. I reach my other hand for her waist and pull her close. She lets me, and I feel like I exhale fully for the first time since I left her hotel room. "I don't know how to be a boyfriend. And I don't know how to open up to people, but I want to try with you, Nicole. And I swear to everything holy, I will never walk away from a fight like that again." I meet her eye to find hers shining and wet, like she's welling up with tears maybe.

"Oh, Nik, don't cry. Not for me. I can't bear to know I'm hurting you again."

She shakes her head. "I'm not hurt this time, you asshole. I'm happy."

"Oh. Well, good," I say. I let my fingers dance up and down her arms, not wanting to lose this physical connection I've craved so deeply for so long. "How am I doing with the groveling?"

"I give it a six," she says.

Smart ass, I think, grinning. "On what scale?"

"One to eight," she says, resting her head on my shoulder.

"I can work with that," I tell her, winding my fingers through her hair and tugging her head back. Before she can say anything else, I lean in to kiss her, deeply and slowly. I use my mouth to tell her all the things I still can't figure out how to put into words. I let my body communicate to her how deeply I've missed her, how badly I need her. How much I want her to give me another chance.

"Be with me," I whisper into her mouth, a plea and a promise.

"I'll think about it," she says, and then she grabs me by both cheeks and pulls me back in for another kiss.

CHAPTER THIRTY-EIGHT
ZACK

 I tell her as she wriggles with impatience. We're standing in our hotel room in Delaware, getting ready to walk over to the start line of the half marathon along the beach.

"It's hard to stand still when my boyfriend is about to stab me with fucking safety pins," she growls, wriggling again and snatching them from my hand. "I'll do it myself."

"Suit yourself," I say, shaking my head and getting to work pinning my own race bib over my Pittsburgh Marathon Relay shirt. I assured Nicole that it's a newbie move to wear the shirt for the actual race while competing in that race.

She wanted us to wear our matching Pittsburgh shirts, which I told her was totally fine since we ran that race last month. Beltane smoked Stag Law, of course. All of us are marathoners. Nicole might like running now, but she's not Usain Bolt. I kept pace with her through most of our portion of the event until she started yelling at me for being anticompetitive and not sticking with the pace she knew I was capable of.

I'm glad I was at the relay exchange ahead of her, after all, because I got to see her face when she charged into the check point to slap hands with Tim. She was so god damned proud of herself, and I was proud of her, too. She wore that race medal afterward and wouldn't even take it off for sex. It kept slapping me in the face as she rode me in her bedroom later that afternoon.

"What are you grinning about," she huffs around a mouthful of pins.

"Just remembering how you tried to give me a concussion with your race medal after the relay," I tell her, taking one of the pins from her and carefully pinning down the last corner of her race number.

"Oh," she says, and then smiles. "I'll probably do that today, too."

"Maybe our medals can clink together while I fuck you in the shower," I tell her, pulling her in for a kiss. I smack her ass and reach for my ball cap on the table. "Come on. We have to get to the start."

Nicole squeezes my hand as she walks beside me. I rub her wrist with my thumb and assure her this is going to be great.

"I've never run more than ten miles," she tells me, her voice quiet as we make our way through the throngs of people.

"Ten is the typical big training run before a half marathon," I assure her. "You've trained your ass off, Nicole. Why would this make you nervous, but you can stand on a stage and ask a room full of billionaires to part with their moldy money?"

She shrugs. "It just never occurred to me that I couldn't convince the billionaires to part with their money."

I pause and turn, putting my hands on her shoulders and leaning my forehead against hers. "Nicole Kennedy, there is nothing you cannot do," I tell her. "Except beat my brother Liam at Scrabble. We have established that you are terrible at that."

She swats at my shoulder. "Dickface."

"I'm going to put my dick in your face in a few hours."

I tease and poke at her until the start gun, and then she's all business. She doesn't chat for the first few miles as we run along the boardwalk. The course wends its way into the state park and, once we grab a sports drink at the six mile mark, she finally says, "I feel great."

"You look great," I tell her, grinning.

"You're not bored senseless running with me? This slow?"

"Nicole, we're not going that slow. And I'm not here to compete against you this time."

"Well, what are you here for, then?"

Easy question. "I'm here to look at your ass in spandex." That gets a laugh from her and in what feels like no time, my girlfriend is shrieking in delight as she crosses the finish line for her first half marathon.

"We are so doing that again," she says, cramming a banana into her mouth at the finish line. "That was amazing."

"Next we do the full distance," I tell her. And before I can catch myself, I say, "If you're going to join the Brady family, you're going to need to work up to the full."

Her face doesn't crumple when I say that. She doesn't slap me or kick me in the shin. She takes a long swig of water and wipes her mouth with her wrist. "Sounds like a good long-term goal," she says, and stretches up on her tip-toes to plant a kiss on my cheek. "You taste salty," she says.

"So do you," I counter, and I lick her forehead, immediately regretting it when I get a mouth full of sunscreen.

Nicole laughs, though, and takes my hand in hers. "Let's go and shower with our medals on," she tells me, practically skipping back to the hotel. "Does this get old? This feeling when you finish a race?"

I shake my head. It doesn't. But that's not entirely why I feel as giddy as she does today. "Seeing you reach this goal feels amazing, Nicole," I tell her, a wash of emotion charging through me as the adrenaline from the race subsides.

"Aw, Zacky," she teases, using my father's nickname for me as she walks backward, grinning. "Glad to help you feel good."

But she does make me feel good. Every day I'm lucky enough to spend with her, I feel good. I feel like my same self, but somehow more. I realized that sparring with her electrifies me. Running with her brings new life to the sport I've competed in for as long as I have memories. Taking Nicole to breakfast in the mornings with my family, and watching them give each other shit like long-lost siblings makes me feel more content than I ever felt possible.

"I love you," I blurt out to her, realizing the truth of that statement with a fierce conviction. I bend down to scoop her into my arms and kiss her, spinning around on the sidewalk as people point and cheer.

Nicole, catching her breath, looks into my eyes for a long beat before she says, "I love you, too, Isaac."

And then, smiling, sweaty, satiated, we rush back into our hotel room and seal our confession with our bodies. We join together, fierce and slick and fast, and I chant, "I love you," as I drive into her, wanting her cells to hear the words, to know the truth of them.

After, she curls against me like a comma, tapping her race medal against mine. "I'd say you deserve a medal for that performance, but you're already wearing one," she teases. I smile, pulling at one of her curls and watching it spring back. "I want to frame these," she says then, her face serious as she looks up into my eyes. "I never want to forget the day I achieved this fantastic thing."

"Babe, I always knew you could do this," I tell her. But she places a finger over my lips and shakes her head.

"Not the race," she says. "No, Isaac Brady, today I swallowed my fear and told a man I love him."

"Who is this man? Do I need to have him killed?" I kiss the finger she puts over my lips again.

She closes her eyes. "Nicole?"

"Hm?"

"I'm not ever going to let you forget who said it first."

EPILOGUE: NICOLE
A WHILE LATER...

 true. I waited until I sucked him off to break the news to him, so he was all calm and post-orgasmic and more likely to listen to me without arguing.

"I need you to move out of your house," I tell him. "Mine is better, anyway, and I'm sick of you not being around on the daily."

He closes his eyes and grins. He thinks I'm just being romantic. I sigh. "Seriously, Isaac, I need your house."

"You need my house?" Isaac cracks one eye open and looks at me, puzzled. "Like, for storage?"

I sigh. This is going to be harder than I thought. Normally, Isaac and I get away with not sharing deep feelings too often. Like once a week we each squeak out something deep and then we fuck after until it feels safe to look at each other again.

I swear I'd been meaning to bring up the idea of us living together. This external crisis just sort of exacerbated the issue. "So," I say, trailing a finger-nail down his chest and loving watching the goosebumps rise on the flat skin of his stomach as I do. "You know my friend Maddie..."

He nods. "That feels good." I twist my wrist so all four of my fingers are tickling his stomach skin. He groans.

"Well, Maddie needs a place to stay sort of urgently. And I want you to give her your house."

His groan changes tone and he rolls onto one side, propping his head up on his hand. "I need to talk to you about that, then."

"What?" He looks serious and grabs my hand, kissing the fingers that had just been tickling his skin.

"Well, you've been hinting about moving in together lately." He looks at me like he's stalling.

"Out with it, Brady. What did you do?"

He closes his eyes and spits his words out rapidly. "I put my house on the market and got an offer right away and accepted it and I close in a few weeks."

I sit up, crossing my hands over my chest. "Well, that's fucking amazing for us. We're going to fucking live together and it's going to be amazing."

"Why does it look like you're pissed off, then?" He raises one brow.

I roll my eyes. "Because of Maddie, asshole. We need to help her."

He wraps his long arms around me and I curl my head against his shoulder. He feels safe, like always. Solid. Terrifying. Exhilarating. "Let me think about it. My dad owns a bunch of rental properties," he murmurs. "Let's try, like, telling each other about these big things and brainstorming together."

I shake my head against his skin. "That sounds like a terrible idea."

"Just awful," he says, biting my ear lobe. I feel him getting hard again, his length rising up against my side as he cradles me in his lap. "This is going to be our bed," he says. I nod. "I want to fuck you in it."

"Yes, please," I tell him, trying to wriggle out of his arms. He pulls them tighter around me, holding me still and using his nose to nudge my face up toward his. He plants a kiss on my lips and we just sit there for what feels like an eternity, kissing and holding each other. I feel vulnerable this way, but also supported.

Neither of us has a strong foundation in healthy relationships or communication. Neither of is good at emotions. But ever since we took the leap and committed to sticking by each other, we've been learning. Together. And my god, there are benefits to learning to love with Isaac Brady.

He slowly lowers me back toward the sheets, his lips dancing kisses down my skin, his hands skating toward my thighs, where I'm slick with need. "I owe you some pleasure," he growls, "after you blew my mind just now."

Feeling good is new to me. But I'm getting used to it. Every day with Isaac is a new opportunity to figure out what I want, what I need, and to plan out how I'll get there. He's always supportive, offering snarky comments for the good ideas and serious-yet-constructive responses when I suggest something harebrained.

I settle back on the sheets, my hands tracing his ears, his hair as he crawls down my body. "That blowie was just to lull you into agreeing to give up your house," I tell him. I suck in a breath as his lips press against my clit and he starts working his fingers inside me. "But that backfired."

"Poor Nicole," he whispers, lapping at me with his tongue. "Always thinking of others, always getting shafted."

He licks and sucks while his fingers pump in and out of me, my hips jerking up to meet him. "I want to get shafted, Isaac," I yell, tugging at his hair. "Right now, please."

He pulls back from me with a grin on his face. "Whatever you say, boss," he says, and buries himself inside me in a single thrust that sends my eyes rolling back in my head.

"Oh god, yes, Isaac. Yes." He drives into me, the angle of his pelvis providing the perfect friction I need. After his tongue primed me for liftoff, it takes only a few thrusts before I'm tumbling over the edge. "I love you I love you I love you," I shriek, coming hard around his cock. I feel my muscles pulsing around him.

He meets my eyes, breathing heavy, and pants, "I get so turned on watching you come, babe. Fuck, you feel so good."

"You, too, Isaac," I moan. "Come with me," I plead. And he does. His eyes boring into mine, I feel his body stiffen as he chases his own pleasure and tumbles over the edge with me. Together.

Psst! If you love these characters, Tim Stag, Nicole's boss, first shows up in my book Sweet Distraction. Nicole first shows up in Fragile Illusion!

SUSPENSION

AN OPPOSITES ATTRACT ROMANCE

CHAPTER ONE
MADDIE

"You've been such an asset to our team the past few years, Madison. Truly." My boss looks like he's going to cry as he slides the letter across the desk to me. Or maybe he's hoping I don't cry? It's hard for me to pay attention to him above the sound of my heart pounding in my ears.

"...severance. And, well, I know you'll have questions about COBRA for health insurance." He swallows. I swallow. Of course I have questions about my god damned health insurance. I spend $500 a month on diabetes supplies *with* health insurance.

"Maddie? Madison?" He looks like he wants to squeeze my hand. I pull my hands back from the desk into my lap and start shaking my head. When we had the company meeting last week announcing a round of impending layoffs, I really thought I was going to be safe.

I've worked at the Post since college—I started with my friend Emma doing grunt work and covering town hall meetings. Now, eight years later, I've got my own beat as a healthcare reporter and have taught myself how to use the back end systems to help with the paper's online content. Hell, people come to me for help putting their stories online.

Phil called me in to his office and I should have known. I should have known when he used a nice voice. This crotchety old blow-hard is always yelling.

"Maddie, honey, you're really sweating. Can I get you anything?" He looks at me with concern and I notice I'm hella thirsty.

"Shit," I say, reaching for his glass of water. I hear my glucose monitor beep a warning at me. My sugars are high. "I'm stressed and I'm hyper. I need to get out of here." I'm yelling, but I also can't seem to control the volume of my voice. This is not good. None of this is good. I vaguely hear my boss—former boss I guess—shouting after me, but I need to move my body.

I barge out the front door of the newspaper office and start circling the building. Laid off. Unemployed. I take some deep breaths, trying to ignore the beeping sounds coming from my glucose monitor. Being unemployed is shitty for everyone, but being unemployed and losing health insurance for a type one diabetic?

I plunk down on the grass beside a garbage can, panicking. With shaking hands, I pull my phone out of my bra and start texting Emma. Only I pull up the wrong message thread and text both her and our other friend, Nicole.

> Got fired. Going to die. Help.

My phone rings in my hand almost as soon as I hit send. I squint at the screen, but my high blood sugar makes it sort of hard to see. I really need my insulin pump to get cranking here so I can calm down.

I press the green circle to accept the call, but it's a group video call, so both Emma and Nicole are squinting back at me as I rest my head on the trash can.

"Madison Parker, you tell me what's going on. Do I need to walk over there and get you?" Emma can't drive because she's epileptic. She and I bonded immediately over our glitchy organs way back in college. We've been glitchy gals for years. I laugh at that idea. "Glitchy gals." I'm about to tell her not to strap her babies in the stroller on my account when Nicole shakes her head.

"Nobody is walking anywhere. I'm coming to get you."

"What about me?" Emma looks insulted that she's somehow getting left out of the pity party I guess they're throwing for me this afternoon.

Nicole rolls her eyes. At least I think she does. My sugars are normalizing a little bit; I can feel it. But the screen is awfully small for a three-way video chat. "Look," she says. "I'm going to make sure Madison is not in a coma and I will bring her to your house. Do you think you can have alcohol ready when we get there, Ems?"

Emma bites a fingernail, pondering. She doesn't drink alcohol, either. See also: epilepsy medication.

"Scratch that. Maddie, can you have alcohol when you're freaking out? I don't know all the rules. Anyway, Emma, we're tapping into your medical weed."

B

I'M NOT sure how long I sit on the grass by the garbage. Eventually, someone hands me a dollar bill as I'm sitting there, and I realize I need to pull myself together and at least start emptying out my desk. Nicole screeches into the parking lot, parking sideways behind my editor's car so he's blocked in. I smile for the first time since I got to work this morning.

"Jesus, look at you," she says, hands on her hips, tapping her stylish shoe. I look down at myself. I'm a little rumpled, it's true. Most days, I wear leggings and a compression tank to hold all my gadgets in place and I top it all off with tunic dresses or long sweaters.

And a fanny pack. I wear one everywhere. I've got a dozen of them. They're just the perfect size to hold all my snacks, and my reporter's note-book, plus my phone and backup insulin cartridges.

Nicole gestures at my dress, all bunched up and draping strangely. My tank is untucked because I was fiddling with my insulin pump. I see now why that passerby thought I was homeless. I sigh.

Nicole starts pulling reusable cloth bags from her purse. "Do you have a lot of stuff to clear out," she asks, raising a brow at me. "We're not waiting for security to clean out your desk or whatever the fuck. I'm getting you out of here." She drapes an arm over my shoulder and escorts me back inside.

She tells me to sit down and pull any personal files off my laptop, handing me an external hard drive that she also has in her purse for some reason. I look at her, wide-eyed with surprise, as she starts pulling my photos off my cubicle walls. As Nicole opens my desk drawers, she starts shaking her head and laughing.

"Seriously, Maddie? All you have in here is snacks and batteries."

"That's not entirely true," I tell her, grabbing my crackers, leaving the batteries for the paper's voice recorder in the drawer and tugging open another. "I've also got my fanny packs."

We share a laugh, my first today, and empty my stash of colorful pouches into one of Nicole's bags. If I'm going to be the weird girl in the black tunics with a fanny pack, I figure the packs should at least be cute.

But really, apart from a few photos and two bags of fannypacks and some food, there's not much physical evidence of me here at work. I start to cry for the first time, looking at the empty walls of my cubicle, realizing how much more I'm losing than just my health insurance. My worst fear has been that I'll become a drain on society. I've spent a lot of time in hospitals. I've put my parents through a lot. I worked really, really hard to make it through college and I thought I was on a really strong path here. Damn it, I like writing about healthcare! I have a really unique experience with healthcare and I think it's made me good at what I do.

"What the hell am I going to do, Nik?" I ask her.

She scoops me up into a hug and just holds me for a bit. "We're going to figure it out," she says. "But for now, you're going to Emma's house to get high."

CHAPTER TWO
MADDIE

I FEEL A LITTLE WOOZY, BUT ALSO HUNGRY SO I'M COUNTING DOWN THE SECONDS until I can eat again once my glucose levels go down. My head throbs from the stress. I keep waiting for Emma and Nicole to come through with the Maryjane they mentioned, but so far, this pow-wow is all spreadsheets and hugs from Emma's kids.

"Ok, so, this is what I've got." Nicole props up the screen of her laptop so I can see all the red, bolded numbers she's gathered together. I squint at the screen, hoping my insulin pump can get itself together here sometime soon.

"You said you're getting three months severance, right? So, I checked, and that will basically cover your COBRA insurance payments."

Emma nods. I tug on the skin of my eyelids, making a crackling sound that used to drive my sister insane.

"Maddie, knock that shit off immediately," Nicole scolds. "I, too, am appalled that health insurance payments are equal to your fucking salary. I almost want to just go ahead and marry you so you can get on my plan." Nicole works with Emma's husband's brother at Stag Law.

It's a whole tangled web of tall, grouchy men. But Nicole's also not serious about marrying me because she's up to her eyebrows in love with her own grouchy guy.

Nicole points at the next row on her spreadsheet. "Now, you'll also be able to collect unemployment, which should cover your cellphone bill and car insurance and your diabetes supplies until you find a job. I've also added a modest estimate for food..."

Emma sets her son on the ground and starts rubbing my shoulders. It feels nice. I take a deep breath, and point out the obvious to Nicole. "That doesn't leave anything for rent."

Emma switches her movements to rubbing slow circles on my back, my favorite, and Nicole nods. "Right. You didn't renew your lease yet, right? You're just going to have to not renew it."

I roll my eyes, which are starting to focus again as my headache finally subsides. "And in this plan, where am I living exactly?"

They both start to say I am welcome to stay with them as long as I want, and I snort. Emma's house is nice, but she's got two really young kids who cry all the time and wake up at five in the morning. Nicole is constantly telling me about the loud, acrobatic sex she and Zack have all over her house.

That might be an option for a day or two, but there's no way I can stay with either of them long-term.

Emma squints, thinking. "What about your sister?"

"Nope." I shake my head. My sister and her wife just signed traveling nursing contracts. They moved all their possessions into a storage unit and hopped a flight to Boston, en route to Chicago and then Austin. "Melissa is living life on the road," I remind my friends.

They don't bother mentioning my parents. After I moved out for college, my parents immediately downsized to a one-bedroom apartment to save money. They've worked hard all their lives, but neither of them has a degree and they don't earn much. I shove down the guilt, remembering how much extra they had to put aside for all my medication and supplies over the years.

Nicole slams the computer shut. "You'll stay with me for now, and we'll figure something out," she says. Emma perks up, noticeably relieved that she doesn't have to host a guest in her house filled with diapers and breast-milk laundry.

"And you won't need to rent a storage unit for your stuff," Emma says. "Thatcher has plenty of room in the studio to store your boxes."

I smile at my friends, gratefully. I know I'm supposed to be more loudly expressing my thanks to them. I just feel empty and hollowed out.

I've wanted to be a reporter my whole life. All I've ever done is write things. When I was diagnosed with type one diabetes in fifth grade, I started researching the disease and writing papers about it.

I was editor of my high school *and* college newspapers, and I was damned proud of myself for landing a job at the Post. My healthcare beat was a huge source of pride and I got to write features as well as short, newsy stories. I did it all.

Newspapers are struggling, though. I don't know any papers in the country that are hiring even entry-level writers.

"What am I going to do?" I moan, sinking back into the couch. I instinctively reach for my fanny pack, but it's empty of snacks now. Half of me wants to start researching open journalism jobs around the world. The other half wants to curl in a ball and cry.

My parents are too pragmatic to offer comfort for something like this. If they lose a job, they call up everyone they know until they find a lead on another one. There's no shortage of custodial or retail gigs, I suppose, but I know they'd be upset if I wasn't out there putting my hard-earned college degree to work.

Emma procures a flask and pours me a finger of whiskey. I guess we aren't smoking her fancy medicinal weed. "It's from that place on Smallman Street," she says. "Thatcher just designed a line of bottles for them."

"It's a gorgeous bottle, Ems." I knock back the drink, coughing as it burns my esophagus, and Nicole rolls her eyes at me.

"My Irish lover would kick you out of the house if he saw you treat the water of life that way." She pours me another shot, but holds up a finger before handing it over. "You have to smell it, and then you sip it slowly to let it work its magic."

I raise an eyebrow at her and check the numbers on my glucose meter. Everything seems like it's back on track, and I give myself a little boost of insulin before taking the glass from Nicole. As instructed, I swirl it around under my nose. It smells sour and smokey, like my mood. When it crosses my lips this time, it doesn't burn so much as it fills my body with heat. Shame, longing, terror—it all swirls around in my stomach with the snacks and the locally distilled fancy whiskey.

I sigh and place the glass back on the table. "I guess we'd better start packing up my shit."

CHAPTER THREE
LIAM

I'M NOT SURE HOW LONG I SPEND STARING AT THE MESS IN THE KITCHEN. I LOVE MY brother, but I don't think I can continue living with him without murdering him. The counters are littered with cereal bowls crusted with rancid milk. There are granola bar wrappers on most surfaces.

I returned late last night from a business trip and, faced with my kitchen this morning, I realize how much time I've spent cleaning up after him. I wonder how many socks I picked up and tossed into his room since we moved in together, or how many cumulative empty sports drink bottles I nudged into the recycling bin at the end of the counter.

"This can't go on," I mutter.

It seemed like such a good idea to live with my brother, initially. He's always been my best friend, and who else would put up with my moody tendencies? I walk away from the filth, deciding I'll get breakfast to go from the cafe down the block. I wonder if it's time for me to live on my own.

I start to think about the logistics of this as I iron my shirt. Cal will probably wear a wrinkled polo shirt and slap some jeans on and call it business casual. There's no documentation at the office mandating a dress shirt, let alone a jacket and tie each day. I just think better when I'm dressed professionally.

I button the shirt, warm from the iron, and start pressing my pants pockets, considering. Cal can afford rent on his own. So can I. I'm a 32-year-old professional. It's nonsense that I live with my little brother, right?

I've never seriously considered living apart from him, though. We're Irish twins, and the longest we were away from each other was my first year of college, when he still spent half his nights on the futon in my dorm room since I went to school right here in Pittsburgh.

It would be hard not having him close by. A change like that requires careful planning and discussion. But I never realized the extent of his sloppiness, or how I contributed to it by picking up after him constantly. I frown at my reflection in the mirror before leaving our apartment. Maybe he and I can find two apartments next door to each other…

℈

I BYPASS the kitchen when I get to the office, not yet ready to run into my brothers or my cousin, Orla. The four of us work for the engineering firm our fathers started together. Beltane Engineering has grown significantly in recent years, and I allow myself the smug satisfaction of feeling responsible for growing the structural engineering division.

Uncle Kellen specializes in civil engineering. Beltane worked strictly with civil engineering projects for two decades, but Kellen took a chance bringing me aboard after I graduated. We now hold contracts to engineer new bridge construction for clients in a tri-state area and we are working on inspection programs for existing structures throughout the entire Rust Belt.

I'm assuming our staff meeting this morning will be a review of my most recent trip, so I take a few minutes to look over my summary notes from visiting railway bridges in Kentucky. I just landed Beltane repair *and* ongoing inspection work for the next five years.

I wasn't expecting a party when I got home, but it would have been nice to not walk into a kitchen full of flies. I sigh, and stack the papers, tapping them on the desk to get the edges lined up.

My uncle and my brother Zack are already in the conference room, whispering about something. Uncle Kellen smiles when he sees me, and he clears his throat and closes the door. "Look," he says, "I know my brother isn't here yet. I wanted to remind you all that the company is coming up on our 35th anniversary." A small smile teases the edges of his normally-stoic lips.

I had not remembered that anniversary, so I'm glad he brought it up. That's something to be proud of, for sure. I nod, looking around the room. Beltane has grown from a small firm that worked with coal mines and dams to a regional powerhouse servicing clients' needs in civil, structural, electrical, and mechanical engineering. Hell, we've even got machine learning specialists activating drones and sensors and all kinds of fancy tricks.

We built a reputation maintaining and repairing existing assets, which is so much more exciting for me. Anyone can design something from scratch, but when you've got to fix something that's already in place? Sometimes you literally have to move mountains to get the job done. I love the thrill of figuring out how, and quantifying why my solution is the most efficient.

Uncle Kel nods his head a few times. "We're going to organize a company-wide anniversary celebration," he says. "And I want to commission a corporate history."

Orla raises an eyebrow. "What, like a book?"

Kellen nods. "Yep. I want this to be something we can give to my brother, but also have on hand to gift our long-term clients, our long-term employees. It'll be a really nice marketing tool to show the breadth and depth of our work to potential clients as we continue to grow. We just need to hire someone to write it." He grins. "Unless you've all been holding back on me, I think it's safe to say our internal expertise is *not* written communication."

There's a few chuckles around the table. I roll my eyes. Most of these engineers crank out truly terrible reports, and nearly incomprehensible emails. We're long past overdue to hire someone permanently to help with editing.

Zack looks like he's going to have a stroke, and starts slapping his thigh. "I've got someone in mind for you, actually." Everyone stares at him, confused by his joyful outburst. "This is just perfect timing!"

"Since when do you hang out with writers?" Orla and Zack never, ever avoid opportunities to give each other shit. But he just squints and points at her.

"Nicole is friends with a few of them," he says, referencing his girlfriend. Who happens to be batshit crazy. Ok, not really, but she's an eccentric, loud person. I can't imagine any of her friends will be well-suited to capturing the spirit of Beltane appropriately. I frown.

But Zack already has his phone held out, showing Uncle Kellen someone's cell number. My dad walks into the room after that and we pivot to new business. I listen to Zack talk about how he and his new partner are programming robots with cameras to inspect the insides of pipes, and working on underwater storage capacity.

Orla talks about the terrible wiring throughout most of the city, and then it's my turn to brag about bridges. I adjust my tie, clear my throat, and slip into my comfort zone: free rein to talk about structures and my plans to improve them.

CHAPTER FOUR
LIAM

I STRAIGHTEN MY TIE BEFORE KNOCKING ON MY UNCLE'S OFFICE DOOR, WHICH IS ajar, but I want to be polite regardless. "You wanted to see me?"

He smiles as he looks up from his paperwork. "Come on in, son. Have a seat." Uncle Kellen calls me and my brothers "son" because we all grew up together. He and Orla moved in with my dad and us after Aunt Helen died. He certainly feels like a father figure to me, especially because we have so much in common. His office is what I would describe as perfect. Everything has a place. Every item in the room serves a purpose, and was chosen to be both functional and attractive. This is a calm room.

I sink into the chair opposite his desk, delighting in the comfortable way it hugs my lower back. "So tell me about Kentucky," he says, folding his hands together.

I clear my throat. I've already been over all the numbers during the staff meeting, so I quickly try to recall the highlights. "We secured several long-term, repeat contracts for bridge inspection throughout the entire coal seam in Daniel Boone National Forest," I begin, but he holds up a hand.

"I know all that. I should have clarified my question. What was it like for you to be out in that role—discussing our work, closing deals?"

"Oh," I say, feeling my eyebrows shoot up toward my hairline. "Well, to be frank, it felt very natural." I don't need to explain to my uncle that I know our inspection program inside and out, and I know that we are flexible, fastidious and efficient.

"Can't help but notice your notes here about the electrical transformer towers out there in the deep woods." Uncle Kellen moves his mouse and pulls up a document where I had been typing random notes in the margins. I hadn't realized I'd emailed him a rough draft.

I don't usually make mistakes like that. "I'm sorry that I sent you that version of the report," I tell him, squirming. This is very unlike me. "I had meant to poke around that line of thinking a bit more before I brought it to your attention."

Uncle Kellen grins. "Let's just say I did some poking myself," he tells me. "It's no secret that our nation's power infrastructure is crumbling."

I nod. "Just glancing at some of the rail systems I visited, I could easily spot damage to towers. Not to mention the wires."

"Take some pretty sophisticated logistics just to get a crew into those remote spots to inspect the structures. Maybe even something like one of Ray's robot cameras." My uncle is nodding his head now. He clicks around on his computer and pulls up his contacts. "You ever try to get a meeting with a public utility before?" He squints at me, studying.

I shake my head. "Well, no. But I did just meet with the railroad. And like I said, I had been planning to do some preliminary research before I brought this to you and Dad."

He waves his hand, dismissing my nerves about the doodles. "Your brief note was all the spark we need, Liam. Now, tell me what you imagined. Just top of your head, big picture idea."

I swallow. This had been all I could think about since I got back from Kentucky, apart from the Cal's filth interrupting my thought patterns. "I propose we inspect the entire power grid for each utility company and make a plan for maintenance and repair, and then engineer those mainte-nance and repair solutions. I agree that Ray should be a huge part of the discussion, and that sensors installed throughout the grid would be instrumental. This could be national," I blurt. Then I look down at my hands.

I think my uncle was implying that I should have been nervous to talk with the railway about what they need to do, about delivering bottom line, come-to-Jesus conversations about structures that have the capacity to facilitate industry...or destroy the supply chain if they fail.

I wasn't nervous, though. I was delivering facts. Numbers don't lie. There's nothing subjective about the maximum load capacity of a bridge, when compared with the heavier-than-average Diesel engines the compa-nies are wanting to use to haul coal faster. Chaos comes from ignoring these structures. But keeping everything in order keeps everything smooth and productive.

"I was hoping you'd say that," my uncle says. He points to a bookshelf where he's got navy binders lined up neatly. "You know what that is?"

"Your life's work?" I'm only partially joking. I'm pretty sure he started keeping his records on the computer in the 90s. Uncle Kellen was an early adopter to digital record keeping, so I imagine those binders go back pretty far if they've got Beltane projects in them.

He stands up and walks over to the shelf, pulling out one of the binders. "This is an inspection program I wrote for the steel industry," he says. He hands me the binder and I take a look at the step by step instructions for analyzing the safety, integrity and function of massive industrial facilities. "We started out writing these protocols for just one client, and this grew to become our proprietary inspection program." He taps the binder. "Anyone in the nation who wants to keep their slag heap up to code is purchasing our intellectual property to do it."

I sort of knew all of this. I know our work constitutes a vital piece of industry. Hell, the entire economy depends on these industries. When the streets of Pittsburgh crack open with sink holes and city buses fall in, there are massive ripples of impact on everything from the city's water system to the service workers who can't keep the restaurants open downtown because their buses are detoured.

I thumb through my uncle's old Xeroxed dot-matrix notes, the blue ink fading with age. I love the fastidious, thorough orderliness of it all. Two pages discussing the acceptable depth of rust on a load-bearing beam. Two more pages about the proper cleaning of dust from an air vent.

"Here's what we're going to do, Liam," my uncle says, leaning back against his desk. "We're going to let your dad do what he does best and start up a conversation with these folks and get them to admit that they've got a problem. Meanwhile, you and I are going to do the work developing the solution they were worried was too difficult to imagine."

"I like the sound of that," I tell him. "Where should we start?"

He holds up a finger. "We're going to start with that corporate history I mentioned."

Certain I misheard him, I tug on my ear lobe. "I'm sorry, what?"

He grins. "Your brother found us a writer for the corporate history. She's great for this project—much more your father's brand of energy than you or me or Zack. I'd like to have her begin with a specific slice of our company history."

I feel my face curling awkwardly in confusion, something I've been working very hard on not doing in client meetings. Orla tells me it makes me seem disapproving. "I'm sorry, but how does that advance the utilities inspection project?"

Kellen grins. "A few decades ago, your father had to go to traffic court over a road rage incident."

I know this story. It comes up at holidays. Dad was late getting home—likely because he was gabbing endlessly with someone in the lobby at work—and tried to drive around a busy intersection. He actually drove up on the sidewalk to get around a car that was taking too long (for his liking) to accelerate.

"In the waiting area for his case, your father got to chatting with someone else who was there for an unpaid ticket." I nod. This is typical for my father.

"Let me guess," I interject. "They became best friends after bonding over the injustice of their citations. And it happened to be a state senator."

"Close," Kellen says, nodding. "It was the CEO of Allegheny Power."

CHAPTER FIVE
MADDIE

"Excited for your first day?" Nicole and I are combing our hair in her bathroom like it's college again and we're in the dorms. I sort of love it, even if I did have to crank my headphones last night to avoid listening to her and Zack.

"Excited feels like the wrong word," I tell her. Zack randomly called the other day as we were moving my stuff into Nicole's house, to say that his company is looking for a writer for a corporate history. I've never done a corporate history before, but I figure writing is writing.

I jumped at the chance. Nicole told me to double whatever I was planning on quoting them for the project, and I just about flew out of my chair when they didn't balk at the number I threw out. "I'm brimming with questions, that's for sure," I say, tying my hair back into a sleek pony tail and smoothing my usual black dress over my leggings and tank.

Nicole winces when I hook on the fanny pack of the day. "What?" I shrug. "You know I need a bag with me."

"Yes, but surely you can choose a nice, elegant cross-body satchel? Something that doesn't fasten with a plastic buckle?"

"I'll wear the black one," I tell her, swapping out my emergency medication and my snack baggies. "Nobody will notice."

Nicole laughs. "They're engineers, Mad. They notice everything."

I shake my head at her. "Not true. I bet you $45 they never notice a

194

woman's clothing or accessories." We walk back to her bedroom to examine ourselves in her full-length mirror.

"Forty-five is an awfully strange number." Nicole slides her feet into an impossible pair of spike heels as Zack bursts into the room, damp from the shower, dressed for work. He pecks her on the cheek and makes to dash out of the house.

"Wait," I shout at him. He freezes. "Aren't we going to ride in together?"

He furrows his brow, clearly considering this for the first time. "I suppose that would make sense." He stands in the hall, considering. "I'm in a bit of a hurry..."

Nicole rolls her eyes. "Nobody cares if you're only eight minutes early today instead of 15. Maddie, why the 45 bucks?"

I slide on my perfectly reasonable, adorably cute black flats and grin at Nicole. "That's what I've got in my bank account after stocking up on my medical supplies and paying my first month of insurance."

Nicole looks like she's going to cry and starts shaking her head. "Do you have money for lunch? Babe, please buy her lunch today."

Zack taps his chin. "I think we're having stuff brought in today anyway," he says. "Noon meeting and all that."

Nicole nods. "Good."

I like the sound of this noon meeting complete with food. I make a note to adjust my snack schedule and estimate I'll be eating by 12:15, so I can monitor my blood sugars. I climb into Zack's truck and zip my pack shut with a flourish.

"Don't you need, I don't know, stuff?" Zack looks at me like I'm missing a limb. "Nicole always has bags and things when we leave the house."

I pat my lap. "That's the beauty of this right here. I'm telling you, it's the perfect bag. I never have to think about it. Got my snacks. Got my phone. Fanny packs are where it's at."

Zack chuckles. We make the short drive to his office and he pulls into a spot in the side lot. "You guys have your own parking lot?" I gape at the prime real estate near the hockey arena. "Your business must be pulling in bank. I can't believe I didn't quote you a higher number."

He laughs at that and swipes his ID to get us in the lobby. Then he looks at me like he's not sure what to do next. The receptionist isn't in yet and I rock back onto my heels.

"Well," he says. "I guess I'll take you for some coffee? And to find my uncle?"

"Kellen did say I'd be meeting with him first," I offer. We start climbing the stairs to the company kitchen. It smells like shitty coffee and powdered donuts. I see a box of the latter on the counter, with only one missing.

"My uncle must have brought these," Zack says, popping one into his mouth in two bites. I make myself busy pouring the coffee and that awful shelf-stable creamer when I hear voices from the doorway.

"You're such a pecking mother hen and I'm sick of your grouchy attitude." I think this is the middle Brady brother, Cal, but I'm still not sure who is who in Zack's family.

"It is not grouchy to insist that you stop leaving food to rot in the sink," the stern-looking one says. His mouth pulls down in a severe line and I can see a vein pulsing in his neck. "I found mold growing in your cereal bowl, Cal. Actual mold."

Noticing me for the first time, the stern one goes wide-eyed and stares. Ah, that must be Liam. "Um, hi," I say, giving a small wave over my coffee cup. I decide to poke around looking for ice for my coffee while the brothers hash it out about their dish duty.

"You definitely are new here," Cal says, leaning against the counter as I stretch to get ice from the bin in the freezer.

"Oh, I'm the writer," I say, plunking the cubes in slowly and hoping the coffee doesn't splash out. This is another reason I always wear black. I cannot be trusted not to spill food, and this keeps me from major embarrassment if I have a research interview.

Cal looks at his brothers, confused. Liam is still staring and Zack is too busy wiping donut powder from his shirt to notice. I offer up, "I'm Maddie? Friends with Nicole? Your uncle hired me to write a—"

"Oh!" Cal snaps his fingers. "Yes. Right. We've met before, right?"

I nod. Nicole and I were out for drinks once and her boo and his brothers stopped by. I remember how they all gave each other shit and I thought it was cute. Well, I guess only the friendly one gives out shit. The grumpy, hairy one mostly scowls. Like now. God, I love a hairy man. He even has hairy hands, and I can see the shadow of a dark beard wanting to sprout from his face.

Looking at his neatly pressed suit, I suspect he hates the unruliness of all that hair. It's not orderly at all.

Zack clears his throat while Liam continues staring. I sip my coffee and stare right back, but then I look down at my dress, worried I spilled something oily. Oily stains show up no matter what you're wearing. Finding nothing, I can only assume he's still angry about Cal's dish mold.

"Maddie, you ready?" Zack starts walking down the hall. I trot along after him, not sure what to expect next.

CHAPTER SIX
LIAM

Cal swats me in the chest so hard I double over, coughing. "What the hell are you staring at?" He stands with his hands on his hips, chewing an entire donut in one bite. I have no idea what the hell just happened here, but I'm shaken.

"Who was that girl?" I ask, staring down the hall toward the direction my brother just disappeared."

Cal blinks at me a few times. "Maddie, she just said, right? Nicole's friend? Writer, apparently?" When I still don't say anything he slides me a donut and shrugs. "We've met her before."

I shake my head. "She didn't look like that before," I tell him.

"Look like what," he asks, cramming another donut in his mouth.

Like something inexplicable, I think. *Like a perplexing blend of amazing and sunshine.* "I don't know," I say, hesitantly. "Like that."

Cal rolls his eyes and wipes his mouth with a napkin. "Well, I've got real work to do. See you at lunch." He saunters off down the hall, tossing his napkin toward the trash. He doesn't stoop to pick it up when he misses, and I remember that I'm fed up with him and his habits.

How is it that we grew up in the same houses, with the same cast of adults, and I wound up anxious and he manages not to care about anything?

The second I sit down at my desk to open my email, a new one pings open on the screen—high priority—from my Uncle Kellen. "Remember the project we discussed. Please come to my office to meet our new writer."

"Shit," I mutter. I had forgotten. And now I realize that Maddie is that writer, and I'm going to have to figure out how to think coherent thoughts with her around. I take the stairs up to my uncle's office and pass Zack on his way back down. He's on a call and offers me a quick salute as I round the corner for the final flight of stairs.

I try to remember the particulars my uncle laid out. We're starting with his connection from the utility company as our first interview for the corporate history. Kellen is going to prep the writer—Maddie—on the background she needs for that personal history and I'm supposed to go with her for the interview. Purportedly for background character information about my father.

The idea of holding my shit together while I figure out why my body is responding to her like I'm having a seizure…"This is a mess," I mutter, rapping on my uncle's door frame and sliding into the room.

Maddie looks up at me and grins. She appears to be offering my uncle some of those fish-shaped crackers that children eat. I frown as he accepts and they both sit there, munching, staring at me. "Hi," I mutter, eventually. "I'm Liam. Brady. I mean, Brady is my last name." *God damn it, I'm an idiot.*

She laughs, and I'm struck by the sound of it. A loud explosion of sound that I can tell was uncontrolled, unforced. Genuine. She's laughing at me. But she doesn't seem cruel? I have no idea what's going on. Her brown eyes radiate delight. "Madison," she says. "Parker. Parker is my last name." She laughs again. This time, I laugh, too. "Just call me Maddie, though."

Uncle Kellen finishes chewing his cracker and wipes some crumbs from his tie as Maddie shoves the baggy back into a pouch she wears around her hips. *So strange,* I think, staring at her lap as I sink into the chair next to her. A woman who walks around with a pouch full of snacks.

I hear my uncle outlining the plan to her and she pulls a small notebook and pen from the pouch, nodding along. I stare, realizing her pouch is a bit like Uncle Kellen's office. Everything has a place. Everything chosen with intention. But what kind of adult woman chooses fish crackers as a snack? "Remind me whether Beltane can lend me a laptop for this project," she looks up at my uncle, biting the top of her pen. "I had to leave mine at the Post and haven't gotten a new one quite yet…"

Uncle Kellen waves a hand. "We can get you a loaner. Liam will get you one."

She sighs. "Oh, good. I really do my best work if I can get typing up the transcription as soon as I finish an interview. Helps me to organize my thoughts. So, tell me the pinch points about this first interview. What shouldn't I ask about, and what should I definitely ask him?"

It's fascinating for me to see the process of her preparation to talk with someone. I hear her mention the audience and purpose, explaining how the purpose of the piece of writing is the most important part. I had no idea writing was such a methodical process. I sit staring at her as she talks, trying to decide what she smells like.

Lavender, I decide eventually. Is it true that we've met? How could I have sat across from her in a bar and not noticed her? What's different about today?

When I think back to the times I've gone out with my brothers in the evenings, I feel like they were all nights I returned from a business trip or a stressful client meeting. Does my work stress cloud my awareness so heavily? I look at Maddie again.

She's not supermodel-magazine-cover beautiful. She's a very different type of beautiful. She's intriguing and real. She radiates honesty and truth. She's certainly memorable. I'm stunned that I didn't notice her before. Everything from her no-makeup face to her black-outfit-covered body is real and...arousing. I'm aroused.

I look down at my crotch to confirm I'm sporting a semi at work. "Huh," I say, and when Maddie and Kellen look at me, I have to pretend I was listening. "I'm just really impressed with your strategy," I say, trying to cover for the fact that I haven't been listening to a thing.

Maddie smiles. Kellen looks at his watch, which prompts me to look at my watch. "Oh," I say. "Well we'd better head over there. Our appointment is in a half hour."

"Hm," Kellen says with a slight frown. "Better take Boulevard of the Allies rather than risk gridlock on Liberty Ave."

"I was thinking that," I tell him, gesturing for Maddie to walk ahead of me. "I'll call you as soon as we're through." With a nod, I follow my new sidekick to the parking lot, where she looks around awkwardly until I remember that she doesn't know which car is mine.

"I thought we'd take a Beltane car," I tell her, pointing to one of the black Saabs my dad bought for important client meetings. Not to be confused with the black pickups he bought for field work. I unlock and start to get in, and then I wonder if I should have held her door open. This isn't a date. I'm not supposed to be attracted to my colleague or to my brother's girlfriend's friend. This is a damn disaster in the making, is what it is.

Maddie clicks her seatbelt in place and looks up at me expectedly. I drape my arm around the back of her chair so I can look behind me to back out of the spot, and immediately wonder if I should have done that, but I'm not sure I can drive in reverse without my arm there, so I just hit the brake and sit, staring, not knowing what to do next.

"Everything ok?" Something in her bag beeps and she unzips it and begins to fuss around, popping more crackers in her mouth.

"Um, you probably shouldn't eat in the company car," I say, pulling my arm back into my own space and gritting my teeth until I get the car headed in the right direction. I'm sweating. I can feel it.

"Sorry," she says, zipping the bag shut again. And then she starts rehashing the plan about Clayton Monroe. My portion of the song and dance is really only important at the beginning and the end, where we need to get him to ask after my father.

I see Maddie changing her energy as we get closer to the Allegheny Power office. I can feel her getting ready for the interview, deciding on her approach. I like it. I hang back silently while the receptionist greets us and takes us up to the top floor of the massive building.

"Mr. Monroe will be in soon," the receptionist says, gesturing toward comfortable leather seats in the conference room. "Please make yourselves at home."

Maddie starts arranging her notepad on the table alongside a small digital recorder, all of which she pulls from that pouch around her waist. I stare at it again, conceding that it's an extremely useful pouch for someone in her role, but it's certainly unusual. I can't think of a professional environment where I've ever seen someone wear a fanny pack.

But then I start considering the tool belts I wear for field work, and I consider that Maddie may have invented a reporter's tool belt. I like how it nips in at her waist, giving me a sense of the swell of her hips beneath it. And, there's my semi again. At a meeting.

I'm still staring at Maddie when Clayton walks in, all bluster and loud small talk. "Liam Brady," he says, pounding me on the back as I rise to shake his hand. "You are the spitting image of your old man. Hope you don't have his lead foot!" He laughs, so I laugh, but it feels forced. Maddie does not laugh, and I decide I like that about her. She smiles, but only laughs when she's actually amused.

CHAPTER SEVEN
MADDIE

seat at the head of the conference table.

"Well, first of all, I'm not that young," I tell him, with a wink. He chuckles and points at me.

"Guess I gotta watch out for you."

"Guess you'd better," I say, and I hear a beep. It's not my beep, though. When it happens again, Mr. Monroe clears his throat.

"Maddie," Liam says through gritted teeth. "I think your phone is beeping. Mr. Monroe's time is very limited..."

I shake my head. "Not mine. My ringtone is the theme song from *Survivor.*"

Liam stares at my fanny pack, like he's not convinced, but eventually, I say, "You know, Liam, I think it might be your phone."

His cheeks flush as he pats his pocket, where his phone is indeed buzzing like mad. "I'm terribly sorry," he sputters. "This is my father. Mr. Monroe, I'm going to step in the hall and take this."

Liam rushes out of the room, hissing hello to his father. Mr. Monroe laughs. "Nervous fella, isn't he? Not like his old man after all, I guess."

I shrug. "I don't really know him that well."

Monroe folds his hands on the table. "Well, what do you know, Maddie from Beltane Engineering."

"Oh, I'm not really *from* Beltane," I start to explain. I'm flustered by the unexpected departure of Liam, unsure if I should tee up the plan or stall with small talk. Small talk is dangerous for me. I'm a blurter. "My friend Nicole is living with one of the Brady boys. Romantically I mean. Isaac is her boyfriend." I feel myself rambling, but am also unable to stop. I was really doing great taking control of the interview until Liam accused me of having my phone go off. "So anyway, I've known Nicole since college because her roommate Emma was my friend. We met in line for disability resources."

Monroe looks at me wide-eyed. "I'm diabetic," I blurt. "Type one."

His face transforms. "Is that right?" He holds out a hand, the fingertips leathery and calloused from decades of jabbing. "Me, too!"

"Really? That's amazing. I don't know too many people in my weird boat."

He chuckles and opens his suit jacket. Patting the pocket, he says, "I carry these injections with me everywhere. Got extras in my desk, in my car. You know how it goes."

I shake my head. "No way, dude. I use a pump! Do you really not use a pump?"

Within minutes, I'm showing him my continuous glucose monitor and I'm a heartbeat away from lifting my dress to show him my pump set on my stomach, when I remember that I'm here in a professional capacity. I drop my hem, in a hurry, but he's still staring at the monitor on my arm. It's the size of a pack of gum, and it constantly sends readings to my phone, letting me know if I should gobble some carbs or bump up my insulin levels.

"That seems like witchcraft," Monroe says, eyes still wide.

"Feels like it sometimes," I agree. "You really don't have a pump? What are you, injecting five times a day?"

He nods. "Alternating legs."

"You really should consider an upgrade," I tell him. "Although, to be fair, I've never had to deal with your way before. I got my pump almost right away when I was diagnosed."

"I don't think any of that was invented when I was young, my dear," he says, staring at my arm and my monitor again. "I'm too old to change my ways."

"Oh, come on, young man," I say with another wink, throwing his words back at him. "Look, I'll show you how it works." I pull out my phone and show him the app. "I'm perfectly balanced right now," I tell him. "What about you? Need some gummy bears?"

He laughs long and hard, but nods. We have our heads bent over the screen, munching the candy, when Liam slinks back into the room, frowning, staring. "Maddie," he says. His eyebrows shoot up, as if he's trying to say "on with it."

"Right! The interview!" I slip the phone back in my pack. "So, Mr. Monroe—"

"Clayton, please," he says, patting my hand with his rhino-hide fingers.

"Clayton," I say, nodding. "I'm going to record, if that's ok? I don't want to miss any of your charming details about your impression of the infamous Mick Brady."

I lean into the convo, then, to Liam's horror, getting Clayton to rehash his meeting with Mick at traffic court and their subsequent friendship at the "naughty driver" classes they both had to take to remove points from their license.

"Can you imagine," he says, "sitting there with all walks of life. All of us in trouble for speeding or driving on the curb or what have you. We all used to go for pizza after. Mick bought, most of the time. For everyone. That's just the type of guy he is."

Clayton smiles, like he's remembering his younger days with fondness.

He tells me some more tidbits about golf outings, but really I think I've captured the personality nuggets about Mick that I need. I glance at Liam, to see if he has what he came for. Kellen hinted that the main secret point of this meeting was to prompt Monroe to call up Mick Brady, who is going to pivot the convo into a business proposition.

Liam is like a brick wall, a frowny brick wall. I set my pencil down on the table. "Thank you so much, Clayton. This was fantastic. Who is the best person for me to contact if I have follow up questions as I'm drafting the material?"

He beams and slides me his card. "You call me any time, Madison. I mean that." He pats my hand again. I smile and stand, shaking his hand while Liam looks perplexed.

"You ready to head out?" I ask, forgetting that I'm supposed to wait for Liam to tee up the ask about calling Mick to catch up.

Liam rises and leans toward Clayton for a handshake, but Clayton turns toward me, tapping his nose with his index finger. "You know, Maddie, would it be ok if I called you this week? I'd like to talk with my wife about that upgrade you mentioned."

He snaps his eyes quickly to Liam and I can tell he doesn't want me to mention anything about our personal connection. "Of course," I tell him.

"I'll be working at Beltane for the next few months, so you can always find me there!"

I keep thinking I've set up the perfect opening for Liam to jump in and say he will have his dad call or something, but he just stands there staring at me. We all finally shake hands and Clayton walks us to the elevators personally.

When the doors slide shut, Liam runs both hands through his hair. "Jesus Christ, what a mess," he growls. "What the hell were you doing in there?"

"Me?"

"Yes, you! With the candy, playing around on your phone. You were hired for a very specific job here, Maddie."

I feel my chest swell up and absorb the rest of the air in the elevator. "Excuse me, but you're the one with your phone going off, bursting in and out of the room and then staring like a silent clown when I was teeing you up to get Monroe to call your dad."

He works his mouth open like he's about to spit a retort at me. "Huh uh," I say, shaking my head. "You're not going to imply that I did anything less than my job here. I got fantastic audio for the corporate history and established rapport with Clayton Monroe where you clearly could not."

I absolutely hate being told what to do. I spent most of my life being told what I can and cannot do by doctors and I'm over it in my personal life. Plus I know I'm right, and I also hate when people don't listen to me.

He sinks against the wall. "You're right," he says. "What was he talking about at the end, anyway? What kind of upgrade is he looking for?"

"It's not really my place to tell you," I say. When the doors slide open, I stalk across the lobby and out into the sunshine. "You know what?" He frowns at me. "It's a nice day. I think I'll walk back to Beltane."

Before he can object, I stomp off down the street, cramming crackers in my mouth as I walk.

CHAPTER EIGHT
LIAM

"Tell me again what happened? And no, I don't care that she was getting cracker crumbs in the company car." My uncle frowns at me disapprovingly as I try for the third time to make sense of what went down with Clayton Monroe this morning.

I feel like I'm on hour 36 of an all-nighter. My head feels inflated and my heart beats erratically. Can this all be related to the mold growing in my kitchen sink? I start to wonder if Cal is actually killing me with his hog habits.

I take a deep breath and go through the main points again. Dad calling during the meeting. Me returning to Maddie and Clayton poring over a cell phone. "He made reference of an upgrade to her, Kellen. Does she know about the plan?"

He shakes his head. "I haven't even mentioned it to your father yet," he tells me. "I really don't think that's what he could have been talking about. We could solve this by asking her."

"No!" I cut him off abruptly and then blush. "I need to pull myself together before I approach her again." My uncle raises an eyebrow at me. "I'm sorry," I tell him and let out a long breath. "What's going on with me?"

Uncle Kellen laughs, which surprises me because I was sure he'd be pissed that I didn't tee up a phone call between Dad and Monroe. Phase One of our plan to inspect and re-engineer the power grid depends on us getting an in with the utilities. "How could I be so stupid?"

"Want to know what I think?" Kellen is smiling now, which flusters me even further. How can anyone smile when so much is on the line? I shrug anyway, and he says, "I think maybe you have the hots for Miss Parker."

"What? No," I lie. How can he tell? It doesn't even make sense that I'm attracted to her, but it doesn't matter because she's several degrees of off limits anyway.

"No?" Kellen raises an eyebrow at me skeptically. "Liam, son, I hope this doesn't come out wrong, but you're generally wound tighter than a cable-stayed bridge."

I snort. "Like those cables, I need all the pieces in my life to help support the load and let me function at my best."

Kellen laughs. "Well, from what I saw this morning, Madison Parker puts a kink in your design. She's like a gust of wind coming in from the bay. Am I right?"

Before I can think, I mutter, "she certainly causes vibrations." When Kellen barks out a laugh I realize I've said that out loud, and I grit my teeth. "I won't let it become an issue. I was...taken aback this morning."

Kellen leans forward and squeezes my shoulder. "I know you won't let it be a problem, Liam. But I also know we need to set Clayton Monroe up with your dad for a call. Let me call Maddie at her desk and get her in here to collaborate on this."

He reaches for his phone. "Um, there's something else I didn't tell you." I fidget in my seat. "I may have yelled at her after the interview and she refused to ride back with me. Said she'd rather walk." I flush. I'm a professional in my thirties. I aced my professional engineering examinations. I've negotiated with railroads. Yet today I fell to pieces because an intriguing woman pulled crackers from her fanny pack and smelled like flowers.

My uncle's eyes look like they're going to bulge out of his head. "Well where the hell is she now?" I shrug. "For heaven's sake, Liam." Kellen stands and grabs his keys, punching numbers into his cell. I assume he's trying to call her and drive to fetch her, although it has been long enough that she's likely close by now.

"It's a nice day," I sputter.

Just then, Maddie rounds the corner, her cheeks flushed from the walk in the sun. She's smiling, although she frowns when she sees me. "Hi, Kellen," she says, ignoring me. "I was hoping we could debrief before I get to transcribing the interview?"

My uncle dismisses me with a wave and I sulk back to my office to formulate a plan to get my shit back together. Along the way, I run into my brother Cal, eating pizza in the hall with a plop of red sauce dripped on the web between his thumb and forefinger.

"Callum, you're such a fucking slob." I growl at him and shove him against the wall.

"What gives, Liam? You're missing pizza by the way." He gestures toward the conference room with his thumb.

"You don't get it, do you? That I'm not joking around when I say I can't live like this anymore. We're not in a frat, Cal!"

Cal squints at me. "I'm going to assume you're hangry right now. We can regroup back at home later." He hustles off toward his own office and closes the door with finality. I pinch the bridge of my nose and breathe deeply.

He's probably right. I need some food and then I need to apologize to Maddie. Then I need to tell Callum we can't live together any longer. Settling on a plan of action, I make my way to the conference room. I nod at Orla and Zack, leaning against the counter in the back, laughing.

They see me and Zack asks where Maddie is.

I shrug again. "She's with Uncle Kellen," I say. "Debriefing."

Zack looks concerned and glances at his watch. "Hm. I promised Nicole I'd get her fed on time today." He pulls out his phone and starts tapping out a text message.

I reach for a slice of pizza on the table. "I'm sure she filled up on fish crackers and candy," I mutter, but Zack swats at my arm.

"Don't be like that."

I remind myself that apologizing to her is phase two in my plan to get back on track. I grab a second plate. "I'll bring her a slice. How's that?"

Zack smiles and nods. Orla chimes in, saying, "Much better, Lee."

My cousin and my brothers have been trying to get nicknames for us Brady kids to stick for years. Zack is short for Isaac. Cal for Callum. Sometimes Cal calls her La-la. They're all trying to get me to agree to Lee, but I'm not interested.

Liam means protector, unwavering. I like that my name already fits into my history. My parents divorced when Cal was a baby and Dad got Zack's mom pregnant with him. My entire childhood was marked by upheaval and chaos. Cal and I spent every-other week in a different house. I was his constant through all that, and Zack's comfort on the days before we'd take off and leave him behind.

Then, when Kellen's wife died and he and Orla moved in to our house, I was again the keeper of the peace. Kellen was comatose with grief. Dad has always been flighty. There were four kids who needed to be fed regularly and kept semi-clean. Uncle Kellen is right that I'm high strung, but someone at the Brady house needed to be. It's the only way the six of us made it through.

I roll my eyes at Orla and head back upstairs with the pizza, only to catch sight of Maddie in the hall on her way toward her temporary cubicle.

"Maddie," I say, walking toward her with the pizza.

She sighs. "Hello, Liam."

Something about the sight of her with her hands on her hips, her brown eyes shooting sparks at me, has my heart racing. I close my eyes and inhale deeply until I feel capable of being professional again. "I come bearing a peace offering." I hold out the pizza toward her. She arches a brow and squints. "And an apology," I add.

She still doesn't move and when I gesture again with the plate, she says, "Well, I'm waiting for the apology part."

Fuck. Me. I'm eviscerated. Done. Ruined for all other women. I want her so badly in this moment and she hates me and I can't have her anyway and I need to go sit in my office and figure out a new plan. I nod. "Yes. I'm sorry, Maddie. I behaved terribly and spoke from a place of heightened temper and panic and it won't happen again."

She smiles. "Forgiven." She snatches the pizza and begins eating, hungrily. "Is there more of this? I'm not really a one-slice kind of girl." Her mood is instantly transformed, like she just needed the gesture of apology, just needed to know I'd humble myself that way.

I swallow thickly. "In the conference room. I can walk you."

"Thank you. I'm still not sure where anything is."

I lead the way down the hall and as we enter the room, our admin Em comes bustling over. "Oh, Liam, Maddie. Good! I was looking for you. Maddie, I have Clayton Monroe on line two for you. He says you're expecting his call?"

She ushers Maddie toward her cubicle and I stare, slack-jawed. I toss my plate in the trash and follow them to Maddie's cubicle.

CHAPTER NINE
MADDIE

to Nicole's place by way of the grocery store. I've felt a little (ok a lot) like a
mooch since I've been staying here, even though Nicole basically forced me
to move in, so I decide to get dinner started for them.

I'm sliding a lasagna into the oven when Nicole bursts through the
front door, all loud energy and fabulous honesty. "It smells fucking
amazing in here, Madison," she yells, kicking off her heels and setting her
bag in one of the cubbies she and Zack installed in the entryway as a
weekend project to celebrate moving in together.

Everything about her house oozes class and sophistication, and she
created every last inch of it herself. I really admire the way she just takes
charge of long-term projects like that and makes them shine.

I pour her a glass of wine as she walks into the kitchen and her face
lights up. "Can I keep you forever? Such service!"

We clink glasses and I sit next to her at the counter. "Tell me about your
first day," she says, reaching for the dish of crackers I set out with the olives.
I tell her about Clayton Monroe—I figure Nicole doesn't work with him,
and she's been around my diabetes drama for a decade now, so she's a safe
haven when it comes to that stuff.

"He called later in the afternoon to ask me more about getting started
with a pump and a glucose meter," I tell her. Then I slam my glass down on
the counter harder than I intended. "Oh, and it was the weirdest thing!

Liam followed me from the conference room when I took the call and hid in a cubicle trying to spy on me."

Nicole frowns and sips her wine. "That's very weird and, frankly, very unlike Liam. Was he, like, crouched on the ground? Maybe he was tying his shoe?"

I shrug. "You'd think! But of course he had loafers on today with his neatly pressed trousers."

Nicole laughs and chokes on her wine a little. "Neatly pressed, eh? So you were checking out his 'trousers?'" She makes air quotes with her hands and sloshes a little wine on the counter.

I reach for a napkin and try to deflect. I don't want Nicole or Zack to know that I was indeed checking out Liam's trousers. And his arms, especially when he looped one over my seat to back out of the parking spot. Or the sexy little vein in his neck that pulses when he yells at me. Not that it's ok for him to yell at me.

"Well what else did the Bradys do all day," she prods. "I've never seen them in action. Well, that's not true. I saw Mick try to run a meeting in Paraguay last year. God, do they all sit around and drink weird tea from gourds like Mick?"

"It just seemed like regular, shitty office coffee." I toss the wine-soaked napkin at the trash and pump my fist when I land the shot. "Kellen is very organized. He's a bit of a silver fox, not gonna lie."

Nicole nods. "Yeah, he smells like Old Spice," she says.

"He totally smells like Old Spice. Anyway, he asked Liam to go with me on the first interview. It seems like Liam is going to run point on the project from the Beltane side of things."

The front door opens and I hear Zack setting down his tools and stuff in a cubby. "What is that smell?" He comes into the kitchen. "God, why don't we cook here more," he asks Nicole, who slides down from the stool to kiss him. I flush and look away, sort of uncomfortable around their intimacy.

They just...fit together. I've never really had that with anyone. I've dated a bunch, but anytime someone starts to get to know me, they either think my diabetes is too much or else my persistent questions and short temper are too much. I'm too much.

"Your brother was spying on Maddie," Nicole says, tossing an olive to Zack, who doesn't open his mouth in time but catches it with his hand.

"Which brother? Cal?" He chews the olive and, finding the pit inside, looks around like he can't figure out what to do with it. Nicole rolls her eyes and hands him a napkin.

"Liam," she says. "He was crouched in a cubicle listening to Maddie's phone call."

He frowns. "That's really odd," he says. "I wonder if I should call him later. There was also something weird at the office earlier where Kellen said Liam yelled at Maddie and she refused to get back in the company car."

He cocks a brow at me and I spring up to check the lasagna.

"Madison? Is this true? Tell me Liam Brady didn't yell at you on your first day at work or I'll be at his house in the morning to bleach his ball hair." Nicole stands behind me and taps her foot. "Oh, that lasagna looks amazing," she says.

I sigh and pull my head out of the oven. "It needs a few more minutes. And yes, he yelled. But then he apologized and brought me pizza. I just realized I'm eating pizza and lasagna on the same day and that's probably not great for my innards."

"Why," Zack asks, spitting another olive pit into his napkin. "Your blood sugar?"

"No," I say, laughing. "Because of all the cheese! I probably won't poop for a week."

Nicole shoves me and starts washing her hands. "Maddie, now Zack knows that women poop!"

He turns bright red, but before he can say anything, Nicole says, "Ok, no more work talk. No more Liam talk. We're going to eat this lasagna and then, Isaac Brady, you may call one family member on the phone for an interrogation." She holds up her index finger. "One relative! Not four. Not even two. I don't want to be up until all hours waiting for you to stop pacing and come to bed."

"Got it," he says.

We sit down to eat at Nicole's table. I realize, after listening to her scold Zack, that I haven't even talked to my family about all this. It's not that I don't have a good relationship with my parents. It's just that, well, they'd expect me to find solutions. If I called them at the problem stage of my problems, they'd want to know what I was going to do to fix them.

After we clean up and Zack calls up his brother to yell at him for being weird, I slide into the sunroom to call home.

"Maddie?" My mom answers like she wasn't expecting to ever hear from me again and I called during something important.

"Yeah, Mom, it's me," I tell her. "What are you and Dad up to?"

I can hear a rustling in the background. "Well, you know, we finally joined a bowling league."

"Really? That's so great. In Lawrenceville?"

She scoffs. "Well there aren't any other bowling alleys in the city anymore, you'll recall."

I roll my eyes. "I know, I just meant...well I'm living nearby the bowling alley now."

I hear a thud and hope she didn't drop a bowling ball on her foot or anything. "You moved out of your apartment?"

"Yeah..." I start to chew on my nails, but then I worry that she can see me and will scold me for it, so I put my hand in my lap. "I got laid off last week." Silence. "From the paper."

"I always hated that rag," she scoffs. "They print a lot of nonsense in there."

"It's still a good paper, Mom. They're just...not doing well financially."

I hear the sound of pins falling in the background and what I assume is my dad whooping for joy. "Well," my mother starts to say. "What are you gonna do now?"

"I don't want you to worry," I say quickly. "I got three months' severance and can keep up my health insurance that long. Nicole actually got me a temporary job already. I'm staying with her. And working with her boyfriend. Nicole has a boyfriend."

I feel myself rambling again and pull the phone away from my ear to check my sugar. I'm never sure if I ramble because I spent my whole childhood being grilled by doctors, or because my blood sugar is low and it makes me loopy. It is, in fact, a little low. Not sure how that can be after I just ate all that damn cheese, but I reach into my fanny pack and pull out some fruit snacks.

"I'm not entirely sure what to make of what you're saying, Madison," Mom says. I don't blame her for getting confused. "You keeping track of your sugars? Cleaning your pump and all that?"

"Yep," I say, mouth full of candy. "I was panicked there when it first happened, but I've got a plan and a budget, thanks to Nicole. I'm writing a corporate history for an engineering firm."

I hear my dad urging my mom to come take her turn at bowling. "Just a minute," she whispers off to the side. "What's a corporate history?"

"It's a book, Mom. I'm writing a book about this company and they're paying me good money. I should be able to find something permanent by the time I'm done with the project."

"A whole book, huh?" She sounds proud, and that makes me feel good.

"Just a minute, I said," she hisses. "Well, listen, Madison, I gotta go take my turn. I'm real proud of you, honey."

I'm glad I waited to call until I had a plan. I hang up with my mother and toss my phone down on the arm of the chair. I step out back and walk over toward Nicole's tank pool. Zack built her one of those trendy animal trough pools and even rigged it up so it can be a hot tub in the winter.

I climb inside—the water's only two feet deep and I can stand in there in my shorts, staring at the sun setting over the river. I'm grateful Nicole and Emma helped me make a plan and put it in action. Where would I be without them?

Alone and broke, in a diabetic coma, I think. I pop another fruit snack in my mouth, and head inside.

CHAPTER TEN
MADDIE

For the rest of the week, Kellen Brady asks me to visit former clients or acquaintances of his brother, Mick. Kellen seems to really credit his brother with building the company into what it is today, even though it's clear from talking to him that Kellen is an engineering genius.

His mind is so calm, so methodical. He can recall specific details from decades prior without having to check, but then he always checks anyway. And he's always right about whatever dollar amount was spent, however many gallons of sludge were rerouted through a pipe. You name it, he can recall the numerical facts about it.

I still haven't even met his brother, Liam's dad. Supposedly they're saving my meeting with him for last so that I don't go into these interviews with preconceived notions. I don't know how to explain to them that between my conversations with Zack and the interviews I've done so far, I already have impressions that Mick Brady is a gregarious observer with a kind heart and, probably, real bad ADHD.

I can always tell if an interview is particularly important to Kellen's vision for the book if he sends Liam with me to supervise. I'm sure he's not actually supervising me, because Kellen has seemed really pleased with the outlines and notes I've sent him to check over.

He seems to have an ulterior motive for all the contacts he includes Liam on. I wish he'd just tell me what that motive is so I didn't have to spend my days wrestling between my annoyance at Liam's grouchiness and my growing attraction to, well, his grouchiness.

Today, Liam asked me to come ready to go into the field, whatever that means. Like, is it an actual field? A flower field? I have so many questions. That's what makes me good at my job. I take off on a hunch until I get to the hidden meat of an issue. I feel ok saying I'm good at what I do. It's been ten years, after all.

I opt for jeans and sneakers today, figuring I can clip my pump on the waist band without being too obvious. Zack lends me a Beltane polo shirt, but it's huge, so I knot it at the side and cover the pump. Liam is waiting for me in the parking lot when I arrive, and I have to take a minute inside my car and just drink him in.

Gone is the suit and tie, replaced by worn jeans, work boots, and a short-sleeved button-down shirt. Holy god, he's probably going to wear a tool belt. I swallow, seeing the smallest bit of chest hair poking out around his collar in the front.

I climb out and walk over to him. "This ok for our outing?" I spin around on my heel and he nods. "I've got a hard hat for you. And ear protection, though I don't think it'll be too loud."

I slide into the passenger seat of the pickup truck and startle when my fingers brush against his as I buckle the seatbelt. He's arranging safety equipment between us on the bench seat. And there's the tool belt.The stuff of fantasies. Not knowing what else to do with my hands, I reach into my pack and pull out a lollipop, the kind with gum in the center.

Liam stares at me for a beat and then explains that today's interview is with a guy named Dave. "He's the harness guy," Liam says. "This is purely for the book. Not a side mission to land future business or anything like that."

"Is that what we were doing before," I ask him, pulling the lollipop out of my mouth. Is he staring at my mouth? I grin at him, and he returns the expression.

"No comment," he tells me. We pull off the road by a fence with access to the underside of a massive overpass.

"Wow," I say, looking up. I can see the scaffolding underneath. I've always known it was there and that workers used the access ladders...I've just never been up close to anything like this before.

"Listen," Liam says, his demeanor stiff. "It's imperative that you follow safety instructions while we are out here."

"Imperative, eh? Are we climbing up there?"

"NO!" He shouts. Then takes a breath. "Please do not climb the structures. Please also follow instructions. This asset has not yet been fully inspected."

"So..." I like the seriousness with which he approaches his work. Like, he really cares very deeply about the rules. "Is a bolt going to fall down and hit me on the head?"

Liam shrugs. "I'll radio for Dave to climb down and talk to us." It's then that I notice there is a man in a yellow safety vest and bright hard hat moving along the underside of the overpass.

"Holy shit!" I can't help but curse as I see the man spring toward the ladder down to the earth. Liam scowls at me, but when the man reaches the ground, he marches straight over and pulls Liam into an embrace.

"How are ya, kid? Good to see you!" He turns to look at me and smiles. He reminds me of my dad. I hold my hand out and he shakes it warmly. "I'm the harness guy. Guess they told you that, huh?"

We walk over to Dave's gear, where he swigs from a water bottle and asks me if I'd like to sit in his office. I do, gladly, and frown at Liam, who stands stiffly, like he doesn't want to lean on anything. Dave tells me he's worked with the company from its beginnings, and hopes to retire here.

"I'm not much for those computer systems and office work," he tells me. "I like being out in a harness, climbing around like a spider." He gestures around him. "This is my view every morning! Except different each day. And not when it rains, of course." He looks at Liam cautiously.

"Of course," I echo. "Do you mind if I record while we talk? I don't want to miss anything."

Dave laughs. "I'll just tell ya again if you do." He tells me about a project where Beltane was repairing a cellular tower once. "We had to climb to the top and measure everything, draw it, reverse engineer it to see if they could put micro discs on it." He beams. "We'd start with one type of job and soon, we were experts on the whole damn structure."

I smile. "Sounds like you're curious like a reporter."

Dave nods. "I guess you could say that." He tells me that he's had the pleasure of helping Mick and Kellen save a client millions of dollars by finding ways to repair a wind-damaged ore trestle rather than replace it.

"Should I know what an ore trestle is," I ask him, breaking out my bag of fish crackers and offering him some.

He smiles. "My grandkids love these things," he says. "Takes me back to when my boys were little. You got kids?" I shake my head. "Anyway, that's how Beltane can compete against people who are so-called experts in that kind of thing."

Dave talks and talks, a natural storyteller. I can tell he's going to feature heavily in the story of this company's reputation as a risk-taking innovator. I glance at my note pad. "I'm supposed to ask you about the fire," I tell him. Dave takes off his hard hat and wipes his brow. Liam frowns at the safety violation. "Don't mind him," I say, patting Dave's hand.

"We get calls sometimes," he says. "We try not to be on the news, but sometimes..." He tells me about a crane explosion, how he helped the team assess what went wrong afterward. He closes his eyes and describes how he could smell the burnt body still in the cab of the crane. I squeeze his hand while he talks and catch Liam staring at me, a strange look on his face.

"They didn't want to hear me when I said what went wrong. They were being investigated by OSHA," he says. "The whole end of the building blew out, and I knew it could have been prevented." Dave swallows. He shares a story of an accident in the same facility from years before, an acid leak. He knew about the leak because Beltane had been on the site to assess something else. "I knew the *history* of that place," he says. "I knew the crane stopped working because there was a dip in the runway, because the foundation was damaged from the acid years before." Dave looks me in the eye. "Back when that happened, I mentioned it to the client. He chose not to listen. Said that was outside my scope of work. I've seen things, you know?"

I nod. "I know. And you're right. History is so important. I think that's why Mick and Kellen wanted me to talk with you. To really demonstrate how Beltane does its homework, looks closer, and remembers."

Dave takes a deep breath. "I don't do site visits anymore," he tells me. "Just bridges now. Just the birds eye view for me."

I smile warmly and assure him I feel safer driving over a bridge he's given his special attention. Liam shakes hands with Dave. "We've kept you from your work long enough," he says, his voice strange.

Dave waves him off. "Happy to climb down and gab for awhile," he says. I get his contact information so I can email him if I have follow up questions and have to run to catch up to Liam, who has already climbed into the truck.

I take off my hard hat and shake out my hair, noticing that Liam is staring at me intently. "What?"

A beat passes, then two. "How did you get him to do that?"

"What?"

"To..." Liam seems at a loss for words. "To talk to you like that. Tell you those things." I shrug. "I've known Dave my entire life. I have never heard him say anything beyond smalltalk unless he was reviewing numbers for a report."

I shrug again. "I don't know," I tell him. "It's just what I do. I talk to people until they talk back."

He starts the car and heads toward the office. He makes a grunting sound and I stare at his hands on the wheel, the thick veins showing through the dark hair I long to touch. I find myself wondering if it's soft or coarse. He mutters something I don't quite catch.

"Pardon?"

His dark eyes flick to mine for a brief instant, liquid and intense. "I said you're really good at what you do."

I'm not prepared for him to speak this frankly, to offer a compliment. I flush. "Thank you," I whisper. Liam Brady is unexpected. I'm not sure what to make of him, but I stare at him driving, deciding I want to figure it out.

CHAPTER ELEVEN
LIAM

ORLA'S SUGGESTION IS A WELCOME ONE FOR OUR AFTER-WORK FAMILY RUN. WE love the tight switchbacks and gentle inclines on the little-used mountain bike trail in Highland Park in Pittsburgh's East End. The trail winds its way through so many areas of the park that people never see. My family, of course, appreciates the engineering of the trail and the way urban infrastructure like wiring and piping wind their way through the park tucked out of view to all but the most adventurous runners.

I send a few thumbs up emojis, hoping to convey my enthusiasm for Orla's idea. And then I remember I'm on a site visit with Maddie. If I take her to the office afterward I'll miss the group outing. I mutter a few curses, trying to figure out how we can cut out early. I look over at her, squatting on the ground with our drone pilot.

I force myself not to notice that Linda handed Maddie the controls, praying silently that she's just looking and not actually driving the device. Beltane started using drones to photograph hard-to-access assets for clients right as that technology was becoming popular. At the time, drone operators needed to go to flight school. Beltane paid for Linda to obtain her commercial pilot's license just so she could operate the flying cameras.

The choice has paid off. Linda is able to physically deliver my dad or my uncle to remote locations, then fly the drone for image analysis. I hear

Maddie's voice as she hands the device back to Linda. "So the real talent is in how you analyze the footage, I imagine," she asks. Linda beams and explains how she's partnering with our newest hire, Ray, who developed machine learning technology to analyze the video.

"Ray's robots can study hours and hours of recordings, find abnormalities, and write up a report for me overnight," Linda says. "Today we're just checking this dam for cracks, though." Maddie watches as Linda brings the drone back down. I realize there's no real way for us to leave the site early, since Maddie is engrossed in the work and it wouldn't be fair to her or Linda if we left now.

Maddie's eyes are wide as she observes, "This is going to be great when I talk about Beltane as the sun rising over the future of engineering. Like, you guys were the early light before dawn with your adoption of this technology."

Linda grins. "You're like a poet, almost."

Maddie shakes her head. "Nah. But it is a nice image, right? What with your logo being the sun and all."

Once we're back in the truck, Maddie fans herself and reaches for her bottle of water in the console. I stare at a bead of sweat making its way down her chest and disappearing beneath the neckline of her flowy top. She always wears black, unless I tell her she needs field clothes. I didn't today, since this isn't a heavy duty dirty work visit.

She catches me staring and scowls. "Why do you look like someone stole your homework?"

"What?"

She rolls her eyes. "You're making a face like someone violated a rule and the injustice of it has you clenching your butthole."

My jaw drops at her candor, and she looks a bit sheepish. "Sorry," she says. "You just look upset. Care to tell me what's wrong?"

I shake my head. "It's nothing. I'm just supposed to go running with my family this afternoon, but I forgot you and I have to—"

"Oh," she exclaims. "Is Nicole going? She can bring me sneakers. I can come, right? Nicole's been dying to bring me so I can be slow with her while you all sprint on ahead."

"Hm," I say. But Maddie has her phone out and taps quickly on the screen.

"Awesome," she says. "Where are we running? Nothing too hilly, I hope."

I drive to the back of the zoo parking lot, heading in as all the minivans and station wagons full of families head out for the close of day. We park in the overflow parking lot where the zoo butts up against the park. There's a trailhead back there, running parallel to the Allegheny River for awhile before we turn up into the park behind the public pool.

I always have my workout stuff with me in the truck, in case I need to run off some steam, or think about a problem, or meet my family to goof off. What I don't do typically is change in front of a woman who intrigues me. I feel my jeans tighten at the thought of Maddie being present while I slip into my shorts and t-shirt. "Um," I stutter. "Are you going to change into something?"

I turn to face her when I park. She unbuckles. "Nope," she says, and to my horror she pulls off her tunic top. But she's got a whole other outfit on underneath it. "I can run in this," she says, gesturing at her tank top and leggings. She snaps the fanny pack back in place. "Guess you have to change, don't you?"

I nod, stiffly, and she climbs out of the truck. "I'll close my eyes, I promise. I can stand out here and warn you if any of these kids' moms are heading your way looking for an eyeful." I glance around her, checking to see if there are women on the loose, chasing their children, and Maddie laughs. "God, you're really easy to ruffle, Liam Brady."

I stare at her and reach for my duffel bag. "I just…"

"It's ok," she says. Then she turns around, leaning her back against the door of the truck. "You're all clear, sir. Feel free to get naked."

I tear off my pants, changing into my shorts faster than I've ever done in my life. I carefully remove my button down and decide my undershirt will do for today's run. By the time Zack and Nicole pull up, I'm carefully folding my work things and sliding them back into my bag, reaching into the side zipper pockets for my sneakers and running socks.

Maddie greets Nicole with a hug and I watch as she swaps out sandals for sneakers. Everyone takes off running into the woods, and I fall back, listening as Maddie and Nicole admire the trail. I don't know why, but it's important to me that Maddie appreciate this space, and I feel a surge of relief and longing when she points out the way the light trickles through the leaves and notices how the vines of honeysuckle threaten to overtake the concrete stairs.

"It's so interesting that the more natural rocky steps are clear, and the ones the people put here are getting taken back over by nature."

Cal catches me staring as Nicole nods along. I jerk my eyes away and sprint on ahead.

CHAPTER TWELVE
MADDIE

On Wednesday, I roll into a parking spot in the company lot just as Liam's arriving. We're meant to visit with some sort of oil tycoon today. Not really. But some guy who is high up at a gas company. Beltane engineered plans for them for a refinery like 30 years ago, and I guess the original structures are still in place. Which I gather is unusual for that type of equipment.

As I climb out of my car, I see Liam squinting at me, looking me up and down. I glance down at my outfit. Standard fare: black cropped leggings and compression tank under a black dress. Black ballet flats. Bright red velvet fanny pack today to go with my red earrings. I even wore lipstick. Well, ok, it's not lipstick. It's tinted chapstick. But it is *almost* lipstick.

"What," I ask, eventually, worried I'll turn to stone under his gaze, trying not to remember the feel of his skin from the other day. How it felt like touching a live wire when I brushed against his arm. I stare right on back at him, in his perfectly pressed suit and polished shoes.

My glucose monitor beeps and I unzip my pack, opting for salted cashews this time. Liam actually growls. "What?" I say it again and try not to shove him.

He shakes his head and strides toward the door to the office. I don't have a Beltane ID, so I always have to either sneak in the door after someone or else wait to buzz reception. Liam almost closes the door on me and then looks alarmed when I shove my hand in the crack at the last minute.

"Don't mind if I join you," I say.

He pauses in the lobby, closes his eyes, and pinches the bridge of his nose with his slender fingers. "I owe you an apology again," he says. "It's just that...never mind." He starts to walk toward the stairs and, clinging to this opening, I follow him.

"Just what?" He doesn't turn. "Liam! Look at me."

He stops on the stairs and turns toward me, fiddling with his tie. "You perplex me," he says.

"What the hell does that mean?"

He squints again. "It means I find you perplexing."

I tap my foot. "I guess I prefer when you phrase your observation as something *you* are doing—finding me perplexing. But what's so weird about me?"

He shakes his head. "Not weird," he says. "Perplexing. I don't know what to expect from you."

I feel a tingling sensation move through my body at this. "Well, it's just me," I tell him. "You can expect just me."

He nods. "I know. And most people aren't like that. Most people have a...a layer or a crust or something."

"So I'm not crusty and that makes you frown and growl?"

"Yes." He turns to continue up the stairs as if that's the end.

I shout after him. "Well, growling is considered rude, Liam. Maybe you could not growl today while we're with the oil guy."

"His name is Clifford," Liam says over his shoulder. "And I will do my best not to growl."

True to his word, he does not growl once on the way to the oil company. Although several of his grunts come damn close. He perplexes me, too. I'm usually pretty easygoing. Why do I find myself snarling at him so often, bristling when he makes observations?

We settle in to the table in the conference room as has become my new routine. I spread out my supplies. A rich dude comes in and shakes hands with Liam. I explain my take on Beltane as a nimble little company with their finger on the pulse of the next big engineering thing that will help their clients.

Clifford nods along at that. "It was clear to me immediately that Mick

Brady had no idea what the hell he was talking about when it came to engineering," Clifford says. "No offense to your old man, there, son."

Liam raises a hand. "None taken. Dad has a sociology degree, after all."

"Yeah, your uncle, though," Clifford's eyes focus beyond my shoulder as he thinks back to their first meeting. "Kellen Brady knew what we needed before he set foot on our site. Hell, I didn't even know what we needed. You gotta understand, 30 years ago, people weren't thinking about what we needed to do to make sure an underground storage tank was still in tact 30 years down the line."

Clifford talks about Kellen and Mick convincing him to use thicker concrete than required, about testing new plastics for liners. Kellen convinced Clifford to plan for regulations that didn't exist yet, and as a result their company could flourish when others around them were shut down for environmental violations. "Beltane gave us our reputation as a safe company," Clifford says. "Not sure Mick knew that, but here we are."

I smile warmly and glance over at Liam, who leans forward. "You know," he says. "You should give my dad a call sometime. He mentioned you guys hadn't played golf in awhile."

I get so excited for Liam nailing his portion of the mission that I forget myself and flash him a double thumbs up. Clifford laughs and I blush. "You like the idea of me calling up Mick?"

I have to think fast and remember not to ramble. "I like the idea of coming along when you two go golfing," I say. My cheeks flush because this is way outside the plan and I'm worried Liam is going to have a stroke. I try to cover. "Just think of the fodder I'd pick up for the book."

Clifford slaps the table. "Yeah, but half of it would be off the record." He winks.

I clear my throat and glance down my notebook. "Well, I think we hit all my questions," I say, chewing the tip of my pen. "I can email you with follow up questions? That is if we're not hitting the links together."

"Who'd be our fourth if we get out there on the green, Ms. Parker?" Clifford pulls a pair of reading glasses from his pocket along with his datebook. I love the sort of older gentleman who still carries around a paper datebook.

"Liam, of course," I blurt without looking over at him. I don't need to. I know he's going to break his promise and growl the entire way back to Beltane.

CHAPTER THIRTEEN
LIAM

I HAVE NEVER FOUND MYSELF SO FLABBERGASTED BY SOMEONE BEFORE. AS WE WALK to the parking lot, I try to think if I've ever even been around anyone like Maddie Parker in my life. My brother Cal is flaky and people consider him fun. He's not perplexing like Maddie.

He doesn't ask probing questions, shirk protocol or eat crackers in cars. Perhaps it's unfair to say she shirked protocol. My uncle never specifically said she wasn't supposed to insert herself when he revealed that I was supposed to be the one to suggest Clifford and Clayton and all the other tycoons ring up my dad for a chat.

"That was unbelievably irresponsible," I say, pulling on to the highway from the ramp near the parking lot.

"What was? Inviting myself golfing?"

"Yes!" I merge into the center lane and head north toward my mother's house. It's Wednesday, and Cal and I always meet her for dinner on Wednesdays. I'm glad our meeting with Clifford was the last one of the day because I don't think I could go back to the office after that.

"Why?" Maddie looks at me as she nibbles the end of a piece of licorice, and I have to snap my eyes back on the road to avoid staring at her perfectly aligned teeth as they sink into the candy. Since when is candy so erotic? Jesus, what's come over me?

"Do you even golf?"

"Of course not," she says, like this is inconsequential. "It's not about golfing, anyway, right? It's about your dad dropping hints about your big secret project, whatever it is."

"Yes, but you still have to carry out the game. The golf is…it's a scaffold for the conversation."

She arches a brow at me and I keep glancing at her even though I need to watch the road. "A scaffold? You don't spend much time away from engineers, do you, Yum?"

She called me Yum. I feel simultaneously irritated because it's stupid and amazed because that's not a nickname my cousin has ever come up with before, and she's tried for a long time.

"Yum?" I ask with a swallow.

"Yeah," she says, biting off another piece of licorice. "Lee-yum. Yum. Yummy. Yummilicious." She laughs. The sound is so contagious that I laugh, too.

"You're right," I tell her. "I do not, in fact, spend much time with people who are not engineers. Are you saying that non-engineers are all like you?"

Another laugh. The car feels full of her laughter, like I can almost see it holding up the roof of the car. It somehow makes the world feel more spacious. "No, I'm perplexing, remember?"

"Hm." I can't tell if she's trying to restart a fight or give me shit about what I said the other day.

"Hey, Yum, where are we headed, anyway? Isn't our office back downtown?"

As we pass the sign for Cranberry, I realize that I have once again let my overwhelm at Maddie distract me. "Shit," I say. "We're…I have dinner with my mother tonight."

"And were you going to invite me formally, or is this how engineers handle such things?"

She gestures at me with the bag of licorice, and I take a piece, even though I don't normally eat candy. I'm surprised by the strawberry flavor as it bursts in my mouth. "This is really good," I tell her, and she nods.

"I, well I got distracted after our meeting with Clifford and I sort of went into autopilot, driving toward my mom's and…if I take you back now I'll be late and I'm not sure what to do, if I'm being honest."

"You could try inviting me to dinner, and then maybe calling your mom to see if it's ok for you to bring a plus-one."

"It all just makes so much sense the way you say it." I spot our exit ahead and signal to change lanes. "Maddie, would you like to have dinner with me and Cal and our mother tonight?"

She frowns. "Won't Zack and Nicole be there? I guess I was assuming I'd ride home with them."

Now it's my turn to frown. "Zack has a different mother. My father…" I drift off, wondering how to explain all of that, but she cuts me off.

"Ah. Say no more, sir. I will not bring up his name…except I'll probably blurt that I'm friends with Nicole. And I live with her and Zack. Does your mom know all that? What's her name?"

The idea of my mother not knowing what's going on with any of the Bradys is laughable. "She knows all of it," I say. "And her name is Sheila."

"Sheila," Maddie says, like she's practicing. "Sheila. Want me to text her from your phone so you don't murder us with distracted driving?"

Before I can answer, she pulls my phone from the console and angles it toward my face. I'm stunned to see she has finagled the face recognition to unlock it that way. "You have your mom listed as Sheila Brady? Not Mom? She never took her name back? Do I call her Mrs. Brady?"

"You should call her Sheila. And everyone is in my phone organized by their actual name. Isn't that how everyone does it?"

When Maddie chuckles and shakes her head, I can tell she's laughing at me and not with me, but she soon holds up my phone, reading, "Ok, I typed, 'Hey, Mom, it's me, Yummy. Ok if I bring a friend from work to dinner?'"

"You did not type the part about Yummy." I quickly pull to the shoulder and yank the phone from her. She of course did not type that and laughs as I frantically scroll around the messages to make sure. The phone buzzes in my hand with my mother's response:

> Of course it's ok. Does this friend have any food restrictions?

"Are you allergic to anything? My mom wants to know."

Maddie shakes her head, biting her bottom lip as I respond. I try not to think about how I'd like to bite her lip, and what it means about me that I suddenly want to bite a woman when I've never once considered that before.

"Hope you didn't spoil your appetite on snack food," I tell her, tossing the phone back in the console and pulling back onto the road. "My mom always cooks enough for an entire flock."

"Flock, eh? Is she a shepherd, Liam? Like Little Bo Peep? Little Sheila Peep?"

I can't help but snicker at that image, and by the time I pull into Mom's driveway, I am laughing. Are we flirting together? Is that how this works? I stopped caring that Maddie invited herself on a networking golf outing, stopped caring about how loud she types on her keyboard when she's transcribing notes in her cubicle. Without thinking, I hop around the car and open her door for her as she looks at me strangely and my mother bursts through her screen door yelling, "Come give your mother a kiss!"

CHAPTER FOURTEEN
MADDIE

"And just who is this," Sheila says, releasing Liam from her embrace and clutching at her chest like my presence is giving her heart palpitations. I know I'm a whole lot, but I suspect her flutters are more due to Liam's typical rigidity than my bright red fanny pack.

I stick out a hand and say, "I'm Maddie Parker. I'm doing some consulting work with Beltane."

Sheila squints for a minute before returning my shake. "You don't seem like an engineer," she says. I smile at her.

"I'm a writer. They've got me crafting a corporate history for their upcoming anniversary."

Sheila starts walking toward the house, gesturing for us to follow. "That idea reeks of Kellen Brady," she says. "I can see him now, outlining exactly how many inches tall he built a tower in 1980."

"Well, that's where I come in," I tell her. "I edit out all the numerical references and spice up the discussion of how innovative an idea it was to build the tower in that specific location."

"Oh I like you," Sheila says. I toe off my shoes in the bin inside the front door, seeing the collection of shoes there. Liam stares at my toenails as he sits on the step to take off his fancy shoes. "Do you consult full-time, then, Maddie? We're always looking for good people."

Liam's eyes flash toward his mother. "You cannot hire Maddie, Mom."

"Why not," Sheila and I both say at once, and then share a laugh.

"My contract with Beltane is temporary," I tell her. "In truth, I was downsized from *The Pittsburgh Post,* where I'd been a reporter since college. I'm working on this project while I find my next permanent position."

"Goodness, with a background in journalism and corporate communications you'd be an excellent fit for us. Liam, you're just going to need to get over whatever it is that's bothering you, because I'm going to recruit this woman."

Liam looks a little like he swallowed a bug, and I do something I'm not entirely proud of. I stick my tongue out at him. It's sort of worth it to watch his eyes widen in shock, but the whole thing becomes moot when Cal plows through the front door.

"Hello, baby," Sheila says. "Did you know your colleague Maddie was joining us?"

Cal grins and shakes his head. "No. That's cool. Mom, did you know she's living with Zack now?"

Sheila hands Liam a bottle of wine to open. "Isn't Zack living with his girlfriend Nicole?" Liam starts pouring glasses for his mother and brother.

"Nicole and I are friends," I say, reaching into my bag to check my numbers before saying yes to the wine. I give myself a little insulin bump and accept the glass Sheila holds out. "When I got laid off, she helped me make a plan to get back on track, which included moving into her guest room temporarily. Zack hooked me up with the Beltane gig." I watch as Liam pours my wine. "That's good, Yum."

Cal and Sheila stare at me, hearing the nickname slip out of my lips. I hadn't intended to call him that in front of other people, but the damage is done now. I bring my glass to my lips to hide my flush as Cal pokes his brother in the chest. "Yum. Fucking Yum. I can't believe we never thought of that one. Lee-Yum, right, Maddie? High five."

We slap palms while Liam starts to protest that Yum is not a nickname for an adult professional.

"All right, boys, set the table," Sheila scolds. "Maddie, you don't have any food restrictions, do you? I know Liam said no, but I wanted to double check."

"That's so sweet, Sheila, thank you. I eat all the things."

Cal loads his forearm with a stack of silverware and china plates. "But you have to check it all, right? You said you have to check the sugar?"

Nodding as I sip my wine, I explain. "Yes. I'm diabetic, so I do monitor things."

Liam freezes in place with the salad bowl, and Cal crashes into his back, holding the dressing and a pepper mill. Liam frowns. "You're diabetic?"

Cal pokes him with the pepper. "Yeah, dude. She was talking about it the other day. You were there. When she explained about the snacks in her pouch?"

Liam starts shaking his head vehemently and Cal nudges around him to the table so he can go back for another armload of food. "I most certainly do not recall this conversation," Liam says.

"It's all right, dear," Sheila pats his arm. "I know you only really pay attention when there are bridges."

Liam sets the salad bowl on the table hard, and then steadies it when it seems likely to topple. "I pay attention," he insists. "I pay attention to Maddie."

My cheeks flush at the implication as Cal chuckles. "I bet you do, bro."

"What's that supposed to mean," he snaps at his brother. I don't like how quickly Liam turned defensive at the suggestion that he pays attention to me because I'm special to him. Before I can think about it too deeply, Sheila puts an arm around each of her sons.

"Enough," she says, guiding them to the table. "Maddie, we're having salmon and there's walnuts in the salad, and I'm so glad neither of those things will send you into anaphylactic shock."

We tuck in to the delicious food and I listen while Sheila grills the brothers about their week. To hear Cal talk, it's been all family runs and engine grease, while Liam paints a picture of tension at home and mounting stress at work as he aims to land some long-term new project.

"You two certainly have different world views," I point out and Sheila nods.

She gestures at Cal with her wine glass. "You know, son, it might be time for you to move out of Liam's space, if you're still leaving your underpants on the floor like that."

"And the sneakers in the doorway," Liam barks out. "They smell like a sewer."

Eventually, Sheila sends her sons to take the trash and recycling to the curb and beckons for me to join her on the back deck. "I'll clean up later," she says.

"Oh, let me help," I start to say, heading toward the sink with my plate, but she takes my arm.

"Please come and sit with me," she asks. "I don't know if any of my sons will bring a woman home again for years."

"Oh, it's not like he *brought me home,* not in that way…" I drift off. Did he bring me home in that way? He said he got in auto pilot and just started driving here from the client meeting, but based on what everyone is saying, Liam doesn't do such things.

His behavior with me paints a different picture. He apparently didn't notice me talking about diabetes, and we've had at least two fights where we've yelled at each other.

"I'd love to know more about why my son looks at you like a deer caught in the headlights," Sheila says, refilling her wine glass and gesturing to see if I'd like more.

"No, thank you," I say, checking my numbers. "I'm in the sweet spot right now."

"Is that some sort of monitor," she asks, looking at my screen.

I show her the readings on my app, and shrug out of my cardigan, showing her the glucose monitor on my arm. "So this guy studies my blood every five minutes and tells my phone what he sees." She smiles. I look over my shoulder and don't see the guys coming back yet, so I hitch up my dress and tanktop to show her my stomach. "This is my external pancreas."

"You're a witty woman, Maddie Parker," Sheila says. "I can see why he likes you."

"Does he like me? I couldn't tell between the frowns and the grunts." I immediately look down as I readjust my outfit, knowing it was a mistake to blurt like that to Liam's mother of all people.

"Take it from his mother," she says. "He's frowning because he can't figure out what to do about his feelings right now."

Before I can expand upon that idea, the guys pour onto the back deck. Cal sits on his mother's lap, making her squeal. "You're much too big to do that anymore," she shouts, swatting at his back.

"You said I'll always be your baby," he jokes, laughing. He plants a kiss on her cheek. "Need anything else from us? I have to head back into the city. Busy day tomorrow and all that."

"I don't need a thing, sweetheart," she says. "Oh, I guess you and Liam didn't ride together, did you?"

Cal shakes his head. "But maybe Maddie should drive the company car home. Liam and I do live in the same place, after all."

I try to mask the disappointment I feel at the thought of driving back alone. I realize I've been saving up little jabs to see if I can fluster Liam, and as I watch him nod and eventually agree with Cal, I remember that it's best if I rein in the flirting. Even if nobody else can recognize my odd behavior as flirting, it's not a good idea to let my thoughts go there. Not with someone from work. Not with my friend's boyfriend's brother.

Too messy.

"Maddie, take my card," Sheila says, rooting around on the counter as she walks us out. She hands me a crisp blue and white oval that reads *Classic Design, for all your corporate needs.*

"You're a graphic designer?"

She nods. "Yes, and I'm sick to death of subcontracting when my clients need writing *and* design. I want to poach you from Kellen and bring you in full time," she says, with a grin.

"I don't know what to say," I whisper, staring down at the opportunity. "I can probably help you with some copy for that slogan, though." And then I wince. *Way to flub a potential job opportunity.*

But Sheila beams. "Email me tomorrow. Please!" Yep, I need to knock off the flirting with Liam Brady.

CHAPTER FIFTEEN
LIAM

"We need to chat, bro," Cal says as we drive home. I stare out the window, trying to figure out what's happening in my head. It feels strange to be leaving without Maddie, even though I never intended to bring her along to my family dinner in the first place. "Liam? Yum?"

I realize I've been ignoring Cal. "What should we talk about?"

He rolls his eyes. "I can think of two main topics, but let's get the easy one out of the way." He turns off the stereo. "We need to stop living together."

"Yes," I answer rapidly. "I think that's clear. Yes."

"Gee, brother, try not to miss me too much," he deadpans. "I'll worry you'll slip into a depression."

"We're adults, Cal, and we...have different habits."

"I guess that's a nice way of putting it. Anyway, I saw someone was looking for a house mate in one of those cool condos in East Liberty. Right by that barbershop where they serve beer!"

I consider that Cal must have started looking into this around the same time I began ragging on him for leaving his mess everywhere. "You don't want to live alone? You can probably afford it."

He shrugs. "I like people."

"Aren't those condos right on top of each other? You could live alone there and it would still be like a college dorm experience."

Cal exits the highway toward our loft. I enjoy living in a remodeled industrial loft. The original duct work is still visible in some of the units, and I love the i-beams and rivets everywhere as memorials to the type of structures that made this city what it is today.

"I hear you saying that *you* want to live alone, Yum. I'm calling you that forever, by the way. Maddie is amazing."

I feel my stomach tighten at the thought of Cal noticing Maddie and taking a liking to her. That's unusual, too. I generally don't look twice at the women Cal goes after. Why does he have to start liking the one who currently has me out of sorts?

"You're right," I concede. "I do want to live alone. Thank you for letting me stay in the loft."

"You gonna roller skate around in there with all that extra room once I move out?" He starts laughing, and I'm glad he understands that that's ridiculous. For one thing, the wheels would damage the finish on the polished concrete floors.

He pulls into the below-ground parking garage at our building. "My new digs will have parking with better air circulation," he says, reminding me that I need to manually lock the door on his ancient SUV. He still has crank-down windows on this thing, and I'm not even sure why he bothers to lock it.

"Did you say there was a second thing you wanted to discuss?" I raise a brow at him as we both instinctively head for the stairs. Our father has always had far too much energy to be confined to an office job, and taking the stairs as often as possible was our normal. The three of us brothers maintain the habit.

Cal leaps up the stairs two at a time, barely looking over his shoulder as he says, "Yeah. We need to talk about how you want to get in Maddie's pants."

"Hey," I scold, putting a hand on his shoulder. "Don't talk about her that way."

He laughs. "So it is like that, is it?"

"Like what? Like you shouldn't be so crass about someone we work with? About a woman who is friends with your brother's girlfriend?"

"Relax, Yum. I was just seeing if I was right. I would never diss Maddie. She's cool as shit." He grabs the carabiner from his belt loop and fishes for the key to our apartment. "I like her for you."

I slide off my shoes and place them neatly on the tray inside the door and stare at Cal as he kicks off his shoes right in the doorway. "Can you not be like that."

"Like what? Like a person who sees that you're so intoxicated by her that you can't even think straight?"

I was not aware other people could see the turmoil impacting my life since she swished into Beltane. Correction. Maddie doesn't swish. She... cantilevers. *Yes,* I think. *She is like a cantilever, jutting out free-form over empty space, solid, barely held in place.*

"See?" Cal continues. "You can't even think of a comeback or a good lie to tell me to shut up."

I wave a hand at him. "It's moot anyway."

"And why is that?"

"She's going to work for Mom. And she's friends with Nicole." I don't mention that she yells at me for growling and thinks I'm a stick in the mud. Because I yell at her for getting crumbs in the car and I shush her if she's singing in elevators when we visit interview subjects for the book. Because I called her irresponsible.

"She likes you, too," Cal says, placing a hand on my shoulder. "For some reason I can't understand." He slaps my back and opens the fridge, drinking orange juice from the carton as he walks with it down the hall toward his room. "I'm going to meet with the condo people after work tomorrow," he says, and then he closes his bedroom door.

I sink into the couch to take stock of my situation. I am distracted at work. I'm making errors both tactical and logistical. This is not acceptable for an engineer. I need to either get myself under control or take a leave of absence. Imagine if I made an error in calculations working on a bridge project for the new rail clients?

I remind myself that my junior teammates are doing the actual calculating these days. Like my Uncle Kellen, I'm in more of a "check their work" position as I help steer the company toward new business strategies.

Whenever I'm working on a new project, I start with research. Tonight, I learned that Maddie is diabetic. Perhaps this situation with Maddie can be approached like my work. I walk down the hall and pull my laptop from my desk and begin reading journal articles about type one diabetes.

Lying on my bed, I start reading about glucose levels and insulin pumps. I read about clinical trials and soon, feel like I could at least hold up my end of a dinner conversation about diabetes.

This is the part where usually, solutions start coming to me. If this was a work problem, I'd have ideas about how to proceed. Rusted beams? I check out new materials or coatings. Shifted foundation beneath a building? I call up my brother, the geotechnical engineer.

Vexing woman I can't stop thinking about?

I think back to our ride to my mother's house, how Maddie's lips looked pulling the red candy into her mouth.

My traitorous mind immediately jumps to wondering how those lips would feel on my skin, whether she would taste like strawberries. I close my eyes and I can smell the faint hint of lavender that hovers around her, mixed with the salty scent of her ever-present snacks.

There's no getting around it. I want her. I no sooner think the thought, than I feel my body respond. My blood pounds, as if my heart is beating out "yes. Now. Yes. Now." The thrumming energy settles in my crotch, where I stare in wonder at an erection that threatens to burst the seams of my very favorite trousers.

I swallow and rise to lock my bedroom door, removing the pants and draping them neatly over the back of my desk chair. I slide my laptop into my desk drawer and lie back on my bed, thinking about how it would feel to run my fingers through Maddie's brown hair, to tug on her ponytail.

I wrap my fist around my throbbing dick and close my eyes, flicking my wrist as I imagine ripping off Maddie's ever-present fanny pack, shoving her against a wall, and spearing her beneath those black dresses she wears every single day.

In my fantasy, she bites my neck and then whispers against my lips, that strawberry-stained mouth begging me to make her come. I groan and almost don't make it in time to grab a tissue from my nightstand as I blast off into my fist.

After, I drift off to sleep and dream of her teasing me, calling me "Yum."

CHAPTER SIXTEEN
MADDIE

"You sure you got everything," I joke. Zack's truck bed is piled high with bags as he and Nicole prepare to leave for an overnight trip. They're going to the Stag Family Getaway along with our friend Emma, her husband, his brothers, their wives, and all their babies.

Nicole always goes to Stag family dinners and such. I've been a few times since I moved in with Nicole, and they all assure me there's space in the giant cabin they all rented. But I've got a very important golf game to attend this weekend.

Zack claps me on the shoulder. "Sure you wouldn't rather come play Sushi Go with Tim Stag than play golf with my dad?"

"Well, I haven't met your dad yet, so I feel like I don't have enough data to answer that question, Mr. Brady." I laugh as he rolls his eyes at Nicole wanting to bring all her fancy bedding along to the cabin. "Go," I tell them. "Have a great time. I promise not to throw a rave."

Nicole clasps my hands, biting her lip. "You know I don't really do the wilderness," she pouts. "Maybe I can go golfing and take really good notes and you can go be witty and drink beer and use bug spray?"

"I do love beer," I tell Nicole. She knows she can't take good enough notes to help me with my creative process. I have to see the men interact, follow up on my hunches. If I'm going to write this book about Mick Brady, I have to see him in his element, see him interacting in a way that's not rehearsed.

I wave as they drive away, and head inside to finish getting ready. Liam has texted me at least 15 times to make sure I have a Beltane polo shirt (I do) and golf spikes (I do not). I have golfed maybe once or twice before in my life and am 100% certain that aspect of the outing will be a disaster.

I wouldn't mind if Liam got up behind me to help with my form, though. But I can't linger on that fantasy. Gotta check my trusty fanny pack for the usual snacks, note taking supplies, and some added sunscreen since we'll be out in the heat for a few hours.

Liam is supposed to pick me up in a few minutes. I crawl into Nicole's closet to see if she has golf spikes, and when I don't find any, decide I'll have to confess my lack of equipment to Liam. Hopefully I can rent the shoes when I rent the clubs.

"Wait, you don't even have clubs?" Liam seems incredulous. He keeps adjusting his collar and smoothing his hands down his cargo shorts. I can't help but stare at his hairy calves. There's just something about really hair legs and chest that does tingly things to my insides. It was hard not to ogle him when we went running the other day. I had to focus really hard on my surroundings so I wouldn't stare at him.

"You didn't ask if I had clubs," I tell him. "You asked if I had shoes."

"And when you didn't answer, I assumed you had them!" Liam is breathing fast and hard. He keeps checking his fancy watch. I see him exhale long and slow. "Ok, if we hurry we can get you to the rental shop and still be on time."

He drives erratically to a golf club north of the city. He tosses his keys to the valet when we arrive and quickly rushes around, grabbing me by the hand and tugging me into the lobby of a fancy country club building. "My colleague needs to borrow some gear," he says to a young kid in the doorway.

People start bending over backwards to help me, until they realize I'm not a member. "She's a guest," Liam sputters, waving his hands around. He seems off kilter, probably because he's not in charge of today. I observe that Liam doesn't do well when he's not in control of a situation. "She's Mick Brady's guest."

"Are you Mick Brady?" It occurs to the staff that Liam is not a member of the club, either, and he rakes his fingers through his hair.

"What seems to be the trouble, son?" A tall man with graying hair and Liam's face saunters into the rental office. "I could hear you hollering from the valet stand!" He notices me and breaks into a grin.

"You must be the writer," he says, bringing my hand up to his lips to kiss my knuckles.

I pull it back before he makes contact with my hand and his eyes widen. Liam, standing behind his father, looks like he's going to faint. "Maddie Parker," I say, tilting my head. "Pleased to meet you finally. And I'm so sorry that we didn't set this up sooner, but I need to borrow some gear today for our golf round."

"Is that so?" Mick breaks into a grin. "I like this one, Liam. She's tough." He looks over at the guy who was waiting on us earlier. "Get the lady what she needs and please escort her outside. We're meeting our fourth in…" He looks at his watch, which triggers Liam to look at his watch again. "Woah. Right now, kiddo!" Mick claps his son on the back. "Stay with the lady and I'll meet you outside with Cliffy."

By the time I figure out how to roll the bag of golf clubs and waddle around in my spikes, Mick and Clifford are loading up a pair of golf carts and laughing loudly. "Maddie," Cliff yells, seeing me approach with Liam. "Great to see you again."

"And you," I smile, pumping his hand while Liam tosses our stuff into a golf cart. "Are we riding together?"

"I sure hope so," he says, and I swear I hear Liam growl until his father shouts, "No way, Cliffy. We need to catch up." Mick beckons Clifford into his golf cart and Liam puts his hands in his shorts pockets and shrugs.

"You can drive first," I tell him, "but know that I am absolutely taking a turn driving the cart."

B

FOUR HOLES in and I haven't lost a ball yet, even though Liam holds his breath each time I swing a club. Mick and Clifford spend three holes talking about old times, and I can see that they both respect each other very much. In between their barbs about each other's gray hair, I can see a warm history that goes beyond just business.

Mick knows the names of all Clifford's relatives and pets. The man is a hopeless womanizer and is in constant motion, but doesn't miss a single detail. He squints at Clifford limping a bit and asks after an old knee surgery.

Liam perks up when Mick asks Clifford about the future of the company. "You thinking of becoming a snow bird," Mick jokes, nudging his old friend with his shoulder. They both seem about the same age—mid 50s

I'd guess—but Mick is trim and fit, obviously athletic. Clifford seems built more like my dad, thick around the middle, like maybe he's spent more time worrying about the board of directors than his cholesterol.

"I'll be ready to slow down whenever you are," Clifford jokes, but Mick shakes his head.

"I've been grooming my boys to take over," Mick says. "Ask Liam here. Kellen and I are too old for those middle-of-the-night calls when a dam collapses or a gas well catches fire."

Clifford sighs. "That fire was a bad night," he says. I mentally comb through my research and recall that Clifford's company had a catastrophic fire about 25 years ago. A few men died and others were very badly burned. This wasn't even the same fire that Dave was telling me about, and the weight of Dave's observations about the importance of their work settles heavily in my bones. Liam and Kellen had told me, sadly, that a proper inspection regimen could have caught the faulty parts on the well.

Beltane and Cliff's company have been working together ever since to prevent that sort of disaster. I'm surprised by how much I'm enjoying this project. There's so much I can't include, with it being a marketing project, but I'd love to be working on a journalistic history. A wave of sadness at the loss of my job crashes over me.

I tune out the men talking about rivets and support beams. I squint off toward the flag at the hole and adjust my stance, getting ready to take my shot. When I look up, I see Liam staring at me. Not just gazing at me curiously while his father talks to a friend, but staring. Intently. I look down at myself: Beltane polo, Nicole's white tennis skirt, cute argyle socks.

I swallow as I realize Liam's gaze is definitely what I think it is: desire. Just then, it starts pouring and I hear a rumble of thunder. I brush my wet hair back from my eyes and look up in time to see a bolt of lightning sizzle through the sky.

CHAPTER SEVENTEEN
LIAM

I SHOULD CARE THAT OUR GOLF GAME ENDED SO ABRUPTLY. I SHOULD HAVE STUCK around to network with my father and Clifford in the club after we fled the thunderstorm on the fourth hole. I should have done a lot of things, but instead I stared at Maddie Parker in her soaking wet white skirt and thought about her ass.

She stood under the awning on the club porch after we sped back, shaking out her shirt, giving me a delicious glimpse of the creamy skin of her stomach as she did so. She ran her hands through her sopping wet hair and I just stood, staring, as her nipples formed stiff peaks that poked through the wet polo.

"I think I should take Maddie home," I say to my father, abruptly turning before he can respond.

"So nice to see you again," Maddie yells as I rush toward the valet and tip him $50 to hurry.

"Take care, dear," Dad shouts after us, signaling for a gin and tonic.

She starts shivering as soon as the AC starts blasting in my car. "We can open the windows instead," I stutter. "If you're cold?"

She shakes her head. "It's too humid. I'll be ok."

"But you're shivering," I say, adjusting the dials so the air conditioner is still on, but at a warmer temperature with no blowing. "Is that better?" I look over and study her arms as the goosebumps recede.

"Wow," she says, looking impressed. "It is better...and it's still not humid." She digs in her bag for the licorice. Never in my life have I seen anything as erotic as Madison Parker chewing on that god damned licorice. I try to keep my eyes on the road and not on her hard nipples in the wet shirt paired with the strawberry candy staining her lips red as she talks. "I sort of just have two settings for the AC in my car. On and off. Blasting and, well, off."

"I'd be happy to walk you through the wonders of variant fan settings," I tell her, and then snap my mouth shut, because what the hell am I doing talking about *variant fan settings.*

I watch as she unbuckles the pouch from around her hips and sighs, setting it in the console, where it drips on my interior. She really got drenched in the rain. I wish I had towels in the car or had thought to grab some for her from the club before we rushed out of there.

"So," she says after she finishes the licorice. "I think I got some really good stuff about your dad for the book. It was good that I was there today."

"Really? We were only there a little while and you didn't ask him any questions."

She laughs. "The questions are never how I find anything out," she says. "The real meat comes from just watching and listening to people in their element."

I turn to look at her, confused. "What will you write about my dad that you saw from a few holes of golf?"

She starts listing all these characteristics about my father, that he's a flirt, has a deep repository for information about the people in his life, is in excellent shape. "I don't understand things that aren't quantitative," I tell her. "I just don't see how you gleaned all that from watching him golf. He barely golfed!"

She laughs again, and I feel the force of it moving the blood cells through my veins. "Well why don't we have you stick to the bridges and towers and I'll stick to the adjectives and participles."

I park in front of Nicole's house and shut off the engine. "I'm sure I used to know what a participle is, but I have no idea."

She pats my hand, and I feel the warmth of her skin, so hot I worry it will sear the flesh from my bones. I look down, sure I'll see a burn, but it's just my own hand there, emptier now that she pulled hers back from it.

"Well thanks for the ride, Yum," she says, grinning at me. "I'm probably going to hunker down and start writing this weekend."

There is no way my lust for her is not visible by this point. Surely she can see it hovering around like a cloud. She pops out of the car and walks quickly toward the house.

The sidewalk is steaming in the heat now that the rain has stopped and the sun has resumed shining. Maddie makes her way through the shimmering ripples and punches in the entry code, disappearing into Nicole's place.

I grip the steering wheel tightly, staring after her, wondering if it's possible for me to be any harder than I am right now.

I hear something beep and, looking down, I notice she has forgotten her pouch here in my car. I remember that she said she keeps her diabetes supplies in there, and I tell myself this is an emergency. I have to chase her into the house to give it back to her. To keep her safe. So I grab it and jump out, trying to remember the code Zack told me to get into his new house.

Of course, I don't think to knock like a normal person.

I tell myself she could be in some sort of diabetic coma on the floor somewhere, and I barge in, yelling her name. "You forgot your pouch!" I shout. "Maddie! Your pouch..."

I drift off when she comes around the corner from the laundry room, eyes wide. "Liam?" She clutches a towel over her chest and I see that she's stripped out of her wet shirt and skirt.

"Christ, Maddie," I groan, unable to stand with her in front of me wearing just her bra and panties. And those are probably damp from the rain, too.

This woman, this infatuating, gorgeous woman, is wet and nearly naked, and I have no restraint left. I'm a writhing ball of need, a wild-eyed madman fueled by lust as I pounce on her.

I back her up against the wall, caging her in with my arms, the pouch dangling from one fist. "Maddie," I rasp out. She looks up at me, her brown eyes dancing back and forth as she tries to make sense of what I'm doing. I feel her breathing against my chest and I rock my hips against her, my dick so hard I'm sure she's going to wince from the pressure.

"Liam," she breathes. "You're so wild."

I shake my head, standing there, pressed against her. "I can't get you out of my head," I say. "Maddie, I...I crave you."

She smiles at that, and with that small bit of encouragement, I duck my head.

I crash my mouth against hers, not thinking, consumed by the urge to taste her. "Fuck," I groan against her lips. She tastes just as I imagined, like strawberry candy and heat. I swipe my tongue along her lips again and again. Our teeth bump together and she laughs against my mouth.

"I'll show you wild," I growl, sinking to my knees and tearing the towel away from her, biting along her chest until… "What is all this?" Kneeling on the ground in front of her, I trace my fingers around two white discs attached to her belly, and a length of tubing that leads to…something.

"That's my pancreas," she breathes, eyes shut and head back against the wall as I keep stroking her skin. "That feels so good," she says.

"What's it really," I ask, dotting kisses above and around each of the circles, careful to avoid the tube in case I hurt her.

"Don't you dare stop touching me," she yells, thrusting her hips forward. I greet her movement with an open mouthed kiss at the top of her waistband. "The circle by your left hand is my insulin pump." She groans as I grip her hips and let my thumbs caress her panties.

"And the other?" I don't look away from her beautiful face, reveling in the look of pleasure she is taking from my touch.

She exhales slowly, moaning as I slide just the tips of my fingers inside the waistband of her underwear. "It basically helps hold the pump and tubing in place," she grunts.

"Tell me what I need to know," I ask, kissing her stomach again. "To make it good for you." She doesn't answer, has a wrist against her forehead as she pants while leaning against the wall. "I mean, if you want to—"

"You need to *not* be gentle." She thrusts against my hand. "You need to know you're not going to break me."

I nod, hearing that, and yank her panties down, caressing one calf as she steps out of them. And then I shove her legs wider apart, my hands on her thighs, and I lick her. A sound emerges from her body, low and deep. Knowing I'm making her feel this good drives me even closer to the edge of madness.

This isn't something I do typically, kneel on the floor at a woman's feet and lick her. But I can't imagine stopping. This is, actually, counter to all of the plans I have in place right now. I pull back a bit, studying the architecture of her body. I trace her folds with a finger tip and, finding her clit, I give it a little pinch.

"Jesus, Liam, where the fuck is this coming from?" She bangs her head off the wall a few times and, encouraged, I let go of conscious thought. Driven by want and by need, I lap at her like she's made of candy. I slide a finger inside her as I nip at her clit with my teeth, vaguely aware that Maddie is moaning my name.

Soon, I feel her contracting around me. Her thighs slam together and her body convulses. "Liam, I'm coming. Oh god, yes. Holy shit, yes." She's breathing heavily and starts to sink down, literally weak in the knees from my work between her legs.

I look up, drawing my wrist across my mouth, feeling her arousal all over my face. "I'm just getting started," I tell her.

Eyes wide, she nods. I stoop to gather up her pouch and, careful of her tubing, I haul her over my shoulder and march toward the sunroom. I move to drop her on the couch, and she wriggles, moving that amazing ass over my shoulder.

I look out the back door at the pool my brother built in the yard. It has deep sides and a shade tent hung over top. Putting one hand on Maddie's legs, pinning her to my body, I slide the door open and drop her into the pool.

CHAPTER EIGHTEEN
MADDIE

I groan, squeezing Liam's ass cheeks as he stalks through the house carrying me like I weigh nothing at all. I have never had someone go down on me like that, like I was a fucking buffet and he was starving.

My crotch is still pulsating.

It's pretty hot that he's frazzled like this. The last few guys I slept with mostly lay still, like they were too afraid of hurting me to get freaky. Liam Brady yanks open the patio door and carries me, naked, out into the back yard. I yelp as he drops me in Nicole's pool.

I look up from the galvanized tub to see him stripping, peeling off his damp clothes while keeping his eyes locked on mine. This is going to be rough and frantic and terrific. I sigh.

I want to see him unravel. I want to fray his edges and see what happens when Liam Brady finally lets go.

"I need you in here with me," I bark at him, peeling off my wet bra and staring at his chest. I toss my bra out of the water and fumble to disconnect my pump. Scrambling in his pockets, Liam finds a condom in his wallet and sets it on the top step leading up to the pool. I watch as he sets my fanny pack next to it.

When I stretch my arm out of the pool to put down my pump, he caresses my hand as he takes it from me, nestling it safely on top of my pack. "Do I need to worry about your tube at all?"

He climbs into the water and slides over me, his weight magnificent.

The pool is a long oblong. There might be room for us to sit beside each other, but it's better this way. With him stretched out above me. Our skin collides like two rivers of hot lava and I love every inch of his hairy, firm skin spread over mine. I chew on his bottom lip as he reaches for my breast, and I yelp when he pinches a nipple.

"Maddie," he says, splaying a hand across my stomach, just resting it on the white discs.

I shake my head. "I clamped off the tube." He pinches my other nipple and I gasp, feeling the hot length of his cock against my thigh while he does. "I need my pack, though," I gasp. "I need to pound some skittles so my blood sugar doesn't crash while we do this."

He looks concerned, and I grip his cheeks with my hands. "I swear, it's going to be fine," I tell him. "Just feed me skittles and make me come, Yum."

"Greedy," he teases, and I feel his erection twitch against my stomach through the water.

He leans over me to reach for my pack and comes back up with the fun-size pouch of candy. "One at a time?" He asks, a mischievous grin on his face. I shake my head and he strokes my bottom lip with his thumb. I stick out my tongue and lick his digit as he uses his teeth to rip open the package.

"You want these?" I laugh long and deep before he tips the candy into my mouth. I chew and moan, both because it tastes good and because he has started licking each of my nipples while he watches me binge on sugar.

Soon, both my breasts are glistening as they bob above the surface of the water in the sunlight as Liam alternates working on each side, sucking and lapping at my body like I'm the candy and he's the diabetic. "Ready to continue, madam?" His low voice rumbles as his chin rests on my sternum. When I nod, he pins my arms over my head and nibbles his way back up to my ear.

"I've dreamed about you like this," he says, his voice ragged as he uses his remaining hand to slide along his erection.

I glance down, at the hot, hard shaft sticking out from a nest of black hair. I long to touch it, and I wriggle against the gentle pressure of his hand holding my arms out of reach. He clutches himself, rubbing his tip along the apex of my thighs. It's so fucking hot I almost come just from the sight of it.

The fact that we're outside, submerged in the cool water, makes it that much more exciting.

"I've wanted you this way," he says, "spread open for me. Moaning my name." His eyes flash when he looks up at me and I feel my heart race. "Open, Maddie." Not sure what he means, I drop my jaw and let my knees float apart, hoping he will invade both my mouth and my center.

I feel his tongue exploring my mouth at the same time his long fingers slide against my aching core. "Liam," I gasp, lifting my hips so his hand slips deeper inside me. "Yes, please," I beg, thrusting up against him.

"Fuck, Maddie." When he looks at me, there is something primal in his expression. "Do you want my cock? Do you want me to fuck you?"

"Yes. Now. Please," I beg, and he lets go of my wrists while he rips open the condom. I slide lower in the water, closer to lying down, but the change in elevation makes me feel a bit light headed. Shit.

I rest my head back on the wall of the pool, closing my eyes. "Are you ready for this, beautiful?"

I've never heard Liam Brady speak this way, using adjectives. I love it. I want it. "Yes," I beg him again. "Fuck me, Yum."

He climbs back between my legs and I wrap them around his waist. He slowly eases inside me and I let out a long, low moan as he fills me, the lubrication on the condom easing his entrance in the water. "Yeah," I say. "That's perfect."

He starts to move, slowly at first, and then I let my heels sink into his ass and he picks up the pace. "Jesus, you feel good," he says. "I want you so much."

"I..." and then I forget what I was going to say. He feels good. This feels good. I know the words to say that, but I just can't seem to think of them right now. I lie still, trying to remember what I was going to say, but I just... can't.

"Maddie?" He looks at me, concern etched across his face. He stops moving and slides out.

"No," I say, shaking my head. "Come back inside." But he doesn't. He frowns, and I hear a beep. "Oh," I say, closing my eyes. "That makes sense. There goes that."

ℬ

MY GLUCOSE METER keeps beeping until I reach around for the snacks I can't seem to find. My fingers shake as I locate the fanny pack and try to get to my backup candy. I yelp when Liam scoops me out of the water. Both of us are dripping as he sets me on the couch in the sun room and runs back outside for my pack and my pump.

"Tell me what to do," he says. "How can I help?"

"I need apple juice," I say. "Frigernator. Friggy. Shit."

Liam jogs into the kitchen and I hear the fridge open. When he comes back, he's got packets of snacks from the pantry, including the fish crackers I love and he hates. I watch as he fiddles with the plastic wrapper on the straw and punches it through the foil disc at the top of the juice box. He meets my eye as he slides the straw between my lips.

I drink for awhile and then swallow, closing my eyes before looking up at him. I feel better already. "Did I fuck up our fuck?"

His eyes go wide. "What? No way. I mean, if you're still up for it..." Liam frowns and stares at me as I sip the juice. I drop one hand to his chest and he watches as I run my fingers through his curly dark hairs. He swallows. "I always want to do that with you, Maddie. Fuck you, I mean."

I sip more of the juice and his gaze softens. "Always, Maddie."

CHAPTER NINETEEN
LIAM

HE JUST SCARED THE LIFE OUT OF ME, AND YET I'M SOMEHOW STILL HORNY AND wild for her. I have no idea what the best next move is, though, but I suspect I should go find us some towels. I hand her the baggy of fish crackers and kiss her knuckles. She smiles.

"I'm going to grab us something to dry off a bit," I tell her. "Don't move."

She laughs. "Yeah, not likely." I take off at a fast walk toward the laundry room, worried that I'll slip and fall if I run. She yells after me. "Please don't put clothes on, Yum."

There's a load of clean towels in a basket on the counter, and I grab the whole thing. I notice the condom, feeling sticky and weird, so I pull that off and toss it in the trash before hurrying back to the couch. "You like the look of all this fur," I joke, rubbing her dry and trying to lift her a bit to absorb some of the water we got on the couch.

"Mmm," she moans, tracing a hand down my chest as she sips from the damn juice box. "I love it." I never want to shave a single hair from my face ever again if it means she will make that sound when she sees it. I settle next to her on the couch, loving how her skin feels against mine, and try to feed her the fish while she looks at me like I've lost my mind. "You hate when I eat these," she says, one brow arched while she chews.

I shake my head. "I hate that I don't know what to do about how much I love that you eat these," I correct her.

I'm about to tell her she fascinates me, when I remember how she preferred when I switch those observations so they're about my thoughts and my actions. "I am overwhelmed by you. In a good way," I add, quickly. Though I'm not entirely sure good is the right word.

I've been totally off kilter since the second I saw her in the kitchen at work, and I suspect that this is the only way to get myself back on track. To give in to my desire for her.

"I usually feel better in about 15 minutes when this happens," she says. "I'm sorry if the beep hurt your ears."

"I barely noticed," I lie, wondering if I'll ever forget how frightened I felt when the thing on her arm started blaring out warning sounds. My dick is deflated for now, despite her hands on my chest. I lie back so Maddie will keep touching me. I make a mental note to grab the other packet from my wallet before we resume activities later, and try to breathe through my eager anticipation for her to feel better enough to keep going.

Maddie offers me a cracker and I open my mouth, capturing her finger when she feeds it to me, wanting to signal to her that I'm very much still here for this if it's safe.

Her pupils dilate and her breathing picks up, so I'm feeling pretty confident she's still into it. "Can we just talk for a little until I'm ready?"

"Of course," I say, tracing my hand along her arm. "I can tell you all about structures and towers and math."

She laughs and asks me about my favorite engineering projects. I roll onto my back to think about it. "Not my favorite that I did," I say, "but I love the Howe Truss bridge along the creek in McConnells Mill state park."

"The bridge there is named Howard?"

I shake my head. "Howe Truss. It's not the name of the bridge, but the type of bridge design. Do you really want to know this?" I look at her, munching crackers and sipping juice, eyes bright and focused on me in the sunlight pouring into the room. She nods. "William Howe was the first to blend iron and wood in his bridge design," I tell her. I trace a finger down her hip. "It's a beautiful, load-bearing system not unlike the bones and tendons of your feet." I rub my hand down her smooth calf, along her ankle and the arch of her foot. "There are vertical and diagonal supports, using tension and compression to hold up the bridge."

She sighs as I stroke her instep. "Will you show me the bridge?"

"Hell yes," I say. "Are you kidding? A hike and a lecture about suspension mechanics? Dream date."

Maddie squints at me and squeezes the juice box, tossing the empty baggie and drink carton on the table before climbing on top of my lap. "I thought this was your dream date?"

My eyes go wide as I take in the sight of her breasts dangling above my chest, her hips rounded as her legs spread to accommodate the width of my hips. "Fuck, Maddie. Look at you."

"Yes, do that, Yum," she says, adjusting the tube for her pump so it's out of the way. "I'm going to leave this plugged in." I nod. "And I'm going to be on top." She presses her hands against the arm of the couch and leans over to kiss me. I wouldn't dream of denying her.

But I do gather her hair in one hand and tug on the tail, arching her head back and exposing her throat. And then I bite her where her neck meets her shoulder.

She rocks her hips, her wet heat so inviting and so fucking perfect as I thrust up inside her, sinking into her while we both groan in pleasure.

Her hands slide down until they're on my shoulders and she grinds against me, meeting me thrust for thrust, seeking out the friction that she needs. I'm desperate to see her come again, face to face this time, to know what she looks like when she's experiencing that level of pleasure.

I slide my hand from her hair and reach between her legs, pressing the flat of my finger against her until I find her clit. "What do you like," I ask, rubbing slowly until she grabs my wrist and, together, we get her there. She wants fast, tight circles, and I watch her face as she unravels, her head dropping back while I continue to pound up into her.

"Liam, yes, just like that," she yells, and she moves her hand up to her breast, her palm against her nipple while I buck up into her, rubbing faster and harder with my hand, loving the sound of my name on her lips.

She stiffens and crows, before collapsing against my chest, "Fuck, yes, Yum, that was amazing." And then she redoubles her own effort, meeting my eye as our bodies slap together. I glance down at the place where we connect, watching myself slide in and out of her and I feel the tingle in my spine, the tightness in my balls.

"I'm close," I pant.

"Yes, Liam," she says. "Come for me. Come inside me. Do it. Right now." And, not able to deny her, I do.

I groan her name and spurt inside her, blasting so hard I'm sure it must be hurting her. But she squeezes her eyes shut and I feel her fluttering against me, pulsing around my cock as she comes a third time, shuddering, collapsing, laughing. "Excellent work, sir," she says. "Whew."

I am wrecked. Destroyed. There isn't anything in the world that could keep me awake for one second longer, and I fall asleep almost immediately.

A few hours later, I wake up to Maddie tugging on my hand, pulling me up the stairs and into her room, where we fall into her bed for another round. Her night stand is filled with condoms, candy and peanut butter packets and we feast on her emergency stash in between, during, and after furious sessions of the wildest sex I've ever had.

Eventually, she yells at me for breaking her vagina, and she smiles and falls asleep. I curl an arm around her and stare at her, more relaxed than I can remember feeling in years.

I don't worry about my brother moving out or the expanded responsibilities at work or slipping away into chaos. I just drift off into the most contented sleep with an intriguing woman wrapped around me, tasting like fruit juice and candy.

CHAPTER TWENTY
LIAM

I HEAR SOMEONE RUSTLING AROUND THE ROOM AS I CRACK MY EYES OPEN IN THE morning. I inhale and remember where I am: in Maddie's bed. Naked. I smile and just sink into her pillows that smell like her hair.

Except she's really rustling around, so I sit up to see what's going on. I zero in on the mess in the room. She has clothes everywhere, piled on the floor and the dresser. I know she's just staying here temporarily, but it looks like her closet ejected its contents.

My own clothes are on the floor downstairs, too, so I try to slow my anxiety about the mess. Maybe she was having trouble figuring out what to wear yesterday and was short on time. And then I interrupted her in the evening...

My dick twitches against my leg, remembering last night. I'm not usually as adventurous. I always make sure my partner has a good time, but I'm not typically pinning arms above heads and biting. I don't know what came over me, but I liked it. It seemed like Maddie did, too.

"Hey," I mutter, seeing her head pop up from where she's crouched on the floor by a pile of medical stuff. "What are you doing?"

"Oh, hey, Yum," she says around a package that she holds in her teeth. "I have to change my set."

I frown. "Is this because of the beeping last night? Are you ok?"

Shaking her head, she says, "I'm totally fine. Today's just my day to change my stuff." She pulls the monitor from the back of her arm in a brisk motion. It seems like it should sting, but she barely reacts, and I'm hit with the scent of an alcohol pad as she cleans the area.

"How often do you have to do all that?" I climb down from the bed and sit beside her on the rug. Both of us are naked, and I kind of love that, just sitting with her this way. I feel like a hairy beast compared to the white expanse of her smooth skin.

I let my hand drop to her leg while she sets up what looks like a stapler and— "Holy shit!" My jaw drops when I realize that she just inserted a needle into the skin on her side, like it was nothing. She looks over at me while she inserts an electronic device into the plastic pouch she just stuck into her body. "Doesn't that hurt?"

She looks at me like I'm the one who is nuts. "I guess, but I have to do it. This is life with the beetus, Yum."

I'm a little taken aback by the reality of what she does to keep herself healthy. No wonder she's able to observe people and parse out the most important bits of information. She spends her entire life observing her body's signals, figuring out what matters.

I feel a little sick to my stomach when she pulls a needle thing out of her stomach, the place I had caressed last night. She cleans residue from the area where the circles were and then lays out a syringe and an array of supplies.

"This is so much," I say softly.

She shrugs again. "If you're not ready for my prickly parts, you don't get to put your prick in my parts." She laughs. I bite my lower lip.

"I'm ready," I say. But maybe it's not true. This whole process feels intense and unfamiliar. I don't do well with change. "I just never saw anything like this before."

She tells me she's filling her insulin cartridge and I watch as she draws liquid from a tiny glass vial. It occurs to me that she's got thousands of dollars of equipment spread out on the floor around her. I watch the news. I know people sometimes fly to other countries to stock up on insulin because it's so expensive here. "How are you buying all that if you lost your job?"

She sighs and lowers her arms. "That's the kicker, isn't it. Nicole helped me map it all out. I was able to get COBRA insurance, but you can imagine I'm pretty eager to hear back from your mom about a full-time job." Flashing me a grin she picks up her supplies again. "Sheila seems pretty great and I looked up her company. She does interesting work. If she has good insurance, I'll be pretty happy there."

I forgot that Maddie was trying to continue working with my family. This whole situation is messy. The room is messy. I'm sticky and messy from sex. She's dropping plastic wrappers on the floor as she works, and I'm sure she's going to clean it all up when she's done, but thinking about it all at once with the reminder that she depends on a job to buy the supplies that keep her alive…I'm starting to feel a bit panicky.

Maddie lines her stapler thing up on her thigh and tells me she's about to inject her set into her leg. I hear a click sound and as I lean in to look, blood spatters my face and chest.

"Aw, hell, I got a capillary," she says, mopping at her skin and carrying on as if she didn't just spray me and the room with human blood.

"Are you a freak?" The words just fall from my mouth before I can think, as I try to wipe the blood from my skin. I stiffen, realizing what I said and when I look at her, Maddie's face is crumpled in hurt.

"I'd like you to leave," she says, fiddling with the tubing until her equipment is in place, and then gathering up the mess. I don't move. She drops an armful into the small trash can and ties the bag shut, then pulls out a red sharps container for the needle I hadn't realized she pulled out of her leg.

"I said get out," she says, standing with her hands on her hips, still nude, still beautiful. But hurt.

"Maddie, I'm sorry," I say, reaching for her hands. "I'm so sorry. You surprised me and I wasn't thinking and I apologize."

She shakes her head. "Out," she says, pointing at the door. She looks like she's about to cry, and it's my fault. I feel like the biggest asshole to ever roam the earth. I hurry down the stairs and see we have trashed Nicole's first floor. I stoop to gather my things, hopping into my damp boxers and cargo shorts.

I don't even pause to make sure I got it all. I can call Zack later to round up the rest. I head out the front door and, seated inside my car, I punch the steering column in frustration, knowing I fucked up. I have no clue how to fix this, or even if I can.

CHAPTER TWENTY-ONE
MADDIE

"I want to stab Liam Brady in his rude kidneys," I say, cramming my laundry in Nicole's washer. She and Zack came back from their glamping adventure to find me stomping through the house, snorting and cleaning.

"You're going to have to tell me the whole story so I can decide if I should talk you down or sharpen the knife for you." Nicole hands me the detergent and I slam the door shut.

"He doesn't deserve a sharp knife. A dull butter knife, right to the spleen." I grab a broom and take off down the hall, sweeping her pristine floors, trying to forget how Liam and I messed them up the other day.

"I thought we were slicing open his kidneys?" Nicole grabs the broom from me and takes me by the hand to her sun room, where she hands me a bag of cheesy popcorn and pushes me down into one of the cushy chairs. I scrubbed the cushions from the couch earlier, but am thankful she doesn't sit there.

She grabs her own bag of popcorn, crosses her legs, and shoos Zack away when he walks into the room and tries to sit next to her. "Go unpack," she tells him. "We're talking about your shitty brother."

"Should I call him?" Zack leans against the door frame looking concerned.

"No!" Nicole and I both shout at once. I glare at her. "You don't need to get involved."

When he raises his brows and walks away, Nicole gestures for me to spill. So I tell her, "We banged."

"Ha! Ok, was it inflexible missionary pistoning with no big finish?" She taps her fingers on the arm of her chair while I shake my head.

"No, the sex was amazing. He's...surprising? Like, all straight edges and sharp corners in real life and growling and biting in bed." I bring my hand to my shoulder, where the skin still smarts from his teeth when he was hammering into me last night. "I liked that part. Also I had a low during, and he was great about it."

"A low? Like when you beep? And forget words?" Nicole and Emma have sat on the floor with me a lot over the years, shoving bread into my mouth and distracting me until I leveled out.

"Yes, with the beeps. But he fed me apple juice and stuff. He fed me candy in bed!" I don't mention that by bed, I mean her pool. I tossed in the chlorine float this morning. No need to tell her *everything*.

"Why are we stabbing him again?" Nicole is sitting forward now, on the edge of her seat at the mention of candy.

"Because this morning he called me a freak." Even saying it out loud hurts all over again. The word I hate the most. The very thing I've feared will always keep me from a loving relationship. Freak. I tell Nicole how I was changing my set and he sat next to me, seemingly interested. "But not like in a stare-at-a-car-crash way, like he really cared about what I was doing."

She nods. "So he was sort of sweet in a weird Liam way and then...he called you names?"

I sigh. "Well I spattered him with some blood," I tell her, staring into my lap. "You know how sometimes I snag a capillary..."

"Oh, honey," she says and climbs into the chair with me, pulling me into her arms. "And he spazzed, because gross and also mess...and then used your trigger word." I nod against her shoulder. "You're not a freak," she soothes. "You know that. You're a steadfast, observant, kind person who always puts the right information together."

"And I'm totally reliant on technology to be alive, and I have freak wires and tubes and I spurt blood on people like a freak."

"I mean, a geek, maybe," she says. I look at her blankly. "You know, those circus people who bite heads off chickens...never mind. He shouldn't call you that, no matter what."

I sit with her awhile longer and tell her I need to go for a hike to clear my head. There's no way I can work on my draft this weekend and maybe not even tomorrow. I can't write objectively when I'm stuck on what happened with Liam.

I walk through the neighborhood, reliving all the hospital stays from elementary school and subsequent tutors to catch up on school work. I always felt very much like a freak having to pass on birthday party cupcakes and punch. My parents used to send sugar free candy to keep in my desk, as if that would help me feel less different somehow. I've always been a freak. I just thought Liam realized that, and wanted me anyway.

Later in the afternoon, I email Sheila the writing samples she asked for and avert my eyes as I wander over to the fridge. Nicole and Zack are cuddled on the couch, talking. I see him looking angry, and I see someone has piled up the rest of Liam's clothes on the hall table, so beeline for my room in case Liam comes over to pick them up. I don't want to see him.

I should have shooed him away when he burst into the house with my fanny pack. I knew it was a bad idea to give in to my attraction to him. But he was so sexy, standing there with my gear, staring at me like I was beautiful.

"Well," I mutter. "I got my rocks off. Time to move on."

By morning, my anger has faded to a dull ache.

I MESSAGE Kellen that I prefer to write from home so I can really stretch my creative muscles to get him the first two chapters I promised. I set to work crafting a story about an innovative pair of brothers ahead of their time, whose greatest gift was their ability to partner with the right people for the right job. Together, Mick and Kellen are an unbeatable force. Ingenuity and a remarkable gift for understanding future trends paired with an innate understanding of engineering principles.

They chose a sunburst for their business crest, I write, *not only because the symbol is the Brady coat of arms, but because Beltane is a Celtic festival that cele-brates a turning point. It represents a blurring of the lines between the human and supernatural world, much like the Brady brothers' gift for understanding what their clients will need in the future.*

By mid-week, I'm deep in the writing vortex and have totally suppressed my anger at Liam. I drive into Beltane to meet with Kellen and go over what I've written so far. Still, I'm shaken to see Liam seated in Kellen's office when I walk in for my appointment. I frown.

"I didn't realize you'd be here," I say. Kellen tilts his head, considering.

"Is there an issue? Liam has been consulting for the entire project so far."

I shake my head and inhale. "Nope, just surprised is all. Let's get started."

I don't look at Liam, except to glare at him once, daring him to offer negative feedback on the writing.

"Um," he stutters. "This is really beyond what I had imagined. Truly."

I frown, but Kellen nods enthusiastically. "Yes, Ms. Parker. This is stunning work. My only note is to adjust the date here on page four."

I feel a strange mix of emotions as I sit through the most enthusiastic review of my writing career. My editor from the Post was never what you'd call appreciative. It was a good day if he didn't use profanity in his assessment. Remembering that just makes me sad about losing my job all over again. What I wouldn't give to have Phil yelling at me right now instead of Liam Brady awkwardly telling me my work is fantastic. *Fantastic for a freak,* I think.

At the end of the Kellen/Liam lovefest, I nod, and back out of the room, heading straight for the parking lot without looking back.

CHAPTER TWENTY-TWO
LIAM

It's been a week since I said the worst thing in the world, and my life is falling apart. My brother has moved out and the apartment is spotless. Dad hung out with Clayton and teed him up excitedly for our meeting about an inspection program for the company electric towers. You'd think this would all signal an improvement, that I'd in fact say I'm at the top of my game.

But I'm not sleeping. I stopped shaving. I know I need to apologize to Maddie for what I said, but every time I come near her, she puts up angry walls so thick I can practically see them. The longer I don't apologize properly, the worse things become when I see her at work.

I haven't even been running with my brothers, and I begged off dinner with my mother this week, setting off a string of daily phone calls about my well-being.

I just don't know how I got here—first, so infatuated with a woman that it impacted my ability to concentrate, and then so rude to her that I made her cry.

I lie on the floor in the living room in the space where the couch once was, the giant overstuffed piece of furniture the first thing my brother hauled out of here when he moved to the trendy condo.

I'm lying there still when both brothers and Orla break in to the apartment and stand above me glowering. She nudges me with her toe. "Dad says you're acting weird," Orla says. "Come running with us."

I look at my watch. It's nearly noon. "Don't you all usually go at eight on a Sunday?"

"We were helping Cal build his new bed," Zack says, crouching behind me and lifting me under the shoulders. "Orla, get his feet."

Before I can protest properly, they carry me into my bedroom and are halfway through undressing me while Orla grabs my running stuff from my top drawer. "Ok, knock it off," I say, squirming away and turning my back while I toss on my mesh shorts.

It's plenty hot today, so I opt for no shirt and Orla rolls her eyes. "What?"

"People are going to think they're seeing Sasquatch," she says.

I spray on some sunblock, smearing it around. "I've literally never heard that joke before, Orla. Thanks."

We walk outside and cross Smallman Street over to the river path. "Let's head east," Zack says, and takes off. We all catch up to his pace and run in silence for a few blocks. Eventually, Zack says, "Based on what Nicole says, you slept with Maddie and then said something super rude and haven't spoken to her since."

"Dude, I knew you were into her," Cal says, shoving my shoulder and causing me to stumble a bit.

"Did you hear the part where he was rude?" Orla's ponytail swishes judgmentally as she keeps pace with us. Orla is about six inches shorter than us, so her stride is much shorter. Yet she is never even out of breath when we're running a string of eight-minute miles.

"Not just typical rigid grouch stuff, either," Zach says. "He called her a freak."

Cal stops in his tracks and we all halt on the path. "You said the word freak? To a woman you'd just been inside?"

The waves of shame wash over me again and I don't bother to explain to them that she had just splattered me with blood, because that's not the point. "Yes, ok, it was terrible and I need help to fix it."

"You need a gesture," Orla says, and she looks both ways and then darts up the access trail that leads from the street to the path. We all follow, confused, as she makes her way up to the strip of shops along Penn Avenue.

She pauses at a red light and turns to face me. "What's she into?"

I shrug as Cal says, "Snacks."

Zack nods. "She always has snacks. For her blood pressure."

"It's her blood sugar, Zack," I interject. And then I sigh.

"Snacks," Orla says, tapping her chin. She veers toward the fancy candy shop and we follow.

Outside, I remember that I'm not wearing a shirt and I frown at my shoes. Cal rolls his eyes and peels his shirt off, handing me the sweaty thing. "You should go. You have to at least pick out your own apology gesture," he says.

"Since when do you know about apologies?"

He shrugs and shakes the shirt at me. I put it on while he leans against the wall outside.

Orla and Zack head for a display of dark chocolate, talking about how women, statistically, prefer this sort of treat.

But I'm struck by a display of different French candies. I pick up a jar of Old Fashioned Lavender Candy from some village whose name I can't pronounce. The shopkeeper approaches me with a smile and asks, "Are you buying for someone in particular?"

I clear my throat. "Yes. And she's mad at me." My brother and cousin turn over to look and crowd around us as the shopkeeper explains that these leaf-shaped hard candies are very special.

"They're made an old fashioned way," she says. "Nothing artificial. Does she have a sweet tooth?"

"Yes," I say immediately as everyone else nods. "And she loves lavender."

Zack tilts his head. "She does? How do you know?"

Orla smacks him. "Because he's into her, you dip. Liam, you should get these. The jar is pretty." I fish my wallet out from my shorts pocket and apologize for the credit card being sweaty.

"Should I give them to her at work," I ask Orla as we start running back toward my place.

She shakes her head. "No," she says. "She doesn't want to think about upsetting personal things at work. She wants to write and she needs to concentrate."

That's a good point. I hate writing reports. It takes me ages to write an email to someone. I can write up the inspection easily. That's just objective, factual. Is the structure sound? If not, why? It's all the rest of it I struggle with.

"I think Zack should deliver the candy with a note that says you'll call her later," Orla says. "That way she'll have time to emotionally prepare and decide if she wants to take your call."

"What if she doesn't want to?" I worry this is all becoming more complicated than I previously thought.

Orla shrugs. "One step at a time. What are you going to write on the note?" We take the stairs back up to my apartment and Orla rummages around the junk drawer until she finds a nice piece of plain card stock.

These made me think of you, I write. *They're unique and...* "How do I say delicate without saying something is fragile? She doesn't want to be perceived as fragile..."

Orla nods. "I get that. She probably deals with a lot of assumptions from her diabetes."

"Oh yeah, she's always talking about that," Zack says. "People are always worried she's going to faint."

I frown at the card some more. *They're unique and spectacular. I owe you an apology. I hope you'll accept a call from me later. —Liam*

I consider writing Yum, but I feel like I probably haven't earned that pet name back from her yet. I slide the package to Zack, already wondering how long I need to wait before I should call her.

CHAPTER TWENTY-THREE
MADDIE

I DECIDE I'M NOT READY TO HEAR FROM LIAM YET. I DO TEXT HIM TO THANK HIM FOR the candy, though, but I don't eat it. I stare at it next to my bed for a few days instead.

Lavender candy. It looks amazing. I'm surprised he could tell that I love lavender. I mean, I use that scent in my shampoo and deodorant, but I don't really use cosmetics or wear perfume. He must have really been leaning in to notice my smell. I think back to my banter with Nicole, about how engineers don't notice things about women, and I grin.

When I do eventually taste the candy, I almost cry, it tastes so good. I let a piece melt on my tongue while I write the third chapter in the corporate history. I'm over halfway done with the book—Kellen had asked for five chapters to cover each of the major phases of the company's development.

I've been deep in the vortex, as Emma and I call it when we're writing and not communicating with the outside world. After a few meetings with Kellen, I retreated to my writing cave and I barely leave my room, listening to my taped interviews again and again, making sure I have every detail, every sensory observation in place to really make the story sing. It's been two weeks since I slept with Liam, two weeks since he called me the name that represents my greatest fear in life.

I think I needed to get these chapters down on paper, to remind myself that I'm an important member of society. I have a skill, and I'm needed by this company, regardless of whether all my organs work properly. I give the chapters a final read, and decide they're all ready to show the client...aka Liam and his uncle.

Unfortunately, I have to do a field interview with Liam to write the final chapter of the book. Kellen says Liam's going to be taking over his role in the business, going to oversee the engineering projects that will carry Beltane forward for the next few decades.

I've been stalling on the conclusion to the book, choosing instead to sit down with Zack and Ray to hear about how they're bringing machine learning and artificial intelligence into their engineering designs and inspection services. I've been trying to come up with a way I can casually write Liam out of his own family business story, and I realize it's time to face the music.

I email Em, the Beltane admin, to get on Liam's calendar for the next day, and I feel a bit like a coward for not at least emailing him directly. I'm sure he feels truly sorry for what he said, but that doesn't mean I don't feel a hurricane of shame and sadness around what happened. I was totally vulnerable with him, and he fed me juice and candy when my body crapped out during sex. But a little blood in the eye was a deal breaker for him?

In the morning, I wake up so nervous, I throw up my breakfast.

Throwing up is not great for a diabetic. It really messes with my insulin and the timing of my eating, so by the time Nicole finds me pacing the kitchen floor, pumping my arms and trying to kick-start my metabolism, I'm sort of a mess.

"Girl, WHAT is wrong?" Nicole makes a circle with her index finger, indicating that my entire person is just as much a wreck as I suspected. When she pulls me in for a hug, I wince. My body feels really sensitive to the touch and I worry I'm going to yak again.

Everything tingles. I can feel each hair in my scalp.

I reach into my fanny pack for one of the Liam candies, since it's the one thing that sounds appealing to me.

"Did you just wince when I hugged you?" Nicole stands with her hands on her hips, frowning. I nod and shrug. I moan as I eat the candy. "God, this tastes so good." I can smell them so strongly. I lean against the sink just sucking on one, moaning.

Nicole stares, and I see her tapping her fingers, counting something. "Did you get your period this week? We're usually synced up. It's period week."

I stare at her. I did not get my period. "I've been in the writing cave," I say.

She frowns. "I'm calling Emma," she says. "You're acting like she did when she was pregnant with Wesley."

At the word 'pregnant,' I freeze. I don't recall Emma barfing or having sensitive skin when she was pregnant. I remember her passing the hell out and having a seizure, wrestling with the decision of whether to move forward with a high-risk pregnancy as a person with epilepsy.

I stand there, a statue, while Nicole pulls Emma up on video chat, like Emma's going to be able to somehow tell anything by looking at me. "How is your sense of smell," she asks, squinting. I shrug. "Do your nipples feel like there's razor blades in your shirt?"

"Fuck," I say, realizing this description perfectly mirrors my experience.

"Stay here," Nicole says, handing me the phone with Emma's tiny face on the screen. "I'm going to run to the drug store and get a test."

"I hope you're literally going to run," Emma says. She looks to me. "Listen, if you are preggo, I'm going to give you the name of my MFM doc. That's maternal-fetal-medicine. They're the people who see the high risk jobs like us."

I just stare at her. I try to remember the sequence of events from the night with Liam a few weeks ago. There was definitely a condom. I remember how he stroked himself before putting it on, how hot that was. But then there was the low episode, and the water and the dripping in the house. "He must have taken it off," I mumble, and Emma stops talking.

"What was that, sweetie?"

I shake my head. "Nothing. What were you saying? What do I do? Should I call my endo?"

Emma and her neurologist are on a first-name basis. They send each other holiday cards. I'm the same way with my endocrinologist. She invited me to her daughter's graduation party a few months ago. I got her to get me special permission to pick up my insulin supplies in bulk before I switched to the COBRA insurance, so I could stock up on everything while I still had coverage.

Nicole bursts back through the front door holding a pregnancy test box like a damn Olympic torch. "Did you seriously run down Butler Street waving that around?"

She shrugs. "Worst case, the neighbors think it's for me and Zack, right?" She looks down at the phone, where Emma is still staring at us while bouncing a child on her hip. "Hey, Ems. You coming in the bathroom with us?"

"Obviously," she says. Nicole marches me into the powder room, which isn't really meant for more than one human to fit comfortably but I make do, sucking on another lavender candy as I line up the stick Nicole hands over. "Most people don't eat in the bathroom," Emma says.

Nicole nods while I pee. "We'll forgive you this time, sweetie." In a haze, I put the plastic cap back on the stick.

"It's probably too early to tell," I say, swallowing a lump in my throat.

"It's almost nine," Nicole says, exasperated.

"I think she means too early in her cycle," Emma says. We have her propped up on the edge of the sink so we can all stare at the test together. "I think I see something," she says, squinting.

"I can't look," I say, burying my face in my hands.

"Oh," Emma and Nicole both say as I feel my stomach churn. I open my eyes and look at the crisp plus sign. "We're going to have a pep talk," Emma shouts. "If I can grow babies with my glitchy brain, you can do it with your jacked up pancreas."

A baby. I stay seated on the toilet, holding the test until the smell of the bathroom makes me sick again.

Nicole hangs up with Emma and backs out of the room, letting me barf in peace. When I stumble out of the tiny room, she hugs me, but not too hard because it still hurts my nips. She offers to sit with me, go with me to a doctor, do whatever I need, but I shoo her off. "Go to work," I tell her. "I need to have a conversation with Liam."

Nicole drops a kiss on my forehead and takes off. Zack is long gone, driving out to a job site early this morning. I don't even take a minute to freak out, because I know once I start panicking I'll be stuck that way for awhile and I don't have enough goldfish crackers for that.

I get dressed and drive into Beltane, marching right past my cubicle and into Liam's office, where he sits behind his tidy desk with its tidy stacks of papers and well-organized bins of tools. Everything in his life is neat and orderly, except for his body hair, and me. The freak who distracts him.

"Hey," I say when he looks up.

"Maddie, I'm so glad you're here. I—"

I hold a hand up and cut him off. "I'm pregnant," I say, cutting right to the chase. No reason to prolong this. I sink into the chair and pop another lavender candy in my mouth, noticing him notice and watching his face shuffle through a range of emotions.

"You can't be pregnant," he says. "You're mad at me."

CHAPTER TWENTY-FOUR
LIAM

I'M FAIRLY CERTAIN I'M HAVING A HEART ATTACK. MADDIE JUST SAID SHE'S pregnant. I want to say, "Are you sure," but of course she's sure. She wouldn't be here with that expression on her face if she only suspected.

Our night together flashes before me: how I took off the condom and intended to get another one, but then I lost my powers of concentration when Maddie straddled me. Not that it's her fault. We were both sober, consenting adults. "You can't be pregnant," I say again.

I rake my fingers through my hair.

"So," she says, gripping the edge of my desk, "You're suggesting that because I am angry with you, my body would...reject your baby batter? That my womb would only open for the sperm of a man with whom my eggs find favor?"

"No." God, I'm such an idiot. "I haven't even gotten to apologize properly yet. I just...this is a bit of a surprise, Maddie."

"No shit," she says, and crosses her arms over her chest. She sits, staring at me. I stare back.

"Everything I want to say feels wrong," I tell her, and she arches an eyebrow at me. I blow out a breath. "Well, you hate me anyway, I guess."

She rolls her eyes. "Are we going to make this about you right now, Liam? Because I'm the one with a human being leeching off my endocrine system as it grows a spinal cord."

I gape at her. "Shit, Maddie. Your diabetes. Are you ok? Is the baby ok? What do we do?"

She seems to soften at this change in direction. "I honestly don't know," she says. "Emma is sending me information about her maternal fetal medicine doctor, and I don't know what that means yet, but if Emma had to have one for her epilepsy, I'm sure I need one for my diabetes."

"Is that someone we call right now? What happens next?"

Maddie shrugs. "I didn't get past telling you when I was making my agenda for this."

I frown, staring at her. Pregnant.

I want to ask ten thousand questions. A thousand scenarios race through my mind at once, and I want to make them all orderly and efficient. This feels like chaos, and my heart is hammering in my chest. I want to hear her promise she's managing her own symptoms and then assure me she will keep our baby safe.

Our baby. I'm already thinking of the baby as...ours.

"I'd like to be with you for appointments," I say quietly. I want to grab her fanny pack and pull up her calendar in her phone and pre-schedule appointments for the next nine months. I want to start googling vaccine schedules and whether diabetes is genetic.

I want to organize folders and notebooks and line them all up like I used to do with my brothers' backpacks. I was usually the only one who kept track of permission slips and whose sneakers had holes. When we were with Dad, he didn't know how to check that stuff. When we were with Mom, I think she just sort of...let me handle it.

I feel myself switching into hyper caretaker mode with Maddie, and I don't like it. An hour ago, all I wanted to do was get her to forgive me and, yes, encourage her to sleep with me again. Because that shit was amazing. An hour ago, it felt good when she helped me loosen up.

Now I just feel like I'm being punished for letting my guard down.

My mouth feels dry. "Can I bring you a drink from the kitchen?" I stand up and smooth down my tie, reflexively.

She shakes her head. "I keep puking everything up except these candies you gave me." She pulls one out from her fanny pack. "Thank you," she whispers. "For these."

I nod and hurriedly grab a glass of water, realizing that I forgot to make sure she'd wait for me. I almost melt with relief when I see her still sitting in my office once I return with the water. She's on her phone, flipping a card over in her fingers while she talks. She beckons me into the room and I hear her say, "I just took the test today, but like I said, I'm a Type One Diabetic."

I can't hear the other end of the conversation. Just a lot of "Mm hm" from Maddie. Finally she gets out a pen and writes down an appointment time. I snap a picture of the card with my phone so that I can make sure to clear out my schedule and be there with her. I'm not even sure what type of appointment this is, but if it's about the baby, I'm going to attend and I'm going to come with questions.

My heart is splitting in slivers here, holding a war between my desire for her as a romantic partner and this new life I need to keep safe. I don't pretend I can do both things. If I unleash my full powers of organization on her, she's not going to want me back. Unless I figure out something different. This is going to be the ultimate engineering project, I feel myself think. No. Not an engineering project. A kid. I have no idea how to take care of a kid.

I sit on the edge of my desk, waiting for her to finish the call. I want to touch her. I need to touch her. But I've lost that right, and I can tell by her body language that I'm not getting it back any time soon.

"Normally, baby docs don't see people until they're 12 weeks pregnant, but because I'm such a freak, I need to get checked out sooner." Yeah, she's still hurt by what I said.

"Maddie," I start to apologize but she holds up a hand.

"I just mean that I'm an unusual case. I'm supposed to call my endocrinologist about this and make plans to adjust my insulin. I'm trying to decide if I want you to come to that appointment."

"If it's about the baby I want to be there." I don't know the first thing about what to do once this conversation is over, but I know I want to be present for every single thing related to this human being that shares my DNA.

She squints at me and eats another of the lavender candies. I feel hopeful that they've won prime place in her fanny pack and that they're the one thing seemingly keeping her from vomiting up all her calories. I vow to order her a case of them as soon as possible. "I'll text you when I know the appointment time with Dr. Cranor."

I nod. "That's my endo," she says.

I nod again. "Of course. Wait. Which doctor were you just on the phone with?"

"The fancy baby doctor."

I nod. Several doctors. This is fine. It's going to be fine. We can color code the entries on my calendar app and I can share the calendar with her if she doesn't have that set up already.

She sighs. "Ok, well I need you to shift gears now and talk to me about work stuff. I have to finish this book so I can stop working here."

I sink back into my desk chair. There's no way I'm going to be able to string together coherent thoughts about my ideas for the future of this company. Not even my notes will save me.

"Come on, Brady," she says. "I know you have shit prepared for our conversation. Pull up your outline."

I blush and tilt my monitor so she can see the bullet points I put together in advance. "My uncle thought I was too young to start meeting with clients," I tell her. "My father had to convince him to give me a chance to go out into the field."

"And what happened? You dazzled the clients with your fun-loving personality?" She starts to record and taps on her notebook with the end of her pen.

I shake my head. "I started talking to coal companies about the structural integrity of their equipment," I tell her. "I'd go out to those sites, and it was like I could just see what needed to be done." I run a hand along my jaw. "That first trip out, I landed us a billion dollars in contracted work to inspect and repair crumbling coal processing gear throughout Appalachia."

That was just a few years ago, and I tell Maddie how it was like a ripple effect. The more I got out there, looking around these sites and talking to the people on the jobs, the more issues I saw that needed our attention. "That's how I got started talking to the railroad industry. I landed those contracts right before we met." I smile at her. She squints at her note pad.

"My father has the ability to instill trust in our clients," I tell her. He's pretty remarkable that way. Some people think he's just sort of a buffoon, but he's always listening, always observing. "Because of that, people are willing to take a risk with us. I mean, we're a small shop. These are big names. The railroad? Hell, Maddie, the railroad shouldn't have taken a meeting with me."

She frowns again. "I thought that one you did without your father?"

I smile and look down. It's true. I landed that project all on my own. "I was able to do that because of the reputation we had with the partnering coal companies, which was because of my father," I explain. "All this new stuff, with the machine learning and the computer science, when we go talk to new clients, we don't tell them we're the best. We ask them if they want to be partners with us to test something new. Dad is really good at framing things about the future and longevity…I'm really good at making sure everything is in order. That everything is safe."

I emphasize the words order and safe, and she seems like she wants to say something, to draw some sort of metaphor to what's happening with the two of us, but she taps her pencil again and continues.

"Kellen says you have a vision for the future? With Clay and the power company?"

"Clay? You guys are on a first-name basis like that?"

She rolls her eyes again. "Look, he called me back about something personal that's totally unrelated to anything engineering. I promise and you need to just let it go." I won't, but I nod. I don't want her sharing something "personal" with one of my dad's friends. It doesn't feel right, and I save that away to figure out later.

"Yes, well, I think I started telling you about the power lines," I tell her, quickly summarizing how I noticed the electrical towers when I was out walking the rail lines. "It's all related. All these industries, they don't operate independently. That's something I tell these folks about their business—some firms might focus solely on coal and be the best damn coal bin engineers out there. But Beltane sees how the coal bin fits into the rail industry and how that fits into the power industry. Our people are checking out inefficiencies at every step along the path."

I rattle on for a bit more about our country's power grid and roaming blackouts. "Each state is individually setting policies on whether these regulated utilities can spend money fixing their infrastructure," I tell her, and I see her eyes glazing over.

"You have a wide angle lens about everything but people, don't you, Liam?"

I'm not sure what to say to her, so I just stare.

"Tell it to me again in a way that makes me care," she says. "I mean, think of me as the audience for this book…a potential client. What should they know about what you're doing right now with the power people?"

I grip the arms of my chair. "We're not just looking at work a month down the line here, Maddie. We invest in our people and our ideas—like hiring postdoctoral computer scientists. His drones can fly out there and find patterns in data we hadn't thought to look for, and each state we get on board can be a model for what's possible." I take a deep breath. "I want our structures to still be standing when my kids go to college."

It's a line I've said a few times in meetings, but as I stare at her, it carries more weight than ever before. My kids...it's no longer conceptual. I have an actual child who will go to college in...19 years. I swallow.

"Ok," she says, looking at me with an unreadable expression. "I think that's enough for today."

CHAPTER TWENTY-FIVE
MADDIE

LIAM TEXTS ME TWICE AN HOUR WITH QUESTIONS. I CAN TELL HE IS AT HOME earning his internet MD, especially when his questions include phrases like "nuchal cord."

"I'm going to block him, I swear it," I tell Nicole. She has, as per usual, offered to help me make a spreadsheet and get a picture of my options. It occurs to me that Liam would probably love to be making a pivot table for me right now, but I'm still mad at him and it feels better when Nicole gives me her special brand of straight talk.

Her spreadsheets feel like they give me a picture of my options, like a guidebook. His feel like to-do lists and boundaries.

"You can't block him," she says. "He's the father of your child and you're stuck with him for 18 years."

I let my head sink to the counter at this. But, I didn't call on Nicole for her syrupy optimism. "Ok, let's keep going with the chart," I tell her.

She takes a deep breath. "Ok, well, obviously you need to nail this job offer from Sheila, because you're going to need so much stinking health insurance."

"So much." Sheila asked for my writing samples and after I sent her my favorite articles plus the first chapter of the Beltane book, she basically asked when I'd like to start. Nicole is coaching me to get her to commit to some numbers and specifics.

"Next," Nicole says, tapping the screen with her fingernail. "Lodging."

She sets her laptop down on the counter. "Look, babe, I adore you. You can stay here exactly until the baby is born. But I'm sorry, I just cannot live with a baby."

I nod. "I know. I wouldn't impose that on you." And I really do know it, but suddenly the thought of being homeless and jobless with a newborn hits me really hard and my eyes start crying without my permission.

"Madison Parker, do not feel like I'm kicking you out into the cold," she says, pulling me in for a hug and letting me snot on her shoulder. "You're a goddess and you're going to be fine. Hell, you probably can put all this Beltane money as a down payment to buy a place," she says.

"Really?" I hadn't considered that. Nicole keeps not letting me pay her rent, so I've just been saving the Beltane money since everything else was budgeted out so carefully anyway.

"I mean, not in this neighborhood. But someplace maybe near Tim." Tim Stag, Nicole's boss and brother to Emma's husband, lives in a family-friendly neighborhood in the east end of the city. I never even imagined myself owning a house. I grew up in apartments. Hell, my parents still rent.

"You think I can afford a house?"

"Want me to make another spreadsheet?" I shake my head, choosing to let that kernel of a dream sit for awhile longer and focus on the imme-diate future. We talk about my car—seems safe enough to put a baby seat into. Nicole has some sort of estimated list of expenses for a baby, and she types CHILD SUPPORT in bold, red letters at the top of the spreadsheet.

That part makes me sad. I always imagined I'd have a family someday, I just assumed it would be a two-adult unit. Two parents, living together, like mine. We never had much, but my sister and I always knew we had security, stability. Cooperation. Someone to take turns with when the kid is in and out of the hospital for years. And my parents obviously love each other. My mom has been sending me pictures from their bowling league, and my dad is grabbing her ass in half the shots.

And here I am, knocked up the first time I sleep with a guy I probably like, making a spreadsheet about how much child support he should pay me. "You want to avoid court," Nicole tells me. "They just plug shit into a formula based on his income and yours. Do you know how much he makes?" She chews on her fingernail. "Do you want me to ask Zack?"

"Nah," I say. "I'm a big girl. I can have these kinds of talks with Liam." Saying it reminds me that I do need to talk to him before our appointment with Dr. Cranor tomorrow, so I thank her for the work organizing my life and promise she can tell Zack my news after I see the MFM doctor and we find out things are ok.

℥

WHEN LIAM PICKS me up for our eight AM appointment, he is just as I expected: nervous, stiff, and carrying a folder. "I've been doing some research," he says, handing me another jar of the lavender candies, which I pop open greedily.

"Of course you have." I pour the candies into the baggy in my fanny pack, tucking the jar in the cup holder on my side. I hope I remember to take it later. Everything about these candies is beautiful, and that includes the packaging. "Thank you for the candies," I tell him. "The baby and I both love them."

Some mornings, when I'm puking endlessly, I stare at the pretty jar of candy in between rounds of barf. I think about how nice it would be to go to France, and lie in a field of lavender with the sun shining on my face.

Back in reality, Liam prattles on nervously about work and parks along 5th Avenue rather than enter the garage. "I get parking validation," I tell him, confused.

He looks appalled. "Have you been inside those garages? Have you seen the blueprints? Do you know how many catastrophic failures there are each year on parking garage ramps?"

"Um, no to all of those except the first." I walk over to the meter and he brushes me aside, entering his credit card. "Is it really dangerous to park in a garage?"

Liam shrugs. "Not safe enough for the woman carrying my child."

"Oh lord, here we go. Liam, I'm not going to live in a bubble." I shove open the door to the medical building and stride toward the elevator. He rushes to keep up.

"Didn't say you should. I'd just prefer you not park in garages. Or use escalators. Unless Cal was consulted on their construction. I trust him." He frowns and studies his reflection in the polished brass on the interior doors of the elevator. "I think."

Dr. Cranor greets me with a hug in the waiting room. I'm her first patient of the day and she waves the medical assistant away, saying she'll snag my vitals herself. She looks at Liam expectantly and blinks a few times until I sigh and say, "This is Liam Brady. He's the baby's father."

He pumps Dr. Cranor's hand and follows her down the hall toward her office. We generally meet in her office, fully clothed, sitting in chairs like humans. It's why I like her and why I'm nervous about starting to see a baby-doctor who will want me in a paper gown and who will talk to my stomach like I'm an incubator and nothing more.

I absolutely detest when doctors would speak about me to my mother in the third person. "Madison has had low sugars this month," they used to tell her. Or, "Your daughter needs to learn to change her set on her own." It's one reason I switched to Dr. Cranor. I always feel like she hears me.

Liam seems unprepared for this low-key vibe, but spreads his folder on the desk. "I did some research," he repeats. Dr. Cranor meets my eye and I nod.

She folds her hands on the desk and encourages him to share his findings with the group. He points to a chart. "The American College of Obstetricians and Gynecologists recommends blood sugar readings of 95 milligrams per deciliter for diabetic pregnant women, before meals," he says, and rattles off a few more strings of numbers before asking, "How can we ensure Maddie remains in those recommended windows?"

Dr. Cranor smiles and pats his hand. "It sounds like you're very concerned about Madison," she says.

"And the baby," he interjects. "Her diabetes impacts the baby."

"I don't love where this conversation is going," I say, flipping his folder closed.

Dr. Cranor puts one of her hands on each of ours. "My philosophy in this practice is very patient centered," she says, looking at Liam. "I've been in consultation with Madison for many years now. How many has it been, Maddie?"

I shrug. "At least 15." I migrated to her office as a teenager even though the children's hospital has adolescent endocrinologists. I met her when she was doing rounds for a study and liked her immediately because she addressed me instead of my mother.

"Shouldn't she have a chart," Liam asks, his knee thumping up and down like a piston, talking about me in the third person like I hate.

I open my mouth and Dr. Cranor pats my hand. "I assume you're aware of Maddie's glucose monitor?" He nods. "That is a chart," she explains. "Maddie can examine trends in her sugars. She can provide granular detail in five-minute increments." She looks over at me now. "Today, I am going to discuss a coordination of care model where sometimes I walk down the hill to Magee hospital and meet with the maternal-fetal-medicine team and you, all together."

"I love that idea," I blurt. "You know how I feel about new doctors."

She smiles. "Just because we are adding more careful monitoring to our routine does not mean my bedside manner is going to change," she says. "Diabetic women have babies every day, Madison. You're going to do just fine."

We talk for awhile about my insulin levels and ramping me up so I can stay in a safe range. Dr. Cranor warns me that I might start to experience uncontrollable lows, and talks about what to do in those cases. Liam takes notes furiously on his phone, his long fingers typing impossibly fast on his screen.

"This will all show up in my chart, right?" I ask. "In my after-visit notes?" Dr. Cranor nods and smiles, and she ushers us out, promising that her administrative assistant will call with a coordinated care appointment time.

"Do I have access to those notes?" Liam flexes his fingers, clearly exhausted from note taking.

"You definitely do not," I tell him. "I'm not giving you access to my medical chart."

"How will I know what I'm supposed to know about the baby?" He looks sort of desperate as he's asking me to give him the ability to read all of my labs, read all my private notes with my doctor. Access a lifetime of my most personal information.

"You can ask me and I'll tell you what you need to know." I glare at him until Dr. Cranor clears her throat and steers the conversation back to the appointments.

To make the most of everyone's time, she wants me to have my lab work and an ultrasound done before the appointment, and she surprises me by writing a prescription for those things.

"I didn't know you could order me things just like a baby doctor," I say. "Can you do my well-woman exams, too?"

"Nice try, Madison. I am signing the order for standard tests and imaging as a member of your prenatal care team. You still have to see someone else for your vulva needs."

CHAPTER TWENTY-SIX
LIAM

I EXPECTED TO FEEL BETTER AFTER GOING OVER MY RESEARCH WITH MADDIE'S doctor, but I feel even more out of the loop than I did before we went in there. The doctor and Maddie have all this access to her readings, and neither of them seem interested in sharing it with me. I feel out of control and in the dark, wondering what's going on with the little grain of rice in her stomach.

Yes, I looked that up, too. Evidently, each week the baby progresses through a different food item. There are all sorts of apps that explain what organs are growing when.

"Are you going in to Beltane today," I ask her as we head back toward the car. She nods, and I'm about to reach to open her door for her, when she spins and vomits on the curb. I freeze, utterly unprepared for something like this. I'm always getting surprised by body fluids with Maddie.

"It's the morning sickness," she says, rummaging in her pouch for a tissue. I'm determined to do better with this than I did with the blood, so I lean into the car and reach for my water bottle, offering it to her. She swishes some water around and spits. "Thanks."

She climbs into my car as if nothing has happened, and I remain frozen in place. "Do we need to go back upstairs to Dr. Cranor?"

Maddie's eyes widen. "For puke? No. Liam, get in the car." She starts eating crackers, slowly for a change. I watch as she fiddles with her pump.

"Are you monitoring your numbers? Can I see?"

She shakes her head. "No, Liam, you cannot have access to my freaky charts. It's none of your business."

I swallow the lump in my throat. "Maddie, I'd do anything to take back what I said that morning. You're not a freak. You're fascinating."

She whips her head toward me. "Like a circus act?"

"No!" I shake my head. "No, like...intriguing. Like nothing I've ever seen before."

"Still hearing novelty act, Liam. I'm not your medical porn source."

This is all coming out so wrong. I blow out a long breath. "Look,"I start. "You move through the world with this amazing confidence and apparent ease, even though you have all this...stuff...going on beneath your fanny pack. I mean, you jab yourself with needles like it's no big deal and puke on the curb and just carry on with your day. That's amazing to me. And your mind works in all these really interesting ways. And you smell like lavender. And I never liked it when someone ate strawberry licorice before, but I can't stop thinking about you doing it."

When I meet her eye, she's holding a piece of the red candy and I grin. "I'm so sorry, Maddie. I'm an uptight engineer and I have no experience talking to real people and I want to try with you."

"Because I'm carrying your baby and you need something else to fret over?"

"No," I shout. And then I catch myself and adjust my tie. "No," I say more calmly. "Because I like you."

She still seems uncertain, but she sits back against her seat and her body seems to relax a little. She reaches for my water bottle and takes another swig, swallowing this time. "I'm glad I didn't share my findings that pregnant women need to drink more water," I joke. "Seems like you're all set with that one."

We seem to have reached a truce, and after a few weeks of silence, I'll take friendly quiet. It's a start.

I navigate through the rush hour traffic on our way to the office. We ride in silence through a few lights before she asks, "Do you know when you're going to tell your family?"

"Hmm." I've been trying to put that off along with exploring my emotions about the whole thing. "Do you?"

She shrugs. "Emma and Nicole know. With my parents, it's better if I go to them after we have more of a plan. I really can't handle it if my mom nags me." She chews on her fingernail. "I need to figure out where I'm going to live before I tell them."

Through all the fretting I've done about this, it had not occurred to me that Maddie was still crashing with my brother and Nicole. Hell, I'm not even sure whether she got that job with my mother. I don't know how to ask her without making her angry again.

"You could move in with me," I say, quietly. "You and the baby. Until you get settled."

I expect her to snap at me and yell about what a terrible idea that is because she hates me, but she's quiet again. "I don't want to do something else temporary," she says, eventually.

"Hmm. From what I hear, it's an all-hands-on-deck situation when a baby is really young," I tell her. "We could help each other. With the baby, I mean. The offer stands."

She nods, still quiet. As I pull into my parking space at work, she finally says, "I'll think about it, Liam."

ℬ

We head our separate ways once inside, and I'm surprised to find my father pacing in front of my office door. "Awfully late to be getting to work, isn't it, son?" He taps at his watch. My father can't stand tardiness. Our business day technically begins at 8:30 and in his mind, showing up past 8:15 is inexcusably late.

"I was with Maddie in the field," I say, vaguely, which is mostly true, especially considering I gave her my assessment of the structural integrity of parking garages. I unlock my office and set my things on my chair. "What's going on, Dad?"

He beckons down the hall. "Come on," he says. "We're meeting with Clayton Monroe." My eyes shoot open.

"You're bringing me at this phase?" This wasn't something we planned for. It's not on our company agenda. I would have prepared and read reports if I'd been aware. Surely I didn't miss something like this on my schedule?

"He called last night to talk about the book. That Parker gal called him for a fact check, he got to thinking about me, I let him know we were sniffing around some new waters. Come on," he says. "We're meeting the board."

"I'm not sure I can handle another curve ball this week, Dad," I tell him, loosening my tie.

"This isn't a curve ball, son. This is business. Adapt or we get outbid.

284

You know that." He frowns at me and tightens my tie again. He studies my shoes and, finding them appropriately shiny, beckons for me to follow him.

Dad arranged a car service to take us, and before I can inhale we are seated in the back seat, crawling back across town. I have nothing with me. Not even a pen to take notes. Not that my Dad has any of that stuff, but most people know by now that he first of all never forgets anything and second, relies on other people to take all his notes for him.

Clayton greets my father warmly when we enter, and Dad drapes an arm around my shoulders. "Clay, you remember my oldest boy?"

"Liam, good to see you again." He peers behind me down the hall, looking for something. "Thought you might have brought Maddie with you again." He seems disappointed. I'm not sure how to respond to that.

Dad's face brightens. "That writer? You want her here, Clay, I'll send for her. Have here here in a half hour."

I open my mouth to assert that Maddie isn't at our beck and call in that way, but Dad winks at me and Clayton shakes his head. "Wanted to give her an update on something is all."

Clayton sinks into his seat at the head of the table and motions for my father to sit. The problem with my father is that he can't sit still and generally arrives at meetings early enough to grab a chair by the door. Anyone watching and paying attention would notice that he gets up to use the restroom or get a drink every 27 minutes.

Dad eyes up the seat to Clayton's left, on the wall opposite the door, and fusses with his tie. *Adapt or we get outbid,* I think at him, wondering if he can hear my thoughts because his eyes snap to mine. "I'm happy to run down the hall and have your secretary deliver a message to Ms. Parker for you, Clay," he says.

Clayton waves a hand. "Nah." He folds open a black portfolio. "I'll just call her later." I stare at his hands as they hover over a sheet of numbers. I don't want him calling Maddie. I don't even know what it's about but I don't like it. He's old enough to be her father. He's mentioned being happily married. I decide her being pregnant with my child gives me a reasonable argument toward feeling protective of her.

The sounds in the room drift out as I stare and worry and wonder if the woman carrying my child will ever smile at me again.

CHAPTER TWENTY-SEVEN
MADDIE

I stand in the entrance to the store, staring. The merchandise is sharply divided down the center, half pink and half blue. It's all so vibrantly opposite. I didn't intend to come in here, not really. I wanted to just check out some prices on things so I could really look at the budget Nicole put together for me.

But here, in the baby store, faced with the reality of everything, I feel like I'm going to pass out. Maybe it's my blood sugar. I pull out my phone and check, but that all looks fine.

Just in case, I reach into my fanny pack for a Liam candy. That's what I've taken to calling them, especially since he had a case of them sent to Nicole's house. *Thinking of you. Around the clock.* He wrote on the note.

I don't know what to make of his note, or of him. So I decided to go look at baby stuff.

I should have looked this stuff up online, but I wanted to be here in person, I think, to touch it all and just...see. I wish I'd brought Emma. I pull myself together and head for the socks. I can write down some costs for one body part at a time, I figure. Except there are garments here that I cannot for the life of me figure out what they do.

I hold up a bag with arm holes, staring, until the clerk walks up. "Those sleep sacks are a real hot seller," she says with a smile. "All the moms rave about them. Except for the ones who prefer the swaddles. Have you seen these with the velcro?"

I shake my head at her, feeling my muscles stiffen. It was a mistake to come in here alone. Liam would have made a chart. Or a list with check-boxes. He would have probably collaborated with Nicole to arrange the chart strategically by area of the store, sorted by body part.

"Do you know what you're having?" I realize the clerk is still talking to me as she hands me a stack of bibs. I think they're bibs.

"Um...a baby?" It feels like a quiz, and based on her facial expression, I got the answer wrong.

She gestures all around the store. "We don't have a ton of gender-neutral things except in the newborn area," she says. "That's where we've got our creams and greens. Come on!" Her voice is perky and she stares at my stomach, which is still flat, but hidden behind my fanny pack anyway.

"You know, I actually am feeling a little overwhelmed," I tell her. I hand her back the bibs.

"Do you need to sit down?" She points toward the back wall. "We have a selection of glider rockers and nursing stools!"

I back out of the store onto the sidewalk outside and make a beeline for a bench. I feel bile rise in my throat and, unsure what to do, I reach for another candy. This just hasn't been my summer. Lost job. Lost apartment. Gave in to my lust for geeky guy at my side hustle...only to have him call me a freak and get me pregnant.

The conception sex was really good, though. I try to decide if it was worth all the puking. I remember the look in his eyes as he knelt in front of me, savoring me. Worshiping me. I've never had anything like that before. Now it seems like I'll never have that again.

I slump back against the bench and call my sister. When we were kids, she was the one who noticed a pattern of something off about my health and convinced Mom to call a doctor. She's told me that my experience inspired her to become a nurse.

As the phone rings, it occurs to me that maybe that's just a more loving way of her telling me I'm such a freak I rerouted her entire life. I move to hang up, but Melissa is already shouting into the phone. "Oh my gosh, Maddie, I'm such an asshole. I haven't called."

"Oh," I tell her, caught off guard. "It's ok. We've both had a lot going on." Melissa is blunt, like Nicole. I love that about both of them. My sister tells me about the new hospital, the temporary apartment where she and Steph are hanging out on their first travel nursing stint.

"We're doing med surge this time," she says. "Lots of dockworkers with compound bone fractures and amputated arms and burns."

"That sounds pretty interesting, actually," I tell her, thinking of the news articles I'd love to write about trends like that in the work force. "Did Mom tell you about my job?"

Melissa clucks her tongue. "Yeah. I'm really sorry, sis. You land on your feet, though?"

I nod, even though she can't see me, and tell her I've got a contract gig and am pretty sure I'll get an offer on a full-time position. "There's something else, though," I start. "And if I tell you, you have to swear you won't tell Mom and Dad yet."

"Huh uh," she says. I can practically feel her shaking her head from here. "Don't put me in that position."

"I'm going to tell them. Just...I need to figure a few things out first."

"Well what could be so bad that you don't want them to know? You already lost your job and moved in with Nicole. It's not like you're pregnant from a bar hookup."

I groan. I don't say anything else and I can hear Melissa breathing. "Maddie? Are you pregnant from a fucking bar hookup? Man, you straights and your poor decisions."

"It wasn't a bar hookup." I hear myself pulling out the small silver lining in my situation, and I realize how it sounds. "I know the guy. I just... don't like him very much right now."

She snorts. "I guess not. Does Dr. Cranor know? Are you physically ok, glucose wise and such?"

I tell her it's been ok, except on days when I puke more than twice. "I'm only like five weeks. I have an ultrasound next week. I think it's next week. I'm so stressed I can't keep my days straight."

"Is this guy going to contribute financially? I don't want to kick you while you're down, but not having the ink dry on this new permanent job is worrisome."

I walk Melissa through what I know. That Liam has said I can move in, that I'm not really sure if I want to, but recognize that it will be easier to have two adults around when the baby arrives. "He says I can stay in the second bedroom in his place," I tell her. I don't mention that I felt simultaneously relieved and insulted when he suggested that. What? I'm not good enough to be in his room? In his bed?

It's ridiculous and unreasonable. I have to assume these thought processes come along with being pregnant. "He's got charts," I tell Melissa, mentioning what a pain in the ass he was at the visit with Dr. Cranor.

"I approve of that," she says. I hear a commotion in the background. I didn't realize she was taking the call from work. "Listen, I have to go deal with a patient who's stuck on the shitter. I want details from your ultrasound, ok?"

"Yeah. Ok." I chew on the inside of my cheek.

"You're gonna get through this, Maddie, and it's gonna be great. Like college." Melissa gave me pep talks when I left home to go to college and was really responsible for managing my diabetes on my own for the first time. Even then, she went to the same university in Pittsburgh, and checked in on me frequently until she figured out Emma and I had each other's backs. Unlike Liam, my sister knew when to pull back from being my nurse to just being my sister.

"Thanks, Mel," I tell her. When we hang up, I still feel listless. I want to call Emma, lie on her couch and have her remind me that people with health conditions get pregnant every day and it's fine. I'm not going to run out of insulin before I get permanent insurance. I'm not going to give birth to a freak baby because diabetes isn't genetic when just one parent has it.

At least I had the sense not to fuck a diabetic guy. I snort out a laugh and then my phone rings. Curious, I look to see it's Clayton Monroe. Huh.

"Hey," I say by way of greeting. I figure, we're past the formality stage since he had me talk him through his first set change over the phone. "How's it going, pump pal?"

"Maddie, I've never been better," he tells me. "Truly!" Clayton proceeds to gush about how much easier each day has gotten for him without constant skin pricks and self-administered shots in the bathroom at work.

"I told you, dude. Robot pancreas is a game changer."

We shoot the shit for a bit, joking about our tubing, and then he catches me off guard. "My wife and I have something for you," he says. "To thank you, Maddie." He sounds a little tearful. "I don't need to tell you how hard things have been for her all these years."

"Aw, Clay. You don't have to do that." I start my reflexive refusal. As a reporter, I couldn't accept anything from people no matter what. I needed to maintain my objective ability to write something critical of them. I guess the same rules do not apply when I'm writing marketing copy for a corporation, but it's a hard habit to shake.

"Have to? Come on," he says. "It's my absolute pleasure. Can you send me your address so I can get it to you?"

I sigh and drop my head back against the bench. What do I tell him? Do I have an address? Finally, I decide to tell him, "I'm actually in the process of moving, Clay. Can you send it to me at Beltane? Or I could come pick it up!"

He chuckles. "You know I always love seeing you! We're in the middle of some intense changes at work right now. I wouldn't be able to give you my full attention. I'll have it sent to you at the office."

I thank him again and hang up, heading home with more questions than when I left the house.

CHAPTER TWENTY-EIGHT
LIAM

MADDIE IS SUPPOSED TO MOVE IN THIS WEEKEND. SHE CALLED TO GIVE ME THE DATE and time for her ultrasound and told me she'd thought about my offer and decided to accept. She was so businesslike on the phone I had to check and make sure I wasn't talking to Nicole.

"I'm having a bed delivered. For my room," she said. I wanted to insist she move into my room, in my bed, and save the second room for the baby, but I just agreed to her request. She also insists on bringing her beloved couch, which is fine because Cal took ours, and she asked for 2/3 of the pantry space so she had room for all the snacks she needs to be eating while she grows a human being.

My child. How could I say no to a request from the woman gestating my child? As soon as we hang up, I drive to the warehouse store and stock up on her favorites. I have no idea if her tastes have shifted with the pregnancy, so I poke around and buy extras until my shelves are crammed with enough packaged snacks to stock a preschool.

All day, when I'm supposed to be thinking about other things, I find myself wondering if the baby will have dark hair like me. I study my hands, my hairy knuckles, and think how much I hope the bean got Maddie's creamy, smooth skin when the genes were being divvied out in her belly.

She's only got one more chapter to write for the Beltane book. Uncle Kellen has her hanging out with Dad later this week. I'm so curious how she will weave in a discussion of his oddities for a book we are supposed to use as a marketing tool for future big clients.

Ray recently told me he wants to branch out and offer some engineering services to clients building space exploration equipment. How the hell are we supposed to get those folks to take us seriously if Maddie is writing about how my dad used to roller skate through the office to work out his nerves?

I sigh and look at my watch. I need to leave to go run with my family and then we're having dinner with Uncle Kellen. I haven't told any of them my news yet. As far as I know, Emma and Nicole are the only people who know about little Baby Brady.

I meet up with Cal and Orla and Zack at the trailhead, and freeze when I see Zack has brought Nicole along. She comes about half the time now and has really progressed a lot since they first met and she didn't even know how to pace herself without passing out.

She narrows her eyes at me, and I try to adjust my pace so I can get her alone on the run and learn what she's told Zack, figure out how long I have until I have to tell my family that I knocked up the contractor...Zack's girl-friend's friend. A woman I shouldn't have gotten involved with. I start sweating, thinking about how things got turned upside down when I let my guard down. When I let myself indulge in my desire.

"When are you spilling the beans," Nicole hisses, pretending to stop and tie her shoe. I pull up beside her.

"I thought I'd tell them one at a time," I say, watching to make sure everyone keeps running.

Nicole shakes her head. "If you don't tell them all at once, they're all going to call each other and it's going to become A Thing," she says circling her fingers for emphasis.

She's right. She stands and we keep running until I see my siblings and cousin pulled over up ahead, craning their necks to see where we went.

"You get a Charlie horse?" Cal starts poking at my leg rather than start running again. I shake my head.

"Liam has something to tell you all," Nicole asserts and crosses her arms, staring at me, tapping her foot.

"Oh snap!" Cal starts jumping and clapping his hands. "Did the candy work? Are you and Maddie a thing again?"

"What? No." I feel frantic and I look back and forth between their confused faces. Nicole gestures for me to continue and Zack frowns at her.

"What have you been keeping from me," he growls. She swats his arm.

I take a deep breath. "Well, the thing is, Maddie is going to move in to my place this weekend," I say, stalling. Once I tell them what happened, I can't take it back. I'm no longer the guy who had everything together, who organized all their medical appointments and made sure they showed up at the orthodontist each week. I'll just be the careless guy who forgot to put the condom back on and got a girl pregnant.

A woman. A woman who isn't supposed to get pregnant unexpectedly because it can risk her health.

Nicole rolls her eyes. "Oh, come *on*, Liam, you big coward."

"What the hell is going on?" Orla walks toward me. "Come on, cuz. What did you do? Did you try to organize her financial statements?"

I close my eyes and take a deep breath. "Maddie is pregnant."

When I don't hear anything, I crack my eyes open to make sure they didn't pass out. All three of my relatives just stand there, staring.

"I got her pregnant," I say, exhaling.

Eventually, Cal starts to laugh uncomfortably. "Ha," he says. "You got me. Liam knocked a girl up not-on-purpose. Funny." As he fake-laughs everyone turns back toward me.

"Oh my god," Orla says. "Is she ok?"

I shrug. "I think so? We're going for some tests this week."

At the mention of "we," my family unleashes a torrent of questions, all speaking at the same time.

Do we know the sex. When will the baby be born. Will the baby have diabetes. Does Dad know. It's that last one that really knocks me over. For years, I've been complaining about my father's irresponsible behavior to my Uncle Kellen. I've been incredulous that a man could succeed so well in business, yet frequently forget to pick his children up from cross country practice.

"I guess I'll tell him and Kellen tonight at dinner," I tell them. I look back and forth between their faces in the fading light. Orla pats me on the back and we keep running. Instead of the usual constant stream of insults, my brothers offer only silence as we make our way along the trail. For the first time in my three decades of life, I have stunned them into silence.

ℬ

AFTER OUR RUN, my siblings stare at me while Uncle Kellen fusses over us and we wait for my Dad to arrive. Kellen furrows his brow, aware something is going on, but I can't bear the thought of having this conversation twice so I try to stall everyone until Dad rolls in.

"Yum-yum, you gotta tell him," Cal says, knocking back a shot of Kellen's every-day whiskey, as if he's the one going through a crisis.

Kellen studies my face and slides me the bottle. "Tell me what, kiddo?" Orla and Zack slink out the patio door and pretend to stretch outside while Cal just leans against the fridge door until he bumps the water dispenser.

"Shit," he shouts, jumping away from the cold spill. "I guess I'll go outside with those guys."

I clear my throat as Cal slinks out and smacks Zack on the ass when he's bent for a hamstring stretch. I wish I could watch the three of them fool around. It feels like I'll never goof off ever again, not that I ever did that more than a few times a year I could let myself relax enough to unwind at a campout.

I swirl the whiskey in my glass and make eye contact with my uncle. Ordinarily, he doesn't approve of just knocking back the holy water of our home country. Whiskey, our Gram has taught us, is meant to be savored. Today, though, I close my eyes and dump the glass into my mouth, sighing as it stings the back of my throat.

"I got Maddie pregnant," I say, staring at my shoes. Kellen must drop the wooden spoon he was using to stir the pasta, because I hear a clatter and a splash. I glance up to see him dancing back from the stove.

"Liam," he says, wiping his hands on his apron. "I was...not expecting you to say that." Kellen drags a hand through his beard and grabs for the whiskey bottle. He pours me another shot and then drinks one himself, right from the bottle.

"Wow, I have not been this caught off guard since your father told me he got Zack's mother pregnant. Of course, he was still married to Sheila at the time..." he drifts off while I shift my weight. I don't need to hear that story again. I've spent my whole life pulling Cal away from those fights, urging him to play hide and seek with me or getting out the loud trucks that would drown out the noises of adults shouting.

"Right," I say. "Well, it's a thing that happened and also I was a jerk to her, so she hates me, but she's moving in to my apartment just because neither of us knows how to take care of a baby alone."

The front door springs open as that sentence falls out of my mouth and my father walks in, clearly having heard pieces of what I said. "Sounds like I need to get caught up," he says, gesturing for the bottle of whiskey.

Kellen offers the recap, Dad looks like he's going to fall down, and then he surprises the hell out of me. He pulls me into a tight embrace, then holds me for a really long time.

"It's going to be ok, son," he says, still holding me. His hug is firm. He doesn't pat or shift. Just holds me. It moves past uncomfortable, past awkward, right on into the surprising thing that I needed. I feel a ball of emotion rising in my chest, splintering out into fear and shame and disappointment in the way I have behaved and my inability to make things right with Maddie.

Eventually, Dad lets go and stands back, keeping his hands on my shoulders and pressing his forehead against mine. "I've been in your shoes," he says. "You might never win back the girl, but you'll always be that baby's Dad, and you've got a whole lot of Bradys here to help you with that."

I choke back some more of the feelings that are creeping up closer to my teeth. I look between my father and my uncle, now both massaging my shoulders. They're like the original bachelor squad, raising four kids together, without women around. I'm not ready to give up hope on Maddie, but it sure does feel better to know that I've got them in my corner.

Maybe the baby part doesn't have to be a chaotic disaster after all.

"You gonna name him Mick?" Dad sticks his finger in the sauce on the stove as Kellen swats him out of the way. I shake my head as he slides open the patio door and starts hollering for everyone else to come inside and eat.

CHAPTER TWENTY-NINE
MADDIE

"You can always come back," Nicole says, pulling another box away from me and loading it into Zack's truck. I know she sort of means it, but she really doesn't want me here once I have a crying sidekick to cramp her style. Zack kisses her on the cheek and slings another bag of my clothes into the truck.

He stands staring at me, sort of awkwardly, and asks, "Can I feel your stomach?"

"What? No," I shove him reflexively, and then remember he's asking because there's a human in there. Huh.

Nicole rolls her eyes. "You can't feel it move yet, Isaac," she says. "Once she's completely round, that's when you can feel it." She looks at me and shrugs. "That's what Emma always said." I survey our surroundings. We've emptied out the room where I've been crashing and unloaded my furniture from Thatcher and Emma's house. It all basically fits in a few truck loads.

Zack and his siblings were very careful not to knock into the cases of glass parts and other things Thatcher had moved to the side to make room for my gear. I feel another swell of emotion noting how many people I've inconvenienced by getting fired and pregnant all within the same season.

I sigh. I guess it's good I'm moving in with Liam. At least all of this is half his fault. He texted me that he told his family at dinner the other night, and then clarified that he told his siblings and his dad and uncle...not

Sheila. I have a meeting scheduled with her later this week to finalize things.

Then, of course, Liam and I have the ultrasound tomorrow morning. Sometimes I hope that the ultrasound shows there's not actually a baby inside me. Maybe the test was wrong and I'm just late because of stress or something. Then I puke on the sidewalk and smell someone's gum from 100 feet away and realize that it's actually true. There's really a baby growing inside Madison Parker.

When we get to Liam's place, he's waiting outside for us, waving us in to the parking garage. I can concede it's medium-endearing that he is so excited, especially when he shows me that he stocked up on snacks. "I don't want Baby Brady to get hungry," he says, offering me a container of fish crackers while Orla and the guys bring my stuff upstairs.

"You mean Baby Parker?" I snatch the crackers and eat a few, taking a moment to acknowledge that this was a pretty cute move. Then I'm nauseated again and dash down the hall to the fancy bathroom, barely making it to the toilet in time. When I turn around to wash out my mouth, I'm startled to see Liam standing in the doorway, his face white with concern.

"It's just morning sickness," I tell him, grabbing the towel from his hand and dabbing at my face.

"Maddie, it's like three in the afternoon," he says, looking like he wants to reach for me, but hesitating and pulling back his arm. I close my eyes and breathe through my nose.

"I don't know why they call it morning sickness," I tell him. "This child makes me puke around the clock. Just constant puking." My monitor beeps to warn me of a low, which makes sense since I just puked up the meager food I'd managed to keep down today so far.

Liam's eyes are horror struck as he steps closer into my space. I fumble with the zipper on my pouch, and I realize he's right there, pulling out my pump and meeting my eye with a question. "It says ENTER FOOD." He looks at the toilet and back at me.

I burst out laughing. I can't help myself. "Yes, Liam. Yes it does," I say, sliding to the floor of his bathroom, still laughing. "I just puked up my fool. My food. You know."

He holds up a finger and jets down the hall. I hear Orla and Cal struggling with the couch in the door way to the apartment, but Liam bolts past them and approaches me with a carton of juice and a handful of the lavender candies. "You need 15 grams of glucose, right?" He looks at me like he's taking a quiz and desperate to get the high score.

I nod. "Have you been reading?"

He seems pleased with himself. "I downloaded the manual that comes with the type of pump you have," he says. "I know Dr. Cranor said we listen to you and how you are feeling, but I need at least a baseline of information about what's going on with the baby or I'm going to lose my hair with worry."

He rambles while I sip the juice and stare at him. I should feel annoyed, because I am certain his actions come equally from a place of concern and trying to control the variables. Aka control me. By the time I get the juice down, my stomach is feeling better and Orla and the guys are peering into the bathroom, clearly wondering where I went.

I wave up at them. "Nothing to see here," I say. "Just a pregnant lady puking up lunch."

Orla wrinkles her nose. Zack doesn't seem convinced and looks to Liam for confirmation. Liam stands and says, "Maddie vomited out all her calorie stores so her blood glucose level and her insulin levels were way out of proportion. She needs regular glucose intake and—"

"Yeah, Liam, they get it. I'm a freak. Thank you. Thank you, everyone, for helping to move my shit." I get myself to a standing position and glare at Liam. "I'll just be in my room, gestating, if any of you'd like to make an algorithm for what I should eat and when."

ℬ

THINGS DON'T IMPROVE after Nicole and the Bradys leave. Liam asks me about my numbers every few seconds. To my credit, I do not harm him bodily, though if looks could kill he'd definitely be dead. Two things have saved him: he's this baby's father and I need his help AND he's hot as fuck when he irons his pants pockets in the morning before work.

It should not be attractive, the way he fusses over the purified water in the steam part of the iron. But it just is. I sit at the counter eating bowls of dry cereal, watching my hairy baby-daddy concentrate on smart seams.

His entire morning routine fascinates me and, again, should not turn me on, but does. He pours himself a bowl of flakey flax cereal and then squats so his eyes are level with the bowl as he adds skim milk so slowly, stirring until each flake is coated but not saturated. Then he stirs for ages before he sits down to eat it.

Honestly, it helps me feel a little better about his obsession with my numbers, because it's very obvious that Liam is particular about absolutely everything. He doesn't just assume I can't control my endocrine system. He is like this about everything. "Hmm," I say, taking a bite of my hastily-poured cereal.

"Maddie?" Liam touches my hand, snapping me back to the present. He must have been talking to me as I watched him get ready, totally zoned out. "You ready to go? For the ultrasound and bloodwork?"

"Right." I hop up and toss my bowl in the sink, giving it a quick rinse and planning to head back down the hall to grab my bag, but I notice Liam staring at the sink. His lips are pursed, like he's trying to decide what to do about the bowl and spoon sitting in there. "You need me to move that to the dishwasher immediately? Is that it?"

He sighs. "Well," he starts. "It does make things easier if we load the dishwasher as we go along, rather than let things pile up. But I see that you did rinse the bowl, and I'm observing that that won't leave an odor or a crust on the dishes."

"Crust?"

Liam closes his eyes and shakes his head. "It's fine." He claps his hands. "Do you think we'll be able to see it? I read that we should expect the heartbeat at this point, but maybe nothing else on the monitor..."

I shrug. I haven't read too much about anything, and Liam keeps me updated each day talking about what food item the baby is shaped like and what internal parts it's sprouted since the last time he asked how I was feeling.

CHAPTER THIRTY
LIAM

I can barely contain myself as we drive to the hospital and make our way to check in for Maddie's labs. Evidently it's unusual for non-gestational parents to come along to the lab, because the phlebotomist looks at me very strangely the entire time I'm seated by Maddie. I can't help but ask him questions as he works, which leads Maddie to roll her eyes. "Don't mind him," she says. "He's always like this. Here." She rotates her arm slightly for him. "Use this vein. You'll get it on the first stick."

He notes her condition from her chart, and they joke about pin cushions and good veins. "I'm a spurter," she says, making the phlebotomist laugh as he snaps the tourniquet around her arm and flicks her skin.

"I'll try not to get a capillary," he says, inserting the needle. I feel regret wash over me, remembering how I'd responded in her room that night after we were together. *The night we made you,* I think, wishing I could reach out and touch her stomach, but knowing such a thing would be unwelcome.

I've really come to think of the little bean not just as an idea, but as my kid. Especially after talking with my dad and my uncle. I think of him as, well, a him. But when I close my eyes, I don't dream about raising him with my dad and my uncle to help. I see Maddie, her easy smile, taking delight in both of us. It's a nice dream, but it feels far off.

I watch the lab staff prepare a handful of vials with labels, and they pull the band off Maddie's arm. Like before, a bit of blood squirts out, but the phlebotomist is quick with the gauze pad and catches it as they both laugh.

Why couldn't I have reacted that way? I could be holding her hand right now, whispering to her how amazing she is instead of sitting stiffly in the chair beside her, mentally helping the staff count vials of blood to make sure they match the orders from Maddie's medical team.

"You ready?" Now it's Maddie standing with her hands on her hips, snapping me back to attention as she gestures down the hall toward the imaging department.

"Yeah," I say, offering my hand to the lab tech. He raises a surprised eyebrow at me and pulls off his gloves before shaking my hand awkwardly. "Thanks for taking care of my...of Maddie," I say, avoiding her gaze as she seems to stare at me, considering something.

We walk together toward the waiting room and I'm pleasantly surprised when we get whisked back to the ultrasound room pretty quickly. I resist the urge to help Maddie up onto the bed and I watch as she pulls up her shirt.

The sonographer stares for a minute at Maddie's pump. "Hmm I think we'll need you to take off your pants, hon. We might have to go low to get around your set there."

Maddie nods and starts to wriggle out of her leggings, but then catches me looking and halts. "Oh," I say, flushing. "Should I leave?" I want her to say no. I want to be here for this, and thankfully Maddie shakes her head.

"No, it's ok. I just...it's fine." The tech hands Maddie a sheet to put over her lap, and all of us relax when she's able to claim a bit more of her privacy.

"Ok," the tech says. "We're going to pinpoint gestational age today, hopefully find a strong heartbeat, and take some pictures of the spinal column."

"To rule out neural tube defects," I add with a question to my voice, trying not to reveal how much I've obsessed over today's scans.

The tech smiles and pats my hand. "It'll be ok, Dad," she says. I want to tell her she shouldn't be saying that to patients before the scan—in case it's not ok—but I'm too overcome by being called "Dad" for the first time. I watch as she squirts some gel on Maddie's stomach and touches the ultrasound wand to her skin.

Maddie snaps her hand out and squeezes mine without a word, and I rub my thumb along her knuckles for reassurance. We both hold our breath until we start to hear a swirling, thumping sound. "Hey, baby," the tech says. "Perfect heartbeat, guys." She moves the wand a bit more and the sound stops.

"What happened?" Maddie tries to sit up. "Where did the heartbeat go?"

I squeeze her hand and reach to squeeze her shoulder, too. "She just moved the wand, that's all," I say, making eyes with the tech, who nods.

"Here, we'll get it back for ya," she says, cheerfully. Maddie relaxes her body when we hear the sound again and I notice how intently she stares at the screen, holding her breath.

"Can we get an audio recording of the heartbeat," I ask, risking running a hand through Maddie's hair to try to comfort her.

"Oh, sure," the tech says, and starts prattling on about technology these days. I give her my email address without taking my eyes off Maddie and the screen, where we can see the little jumping bean...our baby moving around.

"Can you feel any of that?" I whisper into her ear while I brush the hair back from her face. She shakes her head.

The tech pipes in. "She won't feel anything for another ten weeks or so! They love moving around like that when there's enough space." A tear slips from the corner of Maddie's eye as she looks at the screen and she squeezes my hand tightly. I think the tech must bump her tubing, because she winces. My instinct is to search around, fix what's bothering her, correct the problem. But I stay by her side and keep my hand on her forehead, comforting.

After, when we're alone in the room, Maddie eases back into her clothing, adjusting the sheet for privacy. "Is the file in your email," she asks, leaning over my shoulder to look as I pull out my phone. I nod and pull up the video. Once again, the room is filled with the soothing, swirling sounds of Baby Brady's steadfast heartbeat. "Forward it to me?" There is so much vulnerability, so much hope and so much hurt in her voice. I nod and immediately send her the email with the file attached.

"Hey," I say, braving a hand back on her knee now that the ultrasound is over. She stares down at my fingers. "I felt it, too—relief," I tell her, my body sagging with the truth of that. I was relieved everything was ok. So quickly, I've shifted from fear and anxiety about this grave mistake I made to concern and deep caring for the health of this tiny person I helped create.

"Relief?" Maddie stiffens and I draw back my hand. "Why, because you thought my fucked up body wasn't safe?"

"Maddie, that's not what I said." Is she ever going to be able to forgive me for the word I uttered in my panicked, post-sex haze?

She shakes her head violently. "No, but you thought it. You think it every time you demand to know my numbers, every time you urge me to eat the healthier snack when I crave the goldfish." She jumps off the table and seems unsteady on her feet. I reach for her elbow, and she snaps back her arm. "Even now. You think I'm so fragile. So incapable of caring for myself—"

"Maybe it's YOU thinking those things, but I sure as hell don't." I snap at her. "Why are you so convinced I think the worst of you? Did you ever stop to think it's my own fucked up inability to trust anyone that drives my constant worrying?" I stomp toward the door and look back at her over my shoulder. "Jesus, I do all that shit because it's the only way I know how to show you that I care."

I want to stay and keep talking about this with her, want to make her understand everything I'm feeling, but I don't. She isn't going to hear any of my words the way I intend them anyway. She glowers at me, and I march straight out of the hospital. She was already planning to head home on her own after our appointment and I've got to go convince Clayton that he needs a multi-million dollar new infrastructure investment.

<h1 style="text-align:center">CHAPTER THIRTY-ONE</h1>
<h1 style="text-align:center">MADDIE</h1>

I CAN'T GO HOME AND WRITE AFTER ALL THAT. I'M TOO ANGRY AT LIAM AND TOO scared that he's right. Maybe it is me afraid that I'm rotten on the inside. Too off balance to sustain a life in there. I feel certain I've gone hyper, because I can feel the blood pounding in my head, but when I check my numbers, everything is normal.

I lean against the wall of the hospital outside, and immediately realize that doing that here will lead someone to assume I'm having an emergency. I spring back off the wall and without thinking, I dial Emma.

"Madison Parker, you are an ignorer," she shouts into the phone above the sounds of children crying.

"Oh," I mumble. "It sounds like you can't talk. I'll let you go..."

"Hey!" She shouts. I'm not sure if it's at me or the kids. "Not you, Ricky was pulling the cat's tail. Maddie, if I waited to talk on the phone until nobody was crying, I'd be waiting for your kid's graduation."

I laugh at the mental image of me and a little kid in an oversized cap and gown. Where the hell did that vision come from? "I just had an ultrasound," I tell Emma.

She squeals. "That's so exciting. Oh my gosh, I was so stinking nervous the first time." Emma starts to tell me how scared she was that having epilepsy would hurt the baby. "The relief I felt when I finally heard that heartbeat..." she drifts off for a minute, and I think of Liam's words, how I misconstrued them. "Once I saw everything was ok in there, I really felt like...maybe I could do this. Even with my jacked up brain."

At her admission, I just start sobbing. "Maddie? Honey, are you ok?" I try to snort out a response but can't suck in a breath. I'm just snotting and sobbing, sitting on a bench outside the hospital. "Ok, I'm going to send a ride share to come grab you," she says. "Moan if you're at Magee hospital."

"Yessssss," I wail, and I hear Emma whispering something in the background. Soon, a very concerned-looking older man pulls up in a car and I shuffle inside. I fret and cry the whole way to Emma's house and she rushes outside to greet me.

"Come on inside and tell me everything," she says. And I do. I tell her about Liam's charts and his comments. I tell her how he even got rid of the fucking coffeemaker, acting like it was some noble gesture that he's going to give up caffeine along with me.

Emma's kids pat my legs while I cry on the couch and eventually, she says, "Here's what we're going to do."

By lunchtime, Emma has assembled both her sisters-in-law at the house. Alice Stag, a chef, comes carrying a thousand packages of the most amazing-smelling food I've ever sniffed. Juniper Jones, who kept her name, rolls up in a power suit and a mustard-colored minivan. "Get in," she shouts, climbing out to toss her kids' booster seats into the cargo hold of the van.

Emma and Alice hop in and Juniper flicks a button, opening the sliding door and offering me a sticky captains chair. "I've got the van from Ty for a few hours," she says, referencing her husband, who shifted from pro hockey player to pro dad. Most days, Juniper explains, he has Emma's kids and theirs while Emma works on her book.

The three of them talk over top of each other about their children, and it sounds sort of like they have all sons. Based on the interior of the minivan, it looks like all of them like to fling paint and spit out partially chewed fish crackers. I spy a snack cup full of my number one cracker choice, and help myself. "Where are we going," I ask, wiping my face with the back of my hand.

"Pedicures," Emma shouts. "I booked us the whole place." She explains how the salon owes Thatcher a few favors because he did some custom glass work for their space in exchange for credits for his wife to get pampering services.

"I want to barf that is so damn perfect," I say, continuing to crunch the crackers. "Hey, how long am I going to feel like barfing around the clock?"

"Three months," Emma says, at the same time as Juniper growls, "eight months" and Alice shrugs, saying, "I never got nauseated with my babies."

Emma leans across the aisle of the minivan to pat my leg. "Every body and every pregnancy is different." Alice shares a story about how she passed out cold when she was first pregnant with her oldest son, Petey. None of the women in the van had planned for their first kids, but all three of them are living a happily ever after dream life with the Stag brothers.

I snort. "Well I don't have a Stag prince. I've got grumpy grandpa Brady keeping spreadsheets. I'm surprised he hasn't started charting my poops."

We all share a laugh at that, and Alice chimes in, "Do you know, Tim and I had basically only gone on one date when we conceived Petey?" I shake my head. That seems really unlike him, from what I've seen. He's very...well, he's a lot like Liam. Rigid. "Tim wanted me to see some high-risk obstetrician and basically tried to control every aspect of my life as soon as he found out I was pregnant."

My eyes widen. "And you stayed with him? Jesus, this is like a nightmare for me. Constant reminders of how my body is broken, how he doesn't trust me to grow his kid the right way."

Emma shakes her head as we pull up to the nail place. "I don't think that's the intent of how Liam is behaving," she says. I start to protest and she holds up a hand. "I didn't say that wasn't the impact of his actions, but I really think he's maybe acting a little like Tim, a little like Thatcher when they found out we were preggo." She gestures back and forth between Alice and her.

We open the doors to the salon and Emma is greeted with hugs and kisses from the owner. "You all look ravishing," she says, gesturing around the beautiful lobby of the space. "See how the light twinkles through this beautiful fixture?" Thatcher has made a swirling, fiery nest of tubes and soft lights sparkle from within, bathing the space in a soft, warm glow.

"It's very womb-like," Emma observes, and it strikes me that she's probably right about that. We walk through a curtain into a row of pedicure chairs. "Comfy?" Emma asks as I ease my feet into the water. When I nod, she folds her arms across her chest. "Good. Now, we're here to answer every single one of your pregnancy and mama questions, but first you need to tell us what is going on with you and Liam."

I shrug. "I'm living with him because I'm homeless. I don't have a job unless his mother hires me. I'm basically pathetic and fully dependent on him."

"Hmm," Juniper frowns. "It does sound like he's very involved in your life. But are you really dependent on him in a bad way? How many other jobs did you apply for?"

I consider her question. It's true that I hadn't even sent out a resume. Nicole and Zack got me my temporary gig. Sheila aggressively recruited me for the copywriting job I haven't met with her about yet. "I guess his mom didn't know we were sleeping together when she offered me the job," I concede.

"And didn't Nicole say you probably have enough money saved for a downpayment on a house?" Emma flips through a magazine and doesn't look at me as I frown. "So you don't *need* to live with him."

I roll my eyes. "Ok, but if he's going to be involved in the baby's life, it makes sense that we live together, at least at first. And then I have to deal with him explaining which enzymes are in the new non-toxic cleaning products he bought to keep the baby safe."

Alice mock clutches her chest and gasps. "He did what?" The Stag women all laugh and Alice leans forward, admiring her toes. "Listen, I get it. You think it's sexy when he scrubs the shower tile with a toothbrush and—"

"Oh my god, Tim does that?" Juniper laughs. I can totally see Liam popping on a magnifying glass to make sure he gets each speck from the grout.

"Yes," Alice continues. "But sometimes it crosses a line. There's caring and then there's *taking care of*, and it's not sexy to be taken care of. You want a partner, not a parent."

"Yes!" It's like Alice has framed out exactly what's been bothering me. "I want him to iron the fuck out of his boxer shorts, but then with me I want him to—"

"Get them wrinkly." Juniper nods. I nod. We all sigh.

Emma slips a bunch of cash to the nail techs for a tip, even though the services are paid for, and then pulls me in for a hug. "You don't have to explain to me how it feels when everyone treats you like some delicate ornament. That's why we like each other, right?" I nod. "But it's also possible for a guy to admire you and take interest in your condition, not because he doesn't think you're taking care of yourself, but because he's so impressed with how well you ARE."

I furrow my brow, considering that. Liam does seem to admire his uncle primarily because of the accuracy of his work, and when he brags about his brothers, it's generally about their math skills. "Maybe graphs and glucose trends are Liam's love language," Alice suggests. "Like how Tim alphabetizes my spices for me!"

I think of his eager face as he asked Dr. Cranor about baseline numbers, and how he checked into the safety of the parking garage before driving me in there. This is a chaotic situation, and I'm a mess. Emma and the Stags help me see that maybe Liam is a mess, too, only he's the type of guy who straightens his angles more fervently as things get messier.

"You guys are the best and the worst all at the same time," I tell them, feeling a thousand pounds lighter now that I can at least verbalize what's been bothering me. But does knowing what's been bugging me about Liam really get me anywhere toward getting past my hurt feelings?

CHAPTER THIRTY-TWO
LIAM

Maddie isn't home when I get back from work, and she still isn't here when I'm ready for bed. I consider her last words to me, hearing them clatter around in my head. I don't know how to be the man she needs right now. She thinks my fussing means I don't trust her. How the hell do I explain to her that I have nothing else to offer beyond my organizational skills?

Unable to sit still, I stand at the counter with my laptop, finishing up my proposal for Clayton Monroe and Allegheny Power. As I'm studying his latest email to me, I see a notification that he's online. It's very late. Well, for me it's late. I'm supposed to run with my brothers before work tomorrow and then I have to drive to the suburbs for dinner with my mother.

My phone rings. "Clayton?"

"Liam! Good. Was worried the phone might wake your kids or something." I grunt. "You got any kids yet, son?"

Huh. I'm not sure how to answer this question. Am unprepared for how to talk about my personal life with a business associate. I've always deflected conversations about relationships and women, since I've never been involved with either of those. Not in any meaningful way. "No, I," I start to say I don't have kids. But that's not true. "My first is on the way," I correct.

"Really? Fantastic! That's so great. I recently got a new lease on life thanks to your friend Ms. Parker," he tells me. This is all very strange. Clayton sounds emotional. What does Maddie have to do with that? "Listen, I want to tell you not to kill yourself on the details in the proposal, son. This is a good thing you brought to us. A good thing. We need to do it, and I've known your dad for a long time. Your family does good work."

"Wow, Clayton, I don't know what to say."

"Aw, come on," he says. "Say thank you and then tell me you'll personally get the work established with Allegheny Power before you try and expand to West Virginia companies." I laugh at his candor. I can see why he gets along so well with my dad.

"I will be personally overseeing the planning and logistics phase of our work with you," I assure him. "Though we do plan to eventually trust my team with the work."

"Ah, I'm just jerking your chain, Brady. You guys hire great people at Beltane."

I hear the door open and see Maddie slipping quietly inside, like she's trying not to wake me. "Hey, Clay, I gotta run," I tell him.

"Little mama needs some ice cream?" He chuckles. "I remember those days."

"Something like that," I tell him, ending the call and closing my computer. I take a deep breath and close my eyes, praying my words don't set off an angry string of responses from Maddie. "I was worried about you," I say.

When I open my eyes, she's leaning against the counter opposite from me. "I'm sorry I didn't call," she says. "I know I'm typically home in the evenings as I've been finishing the project for your uncle." I nod. "I can see how that was distressing for you. I'll text next time."

"Thank you," I whisper, not sure how to respond to Maddie agreeing with me that my anxiety was warranted.

She bites her lip and fiddles with her fanny pack, then sits on the stool next to me at the counter. "I think I should come with you to dinner tomorrow, to tell your mom our news."

"What? I wasn't going to—" I wasn't going to what? I can't wait another week to tell her. She'd be really angry if my dad knew for so long before she did. Maddie is right that I should tell her. "I want to make sure we deliver the right message to my mother," I finally say. Maddie has been very clear that her tolerance of my behaviors lately has been fully related to baby-daddy responsibilities. Showing up together to talk to my mom feels like the wrong message.

Maddie's eyes flare. "I hadn't considered that," she says. "I don't know yet what I think the message should be. About us."

I start at this revelation. "So...you're not 100% certain that romance is off the table?"

She spits out a laugh. I'd forgotten what her laugh sounds like, and I relax into it. "Romance," she says, in a quiet voice. "Is that what this is?"

"I did hand you a towel after you vomited the last time," I tease, testing the unfamiliar waters of flirting.

"My hero," she jokes. She stares at me in silence for a bit, and I can feel my heart rate speed up.

"Can I take you on a date," I ask her, my voice wavering. "I'd love to show you that bridge." I remember Clayton's question about the ice cream for a pregnant woman. "There's a cute soft serve place nearby."

An eternity passes before Maddie responds, asking, "Is it the kind of place where I can get two flavors swirled together?" I nod, fidgeting with the sides of my laptop so I don't reach out and try to touch her. "All right. It's a date."

I feel all my cells relaxing. I grin and rub a hand along the back of my neck, noting I need to visit the barber for a trim. How long has it been? The idea that I've forgotten part of my regular routine is alarming, until I remember that I was meant to go to the barber the day we met with Dr. Cranor. It feels ok that I prioritized that meeting above a bare neck.

"I'm going to accept your mother's job offer tomorrow," Maddie says, "but I won't tell her about the baby."

I nod. "When can we go on our hike-cream date?" She doesn't laugh at my joke right away and I worry it fell flat, but as she climbs down from the stool she seems to realize that I was being funny.

"Liam Brady, did you just make a portmanteau?"

"I am not familiar with that word," I tell her.

She grins and points a finger at me. "When you combine two words together like that. Hike plus ice cream."

"I had no idea it was an official thing," I tell her, fascinated. "Do you know everything about language?"

CHAPTER THIRTY-THREE
MADDIE

I feel like a cheater. I called Sheila to accept her job offer, didn't mention that I'd need time off in a few months, and didn't tell her I was carrying her son's baby. Nicole tells me that legally, I don't need to disclose my pregnancy at this point, but it still feels sneaky. Sheila wanted to know when I could start and I asked for another week to finish the Beltane book. She told me to go ahead and take two weeks, joking that I'd need a week to unwind after spending that long with her ex-husband.

I don't tell her that Kellen is the bigger pain in the ass right now. Every time I come into the office, he is a worried mother hen, pulling out chairs for me, handing me water. I feel like asking him to get me a fresh sprig of mint for the water, just to see if he will. My hormones are all over the place, but at least I seem to have stopped puking.

Liam and I have reached a truce. I bought a coffeemaker and he didn't comment on it. He hung my fanny packs in rainbow color order on pegs in the entryway and I didn't comment on that. It's just a time of...purgatory. All of us waiting to see what will happen. Trying to make sense of the things we've said, the things we've left unsaid.

"Coordinated care meeting today," Liam shouts down the hall, sounding excited where I'm feeling not quite dread, but almost. I hear him setting up the ironing board in the living room, and wondering again why he doesn't do that in his bedroom.

"Didn't it bother you to be out here doing this when you lived with your brother," I ask, sneaking behind him to get my cereal, admiring the muscles in his back where his thin undershirt hugs his shoulders. I let my gaze fall to his crisp boxers, wondering if he ironed those a few minutes ago or does them all at once when he does laundry. Would they be warm from the iron if I touched them?

Holy shit, I realize. *I have a lady boner for Liam right now.*

"I like to preserve my bedroom for sleeping," he says, concentrating on the insides of his pockets before shaking his pants right-side-out. "Hm. That's not entirely accurate, is it."

"I have no idea," I ask him around a mouthful of colored fruit rings. "That's why I asked about it."

"I have a desk in there and I sometimes do work in there." He pauses to look at me. "I have no logical explanation for why I do my ironing in the living room, Maddie."

"You can change your ways at any time," I tell him, patting his hand. "It's never too late."

He shakes his head. "You don't understand. I have a logical reason for everything! It's all that—" He stills, looking alarmed. He swallows. "Logic and order help keep me calm."

I nod. He steps closer to me, his pants still hanging open waiting for him to tuck in the work shirt he hasn't ironed yet. "My attraction to you is not orderly," he says, reminding me of the night we shared, how his eyes looked wild, how his scruff brushed against my thighs as he knelt at my feet.

Now it's my turn to swallow. "Seems like you were living on the edge before you even met me," I tell him, gesturing to the ironing board. "Sleeping with me was just step two on the road to chaos."

"I think I need a little chaos," he says in a quiet voice, and then I hear a timer sounding in the background. "That's my shoe alarm." He sighs and starts to move the iron along his shirt rapidly. Liam sets alarms for when he needs to start putting on his shoes and grab his bag to leave for work, only today we're stopping at Magee Women's Hospital before I go with him for the final production meeting about the Beltane book.

I toss on a fanny pack from the selection near the door and head to the kitchen to make sure it's stocked with proper snacks. Liam drives to the hospital, circling the parking garage until he finds a space on the roof, which is his compromise since there's not really any street parking near the city's main labor and delivery hospital.

I smile at Dr. Cranor inside and tentatively shake hands with the fancy

O.B. that Emma recommended. "Elizabeth Hudson," she says, pumping Liam's hand after mine. "Thrilled to meet a friend of Emma Stag's."

We all sit around a round table in a conference room with a huge monitor on the wall. Dr. Hudson brings up the video from the ultrasound, which makes my heart swell. Liam reaches for my hand and I squeeze it, loving the sound of the baby's heartbeat. "I was so excited with your blood-work and with the ultrasound," she says. "We're going to want you to alternate seeing Dr. Cranor and myself every two weeks."

I nod. That doesn't seem too terrible. I consider asking if it's normal that I have the hots for my hairy housemate, but then I decide I'm probably mistaking joy at not puking for sexual desire. Dr. Hudson pulls out some pamphlets, which Liam scoops up eagerly, causing her to raise a brow. I'm sure those were for me. "Babies born to diabetic mothers can sometimes have heart trouble," she explains.

Liam's entire body stiffens and I squeeze his hand harder. "We have excellent technology to monitor these things prenatally." She reaches across the table and pats both of our hands. "This heart rate from this first ultrasound is very encouraging. I just want you to be aware of the realities of the next few months."

She goes on to explain something about an umbilical cord, and I can feel Liam taking mental notes for later. Dr. Cranor leans in to ask him, "Would you like us to explain more about that, Liam? You seem concerned."

He nods, and I listen as Dr. Hudson explains how babies need three lines in their umbilical cord and sometimes, babies in a diabetic womb only develop two. I feel increasingly shitty, and panicked, and I reach for my fanny pack, popping a lavender candy in my mouth. I look over and see Liam holding his hand out, gesturing for a candy, and I meet his eye as I hand him one.

I assumed this meeting would send him into a tailspin, that he would yell at me for creating an inhospitable space for his kid. Instead, he winks at me, and I notice that he's got a few days' growth of beard. Even though I'm sitting at a meeting with two important, hard-to-see doctors, and should be paying attention, I blurt out, "You look really nice with a beard."

"Thank you," he says, giving my hand a squeeze. He turns back toward Dr. Hudson and winks at her, and I swear I must be having a low, because I feel faint.

CHAPTER THIRTY-FOUR
LIAM

MY ENTIRE BODY IS SCREAMING IN FEAR AFTER THAT MEETING WITH MADDIE'S doctors. Normally, I would respond to something like this by making statistical models. Roping in one of my relatives to make a chart about risks. If this was a rusting i-beam, I'd map out potential for failure at five years, ten years, twenty years. And then I'd chart out potential interventions.

But this is a baby. It's going to grow. We can't go inside Maddie and add heart scaffolding for a fetus—at least I don't think we can do that—and while the doctor talks, I realize my usual approach isn't going to help right now. Making a graph is not the most efficient intervention. But I see Maddie's hands shaking and realize I can be still, and I can squeeze her hand, and I watch as this simple act seems to calm her, to make her feel better.

Soon, I feel better, too.

After the meeting, we drive to Beltane and sit with Dad and Uncle Kellen to talk about the proof copy of the book: Beltane Engineering, Shining Light on Tomorrow's Challenges. I expect my father to be congratulatory and emotional and for Kellen to point out inaccuracies. I'm stunned when Kellen has tears in his eyes as he thumbs through the pages Maddie had the printer send over.

"This is just beautiful," he says. "I could never have so perfectly described our work and our company philosophy." He dabs at his eyes with a handkerchief from his jacket pocket. Uncle Kellen carries accessories that are both attractive and useful.

My dad, however, wears an unfamiliar expression. He runs his finger along some of the photographs, showing me and my brothers clinging to his legs on a job site. I estimate the photo is from soon after my dad split with Zack's mom, based on how young he and Cal look. It looks like I'm trying to tug my brothers out of the frame, like I was maybe asked to occupy them so Dad and Kellen could pose with a client.

I resolve in that moment that my child won't have to take on any undue burden, that I'll keep adult disagreements civil and out of earshot. That I'll hire a caregiver rather than bring my kids along to construction sites.

"I'd say this work order is complete," I tell the room at large, smiling at Maddie, who looks pleased with herself. As she should. This is excellent work and I'm excited to display it in our lobby, on my desk, and on the coffee table at our home. *Our home.*

I drape an arm around her shoulders. "Kellen, can I assume you're handling the paperwork for Maddie's final payment?" He looks perplexed and nods. "Ok, great! I'm going to take her home and put her feet up. We've had a full morning."

Everyone stares at me, and I understand I'm acting out of character. All my instincts are demanding I hyper analyze and shut myself in my office to plan for the worst case scenario. I've always put myself in the role of rigid protector, even when I was too young to be doing that. But what have my instincts gotten me so far? Living alone with no couch? Frown lines?

I tug Maddie's hand to the parking lot and open the door to my SUV, letting my hand linger on her backside as she climbs inside. She whips her head around, staring at me, eyes wide. Hmm.

I hadn't considered making any sort of physical move with her beyond taking her on a hike-cream date, which we still have yet to do. But I watch as her nostrils wriggle, and I decide I'm also going to ignore my instincts about romantic advancements.

This entire day I've been doing the opposite of the typical Liam Brady routine, and it feels good.

When we get inside the apartment, Maddie leans against the wall to take off her shoes and hang up her pouch. I step into her space, standing so close I see my breath tickling her hair. When she spins around in my arms, I box her in against the wall, an echo of the previous time we were together.

"You're going to need some candy," I tell her.

She looks at me, her eyes wide with surprise, but she doesn't indicate that my closeness is unwelcome. "For what?"

"To keep your glucose levels up while I fuck you," I tell her, zipping open her pack and pulling out a handful of the purple candies.

"Oh," she says, and then she moans as I slide one into her mouth, tracing her lip with my fingertip afterward. "Yum."

I'm not sure if it's a commentary on the lavender candy or if she's using her nickname for me, but either way I lean in and taste her. Our tongues duel around the candy in her mouth and I slip the other pieces in my pocket before planting my hands on her waist. She groans appreciatively as I lean in to her, thrusting my hips against hers.

"You're so hard," she breathes, like she's surprised. As if I haven't been hard for her for months.

"Always, Maddie," I snarl, thrusting against her again. "Always for you." I kick off my shoes and tug her hand, yanking her down the hall toward my room. In the doorway, I ponder the barrenness of the space. Neatly made bed. Bare surface of the desk. I don't even have anything on top of my dresser. It looks like a model dorm room.

I growl as I hoist Maddie up on the desk and stand between her legs. "Oh," she exclaims. And then, "Ooohhh," as I peel off her dress and toss it over my shoulder. I throw it on the floor like I'm some sort of mess expert. Her tank top follows and I drop my mouth to her nipple inside her bra. She thrusts up off the desk, screaming, and I draw back to see if I've done something wrong.

"Holy fuck, Yum, they're so sensitive. That feels so damn good." She writhes beneath me, and I keep sucking, soaking the satiny fabric of her bra as I pinch her other nipple with my thumb. Maddie starts wrestling with the clasp in the back of her bra, seeming desperate to get it off. I snake a hand behind her back and help her, and she gasps when her nipples hit the air.

"Oh, god," I groan, seeing how swollen her breasts have become with her pregnancy. And then I dive back onto them, not stopping until they're both shining and wet from my tongue.

"Liam, don't stop. Don't you dare stop. Oh!" I pinch and I suck and she comes. She seems as surprised as I do when she groans and comes just from me working on her breasts. I reach into my pocket, feeding her another candy while I start to work on my own shirt. "Rip it off," she demands, and I raise a brow at her. "Go on," she says. "Rip it open."

I nod, and send the buttons flying as I rip open my shirt. She laughs and lunges for my belt. When she gets my pants undone, she reaches inside and pulls out my cock, making me hiss from the sudden contact with her warm hand. "I love it when you come undone," she says.

"Get on the bed," I tell her, my voice low. She wants to see undone, I have a whole lot of undone energy to send her way. All the stress of the doctor appointment, all the stress of finding out I got someone pregnant, it all seems to gather in my dick and pulse, demanding a redirection. I finish stripping as Maddie climbs on the bed and stares at me, licking her lips. I toss her the last of the candies. "Don't unhook your pump," I tell her.

"Don't tell me what to do," she says, setting it next to her on the pillow, the tubing snaking up from her taut stomach. Her hips seem wider, and I look my fill as I stroke myself, realizing there's no need to bother with a condom.

"On your knees." Her face transforms. She likes this side of me, and I like how it feels right now. I pounce onto the mattress, draping myself over her back, nibbling on her ear and skating my hands along her body. My hard-on rests between her ass cheeks, pointing straight into the air as I grind against Maddie until she purrs.

"Please," she whispers, eyes closed, weight on her hands. I do as she asks, lining my tip up with the swollen, wet center of her, sliding around a few times until it's clear that I'll be able to slip right inside. "Mmmm, yes." I sink inside her, fully, and then draw back immediately. I watch the supple skin on her ass vibrate as I slam into her and I lean my head around to watch her tits jiggle with the impact.

I feel like a wild beast, like one of the coyotes I came upon in the park one morning when I was out for a quiet run before dawn. Grunting and sweating, I hammer into Maddie as she screams my name and begs me to go faster, harder, deeper. "More," she says, and I give her what she wants. Not caring about the repercussions, for once not plotting out the path toward a solution, I fuck her in my bed until it seems like my spine splits open.

I place one hand on her shoulders, and she lowers to her elbows, pointing that ass higher in the air as I pin her in place. Her face, turned to the side and resting on her cheek, is transformed into ecstasy, and when I slide my other hand around her waist to press against her clit, her jaw drops open in a silent scream. When I feel her contracting around my cock, sucking me even deeper inside, I wail her name as the orgasm rips through my bones. "Maddie," I say again and again, pouring into her until there is no way of knowing where she stops and I begin.

CHAPTER THIRTY-FIVE
MADDIE

I wake up in Liam's bed, naked, with Liam's hand on my belly. He lies on his stomach next to me, his head turned toward me as if he fell asleep studying the numbers on my insulin pump. He probably had.

But as I wriggle and stretch, trying not to wake him, I feel used in very, very exciting ways and I decide I don't care if he wants to ask me about my glucose today. Thinking about my glucose makes me realize I am feeling pretty hungry, though, and then I remember that I don't have an emergency snack stash nearby. I groan and try to thread my way out of Liam's bed.

He wakes up and rolls to his side. "Hey," he says. "Where are you going?"

"I thought I'd iron my underwear," I tell him, looking around on the floor for the garment in question. When he climbs out of bed, presumably to get the ironing board, I laugh and shout after him. "I just wanted a snack. Or breakfast." My stomach growls. "Maybe two breakfasts."

He pokes his head back around the corner and I admire his chest hair again, the way it swirls around his lean muscles. I start wondering if the baby will be tall and lithe like him. "I'll make you pancakes," he says, and disappears again.

By the time I find him in the kitchen, he's found some boxers and nothing else, and is flipping pancakes, whistling. "I like jolly Yum," I tell him, peering over his shoulder at the perfectly browned circles in his skillet. "Those look amazing."

"I only have turkey sausage," he says, frowning as the microwave beeps. "But there's real maple syrup!" I open a cabinet to get out a plate for him to cool the pancakes as he works and he freezes, turning toward me with the spatula in his hand. "I should have said we. We only have turkey sausage. This is your home, too."

"Hm," I say. I want to add on "for now," but I also don't want to spoil the moment, to damage the bridge we've begun to repair between us. So I divvy up the pancakes onto two plates and rinse out the mixing bowl while Liam, still whistling, pours me a glass of orange juice. "I could get used to this," I tell him, trying to remember the last time someone made me a meal.

"You should," he says, kissing my shoulder as he climbs into the stool next to mine. "How soon can you be ready?"

I arch a brow at him. "Ready for what?"

"Our hike," he says. He pulls out his phone and opens the weather app. "Look. It's only supposed to be in the mid-80s today, not too humid. We can splash in the creek if you get hot. And I can show you the bridge..."

He drifts off, his crooked smile so hopeful. "That sounds like an amazing day," I tell him. I fork another big bite into my mouth, moaning at how perfectly the pancakes and sweet syrup hit my need for carbs and sugar. I realize I've eaten all my sausage when I move to stab another piece and when I frown, Liam slides me one of his yet-to-be-eaten links. I swoon. "This is it right here," I tell him. "This is the key to my heart, Yum."

I MANAGE to not jump his bones after I eat, and once he has looked up whether his bug spray and sunscreen are safe for pregnant women, we load into his SUV headed for McConnell's Mill State Park. As we get closer, Liam grows visibly excited when he points out that we "get" to drive through a wooden covered bridge to get to the trailhead parking.

"This is where the horses and buggies used to come to drop grain at the mill, or pick up their flour," he says, pointing at the massive old building that no longer has a water wheel. He hops out of the car and runs over to the bridge, squatting on the ground and pointing. "This is it. The truss structure I was telling you about. This bridge was built in 1874!"

His enthusiasm is contagious, and I listen as he talks about how the mill was one of the first in the country to use roller mills, whatever that means. "Dad and Uncle Kellen used to bring us here hiking," he tells me. "They'd run the trail and we'd try to keep up." He tugs on my hand and looks both ways before pulling me inside the covered bridge. "See how the beams form Xs all along the interior?"

Liam Brady is fully delighted by this structure, and by the longevity that's allowed it to stay standing so long. I don't want to interrupt him telling me about his delights, but I can't wait another second to kiss him, so I stretch up on tip-toe and press my lips to his. I love the feel of his beard against my face, and I nuzzle against him like a cat until he presses me back against the wall. "I can't believe I'm making out in the Howe Truss bridge," he murmurs.

"Play your cards right along the hike, and I'll give you a handy in here later," I tease. His eyes widen, and I realize I've just discovered structural engineering porn exists. Or maybe I invented it. I bite my lip and rub a thumb along his jaw, savoring.

He clears his throat. "We'd better get going so I can buy you ice cream," he tells me. Liam leads the way along the trail that clings to a creek, where we watch as kayakers and white water rafters float down the rapids. We even come upon a waterfall, and I can't help but rush to stand under the rushing, pristine water.

It falls around my face and hair, and I just stand there, loving the rushing, wild rawness of it. "There's nothing more powerful than water," I shout to Liam, who has joined me in the wet.

"You look like you did the first day I kissed you," he says, his eyes dropping to my shirt. I realize with a rush of heat to my center that I must have passed straight on from the puking part of pregnancy to the "ever horny" phase that Emma told me about, where she frequently texted Thatcher to rush upstairs from his glass studio to service her before she'd melt with need.

"Huh," I say, looking around for a cave or alcove where we might find a few minutes of privacy. There have been a steady stream of other hikers passing us in either direction. Spotting no secret nooks, I pout.

"What's wrong?" Liam steps out of the flow of the water and shakes his head, his dark hair flopping like he's in a shampoo commercial. Or a private erotic video just for me.

"I want you," I say, shrugging. "I'm horny as fuck, Liam, and I don't know what to do about it."

His demeanor shifts instantly and he beckons for me to follow him down the trail back in the direction we came. Stepping off the trail and higher into the woods, I notice that the trees grow thicker here, that there are no other hikers. "Where are we going?"

"I know a spot," he tells me, and we duck behind a wide tree. I can hear the water flowing below us, a few kids exclaiming when they see the falls. But we are completely hidden from view up here. I grin as Liam backs me against the tree, and then his mouth meets mine.

Our actions are quick and hungry, needy and rough as he spins me around and yanks down my shorts. I spread my feet as far as I'm able with the shorts around my ankles, and I hear the rasp of his zipper right before I feel the heavy, hard length of him against my damp skin.

It doesn't take long. The thrill of being outside, paired with my overwhelming need, has me screaming into his palm over my mouth within minutes. His breath grows ragged in my ear and he joins me, silencing his cries in my shoulder, his energy sinking into my skin and adding to the electrical fire exploding in my body.

After, soggy and sated, we sit in his hatch in the parking lot of the ice cream stand. He stares at me as I lick my cone, and I wiggle my brows at him. As we head for home, he speeds down the highway.

"Liam Brady, are you violating a traffic rule?" I place a palm on his thigh, loving the feel of his muscles tensing beneath my hand.

"I'm very unlikely to get pulled over at this speed," he tells me. And then, considering, "I'm also very unlikely to drive in such a way as to hurt anyone." He swallows. "Maybe you should take your hand off my leg, though. Just in case."

CHAPTER THIRTY-SIX
LIAM

"What's different about you?" Cal stares at me in the kitchen at work and I realize I'm leaning on the counter, not moving.

"Nothing," I say. "Not really." Nothing except that I think I'm in a relationship for the first time, maybe ever, unless you count a sort of perfunctory experience with my research partner in my college engineering seminar. It didn't take us long to realize we were more excited by eccentrically curved beams than we were by one another.

Cal continues to study me, and I wonder if this morning's lovemaking is somehow visible. I showered afterward, combed my hair. Trimmed my beard but didn't shave it, because my girlfriend says she likes the soft hair, and that makes me want to keep it.

"Is Maddie my girlfriend?" I don't realize I've uttered it out loud until Cal squints over his coffee mug.

"That seems like a question you should maybe ask her? I have no idea." He takes a long sip. "Although, she does live with you and is pregnant with your progeny. So probably? You guys still doin' it or do you have to stop that when a woman is pregnant?"

"Aw, come on, Callum." Orla smacks him upside the head, causing him to slosh coffee on his shirt. I watch in horror as he doesn't respond to move to mop it up.

"What, it's a fair question. Can the baby, like, see the penis during sex?"

My entire family is now standing around the kitchen. They must have all prowled in like cats while I was daydreaming. My father pours himself some more of his fancy gourd tea that he orders from South America. "The uterus is a closed off structure while the baby is in there," he says. "There's a plug at the bottom, and it comes out during labor. Looks like a giant booger."

I should be grossed out by that. Cal and Orla look like they're going to vomit. But instead, I'm itching to go look up how all that works. "What is the biological makeup of the plug," I ask Dad, wondering if this type of scaffolding can be useful in any engineering applications. "Could something similar solve our problems with the oil seeping up near Detroit?"

Kellen nods at this. "You know, Liam, that's not a bad idea," he says. "Zack, can you join Liam and me in an hour to map out some proposals? Let's use our time this morning researching nonporous membranes."

I whistle as I walk to my office, excited that once again my personal life seems to blend into my professional life if I stop hyperfocusing on it. Maddie leaves laundry draped over furniture. Not just in her bedroom, but all over our apartment. But I care about this less than I did with Cal because Maddie also greets me with sex when I walk in the door from work. She says the orgasms are good for me, and I suspect she is right.

She starts her new job with my mother on Monday and says she's using this week to catch up on all the important things she's been wanting to read. Every day this week, I've come home to find her giddy and turned on. So today, when I walk in the door to see her lying on the floor in the living room, I panic.

"Maddie!" I rush over to her, tripping over a pile of books by the coffee table.

"Oh, hey, Yum," she says, sleepily. She drops her book.

"What are you doing down there? Let me see your monitor app." She's woozy like when she's having a low, and glancing at her book title, it seems to be a thriller—the kind of book that earlier this week had her calling me at work so she could let her heart rest in between chapters.

She shoves her phone inside her shirt. "No. Quit being bossy." Maddie reaches for her fanny pack, I assume to grab a snack, but she's not wearing it. Because she didn't leave the house today.

"Did you eat today, Maddie?" I walk to the pantry and grab a few packages of food to bring over to her. She struggles to a sitting position and rips at the bags.

She shrugs. "Probably? Oh, that hits the spot." Silently, I get her a juice box from the fridge and open it for her, sitting next to her on the floor. "Thanks, Yum."

I don't like that she was here alone while this happened, while she seems to be experiencing a dangerous low. "I don't like this," I tell her, working to control my fear and my temper.

"Yeah, well, this is me," she says, shoveling peanut butter into her mouth. "I have diabetes, Liam."

I fight the urge to snap at her, to tell her that she needs to work harder to maintain safe levels, that she needs to think about the baby. "You can't skip meals while you're pregnant," I say, deciding that feels like the most appropriate thing I can insist on.

She glares at me. "I didn't skip a meal. I never skip a meal. I just..." She sighs and finishes the juice with a slurping sound. "I felt my numbers tanking and couldn't seem to make my way to the kitchen." We both sit quietly for a moment, me trying not to scream, her thinking lord knows what. "I've been having a hard time keeping my numbers up this week," she admits.

I rake my fingers through my hair. "Did you tell Dr. Cranor? Why didn't you tell me? I could have worked from home and been here. I could have helped you."

"I don't need a babysitter, Liam. I'm an adult."

"Well you're not really acting like one right now," I spit back at her. "If you're having a health challenge, you need to consult your health team. If you can't stand the idea of keeping your baby's father in the loop, you could at least loop in your beloved doctor you're always talking about!"

"What's that supposed to mean?" Maddie gathers up the wrappers and tries to stand. She grabs the arm of the couch to steady herself and I feel my body clench, worried she'll hit the ground. But she doesn't she marches over to the trash and starts cleaning up the remnants of her day spent reading.

I run my fingers along the spine of the book she was reading, where she's marked certain pages with yellow tabs and I can see her hand written notes in the margins—places she admired use of detail or certain adjectives. She wasn't just reading to escape. Her creative mind is always working. Hell, she probably needed more calories than usual just to keep up with her thought process as she tore through this book today.

"It means it's not just you anymore," I tell her. "It's not you against a world that's different from you." She looks like she might cry. "You have to let someone help you."

Her nostrils flare as she takes in my words. "I don't want a caregiver," she says. "I want a partner."

"Well, tell me how to be that, without you winding up on the floor in the living room," I spit back. Neither of us says anything for awhile. Eventually, I get up and order us pizza for dinner. By the time I finish making the phone call, Maddie has cleaned up all the laundry and books that were peppered throughout the room. The sight of the tidy, orderly space doesn't make me feel calm as it usually does.

I stare down the hall toward the closed door of her room and feel like I'm sinking.

CHAPTER THIRTY-SEVEN
MADDIE

By Monday, things are still a little tense with Liam but we are cheerful together in the morning. "Want me to iron your dress," he offers when he sees me shaking it out as I pull it from the dryer. He is, of course, standing in his neatly pressed boxer shorts and socks, concentrating on a pair of khakis.

"Is it casual Monday for you, Yum?" I gesture at the pants.

He shakes his head. "Oh, no. We're doing a minor field visit with Clay today. I won't be tramping through tall grass, but we are visiting a transformer." He steps into the pants and gets started on his shirt. "I figure this is a nice compromise."

I smile at the short-sleeved button down he's chosen, glad he isn't trying to wear a tie out to inspect power towers. "My dress is a lovely rayon blend," I tell him. "No ironing necessary." I slip it over my head and adjust the chunky necklace I chose to match my orange fanny pack. "How do I look?"

He smiles. "Fantastic as usual." He looks down to line up his buttons, then snaps his head back at me. "Oh crap. You have final contract negotiations with my mom today, don't you?"

I laugh at his aloofness. "I do indeed. I don't really think 'contract negotiations' is the right term. But yes. We're chatting."

He nods and keeps ironing. "And don't forget we're barbecuing with Emma and Thatcher tonight to celebrate my contract." It's possible

Emma is equally as excited about my new job as I am. She mentioned inviting my mother, and I make a note to check if that ended up happening.

Liam frowns. "Hm," he says. Then he shakes his head and bends to put on his shoes.

"What's up?"

"Nothing." He gives his outfit a final smooth with his palms and reaches for his black duffel. I catch a glimpse of his tool belt and hard hat before he zips it shut. He drops a kiss on the top of my head. "I was just thinking about something else." He leans against me, pressing his forehead against mine. I inhale the soapy scent of him.

This feels nice. Comfortable. And then, "Make sure you're eating today? Don't let Mom work you til you forget?"

There it is again. The worrying. "I'm sure you don't mean for that to sound so patronizing," I tell him. "But that's how I receive it. I think you saw that I already had a bunch of oatmeal as a pre-breakfast."

Liam closes his eyes and nods. "I'm trying, Maddie. I'm sorry."

"Thank you." I sigh, watching as he leaves for the office. I decide to go for a walk while I wait for my call with Sheila. I wander down a side street in Lawrenceville, noticing the cobblestones—then I smile, remembering Liam telling me that they're actually called Belgian Block, and it's a completely different material than cobblestones.

I know he's trying. I know he's fastidious. We can figure this all out together. I walk back into the apartment and call Sheila, who picks up on the first ring.

"You excited to get to work with our slogan?" She laughs.

"Just about," I joke back. We chat for awhile about the current work load and she briefs me on some of the clients she's designing for this month.

"We're doing an annual report for an engineering firm—not Beltane." I smile at her jab. "They've asked us to provide content, too, since none of their people know how to describe what they do so investors will care. Then we've got a fun pamphlet for a research team studying the impact of play on early childhood learning."

Her mention of early childhood reminds me that we still have to discuss leave. "Oh, while we're talking about kids," I say, rummaging in my fanny pack to pull up my calendar app. "I'm going to have a lot of appointments coming up. I was hoping we could discuss some flex hours while I manage those?"

She makes a grunting sound that reminds me of Liam. "Flex all the time that you need, dear. I hope everything's ok?"

That's kind of an odd question for her to ask, but I guess all she's had is Liam's side of the story and I'm sure he made me sound like a ticking time bomb. "Everything looks good so far, they tell us." I scroll through the dates. "Looks like I should expect my leave to start in April." I pause, hopefully.

"Leave?" She sounds deeply confused.

I frown. "My maternity leave..." I feel a strange sensation as I realize Liam did not actually inform his mother that I am pregnant with his child. Between the grunts and coughs I hear, Sheila sounds like she is experiencing a wide array of emotions simultaneously.

"Should I infer that you are having a baby?" I nod, though she can't see. "With...my son?"

"I'm going to kill him," I tell her.

Sheila starts to cry. "Please forgive me, Madison. I'm so overcome right now." She takes a few deep breaths and then says, "I'm going to be a Mi-mi. Or am I more of a Gi-gi?" I hear her clap her hands. "April? The baby will be here in April?"

"Sheila," I say, "I am so upset that Liam didn't tell you last week when you had dinner. He assured me he was telling you."

"Wait," she says. "Did he already tell Mick?" I bite my lip and grimace. "I'm looping him in on the call. We're calling Liam."

I hear a bunch of beeping and then the sound of a call going to voicemail. "He's on a field visit today," I say, fussing with my phone to pull up the conference option. "Let me try."

I dial and he picks up after two rings. "Are you in distress?"

"Well, Liam," I start, but his mother cuts me off.

"Liam Brady, you failed to mention that you are going to be a father." I hear silence on the other end of the phone.

Then, "Can we talk about this later?"

"You will come and see me at my office as soon as you are done in the field," she says, and she hangs up on him. "Tell me how you're feeling, darling," she says. I give her a brief overview and I hear her breathe deeply. "Why on earth did he have to inherit his father's communication skills," she asks. "Don't answer that."

"I don't know what to say, Sheila," I stutter. "This all feels really complicated."

"Madison, I'm going to need to compose myself. Can we make a plan to speak later this week? After I've finished yelling at Liam and switched over to just being excited?"

We hang up and I send a string of furious texts to Liam.

> Do you want me to be unemployed? Get over here. I'm mad if you couldn't tell.

B

AN HOUR LATER, after I've paced circles throughout the apartment and considered rumpling all the folded shirts in his drawer, Liam bursts into the front door. "I let my guard down and I forgot something important," he says, staring at me. "This is me, unraveled. This is what happens when I'm not hyper focused on the details. It's a giant staircase, Maddie. It all builds upon itself and I forget to tell my mother I'm having a baby, just like I forgot to move the wash to the dryer."

"This is a little different than musty laundry, Yum," I retort, arms crossed. Liam leans against the door frame. "You're not even going to apologize for making me look like an idiot in front of my boss?"

"Considering you're the employee here, it seems like it was also irresponsible of you not to inform your employer about your life event."

I can feel my blood pressure going up and I reach into my fanny pack for a juice box. "You're right, Liam. I neglected to mention that. Because I assumed she already knew. Because you told me you were telling her." I sip the juice angrily and crush the empty carton in my fist.

Liam closes his eyes and grinds the heel of his hands against his temples. "You don't want me when I'm wound up and so worried about everything I can't concentrate. You don't want me when I'm unraveled."

"I do want you, Liam," I interject. But he shakes his head.

"You don't, though. You tell me the impact of my worrying is patronizing. You want me to leave you passed out on the floor rather than help you get glucose."

I feel my heart pounding in my chest. His words make sense, but I rail against them, feeling a lifetime of experience at war with my sense of reason in this moment. This is all too much for me right now and I stand up from the chair. "I need some time to think," I tell him. "Do not come over to Emma's later. I don't know if I'll come home tonight."

Liam looks wounded but, when I walk past him en route to leaving, he spits out, "Try not to trip and fall over the shoes you left on the floor."

CHAPTER THIRTY-EIGHT
LIAM

I'M NOT READY FOR A RELATIONSHIP. CLEARLY. I'M GOOD AT ORGANIZING THINGS, micromanaging people, and hyper analyzing small details. I am not good at interpersonal relationships. I storm out of my mother's office, angry at myself more than anything else.

I missed observing the first inspection session with our team on the first series of transformers, so I drive straight back out to the power towers, as Maddie called them. I spend the rest of the day re-checking Dave's work, and am then even more angry with myself when of course everything is perfect. Every decimal point aligned, every element scrutinized against the protocols Kellen and I developed for this project.

The apartment is empty when I get home, and neat as a pin. The kitchen smells like cleaners, and I growl, knowing Maddie must have made sure to scrub everything before she left me. Because I'm sure that's what happened. She left me. And I don't blame her.

I'm sure my dad can give me advice on setting up a custody arrangement and fair child support payments when the time comes. It's probably better for everyone if I stick to myself anyway.

I spend the evening watching movies on my laptop, forcing myself to follow Maddie's instructions not to go to her celebration picnic. I guess there's nothing really for her to be celebrating, since I apparently fucked up her job with my mother. By midnight, it's obvious she's not coming home tonight.

I go into her room, feeling like I'm invading her space. It's still littered with clothing and the dresser has stacks of medical supplies on it. I exhale a breath I hadn't realized I was holding. She's going to come back, at least to fetch her extra monitors and needles and things. All is not lost. Not yet.

In the morning, no amount of coffee is enough to energize me as I drive back out into the field. I startle Dave in the parking area near the next set of transformers. "Didn't think I'd have company today," he says, stepping into his harness and preparing to climb partway up the tower.

When I, too, pull a set of safety gear from my duffel bag, Dave frowns at me. "Liam, don't take this the wrong way, but what are you doing?"

Confused by his question, I proceed to investigate the base of the tower. "I'm inspecting this tower, Dave. Same as you."

He slithers back to the ground. "You paying me to duplicate work now? That don't seem very efficient from the client's perspective." He puts his hands on his hips. "I can either move on ahead to the next tower or you can maybe tell me what's going on here. You haven't been doing actual field work in five years and I *know* you don't think you need to recheck my work this way."

I blink at him a few times, considering how to even begin to tell him "what's wrong." *Hey, so I slept with someone I shouldn't have because I was unable to control my lust. Then I got her pregnant. Then I drove her away by being a maniac. So now I'm out here taking it all out on you and making you feel like shit, too.*

"Nothing's wrong," I tell him. "This is just a new project and I promised Clayton I'd oversee it personally."

Dave arches a fuzzy white brow at me. "Oversee a project or micro-manage it? Your uncle know you're out here like this?"

I sigh. "It's true that things have been upsetting at home," I tell him. That seems innocuous enough.

Dave nods and reaches into his tool belt for a bottle of water, which he sips slowly, squinting into the bright sky as he tips his head back. "I've always been a fan of your father's methods, the way he makes it his business to know about his employees' personal lives."

I snort. "You don't just think he's nosy?"

Dave shakes his head. "No, sir, I do not. Mick Brady believes, and I agree, that knowing someone's business can save lives. Take you for instance. It doesn't take a therapist to see that you're pretty upset. Don't look at me like that, Liam. You're practically vibrating."

I look down at my hands, which admittedly are twitching a bit. Dave nods. "Mick has seen how someone who's distracted doesn't necessarily make the most careful observations. Remember...well I guess you're too young, but thirty years ago one of our guys inspected a bridge the day after his wife left him. Moved a decimal point and the thing collapsed soon after."

I've heard this story. Over and over again, actually. "Yeah. The ten-million-dollar mistake." I snort. "Dad didn't even fire the guy."

Dave shakes his head. "No he did not. But he did make him go to therapy before he went back out into the field." Dave turns around and climbs back up onto his post, examining the joints for loose screws or rust or shoddy welding. "You want to talk about it yet?" He shouts over his shoulder, so I at least have the small mercy of not having to meet his eye.

I'm about to answer him when my cell rings, and I see that it's Clayton Monroe calling. "Crap, Dave, this is the client calling."

He waves me away and I walk back toward the company truck. "Clayton," I say, adding a false layer of cheerfulness to my voice. "What can I do for you?"

"How about you come meet me for a coffee and tell me why I just talked to Madison Parker and she was crying."

"I'm sorry, what? You were talking to Maddie?" None of this makes sense. Maddie mentioned helped Clayton before, but it doesn't make sense that she'd be crying in front of him, let alone talking to him today.

I drive to a coffee shop near the Allegheny Power offices and find Clayton seated at a table outdoors, a French press and two mugs on the table. He gestures to me and I pour.

"I was just out in the field with our best inspector, following up on some of the tower work," I sputter. "Things are looking pretty good."

"I'm not here to talk about that, Liam." I swallow thickly. "Maddie told me about the baby." My eyes fly open wider, not comprehending how I came to be having this conversation with this particular client. "Did she tell you I'm diabetic, too?" I shake my head and Clayton laughs. "Well, I did ask her to keep that private."

Clayton explains how he had been managing his diabetes poorly for years, giving himself multiple daily injections and pricking his fingers to take blood sugar readings. Maddie encouraged him to get a pump and monitor like she has. "She does seem to value her external pancreas," I mutter. Clayton nods. "That was very nice of her to support you through that change."

"Yes, well, she's a nice person," he tells me. "I know from experience how she must have grown up with very little control over any of the choices in her life. Visiting the school nurse a dozen times a day while the other kids are playing. Skipping the cake at birthday parties." Clayton looks off into the distance over my shoulder and sips his coffee. "Technology has come a long way since I was diagnosed, and I can tell you she has changed my life, Liam."

I fiddle with my coffee cup, spinning it around in my hands on the table, unsure what to say in response. Clayton says, "I don't need to tell you that she bristles when people tell her what she can and cannot do. But, I can also tell you that my wife nags me half to death about keeping up with my numbers. She wants to put the app on her phone now that I've got this monitor, so she can check in on me."

"I relate to that urge," I say quickly, before I can reconsider tempering the truth of it. "I hate not knowing if she's ok."

Clayton reaches for my hand, startling me. He looks me in the eye. "You know what my wife said after she joked about that app?" I shake my head. "She reminded herself that she has to let me make my own bad choices, just like I've been doing for decades." He tells me about all the times he's had too much to drink at work meetings, nearly gone into a diabetic coma, or not paid attention to his supplies and run out.

"I don't know how to let Maddie risk her health in that way," I whisper. "I don't know how to be ok with her being unwell."

Clayton nods. "I went ahead and told my wife to put the app on her phone, because I know it makes her feel better. And within a few days of me taking care of myself when things went off course, she stopped checking it as much."

I can't think of anything to say in response to that. "I've never had a lot of practice trusting other people," I tell him. Clayton chuckles at that.

"Well, you know I've known your father for a long time," he says. "I can see how you turned out to be sort of uptight to balance him out."

I think about what Dave said earlier, that my father seems like he's meddling in people's business, but his intent is to help them to their safest work and take care of themselves. For the first time in my life, I feel like I see some part of myself in him.

I assure Clayton I'm working on the behaviors that made Maddie cry this week, even if I'm not actually sure how to go about working on them. How do I learn to be supportive without smothering? There's no algorithm for that, that I know of. No checklist to follow. I pay for the coffee and drive back to my office, feeling more lost than before I arrived.

CHAPTER THIRTY-NINE
MADDIE

E MMA DID INVITE MY MOTHER, AND SHE'S MAKING ME TELL HER LATER. T ELL HER everything. She sent me to timeout in the guest room while she walks to the farmers market for cheese, and says I'm supposed to think about why I've been so reluctant to tell my mother I'm pregnant.

This guest room is really the toddler's room, and this is where Emma has offered to let me stay tonight and for as long as I need. Which means Ricky is bunking with Emma and Thatcher, making me feel even worse. I should be running to my parents when I'm in a black mood. I should be crashing on their couch, not making my best friend share a bed with a stinky, incontinent person.

I just can't bear to disappoint my mother in this way. I know what my parents have sacrificed to usher me safely to adulthood and I feel so driven to make good on their investment in me. Obviously they don't *want* to be in their 50s still working to make rent on a one-bedroom apartment.

Mom was out of work for nearly a year when I was diagnosed. She was a constant presence by my side. Never one to cuddle or coddle, she made me do my own injections right from the get-go. But she was always there for it. Nodding. Urging. "You can do this, Madison. You must do this. It won't hurt for long."

What on earth will she think of me when I tell her? Unemployed, single pregnant woman who is also probably homeless. Things are not looking good for me. I haven't heard back from Sheila yet about a start date. I just feel like I'm hiding. In a room decorated with spaceships, sleeping in a twin bed with guard rails and comet sheets. Which, if I'm being honest, are really nice sheets.

Emma shouts her return from the hall. She's supposed to be revising her latest book. Instead, she's fretting over me. I hate this.

"I'm going to make the macaroni salad," I announce, stomping to the kitchen. "Go finish your edits," I tell her.

She grins. "The beta readers loved the draft, Mad! They're so much nicer than Phil."

That gets a laugh from me. "Beta readers...that's like the people who read it after your editor?"

She nods. "So that would be like if Phil read it, you made changes, and then passed it back around the news desk. Only it's a whole book and not just an article."

"I love that they love it, Ems! Can I be a gamma reader? Do you have those?" She laughs and tells me no, but promises me a first copy.

The mood is lighter as I set about making the macaroni salad while Emma loudly edits from her office. She reads aloud while she types, which makes me smile because she's always done that.

Liam tells me I hum while I write, which I found surprising. Not because it sounds improbable, but because nobody has mentioned it to me before. You'd think after years in a frantic newsroom someone would have at least handed me a microphone as a joke. Maybe they were all muttering their own words aloud like Emma and never heard me.

I make the macaroni salad and get started forming patties from the ground meat Thatcher picked up earlier. I am elbow deep in the mixing bowl when he comes up from his studio to shower, and Emma emerges from her office.

"I don't want you to get mad at me," she says, and I immediately drop the latest patty I'm forming.

"Aw, come on, Emma. I thought you were in there editing?"

She shrugs. "I can edit *and* meddle," she says. "I'm an excellent multi-tasker." She nods approvingly at the burgers, waving her hand to waft the garlic and fresh rosemary aromas toward her nose. "These are gonna be good, Mad."

"Speaking of mad..."

"Oh," she says, "Right. Well..."

Nicole bursts into the loft. "I came bearing gin," she says. "It's gin weather. Wait. Neither of you can drink it." She frowns at the bottle, as if she's just remembering that her best friend can't mix alcohol with epilepsy. "Thatchy and I are gonna drink gimlets and dispense wisdom."

"Since when am I wise?" Thatcher Stag emerges from the bedroom and pulls his wife in for a kiss, rubbing his beard on her cheek until she squeals. The whole thing just makes me feel sad and reminds me that I'm not talking to Liam. Emma managed to find a guy who isn't freaked out by her condition, but is also not hyper vigilant and trying to change her. "I'm going to grab the kids from Ty and I'll be back for those gimlets," he says with a wink at Nicole.

"He's really grown on me," she says, watching him leave and starting to mix the cocktails. "Maddie, is your mom going to want a double or a triple when you finally spill the beans?"

Right on cue, my mother arrives at the loft.

I groan at the thought, but I'm glad Nicole is here.

I hear her fumbling with the heavy rolling door and Emma hugs her as she helps her inside. Like I said, my mom isn't a hugger, so she immediately knows something is up.

She plants her hands on her hips and squints at me. "Melissa called me the other day," Mom says. "She's worried."

Crap. I never called her after my ultrasound. I sigh. "I do owe her a phone call, that's true. She should have called me instead of you!"

"A daughter can't call her mother?"

"And why are we having dinner at Emma's house? I thought you were living with Nicole. Last time I talked to you, you were living with—oh, hi Nik." Nicole waves and gestures toward the pitcher of alcohol.

"She and Zack needed their space," I mumble.

Mom rolls her eyes. "Spill, Madison."

Nicole slides her a drink and flops onto the couch, landing on a squeaky baby toy that she doesn't bother to dig from out beneath her.

Like that deflated, squashed rubber giraffe, I sink into a stool and bury my face in my hands. I tell my mother everything and brace for her stern words.

Only, they don't come.

I look up from my hands to see her standing next to me, one hand on her heart, the other pressed to my shoulder with a reassuring squeeze. "Oh, Madison," she says. "Why didn't you tell me sooner?"

And then she totally shocks me by pulling me in for a hug. She did not hug me when I moved out for college. She did not hug me when I landed my job at the Post. We've done a few awkward back pats at Christmas and on birthdays, but this is a deep squeeze like people give when they haven't spent all their spare energy surviving a health crisis and scrimping to pay medical bills.

I decide to just lean in to the pregnancy hormones and I start crying in my mother's arms. "I feel like such a loser," I whimper.

"Loser?" Mom places her hands on my shoulders and straightens her arms so she can look at my face. "How are you a loser?"

"Um, I'm a jobless, homeless single pregnant lady who drove off her..."

"Can we call him a lover?" Nicole shouts this from the couch, where she crosses her legs and sets off another squeak from the toy beneath her ass. "I've always wanted a lover. Baby daddy just sounds so much less romantic."

I roll my eyes. "Anyway, Liam wants nothing to do with me. He thinks I'm irresponsible and that I'm going to kill the baby."

"Did he say those words?" Mom clutches at her chest and presses a hand to my stomach, where the slightest bulge is beginning to emerge.

"Not in those words," I say. I tell her how he keeps asking after my numbers, yells at me about leaving shoes on the floor. "He's so rigid."

Nicole gulps down the rest of her drink and walks over to the counter. "Mrs. Parker," she says, "Did you know I'm living with Liam's brother? He's my lover." She frowns at the pitcher of drinks. "Ok, I hear how it sounds weird now. Anyway, Liam and Zack grew up in a kind of chaotic house."

Nicole tells my mom how Mick Brady went through two divorces one after the other and soon after that, Kellen and Orla moved in. "There was always somebody leaving or dying," Nicole says. "Between the custody transfers and a grieving uncle and an...eccentric dad...no wonder Liam is uptight."

Mom is now rubbing my back, sipping her drink slowly, obviously observing that Nicole made them very strong. "I'd bet your diabetes sets off all his alarm bells," Mom says.

I bite back my response that he, too, sets off my alarm bells. Mom continues. "All those fears he must have had...kids don't do well with instability." Mom takes another sip. "We worked really hard to make sure Melissa understood that she was supported even when I was in the hospital with you."

I remember when Mom would leave for stretches of time to hang out with my sister. I guess I assumed she was just running her to and from softball practice, but Mom talks about how they mostly had long conversations. "She always says she became a nurse because of me," I say.

Mom nods. "It was so important for her to know and understand *how* everything would be ok. She felt more comfortable when she had more knowledge about what was going on with her little sister." Mom kisses me on the cheek.

"Maybe there's a way for Liam to feel comfortable in a way that doesn't make you feel like you're visiting the doctor instead of spending time with *your lover.*" Mom emphasizes this last phrase in a deep, husky voice, making Nicole and Emma crack up.

We set about firing up the grill while we wait for Thatcher and then we all agree Nicole is too drunk to help at all and send her over to a lawn chair. I hear what they're saying, about how all my variables must be sending Liam into a mental tailspin on the reg. I just don't see how we can find a happy medium together.

"You gonna call him," Emma asks, nudging me with her hip while we stare at the trio of gin-drunk adults playing kickball with the Stag kids.

I shake my head. "I don't know what I'd say yet," I tell her, laughing as Thatcher scores a run, beating out his three year old at home plate like it was a fair matchup.

I sleep over in the rocket sheets room, and in the morning I watch as Emma and Thatcher cycle through the entire span of human emotions as they try to get their kids out the door. One of the four of them starts to cry every couple of minutes, but then someone burps and they all burst out laughing.

The spectacle makes me feel simultaneously hungover and hopeful.

"You heard from Liam at all?" Emma and Thatcher are taking turns blowing raspberries on Ricky's stomach while he squeals in laughter. I shake my head, wondering if Liam knows how to blow raspberries.

"Maybe just a text to let him know you're thinking of him," Emma says, handing Thatcher the kiddo and smiling at me. "I believe in you two."

I bite my lip and type the best thing I can think of.

> Hey.

I immediately see the three dots on the screen, indicating that he's writing back.

> Is everything ok? Are you and the baby ok?

Three more dots as I open my mouth to groan.

> That's me being overly anxious again. I'm sorry. How are you doing? Do you have enough fish crackers?

That makes me laugh, so I send him a smiling emoji.

> Plenty of snacks here. See you at our appointment later?

> I wouldn't miss it

he writes, and I know it's true.

> You bringing a clipboard for all your questions?

He sends a laughing emoji.

> Got them all memorized, Maddie.

I move to slide my phone back in my pocket, but it vibrates as another message comes in.

> I miss you.

> You, too

I tell him. And it's true. We need to talk and I need to figure a lot of shit out, especially about my work situation with his mother. But I do miss him. And for now, that feels like a start.

CHAPTER FORTY
MADDIE

THATCHER DROPS ME AT THE HOSPITAL THAT AFTERNOON FOR MY APPOINTMENT. I insisted to both Emma and him that I was perfectly capable of driving myself, but they insisted I be dropped at the door, where a nervous Liam waited with his hands in his suit pockets.

He gives an awkward, confused wave at Thatcher, trying to place him and failing, until I say, "That's Emma's husband. Nicole's boss's brother."

Liam scrunches up his face, putting all those data points together, and eventually smiles tightly. "Hey," he says.

"Hey." We walk inside and down the stairs to the waiting room. Liam babbles about the construction of the curved staircase and bannister, admiring the craftsmanship of the brass that I'd never noticed before this moment. "I like how you really see things that most people don't notice," I tell him.

He smiles and rubs my shoulder as I sign in, and I let him. This is our first visit with Dr. Hudson without Dr. Cranor, and I feel nervous, despite knowing she is someone Emma trusts. "Maddie," she says, when we walk into her office. "So nice to see you again." I do like that we are starting in the office, fully clothed. I remind myself this is a good sign.

Liam offers his hand and Dr. Hudson shakes, then starts going over information from my chart. "Dr. Cranor thinks things are going well for you managing your blood sugar," she says. "Everything looks really good, Madison."

I grit my teeth when Liam holds up an index finger and asks, "Is it normal that she might sometimes experience an extreme low? Where she can't stand up or think straight?"

Dr. Hudson nods and says, "Hmm, unfortunately yes. Diabetics often experience lows during early pregnancy. It can be very hard to balance the endocrine system while the body is making an endocrine system for a *new* body."

I'm not sure how I feel about this conversation. It's true I had that experience and I remind myself it's perfectly reasonable for Liam to feel concerned when he found his pregnant baby-mama on the floor unable to get up. I also deeply resent and fear the idea of other people dictating what I can and cannot do. I start to wonder if I'd feel differently about this if I had gotten pregnant on purpose.

Dr. Hudson continues talking and my thoughts wander to my relationship with Liam, to my physical attraction to him. I wonder if that's enough. Hot sex and an admiration of his keen powers of observation. "So anyway," Dr. Hudson says, "As we discussed, there's a risk that your baby could develop a small ventricular septal defect. I'm recommending a transvaginal fetal echocardiogram, Madison."

"Excuse me?" I'm familiar with this term. Emma had a few of these while she was pregnant the first time, and she said they took two hours. She hated them and cried before each of those appointments, but as Dr. Hudson talks about the risks to heart development for babies of diabetic mothers, I wonder if Emma cried because she was scared for her baby or if the procedure was just so terrible.

Liam holds up a hand. "Can we pause," he asks, and turns toward me in his chair. "Maddie, you seem upset about this."

All I can muster is a nod and a thick swallow. Liam also nods. "Is this type of test absolutely necessary to detect an abnormality?" He puts on his "very concerned" engineer demeanor and crosses his arms over his chest.

Dr. Hudson says, "It's a very low risk procedure. I believe it's warranted in Maddie's case."

Liam frowns and looks at me again. He shakes his head. "Maddie is used to a model of care that involves the least intervention until more is necessary." I stare at him, wondering where this speech is coming from. He looks at me and rests a hand on my thigh. "Would you agree, Maddie?"

Speechless, I nod. Why does it feel different this time when he's being bossy about my body? As I'm struggling to figure this out, Liam continues. "I read a study from Boston that indicates...excuse me a minute." He pulls up his phone and reads, "Where there is access to skilled comprehensive ultrasound services, fetal echocardiography adds little to the care of women with diabetes." He looks up at Dr. Hudson. She squints at him. He continues. "There's another brand new study from Israel that says ultrasound at 13 weeks gestations reasonable to assess fetal hearts in diabetic women."

Liam slides his phone back in his pocket while I stare at him. "You read all that?" My voice is quiet.

He turns to look at me. "I want to know everything about you and the baby, Maddie." His stare is intense. "I'm trying so hard."

Dr. Hudson coughs. "It sounds like you're requesting a literature review before we proceed," she says, and I like how she's coaching me toward something that feels comfortable.

"Yes," I say. "Yes, I'd prefer that approach."

We finish up our visit and I schedule the ultrasound with the caveat that we might switch the imaging depending on what the team thinks after they review the studies Liam mentioned.

Dr. Hudson slides me a new batch of pamphlets before I move to the exam room portion of the appointment. This is a batch all about the horrors of being high risk, complete with illustrations of wide-eyed women.

"I hate these pamphlets," I tell her. "They don't get the tone right at all to connect with their audience."

Dr. Hudson glances over my shoulder, looking at the materials. "You're a writer like Emma," she says. "I forget that sometimes." She pulls a glossy magazine off the small table by her office door. "Our publicity department at the hospital has been hurting." She shows me an article about her and her research. "I hate how they framed the results of my study on women living with substance use disorder."

I quickly scan the article, seeing inflammatory language. "This is supposed to showcase the research here?" I shake my head. "I wrote better copy my first year at the Post."

Dr. Hudson smiles at me. "You should lend us your skills here," she says. "The women's research institute is a scientific nonprofit housed here inside the hospital. We get to do a lot of really cool stuff."

As she talks about the work, I feel myself growing excited. She's right about the research here. On my beat at the Post, I've covered her colleagues' work getting FDA approval for anti-nausea drugs for pregnant women and launching 4D mammogram technology. "Is the institute hiring writers?" I hadn't seen anything open like that, but then I haven't looked.

I went right from unemployment to accepting some nepotism on multiple levels. Dr. Hudson tells me to use her name when I apply for the communications position, and I leave the hospital feeling...fantastic.

I walk next to Liam, nearly skipping as we head toward his car. Without thinking I walk the entire way with him until he says, "Are you, um, coming with me?" He rakes a finger through his hair, which has gotten long again and I like it. It makes him appear less perfectly put together, more approachable.

"Oh," I say. "That's right. We're fighting." I pause. He kicks at a pebble on the roof of the parking garage, where I notice he parked even though I wasn't with him when he arrived. "You were amazing in there," I say.

He looks perplexed. "I was? I worried that was more of the same. Micro-managing you." His voice drifts off and he looks a bit tortured.

"It felt different today," I say. "Like you were using your anal retentive powers for good instead of making me feel like some sort of failure."

"You could never be a failure, Maddie," he says. "I admire you too much to ever think that." We stare at each other for a long while until he asks if I'd like to go get a coffee with him before he heads to work.

"Might as well," I say. "I'm unemployed. I think. I've been ignoring your mother."

LIAM

MADDIE ASKS IF WE CAN SWITCH OUR OUTING TO AN ICE CREAM EXCURSION WHEN she sees the place with the homemade waffle cones. Not certain about ice cream before nine in the morning, I agree anyway because I'm so eager to hear more about why she thought I was amazing during her appointment when I felt like I was steam rolling everyone with my research.

When they won't let Maddie get a mixed cone, I agree to order peach and share with her as she devours her pistachio cone, making sexy moaning sounds I shouldn't be responding to before work on a weekday. I cross my legs to mask my arousal.

"How did you know they'd ask about those specific tests," she asks, leaning over to take a big lick of my ice cream.

I let her, braving a small lick of her cone. I've never had pistachio ice cream before and am delighted by the subtle nutty sweetness within the vanilla. I realize that Maddie gets me to try new things, something that usually makes me uncomfortable. But maybe a little discomfort is a good thing. "I read about diabetic pregnancy each night before bed," I tell her, dabbing at my mouth with my napkin. "I know that fetal heart test is common, but I also read that it takes hours and is very uncomfortable. You know. They go up..." I drift off, not wanting to talk about a doctor inserting a medical device in her vagina while we're sharing ice cream in public.

She sighs dreamily. "They really should let me blend the peach and the pistachio," she says. "Anyway, you were totally right. I didn't like that idea at all and I'm already freaked out enough about the baby being healthy."

"I haven't been to medical school, but I have been to graduate school and I know how to read research papers for a literature review," I assure her. "I wouldn't have brought it up if I felt like it was unsafe to just use the ultrasound."

She nods, looking at me strangely. "I don't think I'm ever going to be able to not read the studies," I tell her. I think about my discussion about Clayton and how he sent his wife his data app, and how she stopped looking at it. I swallow. "I can probably do much better about following your lead about what you're feeling, though."

She squints at me and takes another huge lick of my ice cream. "And no more secrets from relatives where I don't know who knows what," she tells me, swatting me away as I aim for her cone. Then she sighs and offers me the cone, saying, "I need to do better understanding that you're worried about me, and that finding me on the floor is new and upsetting for you."

I bark out a laugh. "Upsetting is certainly one word for it." I nibble off a chunk of the waffle cone and hand her both cones to finish. "If you are going to get low a lot, what's the best way for me to respond? Most supportive I mean?"

She flushes and licks both the cones in succession. "That first night," she says. "You were so amazing." Her expression seems dreamy and I can't tell if it's because of the ice cream or she's remembering our experience fondly. I rack my mind, trying to remember what I did after I carried her inside.

"I fed you snacks and talked to you about bridges," I say, and she nods.

"Yes, Yum. And you rubbed my feet."

I shift toward her on the bench in front of the ice cream shop, where people are starting to walk past us on their way to work and school. "Maddie," I whisper, trying my hardest to seem sexy.

"Hm?" I suspect maybe, shockingly, it's working, because I watch as her pupils dilate and she leans closer to me.

I skate my hand up her leg, fingers edging in between her thighs. "I will talk about bridges with you any time, day or night."

Her head drops back as she laughs, the easy, delighted sounds pouring from her and shattering any remaining tension between us. While she laughs, I dot a kiss on her throat, and then lick a light line along her collarbone.

She gasps and looks at me, snapping her legs close together and trapping my hand between them. "Can we go talk about bridges? Like right now?" I nod. "You know I'm using a euphemism for sex, right," she asks, jumping up from the bench and tugging at my hand. "I'm going to need you to give me sex before you go into work."

I violate some traffic laws as I make my way home, pausing at red lights to taste her mouth, suck on her ear lobe, flick a finger across her nipples. I delight in my ability to make them rise beneath her clothing. "They're getting so big," I whisper, forcing my eyes on the road as I navigate into the garage beneath our building.

We frog march up to the apartment, pausing to make out on the stairs like we haven't seen each other in months. Like we're long term lovers reuniting, rather than two people starting a relationship who've been fighting for a few days.

"Can I get you a snack," I say into her mouth as I fumble to unlock the front door, pressing my bulge against her. The door opens and we fall inside, and her eyes widen as she pulls me to the ground, wrestling with my buckle. I realize her intention as she licks her lips and stares at my cock. "No," I say, "I meant like a food snack. You don't have to—oh shit."

Maddie licks a slow circle around my tip, groaning as she slides me inside her mouth. She is all heat and velvety smoothness as she sucks with increasing pressure until I can't stand it anymore. "Maddie," I whisper, pleading with her. "Please. I can't hold on if you keep doing that."

She looks up at me as I twist a hand gently in her hair, realizing how much I've missed the way she smells, the way she feels, the way she makes me feel. She pops off the end of my cock with a popping sound. "You know I like it when you let go," she says. She moves to dive back on, but I shake my head and growl, flipping us both until she's lying on her back and I'm supporting my weight above her.

"I'll let go inside you," say, kissing her again hungrily, tasting the ice cream on her tongue. She starts ripping at her clothes, trying to unclip her pump from her leggings beneath her dress. I drop back on my knees and help her, gently setting the pump next to her and making sure the tubes are out of my way before helping her peel off her clothes.

"Hurry, Yum," she yells as I wriggle to line myself up at her entrance. She spreads her thighs and I sink inside her as both of us groan. "Oh, god, yes, please."

Her hips buck up to meet mine and together we set a furious pace. Bucking and twisting, writhing and slamming together, we are both soon panting. "Touch me," she yells, grabbing for my hand, which I slide between her legs. She emits a guttural sound as I find her preferred rhythm and when I feel her start to tip over the edge, I join her.

On the floor, inside my front door, where I prefer to stack shoes neatly and hang coats on pegs, I bang my girlfriend so energetically I skin my knees on the polished concrete. As I come inside her, roaring my release, I don't regret a single thing about it. "This is perfect," I pant, peppering kisses on her face. "So perfect."

"Mmm," she moans happily. "It really is."

CHAPTER FORTY-TWO
MADDIE

"I have to call your mom," I whisper to Liam, snuggled in his bed with his head on my belly, as if he's listening to the life growing inside me. He grunts. "I don't think it's good if I work for her."

Liam props himself on one elbow, keeping a hand on my stomach and tracing the white circles connecting my tubing to my belly. "Don't you need the insurance?"

"I've got a few more weeks left on my COBRA plan," I say. "I think I'm going to go for that job that Dr. Hudson mentioned. With the research institute."

I had looked up the organization a little bit more. The job posting was primarily looking for someone to manage the magazine and materials they send to donors and the media, putting the research into language that regular people could understand, but also telling the stories of the people behind the research. "I have so many ideas," I tell him. "Like, we could tell Emma's story, for instance."

Liam kisses my hand. "Or yours," he says. I laugh. "I'm serious, Maddie. I read those pamphlets you hate from maternal fetal medicine. You could write all that stuff to sound more hopeful, the way you wrote about those fires Beltane dealt with." He bites his lip, concentrating. "People lost their lives, and your writing paid homage to how serious that was, but you still made us engineers sound like exciting heroes in that story."

"Hmm," I agree happily. "I did do a nice job on that section, didn't I?"

Liam wriggles up to kiss me on the cheek and then heads to the kitchen, shouting that he's going to invite his mother over for a talk. "You should probably get dressed," I shout after him, loving the sight of his hairy limbs heading down the hallway.

I lose myself in thought as I compose my letter to go with my resume. I realize, staring at the job description, that the hiring manager is someone I've worked with from my job at the Post. As a healthcare reporter in a city of hospitals, I got a lot of press releases sent my way.

"Dear Heidi," I write, remembering the polite and well-organized materials she always sent my way, hoping I'd come to an event and highlight researchers in an article. How do I communicate that I'm looking to switch over to her side of the story-telling team?

I wrestle with the email for a long time, until Liam pokes his head around the corner. "My mom is going to be here in 20 minutes," he says. "Can we start moving your clothing to this room?"

"What, now? This isn't the time for a big redecorating project," I tease. I shut my laptop and head down the hall to the other bedroom. I take note of the big, north-facing windows, realizing there won't be a ton of direct sunlight streaming in. This is a great room for a baby to nap.

I get lost in these thoughts, slowly dressing, imagining a crib in this space, a rocking chair. Imagining Liam in the rocker, explaining how the arched feet of the chair allow the motion as the pair of them gently sway.

I hear voices out front and when I poke my head down the hall, Sheila Brady dashes toward me and wraps me in her arms. "Oh, Maddie, I've been wanting to call, and then not wanting to meddle, but really wanting to call. How are you? Are you still puking? I brought you ginger tea. It was the only thing that helped when I was pregnant with Liam."

She clasps her hands in front of her chest. "A baby!"

Her joy is infectious, and when she and Liam usher me toward the couch, I let them fuss over me and make me a cup of the tea, even though I explain that I haven't thrown up in weeks. "Liam gets me these wonderful lavender candies," I tell her, leaning to show her a jar on the coffee table. I note that Liam has placed the jars of candy all throughout the apartment.

As I'm speaking, I start to feel a little light headed, and I frown, reaching for my phone to check my numbers. My monitor beeps as I'm looking, and I can feel Liam growing tense. "A low," he asks. I nod. He closes his eyes and swallows. "What do you need," he asks, and I exhale, feeling the deep growth behind his question. His body language shows me his concern, but I can see him wrestling with it as he tries to be supportive.

"I'm feeling like a banana," I say. "Hm, do we have soft pretzels?" He's up in a flash, rummaging in the freezer for the box of soft pretzels I had bought a few weeks ago when I first moved in. "Lots of salt," I shout to him.

"Medium salt," he says, and pauses. "Would you consider a medium amount of salt? I know it impacts blood pressure..." His voice drifts off.

"I really feel like a salty pretzel is what I need for my blood sugar right *now,*" I tell him. "You can feed me super bland food for dinner."

Considering this compromise, Liam liberally salts the pretzel as Sheila hustles to grab a banana. She's in the process of peeling it for me, when she looks down and laughs, handing it to me. "Everyone takes their bananas a different way," she says.

"That's true," I point out, peeling it halfway and munching, not caring about the banana strings like I know Liam does. I feel the fruit hit my stomach. I close my eyes while my body adjusts, aware that Liam and Sheila are quietly freaking out.

"Yum, why don't you show your mom the ultrasound video while my body catches up with my robot parts?"

Sheila perks up. "Video? Of the baby?" I sink into the couch while Liam shows his mom the video of our baby, his eyes flicking to me frequently but ultimately unable to look away from the magic on the video. He turns up the volume and the magic rhythm of that heartbeat reminds me that all is well inside me. All is well around me.

For now, all is well.

Liam massages my leg as I feel the sugar kick in. "I trust you to tell me when you need more help," he whispers. "You look better already. You feeling ok?"

I nod my head and rub his hand. "Thank you," I say. "This is what I need."

EPILOGUE: LIAM

"I'm never going to go into labor." Maddie groans from the bathtub as I tug on her hands to help her stand. Our son juts out in front of her, her belly impossibly round and swollen. She is the most beautiful woman I've ever seen.

"You will," I tell her. "He's just calculating the ideal entrance date." Maddie has been taking long soaks in our bathtub after a few visits to Zack and Nicole's place where she loved hanging out in their heated tank pool. We still haven't let on that we basically conceived the baby in there.

"You need to give me your prostaglandins," Maddie says, standing with her hands on her hips while I help her hook her pump back up since she struggles to reach around her belly these days.

I arch a brow at her. "My prosta what?"

"Haven't you been reading my pamphlets?" Maddie swats me with the towel. Her first order of business when she accepted her new job was revamping the high risk pregnancy literature that gets distributed at the hospital. I admit to being distracted and not reading the pamphlets.

"I've been studying the literature about labor and diabetes," I tell her, kissing her belly and watching as an elbow, or maybe a knee, makes its lumpy way across her taut skin. "And I've been spending a lot of time just marveling at this little dude as he moves inside you. I can't wait to hold him," I say, but when I look up, Maddie is still irritated.

"Prostaglandins is the hormone inside your sperm, Liam. It stimulates labor and thins out my cervix and such. I need you to give me your prostaglandins. Right now."

I swallow. "This isn't exactly the most romantic proposal I've ever had..."

"Buck up, Brady. Get your penis up, too. I'll meet you in our bedroom."

I watch, stunned, as Maddie waddles down the hall. I would never say waddle out loud, because that word upsets her, but it's the most accurate description for how she is walking with her sore hips and her off-balance weight distribution. If she's going through all these changes to help our son grow kidneys and eyelids, and she's asking for my cock right now, I feel like the least I can do is oblige her.

"All right," I say, entering our room. But she's still standing naked in the doorway, a stream of water trickling down her leg. "Hey! There we go." A mixture of excitement and relief washes over me when I observe that she's in labor. The past month, she's had four appointments each week, checking the baby's heart rate and amniotic fluid levels. I'm in a constant state of high alert, and am constantly working to temper my urges to put my family in a bubble and keep them safe.

Maddie's blood sugar has been so high lately. I've been trying to follow her lead. It's hard. I want to growl and demand that the doctors just induce her, but I guess that's all moot now. "He's coming, babe," I tell her. "It's time!"

"I don't think so," she says, her eyes wide. She's standing unmoving as I shuffle around the room grabbing her bag and trying to find the dress she mentioned she wanted to wear in labor. "I think I just peed myself."

"You still peeing?" The water hasn't slowed and is making a puddle on the floor. I carefully step around her to grab some towels, dropping one on the puddle and handing the other to her. She sighs and takes it from me.

"I'm scared," she says, her irritated facade slipping a little.

"Hey," I say, grabbing her arms. "Me, too. We've got this, though. Together."

I get her to the car and mutter while I drive. We've spent so much time talking about what she wants in labor, what she needs from me. I'm the protector. I'm the suspension bridge and I'm going to help her get that baby safely to the other side of her womb.

I park in the garage when we realize that's the closest walking path for her, and stick with our plan as we check in. Maddie told me she doesn't want students observing her labor. She doesn't want to be on display that way, and I promised I'd block the door with my body if I had to.

I called ahead, and they're expecting us—one of the few perks of having a high risk pregnancy is that we can bypass the circus in triage. A nurse gets Maddie hooked up to some monitors and immediately looks at me and says, "Her sugars are really high."

Maddie opens her mouth to protest, grimaces as a contraction hits, and I signal that I've got this. "Hey," I say to the nurse, sternly. "You should speak to Maddie, not me. And we know about the sugars."

Maddie groans and the nurse frowns, studying the monitors. "I'm going to see if Dr. Hudson is here," she says, and rushes out of the room.

"Yum," Maddie says, her eyes wide. "I think the baby is coming out. Like right now."

This sounds preposterous, because it's only been about an hour since her water broke. But I remind myself that some women are just fast birthers and some babies are just in a big hurry. A thought occurs to me. "Babe, were you maybe having contractions in the tub earlier?"

She closes her eyes to breathe. "Maybe? I don't know. Ohhhhhhhhhhhh god," she says, circling her hips as she stands beside the bed.

Dr. Hudson pops in the door just as Maddie drops to her hands and knees and growls. No, she roars. "Oh my," Dr. Hudson says, slapping a button on the wall and yanking on a set of gloves. I drop to the ground with Maddie, whose nostrils are flaring.

"My body is pooping," she says with a grunt.

"Baby is crowning," Dr. Hudson says from behind Maddie. She tosses Maddie's dress up over her back and, peeking around the corner, I see a tiny head sliding out of my girlfriend.

"Oh my god, Maddie," I whisper. "You're doing it. He's coming. Right now." I forget to freak out. I don't even need to recite the affirmations to remind myself not to micromanage. The past few months have been so much compromise, so much hard work.

And now, I'm in the zone. I feel like I see everything so clearly, that everything that matters to me is huddled on the floor of this hospital room.

"I love you," I tell her, feeling a tear leak down my cheek as I watch our son slither into Dr. Hudson's gloved hands.

Maddie sinks to the floor and reaches for the baby. Someone reaches around me and pricks the baby's heel and I snap my head around, enraged that we haven't even uttered his name and they're making him cry. It's then that I see the room is filled with people, all looking stern.

"Baby's sugars are very low," someone shouts as I try to block Maddie and the baby with my body. We were expecting this—if Maddie's sugar was high during labor, the baby's pancreas would try to balance that out. We made a plan to get him nursing right away. This is all part of our plan. It was a long plan and I added appendices I studied privately, just because there were so many contingencies and decision trees.

And now he's here.

"He's perfect, Maddie," I say, looking down at his dark hair, his tiny fingers.

"Arlan," she says, the name we were leaning toward. It means oath, and that's what he is. Our promise to keep trying, to keep working for our family.

"Madison, we think Arlan needs to go to the NICU," a nurse says at Maddie's shoulder, a reminder that we still have an audience. Maddie shakes her head.

"Weren't we expecting this?" I ask. We had discussed it at the coordinated care visit, where we had invited a neonatologist to join us last week. "He'll be ok." Maddie shifts around, trying to get her dress over her head and I help her as she places Arlan at her breast.

He squirms around a bit, still wailing, and soon attaches himself to her nipple. "Oh," she exclaims. "This is perfect."

I kiss her. I kiss him, still huddled over both of them on the floor. They are mine to look after right now, both so vulnerable. This is my time to shine, holding all of the potential scenarios in my head, all the responses we discussed as a team. I hear Dr. Hudson's voice in the background, and eventually I turn around. "Could you please page the attending physician from the NICU to come and speak with us?"

I turn back to my family and Maddie beams at me in gratitude.

By the time the chief baby doctor arrives, Maddie is cleaned up and lying in bed with Arlan attached to her breast. They take another reading while he's nursing, and he doesn't cry this time. He just keeps on sucking, holding on to his mother.

"I love you," she whispers into his head. She reaches for my hand and squeezes. "I love you, too, Yum." I am vaguely aware of the NICU doctor explaining that Arlan's levels are just fine and that he can stay right where he is.

I'm only partly aware of the staff gradually emptying out of the room as everything is cleaned up and put away, and I only turn my eyes away from my family when I hear the cacophony of my siblings and parents streaming into the room.

"Oh my god," Orla squeals. "Liam, you replicated yourself." Maddie smiles down at the baby, who does look exceedingly like me. They all ask to hold him and I shake my head.

"I haven't even held him yet," I say, keeping my voice low so I don't startle him. "He's very busy right now." I explain the importance of him staying with Maddie during these early hours. Dad surprises me by agreeing and only when he turns to ask Uncle Kellen if he remembers that with Orla, do we realize that he's not here.

"Maybe he's giving us some privacy," I mutter, kissing Maddie on the forehead. She looks tired. "Want me to kick them out?" I whisper this last question into her ear as my family argues over whether Kellen could possibly still be hanging out with his new neighbor. Apparently he's been spending a lot of time over there, tutoring her son in math.

Maddie doesn't answer, but seeing her tired smile, I turn around to face my family. "Bradys," I say, shooing them back from the bed. "Come back in the morning." With a flurry of rolled eyes and cuss words, most of these from Nicole, they all file out of the room promising to come back bearing pastries.

It's quiet in the room with just the three of us, and Arlan finally releases his latch on Maddie's breast. "Ready to take him," she asks. I'm overcome as she slides the tiny bundle we created into my arms.

"Oh," I sigh, inhaling the scent of him. I pull him tight against my chest. "Thank you," I tell her. "Thank you for him. For us. For everything."

She scoots over on the bed and I sit next to her. Together, we stare at our son and hold each other. "You are beyond anything I could have ever planned," I say. As I take her mouth in a kiss, I try to send her all the words I don't know how to form. "I love you, Madison Parker."

"That feels nice," she says. "I love you, too."

INSPECTION
A SILVER FOX ROMANCE

CHAPTER ONE
KELLEN

You should get out there again, Dad. My daughter's words ring in the air like someone struck a gong. I drop the wrench on the driveway, distracted and overcome by what she's said.

"I mean it." Orla stands with her hands on her hips, shaking her head before stooping to pick up the tool and check it for nicks. She hands me back the wrench and leans over my shoulder, peeking into the hood of her car where we've been investigating a clicking sound.

I blink and lean on the edge of the car, still stunned. "Dad," she says, her voice softer this time. "You've got a lot to offer. And you're all alone here." She gestures toward the house.

"Alone? Did you not sit crammed around my table last night with your cousins and uncle? What I wouldn't give for an evening alone." I'm exaggerating. My brother and his boys are over once a week, Orla a few times more than that. But I'm not lonely. Am I?

"Uncle Mick goes on a ton of dates," she says. "Maybe he could introduce you to someone."

I snort and take the wrench back from her. My brother is a hopeless ladies man. He burned through two wives in four years and has spent the past few decades in a series of month-long expensive flings with women who always seem to hover around, well, Orla's age. "I'm not interested in anything my brother has to say about romance," I say, shaking the wrench at her before leaning back into the hood. "I think I need to adjust your valve train, sweetie."

"Show me," she says. I smile, proud of her endless curiosity and drive for independence. She reminds me so much of her mother. Helen always wanted to know how to fix basic things in her cars, too. I let myself wonder what it would be like if all three of us were out here together, looking inside Orla's "vintage" hatchback. I sigh. Fifteen years. That means the crappy car is the same age as our grief.

I show Orla how to check the pushrod and the camshaft. I hand her the tools and stand close by, quietly offering instruction and then waiting for her to make the adjustments. "Beautiful," I tell her, planting a kiss on top of her head.

She smiles as she lowers the hood and we wipe our hands on a rag before heading into the kitchen to wash up. Orla grabs the green tub of mechanic's soap from the labeled bin on the wall by the door, pushing into the house with her elbow so as not to get the paint greasy. *Who has time to date,* I think, looking at all there is to do to clean up after our project.

By the time I get the garage back in order and everything swept, I'll have just enough time for a run before this week's documentary. I'm working my way through the Ken Burns film series about the history of radio. I make a mental note to log in to the social media site where my film group is chatting about the program and sharing outside resources.

"Dad," Orla shouts, snapping her fingers and waving the soap in my face. "Hello??"

"Sorry, kiddo," I say, taking the tub from her and cleaning my hands. "I was just thinking about my film group."

"See, that's what I'm talking about," she says. "You could meet a nice lady who also likes nerd movies and you two could sit in real life and talk about the impact of alternating current on modern society."

"I talk about alternating current all day at work," I remind her. The engineering firm I started with my brother has grown to include divisions for civil, electrical, geotechnical, mechanical, and structural teams. For the past few months, I've been guiding my nephew through a massive new inspection program checking over the power grid in the Pittsburgh region, and making connections with power companies in a tri-state area.

That's another reason I haven't pursued any sort of relationship. My work is very important to me, and I like to be available to my family in my down time. When Helen died, I was bereft. I totally broke down. I could barely take care of myself, let alone Orla. My brother, newly divorced for the second time, insisted I move in with him and together we raised our four kids as best we could.

"I just want you to be happy, Daddy," Orla says, stretching up to kiss my cheek. Her eyes search mine, checking, as if she can verify my emotions like she might the presence of knob and tube wiring.

"I am happy," I say. And I mean it. Surely this is all a man could ask for. I have an amazing daughter. An extended family who relies on each other. I have a great house all to myself, with two small bedrooms and a basement that doesn't flood. In Pittsburgh, that's really saying something.

"Well thanks for sharing your driveway with me," she says. "And your expertise I guess."

"I just wish they still taught basic engine repair in schools," I chide as she grabs her things. Orla would have come over today to do her laundry anyway. The machines in her apartment building are down in the basement, and only take quarters. Together, we decided that spending that sort of money and making special trips to acquire quarters just for laundry was inefficient.

"You're such an engineer, Dad," she laughs.

"Well I would hope so, after about 30 years on the job."

I watch Orla back out of the driveway, waving, and notice a moving truck swaying down the street. I hold my breath, worried the driver doesn't see Orla, or that Orla doesn't see the truck. But my baby girl brakes, the truck makes a screeching turn into the driveway across the street, and I exhale.

What could I possibly offer a woman right now? The threat of a potential fender bender has me breathing hard and feeling anxious. I decide I'd better get that run in sooner than later. I quickly change and take off down my street, peering over my shoulder to see who it is making trips to and from the truck that could have smashed my daughter.

Shaking my head, I see the stubby ponytail of a woman as she and a teenager carry a sofa toward the house. Moving is tedious work. I should offer to help. I decide I can squeeze in a few miles and still get back before they've unloaded their mattresses.

Then I remember that not everyone packs a moving truck with an engineer's eye. *Kellen, do not loop back to judge their packing choices.* I sigh and cross the four-way stop, heading toward Highland Park. Plenty of time to be a good neighbor. Right now I have to clear my head.

CHAPTER TWO
ELIZABETH

I STAND IN THE PARKING LOT OF THE VAN RENTAL PLACE, STARING AT THE GIANT BOX truck. It looks much too big for me to drive. I wish I'd decided to hire movers. But a small voice inside had urged me to drive the truck myself. To physically be the one to drive my life away from my husband and all his bullshit nonsense.

Ex-husband. I say it out loud again, hoping this time the truth of it sticks. *I am free.*

I wave to the rental guy, staring at me with some trepidation as he taps his pen on his clipboard. Blowing my bangs up out of my eye, I swing open the door and climb inside. I pull the seat up as far as it goes and adjust the mirrors.

Slowly, painstakingly, I make my way to the house I've never liked much. A sprawling brick monstrosity on a rolling suburban lawn, the house is situated in an "upscale" neighborhood, which has never meant much more than uppity rich people moaning about the state of the world as they sip gin at the club.

As I turn into the driveway, I sneer at the topiaries Todd insisted we plant. Looking around, seeing no one, I give the wheel to the truck a quick jerk and I giggle as the front tire crushes the green shrub. *Let the realtor deal with it,* I think.

Jake and Lisa are making piles in the driveway when I pull the truck to a stop. "See," she says, ruffling my son's hair. "I told you your mom could manage perfectly fine."

Jake frowns. "Is a commercial drivers license required to drive a truck of that size?"

I shake my head. "Nope. We're good." We get to work loading our things in the back. It's not much. His bed. The couch. Our clothing. Todd and his lawyer were relentless in cataloguing "marital property" and insisting it all be sold and the proceeds divvied up according to our divorce agreement. Which is fine with me.

Jake hates change, but admits to feeling excited at the idea of selecting his own furnishings with me. We can sit on the floor to eat for a few weeks until the sale closes. Between the three of us, we get the truck loaded up in a few hours. I try not to notice as Lisa sneaks in a few bottles of wine from Todd's collection. "He must have drunk them himself when he went out with Slutty Malone," she says, referring to the leggy blond Todd had been screwing on the side until I discovered them. Now he's screwing her exclusively.

I walk inside, wanting to make sure I get everything this one trip. I don't ever want to come back here. The walls seem to pulse with my years of unhappiness and loneliness, of years of infertility heartbreak and the unraveling of my marriage in the 15 years since Jake finally arrived. I don't care that Todd is trying to wheedle out of paying alimony, not really.

I'm glad to start fresh, start relying on myself. I've got some good leads on jobs and between the child support payments and the soon-to-come proceeds from selling the house, Jake and I will be comfortable. I smile now, excited about the house we're renting.

We drive to the city with Lisa following, winding our way over the Highland Park Bridge and around the impossibly tight turns leading into Morningside, the sweet neighborhood full of elderly Italian families and cute houses with postage stamp lawns. "I grew up in this neighborhood, you know," I say, smiling at Jake while trying to navigate the big truck down the narrow street.

He rolls his eyes. "You've told me that 17 times, Mom," he says. I'm sure I have told him exactly that many. He keeps track of such things. I open my mouth to emphasize some more benefits, but he cuts me off. "I can walk to see Grandma and Grandpa if I want, and I can walk to Rite Aid to spend my allowance and there are three bus lines with regular service."

I laugh at his summary. "See," I say as much to myself as him. "We're going to be just fine here."

I slow down a bit more to make sure I don't miss the house. I see its yellow siding up ahead. Nearly too late, I spot a car pulling out of the driveway across the street. I gasp and make a screeching turn into the small driveway. Checking the mirrors, I see that the small car had stopped in time and is now zooming down the street. "Woooo," I say, turning off the engine. "I do not love driving this."

"Probably because you do not have a commercial drivers license," Jake points out. He walks around the back, eager to work his way through the checklist he's been studying. We prepared for today over and over again, reciting the steps we'd take. Pack our things in boxes, put them in the truck, drive the truck to the new house, and on and on. Jake quickly figures out the mechanism for the rolling door on the back of the truck and seems relieved to notice his things right where he put them.

Methodically, he begins to unload and carry one small item inside at a time. Lisa drapes her arm around my shoulders. She must have pulled up while I was catching my breath. "You've done good, Beth," she says. I nod.

Together, we start hauling inside some lamps and most of the clothing. Jake and I struggle with the couch, but I love how perfectly it fits in the small living room. It seemed such a small piece of furniture under the cathedral ceiling in the suburbs. Here, it fills the room, making the space seem cozy. I turn around the room, deciding where we will put the television and the lamps I'd like to buy, when Lisa nudges me and gestures out the picture window.

"Check out your neighbor," she says. There's a man about my age across the street, stretching long, muscled legs, looking like he's ready to take off for a run. There's something familiar about him and I squint, trying to see if I know the man beneath the graying stubble. "Geeze, Beth, I didn't think you were going to lick the damn glass."

Lisa startles me and I realize I have indeed pressed my face against the window to see him better. But I want to be sure. He grips the mailbox as he pulls back his heel to stretch his quad, and then checks his watch in a gesture I recognize immediately. "I know him," I tell her.

"Can I meet him," she says, staring after him as he starts moving. I swat at her.

"He was my high school boyfriend," I tell her, watching him go.

"Well this just got a lot more interesting," she says, pulling out one of the stolen bottles of Todd's wine. She twists off the cap and drinks from the bottle, passing it to me. I take a swig, thinking about Kellen Brady for the first time in over 30 years.

CHAPTER THREE
KELLEN

I NEVER DID GO ACROSS THE STREET TO OFFER TO HELP THE NEW NEIGHBORS MOVE their heavy things. I got back from my run and kept talking myself out of going over there. So now, this morning, I stand in front of my picture window drinking my coffee, staring across the street through my blinds like some sort of weirdo.

Why didn't I just walk over there and introduce myself? I'm not unfriendly. Most of the neighbors on this street have lived here for decades. Orla and I bought this house about eight years ago, once I felt like I could move out from my brother's house and face the days alone with her. Without her mother.

I think of the boxes in the basement. Helen's things, or what remains of them. She whittled most of it down before she died. Any time she had a good day, she dragged at least one trash bag of clothes or accessories to the porch for the charity pickup.

Maybe that's why the idea of helping a woman move in vexed me so. My phone rings and startles me. It's not yet seven on a Sunday, so it's either a dire emergency at work or else one of my nephews is in a bind.

Quickly walking to the dining room, I see Callum's name on the screen. I wince, and then feel bad for it. The boy is so much like his father. Not even a boy, really. Hell, he's 31 years old by now. "You late for the family run?" I say by way of greeting. Mick, the boys, and Orla hit the pavement early every Sunday. The roads are too much for my old knees anymore and I typically do my miles on the wooded trails in the park.

"Uncle Kel," Cal blurts. "The Bronc is dripping oil again. Can I borrow your driveway in like an hour?"

"Hmm," I tell him. The last time Callum brought that rust bucket over, he left a spill that still hasn't been mitigated. I try to remember what I've got in terms of drop cloth.

"Please? I'll bring you a scone."

They must be running in Frick Park, near my favorite bakery. "Only if they have the chocolate almond kind," I tell him. "I'll see you in a bit."

I set about protecting the driveway and gathering the tools I think my nephew will need to keep his beloved Bronco running for another day. No one in the family can understand his attachment to the ancient SUV, especially now that he lives in a fancy condo where I'm sure the affluent residents don't much like him dripping oil in the parking garage.

I see the teen boy across the street standing at the top of their driveway, squinting around the neighborhood. I give a wave, but he mustn't see because he doesn't return the gesture. Soon enough, Cal rumbles into view and hops out of his vehicle nearly as soon as it groans to a halt.

"Hell, Uncle Kellen, you already got the ramps set up and everything." He grins and tosses me a white paper bag from the bakery. I lean against the garage, munching the treat while he slides underneath his car and sets to work. It occurs to me that the neighbors must think I'm running an underground garage, with all the Brady kid car repairs this week.

"You think after I'm done here, Ferrari will hire me for their pit crew?" He jokes as he works under the car. Callum is a mechanical engineer and has always had a particular love of automobile engines. He was the only Cub Scout in Pittsburgh to win the Pinewood Derby five years in a row. As the adult helping him build his cars, I'm proud to say I didn't have much of a hand in his work.

The boy might be a mess, but he knows his moving parts.

I'm so wrapped up in admiring him, I almost don't notice my new young neighbor stroll into my driveway until he speaks, not making eye contact. "Is that a fifth generation Ford Bronco?"

Cal wheels out from under the car. "Oh, hey, dude. You're damn right it is. 1995." He squints at the teen. "You like cars?"

The boy doesn't answer, but frowns at Callum. "Are you a licensed mechanic?"

Cal laughs. "I'm a licensed mechanical engineer. Will that do?"

The teen's face lights up. He sits on the driveway with his elbows on his knees as Cal slides back under the car. "This was the first Bronco to feature airbags," he says.

I hear Cal groan and I laugh. The airbags are a family sticking point. When he found this car in the junk lot, that was the first thing his father made him replace. His mom still cringes when he drives it, despite my assurance that we found a suitable replacement. I finish my treat while the boy and Cal talk about the features of Rusty, Cal's nickname for his red beast.

"Jake?" I hear a woman calling frantically and look up to see my neighbor dashing across the street. The boy stands up and she clutches at her chest.

"Shit, you scared the hell out of me."

I could say the same thing. I feel like I've seen a ghost when the slim woman with short, graying hair steps closer.

"Is that a euphemism?" He frowns at his mother and I stare at her, not wanting to admit she is who I suspect. She drags him against her for a hug, muttering that he must always let her know where he's going if he leaves the house. I try not to judge, because he certainly looks old enough to wander the neighborhood on his own.

But the woman. She conjures up memories of sunscreen and cotton candy. Of wild nights riding roller coasters, and steamy explorations in my parents' borrowed car. Can it be her?

"Elizabeth?" My voice comes out in a croak as she turns and smiles. It is her, and I know in her eyes that she remembers me, too.

"Kellen Brady," she says. "It's been a long time."

We stare at each other in silence for a long beat as Jake peels out of his mother's embrace and sits back down on the driveway. "Ha!" Cal yells. "Found it. Need to reseal the crankshaft." He rolls out from under the car and stands. "Well, hello there."

Neither Elizabeth nor I moves and Cal looks back and forth between us. "That your mom?" He tilts his chin at Jake, who nods.

"Can I see the crankshaft?"

Elizabeth blinks and shakes her head quickly. "Jake, no. You mustn't bother the Bradys."

"Oh, it's no bother," I say, reaching for her arm to reassure her and freezing with my hand in the air. I can't just casually touch Elizabeth Burns, like the past 30 years haven't passed. Like she's still mine to touch.

She swallows. "Machines, cars mostly, are a special interest of Jake's," she starts.

"Cool," Cal says. "Me too. Obviously." He gestures at the Bronco. Elizabeth grimaces.

"He tends to hyper focus. You really mustn't feel like you need to let him—"

"I have Aspergers," Jake says in a monotone voice, not turning his head as he tries to crawl under the Bronco. "Technically that term does not exist anymore, but some members of the autistic community still claim it as an identity label."

Elizabeth closes her eyes as if she's embarrassed. Cal nods. "Well, it's got ass and burger in the word, so that's fun." He looks at Elizabeth. "Seriously, though, half the guys at our work are probably on the spectrum. If Jake wants to come pick my uncle's brains about crankshafts, it's really fine."

"Uncle?" Elizabeth looks at me, her eyes sharp. "I thought..." She shakes her head. "Forgive me. Let's start again." She holds a hand out toward Cal. "Elizabeth Gaston—"

"Burns," Jake yells, his head under the vehicle.

She nods. "Right. I forgot again. Elizabeth Burns. We just moved in across the street."

Cal pumps her hand. "Callum Brady. I just mooch my uncle's driveway when the Bronc acts up."

She squints at him and thinks for a bit. "If he's your uncle, you must be...Mick's boy. Is that right? Mick?"

Cal and I both roll our eyes. He says, "I apologize in advance for however it is you know my pop." This gets a laugh out of her. I still can't find the words to say anything.

Where to begin? How have you been for the past 30 years? Who did you marry and why are you changing your name back? Do you have other children? May I tell you all about my beloved wife, God rest her soul? Sorry again for anything inelegant I may have done with our bodies as teenagers?

Elizabeth tucks her light hair behind her ears. It's cut chin-length and suits her. Her face is the same as before, but wiser. What must she have seen and experienced since we last were together? I stare at her as these thoughts circle endlessly until she excuses herself and drags Jake home for breakfast.

Once they're inside, my nephew thwacks me in the chest. I look down at his hand, startled again. That's twice today he's frazzled me. "Uncle Kel," he says. "What the hell has gotten into you?"

"Into me?"

His eyes bug out. "You were, like, totally aloof. You didn't even offer her tea or whatever." He starts to clean up his things, handling my tools carefully for once. "Who is she?"

I clear my throat and help him clean up, wondering how best to explain Beth Burns to my nephew. "We used to work together at Kennywood," I tell him, smiling at the memories of my teenage summers driving the train at the amusement park. "She ran the ticket counter."

He grins. "No shit? Teen sweethearts? Is that what it's called?" He shakes his head. "Anyway, why'd you break up? Cuz you met Aunt Helen?"

I sigh and shrug. "There was no reason," I tell him. I think again of riding the rides with Beth after the park closed for the night, after everyone else went home. We'd sit in the back of the Thunderbolt and I'd kiss her as the bottom of the world dropped away, loving the rush of energy that came equally from the ride and the pleasure of being with her.

"I was going away to college," I tell him. "She was going away to college." I hold out my palms and shrug. "We didn't keep in touch."

He raises an eyebrow at me. "From the looks of things, Uncle Kel, you'd like to touch her right now," Cal says.

I smack his shoulder. "Watch your manners, son," I say. *If only you knew,* I think.

CHAPTER FOUR
ELIZABETH

"Beth," Lisa huffs into the phone. "I told you not to buzz. Just come up." I'm meeting her at her office for lunch and always feel out of place when I go someplace professional. I haven't been part of the business world since Jake was born. By the time he was born, after all the years of infertility and struggle, I was already planning to stay home with him.

That choice seemed like an even bigger blessing when I was so sick for so long, and then an even greater blessing when Jake turned out to be…I sigh. My son's mind works very differently from the mainstream culture and it's taken a lot of work and a lot of time to help him be successful.

I walk up the stairs to Lisa's office and tap gingerly on the glass door to her company's suite. She's on the phone and waves me in side. Lisa is ten years younger than me, but we met when Jake and her oldest son, Dhruv, were in preschool. Lisa went on to have two more children in rapid succession, despite the challenges of her oldest having autism like Jake.

I pretty much think she's a superhero who sort of lets me tag along beside her. I smile and sit in the chair opposite her desk. Lisa stayed home with her kids when they were younger but rejoined the work world about five years ago. I've sorely missed our long swaths of time together during the week. This lunch feels like even more of a treat since Jake and Dhruv are at daycamp together and I'm not anxious about getting a call about Jake's behavior. The boys both do better when they have each other around.

"Let me just grab my sunglasses," Lisa says, tossing down her phone.

"Let's sit outside somewhere." I nod and follow as she points to different staff members, letting them know where various projects stand and what she's expecting when she gets back from lunch.

"Project management suits you so well," I tell her, knowing that she runs her household with the same efficiency. All her kids' schedules are color-coded and she's got reminders in her phone for everything from med refills to auto payments to their housekeeper.

"I love keeping these geeks in line," she says. We walk across the way to a new restaurant serving Korean street food. I don't have to remind Lisa that Todd never approved of strong, garlicky foods. Just eating this meal is an act of rebellion, of independence. I smile, enjoying the company and the adventure.

"Talk to me about the silver fox across the street," she says, slurping a bubble tea and pointing a finger at me. "Skip nothing."

I shrug, munching the pickled veggies on our table. "We went to high school together. Burns, Brady...he always turned up in my classes. Things got hot and heavy senior year, but we were both headed off to college."

Lisa squints at me. I roll my eyes. "Neither of us felt like we wanted anything long distance. I honestly haven't thought about him for 30 years." What I don't tell her is now that I've seen him again, seen how he's grown into a sexier, salt-and-pepper version of teenaged Kellen...I can't stop thinking about him.

"Did he swipe your V-card, Elizabeth Burns?" She leans closer as the server brings our food and flushes uncomfortably. I wait until we're alone again.

"He did not," I tell her. I shrug again. "I had done some experimenting before we got together." My insides flutter, remembering the way Kellen and I had been together, though. All desperation and wild passion. "What he lacked in finesse, he made up for in enthusiasm." I hadn't meant to share that last bit out loud, but Lisa throws her head back and laughs.

"Yes!" She shouts. "I love this for you. What's his deal? Wife and kids and such?"

"I'm actually not sure," I say, telling her about the incident in the driveway. "He and his nephew were very kind to Jake, showing him things about the car."

"God, it's hot when people are nice to my kid," Lisa says. "I mean, people should be nice by default, but let's face it. The world is full of assholes."

I nod, digging in to my rice and beef dish. Bibimbop, it's called. The flavors are amazing. Bold and crisp. The vegetables are so bright against the rice. Jake has a very limited diet and strong smells upset him, so when we eat at home it's usually much more bland. I bite right into a pickled spring onion and savor the strong taste as Lisa talks about the various assholes she's encountered this week.

"Hey," she says. "Speaking of assholes, when is Todd going to start his custody?"

I frown. That's been a sore spot throughout this process. Neither Jake nor Todd, frankly, wants to spend much time together. "Todd seems to think he'll earn brownie points at work by having weekend time? I don't even know. He's supposed to pick Jake up after camp Friday. Jake hasn't even seen Todd's new place yet."

"What are you going to do with an entire weekend to yourself?" Lisa leans forward on her elbows. Her weekends are filled with swim meets, frantic errands, and yard work. I know she's rooting for me to have some free time to tell her about.

"Honestly, I'll probably read a book and hold my breath, waiting for Jake to have a meltdown and Todd to call me to come get him."

She squints at me. "I'm thinking sexy buns across the street is single, and you should spend this weekend getting reacquainted with him."

"Lisa," I frown. "The ink is barely dry on my divorce papers."

"Oh come on, Beth. You haven't had sex since you conceived Jake. It's way past time."

My eyes widen. "I'm not about to go have casual sex with Kellen Brady." I may have been a teenager the last time I saw him, but there was nothing casual about him. No, he's not the man you call to scratch an itch.

She slumps back in her chair. "Fine, fine. Let's talk about your career options instead." She arches a brow at me. "You know you'd be a damn fine project manager somewhere, too."

I shake my head. "I haven't had as many balls in the air as you. You slipped right into this role—you said it yourself, that those computer programmers are no different from children who need to get to the orthodontist and soccer practice all at the same time."

We pay the check as she scolds me about downplaying my skills. "Just because you only have one kid doesn't mean you haven't been the goddess of your date book. How many other people do you know who can manage an autism therapy schedule along while arguing with the insurance company about covering medication *and* getting an autistic teen ready for a new school?"

I look down at my lap. When she describes these things it makes it sound like I've been doing so much. "Jake is really excited about high school," I admit.

"This is what I'm saying. You got a *teenager* to be excited about something. You helped him find a school in the city with engineering classes and advanced math, you got him on a tour...you'd be a major asset to any office, is all I'm saying."

"I'll think about it," I tell her.

She points a straw at me as we get our things to leave. "You should spend this weekend starting your resume," she says. "I'm going to call you six times and check until you send me a draft so I can tell you how awesome it is."

CHAPTER FIVE
KELLEN

I've become a hermit. Worse, I'm a peeping Tom hermit. I seem to spend all my time sitting in my living room peeking between my blinds to see if Elizabeth is coming or going. I have no idea why I'm behaving this way and haven't had the energy to sit and ponder what has me so worked up about seeing her again.

There was something jarring about her eyes, once filled with light and laughter and now...so tired. She just seems really tired. I'm tired, too. I wonder about the boy's father, whether he's gone like Helen or just...gone from their lives. It's clear she and Jake live over there alone, although I remember that her parents live in the neighborhood.

I grin, wondering if their basement still has the bright red linoleum floor. She and I used to sneak down there through the side door and make out, careful not to get loud near any of the ducts in case the sound traveled.

I wake earlier than usual on Monday, feeling restless. There are no lights on across the street, and I slip off to work as the sun is rising. I settle in to my office to review the progress we are making with our new endeavors. Beltane Engineering, the company my brother and I started together, recently brought in a guy who studies machine learning.

The whole thing was my nephew Zack's idea. He met this guy in college, Ray, who is showing us all sorts of things about how his sensors can supplement our inspection processes. He's got computer programs analyzing days and days worth of video footage checking out everything from landslides near mining operations to rust on highway overpasses.

It's been a long time since I've been out making calculations. At this stage of my career, I'm doing more big picture work, making sure all the gears are turning. When my nephew Liam got the idea to add power infrastructure to our inspection catalogue, I was simultaneously thrilled for him and his brainstorm and jealous as hell that I hadn't thought of it.

As I stare at our numbers, I realize that my brother and I had planned for our kids to take over leadership of the company...and it's happening. Liam and Zack have found their groove and are proving to be both brilliant engineers *and* good stewards of Beltane.

It should feel better to realize this. How many people can claim this sort of success?

I don't usually think about myself getting older. I know time is passing, obviously, but I don't necessarily feel like an old fart except when these young guys, all filled with brilliant ideas, put things in motion and sort of make me feel left behind. I'm not entirely sure I know what to do with myself if I'm not making sure things are ok at Beltane.

I'm about to slip into some sort of pity party about it when my brother skids into my office. Mick is freshly showered, chewing gum like he's trying to destroy it. "Kel," he says, sinking into a chair, his foot shaking as he crosses it over his opposite knee. "My boy was telling me something very interesting."

Mick vibrates. He's always done so. Mom used to say he was made out of electricity. I know damn well what he's referring to, but I decide to play dumb. "Which boy was that, Michael?"

He reaches in his pocket for a fresh stick of gum. This must really have him agitated if he's going through multiple pieces in a morning. "Is it true that Elizabeth Burns now lives across the street from you?"

"I didn't think you'd remember her." I fold my hands on the desk, willing my body to be calm, trying to ignore the growing tornado inside me as I think about how I'm supposed to deal with this situation.

Mick cackles, sets both feet on the ground, and grips the edge of my desk. "Don't think the time I caught you two in Gram's backyard isn't burned into my brain," he says. "Even this leaky sieve remembers that." He taps on his skull for emphasis. "My niece also tells me she's been pestering you about getting back in the game."

"Oh lord." I bury my face in my hands. It's one thing for my daughter to say these things to me and make me upset. It's another entirely to think the whole family is out discussing me like some sort of highway attraction.

"I know you all think I'm a batty old dirtbag," Mick says, leaning back again with his hands laced together behind his head. "But I happen to think Orla's right about this one. It's been a long time, Kellen. It'll do you good to go out. Meet people. Be social."

"I hate people," I remind him. Mick sucked every extroverted gene out of our mom's womb. I'm perfectly content with my work and my family in my life, even if those two circles overlap quite a bit.

Mick waves that comment away. "Come on, Kel," he says. "What's it been? Ten years? Fifteen? It's not natural for a person to go that long without sex."

"Mick, I'm not talking about this with you." I feel nauseated at the idea of this discussion with my brother of all people. I will admit that he has a small point, in that there really isn't anyone else I could have that particular conversation with. "I think that part of me is…just finished. That's all."

Mick squints at me. It's not really a lie. I haven't felt urges in years. First I was up to my ears taking care of Helen. Then I was grieving and parenting a teen girl all on my own. Nothing like your only daughter getting her period to stifle down any scraps of libido.

But I'm not going to tell him that the night I saw Beth in my driveway, I woke up from a very lucid dream. And I haven't been able to shake the feel of it. My brother spits his gum toward my wastebasket and, thankfully, makes the shot. He and Callum certainly are cut from the same cloth.

"Listen, Kellen, I just want you to be happy. And whole. And I agree with Orla that Helen would want that, too."

"I am happy, Mick." I reach for my brother and pat his arm. "I have a good life."

My brother stands up and walks around the desk, bending over and pulling me into an awkward, long-limbed hug. He kisses me on the cheek. "I love you, little brother."

"Come on, Mick." I straighten my collar as he extracts himself. We make eye contact for a few minutes and I watch him inhale, then exhale back to his usual self.

"I got a date with a pretty young thing this weekend," he says. "Want me to ask if she's got a friend?"

"I'll see you at the staff meeting, Michael," I scold, and I look away from him into my computer monitor. I hear him chuckle as he takes off down the hall.

CHAPTER SIX
ELIZABETH

"I can't believe you're using your one kid-free day to hang out with me." Lisa peals out of my driveway and heads toward the Highland Park bridge. We're heading to the mall together, just the two of us. I try to think if we've ever been able to do this before.

Whenever we've gone to the mall together, it's been for the boys' Pinewood Derby competitions or to take turns watching the kids while we bought them all school shoes. Lisa's husband, Ashish, has all three of her boys out for a bike ride today. Lisa claims she needs new clothes for work, but when she called to see if I was up for a trip to Nordstrom, I suspect she really wants to outfit me for the job search she's certain I'll rock.

"Who else would I spend time with?" I bat my eyes at her and sip my coffee.

"Oh, I don't know," she says, turning onto the highway at the end of the bridge. "Sexy McStretch across the street, for instance."

I cluck my tongue at her. "Geeze, Lisa, we haven't even spoken since that day in the driveway. He keeps really different hours from me, I think."

"I'm mostly kidding," she says. "How did pickup go for Jake yesterday?"

I roll my eyes and tell her how Todd was four minutes late, which of course set Jake on edge. He gets very frustrated when schedules are not kept, and Todd of course refuses to acknowledge that time commitments are important to Jake, even if they're just going to get pizza and watch Star Wars together. "I mean, I know I don't have to explain to *you* how Jake is

379

working so hard on his rigidity." Lisa nods. "But come on! The kid just moved to a new home and you're going to be late?"

We curse Todd together. Jake hasn't checked in yet today, and I try to remind myself that he would call if he felt upset. No news is good news. She must see me twisting my hands together around the coffee cup, because she reaches over and gives my hand a squeeze.

We walk toward Nordstrom from the parking lot and are immediately greeted by sales staff. I expect Lisa to shoo them away, but she asks for the personal shopper. My jaw drops. "Don't look at me that way," she says. "You haven't dressed for an office since you were pregnant."

The personal shopper appears, dressed impeccably of course. She looks like Anette Bening. "My friend here is going back to the world of work," Lisa says.

I grit my teeth. "I thought we were here to boost your wardrobe." Lisa waves a hand.

Anette, whose actual name is June, beams. "A capsule wardrobe is just the thing," she says.

"Say what?" I have a vague memory of hearing this vocabulary word somewhere online in the past, but Lisa's right. I've been wearing faded jeans and turtlenecks for decades.

June walks briskly toward a rack of black pants and points. "We'll get you situated with five to eight pieces you can mix and match so you'll have a week's worth of office wear. What's the office dress code?"

She looks at me expectantly and my jaw drops again. Lisa pats my arm. "We're still in the search portion of the job hunt."

"Oh!" June grins and claps her hands. "Then we need to get you interview outfits, too!"

Two hundred dollars later, Lisa is hugging June and exchanging business cards. I'm impressed and surprised by how far I could stretch my money with June's help. Between the clearance racks and a few store-brand tops, I really do feel like I could walk into an interview on Monday looking put-together. Lisa bought me two chunky necklaces, too, so I can even accessorize differently if I have to re-wear something sooner than anticipated.

"You don't think all this is too young-looking," I ask her, gesturing at myself. She and June agreed I should wear the fitted black pants and scoop-neck green top home. I feel very aware of the shape of my body, on display for all to see. Long, shapeless tops have been my norm ever since Jake's birth.

It was kind of a train wreck, and I ended up having several different surgeries. I've tried to draw everyone's attention, including my own, *away* from my midriff ever since.

"Liz," she breathes. "You're radiant. You're free and you're starting fresh. That body of yours walked the hell out on an asshole and drove a damn moving truck to a new life! It deserves clothes that fit it."

I flush under her blunt praise. Lisa never bullshits. I love that about her. She reminds me so much of me when I was younger. How I was when I was with Kellen. Have I changed so deeply? "You're right," I say, exhaling a big breath. "I have done some great things with this body."

She grins, stopping in front of one of those bath and body frou-frou shops. "I have an idea for your body." She drags me inside, where I'm assaulted by the fruity smells of all the lotions and sprays.

"What on earth?" Lisa stops in front of a bath display table marketing fizzy balls, exfoliating scrubbers and... "A facial massager?"

Lisa scoffs. "I don't know why they don't just call it like it is. It's a damn vibrator, Elizabeth. And you're supposed to use it in the tub while you're all relaxed and smelling good."

I gasp, and then hate myself for doing so. "It's not really for that!"

Lisa rolls her eyes. "You think women really need 'five variant speeds to lift, firm and tone' your *pores?* Please. You're going to buy this and you're going to get off and it's going to be amazing."

I peer at the package. "I'm not even sure I know what to do with it," I admit, biting my lip. How pathetic does that sound? Fifty years old and I'm so out of touch with anything sexual that I'm not sure how a vibrator works. "I've never owned one before."

Lisa nods. "Well lucky for you, this 'facial massager' offers 7,000 vibrations per minute. There's really not much to it, babe. You hold it between your legs and wait for the fireworks."

"I don't know..."

"Then you definitely need it," she says, shoving it in the crook of her arm and grabbing a bag of bath fizzies. "Go home and use it tonight while Jake's gone."

ℬ

AN HOUR LATER, after she drops me off and makes me vow to use the massager, I dump everything on my bed. I stand in the room, sparsely furnished but mine. This week, I managed to find a few pieces of furniture for free online. As autumn nears in Pittsburgh and all the young people move in and out of the universities, apparently everyone purges their household items. My zippy little hatchback managed to get me a dresser and two night stands, plus a dining set.

I realize, despite the hectic busyness this week between getting Jake to and from day camp and setting up our new home, I've been really happy. It feels so strange to not feel like I'm holding my breath or walking on eggshells at home that I hadn't noticed until now.

I pinch my arm, just to make sure I'm awake. Sure enough, this is really my life. On my terms. I walk through the house making sure all the curtains are drawn and the doors are locked, and then I fill the bath.

I feel my heart race as I consider what I'm about to do. How many years has it been? Todd and I haven't slept together since we conceived Jake, and much too long had passed before it occurred to me that that was a problem. By the time I was crawling out from my postpartum depression, I was in fight or flight mode all the time helping Jake. There hadn't been any time for me to think about sex. Even with myself.

I swallow thickly as I plunk the fizzies into the tub and undress. My fingers trail along the scar tissue on my lower abdomen, still numb after all this time. Part of me—a big part—worries that my pleasure parts will be numb, too. But then I remember that I've had a few dreams here and there. The sensations have felt real. Always shy of any sort of big finish, but there was enough there that I'm not totally terrified that my body is broken in that way.

I slide into the warm water and lie there for a few minutes. The fizzing bubbles are nice, and the lavender mint scents are my favorite. I chew on my lip and look around, chastising myself because of course the house is empty and locked up tight. I click on the massager and it tingles in my hand, the vibrations as powerful as the packaging alluded.

I giggle and touch it to my face, and I'm certain that's not at all what this is intended for. It feels so strange on my skin. I can't imagine how it will feel down below. Awkward in the water, I bump my breast as I try to lower the massager to my sex, and I yelp when the vibrating tip catches my nipple. I put it back against my breast, on purpose this time, and a moan escapes my lips. Oh my.

My pulse quickens and I breathe faster, swallowing as I lower the device. I rock my pelvis out of the water a bit. The packaging said it's safe to use in water, but the last thing I need is to electrocute myself. Imagine the headlines: 50 Year Old Woman Dies Trying to Get Off.

When the pink massager connects with my clit, it certainly feels like I'm being electrocuted. But definitely not in a bad way. "Oh my," I say, out loud this time. I move the toy to the side, just above my clit. That feels better. Better than better. I moan. I start to circle the toy, not touching my clit directly but hovering around it until, suddenly and with a rush that causes me to scream, I come.

I come and I come, my legs twitching and water splashing out of the tub onto the floor. Panting and groaning, I come until I drop the massager into the water, and I laugh as I root around trying to find it to shut it off. "Holy shit," I say. I drain the tub and sit in it, staring.

I should have been doing that every day, I decide. "No better time to start," I tell myself.

I dry off and slip into my pajamas. I shoot Jake a text to say I love him and can't wait for him to come home tomorrow. I climb into bed with a smile on my face, realizing it's true. Who knew orgasms made everything so much better? A lot of people knew, apparently, based on the package insert for the "facial massager." I throw the box and the instructions away and fall asleep, content and eager to start the next day.

CHAPTER SEVEN
KELLEN

I WASN'T GOING TO HAVE THE FAMILY OVER ON A WEEKNIGHT. I REALLY WASN'T. There's the new documentary coming out tonight, that I'll have to save for tomorrow, which means I'll have to adjust all my social media notifications since I'll miss the chat and get spoilers if I log in tomorrow. But when my nephew Liam called to say his pregnant girlfriend was craving my special marinade, who was I to say no to that.

I leave the office a bit early to get the meat going and set about preparing for the rush of relatives. With Liam and Zack both partnered off, that means I'm cooking for eight. I smile, pulling two folding chairs up from the basement. Soon I'll have to stash a high chair here for the baby. I love the idea of a tiny baby Brady at my table. I hope Liam and Maddie will let me babysit for them sometimes.

I'm lost in daydreams about having another baby around when my phone rings. Liam. "What's up, son?"

I can barely hear him above the rain. I hadn't noticed the sky, but we are in the middle of one of those late summer storms that comes on quick and fierce. He shouts, "Can you meet us outside with an umbrella? I don't want Maddie to catch a chill."

I hear her in the background in the car, scolding Liam. "Catch a chill? What are you, 80 years old? You do realize the baby is submerged in water, right?"

I chuckle. "I'll meet you out front with my golf umbrella. How far are you?"

I turn the burner off under the sauce for the veggies and look outside to see Liam pulling up. I head out through the garage door, grabbing my largest umbrella. As Liam pulls to a stop, I meet them at the passenger door with a smile. Madison rolls her eyes, but then struggles to hoist herself out of the low vehicle, so I lean in to offer a strong tug so she can get to her feet more easily. She blows her hair up out of her face. "Thanks, Kellen."

"Any time, sweetheart. Here, you take this." I pull up the hood on my rain coat. Liam walks around to the back, grabbing a bag of chips. I'm about to see if I can help him, when I spy something going on across the street.

"You don't understand!" Jake wails, pacing back and forth in the rain in the driveway while his mother stands in the garage, shivering. She looks concerned. "It has to be a back yard barbecue," he shrieks. I see him stomping back and forth, muttering in the rain.

"Won't you please come inside and talk about this, Jake?" Elizabeth looks so distraught. Jake is really stomping his feet now, tugging on his hair.

I jog across the street. "Anything I can do for you two?" Jake whips his head to stare at me, his eyes wild.

Elizabeth sighs. I duck under the garage door to stand by her, dripping on the concrete floor. "Thank you, Kellen, but we're fine," she says, tightly.

"Nothing is fine!" Jake hollers, then starts smacking his forehead.

"He's just upset," Elizabeth says.

"Son," I say, stepping back out in the rain and touching his shoulder. The movement startles him and he looks at me again. "Can you tell me what's got you so upset?"

"I am not your son."

"That's true," I tell him. "I just call young men that. I can't help myself. I don't have any sons."

"Oh." Jake looks at me, blinking the rain out of his face. "I need to have a backyard barbecue. It needs to be today. And Mom says we can't because it's raining, but it needs to be today."

I nod. Elizabeth shouts over the storm, explaining that his autism therapist suggested a backyard barbecue as an example of a social activity they might try to help feel more comfortable in their new neighborhood. "His next session is tomorrow and he was supposed to complete an exercise for homework," she says. To Jake, she yells, "The barbecue was an *example,* sweetie."

He shakes his head, looking upset again.

"Hey, what about this," I tell them. I keep a hand on Jake's shoulder. "I've got a covered deck out back. I'm about to toss some chicken on the grill anyway. What if you and your mother come eat with us, on the deck? Would that do?"

"Is the grill a barbecue? In Canada, it's common for people to refer to gas grills as 'barbecues,'" he says, looking hopeful.

I nod. "I can set out barbecue sauce, too, if that helps?" Jake nods and, without further ado, walks across the street toward my house and in through my garage door. I can't help the chuckle that sneaks out, until I look at Beth, who has tears in her eyes.

"Hey," I say. "Please don't cry on my account."

She shakes her head and wipes her eyes with the heel of one hand. "Thank you, Kellen." She sighs. "I wasn't sure how we were getting through this one. Thank you for finding a solution for us."

"Any time," I tell her, resisting the urge to reach for her shoulder like I had for Jake. "I mean that. Say, I'm going to run back over and get changed. Please let yourself in?"

She nods and I dash back across the street just as Orla, Zack and Nicole are sprinting inside from their cars. With a quick word to my daughter to welcome the neighbors, I dash back to my room and toss my soaked things into the bath tub. I absolutely do not reach for my nicest jeans because Elizabeth Burns is coming over to my house. They just happen to be on top of the pile in my drawer.

I drag a comb through my damp hair and pull on an undershirt. If it was just the family, I'd head back out just like this and throw on an apron. But, I reason, the messy work of the meal has already been done. I can wear a nice polo at least. No reason not to pull myself together for my new almost-neices.

I walk back down the hall and see Beth arguing with Jake about putting on a dry shirt. She sees me and pinches her lips together. "Kellen, I didn't realize this was a special night with your family," she says. "We can't intrude like this."

Cal pokes his head through the garage just then. "Who? Us? Special? Neighbor gal, I hate to tell you but we're real gross and obnoxious."

Beth smiles at his candor. "It's not an intrusion at all," I assure her. To the room at large, I say, "Elizabeth and Jake are going to eat out on the deck. Special project."

"Oh that sounds nice," Nicole says, standing and walking toward the door. "It looks like it's clearing up anyway." Orla slides open the screen door and starts taking plates and condiments outside while the guys start shifting chairs. I've only got four cushioned chairs at my patio table, but nobody seems to mind sitting in staggered height, mismatched seats.

Elizabeth seems a bit shell shocked by all the commotion. I should have warned her that everyone was coming. The Bradys can be sort of a lot when we're all clumped together. But I hated to see Jake upset like that unnecessarily. After all, his therapist gave him homework.

Jake approaches Maddie as he reluctantly pulls on the dry shirt from his mother. He stares at her for a bit, and seems deeply uncomfortable. She smiles and offers him a hand to shake. "Hi," she says, her eyes bright. "I'm Maddie. What's up?"

Jake blinks a few times and bites his lip like he's trying not to say something, then blurts, "Have you been mating with one of the Bradys?" The room goes silent, and I know I shouldn't laugh. I know it. But lord, what a question.

"Jacob Todd Gaston! We have discussed this." Elizabeth is red from the tips of her ears to the knuckles of her hand that she tries to cram into her mouth.

Nicole and Maddie burst out laughing. Jake looks confused and Maddie and Nicole pull themselves together and cough. Elizabeth corrects Jake, saying, "It's more common to say 'are you expecting a baby,' but it's also not polite to ask a woman if she's expecting a baby because we never know what her circumstances are."

Jake seems to contemplate this answer, and looks embarrassed about a social misstep, until Nicole claps him on the back. "I like the blunt approach, kid. Maddie and Liam have been mating like beasts. Their baby boy is coming in just a few months."

I clear my throat. "Jake, would you like to help me gr— would you like to help me barbecue the chicken?" He nods eagerly, and I slip outside with the pan of meat, my new neighbor in tow.

"I want to apologize for laughing in there just now," I tell him.

Jake studies me. "Mom says people laugh when they're shocked or uncomfortable sometimes. Like when I've done something in gross opposition to social norms."

I nod. "That's true. I really wasn't expecting that question, but that might be because all of us already knew Maddie was expecting a baby." I try to use his mother's language, hoping it will set him at ease.

I hand him the tongs and gesture for him to set the meat on the grill, which he does well enough. "Expecting a baby feels like it must be a euphemism," he says. "Expecting it to do what?"

I think about this. "Well, expecting it to arrive. Anticipating."

"Anticipating," he says, nodding. "I like that. Mr. Brady?" He looks at me and hands me back the tongues.

"Please call me Kellen, Jake."

"Kellen. Ok. Kellen?"

"What's up?"

"Your house is my favorite thing about this neighborhood so far."

My heart stutters in my chest at his words. "Wow, Jake. Thank you so much. I'm glad to have you for a neighbor."

He smiles briefly, then looks back at the chicken. "I feel like I can ask all the questions I need."

I nod. "You can definitely ask all the questions you need." I feel overwhelmed by his candor, and so moved that I created a space where he feels safe. I think about how little I did—talk tires with him in the driveway, troubleshoot his problem. It makes me wonder what Elizabeth and Jake's lives were like before they moved here, if such a small thing makes this boy's day.

"Let's go ahead and take some of these off the flame," I tell him, holding up the tray. "You can help me serve the outdoor barbecue meal."

CHAPTER EIGHT
ELIZABETH

I don't normally have an audience when Jake abruptly transitions between meltdown mode and "quirky kid who uses big words that make adults laugh." But somehow the Brady family seems to take it all in stride. They didn't even stare at me when I burst into the house soaking wet, arguing with Jake to put on a dry shirt.

Now, watching Kellen's family fight over the guacamole, I can see how a teenager freaking out about canceled plans would roll right off their backs. They seem so easygoing, even as they tease each other. I lean against the wall taking a few deep breaths to regain my composure. Jake is fine. He's out on the deck with Kellen, studying the dials on the massive grill Kellen is firing up.

He's more than fine. I study him. Jake is at ease out there, comfortable. This family is making my kid comfortable. I feel the hot pull of tears wanting to roll from my eyes, reminding me how rare it is to find spaces where Jake feels like he can be himself. Then I feel the bile rise in my throat when I start to wonder whether all the fancy country club people who felt so important to Todd were just the wrong sort of crowd when it came to welcoming someone who experiences the world differently.

Mick Brady bursts in the front door, shaking the rain from his long black slicker. "Rainbow's forming outside," he yells, by way of greeting, and everyone floods from the kitchen into Kellen's living room to stare out the picture window. There, above my house, is a beautiful double rainbow. The sidewalks steam in the newly blazing sun. I pull up my phone to take a picture, deciding this is the moment the neighborhood became home again.

"Betty Burns, is that really you?" Mick shakes his head, grinning. "My son told me you moved in. You haven't changed a bit!"

I laugh. "Well I hope I've grown up some." I tuck my short hair behind my ears, which I know makes the gray streak more visible. He waves a hand.

"I'd still fight my brother for your number."

I swat at his arm, and immediately wonder why I'm flirting with Mick Brady after 30 years of not seeing him. "Which of these are yours," I ask him, gesturing around the room. Between the curly haired woman, the pregnant woman, and all the tall men, I still haven't figured out just which of these people are Kellen's children.

Mick grabs a beer from the fridge and gestures toward me. I don't typically drink beer, but I say yes and twist the top off the Killian's Irish Red. The Bradys have always been into their Irish heritage. Mick takes a swig from his and points to the long-limbed young men. "Those three goons are my sons," he says. "Two of them managed to find women who aren't sick of them yet. That one there is carrying my first grandson. Can you believe I'm gonna be a Pop-pop?"

"You settled on Pop-pop? Not Pee-paw or Pappy?" It feels good to joke around with him. He was always easygoing and fun when he was around. He was already in college when I got together with Kellen, but he came home that summer and always tried to mooch free admission into the amusement park when I was at the ticket counter.

Mick drops his head back in laughter. "I ain't no Pee-paw, sweetie."

"She's not your sweetie, Mick." The curly haired woman leans past him for a beer and offers me her hand. "I'm Nicole. I live with Isaac." She gestures toward Mick's dark-haired son, currently smacking his curly-haired brother away from yet another snack. Looks like a cheese dip this time. "Is it true you used to date Uncle Kellen?"

She stares at me without blinking. Her forthright question stuns me for a minute, but I realize this must just be how she is, because the room suddenly stills and everyone stares at me. "Um, yes. A very long time ago. Yes, Kellen and I dated. As teenagers. A lifetime ago." I realize I'm rambling and take a pull of my beer.

The pregnant woman my son accosted smiles. "And you and Jake just moved in? How fun. Across the street from your old flame!"

"Maddie, you can't just say old flame about Uncle Kellen." Her partner —that must be Mick's son Liam—frowns and massages her shoulders. Maddie shrugs.

"Has he always smelled like Old Spice?"

"Oh, good question," Nicole chimes in. "He's rocking that old man smell right now."

Mick pouts. "You guys talk about how Kellen smells? What about me? I've got this new cologne from Iceland…"

"Mick," Nicole puts her hand on his shoulder. "You smell great. This is about Kellen right now."

I'm saved from embarrassment when the man in question slides open the back door. "Chicken's ready," he says, gesturing for us to follow him outside. Everyone does. My son is holding a pair of tongs, serving the Bradys as if he doesn't typically pretend to gag when I cook anything that has an aroma. I don't know what witchcraft is happening over here, but I'll take it.

Once everyone is sitting down and has all the proper utensils, Nicole shouts over the din again. "So, Elizabeth, what's your passion?"

Jake looks at me, fork midway to his mouth. I gasp. My son hasn't tasted a food with a spice on it in…I don't believe he has ever tasted a food with a spice on it. "Jake," I say. He looks at me, bites the chicken, and grins. His eyebrows move enthusiastically as he crams another bite into his mouth. "Jake is my passion." They all look at me, and I explain, "It took me years to conceive Jake and, well I'm sure you heard me say by now that he is on the autism spectrum."

"I have Asperger's syndrome," he interrupts.

I nod. "Yes. And I've really dedicated a lot of effort to his therapies and working with his teachers to make sure everything goes smoothly at school." I shrug. "It's been my focus for a long time."

"What about Jake's dad?" Callum asks the question and his brothers groan. Zack smacks the back of Cal's head. "Hey! What? It's a fair question. Shouldn't dads help with therapies and school shit?"

Kellen clenches his teeth and I take a deep breath, ready to respond. But Jake butts in. "My dad thinks therapists are full of shit," he says. "That's a euphemism, although the human colon can hold up to 40 pounds of feces." I take a deep breath and count to ten inside my head. I'm used to my son being blunt. I'm not used to him repeating his father's shortcoming aloud. It stings for me to hear what Jake has been hearing his whole life, spoken with as much emotion as the weather report. Jake continues eating his chicken.

Nicole makes a disgusted face. "Therapists full of shit? Seriously?" She throws her napkin on the table. "I'm glad you two are living here now away from that energy," she says. "Elizabeth, it sounds like you made sure Jake had everything he needed."

Maddie's eyes light up. "My mom was like that," she says. She gestures toward her stomach. "I have Type 1 Diabetes. Every year my mom had to basically give a health seminar to my teachers."

I nod. "Yes, the training and awareness around here, especially in the suburbs...it's...lacking."

Maddie points her fork at me. "Do you ever work with the FARE center? Family Advocacy and Rights...something? They were such a help, even when I went to college. Helped me figure out how to get in touch with disability resources and stuff."

"Aw, babe, that's so great that you had an organization who helped you." Nicole clutches at her chest. "Emma sure didn't have anything like that." She looks at me. "We've known each other since college. Emma is our other friend, and she has epilepsy, but her parents did *not* know the things it sounds like you knew to get help for Jake."

I look up to see Kellen staring at me with an odd, unreadable expression on his face. I take a deep breath. "I'm sorry your friend had to experience that. I've certainly learned a lot the past 15 years."

Maddie's eyes light up as she holds up her phone. "Oh my gosh, they're hiring," she says. "I just wanted to get the name right. Family Advocacy and Rights Education. They're hiring. You'd be so great at that."

"At what?" I'm so stunned I don't even remember my manners. I fidget with the napkin in my lap.

"Parent coaching," Maddie says. She nods. "Looks like it's a part-time role doing phone support, helping parents and guardians when their child is diagnosed or is having trouble with school and such. Did you know this is, like, a service families have? I didn't know it was a free program when my mom called them all the time."

Nicole, Maddie, and Liam enter a heated discussion on the benefits of tax-supported programs for families while Mick and Kellen drift off into another topic with Kellen's daughter, Orla. Jake and Cal are talking about car parts and I take advantage of the lull in attention to internally freak out about the opportunity that just fell into my lap.

A job opening! The perfect job opening. Can it really be true that there's a job for people to help guide other parents through the earth-shattering experience of diagnosis and getting started with autism therapies and navigating school systems for kids like Jake?

I glance up at the sky again. The rainbow is no longer visible, but the magic of this family still hovers in the warm air like a hug. Never in my wildest dreams would I have imagined that Kellen Brady would enter my life again in any capacity, let alone as friend to my son. And now his niece-in-law has just dangled a fruit so tempting, I almost excuse myself and go apply for the position.

I decide there's no harm in staying put for a little while longer. After all, how often do I get to enjoy a good meal with kind company who convince my son to try new things? I laugh, still not believing this life is real. That it's mine. This time, when Kellen catches me smiling, I almost suspect there's more heat to his gaze. I look away, squeezing Jake's shoulder as he earnestly tells the deck at large, "this is the best outdoor barbecue I've ever had."

CHAPTER NINE
KELLEN

 documentary. Everything feels off about the experience, though, because I'm not chatting about it online as I watch with a group of fellow enthusiasts. I'm sitting alone on my couch in sweatpants, fidgeting as I stare at the screen.

My mind wanders back to the family dinner the other day. Between the rain and the squabbling, it seemed like the typical wild Brady gathering. I'm struck by how Elizabeth and Jake fit right in to the whole scene. She seemed embarrassed by her son's frustration over canceled plans, and I had pointed out that my grown nephews almost came to blows over the last scoop of guacamole in the dish. Who cares if a teenager needs to yell a bit when things don't go his way?

The truth is, I know a lot of people care. Mick and I are well aware that the family we've built is eccentric. We don't mix well with others. For some reason, major clients accept his quirky personality and I like to think that my engineering skill has done an okay job securing their trust in us as a company. But personal stuff? Who wants to mix it up with an old man whose favorite pastime is watching geeky documentaries?

Elizabeth had a good time yesterday, I think. I push those thoughts aside and focus on the soothing voice of the narrator, explaining all the ways that radio changed the world. I glance out the window and see Elizabeth's parents walking up to her front door, carrying a huge basket of flowers. I had forgotten, again, that she grew up in this neighborhood. No wonder she chose this as a landing place for her and her son.

Jake comes outside and I see him giving his grandparents a tour of the yard. He lugs the flower basket in one arm. Through my open window, I hear him say, "Mom isn't home yet from her errand. I'm not supposed to let anyone into the house when she's not here." I chuckle. Orla was sometimes really literal in that way, especially when it came to safety rules. Attention to detail like that makes her a good, safe electrical engineer.

Of course, Orla is able to see nuance in a way that Jake obviously struggles with. I'd like to ask Elizabeth more about his autism. I flick off the documentary, realizing my heart isn't in it and I'm no longer interested, and I look at my picture window in time to see Jake waving at me with both hands, flowers flying out of the basket on his arm.

"This is my neighbor," he says. "He invited us for a backyard barbecue and it was a successful social outing."

I wave at Mr. and Mrs. Burns, who wave casually, and then do a double take. I head toward the front door, knowing it would be rude not to go out and catch up. "Kellen Brady, is that you?" The Burnses have to be pushing 80. They still seem like they're in good health, though Mr. Burns is pulling his shorts up higher and wearing socks with his sandals now.

"Mr. and Mrs. Burns, delighted to see you again," I say, shaking their hands with both of mine. "I'm sorry I didn't look you up sooner. I had forgotten we were neighbors."

Mrs. Burns wags a finger at me. "You're an adult now, Kellen. You can call us Steve and Anna."

"I'll keep that in mind," I say. "Fine grandson you've got there."

Anna beams. "Isn't he a delight. Steve is trying to get him to let us inside until—oh, there she is. Elizabeth! Tell your son to let us inside. Your father is getting eaten alive by mosquitos."

Elizabeth emerges from her car with a shopping bag, grinning. "Jake, sweetie, why won't you let your grandparents inside? How long have you been here?" She directs this last comment to her parents and then, noticing me, gives me a slight nod of her chin.

"I'll just head back on inside," I start to say, turning, but Steve hollers.

"Ah, come on. We haven't seen you in 30 years, kid. Come tell us if all those big plans you had worked out."

Five minutes later, I'm seated on a folding chair in Elizabeth's dining room, where she hasn't yet acquired furniture, passing around pictures of

Orla on my phone. "She works with Mick and me at Beltane engineering," I tell them. "She's whip smart and full of sass."

"She's a beautiful girl, Kellen," Anna says, patting my hand. Elizabeth glances at the photos and smiles, nodding. Anna squeezes my arm. "And what about Mrs. Brady? All this talk of Orla. Where's that wife of yours right now?"

I'm supposed to be used to this question. Normally, I do ok. For the past five years or so, I've been able to take this question in stride, but it's not usually coming from people who knew me as a teenager. I swallow, feeling tears well up. God, it's like my first night at a support group. "She's uh," I start, and swallow again. "Helen passed away some time ago. Cervical cancer."

There's a heavy silence in the room. Elizabeth stares at me. I'm not really able to control the muscles of my face, so I stare back. I feel the tears return to their proper place in my ducts and I smile, tapping the phone. "Orla looks just like her."

"I'm so very sorry," Elizabeth says.

"Thank you." I inhale, exhale slowly through my nose. "I bought this house about 8 years ago," I explain. "Orla and I lived with Mick and his boys for a while after Helen died. You remember my brother Mick?"

Steve shakes his head, but Anna rolls her eyes. I chuckle. "He's still the same."

"What was it like living together? You two boys...and a young girl..."

I'm used to this question and it doesn't phase me at all. "It was the best time of my life," I tell them honestly. "And also the worst." Mick had been through two divorces in a row, was raising three boys who were basically Irish triplets. "Neither Mick nor I had any idea what the hell we were doing, and I was pretty sick with grief," I say. Anna squeezes my hand and I smile. "But we had each other. All of us did. We're all so close now."

Elizabeth adds, "Kellen works with his family, too. They have an engineering firm."

"Do you now?" Steve perks up. He was always interested in my fascination with physics. Maybe he hoped it would rub off on his daughter. She always tended more toward art and literature.

"It's nice working together, all of us," I tell him. "Mick's boys, Orla, Mick and me...we've got a bunch of others on staff, too, so we aren't at each other's throats all day. People tease us, but we do good work," I assure them. "Beltane Engineering has good synergy."

"That does sound nice," Elizabeth says. "I'm glad you all have each other like that."

She starts to put away the chips and cereal from her grocery bag, and I rise from the table. "I should get going," I say, hoping they'll insist I say, and then immediately feeling embarrassed by how desperate I am for company all of a sudden.

"We're just getting caught up," Anna says. "I'm sure Elizabeth can offer you a snack if that's what you need. Bethy, get the man a cookie."

"Oh, no thank you, really."

From this angle, standing at the table, I can see Elizabeth bent over to put the snacks in her pantry. For the first time in many years, I feel the zing of heat churning through my veins, straight to my crotch. *Good lord, man, control yourself,* I think, noticing with uncomfortable certainty that I have a hard-on in my neighbor's kitchen with her son and parents present.

Concerned with how visible this situation will be through my sweatpants, I sink back down into my seat. "Water would be great," I manage to croak out. Someone hands me a glass and I gulp it down, trying to forget the way I felt just now, staring at the round swell of Elizabeth's hips in her dark jeans. This is not how I expected my evening to go at all.

I have no idea what to do about any of it.

CHAPTER TEN

ELIZABETH

"It's 3:06, Mom." Jake has both palms on the glass of the storm door, staring out at the street where I know Todd is not going to arrive any time soon. Damn him and his selfish horse shit. I should never have relied on him for anything.

"I know, babe," I tell my son. I pick at my shirt, adjusting one of the "capsule" outfits that Lisa and June declared interview appropriate. I don't actually have an interview, but I plan to go drop my resume in person at FARE and want to look nice. Of course, I can't go do that if Todd doesn't come meet his fucking custody responsibilities.

We both stand there for another five minutes, our breath becoming irregular. I'm sure Jake's heart is racing as much as mine. "Are you calling him?" My son looks at me so intensely. I have no desire to call Todd, because I am sure I'll regret what I say to him if I get through, but I nod to Jake and pull out my phone. I dial.

"Right to voicemail, Jake." We both sigh. Then he screams.

"I don't even like him. His new house smells like fragrance and I don't like that person he's living with because she smells like hairspray and all the food has *tomatoes* in it." Jake yanks open the front door and steps into the front yard, where he screams again and then plunks down on the grass.

I close my eyes and wait for inspiration to come to help me salvage this day, but it doesn't arrive. Until I open my eyes and see Kellen crossing the

398

street, a lawnmower abandoned in his driveway. "Hey, Jake," he says, his voice kind. "Something bothering you today?"

"Yes!" Jake doesn't elaborate. I smile because he did indeed answer Kellen's question. Kellen also grins, and I feel warmth spread through my chest, where I hadn't quite realized an icy chill had settled.

"Would you—now wait. Let me get it right. I'd like to see if I have an idea to help. What's bothering you?"

Jake seems to ponder Kellen, who sits down next to him in the grass and waits, patiently. *Why can't Jake's actual father be this patient with him,* I think, and immediately hate myself for having such thoughts. There's just so much to unpack there. I listen as Jake complains that his dad is late, is not answering his phone, and has basically ruined Jake's entire life.

Kellen looks up at me and nods. I wave. "Your mom is pretty dressed up. She looks like she had some plans go awry, too."

Jake considers this and looks at me. "She is dressed atypically, yes."

"You got somewhere to be, Beth?" With his legs bent, arms dangling as he and my son fidget with the clover growing in the yard, I can easily pretend, just for a minute, they both belong there, together. Father and son, making sure I get out the door okay. It's a fantasy, totally unrealistic and a dangerous path to let my thoughts wander.

"I had an errand to run," I say, waving my hand. "But I can go another time. I don't want to leave Jake while he's upset."

Kellen is quiet for a moment and Jake yanks a clump of dandelions from the yard, hurling them toward the street. "I see that your grass is a bit long," Kellen says. "Is the landlord supposed to mow?"

I bite my lip and shake my head. I haven't gotten around to dealing with the lawn yet. Every time I think I'm getting caught up with this new life, I'm reminded of another thing I didn't do. Or couldn't do. How hard is it to get a lawnmower and take care of this small amount of grass? Evidently hard enough that I failed to do it.

"Tell you what," Kellen says, standing and extending an arm toward Jake. "Why don't I show Jake here how the lawnmower works. You have a knack for mechanical things, right?"

"I understand how combustion engines function to operate the blades." Jake rolls his eyes, like Kellen just suggested he didn't know something simple like counting to five.

Kellen chuckles. "Well then we're halfway through already. Beth, you can run your errand and by the time you get back, we'll have covered safety tips as well as mechanics."

"Oh, I can't let you mow my grass, Kellen," I spit out automatically, accustomed to saying no to help. I may have known Kellen as a teen, but I'm not ready to leave my son alone with him, not when Jake's been upset. Most of the time, the well-meaning person offering assistance isn't really qualified to help me get Jake to the car or coax him to move if he's blocking a door and gets upset. I've just gotten used to being on call. All the time.

"I'm not going to mow it," Kellen says, scoffing. "Jake will."

My mouth drops open to protest, but Kellen holds up a hand. "I've taught four teens how to use a lawnmower and haven't had a lost digit yet. You go on and run your errand and then stop somewhere for a cup of tea by yourself."

I swoon, right there on my porch. If I hadn't been leaning against the door to my house, I would have fallen right to the ground. That is the most romantic thing anyone has ever said to me in 50 years, and that includes the first time I knew Kellen when he used to say beautiful things to me before we'd kiss.

I touch my lips, remembering the feel of his soft lips against mine. He had smooth cheeks then, no chest hair poking out from his shirt collar. I shake myself back to reality and sigh. He's right. I should run my errand, but I also should stay home and make sure that Jake doesn't relapse into the red zone and hurt himself.

Kellen seems to watch me working through this thought process. He squints. "What if Jake calls to check in every ten minutes until you get there? He's got a phone, right?"

Jake rolls his eyes and pulls out the phone in question. "Mom, it's fine. I want to use the lawnmower." He doesn't look back at me, walks right across the street toward Kellen's garage in that way he has of shutting off the switch, like the lightning storm never even happened.

"I swear I've got this, Beth," Kellen says. "Go run your errand."

I try not to cry, and I close my eyes. I tell him, "When his shoulders get tense, that's his tell that he's starting to get very upset. Promise you'll have him call me right away?"

"I will study his shoulders with all the care I give a dam about to break." Kellen holds one hand over his heart and one hand in the air, like he's saluting me, and I feel something shift in my chest. Maybe this can be okay. Before I can talk myself out of it, I run back inside to grab the folder with my resume, along with my purse.

When I get to the driveway, I see my son crouched next to my former lover, leaning over the lawnmower and talking about "rigid rules and flexible rules," and I know for sure that I'm going to have to use my facial massager later, because my god. This man understands how to talk to my son. And it turns me on.

ℬ

"MAY I HELP YOU?" There's a pleasant woman at the reception desk when I find the FARE office in a row of old industrial buildings.

I put on my most confident smile and lean on the counter. "I hope so," I tell her. "I'm interested in applying for the open position I saw online. For the parent coach? I've got my resume and cover letter here." I open the folder and hand her the documents, but I can tell by the look on her face that I've made a blunder somehow.

"Oh," she says. "I'm so sorry. We actually just filled that position." I will myself not to feel defeated. It was a pipe dream job, anyway. In no universe would the perfect part-time job open up and fall at my feet that way. Not that easily.

I nod. "I understand. Bad timing," I say, pulling back the papers. A door opens behind the desk and I see a woman who looks vaguely familiar.

She hangs up her cell phone call and does a double take when she sees me. "Elizabeth Gaston!" She points at her chest. "Do you remember me? Karen Wolfe. Our boys were in social skills together. Gosh, it's been almost ten years now."

I do remember her, now that she says that. I smile and shake her hand. "It's Elizabeth Burns now," I say. "It's so good to see you."

"What brings you down here? We don't get many visitors here at the office." I learned from their website that most of their trainings are in schools, for teachers and staff, but sometimes in community centers when they host events for families to attend.

"I was actually here to apply for the coach position, but I just learned that I was a little too late." I shrug and try to seem casual, even though I'm ready to cry inside.

Karen makes a disappointed face. "Oh, gosh. That's too bad. I always love when we get parents on the team who really *get it*. You know? Of course you know. How is Jake?"

I shrug. "Pissed off that I ruined his life by moving him to a new neighborhood with new smells and different furniture." We share a belly laugh about that. I seem to recall that her son has an aversion to the color yellow and can't even be in a room if someone else is wearing a yellow shirt. "Is

Evan still struggling with yellow?" I clutch the folder tight against my chest, hoping I haven't struck a nerve. That one would be a really hard aversion to manage, especially in Pittsburgh where half the city dons black and gold clothing every Friday in support of the baseball, football or hockey teams.

Karen beams. "You remembered! Oh man, that one was a hard one. We got the most wonderful behavioral specialist and she took him to the football stadium—you know most of the seats there are yellow. Gold. Whatever. She did all this desensitization work with him and of course he still hates yellow, but is able to at least attend class with other kids who wear a Steelers jersey or something." She shrugs. "I'm so bummed we don't have anything here for you."

"There will be other opportunities," I say, echoing things I've heard Lisa say before. Echoing the statements I say to my own kid when he's suffered a disappointment. If I say it often enough, maybe the sting will wear off my own disappointment.

Karen makes a face. "Well," she says. "Why don't you leave your info with me. Got a resume? Of course you do. Anyway, we partner with so many organizations. It's the time of year where there's so much turnover as schools are getting started...why don't I pass your info along if I see something?"

"Oh my gosh, Karen! Yes. Thank you." I hand her the folder. "That would be amazing. Truly." She hands me her card and tells me to call, and not just about Jake. I slide it into my pocket, not wanting it to get lost in the cavern of my purse.

I walk back to my car, reminding myself that this was a reach job anyway. I have no real training or qualifications, just 15 years of advocating for my kid to get the services he needed and the insurance coverage necessary to pay for it. It's not really like I lost the job. Karen seems like she has really good connections.

I slide into the driver's seat and look around. There's a comic book shop nearby, a few dive bars. Kellen urged me to go get a tea, but I've been gone nearly an hour by now. Surely he and Jake have finished mowing the grass. I realize I didn't even leave Kellen my phone number in case of an emergency. What if Jake didn't charge his phone? Jesus, I didn't even call to check in like I said I would. Panicked, I start to drive toward home, telling myself Jake has my number and both of them know where my parents live, and my parents have my number, too.

"This is fine," I tell myself. "It's fine. You can run an errand and leave your teenaged son at home. This is fine."

My phone pings while I'm at the light. I look down to see a message from Jake: ***Can I mow lawns 4 $$? Kellen says I can use his mower.***

I feel a deep relief that spreads through my veins like warm chocolate. I'm almost high on the sugary sweetness of this feeling—Jake cooled down from being upset and moved on with his day.

The light turns and I swing over the Hot Metal Bridge back toward my end of the city. I'm driving along and I see a jumble of furniture by the curb as I get to a neighborhood where a lot of college students live. Remembering the bedroom furniture I recently picked up, I slow down, hoping maybe I'll score something for the dining room.

All the chairs I see are stained or broken, but my eye catches a flat black...something. "Works! Free!" Someone has written a sign with black marker and taped it to the object. I park and get out, peering down. I realize it's a portable treadmill.

It's small and pretty basic, but I think about all the times Lisa has told me stress lives in the legs. She started power walking whenever she had a call home from a teacher, pacing until she felt calm enough to carry on with her day. Soon, she was putting in 30 miles a week, sometimes with one of her kids running behind her, complaining about her pace.

I don't have a supportive husband at home like Lisa, to take the reins with the kids while I go blow off steam. I decide this treadmill is the perfect solution. I won't have to leave Jake if I'm anxious that he's on edge. I can stomp out all my rage. Maybe I'll even work up to jogging. How many years has it been since I exercised?

I wrestle the treadmill into my hatchback and head home, a smile on my face. When I pull in the driveway, I see that the yard has been neatly mowed. Jake is inside on the couch playing a video game. "Hey," I say, ruffling his hair. He bats my hand out of the way, not looking up from his game.

"I'm in the middle of a round," he says.

I roll my eyes, drag the treadmill into the room, and plunk it in front of the TV. I sink into the couch next to my son and pull out my phone to search for the instruction manual for this model.

CHAPTER ELEVEN
ELIZABETH

I LOVE MY NEW TREADMILL. I LOVE THAT I FOUND IT, I LOVE THAT I CRAMMED IT IN the car by myself, and I love how I feel when I use it. I can tell it's poor quality, but it's so portable. I can move it around all the different rooms of my house, using it in front of the television when I'm watching, or in my bedroom with my headphones and an audiobook when Jake's playing video games.

I see how Lisa worked her way quickly up to 30 miles a week. I am walking at least two miles a day right now as my son starts a new high school, I adjust to life on a new budget, and I wait to receive the money from the sale of my marital home.

I start to notice other changes that feel related to the treadmill. I'm more comfortable wearing the capsule wardrobe that reveals the shape of my body, now that I'm focusing more on how my body feels walking around in the world. I can feel each of my muscles now, and I'm not sure if it's because I activated them or because I think about them as I walk.

I also feel myself making other impulsive decisions, without analyzing them first. Without second-guessing myself. Which is how I find myself walking across the street lugging a high chair. I saw it by the curb as I went to collect a second-hand dining set I found online. It's a name brand high chair that had just a few scuffs I polished out in my kitchen.

I place the chair on the brick stoop and knock on Kellen's door. Even though I should be used to seeing him every day, it takes my breath away a little when he answers. He's so handsome and kind. His dark eyes always seem so honest. "Hey," I say, greeting him, loving that his smile widens. "I wanted to thank you for being such a great neighbor."

"Oh, Beth, that's not necessary," he starts. I hold up a hand.

"I heard you say something about wanting to keep a high chair here, so Maddie and Liam's baby can eat with the family. And, well, I saw this..." I gesture toward the chair. Kellen pushes the door open and steps outside, hands on his hips. I shrug. "I grabbed it for you. I know it's second hand, but you know how babies are."

"They're a mess," he says, laughing. "God, Orla used to throw food everywhere while she ate. Callum still does." We share a smile, likely both remembering the great guacamole fight from the family barbecue. "Beth, this is...well, it's perfect," he says.

We stand in silence on his stoop, staring at a piece of baby furniture. I like everything about his response, although I feel a brief twang of sadness that I didn't get to see him as a father to young kids. I remind myself what I'm actually doing is grieving the loss of a great father for Jake, not wishing Kellen away from his life experiences.

He looks up at me and takes my hand. "I hope you and Jake will be here for many more dinner parties once the baby arrives," he says.

ß

My high from the encounter lasts nearly a week. I see Kellen outside almost daily. We wave and shout back and forth about the weather, but I don't approach him again. I just sit around and think about him instead. I think about the name of his company, Beltane, how it's a Celtic festival of fire and new beginnings.

That leads me down a rabbit hole of Celtic astrology. My father's family, the Burns family, has Irish heritage, too. We always sort of thought everyone in the U.S. was a little bit Irish. Not like the Brady family. Kellen's mom was a first generation American and his family used to go visit their relatives in Ireland all the time.

I stumble onto an article about the moon, and how the Celtic druids believed the full moon closest to your birth determined personality traits. It's all ridiculous, probably, and I know Lisa would tease me if she could see me wide-eyed and staring at my laptop, but I see that my own October birthday aligns with the Exploring Moon and the ivy.

My Celtic horoscope talks of big transitions, of internal strength and the pull of relocating in the face of struggle. I start to cry as I read about ivy, a vine that overcomes despite all odds. "Life can be difficult," my internet spirit guide says, and I know it's generic and silly, but for the first time since I left Todd, I feel seen. "You endure troubling times with silent perseverance and soulful grace," I read aloud.

I snap the laptop shut and do something else impulsive. I drive to a tattoo parlor and ask for an ivy tattoo, just a small one, black ink only, on my hip. Where only I can see. I lie on the table as the artist transfers a sketch onto my body. The needle burns more than it stings, and I relish the sensation, searing this meaning and awareness into my body forever. "I persevere," I whisper. *I take root and cling,* I think as the tattoo gun inks my birth rite and heritage into my skin.

I drive home with instructions for care and healing, and I tell no one. It's my secret. My affirmation. And I love it. When I get home, I fast-walk two more miles, loving the quick glimpse of my thigh beneath my shorts with every step.

CHAPTER TWELVE
KELLEN

AGAINST MY BETTER JUDGEMENT, I AGREE TO GO ALONG WITH ORLA AND MY brother and his boys for a family run. They've all been very busy with new projects at work and we haven't had dinner at my house for a few weeks, so I'm eager to spend time with them. I just doubt it's a good idea for my joints to run on the paved trails they prefer for the weekend morning long runs.

"Doesn't this kill your knees," I ask my brother, who is practically sprinting five miles into our route. I'm starting to feel a cramp in my foot and my knees aren't exactly sore, but they don't like this impact. My brother is three years older and should be more rickety than me, but he's bouncing along like an impala while the kids fall in behind us.

"I've got these gel inserts in my shoes," he says, pointing at a designer sneaker that looks like something a professional athlete would wear to a nightclub. I grunt a response and slow up a bit, wondering if that will help.

"You still living that hermit life?" Orla nudges me with her shoulder and grins, tucking her long hair back out of her face.

"Hardly," I tell her. "You know exactly what I've been up to at work, madam." Orla is consulting on the electrical grid inspection program that Liam got started. They're helping to write up proprietary protocols as Beltane looks to expand beyond the Allegheny region.

She pouts at me. "I can't decide if I want you to pick me to go on site visits in Tennessee or if I think you should go so you can spice up your routine a little."

I grin at that. "We haven't been to the Smokies in a long time." That was one of the last family trips we took together, before Helen was too sick to travel. I remember how the air felt crisp there, the sunsets magical as I watched them with both my girls. And then, as has been happening more frequently lately, I feel a pang in my chest and a lump in my throat. I miss Helen. I miss doing things with her and talking about nature together.

Orla nods. "If we go again, I'd want to actually camp this time."

"What do you mean?"

She balks, flicking her hair again. "We stayed in a lame cabin with electricity," she scoffs. "Mom hated camping and you always said cabins were a compromise."

"Your mother didn't hate camping." Did she? I seem to remember camping frequently.

Orla laughs. "Um, yes. She did. She liked the views and hated the bugs. Remember?"

As Orla says it, I do remember Helen saying that. "Well, anyway, it's been a long time since I stayed in either a cabin or a tent," I tell her. "You're right."

"So plan a camping trip," Orla says. "Shake the mildew off the tent. Lie on the ground until your hips ache."

"Who will go with me, though?" I look around at Liam and his pregnant girlfriend. Zack's girlfriend Nicole is decidedly not interested in nature. Maybe Cal or my brother feel like checking out the leaves some weekend.

"Well, I'm out, because you're going to send me to Appalachia, and Uncle Mick is going to be there to woo those power company guys."

Right. My brother is the face of the operation, the guy who is good with the customers. When I don't say anything for a spell, Orla glances over at me. "What about your neighbor?"

"Who? Mr. Beckas?" The Greek couple next door to me are in their late 80s. They're the type of Greek neighbors who roast a lamb in their back yard on Orthodox Easter, and they always share. But they don't strike me as interested in camping.

Orla rolls her eyes at me. "Elizabeth, silly. God, Dad, you're 50, not 100."

"What's that supposed to mean?" I try not to focus on my foot, which is starting to really throb now.

"It means you should ask Elizabeth if she wants to go camping. Take her to see the hemlock grove in Laurel Hill." Asking Beth to go on a hike to see the ancient hemlock forest sounds like a nice idea, actually. It's such a mysterious, supernatural type of place. I bet she'd really enjoy the energy there. But then Orla says, "Maybe kiss her while you look for shooting stars."

I freeze in my tracks. "Orla," I say. "Enough." She opens her mouth to say something else, but then snaps it shut and shakes her head, running off to join her cousins.

Distressed by our conversation, I beg off the family outing to the diner after our run and head home to ice my foot. The pain eases up some, but by evening I'm experiencing shooting pains when I stand on it to heat up my dinner.

"Figures," I say, pulling out my laptop to look up what sort of doctor I might need. Orla and I made a vow to Helen that we wouldn't ignore health concerns. Even though she always went for her well-woman visits, she never spoke up about the abdominal pain she was experiencing until it was too late. By the time my wife's cancer was discovered, she was well past the point where treatment would have been effective.

I inhale and think. The likely culprit is probably running, but sometimes a sore joint could be a hint that something else is wrong. When your wife dies of cancer in her 30s, it's easy to assume every ache and pain is simmering cancer. I decide the foot pain is probably just a muscle or joint pain, and groan when I look up "foot doctor." *Podiatrist* just sounds like an old-man word. I remind myself that it's a gift to be old, to live long enough for aches and pains. I click on the podiatrist who offers online scheduling so I don't have to wait until Monday to call.

I stare at the appointment confirmation email. Here I am with a podiatry appointment. Sure, this is the perfect time to ask my former girlfriend if she wants to spend a romantic night with me in the woods. Maybe we can bring a cane and some adult diapers while we're at it. Really turn up the sex appeal.

Orla's comment earlier about the shooting stars reminds me that I have kissed Elizabeth by starlight before. We never went camping together, but we went out exploring after dark plenty of times. Back then, there was less light pollution in the city. We could wander deep into Frick Park and sit by a creek, listening to the rushing water, making out in the moonlight.

It felt daring to break city ordinances about parks closing at dusk, and it felt good to kiss each other in the open air, our warm bodies pressed together, so young and curious.

Sitting on my sofa, alone in my house, I realize that my body has once again responded to thoughts of Elizabeth Burns. I move my computer to the side and look down at my pants. My own body has become a stranger to me in this way, like maybe it's somebody else's erection throbbing and twitching in my lap.

Swallowing, I close my eyes and reach into my sweats. I gasp as I touch myself, my skin hot. My breath quickens as I pull up the memories of those makeout sessions with Beth. I recall how young we felt, how alive. The thrill of pleasure, still new to us as teenagers. My hand closes around my cock as I remember sliding my palm up Elizabeth's shirt, my tongue plunging into her mouth.

I remember her breathy gasps as I pinched her nipples. She didn't even wear a bra back then, and I didn't know enough to realize how sexy that was. My hand moves faster, fist clenching tighter, pressure mounting. I start to wonder if she wears one now, imagining her body in black lace, bare for me. Here in my house.

I shudder and my abs clench as I come on my chest, gulping for air as the orgasm rushes over me like a tidal wave. I look down at my sticky hand in surprise, knowing I'll repeat this action again and wondering if Beth ever does this same thing.

CHAPTER THIRTEEN
ELIZABETH

I'M DEFINITELY LIMPING. I SEE LISA LOOKING AT ME SIDEWAYS AND WINCE. THE TWO of us usually power walk laps around the block while our boys are in chess club. I asked Jake if he still wanted to participate since we don't live up this way anymore, but he looked at me like I'd just killed his puppy or something. Shows what I know about teenagers.

Lisa takes a swig from her water bottle. "Why in the hell are you walking like that," she asks, seeming concerned. It's been a few weeks since I brought the treadmill home. Between Jake starting his new high school and Todd being an asshole and my growing frustration at not having a job, I've been pounding out a lot of miles on that thing.

And it would seem you get what you pay for.

I choose not to tell Lisa I trash picked a shitty foot-breaker. "I've been running in bad shoes," I tell her. "I think." We sit on a bench and I pull off my sandal, rubbing my foot. "It usually only really hurts in the evening once I lie down."

Lisa nods. "You need to see Ashish." I roll my eyes. Lisa's husband is an orthopedic surgeon who works with professional athletes.

"Ashish? Really? For a sore foot? I just need some Advil," I tell her, pulling up my purse and searching around for some. Ashish probably books out months in advance unless you're a hockey player.

"At least let me asks him who he thinks you should see?" She already has her phone out and is calling. He answers immediately. I love that about them. Even this high profile surgeon answers her calls unless he's in the O.R. Even if she's just calling to tell him she's overwhelmed with the boys. My thoughts drift back to Kellen, the way he's been showing Jake how to use the lawn mower and weed whacker, so patiently. *I bet he'd answer if I called upset about Jake,* I think.

Todd used to chastise me, even if I was calling to say we were headed to the emergency room because Jake smashed his hand in the ball return at the bowling alley when he got too excited studying how it worked.

I chew on my cheek, rubbing my foot, while Lisa chats with Ashish. "Did you eat dinner," she asks him. It'll be past eight til she gets home after the boys are finished. I hope to be in bed with a painkiller by then. *Okay, so the foot is pretty bad,* I concede, mentally.

"He wants to talk to you." Lisa waves the phone in my face and I sigh, taking it from her. A few seconds later, he texts me an appointment time with a podiatrist he's friends with. "He's going to fit you in tomorrow," Ashish says. "You're too important to be crippled by a foot injury, Elizabeth. Your feet withstand hundreds of pounds of pressure every step. The bones and tendons form an intricate network. It can be very debilitating if something gets left untreated."

"Yes, doctor," I sigh, feeling a little petulant. I'm definitely not accustomed to prioritizing my health, which is part of the reason getting the treadmill felt so delicious. It was such a great idea to take care of me! And now I messed all that up by walking too much or wearing the wrong shoes or...something. By the time we hang up, Lisa has somehow procured milkshakes from one of the nearby shops. She passes me one and we spread out on the bench outside the library, waiting for the kids to burst out yelling about strategy.

"It's good you got a treadmill," Lisa says. "That shows you're ready to start doing more things for you."

I nod. "I realized I'm not going to feel comfortable leaving Jake to go and exercise. Not yet, anyway. Even though he's doing great. But if I had something at home, I figured I'd do something good for my body."

"I love it! I'm inspired. Let's get your foot better and make a plan to do more movement things together."

"I'd like that!" And I mean it. We can drag our kids with us, or Jake feels comfortable at Lisa's place if Ashish is around to keep an eye on them. I hear the library door open and I stand to greet Jake, wincing again. "Yeah," I say. "I'm also glad you're making me talk to a foot doctor."

B

THE NEXT AFTERNOON, I slip into sweats in case I need to get undressed for X-rays or something. I pull into the parking lot of the podiatrist's office, happy my friend recommended a place just outside the city where parking isn't as much of an issue. Everything hurts worse today and I'm not sure how I'd make it if I had to park a few blocks away!

It seems like the waiting room is full of old people. I'm no spring chicken, but these are bonafide old people with pouffy hair and canes and compression socks. *Oh god, what if I have to start wearing compression socks?*

Eventually I get called back and Dr. Sam has me hop up on his exam table. As I explain what's happening he holds up a hand. "Let me guess," he says. "Hurts worse at night? Sort of throbs all the time?" I nod. He nods. "I see it all the time with postmenopausal women."

I feel a lump form in my throat. Does it even count as menopause if it's surgically induced from a hysterectomy? Dr. Sam continues, explaining that the loss of estrogen lowers bone density in the feet. "I can't tell you how many women your age I see with stress fractures," he says.

"Wait. Fracture?"

He nods. "Oh yeah. I'd bet my farm on it. I don't really have a farm, but you catch my meaning." He gestures for me to lift my foot and he starts poking around. "We'll do an X-ray to be sure," he says, "but I'm putting in orders for a walking boot and I'll have one of my assistants get you fitted after we read the X-rays."

Within a half hour, I'm thunking around the waiting room in a huge black walking boot, wondering how in the hell I'm going to get my car home. Because guess what? I can't drive. Todd is going to love hearing this. I'm so irritated that I almost don't notice Kellen Brady standing at the desk, asking a question about a big white and blue splint-looking device.

He turns toward me and beams. "Beth," he says. Then he looks down and frowns. "Not you, too?"

I lean on the wall. "Stress fracture," I say with a sigh. "What are you in for?"

He rolls his eyes. "Plantar fasciitis. Just saying it makes me feel old. You getting gel inserts for your shoes?" He gestures at the pile of things on the desk as the receptionist hands him back his credit card. Kellen gathers it all into the bag they hand him and limps over to me.

I swallow, thickly, knowing I'm going to have to ask him for a favor here. "Hey, are you heading home?"

He nods and looks at my foot again. "Need a ride?"

"If it wouldn't be too much trouble—"

He interrupts, holding up a hand. "Don't even think about it. Happy to do it. I'll send one of the kids to come fetch your car later if you want?" Before I can answer him, he barrels on, saying, "I call them kids, but they're all in their 30s now. Well, not Orla. She's 25. Still not a kid."

I smile at that. "She can be your kid," I tell him. "I'm sure Jake will always be my kid." He nods and holds open the door for me as I wobble out, still unsteady on my boot.

CHAPTER FOURTEEN
KELLEN

*OF ALL THE GIN JOINTS...*I still can't believe I ran into Beth at the podiatrist. I'm wearing ratty old clothes since I didn't know what I'd have to take off or put on. And now she knows my old-man secret. Yet still, I find myself telling her more about it, how I have to wear the splint at night when I sleep and take ibuprofen for weeks.

She doesn't seem grossed out by it, though. Just nods along, telling me about her own foot-care regimen. "I don't know what I'm going to do about Jake," she confesses, worrying her lower lip and tapping her fingernails on my console.

"What about him? Doesn't he take the bus to and from school?"

She nods. "Yes, but now I don't have any way to get to him if they call and he's having a meltdown. You know, if I don't get there fast enough, they call the cops."

"The cops?"

"Oh, don't get me started. Nobody knows what to do with an autistic kid once he starts screeching, and they usually try to pat him or hug him and he flails out...and they call the cops."

"Jake has had the cops called before?" I just can't picture it. The kid has always responded to quickly to me, even that day he was so upset in the rain.

She shakes her head. "Not Jake, no, but friends of ours." She stares out the window. "I've always managed to get there quickly if he gets upset. It's why I never went back to work."

I think about how very hard she has worked to help her son succeed, to keep him from harm, and I tell her, "I'd say you've been working plenty."

She smiles at that. "Doesn't help me get to Allderdice High School from Morningside if there's a problem," she says.

"I assume his father isn't a resource?"

She snorts out a laugh at that. "Uh, no. I don't even think I ever wrote Todd down as an emergency contact, even before we were divorced." I have nothing to say in response to that. It's unthinkable to me, a parent not willing to go to bat for his child. Mick and I may have traveled a lot, but the kids always knew one of us would be available. The older boys had their mother, too.

I grind my teeth together, wishing I could ask Elizabeth to list me as an emergency contact for Jake. But I don't know her well enough, not anymore. That would be inappropriate. They're not mine to take care of.

The thought rattles me. Why would I want to take care of them? Where had that even come from? Based on the state of my own feet, I'm not doing the greatest job taking care of my own damn self, let alone Beth and her boy.

Eventually, she says, "I guess I'll just have to ask my parents to be on call for a few weeks until I'm allowed to take the boot off to drive," she says. Then she sinks lower in the seat of my car. "Ugh, telling them I have a stress fracture is going to open up a whole bunch of scrutiny. They're going to come take my temperature," she says. I laugh, because she's right.

"They'll probably bring a gallon of chicken soup."

She snorts again. "Wait til I tell them you have a hurt foot, too. Distract them a bit. Spread out the panic."

"I'd eat the soup," I tell her. "No. That's not entirely true. I'd put it in my fridge, and Orla or Cal would come take it."

We both share a laugh at that and I pull into her driveway. I don't want her to have to walk too far. I'm sure her foot must be hurting her.

"Thank you so much, Kellen. Truly." We both get out of the car and lean on the railing leading up to her steps.

"Give me your keys," I tell her. "The boys can go get your car later after family dinner."

"Oh, that's too much," she protests. "I just..." She drifts off and stares at her house. Takes a deep breath and fishes in her purse, shaking her head.

"Thank you," she concedes, handing me the key ring. "I'm working on saying yes to help."

"Oh yeah?"

She nods. "It's new to me, having help offered. And even newer for me to accept. Ever since I walked in on Todd with that stupid, vapid asshole woman…" She drifts off. "You don't want to hear about that. Anyway, I'm here now, living in my own house, and I'm saying yes to your generous offer to have your nephews fetch my car."

"You and Jake should join us for dinner," I blurt, before I can think twice about it. The words just fall from my mouth, right after she told me she felt overwhelmed by my offer to fetch her car. "I'd like it," I say, and it's true. "I like spending time with Jake. He's so curious. And," I pause, clear my throat, and fix my gaze directly on her eyes. "I like spending time with you, too, Beth. It's good to see you after all this time."

Her eyes well up, and I worry I've overstepped. She confessed a lot here in the past few minutes—her dirtbag husband not only isn't there for his kid, but he was sleeping around on an amazing woman like Elizabeth. I worry about what I'll do if I ever lay eyes on him. When she still doesn't say anything, I add, "You don't want to stand around and cook dinner tonight on that boot. And I don't want to stand and cook, either. I'm ordering out. Burrito bar." I decide it as I say it, knowing it's a fantastic idea because I'll have leftovers for a few days and not have to worry about my lunches.

She brightens at that idea and reaches into her bag again. "Let me chip in," she says as I start waving her hands away. "Please, Kellen." She thrusts a few twenties into my sweatpants pocket as I'm protesting and we both look down at her hand in my pants. I cough and adjust my stance, but based on the look on her face I'm too late.

My body definitely noticed her fingers near my cock even if my brain was busy trying to refuse her money. "Thank you," I tell her. "I'll order extra guac and make sure your boy gets his fair share."

She nods rapidly. "See you around six?"

"Sounds perfect," I tell her. I hurry back around to my side of the car and reverse across the street and into my garage. I shut off the engine and exhale long and slow. I'm going to need a few hours to calm down.

CHAPTER FIFTEEN
KELLEN

I wake up with a cramp in my calf and remember I'm wearing my night splint for the old-man foot. After dinner last night, I was hurting something fierce. I kept walking around the kitchen like nothing was wrong, making sure we had enough plates and spoons, helping Jake get the right soda since he had opinions on the sell-by dates.

I took a lot of pain relievers before bed and fell asleep feeling old and decrepit. Sighing, I remove the hard plastic device and limp my way through my morning routine. It feels strange to go to work without exercising, like I'm starting the day without breakfast. But I haven't figured out a low-impact workout option yet, so here we are.

I'm even earlier to the office than usual and am surprised to find Orla in the kitchen staring dreamily at her coffee. "Hey, sweetheart," I say, greeting her with a kiss. I have an urge to pat her on the head and tug on her blond ponytail, but I resist, reminding myself that she's an adult now.

"Morning, Dad." She smiles and starts drinking her caffeine. I rock to one foot and wince, remembering the pain in my arch too late to avoid discomfort.

"Say," I tell her, sinking into a plastic chair in the kitchenette. "I've been meaning to check in with you. I was going over some of my paperwork." She pulls up a seat at the round table nodding. "You know you'll inherit everything—"

"Dad, Jesus. Not at work. Come on. You're 50."

"Yes, well, your mother was 35." My retort jars her and she snaps her mouth shut, nodding. "Anyway, I was thinking of leaving the tools in the garage specifically to your cousin Callum. He uses them regularly and you don't seem interested..."

I drift off as she stares at me. "Dad," she says, setting her mug on the table. "You are not going to itemize your estate. You need to stop."

"Preparation is a gift, Orla. This is a kindness for you."

She shakes her head. "Having the paperwork in place is one thing. You're a healthy man who gets his checkups regularly. You're in perfect health."

I want to rail back at her about my foot, about how this slow degradation of my body surely indicates the creeping arrival of the Grim Reaper, but Orla isn't finished. "Dad," she says, grabbing my hands and looking into my eyes. "I'm not just talking about itemizing. You're not living your best life. You're holed up." I shake my head. Orla nods hers. "You are, Dad. But you know what I saw? I saw your entire face change when you were talking to your new neighbors. I saw you make that kid's entire day better and yesterday I saw you convince him to taste sour cream on his burrito."

"The flavor really ties the meal together," I mutter.

She nods. "I know it. Now Jake does, too. When's the last time you spent time with someone new like that? Really got to know someone?" I sigh. I feared she'd start in on me again about dating, but Orla raises a valid point. "Those film nerds you talk about are all on a chat group online," she says. "You could totally be getting together in person for that hobby, but you're not." She sips her coffee and I stare at her. "If you want me to be ok with you giving Cal the tools, then I want you to promise to start doing more social things outside the family."

I snort a laugh. "What a firecracker you are. Who raised you?"

She winks at me. "A guy who was dealt some bad cards and coasted on fumes for a lot of years."

"You're mixing metaphors, darling."

She stands and puts her empty mug in the dishwasher. "Yeah, well, you're festering away." She plants a kiss on my forehead before I can come up with a retort and makes her way to her work space. I try to focus on my projects. Liam and I have meetings coming up to pitch inspection services to a few different power companies.

These are warm calls. My brother already went out there and wined and dined them. He's the one with all the pop culture knowledge, who can strike up friendly conversation. I go in and talk about technical details. I can do that with half a mind. Have been for years, with barely any small-talk before or after.

It bothers me that I think Orla's right about the social aspect of my life. I've been very focused on my family for…a very long time. I haven't felt lonely. There's too many Bradys in my business—literally at my work place. I chuckle at the thought of loneliness. Glancing at my calendar for today, I see I'm in meetings straight through for hours.

No, I'm not lonely. But Orla's right about one thing. I'm not social. And she's also right that I enjoy getting to know Jake. I swallow, remembering my time in the shower this morning where I yet again played out fantasies with Elizabeth. The room heats up as I recall how savagely I touched myself, thinking about the scent of her in my car the other day.

She and I haven't had any real conversations, not privately. She's been to dinner with my entire family and I've taught her son to mow the lawn, but apart from that car ride I haven't sat and talked to her. It seems disrespectful to use her in my fantasies and not at least take her out to dinner. Maybe Orla's onto something.

Before I can talk myself out of it, I pick up my cell and call Beth. She answers breathlessly, like she's just been struggling with something. I look at the time. "Oh, crap. Are you driving Jake to school?"

"No, no," she huffs. "I walked him to the bus stop this morning." I hear the mismatched clunk of her walking cast as she thunks back home.

"Should you be doing that? With your foot?"

"What can I do for you, Kellen," she counters, an edge to her voice.

I close my eyes and swallow. "I wondered if you'd like to have dinner with me this weekend." There's silence on the other end of the call. I worry it got disconnected until I hear the throttle of a motorcycle passing near her. "Beth?"

"I…um, yes."

"Yes?"

"I guess you can't see me nodding, can you." She laughs. "I am *interested* in having dinner with you, but I'm concerned that Jake's father won't show up."

I don't want to reveal the sinking disappointment I feel at this reminder that, though we are both adults, we are not both independent in the same way. "Well," I respond. "If that happens, why don't the three of us eat together."

"Are you sure? Jake is very particular about his Friday night routine."

"I like spending time with you both," I say, truthfully. "But I'd be lying if I said I wouldn't prefer to have you to myself."

I hear a quick intake of breath as Elizabeth gasps, and I worry I've said something inappropriate. I hear the sound of her unlocking her door, clunking inside with her boot. "Well," she says. "See you Friday? Maybe I can text you whether Todd shows up?"

"I could just watch from inside my window."

"Right. And that's not creepy at all, Kellen."

I chuckle, knowing of course I'm going to watch her driveway from my window. Who could help but do so? "I'll see you around the neighborhood," I tell her. As I hang up, I think I hear her sigh contentedly.

CHAPTER SIXTEEN
KELLEN

Todd does not show up. I resigned myself to this as soon as Elizabeth reminded me of the expectation. I spent the entire day fretting about it, realizing Orla was absolutely right about my need to put myself out somewhere socially. Who could I even talk to about my nerves for this evening? A date. I haven't gone on a date with a new woman in 30 years.

Does Elizabeth count as a new woman? I decide that she does, even though I have nobody to confirm my suspicion. I don't care to discuss these things with my brother. It feels inappropriate to call my daughter or one of my nephews.

So I'm left on my own to agonize over what to wear if we stay in, and whether to change that up if we go out. I even leave work early to pace in front of my closet, eventually deciding on a pair of dark jeans my brother bought me in Europe, paired with today's dress shirt from work. I move my pacing to the living room around four, when I peer out the window to see Jake pacing in the driveway.

I see Elizabeth talking to him from the steps. I imagine she's letting him know she loves him. That he can still have a fun weekend. I feel such deep anger for Todd Gaston, a man I haven't met but would like to strangle. I realize I'm angry on behalf of fathers everywhere. I stand in the picture window with my hands on my hips, looking out until Elizabeth meets my eye from across the street.

She mouths, "Creeper," and smiles, so I decide to just head on over there.

"Hey, neighbors," I say, extending my hand to pat Jake on the shoulder, but then catching myself and remembering he might not like that. I've always been physically affectionate with Orla and my nephews. They joke about Brady hugs. But I know not everyone appreciates that sort of thing. I wave awkwardly instead. "What are you two doing this evening?"

Elizabeth opens her mouth to say something, but Jake flashes his eyes at me, angry, and says, "It's Friday. On Fridays I eat pizza and watch Star Wars."

I nod. "Which episode?"

He rolls his eyes at me. "I'm on Last Jedi. I watch one each week and then go back to the beginning."

I put my hands in my pockets and raise a brow at him. "Do you loop in Rogue One?"

Jake sinks down on the steps next to his mother, shaking his head. "Obviously not. How could you even ask that?"

Elizabeth hides her smile behind her fist. I try to cover. "I was just making sure we were on the same page." He rolls his eyes again. "Would you and your mother like to come have pizza and watch at my place?"

"Will you order pizza with pineapple?"

Sensing this is another test, I purse my lips before I reply. "Only if you like it that way."

He nods. "Come on, Mom. Does this count as a dinner party? I'm meeting so many requirements for Miss Amy this month."

Without waiting for us, he charges across the street and lets himself into my house. Elizabeth moves to shout after him and I touch her wrist. "I'm happy to have you both over," I tell her. "Truly."

Half an hour later, we are all seated on my sofa with an extra-large cheese pizza on the coffee table. It's not lost on me that I'm an old man with a podiatrist taking advantage of the early bird dinner special, but Jake seems thrilled to get a head start on his exciting Friday evening.

I try to hide my disappointment that Jake sat between Elizabeth and me on my couch, but if I'm really honest, I'm too nervous to make a move on her anyway. She asks questions about the movie periodically, and he shushes her, not wanting to miss a thing. He mouths the dialogue along with the characters, showing me this probably isn't the first or the last time Elizabeth has seen the movie, either.

I lean behind Jake, who is sitting ramrod straight, engrossed in the TV. "Can I get you a drink," I ask Elizabeth. She nods emphatically and smiles. I like how I feel when she smiles, and I like knowing I can make a woman smile after all this time. There's something magical about knowing I brought her pleasure. Then the thought of pleasure takes my mind into other forms of it and I quickly stand and head toward the kitchen before my thoughts spiral out of control.

I pour a few fingers of whiskey for each of us, grab the freshest soda in my fridge for Jake, and settle back into the sofa, raising my glass to her in a toast before slowly sipping my drink. "You and your whiskey," she says, smacking her lips as Jake shushes us.

Elizabeth winces as she swallows her drink. "The second sip goes down smoother," I tell her, raising my eyebrows as I savor my own second sip. The drink warms my insides, calms my racing heart a bit, even as the action on the screen intensifies. I feel my pulse throbbing in my veins as I watch Rey and her nemesis fight, then nearly kiss.

Eventually, the movie ends and Jake stands up, clapping his hands. "Whew," he says, turning to face us. "Mom, can I go play Xbox now?"

"What?" She looks taken aback, like his question jolted her back to the room and her thoughts, too, had been elsewhere.

"Xbox. Can I go play? Zack and Fred from school said they would be online tonight and you emphasized how important you thought it was for me to build social relationships."

"You met friends at school?" Elizabeth's mouth hangs open and she clutches her drink to her chest.

Jake rolls his eyes again, reminding me how often this happens with teenagers. "Yes. And they're on Xbox. Let's go home. I'm going to play."

He heads toward the door but realizes she hasn't stood to follow him. She looks at me, obviously not ready to call it a night. "I could..." I don't want to invite myself to her house. That's too forward. But I'm not ready for our night to end, either. None of this has gone how I was expecting. I run my fingers through my hair and scrape a hand along my jaw, where my beard has come in nearly white.

"I'll be over here, sweetheart," Beth says. "You go and play, but come get me if you need me."

"Mom," he says, heading out the door again. "I'll just text you. Duh." The silence rings after the door shuts behind him. We both lean a bit to stare out the window and watch the lights turn on in Elizabeth's living room as Jake settles onto their couch, firing up the video game system.

Eventually, I realize that we are seated with my arm around the back of the couch, just above the line of Elizabeth's shoulders. The smell of her is everywhere around me. Yes, I smell pizza and whiskey, but I also smell her. Sunshine and citrus like always, but something else. Something new and mature and wonderful. "You smell nice," I mutter, before I think better of it.

She flushes. "You've always smelled nice," she says. "You smell better now."

"Is that right?" I bring my glass to my lips again as she nods.

"You stopped wearing that awful drugstore cologne," she says, smiling into her own drink. We sip in silence for a bit, evidently smelling each other. I don't feel drunk, but I am definitely affected by the alcohol.

"Maddie says I smell good," I tell her.

Beth nudges me with her shoulder. "She clearly has good taste." I feel a pulsing tension in the air, a current between us. "I'm glad you asked us over tonight," she tells me.

"I was very glad to have you here," I tell her, truthfully. "Both of you. Truly."

"I can tell," she says, and drops a hand to my knee. We both lower our eyes to where her skin warms through the denim. "I love that you like my son."

She doesn't move her hand, so I move my arm closer to her shoulders, half on the couch and half draped over her slim body. I can feel the heat circulating through her veins, too. "I like both of you," I tell her. "Of course your kid would be great. He's *your* kid."

"Orla is wonderful, too," she says. "I admire her spirit."

I lift my glass toward her. "To great kids," I say. We clink glasses and drink, and I stretch to put my glass on the coffee table. "I don't want to talk about kids anymore, Beth."

She swallows thickly and looks out the window. I follow her gaze and see Jake illuminated by the blue light of their television. He's wearing a headset and shouting animatedly as he leans to and fro, holding the video game controller.

Elizabeth's eyes return to mine and I lean closer to her, dropping my other hand to her shoulder so she's sitting between my arms. "It's been a really long time since I did anything like this," I tell her.

She snorts. "Uh, yeah. Me, too."

I close the distance between us and kiss her, feeling my lips melt into hers. It's familiar and new. Strange and magnificent. As I move my lips, deepening the kiss, my thoughts flit between how this feels so different from kissing my wife and how I shouldn't be thinking about my wife when I'm kissing someone else.

Elizabeth's tongue slips into my mouth, dotting against mine. I groan, tasting her. We both taste like whiskey, like heat. Like discovery. She puts both her hands on my shoulders, too, pulling us close against one another.

I adjust my legs and she's kneeling between my thighs, kissing me, moaning. I hear nothing, see only her as she seems to fill my entire body with her wanting. Elizabeth is pressed tightly against my chest and I feel the heavy weight of her breasts. I think I can sense the hard pebbles of her nipples and the realization of that has me gasping for breath.

I break the kiss, resting my forehead against hers. "Kellen," she breathes. "I want you."

"I want you, too," I say, kissing her again, and then stopping. "I don't know if I know how."

She shakes her head. "I don't know if I do, either."

I hold her then, and she rests her head on my shoulder, the two of us panting. Eventually, she pulls back and kisses me on the forehead. "I should go home," she says, rising from the couch, slipping through my fingers like rainwater.

I rise along with her. "When can I see you again?"

She laughs, smoothing out her jeans and adjusting her short hair. "The next time you look out your window I guess."

I frown, gesturing at her walking boot. "I'm walking you home," I tell her. "This is still a date, after all."

She nods. "I'll accept that." We navigate our way down my steps, and between her cast and my sore foot, we actually seem to need the physical support when we clasp hands. And we walk that way across the street, holding each other's hands until she gets her front door open.

"Good night," I tell her, lifting our clasped hands and kissing her knuckles.

The smile she gives me stays with me until I fall asleep.

CHAPTER SEVENTEEN
ELIZABETH

I touch my lips with the pads of my fingers. I can still feel him, still taste him. The thrill of making out with Kellen is overwhelming, and when I get inside, I can't even manage to say goodnight to my son. He doesn't notice anyway, thankfully. Just grunts as I walk past on the way to my bedroom.

I can't remember the last time I felt this alive. Between Kellen happily conversing with my son, just bantering with him about Star Wars like it was a regular Friday night...and the whiskey. And the feel of his body pressed against mine. I might swoon.

I sit on the edge of my bed, vibrating. No, wait. My phone is vibrating.

"Lisa," I hiss into the phone. "Holy shit!"

"You better tell me everything. Are you naked right now? Oh my god why are you answering the phone?"

"Todd didn't show up. Obviously." I hear her hurl profanity and it sounds like she's throwing something. She's probably doing dishes while we talk. Lisa only buys plastic plates and bowls so she can slam them around for emphasis when she fights with Ashish. "But we kissed," I blurt out.

She squeals. "Oh, Liz. I'm so stinking happy for you. Was it awesome?"

I flop back on the sheets, the muscles of my cheeks straining from all the smiling I'm doing. "Unreal," I tell her. I describe how Kellen was so awesome with Jake, so friendly.

"Good men being good with kids is like the ultimate turn-on," Lisa says, and I know she's doing dishes now because I hear her bang the counter.

"It really is." I feel a bubble of shame, not for the first time, at not seeing Todd for a dirtbag sooner. What kind of man can't be bothered to get to know his son? "I haven't even had to *explain* Jake to Kellen, Lisa. He just seems to understand how to talk to him."

"Well," she says, "I feel like there's a stereotype about engineers being on the spectrum anyway. He's probably used to it."

"But also, he's charming. He makes my kid smile. And I know Jake feels comfortable with him, which makes me feel comfortable..." I drift off, not sure if I should tell her just how comfortable I was getting tonight. I was so close to orgasm, just from rubbing my chest against his.

I've been using my facial massager almost every day since I got it and it's like I uncorked a river of sexual energy.

"We need to go get you lingerie," Lisa says, matter of factly. "I'm taking Jake overnight next weekend and you're wearing black lace panties and doing all kinds of things in and out of them."

I roll my eyes. "I'm not going to the mall again," I tell her, and then wonder if I can maybe order a few things online. It can't hurt to try, right?

"Also? Don't be upset because I didn't use names, although I'm sure he knew who I was talking about. Anyway! I was talking to Ashish about sex."

"I'm sure you were."

"No, I mean I was talking to him about ladies having sex after menopause. Which gave him quite a start, because I'm not quite at that phase yet."

"Quit rubbing it in how young you are."

"I have an old soul," she says. It's true. I've never felt like she was an entire decade younger than me when we have so much in common otherwise. "So. Ashish says the physical therapists at work talk about this all the time. They actually see a ton of women for pelvic floor therapy."

I sit back up in bed. "You know I had that for a long time after my hysterectomy. After Jake's birth." It was the only contact another human made with my nether regions since his conception.

"I remember." She makes a sound of compassion. "And *anyway* apparently women of a certain age who have gone a long time without visiting pound-town get, like, thin vagina walls."

"Thin walls?" It's hard for me to quantify if this should feel as scary as it sounds.

"Thin walls. Basically, your pussy is like a muscle? And you need to work up to inviting his sausage into your bun."

I snort-cough. She's so crass when her kids aren't around. I love how open she is, how open I feel when I'm around that freedom of expression. "Oh my god, Lisa. You're killing me."

"I'm serious. This is a real thing. You should also call your OB because there's a cream you can use to help things along."

I groan. The last thing I want to do right now is talk to another human being face-to-face about how long it's been since I've had sex. But then I remember the feel of Kellen's erection near my fingertips when I shoved the burrito money in his pants pocket. I remember the hard length of his body pressed against me on my doorstep after our date.

I definitely want to explore this type of behavior with Kellen, and it sounds like I need to do some homework to get my body ready for that. I look down at my secret ivy tattoo and remember: I persevere.

I hang up with Lisa and promise to call my doctor about the cream. But first I grab my laptop and order some lingerie online. Just a few things. Just a few dozen pairs of lace panties in different styles because I have no idea what will feel comfortable or what Kellen will like.

Looking around, as if someone could see what I'm doing, I pull up the search engine and start looking into the estrogen cream Lisa mentioned. The results make me cringe, referring to a woman's "intimate area" and "the change of life." But the overall message is clear: I need to approach this slowly and use some sort of product or else my best case scenario is a raging yeast infection.

"Well that's a sexy conversation to have," I mutter, trying to imagine sitting Kellen down and explaining that, due to my old crone situation, my honey pot has literally dried up and might rip if we try anything physical too soon.

I toss the laptop across the bed, wondering what comes next. I felt how eagerly he was touching me tonight, how he was yearning for more. How can I tell him we need to go slow? I take a deep breath and try to remember that it's been awhile for him, too. "He hasn't been with anyone since his wife," I remind myself. "This is new for him, too."

I toss and turn for awhile, fretting. I can't stop my thoughts from churning out mean ideas. Like I brought this all on myself by not doing something about my sex life a decade a go. My cruel inner voice tells me I drove Todd into the arms of all those women he apparently was sleeping with for years. And then my rational mind sets in again and I remember how hard I was focused on other things, how many other amazing things I did, like helping Jake navigate a world that's not quite ready for him, or forging this fantastic friendship with Lisa.

"You got out when you were able," I mumble, quoting the therapist I visited when I was starting the divorce proceedings with Todd. "I'm like the explorer moon," I repeat and touch the healed tattoo. In the grand scheme of things, telling a man we need to go slow and use lube shouldn't be nearly as hard as, say, getting an autistic child to agree to his flu shot.

So why does this feel so much scarier?

CHAPTER EIGHTEEN
KELLEN

In the morning, I want to call Elizabeth. I want to walk over to her house and kiss her again, to see if last night was a fluke or if I really am feeling this alive. I wake up, peel off my night splint, cursing the ligaments in my old foot, and decide there's no reason to sit alone in my house when she's right there, across the street, likely drinking coffee while her son plays more video games.

I brew an extra cup and head across the street carrying two steaming mugs, tapping on the glass of her storm door carefully so I don't spill. This is unlike me, an uncalculated, unplanned move. What if she's not up yet. What if she is in her robe. A million terrifying thoughts circulate as I wait on the porch until I hear the snick of the deadbolt being opened.

I grit my teeth until I see her face light up. "Kellen," she whispers. She opens the door further. "Jake's still in bed."

"Oh. I hadn't thought of that," I admit, staring down at the coffee. "I just...would you want to drink a cup of coffee with me?"

She sets a mug of coffee down on the table inside the door. Of course she had already made her own. I'm feeling ashamed of my rash choices, questioning my sanity, but she tugs my elbow. "I'd love that. Mine's gone cold, anyway," she says, taking one of the mugs from me. We make our way to the dining room, her thumping in the walking cast and me stepping gingerly on the gel inserts I've had to put in all my shoes.

I hadn't considered my day past this moment, apart from kissing her again, so I sip my drink nervously, waiting to see if she'll say something. Her cheeks bloom with a beautiful pink, and I wonder if it's the heat radiating from the drink or something more. "I had a really nice time last night, Kellen," she says.

She slides a hand across the table and grips mine. I stare down at our entwined fingers. "That's an understatement, Beth." She squeezes my hand. And then, like water over a dam, I just start talking to her. "It's been so damn long since I had these kinds of feelings, since I had this kind of wondering about a new person. I..." I look over at her and she's smiling.

Not a pitying type of smile, but a happy one. "You make me feel really alive," I say, finally.

"That's a really nice compliment, Kellen." She leans around the table and kisses my cheek. She makes to lean back into her seat, but I snake an arm out and around her shoulders, pulling her closer. I let go of the coffee mug and cup her chin, tipping her beautiful face up toward mine so I can kiss her mouth. And then I keep on going. *Yep, definitely alive.*

I lose control of my faculties and am about to pull her into my lap, when she draws back. "I need to talk about...this." She gestures between us.

My mouth snaps shut. As if she is reading my thoughts, she shakes her head. "No, I mean, yes. I want to do this. I want to be physical with you, Kellen. God, I want to do that." She blushes again, then swallows. "But there are some mechanical obstacles. Logistics?" She shakes her head. "This is coming out wrong."

"You can tell me," I assure her. "I'm not going anywhere." To emphasize my point, I put my sore foot up on another chair in her dining room. "I'm literally not going anywhere until I take some more ibuprofen."

That gets a smile from her. "What I am trying to say is it's been so long since I was intimate with anyone, and well, you know how old I am. We need to go slow is all." Her eyes widen, a hopeful look on her face. "Really slow. With...penetration stuff."

Understanding dawns on me. I tingle with embarrassment because I had not taken the time to consider what changes women must experience in that department. I'm briefly struck by the thought that Helen never even got the chance to worry about that, but I push that aside and reach for Elizabeth's hands. "I'm good with that," I tell her. "I just like being near you. I like how I feel when I'm with you, Beth."

She bites her lower lip. "Same, Kellen Brady." I hear a stirring down the hall, the telltale signs of a teenager reluctantly getting out of bed.

I don't know if it would be upsetting for Jake to come out and find me here, whether that would be so unexpected it would set him off. I stand. "Have dinner with me tonight again," I say. "I'll order in, or if there's somewhere Jake likes we can go out."

She stares down the hall, where we can hear him grumbling as he slams drawers open and closed. "Maybe Jake wants to visit my parents for a bit this evening," she says. Then she grins at me. "That way we could..."

I nod. "I'd like that very much," I tell her. I bend down to kiss her cheek and snatch the empty coffee mug from her hands. "My lady," I say, saluting with the mug. "See you around..." I raise my eyebrows, waiting for her to fill in the time.

She sighs. "My parents eat at like 430," she says. "They're ridiculous. I'll try to have Jake over there by then, so..." she drifts off. "Maybe we can do something before dinner, too?"

"We're becoming a pair of regular early bird specials," I say. "I'll see what I can come up with."

ℬ

I EMERGE from her house to find Callum in the driveway, sweaty from a run, sliding underneath his Bronco. "Over for an early visit with your neighbor?" He stares at the two mugs in my hand, like he's hoping to read more into that situation but can't quite find a way to insinuate something untoward.

"You mind your business, young man," I tell him. I squat next to the vehicle and peer underneath. "What have we got going on today?"

CHAPTER NINETEEN

ELIZABETH

I REALIZE THAT ALL THE THINGS I BOUGHT ONLINE WILL OF COURSE NOT BE ARRIVING today in time for my date with Kellen in eight hours. I groan, realizing I'm going to have to go shopping again. I know I just told him we have to take things slowly and there's no earthly reason to suspect he might be anywhere near my underwear, but the thought of going on a date in my current sagging stash of lingerie makes me shudder.

Somewhere in the past decade, I slipped into my mother's worst nightmare: I have nothing but gray, threadbare bras and panties with withered seams. "Jake," I shout down the hall. "Do you need anything at the mall, babe? I need to buy some things."

"Ugh, I hate shopping," he groans. "I'm supposed to be online today with Mitchell."

"I didn't say you had to come along. I asked if you need anything."

By the time I get out of the house with his list I'm confident the stores will at least be open. I decide that purchasing these things has very little to do with Kellen, actually. Even if he doesn't end up seeing the pretty lace underthings, I am buying them as an act of self care. I care enough about myself to buy bras without the wires bursting through the fabric, to buy underwear that wouldn't bring me shame if the paramedics ever had to cut them off my unconscious body.

While I'm in the department store searching for the undershirts Jake likes, with no tags or raised seams, I decide to splurge on a long dress for myself and a bra/panty set for tonight.

The dress, a flowing black maxi with an asymmetrical neckline, covers the walking boot. The new bra hoists up my bust so I can barely tell that it sags practically to my navel. I stare at myself in the full length mirror for a long time, accepting that I don't look a thing like the frumpy, flustered mom I've felt for the past decade plus.

"I look so good," I say out loud, realizing that I'm still Jake's mom, and so much more. I'm the woman who stood up for herself, the advocate who stands up for her son. "And I'm the woman going out on a date with a sexy man tonight," I mutter, bagging everything up and heading to the checkout.

My parents are delighted at the opportunity to have Jake over to their house, and Dad even pipes in that he's going to drive the two of them over to some sort of event at the board game store. "That sounds perfect, Dad," I tell him. I expected Jake to resist when I told him he's going to his grandparents' house, but he surprised me by asking if he can go down there immediately rather than wait until 4pm.

"Well, I can't see why not," I start to say, staring at him. This isn't the sort of day I'm used to having, where an attractive, kind man brings me coffee, asks me to dinner, childcare appears, and my usually-rigid son rolls with the punches. I feel myself holding my breath, waiting for the catch. We are not "loose plans" people. As I return from my unplanned errand, my body waits for the meltdown or the call from someone that will throw everything into a tailspin.

I'm so used to planning for the worst and feeling relief at any scrap of a nice time. It actually feels a bit unsettling to arrive home to a pleasant kid, a house that's not on fire, no trace of a meltdown in sight.

Instead, Jake tells me, "I want to use Granddad's account to get another copy of the Roblox promo skin."

"Another copy? What?"

He rolls his eyes at me. "There's a free promotion through our cell phone service. I'm going to ask Granddad if I can have his code, too. Can I go now? I'll walk."

He tosses on a hoodie and heads for the door without glancing back at me. "Text me when you get there," I shout to his back, but he's off. I want to chase after him, to make sure he knows the way without getting lost, even though of course he knows. He probably knows exactly how many sidewalk squares he'll cross between our two houses. And he's determined to go now. There's evidently some sort of free video game code and his body is drawn to it like a beacon.

When he's gone, I take in the stillness in the house, how it doesn't feel oppressive or frightening. It just feels content.

ß

WHEN KELLEN RINGS my bell a few hours later, I'm more relaxed than I've felt in years. I spent hours alone, reading a romance novel that made me blush. *So this is what it's like,* I think, marveling at how quickly I feel like a goddess, how little down time it takes to help me feel like my lungs fully expand. I'm so used to being on, so used to being fully attuned to Jake's specific needs. Is it possible that all of the therapies are kicking in? That he's navigating the world with less assistance?

Did I not notice things getting easier before the move or has it really been this sudden? "Beth?" I hear Kellen's voice on the other side of the door and realize I'm standing in my hall, talking to myself.

I pull open the front door and the sight of him takes my breath away. He's standing there looking unbelievably sexy in dark jeans, a button down shirt, and a blazer. And he's holding flowers. I literally swoon, sagging against the door frame. "Kellen," I breathe.

His jaw works up and down as he stares at me, and I smile when he says, "I feel the same way. You look breathtaking, Elizabeth."

We stare at one another for a few beats and then I reach for the flowers. "Let me put these in water," I say, hobbling to the kitchen and plunking the flowers in an empty water glass I pull from the sink. I don't have a vase, but I can't find it in me to care.

I get to go out with this man, looking like this, looking at *me* like that. He reaches for my hand and we walk back across the street to get in his car. "How do you like mussels," he asks. I melt into his interior.

"My favorite."

"I normally walk to Park Bruges," Kellen says, putting his arm around my seat as he backs out of the driveway. I'm immediately taken back to 30 years ago when I used to swoon when he'd do this, driving us somewhere in his parents' car. It gives me comfort to know that some things like this don't change, even when people have lived a lot of years of a lot of struggle and change.

"Next time we'll walk," I tell him. "When our old feet are up to it."

It's less than a mile drive, and Kellen is able to find a parking spot near the restaurant. It's early enough that there's no crowd inside the sunny little cafe. "I've never eaten here before," I tell him. "I've heard of it, though." The restaurant is famous for their Belgian beers, their fries and their mussels. Kellen slinks an arm around my waist, drawing me out of the way as an employee rushes past with a hand truck holding two barrels.

"Careful now," he says, his breath tickling my neck. "We're here at the same time the food's getting delivered."

I shrug. "It'll just taste that much fresher, right?"

CHAPTER TWENTY
KELLEN

I'm not sure how many hours pass at the restaurant. Elizabeth and I have each had a few drinks, shared several pounds of bivalves, and are holding hands on the table. I keep staring down to make sure it's really my skin against hers. A living woman. Someone I admire. She strokes my palm with her thumb and I feel the motion in every cell of my body.

"Tell me about your job search," I say, dipping a piece of crusty bread in the buttery sauce from our dinner.

She frowns. "It's a bit stagnant right now. I'm being really particular," she says, and shrugs. "I can get by on the support from Todd."

She hesitates, and I jump in, saying, "As it should be. Fucker."

She squeezes my hand. "Yes, he is that. But it's more like...I put up with bullshit for so many years. I just don't have it in me to devote my time toward something that's not dramatically fulfilling."

"I love that," I tell her. "Life is definitely too short to put up with bullshit."

Elizabeth pulls her hand back, tucks her short hair behind her ears. "I am so sorry about your wife, Kellen."

"Thank you." I sigh. "Orla thinks I've been just waiting around to die."

She laughs. "I don't get that impression at all," she says. "I've met your family. It's a pretty wild bunch."

"I agree," I tell her. "It's just...she's a little bit right. I haven't exactly been grabbing every opportunity, seizing the day." I adjust my legs on the bench and my foot comes in contact with Elizabeth's calf. I don't pull it away and she doesn't move her leg. "I've been..."

"Stagnant?" Elizabeth raises her brows at me and presses her leg into my foot. I nod.

Suddenly feeling anxious for reasons I can't describe, I clear my throat and pull back my leg. "Elizabeth, I love talking to you," I tell her. As the afternoon gave way to dusk, she and I sat here discussing history documentaries, our shared love of very dark chocolate, and Dolly Parton podcasts. She opened up about some of the struggles Jake faces in schools when rigid teachers can't seem to follow the impact of their strict rules on a young man who just requires more and different explanations than other kids. I spent at least an hour of our conversation wanting to quit my job and go become a high school teacher so I could give Jake and kids like him a safe place to learn about physics.

"I love talking to you, too," she says. And she flushes again. "I keep thinking about what we discussed..."

She doesn't have to remind me which discussion. The one this morning, where she was so open about needing some careful attention before we can be physically intimate. "I..." I clear my throat and close my eyes, deciding blunt honesty feels best, even if I can't brave the look in her eyes as I admit what I've been thinking all day. "I'm worried I'll hurt you and am equally worried my own performance will be absolutely terrible if we...make love." I hesitate on the phrase "make love," because I don't know that I've ever used those two words together.

Helen and I enjoyed a healthy sex life in the beginning, but didn't exactly discuss what we were up to. Teenage Elizabeth and I didn't use that sort of language either for our stolen moments of exploration and fumbling.

When I open my eyes, Elizabeth's are dancing between mine, her expression hopeful. "Last night was wonderful," she says. I nod. "We could go home and...build on that?"

I slap a wad of cash on the table and spring up from the booth at her words, extending my hand to her. She laughs. "You like that idea, do you?"

"I'm terrified and insatiable."

The one mile drive home takes far too long, with pedestrians moseying through every intersection and a neighbor navigating a boat trailer down our narrow residential street. By the time I park in my driveway, I can practically hear Elizabeth's heart racing. Or maybe it's mine. I hurry around to her side of the car, opening her door for her and fumbling with the garage light to enter my house.

She bites her lip as I help her up the stairs and, as soon as we are in my kitchen, I gather her in my arms. "Beth," I whisper, pushing her up against the closed garage door. She shudders as I pepper kisses down the length of her neck and the taste of her skin is so overpowering, I forget how nervous I am that she is fragile.

She gathers the front of my shirt in two fists and pulls me against her body, pressing her lips against mine fiercely. "I want to lie down with you," she pants. "I want to feel you lying on top of me."

"Yes," I breathe, marching down the hall, tugging her closely behind me. We stumble a bit en route to my bedroom, but she starts to giggle so I stamp down the worry that I'm somehow harming her injured foot.

When we get to my bedroom, Elizabeth crawls onto my bed and lies on her back, patting the blankets next to her. "Come closer, Kellen."

I obey, trying not to fret that I'm still wearing shoes, that there has never been a woman in this bed since I bought it, that I am liable to come in my pants at the first hint of friction.

I support my weight on my forearms and kiss her as Elizabeth snakes her arms around my neck, along my back, fingers in my hair. "You feel so good," she says between kisses. "You smell so good."

I want to parrot her words, unable to come up with anything coherent. I'm drunk on the experience of being here with her. I'm near tears as I savor the feel of my body spread on top of hers. I'm so hard I worry about the structural integrity of my pants, and I rock my hips just to see what will happen.

"Oooh, yes," she moans. "More." Elizabeth bites my lower lip, pulling my face closer to hers. I shift my weight so I can touch her face, and I rock my hips slowly against her. Her dress has rucked up past her knees as she opens her legs to allow me to settle between hers.

I feel the heat of her through my clothes, warm and safe. I continue rocking and adjust my torso again so my hand is free to massage her breast. "Oh!" Elizabeth yelps. "Oh, Kellen." I glance down, my hand on her breast, squeezing, thumb dusting across the pointed peak of her nipple, and I feel Elizabeth's hips churning beneath me.

"Kellen, I think I'm...oh, god, Kellen I'm coming." I'm so surprised, so delighted by this news that I thrust once, twice more and I'm there with her, coming in my jeans just from dry humping and squeezing her boob.

We meet each other's glance, mouths agape, and both of us burst out laughing.

I roll off of her and tug her against my side, careful not to press her dress against the wet stain spreading from my crotch. "That was undignified," I whisper into her hair.

She props her head on her elbow and stares at me, looking extremely satisfied. "Who cares about dignity," she says. "It just felt so damn good, Kellen." She bites a lip. "I couldn't help myself." She traces a finger along my jaw. I turn my face to kiss her palm. "When did you grow the beard?"

I keep my hand around her wrist, seeking the skin to skin connection with her. "It's been years," I say. "Maybe since I bought the house? I think it started during a time when something had to give, and that thing was daily shaving." I drag a palm along my cheek, the crackling sound of my skin in the short hair filling the silent room. "What do you think of the gray?"

"Honestly?"

I grin. "No. Lie to me."

She swats at my shoulder with her free hand and I snag her palm against my body again. "It looks amazing, Kellen." Elizabeth sighs. "You're like...exactly what you should look like as an adult."

We're quiet for awhile until eventually, I tell her, "It's not what I expected. Adulthood, I mean."

She nods. "That's true enough." She squeezes my hand with hers. "There are moments that take my breath away, though, Kellen. And I just want to pinch myself to see if it's real."

I lift my hand from where it's connected with hers and pinch her bicep. "Definitely real," I tell her, kissing the spot. Then I press my lips to hers again, kissing her slowly. "Definitely a dream, too."

CHAPTER TWENTY-ONE
ELIZABETH

I DON'T HAVE TIME TO DWELL ON THE MY AMAZING EXPERIENCE WITH KELLEN. IT'S obvious he and I have a lot to build on and I want to repeat what we did together, but Jake has a chess tournament this week and he's perseverating. That means every few seconds, he asks to review expectations again. And again.

"There's only one winner, but every participant receives a keychain," he says, his eyes looking hopeful.

"Right. A chess piece keychain," I assure him. "Just like last year."

"But last year's pieces were red. And they were green the year before. So it's not just like it." Jake tugs at the collar of his polo shirt, frowning. We've been working very hard to find him an outfit that meets the parameters for the tournament but doesn't bother his sensitive skin. "This itches," he says. "It's burning. I can't wear it."

"Jake," I squeeze his arm. "Hear me out for a minute. What if you wear one of your preferred t-shirts under the polo? Then you'll have a nice soft collar but still meet the dress code."

"That sounds sweaty," he says, shaking his head. "I'll be sweaty."

"I'm sure they'll keep the temperature reasonably low in the library," I try to assure him. "Event planners usually set the temp lower when they're expecting a crowd."

As Jake ponders the potential of this tidbit, I concentrate on my breathing. When he's anxious like this, worried about something, the energy of it fills the room. Everything feels tight. My temper gets short. He and I have been working on it. We're always working on everything. Repeating the expectations helps him feel more in control because there are so many things he can't control, like the outcome or whether someone at the tournament will show up wearing strong perfume that will make him gag and derail his concentration.

Jake concedes my point and sets out a t-shirt, a polo, and a pair of pants with the least itchy seams I could find. "And I have good news about the socks," I tell him. We subscribe to his preferred brand of socks since he's so hard on them and they wear out quickly. "I was able to bump up the delivery, so your new package will arrive tomorrow."

I don't tell Jake that I never got through to his father and I have no idea whether he will turn up at the tournament as Jake requested. I can't tell if Jake actually wants to see Todd there or if he feels like he needs his dad there in order to fit in. Dhruv will have two parents present, so Jake might fear he will stand out if he does not.

"I don't like competing against Dhruv," Jake says.

"Oh, I know, sweetie. But if both of you play your best, that's the important thing. Building skills, right?" Jake looks at me like I'm naive, and I laugh. "Okay, okay, I know you both really want to win. But learning how to lose gracefully is also an important life skill."

He stomps off to his room to study, and it's unclear to me whether he's studying chess strategies or school assignments.

ℬ

I PICK Jake up from school early the next day, leaving my walking boot at home. I keep telling myself it's not my modesty that keeps me from wanting people to stare at my leg. I just want as much as possible for Jake to feel like I'm not distracting him. He and the kids from his regular chess club are competing against teens from all throughout the county. It's such a nice tournament, from my perspective anyway, because the atmosphere seems friendly.

We find Lisa, Ashish and Dhruv and get ourselves checked in. The boys don't look up from their phones to greet each other as they normally would, and Lisa and I share facial expressions communicating that we're both going through the stress of our kids' anxiety.

After the boys check in and go off with their coach, Lisa and Ashish and I try to find some seats. The players are broken into brackets and the first match kicks off. The parents all sit around sipping drinks, speaking in hushed whispers as the brainy teens compete. "No Todd, eh?" Lisa wrinkles her nose. I shake my head.

"It's probably better this way," I tell her. "Lord knows I don't want to sit near him and his presence might distract Jake, you know?"

She nods and our conversation drifts between each of their jobs—stressful—and my job search—stalled. "But hey," I say with a shrug. "I didn't have to use any PTO to be here today!"

No sooner are the words out of my mouth than we hear a commotion at the door. I groan, knowing before I turn my head fully that Todd is the source of the racket. I groan louder when I see that he's brought the strumpet with him.

"Oh no, he's not trying to come over here," Lisa huffs, following my gaze. Todd and the tramp are noisily weaving between spectators. They're dressed to the nines, clearly en route to a formal event and thinking they'd make some sort of pit stop for appearances.

I glower at them, suspecting they're heading to one of the grand hotels nearby for a fundraiser. "There's not even a valet," the tramp says, flouncing into a seat a few rows behind me, deliberately avoiding eye contact with both me and Lisa.

Lisa can't help herself. She turns in her seat. "Of course there's not a valet," she hisses. "It's a teen chess tournament at the library." Some other parents sitting nearby chuckle. Tramp makes a duck face and squints at my friend.

"Elizabeth," Todd says, his voice devoid of emotion. "Your description of this event was misleading."

Is he trying to get a rise out of me? I trace a finger along my slacks where they hide my ivy tattoo. *Persevere,* I think as I turn in my seat and force a smile on my face. "Which part?"

"Pardon?"

"Which part of my description was misleading?"

He rolls his eyes. "You suggested this was a prestigious opportunity for our son. You indicated a full showing from the county."

I will not react strongly, I tell myself. "I believe my exact words were 'Jake is competing in the county teen chess tournament at the library.'"

Ashish gives me a thumbs up from the other side of Lisa. And then we all turn our heads because one of the players roars. I know it's Jake before I locate him. And then I see him, tugging on his hair and muttering, "No, no, no, no, no."

He meets my eyes and I bite my lip. Should I go up? Is this salvageable? It seems too soon for him to have lost the match already, and I know each teen plays two matches before elimination.

I feel a hand on my shoulder, firm and uncomfortable, and I whip my head around to see Todd's enraged face an inch from my own. "Are you going to let him humiliate himself like this? What have you been doing since you decided you were too good for our marriage?"

I stare at my ex-husband for a second, and I realize I feel bad for him. He's so wrapped up in other people's perceptions of him that he is truly not able to see anything beyond himself. I turn back toward Jake and my heart swells when I see the chess coach has approached him. The coach uses hand gestures mimicking deep breaths and gives Jake a thumbs up as my son nods and puffs out his cheeks on an exhale.

I actually clap my hands when I see Jake pick up a chess piece and make another move, meltdown avoided. Lisa squeezes my hand and Ashish yells out, "Yeah! Nice, Jake!" I laugh as my son flushes and holds his hands over his eyes, embarrassed not at his outburst but at Ashish's. "Did you see that?" I lean across to my friends, who nod. "He worked it out."

"He totally did," Lisa says. "Who is that coach and can we take him home with us?" I'm so caught up in my celebration of Jake's progress that I almost forget Todd is sitting here, all judgmental and missing the point.

Almost.

"Are you kidding me right now, Elizabeth?" When I turn to face him again he has his arms crossed and looks like he just lost out on a merger.

I raise an eyebrow at him by way of response, wondering what ever drew me to him in the first place. He's bitter and mean, and I lived in a house with him for nearly 20 years. "Gross," I mutter.

"You're not going to reprimand him?"

"Reprimand?" I feel Lisa stiffen in the folding chair next to me and I squeeze her hand. "For what exactly? Having emotions? Feeling strongly about his performance?"

"His behavior is unacceptable," Todd growls, gesturing around the room. No sooner does he say so when I hear another teen groan. This one bangs his fist on the table before he tips over his king, ceding the match to his opponent. I don't point this out to Todd.

"People groan when they're disappointed, Todd. Maybe you missed the part where our autistic son put his strategies into use and calmed down so he could keep playing?"

The tramp looks confused. "Autistic? I thought you said he was just weird," she says to Todd, twirling her hair around one finger. "I mean, he is weird for sure. I didn't know he was *autistic.*"

Todd springs to his feet. "Jesus, Elizabeth, do you need to air our private business like this?" *Private?* I look at Lisa, who shrugs. Todd extends his hand to the tramp. "Come on, sweetheart. We need to be going to the gala anyway." She shrugs and stands, adjusting her gown before she starts to squeeze her way down the aisle of chairs.

"Do you...are people around you not aware that Jake is autistic?" I can't imagine how or why he would keep such a thing to himself. Jake certainly volunteers this information given the opportunity. I guess his father doesn't ever give him the opportunity, and I immediately feel sad for my son, that I subjected him to spending time with someone who tries to hide him.

"I was under the impression you were spending your time trying to fix all of that," Todd grunts, shouldering his way out.

When he's gone, I look over to Jake, who is still deep into his first round. I locate Dhruv, who is rocking in his chair and tapping the table, but also seems to be contentedly playing his match. I turn to Lisa and say, "Did that just happen?"

"Did your scumbag ex-husband reveal that he thinks autism can be cured, all the while telling everyone his own son is weird? Oh yeah. That happened."

I feel a giant lump in my throat, pulsing inside me. I don't know if it's the physical manifestation of my rage, or my disappointment or my heart breaking for Jake. I don't know what it is, but I know I can't process it right now. I'm here to watch my kid—my brilliant, funny teenage kid—compete at something important to him.

"Babe, give me my bag," Lisa says to her husband, gesturing for her purse under his chair. "I want to grab a knife and go slash Todd's tires."

"Lisa, honey, you can't just say things like that," Ashish says, draping an arm around her shoulders and squeezing her arm. Looking to me, he says, "Let me know if you need a witness at court when you adjust your custody agreement."

"Oh fuck yeah, babe. God, it's hot when you do that," Lisa says. "That asshole should never have access to Jake again, Liz. You want me to subpoena all the other parents here?"

This gets a laugh from me, and I'm thankful, because it pushes the lump down inside a bit. I make eye contact with our boys again. Seeing they're carrying on unphased, I shake my head. "Thanks for the offer, Lees. I'll let you know what my lawyer says tomorrow."

ß

JAKE AND DHRUV make it through the second round and are both eliminated. I worry the seam on my slacks when I see Jake tip over his king, but then I feel elation and relief when my son smiles. He stands and shakes hands with the teen across from him and walks over to me, holding out the bright blue bishop keychain.

"I asked my opponent for his contact information," Jake says. "He's a worthy adversary."

I pull my kid in for a hug and laugh. "That's a fantastic attitude to have, Jake."

"Does this complete the unit on sportsmanship," he asks, looking at me. I ruffle his hair.

"I'd say so," I tell him, and then I tilt my head towards our friends. "Come on, babe. Let's go get burgers and shakes."

"And fries," he says. "The crispy ones. Not the mushy ones that are undercooked."

"Of course," I tell him, linking my arm through his, and pulling it back when he brushes it off. I'm elated by his victory today—I don't care a fig about his chess performance. He tamped down a code red emotional fit and lost gracefully.

This progress has been so hard-earned, so gradual. As the five of us sit down in our favorite burger joint, I take stock of the progress Jake has made since we moved. He's thriving, I realize. I make a note to point it out to his therapist the next time we talk. I can worry about Todd later. "To sportstmanship," I say to the table, raising my milkshake in toast.

"To sportsmanship," Lisa and Ashish say, enthusiastically clinking glasses with me. Dhruv nods and says, "The custom of toasting can be traced back to the ancient Greeks, when honoring the gods."

Jake likewise nods, and eventually raises his glass. "We are like the gods of the game of kings." The boys clink glasses. Jake looks at me and grins. "Was that a euphemism? Did I do it right?"

"You did perfect, baby," I tell him, tears in my eyes. "Just perfect."

CHAPTER TWENTY-TWO
KELLEN

W*HEN CAN* I *SEE YOU AGAIN?* I TRIED TO RESIST SENDING THE TEXT, BUT THE absence of Beth this week stings. I've called a few times, and she's been distant. I can tell something is wrong, but haven't been able to get her alone to discuss it.

I'm glad I sent the message, though, because I immediately see the three dancing dots on my phone indicating that she's typing something back to me. Something that's taking her quite awhile.

Enough of this. I call her. "Beth," I say when she answers. "Please talk to me."

"Kellen." Her voice is heavy. It sounds like maybe she's been crying. She sighs. "I could really use a friend right now."

"I'm your friend," I assert. "I'm definitely your friend. What can I do?" She agrees we can have dinner together tonight at her place, and I stop for a very specific sandwich order she messages me. I don't begrudge Jake his particular order. In fact, his sandwich sounds so good I special order myself a similar one. I never thought to combine butter with pickles and ham, but I'm looking forward to tasting it.

I show up with the food and Elizabeth looks tense as we eat. She keeps flitting her eyes to the clock, nervously spinning her fork around in circles on the table.

"Hey, Jake, I want to thank you for teaching me about this sandwich," I tell him. "This is really good."

"It's French," he mumbles around a mouthful of sandwich.

I nod. "Yes, I gathered that when I picked it up from the French bakery." I toss him a wink. I was surprised Elizabeth mentioned the tiny bakery on Butler Street, since I hadn't known they made sandwiches. I also hadn't imagined there was something there Jake would agree to eat, given his limitations on flavorful food. When I asked her if I could grab something for us all to eat, she hesitated initially. I could tell she was anxious about making a special request for Jake.

I gesture at Jake with my water glass. "I just want you both to know I am enjoying my JG special. That's what I'm calling the sandwich."

Elizabeth smiles at that and takes a bite of her own, chasing it with potato chips. I wish I could do more to show them that I'm very comfortable with different ways of looking at the world. "You know," I start to say as they both look up at me, distracted. "My nephew led a meeting today at work. This is Zack I'm talking about now. He brought a new person in to work at the company who programs computers to learn things. Anyhow, this guy looks at the world and sees it so differently from me. And it makes him a real asset to us because he's already identified a lot of problems for our clients. Then we figured out ways to fix them."

"Like what kind of problems," Jake asks, seeming interested.

I explain how a lot of our industrial clients were experiencing landslides that meant they couldn't get vehicles on their access roads. "This guy, Ray, put cameras on city buses that drive the same routes every day, so we could study the footage over time and his computer program learned how to identify when the ground is unstable."

Jake's eyes light up at this. "That is very sensible. What else can the bus cameras monitor?"

I grin. "I'm glad you asked, Jake. That's what we're figuring out right now, in fact. So many possibilities. Liam—"

"The one who is *anticipating a baby* with Maddie?" Jake's interruption surprises a laugh out of me.

"Yes," I tell him. "The very same. Anyway, Liam is very interested in power lines." I spend the next half hour telling a very interested Jake all about Liam's pet project at work until I notice that Elizabeth has tuned out and seems to be fussing over something internally. Eventually, Jake excuses himself to go play video games and Elizabeth looks relieved when he shuts himself in his room to play on the computer instead of their living room system.

"Hey," I tell her, walking around to massage her shoulders. "What's up?" I don't like this, having to pester and dig to find out what's bothering her when it's so obvious something is wrong. I wish she would just tell me openly, let me share her burden, whatever it is.

"I am going after Todd for full custody," she says, nodding her head like she needs to work on convincing herself this is the right choice.

"Oh," I encourage. "Well, that seems appropriate." Is that over stepping? The man hardly shows up for his custody time anyway and all that does is upset Jake.

Elizabeth shakes her head. "He's not happy about it," she says. "I just don't understand what his motivation is, and that makes it difficult to know how to act here. Like, he doesn't *want* the responsibility of parenting Jake, but he also doesn't want the stigma of losing custody of his child. I think. I think that's where I've landed about it."

I sit down in the chair next to her. "Oh, Beth. That's a lot." I hesitate offering the only insight I have into court and custody situations, from Zack's mother thirty years prior. "Mick's second wife was sort of like that. Maybe not a direct comparison. She was happy enough to take a settlement check and high tail it out of Pittsburgh."

Beth's eyes seem sad and she squints, nodding. "That doesn't seem quite the same sort of thing. Although, I think I'd like it if Todd did just move away. Maybe that would feel more final or something."

We sit in silence for a long while after that, occasionally listening as Jake whoops or growls from down the hall. I massage her wherever she seems receptive to my touch and I feel like a real slime ball because I keep thinking about how much I'd love to sneak across the street to my house and throw her on my bed to massage her properly with my tongue.

Eventually, she looks at me, really looks into my eyes and the intensity of her stare floors me. "You said you want to be my friend," she says. I nod. "Take my mind off all this," she says. She stands up and puts her hands on my shoulders. I tilt my head up to look at her and she bends to kiss me, desperate and hungry. I moan softly as she kisses me and then my eyes fly wide as she bites my lip.

My instincts are screaming to slow this down, to talk to her and sort out what's really bothering her. But the sexual part of me that has lain dormant for so many years is roaring in response to her touch, her scent.

"Make me forget," she whispers. So I do. I make her forget until I, too, forget what drew me over here, which was that I wanted her to let me in to her worries. I can't help but feel there is something she's holding back. But by the time we hide in her garage, frantically wrestling to get her up on the washer so I can slide my hands down the front of her jeans, well. I forget everything else and sink into the physical sensation of being with her.

CHAPTER TWENTY-THREE
ELIZABETH

It's like Kellen and I knocked over a hive, and a swarm of energetic passion bees buzzes between us. Every evening after he gets home from work, he comes over and we make out. Once Jake gets situated in his room with his video games in the evening, I sneak over to Kellen's and we make out.

I'm shocked at what a stress relief it is to sneak around and make out with my...is he my boyfriend? Do 50 year old women say the word "boyfriend"? I feel a slight twinge of guilt that I'm not actively working on more with him than the physical stuff, but as I spend my days sending messages back and forth with my lawyer and prepping to fight for Jake, the physical release is what I need most.

We kiss and we touch and he makes me come without ever taking off my clothes. I give him hand jobs in his kitchen, both of us fully dressed with just his zipper opened. It's messy and raw and everything I need. After a week of this petting and pawing, I thought I'd feel less obsessed but I find I can barely concentrate throughout the day. I think about showing up at Kellen's office wearing nothing but a trench coat. I think about positioning myself naked on his bed so he comes home from work, slides off his tie, and startles, finding me there in his bed.

But of course, reality shows up. Kellen's family needs his guidance and security. Jake needs my help with his Spanish homework. Lisa needs me to listen while she vents about her sons peeing on the bathroom floor. And walls.

I have no idea how that happens. Jake isn't exactly tidy, but he's not peeing on my walls.

"Anyway," Lisa says after she screams at the men in her house. "Enough about my piss walls. What's going on over there."

I debate what to tell Lisa.

I still haven't been fully up front with her about Kellen because I don't yet know what we are to each other. We've had stolen time alone together, sneaking like teenagers. But we haven't had intentional time, planned to be together, where I can talk to him. Maybe I'm to blame for all of that because I keep reaching for his pants when we are together.

"I have no idea if Todd will show up for his custody time on Friday," I eventually tell Lisa.

She scoffs. "Of course he won't. Fucker. What's the next thing that happens with court?"

"I don't know, actually. I'm sort of thinking Todd will want to make a big show of being an involved dad now? I don't know. I just don't know. My lawyer was sort of vague about what I should expect. I hate this."

"You're telling me," she says. "My eyes are burning from the ammonia smell."

"Are you still talking about the piss?"

"Yeah, I mean the human piss stain that is your ex-husband," she says. She's quiet for a bit and I think she's maybe scrubbing or spraying a cleaner around. "So did you bang the silver fox yet?"

"Lisa! No," I respond quickly. Though I wish I had slept with Kellen. I want to get naked and rub my skin against his and feel that beautiful, raw fullness of having a man inside me.

"Have you been using the cream?" She doesn't miss a chance to emphasize vaginal health. "Get Jake one of those gamer headsets for his Among Us rounds and bag the fox."

"I'm working on it," I say, and we hang up because I hear Jake mounting the steps on the way home from school.

I can tell by his face he's upset about something. "What's up, babe?"

He growls at me. "I have an 89% in Physics."

I close my eyes and take a deep breath. Jake is a perfectionist. If he feels he should be getting a higher grade than that, he will become mired in frustration and things will snowball until he's not able to complete any of the work. "Is there a concept you need help with?"

"You said you don't understand any of it. You said I surpassed you years ago with math and science." I nod. Jake shoulders past me into the kitchen and gulps down a glass of water. "I am trying to use my strategies."

"I know you are, sweetheart. Let's talk this through. Was it one assignment that took your average down or a slow creep?"

He takes a breath, closes his eyes. "Slow creep. I have been missing approximately five points per homework assignment."

"And it's actual wrong answers, not something like rushing and forgetting a decimal or something?"

He rolls his eyes and I'm worried I lost him. If he thinks I'm nagging or scolding, rather than seeking information, he will detonate. I decide it's time for another partner session with Amy, his therapist. He's been seeing her alone lately and I haven't been privy to any new strategies or triggers. Jake grips the edge of the counter. "I'll never get back on track. I will never get accepted into MIT. I will never be a scientist."

"Oh, Jake, I know it seems that way. Let me think for a minute about what we can do."

"Why don't you know more about physics?"

I snap at him. "Because my degree is in marketing." I take a breath. "This isn't useful. Can I see the assignments?" Jake kicks his backpack across the floor and starts pacing. I rummage through until I find his physics folder.

I have no idea what I'm looking at among the mess of shapes and equations, but one of the word problems catches my eye. Something about calculating the talus slope of a dirt retaining wall. "Kellen," I mutter. "Kellen works with this stuff all the time."

Jake's eyes light up. "I'm going over there," he says, reaching for his bag. He yanks the folder from my hands. "He said I can knock on his door any time. This is any time, Mom. Right now."

By the time I gather my wits, Jake is across the street and tearing up the steps to Kellen's front door. He's not home from work yet and I watch as Jake realizes this and plunks down, seated on Kellen's steps.

I pull out my phone, thinking to text Kellen at work, but I decide I want to hear his voice and call. He answers almost right away. "Hey, there," he says in that deep voice I love to hear close against my ear.

"Hey," I start. "I have a favor to ask."

"Anything, Beth. Shoot."

I sigh. "Well, Jake is upset about something from his physics class. I don't even know where to begin and—"

"I'd love to help him!" He sounds like he means it, too. I love this about Kellen Brady. He's not nice to us because he wants to get in my pants. He's just nice to us. He's nice. And that makes me want to let him in my pants. *Focus on your kid,* I remind myself. Kellen shuffles some things around in the background. "I'm packing up for the day," he says. "I was in early this morning and, well, I run this joint. I'll be home in a half hour."

"Please don't feel like this is a priority. You don't need to rush or cancel things," I start into familiar patterns. If, in the direst of emergency, I ever called Todd, he made sure to emphasize repeatedly how many opportunities he was missing to get ahead at work. How much face time with a client or superior.

"Beth," he says, his voice firm. "You and Jake *are* a priority to me."

I sink into the wall. Yep, Kellen Brady makes me dizzy. "Ok, then," I whisper. "I'll let Jake know."

Jake decides to wait on the steps for Kellen, who pulls into the driveway 21 minutes after we hang up. I see the smile on his face as he gets out of his car and watch as he extends a hand to ruffle Jake's hair. I'm stunned when my son squeezes Kellen in a hug.

It's not that Jake is not affectionate. It's that his affection is very hard earned. Where Kellen seems to use affection as a means of communication for the people in his life, Jake reserves his hugs for moments of deep importance. Kellen glances over at my house and sees me watching from the window. He beams and when Jake pulls back, Kellen gives me a thumbs up as they walk inside.

I decide to make dinner for three, wanting to both demonstrate my appreciation and to do something kind and nurturing for Kellen in return for this amazing thing he acts so cavalier about. I'm no wizard in the kitchen, but I can whip up a pretty mean chicken parm with a homemade bright sauce.

I'll set aside a plain chicken breast and some of the noodles to butter for Jake. Kellen and I can eat the flavorful stuff.

Every brush of the lemon across the zester, every sprinkle of basil into the skillet, I think about my gratitude. I'm thankful for the tingle between my legs, for the knowledge that my body still functions in that way. And most of all I'm thankful that my son has at last found a man he admires who he can turn to when he has a challenge.

An hour later, I'm plating the breaded, cheesy chicken from the broiler and lugging the sauce and noodles across the street in my biggest tote bag, slowly with my boot so I don't spill anything. I let myself in the front door and freeze in my tracks at the sight of my son, bent over the dining room table with his head almost touching Kellen's.

This is the image I've longed for. Affection, shared respect. My son calmly working on his homework with a man who is happy to help him with it.

Jake mutters to himself, working on a problem and Kellen smiles, patiently. Calm radiates from him along with...is that pride? Jake beams, slamming his pencil down on the table. "I'm certain it's perfect," he says. If my arms weren't full of food, I'd clutch my heart, because he's right.

CHAPTER TWENTY-FOUR
KELLEN

I FORGOT HOW EXCITING IT IS TO WATCH A TEENAGER GRASP A NEW CONCEPT. JAKE had mixed up his formulas for friction and gravity, but as soon as I got him on the right track, he was racing through his homework problems like they were rudimentary, rather than advanced physics.

"You're a freshman in high school?" Elizabeth had failed to mention that her son was a damned genius. "I didn't even take physics until my senior year." *The year I met your mother.* I shake that thought right off.

A sound from the front room pulls my attention, and I look up to see Elizabeth struggling with a bag and a huge pan. "I made dinner," she says. I hurry over to help her and notice that Jake is still sitting at the table.

"Come on and help," I tell him. He looks startled at the suggestion, but rises and stands in the living room.

"Jake, can you put this pan on top of the stove?" Elizabeth gently prods him and I realize he must not be processing what to do in this, an unusual situation for him. I recall how important it was for him to eat in the back yard and realize he and Elizabeth must not carry food to other people's houses very often.

There's a lot I have to learn about how Jake experiences the world. There's a lot I have to admire about how Elizabeth works to guide him.

"This smells amazing," I say, clearing off the table and ushering her into a seat as I fetch plates and silverware.

"Chicken parm," she says. I halt in my tracks. I hear Elizabeth chattering, talking about how it's her go-to meal when she wants to impress someone. "Big flavor, low effort," she continues. "Jake, can you grab me a glass of water? Thanks, honey."

Chicken parm was the meal Helen requested on her last good day. She smiled at me and Orla and suggested we make it together. Our family favorite. It was Helen's go-to as well, for all the reasons Elizabeth listed. Orla and I have avoided it since.

That meal was sacred for us. A last supper. I can remember every facial expression, every time one of us flung bread crumbs at the other as we coated the meat. We all knew it was the end.

"Everything ok, Kellen?" I realize Elizabeth has risen and come to my side, where I'm standing in the middle of the kitchen, holding a stack of napkins.

"Oh." I feel tears in my eyes. "I just…" I look at her lovely face, so hopeful, so kind. "It's been a really long time since someone cooked food for *me,*" I say. I can tell this was the right answer, because Elizabeth beams.

"I wanted to do something kind for you." She walks back to her seat at the table and I slide into the chair next to her, squeezing her hand.

Elizabeth and Jake start eating and I cut into the meat slowly, twirling the pasta on my fork to form the perfect blended bite. I close my eyes, feeling conflicted, hoping the meal doesn't taste like Helen's recipe.

It does not. This food is spicy and bold, garlicky with a zing of basil. Not at all like I feared. The relief is palpable. I can do this. I can create something new with Elizabeth, enjoy the experience of receiving someone's kindness.

"Hey," she whispers, leaning close to me. "What's wrong?"

I reach under the table and squeeze her leg, shaking my head. "This is wonderful," I tell her. "Thank you."

She sits back up, as if she can tell I'm holding back on her. Shit, this is hard to navigate. I clear my throat. "I was just having a small moment of grief about Helen," I tell her, shrugging. "She used to make chicken parm."

Elizabeth clenches her hands into fists. "Oh, Kellen, I'm so sorry," she fusses. Jake looks up at us, surprised.

"Nothing to be sorry about," I assure her, squeezing her leg again. "I really am glad to have you here and it truly is nice to have someone cook for me."

We eat in awkward silence for a bit until Elizabeth asks Jake if he feels better about his physics class. "I can still get a 94 by the end of the semester," he says, nodding. "Kellen can help me if I stray again."

I laugh. "I'll help you any time, Jake. Really. I like this stuff."

"Did you use physics in your work today?" And with that question, the air clears and the three of us are off on a deep dive, discussing the engineering projects I'm supervising. It feels so natural and easy, so right to be having this conversation here in my house, with my hand roaming around Elizabeth's body. It's hard to believe a month ago, I was convinced my life was fine as it was. I look at the room, how rich and full it feels. I feel emotional in a way I can't describe. I feel gratitude.

The front door bursts open and Orla walks in, lugging her laundry and rumbling about parking. She looks up and sees the scene in the dining room, and I watch her realize what's happening. I know exactly what she sees, but this is the first I'd considered her reaction.

Elizabeth's face brightens. "Orla, please join us," she says. "I made plenty. I wasn't sure which days you come eat with your dad."

Orla walks a little closer, looks around the kitchen and dining room. "Is that chicken parm?" Her voice is cold and I can tell she feels betrayed.

I nod. "Elizabeth made dinner while Jake and I worked on his homework," I tell her, my voice drifting off at the end.

"Chicken parm?" She puts her hands on her hips and I see tears well up in her eyes. I'm not sure what to do about any of this. "May I speak with you in private?"

I glance at Elizabeth, who seems perplexed and hurt, and I place a hand on hers. "Please stay," I tell her. I gesture my head toward the back deck and Orla stomps outside to the far end of the railing. I follow my daughter, gently sliding the door closed. "What's wrong?"

"Chicken parm, Dad?"

"Orla, I didn't know she was making dinner and it would be unspeakably rude to refuse it." Orla breathes through her nose, her nostrils flaring. "Honey, it's not like I sat down and explained every grief trigger to her."

"No shit, Dad. You've been with her for like five seconds and you guys are what? A cozy instant family?"

"What? Orla, did you not encourage me to 'get out there'?" I throw her words back at her, trying to keep my voice down and not wanting Elizabeth to hear.

My daughter moves her hands to her hips. "I meant like go to bars and get laid, Dad. I didn't think you'd..."

"You didn't think what, Orla? Please don't be crass. I am not now and have never been someone who goes out and sleeps around."

My heart sinks when I see tears falling down Orla's cheeks. I step toward her and pull her into my arms. "Baby, what is it?"

She shakes her head, then rests her forehead on my shoulder. "I didn't know it would feel this way to see you with someone."

"You've seen Elizabeth here for meals before." Has so much really changed since the last time we were all here for post-podiatrist burritos?

"Dad, do you know what it looked like when I walked in?" She meets my eyes, her head tipped back, tears welling up again. And I do know what it looked like, because it felt amazing.

"It looked serious," I tell her, nodding. "Honey, it feels serious. You were right about everything, Orla. About me needing to feel alive again, needing company. Needing to do things on week nights that don't involve my nephews."

She steps back out of my hug and starts pacing the boards of my deck. "It's too fast, Dad. It's too convenient. Your high school girlfriend and her kid move in across the street and you're just what? The kid's new Dad? Playing house?"

"Orla, you're crossing a line." She closes her eyes. "I'm setting a boundary and asking you to go process what you're feeling and come back when you can speak rationally about what's bothering you."

Orla flings her arms up in the air. "You're such a god damned cyborg sometimes. It's like living with Liam."

"You haven't lived here for years, Orla. This is always how we've approached problems."

She rolls her lips between her teeth and I watch her counting to ten internally. "You're right," she says. "I need to process. I'll come back. We're not done talking about this."

Orla stomps off through the house and out the front door. I note that she doesn't grab her basket of laundry. I sigh and look to the kitchen, where Elizabeth is drying her hands.

"You shouldn't have cleaned up," I say, looking around. Everything is put away. Jake is gone. The kitchen is just as it was before they arrived today—sterile and photo-ready. Nothing out of place. Nothing spicy or vibrant. All the things Beth has brought into my life.

"It's ok. I felt..." Elizabeth sighs. "I put the leftovers in your fridge. You're the only person I know with an organized Tupperware cupboard." She huffs out a laugh.

I swallow. "Orla just needs some time to adjust. I haven't dated anyone else..."

Elizabeth nods. "I know, Kellen." She leans in and kisses my cheek. "It all feels fast."

I grab her hand and bring it to my lips. "It is fast, but it's also not fast enough. Beth, I'm...you make me feel so alive," I tell her. "You and Jake. Both of you. I need you," I tell her. "Orla will come around."

Elizabeth cups my cheek. I can't get a read on what she's feeling. "This was a lovely day," she says. She stretches up to quickly kiss me, a brief, chaste pressing of her lips against mine. I want to prolong it, to press her against the wall or sneak into her kitchen like we've done every night since our Star Wars date. But she retreats, both physically and emotionally.

"I'll text you tomorrow," she says and makes her way toward the door. When she's gone, I open the fridge and stare at the leftover forbidden meal. I open the lid to the container and inhale, savoring the smell one last time.

I think about Orla, about her sense of betrayal at seeing me all in for this relationship. It did feel like an instant family. Elizabeth and Jake fold into my life as if they've always been there. But they haven't always been there, and my obsession with this new phase has hurt my daughter.

I dip a finger in the dish, tasting the lemon and black pepper one last time, and then I throw the food in the garbage.

CHAPTER TWENTY-FIVE
ELIZABETH

I'm sorry about this evening. I pace around my house, cleaning and doing laundry and trying not to call Kellen. I can't stand that I've caused a rift between him and his daughter. I got so swept up in the fairytale of this amazing man helping my kid, helping me. God, what must his daughter have thought, coming upon us cozied up in her father's dining room. Eating their grief trigger, apparently.

"Instant family," I heard her yell from the deck. Is that what is happening here? Jesus, after the shit with Todd did I just want to...play pretend with Kellen? Everything with him just feels so right. Maybe that's just in comparison to how drastically, shamefully bad things were with Todd?

Kellen doesn't immediately respond to my text and I fight the urge to run back over there and check in. But I also feel like I have ants living in my skin, so I call Lisa to see if she has any guidance.

"I was on my own for a heartbeat, Lisa. What am I even doing?"

"First of all, you're having tons of orgasms, is what it sounded like when we last talked." I hear her moving through her house, picking up food packages and other crinkling plastics. Lisa doesn't have time to sit and chat on the phone. She wraps our conversations into the things that need to be done.

It's what I relate to most about her. Both of our lives have been so intense. We're always one small domino away from the entire set crashing down. The difference is that Lisa has Ashish to rely on.

"Second, you've been on your own for a long ass time, babe. You've just been fending on your own under the pull of a gaslighting philanderer."

"Hm," I huff out. I had not considered this angle before, not until I started getting a whiff of what things could feel like when I get a chance to refill my own batteries. "I didn't move here to jump into a serious relationship, though," I sputter back as the anxiety kicks back into high gear.

"You haven't even had a sleepover yet. Keep waiting on that, by the way, until you've used that cream a bunch and gotten your cave walls nice and sturdy before anyone goes spelunking."

"Spelunking!" Where she comes up with this stuff I'll never know. I never have the energy to spout out anything witty.

"Anyway, listen." I hear Lisa open the trash can and cram in the crinkly plastics. "I don't think you're moving too fast. I think his daughter maybe needs to do some work around the idea of her father dating again."

I don't know if Lisa is entirely right, or if Orla had fair points. "We do live across the street from each other," I say, quietly. "If things go belly up, it could get very awkward. I really should have thought more about this. Jake is invested now."

I think about the last time Kellen and I parted ways. Nothing was dramatic. Nothing was heart rending. We both...moved. Not just moved on, but literally moved. It's easy to not be awkward around someone when you don't see them for 30 years.

I'm about to open up this line of discussion when I hear a knock at my front door. *Kellen*, I think. Who else would knock on the door in the evening like this? "Maybe it's the paper boy," Lisa says, and I realize I've said that last bit out loud. "Just kidding. It's obviously him. Go talk to him. Call me tomorrow. Remember the cave grease."

"Ugh, Lisa, it's not grease."

"Bye!"

I pad to the front door in my slipper and walking boot. Sure enough, Kellen stands illuminated by the porch light whose bulb he helped change the other day. He's right, the warm glow makes everyone look friendlier.

"Hey," he says when I open the door.

I pull it all the way open and tilt my head toward the living room. "Come inside."

Kellen shakes his head. "I just came over to invite you on a bike ride," he says, grinning.

I haven't ridden a bike since well before I was pregnant with Jake. "I don't know if I remember how," I admit, slumping a bit against the door frame.

"Isn't there a saying about that," he jokes. He reaches out a hand and rubs mine with his thumb. "I was thinking about it, because I really want to go for a long walk with you, or a hike, but we've both got bum feet. But we could ride on the bike path, I think."

The podiatrist had mentioned cycling as a good opportunity for me to get some cardio without putting too much strain on my stress fracture. Even said I could take the boot off for something like that. I just hadn't given it any thought because I don't have a bike. Seeming to anticipate this argument, Kellen hooks a thumb over his shoulder and points at the garage. "I've still got Orla's bike in there. And Callum owes me some favors, so I thought I'd ask him to give mine and hers a tune up. What do you say?"

From the pocket of my sweater, I hear Lisa's voice blurt out, "Yes. She says yes. I'll hang with Jake. He can come sleep over with Dhruv!"

"Oh my god." I frantically reach in my sweater and my hands shake as I pull out the phone I evidently didn't hang up properly when I walked to the door. Kellen laughs as I stab at the red icon to end the call. "That was my friend Lisa."

"I gathered," he says. He puts his hands in his jeans pocket and grins, and the dim warm light seems to transform him into a teenager again rather than the silver haired, mature man he's grown into. "So what do you say?"

"I just...isn't it bad form for me to borrow Orla's bike? After what happened this evening?"

Kellen shakes his head. "If Orla wanted her bike, she'd have it in the storage unit in her apartment building. And she wasn't upset about you this evening, Elizabeth. You have to know that. I think there are some grief emotions coming up for her that she didn't anticipate."

I nod, and bite my lip, uncertain. "She's not entirely wrong about things being intense, though," I say, my voice trailing off.

Kellen nods right back at me. "I can handle intense, Beth. So what do you say to a bike ride with me?"

I wish he'd kiss me, but know he won't tonight. And that's not what he asked, anyway. "I guess it's a date," I tell him.

He pumps his fist in triumph. "Yes," he says. "I was hoping you'd say that." Laughing, he kisses my knuckles and I feel the familiar tingle, the sense of flying and falling at once. "Talk to you soon," he says, and he heads down the steps, favoring his hurt foot as he walks home. And even in the semidarkness, the warm glow of that bulb he recommended shows off his lean, muscular frame.

Yes, I think. I can savor this nice thing in my life. For once, I can enjoy something without having to worry about the fallout. I'm going to ride that damn bicycle, I decide, and I'm going to ride Kellen Brady, too.

CHAPTER TWENTY-SIX
KELLEN

My nephew shows up late. I don't like this. I know my way around a bike just fine, but that's not the point. I didn't specify that I was on a schedule for today, and that's not the point either. I did ask if he could be here by eight and he'd said yes. In our family, we prioritize each other.

"Cal, you're looking rough, son." His eyes are a little bloodshot and he doesn't seem to have showered. "Things going okay in your new apartment?"

He sighs. "It's a *condo,* Uncle Kel. That's what Logan keeps insisting we call it. Drives me freaking insane. Anyway, I'm sorry I'm late. I don't want to be that guy."

I feel relieved with his apology. "Thanks for being here, Cal."

He nods and walks a lap around the two bikes in the garage, considering. "These haven't seen the light of day in a long time, huh? You going out with Orla?"

Callum starts oiling the chains on the bikes, checking out the brake cables and muttering as he struggles with an Allen wrench. "You never answered me, Unc. So I'm guessing it's not Orla, considering she's with Liam en route to Kentucky to present to the power line people."

I don't like that Orla left town with things still unsettled between us. I don't have time to dwell on it because Cal looks up at me with a grin. "You going on a romantic ride with the neighbor lady?"

I scrape a hand along my jaw. It's not that I'm hiding things from my family. "It's very new, Cal. I'm still figuring everything out."

He nods. "Does Orla know you're seeing her? I mean seeing her like *that*. Obviously we all know she lives across the street. Man, how's that going to work when you guys move in together? I guess she's renting."

"Callum, you're rambling." I squat beside him and help him peel the rubber tire off Orla's bike wheel so he can change the tube. I ruffle his hair like I've always done. It reminds me of mine when I was younger. Dark. Unruly. Too long. "We're just spending time together, son."

We finish up the bikes and he asks if he can nap on my couch, which is a surprising ask but I shrug. I like that he feels at home here. I get the bikes and bike rack loaded on my car and head inside to get ready. I pace around the living room as Callum snores, wondering why he doesn't just head home to his condo, and waiting for Elizabeth to return from dropping off Jake.

I consider Orla's argument and Cal's discomfort. I try to assess the situation objectively and consider making a rubric. That's what I'd do if it was an engineering challenge at work. Mentally, I consider family obligations, and those are not impacted by my pursuing a relationship with Elizabeth.

I consider the impact on Jake, and I don't want to think too highly of myself, but I seem to be getting along with him very well. I have no intention of being awkward or hostile with Elizabeth, no matter what happens. If my brother can maintain a cordial relationship with the ex-wife he cheated on, surely I can successfully live across the street from Elizabeth and Jake even if things turn sour between us. I'm certainly not going to cheat on her, although that reminds me we should probably have a conversation about being exclusive. Just to be explicit about it.

I bring a fingertip to my lips, remembering the feel of her skin beneath my kiss. Adult Elizabeth radiates calm and strength. Her skin seems to vibrate with a wisdom I find alluring. I give a lot of thought to the question of whether Orla's right that I'm pursuing her because it's convenient, and I dismiss that immediately. I'm interested in Elizabeth because she's Elizabeth.

I see her car turn into the driveway from dropping off Jake and I spring to action, grabbing the messenger bag of water bottles and snacks that I put together. As I cross the street to greet her, she beams, and I know I'm also smiling like a kid. "Hey, you," she says, stretching up on tiptoe to kiss my cheek. "Am I dressed ok?"

She spins around in her black leggings and turtleneck. My eyes are drawn to the shape of her backside and I swallow, knowing I'll spend my day staring at it as I ride behind her. "Perfection," I tell her, guiding her toward my car. I drive to the trailhead for a portion of the Great Allegheny Passage trail, and Elizabeth helps me get the bikes set up once I park.

"This trail really goes all the way to D.C.?" she looks toward the southeast, incredulous.

I nod. "Used to be a railway, so it's mostly flat the whole way. Someday, I'd love to ride with you. We can stay at bed and breakfasts on the way. Or camp."

"Let's just see if I can ride without tipping over and we'll build from there," she says, laughing. She tests out the brakes and timidly climbs on the bike. "God, it's been so stinking long since I rode one of these."

"You can do it," I tell her, clipping my bike shoes into my pedals and starting a slow, wide circle to get acclimated to the paved trail.

Elizabeth takes a deep breath and presses off with her foot on the pedal. She wobbles a little and then squeals in delight as she starts riding forward. "Kellen, we're going. Can't stop now!" She laughs, the sound tinkling through the morning autumn air, and I fall into pace behind her. The view is spectacular, and I don't mean the foliage or the riverbank.

"What happens if we need to turn? I'll tip over," she says.

"Well," I pull up next to her so I can concentrate without getting distracted. "For one thing, there aren't really any turns on the path. For another, you're doing great, Beth."

Keeping her eyes on the path ahead, she pedals, her knuckles a little bit white on the handlebars. "You're the only one who calls me that, you know," she says, not taking her eyes off the path.

"I can't help it," I tell her. "It's how I think of you."

Elizabeth flexes her fingers, lifting one hand and then another to gently shake it while the bike keeps moving. "I like it," she says. "Woo, we're really doing this!"

We ride for a few miles, past the training center where the professional football team trains. We ride past the shuttered steel mills that built Pittsburgh's reputation as a manufacturing jewel. We pass the bridges and trusses that brought Beltane its first major clients.

"Holy shit, Kel, is that Kennywood?" Elizabeth skids to a halt. I don't point out to her that she has successfully stopped the bike and not tipped over. I pull off to the side with her and unclip my feet, reaching to drink some water.

"It is indeed." We stand there for a good long while, gazing up at the roller coasters we used to ride together. The park must be open for the weekend, because a car of screaming passengers flashes past, just on the other side of the trail from where we stand.

"We had some good memories working there," Elizabeth says. She runs the back of her hand across her forehead and guzzles the water.

"I'm making some good memories with you here now," I tell her. I can't hold back. I'm so impressed with her tenacity, her willingness to try something she was nervous about. I lean in to kiss her, tasting the salt of her exertion on her upper lip. "Thank you for trying hard things with me."

I can see happiness radiating from Beth's eyes. "Come on," she says. "We can't stop now!"

We cross a rail bridge and then another, stopping to see a bald eagle nest above the crumbling frame of an old steel mill and admire our view of the new robotics manufacturing center being built across from it. "Pittsburgh's renaissance," I mutter.

"What's that?"

I swat a hand, dismissing my comment. "People in engineering. They're calling all the new robotics centers and tech startups 'Pittsburgh's renaissance,'" I tell her.

She brakes and comes to a stop, cupping her hand on her forehead to try and see the eagle. "I like the sound of that," she says. "A revival. Like us." Her cheeks flush as she looks at me, and I don't have to guess where her thoughts have traveled.

"Come on," I tell her. "Let's bike back and revive other things."

CHAPTER TWENTY-SEVEN
ELIZABETH

I can hardly wait to get back to Kellen's house after our ride. I feel like I'm on fire in the best possible way. My muscles are shouting, my heart is racing. "I feel like I can do anything," I tell him, gripping the interior of the car as he rubs my thigh at a traffic light.

"You can do anything," he says, grinning. "That's what I like about you."

I snort. "If that were true I would have moved out a long time ago." My stomach clenches at the thought of leaving Todd years earlier than I had, of perhaps getting all that time with Kellen instead of standing alone in my living room crying because I felt overwhelmed caring for Jake with no one to talk to about it.

"Well I'm glad you're here now," he says, turning into the neighborhood that already feels comfortable, like home. Most of the time, I can almost pretend I never left Morningside. Up the hill from my parents, across the street from the man who makes me smile.

Kellen pulls all the way into his garage, muttering something about his nephew leaving a grease spot from where his Bronco had been parked. All thoughts leak out of my head when Kellen pulls open my car door and tugs me into his arms. He kisses me, moaning softly as he pulls me in tight against his body.

"Oh," I say when he pulls back, because what else is there to say as my nerves tingle and my heart flutters.

"I've been staring at you in those leggings all day. I have to touch you," he says, backing us up the steps into his kitchen. I nod enthusiastically, diving back into his arms to kiss him in return, trying to drum up the confidence that let me shove off on the bicycle even though I was nervous. Even though I hadn't done it in awhile.

Instead of stopping in the kitchen to make out as we had a few other times this week, Kellen backs us down the hall toward his room. This is what I've been thinking of for weeks. Since the day I moved in and saw him, if I'm being honest. He backs right up to the edge of his bed and sinks down onto it, pulling me with him. "You'll tell me if something is uncomfortable?"

"This feels amazing," I tell him, nestling in between his spread thighs, loving the feel of his chest beneath mine, both of us wearing thin workout clothes that reveal the firm expanse of him. The last time, we were both so nervous. Today it feels thrilling, familiar and simultaneously brand new. Kellen slides his hands down inside my waistband, his fingers teasing and stroking, petting and driving me wild.

I reciprocate, sneaking my own hands up inside his shirt. He moans into my kiss as my fingers explore the planes of his stomach. I feel chest hairs that weren't there the last time I touched his abdomen. I feel the long muscles that were. His breath quickens as my hand creeps lower and I finally rub my palm over his hard length, pulsing beneath his sweats. "Kellen," I breathe. "You're so hard."

"I'm hard for you, Beth. Jesus, look at you." He starts to lift my shirt. I raise up from his chest to let him, and then I lose my nerve.

"I...don't know if I'm ready for you to see," I tell him, sitting up on the bed. I cross my arms protectively around my middle. It's daylight. I feel exposed. "I'm a bit mangled," I mutter, trying to garble the word hysterectomy. I don't need to go into detail about the subsequent surgeries I had to have after my pelvic floor collapsed following my emergency cesarean when it seemed like I might bleed to death delivering Jake.

Somehow I don't think Kellen would find that very sexy. But he sits up and cradles me in his arms. "Elizabeth." He nibbles my ear lobe as he continues to caress and kiss me. "You think I'm expecting the same teenage girl I kissed in high school?" I shrug. "I want you, Beth. I want you as a woman, as a mature, brave fighter."

He meets my eye and lifts his brows as his hands gently grasp the hem of my shirt, as if he's seeking permission. I bite my lip and nod as Kellen lifts my shirt and I sit there in my bra, my stomach on display. The dimpled, scarred mess of it. Kellen dips his head and traces his tongue along the vertical scar beneath my navel.

"Beautiful," he whispers. "This body gave life, Beth." He licks and kisses my stomach and my hips start churning in his bed. I fall back against the pillows and he continues to stroke and lick. "Your cells self-engineered a way to repair the damage," he mutters.

This gets a laugh from me. "You're such a nerd," I say, my fingers in his hair. And then I gasp as he tugs down my leggings. "Oh," I moan. Kellen takes his time, his long fingers tickling trails of sparks down my calves as he slides off first the leggings and then the new panties I wore, despite their being the wrong choice for a bike ride.

"What's this," he says, his mouth hooking into a grin as he holds up the black lace boy shorts he tugged off my quivering body. I bite my lip. "What's *this?*" I feel his fingers trace my tattoo.

"That's my ivy," I tell him, reaching down to trace it dreamily.

"You got a tattoo?"

I nod. "I wanted something just for me. A secret."

"Oh, Beth," he says, his eyes darkening as he shucks his shirt and crawls back onto the bed. "You turn me on so much."

And then I gasp as he dips his silver head between my legs, spreads my thighs apart, and licks my center. "Kellen!" I feel my arousal seep out at his actions, slick and hot. And then I lose my ability to see or speak as he nudges my clit with his nose, slides his tongue inside my body, parts my folds with his gentle fingers.

My hips are bucking up toward his mouth, and my nerve endings are exploding, sending fireworks throughout my entire body. "Oh, god, oh yes. Please, Kellen," I mutter, begging him for what I do not know. But god, does he deliver it. He sucks and bites, presses and rubs until I forget to be worried that 50 year old women don't do things like this. "Kellen, I'm going to come," I sputter.

"Please do, Beth. Come on my tongue. I want to watch you." With one final pinch of my clit and lap of his tongue, I fall over the cliff. I scream and bunch the sheets in my fists, writhing and churning and coming long and hard. Before I can catch my breath, he's on top of me again, nestled between my thighs now, kissing my jaw.

"That was so sexy, Elizabeth," he says, thrusting his hips against mine to demonstrate exactly how turned on he is from making me come like that. We kiss, and I can taste myself on his mouth. My hands are everywhere on his body, nails scraping along his shoulder blades. I'm not sure if I'm ready to have him inside me, but I'm also not sure I can bear to go another second without him in there.

Until my phone rings.

"Leave it," he growls, pinning my arms above my head in a move that would turn me on if it weren't my special ring tone for Jake. The phone rings and rings in the pocket of my leggings, even though I put it on do not disturb. I have my settings tweaked so that Jake can always reach me.

"If he's calling from Lisa's house, it means something's wrong," I say. Kellen's body stiffens, but he releases my arms as I roll out from under him. I can tell by his face that he's disappointed, but my son comes first for me. Always. I'm disappointed that he would make me feel bad for it.

"Jake," I say, stabbing at the screen to pick up the call. "Baby, what's wrong?"

"Lisa bought generic soft pretzels for lunch," he screams. I can hear him pacing. "There is nothing here I can eat. We were supposed to have soft pretzels."

I sigh. "Did you ask her for any other options? What is Dhruv having for lunch?"

We go back and forth for a few minutes about Lisa's lack of the proper brand of every food until I ask him to put her on the phone. Lisa is horrified to learn he has called me in the middle of my date. "Liz, I swear to you, Ashish is three minutes away with the right brand of both pretzel and cereal. Please go back to what you were doing and let me handle this. I've got you."

"Is Jake aware that the food is coming?"

"Elizabeth, I've got this," she insists. I can hear my son freaking out in the background. I squeeze my eyes shut and feel a tear slip down my cheek. I want to believe that she can get him calmed down, but he sounds so upset.

"I'm here, Jake," I hear Ashish's voice bursting into the house. "I've got your lunch, dude."

And then, like a light switch, my son stops shouting. Lisa says, "he's already got the pretzel in the microwave, Liz." I nod, but she can't see. We hang up with her assurances that she will make Jake talk to her before calling me again.

When I look up, I see that Kellen has put his shirt back on. He drapes a blanket over my shoulders and I know our romp in the sheets is over.

"Talk to me," he says, leaning back against the headboard.

"I'm so sorry," I start. I feel all the arguments I've had for 15 years coming up to haunt me. "I know he's too old to be upset about his lunch, but he's got a disability. His brain goes into fight or flight mode when things aren't as he expects them to be and he just—"

"Elizabeth, I know." Kellen bites his cheek and squints. "But why couldn't Lisa handle it and let you have an afternoon away for once?"

I stiffen. "I don't get to be off from being Jake's mom," I tell him. "I'm all that he's got."

He shakes his head. "That's not true, Beth. He's got Lisa. And he's got me. I'm not going to judge him for getting upset."

"Well it seems like you are, Kellen." I stand up, pulling the blanket tight and stooping to gather my things.

"I'm upset because you don't get to ever be off," he says. "You don't get to prioritize anything *but* Jake. It makes me angry."

"Well," I start, considering his words. "That's not what I was expecting you to say."

"You've been on your own against the world for too long," Kellen says, crossing his arms now. "I don't know how to help."

"Well I don't need your help," I spit at him, even though it's not true. I need his help and I need his affection and I need his friendship, and all of those realizations make me upset.

"Maybe I need to be needed," he counters, and the truth of our dual troubles rings in the air. We stare at one another for while. I step back into the leggings. I can't find the panties. I tug on my shirt and tuck my hair behind my ears.

"I'm going to go home and take a shower," I tell him. He nods, and when he doesn't spring up to stop me, I sigh and walk home alone.

CHAPTER TWENTY-EIGHT
KELLEN

I don't like this at all. I don't like that Elizabeth and I were interrupted yesterday when I was in the middle of something so amazing with her. It feels childish to pout about it, but it's been 15 damn years since I was with a woman in that way. I felt like we had everything set up to be successful. Her friend had her son.

She's not just some regular babysitter. Lisa has a son with autism, too. If I'm honest, I'm disappointed that I let myself get my hopes up so high for something like a sexual encounter. Elizabeth was pretty clear that she wants and needs things to go slowly in that regard.

I stomp around my living room tugging at my hair. This isn't like me. I don't act rash. I don't upset people. I've spent decades being the voice of reason in my family network, taking care of Mick and Mick's kids as much as my own. I didn't get this far in life by having temper tantrums, yet that's exactly what I'm doing right now.

Because, shit. I'm still bothered by what happened. It's true what I said. Elizabeth never gets a break. I'm mad for her. I'm mad that she can never be off. I stop pacing in my hallway as I realize that deep down, I might actually be mad that she can never fully prioritize *me*.

Am I okay with that?

"That's something to think about," I mutter.

I decide to head into the office even though it's a weekend. I can't think here, when my whole house seems to smell like Elizabeth. I've been neglecting these projects I'm supposed to be grooming Liam to take over. Hell, I didn't even call Orla to check in before the two of them left for Kentucky this weekend. I was still too worked up over my fight with her Thursday evening.

I'm losing control, and that's not good. Control is the only thing I have going for me. That feels off, so I sit back and take stock. Family. Work. I have those things. They can reciprocate and we can prioritize each other. I need the work, and the company needs me.

I manage to pore over a few files of employee projects, noting inconsistencies and taking a red pen to some of the reports from our junior engineers. Eventually, I take a break and sit back in my desk chair to consider Jake. My argument with Beth yesterday sticks into me. I don't like that Elizabeth doesn't feel able to trust anyone else to support Jake.

He's got a sharp mind, very detail oriented. It makes sense that he applies that same mathematical fastidiousness to all aspects of his life, including what he eats and how he spends his free time. What will it take for Beth to trust me if she can't trust her best friend of ten years, who also has an autistic son?

I scratch at my stubble, considering how some of our staff members remind me a lot of Jake. I don't have access to their personal health files, but I'd bet a lot of these engineers are on the autism spectrum, too. *So how is it that they manage to succeed in a work environment where the unpredictable often happens,* I think.

Sure, these are adults and Jake's a teenager. That has to account for some of it. But I start wondering how they get here, to this adult ability to roll with things that maybe used to send them into a panic. That would perhaps get them so upset they call their mother while she's trying to get it on with a handsome suitor.

I roll my eyes at myself for thinking the word suitor, but I start tapping around my search browser until I discover an ad for an autism coach. "Huh," I say aloud, leaning closer to my monitor and reading about this concierge service, pairing teens and young adults with a trained coach who helps them navigate social situations and build skills for independent living.

They have a link on their site for an advocacy organization, a group where adults with autism get together for social outings, to discuss issues impacting them, to share resources. Like a club, I decide. Nothing too different from the support group I attended after Helen died.

I reach for my phone and call Elizabeth. I'm worried she won't answer, but she picks up after a few rings. "Hey," she says.

"I was studying services for adults with autism," I tell her.

"Oh?" There's an edge to her voice, like she's not sure what to feel about this revelation.

"I was," I say. "And my takeaway is that there is a network of people out there who really care and understand."

"I guess you can't hear me nodding," she says after she's quiet for a bit. "I know you want me to be able to rely on more people. I'm working on it, Kellen."

"I know you are, Beth. You're working harder than anyone I know."

Another silence before she says, "Thank you for acknowledging that. I don't think I'm anywhere near being able to take some time off."

"Well," I shift in my chair and flip my notebook shut, closing my laptop with one hand. "I was wondering if you and Jake wanted to come with me to this event I found online. It's kind of a meetup for adults with autism."

"Oh," she says. "Kellen, thank you for looking into that." She pauses. "Jake already has a number of social skills groups and a therapist and—"

"I just thought you'd want to meet some adults who have made it past these tricky years you're navigating with Jake." This time the silence feels pointed, even over the phone, and I can tell I've overstepped somehow.

"Kellen, the adults at that group aren't past a tricky time. They're all working very hard to navigate a world that overwhelms them." She sounds like she's disappointed in me, and I hate this.

"That came out wrong," I try to tell her, but she cuts me off.

"You have to understand that all the therapies Jake does, all the support I'm finding for him, it's never for a cure." I try to interrupt her, to say I didn't really think there was a cure. But maybe I did think that it was something that sort of passes with adulthood. Nobody at my office is ever flipping out the way Jake does.

"Jake is who he is," Beth says. "I'm working to provide ways for him to open doors for himself." There's a pause, and I want to tell her I know that, but she charges on. "Besides, I don't know that the public would necessarily be welcome at an event like you're describing."

"Not the public," I start to explain. "You and me and Jake."

"Hm," she says. "Again, I appreciate you starting to research this stuff."

"I messed up somewhere, didn't I?"

"Oh, Kellen," she breathes. "Your impulses are so caring and good. I can feel that, I can. I wish that Jake's father would take such an interest in better understanding what he's experiencing."

I run a hand through my hair, questioning whether I should admit my motivations. Fuck it. "I mostly wanted to understand what *you* are experiencing," I say. "I guess I figured...Jake is going to be fine."

"Hm," she says again. I can almost hear her trying to figure out the right thing to say next. "How about if you and I do things together that we both enjoy and let's follow Jake's lead if he wants to include you in any of his therapeutic activities."

Ouch. I recoil as if I've been slapped, even though I have no right to take these words so personally. Even worse, I think Elizabeth can sense that I've been hurt and I can hear her slip into the role of trying to comfort me from the consequences of my own choices. "We visit an autism resource center north of Pittsburgh, up where we used to live," she says. "I'm sure Jake would love to show off his new favorite physics coach during his next teen group meeting..."

Of course Elizabeth would be plugged in to resources for Jake. I'm not sure what I was thinking, searching for coaches and adult groups. "I'd love to be included in Jake's group," I say, feeling humble.

"I'm going to get going, Kel. I'll talk to you soon, okay?"

We hang up and I'm left feeling deeply unsettled. I know I've messed things up, and I don't know how to fix it.

CHAPTER TWENTY-NINE
ELIZABETH

You got this. Lisa's text bolsters my resolve as I head into the family court building. Today is some sort of hearing in front of the family court judge, and I'm told Todd has decided to represent himself going forward. I smile, remembering my lawyer's triumphant cackle when she learned that Todd fired his lawyer after he wasn't happy with the turnout of the division of marital property.

I wish I could have told Kellen about today. I was so taken aback by his call, so confused by his words. I do love that he was researching resources in Pittsburgh for autistic people, but how could he and Todd *both* hold the similar harmful view that people somehow outgrow autism and all the challenges that go along with it.

I stab the elevator button and shake my head. I need to change my mindset. I've been working very hard not to focus on the challenges, but to think about the unique way Jake is able to approach problems due to the way his mind works. This just makes me remember how Kellen talked about his colleagues and their innovative way of solving challenges. "Gah," I growl. I smooth my hands down my outfit, one of the professional sets from the capsule wardrobe.

I pat my thigh with the tattoo, glad all over again that I got it. It's like a secret talisman to help me do hard things. I'm different than I was a few months ago, and I'm strong enough to face whatever waits for me in this meeting.

My lawyer, Erin, stands in the hall staring daggers at Todd. Erin wears killer heels and a tailored pantsuit and looks like she can make people weep. This is why I hired her. Lisa and Ashish helped me find her. "Liz," she says, nodding. "This is about to be amazing. I promise."

I glance over at Todd and sneer. We all get called inside and I spend the next hour rolling my eyes. Todd is filing a motion to get 50/50 custody, increasing his hours with Jake in response to my filing for full custody and support.

"He hardly ever shows up for the time he does have with Jake," I shout eventually, slapping the table and earning a stern head shake from Erin. I bite my lip and sink back into the chair. Nobody is listening to reason. I hear Todd outlining some nonsense about me actively working to alienate him. He's presenting himself as a doting father driven to stray from his cold, depressed wife.

My knuckles are white as I squeeze the edge of the table. Erin hisses out of the side of her mouth, "Say nothing. This is expected. Let him dig a hole."

Todd steeples his fingers on the table, looking so smarmy I feel myself wanting to slice his face with the fancy pen sitting on the table in front of him. I only half listen as the judge explains that we both need to attend a seminar about co-parenting. *Like hell Todd will show up for anything like that*, I think. Eventually, I'm startled to realize Erin is nudging me to leave the room.

"What the fuck, Erin? How dare he? How dare he bring up my post-partum depression! I was left home alone to recover from an emergency cesarean and hysterectomy, to simultaneously parent a colicky newborn with absolutely zero help." She nods. "He only took two days off work," I shriek. Erin tugs my arm and pulls me into an open supply closet.

"Lizzy, we're not going to lose our temper in public. I know all this shit is hard to hear. I know." She rubs my arm. "I promise you he did not come out of there looking good." She assures me the next hearing will be the end of things, when she will present all the dates and times of missed custody as well as Jake's own vehement wish not to go sleep over at his father's house.

I drive home, feeling dejected. I stare at the treadmill, knowing I might feel better after a pounding run—or at least a vigorous walk—but I can't even do that with my injury. All I feel capable of is sinking into the couch.

I keep hearing Todd's words, the way he was twisting my parenting to make me sound like a helicopter parent, some sort of spoiled housewife out to ruin Todd's life.

I look out the window to see Jake climbing the hill on his way home from school. My survival mode instincts kick into gear. I feel myself shutting down all my own needs and active emotions. My body prepares to emphasize him and his needs.

And then I watch as he turns toward Kellen's house. He rings the bell and starts fishing in his bag, pulling out what I recognize as his physics folder. He grins when Kellen answers the door and beckons him inside.

I have no words to describe the deflation I feel in this moment, no explanation for why this feels like such a rejection to me. But before I know it, I recognize the sound of gasping sobs escaping my body. I sit on the couch and just sob and scream in a way I haven't yet done. Not when I caught Todd with his mistress. Not when I woke up from surgery to learn I'd never have another child.

I cry for all of it, until I feel empty and I have no idea how to fill myself back up again.

CHAPTER THIRTY
KELLEN

MY ARGUMENT WITH ELIZABETH HAS ME DOWN. I EVEN CALLED MY NEPHEWS AND canceled family dinner this week, although Orla told me she's still coming over to do her laundry. I suspect she's coming to fret over me. Or maybe to yell some more.

When my doorbell rings, I assume it's her, ringing because her arms are too full to open the door. But I see Jake standing out there clutching his physics notebook, looking eager.

"Kellen," he shouts through the glass storm door. "I need assistance understanding Faraday's law."

Like magic, my mood elevates. I push the door open and Jake greets me with a hug. "We've begun discussing electromagnetism," he says, barging past me toward my dining room. He starts spreading out his things before I get my bearings. I love his enthusiasm and focus.

I sit next to him and ask him to tell me what he's learned so far, and Jake regurgitates the textbook definitions of the concepts and formulas he needs to solve the problems he's been given for homework.

"Can you tell me what this means in your words," I ask. He looks at me puzzled.

"Those were my words," he says. "I spoke them."

I nod. "Ok. Let's look at this first problem and see if you know how best to approach it. *'A UHF television loop antenna has a diameter of 11 cm. The magnetic field of a TV signal is normal to the plane of the*

482

loop and, at one instant of time, its magnitude is changing at the rate 0.16 T/s. The magnetic field is uniform. What emf is induced in the antenna?"'

Jake looks up at me expectantly, blinking. "Ok," I tell him. "Where do we start?"

"That's why I'm here," he says. I chuckle.

"You know," I tell him, "This is the work my daughter Orla does every day. She's an electrical engineer."

"Are all of the Bradys licensed engineers like Callum?" He chews on the end of his pencil methodically and I nod.

"We are. Well, not my brother. All the rest of us, though!"

"I wish I had relatives who knew about physics."

"Well," I tell him. "You know you're welcome over here any time, Jake. We'd all love to talk physics with you."

The front door opens as I say that and Orla staggers in with her laundry. "Oh," she says, seeing Jake at the table. She pinches her lips together and says, "So you canceled dinner with us to hang out with—"

I cut her off before she says something she will regret later. "Jake came over and asked for some help with his homework," I tell her. "Faraday's law."

Her face brightens a little but she still seems upset. I meet Jake's glance and say, "Can you get started with an attempt at this problem? I need to help Orla get her laundry started."

Jake nods. "It can be difficult to decide which clothing goes together for loads of laundry." He bends over his notebook, still chewing the end of his pencil.

I walk toward the basement steps and beckon for Orla to follow me to the laundry area. We each carry a basket down the stairs and she dumps her clothes in the machine, not looking at me.

"Want to tell me what's bothering you?"

She shakes her head. But then she turns and leans on the machine, palms up in frustration. "Did you seriously cancel family dinner this week but make plans with your new family?"

"Orla, I did not know Jake was coming over. Not that it's much of your business, but I canceled family dinner because I had an argument with Elizabeth and, well, I'm rattled by it."

"You had a fight and didn't ask all parties to sit down and discuss immediately?" She nudges me with her shoulder, then sighs. "We didn't finish our conversation from the other week, did we?"

"We did not." I drape an arm around her shoulder. "Do you want to start or should I share first?"

Orla squeezes her eyes shut tight and starts talking. "I didn't know it would feel this way to see you with someone else," she says. "You've been... you've been all of our dad for so long. Like, you're the one who talks everyone down from stupid decisions and dishes out wisdom."

"That's not going to change, Orla."

"I guess I know that. I just...where does it leave me if you've got a girlfriend and a new kid?"

I huff out a laugh. "I don't know if Elizabeth wants to be my girlfriend right now. But that's not the point," I add quickly. "You're my most important person, Orla. That will never change. Why do you think I'm in the basement with you in my house helping you wash your unmentionables?"

She leans her head on my shoulder. "I miss Mom," she says. "Like, I miss the idea of her, and having a mom and all that."

"I miss her, too," I say. "I'll always miss her. I'm not aiming to replace her, Orla. Elizabeth is...she's different. And she makes me feel good, and I'd like to figure out how to earn back her esteem."

"Her esteem? Jesus, Dad. No wonder you've been single for so long."

"That's enough of that," I tell her, and I can tell the mood has shifted. I sigh. "Want to come upstairs and help me explain electromagnetism to a teenager?"

She purses her lips for a minute and squeezes her arm around me tighter. I match her embrace. "That actually does sound really interesting," she says.

We head back upstairs and both sit at the table with Jake and his high school physics textbook. Orla is enthusiastic, animated while she explains the concepts to Jake. She pulls a pencil from her shirt pocket and starts scratching out multiple approaches to the problem on some scrap paper, and Jake's jaw drops.

"You are so much better than my teacher," he says, looking at her in admiration. "You really make me want to master this."

She looks smug. "You'll have to come shadow me at work sometime," she tells him, and I feel glad that she clearly means it. Jake works his way through a few more problems, needing less assistance each time, until he finally slams his notebook shut and rises to his feet.

"You heading home?" I lean back in my chair, my fingers laced behind my head in a posture I'm always chastising my nephews for. Jake nods and walks out of the house without saying goodbye.

Orla raises her brows and turns to me. "He's very...blunt," she says.

"Takes one to know one." I wink at my daughter.

"That's fair, I guess. I'm glad we aren't a family that dances around delicate topics." Orla sighs and blows her hair out of her eyes. "So tell me more about what happened with your lady friend, Dad."

"You sure? Because my hope is that I get back to a place where you see her here at my house more often."

She nods. "I mean, I'm not running out to buy her a Christmas present early. But I want to be supportive." She winks. "I did urge you into this, after all."

I squeeze her hand and fill her in on my argument with Elizabeth. "I didn't appreciate what it really meant for Jake to follow such different social rules," I tell her. "I wish I could take back what I said to Elizabeth about autistic adults being past their challenges."

Orla considers me and then pulls out her phone. She taps around for a bit and I see she's pulled up the advocacy site I had naively mentioned to Elizabeth. "This group does workplace trainings," Orla says, showing me a section of the website I had not visited. "You can pay them to come in and talk about making the office more inclusive, helping with some understanding of autistic brains."

"Huh." I squint to look at her phone screen. "We should do that at Beltane."

She nods. "Obviously. Want me to schedule it?"

I shake my head. "I'd like to do it," I tell her. "I am the president of the company after all." I ruffle her hair. "What are you making your old man for dinner?"

CHAPTER THIRTY-ONE
KELLEN

I'M ABLE TO SCHEDULE THE WORKPLACE TRAINING WITH THE AUTISTIC ADVOCACY staff for Friday. I spend the entire week looking forward to it, poring over their website and reading about differences in autistic brains compared to neurotypical brains. Neurotypical is a new word for me. I send a company wide email inviting everyone to the training Friday and have our administrative staff reschedule all appointments so everyone is able to attend.

I arrange for a walk through with the trainer after the session, where we will look over the physical work environment and talk about changes I can make there as well. By the end of the day, my Beltane team has listened to countless stories from employees sharing their experiences and created a monthly speaker series plus some support groups for people to vent and get support. I order light diffusing covers for the fluorescent lights and high quality noise canceling headphones for every employee, should they choose to wear those during the work day.

I'm surprised by the number of my employees who self-identify as being autistic and who, like Jake, use the word Aspergers to describe themselves even though that technically doesn't exist anymore. I leave the afternoon so energized, excited to put words to one of the elements that gives Beltane an edge when it comes to meticulous inspections and innovative, outside-the-box thinking about client challenges.

I drive home eager to knock on Elizabeth's door, to ask her to please have a conversation with me and listen to all that I've learned. I know she likely already knows all of this information, but I want to let her know that I understand Jake's autism isn't going anywhere. I know he's learning techniques to navigate this world, and I know that Elizabeth is his soft landing space.

I want to tell her that I'd like to be a soft landing space for him, too. That maybe between the two of us, we can support him and she'll feel less... I don't even know how to finish that thought, but I don't get the chance. I pull into my driveway and see a commotion across the street.

A man stands in the yard, shouting. It must be Todd Gaston, and I sneer at the thought of him coming here. I get out of the car and decide to stick around, just in case. Just in case of what, I don't know, but things are getting heated over there.

"You're coming with me and that's final," Todd shouts at Jake, who shakes his head and backs up closer to his porch stairs. "I have legal rights to spend this weekend with you," Todd sneers, and Jake starts screaming back at his father.

"I don't want to go with you. No, no, no!" He sinks to the grass and starts rocking back and forth, his hands slapping at the yard. It's painful to see him so upset and I'm about to walk over when Elizabeth bursts outside.

"Enough, Todd. He doesn't want to go with you."

The asshole shakes his head, grinning cruelly. "Of course not, after you poisoned his mind against me. I'm recording this entire thing, you know. Let's let the lawyers see how our child is frightened of his own father, thanks to whatever bullshit lies you've been feeding him."

"Please do record this, Todd," Elizabeth says, walking over to Jake to comfort him. "Make sure to send me a copy, too." She places a hand on Jake's shoulder and he swats her hand away. "Sweetheart, do you want to go inside?"

Jake starts to scream, a low keening sound. I walk over toward him, unable to stand by while he's suffering like this. "I think Jake has had enough," I say to Todd. He snaps his head toward me.

"Who the fuck is this, Elizabeth? Mind your own business," he spits at me. I ignore him and squat so I can make eye contact with Jake. Jake is the one who matters right now.

He sees me and crawls over toward me on the lawn, surprising me by wrapping his arms around me. I hold him and rub his back as Elizabeth looks at me with tears in her eyes. I reach a hand for hers and squeeze, and I see this is the moment where Todd figures out what I am to her, what I have become to his family.

"You want full custody," he screams at her. He starts flailing his arms around, still holding his cell phone like he's recording. "You think you're fit to care for a disabled child while you're out fucking this guy? Whoever the hell he is."

"That will be enough of that," I tell him, disentangling myself from Jake's limbs to stand up. "You need to head on out of here and regain your composure. If you ever had any."

"Fuck you," Todd glares at me. "You're behind all this? You encouraging her to bleed me dry? She sat around for years, spending my money and refusing to fuck me. She'll stop fucking you, too." He opens his mouth to keep going, but I stand firmly in his space, an inch away from his face.

"Get out of here," I growl at him, my voice low, enraged. "You will not speak that way in front of a child and you will not speak that way about Elizabeth."

He laughs, a cruel sound. "You're the manners police?" Todd dusts off his slacks and shakes his head, walking toward his car. "I'll see your ass in court," he shouts. "You're going to lose everything and my son will get placed in a proper treatment center for people like him. Enough of this freak show."

He gets in the car and races down the street. Jake's eyes are wild with fright and anger. He stomps into the house and slams the door. Elizabeth moves to follow him.

"Beth," I say, "Please, wait. Please talk to me."

She shakes her head. "I have to go to him," she tells me. I see a tear roll down one cheek. "I have to calm him down and I have to call my lawyer to document this before his fucking lawyer sends some sort of injunction."

"Let me help," I plead with her, following her toward the house.

"We're not a project for you, Kellen," she shouts. "I have to go protect my son before I lose him."

"Elizabeth, I'm not going anywhere," I tell her. "And I won't let you lose him. Let me help you."

She's crying real tears now and she ignores them as they roll down her cheeks. She makes her way toward the steps. "I can't make room in my life for anything but Jake," she tells me.

I think of all the ways I could be helping right now if she would just let me in. I could call the lawyer and give a statement. I could make them dinner while she works with Jake to calm him down.

But she doesn't let me. She goes inside and I hear the deadbolt turn as her footsteps fade down the hallway. I'm left outside alone.

CHAPTER THIRTY-TWO
ELIZABETH

IT TAKES ME HOURS TO CONVINCE JAKE THAT HE IS NOT GOING TO HAVE TO GO LIVE IN a treatment center. I explain that there isn't even such a thing for teenagers with his specific abilities. "Jake, you're thriving in school. You're in all honors classes and competing in chess and you're about to graduate advanced social skills at the center."

We've had this same conversation 15 times this evening and I'm drained. I'm exhausted, but he needs to hear it again, to internalize the truth of it, so we go through it again. Finally, Jake looks at me. "What did Dad mean about you fucking the neighbors?"

"Oh, Jake, honey that was just angry talk."

"Fucking is mating, isn't it?"

"Sweetie, you really need to stop referring to mating. It's just not a word you should use with humans. That's a rule for you to write down in your book, okay?"

He nods, but continues. "But are you fucking with Kellen? You're not expecting a baby. You said your body can't gestate anymore babies."

I close my eyes and swallow. "Kellen and I are friends," I tell him. He rolls his eyes. "And Kellen and I...were...I'm interested in kissing Kellen and being affectionate with him."

"He's very nice," Jake says.

"That is accurate," I tell him, adopting one of his favorite phrases. "And I'm very glad you have him as a friend. Especially for the homework help."

"He was nice today. When Dad was yelling."

I nod. "That's very true, babe."

Jake seems to settle finally and, since we missed Star Wars night, I let him watch it on his laptop in bed.

I make my way to the kitchen, wishing I had alcohol in the house. I consider asking Lisa to drive over with a bottle for me. I consider walking across the street and begging Kellen for some of his whiskey, but I've lost the right to ask him those sorts of favors.

He wants a level of intimacy from me that I can't offer. He wants me to keep him in the loop, to help me with this whole mess. I can't be his project. How can I focus on anything else at all when I've got to protect Jake? It was fun to feel distracted for a bit with Kellen.

I let myself think for a minute that we could move from distraction to something real. But I don't get to let my guard down and enjoy a relationship. This is what I've got right now. I sit at the table and start a long email to Erin. When I hit send, I head to my bedroom and fall into a fitful, dreamless sleep.

B

SATURDAY EVENING, Jake and I have to prepare for his social skills celebration. Jake and Dhruv attend a lot of classes at the family center north of the city. Autistic teens work on all sorts of skills, like compromise and reciprocal conversations. This quarter, they've focused on strategies to calm down when faced with something unexpected.

"I've decided what example of success I will share when it's my turn to talk," Jake tells me. The program includes each member sharing a story, which is also meant to inspire the incoming class of teens who generally assume their challenges are insurmountable.

"Which success is that, babe?" I assume Jake's going to talk about the chess tournament, where he was doing poorly and accepted his loss with grace.

"I made a new friend," Jake says, shrugging. I nod, conceding that this is indeed a big victory. New people come with new and unfamiliar expectations. I assume Jake is referencing someone from high school, since he's talked so much about his new video game companions.

We pull into the lot and start to walk toward the building when I see Kellen Brady standing there with his hands in his pockets. "You came!" Jake jumps up on the curb and approaches Kellen, beaming.

"Couldn't turn down such a dazzling invitation," Kellen says. I'm so stunned to see him here that I freeze. I stand in silence, just starting at Kellen as Jake starts bouncing impatiently.

"Mom," he says. "We are not going to get a desirable seat."

"Why don't you go in and save us three," Kellen suggests, dropping a hand briefly on Jake's shoulder. Jake frowns.

"Is saving seats fair? Does that violate a social custom?"

"We'll be right behind you," I say, gesturing with my head. Jake nods and goes inside, grabbing programs from the table and making a beeline for the common room. All the chairs will be placed in a circle around the room so everyone can see everyone else. There's only five teens in the group, but Jake has ideas about the most desired seat in the circle. Who am I to argue?

"Jake texted me to invite me," Kellen says, hands in his pockets, looking awkward. "You said I'd always be welcome if Jake wanted to include me..."

I nod, quickly. "I...just didn't know he'd done that." So much is unsaid between us and I'm still rattled by the argument from the other night. "I don't know what to say, Kellen."

He breathes out of his nose and leans on the building. "What if you don't need to say anything just now," he suggests. "What if I just sit beside you and you know I'm here for you when you're ready?"

I feel a lump in my throat again and start to wonder if eventually I'll choke on all these big emotions that have been surfacing for me lately. "But why, Kellen? Why are you here?"

He grins. "I can't stay away, Beth," he says. "I feel more myself when I'm with you."

I feel a flush spread over my body, a warmth I can't identify. I feel the same, safer with him, like things make sense. "I don't want to be a special project for you, Kellen," I tell him, swallowing down the lump.

He shakes his head. "You're not a project, Beth. You're my inspiration." He reaches for my leg, his fingers tracing the spot where my ivy tattoo marks my thigh. "I've been thinking about what you said about that ivy, how ivy can indeed spread and thrive on the ground. But you know what? If it wants to climb, it needs a trellis. It needs support."

I feel a tear sneak out and I roll my eyes at how often I've been crying this week. "God, that's a nice metaphor, Kellen." I huff out a laugh.

"You're sure it's not a euphemism?" He hooks his mouth into a grin and reaches for my hand. "Come on," he says. "Show me what this place is all about."

We head inside and find Jake spread eagle, his hands and legs blocking off a chair on either side of him. Kellen and I sit, flanking him, and Kellen wraps a long arm around the back of the chair, cradling both Jake and I in his safe embrace.

The group facilitator reviews the kids' achievements over the past few months, talking about how hard it can be for autistic teens to face the unexpected and carry on when so much around them does not make sense. "But these guys did it," she says, "And you're about to hear their takeaways."

The teens share their victories, describing brave forays into sports tryouts and after-school job interviews. When it's Jake's turn to talk, he stands and describes his move to a new neighborhood and a new school. "And that's where I made a new friend," he says, gesturing to Kellen. I listen to my son describe what it meant for him to meet someone who helps him problem solve. "He helps with homework and knows what to do when my plans get canceled," Jake shares. "And even though my mother is not engaging in sexual intercourse with him, he still shows up when it's important."

My jaw drops and I hide my face behind my hands. I feel Kellen adjust in his chair, clearing his throat. "Thank you, Jake," Miss Amy says when Jake finishes speaking. "We're all so glad you formed a new friendship this fall." She starts to lead a round of applause and I feel the chair shake as my son sits back down.

"Thank you for attending tonight, Kellen," Jake says as he sits.

"You bet," Kellen tells him, and I see his jaw set as he tries to maintain control without laughing.

THE CEREMONY ENDS and the teens disappear to play air hockey in the lounge, leaving the parents to swarm over to me. A collective laugh bursts from everyone in the room as they all seem to say "intercourse," together at once. Miss Amy places a hand on my shoulder and assures me they'll discuss healthy sexual relationships in the winter session.

"He'll be here for it," Kellen says, and then turns toward me. "I'm sorry," he says. "That's not for me to determine."

"Oh, he'll be here," I say. "Not sure if I'll be able to show my face here again, but Jake will be here."

"Aw, come on," Amy says. She winks at Kellen. "There's not a person here tonight who isn't rooting for you to change your mind and mate with this fox."

I wish the earth would open up and swallow me, and I'm relieved when the other parents leave us alone to go grab cookies and lemonade. "So," Kellen says, brushing my hair back from my forehead. I feel a trail of sparks behind his touch.

"So," I say. I sigh. "This is all really new for me." He nods. "It really matters to me that you showed up tonight. And the other afternoon. You weren't meddling."

"I'm here, Beth. I'm here for you and Jake."

"I feel like I don't have anything to offer you," I tell him, voicing my fear, realizing as I say it how true it is.

He shakes his head. "How about you just offer yourself," Kellen says, and leans forward to press a kiss against my forehead.

His lips feel so safe, so soft, so loving. "God that feels good," I blurt, closing my eyes and leaning against his chest. He tilts my head back and kisses my lips, his tongue sweeping between mine. It feels familiar and exciting and I moan, returning his kiss, pressing my fingers against his chest until I feel his heart racing, just like mine.

My phone starts to ring in my pocket and I groan as reality sets back in. I can't give Kellen myself. "Answer it," he says, reaching for my pocket. "I can wait."

I look into his eyes and see that he means it, that he's willing to stand by while I address whatever crisis awaits me on the other end of the line. He nods. I bring the phone to my ear. It's Erin.

"You're going to be so excited," she tells me. "Our hearing is first thing Monday. And we got the judge I'm excited about."

"Monday?"

"Yes, and this is great news, I promise." Erin tells me to be at the court building by 8 on Monday and I chew on my lip while she talks. Kellen massages my shoulders, and I lean into his touch.

"This could all be over in a few days," I tell him.

He grins at me. "It's going to be a relief," he says, giving my shoulders another squeeze. "I can feel it." He helps me round up Jake and kisses me goodnight while Jake groans from the passenger seat.

"Thanks again for including me tonight, J," he says, leaning in across me to shake Jake's hand.

"Just stop kissing my mom in public," he says, rolling his eyes.

CHAPTER THIRTY-THREE
ELIZABETH

I DON'T SLEEP WELL THIS WEEKEND. FOR ONE THING, ANY TIME I HAVE TO ABRUPTLY change Jake's plans, it's fraught. I'm so tired, mentally, and he needs to ask me a lot of questions over and over again to feel reassured about what to expect on Monday.

"What is the statistical likelihood Dad will send me away?" He looks so young, so vulnerable. I pull him into my arms and promise him I will never let that happen. I do it again and again, right up until we park in the garage downtown, both wearing our most uncomfortable professional clothes, and we walk hand in hand toward the courthouse.

Erin is waiting for us in the lobby, greeting us warmly and abruptly in a way that oddly sets Jake at ease. "That flaming asshole doesn't even have a lawyer," she snorts. "Sorry, kid," she adds as an afterthought, but Jake just shrugs.

We enter the elevator and make our way to the courtroom. The hall is crowded and bustling with people in suits, angry parents, a few sullen kids. Erin pushes the open the door to our hearing room and I take a deep breath before crossing the threshold.

There, standing stoically in a dark grey suit, is Kellen Brady, grinning. My jaw drops and my heart swells a little bit. I didn't even call him this weekend, or leave my house, or really leave the fetal position. It never occurred to me to ask him to come with me, but seeing him here I feel... hope.

"Hey, Beth," he says, leaning in to kiss my cheek. I hear Jake grumble beside me and Kellen tosses him a wink. He reaches a hand out toward Erin. "Kellen Brady."

She raises her eyebrows and looks him up and down. "Erin Long," she says, pulling back her hand and turning toward me, then back to Kellen. "You, sir, are what we call an upgrade."

Kellen blushes and shifts his weight. It's then that I notice he's not here alone. Grinning behind him are Callum and...Orla. Jake hustles over to them and beams. "What are you guys doing here?"

Cal shrugs. "We had nothing better to do, so we thought we'd hang out and then take you with us to check out all the robots at our office."

"You have robots in your office?"

Erin taps my shoulder and gestures toward the front of the room. "Come on, guys," she says. "Let's do this thing."

My head swims as the judge enters and the court staff give their spiel. I barely look over at smarmy Todd, sitting by himself seeping audacity. I think about Kellen here, even though I ignored him all weekend. Orla came. Orla!

I'm rubbing circles on Jake's back without thinking as Todd stands up. Apparently he gets to go first since he is filing today's motion. He waves around a USB drive, saying, "I have compelling video evidence here, your honor." Erin rolls her eyes and grins as he begins to play the video on the monitor in the front of the court. I cringe as Todd starts yelling, and I hear Orla and Cal growl at the part where Kellen shows up and tries to calm things down.

Once Todd starts yelling about sending Jake away, the judge holds up his hand. "That's enough, Mr. Gaston," he says, sternly.

"Your honor? I think you need to see the rest of this to—"

Judge Palowski takes off his glasses and sets them on the desk. He crosses his arms across his chest. "Mr. Gaston, are you aware that I also have an autistic teenager?"

Todd stammers. "I was not aware of that, your honor."

The judge nods his head. "I do indeed, and I have to tell you that I do not appreciate the notion that your long-term parenting plan is to send your son away to an institution that doesn't exist."

Todd clenches his jaw and I squeeze Jake's arm. The judge picks up his glasses and puts them back on and leans forward, pointing at Jake. "Jacob, do you have any desire to spend time with your father?"

"I object!" Todd stomps his foot and the judge glares daggers at him.

"Jacob," Judge Palowski says again. "What are your thoughts on all this?"

"I want to stay with my mom," he says, and I feel a sob crawl up my throat. I breathe rapidly through my nose, trying to calm down.

"I suspected as much." The judge starts writing in his book on the table. "I am awarding Ms. Burns full custody in this case and adjusting support payments accordingly." He looks up at me and smiles. "Case adjourned."

"Yes," Erin pumps her fist and turns to me for a high five.

"I don't understand," I tell her, frowning. Kellen, Cal and Orla hustle forward as Todd is escorted out of the room by the clerk.

"I'll make it simple for you," Erin says. "That oozing hemmerhoid came in here guns blazing and demonstrated exactly how much of a pile of feces he is. He's now being guided through adjusted paperwork to pay out the ass and leave you guys alone."

Cal grins and elbows Orla. "Oh, I like her." Orla nods. Kellen shushes them and squeezes behind the table to put his hand on my shoulder. Only when I feel his firm touch do I realize I'm barely able to stay standing.

I don't say anything. I can't speak. I need to make sure I understand what I'm hearing. "So Jake and I are free?" Kellen beams at my words, pulling me in tighter as I try to listen to Erin.

"Free and fully funded. It's coming right from his paycheck into your debit account," she says. "Congratulations, Liz. Hope I never see you again." I laugh at her candor and thank her for her work on the case.

She winks at Kellen. "Definitely an upgrade, Liz." And she's gone.

I turn around and look into Kellen's eyes. "It's over," I tell him. He picks me up and spins around, holding me in the air, and when he sets me down he pulls me in for a kiss. I hear the other Bradys whistle and Jake protest and when I disentangle myself from Kellen's embrace, I feel like I should be embarrassed, but all I can think about is how happy I feel.

CHAPTER THIRTY-FOUR
KELLEN

After I leave Jake and Beth at the ceremony on Saturday, my mind is reeling. I am still not sure if we're okay after the things I said to her, but I also know she has to prepare for her hearing on Monday, so I don't want to distract her with my own selfish needs to be comforted.

By the time my family shows up on Sunday for dinner, they panic when they find me sitting around in sweatpants watching television. I barely respond to them being here, unable shake off the deep desire to help Elizabeth, paired with my equal desire to show that I believe she can help herself when she needs to.

I considered going over to her house a thousand times, wrote a rubric about my options, and eventually sank into the couch catching up on the radio documentaries that suddenly no longer seem interesting to me.

Mick takes a look at me, orders pizza, and insists the Brady family intervene somehow. They all want to storm the courtroom when I tell them about the hearing Monday, but surprisingly it's Mick who speaks as the voice of reason about that suggestion.

"She can't show up in there with a circus in tow," he says, shaking his head. "We'll just name delegates who can behave."

"Oh, well Isaac is out then," Nicole says, elbowing my nephew in the ribs. "And me. Don't let me near that scum bag. I will not be couth."

"Is couth a word?" Maddie is pacing the room, rubbing her bulging stomach. "I know about uncouth. Anyway, I could spew this baby out at any time so Liam and I are a no for tomorrow."

"I'm not going back in a family courtroom ever again," Mick says, starting to clean up all the paper plates and napkins. I stare at him, cleaning up my house, speaking with experience about custody proceedings. "We should bring the kid back to Beltane afterward, though. Isn't he an egghead?"

"Is egghead an insult?" Nicole frowns at him. "It feels like it could be insulting."

I roll my eyes at them all, but I love that they're doing this. They're treating Elizabeth like she's one of us already and it's so meaningful to me I almost start to cry. Nicole hands me a beer and says, "Here's what we're gonna do. Isaac and Ray are going to plan a nerd-gasmic robot adventure for Jake and Orla and Cal will be Brady ambassadors along with Uncle Kellen."

They all nod and wedge themselves with me on the couch. Sitting here, together with them all, I know things are going to work out. Mick claps his hands and stands up. "Well, I've got a date," he says. "Good night, you beautiful babies. Nobody show up in court wearing sneakers." He glares at Callum and backs out my front door.

℔

AFTER THE HEARING, Orla and Cal bustle Jake away. Elizabeth, holding his tie and blazer, still looks shell shocked. She stares after them, tears rolling down her cheeks in the hall where the staff ushered us after the hearing. They really pack those courtroom schedules, and the next deadbeat ex-husband is due to get his comeuppance a few minutes after Elizabeth's.

"Let me drive you home," I whisper into her ear. "My car is at the Beltane lot and I walked." I shrug and reach for her purse, and she hands it to me. I pull out the keys and place my hand on the small of her back.

We walk to the garage and she sinks into the passenger seat of her car and looks over at me. "Did all that really happen?"

"Sure did," I say, pulling her garage ticket from the visor above my head and inserting my credit card in the machine at the exit. "And from the sound of things, Jake is having the time of his life at my office."

"But you're here with me?" She rests her elbow on the window and her head in her hand, turning toward me. Her expression shifts from one of stunned surprise to a heated gaze emitting a very different energy.

"I'm here with you," I tell her. I pull onto Bigelow Boulevard and reach for her, needing to connect with her skin. We touch the rest of the way to her house, her breath coming faster and my patience waning as the lights seem to stay red forever.

I pull into her driveway and follow her into the house, where she heads down the hall and looks at me over her shoulder. I step closer to her, into her space. I can see her chest rise and fall and I place a finger on her chin, tipping her face up to look at me. "I was so proud to be there with you today," I tell her. She smiles.

"Thank you so much for showing up today," she says, her voice shaky. "I can't begin to tell you what it meant to see you and your family there."

"Well," I put my hands on her hips. "How about if you show me then?" She stretches up on her tiptoes and captures my mouth in a kiss. I'm happy to receive it, opening my mouth to receive her tongue as she explores. We kiss in her kitchen, my hands roaming her body, fingers lingering on her backside, and when I squeeze a proper handful, she pulls back.

"We should probably be quiet," she says, and starts walking down the hall, tugging me by the hand. "The neighbors are out raking leaves..."

"I won't make a sound," I whisper, following her as I toe off my shoes and start to work on the buttons of my shirt. When we get in her room, she shuts and locks the door and pounces on me, shoving me back so I fall on her bed.

She climbs on top of me and flattens me in a kiss, shoving my hands out of the way as she pulls open my buttons. She groans when she encounters my undershirt, as if she's as anxious as I am to feel our skin pressed together.

I clutch her waist and roll us so that I'm on top of her, nestled between her legs. I reach over my neck to pull off my undershirt with one hand while I kneel on the bed. Elizabeth reaches up and works on the waistband of my slacks.

"I want all of you, Kellen," she says. "I don't want to stop halfway."

"Same, Beth," I tell her, gently lifting her shirt and easing it up as she lifts up to let me pull it off her head. "You let me know what feels good, though." I don't want to let my barely-contained lust to hurt her in any way.

"All of it feels good," she says, wriggling out of her pants. We strip each other until we are bare, and I'm kneeling on the bed with my cock in my hand, stroking it as I look down on her magnificent body.

She reaches a hand for her breast, and I'm worried she's going to try to cover herself from me again, but she stares at my crotch and fingers her nipple, like she can't help herself. She's pleasuring herself, and it turns me on. A lot. "Oh, Beth," I growl. "Do you like what you see?"

She bites her lip and looks up at me. I dive down on top of her, spearing her mouth with my tongue, filling my palm with her breasts. I feel her nipples tighten beneath my touch and I groan as she snakes a hand around my erection.

Gasping, she pulls back. "I have lube in the night stand," she breathes. "But I don't have condoms."

"I haven't been with anyone in over a decade," I say into her neck. I glance up and meet her eye.

"Me neither," she says. And then she laughs. "And I can't get pregnant." She pulls her hand back from my chest where she's been tracing a nail through my graying hairs. She opens her drawer and pulls out a tiny bottle of lube. "We should just go for it."

"Oh god," I moan. "Yes, Beth." I take the bottle from her hand and set it beside her head on the bed while I continue my exploration of her beautiful body. I lick each nipple until the glistening tips are standing erect as Beth's chest rises and falls with her panting breaths.

She moves her hands to my ass and massages. Her touch is warm, exploratory. "Kellen," she moans. Beth thrusts her hips up and I feel her center against my hard-on, warm and welcoming. Bracing my weight on one arm, I pop open the cap to the bottle and pour a drop on my finger.

"You'll tell me if something doesn't feel good?"

"It all feels good, Kellen," she says, her hips churning beneath me. I reach down between her legs with my lubed up finger, parting her as she sighs. "Oh," she moans. "Yes." My finger slides inside her body and she's so tight, so slick and hot. I add another finger and feel her bear down as I stroke in and out.

This experience is familiar, like a far-off dream, but also feels so new I want to savor every instant with her. I want to see what makes her feel good, to watch her face transform.

Beth moans my name as my thumb presses against her clit. I look down at her lovely face, her eyes closed as she moans and wriggles on the bed. Her hands fall off my body and clutch at the sheets as I increase my speed and pressure. "Kellen," she cries.

"Ssshhh," I remind her. "We have to be quiet, remember?" I press my mouth against hers to swallow her moans as she bucks beneath me and I draw an orgasm from her with my fingers. Her pleasure is a gift to me. She's bare to me in every way, vulnerable and open. I'm incredibly turned on.

As she gasps for breath, Elizabeth grabs for my cock and rubs her thumb around the sensitive tip. I feel a drop of pre-cum slick beneath her hand and I groan. "Please, Kellen," she begs. I don't make her say it twice. I reach for more of the lube just in case, and she watches as I drizzle it on my hard length. "So sexy," she says, extending a hand to help me as I spread the liquid around.

I adjust my weight and align myself with her center as she keeps her hand on me, sliding her fist up and down, slick and perfect. I press a kiss against her mouth as I slide carefully inside.

"Oh, god," she and I say together. I feel her around me everywhere. Every nerve in my body fires for this experience as I sink into Elizabeth's welcoming heat. I intend to lie still, to let her acclimate to my presence inside her, but Elizabeth starts to rock her hips. She starts to take control, digging her fingers into my butt as she lifts up from beneath me.

"You like that, Beth?" I grin, propping myself on my forearms as she pulls me in deeper, faster, harder.

"So good," she moans. And I want this for always, us together, open. No limits. No barriers between us. I want to be here for her difficulties and I want to be here to make her feel good. I join her motion, and the two of us rock together, our old bodies finding a new rhythm. "Right there," she breathes and then she starts to moan. "Harder."

"Beth, are you sure you—"

"Shut up, Kellen," she snaps, and she rocks into my pelvis, grinding against my pubic bone. "I'm going to come again. I'm going to come!"

I pick up the pace and she joins me every step of the way until we are both tumbling over the edge. I come, the hot ropes of my release filling her as she shouts my name and claws at my shoulders. And then I collapse on top of her, feeling so complete I might cry from the relief and the beauty of it all.

Some time later, maybe it's an hour or maybe it's ten, she wriggles out from beneath me and kisses my cheek. "I need to use the restroom," she says, but I shake my head. "Let me help you," I say.

I yank on my boxers and pad down the hallway. In the bathroom, I find a washcloth and soak it with warm water.

I bring it back to the bed and nudge Elizabeth's thighs open to clean her, peppering her stomach with kisses as I do.

"I can't believe I'm sleeping with a tattooed woman," I say, tracing the leaves again on her thigh. "You're such a rebel."

"Hm," she laughs, flicking at my nipples.

"Better watch out with that behavior or we'll be going again," I tease. I toss the washcloth into her hamper, making note to help her get a load of laundry started later on so nothing gets mildewed. I snuggle into the bed beside her, wondering if it's inappropriate if I ask to stay over tonight.

I can't handle the thought of sleeping away from her, not after what we just experienced together.

"That was so perfect, Kellen," she murmurs, taking a long whiff of my armpit.

"Did you just sniff my pits?"

"I did. You smell so good. Even your sweat smells sexy to me."

"I'm not sure how to feel about that, Beth." I puff up the pillow so I can more comfortably slip an around around her shoulders and pull her close.

"This is what I want, Kellen," she says, those fingers tracing my chest again. "I don't want a white knight to save me."

"I've been thinking about that," I tell her. "And I decided you don't need saving." She smiles and I kiss her nose. "But I'm happy to be here with you to celebrate your victories." Another kiss. I clasp her hand in mine and bring her knuckles to my lips. "I hope you'll let me be here beside you for support if things are hard."

She nods, tears welling up in her eyes. "I'd like that, Kellen. I would. I'm working on it."

"We can work on it together," I tell her. And we drift off to sleep in each other's arms.

CHAPTER THIRTY-FIVE
ELIZABETH

I WAKE UP IN A HAZE NEXT TO A SLEEPING KELLEN, A FIRST FOR US. THE LIGHT HAS shifted, but I have no idea what time it is. I roll on my side and smile at his sleeping form. He is every bit the silver fox Lisa described him as. I trace a finger along his sturdy jaw line, reach for his hair that used to be unruly and dark. Now it's clipped short and graying. I want to spend an eternity admiring his beautiful form, but I know Jake will be home soon.

I find my phone and see a series of messages from him, telling me something about a Brady crisis and he took the bus to his grandparents' house. Then he sent a few dozen photos of different robots that can apparently crawl inside pipes or fly up inside generators to complete safe, accurate inspections.

I dial his number and it rings ten times, an eternity, before he finally answers. "Mom?" He sounds like he's clanging pots around the kitchen. I hurry out of bed to the kitchen, thinking on the fly, panicking.

"Do you need me to come get you, honey?"

"What? No. Grampa is giving me another code for a Roblox skin. From his cellphone service." I hear another clang as I take stock of what's going on. My son had an adventure with robots, took a bus to see his grandparents, and I got to spend an entire day in bed with a silver fox.

"Beltane Engineering is the place where I want to spend my life," Jake tells me, rattling on about the computer servers and design software they have there.

"I'm so glad, sweetheart," I tell him. "Did you want to talk about anything that happened in court today?"

He groans. "No. I want to tell you about the drones they have. Did you know I can get my drone pilot license and work for them this summer? The Bradys said they would hire me without an interview. If I passed the test. Can I have your credit card to register for the test?"

I laugh in delighted surprise. "How about we table that until I have time to settle down," I tell him. "There's just been so much today and—"

"Fine, ugh." He makes another clanging. "I'm going to play Roblox here for awhile. Grampa wants to learn about Bee Swarm Simulator."

I sputter a laugh, feeling a bit of the whiplash I'm used to when parenting this teen and realizing this is it. We get to work through these things together, every day, without worrying about an unreliable father throwing a wrench in his gears.

I pad back down the hall to check on Kellen and hear a persistent vibrating from the floor near my door. *Brady crisis,* I think, remembering what Jake said.

I stoop down to pick up Kellen's slacks. "Kel," I whisper, waking him with kisses. "You're blowing up."

"Ungh," he groans, rolling away from me. "What time is it?" I must have really worn him out. I sneak over to his pants and pull out his phone. "It's about 5," I tell him, smiling that we spent an entire day together entwined in my bed. He must have had his phone on do not disturb mode, because all the messages seem to pour in at once.

"Kel, you have about 100 text messages and a bunch of voicemails." I toss him the phone as he sits up, looking concerned. And then his face transforms into joyful elation.

"Maddie had the baby," he says, showing me the screen. "Arlan."

"Oh, that's wonderful," I squeal, reaching for the phone so I can look at the pictures Liam sent. "Is it ok if I scroll and look?"

"Yes! Scroll. How many did they send?" The two of us look over the pictures and read through the messages, laughing at the increasing levels of panic from Callum as he narrated Maddie's labor via text.

"Does anyone mention how Maddie is doing? Isn't her diabetes a risk during labor and delivery?"

Kellen frowns and keeps scrolling. "There are no updates after the baby pictures," he says. He stands up from the bed, tapping at the phone. "I have to find out." He looks anxious and fumbles with the phone a bit.

"Here," I say, reaching for it. "Let's call Nicole. Do you have her number?"

"Oh that's a good idea," he says and I see him open his family group text. He navigates to Zack's girlfriend's name and dials, then we both draw back from the phone as she squeals out a greeting to us.

"IS'NT IT AMAZING?? Oh my god, Uncle Kellen, you should see this baby. Wait. Why weren't you there? You sly dog, are you with Neighbor Gal?"

He clears his throat. "Elizabeth needed a ride home from court this morning," he tells her.

"Aw, that's so great that you think I don't know you were banging her all day," she says. "I know exactly why Cal and Orla really whisked Jake off to Beltane after the hearing."

I blush uncomfortably, hearing every word she shouts even though she's not on speaker phone.

"Nicole," Kellen interrupts. "How is Madison?"

"Oh, dude, she's ravenous," Nicole says. "I'm at the bakery for her right now because she's hypo." Kellen turns to me and mouths "diabetes jargon" as Nicole keeps gushing about Maddie and the baby. "You should come to the hospital and squeeze that baby while everyone else is out getting food and shit." I nod vigorously and the two of us plan to drive to the hospital.

I send Kellen home to shower and change so I can arrange for my parents to keep Jake for awhile, who is apparently roaring away teaching his grandfather to play video games. He barely acknowledges my comment that I will be leaving him with his grandparents for a bit when they hand him the phone. I hang up and quickly get myself ready and Kellen pops back into the kitchen, smelling fresh and looking excited.

"Maddie loves goldfish crackers and candy," he says. "Can we stop at the grocery store on our way? To get her some?"

"I can help with this," I tell him, heading into the kitchen. I open the snack cupboard and, like Vanna White, indicate the cornucopia of individually packaged snacks in there. "Behold," I tell him as he cracks up laughing. "Jake's approved school lunch supplements."

"It seems like he and Maddie share a similar palate," he says, as I shovel the snacks into a gift bag. We drive to the hospital and sign in, and I can tell Kellen is an anxious mess as we wait for the elevator. I squeeze his arm and steer him down the hall toward their room.

Liam looks up as we press the door open and his face lights up when he sees us. "Uncle Kellen," he whisper shouts. "Arlan is here." Liam looks like he's been awake for weeks, even though it sounds like the baby came quickly. Liam has dark circles under his eyes, but the way he gazes at his family...he just radiates joy.

I feel my heart clench at the sight of this man, so enamored by his son and his beloved. "I'm just so grateful," he whispers, and Kellen nods, tears in his eyes.

"I remember that, kiddo, looking down at Orla's tiny body, the gratitude I had for her mother bringing Orla here to me." Kellen and Liam embrace and I'm overcome at the love in this room. Before I can think better of it, I'm crying right along with them, grateful to be included. I linger by the door, fiddling with the gift bag until Maddie looks over at me.

"Hey," she says, beckoning. "Come see what I did!"

I approach the bed and offer the gift bag. "We brought sustenance," I say, and then I realize Maddie is feeding Arlan. "Oh," I exclaim as I see his jaw working hard. "Look at his wonderful latch."

"Is this right?" She asks, reaching for the candy with one hand and fumbling Arlan's head. "It feels right, but I honestly have no idea."

I nod and lean in, stroking the baby's ear and showing Maddie how to tell when Arlan is swallowing. All these years later and I can still remember just how it felt to have a baby attached to my body on the outside, depending on me for food.

"I feel it all the way to my toes, when he's sucking like this," Maddie says, and I nod. I feed her M&Ms while she focuses on Arlan and eventually, I look up to see Orla opening the door. She holds a bunch of balloons, and halts in her step when she sees me snuggled up cozy with Maddie and Arlan.

"Hi," Orla says, hesitating. I drop a kiss on the baby's sweet head and stand up.

"Hi, Orla," I say, stepping toward her. "I'll step out so you all can visit," I say. But she shakes her head.

"No," she says. "You should stay." Orla gestures toward Maddie and the slurping baby. "You know more about this stuff anyway. We need your expertise."

We convince Liam to head home and shower by telling him he needs to grab more chapstick and deodorant for his baby's mother. Maddie drifts off to sleep after Arlan finishes eating and my heart melts as I watch Kellen cradle the baby in the rocking chair, murmuring into his tiny head as he rocks his grand-nephew to sleep.

Orla is also watching and I smile at her. "He looks good in grandpa mode," I say, winking.

"Oh, christ, please don't start in on me about getting married," she says, and I laugh.

"I would never." The two of us sit in a sort of awkward silence as Maddie snores, her IV and monitor beeping rhythmically and Kellen rocks Arlan in time with its chorus.

I clear my throat. "Orla," I say, "I just feel like I should tell you that I... well, I really care about your father." She nods and shrugs. "But I would never do anything to compromise the relationship you have with him." She swallows slowly, stiffening. "I can't tell you how meaningful it is that you came to the hearing today. And I know I could never replace your mother." I start babbling now, unsure what to say, but feeling like I need to communicate my intentions to this woman. "I would never try to do that, either. But I hope that you and I could be...friends seems like maybe a weird word. But I hope you and I can be...something."

Orla's eyes brim with tears, and I'm taken aback because every time I've ever seen her she's been so tough, so brusque. "Thank you for saying all that," she says. "Your son is pretty amazing, and we were all happy to be there to support you two. Anyone with eyes can see that my dad is crazy about you." I smile. She sighs. "And if I'm honest it's really nice having a woman around sometimes. Like, an adult woman." She gestures around the room. "Maybe we can band together and balance out these farting cretons."

"I'd really like that," I tell her. "I like having a woman around, too." Kellen looks up from the rocking chair at the two of us and I give him a small smile, which he returns.

Not long after, Nicole and Zack and Mick hustle into the hospital room and I find a corner of the room behind a curtain, running out of space. I feel the heat of Kellen's body behind mine and he leans in to kiss my neck.

"Ready to head back," he asks, and I nod. We walk to the parking lot holding hands and I lean my head on his shoulder.

"That was really special, Kellen," I tell him, squeezing his hand.

"Well," he says, "You're really special to me. I'm so glad you were with me there to meet Arlan." He kisses me on the cheek. "And I'm really glad you got to talk with Orla a little bit."

I smile. "We're a ways off still from going to the mall together, I think."

He laughs. "Well, you know, she did help Jake with his electromagnetism homework the other week."

My eyebrows shoot up in surprise. "I did not realize that." I smile at the thought of my kid and Kellen's daughter spending time together. Like maybe we really can form some sort of...

"I'd like to build a family with you, Beth," Kellen interrupts my thoughts, stealing the very words from my mind and expressing them out loud. "I know it will be messy and loud and all of us will have to work hard to communicate our boundaries. But I'm all in."

"Oh, Kellen, me too," I tell him. I jump up into his arms as he spins me around in the parking lot, pressing his mouth to mine. I don't know what tomorrow will bring, what new challenges Jake and I will face. But I know we aren't alone in facing them.

We're here, with this quirky gang of linear thinkers who all evidently love helping my son with his physics studies. As Kellen moans softly against my kiss and I press my body into his, I know that we can build something good together.

"Will you be my trellis, Kellen Brady?" I ask him, burying my head into his shoulder as he finally sets me back on the ground.

"I already am, Beth. Now take me home so we can wind our roots together."

"Was that a euphemism?" I laugh as I unlock my car and he slides in the passenger seat.

"You bet your ass it was."

EPILOGUE: KELLEN
TWO MONTHS LATER

I MAKE MY WAY BACK TO THE TENT WITH THE HOT COFFEE, HOPING I'LL BE ABLE TO nudge Elizabeth awake with a steaming mug. She was so excited when Jake arranged to stay with her parents so the two of us could "have an excursion" together. Pittsburgh has been experiencing a warm snap and so, even though it's nearing Thanksgiving, we booked a spot in a state park to go camping. Elizabeth was gung ho to camp on the ground in a remote spot, have us walk in all our gear.

But when we loaded the backpacks and took a practice walk around the block, I felt the sting in my foot and knew it wasn't a good idea for me. So we compromised and borrowed Orla's air mattress to wedge into the tiny tent. When I approach from the picnic table where I've left the camp stove to cool, I'm greeted by the sight of Elizabeth's backside in black tights.

I nearly spill the coffee as I ogle the beautiful round shape. She's on her hands and knees, crawling around the tent looking for something when she hears me approach. She turns over her shoulder and smiles, and I'm so overcome with lust I have no choice but to plunk the travel mugs on the ground and climb inside the tent.

"Stay where you are," I tell her, wedging myself behind her, rubbing my hands over her warm skin. The November air was just cool enough to snuggle under the blankets but not so cold that we see our breath this morning.

"Where have you been, mister," she asks, dropping down onto her elbows as I massage her backside. "That feels nice." And then she gasps when I pull down the leggings and whatever she has on underneath them.

I reach between her legs and find her wet for me, and I growl at her. "I'm wild in the wilderness," I whisper. I'm immediately, painfully hard and her small noises arouse me further as I root around inside my pants to pull out my cock.

"Kellen Brady, are we having wakeup sex?" Beth actually giggles, but sucks in her breath as I slide right into her. We've been working hard over the past month to build up her body's stamina where sex is concerned. I've been more than happy to help her with this therapy for her most intimate parts.

"God, Beth, you feel so good," I pant into her ear, leaning over her as I start to rock in and out. I've never had this type of experience camping and I'm filled with regret that I missed out on 50 years of rutting in the outdoors.

"I love how you fill me up," she says, and I know she means both physically and emotionally. But right now, I'm focused on the physical part.

I grunt like a caveman as I thrust as hard as I dare, my hips banging off her generous curves. I want to respect that this is still very new for both of us, but Beth turns over her shoulder and blows her hair out of her eyes and says, "Harder, Kellen. Faster."

"Oh god," I groan as she slams her body back to meet mine. Together, the two of us set a frenzied pace in the tent until we are both tumbling over the edge, crying out in the woods among the birds and all the wild things trying to hibernate. I spill inside her as she moans my name and collapses onto the floor of the tent, sated.

A few minutes later, we're cuddled together on the air mattress sipping the coffee. "You know," she says, "I really think that diversion was perfect. This is just the right temperature now."

I nod, agreeing with her. We don't always agree like this, but we did make a promise to always talk things out. She draws the line at my rubrics a lot of the time. I call her out when she's evading discussing something important.

We've had so many long talks this fall. So many deep conversations on her couch, on mine. She's been so helpful when Maddie needs breast-feeding advice and has stood by my side as I've implemented both policy and physical changes at work to make our space more inclusive not just for autistic employees, but engineers of all abilities.

I'm so grateful for Beth and Jake and the ways they've opened my eyes to the brilliant staffers I had inadvertently been leaving out of the conversation. Which is why I wanted to bring her here specifically, to this state park, home of an ancient grove of hemlocks.

After our coffee, Beth gets cleaned up and we hike out to the trail. "This is amazing," she comments, inhaling deeply. I haven't been here for many years, but I know what she means. The air feels different here. It actually feels mystical, like anything could and has happened among these branches.

"I've been thinking about your tattoo," I tell her, leading her through the shady grove. "And then I was thinking about this grove, how I've always loved it here."

"Oh yeah?"

I nod. "The druids say hemlocks symbolize shelter, protection and healing."

"Hm," she says. "That fits." She spins around on the path, looking up into the soft, fir branches. "It's beautiful, Kellen. Thank you for bringing me on this excursion."

I squeeze her hand again. "I've been wanting to tell you something," I whisper, leaning in close and pulling her up to one of the massive trunks.

She looks up into my eyes and I know she knows what I'm about to say, but she lets me say it first anyway. "I love you, Beth." I kiss her. "I love your passion and your strength. I love your determination. You inspire me and I love you."

"Oh, Kellen," she says, her hands coming together in front of her chest. Like a prayer. "I love you, too."

I kiss her there, beneath the protective shade of the hemlock grove, and I promise to be her steadfast partner as long as she'll have me. We eventually make our way back to our campsite, arms around each other, pressing our bodies tight together like vines entwined.

Beth's phone rings as we crest the hill, the small space in the state park where we evidently have cell service. She looks at me. We'd agreed to avoid our phones for this trip if possible, with emphasis on the "if possible." I nod and reach for her pocket. "Go ahead," I say. I kiss her cheek. "I'll wait."

She looks at the number on the screen. "It's Jake's autism center," she says, arching a brow at the phone. "Hello? Amy?"

I watch Beth's face as she talks to the counselor from the social skills group. Beth nods, smiles, nods some more, and then gasps. "Oh. Oh my. Oh, Amy, yes. I'll take it."

She nods a few more times and says she'll be sure to phone when we are back in an area with reception. Then Elizabeth hangs up the phone and starts jumping up and down clapping her hands. "Kellen, I got a job!"

"What? That's fantastic. What's the job?"

"I'll be the program coordinator at the center," she says, squealing again. "Amy called as soon as Mandy gave her notice. It's a part time job and I can work remotely a lot of the time and oh! Kellen, it's just the perfect space for me."

I laugh, catching her enthusiasm. "I'm so happy for you." Beth does a little shimmy in the sunlight and I stare, wanting to capture this memory, her happy face on the day we first exchanged "I love you's."

"This is my favorite camping trip of all time," she tells me, linking her arm through mine again.

"Agreed," I tell her. And then I wink. "Let's go back to the tent and celebrate."

And we do.

Gasping, moaning, sighing, we celebrate together. We celebrate our love, Elizabeth's job, our families. We celebrate the life we're building together. It's not the experience either of us was expecting and it hasn't been easy. But we're here, together under the stars. "I love you, Beth," I whisper into her ear as she falls asleep in my arms.

"I love you, too."

VIBRATION
AN ACCIDENTAL ROOMMATES ROMANCE

CHAPTER ONE
CAL

I shouldn't be upset that my family is missing my birthday. But here I am. Pissed off.

I'm turning 31. I'm an adult. But as each of my brothers and my cousin text me in turn to say they're out of town or have an essential work function they can't miss, I wallow a little deeper into the sting.

The final straw comes when my mom texts me to ask if we can move our standing weekly dinner date to the weekend. She's presenting to a new client, and I get that that's important.

I feel like a brooding baby as I throw my phone across my office after reading my mom's text, and then I decide I'm not doing anyone any favors being here at work anyway. I grab my phone, fish around for my keys, and walk out of Beltane Engineering without saying goodbye to any of my traitorous relatives.

The shitty part of working with my family is that when they do something like this—collectively put me as a last priority—I can't really get away from them to cool down. This place is crawling with Bradys, all doing something more important than sitting down with me for one fucking evening to say they're glad I'm on this earth.

I realize this sounds ridiculous, and I'm working on it. That's why I'm going somewhere else to clear my head.

Once I'm outside, I don't know where to go next. I have no plan. What does a 30-something do alone on his birthday? I realize I don't have too many friends outside of my family, and that pisses me off even more.

Don't get me wrong. My family is awesome. We're Irish and there's a bunch of us, especially now that my younger brother has a live-in girl-friend. Shit, I bet Nicole would be a blast on a birthday bender. She seems like someone who could drink me under the table.

But it's the middle of the day and I'm not about to call my brother's girlfriend at work. She'd probably come kick me in the balls with her spike heels.

I climb into my car and clench my teeth, hoping she starts. I drive a vintage Ford Bronco, bright red, and I've rebuilt her myself with some customizations. What's the point of being a mechanical engineer if you're not going to soup up your ride a little bit, right? It's just that I've been having a ton of trouble with some of the substitute parts I've had to order for the engine. It's getting harder and harder to find original components these days.

Big Red roars to life, and I rev her engine a few times in the parking lot, hoping I disturb someone inside, and then feeling bad about it. This shit always seems to happen to me, though. My parents told us they were getting divorced on my birthday, years ago. Who does that? I was a toddler, but the whole thing scarred my brother so much that my birthday has always been clouded in this sense of unease. No wonder they all schedule trips and client shit for this week.

For a long time, I thought I killed my parents' marriage. My brother Liam and I are Irish twins, born less than a year apart. That can't have been easy, but I know now that my parents are just really incompatible. Plus my dad couldn't keep it in his pants. I'm a lot like him that way. I come by it honestly, I guess.

Pittsburgh's streets are pretty quiet for a weekday. I crank the radio and roll down the window, feeling the sun on my elbow as I let it hang out the window. This is nice. I needed this thinking time.

I give myself a pep talk: my family aren't being assholes on purpose. We're all engineers and lots of projects really get cranking in spring because the weather turns decent. My family didn't bail on me because they've been cursing my birth for thirty years. It's more that they tend to supervise industrial job sites that can't really excavate a mine shaft when the ground is frozen or saturated with early spring rains. It's just shitty timing.

I head north along Route 28, stopping at the drive-through beer distrib-utor. I buy a cube of cheap, shitty suds and make my way toward the marina along the river, where my dad docks his boat. Don't mind if I do jump-start his precious watercraft and treat myself to an afternoon cruise.

I get the *Erin Go Braless* going and head up the Allegheny River at full speed, even in the no wake zone, until I remember that the high school kids might be practicing crew or something and slow her down. See? I'm not totally irresponsible. I crack open a few beers and guzzle them down quickly before I decide to see if I can turn donuts in the narrow river.

Indeed I can.

Feeling listless now, increasingly bored, I continue on up river. I'm well outside the city now, approaching the junction with the Kiski River. I slow down for a minute and pound another beer, admiring the confluence where the two bodies of water collide. There's a distinct line where the brown water of the fast-moving Allegheny meshes with the almost-turquoise water of the Kiski.

I think about how they're connected, two parts of the same body of water, like a family. But the Kiski is so different. Another color. Another direction. Another way of moving things. I start wondering if the Allegheny ever notices that the Kiski is struggling, if they fight as they try to cooperate, and then I chug another beer because it's insane to be thinking of rivers as if they had feelings.

I pull back on the lever and the boat catches a wave or runs over a log or something, jolting me so that I drop my beer. I take my eyes off the water just for a second as I stoop to pick it up, frantically feeling around until my fingers find purchase. But by the time I stand up, I know I'm well and truly screwed. The boat is hurtling toward a small island.

I try to slow down, I try to duck, but it's too late. There's a terrible crashing, crunching sound, a jolting crash, and the world fades to black.

℔

WHEN I OPEN MY EYES, I can't tell which way is up. Everything aches, but nothing as much as my head. I slowly realize I'm dangling upside down and the throb I feel is probably the blood rushing to my head. I try to get my bearings, see that I'm somehow caught in a bunch of tree branches. I grip a branch and tug and, feeling that it's steady, I use it to get myself upright.

"Holy shit," I say, looking around me. I'm hanging off the side of my dad's boat, which I've somehow managed to crash into the upper portion of a tree. I'm still half buzzed from all the beers, and I know there were a lot because I see all the silver cans glinting in the sun as the boat rocks in the tree branches.

But I know I should get to the ground and away from this disaster. I pat my pockets and am shocked to feel my phone is still in my jeans. I shimmy out of the tree and try to back away as my sneakers sink into the wet ground. This isn't an island so much as a piece of land that's been flooded. The tree isn't sticking very high out of the water, but only because the water comes up about a foot above the soggy sludge.

I take a few careful steps back. My head is swimming with panic and alcohol, but even in this sorry state, I know I have no choice but to call someone for help. I pull up my contacts. All my recent calls are to girls whose last names I don't know. Waitresses and bartenders, mostly. My bank teller. I'd really like to call my Uncle Kellen, mostly because he wouldn't yell at me like my dad surely will. But Uncle Kel is out of state with my brother Liam for work. Hence my fucked up pity-party.

I sigh and blow out a long breath until my entire body feels deflated. There's nothing to be done. I close my eyes and dial, and my dad picks up after the first ring. "This better be an emergency."

"Dad." I swallow. I can feel his impatience, and I know that's only going to get worse. "I fucked up."

CHAPTER TWO
CAL

My father doesn't say a single word to me. He shows up with a crew of old guys and a tugboat and they yank the boat out of the tree before tossing me a ring and making me swim out to meet them on their boat. I realize it's ridiculous, but I try to swim with one arm and keep my phone out of the river, needing to salvage at least some aspect of my life. The guys make a few comments about me being dumb as a bag of rocks, and I don't have it in me to argue with them. Soon, they leave me alone to sit by the rail as we chug back toward the city.

I hear my dad working out a barter with the tugboat guys, I guess to cover the tow and repairs. I nearly gasp when my dad offers up season tickets to the Iron Men, but then I remember that my dad is buddies with the owner of the professional football team. I snort. Typical Mick Brady. Giving away something he likely got for free, in exchange for something huge like this.

The light is fading and the air on the river is cold as I sit there in my soaking wet clothes, wondering if my phone is ruined forever as I shiver. We coast past the marina to the boat repair shop and I wince at the rumble of the loud garage bay doors going up.

"I'll be in touch about those seats," my dad says, shaking hands with the boat guys and giving them a wink. "Appreciate you guys keeping this between us."

I shiver with my hands in my pockets while they make small talk and when my dad starts walking toward his car, I make to follow him. As soon as we're out of ear shot of the boat repair guys, he turns and holds up a hand.

"You won't be messing up my interior today, Callum. We'll discuss this later." He climbs in his car and drives off, the gravel crunching under his tires.

This feels pretty shitty, not gonna lie. Right about now I'm thinking I'd rather just be pissed off back in my office than standing here soaking wet with no ride. I don't know where we are precisely, but I know it's miles from the loft apartment I share with my brother Liam.

My phone won't turn on so I can't call a lift and I'd rather walk home than go ask the tow guys for anything else. So, dejected and ashamed of myself, that's what I do.

B

I wake up in the morning to the sound of my brother muttering and clanging pots and pans. I groan. My head is pounding and my legs ache from walking three miles in wet sneakers. I don't even know when I got home last night, but I sure as shit didn't have the energy to clean up the apartment, which I'd let get pretty out of control while my brother was away on business.

Chalk this up as another reason Cal Brady is the family fuck-up, I guess.

Eventually, my brother leaves for work. I'm sorry I missed the daily opportunity to make fun of him for ironing the insides of his pockets, but not even that can make me feel better today.

I make my way to the office thanks to ibuprofen and breakfast burritos, the grease in my belly doing wonders for at least a few of my issues. Nothing eases the ache when my father won't make eye contact with me at the morning team meeting. I try to follow him to his office to talk about yesterday, but he closes the door in my face.

I guess I deserve that.

For two days, my father ignores me and my brother rides me hard about being a mess, despite my best efforts to come home and clean up the apartment.

"Callum," Liam bellows from the bathroom. "What in the hell did you leave rotting in this trash can?" He stomps down the hall toward the trash chute with the wet clothes I threw out after walking home covered in river sludge. I don't say anything to him, because last week he yelled at me for wasting resources when I threw away a plastic bag of trash that was only half full.

I get the same response when I try to run the dishwasher, also half full, and apparently not loaded in an efficient manner, and I walk away before I raise my fist to my brother's face.

I feel like I'm going to snap if I don't do something drastic. I drive to work and storm into my office where, instead of pulling my dad aside to ask when we can talk, I pull up apartment listings online and fantasize about moving away from my family.

The first listing I see catches my eye.

ℬ

ROOMMATE WANTED: *Immediate Opening*

Large, sunny bedroom available in shared Bakery Square condo. Building has on-site gym, parking garage, secure entry. Balcony overlooks Mellon Park. Utilities included. Serious candidates contact Logan Miller.

ℬ

HUH. I sort of thought I was doing this just to mess with Liam's head or something. But the pictures of this condo are pretty sweet. I start thinking about how I've lived with Liam my entire life and never really got to experience living it up with bros who aren't related to me. His first year of college, I spent a lot of nights in his dorm room and we lived together the whole time I was in undergrad, too, even when he started working.

How would it be to live with people who don't view me as the black sheep of the family? Would it ease some of this tension if I moved out? I mean, I know I'm going to have to face the music with my dad here eventually, but what if I put up some sort of barrier with my family so I can try to get my head on straight?

Bakery Square is a really cool neighborhood. There's like five cool bars across the street from this place, plus a million restaurants and I could walk to Whole Paycheck if I felt the need to stock my fridge with fancy cheese.

The one picture of the balcony is obviously taken from a seated position, and I start thinking how nice it would be to kick back after work, maybe smoke a J on my balcony, watch the honeys play soccer in the park... in just their sports bras.

Then I think of my damn brother ironing his underwear in the living room. Do I really want to leave him alone with himself? I mean, if he's not ragging on me to shine my shoes properly, is he even living?

I start to consider walking to his office, making nice with Liam and confessing what happened on my birthday with Dad. That's the mature thing to do, right? Fess up and ask for advice to move forward? I don't want to just do yet another impulsive, stupid thing and move out.

By the time I work through this train of thought, I'm halfway to the office kitchen and can smell donuts. When I get there, I start laughing because Liam is staring slack-jawed at a chick I know. She's Maddie, my brother Zack's girlfriend's bestie. I have no idea why she's here at Beltane Engineering, but I remember her because she always wears a pouch around her waist and, last time I saw her, she told me she keeps her snacks in there.

See, this is the kind of brilliance I miss out on living with my family. Brady men just do not have snack pouches. I give her a high five and we eat donuts for a few minutes, shooting the breeze while Liam gawks at her. Maddie and Zack eventually head out of the kitchen and Liam is still standing around catching flies in his open mouth. I swat him in the chest. "Dude. What the hell are you staring at?"

I cram a donut in my mouth as he points around, flustered, asking me who the girl was. "Who, Maddie?" I'm talking with my mouth full, but he just gave me a lecture about being a slob while he ogled a woman, so I don't bother to cover my mouth. "Nicole's friend...writer?"

He blinks. I swallow the donut. "We've met her before."

Liam shakes his head and I reach for another donut, the chocolate cake one I'm pretty sure he was going to take. Screw him.

I smirk when he glares at me.

Liam says, "she didn't look like that before," and I know he's got it bad for her. I laugh, tucking away this information for future use.

But I can also tell that the window has closed for me to confide in him. The kitchen gave me clarity. Liam's not going to be on my side and he's probably just going to scold me about the whole boat situation, like he scolds me about frosting on my shirt and loading the dishwasher "wrong." He fidgets with his tie a few more times and looks like he's going to say something to me, but I just shrug.

"Well, brother, I've got real work to do. See you at lunch." I head back to my office and look at the pile of work on my desk. More of the same. Writing up some more reports on motors for industrial fans. I flip open my laptop and the condo listing is still sitting on my browser.

No communication from my father. No serious assignments for

someone who's been a practicing engineer for nine years. Just busywork, funneled off to the kid they had to hire because he shares a last name with the owner.

I stare at the real estate listing and click the link to start up an email. *hey, logan, saw ur ad for a roommate. am definitely interested and can move in right away. i've been to those lofts before—it looks like a kickass place to live.*

As I think about it, I remember when our company did some inspections on the property when the HVAC and electrical systems were installed. It's a cool-ass building. With no family members. I nod, continuing to type. *so I can move in any time that works for you. i've got a couch and a bed and don't take up a lot of room otherwise. email me and i'll sign whatever.*

cal e brady

NOT SURE WHY I stick the E in my signature, but it felt more mature somehow. Callum Eamonn Brady is just about the most Irish name a guy could have, but also feels like the sort of name a kid would have. Or maybe I just feel like my family thinks of me as a kid. To them, I'm Callum, the slob. The chill guy with no real responsibility. To Logan, maybe I'm Cal E. Brady, professional adult. Enthusiastic roommate.

I wonder if he likes beer?

I make a mental note to grab some to celebrate whenever he sends me the lease info, and then I sigh and dive in to my boring paperwork. Still no word from my dad. It's going to be a long day.

CHAPTER THREE
LOGAN

I CHEW ON THE END OF MY FINGER AS SOON AS I CLICK SUBMIT FOR THE RENTAL listing. I have to make sure nobody from the office comes across it. Not that any of them would be looking, but I know they'd call my listing number just to tease me if they found it. They always seem to find something to tease me about.

My watch chimes the hour, letting me know I'm on company time officially, so I put away my phone and get to work.

I love my job, even if the other people here are just like everyone else... mean, vindictive, and eager to claw each other's eyes out to get ahead. I know they all think I'm weird, but I have learned I can't let that stand in my way. I'm here because I'm really good at financial analysis. I'm allowed to say I'm really good at financial analysis because I have an Ivy League degree in that subject.

"I am not high falutin," I mutter. This is objective fact.

Living above my means in a condo I can't quite afford is a different matter.

Always wanting what you can't have, I can hear my mother's voice saying. I shouldn't have bought the condo so soon. I know that now. It's just that I was struggling to find a roommate while I was still in Philadelphia and the relocation expert from HR pointed out all the benefits of buying something compared to renting.

It's not like I had anyone else to give me advice about this sort of thing.

My classmates in grad school were paying for their degrees with generational wealth and my single mother has been raising me on her own since she was a teenager and her family cut all ties.

I'm not out running up credit card debt on makeup and couture. Starting back with my first paycheck, I've been sending enough money home to my mom to cover her rent so *she* can finally let go of the second job. But I don't think she quit yet. I think she's still skeptical that all this is real.

I try not to think about the roommate listing while I dive into my first client portfolio of the morning. I was recruited to be an analyst here in Pittsburgh in my last semester of graduate school. I love the idea of being closer to Mom. I originally bought the two-bedroom with thoughts that maybe she'd come stay with me, or at least visit sometimes. It hasn't worked out yet, though. As it turns out, I can't quite afford to pay her rent *and* the mortgage on a posh condo in a trendy neighborhood.

I remind myself that this is a college town. There are plenty of young professionals who will be eager to find a tidy, quiet roommate like me. "It's just a cash flow problem," I whisper. "I am not living outside my means."

I talk to myself. A lot. I have to try and find my way forward as I straddle two worlds. One of my feet is always stuck in the sidewalk cracks in the neighborhood where I grew up, while the other reaches around in the dark, trying to find the right way ahead. So far, I'm my only guide.

I look up at my diplomas. Right now, they're in a cheap frame from the dollar store, but eventually I'm going to have them framed with those nice mats I see fancy people have. I, Logan Miller, earned full scholarships to Temple and then to Penn, and now I'm sitting in my own office, working as an analyst at a hot financial firm in Pittsburgh. "Not a cubicle," I mutter, admiring the view of the river from my small window. I've got an office, with a door.

I'm lost in these thoughts when said door whooshes open. Marie, my supervisor, bursts in. "Let's go, *Logan*," she sneers, emphasizing my name. "Staff meeting with top brass."

Hm, that's very unusual. Top executives typically are scheduled out well in advance and meetings with them come with agendas and "save the date" notices from their administrative staff. I close my computer and grab my clipboard and notebook, tucking a pen behind my ear as I follow Marie to the large conference room.

The space is buzzing when we arrive. All the analysts and sales staff clamor to find seats at the table before Mr. Alexander, our director—or is he the owner, I wonder—walks in with a pair of assistants at his heels. He types on his phone as he walks and hands the device to one of the assistants, while the other hands him a folder. I can see talking points paperclipped to the top of the folder, but can't make out the text.

"All right," he says, and the room goes silent. "I know this is an unusual meeting and you're all curious why we're here." He looks up from his notes and around the room, where everyone is rapt and staring. "We have just received a signed contract to manage the investments accounts of the Rudy family."

Jaws drop around the table and some of the analysts slap each other high fives. I have no idea what this means, so I put my business smile on my face—a practiced expression I've learned to wear in professional settings until I figure out what to do with my emotions. I write

RUDY

on my note pad as Mr. Alexander starts talking about how this high profile account means a lot of prestige for the firm. "I'll be looking for my best analyst for this account," he says, looking slowly, pointedly around the room, nodding periodically.

I feel a flutter of hope at this statement. I might not know who this family is, but if they've got a lot of money to invest, I know I can help them do so profitably. Could Mr. Alexander possibly pick me, a brand new employee fresh from graduate school, to work on an account that is clearly meaningful to the company?

"As this is a high profile account, I'll be meeting with all of your supervisors in the coming weeks to determine the best team to service the Rudys. If I'm not being clear, that means pull out the stops for customer service. No limits on the budget for wining and dining." Everyone starts murmuring and whispering and Mr. Alexander holds up a hand. "We will also be planning our regular gala to close out the fiscal year. All of our top clients will be invited, and you will be expected to attend and help them celebrate all the magic we have made together this past year."

More murmuring from around the table, and sinking dread from me. I don't do well at events. I worry constantly that everyone can tell I grew up poor, that they can smell it on me no matter how fancy a dress I buy or how carefully I walk in my heels. I am an analyst for a reason, and that is because I do not do very well talking to people. The account managers schmooze the clients, share the information I give them, verify the plans I map out. I sit in my office with my forecasting software and my multiple monitors and I run numbers.

I like numbers. They're predictable and they don't disappoint. They do not involve emotions.

Mr. Alexander ends the meeting abruptly, disappearing down the hall with his staff close behind, and everyone erupts. I bite my lip, unsure whether I should stay and eavesdrop to figure out what's going on, or slink back to my office and keep going with my reports.

Devin, a guy who has so far been the least mean to me, catches my eye. "Isn't it great?"

I bite my lip, considering. Devin has not outwardly mocked my name and did not laugh at me the day I came to work wearing two different (but similar!) shoes by accident. I nod and decide I can trust him to fill me in on this. "Actually, you know, I'm not from Pittsburgh. Can you tell me who the Rudy family is?"

His eyes bug out of his head. "Oh my gosh, seriously? They own the Iron Men. The pro football team?"

I grimace. "*That* Rudy??" This city is absolutely obsessed with its professional sports teams, and I grew up about an hour away. Football and hockey were the lifeblood of my hometown—an economically depressed, post-industrial area. I understand the allure of professional football. It brings people together and gives them hope. I can't believe I didn't make the connection. This family must have more money than God.

"Man, Logan, where have you been?" He shakes his head. "It's gonna be a bloodbath battling for whoever gets that account."

In high school and college, I was always waiting tables while football games were on in the background. Sports were the soundtrack to my life. It seems surreal to imagine I might brush up against this world in real life.

Devin shrugs. "Well one of us is going to be working a lot on this account, that's for sure. You think we'll get box seats at the games?"

I'm about to shrug and tell him I have no earthly idea when Marie clears her throat. "I see that you're busy gossiping about the new client," she says, narrowing her eyes at me (not Devin), making me wonder for the millionth time whether I just always seem to land in jobs with miserable colleagues or if people really are this grouchy. I guess I thought once I was working somewhere with a decent paycheck, my coworkers would be happier people. "Shall I tell your current clients to wait for their financial reports or would you like to explain to them why you put their work on hold to talk about *other* clients?"

Marie truly is impossible to please. I know she supervises at least three other people at this table and manages all their accounts, and they're all actively squealing about the Rudy announcement. She must be able to be nice to clients, or else she would never have gotten to this position. What do I need to do to get her to use some of that kindness with me? I breathe slowly through my nose and stand up. "I apologize for lingering after Mr. Alexander ended the meeting," I say, and I walk out of the conference room before she has a chance to say anything more.

I close my office door and try to gather my thoughts. I conclude that expressing interest in a new and much-desired account would put a target on my back socially, and company culture is already pretty rough for me. I've only been here a few months. Better to build rapport and do good work with my current client portfolio.

I hear a ping from my purse and realize I forgot to turn my phone on silent. I'm glad I left it behind when I went to the meeting. I would have been mortified if it chirped while Mr. Alexander was speaking.

I slide my phone out of my bag, intending to power down until my lunch break, but I see that I've got a new email.

Someone named Callie is interested in the apartment. I feel relief melting through my bones at the thought of the financial cushion I'll get from the rent check. Callie offers to move in immediately, making me suspect that she's also dealing with some sort of stressful situation. Through my closed door, I hear Marie in the hall talking to another analyst. "We've got this in the bag, guys. No worries. It's not even a competition. You're the best analyst we've got and clients love me face to face." I hear them agreeing.

I'm not even sure who she's talking to, but I know it's a guy. There are very few women who work here. I knew finance was a male-dominated field. I had an advisor during undergrad who used to try to give me pep talks, tell me I had the right mind for this line of work but I'd have to hurdle over men who don't know how to behave around women.

I start to daydream about how my work life could be better. If Marie and one of the jerky were assigned to the Rudy account, maybe they'd be so busy that I'd get shuffled to another team. People who respond when I wish them a good morning, or invite me to join their conversation rather than walk away as I approach. Maybe I'd have a boss who was more supportive, more like the teachers I had at Penn.

My professors were tough, but kind. I had brief internships in a few different companies in Philadelphia throughout my coursework. The people there were a mixed bag—many of them as miserable as my colleagues here, but some had a certain spark, a love of their work.

I'm sitting clutching my phone, remembering the week I spent shadowing in a tech startup, when Marie bursts into my office. Her eyes widen as she sees me sitting with my phone in my hand. "God, Logan, I can't believe I have to micromanage you like this. Why are you not working? Seriously? Get your ass in gear so I can send the Emersons their third quarter forecast."

I have no response. She has indeed caught me not working. I could remind her that I'm salaried and often work a few minutes late or come in a few minutes early. It's okay if I take a break, surely. But I don't say any of that. I swallow and nod and pull up my software, clacking on my keyboard until she huffs out of my office and stomps into her own.

I feel so alone and confused. I wish for the thousandth time that I had girlfriends I could call about this. Everyone on television would be whisked away by a best friend for pedicures...or shots. A best friend could tell me Marie is rude, to brush off her comments and focus on the prize.

It's just that I'm not so sure I know what the prize is, actually.

My chest aches and I feel so out of place. I feel a tear form at the corner of my eye and I flick it away and shake my head. Nope. I chose this. I can do this.

I pick up my phone and dial my mom, needing some sort of comfort and reassurance. "Lo?" I hear a lot of commotion in the background. Of course she's at work. I check the time. Should be in between breakfast and lunch rush.

"Hey, Mom," I say, biting my nail, and then stuffing my hands onto my lap as if she could see me doing that. "You doing okay?"

"Eh, you know. Party of six left a ten percent tip this morning. Felt like chasing them down the sidewalk but it's raining here. You know how it is."

"Why do people do such a thing? I hate that for you." She makes a grunting sound and I listen to the familiar noises of the back of the restaurant. Pans clatter, the dishwashers make jokes. Sounds like someone's playing music. "Did you get the check I sent, Mom?"

"Logan." She sounds upset. "You can't be doing that, baby. You need backup money."

"I told you, Mom, I can spare it," I lie. I can't quite spare all that I sent, but I wanted to pay her full rent. Let her drop the warehouse job, maybe live a little. She's only 40. She shouldn't have to work herself to the bone around the clock.

Mom sighs. "I just...this is all very new. You're very new there. You know how it is with new people at work. You have to pay your dues and we don't know if you'll still be there a month from now."

I close my eyes. "You didn't leave the warehouse, did you?"

Another sigh. "Baby, I can't just give up a good job on a hope and a promise. I have a lot of seniority there."

"Well they should pay you more, then," I snarl and she snorts.

"That'll be the day, Logan, won't it? Hey, what time is it? Are you calling from work?"

"I'm taking a break," I tell her, reminding myself to stay late and make up the difference today. I hope Marie doesn't wander past. God, what if she's listening at the door. Is that really how people behave in professional offices? "I guess you're right," I say. "Things aren't exactly what I was expecting here. Not really."

"You causing trouble with your questions? You always had so many questions." I'm not sure what I was expecting when I called my mother. This is always how it goes with us. No room for coddling. Tough love.

"I'm trying to keep my head down, Mom. I'm trying."

"Well, I do appreciate the money you sent, honey. I really do. I'm real proud that you got a paycheck big enough to send me that kind of change. You just keep working hard and keep in their good graces."

"I will, Mom."

She hangs up abruptly when someone calls her name. I remember being surprised in college to overhear some of the girls in the dorm talk about how the culture at restaurants was brutal. That was the word they used. Ever since I was old enough for a work permit, I've been working in restaurants. It felt very illuminating to hear someone use that word, to give voice to the type of energy I felt waiting tables. Brutal.

I wish I could go back and find them and tell them things aren't much different in business. My feet hurt less but I'm still holding my breath a lot.

My phone pings again. Another email from Callie. No, cal e. Maybe she spells it weird, which is fine because I'm a girl named Logan. What a pair we could be, right? Maybe Callie could become my best friend and we could do spa nights with those mud masks on our faces to soothe our pores. I could tell her how much Marie makes me feel like garbage and she'd say something witty to make me feel better.

I look at her emails again. There's something comforting about the way she avoids capital letters, and I decide it means she doesn't take up much space. To me, this signals that she is considerate. And clearly in a bind to live somewhere else, based on her enthusiasm.

I silence the voice telling me it's a terrible idea to sign a lease and live with someone I haven't met. I ignore the niggling fear that I'm risking a personality clash. I take a deep breath and send her the generic lease agreement I found online and when she returns it, initialed and signed, I do a little dance.

Things are looking up.

CHAPTER FOUR
CAL

I LOOK UP FROM MY PAPERWORK WHEN MY PHONE PINGS, LETTING ME KNOW I'VE GOT a new email. Sweet. Logan sent one of those e-document lease agreements. He seems like a guy who has his act together. It briefly occurs to me that I could be setting myself up for a terrible living experience, but I'm a pretty chill dude. I've got divorced parents, weird brothers and a female cousin who is basically the bratty sister I've always needed to let me know when I screw up.

This will be fine. I can tell.

I stand up and stretch, noticing a dull ache in my limbs leftover from the boat crash. I've been sitting way too long. I hate being at a desk. Most days, I wish I'd gone into civil engineering like my brothers. At least then I'd be out in the field on the reg, climbing poles and checking out mine seams. Who knew mechanical engineering involved more paperwork than it did getting my hands on mechanical engines?

I remind myself it'll likely be a long-ass time before my dad trusts me with any hands-on work. We still haven't talked about my birthday.

Well, moving out of my apartment ought to get my blood flowing at any rate. It's true what I told Logan. I pretty much just have my clothes, my bed, and my couch. Shouldn't take too long to throw all that together. I will need help to get my bed in Big Red, though.

I poke my head out my office door to the cubicle farm. I'm painfully aware that I really only have an office because my dad runs this place.

Despite passing my professional exams, I'm basically a paper pusher here, like all these guys with no privacy. I look around, trying to find one of the interns.

"Yo, Drew." I lean against the wall of his cubicle and feel it wobble a bit under my weight. I straighten up as he turns around. "You wanna earn a quick fifty bucks after work today?"

He arches a brow at me. I remember what it was like to be in college. I also know what we pay our interns, so I definitely understand why Drew starts nodding before I even tell him what I need.

"It shouldn't be more than a few hours," I tell him. "I need help getting my couch up on top of my Bronco and maybe a hand taking my bed apart. I don't have much stuff."

"Sounds like a plan," he says. "Did you drive today?" I laugh. I also remember what it was like taking the bus to and from campus every day, although I'm sure my dad and uncle would prefer if I didn't park Big Red in the company lot. She's not much to look at, a little bit like me, rough around the edges, full of big ideas. Not content to sit parked among the neat and tidy company cars without dripping a little.

Around four, I grab Drew and we head to the loft I've been sharing with Liam for a few years. Of course, the place is spotless. I know Liam thinks he's doing me all sorts of favors, picking up after me all the time, but truthfully, he drives me insane the way he's always rearranging the cupboards so I can't find anything. Like, I'd probably remember to pick my running shoes up out of the entryway if it didn't take me so long to find my protein powder to make a recovery drink after my long runs. I have high hopes this won't be an issue living with Logan.

Drew and I get my clothes in trash bags pretty easily and the rest of my personal stuff in my duffel bag. I borrow a handful of bungee cords from my brother and the two of us get my couch settled in on top of Big Red. It doesn't take long to disassemble my platform bed.

"I can't decide if it's awesome or sort of pathetic that my entire life fits inside my car," I say to Drew, who shrugs.

"You don't even have video games?" He looks around the living room as I do a final sweep of my bedroom. I remember that I do actually own a suit, but since my room here didn't have a closet, it's hanging in my brother's. I feel a pang when I see that he's hung it carefully in a garment bag for me, obviously cleaned after the last time I wore it to a company event.

"We aren't really gamers," I say to Drew. I grab the suit, remembering that I'm not moving to the moon. "We mostly wrestle with each other over the guac at family dinners and go running together." I shake the duffel bag with all my running gear.

I take one final look around the loft and then toss my keys on the counter before I pull the door shut behind me. Drew and I drive to the East End, rocking out to some jams as we sit in traffic with the windows rolled down.

I pull into a loading spot in front of my new digs and ring for Logan, who buzzes us in. I'm not sure what to expect, but it's definitely not the chick who opens the door when Drew and I get to the apartment with our arms full of trash bags. "Are you Logan's girlfriend," I ask at the exact same time the girl asks me, "Are you Callie's boyfriend?"

I crack a smile. "Boyfriend? Me? Nah. I'm single. Where's Logan? I want to meet my new roomie." I crane my neck to see around her, catching a whiff of her shampoo as I do. She smells very...clean. Her hair is all smoothed back in some sort of twist and she's wearing all black. She must work in a stuffy office with a dress code.

"Um, where's Callie," she asks, putting her hands on her hips, causing me to notice how the material of her blouse pulls across her chest.

"Callie?"

She rolls her eyes. "I'm Logan Miller...and Callie Brady answered my ad for a roommate?" She frowns at the bags in my arms. "Are you helping her move?"

Drew starts laughing and tosses his bags inside the door. "Oh, snap, Brady," he says, bending at the waist to catch his breath. "You're screwed."

I suck in air through my teeth and consider this woman. "I am Callum Eamonn Brady," I tell her. "And you've got a dude's name."

Her eyebrow shoots up. "Well, you've got a woman's nickname."

"My nickname is Cal," I tell her, tossing my trash bags in the door on top of the ones Drew dropped. "Cal, space, E, space Brady. What's so feminine about that?"

Logan rolls her eyes at me and throws her hands up in the air. "I should have known better than to trust someone who doesn't use punctuation or capital letters in their email," she shrieks. "What the heck are we supposed to do? You can't live here."

This is definitely not what I expected. But after the week I've had, I'm definitely not up to moving my shit back home and having to beg my brother to let me inside the door.

I walk inside the condo, checking out the space. There's tons of room here and really good light. "I use punctuation," I mutter, walking down the hall. I stop in front of the empty room. I grin at the view of a bunch of kids playing soccer in the park down below. It's nice here. "Drew, let's bring up the bed next."

I start to walk back out, looking around for something to prop the door open. Logan follows me, her dress shoes clicking on the polished concrete as she hurries. "What are you doing? You can't move in. I can't live with a… with a man!"

I flip the deadbolt so the door won't slam and turn to face her. "Listen, toots. You have nothing to worry about from me. What you see is what you get. Just cause I have a peen doesn't make me any more of a threat than whoever you were expecting when you signed a lease without meeting your roommate."

I hear her groan as Drew pushes the button for the elevator, still laughing. He and I hustle with the rest of my stuff and, in about three more trips, have everything I own deposited in heaps around Logan's formerly-tidy condo. "You're something else, Brady," he says, holding out his palm for his cash. I fish around in my jeans for my wallet and shake my head as I count out the bills.

"This is really no big deal," I tell him.

He looks toward the balcony, where Logan is pacing and tugging on her hair in frustration. It falls out of the twist and slithers down her shoulders, long and brown and shiny. "Sure, man," Drew says. "It's no big deal at all to be living with a hot librarian."

I grin at him. "You get that vibe, too?" Drew heads out and I adjust the couch, moving Logan's armchair to the side so the couch faces the TV she mounted on the wall.

I flop back with my hands behind my head as my new roommate slides open the balcony door to come back inside. "So," I ask her. "What's your deal, Logan-the-girl?"

CHAPTER FIVE
LOGAN

"I'm not a *girl*," I huff at him, feeling very childish indeed when I do. Cal has certainly made himself right at home, which is unnerving and calming all at once, somehow. "What are you doing?"

He grins at me and I stare at his perfectly white teeth. He has the kind of teeth where you can tell his parents sent him to the orthodontist. I'm always very self conscious about my smile. I was probably the only teenager around who wished for braces while everyone around me was groaning about not being able to chew gum.

I add invisible braces to my mental wish list for when I get my finances sorted out.

"I'm relaxing, Logan. Kicking back on the couch in my new apartment. What's it look like?" He laughs and sits up, stretching, and I stare at him as his t-shirt lifts, revealing a sliver of flat, tan abdomen. I take in the long lines of my new roommate, the veins in his forearms, the way his too-long hair curls around his ears and at the nape of his neck.

After a bit, he groans and stands up, stretching and giving me more of a view of his stomach. I can't look away. I cannot live with someone who looks like this. It's indecent. He stoops to pick up some of the trash bags that evidently contain his belongings, and I watch as the muscles in his neck flex with his effort. "You like watching me work hard?" He shouts over his shoulder as he walks down the hall toward his room, and I follow, drawn to him. This might be the longest time I've spent alone with an adult male.

What am I thinking, allowing him to unpack? To actually move forward with this ridiculous arrangement? I can't live with a *man*. Not a man that looks like...well, like men are supposed to look, I decide.

I'm not a virgin. I've given sex the old college try. That doesn't mean I'm going to have sex with *him*. Maybe it's like Cal said—him having a penis doesn't automatically make him a bad choice for a roommate. No, it's more that I don't know him. We haven't discussed our lifestyles. What on earth was I thinking, sending him a lease agreement before I met him?

"Hey, Logan, can you hold this for me?" Cal's voice carries me back to the present and I look in the door to his room. I'm already thinking of it as his room. He's kneeling in the middle of a pile of boards, holding a wrench... thingy. "I could use a hand just keeping this steady. If you're willing?"

His face is so earnest, like there's truly nothing else he wants or needs than a steady hand to help screw two boards together. I feel myself waiting to try to figure out the joke, holding my breath to see which social norm I've violated, but none of that happens. Instead he just lifts his eyebrows higher and higher in anticipation of my answer.

"Let me change out of my work clothes quickly," I say, dashing down the hall to my own room before he can respond. I hang my slacks on the hanger carefully, toss the blouse in the hamper, and yank open my drawers, searching for something I won't mind ripping.

My wardrobe is nearly 100% office wear at this point. I had to devote my entire clothes budget to finding a set of things I could wear to work every day without looking like I'm repeating the same five outfits each week. I glance at my drawers and decide my old uniform from waiting tables will have to do for assembling furniture, and I yank on some ripped jeans with a diner t-shirt.

"All right," I say to Cal, noting that he's setting up his bed on the wall he shares with my room. Our heads will be inches apart, separated only by some drywall. I bite my lip, urging my brain not to linger on thoughts of Cal in bed. "Tell me what to do."

He lines up a board and tells me to hold it steady as he quickly cranks in a few screws. I see that the wrench tool is hooked up to his keychain, which is attached to his belt with a chain, but not like it's for show. His tools seems well worn, in a good way. We make our way around the rectangle and I see that his bed goes on top of a set of drawers. "That's pretty smart," I say, marveling at how quickly the whole thing comes together.

"I'm a smart guy," he says, grinning again. We talk as he screws, sharing the basics of our jobs. "I can already tell you're a lot like my brother Liam," he says with a nod. "You like things to be particular, right? I can almost feel you itching to organize my sock drawer once I get this thing put together."

I huff out a laugh. "Okay, fair. I do keep a tidy house." I bite my lip and frown at the heaps of bags he seems to have kicked all around the room. Surely he's not going to just leave them like this. "So you've got brothers? Was the person who helped you today one of your brothers?"

"Drew? Nah, he's an intern. My brothers wouldn't help me move in to an apartment sight unseen with a stranger." His eyes flare and he grins again. It's an expression that seems to come easily to him. "I think I just needed to do something I knew they'd hate. I don't know."

"How many brothers are there?"

"Just two. We have different moms. My dad was a bit of a lech."

"A what? Different moms?"

He nods and beckons for me to hold one last board and I realize I'll have to climb on top of the bed structure, very close to where he kneels with the tools. I make my way over to him and he smells like sawdust and a little sweat. I'm surprised to realize I like it. Cal says, "Yeah, so my dad, Mick, cheated on mine and Liam's mom with Zack's mom. Zack is just about a year younger than me. His mom skipped town. It's a whole shit storm. So then my dad's brother, Uncle Kellen, moved in with us with my cousin because *his* wife died of cancer."

I scoop up the last of the screws and hold them for Cal as he talks, loving the feel of his rough fingertips against my palm when he takes the tiny fasteners. "That's so sad," I say in response to his story.

"Yeah. I remember my Aunt Helen. She was pretty great. But, I will say, it was awesome having Orla and Uncle Kel in the house with us. She's more like a sister than a cousin, and it's sort of like we all grew up with two dads."

"That's two more than I had," I blurt before I can think twice about it. I slap my palm over my mouth, so shocked that I would share such a thing with someone I just met. I make it a point not to talk about my past, not to be the white trash swan who rose from the slums to get herself educated.

"Single mom, huh?" Cal doesn't seem like he harbors any judgement or fascination with what I've shared. He just takes it in as information, like it's perfectly normal to have either two fathers or none.

I nod in response to his question. "He never even stuck around to meet me," I tell him with a sigh. Cal stands up from the finished platform of his bed and turns to face me. He plunks a heavy hand on one of my shoulders and looks me in the eye and I feel like I might combust, between the heat of his skin and the burning honesty of his gaze.

"Well he sure did miss out, Logan."

Before I can respond, he turns to hoist his mattress up from the ground. He seems to have duct taped it into a long tube, I guess so it would fit in his moving truck better. He fishes in the back pocket of his jeans and extracts a pocket knife this time and I stare in wonder as he slices open the tape around the mattress and tosses it on his bed. I've never seen a man move like this, so sure of his body in space, so at ease in his movements.

Cal straightens the mattress on his bed and then lifts his shirt to wipe at the sweat on his forehead. My eyes bulge when he pulls the shirt off and tosses it in a corner before he flops down on the bed, limbs spread wide like a starfish. "Whew. There's that done," he says. Then he pats the mattress next to him. "Why don't you come sit and tell me about how hard you always work to help your mom out."

I stare at him, frozen in place. "How do you do that," I ask him, studying his face, trying not to stare at his naked chest.

"Do what?"

I gesture around the room. "Just say something of huge significance, with no warm up, like it's not a test."

"There's no test, Logan," he says, patting the bed again. "But I am going to want to know how the hell you ended up with a dude's name."

CAL

"Hm," Logan says for the tenth time this morning. It's my third day in the condo and we haven't talked much since I moved in. She works long hours and I've been crazy busy with paperwork since both my brothers went out and brought in a bunch of new business to Beltane.

I try and linger at work to see if my dad will summon me, but he doesn't. Which probably means he's saving up for some sort of family-only confrontation.

I look across the room to where Logan stands with her arms crossed, chewing the tip of one finger and frowning at me. "Hm," she says again. I glance at the counter, where I can see that I've spilled some milk when I was pouring my cereal. And then I notice that I didn't rinse out the bowl when I went to take my shower, so yes. I can see that it has formed a bit of a crust in there.

"I'll clean up the kitchen before I take off," I tell her with a wink. "Scouts honor."

"You were a Boy Scout?" Logan seems surprised as she leans to buckle her shoe. She wears these adorable little heels with a strap, with no socks, and I love how she carries them pinched between her fingers until she's just inside the doorway.

"Well, I stopped after Cub Scouts," I tell her. "But I wore the hell out of that uniform in elementary school."

Logan looks down the hall, squints, and says, "Hm," again, then leaves.

I sigh. I haven't unpacked all my bags yet. I know she's got to be bugging about the heaps all around. Shit, I'm going to have to do something about that, which means missing my run today. As soon as Logan takes off, I drag a sponge across the counter and fill my breakfast bowl with water to soak.

Heading down the hall, I quickly gather up all the bags and, not bothering to fold or sort, I just shake their contents into the drawers of my bed. I glance into the bathroom and then rush in there to pick up the towel I left bunched on the sink. "Crap," I mutter, looking down at the towel. It's Logan's. I don't own any towels and have been borrowing hers since I moved in. I really need to get my shit together.

I give the apartment another quick look and decide it's much improved, so I stuff a granola bar in my bag and head out to Big Red. By the time I get to work, I have an email from Logan. I want to laugh when I see the subject line: House Meeting, but when I open the message I grimace. She's typed up an agenda that includes items like "communal belongings" and "shared household responsibilities."

I'm still wincing at the email when Liam and my uncle come up behind me in the lobby. "How's the new dwelling, kiddo?" Uncle Kellen is like fifty percent cool and sixty percent as uptight as Liam and, apparently, Logan.

I roll my eyes and hold up my phone for them to see. "I feel like I have to be on my best behavior all the time," I tell them.

Kellen nods approvingly at the screen. "This meeting seems like a great way to establish boundaries," he says.

Liam snorts. "Welcome to adulthood, Callum. You'd better accept the meeting invite." He and Kellen snicker as we all take the stairs up to our respective offices. Normally I'd duck into the kitchen with them to shoot the breeze, but I'm irritated. Logan is well within her rights to be pissed at my mess and that I took her towels without asking. But why can't she just say so? All this chin tapping and silent planning is going to drive us both up the wall.

I've already got my dad giving me the silent treatment, leaving me to marinade in my shame. I do not need this shit at home, too.

I click "decline" to her meeting invite and stuff my phone in a drawer, where I ignore it for hours.

ℬ

After work, I head for home and, honestly, I've forgotten about this morning and the whole meeting thing until I unlock the door and see my roommate sitting at the counter with her head in her hands. When she looks up at me, she's not angry like I expected. She looks sad.

"Hey," I say, feeling like an asshole and powerless to do anything about it.

"You declined my meeting request," she says, shaking her head. "I just..." She waves around. "We need to talk, Cal."

I slide into the stool next to her and sigh. "You're not wrong about that, Logan. And I'm sorry. I've been a slob. But seriously, it's better for me if you just say so rather than ponder it for a week and invite me to a meeting about it in my own home."

"*Your* home?"

Here comes some of the anger I was expecting. And honestly, I feel like I know how to handle that better. "Yeah, my home," I tell her. "I signed a lease. I sent you a check. I live here. If you're pissed about me leaving my crap laying around I want you to say so, and eventually if you do something that pisses me off, I promise to tell you, too."

Logan's mouth works up and down like I was just speaking to her in a foreign language. "Hm," she says again, and moves to tap her chin.

"Oh no," I say, grabbing her hand. I tug her to her feet and nod my head toward the door. "Come on. We're going across the street for a beer and talk this out like men."

That gets a laugh out of her. I don't need to tell her nobody would ever confuse her for a man, except me. I also don't release her hand as we make our way across Penn Avenue to the new restaurants that made me want to say yes to this condo in the first place. There's a whole food court, basically, of high end choices all under one roof. I finally let go of Logan to gesture around. "What's your favorite? I love it all, so you pick and I'll buy."

She shakes her head. "No," I tell her, placing my hand on my heart. "This is me atoning. I'm getting dinner. Now, tempura or tostadas?"

She shakes her head again and bites her lip. "I...have never had either of those before."

Now it's my turn for my jaw to go slack. "Never? Like not once? Where'd you move here from?"

I know Logan said she grew up without much money to spare. It makes sense that she wouldn't have eaten out all that much. But I swear she said she went to college and grad school in Philly. "Don't they have Japanese food in Philly?"

"Growing up, I thought Olive Garden was the fanciest restaurant around. We mostly ate leftovers the diner sent home after my mom's shifts." She shrugs and I wave a hand.

"Nevermind," I tell her. "I'm buying you some of everything." She starts to mutter about it being too much, but I assure her I eat like a horse and would have ordered extra stuff anyhow. I grab a few things from the Japanese and the New Mexican food stands and order us a few different beers.

Settling in to the wooden table, plunking our multiple order numbers on the end so the servers can find us, I rest my cheek on my fist and meet her eye. "So. Roomie. I need you to tell me exactly what has you pissed off about the apartment."

Logan squints and sips at her beer. "Oh," she says. "Wow, this is really good."

I nod. "Yes, I have excellent taste in beer," I tell her. "But you have to say it. You have to say 'Cal Brady, you gotta pick up your shit.'"

She smiles and takes another sip of beer. "Come on," I urge. "Out with it."

She sets her glass down a little harder than I think she intended and some of the beer sloshes out. She hurries to dab at it with a napkin. "Okay, so, Cal, it would be great if you could rinse your dishes before you put them in the dishwasher."

I pat her hand. "Yes. See? That's a totally reasonable ask. I will definitely work harder to do that, Logan. And I'm going to order new towels, too, I promise." Her eyes widen. "Oh, yeah," I say. "I've been using yours. Like every day." I wink at her. "How many weeks do you think it will take for me to get you to ask me outright, 'Cal, can you stop wiping your ass with my good towels?'"

Logan throws her head back and laughs long and hard, tears forming at the corners of her eyes. As she tries to catch her breath, the server arrives with some of our food. I gesture for Logan to pick first and she reaches timidly for the batter dipped shrimp, as if that could taste anything other than amazing.

Logan dips the shrimp in the teriyaki sauce and pops it in her mouth. I watch as her pink tongue sweeps out along her lower lip and then her eyes flare. "Oh my god," she says, with her mouth full, and then reaches for another shrimp. "This is amazing!"

I grin, grabbing a shrimp and holding it up toward her to toast. "This is the start of a beautiful cohabitation," I tell her. "I'm gonna show you the world, Lo-lo."

CHAPTER SEVEN
LOGAN

I FEEL UNSETTLED. THIS MORNING, AS I STUDIED CAL SHOVING LAUNDRY IN THE washer with his foot, I knew he wanted me to just tell him what was upsetting me, but the truth is I don't quite know. He lives here now. It makes sense that he would be fully in the space. It's just that Cal is so loud. Not physically noisy, but his presence is loud. He's everywhere, humming in the shower, laughing out loud at television shows in the evening. He wears bright colored t-shirts and sneakers he calls his "Chucks."

It's been a few weeks already, and I cannot get used to the way he just makes himself known in the condo. I lean against the wall of the hallway, watching as he looks at his phone while he eats his breakfast. He laughs and slaps the counter. I realize I've never done this, most likely because I always knew that my mother had to sleep.

The more I study Cal just freely being, the more I realize how long I've been holding my breath. My mother always worked more than one job and I spent my entire life avoiding making noise in case she was trying to lie down. Teachers never called my house because my behavior and academic performance were impeccable. I didn't act wild or play rough and if some-thing was funny on the TV, turned down low, I bit my lip and just smiled rather than laugh out loud.

"Hm," I say, the power of the realization stirring up a wave of emotion. There's nobody here needing their rest, and yet I still don't put on my shoes until I'm near the door, in case the sounds of my heels on the floor might disturb somebody.

"Don't start with the 'hm' again, Lo-lo." Cal points his spoon at me. "Just spit it out. What did I do this time?" He looks down at the counter. "I didn't even make a milk puddle. Yet."

I shake my head at him. "It's not that. I just...remembered something." I bend over to fasten my shoe. I don't have time to talk all this through with Cal while he's moaning in appreciation as he shovels Cookie Crisp into his mouth. I have a work meeting about the Rudy accounts and the upcoming gala event. "I'm running a bit late, but I'm not mad. I won't schedule a meeting with you."

With a clatter, Cal tosses the bowl into the sink and turns on the faucet to rinse everything. I swear, he rattles the dishwasher tray as loudly as he can while he sets his dishes in there for when we run it later. "I can order some dishes and stuff, too," he says. "Yours are really nice. Honestly, I don't even know what to type in. Is there, like, 'apartment starter kit for immature men' or something?"

I smile at the row of plates in the top rack of the dishwasher. "I found those used online," I tell him. "Someone was leaving for the Peace Corps and unloading her whole apartment."

"Aw, dang, Lo." He gestures at the pots and spatulas and things I have hanging on hooks. "You literally got a start-up pack." Cal shakes his head. "Hey, you want a ride?"

I normally take the bus to and from work. One of the perks of this condo is the proximity to the dedicated busway, so the commute downtown takes under 10 minutes. "That's a kind offer, Cal," I tell him, "but I think the P3 can get me to my building sooner than Big Red at this time of day."

"Fair enough," he tells me, stooping to grab his messenger bag by the door. "I can at least accompany you to the elevator."

I ride to the ground floor trying not to think about how nice he smells this morning or how interesting it is to me that he can go to work in ripped jeans and a flannel shirt. I know he has a "real job" as my mother would call it, and he's mentioned more than a few times that he has more money than sense.

The truth is, Cal is a marvel to me. Easygoing, comfortable in his skin. Financially secure enough his entire life that he never worries about anything. It's sort of like I'm watching a documentary about how other people live, but instead of being on television, he's right here with me in the elevator, smiling and smelling like aftershave.

I'm still thinking about him when Marie calls our team meeting to order. Devin sits beside me, taking notes. I've already decided not to bother trying for the Rudy account, and things have been much smoother for me since I holed myself up in my office and ran financial scenarios for the "lowly" clients with only a few million dollars to invest. I've put together some pretty exciting investment forecasts this month and feel proud of that.

I smile, remembering how one client wanted to focus on companies promoting sustainability but still turning a big profit for investors, and how excited they were when I put together a portfolio that met both of their bottom lines.

"Logan," a voice hisses by my ear.

"Huh?"

Devin kicks my shoe and I whip my head up toward Marie, who is smiling cruelly. "We were discussing the optics of our analysts bringing a plus-one to the gala," she says. "Since you're the only female analyst we weren't sure how it might look to the wives of our male clients if you were to arrive without a date."

Someone at the table makes a comment under their breath I can't quite make out and my cheeks heat as I realize they're making fun of me, or implying that I would hit on the clients, or maybe both. "Excuse me?"

One of the guys...why can't I remember anyone's name? He sits forward and said, pointedly, "I said what's it matter? You're too uptight to steal anyone's husband."

Fuming, I ball my hands into fists. I'm about to snap back at him that half my clients are actually women, when Marie says, "I don't suppose you could manage to pay someone to escort you? It's really better if we promote the idea that we're a family-friendly organization. Besides, everyone else will be paired off. It would really mess up the seating arrangement if you showed up alone."

"Well," I almost shout. My eyes flare. My heart rushes. "Considering I live with my boyfriend, I'll make sure to include him on my RSVP."

The room goes silent and they all stare at me. That's probably the loudest I've spoken in a really long time. It felt good, actually. My mind races as I try to figure out what I need to do about everything that just happened here. This feels like an issue for Human Resources, but I can't help but recall Marie's comment that I'm the only female analyst. I'm not going to do myself any favors by reporting the unsavory remarks here today. It would be entirely obvious it was me, and I'm pretty sure I'm still within my probationary period where the company can let me go without severance.

It takes a few minutes for me to remember that I also just told a blatant lie about Cal being my boyfriend and that I've now roped him in to coming to this stuffy event with me as my date. Oh god, he's going to have to pretend to be my intimate lover. I bury my face in my hands, unaware if the meeting has carried on without me.

Eventually, Devin kicks my shoe again. "Hey," he says. "What was all that about?"

I look over at him. "Maybe you can explain it to me, because I certainly have no idea. Marie is always mean to me." Then I slap my hand over my mouth because I don't want to be someone who speaks ill of my superiors at work. No good can come of that.

"Do you really live with your boyfriend?" Devin seems stunned by this information. "You never talk about him." I clear my throat and explain that I never talk about anything personal at work at all. "I guess that's true," he says. Then he pauses. "Some of us grab 501's after work on Fridays. You should come."

"501's?" My mind races, worried there's a company policy he's referencing or something. Devin laughs.

"Yeah. You know, work ends at 5. So at 5:01..." Devin's eyes widen as he realizes I still don't quite know what he's talking about. I sigh. He sighs. "Immediately after work we grab a beer on the North Shore." He pats the table twice. "You should come," he repeats.

I stare at him until he starts shaking his head and walks out of the conference room, whistling.

CHAPTER EIGHT
LOGAN

WHEN I GET BACK TO MY OFFICE, I FUMBLE AROUND FOR MY PHONE AND SEND A message to Cal.

> I need to tell you something. Will you be home after work?

Almost immediately, I see the three dots appear, so I know he's using his phone during work hours. I have to remind myself that some people don't stash their phone away while they're on company time. My phone pings with his response.

> CALLUM E BRADY:
>
> wus up? I am downtown anyway for an inspection.
> Buy me lunch?

> That works.

ℬ

I TRY NOT to think about the perfectly good lunch I already have packed in the company fridge. It'll keep for dinner, I decide. Despite the conversations Cal and I have had about honest communication being the ticket to living together, I decide the better move ahead is to ask him to carry on this ruse with me than to go to my bitchy supervisor and explain that I don't actually live with my boyfriend and don't have a plus one to the gala.

Then I look over my shoulder in case she's standing nearby and can hear me use the word bitch in my thoughts.

I dive in to some reports I've been working on until someone raps on the door to my office. I look up, surprised to see Cal standing there, wearing his usual attire. In my stuffy, professional office. "Oh my god, I would have come down to meet you," I hiss at him, scrambling to my feet and closing the door behind him.

"What's the fun in that?" He grins. He does have a dazzling smile. I shake my head as he crosses his arms and leans against the wall. "So what's up?" I bite my lip and wince. "Is this about the dishes and towels? I swear, I'm going to ask my mom to help me figure all that out."

I shake my head. "No, Cal, it's not that." I sink into my desk and hide my face in my hands while I give him the brief rundown. He leans forward, his palms flat on the desk.

"Let me see if I've got this right. You want me to pretend we're banging and shacking up, and I'm going to be your date for a fancy party with professional athletes and millionaires?" He sounds like he's trying to be stern, but he's still smiling, so I'm not sure what to say in response. I just nod. "You'd owe me, Lo-lo," he says, his grin growing.

"Yes," I tell him. "Anything."

He nods. "I'm gonna hold you to that. Come on and feed me already. I was serious about you buying me lunch." He gestures toward the door and I grab my purse, walking through the door he holds open. Then I gasp when I feel his hand around my waist. My eyes widen as I look up at him. "What?" He squeezes my hip with his long fingers and my body feels like it's lit on fire. He starts ushering me down the hall and I see people staring at us through open office doors, through the blinds in the conference room. "When I visit my girlfriend at work, I'm not going to *not* squeeze her ass," Cal says, and then he winks at me.

I swallow, trying to regain my composure as we walk past reception. Jeanine at the desk beams at Cal, who shoots finger guns at her and says, "Thanks again for getting me to my girl here."

She waves as the elevator dings and the doors glide open. Cal grabs my hand and tugs me inside. When the door slides shut, he says, "I'm already good at this."

I nod vigorously, because he really is very good at seeming like he knows me intimately. The problem is that my body is responding as if it really does want him to keep exploring. I sigh deeply and lean against the wall as the elevator makes its way down to street level. Cal leans on the wall next to me, studying me. "You're messy, aren't you Lo-lo," he says. I arch an eyebrow at him.

"I don't mean, like, towels on the floor spilling cereal milk like me, messy. I mean like you've got yourself into an interpersonal mess and you have no idea how to clean it up."

"Well," I tell him, tugging on my skirt to try and straighten it as we walk through the lobby. "That feels accurate, if blunt."

ℬ

WE EAT BURRITO BOWLS, his with multiple types of salsa and the fajita toppings *and* guacamole, mine feeling very bland in comparison. It would never occur to me to ask for multiple salsas if they didn't offer that. Cal of course moans appreciatively with eat bite. "I like the bowl because there isn't a good fillings-to-tortilla ratio here and the tortilla is too chewy," he tells me. "Why do *you* get the bowl instead of wrapping it up?"

I look down at my dish. "I don't actually know," I tell him truthfully. It's how I've always ordered here. "The lid makes it easy to wrap up and eat the rest later."

"The rest? You're not going to finish it?" Cal has devoured nearly the entire thing in the few minutes since we sat down. I shake my head, horrified at the idea of all that food sitting in my gut while I'm trying to concentrate at work. He pats his stomach and belches. "Shoot, I could eat yours right now, too. I'm always hungry though. My mom calls me a garbage disposal."

He wads up his napkins and starts to tidy up his trash. "Oh, hey I forgot," he says. "I won't be home after work. I eat dinner with my mom on Wednesdays. Generally we all invade Uncle Kellen's house another night of the week, too, but that tends to fluctuate based on who's having a crisis."

I listen as he describes his family, marveling again that such a group of people could be real. I always assumed those sorts of families only existed on television or in books. Those fictional families were my only company growing up. I have no idea how I'd act around cousins and uncles and siblings.

"I can't believe that's really your family," I blurt, and then blush, not meaning to interrupt him.

"What? You don't have family drama?" Cal grins and tries to reach for my leftovers. I swat his hand away.

"It was always just me and my mom," I tell him. I sigh. "I was so excited when I thought Callie was moving in because I wanted to do spa nights with her and vent and have her give me advice."

He nods. "I can see how I would be a big disappointment with those expectations." He grins and I shake my head again. Then I startle when he reaches across the table and takes my hand. "But Logan, you can vent to me. And my advice is shitty, but I'll give it to you if you ever want to hear it."

I swallow, noting the sincerity in his eyes. "Thank you, Cal. For the offer. And for agreeing to pretend to be my date. For all of it."

He grins again. "Just don't ask me to do that spa night stuff. I'm not painting my nails."

"What about the mud masks, though? Maybe while you're watching Avengers?" It feels so natural to banter with him like this. Is this flirting? I just like making him smile and it does feel good to be honest and open with Cal.

"Hey," he says, sitting up straighter and letting go of my hand. I instantly feel the loss of heat from his warm palm. "Speaking of being open. Did I tell you my brother Liam knocked up the girl he's been seeing?" Cal shakes his head, laughing. "Everyone thought it would be me sailing that boat, but Liam—he's the uptight one with a stick up his ass—he has bought me so much leeway. I can break my femur paragliding and they'd all say *well, at least he didn't get anyone pregnant like Liam did.*"

"Is it really such a bad thing?" From the sound of things Liam has a stable career and can provide a good home for a baby. I can't imagine this sort of thing is super devastating to people with money.

"Oh, no way. It's totally fine," Cal says, waving a hand in the air. "It's just...wait til you meet Liam. He alphabetizes our cereal boxes. So the idea of him being careless is just funny. We're just giving him shit."

I decide I'm well past comfortably full and start to wrap up my lunch to take with me. "I can't believe you're really not going to eat the entire thing," Cal says, tossing his napkin into the compost. He turns to face me as we squeeze through the door to the busy sidewalk. "Want me to walk you up? I can kiss you in front of that receptionist. Give you the full onion breath experience?" Cal waggles his eyebrows and I shove him in the chest.

"Ugh, you're so gross." I roll my eyes but I can't help smiling at him. He's kind of delightful. "Thank you for the offer. I'll see you later."

CHAPTER NINE
CAL

Liam made me swear not to tell our mom the time bomb news that he knocked up Maddie. The only reason I even consider keeping my mouth shut about it is because he explained that there's a lot of health concerns with Maddie's diabetes. I don't have a degree in medicine, but I guess you don't have to in order to understand that sounds risky.

I was super interested, professionally speaking, in Maddie's insulin pump. The last time I saw her, she was showing me the mechanism for how it delivers insulin through a tiny needle that just sort of hooks in to her skin. I feel a fleeting disappointment that I'm not working on research and development for a device like that. It's a familiar feeling these days.

I spiffed up Logan's hair dryer for her so it's like a turbo blaster. That's about the most mechanical engineering work I've gotten to do this month.

I like working with my family at Beltane, but industrial inspections just are not very fulfilling for me. Sometimes I have conversations with guys on job sites and they're, like, changing the world. Me? I'm checking out efficiency in furnaces on factory floors. Sure, sure, I'm making sure employees don't asphyxiate. It'd be nicer to make sure diabetic people can have healthy pregnancies.

I arrive at Mom's before Liam. I'm worried that if I go in there, I'll either blurt about Maddie or else Dad will have told her about the boat and she'll freak out. So I pause outside to make sure all the railings on her porch stairs are secure. That's important, right? I examine the paint on the metal rail until Liam pulls up. "Thank god you got here, man," I shout at him. "I'm not about to go in there alone with a secret—"

I'm cut off by the front door springing open and my mom exploding out onto the steps. "What took you both so long? What's this about a secret?" She stands with her hands on her hips and brows furrowed while Liam looks like he wants to strangle me.

I sigh dramatically. "You caught me, Mom. I was just about to spill the beans to Liam." We walk inside and she thrusts a bottle of wine into my hands. It's a twist off, so I open it for her and make a show of pouring her a full glass. "Turns out, my new roommate?"

"Ah," she says, starting to drink the wine. "Yes, Logan. Finance guy?"

I nod. "Almost. Logan is actually a girl! But it's cool. She and I get along great and it's fine."

Mom squints at me and Liam looks like he might laugh for the first time since he found out Maddie was pregnant. "You're living with a woman? That you just met?"

I wave a hand at her and take a swig from the wine bottle as she squeals at me, a disgusted noise that makes me laugh. "It's not like that. I'm telling you, it's totally platonic. She's even making me buy my own towels because I was using hers."

"Callum Brady, that's disgusting," Liam says, reaching for the wine bottle. I hand it to him and he pours his into a glass, taking a long swig.

"Yeah, well, I've also been using her dishes. I wanted to ask you about that, Mom. Where should I get dishes and shit?"

"Shit? Really? You're going to curse at your mother after you just told us you're living with a woman we haven't met?"

"Would you want to meet my roommate if he were a...he?"

"Yes!" Mom sounds really exasperated, and I feel saved by the bing from the oven timer. "There's dinner. Boys, set the table."

Liam makes a face and hands me a stack of plates, which I turn upside down to look at. "These are nice, Mom. Seriously, where should I get stuff?"

One slips off the bottom of the stack as I flip them over and it hits the floor, but doesn't break. "Woah."

Mom nods. "Fiestaware," she says. "That's where all your things are from. But it sounds like you left everything at your brother's loft?"

"I assumed all that stuff was his," I say with a shrug, rinsing off the plate.

"It is all mine." Liam folds a napkin neatly at each of our place settings. Of course he's folding the napkins and I don't even know where to buy napkins. I wonder if our parents were all so messed up with the divorce that they forgot to teach me that etiquette stuff. "I went to the factory outlet and bought a whole set."

"Oh," Mom exclaims as she carries a casserole pan to the table. "That's a great idea. The factory outlet could be so fun. They have a tent sale coming up. You know, I don't have any daughters. Maybe Liam's friend Maddie would want to go? Oh, and your brother Zack's girlfriend. What's her name? Isn't she friends with Maddie?"

Liam turns ashen at the mention of his lady friend. "Nicole," I add, helpfully. "Nicole and Maddie are best friends, it's true. I bet they'd love to go shopping with you, Mom. But Logan has her own dishes already. It's me who needs them, remember?"

Mom waves a hand. "I'll buy them for you. And she can get some different bakeware. They have butter dishes and sugar bowls. All that stuff!" I make eyes at Liam, wondering when Mom turned into a walking catalogue for kitchen shit, but he looks like he swallowed a worm, and I remember that we're hiding the big secret that he got Maddie pregnant.

"So back to Logan," I start, wondering if I should fill them in that I'm going to play the part of her date for that work thing. But as Mom looks at me so hopefully and Liam looks at me so gratefully that I've pulled attention from his issues...I decide I actually don't want to go into all that with them. I take a bite of casserole. "This is really good, Mom."

"Thank you, baby," she says, patting my hand. "Logan?"

I nod, swallowing. "Yeah. Well she's not from around here and her family isn't tight. So she'd probably dig that dish sale. Hanging out with you, I mean. And Nicole. Maybe? Nicole's kind of mean. Maybe Orla should go. Would that be weird?"

Liam frowns. "I think it sounds unusual."

Mom waves a hand. "I'm still Orla's Aunt Sheila even if I divorced your father. Give me everyone's email and I'll set something up."

I make a face. "I don't have Nicole's email, Mom. I'm telling you, she's mean."

Mom points at me with her fork. "If you want my help getting dishes for your new love shack, you'll get me some shopping buddies." I open my mouth to protest. She gestures with the fork again. "I mean it, Callum Eamonn Brady. Now eat your dinner."

I nod. "Yes, ma'am."

CHAPTER TEN
LOGAN

THE REST OF THIS WEEK IS SO STRANGE. I START PAYING ATTENTION TO EVERYONE else on the analyst team, and I decide two things must be true. First, they are all really awful people, except maybe Devin, but he doesn't ever say anything to challenge the sexist, mean things they all say so the second thing I decide is that I need to be wary around him even if he seems nice.

Friday comes in like a freight train with deadlines and presentations to the higher ups. We're about to start the third quarter and I worked like a fiend this week starting to get end-of-quarter reports together for each client in my portfolio. I get everything prepared to present in both bar graphs and pie charts, knowing some of the company leaders need that visual element to understand at a glance what impact we've made for the clients.

I wear my fanciest suit, but pack something more casual to wear later in case Devin was serious about happy hour. There were a few times in college where people from class would invite me to a party and give me an address, only for me to show up at a daycare or cemetery. I think I give off a vibe that I'm desperate for friends.

But I don't need friends at work. I'm here to do a very specific thing, and I remind myself that I'm good at it. When it's my turn to present, I enter the zone. When I first started grad school, I couldn't even stand in front of the class, I'd get so nervous about how my speech sounded or that it would be obvious I had no idea what I was talking about. But I took advantage of every mock interview and mock presenter opportunity at Penn and gradually learned to have confidence. Well, during presentations anyway. Right now, I put all my strategies into play.

I focus on the clock at the back of the room, so it seems like I could be making eye contact with any and everyone. "It's been a good quarter," I start, offering some summary remarks as I pull up the slides on the huge monitor. I noticed some of the other analysts had trouble earlier, so I'm glad I had remarks memorized that I can deliver while I'm clicking around.

"I advised most of the clients in my portfolio to increase their investments in biotech this quarter," I state and I grin when the graph comes up on the screen. "As you can see, this turned out well for everyone."

ℬ

After the meeting, I feel excited. I decide to do something to celebrate this afternoon even if there's no drinks with colleagues. I don't even really like them that much anyway, so I'm not going to let it sting me if this was a bait and tease situation. I'm about to text Cal and buy us some mud masks for spa night when Devin catches up to me in the hall. "Hey," he says. "Hold up."

"Hey," I say, nodding and pausing outside my office door.

Devin puts his hands in his pockets and shakes his head. "How did you get Truman to up his investment in that diabetes treatment company?"

My eyebrows shoot up. Nobody here ever asks me to collaborate or talk about strategy. "Oh." I bite my lip. "Want to come in my office and I'll show you some stuff?" It had been a real triumph getting Marie to agree to share my advice with the clients. More than once, I wondered if she was resisting because she wanted me to look bad, but even Marie responds to black and white data. I bring Devin around to one of my monitors, where I keep an RSS feed of news articles scrolling all day. I have financial statements and predictions on the other screens.

I point to a string of articles from university research publications. "I had seen this patent come through for a new medication pump that's twice as efficient as the market standard." Devin's brow furrows.

"You understand that kind of thing? I thought your degree was in finance."

I shake my head. "Oh I have no idea about bioengineering. But I know which are the major scientific journals, and when I see the scientific community excited about something, I study similar trends in the market after patents are awarded and advise my clients accordingly."

I take a deep breath after saying all that, and Devin's eyes are wide. "You're putting all those things together? How do you have the head space for all that?"

Thinking he's teasing, I laugh, but then I realize it's a serious question. "Isn't that what all of us do as analysts?"

"Logan." He gestures around my office. "You're very likely a damn genius, you know that?"

I shrug. "It's probably just that I know how to use the different databases available..." I can tell Devin is astonished, and I don't want to come across as bragging, so I try to change the subject.

"So, um, is the offer still up to come out for 501s?" I flush immediately, knowing I probably sound totally desperate. Which, I am desperate, really. All I've ever done is work, and usually the people around me seem to know a bunch of undocumented rules about how the real progress happens in social situations. I need to go get these beers and learn how to be normal.

Devin's face shifts to a grin. "Sure is," he says. "I'll bang on your door on my way down."

ℬ

ALL THE OTHER junior analysts are tall and male, so they keep a brisk pace as we head from our office building across the Fort Duquesne Bridge to the bar. The guys cross North Shore Drive at a rapid pace and the light turns yellow as I'm huffing to the corner, struggling to keep up even in my flats. "You can make it," Devin yells, stepping back out into the street when he sees me on the opposite corner.

The other guys pause and look back, like they're startled to realize I've joined them. "Come on, Logan," Devin beckons, and I feel a rush as I hustle across the street as the light turns red. I just jaywalked. During rush hour. I feel an odd thrill at the idea and smile, forgetting how irritated I felt that they all walked so far ahead in the first place.

"You're coming in?" I think his name is James. He seems like he doesn't really believe I'll do it, but I nod and shrug out of my sweater, tossing it over my arm as we enter the crowded bar. James pushes ahead, spotting a tall table that's still available. All the guys drape their suit coats over the tall stools but don't sit.

Someone produces a tray full of shots and I stare at the liquid, which smells like those awful cinnamon brooms people sell near Halloween. "It's a fireball," Devin says with a shrug. They all lift their glasses, so I grab mine.

Ian, at least I think his name is Ian...he clinks his glass against mine and says, "To adventure." There's something about the look on his face that tells me he's probably teasing me. Like it's not an achievement at all to run a red light or go out for drinks with practical strangers. I'm way outside my comfort zone, but I tap my glass against his and meet his eye as I repeat his words.

When I pour the alcohol in my mouth I vow not to cough, but my eyes practically bulge out of my head as the burning liquid sears my esophagus. Whatever a fireball is, I never want one ever again. Ian shakes his head and blows a raspberry, slapping the table and flagging down the server. I listen as the guys all order pitchers of beer. I certainly hope whatever they're drinking next doesn't taste this awful.

My phone buzzes in the pocket of my sweater and I pull it out to stop it vibrating on the metal chair. It's a message from Cal.

> Hey Lo-lo, want to race home? You on your busway, me in Big Red?

I smile and let him know I can't today because I've gone out for drinks with colleagues. And then I cringe because "colleagues" is so lame when I should have said "the guys from work" or something.

> Look at you go! How you getting home later?

I send him a shrug emoji and slip my phone in my pocket, looking up just as Devin starts telling the guys about my diabetes tech research. "Logan basically knows everything about everything," he says, and I try not to concentrate on Ian's frown.

I shrug. "You can set up alerts so you get emails if anything newsworthy is happening in any of the industries where your clients are investing," I say. "It just means I spend time reading my emails while all the forecasts are populating."

I bite my lip and take a sip of the beer, wishing I knew some other way to talk to them, wishing that being good at my job didn't make me such a loser socially.

Ian takes a long pull on his plastic cup and says, "You've been here like a minute and you're already the top candidate for the biggest white whale client we've had."

My eyebrows shoot up at this comment. "Me? Oh, no I don't want to be considered for the Rudy account." I shake my head, taking another sip of beer. Trying to look cool.

"You really have no idea, do you?" Devin looks at me the way I look at my news feed in the morning: like discovery awaits.

"No idea about what?"

But before he can respond I jump, feeling an arm snake around my waist. I turn my head up to see Cal standing at my side, and I can't help the smile that takes over my entire body. I instinctively melt into him, feeling twenty times more at ease suddenly.

"What are you doing here?"

Cal winks at me and takes my beer from my hand, downing the rest of it as I stare at him. "You have location sharing turned on in your phone," he says, wiping his mouth with his hand and then dropping a kiss on the top of my head.

I flash a glare at him until I remember that he's supposed to be my boyfriend, because I asked him to pretend, which is why he has his arm around me now, his fingers tracing small circles along my hip. "Oh," is all I can muster as Devin shoots out a hand to introduce himself.

"Cal Brady," he says, nodding at each of the guys. "I hope you're taking good care of my girl here."

CHAPTER ELEVEN
CAL

The second I walk into this bar, I can tell Logan is uncomfortable. Her posture is all stiff sitting in the stool and I can see her fiddling with her cup of beer. She probably doesn't even like commercial beer. Well, if you can even call the piss these assholes are drinking *beer*. Looks like pale yellow water.

I stalk my way over to her, brushing past servers I usually chase down after a hard week of crunching data for my dad. I don't even have to try to pretend when I get across the room to Logan. I feel like some sort of caveman as I watch those guys looking at her, like they can't decide if they want to destroy her or fuck her. Pricks.

I can tell I interrupted one of them about to say something shitty, but we go around and do the small talk thing. "So, Cal Brady," one of the assholes says my name like he's so much better than me. "What is it that you do?"

I shrug. "A little of this, and a little of that," I tell him. "I mostly do Logan, here, when she lets me." I don't even feel sorry for saying it because the color red that she turns is pretty spectacular. Plus she sinks into my side a little deeper and I can feel the shape of her boobs pressed against me. I need to pull myself together and remember this is just an act since she asked me for a favor.

"Cal is a mechanical engineer at Beltane," Logan says. "He's got a particular interest in engines."

"Engineering, huh? You probably know my clients over at Beagle." One of the assholes has my attention now and I whip my head toward him.

"Beagle? Like the autonomous vehicle guys?"

He nods and Logan whispers *James* into my ear. I try not to pay attention to what it does to my body when I feel her breath on my skin. "James, is it? You work with Peter Harris and the guys at Beagle?"

James nods. "Yeah, man, he's really cool. I work with his personal account, though. Not the business or anything."

Another douche pipes in, saying, "well if Logan really just wants the small clients, maybe you can trade her for the Rudy account."

That gets a round of laughter from the table and I have no idea what any of them are getting at. Two things are abundantly clear here: these guys do not like Logan and I have to get an introduction to Peter Harris.

Beagle is named for Darwin's ship, the one that safely and swiftly carried its genius cargo around the world and artfully sailed through the London Bridge. They make autonomous vehicles that focus on safety and they're known for their algorithms. Peter Harris has never had a traffic mishap on his test routes. I salivate at the idea of work like that.

I try to change the subject. "Beltane doesn't really work with anything new tech like autonomous vehicles, but my brother did bring in some machine learning stuff." I shrug. "I mostly work with industrial sites."

They don't even pretend like they care and soon, Logan and I are just spectators in their big circle jerk. I start to play with her hair, twirling it around my fingers because it feels nice. She smells nice, too, like she's been walking outdoors. She sips politely at her drink for a bit before I say, "Well, babe, you about ready to head home?"

Logan looks utterly relieved as she nods, hopping down from her stool immediately. "Thank you for inviting me, Devin." She smiles at the least-jerky dude, who rolls his eyes and grins. "This was nice." Logan is a terrible liar, but some of the guys wave and I guide her out of the bar, keeping my hand on her hip even after we get outside. Then she doesn't push me away so I keep it there.

"Your co-workers are bunch of dickwads," I tell her as we approach Big Red parked along the street. I'm lucky I don't have a ticket, since it looks like this lane was supposed to become a driving lane for rush hour. I wrench the door open and help her up inside.

"I'm really glad you said that, because I wasn't sure if it was just me," she says, puffing out a big breath.

"No, Lo, they are just shitty people. How can you stand them?" We spend a few blocks talking about how she always feels a weird tension in the air at work and how much she hates not understanding where it came from.

"I guess I just sort of thought finance was a stressful industry."

She's quiet for awhile and I pat her leg. She turns to look at me. "Want to know what I was going to do tonight before I went to the bar?"

"Hit me."

She grins. "I was going to buy us some face masks and see if you wanted to do a spa night. I kicked ass in a presentation today and...I just wanted some pampering."

I don't even know what is in those face masks girls use, but I honestly don't see how anyone could say no to Logan if they saw the look on her face right now. "We can stop," I tell her, putting on my blinker and parallel parking near a drug store. "Do they sell these things at Rite Aid?"

She shakes her head. "No, it was silly. You said you didn't want to do spa stuff."

"Ah, come on, Logan. I was only teasing. I'm not too macho to be pampered." I reach across and unbuckle her seat belt. "I'm sure they sell all these things in manly scents, too, right?"

Logan shrugs and grins. "I'll be right back."

"No nail polish!" I shake my finger at her and she shakes her head, smiling, as she runs inside.

ℬ

SHE COMES BACK ten minutes later with a bag and we head home. Logan tells me to change into sweats and get barefoot, so I do and we settle on the couch.

"Okay," she says, and then she claps her hands. "I can't believe I'm really doing a spa night with my roommate!"

"It's my first time, too," I deadpan, and she elbows me, but I like that she shifts closer to me on the couch.

"I got us peel off face masks and exfoliating foot masks."

"Foot masks?"

She nods. "They're baggies with, I don't know. Chemicals inside. Take off your socks." I watch as Logan peels open the packages and I cough at the strong smell when she hands me the white, crinkly baggies.

"We're supposed to put these on and leave them for an hour." Logan wiggles her foot inside the bag and giggles. "It's cold and slimy."

My big foot barely fits inside and we both laugh and struggle to wrap the tab around my ankle. "Maybe I'll only partially exfoliate," I joke. We prop our heels up on the rustic crate Logan uses for a coffee table and drape goopy sheets on each other's faces.

I swallow as I feel the pads of Logan's fingers pressing into my cheeks, her thumbs dancing above my eyebrows. I try not to linger when I apply hers for her. *She's your roommate,* I remind myself. *Off limits.*

Eventually, we get to the hurry up and wait part of spa night and Logan tells me it's time for us to dish. "What should we talk about?" She's so cute and enthusiastic. I don't get why people have evidently been so mean to her all the time. I think she's great. I need to introduce her to my family stat so she at least can get to know some Pittsburghers who aren't total assholes.

I shift on the couch and tilt my head so it leans against hers. "I figured out what I want as my favor."

She looks at me, hopefully. "Please don't say something terrible right now."

"Nah, I just want you to introduce me to Peter Harris."

"The Beagle guy?"

"The Beagle guy." Logan's phone timer goes off and we both peel the masks off our faces. "This feels really weird, by the way." I offer to throw out our garbage since I don't want our house covered in frou-frou goop. Funny how I already think of Logan's condo as our home.

I almost wipe out when I stand up with the baggy on my foot but I get it together and slide back from the trash. "I'm gonna tell you a secret, Lo-lo."

"Please do," she says, leaning an elbow against the arm rest.

"I hate working for my dad."

"Oh," she says. "I could sort of tell that you don't love your job right now."

"Shit, is it obvious? Hm, one of my brothers would have said something if they could tell. I think you're just really observant. Anyway, I'd love to work in an industry like autonomous vehicles. How fucking cool would that be?"

Logan nods and looks like she's thinking. "Wouldn't that be more for computer engineers, though?"

I shake my head. "Oh my god, no way. First of all, mechanical engineers would be the guys who—"

"You should say people," she interrupts. "Surely it's not all men, right?"

I snort out a laugh. "Right. People. The people who have to modify the car engine so it talks to the computer program controlling it. I mean, think about it." I mimic turning a steering wheel. "Someone who understands engines and moving parts has to be the one to plug this bad boy into a computer system that would operate it. Right?"

Logan shrugs, but I'm on a roll, just imagining what it would be like to have my hands on car parts all damn day and get paid for it. "I mean, just think what I could do with the coolant systems...adaptations to the chassis..."

Logan pats my hand and I look down, surprised to feel my whole arm tingle at the contact. "I don't know anything about any of that stuff," she says. Without thinking, I pick up her hand and kiss her knuckles and her eyes go wide.

"I like you anyway," I tell her. And damn it, it's true. But then I realize it's also just another example of how I act before I think. Impulsive. "So what do you say? Seem fair to introduce me to your buddy James's client?"

Logan smiles. "If anything, I'm getting off easy. Are you sure that's all you want in return for..." Her voice drifts off as the foot bag timer goes off. I stand up again and offer her a hand, noticing that the top of her head only comes up to my shoulder. My brothers and I are tall and lanky, like my dad and uncle. Even Orla is 5'-10", which I know is tall for a chick. Not sure why I'm noticing Logan's body. Maybe it's because we're focused on face and feet and exfoliating, whatever that means.

We waddle down the hall together to the bathroom and she bends to peel off her foot bags. I lean past her, getting a whiff of her as I grab some towels from the shelf. "In return for what?" It's still new to be in close proximity to her like this. I like how I can see her face moving around. I think I can see her pulse moving in her throat.

She shrugs. "You know, for acting like you're my boyfriend."

I step into Logan's space and I watch as her chest rises and falls with her breath. "This is really no hardship, Lo-lo," I tell her. Then a thought occurs to me. "Have you...had boyfriends before?" She shakes her head and frowns. "But you've had sex, and stuff, right?" I scratch my head but don't step back from her space. "You're not a virgin?"

CHAPTER TWELVE
LOGAN

like all I can smell is him, and all I can hear is my blood moving through my veins. "I'm not a virgin," I tell him.

Cal leans his shoulder against the tile, still somehow surrounding me with his long legs and his arms are on either side me as he holds a washcloth. "You don't strike me as the fuck 'em and leave 'em type, Lo. No boyfriend? Not the captain of the debate team or something like that?"

I snort out a laugh. "Um, no. I never had time for dating, but sex felt like something I should try."

"Something you should *try?* Jesus, Logan, the things that come out of your mouth."

I swallow and tuck my hair back behind my ears. I feel disheveled. On display for him here, from the inside out. I clear my throat. "My mom didn't have time for much, but she made absolutely certain I understood that getting pregnant would lead to a very, very difficult future for me." I hear myself telling Cal about our lack of safety net, how we didn't have extended family who helped with babysitting or rent money or anything like that. "She got pregnant with me in high school...and never graduated. So I—" I close my eyes and take a deep breath and tell my roommate my weirdest secret.

"I figured out what date on the calendar would allow me to still graduate high school even if I got pregnant by accident, obviously accounting for any potential prematurity."

"Obviously," Cal says. He leans back against the sink with his arms crossed, face rapt. I wish we weren't having this discussion in the bathroom. Or at all.

"Right, so I knew no matter what, at least I'd graduate high school and I..." I pause and look at Cal, who is fascinated, eyebrows raised, waiting to hear the rest of this story. "I chose someone from physics class. He had a car, so I knew we could use it to...you know."

"Did you give him a blowie after study hall, Lo?" Cal grins.

I roll my eyes. "No." I shove his chest. "He...deflowered me."

"Oh my god you did not say deflower."

I nod.

"So you didn't want to date Mr. Bunsen Burner after that thrilling ride?"

I make a face. "I don't know if thrilling is an adjective I'd choose." The sex had been really disappointing. Not painful, but it certainly didn't feel good. I spent the entire time contemplating the superior, exhilarating thrill of sledding down the stairs in my apartment building with the neighbor kids when our parents were all at work in the summertime.

"I tried again in college," I tell him. "And grad school." I shrug. None of the boys I chose, the ones who seemed organized and put together—none of them made me feel safe. The utter terror at getting pregnant before I met my life goals was always so overwhelming I just couldn't relax, so I mostly lay there biting my lip and waiting until I could get back to reading my book. "It just isn't for me, I don't think."

"Oh, Logan." Cal's face shifts and he steps closer to me again. I feel his breath on my face. "I fucking hate that it wasn't good for you." I can see his nostrils move as he breathes and his scent is intoxicating. I certainly never felt this way around anyone from physics class, but I don't think I need to tell this to Cal.

"What do you mean," I ask him, thinking again of that moment during my third attempt where I realized it's all just a lot of hype. Fiction. Like the idea that people live happily ever after. Even with my hand, the pleasure I can find is just okay. When I try, I can feel myself approaching a pinnacle sometimes, but there is no toppling over. No explosion or fireworks. I'd rather be forecasting.

He steps closer to me again and touches my face. My eyes go wide at the feel of his gentle touch. "If it were me, it would be good for you, and you wouldn't have to ask what I mean," he says, his breath ragged.

I feel overwhelmed and hot, flustered and I start to panic a little bit. He's too close, and too big and too off limits. We live together. "I need to go to bed," I tell him, ducking out from under his arm and walking toward the door. "Thank you for doing spa night with me. And picking me up and stuff."

I hustle down the hall to my room, closing the door before I can tell whether he's followed me. Of course, he's right behind me because we live together. He's my roommate. My male roommate. I'm starting to realize that I made a huge mistake letting a man into my personal space, because now I can't go anywhere to escape him.

"Lo, I'm sorry," he says through the door. "I shouldn't have gotten in your space like that." I hear a thunk, like maybe he's resting his head on the door. I stand in the middle of my room trying to catch my breath. I nod but he can't see me, of course. "Are we cool?"

I try to speak but no sound comes out. I clear my throat and try again. "Yes, Cal. It's fine. I'm just really tired, okay?" He doesn't say anything. "I'm going to go to bed." I stand in the dark in my room, listening, until I hear his footsteps pad down the hall.

CHAPTER THIRTEEN
CAL

I FEEL BAD THAT I MADE LOGAN UPSET, BUT IF I'M HONEST, I'M GLAD SHE SHUT herself in her bedroom. I don't know what the hell has come over me. When I saw her at the bar like that, looking unbelievably sexy and uncomfortable, something shifted. I wanted to protect her from those assholes. But I also found myself thinking impure thoughts about my roommate once she got talking about her background.

I snort, disgusted that I'm feeling proud of my restraint for not pressing my lips to her throat. My family is really right about me. I give no thought to the consequences of anything. Meanwhile Logan maps out every possible consequence of sex apart from pleasure, apparently.

What the hell kind of jerks was she propositioning that couldn't even get her off? She didn't come out and say so, but I'm pretty sure her facial expression said it all. No guy has ever made Logan come. That's a crime against humanity.

I'll never admit this if she brings it up to my family, but I kind of liked our little spa session. Not that I'm going to go out and buy that makeup stuff, but it was nice sitting next to her and just talking. We told each other stuff. Real things. I feel a lot closer to her, which makes it even worse that I keep thinking about kissing her and sniffing her hair.

B

MY FAMILY IS DOING A LONG RUN this Saturday, so I sneak out of the condo in the morning. Logan hasn't gotten up yet, and I figure she can use a day without me in her business. But then when I leave, it's weird driving to meet my brothers without Liam beside me in Big Red. He and I lived together for so long. It was always the two of us going out to find Zack and Orla. Now each of us is arriving alone. I don't love it.

Today we're meeting in our secret trail in Highland Park. It's not technically a secret. I mean, it's a public trail in a huge city park, but it's one of those hidden ones not many people know about. The four of us Brady kids used to sneak there when we were younger and pretend we were alone in the wilderness. I spot my family near the trailhead waiting for me and I slap my brothers on the back like I haven't seen them in a year.

"Impregnate anyone new today, Liam?" It's fun to tease him about this because his face turns an amazing shade of purple almost immediately.

He punches me in the shoulder. "Defile your female roommate yet, Callum?"

I'm about to come back with something witty when I realize that I sort of almost did. Before I can respond, my dad and uncle walk up behind us. "What's this? Roommate?" Uncle Kellen leans on my shoulder to stretch out his quads. He ruffles my hair. "I thought your new roommate was a guy named Logan?"

I shrug. Dad just glares at me. "Turns out Logan's a girl in this case." My uncle makes a concerned face and my dad snorts.

"Who knew all three of my boys would be living in sin?"

Orla pretends to vomit. "Come on, Uncle Mick. Don't be a hog."

I nod, stretching my own legs. "It's really not like that with Logan, guys," I tell them. "She's...well you just have to meet her."

Uncle Kellen pats my arm. "Good idea. Bring her to dinner tomorrow." He takes off into the woods at a fast clip. Every week, I forget that he and my dad are in amazing shape even though they're in their 50s. They don't ease into our runs, because they don't need to. They're like gazelles and I feel my muscles protest as I work to keep up.

"I don't really know if Logan wants to be subjected to a Brady family meal," I say as Orla snorts.

"Well, neither do I, and I still manage to show up," she says, laughing as her ponytail swishes. She passes me on a tight turn and I almost slip off the edge of the hill.

I sprint to catch up with my dad and try to signal that I want to talk to him, but he keeps his eyes ahead on the path and trails Uncle Kellen.

We finish our run and by the time I get back to Big Red, Dad has left and Uncle Kellen has already cooled down from his workout. He's not even breathing hard. "Bring your friend to dinner, Callum," he says and points a finger at me. "Nobody should eat alone."

I GET BACK to the apartment and find Logan sprawled out at the counter with at least three laptops open. Her eyes dart back and forth between the screens and she's typing furiously on the biggest laptop. "Hey," I say, tossing my keys on the counter and kicking off my sneakers.

She looks up and grimaces. I pause, then I bend and pick up my sneakers, lining them up neatly in the bin by the door. "Hi," she says, and bends her head back into her work.

"Are you trying to take over the world there?" I grab a banana and walk behind her, squinting at the graphs and numbers flying by on all of the monitors.

She shakes her head. "Just trying to get ahead of these reports for my clients," she says. With a few more clicks she rests her hands on her laps and sighs, turning toward me. The energy between us feels normal right now and I'm grateful. I slide into the stool next to her.

"I'm really happy working with these clients personally on their individual financial plans," she says. "The other guys all want to be the one to manage this big, new account we've got and I just...I don't need that pressure."

I nod and eat some more of my banana. I talk with my mouth full, which I know is bad manners but usually I lose my ideas if I don't spit them out immediately. "It seems like you've got the skills they probably want for the big cheese, though, Lo."

She rolls her eyes. "I have my entire career to make big moves," she says. She waves a hand and starts closing the lids to her laptops. "I want to establish rapport at work this year. I'm building a foundation. Getting situated in my new town. You know how it is."

I have no idea what she's talking about, but it sounds like she's trying to lay low because these jerks are mean to her. I grunt at that thought and bite back all the rude shit I want to say about those guys. "Speaking of getting situated," I say, "My uncle invited you to family dinner tomorrow."

Logan's eyes flash. She looks like I just asked her to eat uncooked squid or something. "Family dinner?"

I nod. "Yeah. Me, my brothers, Orla, my dad...everyone. It's super casual. Uncle Kellen's a really good cook." Logan looks over at the stove, which is still a little crusty from my last experiment with boxed pasta mix from the other night. Note to self: ask Uncle Kellen what cleaner will unglue that gunk from the stove.

Logan still looks terrified, so I pat her arm, then I feel those weird sparks and yank my hand back. "I promise, everyone is really nice," I tell her. "Well, that's not technically true. Zack and Liam are grouchy and Orla's kind of irritable." She blinks at me. "Also Nicole will probably shriek a bunch of profanity. But Maddie is nice."

Logan looks like she's going to hyperventilate. I grab a piece of paper from her note pad. "I'll make you a chart," I tell her, starting at the top.

"Dad—I guess you'll call him Mick—and Uncle Kel are brothers. They run the company where we all work. Uncle Kel is a widower. Dad is a sleaze. Zack and Liam and I belong to Mick. Orla is Uncle Kellen's daughter."

Logan nods as I write all their names. "This sounds familiar. Thank you for the refresher."

"Okay, so Nicole is Zack's girlfriend. She's a real pistol. I'm super glad she tolerates him. Maddie is her best friend. My brother Liam knocked her up the first time they slept together." I point my pen at Logan. "Always use condoms, Lo-lo. Bag it up every time."

"You don't need to tell me that," she says.

"Oh, shit, I forgot about your whole situation." I put the pen down. "I'm such a jerk. We like to give my brother a lot of crap, but honestly, our family is super here for this baby. Liam has lots of support. Swear to god."

Logan tears up a little bit at this, so I hand her the Brady family tree. Her eyes are so big and searching, and she was totally honest with me yesterday about her terrible sex choices. I feel like I can come clean to her about the boat. She listened when I said I didn't like working with my family. And god, it'll feel good to just *tell* someone. "There's something you should know before we go," I tell her. "Just in case someone mentions it. I..."

It feels really crappy to be bringing this up to her all of a sudden and I start sweating again. "What is it, Cal?"

"I did something really stupid before I met you and I haven't faced my reckoning yet."

"Your reckoning? Is this a historical novel?"

I roll my eyes and give her the summary of what happened. She looks utterly horrified. "Dad hasn't said a single word about it, Logan. His silence is the worst thing. My family isn't like that at all," I tell her. "I'm worried he's waiting for everyone to be present before he brings it up and just roasts me. And I deserve it. But honestly, the not knowing and the anticipation of it." I drift off and mimic an explosion.

"That sounds terrible," she says, biting her lip. "It sounds like your family talks through everything, whether you want to or not."

I snort.

"What if you emailed him a meeting request? Put the boat incident on as an agenda item?"

I laugh harder than I have since my birthday at the thought of sending my dad a calendar invite. "Oh sweet Jesus, Logan. My family is going to love you."

"That's sweet, Cal. But really. You need to talk to your dad. What if you call him?"

I feel a lot better having told someone, but I also know that this psychological torture is all part of my consequence somehow. I plunk a hand on her shoulder. "I'm going to go shower and stuff. Dinner's at five tomorrow. You in?" She nods and I walk out of the room before I say something else insensitive.

CHAPTER FOURTEEN
LOGAN

I sit in Cal's car tapping my nails on the pot of the plant I bought across the street. Cal insisted we don't need to bring any food and that his family is really particular about alcohol, but I couldn't show up with just myself no matter how many times Cal rolled his eyes. My mother would probably drop over dead if she thought I was going to someone's house empty-handed.

"Are you sure your uncle likes succulents?" I look at Cal hopefully as he shakes his head and weaves in and out of the traffic along Penn Avenue. We're running a bit late because Cal didn't want to interrupt me when I was working and I was waiting for him to tell me it was time to leave. I always feel better when I use alarms and timers to get places on time, but Cal says it's okay if we are the last ones to arrive.

"He loves everything," Cal says, then punches the horn as someone slows to a stop at a yellow light. "We could have made that."

"It'll be okay," I tell him, and myself. I can tell he's anxious to be around his father, and I bite my lip so I don't encourage Cal to just bring up the boat situation. I don't want to touch him again, even reassuringly, because I'm still not recovered from the throbbing sensations that wracked my body Friday after our spa night. It seems like neither of us is going to talk about it, and I'm glad. Better if we just pretend nothing happened and go back to being jovial roommates.

A nagging thought eats at me that not talking about things seems like a pattern for Callum Brady. He was gone when I woke up yesterday and made himself scarce most of today. But then I remember that he's actually really suffering because his dad won't discuss the accident. Maybe none of the Bradys are any good at communicating? Maybe he just stinks at initiating conversations?

Cal parks in his uncle's driveway and dashes up the steps to the front door, so I follow. He's met by a chorus of shouts and I concentrate on my breathing as a swarm of people press around the door frame, staring at me. "Is she here?" A woman's voice comes across the din and I wonder if this is Nicole. *Partner to Zack. Tends to swear.* I mentally run through Cal's notes about his relatives, hoping I don't make a blunder.

A curly haired woman charges through the group of lanky men and thrusts a drink at me. "Here, you'll need liquid courage for this," she says, taking the aloe from me. "Aw, Uncle Kel, she brought you a plant!"

I'm ushered through to the back patio, and handed a plate of cheese and fruit. A tall man with dark hair and Cal's face sits opposite me. This must be his father. He cracks pistachios into a napkin and nods at me. "Mick Brady," he says. "I hear you wound up with my Cal for a roommate."

"Something like that," I tell him. There's no trace of anger in his face as he brings up his middle son. It's very strange to me when people can compartmentalize their feelings. I feel wary.

Nicole slides into the chair next to me. "I hear you're a financial analyst," she says. I nod and Nicole squints at me. "All those finance guys are horrifying." Nicole sips her alcohol—I'm thinking it's whiskey—and shakes her head.

She looks like she's going to say more, but Mick cuts in. "Finance, eh? You work with investments?"

I nod and swallow my bite of cheese. "I focus mainly on individual accounts. Not hedge funds or anything like that."

Mick leans back in his chair and pops a green nut into his mouth. "I'm going to be a grand-pop soon. Did you hear about that?" I nod. "Give me your card. I want to set something up for Baby Brady. Gotta look out for his future."

"Mick, you don't know if it'll be a boy," Nicole says.

He waves a hand. "We don't make girls," he says, gesturing around the deck.

"Um, hello? I'm here." A woman who must be Orla walks out onto the deck clutching a dish of guacamole to her chest as Cal tries to reach around her and steal it.

"Well, honey, you're the exception," Mick says, blowing her a kiss. Orla rolls her eyes and plunks into the chair next to him.

I assume Mick is just making conversation about coming to see me at work, but he asks again for my information. "Oh," I say, blushing and biting my lip. "All my stuff is inside. I have a card in my purse somewhere..."

When I got swept into the house, one of the Bradys took my purse to some bedroom and I haven't seen it since. Thankfully, Cal comes to my rescue, telling his dad, "I'll text you Lo-lo's info, Dad. Wait til you see the butt-holes she works with."

I want to bury my head in my hands and really wish Cal would talk about something else, but his face is so hopeful as he waits for his father to acknowledge him. I don't like how his family's attention is turned toward me, but I guess that's better than Cal getting reamed out in front of his family. Nicole gestures at me with her drink. "It doesn't surprise me in the least that you work with a bunch of monsters in finance. I was at a tech startup before I moved to Stag Law." She practically growls. "So much patriarchy. God."

Nicole leans back as Zack stands behind her and rubs her shoulders. I'm not sure when he came outside but he brought a tray of beers with him and Cal hands me one, twisting off the top as he does so. I try not to look at the muscles in his forearms.

Nicole continues, with a mouthful of potato chips. I can see why Cal likes her. "If you get sick of testosterone city over there, let me know. I have contacts with this kick-ass group of female entrepreneurs. Startups are *always* looking for an MBA."

"Aren't startups risky?" I peel the label off my beer bottle nervously, really wishing the conversation would drift away from me already. How is it that this entire party full of people is focused on me and Nicole?

She shrugs. "You've got an Ivy League MBA. It's not like you'd be unemployed long if something went belly up. You should think about it. These tech companies always have someone good with ideas and someone good at networking, but never anyone who understands the financials. Come have drinks with me sometime and I'll introduce you to folks."

"Since when do you have friends other than Maddie and Emma?" Cal throws a napkin at Nicole, who gestures at him with a fork like she's going to stab him.

"Well, Callum, these aren't friends per se. They're women in business. Networking connections." She jabs something on her plate with the fork. "We vent a lot. Oh! And we're doing a book club."

"Not this again." Orla shakes her head, but Maddie perks up and reaches for her bag next to her chair. She pulls out a very tattered paperback.

"Orla," she says, "I'm telling you it's so good." Maddie hands me the book—*The Redcoat*—and fixes me with a pointed stare. "Logan, you need to read it."

Liam and Zack roll their eyes. Zack leans back against the railing on the deck, shaking his head. "I never in a million years would have pegged my girl to be into reading romance novels."

"So sappy," Liam agrees, and starts making kissing noises. Maddie and Nicole look like they're going to murder their Brady boys.

"Listen to me, assholes." Nicole seems fully enraged by now and I notice Mick shifting uncomfortably in his chair, peering inside like he's hoping Kellen comes out soon with the food. Maybe that's just me. But I guess I'm glad they're all focused on something else. Nicole actually stands up clutching the book. "This is a sweeping tale about relationships and love and honor and caring for other people. Plus it's about revolution and history and fighting for what you believe in. Isaac Brady, if you want access to my honeypot ever again, you will read this book until you know that reference."

Zack (I recall Cal telling me Isaac goes by Zack) points at Nicole and says, "If I want to learn about the revolutionary war, I just need to go to the Fort Pitt Museum down at the Point. You can keep your kissing book."

Liam moves to offer him a high five, but Maddie throws her copy across the deck and pegs him in the face. "The book highlights all the gritty realities of parenthood, too," she shouts. "The love story is just part of it. This is really about the human condition."

Cal leans closer to me as they all continue shouting at one another. "I feel like we should both read this book. It must be good if Nicole is making threats and Maddie is throwing shit."

I nod as he pulls out his phone. "Oh," he says, showing me. "There's an audiobook! Should we listen?" I like the idea of us reading the book together, discussing the story over food. Cal might not be Callie, but I'm really starting to see how this living arrangement offers everything I'd been fantasizing about. This family is strange and loud and evidently needs a lot of work on their communication skills, but I feel so thrilled at how readily they're including me. My cheeks start to hurt from smiling as I help Cal check the audiobook out from the library.

He downloads the book and slides his phone in his pocket. Uncle Kellen brings out a huge pan of food and chaos erupts as everyone digs into the casserole. I'm able to settle back in my seat, no longer the focus of attention, and just observe. The Brady family is awesome, frankly. They tease each other but obviously help one another with everything from opening beers to taking care of each other's cars.

I've never had anything like this. The silent treatment Cal mentioned, I can relate to. But I don't really see evidence of that. Right now, the Bradys are all shouting and joking and complimenting Kellen's cooking. Every now and then, a family like this would come into the diner when I was working. I'd hang back and watch as they shared food with each other, offered helpful suggestions to each other's challenges.

They all seem comfortable and relaxed. I feel like I've been clenching for my entire life, anxious I'll flounder and start a chain reaction that would leave us homeless.

We were always balancing on the edge of a razor, always one small emergency away from not covering our bills, even with me chipping in with my part-time job. I sit on this deck and imagine what it would have been like with more people to share in the work of keeping it all together. I wish my mom could be here now, relaxing. *She's probably at work,* I think.

Cal squeezes my shoulder and mouths "are you okay?" I nod and smile, because I am. I am doing better than okay, despite all the challenges I faced. I just wonder when I will be able to let go and enjoy it.

CHAPTER FIFTEEN
LOGAN

Monday morning, Marie bangs on the frame of my office door, which I kept open today for some reason. "What did you do," she asks, tapping her foot.

I try to imagine what she's referring to and I squint, thinking through my to-do list from the morning. "I ran a forecasting model for a few of my accounts," I tell her, and start to fumble around with the papers on my desk when Marie makes a sigh-groan type noise.

"I mean what did you say to this new client? I've got a Mick Brady here refusing intake procedures and insisting he meet with you directly."

"Oh," I say. "I didn't know he was serious about coming in. He's—" I remember that my colleagues think Cal is my boyfriend. "He's my boyfriend's dad."

Marie presses her lips together and glares at me. "Well as your supervisor, I'm telling you to tell your father-in-law he has to stick with protocol. You are not involved in client relations, Logan. You run the numbers. Did you think you'd get a referral bonus? Seriously?"

I open my mouth to say something when Cal's dad pops his head into my office. "There you are, Logan! Told you I'd be by to set something up." He elbows Marie. "Did Logan tell you I'm gonna be a grand-pop?"

Mick squeezes past Marie and sits down across from me at my desk. She is flustered, because this definitely isn't how clients usually come on board. "Mick," she says, smoothing out her suit jacket. "I thought I was meeting you in the conference room to talk about the perks of investing with us!"

578

He waves his hand at her dismissively. "I don't need to know the perks. I just want Logan to set something up for my new grandson."

Marie grits her teeth. "Logan wouldn't know how to do the setup for something like this, Mick."

Cal's dad's face shifts and he tilts his head to the side as he reaches into his suit pocket. He pulls out a fat envelope and throws it on the desk. *Oh my god, he brought cash.* I steeple my fingers, pressing them together firmly and breathing deeply. Mick gestures to the packet. "Sweetheart," he says to Marie, "Why don't you go take care of that for me while Logan handles my business." She stares at the money. Mick leans closer to her. "It's probably better if you call me Mr. Brady," he says. "Mick is what my friends call me."

Marie turns beet red and I try to savor the sight of her. I know I'll suffer for this later, but right now, in front of a client, she's totally trapped. I bounce my knee up and down anxiously until she scoops up the bills. "I'll just...figure out what to do with this," she says, and backs out of the room.

Mick leans back and pushes the door to my office shut. "She's a real piece of work," he says to me. "I don't know how you stand being around that sour puss all day. I'll tell you, I didn't make it this far in business without learning how to read people and this office has a bunch of duds." I swallow and nod. I'm still not done savoring the look on Marie's face when Mick told her off.

But all that evaporates when I remember what Cal confided in me and how Mick is giving him the silent treatment. Supposedly. Do I come clean that I know about it? I have no idea how to proceed here, so I just stare at him. "What's eating at you, kid? You worried I'm going to say something awful about Callum?"

I swallow, not sure what to say. He leans back in his chair.

"My boy and I are going to have a conversation about that eventually," he says. "I assume you know what I'm referring to."

I nod.

"I haven't quite worked out my feelings about what happened there," Mick says. "Don't you worry about. He and I will be just fine. Like I told you, I can read people. That doesn't always mean I can read them immediately." He takes a deep breath and I can tell we are both thinking of Cal. "This family has gone through worse." I nod again, wondering if I'll ever recover from the contrasting emotions today has brought. "So," Mick says, "tell me what you've got in mind for Baby Brady."

"You mean now?"

He laughs. "Well sure. I'm here, aren't I?"

I take a deep breath and spin one of my monitors toward him. "You know you caught me off guard, Mick."

He leans forward and winks. "Yeah, but I bet you have ideas anyway."

When I laugh, my feeling of relief is genuine. He's right and I like this much better than trying to figure out Marie and her moods. Financials are much more in my comfort zone. "You've got at least 19 years until he or she will need any of the funds," I tell him. "We can comfortably assert a little risk. I'm really liking some of these biotech opportunities in India."

Mick and I pore over my prediction models and set up a nice little fund plan for Liam and Maddie's baby. It occurs to me that I didn't even realize this was a thing people did until recently, and here I am having a conversation with someone wealthy enough to do it. And he trusts me to help him!

"Want some pistachios?" Mick reaches into the same pocket where he stored his cash and procures a single serving package of nuts. He is without a doubt the strangest person I've encountered since moving to Pittsburgh, but I get the sense that like Cal, he's just absolutely showing me his honest self. And right now, he wants to eat a snack and talk about investments.

"Sure," I say. We end up chatting until he stands, pulls me in for a hug and says he has to leave.

"I like you, Logan," he tells me. "You're going to be good for Callum, I can tell. You gotta stand up to the sour pusses around here, though." He gives me a salute and takes off before I can remind him Cal and I are just friends. I slump into my chair and exhale, exhausted by the hurricane he just set in motion.

Later, on the ride home with Cal, I want to tell him everything about the day, but he reminds me we are about to reach the point in our audiobook where the redcoat soldier and his colonist lady get married in secret. "Remember that I waited for you, Lo-lo," he says, pulling out into traffic after picking me up from my building. "I could have listened to this entire thing today at work."

I roll my eyes and try to convince him that he needs to hear me out about my meeting, but he turns on the recording and starts saying, "La, la, la. I can't hear you!"

The narrator mentions a belt hitting the floor and Cal snaps his mouth shut.

"Shh," I say, swatting at his arm. And then the two of us stare at each other as the McClintons consummate their marriage. Repeatedly.

"This is a dirty book," Cal says, eyes wide as he merges onto Forbes Avenue.

"Shh," I say again, shifting uncomfortably in my seat as I listen to the narrator describe intense passion between the main characters. At one point, Cal pauses the story and looks at me, eyes wide.

"I'm not sure why I don't hang out with Nicole more often," he says, fanning himself. "Did you know this was a dirty book?"

I shrug and reach past him to push play again so I can hear what happens next in the story. For once, I'm glad there's traffic so we can continue listening. Linus McClinton asks his new bride if it's normal for a man and a woman to feel such a connection, and I feel myself tense.

This is always the part where I tune out of a romantic movie or novel. I've never felt such a thing, not even an inkling, and I want to cringe when fictional characters suggest that true love is out there for the grabbing. I nod in relief when Sally confirms that what she and Linus are experiencing is unbelievable. Surreal. "Thank you," I say to the car at large.

Cal slaps the pause button as he pulls into the garage of our building. "Hot damn," he says. When he pulls his Bronco into the parking spot, he slithers down in the seat, looking limp. "How can you just sit there like that? All unaffected?"

"What do you mean?"

Cal looks at me like I have two heads. "Logan, we just listened to the sexiest love scenes and you're..." he gestures at me and mops at his brow again.

I shrug. "It's like Sally said there at the end. What they have is extraordinary. It's a fiction. A fantasy."

Cal raises a brow at me in the dim light of the parking garage. "By fantasy, do you mean you'd be down for some inspired role play? Because I could get a musket."

I swat at his arm. "I already told you. All that stuff, it doesn't affect me."

"What stuff? Sex? You mean to tell me you don't have a lady boner after listening to that?"

I recoil away from him and open the door to the car. "A lady boner? Ew, Cal."

He rolls his eyes and tosses me my bag, shouldering the driver-side door shut and following me to the elevator. He leans on the wall facing me as we wait for it to arrive. "You can't tell me you weren't affected by listening to that, Logan." His voice is lower, somehow, his eyes darker than usual.

I do feel something, but I don't know how to identify it. My neck is sweating and I can feel the blood in my ears throbbing as Cal raises a hand

and tucks my hair back from my shoulder. My mouth feels like I swallowed peanut butter too quickly. But none of these symptoms matches anything I've read about or heard described in the so-called dirty book so far. I don't know what this is.

The elevator bings as the doors slide open and I climb inside, licking my lips and trying to swallow. Cal looks at me strangely as he saunters inside. I take a deep breath. "Thank you for the ride," I tell him.

"No sweat, Lo-lo. Want to keep listening while we make dinner?"

The next few chapters of the book involve a shooting and a dangerous encounter with the rebel army, and I notice it's much easier to be around Cal while we're listening to that.

CHAPTER SIXTEEN

CAL

Liam and Maddie finally tell my mom about the pregnancy and she stops hounding me about taking Logan shopping for dishes. For about two days. Then, my phone starts blowing up every hour until I promise that I'll bring my roommate along the next time Liam and I meet Mom for dinner.

I'm not sure why I thought a nice little dinner for five would be less of a production than sending the womenfolk shopping. But Logan has spent the entire ride so far fretting even worse than when she was meeting the Brady crew last weekend.

"She didn't tell me what she was making," Logan says, nervously twisting the bottle of wine in her lap like it's coated in sand paper or something. "I don't even know if white wine was the right choice. But the woman at the store says most people enjoy a nice sauvignon blanc. Am I pronouncing that right? Cal. You have to swear you won't let me pronounce things wrong and sound like a hick in front of your mother."

"Jesus Christ, Logan! You're fine. It's fine. Calm down."

She snaps her head back like she's been slapped and I feel like shit. "I'm so sorry," I tell her, shifting down into fourth as the traffic crawls along up 279 from downtown. "God, Logan, everything I say and do lately just turns to shit."

"What's wrong?" She frowns, looking concerned, and starts twisting the wine bottle again.

I slap at the steering wheel. "I'm all worked up about what you said my dad said in your office," I tell her. "I also don't know if my mom knows what happened. They still talk. And I don't know what the hell she really thinks about our whole…situation. I'm damned if I do and damned if I don't with that."

"What do you mean?" Logan's eyes are sometimes so wide and innocent I feel like I'm sinning just being in the same room as her. I think back to how I was creeping into her space after spa night and I feel like even more garbage.

I take a deep breath. "If my family thinks we're sleeping together, then I'm impulsive and dumb for moving in with a woman and getting into her pants. If we're not sleeping together, then I'm dumb and immature because you're amazing and I haven't settled down yet and I'm still going out and getting wasted on my birthday, crashing boats into trees."

"Cal," she says, reaching for me. I pull my arm out of the way, not ready for the kindness of her touch right now. "It's been over a month now since you moved in, since the boat thing. You've been a pretty good—"

"I'm the grunt boy at work, Logan. Nobody trusts me with anything resembling real engineering. And I obviously can't be trusted with anything more than paper pushing. You work with people who are assholes to your face. Me? I work with people who will never, ever stop viewing me as the good-time guy. I'm great at parties. Terrible when things get real."

I exit the highway and turn toward my mom's neighborhood. She moved to some swanky suburb after she and Dad got divorced and commutes every day to her office in the city. I watch Logan's face as she assesses her surroundings. Luxury cars, immaculate landscaping.

"I've been real with you," Logan says, pulling her eyes away back into the Bronco and toward me. "I've told you things I never told anyone else."

"Well," I mutter. "Fuck. Thank you for that. You're the only one." She smiles and stares back out the window as I swerve around the floral dividers that are centered in each intersection of Mom's neighborhood. Things are really starting to bloom now. Everything looks great on the surface.

"Cal," she says, her voice quiet. "I think you need to be real with your family, too."

I grit my teeth and shake my head, not able to think about the emotions threatening to rip me apart right now. I pull into Mom's driveway behind Liam's parked car. "You ready for this?"

She smiles and nods, slithering out of the Bronco. I really should get her a step stool or something so it's not such a big drop for her. Logan gets about two steps toward the door before my mom bursts through it.

"They're here! Liam, come get her coat. No, wait, stay there with Maddie. Your brother can help her. Logan!" Mom claps her hands together and clutches her chest. "I never thought my Callum would ever bring a woman home to meet me." She actually starts crying.

"Mom, it's not like that," I remind her. "Remember? Logan is my roommate."

Mom waves her hands around. "I'm going to be a grandma," she says, draping an arm around Logan's shoulders. "You'll forgive me for being emotional. Oh my god, I didn't even introduce myself. I'm Sheila Brady. You must call me Sheila."

Liam and I exchange a glance and I crack a smile when he rolls his eyes. Thankfully, Maddie interrupts the sob fest and starts asking Logan how far we've gotten in the audiobook. Eventually, Mom slows her roll and we're soon sitting around the table with snacks and drinks while we wait for a frittata to crisp under the broiler. That's a phrase I wasn't familiar with at all, because my entire life my mother has made really bland diet food or else ordered takeout, but now that Liam and I are bringing women around, she rolls out the red carpet.

Maddie fans herself with a napkin and shakes her head while she tells my mom about *The Redcoat*. "The McClintons are going through all this strife because Linus is a redcoat. But he's starting to see that the rebels have a valid beef with the British. And Sally is helping him through parting ways with his brothers in arms."

Liam scratches at his stubble, looking intrigued. "I thought this was a kissing book?"

"Oh," I interject. "That's in there, too. Woo! Man, is there kissing. But yeah there's also all this stuff about the battles and loyalty and—"

"And doing the right thing," Logan says, nodding. "I can definitely relate to Linus sort of figuring out he's working for the wrong side..."

"Logan's co-workers are terrible people," Maddie says to Mom. She gestures with a carrot stick and tells Mom about Dad's visit to Logan's office—a meeting that has quickly become a treasured part of our family lore.

Logan, her face a little flushed from the wine, leans forward and puts her elbows on the table. On second thought, as I study her, she's more than a little tipsy. "Can I tell you a secret?" Mom and Maddie are rapt, and I'm worried because Logan never gets personal with people. Other than me, I guess. "They said I had to bring a date to the gala because the clients' wives would think I was trying to get in their husbands' pants."

Mom gasps. Maddie pulls a bag of candy out of her fanny pack and passes Logan a piece of licorice. "That's pretty fucking bad," Maddie says, patting Logan's hand. She gestures at me.

"Cal is coming to protect me," she says, and slaps the table. "Just gonna make sure I don't steal all those greasy rich men right out from their wives' noses. You know me!"

"Hey, Mom," I interrupt. "Can we maybe get some food into Logan here?"

Mom orders Liam to get the pan out of the oven and leans forward, gripping Logan's forearm. "Logan. Sweetheart. That is a Human Resources nightmare. People said these things to you at work? During work hours?"

Logan's face pales at Mom's mention of HR and she starts shaking her head rapidly. "It's not like that. I'm just new there is all. Finding my feet. I don't want to rock the boat..." Her voice drops off and Mom and Maddie move their chairs closer and start hugging her. Logan starts to cry.

I look at Liam, panicking. I have no idea what to do with a group of women crying. This is literally the first time something like this has happened in my life and I feel helpless. Liam shrugs and makes a "don't ask me" gesture and I roll my eyes at him, and clear my throat. "Hey, so, I'm going to be Logan's date for this thing and sniff it out. Plus Nicole is helping Lo-lo connect with some networking opportunities."

Mom starts shaking her head. "This type of behavior needs to be nipped in the bud."

"Hey," I say, patting my mom's arm. "If Logan's ready to make that move, we'll help her."

Logan blinks away her tears and just looks back and forth between all of us. Liam serves her a slice of frittata, acting like he heard of that food before today. Logan takes a bite and closes her eyes, saying, "You're all being very supportive. I'm sorry to ruin your dinner getting over-emotional."

"Nonsense!" Mom takes a swig of wine. "You didn't ruin a thing, darling."

"I really just want to get situated. This was a big move for me to a new city. I know I should be grateful for the job offer and the opportunity."

Maddie snorts. "Grateful? Please. They're the ones who should be grateful you're lending them your skills. I heard Mick talking about the investment package you set up for him."

"Really?" Logan and I say this at the same time and I'm glad to see she smiles, noticing that.

Maddie nods. "We were presenting him with the final version of the corporate history." She turns to Logan. "I'm writing a corporate history for Beltane. It's how I met Liam. Anyway, he was trying to deflect because praise makes him uncomfortable."

"Oh, it absolutely does not." Mom looks like she's going to smash her wine glass when Maddie says that, but Liam rests a hand on Mom's shoulder as Maddie keeps talking.

"He's pretty blustery but I think deep down he's very moved by what his colleagues all said about him. Even the people he's had to fire over the years said really respectful things about how he handled that."

None of us has anything to say in response to that little bomb Maddie dropped so I dive in to my dinner, wondering what to make of all of this. I'm relieved when Maddie and Mom pivot back to talking about the *Redcoat* book.

℔

Logan is quiet on the drive home after I told her to stop telling me she felt embarrassed for the things she said. "Seriously, Lo," I tell her. "Mom is on your side and you already knew Liam and Maddie were on Team Logan."

"But why," she asks. "Who am I to earn their advice and their loyalty like that?"

I shrug, even though it's dark and she can't see. "You're my friend," I tell her. "That makes you an honorary Brady."

More silence. But then, "I've never been on anyone's team before."

"Well, now you're stuck with us," I say, chuckling.

"As long as I don't fuck up too badly? Like crash one of their cars?"

"Ouch, Logan. What the hell?" I stare at her, shocked that she'd bring that up this way.

"I just feel like your family doesn't even know you and your dad have this rift. And you haven't even told them you hate your job. How can I let my guard down if their own blood relations aren't immune from being shunned..."

"I'm not being shunned, Logan. My dad's going to tell me I disappointed him and I'm going to feel like shit and I'm ultimately going to stop acting like an idiot. Hopefully." I shrug again. "Plus you'd never do anything that dumb. You're like Liam. His worst 'mistake' is making my parents into grandparents and they're both delirious with joy about it."

"Cal?"

She touches my arm again and I wonder if her skin will ever stop making mine sizzle like that. "What's up, Logan?"

"I'm nervous about this weekend."

"Just keep your eyes on me, doll. That's why I'm there, right?" I pat her leg and then yank my hand back to the steering wheel where it belongs. It's awfully complicated trying not to flirt. Like Logan, I wonder if I'll ever find my footing, as she calls it.

"Do you think you might want to go to HR like my mom suggested?" I swallow thickly as the question hangs in the air. I can practically feel Logan panicking at the question. "Hey," I tell her, hearing her breathing quicken. "Forget I said it. You don't have to do anything that makes you uncomfortable. I'll be by your side at the gala but I'd be at your side no matter what, okay?"

She nods, but the energy is different in the car. I crossed a line somehow and I don't know how to get us back on track. Things were easier when I didn't care what anyone thought.

CHAPTER SEVENTEEN
CAL

THE NEXT FEW DAYS HANGING OUT WITH LOGAN ARE SO CHILL THAT I ALMOST forget I promised to take her to her work party this weekend. We've been listening to our book. It's hard for me not to listen ahead when I'm out for a run or doing something with my family and Logan's not around, but I try to imagine how I'd feel if she listened without me.

Plus I love listening with her. We're always pausing and talking about the story. It's funny, the things she and I both notice and relate to. Most evenings, we sprawl out on the couch with popcorn and listen to a few chapters. Honestly, it's been really cool getting to know someone who hasn't been there for my entire life story. It'll be nice to hang out with her at this work thing.

Saturday morning, I meet up with my family for our usual long run. Nicole actually decided to come this time and she's all put out that I didn't bring Logan. "Callum, I was going to yell at her to come with me to the networking thing next week. She never did email me." Nicole points a finger into my chest like it was me who forgot to email.

"I don't really think she's much of a runner," I say, shrugging and bending to stretch. "Besides, she's going nuts getting ready for the gala thing tonight." Logan looked like she was going to cry when she told me a bitchy woman at work said something shitty about her hair. I think Logan's hair is beautiful. That's just objective fact. She was feeling self-conscious about it, though, so Logan was planning to go get all done up at one of the salons near our condo this morning. "I'm really hoping I don't punch anyone tonight," I say, before I remember that my family doesn't know I'm acting like Logan's boyfriend for work purposes.

"What's tonight? Can I punch someone?" Zack looks like he's in a black mood, and I start to wonder whether Nicole held firm to her promise of keeping her honeypot to herself.

I shrug as we start running through Frick Park. It seems like all the tadpoles born this spring have become super loud frogs overnight, and for a while we're surrounded by the sound of our sneakers on the path and a bunch of croaking amphibians. It's sort of nice, especially considering we're still inside the city.

"Hello? Cal? What's tonight?" Liam and Zack flank me while Nicole and Orla move on ahead. I can hear them talking about the Redcoat book, and I wish I could ditch my brothers and join that conversation instead.

"Ah, Logan's co-workers are a bunch of assholes," I tell them. Liam knows, of course, after that whole emotional dinner fiasco with Mom. I guess he and Maddie didn't talk about it with Zack and Nicole. "I'm going to her party with her. Free food and all that." I try to play it off like it's no big deal and am surprised when Zack nods.

"Oh, right, Dad told me about that."

"Dad?"

Zack looks over his shoulder, like he's checking for his girlfriend. "Yeah," he says. "You know, Dad went and opened an investment account with Logan. For the baby."

I knew second-hand that Dad opened an account with Logan, but it hadn't occurred to me that he shelled out enough to get invited to the gala event. I know Dad has been doing okay the past few years, especially since my brothers have opened up new income streams for Beltane. "Did you know Dad was swanky-schmooze-invites rich? He has that much money to toss around?"

Liam nods. "He won't tell me how much, but he did agree that the people from Logan's work are a pack of assholes. Hey, you think you'll be sitting with Dad?"

Shit, I hope not. It won't be easy to play the part of Logan's boyfriend with my dad interrupting me all the time to ask questions about hygiene or herbal supplements or whatever weird interest he's got right now. If he decides he's speaking to me tonight. He probably will, because people will be looking. I laugh at my brother's comment and the path starts heading uphill, so none of us are really talking anymore as we focus on our breath.

I figure it's better this way. I don't want to say anything else that will tangle my responsibilities. I wish Logan had told me my dad was invited to the fancy party. I probably also should have remembered to have my suit dry cleaned.

By the time I get home, it's way too late for that option, but I borrow Logan's iron while she's still out at the salon, and I think everything turns out ok. I decide I'd better not put the suit on to eat lunch in case I spill something, so I'm sitting in the living room in my boxers, post-shower, eating tacos from across the street, when Logan bursts into the apartment.

I almost drop the delicious meat on my chest when I see her. The stylist did something to make her hair bouncy, and I can tell she's got makeup on, even though she doesn't look fake. She just looks...fancy. "You look really elegant," I tell her, nodding and licking taco sauce off my fingers while she peels off some sort of foam shoe. "What's all that?"

She grins. "I got my nails done," she says. "They give you these foam flip flops so you don't mess anything up walking to your car. Of course, they weren't expecting me to be walking home a few blocks...but they still look ok!"

Logan extends her leg, pointing her toes and wiggling them all around and I've never really been a foot man, per se, but hot damn, she looks sexy right now in her shorts with those dark purple toes and nails. And the fancy hair. Damn. "They look awesome," I tell her, standing up from the couch and then sitting back down immediately when I remember that I'm only wearing boxers and the toe action has caused a little stretch and lift down below.

She bites her lip and studies the fridge, settling on a cup of yogurt and a banana from the counter. "I'm starving, but I don't want to smear all my makeup," she says, daintily licking her spoon and biting the fruit. My crotch situation is not improving as I watch all this happen.

I clear my throat. "I had the same concern about getting food on my suit," I tell her, gesturing to my semi-naked couch outfit. I grab a throw pillow from the corner of the couch and toss it on my lap, leaning forward on my elbows. "What time do we have to leave?"

"Five," she says around a mouth full of banana. "I'm going to finish getting ready, okay?" And she's off down the hall before I can respond. Shit, since when does the sight of Logan send me to half mast? Check that. Full mast. Gah. I guess that sort of thing is inevitable when you live with a chick and you're also attracted to chicks. I should stop saying chick. Orla is always on me about that.

Eventually, I make my way to my room and into my suit. I know I told Logan I'd dress the part for a fancy-people party, but I just don't have it in me to wear stuffy dress shoes. That's Liam's thing. I tug on my dark green tie and smile down at my brand new, matching Chucks. I know Logan's wearing green tonight, so we'll match. Sort of like prom, I guess.

I'm in the middle of wondering whether she went to prom and whether her date tried to match her dress when she backs down the hall half naked. "Hey, Cal, can you help me?"

I freeze in my tracks, just staring at her skin on display. She's not wearing a bra and the smooth expanse of her back moves as she breathes. Logan has her salon curls swept up with one hand while she tries to hold the pieces of her dress together with the other. I say nothing, trying to move my eyes toward the ceiling so I don't look down the dress in search of her ass.

"I can't reach the zipper," she says, wiggling the fabric around in her left hand, still not looking at me.

I make a grunting noise, because that's all I'm capable of right now, and swallow, reaching for the dress. The shiny fabric is silky smooth as I root around in search of the zipper. I find it, somewhere in the middle of her ass, and my fingers linger as I tug the zipper into place. *Fuck, this is hot,* I think, fumbling around for the hook at the top.

I put one hand on Logan's shoulder and pop the hook into place, noticing that the dress forms sort of an X in the back. It's elegant and shim-mery and clings to curves I hadn't noticed before today, not like this. I start to wonder what she tastes like under all that hair, with her big brain and excellent hygiene. And then I have to know. I have to taste her like I have to breathe. Before I can control myself, I lean forward and kiss the nape of her neck, where she's holding her hair out of the way.

She drops her hair with a little gasp, spinning around in my arms, which I don't retract. When she meets my eyes, she looks frightened and I feel like shit. "I'm so sorry," I whisper. I shake my head and reach for her hand. "Forgive me, Logan. You just looked so...pretty."

Her mouth forms an "o" and she blushes, looking even more beautiful. And then she smiles and I feel like the sun is shining down on me. We stand there in the hall, staring at each other, all dressed up. Eventually, Logan says, "Thank you, Cal. You look amazing, too." Her smile shifts and she squeezes my hand back, before dropping it. "Let me grab my bag and we can call for a ride. You ready?"

"Yep," I say, even though I'm thinking I have no idea what I'm doing. Not one bit.

CHAPTER EIGHTEEN
LOGAN

CAL TAKES MY HAND AS WE WALK INTO THE GRAND ENTRANCE OF THE UNION Station building. My breath catches when I realize how much I enjoy holding his hand. I'm still a little shaken by his kiss at the condo, not because I didn't like it, but because of how much I did. I can still feel the whisper of his touch on my neck, like his lips branded my skin.

I look up at his face, trying to make sense of the joy I feel at the idea of him branding me. Claiming me as his. Cal gestures up at the arched bricks and beautiful glass of the building. "Can you imagine getting off a train here? So cool, right?" All I can do is nod, feeling dwarfed by the grandeur of it all.

Cal pats one of the brick columns. "My uncle and brothers would have a field day if they were here. They'd want you to understand, structurally, everything that makes this place special."

I look up at him, confused. "But you don't want to do that?"

He shrugs. "You know, buildings don't do it for me, Lo-lo. I'd rather tell you all about an engine." He tugs me through the entrance, where the restored, original benches are still placed around. The elegant train station is now a tower of high-end condos, but the ground floor is used for events. I feel out of place, like I've got a third-class ticket sneaking into the first-class lounge.

I watch as my colleagues see me arrive and then turn back to their drinks and conversation partners. That's fine. I wasn't expecting a warm welcome here. But...it does sting. It's such a contrast to the way the Brady family, for instance, has welcomed me. Steadfast at my side, Cal leans in to ask me, "When can I meet the Beagle guy?"

I blink at him. I had totally forgotten about that. Then I feel bad, because he's talked so much about wanting to "talk tires" with the founder of that company. I know it's a big deal that Cal confided in me that he's been unhappy at work, that he wants to try something different and longs to work someplace like Beagle A.I. I've been so selfish, bogarting conversation about my own work situation instead of helping him get ready to dazzle Pete Harris. I nod and bite my lip. Cal raises a brow and gestures his head toward the bar.

"Let's get us some fancy drinks and then you can go insert yourself in the conversation." He smacks my butt when I don't move and I'm so surprised that I burst out laughing. Loudly. People turn and stare, of course.

I flush and Cal just grins, steering me toward the bar with his arm around my waist. I realize how much I like the feel of that. He's so warm and confident. It does interesting things to my body to feel his touch, and I notice that a lot of the women here are staring at us. We get in line for drinks and I study Cal's appearance. He looks amazing, actually. His unruly hair is combed and he must have some product in it because it stays put, the gentle waves framing his face without looking sloppy.

His suit fits him really well and even though he's wearing his standard sneakers, the look works for him. Even in a room full of wealthy, refined people, Cal seems comfortable and at home wearing sneakers with a suit. I can barely breathe I'm so anxious about tripping on my dress. Cal starts to circle his thumb along my hip where his arm snakes around my waist and one of the women serving appetizers on a tray gives me a tight-lipped glower. Well, that's par for the course for me. I'm used to getting the stink-eye. Not typically from service industry professionals, though.

"Lo?" I realize Cal has been talking to me and I bite my lip again. "What do you want to drink, sweets?"

I make a face. I don't like being called those kinds of pet names even though I don't really think Cal means anything patronizing by it. Too many diner customers used to take liberties and call me that and try and touch me. I realize people are waiting in line behind us, probably staring at the dumb girl who's holding up the line. "Whatever you're having," I blurt, remembering that Cal always seems to know what tastes good. He arches a brow at me as the bartender slides two tumblers of liquor toward us. Cal drops some cash in the tip jar and I feel bad that he's doing me the favor of being my date, and yet he's the one paying for the tips.

"I'll get the tip next time," I tell him, quickly grabbing the glass and moving it toward my mouth.

"Woah, woah, Lo-lo," he says, putting a hand on my wrist to stop me knocking back the shot. "This is a fine Irish whiskey, girlfriend. We sip and savor."

"Good save, son." A hand claps onto my shoulder and I look up to see Mick Brady standing between us, an arm around each of us. "Glad to see I've taught you at least one important thing in this world."

"Hey, Dad," Cal says, gesturing toward his dad with his glass. "You probably taught me a few things."

"Well," Mick says, "Whiskey is the most important part at a shindig like this anyway." Mick nods at his son, pulls his arms from around us and rubs his palms together. "Tell me who's here. Who do I know?"

Cal just shrugs. I can tell he's uncomfortable being here with his father, and also being here with me playing pretend. Mick doesn't seem to notice anything amiss, though, and I'm glad Cal and I have established friendly rapport with his family. I decide to give Mick an overview of the room. "We've got the Stanton family over by the fondue," I tell him, and then I squint as I study the space, looking past my colleagues and trying to identify our clients. "Oh, and the Kellys are here. Do you know them? Their law offices are near Beltane."

"Old Kelly and I go way back," Mick says, nodding. He glances around. "Tell me, Logan-the-girl...is it okay to call you that? That's how Cal first mentioned you." I don't get a chance to answer as he rushes on. "You got anyone here from any public utilities? Did Cal tell you that's our focus these days?"

I shrug. "He didn't mention it. I'm not really sure where people work unless they're on my client list," I tell him. "I could probably ask around for you, if you want?"

Mick waves a hand and takes his son's whiskey from him. "No need. I'm going to mingle. See what I can drum up." And he's gone before either of us can say another word.

"That seemed like an okay interaction with your dad," I say, looking over Cal's shoulder and watching as Mick sidles up to a pair of older men who seem delighted to see him. "He seems to know everyone."

Cal puts his hands in his pockets and looks upset. "He does know everyone," he says. Then he shakes his head. There's a strange silence between us until he gestures toward my drink. "So first, you want to smell the whiskey. Go on."

I give it a sniff. It smells warm, somehow, and sharp. But not unpleasant like the fireball the guys handed me at the bar the other weeks. "Open your lips a bit while you sniff it," Cal says, stepping closer to me and watching. My mouth falls open as I inhale, the scent mixing with his aftershave and making me feel a little woozy, if I'm honest.

"Now sip it slowly," Cal says, nodding. His eyes have gone intense, deeply brown so they're nearly black as he watches my mouth. I've never had someone study me as I eat or drink before and I'm self conscious, worried I'll cough and sputter like I did at the bar. "Hold it on your tongue and let it spread through your mouth," he says, his voice low and deep. I can see a vein moving in his neck above his collar and I like watching it, like seeing him swallow. I don't feel like I'm pretending with Cal right now. But I also don't know how to describe whatever this is. I tip the glass into my mouth and my eyes flare at the feel of the alcohol. It tingles a bit, but doesn't burn.

"Breathe through your nose." I do as he asks, sensing that he wants to reach out and touch me, and wishing, strangely, that he would. I remind myself that his father is here. And this is a professional function. I swallow the whiskey. "Tell me what you taste," he says, his face so close to mine. So close.

"It's smooth," I whisper. "And warm." My breath is coming so fast, I feel like I just worked a rush hour shift at the diner. I'm surrounded by Cal, by his scent, by his arm on mine. The warmth of the drink is spreading through me now, but it's not unpleasant. I don't feel afraid of these feelings like I did in the parking garage that time. Ever since Cal kissed my neck, I've been...craving him. Cal shifts closer to me as I raise the glass again to take another sip.

"Logan! There you are!" I'm startled by the voice of Mr. Dolan, one of my favorite clients.

"Jim! How nice to see you." I smile and raise my glass toward him. "I'm so glad you could make it tonight."

"Wouldn't miss a chance to hang out with you, my dear. Say, who's this fella?"

Cal grins and extends his hand for a shake, and I'm conflicted, because I already miss the feel of his big hand on my arm. "Cal Brady," he says. Then he winks. "I also wouldn't miss a chance to hang out with Logan."

"I've been following those companies you mentioned," Jim says, nodding at me and scratching his chin. "I feel like you've got a sixth sense about investments. My portfolio is way up from last year!"

"I just do what the algorithms tell me," I tell him, smiling into my drink. It's somehow less delicious without Cal's hot gaze on my lips.

"Don't sell yourself short, Logan," he says, just as another client wanders over.

"I wanted to say hello before there was a line," she says, her laugh tinkling over the sound of the live band playing jazzy music. Mary Emerson is extraordinarily wealthy and hers is the largest account I've been given in my short time with the firm.

"I'd always make time for you," I say. I extend my arm thinking she will shake my hand, but Mary pulls me in for a hug.

She turns to Jim and says, "I just doubled my investments with Logan after I saw my latest dividends statement. I spoke with my brother in New York and he's thinking of stopping in for some financial advice, too. Logan is magical when it comes to these things."

"That's what I was just saying!" The two of them start chatting about how pleased they are that I'm looking after their financial future and I allow myself a small moment to feel proud that I've made such an impact on each of them. It feels good, especially when they talk about scholarship funds they're setting up with some of their earnings. I like knowing that someone will be able to go to college who wouldn't have been able to otherwise, like me.

"They love you, Lo-lo." Cal's breath on my ear makes me shiver and I glance up to see yet another version of his smile. This one is joyful and sultry all at once somehow and I think the whiskey might be getting to me, because his expression no longer seems friendly. It seems like he's interested in something more seductive.

I'm torn between leaning into his touch, because I crave it, and not doing that because Cal's father is here. Just then, I spy James over Cal's shoulder, talking to a group of people. "Hey," I say, nodding toward James. "You should go talk to your Beagle guy."

Cal grins, pure friendly this time. He runs his hands through his hair and smooths out his suit. "Gah. This is exciting. Do I look okay?"

I laugh. "You look fantastic." And then I suck in a breath when he plants a kiss on my cheek, an echo of his kiss a few hours before. I watch as he makes his way over toward my colleague until Mary squeals.

"Logan! What a delightful young man you've found," she says. I flush, remembering that of course Cal is putting on a show because he agreed to.

"Thank you, Mary. He is."I don't meet her eye as I watch his face come to life meeting James's client. This must be the engineer Cal had been gushing about because he's gesturing with his hands, grinning widely. And then he catches my eye from across the room and winks again. Mary seems like she's going to swoon.

"I can practically feel the passion between you," she says, and I should feel relieved by Cal's acting ability. He's obviously done his part being convincing. Because the company wanted me to seem like someone in a stable relationship to convey confidence to our clientele. Surely that's what Marie meant to say when she allowed my co-workers to belittle me and talk about my personal life during a meeting.

I think back to a time I had been selected to go on a trip to meet some lawmakers in high school. The other kids chosen were popular, and none too kind when they realized I was getting my ticket and my professional outfit paid for from a special fund at school. I made the mistake of telling my mother how mean they were to me, the things they whispered about my crooked teeth and discount-store suit. "You get what you get, and you don't get upset," my mother hissed as she handed me bus fare so I could get to school early enough for the field trip departure. I think about the impact of that lesson—that I should feel gratitude for whatever I'm given and look the other way if people act like...well, like they act at my current work.

My entire life, I've been taught not to get upset. Not to make a scene. Not to acknowledge my feelings and to just be grateful. And now that I've realized how wrong that is, it's like I can't put back the veil. I look around this room and the only thing in it that makes me feel good is Cal.

Suddenly I don't want to be here anymore. I don't want to be here with Cal under false pretenses and play into the hands of people who would suggest my behavior toward my clients is anything but professional. I don't want to contribute to Cal's rift with his father.

I watch as Cal reaches into his suit jacket and hands his card to a man I assume is Pete Harris. The look on Cal's face conveys total sincerity, hopefulness. I stiffen and sigh. I've come this far. I can help Cal get something he wants. I turn back to my clients and smile.

CHAPTER NINETEEN
CAL

"Seriously, man, it's great to meet you." I know I sound like a fanboy, but fuck it. I definitely am. "I can't believe we never ran into each other at school." Turns out Pete Harris and I were in college at the same time, although he was a year ahead of me. It was a small enough engineering program. I must have been too blinded by partying to notice the people around me.

This guy founded a multi-million dollar artificial intelligence empire while I what? Fucked the servers at my favorite sandwich shops for nine years and did whatever grunt work my family sent my way. This guy took initiative.

Pete and I drift away from Logan's asshole co-workers to grab another drink for him and an actual drink for me, since my dad took mine. "I really wasn't going to come tonight," he says, rolling his eyes. "Bunch of rich folks gushing about how their financial advisors are making them richer."

"Good networking opportunity for Beagle, though, right?"

He grins. "Why? You know someone looking to invest?" I'm about to laugh and remind him that I am hardly in a position to talk with rich folks about their money, when I see James and his date sliding toward us. Pete groans. "Ah, crap, they found me again."

"Yeah, that guy definitely sucks," I agree, glaring daggers at James as he approaches us with a fake smile on his face.

"Calvin, right? Great to see you again. Where's Logan?"

"It's Cal, and she's with her admirers." I smile, noticing how Logan is swarmed by satisfied clients, who seem to be pulling in other party guests to gush over her big ass brain and the ways she applies it to their finances.

"She? A girl named *Logan?* That's so weird." James's date wrinkles her nose as James snickers.

My eyes snap over to her. "My name is Callum Eamonn," I say. "Is that weird, too?" She laughs again, thinking I made a joke I guess. But I don't smile and her face shifts.

I set my glass down on the table and turn toward Peter. "I've got to go rescue my girl from the masses," I tell him, jerking my head over toward Logan. I reach into my pocket for the single business card I printed for just this occasion. I didn't want to give him anything branded with Beltane in case my father got word that I'm having this conversation.

I look down at the neat black letters of my name, my professional certifications and my email. I remember how much harder it was for me to pass my professional engineering exams than it was for my brothers and Orla. I never use the P.E. in my email signature or anything at work. It's a bit of a sore spot, actually, because my dad didn't want the company to foot the bill for me to sit the exam. Uncle Kellen had to remind my father that it looks good for Beltane to have a deep roster of engineers with professional credentials.

Neither of them made the arguments that I should be able to take the exam for my own career development, of course. And, if I'm being honest with myself, I haven't done anything to make good on that investment for them. I sigh and push those thoughts right back down as I slide the card to Pete. "Hit me up sometime," I tell him. "I'd love to hear more about those fuel sensors."

Pete takes the card as James frowns warily. "I'll do that," Pete says, sticking my card in his jacket pocket. That makes me feel better than if he'd put it in his pants pocket, for some reason. Seems more serious. "Good luck with your Bronco," Pete says, shaking my hand. The fact that he remembers which model car I drive tells me he was definitely into our conversation earlier.

I was totally geeking out, telling him how long I've been working to refurbish the fuel lines in my ancient Big Red. I try not to dwell on how amazing it would be to sink my fists into a similar project with an autonomous vehicle.

Feeling high on the encounter with Pete, I slide back over to Logan, whose cheeks are rosy and who seems uncomfortable from the past hour of praise she's been having to "endure." As I walk toward her, I notice a whole bunch of tightly pursed lips from other folks from Logan's company. I can't believe they're all actually this petty, giving Logan this much shit because she's obviously really fucking good at her job.

My dad's always talking about how some people surround themselves with people who challenge them and other people are so desperate to cling to their piece of the pie, they shove down others around them. Logan has landed at a company that's trying to hold her head beneath the water.

She absolutely shines because she's totally genuine and the clients can all tell. I'm sure they can also tell the rest of these finance folks are miserable.

I've had just about enough alcohol to speak up about it, but then I hear my dad. "This is the gal I was telling you about, Rudy. She lives with my boy Cal. Remember my middle son?"

Dad sidles up to me with a guy his age at his side. He looks familiar but I can't place him. "Denny Rudy," he says, shaking my hand. There's a bit of a hush at the mention of his name, and the people surrounding Logan all fizzle out of their conversations as they turn to look at the man pumping my hand. "You look just like your old man did at your age, Cal," he says, then he points to my dad. "I always was telling him to get a haircut."

Dad laughs and runs a hand along his thinning, short hair. It's gone completely white in recent years and the look is pretty good on him. I'm glad he didn't dye it like he always said he was going to. Dad looks at Logan. "Have you met Denny yet? I know he said he just signed on with you guys."

Logan pales a little and shakes her head. Then takes a big breath. "So good to meet you, Mr. Rudy. I don't think Mr. Alexander has finalized the team for your portfolio yet."

"Mr. Rudy was my father," he says, holding his drink toward her in a toast. "Please, call me Denny. Micky here was just telling me you're a genius."

"Oh, she absolutely is." The woman who had been gushing over Logan earlier chimes in, and the crowd that had been yakking her ear off all starts murmuring in agreement.

Dad perks up. "Rudy, I've got Logan here taking care of my grandson's future. Did I tell you I'm gonna be a grand-pop?"

"You already? Which kid is it?" Denny looks at me and I start shaking my head.

"My brother Liam," I say. "Sometime next spring."

Denny starts pulling up pictures of his own grandkids on his phone and showing them around to Dad and the other people nearby. I lean in to Logan. "They're drawn to you like moths to a flame, Lo."

Logan waves her hand at me like she's trying to shoo me away, but I just step closer to her. "Seriously. You're the main event tonight. Hands down."

She looks down at her drink and nods. "Is anyone from the office looking? I'm really trying not to make waves."

I take a look around the room, and basically everyone in here is staring at Logan, my dad and Denny. Logan's co-workers from the bar are all staring major daggers at her and I remember that they're all vying to be the account managers for the Rudy family. It all clicks together and I remember that this guy owns the Iron Men, a professional football team in a city where football is church.

I know Beltane keeps a set of season tickets my dad and uncle use when they're trying to woo new clients or impress existing ones. Or, I guess, trying to buy off boat repair guys. I somehow forgot my dad is apparently besties with the team owner.

I try to distract Logan and ask, "Hey, Dad, how do you and Denny know each other anyway?"

Denny throws his head back, laughing. "What was it, Mick? Thirty years ago? He was being a loud mouth during the mayoral race." My dad cracks a grin.

"There were some issues with the tax structure for small businesses then," Dad says. He shrugs. "We were just starting out and I favored the candidate who was easy on the wallet, taxwise. I met Denny here at the victory party after the election."

Denny tosses an arm around Dad's shoulder and tells the crowd how Mick Brady has always known how to have fun, so he asked Dad to come along when the Iron Men had an exhibition game in Japan. *Always knows how to have fun.* The words sink in deep. The exact same words people say about me, paired with *never knows how to be serious.*

Christ, I'm turning into my father. What am I? Two years away from two baby mamas like him? I stare at my dad while everyone keeps talking, remembering that much like Pete Harris, my dad is the ultimate entrepreneur. He and my uncle were younger than me when they started Beltane. Denny shrugs and keeps talking about taking my dad to Japan. "We wanted community and business leaders to go with us on the trip and sell Pittsburgh as a good place for Japanese companies to do business."

Denny gestures at me with his drink. "Your dad was in charge of making sure everyone had a good time even if they didn't speak the same language."

"I did a damn fine job of it, too," Dad says and Denny laughs again.

"At one point, Mick was up in the cockpit flying the plane," Denny says. "And before you ask, no. He absolutely does not have a pilot's license."

"You were flying the plane?" Logan is riveted, and looks horrified at the thought of my dad taking the controls. This story just sounds like par for the course for my dad. Him shooting the shit, silently observing everyone. I'm sure he left the experience with a million new contracts for Beltane, solving problems people revealed on the sly when they thought they were all just talking about sushi. When I take the controls, I just crash into trees.

"Mick Brady works his way into doing things most people wouldn't even think to ask about," Denny says. "But damn it, the man knows how to build lasting relationships."

"Aw, shucks, Denny." Dad nudges his shoulder. "You're just trying to butter me up so I go easy on you on the back nine."

I'm desperate to get away from this. Once they pivot to golf, I know they'll be here for hours, so I lean in to ask Logan if she needs another drink. She nods, and I go grab us something lighter since I feel like I already had too much whiskey. I'm heading back with a pair of highballs, extra soda, when I see some douchy guy talking to Logan.

He's young and looks mean, so he must be a coworker and not a client. She bites her lip and looks like she's in agony. She's mentioned a few times that she's always expecting people to be pranking her, pretending they want to do something social with her and setting her up to look like a fool when she says yes. I'm sure these fuckers are pissed off that she's getting so much attention from the white whale client, especially since her office seems like they're more interested in brown-nosing than putting the best person on the job.

"Hey, Lo-lo," I say, stepping between her and the douche.

"Can it wait? I was just asking Ms. Miller here for her secrets." He winks at me dismissively and I ball my hand into a fist at my side.

I set the drinks on a high table nearby and reach for Logan's hand. "Sorry, dude. Logan saves all her secrets for me." I wink right back at him and he glowers. Who even knows what he was about to say to her if he got her alone. I give Logan's ass a squeeze and I see my dad notice and give me a strange look. I don't really care right now that my dad and his golf buddies are here to witness me getting hot for my roommate.

If I wasn't already half-stiff at the sight of her in that damn dress with no bra, I'm definitely rest of the way there seeing how every client she works with seems to idolize her. Competence porn, I think the phrase is. I'm watching it, and Logan's the star of my fantasies right now. *Never thinks about the consequences. Acts before he thinks.* I know I'm traveling a dangerous road with Logan. I've known it since the day I moved in and I guess what they all say is true. But I don't care. I have to touch her right now. Have to.

"Come on, Lo," I say, pulling her toward the dance floor in the middle of the space. Hardly anyone is out there. A few older couples reliving their youth as the band plays some jazz.

"Nice to have met you, Denny," Logan says as I take her away.

"You kids have fun," he says, already turning back toward the crowd of suits. I'm amped up on adrenaline from meeting Pete Harris, rattled about meeting my dad's friend, and I've had just enough whiskey that I'm not thinking too hard about the ramifications of pulling Logan tight against me while we start to dance.

Her eyes go wide as I tug her in close and spin her slowly around the room. "You smell nice," I tell her, in the most inadequate possible response to the fully intoxicating aroma of her. She smells like whiskey and mint and I can tell she dabbed on some sort of perfume because I inhale something musky right near her ear. It doesn't feel wrong. It feels incredibly right, actually, to be holding her. Thrilling and sexy and perfect.

Logan rests her cheek on my shoulder as we move, her fingers clasped tight in my left hand and I remember again that she's not wearing a bra. I concentrate until I can feel her nipples pebbled against me through my dress shirt. With the hand around her waist, I squeeze her a little tighter against me, wanting her to feel how hard I am right now. When she gasps, I know she's figured it out and she looks up at me, her face full of questions.

"Do you want to get out of here, Lo?" I need her to say yes. I need to take her back to our place and fuck her and get it over with, because we're done pretending to be together after tonight. At the moment, I don't care if she makes me move out tomorrow, if I have to go stay with my dad or my uncle or sleep in my car. I just need to do something with all this energy I feel when I look at her or think about her or, Christ, feel her luscious ass with my finger tips as we dance.

"Yes," she says, and a wave of heat and relief rolls through me. I don't hesitate for a second. I barrel toward the door, pulling her along without a glance back.

CHAPTER TWENTY
LOGAN

 presses me up against a brick column, his chest heaving as he breathes. I don't know how to describe the look in his eyes, except he seems like he's starving, and I'm what he wants to eat.

"Do you know how sexy you are, Logan?" He brings a hand up and strokes my face and his touch sends sparks shooting through my body. I shiver and lick my lips. "Oh, Logan," he says, more of a growl.

A car pulls up and he looks as it slows to a stop. He opens the back door for me and I slide across, then yelp when I realize he's slid in right up against me, not even saying hello to the driver. "Cal," I hiss. "You have to wear a seatbelt."

He wriggles beside me and finds the center seatbelt, clicking it into place and leaving his hand between us, fingers rubbing at my upper thigh. He slowly manages to bunch up the material of my dress and reaches across with his other hand to slide a palm up my leg. "This dress is killing me, Logan." Cal's voice is deep and smooth as the whiskey he gave me earlier, and makes me feel just as warm inside.

I'm still shocked that he seems to be on the same wavelength as me. That he is attracted to me the way that I've figured out I am definitely attracted to him.

"What happens if we do this," I ask him, biting my lip, clutching the arm rest on the door on my side of the car, afraid that if I touch him I won't be able to stop. Terrified he will look at me and laugh, asking what I mean by 'this.'

Cal shrugs. "We figure it out," he says. "All I know is I can't go another second without tasting you." The words are barely out of his mouth before his lips crash against mine. His jaw moves slowly and he moans into my mouth. I feel like my skin is on fire, like a lump in my throat has exploded and the energy of that is radiating through my body into Cal's. I press my lips back against his, curious about the sensations this is building in my body. I feel my heart racing, even faster when he slips his tongue inside my mouth.

I gasp at the feel of it, wet and hot, exploring. He isn't just tasting me right now. He's claiming me with his mouth, moving in to the space of my body. And I like it. I like it so much I forget to worry about the driver seeing us. I forget to worry about what it might mean to let go of control in this situation. I pick up the hand I had fisted in my lap and squeeze Cal's leg, loving the feel of him beneath my fingers.

He moans again, and I love thinking I produced that sound by touching him. I'm startled when the car slows to a stop and the driver clears his throat. Cal pulls back and grins, a megawatt smile that leaves me as breathless as his kiss. "Sorry about all that, man," Cal says, slapping some cash in the driver's hand before he backs out of the car and leans in to reach for me. "I'm actually not sorry."

I stumble out after him, tripping and wobbling in my heels as he gives up on the elevator and pulls me up the stairs, through the door of our condo at last. "Cal," I breathe, feeling the world turn upside down as he scoops me off my feet and plunks me on the counter.

"I wasn't done tasting you," he says, peeling out of his suit coat and loosening his tie. I liked how he looked in the suit, but I love seeing him now, disheveled and glassy-eyed, standing between my legs. It doesn't feel forbidden or even like a bad idea. It just feels necessary.

"Oh," I say. "Oh. Yes, Cal." He starts licking my throat and I clutch his shoulders, groaning when I feel his teeth nipping at my skin.

"Take off that dress, Logan," he says.

"I...can't. I needed you to help with the zipper before, remember?" I lean back, gripping the edge of the counter with one hand and trying to twist my arm behind my back.

"Fuck it," he growls and tosses my skirt up around my waist. Cal drops to his knees on the floor and looks up at me, his nostrils flaring.

"What are you doing?"

He grabs my legs and drapes them over his shoulders. "Raise your hips," he says, and I do, gripping the edge of the counter again and then yelping when he yanks my panties down. He runs his hands along one leg, pulling my ankle out of the black panties I bought just for this party. My only fancy pair. Not caring about the panties around the other ankle, he starts kissing my inner thighs.

"Oh," I moan, realizing his intentions as he licks higher and higher, alternating sides as his fingers creep closer and closer to my center. "Cal," I say. "Nobody has ever…"

"Oh, I know, Lo-lo." He growls into my crotch and then I feel his long fingers make contact. He touches me so lightly. It drives me mad. I want more, more friction, more everything. I'm on the edge of something and I'm going to burst out of my skin if he doesn't help me get there.

"I want…" I have no idea what I want. I'm transformed into a writhing ball of need as he teases me and I don't know what I need, except that I need it desperately.

"Tell me," he says, stroking me. "Tell me what you want, Logan."

My head falls back as he rubs and a finger slides inside me. That, I realize, is what I want. Exactly that. "Oh, I want…inside me…please, Callum. Please."

"You don't need to beg, Logan." He slides a finger deep inside and I think he adds another as he presses a kiss to my stomach. "You're so fucking wet," he says. "You feel so good. You're gonna come so hard on my tongue, aren't you?"

I don't answer, and he doesn't wait. He keeps his fingers pumping inside me and I shriek when I feel the warm, flat glide of his tongue licking my center. "Oh yes, do that," I groan, my hips jerking up off the counter. Everything he's doing is new. The other guys I was with were so timid, but Cal is confident in his movements. And god, he should be confident. He takes me up to the point of pleasure I've manage to build on my own with my fingers in the past. But unlike my frustrating solo sessions, there's just *more*. Somehow there's a new level of good feelings, and Cal propels me up toward it. At first I feel afraid I'm going to tip off into nothingness and I squeeze my legs against him.

"I've got you, Logan," he murmurs. I raise my head again and look down, seeing him with his face between my legs, his eyes closed and his face relaxed in pleasure. He seems to be enjoying this as much as me. "You taste amazing," he mutters, lapping at me like an ice cream cone. When he twists his hand and crooks a finger inside me as he licks, I feel a flood of something release within me. He chuckles, pleased. "Oh, yeah, Logan. Let me have that honey."

My eyes widen in shock, and then roll back in my head from the feelings I'm experiencing, starting in my core and spreading through ever cell of my body. He pulls his hand out and I whimper, lifting my head again just in time to see him diving inside me with his tongue, licking and sucking and groaning in pleasure as I feel something new building in my core. "Oh, oh, oh." I'm not in control of my words any longer. My body just produces sounds that pour out of me as I churn my hips against Cal.

"That's it, baby. Ride my tongue." Cal adjusts his position and nudges at me with his nose. "Come for me, Logan. Let me feel you come on my face and I'll feed this hungry pussy my cock."

"Oh my god," I shout, feeling each of his dirty words rock through me. I realize I want everything he has just described, and had no idea I would ever want such things. But now I'm desperate for it. He keeps telling me to come and I don't know how to do as he asks, don't know what to do other than be here experiencing the way he seems to know how to activate my nerves. Never have I felt cherished like this, wanted like this. Known in this way.

I need..."Press harder," I shout to him, letting go of the counter with one hand to press against my body, just above where he's teasing. My fingers swirl greedily as I search for pleasure. I rarely do this. Sometimes I wake up from a lucid dream, finding my hand down my pants in bed as I wriggle around chasing a sensation I can't identify. But it never seems to pan out.

I'm feeling it now, but bigger and it starts to spiral as I rub myself. For the first time, I'm taking what I want. I'm shouting and groaning and god! It feels so good. Suddenly, I feel Cal's hand on mine. "Show me," he says, continuing to bite and kiss and suck at my center as he adds the pressure with his thumb. "Show me what you need."

Nodding, I press his thumb hard against my body and arch my back. He digs in harder, just like I need, and I bend until I feel like I might snap. Panting, shrieking, kicking, I come apart as Cal licks and bites at my skin. My body crumbles to bits, blown around by the hurricane of my firing nerves. I gasp and writhe and experience a blinding, perfect stillness behind the greatest pleasure I've ever known. The tingling waves subside and I come back into my body just in time for waves of embarrassment to crash into me instead. What the hell was I just doing? With my roommate?

"Logan," he says, standing up and leaning over me on the counter. "That was sexy as fuck."

CHAPTER TWENTY-ONE
CAL

I'm not waiting a second longer to dive into Logan Miller cock-first. She doesn't seem capable of walking, so I scoop her up off the counter and carry her down the hall to my room while she sort of sags in my arms.

"I don't know why I was spasming like that," she says, hiding her face in my shirt. "I'm so embarrassed!"

I plunk her on the bed and leap on top of her. "Logan," I scold. "Do not ever be embarrassed about that. Are you fucking kidding me? You came so hard on my face that I could feel it in my dick."

She looks up at me, her brown eyes wide and searching, confused. "I don't know what that was," she says. "Nothing like that has ever happened to me before."

I start pulling off my belt and stripping out of my clothes. "That's because nobody has ever fucked you properly," I tell her. And then I remember our conversation in the car when we first started listening to those audiobooks. "I told you I'd make it good for you."

Her cheeks turn red and she watches as I peel off my suit pants. "Take your dress off, Lo." I palm my cock through my boxers as she does what I ask. My roommate has been hiding a hot little body behind all her boxy suits and smooth ponytails. Now, though, she's spread out on my bed with her hair all wild and her skin glowing from a bangin' orgasm.

I kneel above her, admiring, until she starts to squirm. "Cal," she breathes.

"Go on and touch me, Logan. I want you to." She nods and reaches for me, her hands running along my chest, nails parting the hair on my pecs as she traces her way down.

"You feel so firm," she whispers.

I dip my mouth to suck her nipple into my mouth, groaning. "Mmm and you feel so soft," I tell her, settling between her legs and smiling when she wraps them around me. "We feel really good together, Lo."

She sighs as I play with her nipples, pinching and sucking, cupping her tits in my hands while I hold myself up on my forearms. Her eyes fly open when I bite down on one dark peak and I grin, waiting a beat to let go. "Where did you learn to do these things," Logan asks me.

I shrug. "Most recently, from that damn audiobook," I tell her, sliding my palm down her stomach, in between her legs, and bringing my finger back to my mouth. "Fuck, Logan, I can't get enough of the taste of you." As if to prove my point, my cock twitches against her hip and I moan when she reaches for it. "Yes, please," I say when she begins to trace the tip hesitantly with a finger.

Feeling a bead of pre-cum on the tip, Logan freezes. "Do you have condoms?"

I nod, shifting my weight to reach for one of the drawers under my bed frame. I fish around until I come up with the foil packet. I move to open it, but Logan grabs my wrist. "Is it expired? Does it have a date on it?"

I remember how touchy she is about unplanned pregnancy, so I rock back to sit on my heels and hold her hand. "You can check it out and then you can be the one to roll it on me, okay?"

Logan reaches for the packet and bites her lip, tracing the date on the back and ripping open the foil. She looks up at me, her big brown eyes equal part trusting and vulnerable. "I'd never do anything to hurt you, Logan," I say, kissing her knuckles. "It's okay if you don't want to do this." I hope like hell she still wants to do this, but I know it won't be any good if she's not 100 percent on board.

"I want you," Logan says. I feel relief roll through me, and my dick twitches in my hand as I slowly stroke myself, waiting for her to make the next move. She takes a deep breath and sighs and then rolls the condom down my shaft. I shudder at the pressure of her hand on my aching cock. "That feels so good," I tell her.

"Really? You like this?" She gives me a squeeze and I nod, lying down on the bed next to her as Little Cal twitches flat up against my stomach. Logan seems intrigued, drawing one finger all along my chest and squeezing the root of my cock with her other hand. My eyes flutter shut when she gathers my sac between her fingers.

"Oh, fuck, Logan." I don't normally like having my balls fondled, but there's something about her touch, a combination of just the right pressure and the dueling sensation of her nails on my stomach. It has me on the edge.

"Can I be on top?" She pauses what she's doing to meet my eyes, which fly open as I nod.

"You can do whatever the hell you...want..." I sigh out this last part because Logan slings her leg over my hip and uses her fist to line me up at her entrance, then slams down onto me in one quick bounce.

"Ooh, Cal, this feels so good," she says, leaning her hands on my chest as she starts to move. I like this side of Logan, super aggressive. Hot and slick, sure, but sexy because she's so into this. "I want this," she shouts. "Yes." I'm just lying here loving the view as Logan swirls around in tiny arcs that send her tits jiggling, her nipples bright pink beads. I reach up to grab them and she tosses her head back, grinding down against me. "Ooooh," she keeps shouting. "So good. I'm so...full."

Something about that word turns me up a notch and I sit up, wrapping an arm around her waist so I can pull her against me while I put my weight on my other arm behind me on the mattress. "You like when I fill you up with my cock, Logan?" She bites her lip and nods as I thrust up into her. She bears down and together, we work up a sweat. "Let me see you come again, Logan," I tell her, my fingers digging into her thigh.

"I can't," she says, even as she presses tight against my chest so her nipples get in on the friction. I love the feel of those hard pearls rubbing into my skin.

"Yes," I grunt. "You can, Logan. Mm." She wraps her arms around my neck and kisses me, her tongue diving inside my mouth now, so confidently. So needy. I slide my arm from around her waist and reach between us, finding the hard nub of her clit and pressing into it like she showed me in the kitchen. "Take what you need, Lo. Take it. Come on."

Logan nods and grinds against my hand as I drive up into her. I can feel her pulsing around my cock and I'm glad for the condom. I want to last, but with this view, with her letting go this way to find her pleasure? I'm about to burst.

She pulls back, mouth dropping open into an oh while she moans. "Oh god, Callum." I love hearing my name in her mouth while she comes. I feel it before she announces it, her pussy clenching down on me so tightly in waves as she shouts my name. Eventually, I can't take it anymore and I thrust up one final time, my orgasm ripping through me and my release filling the condom as Logan stares down between us at the place where our bodies are joined. I move in and out a few more times as she watches, loving the sight of my cock, slick with her honey, disappearing inside her amazing body.

"Look at us," I say, keeping my eyes on her stretched around me. "Look how fucking good we look, Logan."

We sit in silence for a few minutes, both of us exhausted. I feel my lips turn up in a smile and finally, I tuck her hair back from her face. "That was amazing," I tell her and peck a kiss on her forehead before pulling her in tight for a hug as I sink back down onto the bed.

I'm too tired to pull out and not ready to separate from her, which is weird because usually my skin starts to crawl right about now once I've been with a woman. I already know Logan a lot better than most of the women I sleep with and it just feels nice to be here with her. Comfortable. Maybe there really is something to this mind-body connection concept.

"I didn't know," she whispers, flopping her head back on the pillow. "I didn't know it would be like this."

"Whoosh," I breathe. "Happy to clear that up for you." I tap her butt and pull out, and she whines a little as I slide away to take care of the condom. I dash across the hall and grab a washcloth from under the sink. "Hey," I say, awkwardly offering it to her. "I wasn't sure if you wanted to clean off or anything."

This part feels weird. I guess this is the part Logan was worried about, the whole "what does it mean" question. What comes now? I have no idea, except I'm tired as hell after that performance. I gave her everything I had, that's for damn sure. And even as I feel physically drained, I feel like she filled up some place inside me I wasn't expecting. It felt so amazing to have her trust me like that, to have her let down her walls for me. I don't know what to say or do, so I just stay here.

I settle back down on the bed beside Logan, playing with her hair as she dabs at herself. I love the smile on her face and knowing I was the one who put it there. It's so soothing, feeling the dark silky waves slide between my fingers. Logan eventually nestles back down beside me, and I keep stroking her hair.

The next thing I know, she's waking me up in the dark with her hand around my dick again.

CHAPTER TWENTY-TWO
LOGAN

I WAKE UP IN BED WITH CAL AND ALL THE MOMENTUM I FELT EARLIER, ALL THE resolve to start focusing on my feelings and needs—it simmers until I feel my crotch throbbing. I...need Cal again. Silently, I reach for him and find him erect in his sleep. I start to run my hand along him and his eyes fly open. He rolls on top of me, grinning, and it's different this time.

Things were all heated and passionate leaving the work party. We seemed desperate in the kitchen and again when we first got into his room, but the second time is more...tender I guess.

No more dirty talk. Lots more kissing and it feels really good to have him on top this time. I had been thinking that since the guy was on top all the other times I had sex, it might have just been the position that was lackluster for me. But Cal explodes that myth, too. Never could I imagine the bliss of just lying beneath him, feeling the weight of him and the heat of his skin spread out over mine.

Cal insists on bringing me to orgasm twice before he comes, using his fingers and adjusting the angle of his hips until he can tell I'm coming even if I don't say anything.

And then he falls back asleep petting my hair again. God, I like that. As dawn breaks, I lie in his bed pondering all the new things I just learned about my body.

Cal tore me to pieces with pleasure four times last night. I've never even succeeded in getting there once on my own. I realize now that whatever I was doing was just not complete. Every time I would try, I felt this increasing urge, almost like I had to pee, and I could tell there was something else just out of reach that I could never quite find. But I thought that was it.

And I was shockingly wrong. There is so much pleasure inside me. I had no idea.

What does it mean that my roommate helped me get there? What does it mean about all the other aspects of my life where I've held back? Something has shifted tonight. I don't know if Cal fucked me to a spiritual awakening or if I just had some sort of epiphany thanks to his family and him supporting me, but I feel like I've seen a different way of being and I don't know what to do with myself.

I try to climb out of bed so I can go sit in the living room with a cup of tea and think about it. I'm unable to move, though. I look down to see Cal's arm locked around my waist like a seatbelt, holding me against him while his chin nuzzles into my shoulder.

I come to full awareness and feel his breath tickling my ear as he sleeps. This is my first time waking up beside someone in this way. It feels nice, and comforting, and concerning all at once because Cal is not supposed to be my lover. He's not actually my boyfriend. Cal is my roommate—my tenant, actually, whose rent money I send home to my mother for *her* rent money so she can cut back to just one job. I sigh.

This feels wrong. There's a power differential here, and that's not okay.

"Cal," I say, shaking his arm. He grunts and digs his chin in a little deeper. I remember that we are both naked as I feel his erection thickening along my butt. What a predicament. "Cal, let me up," I hiss and he blinks and wiggles, slowly becoming conscious.

"S'wrong, Logan?" He cracks one eye open and studies me. He loosens his grip on me but doesn't retract his arm. "Don't you want to cuddle?"

I actually would like that very much, I realize, but it's still a bad idea, so I shake my head and extract myself from the bed. I stoop to gather up my dress, remembering with a flush that my panties are on the floor in the kitchen. Cal rolls over and mutters something and I soon hear him softly snoring, telling me he's fallen back asleep. He normally gets up early to run on the weekends, but I guess he was planning to skip that today.

I run down the hall to my room, feeling strange moving through my own house naked, and I take a shower. As my hands move over my body I remember last night in vivid flashes of heat. I scrub my skin, but feel Cal's mouth and fingers on me instead, causing me to rush and get dressed. It won't do to linger on those thoughts.

Voices sneak into my thoughts, the older women who waitressed with my mother at the diner saying to her, "It don't do no good to linger." Sometimes a handsome customer would leave a note or a phone number along with his tip, but my mother never called.

Men are too much trouble was the mantra of my youth.

I gather up the panties from the floor in the kitchen, stuffing them in my back pants pocket as I spray cleaner on the counter and wipe it down, trying to turn off the memories of me thrashing around up there like a rabid animal while Cal's face was buried between my thighs. I make a cup of tea and drink it and Cal still hasn't emerged from the bedroom, so I decide I'll open up my laptop and check through my work emails. Maybe I'll review the market analysis and get a jump on this week's client work.

Right now, the sex and the decision to stop letting people at work steamroll me feel related. But the more I think about it, the more I decide they don't have to be. Cal and I were scratching an itch last night. Both attracted to each other. He said a few times that he wanted to show me what it meant to have good sex. Mission accomplished.

We should focus on our friendship. His family is helping me stand up for myself at work, after all. His mom seemed serious about helping me contact HR. I can help him mend fences with his dad. We can't work on those things if we're also navigating a romantic relationship while living together. It's too much.

I sip the tea, feeling better now and in control again. Cal is my friend. I need to focus on making changes at work. Yes. This seems like something Sally and Linus McClinton would approach together. But then I remember that Sally and Linus are lovers and *The Redcoat* is a romance novel. I shake my head and try to focus on my inbox.

I nearly drop my mug when I see the number of emails flashing at me. Half of my clients sent notes about enjoying spending time with me at the event last night, and the other half sent messages mentioning they'd been talking to one another and are interested in increasing their investments to match some of the portfolios I set up for their friends.

For a social event, last night seemed to prompt a lot of business conversations. Maybe that's normal. I'd probably know if I felt like I could approach my co-workers to ask them. Scrolling down further, I see a message from Dennis Rudy with the subject **New Account Manager.** I bite my lip and open the email, seeing that it's addressed to Mr. Alexander, the big boss, and I'm copied.

The message is brief and to the point, addressed to my boss's boss and sent late last night. "Nate, lovely event this evening. Enjoyed meeting my new account manager. Mick Brady and Mary Emerson assure me she's top notch. Have your people call my people to set up a time. DR"

I stare at the screen, not sure what on earth to make of this. I snort out a laugh at the folly of thinking I could fly under the radar at work, sitting quietly in my office and just analyzing the best path ahead for my clients. Without even trying and without any awareness, I seem to have landed the white whale. I also know that this news is not going to do me any favors socially. I feel like a pariah at work. Devin is sort of decent to me, but everyone else just acts like I'm an unwelcome backpack they have to carry through a theme park.

I close my eyes and bring up the voices of Cal's family, assuring me that my employer should be supportive and creating a collaborative environment. Such a different message than I've received my entire life, from a mother doing her best to overcome a mountain of hard luck.

I've been thinking about Mick's comment in my office, that I need to stand up for myself at work. I'm not even sure what that would look like. I know all the rules of the game when it comes to actually calculating what's best for my clients and their individual tolerance for risk. But when it comes to my colleagues? There seems to be some sort of playbook full of terminology and behaviors that nobody gave me. I've felt unprepared for every social interaction my entire life, and there's nothing I hate more than feeling unprepared, whether that's for a dinner party or a class or a meeting at work.

But I can't control how my coworkers act, or evidently Dennis Rudy's preferences for who manages his account. What I can do is prepare to walk into work on Monday ready to talk numbers with Mr. Alexander. I've spent the past five years honing my analyst skills. I need to let go of worrying about the other stuff and focus on what I do best.

I take a deep breath, read Mr. Rudy's email again, and decide I'm going to spend the day researching him, his family, and his financial holdings. I know tomorrow will bring a boatload of unpleasant interactions with my co-workers, but at least I can go into the inevitable meeting with Mr. Alexander ready to take off running.

CHAPTER TWENTY-THREE
CAL

SHE LEFT. I WAKE UP EXPECTING TO SEE HER STILL HERE IN MY BED, BUT I REMEMBER that she left sometime in the middle of the night. What in the hell do I do with that? If I'm honest, I have no idea what I would have done if she was here when I woke up. But somehow knowing she was freaked out enough to leave makes me feel more alone.

I'm afraid to leave my bedroom. I lie in my bed for hours longer than I want, hoping I'll hear Logan leave the condo so I can grab some food and mope. I feel like the worst kind of scumbag after giving in to my irresponsible lust for her. I can practically feel all my brothers telling me this was careless and impulsive. Typical Cal, giving in to a desire just because it's there, tempting me.

But damn it, last night didn't feel impulsive. Nothing about that was anything like previous encounters where I fucked first and dealt with consequences later. I don't think the intensity I felt last night was one-sided, but of course I didn't have a conversation about that with Logan.

I got into this mess on a whim, signing a lease without meeting my new landlord-slash-roommate. God, what if she throws me out now? What did she say earlier when she woke up? I cringe, remembering that I asked her to cuddle.

Eventually, I don't hear anything for a long enough time that it seems safe for me to at least go to the bathroom. I pee for what feels like a decade and make my way into the kitchen, freezing when I see Logan on the couch with her computer, typing furiously and nodding her head along with whatever's flowing through her headphones.

I consider just dashing out the front door like a coward, but two things pull me over to sit on the couch beside her. First, I'm worried that she's listening to our audiobook without me. Second, I know I have to talk to her about what we did last night, even if it sucks and feels too big and too uncomfortable.

I plunk down next to her and nudge her with my shoulder, realizing that I should probably have put on a shirt or at least some pants before approaching this conversation. I sigh, shaking my head at myself while she pauses whatever she's jamming to. "Oh, sorry," she says. "I didn't hear you come out." Her eyes widen when she sees that I'm just wearing boxers and I try to stuff a pillow on my lap and reclaim a tiny shred of dignity.

"Just making sure you weren't listening to the McClintons without me."

"I would never!" She seems insulted as she pats my arm. "Although, can we listen to a chapter? I'm dying to know what happens in the battle."

Nicole convinced us to crank up the audio speed to 1.5 so we could ingest more on our commute and then Logan and I agreed we could handle 1.75 speed. We've been flying through and are almost done with book two at this point. The Revolutionary War is in full swing since we heard the spicy bits on our commute. Linus is about to swear allegiance to the colonial army, about to leave his red coat in the mud back at the British camp. I grin, loving how into this story we both are. "Sure, Lo, but I just wanted to... you know..." I scratch my head and she stares at me. "Are we cool?"

"Oh," she says, closing the laptop and setting it on the coffee table. "I think so. It was just a one-time thing, right?" She shrugs and I feel a lump of dread press down on my shoulders. She's right, sure. It would be dumb to dive into something romantic when we're just getting to know each other as roommates. But damn it, something about hearing her say it was a one-and-done makes me want to drag her down the hall and take her again, even though I absolutely know the right thing to do is keep things friendly between us.

I take a deep breath and nod. "Right. One night."

We stare at each other for a bit, not talking, until Logan grabs her phone and queues up the audiobook. I sit next to her, wanting to drape my arm around her shoulders while we listen, but keeping my posture stiff and awkward so we don't touch.

The story hits an exciting part involving surgery after a battle, when the audio cuts out and a robotic voice announces "Incoming text message from

Nicole Cal's-brother's-girlfriend." I bark out a laugh at Logan's contact label.

"She'd shit if she knew you were identifying her by her relationship status," I say, finally nudging Logan with my shoulder, like I always do when I'm teasing her or giving her shit. Logan rolls her eyes.

"I know, I know. I keep meaning to ask you what her last name is. Oh!" She waves a hand to shush me as the phone reads the message to us.

"Bitch, please tell me you are coming to Brady family dinner tonight? As you know I am hosting. Don't plan on swimming in the pool. Apparently Liam and Maddie fucked in it."

Neither of us seems to know what to say in response to that message, and we stare at each other for a long time before we both burst out laughing. The air feels better after that, like we're back to old times. "What time is dinner?" Logan frowns at her laptop. "I have a big meeting tomorrow I need to prepare for today."

I glance up at the clock above the television. "Lo, it's only noon. You've got at least four hours before we have to head over there."

She nods. "Okay good. I want to go over everything at least once more so that I don't get nervous tomorrow morning." She tells me how she's been volun-told she'll manage the big account with my dad's golf buddy Denny. Personally, I think it's great because Logan is clearly amazing at what she does and the clients think she breathes sunshine and farts gold coins.

"Listen," I tell her. "Nicole Kennedy is just the woman you want to give you a pep talk before that sort of thing." I pat her leg and stand up so I can go change and hopefully get a run in before we leave. "I'm glad you're coming along tonight. Honestly, it'd be weird going to family dinner without you after...everything."

She smiles sort of stiffly and reaches for her laptop again, and I head back to my room to get dressed.

It's a warm day, and I decide not to wear a shirt. I also realize as soon as I step into the hall that I've forgotten my keys, but at least I've got my phone on me so I can call Logan to let me in when I get back. I try not to dwell on the fact that I'm such a big cliche. I've always been like this, and I know that because it's the huge family party line. Cal's irresponsible. Cal's always making a joke, good for a laugh, but not someone you rely on.

Growing up, when Mom left Dad, shit was super tense at home. Liam was already the surly kid. Then Zack showed up, and then his mom left, too. Everyone was sulking around being bossy all the damn time. Me and my dad, we're just wired differently I guess. Only thing is, everyone views my dad's quirky shit as some stroke of genius where every story about pistachios eventually winds up being related to him investing in efficient agricultural engineering technology or some shit.

When I fuck up rushing through the math on an inspection report because I can't stand it another second? I'm just being careless. Dad was friendly enough last night that I'm thinking he might be over the boat situation, but that still doesn't change the fact that I'm more *tolerated* at work than valued.

I have to tread carefully if I'm going to actually have a conversation with Pete Harris outside of the fancy party with Logan. I want to make a career change so bad I can smell the idea burning in my gut. But I just don't see a way to do that. I work for my family, with my family, in a city where my family apparently knows literally everyone.

Leaving Beltane would look like just another impulsive, reckless Cal move to them. I shake off that thought and turn to run back toward the condo. I can't worry about leaving Beltane yet. Hell, I don't even know if Pete is hiring. I gotta get through family dinner first.

CHAPTER TWENTY-FOUR
LOGAN

Cal drives us to Nicole and Zack's house for Brady family dinner and when he lets himself in the front door, we're slammed by a wall of noise from inside. "Are there way more Bradys here than last time?" I was worried coming here would be strange, like his entire family would be able to tell we had slept together, but Cal hasn't really brought it up, so I think we are carrying on as if it had not happened.

Maybe it really was a one-time thing. Similar to the one time Cal and I rented bicycles and rode around some of the trails for an hour. Did we discuss that afterward? Not really.

It's better that way, and I really liked going to the last Brady function. I barely paused from my meeting prep to eat today, and I'm feeling a little woozy, so I'm not sure what to make of all the loud yelling and...is that crying? Before Cal can answer me, a pair of sock-clad kids streaks up the hall and they slip on the hard wood floors, falling in a heap at our feet, punching each other.

"All right," Cal exclaims. "These are definitely Stag kids."

"Stag? Like baby deer or like..."

Cal surprises me by bending down and picking up the boys, one in each arm. "That's enough, you two. Which ones are you? Huh?"

The kids are still scrapping, reaching around Cal and trying to get in a few more smacks. A man comes around the corner and I gasp, reaching out for Cal's arm. "Oh my god. Ty Stag is here." I turn to face Cal. "YOU KNOW TY STAG?"

I don't follow a lot of professional sports and I never made time to go to any games. Not that I could have afforded the tickets. But growing up in Johnstown, PA, everyone lived and breathed the Pittsburgh sports teams. Ty Stag took the Fury to a few championship wins before he retired to be a stay-home dad.

I'm standing there staring at the man with my mouth hanging open when he walks up to us, gesturing for his kids. And then, like an idiot, I place my hand in his outstretched one, pumping it up and down. Ty grins and I pull my arm back. He says, "Pleasure to meet you…Cal's friend?"

"Oh, sorry, man." Cal hands Ty the children, who climb up Ty like he's a tree. "This is my roommate, Logan Miller. Big fan of yours apparently."

"Well, like I said, pleasure to meet you." He tilts his head to the side, studying me. "Did you not know this was a double family dinner?"

"Nicole did not mention that, nope." Cal reaches out and ruffles the hair of each of the boys, who I can now tell look exactly like their father.

"Ah," Ty says. "Well, Nicole double booked herself for family dinner, so she just invited both families." He shrugs. "Happens sometimes." He turns and walks toward the epicenter of the noise and I follow behind when Cal does.

Ty disappears into the crowd and Cal moves to walk toward his brothers when I grab for his shirt. "Wait," I say. "You can't just leave me alone. There's a celebrity here."

He blinks a few times and then shakes his head. "Sorry. You just fit in so well with my family last time. I honestly forgot you don't know all this. Okay." He puts an arm around my shoulder and I tell myself the heat I feel from our connection is just due to the house being warm. Cal points across the crowded room.

"Over there is Nicole's boss, Tim Stag. He owns Stag Law and his wife Alice is the pregnant one over there." He points to a curly-haired woman standing and gesturing at Maddie's stomach. "Tim and Alice have at least two of the boys roaming around here. Then we've got Emma and Thatcher Stag. She's the redhead and he's the man-bun. They've also got two boys. Wow. I'm just realizing how many boys there are. You met Ty and two of his. I think he and Juniper maybe have another one? It's probably a boy."

When I look at Ty he has a third child on his shoulders, and he's laughing animatedly with Liam, offering him some of the children to hold. Liam doesn't accept, which makes Zack laugh. I see Nicole over in the kitchen with Uncle Kellen, stirring a giant pot of food, and Mick is in deep conversation with a tall woman who seems really familiar.

I gesture toward her. "Who is that?"

"That's Juniper. Judge Juniper Jones," Cal says.

"Oh, I've read about her," I tell him. "In graduate school, actually. She's an Olympian. And grew up in the foster care system." I remember taking a "women in business" elective and Juniper was featured as a case study for her work with women's sports teams, helping them to get fair funding. When I read Juniper's quotes about having grown up struggling financially, and how that experience informed first her legal practice and now her work on the bench, I felt so inspired. Like I wasn't the only woman to reach up for something different.

I sigh. I can't believe these are the people Cal hangs out with casually. Celebrities. Career professionals. It all feels so foreign. I'm on the verge of a panic attack about it when Nicole sees me and squeals. "Oh, Logan! You made it!" She rushes around the counter and pulls me in for a hug. "Did this doofus introduce you?"

"Oh, he told me who everyone is, but I didn't get to--"

"Hey, everyone!" Nicole whistles and cuts me off. The room goes silent, except for the kids, who are somehow all trying to physically maim each other. "This is Logan. She and Cal are *just friends*." She throws her head back and cackles. I turn beet red at Nicole's joke, but nobody seems to notice.

There are a few snorts of laughter and the Bradys tip their glasses in my direction, and then the talking resumes. Nicole procures a drink from somewhere and hands it to me. "Kellen took over with the spaghetti, and Alice brought all the salad and bread and stuff, so now we just get toasted and watch Liam and Maddie squirm while all the Stags offer them parenting advice."

"Oh that sounds uncomfortable." I take a sip of the drink. "Wow. This is amazing. What is it?"

"My friends I was telling you about? Those ladies who take no shit? One of them owns a bar and is teaching me some things. I'm telling you, you need to hang out with me. Have you been reading the book?"

Cal reappears over my shoulder. "Nicole Kennedy, you sly dog. You've got us totally hooked. We're about to finish up the sequel."

"You went ahead! No fair. You're supposed to wait for the group," she says, and then she and Cal dive into a heated discussion of revolutionary politics in the 18th century. I sip my drink and nod along with them until Kellen announces that dinner is served.

"Come with me," Nicole says, tugging me to her sun porch. "Trust me. You want to wait out the rush back here until all the kids get released into my back yard. Did you see what my Isaac did back there?" She gestures out the window at the beautiful landscaping with a view of the river, telling me how she met the Brady family when half her yard dropped away in a landslide, which the youngest Brady boy repaired for her. "Like I said earlier, though, don't go swimming until I disinfect. Liam told me they conceived the baby in my stock tank pool. I'd hate them if I didn't think that was pretty bad ass."

By the time we talk through the features of the trendy, Pinterest-worthy galvanized steel pool complete with white rocks and a hot tub feature, the scrum at the spaghetti buffet has died down and we can grab our own plates.

I sit down next to Nicole and am surprised when Mick slides into the chair next to mine. Nicole has set up a bunch of folding tables and chairs in a U shape to accommodate everyone and it feels simultaneously formal and totally laid back as everyone digs in and continues their loud conversations. Mick grins at Nicole. "Nicky, did Logan here tell you about her big work news?" She arches a brow at him and he waves his hand. "Aw, come on, if an old man can't call you Nicky what pleasures do I have left in life?" I assume his "news" is that he came on as a client at my firm, but I'm stunned and touched when he explains that his buddy Denny Rudy insisted on me being the analyst who handles his investments.

Nicole grips the edge of the table with both hands and beams. "Logan. That's fucking amazing. You're such a bad ass. Way to go with your finance skills." I bite my lip and hope they'll move on and talk about something else.

"I'm sure it's just because Denny is friends with Mick." I force out a laugh. "Nepotism."

"I didn't tell him a thing, Logan. The broads at that shindig think you breathe diamonds, sweetheart." Mick grins and shakes his head, then leans the other way to talk with Tim about the joys of having three sons.

But of course I can't stop thinking about whether what he said is true. I feel tears threaten at the idea of my clients saying such nice things about me. I absolutely cannot fall apart like I did in front of Cal's mom. That was a mess.

Nicole leans toward me. "What's with the face? Talk to me."

I take a deep breath. "I'm really new at work," I tell her. "I'm not trying to rock the boat. Getting this big client? It's going to make people really jealous." I realize how juvenile it sounds as I'm saying it, but the atmosphere at the office has been so heavy and I already have enough heavy shit in my life without having to walk on eggshells each time I open my office door. All of my resolve from early this morning slides away in the light of day and I'm back to feeling like a tourist in my own life.

Nicole sneers. "Well fuck them, then. If your colleagues wanted better clients they should be better at their job."

I blink at her a few times and burst out laughing. I've never been around anyone young who is as blunt as Nicole. It's refreshing. She's like all the old ladies my mom worked with...but not bitter. "I wish I could take that attitude about it. It's just so hard. I had really been hoping to lay low this first year, really get myself settled with the accounts they gave me when I was hired. I had hoped to let the other guys sort of duke it out over the Rudy account..."

I trail off, hearing what I sound like. For someone who worked as hard as I did to maintain perfect grades and keep my scholarship, and then repeat the same process for my fellowship in graduate school, it sounds ridiculous to hide. I sigh as Nicole rolls her eyes. "You said guys? You work with mostly dudes, right? Enough said. Let me guess. The few women who do work there are total assholes to you?" I give a little nod and Nicole barrels on ahead. "I already told you, I worked in tech. I am very familiar with this episode of the patriarchy show."

She slugs back the rest of her drink and points at me with her fork. "You need to come to Bridges and Bitters for Foof."

"Foof?"

Nicole nods. "Fresh outta fucks. F. O. O. F. Foof. It's a group of women committed to releasing our last fuck into the breeze and grabbing life by the horns. But instead of slamming all the doors shut behind us, we help other women release their fucks, too."

"Oh my gosh, Nik, are you talking about Foof again? I really need to get back to one of the meetings." Emma Stag had been pacing behind us holding one of her sleeping sons over her shoulder and paused behind Nicole. She sort of waves at me with one hand. "I'm Emma. I haven't gotten to meet you formally yet. I'm up to my elbows in baby mucous, but Foof totally supported me when I broke up with my publisher and started self-publishing my books a few years ago."

Nicole beams and takes a big bite of her dinner. "Asshole publisher tried to say our Emma here was only worth a $100 marketing budget. What was your latest royalty check, Ems?"

Emma sort of hides her cheek behind the baby's head, but I hear her say, "I was able to hire an assistant to help with my administrative work since I'm technically still on maternity leave."

"That's incredible," I say, looking around the room. "Everyone here is so accomplished. I feel out of place."

"Uh, hello? Did you not just woo the owner of the Pittsburgh Iron Men with your brain powers?"

I shrug and bite my lip, unaccustomed to talking about my achievements at work. I have a feeling it's going to take a lot of work to feel at ease among Cal's family. But as I look around the room again, blushing when Cal winks at me, I decide the effort will be totally worthwhile.

CHAPTER TWENTY-FIVE
CAL

"Hey, Uncle Kellen." I wade toward my uncle where he's helping Alice navigate food prep. I wave a grocery bag at him. "I found this old car manual when I was unpacking my stuff. Thought maybe Jake would dig it." The kid across the street from my uncle is obsessed with engines. Reminds me of me in some ways. And my uncle has the hots for the kid's mom, so I figure everyone wins when I saved this old Bronco manual from the landfill.

Kellen's face totally shifts and he smiles at me for the first time in weeks. "That's really thoughtful of you, Callum."

I shrug. "Where's your stuff? I'll set it down for you so you don't have to clean your hands." He's got tomato sauce splattered all over his front and he chuckles, shaking his head a bit as Alice whirs past with something fragrant.

"Thank you, son. I'll let him know it's from you."

I make my way to the heap of coats and bags in the laundry room and find my uncle's stuff before heading back into the dining room to grab a beer. While I'm making amends here, I decide I'm going to go stand near my dad and refuse to move until he talks to me.

Maybe I should apologize to kick things off. I don't freaking know anymore.

I grab a beer for me and a tea for my dad as a peace offering, but then I get distracted when I hear Logan laughing. I'm drawn toward the sound of her voice, captivated by the look of her talking to all the important women in my life. I hadn't expected to feel anything at all watching her interact with my family, but she sits there having a heart-to-heart and I can hear the women periodically shouting encouragement to Logan. And now I find myself here next to my dad with a hard on.

This makes no sense. I tell myself my body is still experiencing aftershocks from last night.

"Hello? Callum?" Dad snaps his fingers in my ear and I turn toward him.

"Sorry, Dad. What's that again?"

He sighs. "Where's your head today? Did you tie one on last night after the party?"

"No, Dad. I'm just distracted. It's loud in here."

"That's true." Dad glances at the herd of baby Stags fighting in the back yard. "Twenty bucks says one of them is bleeding before Kellen and Alice serve dessert."

I wave a hand, mimicking one of my dad's old-man moves. "That's not a bet. That's a certainty." Honestly, it's good to have him talking to me again. I should say something to him about the boat incident, but it feels so calm right now just chatting with him while I stare at Logan. So instead, we stare out the back patio door as one of the kids face plants in the rocks around Nicole's pool. The kid bursts into tears and Ty and Thatcher hurry over to his side. "See?" Dad smiles as Ty pulls a pack of bandages from his jeans pocket.

"So anyway, son, like I was saying, I'm concerned about the long-term project over at the steel plant." I know the project he's referring to. Beltane has a guy working there full time to monitor the equipment, check everything out. These machines are the size of city blocks and having something go down could cost millions of dollars a day.

"Something isn't sitting right with me about Tony's reports."

I raise a brow at my dad. "Since when do you look at the paperwork?"

"Don't get smart with me. I talk to your uncle. I'm telling you, Tony needs someone to look after his work."

"You want me to go ride herd on Tony? He's got ten years on me, Dad."

My dad frowns. "I didn't say ride herd. But the last time I talked with him, Tony was going through a rough patch at home. I worry what that means for his concentration. And he's all alone there." Dad swallows a big gulp of water and smacks his lips appreciatively. "I'd like you to shadow him this week. Your uncle is aware."

I don't bother arguing that I have no desire to spend a week in a steel plant measuring the rust on I-beams. I'm being banished there and it occurs to me that this is him telling me what's going to happen as a result of the boat crash. I'm the family fuckup working for a pair of men who still think of me as the kid who missed the school bus or spilled food on himself at a scholarship interview lunch. Or, you know, the 31 year old man-boy who stole a boat and crashed it.

I'm not in a very festive mood by the time I finish eating and I have no real desire to linger. I see all the Stags gathering up their babies and hope that means a ripple effect of mass departures so we'll all cut out early. Those hopes are dashed when Emma, Juniper and Alice all settle into Nicole's couch, explaining to Logan that Ty is driving the Daddy Wagon and leaving all the girls behind to catch up.

Emma, Maddie and Nicole all went to college together, and they get along really well with Orla, Juniper and Alice, and it's nice seeing them tug Logan over to their circle. But why do I care? She's my roommate. She doesn't need to be best friends with my family. Shouldn't she make her own friends? I carry my plate to the kitchen, where my brothers are washing dishes and giving each other shit. I don't even linger to join in, wandering over to the girls instead. "Hey, Lo, you ready to head out?"

Her face falls a bit, but she sighs. "I really should. I want to be well rested for tomorrow."

"Just remember, you got this," Maddie tells her, rubbing her own stomach like it's a good luck charm.

"Fuck those bitches," Nicole says, winking dramatically. "Come to Foof this week."

"Do I want to know what she's talking about?" I steer Logan toward the door. I see my dad has slunk away without saying goodbye to anyone. Or maybe he just skipped saying goodbye to me. Good. I don't feel up to talking to him, but I'm a little irritated he beat me to the Irish farewell.

"Oh, they were giving me a pep talk for tomorrow," Logan says, climbing into Big Red and struggling as she tries to pull the heavy door closed.

"Watch your fingers," I say, taking pity on her and give it a slam. "What's tomorrow?"

She rolls her eyes. "Um, remember? I'm meeting with Mr. Rudy and everyone at work will know they didn't get selected to manage his account? And they'll all hate me worse than they already do?"

"God, Logan, I hate all those assholes so bad. Have I told you that?" She bites her lip and looks out the window. "They just aren't nice to you. I mean, at first I wasn't sure if they were just being weird because I was around, but seriously screw them if they're going to act like children. They're impacting the bottom line of their company if the clients get wind of this sort of behavior."

It's not lost on me that my father could say the same thing about my own mopey attitude. My mood blackens as I realize *I'm* Logan's shitty coworkers in this analogy. What did I hear Nicole say? They should be better at their jobs if they want to be assigned better projects? Maybe I'm not as good a mechanical engineer as I thought I was.

"I'm feeling pretty good about my approach for tomorrow," Logan says stiffly. "I don't really want to talk about that anymore."

"Fine by me," I say, snapping on the audiobook. We're at a part of the book where everyone is at war, and characters are dying left and right. It all feels fitting with my mood and I grunt as I shift into fourth gear and speed toward home.

CHAPTER TWENTY-SIX
LOGAN

Nicole advised me to wear a fitted suit today with heels and red lipstick. She even gave me a tube she said would be a flattering shade, since I confessed my makeup all comes from the dollar bins at the drug store. She also told me to make sure I get myself off because "there's nothing like an orgasm to recharge your power vibes."

I think I probably blushed redder than this lipstick when she said that. Thankfully, I'm pretty recharged in that respect from this weekend. But I already decided not to think about that right now.

The women in Cal's family are just what I need in my life, and I'm grateful I get to spend time with them. It's this thought that keeps my eyes averted as he wanders around the apartment in his underwear this morning, skin glistening from his shower.

Nope, not going to pair that image with memories of what we did the other night. For the first time in my life, I have friends who are confident. Nicole is blunt. She literally told me to apply my own expertise to my budget and stop acting like I'm poor.

She's not wrong. I slick a comb through my hair, aiming for a low bun while I remind myself that I've fully stocked a six month emergency fund and am sending Cal's rent payments to my mother. I keep meaning to call her and make sure she quit her second job. I take a moment to recognize that my fear of this "good fortune" disappearing comes not from a rational place, but from my mother's fears. From her lived hardship.

I hear a rap on the door to my room and mumble out a noise since I've got bobby pins in my mouth. Cal pokes his head in the door. "Just wanted to remind you I'm working on a job site this week so we can't ride in together and...woah."

I turn toward him, plucking the final pin from my mouth and smoothing the sides of my hair. "I remember, thank you, Cal." I smile and twirl around. "How do I look?" I expect him to wink and say something crass like usual, but he stares at me for a few beats without speaking.

"You look absolutely fierce," he says finally, with a small smile.

"Thank you, good sir. See you tonight?" He nods, still looking a bit shell shocked as I click past him in my heels and head for the bus. And then I realize that I let myself put on my shoes before the doorway. I'm starting to unfurl a bit at home. The power of that fuels me toward my office, even though I'm still nervous about what awaits me there.

When I get to my building, I take a deep breath. Marie will likely meet me in the hall. She will greet me with a mean facial expression and her body language will convey her truth. I remind myself what Nicole, Maddie, Emma, Juniper, Orla and Alice all emphatically reassured me: it's inappropriate for my supervisor to be angry that I'm good at my job. That's on her.

I start thinking about Linus in the book series. In the beginning, he's just doing his job and feels honored to serve his king and country. He slowly starts to realize the administration he's fighting for aren't really all that noble. I'm starting to feel a connection with Linus, torn allegiances. Where Linus has Sally urging him to do what's right, well, I've got my roommate *and* his family.

The elevator doors slide open and I walk confidently toward my office, setting my bag on my desk and turning to hang my coat on the hook. I hear someone approach and know it's Marie. "I don't know what you think you're playing at," she says, standing in my door and tapping her foot.

"Good morning," I say, not meaning it. Rather than ask her what she's referring to, I walk around my desk and pop open my laptop. I'm expecting Mr. Alexander's administrative assistant to reach out about a meeting, and I grin when I see an email from her at the top of my inbox.

I hear Marie inhale through her nose. "You know damn well that Carl and Jason were working toward the Rudy account. What did you do? Flash him your tits Saturday night so he'd pick you?"

I frown. "I'm not going to dignify that with a response, Marie. Perhaps Carl and Jason should have worked harder to earn their clients' endorsement." I type a response to the email invitation, clicking accept with an enthusiastic tap of my index finger. I can do this. I can push back against Marie's words. I am like Linus McClinton, brave and strong.

But Marie doesn't apologize like she did in my fantasy of this scenario. She leans forward on my desk and snorts. "Client endorsement? Please. You're fucking the son of Rudy's golf buddy. Don't kid yourself, Logan." She tosses a file on my desk—this week's meetings and report expectations. "Good luck keeping up with your client list while you manage the Rudy account. Wouldn't want to shuffle anyone off to an analyst who isn't *endorsed.*"

She huffs out of the room as her words sink in. I'm going to maintain my full load of clients while also managing the complex investments of one of the city's most wealthy families.

I'm never going to sleep again.

By the time I make my way to Mr. Alexander's office I'm wobbling in my heels and biting my lip. It's too late to check and make sure I didn't smear the lipstick.

"Logan," he greets me brightly. "Come on inside." I follow him to his desk and he sinks down behind the massive wooden slab that's larger than the table Cal and I have at our apartment. I notice that his guest chairs are plush leather, a stark contrast to the plain, plastic chairs we have in our offices. As I sit, he says, "you know, analysts like you have gotten me where I am today. I hope you know how much we value your skills when it comes to forecasting trends."

I smile and nod, still reeling from Marie's sharp tongue. "Thank you, sir."

"I've known Denny Rudy for a long time," he says, "and Mick Brady, too. I hadn't realized his son was a particular friend of yours." I purse my lips, uncertain what he assumes about Cal.

"Anyway," he says, "Rudy said he got a good feeling about you from meeting you Saturday night." He leans forward and steeples his fingers. "Look, I'm not new at this. You're the new kid in town and I'm sure it chaps all their asses that you're getting this sort of opportunity," he says, gesturing around as if he's aware that everyone else here is indeed mad at me. "I'm not going to get involved in schoolyard drama, but if any of them pulls shit that puts our reputation at risk, I want to hear about it."

I swallow and try to control my facial expressions as I nod back at him.

He grins. "Great. Well, Marie is going to be managing the client relations and you can start working your magic. We're looking at a few million to play around with...to start!"

I nod. "I actually prepared a few scenarios this weekend. I have some options to send, depending on his risk tolerance this quarter."

Mr. Alexander grins. "Risk tolerance is high. Nice work, Logan."

"Thank you, sir."

❧

AFTER MR. ALEXANDER DISMISSES ME, I am feeling a small resurgence in my confidence and try to maintain that as I walk back to my office, ignoring the creeping dread of too much work and not enough time. I want to message Nicole and the girls and give them an update, but I made a commitment not to do personal communication on company time. No sense shifting from that now, especially when I have even more work than before. I hurry back to my office, successfully avoiding contact with anyone else, and I shut myself in to dive in to the work.

CHAPTER TWENTY-SEVEN
CAL

I FLASH MY BELTANE BADGE AT THE ENTRANCE TO THE STEEL PLANT AND PARK IN THE visitors area. It's nice wearing boots and a hardhat to work for a change. I've always hated sitting at a desk in an office. I'll be damned if I tell my dad that I'm appreciating the change of scenery, though. I still don't understand quite why I'm here. Big deal—Tony's having trouble at home.

I'm having fucking trouble at home and it's not impacting my work.

I whistle as I walk inside to find Mr. T. housing down donuts behind a cluttered desk. "Hey, man," I say, leaning on the door frame. "We're gonna be buddies this week I guess." He grunts. After a while, it's pretty clear that he has no plans of getting up from his chair any time soon, so I grab a tablet from his desk and head out onto the floor.

It's kind of amazing being here. With my ear plugs in, I can still hear the roar of everything but there are no distractions. I wander up and down the line, just looking. I decide to take a full lap of the plant before I even open the inspection software to take a look. I'm not sure what my dad was most concerned about. God forbid he send me with notes.

That's more Kellen's bag, but I forgot to check in with him this morning. I remind myself to check my email when I'm back somewhere with wi-fi. I pause in front of the coal conveyor bridge. This is the main thing, I recall. It's not some dinky little footbridge. This sucker is so big a car could easily drive across.

It's hard for me to imagine a structure like this failing. These are usually so overbuilt. This one's been in service for a few decades, though, so I take a careful look. I admire the track that has the deep pockets, moving coal from the hopper to the furnace. The mechanics of this equipment are a beautiful thing. Everything is pure simplicity.

I hear a groan as the belt crosses the middle of the structure and I frown. I should not be hearing anything above the other noises in here, on top of my ear plugs. I pull up the inspection software and see what Tony's supposed to have been monitoring. Everything seems in order. Hell, I don't even have to calculate anything. This algorithm Uncle Kellen wrote for the inspection program does it all automatically if I just plug in the readings from the different instruments.

Something doesn't sit right with me, though. I find the foreman and ask about the groaning, but he just shrugs and says the sound is part of the job. We're communicating mainly through gestures because of the noise.

I should go back in the office with Tony and watch some monitors, but something nags at me. The furnace sits at the far end of the structure and the belt is bringing coal from the trap door in a huge bunker. Both ends of the bridge seem sound. It's that middle section.

The thing is the length of a football field. The support columns are the size of tree trunks. I go through the list and I check for rust, for signs of corrosion. I don't notice anything dripping or leaking. But when the conveyor belt groans over my head again on its way to the coal hopper, I decide I have to at least call my uncle. He'll know what to do.

I march back to the office, where Tony is actually working on reports, although his desk is still an ungodly mess. I can definitely see what my brother and Logan are talking about here. I'm just a few years away from this, a place where sloppy crosses from charming into scary.

"Tone," I say, plunking my hardhat down on the floor beside me as I perch on a stack of papers to try and sit. "What can you tell me about that coal conveyor bridge?"

"Other than it's been there thirty years?" He shrugs. "Seems fine."

"Does it always groan like that?"

Another shrug. I blow out a breath, wishing I'd taken one of those donuts from his desk earlier. "My dad tell you why he sent me out here?"

Tony waves a hand. "He was in the other day talking with the top brass. Something about drones." I nod. Dad and Uncle Kellen are very interested in getting drones and sensors doing most of our preliminary inspections.

Makes sense, since they could tell things I definitely can't. Like the temperature of that conveyor belt after it passes near the furnace.

"What do we know about the age of the belt? How often is that sucker replaced?" Tony roots around for some papers and we study the numbers together. On paper, everything should be fine. At any rate, this isn't necessarily something Tony would be missing because of a domestic dispute distracting him.

I shoot my uncle a text and he calls Tony's office phone almost immediately. "I'll get it," I tell him, snatching the oily handset with my sleeve pulled over my hand. "Hey, Uncle Kel."

I tell him what I've seen (mostly everything is fine) and what my gut tells me (something is off about that conveyor bridge). "Here's what will happen," he says, sighing. "I'll have to go to the plant manager with your hunch, and he will tell me that he cannot risk a multi-million dollar pause in production for a hunch."

"Can they even pause?" From my brief stroll through the steel mill, I gathered it would take hours just to slow the machinery. This isn't like a small factory spitting out rivets. Just stopping the turbines is a whole process. A beautiful, mechanically wonderful process I'm dying to examine, but obviously nobody's going to do it for shits and giggles.

"No, son, they can't. Not unless it's a crisis. Hang out a little longer and see if you can get me some hard facts," Kellen says. I wander back out with my ear plugs, talking to a few employees here and there. I ask if anyone changed any settings on the furnace, if there's been a new batch of coal. I can't point to anything that would have changed, and nobody but me seems bothered by the conveyor belt.

At the end of the work day, I head home because I'm ravenous. I never did find any lunch. I can't cook worth a damn, so I go across the street to order something. It seems like no time has passed since I took Logan here for her first enchiladas, but it's been almost two months.

I consider how tight she is with my family, how much I like spending time with her just goofing around, talking about that book series or checking out new beers. *And licking her pussy.* The thought flashes through my head before I can stop it. Suddenly, I'm in line for takeout with a fully erect dick, thinking about how she looked this morning.

I shift uncomfortably, sticking a hand in my pocket to try and adjust things while I wait for my order. I start to recite equations, think about the melting points of various metals. By the time they call my order, I can almost walk without my zipper grating my skin.

I hustle back across the street and into the condo, tossing the bags of food on the counter. Logan isn't home yet and I absolutely have to take care of the situation in my pants, so I sink into the couch, unzip, and reach inside.

CHAPTER TWENTY-EIGHT

LOGAN

I WORK UNTIL MY EYES START TO CROSS AND THE NUMBERS ON MY MONITORS ALL start to blur together. I've run more reports and analysis today than I did in my entire final year of graduate school. With a deep sigh, I decide I have to head home and at least change into sweats before I keep working. My mouth waters at the thought of food, since I didn't stop for lunch.

I feel a flutter of nerves when I open my office door. I don't want to face more of my co-workers. Somehow I used up all my reserves standing up to Marie, and I didn't even do that as well as I'd practiced. But the good news about working late is that most people are already gone, and I'm able to make it down to the street without talking to anyone.

That puts a skip back into my step and, just my luck, I arrive to the bus stop just as the express is pulling up. I even manage to snag a seat in the back, and I grin when the bus pulls into the stop near our building just a few minutes later. If only Cal and I were racing today, I would have totally won and he and his bucket of rust would still be sitting at the light downtown.

I shouldn't make fun of his car. He loves that thing. Thinking of Cal's car reminds me of his family dinners and listening to audiobooks as we ride together. Which has me thinking of our night together Saturday. I wriggle around in the elevator, remembering his face between my legs. Him between my legs. Everything about that night was so far beyond my expec-

640

tations. It was like...well, it was like all of the sex I read about or saw in movies.

My skin feels charged with electricity as I open the door to our apartment and then I freeze, because I'm not sure if I'm imagining things or if Callum Brady really is sprawled out on the couch, touching himself.

After a few strokes, he emits a soft groan, and I know it's really happening. He sits with his eyes closed, his head thrown back on the cushions as his right hand moves furiously in his pants. His jeans are barely unzipped and he's wearing dirty work boots in the living room.

I shake my head and slowly close the door, trying not to worry about the boots. I need to focus on the illicit image in front of me. I need to figure out my feelings for him. No, I need to watch this unfold. I lick my lips, watching the muscles in his neck tighten as he clenches his jaw. His hair is sweaty and disheveled. I see a hard hat on the counter and have to fan myself. Why is this turning me on so much?

I start to worry that it's inappropriate for me to be standing here, spying on him like this when he's not aware I'm here. But I can't seem to force myself to move or call out to him. Until he moans my name.

Logan. It hangs on his lips like a prayer as he squeezes his own leg with one hand, the other moving fast and steady up and down his shaft. He's imagining me while he does this. I set my bag down and walk toward him, hoping he will open his eyes, but he is too deep in concentration now. His breath comes in bursting pants, and he keeps his eyes squeezed shut as he pleasures himself.

I sink to my knees in front of him and focus on the shiny head of his erection bobbing above his index finger as he squeezes. I place a hand on each of his thighs and finally, his eyes shoot open. "Oh, fuck, Logan." His eyes are wild and panicked, like he is also uncertain whether this is real.

"It's okay," I say, and then I dip my head, my tongue poking out hesitantly. I want to taste him, and I push his hand aside so I can wrap my own around his base.

When my tongue connects with his skin, licking delicately around his tip, he groans so loudly I can feel it in my teeth as my mouth slides around him and then back off. "Is this all right?" I look up at him, questioning, as I kneel between his legs with his shaft in my hand.

"Christ, yes, please, Logan. Oh god yes holy shit." He sputters and curses as I lick him again, more aggressively this time, tasting a salty rush as a bead of fluid seeps from his slit. Cal starts panting like a Lamaze instructor and I ease him into my mouth, loving the firm feel of him, loving the reactions I'm drawing from him.

I've never felt power like this, never felt sexy like I do now. I came home to find this man pleasuring himself to thoughts of me, and the high of that has me moaning right along with him as I bob my head up and down. I feel one of his hands rest softly on my neck, his fingers playing with my hair. "Oh, Logan. Holy god, woman."

His hips thrust up off the couch and he grows harder in my hand. I shift my weight so I can bring my other hand to his balls, remembering the feel of that soft, saggy skin. Cal obviously enjoys that move as he shouts a staccato noise I'm sure the neighbors upstairs can hear, even through the thick floors and insulation. "Sweetheart, I'm close," he says. "You'd better stop."

But I don't want to. For the first time, I'm desperate to feel a man unravel in my hands, to taste his orgasm and lick every drop of it from his body. I'm going to take what I need, damn it. This isn't like the other men who flopped on top of me until they went slack. This is Cal Brady, firm and solid and charming and real, crumbling to pieces beneath my hands and under my tongue. I increase the suction of my mouth, feeling him hit the back of my throat once, twice before he sobs a moan and shudders beneath me. Cal spurts into my mouth and I'm stunned to realize I enjoy the splash, the salty essence of him.

As he sags into the couch, I pull away from his lap, wiping my mouth with the back of my hand as he did after making me come with his tongue. "That was amazing," I whisper, not sure what to do next.

He barks out a laugh. "You're damn right it was. Come here." And I squeak as he pulls me into his lap, adjusting me so I'm not touching the sensitive skin of his still-erect penis. "Are you seriously here right now? Did that really happen?"

I nestle into his shirt, loving the sweaty smell of him today even as I worry about stains on my power suit. I don't want to worry about the implications of this. I just want to experience this with him. Before I can answer, Cal is kissing me again and I'm returning every twitch of his lips, our mouths moving together, tongues exploring. He groans softly into my mouth and I discover that I love nothing more than the small sounds he makes when we're together physically.

I hear his stomach gurgle, but he doesn't pull back, just keeps kissing me and winding his fingers more tightly into my hair. I glance down and see he's still hard beneath my hip. "Your belt is poking me," I tell him.

He nips at my ear lobe and says, "That's not my belt, babe." It's my turn to laugh as he drags his cheek stubble along my skin, teases his tongue along my jaw. "I was imagining you," he says between kisses. "And then you were here."

I'm about to tell him it was meant to be, when his stomach gurgles again. "You're starving," I say and then gasp as his thumbs circle my nipples through my blouse.

"For you," he says, but there's another groan from his GI tract. "Ugh. Okay, yes. For food, too."

With a sigh and a kiss to the top of my head, he eases out from under me and walks to the counter, rummaging around in the takeout bags. "I got enough; we can share," he says, coming back to the couch.

"You're just going to walk around with your..." I gesture at his crotch, where he's got his pants unfastened and his underwear shoved down right below his balls.

"With my dick out? Damn right, Lo-lo. He needs to dry out. You got him all wet." I bite my lip as he sinks back into the sofa next to me. "Anything else wet that needs to air out? Hm?"

I flush, which is ridiculous because he's had his mouth on every part of my body. There's something about finally discussing it with him that has me squirming, reminding me again how badly I've missed out on having close friends or, really, any opportunity to discuss anything personal. Mentioning a strong feeling to my mother was a sure way to get shushed. Cal hands me a container of chips and guac and I dig in as he attacks the enchiladas.

We cram food in our mouths, switching containers without talking, until he asks me how my day went. I shrug. "The suit helped," I say, and then I melt a little bit when he dabs at the corner of my mouth with his thumb, sticking it in his own mouth afterward to lick off the drop of cheese sauce. "I basically have twice as much work now," I confess and gesture at my work bag. "I have a bunch of reports I need to finish up tonight so I'm ready for client meetings tomorrow."

"They just added fancy-man to your work load? They didn't, like, move your regular folks to someone else?"

I shake my head. "And I guess it makes sense? I couldn't name a client I'd want to give over to anyone else at work, to be blunt about it. Maybe your dad."

Cal snorts. "Like he'd stand for that." He tells me about the steel mill and the groaning conveyor belt. We clean up the cartons together, him still with his pants unfastened, and I cannot stop laughing at the sight of him shoving bags in the trash with his underwear bunched up like that.

"You think I'm funny, Logan Miller?" He arches a brow at me, a gleam in his eye. I nod. "What if I decide to punish you for laughing at me?" He's on me before I can react, his tall body spinning me so I'm facing the counter. "What should I do about you?"

My breath hitches as I lean into the counter, enjoying this game, this side of Cal that I first saw Saturday night. I splay my fingers wide across the granite, palms flat as he sucks on my neck and pulls my hair loose. It tumbles around my shoulders for an instant before he gathers it in his fist and tugs my head back toward him, exposing my throat. "Maybe I should spank you," he breathes and I swallow, nodding, because that sounds like exactly what I want right now.

Cal gets to work unfastening my pants, yanking them down. "Step out of the pants," he says, helping to peel them off but keeping my heels on. He breathes slowly through his nose as he slides my panties off in the same way, and then I'm bare from the waist down, bent over the counter while he stands behind me, silently.

"Mmm," he groans as one palm massages my ass cheeks. "Now who's exposed?" He keeps kissing my neck as his hand massages, kneading harder while his other hand pinches my nipples into desperate peaks through my blouse. "You make me wild, Logan," he says, and then he bites me at the same time as his palm cracks across my flesh.

I scream, not in pain but in pleasure as it ripples through my body. All my senses fire at once as Cal keeps pinching and smacks the other cheek before his fingers reach between my legs where I'm hot and slick with wanting. "I found something wet," he says, stroking me as I moan and purr in his arms. "So fucking wet."

Cal slips a finger inside me and moves his other hand from my nipple to offer a finger to me, and I greedily suck it into my mouth, needing to feel full in both places as he strokes. "Hungry girl," he says. "And I just fed you..." Another crack as he smacks my ass again, and then the other cheek. I'm so grateful that he's spanking both sides equally so I don't feel unbalanced, but as soon as my thoughts drift to this distraction, I start moaning as he slides fingers back inside me.

Cal pulls his finger from my mouth and moves his hand to my hip, steadying himself. His mouth stays near my ear and I love the feel of his breath tickling me, his dirty words right up close to me. "So wet," he keeps saying, "so hot."

"Cal," I pant, bearing down on the finger he has inside me. "I want...I need..." I can't form words for what I want, but all I know is that I do. I want. I need. I'm writhing against him now, my palms sweating and sliding on the counter.

"Logan," he says, his hand firm on my hip. "Do you need to be fucked?"

"God, yes, Cal. That's what I need." I whimper as he pulls his finger out from inside me. "Oh, please."

"Tell me you want my cock," he says as I hear him rustling in his jeans, reaching for a condom. I hear the crinkle of a packet and he takes his hand briefly off my hip. I don't turn to look, frozen in place by the sensations he's stirred up. "Ask for it, and I'll give it to you, Lo."

"Please," I breathe, and then his hand is back on my hip, his body pressed against my back. He presses on my shoulders and I arch my back, presenting myself to him, sliding the slick heat of my center along his finger.

"Please, what?"

I take a deep breath and, eyes clenched shut with desire, I shout out, "Please, Cal. I need your cock inside me."

I barely have the words out before he slams into me, forcing my hips against the edge of the counter. It feels so big, so delicious, rasping against my inner walls and making every nerve in my body fire at once. I see stars as he circles his hand on my clit while he thrusts. Cal sinks his teeth into my neck and I come, moaning and shrieking, wobbling in my heels.

He doesn't ease up, keeps pistoning into me, grunting my name, tugging my hair, biting me. He is savage and I love every second of it. Just as I'm coming back into my body, I feel him swell even larger inside me. Cal grips me by the hips and pulls me against him. He's so deep inside me I worry he will poke out through my belly, but as I feel him throbbing, I start to come again.

"Cal, I'm..." I shriek again, sagging against the counter as he slumps over my back, pulsing his own release inside the condom while I spasm around him.

We stand like that together. Lean? We exist together against the counter until my knees actually do buckle. "Come on, Lo-lo," Cal says, scooping me up. "Let's get you to bed."

CHAPTER TWENTY-NINE
CAL

How does this keep happening? Am I really the selfish idiot my family says? Honest to god, that was exactly what I needed after a long day at work, and the fact that it was with Logan makes it all the better because we get along so damn well. That was the hottest fucking thing. It's like I conjured Logan right out of my fantasies. She literally walked up to me while I was imagining what she'd look like with her mouth wrapped around my cock.

She snores quietly next to me in my bed and I feel a little bit bad that she fell asleep before she could finish her work, but fuck that company. They can't just dump double work on her because all the other employees are too shitty to handle her clients. Shouldn't they want to hire a full staff of people like Logan? I guess she is uniquely brilliant.

I hate how stressed her job makes her feel. Like, I get that she grew up poor and needs to send money home to her mom, but does she really think she's a week away from being evicted? How much of an asshole am I if I feel glad that jumping into bed with her helped her kick back and have a little fun for a minute. She carries so much emotional weight around with her.

I sigh. Logan doesn't need my brand of fun. I roll onto my side and stare at her. She's so relaxed when she's asleep. Logan is beautiful. I love the lines of her chin, the slope of her shoulders. I really love the way her hips swell up from her narrow waist.

I reach out to touch her, just needing that connection, and I drift off to sleep with my hand on her skin.

B

IT'S STILL DARK when I start hearing my phone ring furiously, again and again. I think it's in the living room, rattling around on the coffee table, and I groan as I stumble over to it, knowing it's not going to stop ringing at this point.

"Uncle Kel?"

"Callum, you need to tell me exactly what happened at the steel mill today."

Shit. He's using his stern voice. "I told you everything I could figure out," I tell him, scratching myself as I try to wake up.

"And you left? Without concrete evidence to support your suspicion?"

What the hell did he expect me to do? Stay there all night to see why the belt was groaning? "Yeah. I came home at the end of the day. I hadn't eaten. I was spent. Doesn't Dad always say those basic needs are the most important element of a good—"

"Callum, the fucking bridge collapsed and I need you to meet me at the site as soon as humanly possible."

The line goes dead and I stare at my phone. Did that just happen?

I turn when I hear a shuffling sound and see Logan padding into the room. She's wearing my t-shirt and I feel something happen in my chest at the sight of that. "What's wrong?" She walks toward me and reaches out an arm to touch me, but hesitates.

I shake my head. "Something collapsed at the job site," I tell her. "I gotta go in to meet my family." I start rooting around for my jeans and a clean shirt. Logan stands at the door holding my hardhat, her eyes puffy from interrupted sleep. It's such a nice gesture and I don't quite know how to respond to it, so I cram my feet in my boots without tying them, and bend down to kiss her on the cheek before grabbing the hat and heading to the parking garage.

Damn, I had no idea the bridge was on the point of collapse. I just figured I'd go in this morning and stare at everything again with fresh perspective. As I drive, my mind wakes up fully and I consider what's likely going on down at the job site. I think my uncle would have told me if anyone was killed. God, I hope nobody was killed. It's one thing to cost a client millions of dollars in lost work time. Loss of life is something else entirely.

There is a whole army of security at the site when I pull up to the gate and I have to dig around to find my Beltane badge. Someone directs me where to park and I see my uncle and my father standing under a huge light with a bunch of very angry looking corporate dudes.

The whole place smells like acrid, burning stench. Like metal and rubber caught fire or opened up the pits of hell. The sounds of creaking metal and generators overpower all my senses and I wish I had grabbed ear plugs from inside Big Red.

I hang back, but my uncle sees me and stomps over to me. He doesn't speak, but I can see his nostrils flare. I try to remain calm here. I did my part. I told him what I saw, what I suspected. He clearly chose not to inform the client, or else they chose not to respond.

My dad is not as calm. He marches right over and shoves me in the shoulder, hard. "What in the hell is the matter with you? Did I raise you to be an idiot?"

"What the fuck, Dad? I called Uncle Kellen. I told him something was off."

Kellen pulls up a spreadsheet from the inspection application on his tablet device. "You didn't notice this?" He taps at the column of temperatures.

"Of course I fucking noticed that. That was the first thing I checked, to see if the heat was warping the belt."

Kellen double clicks the column and it gets larger. "All the numbers are the same, Callum. Tony dragged the same number down the entire column."

I frown. "It should be the same, though," I tell them. "Shouldn't the furnace have the same output given a consistent input and air circulation?"

My uncle shakes his head in disbelief. "Down to the tenth of a degree? Every single time? Grow the fuck up, Callum. We sent you in here to supervise this. It was your job to notice that he wasn't actually taking this measurement. Tony was phoning it in and now the client is losing a million dollars every few seconds."

I've never heard my uncle raise his voice before, let alone curse. Not like this. I literally have nothing to say in response to him. I just stand there for a long time, and I must not have noticed that my dad had walked away because I see him stomping back up to us with someone else in tow.

"Edward, this is my son, Callum." Shit. Is he going to feed me to the wolves right here? I actually feel like I might shit my pants, especially as I hear a terrible roar of machinery from inside the plant. Edward squints at me and runs his hand through his hair. My dad clears his throat.

I stick out my hand. "Nice to meet you...sir." I have no context for who this guy is. If my family is going to give me this much shit about a situation they really need to brief me more fully. I can't imagine Liam would ever walk into a scenario like this, but I guess Liam would have asked questions about the temperature column.

My dad's eyes flash anger at me, and I clench my jaw. "Callum is going to personally oversee the design and repair of the system," he says. I whip my head around to stare at him. Dad continues. "I give you my word that my own son is on this, because I know you know the Brady name equates to excellent engineering."

Edward looks me up and down and gives a curt nod, then turns on his heel and marches back over toward the mayhem.

Nobody speaks. None of us move. Finally, my dad raises a hand, and I flinch, worried he's going to actually hit me this time. But he points a finger at me. "I was embarrassed tonight, son."

I blink at him a few times. "Why are you putting me in charge of fixing this?"

He inhales deeply and lowers his hand. "Because this is your mess to fix. Make it right."

And without another word, he and my uncle walk back to their cars and drive away.

CHAPTER THIRTY
LOGAN

I SHOULD GO BACK TO SLEEP, BUT BETWEEN MY CONCERN FOR WHATEVER EMERGENCY pulled Cal away and the nagging pull of unfinished work, I find my mind is on fire. I make a pot of tea and pull on the sweatpants I had imagined wearing before...well, before tonight went off the rails.

Snuggled into Cal's shirt, I grab my laptop and nestle into the couch. Before I left the office, I determined that the bulk of my clients were at the same investment level and approximately the same age, which usually indicates they share a similar willingness to take financial risks.

I never wanted to offer anyone a cookie-cutter approach, but given the complexity of the Rudy account, I've decided that the best way forward is for me to recommend a very similar investment strategy for my other clients. I tell myself this is okay, because at the gala they all seemed interested in each other's portfolios.

By the time the sun comes up, I've selected a few safe choices and made note of a really interesting opportunity. I write a note for myself to look into this one local business that keeps turning up in my research, and then I close the laptop to stare out the window.

Cal's scent permeates this shirt, and I can't stop thinking about him now that he's not here. This isn't some perfumy fake smell. He wore the shirt all day to a job site, and I smell both his deodorant and a little of his sweat, and I try to understand why I like it so much. Nothing about the way my body responds to him makes sense.

I'm upset that once again, I dove into a physical experience with my roommate before we've had a chance to talk about things. I want to have a plan with Cal, talk through worst case scenarios. I want to make lists of expectations if we're going to have this sort of relationship. And yet, what I enjoy most of all is the unexpected and unplanned rush I feel each time he kisses me or touches me or slides inside my body.

I press the back of my hand to my cheeks, feeling the heat bloom there as I remember how completely I let go with Cal, sexually. It felt so wrong, but so absolutely right all at once. And I was so brazen when we were together, telling him just what I wanted, what I *needed.*

I don't know if there was ever another time in my life where I desperately needed something and asked for it...and got it. My mind races while I try to make sense of it, what it means going forward. He seemed to agree with me when I said it should have been a one-time thing, but then he also slept with his arms around me after he speared me with his musket in the kitchen. I giggle, remembering his Redcoat joke. Reluctantly, I rise to turn on the shower. I peel off his shirt, folding it and placing it on his pillow, and slip into the warm water, trying to reorganize my thoughts to begin my day.

The apartment feels empty without Cal here this morning, and it feels strange to leave for work without any of his questions, comments or observations. I consider sending him a text, but I don't want to distract him if he's in the middle of dealing with an emergency. Even the vibration of a cell phone can pull me right out of the zone if I'm concentrating. It's partly why I leave my phone off in my bag while I'm at work most of the time.

I catch the express bus toward the office, and smile when a text comes in from Nicole.

> You never told me how it felt to burn your bitch boss to ashes with your words.

> It was a medium successful operation,

Nicole immediately responds with a finger wagging GIF.

> Logan. You need Foof. I'm calling an emergency meeting for tonight.

> Oh, no, please don't bother anyone. I did stand up for myself and I have a plan.

NICOLE KENNEDY:

> Too many fucks are being devoted to this. You're
> coming to the bar tonight at 5:01. Do I need to send
> a car to fetch you?

Apparently everyone but me knows about 501's as a concept.

> Really, I'm okay. Your pep talk was so great.

I hate to think about my roommate's family pulling together over this, especially if there's some sort of all-hands-on-deck situation with a Beltane client.

Nicole sends an eye-roll GIF and types:

> I'm sending a car. Which I will also be inside. Do not
> make me come up and drag you outside.

I have to admit, it does feel nice that someone cares this much that I'm having a rough time at work. I bite my lip and type back

> OK

before I hop out of the bus and shove my hand out just as the elevator doors are closing in my building.

Of course, Marie is inside the car. Her eyes flare when she sees me and it looks like she's about to spit coffee at me. I wince, wondering if she'd really do that. I say nothing, and she says nothing until the doors open and we approach her office door. "You have Ms. Emerson at two o'clock and Mr. Dolan at two o'clock," she says curtly.

"A joint appointment?"

"No," she snaps. "They each asked to meet you individually."

"Marie. Why would you schedule them both simultaneously? How is that supposed to work?"

"Figure it out," she snaps, and slams her office door.

Okay, maybe I really do need Nicole to summon her cavalry. I ease into my office and try to decide a course of action that won't impact Mr. Alexander's bottom line. I don't want to have to reach out to him only a day after I took on the new account.

I stare at my desk for a few minutes, thinking. This isn't so different from when Linus needed to arrange a meeting with town leaders in *The Redcoat*. My fictional hero was dealing with volatile people on the brink of starvation and revolution. My clients seemed to get along the other night at the event. Pretty sure I heard Ms. Emerson ask to hear about the same opportunities as some of the other clients. Like Linus, I can help them find common ground, right? A mutually beneficial arrangement...

Interpersonal relationships with clients is not part of my job expectation, and for good reason. My brain does best with numbers. But I decide to build on the rapport and energy I had going Saturday night and just roll with the double meeting. I pull up some of the analysis I was working on at home. I type up some bullet points for what I plan to say to the clients, print out some visuals, and touch up my lip gloss before I make my way toward the conference room.

I channel my inner Nicole and do not glance to either side as I walk down the hall full of colleagues who are jealous of me and a supervisor who is setting me up to fail here this afternoon. I paste a huge smile on my face and walk up to both of my 2pm meetings.

"Jim! Mary!" I fake enthusiasm when I see them sitting with their coats in their laps. Is the receptionist against me, too? This is really unacceptable. "Let me grab those coats from you. Do you want to make your way into the conference room and I'll join you?"

Mary looks at Jim and back at me. "Both of us? I thought *we* were meeting, dear..."

I wave a hand as I scoop up the expensive coats from their laps. "I'll explain everything in just a moment."

I hurry over to reception and plunk the coats on the desk, causing Jeanine to startle and look up at me, then wince. I grit my teeth. "You will take these coats and then come offer the clients refreshments as per usual or I will not hesitate to march directly into Mr. Alexander's office." I don't wait for her response. Maybe I'm channeling Nicole without needing tonight's Foof meeting. Maybe I've just had enough?

I slide into the conference room and sit between Jim and Mary, who have each taken a seat at opposite heads of the table. "I was so glad when Marie told me you had each requested a meeting," I lie. "Ever since Saturday evening, I've been wanting to discuss an opportunity with you."

I pull up two packets and slide the print-outs toward them. "You know I look very closely into the companies where our clients invest. Any and all information about spending and hiring, and I'm studying it night and day."

I rifle through the pages of my own packet, holding it up like a librarian at story time so they can each see. "Each of you is heavily invested in healthcare and life sciences," I tell them.

Jim nods and aims finger guns at me. "Yeah, thanks to your good advice!"

I nod back. "Well, you know, I do tend to recommend the same good investments to all my favorite clients." I'm really laying it on thick, but they seem to be eating it up, so I carry on. "Notice anything on the budget lines for each of the companies?" I don't wait for an answer, charging ahead. "Trick question." I wink, channeling Cal's fun energy. "I highlighted the interesting part for you."

Jim and Mary squint at the paper, where I've pulled snapshots of the main budget items for a few different labs, most of them spinoffs from the research universities and medical school nearby, and all of them places each of them are already pretty heavily invested. Mary taps at the paper. "What is Vinea?"

"Great question," I say. "That exact question had me up most of last night." This is true. I noticed all our chemistry, healthcare and biotech companies where many of my clients invest are utilizing Vinea. "I did some research and best I can tell, it's a pretty new venture actually based locally here in Pittsburgh. The founder built the company from her dorm room in college."

I flip my packet to a page featuring a smiling blond, printed from Vinea's website. "I'm going to place some calls, but hear me out. Vinea is actively seeking investment funding. All of these trusted companies are already using their services."

I pause for effect here, trying to draw on my presentation skills from my MBA courses. Mary and Jim seem confused. "What if you invested some seed money into Vinea?" I'm not sure if it's possible for my eyebrows to shoot any higher into my hairline while I smile and wait to see what they think. I actually don't even know if this is something we're able to facilitate as an organization. This is very different from buying into a mutual fund and building an investment portfolio.

But here I am, figuring out what to say to the clients. I remind myself that I'm in this room right now because my supervisor acted inappropriately. I clench my toes inside my shoes, hating Marie with every hair on my head. Mary looks at Jim. Jim looks down at the papers. "It feels risky to me," he says, looking like he wishes he didn't feel that way. "In my younger days I took chances on new companies..."

Mary nods enthusiastically. "I completely agree." She pats my hand. "It's not that I don't trust your instincts. I actually had come to talk about moving along that risk scale you showed me months ago. Siphoning to more stable funds?" Mary bites a lip and I guess she doesn't want to admit her real age or financial circumstances to Jim.

I force myself to smile. "I completely understand," I tell them. "And I do want to apologize again about the scheduling confusion today. Mary, I'm happy to move you up the scale as we discussed earlier." I turn toward Jim, who keeps staring at the papers. "Is there anything I can do for you today since you came all the way here?"

B

A few minutes later, I usher both of them to reception, insisting they keep the packets to look over if they change their minds. I storm back into my office and slam the door, sinking into my chair and hoping neither of those clients complain to anyone higher up.

It's one thing for them to laugh and joke with one another at a party, but discussing their portfolios in front of each other? They could easily walk, and Mr. Alexander would want to know about this. But I can't bring myself to run to him with this issue. The time for that would have been before the meeting. At this point it would truly be my own fault if either of those clients raised a complaint about my little presentation.

"I can't go on like this," I say aloud. I massage my temples with my palms, realizing how badly I really do need advice from Nicole and her friends. Five-oh-one can't come soon enough.

CHAPTER THIRTY-ONE

LOGAN

I DECIDE TO WAIT FOR NICOLE OUTSIDE. I FEEL LIGHTER JUST STEPPING OUTSIDE THE doors to my building. I suppose this is how my mother has felt for years when she leaves work. Even the skin on my scalp loosens up. A whisper of guilt climbs my spine as I think about her having no options and working so hard so that now I have options. I have options. I have to keep reminding myself of that.

I laugh when I see a fancy black car slow to a stop and Nicole leans out the back window, her curly hair flying around in the wind. I've noticed that it's always windy downtown in Pittsburgh, probably because of the rivers. My own straight hair whips me in the mouth as I slide into the car next to her and lean my head back on the headrest.

"You look like you still have fucks, Logan Miller. You need to release the fucks if you're coming with me today."

"It's just really complicated," I start to explain but she claps her hands in my face, startling me.

"No fucks. Fresh. Out. Of. Fucks. These women are serious about reducing bullshit. Hey!" She directs this latest comment to the driver. "There's still a sinkhole on 10th. You need to go up Liberty Ave or we'll never get there."

He turns around in his seat and makes a face at her, but she points a finger at him. "Liberty," she repeats, and he rolls his eyes and puts on his blinker. Turning to me, Nicole reiterates, "You cannot have any fucks, Logan, or you will never get anything done."

Nicole tosses the driver a twenty when we stop in front of a cute building on Smallman Street. Nicole could definitely have walked here from her house, so I feel extra grateful that she made the extra trip to come retrieve me in a car. Inside, Bridges and Bitters looks less like a bar than it does a fancy Victorian parlor. The chairs and benches have velvety cushions. There are beautiful carpets throughout the space, and a dark mahogany bar takes up the back wall. Everything is illuminated by those lights that look like old gas lamps.

"This space definitely gives a lot of fucks," I whisper to Nicole, looking in awe at the elegant design.

Nicole nods. "You *should* give fucks about your career. Esther gives a ton of fucks about this place. Foof is mostly about giving no fucks when it comes to nonsense."

"We really should make shirts." A woman in a beautiful red dress winks as she reaches toward Nicole for a hug. She thrusts a hand toward me and says, "Esther Storm. I own this joint."

"Logan Miller," I tell her. "Your space is amazing." I notice the pride evident in her face as I gesture around.

"Logan is releasing her fucks with us." A familiar voice comes up behind me and I turn to see Juniper Jones shaking out her short, dark hair.

There are just a few patrons in the bar, and Esther points a thumb toward the back wall where the bar is set up. "Go on in," she says. "I'll bring a tray in a minute." I see a hall to the left of the bar and we round the corner. I'm expecting it just to be restrooms and maybe an office, but I gasp when we approach an elegant banquet room.

The crystal chandelier sends rainbows and sparkles of light bouncing off the walls and I watch with delight as Nicole sinks into a vintage settee, looking very much like she'd fit in on the *Titanic*. I squeeze in next to her as she kicks off her shoes and I watch as a stream of confident women make their way back into our hideout. Orla slinks in and somehow doesn't seem out of place dressed as if she were climbing around a dusty job site all day. I'm sure she *was* doing that.

After a few minutes, Esther returns with a silver tray of fancy drinks and someone stands and taps her ring against the stem of one of the glasses. "Ladies of Foof," she says. "We have a newcomer."

I should feel embarrassed. Normally I would with all this attention lobbed at me, but I already know Nicole and Maddie, and I sort of know

Juniper. I can feel the three of them forbidding me from feeling uncomfortable. The blond woman smiles and says, "Esther, you introduce yourself first and tell us what we're drinking today."

Esther gestures at the tray. "I'm Esther Storm, proprietor of Bridges and Bitters. Yes, Storm is my real last name." Everyone chuckles. "Today, you're enjoying a Transitiontini. It's local vodka, ginger liqueur, pear juice, Luxardo, morello cherry, half a lemon squeeze, a splash of syrup, and let's get these fucks flying already."

Esther sips her drink and smacks her lips. The blond woman does the same. "Amazing flavor combinations, babe. As per usual. I'm Samantha Vine, data scientist."

I hear from a personal trainer named Piper and a romance novelist named Chloe before all eyes turn to me. "Hi," I stammer. "I'm Logan and I work at—"

"Nope." Nicole shakes her head and takes a sip of her drink. "Not 'I work at.' What *are* you, Logan? Remember Foof. It's the sound of your fucks floating away, Logan."

I nod. "Okay, I am a financial analyst. And I'm new at...expressing my feelings."

"Nice," Juniper whispers.

Samantha points at Juniper. "Before we learn about how Logan is freeing her fucks, I want to hear an update from Juniper's re-election campaign. Last time, some asshole was upset about her clothing choices?"

Juniper rolls her eyes. "The trolls are out there in force. They were commenting on my pant suits as unfeminine the last time I was here but this week I'm catching flack because my husband stays home with our boys."

There's a collective gasp around the room as people murmur angrily in response to Juniper's comments. She nods her head and rolls her eyes. "My clerk literally fielded a call today from someone wanting to know if I'm proud of myself now that I've emasculated my husband."

Juniper goes on to explain that Ty wanted to go to the caller's house and beat him up or at least speak to the press about how much he loves being around for his kids. "Ty's dad wasn't in the picture when he was young," Juniper says. "Being a father is really important to him. But fuck that caller."

"What did you say in response?" I blurt out my question, on the edge of my seat and forgetting I'm new here. Nobody seems to recoil at my outburst.

Juniper grins. "I asked to hear my opponent's thoughts on having a stay-home spouse caring for their family, and kept pushing him to clarify why he hadn't asked my male opponent that question. Eventually the jerk hung up."

There's a round of cheers from the room and lots of clinking glasses. Maddie nods fiercely and pats her belly.

"That's such horse shit," Samantha says and everyone takes a breath. She turns to me and smiles. "Juniper has had a lot of practice freeing her fucks from her last time running for judge. But Nicole says you're new to the art. Let's hear it, Logan."

I bite my lip. Nicole pats my leg. "I'm going to summarize to save time. Logan is a bad ass analyst fresh out of an Ivy League MBA program. Obviously she got swooped up by a big firm to come work here in the city of bridges. Her coworkers are a bunch of whiny man-babies who can't handle it that someone with a vagina is smarter than them and they treat her like shit at work." I open and close my mouth, feeling like I should refute her, but she keeps flaring her nostrils as she talks and honestly, she's not wrong.

I pick up the thread, explaining that the firm landed a huge client, who ended up requesting me personally to handle his account. "So now, they're dumping grunt work on me and, like, the receptionist isn't taking clients' coats? They've left me to operate alone and are sort of refusing to work with me in any supportive role. And my big boss said I should let him know if there were shenanigans that impact the bottom line and honestly I don't know when to go to him or how I should proceed with just...doing my job."

I take a deep breath. I feel like I can't stop talking now that I started and the room is full of gasps and shocked faces, making me feel like I'm not insane, and I realize I maybe thought my feelings were off since I was the only one who seemed to feel them. I wish I'd listened to Cal and his family sooner.

I swallow and turn to Juniper. "We studied you in grad school. I was so awed by your background, how you came through the foster system. I grew up with a single, teen mom." I spill my guts, telling these women how I've spent decades learning to tamp down any strong feelings and act grateful for anything I get. Anything.

Juniper comes and hugs me. She clasps my hands. "Those are heavy lessons to unlearn. I'm here to tell you, you are *worthy* of success."

"Hear, hear." The women in the room clamor to agree with Juniper, shouting words of encouragement.

"So," I say, shrugging and sipping my drink. "I don't know what to do."

"What's your worst case scenario?" I think it's Chloe asking. I wonder if she's going to use my story in one of her books or something. I bite my lip in fear at the thought, but everyone else nods.

Another deep breath. "Well, like I said, I was raised by a single mom. Anyway, things were always hard for us. Mom always had two jobs, and I always had a job. Anyway…I keep saying anyway. I had scholarships for school, so I don't have loans. I just want to be able to take some of the burden off my Mom. I've been paying her rent." I feel myself getting choked up as I talk. "If I lose this job I won't be able to do that for her. Or me I guess."

Samantha's face is sympathetic as she leans forward on the table, stretching to grab my hands, which feels odd but I let her. "You know you won't be destitute if you leave a shitty job, right? Someone else will snap you up immediately."

I do know that, rationally. "It's a lot of years of housing and food inse-curity to overcome with rational thinking," I say quietly. I take a shaky breath. "I know I have an attractive degree, but I also know what it feels like to be evicted. I feel like…everything I bring home I have to hoard away just in case."

"Logan's still living like she's poor," Nicole butts in. My eyes widen at her blunt speech. "You do, babe. You've got an emergency fund, you've got friends with awesome houses with guest rooms. Hell, if things get really bad you know you can live in the back of Cal's disgusting Bronco."

Nicole looks around the room. "I think she needs to jump off of that shitty company. There's really no way to salvage that toxic climate."

Toxic climate is a new phrase for me, but it hits home immediately. "Shouldn't I try to fix the problem, though?"

Piper taps a fingernail on her lip, considering. "I put a lot of effort into working on communication with the staff at my former place of work. It was a similar thing. I kept getting more personal training clients than the other trainers who had been there longer."

"And who also had dicks," Orla blurts. Everyone rolls their eyes.

"Right. It was a bunch of men threatened by me." She shrugs. "I tried HR, I tried professional development, but honestly the other people there weren't interested in changing and there was no pressure from manage-ment for them to do so. I was bending over backwards to improve that work atmosphere, and they didn't give a rat's ass. So I quit and took my clients with me. Thanks to moral support from Foof, obviously."

Samantha grins. "Best move you could have made."

I look around the room at all the supportive faces. "I'm not...ready for private practice, though. I don't really want to do that. I enjoy working for a company, being part of a larger team."

Piper leans across the table to meet my eyes. "Are you ready for an agonizing process of working with Human Resources and sitting across from your colleagues as you all attend civility trainings?" I shudder at the thought and shake my head.

"Then you need to find a recruiter and work for a better company," Nicole says, beckoning the newly appeared server for another tray of drinks. "That's my homework for you I think. Call a head hunter."

"What about my clients?"

"That's a fair question," Samantha says. "If the clients are unhappy with your firm after you move on for a better opportunity, they'll move to another one. You can't keep yourself miserable just because you like your clients."

I hadn't considered that, and I sit for a minute sipping my drink, my head swirling. There's so much confidence in this room, so much assurance. Maddie talks a little bit about her own career challenges. She was laid off from the newspaper, has no safety net other than the women in this room, and doesn't want to be financially dependent on Liam. She catches my eye and says, "My parents worked shitty jobs and shift-work, too. My first couple paychecks at the paper were...more money than I'd ever seen before in my whole life."

I relate to her words so deeply I feel a little tingly. Maddie nods her head at Nicole. "This one here forced me to make a budget and tape it to the fridge so I could remind myself I really, truly did have spare money to spend on fancy fanny packs."

Everyone laughs as Maddie pulls a stick of gum from the pouch around her waist. She shares a few job leads she's chasing and lets everyone know she decided not to work with Liam's mom. "Things are actually going way better with us now that that's settled," she says. And then she winks. "But I know we're not talking about that sort of fucks."

"We'll get back to that sort of fucks," Samantha says. "I need to butt in and say that I definitely took the Nicole spreadsheet approach and decided I'm going to pursue funding more aggressively. Vinea is ready to spread, I think."

"Wait, did you say Vinea?" I snap my mouth shut, not meaning to interrupt. Is this seriously the founder of the company I was researching earlier? Is Pittsburgh that small? I tilt my head, feeling my drinks a little bit, and study the attractive, kind woman across the table from me. It is her. The woman from the photo online. I'm not sure how I didn't put it together earlier, but I chalk it up to me being nervous.

Samantha nods. "Yep. Sam Vine. Vinea. Cheesy, I know, but like I always say, I want my solutions to spread like a vine and dig their tendrils into every lab, every research project."

She talks about her team she's putting together and the successful launch of their new product. Samantha created a cloud-based tool for scientists to track, measure and forecast their scientific work. "There is so much repetition in labs," she says. "Plus these idiot geniuses keep misplacing data. And doing shit on paper. Paper!"

"Liam hates paper," Maddie blurts and gets a round of hearty shushing.

"Literally nobody cares about him right now," Orla says, leaning toward Samantha. "I want to hear about Samantha's funding."

"Well, I mean, that's my work right now. Finding the millions of dollars. I..." her eyes sparkle and she looks around the table. "I think we can get a billion. Foof!" She blurts the term like a battle cry and slaps the table. "I *know* we can get a billion."

"I agree," I say, causing everyone to turn and look at me. I shrug. "I was looking into the budgets of the companies where my clients are currently invested. Vinea is a line item on basically all of them. You're already in use by the big players that attract the attention of the big investors."

Samantha blinks a few times and then points at me. "We need to have a chat."

CHAPTER THIRTY-TWO
CAL

I don't know where to start. Uncle Kellen fired Tony as soon as he found the drag-and-drop temperature shit. I don't have project management experience, not like this. I don't know what my budget is, who our suppliers are. I know literally nothing except that I'm surrounded by actual hellfire and I've been left here to burn.

The guys cleaning up the mess on the floor seem to have their marching orders, so I go into Tony's office. I try to channel everything I've ever heard my dad and uncle say about business. My dad's big thing is looking at people's trashcans. He has a theory that if a company isn't managing something simple like regularly emptying the trash, then there's something really wrong at every step of the process.

Sure enough, Tony's trash is full and has flies hovering around it. Not knowing what else to do, I start cleaning up his office. At first it's easy to find the obvious trash and food wrappers, and I bag those up and find a Dumpster outside. But then, I don't know what to do with the papers everywhere other than fucking read each of them. Tony's office has filing cabinets, but he doesn't seem to use them or organize anything in any meaningful way.

I start to suspect my dad sent me here initially knowing I'd wind up having to clean this office and that would be my penance for the boat thing. Since the heaps on the desk are useless anyway, I take an arm and sweep them all to the floor so I have a clean surface to start making piles. And then I just start organizing shit as best I can.

I find inspection reports, and realize I can sort those by machinery type, so I start making stacks. Then I find repair contracts and purchase orders for components of the different machines. I really start to feel like I'm getting somewhere. The sun is up before I stop for air.

$$\text{B}$$

I OPEN the door to the office and see that it must be a shift change. Workers are filing into the office area to punch in and stash their lunch boxes. I follow the line to see if there's at least a vending machine where I can buy something crappy to fill my belly. I grab the least disgusting sandwich and look around, noticing that people are staring at me. "Hey, everyone," I say, waving and trying to swallow the dry sandwich. Overly dry is better than soggy, I guess.

"I'm, uh, here to fix the bridge."

More than a few of them make a face, like that's the most shocking and upsetting news they've ever heard. I can't help but agree with them. "I'm Cal," I say and gesture around. "I met some of you yesterday, I think. Anyway, you're all the experts of how this place works. I hope I can learn from you while I find my bearings."

Someone snorts. "You gonna pay us overtime for training you?" There's a round of agreement and people bang on the table supportively.

"I wish," I tell them, feeling like Linus McClinton in *The Redcoat* when he had to appease the angry villagers. I know these guys are stressed, too. Hell, they work here every day. In the book Linus kept trying to find ways to relate to everyone, find the right levers to pull that helped people agree. I say, "The sooner we get this place back up and operating, the more secure your jobs are, right? Hopefully we can find some common ground." The mention of job security shuts everyone up, but honestly they're all getting laid off if the company keeps losing money this way. Bankruptcy is always a looming threat for industries like this.

I nod and make my way back to Tony's office, starting in on a new heap of paperwork in my sorting journey before I finally locate the name of the company who last serviced the bridge. "Fuck yeah," I shout, wiping off Tony's office phone and calling the number on the invoice. "Now we're getting somewhere."

ℬ

AN HOUR LATER, my new best friend Frank is here with a crew to haul away broken shit and assess which pieces of the bridge are salvageable. Frank knows exactly what to do, and I'm so grateful I could hug him. But I don't, because I know that getting started on the repair work here is basically the least of my concerns. I commit to getting Tony's office in order before I leave here today, but take the time to fire off an email to the head of the mechanical department at Beltane. I know dad put me in charge of overseeing this, but if he wants this to go well I'm going to at least need advice from people who have managed this sort of project in the past.

I work until it's dark outside, which is a pretty long time considering it's summer and I'm sweating up in a barely air conditioned office. Frank introduces me to his second-shift top dog and I make sure they both have my cell before I take off. I have got to get some sleep or I'm going to be useless in the morning.

The condo is dark when I get there, and I'm too exhausted to call Logan and figure out if she's okay. I know she's got some shit going on at work, too. I make myself a sandwich and pass out. When my alarm goes off at five, I feel groggy and hungover. I down a bunch of aspirin and start shoveling food into a bag to take with me today. I cannot continue living on that vending machine and skipping meals.

I look down at what I have in the cupboard—mostly bars and peanuts. I feel like on one hand, I should rush back to work and be there, but then something else tells me I need to pause for a minute and make a plan. This isn't going to be a sprint repair where I pull one late night and then make up for it over the weekend.

I cringe when I look in the open cupboard and notice that I still haven't contributed any dishes or towels to the kitchen. I think back to Tony, just sitting in piles of disarray. Sloppy. This isn't who I want to be. Okay, one thing at a time.

I stop at the 24-hour grocery store and fill a cart with non-perishable stuff that doesn't seem too unhealthy. There's a lot more options than I thought, between dried fruit and nuts and these little quinoa pouches that are basically adult baby food. From the parking lot of the store, I pull up the Fiesta website on my phone and see there's something literally called a starter set. I get why my mom was keen to go to their clearance sale, but sometimes a guy just has to pay full price to solve a problem. I order the starter set in the sunflower color, because it makes me think of Logan, all bright and cheerful.

I email my mom to say I took care of the dishes, thanking her for the lead on the brand name, and tell her I won't be able to make it to dinner this week because of a crisis at work. Then I set some reminders for myself to drink water, turn my phone on Do Not Disturb, and drive back to the work site ready to keep sifting through the ashes.

CHAPTER THIRTY-THREE
LOGAN

 the night. Samantha beckons for me to follow her out to the bar, where she asks Esther to pour us "something celebratory."

I climb into the stool next to her, noticing that there's a foot rest at exactly the right height so my legs aren't dangling as I sit. Sam sees me noticing, and nods. "Esther thinks of everything," she says. "This is a place where women are centered." She gestures toward a series of hooks beneath the bar and I realize I can hang my bag there, right where I can see it, but don't have to hold it.

All these little touches make me feel so comfortable. I can absolutely see why Nicole loves it here, and I'm so grateful she included me in this circle. Sam rests her elbows on the bar and turns toward me. "I'm just going to get right to it. I want you to work for me."

I almost spit out my drink. "What? We just met!"

"Maybe, but you didn't 'just meet' my business, you obviously have a sharp eye for financial analysis, and you come with Nicole Kennedy's blessing as a boss bitch. I need someone with your skill set."

I recall how Nicole said most startups have ideas people and hustlers, but always need to find someone with an MBA to round it all out. "I..." My instinct is to insist I can't possibly walk away from my job and my clients. My instinct is to tell her I need the stability of an established company and the health insurance and so many things. But what has that gotten me so far? A situation where I walk around with my entire body clenched and a sense of dread every time I open my office door.

It's like Sam can read my thought processes, because she says, "I'll match your salary. We've got a decent health plan at Vinea. You've seen for yourself that my software is the real deal, Logan. I'm not being cocky here. I know there's a problem in the world of life sciences research, and I know Vinea can solve it. You know it, too."

I swallow and take another sip of my drink. It's something light this time and it might not even have any alcohol in it, but it's refreshing and the pause lets me gather my thoughts. "I do know it, Sam," I tell her. "But I'm not sure if I'm ready to make that move."

"Come build something extraordinary with me," she says. "Do you really want to spend your career being nice to assholes while you apply your skills to build other people's dragon hoards? Come help build the tool that lets scientists discover the cure for cancer and transform regenerative medicine."

I sigh. This woman sure knows how to lead a sales pitch. "I thought computer programmers were all socially awkward," I tell her, laughing.

She takes a big swig of her drink. "I told you, I'm a data scientist." We laugh together and Sam beckons Esther for her bill. Esther swats her hand like Sam's money is no good here and Sam snorts, fishes in her purse, and slaps a fifty on the bar. "Come on," she says. "We have to run before she tries to give the money back."

Feeling elated and overcome, I grab my purse and follow her out the front door. The steamy summer air hits me when we reach the sidewalk and I have to pause and catch my breath from the drastic change. "Call off sick tomorrow," Sam says. "Let me give you a tour of Vinea and make you a proper offer. You can have Juniper look it over if you're worried."

I have never called off before. My mom never had healthcare or paid sick days. Calling off always meant missing pay. For the first time, this really feels like a past tense worry for me, like I've finally internalized that this is no longer something I have to worry about. I've got personal days and paid sick time and vacation time at my job now, and most likely any job I'll get from here on out.

"I signed a non-compete when I moved here," I tell Sam, biting my lip and watching as she uses her phone to call for a ride.

"Where do you live? We can share a car," she says, ignoring my comment. It turns out we're both in the east end of the city, and my heart soars at the thought of having a friend live nearby. As we slide into the back seat of the SUV that pulls up outside the bar, Sam finally acknowledges my last remaining worry. "Wouldn't a non-compete clause just prevent you from joining another investment firm? I'm not hiring you to do that, Logan. I'd be hiring you to lead and build my finance team."

The car pulls up in front of my building and Sam hands me her card. "Call me when you wake up. We'll talk. If you want, I'll have someone from legal take a look at whatever contract you signed. Let's make this work."

I nod my head, only slightly, and Sam grins as the car pulls away.

My emotions are swirling, my thoughts racing. Can I really do this? Leave a sure thing I hate, to take a chance on something I might love? I own my own condo. I have a job with growth potential in a company that pays well. I have a graduate degree. I think about my goals, and realize that they've all failed to take my happiness into account.

The only parts of any of it that I enjoy are the thrill I get when one of my predictions pans out...and my roommate. I take the elevator up to my floor and see that Cal must have come home. His boots are in the tray and he left the light on over the stove. I smile, remembering how my mother used to do that so she didn't have to turn on the big kitchen light and risk disturbing me since the door to my room never quite shut all the way.

I think about something Juniper said at the bar. If the people at my job right now feel like it's totally okay to talk about my personal life and accuse me of going after clients romantically, it's going to take a huge effort to shift the needle on office culture. Samantha Vine is an entirely different sort of leader, and likely runs a company with an entirely different feel. I nod my head, determined to do this thing. It feels scary, but it feels right somehow.

Glancing down the hall, I see Cal's door is shut tight. I'm glad he's getting some rest. He must be exhausted and, frankly, so am I. I take a magnet and pin Sam's card to my fridge and pull out my phone to dial Marie's work line. When her voicemail picks up, I say I need to use a personal day and don't feel up to coming to work in the morning. It's not even a lie.

I know better than to call my mom for her support about this. Better to let her know once the ink is dry and I've made a change than to expect her to pep me up for a meeting like tomorrow. Instead, I email Sam's Vinea address from my phone to ask what time works for her in the morning, and I smile when she responds almost instantly, telling me to be there with a smile on my face at nine. My heart soars and I wish I had someone to celebrate with. I wish for a moment that Callie had been real, and that she and I could jump and hug and clap our hands about this opportunity.

But, then I wouldn't have met Cal and I wouldn't even be in the position to make this change in my life without him. I know that if I went in and shook him awake, he'd give me a high five. I could probably convince him to have sex again in celebration. But I also know that he needs his rest so he can be on top of *his* game at work right now, so I just smile and pat his door as I walk past his room. I head off to bed feeling satisfied for the first time in a long while.

CHAPTER THIRTY-FOUR
CAL

I'M NOT EXPECTING MY COUSIN ORLA TO SHOW UP AT THE STEEL MILL, SO I ALMOST drop a pile of files when she inserts herself into my new office. "Jesus, Callum," she snorts, plunking her messenger bag on the chair. "You need me more than I thought."

"Who sent you?" It comes out like some sort of threat in a thriller movie, and I realize I'm pretty darn tired. I start looking around for my snack stash to see if I've got anything caffeinated.

"I heard my dad and Uncle Mick talking about this disaster," Orla says, rooting through her bag and, finding a banana, handing it to me. The smell of it when I crack open the peel has a hypnotizing effect and I sink into my chair, which groans. How did Tony work in these conditions for so long?

"So anyway, you emailed the head of mechanical, which is great. But obviously you're also going to need to consult with someone from electrical. That's me." She pulls out her iPad and loops a set of ear plugs around her neck. "Tell me where you are right now and I'll tell you who you need to call to help get this fixed."

"Dad told me I had to do it," I sigh, smashing my forehead down against the desk, which I've finally managed to clear off.

"Did he say you personally had to do something outside your skill set? Did he really say you, Callum Brady, were meant to tighten every screw and solder every joint on that bridge?" I shake my head. Orla sounds an awful lot like my Uncle Kellen, just with more ire behind her words. "What's the number one motto at work, Cal?"

I just blink at her a few times, too tired to argue and not really sure if this is a rhetorical question. She rolls her eyes at me. "Hire the right person for the job," Orla says. She starts screwing the ear plugs in and slips a set of safety goggles on her face before flipping her ponytail so it sticks out of her hardhat. "You coming with me?"

I trail behind her as she starts talking to the crew working on the conveyor. They're definitely nicer to her than they are to me. For as long as I can remember, Orla has been the only girl in any of her engineering environments. Even at a huge school where tons of women enrolled in environmental and mechanical and civil engineering, the electrical specialty was a huge sausage party. Orla always says she has to be mean so they don't turn on her. Watching her now, I'm certain everyone listens to her because she's so damn competent. Expertise seems to swirl around her like a current.

"Why aren't you in charge of everything?" I marvel at how quickly Orla checks over the specs for repairing the wiring in the damaged conveyor.

"You're asking the right questions at least," she shouts as someone nearby starts sawing apart the crumpled metal to be hauled out of here. "Look, Cal, you can still oversee this project personally but you need a project manager who's used to working on projects that span multiple departments. I think you need to tap Dakota."

I wince. "She's Uncle Kellen's favorite person at work. There's no way he's going to let her go from whatever else she's working on."

Orla looks at me like I'm the stupidest person she ever met. She's probably right. "Cal. This is a steel client. Do you know how many zeroes they add to the Beltane revenue? You're an idiot if you don't think Dad is waiting for you to call Dakota over here."

"Did your dad send *you* over here, Orla? Is this some kind of test?"

"Of course it's a test. But no, like I said, I'm here to oversee the electrical. Because unlike you I aspire to climb the ranks at work and run the department some day and I need to seize opportunities like this when they come up."

"What the hell is that supposed to mean? You think I want to sit and file paperwork for my entire life?"

She shrugs. "You never do or say anything to suggest otherwise. I just thought you were content."

What is she even talking about? I've complained about my lack of responsibility at work for years. Years! "You can't tell me you don't know I hate inspection write ups."

"Big deal. You hate them. What initiative have you taken to do anything else?" Orla turns as she notices a beeping sound from across the room and sighs. "I gotta go look into that. Call Dakota. Trust me."

I'm a little shaken up by this whirlwind visit and I start to wonder if I imagined the whole thing. Like maybe I'm just exhausted and she's some sort of hallucination sent to make me question my entire existence? Do people really think I'm just content? I drag my hands through my hair and look around at the chaos that is my new home until I restore order. Somehow.

"Right," I mutter. I literally don't know Dakota's last name or how to look up her number. I have to call the freaking front desk and ask Em to connect me. Dakota picks up right away. "Hey, Dakota. Cal Brady."

"Oh. Hey!" She doesn't sound surprised to hear from me.

"So I'm sure you've heard about the conveyer collapse?" I bite my nails as she tells me that everyone at work is scared to breathe too loudly around my dad and how Uncle Kellen showed up today with his top button undone. "I swear he's a minute away from rolling up his sleeves," she says. I should laugh. If I were less terrified and overwhelmed I'd probably laugh at the thought of my uncle looking rumpled.

"But yes," Dakota continues. "I was sort of expecting your call. I can be there in an hour but I'll email you some cascades and punch lists right now."

My phone bings with an email notification as she speaks. "Wait. You have all this stuff ready to go?"

"Like I said, I was expecting you to call. I know this project predates me, but I pulled up the notes from my predecessor, which wasn't easy because everything was all hand written then. That bridge was reaching the end of its life. But I guess nobody quite expected...this."

"Thank you for saying nobody expected it," I breathe out. "My family acts like I'm a royal fuck up for not expecting this." That's not entirely true, I remind myself. I feel bad for putting her in a position where she has to comfort me. I hang up with Dakota, who says she will get here as soon as she can.

I look through all the organized charts she put together of who specifically is responsible for what, on what timeline. Glancing down the list, I'm relieved to see calling in Frank was the right move and it seems like his crew is on schedule for the repairs. Dakota even has notes on here for when

I'm supposed to email updates to my uncle to sign off on. It's strange to see my name in so many different slots on this list, as point person and the decision-maker. Like I just told Orla, I've been desperate for more responsibility. Now that I have it for something like this, I feel really inadequate.

In my office, which seems less dreadful now that I've finally filed all the piles of crap lying on every surface, I sit down and really study the lists. I think about the past few weeks leading up to this moment, starting with my birthday. I'm not proud of anything I've done recently. All of it has been impulsive, reckless. God, especially sleeping with Logan. I feel like an utter slime ball for messing with her trust that way, just because I felt horny and couldn't control my urges.

Tamping down those feelings of self loathing, I look at Dakota's spreadsheet and find the first task with my name on it. Of course, she has hyperlinks to the schematics of each machine component on the manufacturer's website. I pull up my design software and, for the first time in a really long time, get to work actually engineering a solution to a problem.

CHAPTER THIRTY-FIVE
LOGAN

The air feels different at Vinea. I decide this must be because the offices are in a brand new building with tons of south-facing windows and the whole space is filled with light. As the receptionist walks me to meet Sam, I notice that all the employees on the floor have privacy walls that move up and down in their work space, depending if they're on the phone or collaborating on a project.

Everyone has a happy expression on their face and seeing the contrast to the energy at my current office takes my breath away. I'm actually winded when Sam pulls me in for a hug as she greets me before saying, "Sorry. I know I'm supposed to ask first if you're a hugger. I'm a hugger. I'm so happy you're here!"

We sit down in her office, which looks an awful lot like my living room in the condo. She's got a couch and a fridge, a table and chairs. Her own desk is a small one off in the corner, with one of those yoga ball chairs and a floor lamp. Everything in here screams comfort and approachability.

"I've got some paperwork," she says. "I want to talk numbers with you and tell you what I need most, and then I want to hear all of your worries so I can address them."

Sam shows me the Vinea software I've seen appear as a budget line item for so many of the companies I've suggested my clients invest in. We watch a promotional video explaining how the software works. "Wow," I say as the short clip ends. "I was expecting a lot more jargon there."

She beams. "The target audience for that isn't the scientists who will use the software," she explains. "This one is aimed at investors we need to convince to fund the software." Sam tells me she hired a great PR firm with staff members who have degrees in the hard sciences. "They can translate all my data-brain dumps into gold nuggets for rich people to scoop up." Sam winks.

"But like I said, I need a numbers gal. My focus is on the solutions, on coding them and building them out so they're tailored to research institutions, startups, and huge biotech firms. I've got people doing my hustling. I need someone like you to manage the forecasts."

She slides me a contract and my eyes bulge when Sam taps the highlighted salary figure. "That can't be right." I slide the contract back to her. "That's more than I'm earning now. Way more."

"That's industry standard for someone with your degree," she tells me. "This would be a promotion, Logan. In every way." She thumbs through the contract, looking for something. "Ah. Here. Last night I asked my legal counsel if there would be any concerns about poaching you. Did you bring your contract? My MJ can check it to be totally sure, but said this is a totally different industry and your non-compete clause shouldn't be an issue at all."

My jaw works up and down as I take in everything she's saying. "Our HR person can review all the nitty gritty with you. We've got a gym on site and showers and all that crap. You can work from home if you want. We serve lunch and breakfast here every day, on site childcare, PTO...you'll probably understand the retirement options better than I do."

Sam leans back in her chair and takes a sip of water. "Tell me your worries, Logan. 'Cause I want you here."

AN HOUR LATER, I have exhausted every nervous concern I can think of and Samantha grins at me like a Cheshire Cat. "I don't want you to sign today," she says. "I want you to go show all this to Juniper or whichever lawyer you like, and I want you to sleep on it. And then I want you to sign it electronically so we don't have to go through the extra step of scanning it. That's so annoying and I hate physical paper. You saw that in the promo video."

I laugh. And then I bite my lip. "Honestly, all of it sounds too good to be true, Sam. Friendly colleagues. A pleasant work environment..."

Sam rolls her eyes. "You've obviously never worked anywhere run by women before," she says. "I take leadership very seriously. I take classes on this shit because it's important. Building a sense of belonging for everyone. Did you notice there's no stairs in this building? I don't ever want to have to retroactively add a ramp to accommodate someone who uses a mobility tool. My ideas can't change the world if I'm not looking at *everyone* who lives in this world. I don't just talk about equity and inclusion. I pay cold, hard cash to experts to help me bring diverse minds to the table at the planning stage of everything." Sam grabs my hands and looks into my eyes. "Vinea has the potential to be something amazing, Logan. I know it. I want you to help make it so."

Woosh. This feels so different from when I visited the recruiting events in grad school. The companies I visited seemed to care more about my GPA and the prestige of the school than the skills I was building. Samantha seems like she can see through my skin, and, shockingly, likes what she sees in there. I'm not used to feeling appreciated.

I leave the Vinea campus—it's weird to me to use that word for a workplace, but it definitely has the collaborative, inquisitive feeling of a place of learning—and feel unsettled. I don't know what to do with myself, but know I can't go home in this state of mind or I'll do something rash. I take a few deep breaths and then pull out my phone, deciding it's close enough to lunch that maybe I can catch Nicole and pick her brain while she takes a break.

She answers after one ring. "Oh my god, did Sam woo you? Are you going to work for her? You have to tell me everything."

I laugh. "She's trying her best. Hey, do you have a few minutes?"

I hear a loud clanging sound in the background. "Ha! I've got thirty. Where are you? Want to come for lunch?"

I hustle across the Rachel Carson bridge to the Stag Law office building, where Alice is apparently just serving lunch for the entire company. Nicole meets me at the door and rushes me into the cafeteria, where she snags Alice from behind the serving line. "It's sandwiches today, Al," Nicole says. "Let everyone just take their own shit. You have to come sit with us and hear Logan's scoop."

Thrown off guard once again by their friendliness, I find myself seated in a cozy booth with a tray of sandwiches and fruit. Nicole even drops a pickle onto my plate. The scene is both an echo of and totally opposite from the diner where I spent my formative years. How many times did I serve lunch to groups of colleagues like this, talking about something important in their world. And now it's me, sitting down with successful career women, biting into the pickles instead of serving them.

"I still feel anxious about what leaving will mean for my clients," I confess as Nicole nods.

She folds her fingers on the table and clicks her tongue. "Our clients here are like family," she tells me. "I don't even really have any business connecting with our clients and I still love all of them. So I get that. But you know what? Sometimes our lawyers leave and go on to better things—like being elected judge—and we find someone else new and lovely to take on those clients."

Alice beams. "Tim agonizes over reassigning clients when someone leaves. Hell, it's hard enough for him to delegate clients to his staff to begin with. He'd be a total micromanaging monster if we didn't have Donna here to yell at him."

"Um, and me, thank you very much." Nicole throws a grape at Alice.

"Yes, of course. You yell at Tim very effectively." Alice looks at me. "Nicole is always right, you know. Even if it doesn't feel like it at first."

"The only actual question here is whether you want to be a total Big Swinging Dick and take all your current clients on as angel investors for Vinea."

My jaw drops. "I would never do that," I tell them. "That feels really slimy."

Nicole shrugs. "Then you'd better go give them your notice and get to work for Sam. It's your boss's problem if he doesn't have anyone else capable of making your clients happy." We eat together for awhile and Alice talks about how the baby is kicking her in the organs.

Nicole rolls her eyes and says she doesn't care about babies, but I suspect she's not being totally genuine about that. Before I can decide whether I should ask if she and Zack have talked about kids, Nicole asks to see my contract.

"You should have Tim look at it," she says. "He will make a referral if he thinks you need a more specialized opinion."

"That would be amazing," I tell her, swallowing the last of my lunch. "I really appreciate the help."

Alice pulls Nicole in for a hug and kisses her on the cheek. "We help each other out in this family," Alice says. "And family for us includes everyone we care about." Alice reaches out and squeezes my hand. "I hope you know that includes you, too, Logan."

This time, I don't succeed at holding back my tears. "I don't know how to tell you what that means to me," I say. "I haven't had a lot of people on my side in the past."

"Well," Alice says, slamming down her juice glass. "From now on your bigger problem will be holding us back if someone is mean to you."

As Nicole spies Tim and barks at him to come over, I say, "It feels like my whole life is changing."

Nicole rolls her eyes. "Well, good," she says. "You were overdue for a shakeup."

CHAPTER THIRTY-SIX
CAL

I haven't been home during daylight hours in days. I've texted Logan a few times just to let her know I'm still alive, but I'm barely hanging on and I'm desperate for some rest by the time the whistle blows at the end of the day shift on Friday.

I find Dakota and Frank and let them know I'm going to head out. Dakota grins. "No reason for you to stay, Cal. We're right on schedule." I feel frozen in place even after her go ahead and I scratch the back of my neck while I watch her clicking around on her tablet device.

She eventually slides it into her bag and looks startled to see me still standing there. "I'm heading out, too. Seriously. Things are okay here." Frank nods in agreement, waving as he makes his way toward the second shift captain. We're working three shifts a day on this situation, weekends, too, but Dakota says the line will be back up and running in a few days.

"Go home, Callum. Take a shower. Go to bed early. I'll see you back here at nine tomorrow."

"Not six?" She laughs and waves, heading to the parking lot. I blow out a breath and follow her, heading home.

There's a huge package for me in the lobby, so I heave it up on my shoulder and make my way into the apartment. Slicing it open, I see that it's the dishes I ordered. "Hey, now," I say, tossing down my stuff and unpacking the box.

I'm reaching up to put the dishes in the cupboard when I hear the door open and Logan rushes inside. "Oh my gosh. Is it you? In real life?" She looks happier than when I last saw her, which I remember was a few hours after I was inside her.

God, what a mess. "It's me," I say, and hold up a dish. "Finally doing my part here." I stretch up again to put the dish in the cupboard and am startled when I feel Logan wrap her arms around me. I nearly drop the plate when she reaches up to try and kiss me.

"Hey, now," I say, stepping back. I see her face crumple, so I hold out my hand. "Lo, I'm sorry." I lean back against the counter. She looks like she's going to cry. "God, I fuck everything up. Come here." I try to hug her, but she's stiff and feels like she's holding her breath.

"I'm sorry," I say. "I've been—"

Logan shakes her head and cuts me off. "No, I'm sorry. I know you're tired. You've got a lot on your plate."

"Plate? Get it?" I hold up another dish and wave it at her. She cracks a smile, but I can tell some of the light has gone out in her eyes. I've really messed things up with her. And, I mean, obviously. I slept with her and then haven't talked to her in days. Days. Jesus, I'm a dick.

She climbs up on the counter next to me and pulls her knees up to her chest, looking like a young girl. "So what happened at work? I know it was an emergency, but..."

I lean against the counter next to her and give her the overview. "It's been bad. But is it wrong that I'm feeling okay about how things are shaking out this week? Now that I've got Dakota and Frank and even Orla all working together, it feels really...invigorating."

Logan smiles. "That's really great, Cal. Why would that be wrong?"

I shrug. "I know my dad thrust me into this hoping I'd fail so he could, I don't know, finally fire me or something and send me away."

She reaches for my arm. "I don't think that's true, Cal."

I shake my head quickly. "No, it is. I mean, why would he and my uncle plunk me in such a big role otherwise? They've been giving me shit work to do for years."

"What if they knew you were up for the challenge?"

I lean my head back on the cupboard and close my eyes. "I don't think so. But you know, it does feel like a challenge. In a good way." I tell Logan about my idea to make the new conveyor less vulnerable to temperature changes from the furnace. "I've been reading about some new material coatings," I tell her. "Even called in some of our guys with a chemical background. And I'm working with them on engineering a new design for the mechanics. It's actually pretty cool."

"That sounds right up your alley," Logan says, relaxing her body a little. "Tell me more."

And so I do. I tell her about this new vendor I found who is making cool sensors. "We're going to put in these tiny stickers with wireless sensors all along the conveyor and a bunch of other parts of the steel process, actually. These sensors are heat resistant, and I believe they will prevent this sort of thing from happening again. I haven't spoken directly with my uncle, but Dakota sent in the budget and everything has been approved." I shrug. "I just hope the client is happy."

Logan seems to be hanging on my every word, which reminds me how good a roommate she is. She's always listening to me and supporting me. It's another reminder that I can't be stomping all over her goodwill. I absolutely cannot look at her cleavage while she's perched on the counter next to me. I start putting the dishes away again so I'm not tempted to ogle her.

"You didn't have to buy all new dishes, Cal," she says. "I don't mind sharing with you."

I shrug. "I like feeling like I'm contributing here." She climbs down from the counter and wraps her arms around me again.

"You definitely contribute," she says, looking up at me with huge eyes. And then she reaches again to try and kiss me and I jerk my head back, because I can't keep going there with her. Not if I want to be able to sleep at night.

I watch her smile melt, and I don't know what to say, how to explain to her that I need to grow up, that I can't keep being the guy who bonks his roommate just because it feels good. The guy who crashes boats and fucks up checking measurements. "Logan," I whisper, swallowing thickly as I see that I'm hurting her. "I can't do this. I think we made a mistake getting physical."

She stiffens and backs away, smoothing out her shirt and shaking her head. "Of course," she says. She starts nodding and grabbing dishes, stacking them on the counter. "I'm sorry for crossing a line, Cal. It won't happen again."

"Hey," I say, reaching for her arm, but now it's her turn to jerk out of the way.

"I'm actually going to change. It's been kind of a long day and I might just go to bed early." She bites her lip. "Are you around tomorrow?"

I shake my head. "I have a few more days of intense work on the conveyor."

She nods. "Okay, well I'll see you around." She hurries down the hall and slams her door closed before I can think of something to say to make her feel better.

"Shit," I say, slapping the counter where a week ago I had her screaming my name in pleasure. Even when I try to do the right thing I fuck it up.

CHAPTER THIRTY-SEVEN
LOGAN

I feel so foolish. I walked into the apartment so high and energized by my week. I heard back from Tim and went over my Vinea contract. I even talked through a few different things with Sam and was so excited to see Cal and just tell him everything.

And then I had to mess everything up and try to kiss him. I just equated my happiness with our physical experiences in my head. Clearly that was a huge mistake. Isn't that what Cal called our hooking up? A mistake?

I feel tears rolling down my cheeks as my heart pounds in my chest. I hate feeling this way. It's like when people manage to rip the rug out from under me in social situations. I'm always caught off guard. I always think I understand reality and am reading people accurately.

I really thought things were different with Cal. We shared something so intense. Maybe it wasn't intense for him. He certainly has more experience in that arena. It occurs to me that maybe he slept with me out of pity. How many times did he mention that he couldn't believe I'd never had a good sexual experience?

I hear him continuing to slam things around in the kitchen. It's clear that Cal enjoys living here with me. He invested in domestic stuff he never had before. He just wants to keep a boundary when it comes to physical stuff. I choke down the lump in my throat, knowing he's probably wise to set that limit. After all, I'm just starting to fall in love with his family. I need them. Romantic relationships fizzle, but friendships stick around. Or so I've heard.

I wipe the tears from my face, wondering if I'll ever really be able to trust someone with my feelings and my secrets *and* my body. I swallow thickly and shake my head. One thing I do know I can control is my work. I have everything in place and even now while I'm questioning my sanity, I can still see the right decision for my career.

I pull out my laptop and digitally sign the contract with Vinea and send that back to Sam. Next, I email Mr. Alexander, skipping right over Marie in the chain of command, to let him know I've accepted an offer as the finance director at a research company. The email could serve as my notice, but I believe they'll want me gone effective immediately since they won't want me to poach clients or anything.

I fall asleep feeling empty and full at the same time.

My phone rings at six. I slept fitfully, wondering when I'd start getting calls from work. I recognize the number as one from my office, but don't have it saved in my phone, so it's not Marie. "Hello?"

"Logan." It's Mr. Alexander. "Your email comes as quite a shock." He seems distraught, which isn't entirely unexpected. I take a deep breath and remind myself to stick with the script. I actually have a script that I put together with Orla, Maddie and Nicole via text messages all week. It's my first time being part of a group chat, in fact.

"I was offered an opportunity that was too good to pass by," I say. "This is a big move for my career, but as I mentioned, I'm happy to stay on and help transition my clients to other analysts."

Mr. Alexander sputters and it sounds like maybe he slaps a piece of furniture. "Is this about money? I can match a salary increase."

I shake my head. Maddie predicted they'd offer me more money and she urged me to just stick with facts. "I'm sor—" I start to apologize, and then I remember Nicole adamantly insisting that I should never apologize for following my career goals. I clear my throat. "My new position is a vertical move, Mr. Alexander. It's a real opportunity for me as an analyst."

"Rudy is going to lose his ever-loving mind," he says with a growl. "To think about all the work that went into landing him...and he was adamant that you be the one to work with him. What can I do to persuade you to stay?"

I sigh. "Mr. Alexander, the culture at your company is not a good fit for me."

"I told you to come to me if those imbeciles threatened the bottom line," he nearly roars. I wince and hold the phone out from my face.

"It's very early and I have plans today," I say, faking more confidence than I feel. My arms are shaking with adrenaline from this confrontation, but I'm glad it's happening over the phone and not in person. "Please let me know whether you'd like me to help with the transition or whether I should come collect my things on Monday."

Now it's his turn to sigh. "You know you can't maintain access to accounts if you've already signed with another company, even if it's not a competitor. I'll have security box your personal belongings and you can turn in your badge and computer Monday morning."

He hangs up. I start shaking in earnest. I really need a friend right now to reassure me that I've done the right thing. Why should I be responsible for Mr. Alexander's frustration at work?

Because I always feel responsible when people around me are upset. Strong emotions have always been forbidden to me. I open the door to my room and pad down the hall softly to see if Cal is awake. His door is open, and my heart swells, hoping I can at least confide in him, hoping he'll make me laugh and maybe take me out for pancakes.

But his room is empty. When I look by the front door, his boots and bag are gone. I'm all alone, like always.

CHAPTER THIRTY-EIGHT
LOGAN

NICOLE STARTS TEXTING ME AFTER I'VE COLLAPSED INTO THE COUCH, FEELING empty.

I consider just throwing my phone on the floor and trying to ignore the world for a few hours, but avoiding other people is my old M-O and making changes the past few months has felt pretty good. Apart from today. God, I'm a mess. I dial Nicole's number.

"Spill," she says, and I hear shuffling sounds in the background, like she's jumping out of bed and bothering Zack.

I take a deep breath. "Mr. Alexander did not take my resignation very well," I tell her. "He called everyone else at work imbeciles, too. Which, they *are,* but the boss shouldn't say those kinds of things. Right?" I expect Nicole to retort with something snappy and crass, but she takes a deep breath on her end of the phone and there's a pause.

"Hey, Logan, I know that kind of shit is not easy to hear. Can I take you out for brunch and we can talk about it?"

"Brunch?" I'm rattled by the idea of going out in public. I'd have to do something about my face, for starters. "I don't know, Nicole..."

687

"Hm," she counters. "Why don't I come to you. Text me your address. I'll order takeout. Is Cal there? I'm not getting enough to share with him. He eats like a hog. Oh! I should see if Emma and Maddie want to come over. They're really excellent listeners."

I hear muffled noises as Nicole talks and I can almost see her throwing on clothes and grabbing her bag. I hear the beep of a car alarm and her voice skips briefly when Bluetooth picks up her call. "I'm on the move, Logan. I'm hanging up so I can use my voice to text and deal with everything. Did I tell you that fucking voice in my phone finally understands all my cuss words?"

I can't help but sneak a small smile when we hang up, although it's short lived. I take stock of myself and decide I need to at least wash my face and put on a bra if an undetermined number of Foof ladies are coming to my house. God, where will everyone sit? Cal and I just have the small table and a few stools at the counter.

What if they want to sit on the deck? I only have one flimsy camp chair out there. I can't believe I'm about to host my very first social gathering of my adult life and I'm sitting here like a total slob.

The intercom beeps, jolting me back to awareness from my anxiety fit. "Nicole?" I don't expect the loud "woo!" I hear back, and I smile, pushing the button and opening the front door. A minute later, I see and hear Nicole, Maddie, and Emma with my new boss with Juniper Jones bringing up the rear.

"Piper's exercising, obviously, and Chloe has an emergency meeting with her cover designer. Something about man nipples getting censored." Nicole plunks bags on the counter as she talks. "Orla is apparently with your roommate at the factory. Do we still say factory? Plant? Oh, and we don't call Esther before noon. Remember that. Girlfriend owns a bar and works 'til two in the morning."

Juniper waves a bottle of champagne and asks for a dish towel so she can uncork it. "How did you all get here so fast? With food?"

Juniper shrugs. "I'm knocking on doors today in the east end anyway. Nicole talked me into a pit stop."

Emma sprawls out on the couch. "I just wanted to get away from my kids. I love them. Also I'm sick of them."

"And, as you know, I live near you. Now we're best friends *and* co-workers, so you have no hope for any work-life balance." Samantha starts pouring orange juice into glasses from my cupboard, muttering that this would all be better with actual champagne flutes. "Look, Nicole's text said you're upset about some nonsense with asshole men. And I want to hear about that. But first..." She hands everyone a glass and stands in the middle of my living room, smiling in the sunshine from the patio. "We need to celebrate, Logan. I'm excited. You're bringing amazing talent to my baby. Obviously in this metaphor my company is my baby. No offense to human babies."

"None taken," Emma and Maddie shout. Juniper just rolls her eyes.

"So, Logan Miller, here's to freeing your fucks and taking a leap and helping me out."

"To Logan," everyone says, and they all clink glasses. I feel overwhelmed. I feel so celebrated and seen and it's just too much for me on top of my boss yelling and Cal's rejection yesterday.

So instead of drinking my mimosa, I sit on the stool at my counter and start crying.

"Oh dear," Maddie says, reaching into her fanny pack and pulling out a tissue. She walks over to me and pulls me into a hug. "Come here, Logan. Let it out. I've got you."

And, nestled in her surprisingly strong embrace, I do. I cry until I'm not sure why I'm crying. All the stress of the past few months at work starts leaking out in my tears. All the anger that life was so hard for my mom, that she had so little support. All my confusion at my complicated feelings for Cal. I cry it all out while Maddie hugs me and everyone stands around me drinking and watching.

When I stop, I take deep breaths and Juniper slides me a plate of food. "You should eat something," she says, and I do.

Samantha leans on the counter with her elbows, taking bites of quiche and chugging her mimosa. "God, I hope I never make an employee cry based on our office culture. Can this guy seriously not tell that his employees are miserable?"

I shrug. "He never really mingles. I only ever saw him at big meetings."

Sam taps her chin. "Do you think the Vinea people are sick of seeing me? I see everyone, like, every day."

Nicole snaps her fingers. "You are not going to allow this man rent-free space in your head, Samantha Vine. You're the best boss to ever boss anyone around. Apart from me. And Juniper. Obviously."

Juniper winks. "I'm wondering, apart from him being an asshole of course, if Logan is suffering from imposter syndrome."

"Say what now?" Maddie grabbed all the sweet crepes from the brunch buffet Nicole brought and keeps swatting Emma's hand away when she tries to taste the Nutella confection.

"Imposter syndrome." Juniper looks at me sternly. "It's when you feel like a big faker when something good happens to you, like you don't deserve it or you haven't earned it properly."

My eyes widen as she speaks. Juniper nods. "Look, I know you know I grew up in foster care. When I went to college, I had a lot of that. Hell, I wound up living with a man who didn't deserve me just because he was the first one to be nice to me. Imposter syndrome makes you doubt that you have earned your success, even if there's rational evidence that you're awesome."

Nicole snorts. Juniper continues. "So instead of running around Boston demanding everyone bask in my brilliance, I felt like I was lucky to be there. Like I was a minute away from someone discovering that I was a fraud."

"Oh my god. Yes. Yes!" I lean forward. "You're describing my life right now. Why am I like this?"

Juniper shrugs. "We have a lot of systems that really suck at taking care of people. If you care to read my judicial platform, I can show you how I'm working to improve these things from the bench. Like...making it harder to evict people and making it way harder to raise rents unfairly."

I clutch at my chest. "What my mom would give to have had you overseeing her case for half my life."

Juniper grabs my hands. "Logan. Nothing about your background means you are unworthy." She shrugs. "You just need to tell yourself every day that you're amazing. You do amazing things. You have amazing friends."

"We *are* amazing," Sam says with her mouth full of food. She swallows and grins.

I feel a lump forming in my throat again. "You're my friends?"

"Oh, Jesus Christ," Nicole shouts. "Of course we're your friends. Juniper, how do we help her with this syndrome?"

She shrugs. "We just keep showing up when she needs us."

Everyone is quiet for a few minutes, just eating and drinking our mimosas. It's overwhelming, but feels really nice. Comforting.

"Maddie, I don't care if you're pregnant, you have to let me try at least one of the chocolate ones." Emma dives across the table to grab the last bite from Maddie's fork. They both laugh as Emma wrenches the fork out of Maddie's hand.

"Liam would die before he'd share silverware with someone," Maddie says, reaching for a scone since Emma took her crepe.

"And yet he licks *your* fork for hours," Nicole says, laughing at her own joke. She turns toward me. "The Brady men are good with their tongues," she says, slapping high five with Maddie across the table.

I blush, remembering how true this is. I don't say anything, but Juniper shouts, "Oh, Stag men, too."

"Cheers to that!" Emma raises her glass.

Samantha stares at me. "Well I'm not fucking a Stag or a Brady, but I want to know why Logan is making that face right now."

"I'm not making a face," I say, too quickly. "I'm just...thinking of *The Redcoat,*" I lie.

Nicole sits back in her chair and crosses her arms, staring at me. "You guys totally fucked," she says, nodding.

I feel my heart rate increase again, just when I was starting to calm down after all the emotions this morning. I really don't want to talk about this with Cal's brothers' girlfriends. I start shaking my head rapidly, but I don't want to lie to them. Not after that big speech about how they will be here for me, because they're my friends.

"It's not like that," I mutter, but then I start crying again so I quickly try to hide my face inside my mimosa.

Nicole leans forward. "Not like what? Like, no Cal didn't ram his rod in your musket or..." she drifts off and I stare at her, then Maddie. Everyone is silent, staring and waiting for me to say something. God, even my new boss is here waiting to see what I'm going to say.

I close my eyes. "He said it was a mistake," I whisper.

"Oh, Christ, here we go," Juniper says. She opens another bottle of champagne and starts filling everyone's glass.

Maddie wraps her hand around the top of her glass and reaches for the juice. "First of all," Maddie says. "These Brady men say a lot of really dumb shit."

I shake my head. "He thinks it's better if we're just roommates. And." Something occurs to me and I start crying again. "I'm the one who told him it should have been a one-time thing! I said that. But then we did it again."

Maddie nods. "They're irresistible. I get it, babe."

"He's trying to focus on this big emergency at work and making up with his dad and..." I look around and bite my lip, worried about spilling too many secrets to Cal's family. "He just made me feel really good and I am the one who went back on what I said. But he was saying my name so I... thought it meant something. But I read it wrong."

My breath hitches as I exhale.

"Oh, Cal, you beautiful moron," Nicole mutters.

"Please don't call him that."

"Oh, honey, if he says it was a mistake to raid your honeypot, then he's definitely a moron. Do *you* think it was a mistake?"

I shake my head rapidly before I can think about the best response. "No. It was...it was all I wanted to do after I signed my contract with Vinea. And I really wanted to talk to him after I put in my notice at work and he's just... not here."

"He does seem to run off when there's something big to discuss," Maddie says. She sighs. "That whole family...they haven't had a lot of practice communicating."

"Plus they're engineers."

Sam perks up. "What's that got to do with anything?"

Nicole shrugs. "They're so busy thinking about efficiency that they never pause to consider the human, emotional aspect of anything."

"Liam does like a nice, efficient conversation," Maddie says. "He makes checklists about potential topics." She grins.

"I make checklists," I shout. "I even sent Cal meeting invites with an agenda."

"Yeah, you should probably move in with Liam," Maddie laughs. "But seriously. I think Cal's always tried to be the diffuser. Always cracking a joke to ease the tension. That sort of thing."

I swallow. "I guess I'm too much bad energy for him," I say, prompting Juniper to grunt.

"Nah uh. That's imposter syndrome again. What if he said that for a dumb reason? Like when Ty and I first got together, I rejected him because he was my boss's brother. Nevermind that he was my greatest supporter and made me feel like a goddess."

Everyone sighs collectively as Juniper talks about how much she loves Ty. I remember the media clips from when Juniper won gold at the Olympics. The entire internet was on fire talking about how obviously smitten Ty was as he celebrated her win.

I really thought Cal was looking at me that way the night of the gala. Maybe Juniper's right. "I guess I need to talk to him," I say and slump down in my seat. "If he ever comes home."

Maddie winces. "Liam says things are pretty bad at the steel mill. Like... really bad."

Nicole points an index finger at the ceiling. "These disasters aren't forever. Not that it's the same scale, but my backyard sliding into the river was really bad and the enginerds were deeply engrossed for a long time. And then they weren't, so we could talk it out. This will pass, Logan."

Sam bangs her glass on the counter. "Well, that's enough talking about angry men who aren't good at feelings," she says. "Back to Logan's celebration. What are we doing this afternoon?"

"Um, hello?" Juniper waves around a pile of campaign literature. "How about you all help me get re-elected."

Samantha knits her brows, considering. The thought of knocking on other people's doors right now terrifies me, and not just because my face is puffy from crying. But Maddie leaps to her feet. "Yes. Duh. Of course we'll help you, Juniper. Now can you explain what exactly you are trying to do? Because I actually have no idea."

In the end, Juniper convinces us all to come to her campaign headquarters since none of us ever knocked on people's doors before. When we arrive, there's a flurry of activity as Juniper's campaign manager organizes volunteers into groups based on which neighborhoods they'll visit.

Someone has taped talking points to the wall, giant bullet points of Juniper's philosophy as a judge: compassion, empathy, fairness. Nicole and I get assigned to fold and organize information packets, while Sam, Emma and Maddie hit the streets to talk with neighbors.

"This is amazing," I tell Nicole. "Everyone is like a big team here."

She just nods. "Women of Foof stick together." She squeezes my hand. "It won't always be you feeling overwhelmed and needing support. It's all reciprocal."

I eavesdrop on a few phone calls, listening to campaign staffers talk to voters about what issues matter to them. I start crying when I read about the impact Juniper has made on evictions in Pittsburgh. She set up a program where people who struggle to make rent are connected with social services. There are even grants for single mothers to help cover the gaps.

I realize that in accepting her help to further my own career, I have connected myself to Juniper's mission. And now I'm helping her help families like mine. The whole morning fills me with hope. Suddenly, my former boss's harsh words sting less.

I stand up from my completed pile of folded and organized pamphlets and walk to the head volunteer. "I want to do more to help," I tell her. "Where do I sign up?"

CHAPTER THIRTY-NINE
CAL

I grab my hair at the roots and silently scream after Logan storms out of the kitchen. I had no idea it was possible to feel so deeply, thoroughly like garbage.

I'm in a weird place with my family, work is a shambles, and I just hurt my roommate, who has been the most supportive person in my life the past few months. I punch the counter until my knuckles split, not knowing what else to do with my frustration.

How long has it been since I went for a run? I know I'm supposed to be resting before going back to the mill, but I feel like I have hornets inside my skin. I rip off my shirt and yank on a pair of mesh shorts and my sneakers, making sure I put my ID and my key in the zip pocket.

I tear out of our building into the dark, not stopping at intersections, but just turning right each time until I'm able to cross streets without waiting. I don't know how much time passes or where I'm headed. I think about how badly I want to change and how much I have no idea what to do about it.

Before Logan, all I really cared about was restoring my Bronco, and I pound the pavement thinking about how pathetic that makes me. When I feel like my legs are about to give out, I stop to get my bearings. I'm actually not too far from home. If I cut through the park I can be there in a few minutes.

It's after midnight when I make my sweaty way into the apartment. I shower as quietly as I can, not wanting to disturb Logan any more than I already have. I notice that of course I still haven't replaced her towels and I scoff at myself as I use her nice linens to dry off.

I'm not sure that I actually manage to get any sleep, and it's not yet light out when my alarm goes off, so I head back to the steel mill still feeling like death. Frank and Dakota arrive as I'm parking, and my mood shifts a little bit. I like working with these two. Dakota's a smart ass, and she's confident in her work, which makes me feel better about my contributions.

I smile and walk over to Dakota's car, bending to help her with the crate of paperwork she's trying to haul in. "Hey," I say. "What's with all this?"

She beams and hands another crate to Frank. "Final approvals on designs," she says. "You sign, Frank builds, and off we go."

"No shit?" It seems crazy that all of this work would be ready to go so soon. It feels like it's been a month since the collapse, but I know it's only been about a week. I think. I'm not exactly certain what day it is today.

We carry everything to my office and Dakota walks me through what to sign. "Kellen approved all this," she says, waving at a stack to her left. "He didn't even send it back for revisions, Cal. That doesn't happen often."

"So that's a good thing?"

She blinks a few times. "Uh, yeah."

Frank rifles through a summary sheet on top of the stack Dakota handed him. "We can assemble this today," he says. "Our machine team finished up late last night, according to the third shift report." By the time we work our way through the stack, Dakota says she thinks we can get the line back making steel before Monday.

Monday. In a few days, this whole nightmare will be over and I can get back to...what? Paperwork? Bad decisions?

Dakota and Frank head out of my office, leaving me with instructions to update Dad and Kellen. But I don't know how to pick up the phone and make that call, so I just sit and stare at the wall. Before too long, there's a knock on my wall, and I look up to see my father leaning agains the doorjamb, dressed for a run.

"Am I hallucinating?" I rub my eyes with the heels of my hands, and stare back down at the paperwork I was supposed to report out to him.

"Nah. I needed to stop in and check on this mess. Thought I'd wrap it into my morning sweat. You know, it's not good to skip a workout. Keeps the ticker healthy."

Dad doesn't sit, because he hates being still. He stands across my desk looking at me, snapping his gum, waiting for me to talk, I guess. "I was about to call you and Uncle Kel," I say, swallowing and gesturing at the papers on my desk. "Dakota and Frank say we could be up and running Monday morning."

Dad breaks into a grin and slaps my desk. "That's some good news, kid. That's good news indeed. Kellen worried it'd take a month to deal with this nightmare."

"Kellen approved all the designs last night, apparently," I say, biting my lip. I wonder why my uncle didn't report out to my dad.

"Kellen doesn't approve just any old designs." Dad walks around the desk and leans on a filing cabinet, gesturing for me to hand him the summary report. He studies it, snapping his gum and nodding, before setting it back down on the desk. "You know why I was upset about my boat, Callum?"

I groan. "Dad, I'm so sorry about that. I don't want to make excuses but it was my birthday and everyone bailed and—"

He holds up his hand. "I didn't say I was upset at *you*, kiddo. Now let me talk." I lean back in my seat and snap my mouth closed. Dad lets out a long sigh through his nose. "You're a lot like me, you know?" I nod. "I never could stand it when the mood got heavy. But I also couldn't sit still long enough to ever do a good job in school. They didn't have ADHD when I was coming up."

I roll my eyes. "I don't have ADHD, Pop."

He waves a hand. "I'm talking about me, here. Your uncle is the only person in my whole life who never gave up on me, you know that? Why do you think I wanted to go into business with him? My kid brother has been my hero."

I think about how important my brothers are to me and nod, wondering why I never stopped to think about the bond between my dad and my uncle before. Dad keeps talking. "I wasn't a good husband. I'm a lousy boyfriend. I had no idea how to be a father. But I'm damn good at reading people, and your uncle and I make a good business team."

"Dad." I want to tell him he was a great father, or say something reassuring, but he holds up a hand and keeps talking.

"You aren't as serious as your brothers and your cousin, and I think that's made you think people don't take you seriously." Dad leans forward and puts his hands on the desk so his face is close to mine. "But son, there's value in being the peacemaker, in being the person who helps break the tension." I swallow, considering his words. "Do you know what it meant to that kid Jake that you gave him that old Bronco manual? That kid's own father doesn't even show up to hang out with him, and Kel said Jake's showing that manual around school and using it for his research paper. So."

Dad stands back up and wraps his gum in a tissue, reaching in his pocket for a pack of pistachios instead. "The boat. When you called me, I was upset that we had all let you down on your birthday. You didn't tell us how much that day mattered, and I was angry because we shouldn't have needed to be told. Beltane is an important thing to this family, but we can't it be more important than the people in it."

Dad pauses to munch his nuts while I swallow, feeling the room close in on me. "I don't know what to say," I tell him, pursing my lips.

"I mean, of course I'm pissed that you wrecked my boat, kid. Cost me my season tickets to the Iron Men. Thank that girlfriend of yours for reconnecting me with Rudy, why don't you? He gave me another set."

"She's my roommate, Dad."

He rolls his eyes. "You're still an idiot," he says.

I know he's joking but I feel like the exhaustion of the last week combined with feeling overwhelmed at his earlier speech just combines until I burst out of my seat. "Of course I'm an idiot," I shout. "I'm a fool who crashes his dad's boat and ruins all my shirts with food stains and goes home to fuck my roommate instead of figuring out that Tony was fucking up all the data here."

I start pacing around the office, shouting. "I let myself push paper at work for nine years rather than demand anything more challenging until you thrust my ass into catastrophe cleanup at a steel mill that stinks like hellfire. My life is a total shambles and I have no idea what happens now."

Dad grunts. "I knew you were sleeping with Logan. Your uncle owes me fifty bucks."

I throw my hands in the air. "Jesus Christ, Dad. Why are you here? Are you seriously here to kick me when I'm down?"

To my surprise he steps forward and wraps his arms around me. I stiffen, unsure what to do next, but he just keeps hugging me until I sort of relax into his shoulder. "Callum. Your life is not a shambles." I shake my head. "You helped your brother make peace with his pregnant girlfriend. You fixed your mother's porch railing. Between you and me, I think you helped your uncle get lucky with his neighbor lady."

"God, Dad," I say into his shirt. "You're going to make me puke."

He releases me from the hug but keeps his hand on my shoulder. "I put you in charge here because I knew you could fix this situation. I see now that you've been waiting for permission or approval when it comes to Beltane. And that's on me, for making you think this company was so precious to me that it can't handle a setback."

I groan and sink back into my chair, slumping forward to put my head on my desk. "Cal, go home and take a nap. Tell Logan you're into her. Kiss and make up for being an idiot. Then meet me tomorrow morning at the Duquesne Club. We're going to pitch old Eddie a long-term solution here for the mill. I think you're gonna like it, kid."

I lift my head a few inches and raise a brow at my father. "Please don't be cryptic with me now, Dad. Can you just tell me straight what to expect tomorrow?"

He laughs. "What's the fun in that?" He laughs again as I moan. "Okay, okay." Dad tells me he and Kellen were intrigued by the vendor I found who uses the sensors and drones. "We already have a drone pilot at Beltane," he says. "Why should we keep buying other people's hardware when we've got mechanical engineers in house?"

My eyebrows shoot up. "What are you getting at?"

Dad tosses me a pouch of pistachios, which I start munching as he talks. "We want you to help us make our own drones and sensors, custom for the work we're doing. That machine learning guy your brother brought on board says he can get these things programmed if you can get them flying."

"You talked to Ray about this?"

Dad snorts. "What do you think we've been doing all week—sitting around eating snacks? Don't answer that. Anyway, Ray says he can write an algorithm, which your uncle tells me is basically a punch list for computers. You've just spent a decade inspecting pipes and towers and mines. Hell, Cal, you know better than anyone all the different environments where it's safer and more efficient to use a machine to keep an eye on things than it is to send one of our folks in."

My eyes widen as he talks, because he's right. I've been making mental notes for ages about how much sooner we could capture a problem for our clients if we weren't relying on human eyes to physically inspect their buildings and machines and structures.

"Go on home and clean yourself up," Dad says. "And don't wear those damn sneakers of yours to this meeting on Sunday. Shined shoes, son." With a final slap to my desk, Dad scoots out of my office, leaving me reeling in my creaking desk chair.

CHAPTER FORTY
CAL

WITH NOTHING FURTHER TO DO AT THE STEEL MILL FOR THE DAY, I DECIDE TO TAKE Dad's advice and head home. I stop at the drug store for a sports drink, needing to hydrate and think about tomorrow. What a mind fuck. It's been so familiar, for so long, to assume my family just thinks I'm this big screw up. From the sound of things, Dad says they all actually appreciate me cutting through the tension, even if they won't admit it. Okay, even if Liam won't admit it.

Logan's been on me to talk to my dad for months. Now, hearing all he had to say and getting ready for my meeting tomorrow, I wish I'd listened to her earlier. I wish so many things with Logan. Most of all that I hadn't caused the look of hurt on her face in our kitchen last night. She's the first person I want to tell all my news today, and I know she had something to tell me about work. I feel shitty that I didn't get to talk with her about it.

I know my dad thinks I should be straight with her, but I still don't know if it's a good idea to get involved. I have a pretty precarious grasp on adulthood without tossing in a complicated romance with my landlord. Hell, she's the one who first said it should have been a one-time thing. But then she's the one who came to me...because I was jacking off moaning her name on the couch.

Gah! My head is so fucked up.

I do need some sort of gesture to make nice with her, though. I decide to wander over to the beauty products section and see if I can figure out what

I'd need to buy to have another spa night with her. How good would that feel to put those foot things on again and pass out on the couch together? We could listen to *The Redcoat* sequel and pig out on fried shrimp while we open our pores or whatever Logan liked from that face goop. Like nothing complicated had ever happened to us.

Unfortunately for me, there are about 50 different flavors of face goop to choose from and I furrow my brow, staring, until another customer must feel bad for me because she asks, "You need a hand?"

"Ah, yeah. I'm trying to do a spa night with my girl...my friend. Anyway, she likes those foot baggies and the face...things."

The shopper laughs. She reminds me of my mom. Somehow, despite my terrible explanation, she hooks me up with a set of lavender mud masks and a set of intensive foot masks, which this lady says will make our feet peel. Which this lady further explains is a desirable outcome for a spa night pedicure. I stop internalizing once I get to the word "relaxing" on the package and check out, hoping I can relax Logan into forgiving me.

When I get to the apartment, though, she's nowhere around. I try calling, but her phone goes right to voicemail and she doesn't respond to my text asking if she is up for a spa night. This sucks. I sigh, looking around the condo. There's a bunch of garbage in the can, which seems unlike Logan to leave, but I bag it all up and toss it in the chute in the hall. I come back inside and decide I can probably clean up a bit since I haven't been pulling my weight in that arena.

I find all the cleaning stuff under the sink and scour the counter and stove and faucets. Still no Logan. Sick of checking my phone looking for her, I decide to brave scrubbing the bathroom. Once I get the shower and toilet scrubbed, I remember that I still need to get some towels. But I don't want to leave and risk her coming home and me not being here. I pull up one of the delivery apps on my phone and see that I can get someone to run basically any errand for me, so I pay out the nose for some guy named Raul to get me a set of towels, washcloths, and a few pints of ice cream from Target. I envision my mom's place and remember she has candles sitting around, so I add a few of those onto my order figuring Logan will like the ambiance. She's had a stressful few months.

I scrub, dust, and vacuum the entire condo. I even wipe down the inside of the washer, and I feel good about how nice it looks around here.

By the time my order arrives, I'm hungry again, so I call to have Japanese food delivered, too. Just as I get the candles lit and the tempura plated, I hear a key in the lock and my heart jumps a few times in my chest.

I look up from the table as Logan comes in the door and the sight of her takes my breath away.

Her skin is all rosy like she's been outside for awhile, and she just radiates happiness. She's calm as she sets her water bottle on the counter, but, looking around the apartment, she seems confused. "Cal?" There's a huge question in her voice. "What is all this?"

I shrug. "I missed talking to you all week," I tell her. "Something really good happened at work today and I thought maybe we could celebrate with spa night. Just Logan and Callie." I wink and love seeing her smile.

"That actually sounds amazing," she says. "My feet and back are killing me."

"Oh yeah?" I'm about to wonder what she was doing all day to cause that when she sinks onto the sofa and drops her head on the back.

"Tell me your good work news, Cal," she says, grinning. So I grab a plate and carry it over, sit beside her, and tell her everything. I tell her how I finally talked things through with my dad and how the crisis at the steel mill is averted. I tell her how I'm meeting with Dad and the big cheese tomorrow to talk about a new direction at work. "And it's exactly the kind of work I want to be doing, Lo-lo." I have to resist the deep urge to reach for her hair and twirl it around my fingers.

When she turns and smiles at me, I swear I can feel all my worries melt away. I've never seen a look of such pure admiration pointed my way. "Cal," she says, squeezing my hand. "I'm so glad to hear that you and your dad talked. Gosh, I knew it would be something good once the two of you just sat down and hashed things out."

I nod, struggling with a lump of emotions in my chest, remembering again how he told me he wants me to head the project engineering the drones from scratch for Beltane. "What's your work news," I whisper, glad she hasn't pulled her hand back, but worried about it all the same. If I'm going to be serious about not hurting her, I need to focus on not stringing her along. We can't be friends who secretly fuck. She deserves so much more than that.

"Can we do our spa feet before I tell you?"

"I thought you'd never ask." I reach to grab her plate and stack it with mine on the coffee table while Logan rips open the foot mask bags. The scent of the lavender overpowers the fried shrimp smell in the apartment, blending with the citrus candles I lit. It definitely smells girly and, I'll admit it, nice.

I laugh as we both groan when we peel off our socks. "I know what I was doing all day, but what's got your dogs barking?"

Logan's smile seems like it stretches all the way to her ears, still pink and a little sunburned. "I was volunteering for Juniper's campaign today." She slides the foot baggies on and props her feet on the edge of the coffee table. I scooch it a little closer to the couch since I know her legs aren't as long as mine. Soon, both of us have our feet propped up. Logan snuggles in to the couch and says, "Cal, it was the most invigorating thing. All the Foof ladies were there—those are all Nicole's networking friends. My friends, now, too, I guess." She blushes and smiles again.

"Of course they're your friends," I tell her. "So Juniper's volunteers are pretty cool?"

She shivers. "She put so many programs in place. I can't believe how awesome she is. I mean, I can believe it. Cal, she helps families facing eviction. There's all these social services Juniper brings right into the court house so if someone is facing an eviction trial, they can connect with these grants and the landlord is able to get paid and the families can get a little cushion to get back on their feet."

"You know, I think I knew she did that kind of thing. I remember Ty bragging on her one time when she missed a family dinner and Nicole was trying to give Juniper shit about it." All my instincts are screaming for me to touch Logan while she tells me this stuff, to reach out and just massage her shoulders where she's pinching at a sore spot on her neck.

"I realized that I've been so lucky to get where I am, and I can give back in ways that really help families like mine. Cal, it was the most freeing thing. All this guilt sort of melted away, especially meeting some of the people Juniper has helped. They were volunteering. Hey!" She squeezes my arm. I stare down where her hand touches my skin and swallow. "Will you come with me tomorrow? I want to help her knock on some doors."

"What time tomorrow?"

"Oh, right, you have that thing with your dad. Well I kind of want to go all day, but there are shifts through seven since it doesn't start to get dark til around then."

I grin and re-cross my legs, wiggling my toes in the foot baggies. "I'll come right after my meeting with Dad. I'll even be dressed nice, so people will take me seriously."

Logan nudges me with her shoulder and then doesn't scoot away toward her end of the couch. She's initiating a lot of physical touch and I'm going to have to crush her joy again and talk to her about it. We have to set up some boundaries. I don't know if I can trust my dad that it would be okay to move ahead with all these changes at work *and* pursuing something romantic with Logan.

"Hey," I tell her. "You didn't tell me your work news yet."

"Oh my gosh, that's right. Well I accepted Sam's offer! I'm going to be the chief financial officer at Vinea."

"The data chick? Nicole's friend?"

Logan nods and claps her hands. "I heard back from all the lawyers and the contract is solid. I gave my notice at work. Oh my gosh, Cal, it was a nightmare. Mr. Alexander was so angry." Her eyes waiver and she bites her lip. "I came out to try and find you after I talked to him, but you had already left today."

"Oh, Logan, I'm sorry I wasn't here for you. Shit. What did he say?"

She shakes her head. "It's okay. Foof came over. They brought brunch and hugged me and..." She smiles and shrugs.

"I guess that explains all the extra trash I found. Look at you having chick parties with your lady friends."

She beams. "We basically went from a Logan pep talk to pressing the flesh for Juniper." Logan winces. "That was Nicole's phrase. It doesn't feel right when I say it."

I can't help myself and I do reach out and run my fingers through her hair. Her breath catches as my fingers move through the silky strands. She feels so nice, curled up against me and her hair feels so smooth and soft. I swallow thickly. "I like it when you say things the way you feel," I tell her. She nods.

"So, Monday security will box up my things and then." Logan shrugs. "I don't start with Sam for two weeks. I'll probably visit my mom and just spend a lot of time helping Juniper." Logan tells me how volunteering closed up wounds she didn't even realize were bleeding in her heart. Her words are so pure and honest, and I know she must trust me so much to say these things to me.

"I'm so glad you found those gals," I say. "It's great to see you so excited."

Logan takes a shuddering breath, closes her eyes for a minute, and says, "So you said you got face masks, too?"

I hop up carefully and hold my hand out to her. We hold on to each other as we slip and slide down the hall in the booties, laughing hysterically each time one of us wobbles. Once we get to the bathroom, I show her the packets of face goop. "I'm told these are very relaxing," I say, offering a pack to her. She smiles and together we stand in front of the mirror, smearing the stuff on our faces. Logan and I keep looking at each other and laughing. This kind isn't like the first pack she got us that we just plastered on in one sheet.

I have to rub the mud around on my face. Logan pulls her hair back in a ponytail, telling me when I miss a spot. "Where?" I say, leaning close to the mirror, and she shoves the back of my head so my face hits the mirror. She grips the counter, laughing as I try to regain my balance and slip around in the socks. "You big jerk. I just cleaned in here!"

Logan is laughing so hard she starts coughing and I want to reach for her to shove her back, gently of course, but I lose my balance and fall on my ass in the bathroom. "Oh my god, Cal!" She shrieks as she reaches for me and winds up on top of me on the bathroom floor.

We lie there a few beats in silence, both of us trying to catch our breath. She reaches for my face and I catch her hand in mine, pinning it to my chest. "Cal," she whispers. She takes a deep breath, her face covered in purple goop. "I..." She sighs. "I disagree with your assessment that being intimate was a mistake."

I feel nauseous. My closest friend is sprawled on top of me, and I've seen her naked. I've made her come and she's brought me the most intense sexual experience of my life, and I can't—

"Cal, I know you're thinking a mile a minute." She interrupts my thoughts and places her palms on the tile on either side of my head. "I also know your whole family thinks you and I should be together and—" Logan pouts, her brow furrowed behind all the goop. "I will terminate your lease if you don't kiss me. Right now."

CHAPTER FORTY-ONE

LOGAN

I can't believe I just threatened Cal. What sort of awful human being am I to threaten to toss him out if he doesn't kiss me? Jesus, he could take me to court over this. I wriggle on top of him to try and find leverage to stand up, but between the bags on my feet and my palms sweating, I just wind up thrusting around on top of him on the floor.

"Christ, Logan," Cal groans. I feel him stiffen beneath my hips and I gasp. "Will you lie still a minute?"

I freeze, my body riding up and down as his chest moves with his breath. I can feel his heart pounding and it's so hard to take him seriously when his face is covered in purple goop. But I know that I am also covered in mud mask, and damn it! He's being a scaredy cat about us.

Cal must have insane core strength because he wraps his arms around my waist and manages to sit up. I wind up kneeling around his hips, my hands still on his shoulders. He opens his mouth like he wants to say something, then closes it again. "Logan." His voice is like gravel. "With you...I've never felt anything like I did with you."

"Cal, we are amazing together. I know you felt it."

"It was like dynamite, Lo-lo." He takes a deep breath. "But I don't know if it was worth risking what we have."

"What do you mean?" I snap back, trying to disentangle myself from him but between the mud masks and the slippery bags on our feet, I just wind up grinding against his lap until he groans.

706

"Lo, I mean that I want you more than I've probably ever wanted a woman in my entire life. But our friendship? Is so important to me. Lo, I can tell you things I've never said. Not to anyone. When my dad left my office today, you were the only person I wanted. When you talk to me, things make sense, Lo."

"Cal." I start shaking my head and take a quivering breath. "I feel all of that, too. But don't you think that just means we'd be right together? As a couple and not just as friends?"

"I've never been in a couple before, Logan. I have no idea how any of that works."

I shrug and cup his cheeks, not caring that his face is covered in goop. "I don't know how it works either, Cal, but I know that it all works better when you're by my side."

Cal hooks his mouth into a grin, cracking the mud on his face. "It sounds better when you say it that way, Lo." He reaches for my hand, squeezing it. "Being with you...I don't want it to just be another impulsive thing I get judged for later."

I take a deep breath and close my eyes, swallowing and feeling the mud mask crack. "Cal, why is impulsive always bad? Was it impulsive for you to buy all this spa stuff for us tonight?"

He blinks rapidly, his face shifting as he ponders that. "I guess it was." We sit together, until our breathing syncs up. "This? You and me? It feels really big and Logan, I'm a little afraid, if I'm honest."

"Well good news," I tell him. "I'm afraid of basically everything. But I did a whole bunch of scary stuff this month and it's all working out so far."

He chuckles and we're pressed so closely together I feel the rumble of his laugh in my own bones. "So what you're saying is you're down to fuck because it'll be scary, but in an exciting way?"

I nod, curling my bottom lip in and then scowling when I taste the face goop. He starts to laugh and then reaches up and touches his cheek. "This stuff feels really weird. Can we wipe it off?"

He looks down and his t-shirt is covered with purple streaks of mud. Both of my hands are caked in goo. "I think it's probably been seven to nine minutes," I say, laughing.

"How's this for an agenda," Cal says. "How about we take these bags off our feet and wash up?"

"I thought I was jumping your bones."

He leans forward and rips the baggies off my feet and tosses them into the trash. Then he grins a mask-cracking smile as he starts peeling my shirt off. "Cal!" I want to protest about him getting mud on my shirt, but he leans back and peels his shirt off, too, and I'm distracted by his abs.

"Lo, take off my foot booties so I can get us into the shower." I nod and do as I'm told, and then squeal as Cal jumps up and cranks on the water. The bathroom fills with steam and he starts kicking off his clothes. I yelp when he jumps forward and his eyes flash as he starts peeling off my clothes, too. I should feel nervous, standing here in front of him naked with my face covered in purple mud. But I don't. I feel fully myself, turned on, but comfortable in my anticipation of what is about to happen.

Cal backs into the shower and tugs me in by the hand. I look up and he starts gently rubbing the mud off my face in the water. I reciprocate and love the feel of his skin beneath my hands. It's been just over a week since I touched him this way, for more than an instant, and my body has missed his touch like it misses air when I hold my breath.

After a few minutes of scrubbing, Cal's face is fresh and clean in the spray, and I extend up on tiptoes, hoping to finally kiss him. "Logan," he whispers. "I'm going to fuck up. Probably really often."

"Me, too, Cal. But we'll talk about it each time. I can set regular meetings for us to check in if you want."

That gets a laugh out of him and he pulls my body flush against his. My nipples pebble against his chest and I feel the supple heat of his body as his legs surround me, his erection pressing against my belly. Finally, he leans forward and his lips connect with mine. Our mouths move together, both of us groaning under the spray. His tongue slips into my mouth and I open wider, welcoming him inside me as I jut my hips against his. I bite softly on his lower lip and he growls in response, hefting me up into his arms and backing me up against the tile.

"Oh!" I gasp as he licks along my jaw, lewdly thrusting his hips against mine.

"I love how your body is so responsive," he says, his fingers curling around my hips to spread my ass cheeks apart. The tips of his fingers find my center and I moan in pleasure as he begins to stroke and tease. I rake my nails along his pecs, nibbling on his lips and ears and anything else I can catch with my mouth as Cal starts to split me open.

With a forward thrust, he lowers my feet back to the ground and sinks to his knees in front of me. "I have missed tasting this pussy, Logan," he says, spreading me apart with his thumbs before diving into me with his tongue. My head falls back against the tile and I moan, rocking my hips as he licks me greedily. "That's it, babe. Fuck my face." He starts moving his tongue in and out of my channel as I stare down at him. The sight of him on his knees in front of me, devouring me as his cock grows harder and harder...it drives me out of my mind. Before I can control myself, I follow his instructions, rolling my hips along his tongue until I find the rhythm that feels right. I lean forward until his nose presses in against my clit while he licks, his fingers digging in to my thighs.

I curl my fingers into his hair, letting the water roll off of us as I hold his face tight on my body until I am spiraling over the cliff. My orgasm rips through me until I feel like I'm going to collapse. Just in time, Cal stands up and lifts me up, shutting off the shower and setting me gently on the mat outside the shower. Before I can start shivering, Cal reaches for a fluffy towel and wraps me up tight.

"Where did these come from?" I finger the cotton as Cal dabs his own towel against his dripping hair.

"I really need to do better at oral if you're thinking about towels right now, Logan." Cal's grin is wicked as he throws his towel on the ground and yanks mine off my body. He tugs me down the hall into his room and backs me up against his bed. I let myself fall onto the mattress and scoot up to the headboard as he dives in after me.

We lie there together, kissing and touching and petting, until I remember that Cal hasn't come yet. I reach down, feeling his stiff, hot shaft and moaning as the movement lines the tip of it up against my center. He feels so good and smooth as he brushes my slit that I gasp and my hips involuntarily jerk. Cal moans. "Logan, you're so damn wet. God, you feel so good brushing along my cock like that. Fuck, baby."

Cal leans over me, reaching for his drawer. He rustles around with one hand, using the other to cup my breast, but he grows frustrated and crawls up on his knees to dig in the drawer beneath the bed. "Fuck!" He sits back on the bed and starts pulling on his hair. "Logan, I don't have anymore condoms."

His chest heaves as he looks at me. He sinks onto the bed next to me, staring sadly down at his crotch. I swallow, afraid of what I know I'm about to say next. "I'm on birth control," I say. "I got the shot."

Cal starts shaking his head. "I don't want to do anything that makes you uncomfortable, Logan. I know how important it is to you to not get pregnant."

I think about his brother and Maddie, how on the one hand it seems like Brady men have super sperm, but on the other, they're sticking together and supporting the growing young family. "I'm not a teenager," I say to myself as much as Cal. "I can trust the shot and trust you if it doesn't work."

He smiles. "Are you sure? Because I gotta tell you, Logan, the thought of sliding into you bare is making me hard as fuck."

I look down and verify what he says. Cal is throbbing and huge, so hard I almost worry about him fitting inside me. "Let's do it," I say. "I trust you." I smile at the thought of how good it will feel to try, and before I can blink he's on top of me again, lining himself up at my entrance as he looks into my eyes. He slides slowly inside me. "Oh, god, Logan, this feels so good. We are so close together right now."

I feel almost like I'm going to cry, it's so intense. I love moving with him this way. He is hot and smooth and so slick inside me. Both of us groan as he glides in and out and I love looking down and seeing his body connected to mine, deep inside me physically and emotionally. "I'm so close already, Logan," he growls, thrusting slowly until his crown bumps against my cervix.

I arch my back at the contact and adjust the angle of my hips, my mouth falling open into an oh as the new position has him stroking my clit and a perfect spot inside me all at once. "Logan," he breathes as I moan his name in response. I start to twitch as another orgasm builds and then I'm lost to pleasure, wrapping my legs around him as he palms my breasts and strokes long and hard.

As I begin to spasm around Cal, he shudders and moans my name. I feel him grow inside me and then his body stiffens and I can feel him coming. I love watching Cal come to pieces, shuddering and spilling into me with my name on his lips. Long, hot spurts pump inside me as Cal buries his head in my shoulder and cries my name over and over.

Both of us lie still, catching our breath, recovering. Then, Cal pushes up on his forearm and pumps in and out of me a few more times, grinning. "I'm going to be oozing out of you all night, Logan Miller," he says and my jaw drops. This is a new level of filthy from him and...I like it.

"You're very proud of yourself, sir."

He pulls out and reaches between my legs, spreading his come around with his finger. "I am proud," he says, kissing me lightly. "I throw the best spa nights ever."

I laugh around his mouth as he deepens the kiss.

"I'm serious!" He slides a finger back inside me. "Have you ever felt this relaxed? Your skin is glowing Logan." I don't think it's possible for me to come a third time, but as Cal rubs me with his own release, I feel my legs spread open even wider. Shuddering, gasping, I feel the pleasure building yet again while he smiles down at me, stroking my core with his long fingers until I tumble over the edge in his arms.

CHAPTER FORTY-TWO

CAL

FALLING ASLEEP CURLED UP WITH LOGAN IS ALMOST AS GOOD AS BEING IN BED INSIDE Logan. When her eyes creep open in the morning and meet mine, and her face lights up with a smile, I decide actually this is better than making love. This is...being together. And I thought it would feel terrifying, but it just feels amazing.

"Hey," she whispers.

"Hey," I say back, and I reach out to wipe a tiny smear of face mask from near her ear. "I missed a spot last night."

She nods. "So you're not the best at spa nights, then?"

I smack her ass playfully and pull her in tight against me. "I'm the best at spa night and if you say otherwise, I'm going to hog all the supplies next time."

We argue about it playfully for a while, and then we roll around in the sheets a while more. Eventually Logan says she has to get ready to go to her volunteer shift. I check the time, panicking, but it's still early. I'm not meeting my dad for a few more hours.

I decide I'd better wash my sheets after all that activity and I'm bent over loading the washing machine when Logan comes up behind me. "Cal, what all did you do yesterday?" I close the door on the washer and stand, feeling nervous that I already fucked up after less than a day in a relationship.

Logan holds an armful of towels and gestures around the apartment. "You bought towels and candles and...did you clean? Everything?"

"Oh," I say, feeling relief wash over me. "Yeah. I told you I was going to pull my weight. I didn't want you sending me another meeting invite."

"What if the meetings are more fun than you think?" I like this side of her. I like everything about her. She plants a kiss on my cheek and adds some towels to the wash. Then she looks around the apartment, happily. "It really feels like home now," she says.

I squint, seeing how my stuff sort of blends with hers for a look that seems put together. "It always felt like home to me, Lo-lo. From that first day."

"Hm," she says, tapping that foot of hers and looking around. I pinch her behind and kiss her on the cheek. "I think I just needed to get used to the idea," she says.

"That feels right."

Logan heads to her volunteer shift, promising to leave her phone turned on this time so she can at least get my texts. I tell her to turn on her tracking app so I can find her if she's out knocking on doors, without me having to call and interrupt her if she's talking to someone. I suit up and head into the Oakland neighborhood near all the universities, to meet my dad at the swanky club.

I hate that he takes clients here. Orla told me they only recently started letting women in at all and I make a mental note to tell my dad he should check out that bar Logan's been visiting. I find Dad and Edward as they're about to be seated, and the three of us grab mimosas from a tray on the bar.

"Mick, I certainly hope you have something to tell me worth toasting," Edward says, frowning as he sinks into his chair.

Dad waves his hand. "If it was bad news I'd have met you at the plant again." He hooks a thumb at me. "My kid here got you situated and you'll be up and running again by morning." Edward looks like he's about to melt in relief at that news. I let out a breath I didn't realize I was holding, seeing his response. Dad keeps talking. "But I could have told you that on the phone." He winks at me as he takes a big swig of his drink.

"Eddie, my Cal here was telling me some very interesting things about sensors. They're the way of the future for old dinosaurs like us."

For the next hour, my dad prompts me to explain how the little sensors can adhere to all the parts of the machines throughout the steel plant and take human error out of the equation when it comes to monitoring the condition of all the parts and pieces of the steel making process.

"Basically, instead of us coming in to check on things once a month or whatever interval, these babies are sending a constant stream of data. Around the clock."

Edward squints, considering. Dad gestures for me to keep going, so I do. I tell him about the drones and how they can get closer to the heat sources, deeper inside smoke stacks, further inside the coal storage. Dad takes over again when I start using the salt shakers to demonstrate what I'm talking about. He says, "Eddie, we've got artificial intelligence experts at Beltane. And now that he's got you back on track, my boy Cal is going to be engineering our own custom drones for our bigger clients. The ones with the most complex needs."

ℬ

Out in the parking lot a few minutes later, Dad pats me on the shoulder. "That was nice work in there, Callum."

"Thanks, Dad. I can't believe you got him to hire us to do predictive maintenance for them. Ray is going to shit when he gets to design that algorithm!"

Dad shakes his head. "Cal. Son. I wouldn't know predictive maintenance from a garbage truck." He pokes me in the chest. "*You* got him to hire us for that, kiddo." Dad smiles and keeps patting my shoulder. "You bringing your girl to dinner with your uncle later?"

"Oh, crap, Dad, I can't tonight." I forgot to tell my family I'd be missing Brady Family dinner today. "Logan asked me to come help her with something for Juniper Jones. You know, Nicole's boss's brother's—"

Dad waves a hand in my face. "I know who Juniper is, you goof. Go on and help her. And tell your mother hello for me when you see her this week." Dad kisses me on the forehead and spins on his heel as the valet brings his car around. I wave as he drives off, and then I pull up Logan's location on my phone as I walk to where I parked Big Red down on the street. I would never trust a valet with my baby like that.

I find Logan's blinking location dot in a neighborhood pretty easily, so I park the Bronc and head out to meet her. I didn't text her that I was coming, and when I spot her, I'm glad I get to watch her without her seeing.

She stands on the corner talking to a woman with a young girl hiding behind her.

I walk closer, and I can hear Logan talking about her own experience. "I was raised by a single mom," she says to the woman and the little girl. "And we struggled. So much! So I know what it's like when people in charge don't care. And let me tell you! Juniper Jones cares." Logan shows the woman the list of programs Juniper brought into the court system. They go over the pamphlet together and when Logan waves and starts to walk away, the girl actually runs out and hugs Logan's leg.

I pop out from behind the hedge as Logan is working to pull herself together from her encounter. "Hey," I whisper. She beams at me. "You were great with them," I say.

"I feel great," she says. "Everything is great!" I love seeing her so happy, so light.

We make our way through the apartment complex, knocking on doors and talking to renters, or just leaving pamphlets if nobody is home. I don't know how much time passes, but I feed off Logan's energy, watching as she gets more excited with each person we talk to.

Juniper apparently gave Logan cards to hand out if people need housing support right now, before it gets to the point of going to court for an eviction, and Logan hands out a handful of those. I smile as she gives the families her personal cell number, offering to help them with the forms if anything is confusing when they try to sign up for help.

"Hey," I say, stroking her cheek while she catches her breath after one of those conversations. "You're really helping people today, Logan. You're making a difference."

"Oh, Cal!" She wraps her arms around me and buries her face in my chest. "That's all I hope for. I had no idea I could feel this good. This useful!"

"You're just getting started, Lo-lo." I squeeze her hand. "When I moved in, I told you I was going to show you the world."

She grins. "I remember."

I bring our clasped hands to my mouth and kiss her knuckles. "I was so wrong, Logan. It's you showing me. You're showing me everything." We're quiet for a few blocks, hitting a bunch of homes where people don't answer the door. We pause at the street corner so Logan can check over the street list, and she tells me we have just one block left before it's time to head back to JJHQ.

We make our way up the brick path to a house with a pretty sweet electric car in the driveway. I'm checking out the wheels when Logan knocks on the door, until I hear the voice of the guy who answers it. "Pete?" I whip my head around when I hear Logan recognize Pete Harris, my hero.

"Hey, Callum, right?" He steps out onto the porch and closes his door behind him. "What are you guys doing here?"

Logan waves the flyers around to show him, but I cut in. "We're out campaigning for our friend Juniper. But we can just leave this stuff and get out of your hair." I don't want to bother this guy or bore him if politics aren't his thing. It's one thing talking to strangers about this stuff, and another to be here asking a guy I wanted to work with if he'll vote for my friend.

"Juniper Jones? She's awesome," Pete says. "She was on the bench when Beagle had to dispute a traffic situation." He waves a hand. "It was a whole thing. She's running again?"

Logan nods and hands him a flyer. "Hey, man, it was good running into you," I tell him, meaning it. "I never did reach out but we should grab a beer sometime."

Pete nods and salutes me with the pamphlet. "Definitely."

It's so strange to come away from that conversation feeling like I finally have something at work worth talking about with him. Like, maybe Pete can just be my engineering friend instead of someone I want to use as a hiding place to run away from my family. My family, who is creating a whole new experience at Beltane that aligns with my passions, even if it doesn't involve automobiles.

I feel like skipping as we finish up and make our way back to Big Red so we can drive to meet the rest of the crew. Logan is practically vibrating in the car, high on the sense of community she is building here.

When we walk into the office Juniper rented for headquarters, the smell of food hits me in the face and I realize I haven't eaten since brunch with my dad hours earlier. My stomach gurgles as I look around. I see Ty Stag and his brothers in a room off to the side. It looks like they stayed behind to babysit about a million kids.

"What's all that," I whisper to Logan, gesturing toward the makeshift daycare.

She giggles. "The campaign wanted young families to feel like they could volunteer without worrying about their kids," she says as Ty pretends to be a zombie and starts chasing his giggling prey.

"We thought you two would never make it back!" My uncle's voice rises above the cacophony and I turn, startled to see him and my dad serving at the buffet line of food.

"Uncle Kel?" He grins as he serves a piece of chicken to a young volunteer.

"Your dad mentioned why you weren't coming to family dinner today," he says as my dad scoops out baked beans and mac n cheese. Kellen shrugs. "We thought we'd bring family dinner to you!"

Logan claps her hands in front of her chest. "That's just the most amazing thing," she says. "Thank you, Kellen. And you, Mick!"

She runs around to hug them both and I stand with my hands in my pockets, grinning as my dad winks at me. I see Nicole and Zack come in the door followed by Maddie and Liam. My face lights up when I also see my uncle's neighbor and her son make their way over from a table where it looks like they've been folding pamphlets.

"Everyone's here," Liam says, nodding sternly and stating the obvious when Orla emerges from the childcare room looking like she's been to war. We all stare as Uncle Kel's neighbor, Elizabeth, gives him a shy peck on the cheek after he offers her two pieces of chicken at the buffet.

"Everyone is definitely here," I say. Logan comes back and inserts herself at my side. Without even thinking about it I drape my arm over her shoulder and squeeze her close at my side. She kisses me on the cheek and I grin.

My family doesn't even give me crap about it, but Zack nods his head at me sternly until Nicole swats him and winks, giving Logan a thumbs up. Juniper stands on a chair and starts thanking everyone for their work until Nicole whistles and leads everyone in a round of applause for Juniper.

I smile as my family whoops and hollers. I love how they showed up today, how they've all embraced Nicole as part of the family as much as anyone with the actual Brady last name. I love the way the Stag family adopted Nicole and then blended into the Bradys, how we've become this massive network of people who show the fuck up for each other eventually, when it matters.

And then I look over at my roommate, looking sun kissed and gorgeous as she bumps shoulders with my dad and steals food from my brother. She makes her way back to my side and my blissed out feelings start shifting toward other sensations.

"Hey," I whisper to Logan. "I have an idea."

She reaches past me to grab a roll and bites into it as she makes a "go on" gesture with her other hand.

I hook my finger into the belt loop of her jeans and tug her closer to me. "I think we should listen to *The Redcoat* as we walk back to my car and then go home and act out the naughty parts."

"Oh my gosh," she squeals. "I love that idea."

But instead of putting on the audiobook in the car, Logan is bubbling with excitement and starts to talk. "I loved everything about today," she says. "I loved how it made me feel good and I loved how your whole family showed up."

"Well, my family loves you," I tell her. And then I realize something, and once I think it I know I can't go another second without saying it. "And I love you, Logan." The truth of it rings in the air, in her eyes as she smiles back at me. "You complete me. Or anyway, you make me better. And I look forward to just sitting next to you every day and...well, I love you."

"Wow," she says, slumping back against the seat. I pull the car over and turn to look at her. "Nobody has ever said that to me before," she whispers.

"I've definitely never felt this way before," I tell her. For a second I'm worried she isn't going to say it back to me, but I think of her face this morning, of the beautiful way she looks when she's asleep in my arms, the way she clutched my arm in excitement as she figured out how good she feels when she's giving back to other people. I know she cares about me and I know she's right here with me in this, even if she's not ready to say it yet. So I say it again. "I love you, Logan. I love you."

A tear rolls down her face and I reach to brush it away with my thumb. She turns her cheek into my hand and kisses my palm. "Cal," she whispers. "I feel so safe with you. I feel your love." She smiles at me in the dark, her eyes glittering beneath the street light. "I love you, too."

I pull her in for a kiss and I hold her until the windows start to steam. We pull apart and I drive the rest of the way home, ready to keep on showing her how much I love her, ready to repeat it as often as I can.

EPILOGUE: LOGAN
ONE YEAR LATER

"Callum, you have to stop." He nips at my skin as he crawls around our bed as I try to swat him away from me. "Cal, you're in the wedding party."

He groans and stands up, scratching his bare butt and making me laugh. "I still can't believe Nicole and Zack are having an actual wedding," he says as he heads toward the shower.

I pad down the hall to the office to wait my turn for the bathroom. Lord knows, if I try to climb in there with Cal we will never even get to the venue. Cal built a Murphy bed in what used to be my bedroom. If my mom ever agrees to come visit, we can pull the bed down and the whole desk just folds underneath.

Mom finally let go of her second job at least, once I sent her a check made out to her landlord to cover the entire year's rent. Cal keeps reminding me Mom has been balancing on a razor blade for so many years, it's going to take a long time for her to exhale. Meanwhile, after Juniper got re-elected I started volunteering with the organization here that provides emergency grants to single parents for rent. I pop open the software from our latest fundraising campaign and clap my hands when I see how much we've brought in to help these families.

Cal sneaks up behind me and rubs his wet hair against my neck, making me squeal. "You're up for the bathroom, Lo-lo," he says, starting to peel off my robe.

I spin in his arms and plant a kiss on the tip of his nose. "Later," I say, tugging it back closed. "Today's about your brother." He follows me down the hall, trying to peek until I close the bathroom door in his face.

"He better watch out or I'll make our wedding a whole weekend project," he shouts through the door. Cal and I joke about our eventual wedding all the time. Over the past year, we've worked so hard at communication. Being with Cal is easy. Talking with Cal about my fears? About the worries brewing in my own head? That is something I practice every day.

But by the time Cal tugged me under the mistletoe at his family's Christmas party, and the whole Brady crew applauded, I knew we were a permanent pair. It just feels like he belongs in my life. We'll figure out the best time to make it official. "I love you," I tell him as we approach Heinz Hall. The wedding planner sweeps him away with the rest of the wedding party and I head off to find my seat.

Samantha waves and beckons me over, pulling me in to a hug. "You sitting with Foof for this shindig?" She gestures around her, where Esther and Chloe and Piper are dressed to the nines. Juniper is officiating, and gives me a wink from up at the podium as she organizes her notes.

"Nah," I say with a shrug. "I'm over with Cal's uncle and cousin and such. But obviously we'll hang out at the reception."

Sam shoos me away with a wink and I squeeze into the front row, where Uncle Kellen and his girlfriend are taking pictures of everything. They're adorable, Kellen pointing out all the exciting features of the building and Elizabeth telling him she loves that he notices that. She smiles warmly at me and squeezes my leg as I sit down. "Isn't this terrific," she asks.

And it is. It's terrific to see Zack overcome with emotion, and Nicole being sincere as they promise to always care for each other. It's terrific to see Mick and his three boys looking so genuinely happy during photos after the ceremony. But the most terrific part is Cal pulling me close to him for a dance during the reception.

I laugh as he tugs me over toward our family, who are all flailing their limbs as they dance with Nicole and Zack. "I'm keeping my name," Nicole shouts as she spins and smiles.

"What if I take yours?" Zack pokes a finger at his wife's ribs, a look of delight in his eyes. They start to argue about whether Nicole will let him become a Kennedy, and it's great to see them teasing each other, the balance they have between fun and serious. I feel like I have that same balance with Cal.

I rest my cheek on his chest, feeling the heat radiate off of him as he laughs, and he runs his fingers through my hair like he often does. "I love dancing with you," I tell him.

"Good thing we did a foot treatment the other day," he jokes. "I'm on top of my game." He twirls me around a few times and then tugs me behind a marble column, planting a searing kiss on my mouth. I moan into him, twisting my fingers into the lapels of his suit.

"This isn't a game," I tell him. "This is real life. And it's more than I ever dreamed of."

"I'm not good at saying that sort of thing, Logan," he says, running his lips along my jaw. "But I definitely agree." He presses me closer to him and I feel just how excited he is.

"Behave!" I scold, and then kiss him again. "I love the things you say, Callum Brady."

"How long do we have to stay?"

"Let's see. At your brother's wedding? Until it's over." He groans and rests his forehead against mine. "Hey, cheer up," I tell him. "Nicole has a cookie table. Why don't we go get you a half dozen to distract you?"

Cal perks up at the mention of baked goods and we search the lobby, finding an overflowing buffet of every kind of cookie imaginable. Cal reaches in with both hands, delighting me with his excitement. I almost don't notice a flash of red dress rushing through the front doors.

"Hey," I nudge his shoulder. "Wasn't that Orla?" We look outside in time to see her dash across the street, tugging a man behind her, a determined look on her face. "Who's that with her?"

Cal squints and nibbles his cookie, considering. "That guy is a client. Or his dad is. Anyway, it looks like Orla missed the memo about Bradys staying til the end of this thing."

"Did she just grab his crotch?"

Cal winces and nods. "Come on," he says, pulling me back inside the reception. "I need to go gauge out my eyeballs and clear that memory."

I look around the reception, where all my friends are smiling and waving, where our family is hugging and laughing, where the room vibrates with joy. "We'll build new memories," I say to Cal. "Every day. Together."

"I like that," he says. Hand in hand, we walk back toward the party, where we are welcomed with open arms.

ℬ

EPILOGUE: LOGAN

The Foof ladies each get books, too!
The Bridges and Bitters series kicks off with Samantha's story,
Fireball: An Enemies to Lovers Romance.

CURRENT

A SECRET BABY ROMANCE

CHAPTER ONE

WALT

JUNE

"TRIP, PUT ON A SUIT. I NEED YOU TO COME WITH ME TODAY. I'LL TEXT YOU THE address." My father doesn't waste time with pleasantries. Not with me, anyway. He hangs up the phone abruptly. I could have had plans today. I could have been out somewhere. He has no idea and he doesn't care. Something evidently came up and I'm needed to show my face and preserve the family brand.

I look at the address my father sent: Heinz Hall downtown. I remember something vague my mother had said about going to a client's daughter's wedding this weekend. The fact that I'm being called in as a pinch hitter means Mom is either faking a dizzy spell or she mixed up her Benzos with her vitamins this morning.

I could tell my father to fuck off. I could get in my car and just drive away. I have a college degree—I could probably get a job doing something and support myself. I used to watch YouTube videos about people who just live in a van and drive around the country, working on farms in short bursts to support their wanderlust. I don't have the first clue how to do anything on a farm, and we've always had plenty of money to travel in style. I don't have wanderlust so much as...a deep and burning desire to escape the Sheffield name and all that goes with it.

But if I'm honest, I can't escape the hope that eventually, my father will smile at me and maybe tell me I did a good job at something.

Depending who you ask, my parents are model citizens. They're

725

involved in philanthropy and sit on boards of directors for charities. They invest in their communities and our last name shows up all over kids' baseball jerseys and soccer fields we've patronized. But behind closed doors, my mother criticized my sister's appearance incessantly. My father spent the past 25 years both telling me I'm worthless and insisting I need to step up and take the helm of the family empire.

The promise of that is intoxicating. Taking the helm. What would that feel like?

I step into my closet and start putting on my tailored suit. It's like a costume. When I'm wearing it, I'm Trip Sheffield, heckuvaguy. I shake hands too aggressively and laugh too hard at old men telling sexist jokes. When I say something, it has no substance or else it makes women uncomfortable.

I tighten a perfect Windsor knot in my tie, hating my reflection in the full-length mirror. Maybe it's not entirely fair to say the suit is a costume. I'm never *not* wearing tailored couture. The last time I tried to be me, I was in high school. I was a day student at a posh academy where boarding students came from all over to "prepare for a lifetime of success."

I was, of course, expected to participate in respectable sports like lacrosse, golf and tennis. I was expected to take courses in business and economics. But one day I enrolled in an acting class. I figured I spend my entire life acting like Trip Sheffield. What if I tried something else?

ℬ

I STARE INTO MY REFLECTION, remembering the twitch of my father's neck muscles when he personally drove to campus to inform the head of school there had been an error in my registration. To anyone else, he was an attentive father, taking time from his corporate life to see to his son's education. I saw the way his entire body clenched, felt the sting of his fingers digging into my arm as he walked me to his car.

I learned two things that day. First, whatever hold the Sheffields apparently had on the upper class is apparently precarious, and second, our friends and neighbors are evidently utterly unforgiving of any activity that carries the slightest whiff of not meeting expectations.

ℬ

I ᴛᴜᴄᴋ my phone into my jacket pocket and sigh, hoping I'm not late to meet my father.

B

Hᴇ ɢʀᴇᴇᴛs me with a nod and starts walking inside. "Hey," I say, causing him to stare at me disapprovingly. "I just...can you brief me before we go in?"

He rolls his eyes. "Mick Brady's son is getting married. Owns Beltane Engineering. They're consulting on the Garfield project for us. You recall your responsibilities to this property?"

"Sure, Dad. Of course. This is just a little last minute for me is all."

"Yes, well. Your mother wasn't feeling well today." I don't ask after her. There's no point really.

"Anything I should be aware of before we go in?" I arch a brow, glancing around his shoulder to see if I know anyone.

My father licks his teeth and waits a few beats before saying, "The broad comes from a well-connected family in the south hills. There will be a lot of important contacts here today, but they're here for a wedding. Don't bring up business. And for the love of god, don't try to talk about your bakery."

I hold up my palms in a surrender gesture. "Of course not," I sputter. My father gave me a task for his company's new project in the Garfield neighborhood. I keep clinging to hope that this will be my big opportunity to prove myself to him, but most of the time he doesn't seem to remember he assigned me a project to lead.

There had been a project planning meeting, and he asked for ideas to round out the development. I spit out the phrase "keto bakery" in a panic after scrolling through social media on my phone in my lap. I plunked in the terms "powerful influencers" and "market trends" and managed to get the nod from our investors. I'm supposed to be creating a trendy, new customer magnet as part of some big project my father has going in that neighborhood.

That's what our family business does. We develop new commercial projects, secure investors, sell the businesses, reap the profits. Only I'm not sure how any of it really works. I mostly take credit for the work our interns are doing.

Dad shakes a bunch of hands as we walk inside and take our seats just before the ceremony begins. I tap the program on my leg nervously as the wedding party files past. And then a woman catches my eye, because she looks as uncomfortable as me.

She's tall and gorgeous, and she moves like she's not used to wearing a dress. I look at the program, and almost everyone has the last name Brady, so the man with his arm hooked around her is most likely her brother. I find myself feeling relieved that he's not competition, as if a woman like that would ever look my way.

Her full lips are painted a deep red, the color of ripe cherries. Her long, golden hair is looped into a braided crown, and she is absolutely regal moving through space, like she owns every atom. She turns her head to scan the room and looks through me, past me, like I'm just a face in the crowd.

I stare at her for a half hour, not even aware when the wedding ends until she files right on past me again and I watch as she walks directly toward the bar across the hall, in the space reserved for the reception.

I feel my father's hand on my shoulder, an ounce more firmly than is comfortable. "You see that tall drink of water over there?" Dad points at the bar and my heart sinks when I realize he's gesturing at the regal beauty from the ceremony. "She's one of the Brady kids and I'm doing business with her family. Why don't you go over there and show her some of the ol' Sheffield charm?"

It's not really a request. I exhale slowly, wishing it weren't so easy to let my slimy persona slide into place. I nod at my father and walk toward the bar.

CHAPTER TWO
ORLA

 the wall in the dressing room as my friend Nicole smooths out the skirt of her very fancy wedding gown. My cousin's bride-to-be twists to the side to check herself from multiple angles.

"Isn't it wonderful?" Emma Stag, one of Nicole's friends, claps her hands, perched on the edge of a stool so as not to mess up her hair or gown. Nicole and Emma both have unmanageable curls, and the wedding stylist tamed everything into elegant up-dos.

I pat my braids, hoping they don't stand out as homemade. My mom died when I was ten, and she was sick for years before that. I had bowl cuts until high school and grew up surrounded by Brady boys. There was nobody to teach me I was supposed to care about up-dos, let alone teach me how to create them. Nicole sometimes offers to do fun things with my blond waves, but she's marrying Zack today and I didn't want to distract her. It was better for me to figure something out on my own. This braided concoction is the result of hours scouring internet tutorials, and as I look around the room at these gorgeous women, I feel self conscious. But then I remember that I'm a badass engineer and I blink those feelings quickly away.

The bridal party is all decked out in black gowns everyone promises they'll wear again, and I have to admit that as far as dresses go, this one is pretty decent. Nicole knows I don't really go for dresses, but our gowns have pockets, one of those ruched up designs that flatters everyone's waist, and a neckline that lets me actually wear a regular bra.

I can already feel myself maybe agreeing to wear it to the next work function my dad deems formal. Another perk of being an engineer: ripped jeans and flannel shirts are the norm on a job site. I have to care about my clothes a few times a year, tops.

ℬ

"But look at the shoes," Nicole says, showing off the deadly looking spike heels that make her calves look terrific. As my thoughts wander, I almost forget I asked her about her fairytale princess wedding. "And there's a cookie table."

"Who doesn't love cookies?" Nicole's other bestie, Maddie, lives with my other cousin, Liam. They have a kid together and everything, but even before she was a mom, Maddie was the queen of snacks. She's even got a fanny pack to match her bridesmaid dress, since she uses those bags to hold her diabetes supplies...and cookies, apparently.

The Brady guys are technically my cousins, but really they're like brothers. Our families lived under the same roof for years. The three of them even greeted my prom date with glowering expressions and threats of violence.

Despite all that dysfunction, everyone in my extended family is happily partnered, and I hear about it no fewer than forty times a week. My dad seems more excited about his imaginary future son-in-law than he does about his existing daughter.

Okay, that's not fair.

But he and his girlfriend do keep asking pointed questions about my love life, and I try to steer them back toward questions about electrical systems.

Everything seemed a lot easier before they all remembered that I'm a woman. I silently curse my cousins for all managing to find true love before I was ready to even start looking. Now there's all this pressure on me, in addition to the building pressure for me to advance in my career, pass my exams, and start taking on my own electrical engineering projects. Dad wants me to take the helm for the company's new power plant projects, and he seems to pivot between asking about my love life and making sure I'm up on all the new codes for high voltage transmission lines.

ℬ

THE WEDDING PLANNER swoops in to the room, clapping her hands and telling us all to take our places. I have to admit, it's pretty cool that Nicole and Zack are getting married in Heinz Hall. This place is like a dream for a gang of civil engineers. Sure enough, as I sneak my head around the corner to peek at the aisle, I see my relatives all pointing out architectural features and admiring the load-bearing columns in the historic Pittsburgh concert hall.

The crowd is full of my dad and uncle's clients and golf buddies, who seem to overlap with Nicole's parents' clients and golf buddies. I worry there won't be a single person here that I can tolerate outside my relatives, but then my eye drifts to a group of women wearing varying shades bright red, sitting in the middle on Nicole's side. I instantly relax. The ladies of Foof will keep me sane at the reception.

Fresh Out Of Fucks, they call themselves. Nicole introduced me a few years ago when she and Zack first got together and I was really struggling with being the only female engineer in a world full of men who all think they know more than me. Foof gets together every few weeks to strategize about the best ways to overcome our problems. Sam Vine, who owns a kick-ass tech startup, talks about Foof like we're witches, gathering together over a cauldron to combine our powers.

Mostly, I just appreciate the support. I never have to explain anything there, not really. It's amazing to have female influence like that. I grew up in a house with five men. On the one hand, I never had any opportunity to doubt that I belonged in the world of engineering. On the other, I was at least 18 years old before I realized it's not normal to be able to identify your cousins based on the smell of their farts.

ℬ

AFTER THE CEREMONY, I grab a drink and make a bee line for the ladies in red. "Orla!" Sam sings out my name and shakes her glass at me. "You look terrific. Did you take my advice about the shape wear?"

"I told you I don't do shape ware," I tell her, rolling my eyes.

"You're missing out. It just smooths everything." As she gestures up and down her abdomen, I catch sight of a guy staring, and I roll my eyes again.

"You're attracting attention," I say, my voice a little quieter. Sam waggles her eyebrows, like she knew and that was the point. Sam laughs and shimmies as Logan, another Brady girlfriend, makes her way toward us.

"Oh my gosh, Orla, you look beautiful. This whole thing is just beauti-ful." Logan claps her hands and bounces on her toes. "Cal won't stop talking about the architecture of the building." At the ripe old age of 31, Cal's six years ahead of me in age and a few decades behind me in common sense.

Except when it comes to girlfriends—Logan's pretty great.

"Let's talk about something more important," Sam says, steering us both across the room. "Nicole mentioned there was a cheese sculpture." The food at this event was actually something I got excited about when Nicole was describing it over the past few months. Wait staff circulates the room with all sorts of things wrapped in bacon, tiny cups of shrimp, various flavored meats.

"I think she commissioned an actual chalet made of Swiss cheese," I say, snagging a skewer of chicken satay from a waiter, who grins at me suggestively. I consider kneeing him in the balls, but I don't want him to drop the meat. I might want more of this later.

Sure enough, we approach a table that would fit in at an art gallery. It's like a model railroad village, but all the structures are made from different cheeses, and tiny knives invite would-be destructors like Foof to tear down the walls.

"Now we're talking," I say, setting my drink on the edge of the table and reaching for one of the knives. My tongue pokes out in anticipation while I consider where to start. I twirl the cheese knife, pondering. Should I slice into the roquefort sheep farm or the gouda windmill?

"You can handle my knife like that any time." A deep male voice cuts into my decision space and I whip my head around to see who said some-thing so gross. The guy who was staring at me and Sam earlier, who looks like a Ken doll, gestures lewdly in the vicinity his crotch and then winks. I absolutely hate winkers.

"Pass," I say, jabbing the knife into an Italian villa made from asiago.

Undeterred, Ken-doll leans on the edge of the table and watches me. "You really know your way around a hard blade," he says. "Any chance you'll save a slice for me?"

"Unlikely," I say, and I turn away from him, grabbing my cheese and my drink and finding my friends, who have migrated toward the fruit table. Nicole did say we should all stretch out our stomachs with the appetizers to make room for the feast she's got coming our way. I'm here for it.

When I get back to my friends, Logan and Sam are conspiring about introducing themselves to some of the rich old buzzards here at the reception. Sam hired Logan as the CFO at her company, and the two of them are inseparable.

I'd kill for a female best friend at work. Sure, we've got Dakota, but our project manager is mainly in the office and I'm typically out on job sites. I munch on my cheese and listen as they rank the rich guests by their likelihood of becoming investors in Sam's business.

Soon, I realize they're not going to stop talking about work, and I have nothing of substance to offer in the conversation.

As my mind wanders, Ken-doll keeps looking at me and licking his lips. I glare at him, but then I decide his lips are actually kind of pillowy. He's really fucking hot, but he knows it and that makes him seem gross.

I look around for Maddie and Emma, hoping they'll distract me, but when I find them, they're both gushing about how great it is to have a day off from their kids, and I feel left out of that conversation, too.

Unlike Sam and Logan's work talk, Maddie and Emma's mom-talk causes my chest to tighten and the blood in my temples to pulse uncomfortably. I know they're entitled to a break, but it stings a little to hear them expressing relief about it when I know my mom sobbed for months when she learned her cancer was terminal. All she wanted was more time to be a mom.

⸱

I DRIFT over to where Nicole and Zack are chatting with their guests. Zack, usually the grouchiest guy around, is actually smiling as he fiddles with his new wedding ring. It glints silver in the lights in the hall. I'm about to have my turn hugging them when Nicole's sister steps in my path. "Oona, right? Wasn't it a beautiful ceremony?"

"It's Orla," I remind her. She knows damn well what my name is, because my dad said I had to play nice and work with her to plan Nicole's shower. Thankfully, she took charge of that whole thing, but she still had to type my name in the "to" line of every group email.

"Orla, of course." Her smile is as fake as her nails. I never have any idea how to behave around fake people. I grimace and poke my cheese with a toothpick. She leans closer to me. "Soon it'll be your turn! Do you think you'll choose a non-religious ceremony as well?"

"Uh. Yeah. Because we are not religious." I know it's a faux pas to say that, but why is she asking me about my wedding at her sister's wedding? I spin away from her as she blinks, and make my way back to the snacks.

A server passes by with bacon-wrapped-dates, and I pluck one from the tray, cramming the sweet and savory goodness into my mouth. "Um, god, that's good," I say involuntarily.

"Aren't they, though?" This time I'm intercepted by my dad, who seems to be making his way toward the bride and groom. I look around his shoulder to make sure Nicole's sister is gone before I fall into step alongside him. He drops a kiss on the top of my head. "You look beautiful, sweetheart."

"Thanks, Dad. You clean up nice, too." Dad always wears suits to work, so this slightly fancier suit shouldn't make much difference, but with his silver hair cut short and his beard trimmed, he looks damned sophisticated.

When I look up at Dad's eyes, I see they're a little watery. "You gonna make it?"

He dabs at his eye with the heel of his hand. "Oh, yes. I'm just thinking how much your mother would have enjoyed seeing your cousins all grown up. And you, obviously. Anyway, I was just missing her today."

I feel a pinch inside my torso, like my spine has locked itself into place. I have to breathe very carefully as I work to maintain my composure. This is all feeling like too much. I just wanted to hug my fucking cousin, and even that has meant a journey through emotional minefields.

"Hey, Dad, I'm just going to grab a drink." I squeeze his arm and try to turn out of his grip.

"You've already got one, Orla-bear." He taps at my glass. I chew on the inside of my cheek.

"I meant water, Dad. Best to alternate. Haha. Gotta pace myself." I force a smile and he nods.

I walk away, not knowing where to go. I can't seem to find any of my friends and my relatives are all scattered throughout the room.

A huge combination of uncomfortable feelings has my head throbbing a little bit, but when I look up at the bar again, Ken-doll is standing in my space. "You look lost, little lamb," he crows. "Want me to help you find your way?"

I roll my eyes. "Are you always this pompous? Little lamb? Come on."

He blinks. "I was just referencing the cheese sheep you destroyed over there." He shrugs and reaches for my plate, and plucks up the remains of a tiny cheese-sheep. Then he opens his mouth, sticks out that tongue, and eats my cheese.

I should hate him. I should punch him. Any other day, I'd stomp on his foot and tell him to get lost. I can't put my finger on it, but I know this is an act for him. It takes one to know when when you're putting on a show, after all. I squint at him, wondering what's beneath this shell. He grins and suddenly, I have to know.

I very calmly set down my cheese, smooth out my skirt, and grab his hand. A solution to my wedding discomfort has presented itself to me. I'm going to walk away from this crowd and get sweaty with this sexy, gross douchebag.

"All right," I say. "Let's do this."

His eyes flash a brighter blue. "Come again?"

"I plan to," I say, tugging on his arm. "There's a hotel across the street."

CHAPTER THREE
WALT

I'M IN WAY OVER MY HEAD. I DELIVERED MY SMARMIEST, MOST TERRIBLE LINES TO this chick like I always do, hoping like always that she'd be so turned off that she'd continue to avoid me all night. Because then I could pretend that I gave it my best effort. I played the role. I'm a Sheffield, after all. I need to come on to beautiful women at fancy parties, acting like I expect them to sleep with me.

But they don't usually do that.

I work very hard to repulse them before they can figure out what a disappointment I am.

"Hold on a second, sweetheart," I say. She freezes in her tracks and whips her head around to glare at me.

"Do *not* call me that," she barks.

"Okay, okay. But what should I call you?"

"You're going soft on me now? After offering to let me wield your knife?"

I swallow and run a hand through my hair. "Baby, you know how it is. Women like—"

She holds a palm up. "You can stop with the pet names right the hell now. And don't you dare tell me what women like." She starts walking again, dragging me out of the venue into the windy Pittsburgh afternoon. I guess this is happening? "My name is Orla fucking Brady. And just for that last comment, you better make me come at least twice."

"Come?"

"At least! Twice!" She shoulders the revolving door to the hotel across the street and the bellhop springs to attention as she stalks through the lobby. We get to the elevator and she stops, hand on her hip, looking up at me. "Well? You need your room key to call the elevator."

"I don't have a room," I mutter. "I live two miles away..."

"Ugh, I hate you," she mutters, rummaging around for a pocket miraculously disguised in the side of her dress.

"Join the club," I mutter, watching as she pulls out a key card and summons the elevator before sliding the card back into her pocket. I have no idea why, but I'm painfully turned on right now.

Orla fucking Brady is taller up close than she looked up front at the wedding. Her arms look fit and toned and her body seems firm and commanding in her bridesmaids dress. I've had a hard-on for her since I saw her walk down that aisle a few hours before.

Now that I'm here at a hotel with her, and she's demanding orgasms, I'm not quite sure what to do about it. We walk into the elevator and she leans back on the polished brass railing against the wall. "You going to tell me your name? Or should I call you baby and sweetheart?"

"Trip," I spit out. "Everyone calls me Trip."

"Everyone calls you that or that's your name?"

The doors slide open and she pops off the wall, nodding her head for me to follow her down the hall.

"My name is Walton Henry Sheffield the third," I tell her, and she halts in her tracks.

She turns to face me, one eyebrow arched. "No," she says. "I'm not calling you that. That's ridiculous."

"Well, like I said, everyone calls me Trip." I'm starting to get annoyed, but I also find that my attraction to her increases along with my irritation. I'm not annoyed at *her* so much as I'm hearing her validate a secret thought I've been wanting to voice all my life.

"Wally," she says, pulling out the key card again and sliding it into the notch on her room door. "I'll call you Wally."

I step into the room and Orla places two hands on my chest and shoves me at the bed. Taken aback, I fall and she straddles me on the mattress. Her thighs are pressed firm against mine and that skirt bunches up, revealing the long, tan lines of her legs. My hands move automatically to caress them. Being here with Orla feels daring. I imagine my father scanning the reception, wondering where I've gone. Fearing I'm saying something that will impact his reputation. Instead, I'm in a hotel room getting shoved around by a grouchy, Celtic goddess.

"Well, Wally? I believe you offered me the use of your knife?"

I snort out a laugh. "You gonna slice my throat with it?"

"Are you saying you want me to choke you with your own dick, Wally?"

I feel a burst of energy and a surge of lust, and I thrust up off the mattress, flipping us both over so I'm on top of Orla, nestled between her legs. I jut my hips against her, feeling the warm heat at the apex of her thighs. She wants me, too, I remind myself. She's into this for some reason.

I'm totally overcome, outside my normal comfort zone. I'm typically timid with women in bed. Frankly, I don't think I'm very good at making things good for them. But for some reason, this woman rejects my Trip performance. I can be anyone I want right now.

And I want very badly to be a man who makes Orla-fucking-Brady feel good. I lick my lips, staring down at her chest, and take a deep breath. "I'm going to stuff my dick into your pretty little pussy, Orla-fucking-Brady," I tell her, and her eyes turn molten. I press her wrists above her head with one hand as I unzip my fly. "Does that sound okay to you?"

"Finally, Wally," she says, smiling. "That's exactly what I want to hear." I manage to undo my belt buckle and yank down the zipper on my slacks as Orla watches, wriggling. I pull my cock out from my boxers and tap it against her thigh a few times.

"Keep your arms above your head," I command, releasing her wrists. I've never told a woman to do this before. I had no idea how fucking powerful I'd feel when she listens. My cock jolts in my hand as she nods her head. I use my free hand to yank down her panties, and I throw them on the floor behind me.

I start tracing a path up her leg with the tip of my cock and let my other hand trace along her body on my way back to her wrists. Her tits are amazing, firm little apples, and I groan as her nipple hardens under my thumb. I pause there, at her breasts, circling the bump through the fabric of her dress and I move across her chest to give the other nipple my attention as I jerk myself off slowly.

"Oh god, Wally, I didn't think you'd actually be good at this." Orla moans and writhes on the bed. I let go of my shaft and reach between her legs, my fingers finding a hot, wet paradise. I'm really not a confident person. My entire family treats me like I'm an idiot. I've spent my whole life building up a fake, slimy wall when I interact with people so I don't have to reveal anything true about myself. And usually, when I do get a woman to come to bed, I fumble around with all the mechanics.

So I'm not entirely sure where the inspiration comes from when I circle my index finger inside Orla-fucking-Brady, pull out the glistening digit, and bring it up to my lips. I've got her wrists pinned above her head again with one hand and I lean close to her face as I lick her moisture off my finger. "Delicious," I whisper. And it's true. She tastes like danger and confidence and wanting, and I'm starving for it.

I sink to my knees between her legs, letting go of her arms as my fingers dig into her thighs. I push them open, rucking up her skirt and baring her for my delight. The scent of Orla's pussy greets me, earthy and salty. Maybe a little mean, like her. I meet her eye as I stick out my tongue and lick her, hard.

"Fuck, Wally. Oh, god," she shouts as I carry on, lapping at her. I've never done this before. I feel Orla shudder beneath me and I'm forlorn that I've missed this opportunity to bring a woman to this state before now. I groan against her tender flesh, and the vibration causes her to buck up against my face.

I peel back Orla's petals with my thumbs as my fingers stroke her upper thighs, and I lap and suck at her pussy like it's something new. Something miraculous. Because it is. I've never been this close to a woman's center. Everything here is complicated and foreign, which is fitting because women seem complicated and foreign to me.

And yet, *this* pussy and *this* woman seem to respond very positively to my attention, for the first time in my life. "Do not stop doing that, Wally," she pants, as I nudge her with my nose, continuing to lick. I feel my erection bobbing against my stomach, a bead of moisture forming on my undershirt.

I swallow and gaze at this stranger spread before me. She's wild now, frantic, her hips reaching up as I move my face away, removing the friction she needs. *She's desperate for me,* I think, and the thought is a heady drug. Never has someone been wild, unhinged for me. Just for me. Not for my money or my family or my connections. Never has someone rejected my public persona, seen the real me and...liked it. "Please," she whimpers, and her hands claw at my hair, trying to pull my face closer.

"You need this." It's both an observation and a question as I delicately trace a finger beside her clit.

"Oh, yes, please, Wally," she moans. "Please!" As she begs, I slide my finger inside her and alternate stroking her clit with my thumb, and blowing on it, and then I feel Orla-fucking-Brady come apart. Her body clamps down on the finger I slide inside her, and she screams, her nails digging into my scalp as she tries to hold me closer against her body.

I leave the finger inside her and press hard against her clit with my thumb as she thrashes around, until she returns to her body, when I expect her to yell at me to get the hell out of her hotel room. Instead, she looks at me with sex-drunk eyes and says, "Where the fuck have you been all my life?"

I shrug and rock back on my heels, looking down at my erection, which has turned purple as I grow harder than ever, relishing in the image of Orla coming. I blow out a breath when she doesn't kick me or tell me to leave.

"I believe you requested two of those," I tell her, raising my brow at her and stroking my cock again. She looks down at it and nods. I'm a tall guy. I have big feet. My body is proportional. But I still feel like some sort of Nordic god as Orla ogles my cock.

"I have an IUD," she blurts.

"Okay..."

"It means I can't get pregnant, asshole," she says, and starts trying to wiggle away from me.

"Where are you going?" I grab her hip and hold her still, tracing my cock along her thigh again. I love the feel of her skin against my sensitive tip.

"I haven't been with anyone in almost a year," she says. "I'm clean."

"Actually, I think you're very dirty." I reach a lazy hand up to play with her tits again and she practically purrs as I pinch her nipple. *Interesting*.

"Oh, god, I hate that you're so fucking good at this," she groans, arching her back up off the mattress toward my fingers as I retract my hand. "You keep bringing me to the edge and then moving the fucking edge. Jesus, Wally. Why do you even bother with those terrible pickup lines when you're—"

I pinch her nipple and she screams. I think about her words, that I'm good at bringing her pleasure. "Are you ready for my cock, Orla-fucking-Brady?" I raise a brow and look at her, with her braided crown a mess as she runs her palms down her regal cheeks.

"Yes, damn you. Please fuck me with that monster cock."

"Hm." I crouch back down, kneeling between her open thighs. I reach around for my wallet, procuring a condom. "Should I wrap up?"

Orla pants and stares at me. "Probably," she says, her hands grasping at the sheets, impatient. I roll the rubber on slowly, wincing at the sensation.

If she says anything else about her orgasm, I'll come in a heartbeat. And fuck me, that pussy. That wet, hot, puffy pussy of hers is still contracting a little with her post-orgasm shock waves. I can see it winking.

A thousand fantasies flash through my thoughts before I land on what to say next. "On your knees, then."

"What?"

I grin. It's like Orla desperately wants me to do all the things I've always desperately wanted to do in bed, but never had the opportunity to try. I grip her hip and flip her over as she squeals. "I said ass up, Orla." I toss her skirt up even higher and give her rump a smack as she adjusts herself on the bed.

Standing behind her, massaging that round, firm ass with one hand, I line myself up with the other and slam into her. I hiss, because it feels so good I might blow right away and I know I need to get her off one more time or she's going to know I'm a fraud.

I puff out my cheeks as I exhale, slowly stroking into her until my hip bones bump against her ass cheeks. She starts pressing back against me, meeting me as I drive into her. "Fuck yeah," I say. "You like that?"

"You know I fucking like it. God, your cock feels amazing. I can practically feel it up in my rib cage." She's right. I'm so deep inside her at this angle. She's wrapped tightly around me like moss on a rock, and just as slippery. Orla starts rocking her hips up and down and back and forth until the two of us are sweating and grunting in a race to see who comes first.

"Touch yourself," I command, reaching around with both hands to massage her breasts as I pump into her. She slithers a hand between her legs and I watch her wrist flex as she works frantically to get herself off.

Orla moans and stiffens and I feel her contracting all around me. God, the pulsing squeeze feels like nothing I've ever experienced. She shrieks and tells me she hates me as she comes and her shoulders sink into the bed. Her hips arch up higher and with this new angle, I'm deeper than ever before.

I pound into her, grunting like a savage until I feel my balls tighten and know I'm about to blow. With one more thrust, I know I'm close. I feel my release, it's so close. My cock begins to pulse inside her and I'm in ecstasy... until I'm really not.

I feel a jabbing sting, like something stabbed me in the head of my cock, and I fly backwards.

"What the fuck?" I scream in simultaneous pain and bliss. I wrap my fist around my cock, which spurts as I come even in the midst of my pain. I rip the condom off, and I'm still coming as I drop the sloppy latex on Orla's back. My mess oozes out of it as she squeals and I see a bead of blood at the tip of my cock.

She looks at me over her shoulder, her face confused. "What?"

"You stabbed me," I mutter, staring down.

"What?" She brushes the hair out of her eyes with her forearm, panting. "What are you talking about." Orla shifts around on the bed as I stand there with my quickly-shriveling penis in my fist. "Oh," she says, her eyes going wide. "Huh."

CHAPTER FOUR
ORLA

Of course Sam and Maddie catch me sneaking back in to the reception. I try to play it cool like I've just been in the bathroom for a long time, but Sam squints and leans toward me, sniffing. "Orla." She puts her hands on her hips and leans close. "You smell like man."

I groan, but grab a flower from a nearby vase and sort of smear the petals around my throat and wrists. "Better?"

She laughs at me. "No. Now you just smell like man and have crushed flower parts on your neck. Who did you do?"

I shrug, scanning the room for Wally but not seeing him. He moaned for a long time about his dick getting stabbed and I eventually left him in the bathroom to come back to the wedding. I sort of hoped he'd be down for another round later. That Ken doll is a sex god and I'd like some more of that, please.

He was a whole different person in my hotel room, and...I liked it.

It felt daring, risqué. Something my father would frown upon. Something a man would do without thinking twice.

"Oh my gosh," Maddie says, reaching for her fanny pack and procuring a lollypop. "Is he here at the party?" She stands on tiptoe and starts looking around the room.

"I think he left," I whisper, reaching out for champagne from a passing server. I sip my drink and try to use my eyebrows to convey *I totally wore him out.* But that's only true in the sense that I might have somehow broken his precious winky. It's me who feels wrung out inside. Only I'm not wrung out. I'm feeling electric and alive, like I can do anything.

"So something weird did happen during," I tell them, biting my lip. They lean in. "Did you ever, like, stab a guy's dick with your IUD?"

Maddie drops her plate of food on the ground, and it shatters. A server comes rushing over with a tiny broom and dustpan while Maddie and Sam both stare at me, slack-jawed. Sam grabs my elbow and drags me away from the mess as Maddie totters after us. "Tell me exactly what just happened," Sam says. "I want to know everything."

"So you never had that happen?"

Maddie closes her eyes and raises a hand in the air. "I just need, like, one more minute before I can breathe again," she says. "I'm picturing it silently at the moment. Was there blood?"

"Well, just a little," I tell them, explaining how he sprang off of me the moment it happened. "I mean at least he came, right? Despite his tiny flesh wound."

Sam nods, squinting, holding on to the wall for support. "I'm going to go ahead and say that's unusual, Orla."

"Mm hm," Maddie agrees. "But really? How terrific is that? Your pussy bites back. Do we feel bad for this guy? Or are we happy it got him out the door sooner? Where are you on your journey with this man?"

I consider, gulp down the rest of my champagne, remember how Wally caught me in a moment of weakness, when all my demons were trying to make me uncomfortable. I'm not sure I have the stomach to go after someone who acts smarmy and entitled in public, even if he turns terrific behind closed doors. "This was an efficient way to end the encounter," I tell them. Sam's laughter echoes above the live band performing at the reception.

But then she grabs my arm. Looking at me sternly, she says, "Seriously, though, you should swing by a clinic for an STD panel."

I groan. I had been trying to suppress worrying about that. "Yeah." I reach for a cookie from my friend's plate and take a bite, shrugging. "It was worth it."

B

MONDAY MORNING, I have a sour stomach. I'm meeting a new client today first thing after a quick briefing meeting at the Beltane offices. My dad is trusting me to take the lead on the electrical for a new commercial eatery and I've never done this before. But I have to sweat all my nerves out at home because I don't let people at work see me this way. One sniff of doubt and they'll all be clamoring to put a man in charge.

I skip my Brady family group run this morning and take off on my own, pounding out an 8-minute mile pace until the endorphins chase off my nerves.

I stand in my bathroom and remind myself I took charge at the steel plant last year when they had a machinery collapse. If I can supervise the repair of a thirty-year-old conveyor system, I can get a few ovens and deep freezers up to code. In an old laundromat. No big deal. "No fucking sweat," I say out loud to my reflection.

This will be the last project I have to tackle under supervision before I can sit for my professional exams. Just a few more months, and I can become a licensed professional engineer. I can practically feel my ovaries cheering for me.

I breeze through the planning meeting at the office and take a company car to the Garfield neighborhood where the client is redeveloping an entire city block. They're putting in an upscale brew pub, hot yoga studio and, apparently, a keto bakery. I had to look up the word keto, and I'm not really interested, but Dad reminded me yet again of my upcoming exams and my long-term plans for career growth.

"Even if they don't eat grains, they still need their wiring up to code," I mutter. "A circuit breaker is a circuit breaker."

I park a block away and my boots crunch on the crumbling sidewalk as I make my way to the building. I pause to pull out my tablet and make a note to ask Dakota about the timing of new plumbing and wiring compared to when the concrete guys are scheduled to replace the walk. I'm not even sure if Beltane has been hired to oversee the entire job or just the electrical. Come to think of it, there are a lot of unchecked boxes on this job sheet. I'll have to touch base with my dad and Dakota after I meet with these folks.

When I reach the door, I find it locked. I frown. I know the space isn't currently in use, but it's got an active work permit. I assumed it would be crawling with contractors, especially if they're at the stage where they're bringing in the electrical engineer for a consult. I lean against the front window to peer inside, and then scream when I hear someone speak an inch away from my ear.

"Didn't know they'd be sending in a little lady for this discussion," says an all-too-familiar voice.

I whip my head around to see Wally, looking unforgivably sexy in a dress shirt and slacks, standing next to a bored-looking, much-less-sexy colleague. "Jesus, Wally, you shouldn't sneak up on people like that."

He's taken aback when he recognizes me. I snort. "How's wee Wally faring?"

His eyes widen as his colleague frowns. I stick out my hand. "Orla Brady. Beltane engineering," I tell the new guy, and then I turn to Wally. "You're supposed to be showing me the plans to convert this place into a commercial kitchen?"

I watch as Wally transforms his face from human back into smarmy-cyborg. "My assistant should have sent you the plans electronically," he says, trying to sound condescending. I see the subtle move as his eyes dart to his colleague and back to me. Wally rolls his eyes and says to his colleague, "This one probably had trouble with the attachment." He hooks a thumb in my direction. "Like I told you this morning, we're just waiting for the engineers to quit dragging their feet on this."

"You can cut that crap out right now, Sheffield," I tell him. "You know perfectly well you only obtained the license for the diagramming and vector drawing software over the weekend. We're reviewing the plans today in person based on the concept your architect submitted Friday."

The boring suit guy looks impressed, then turns his head toward Wally, waiting for a response. Wally maintains his waxy grin. "Like I said, you were sent the plans as an attachment."

"If that's true why would I be here in person? Why are you here right now, Wally?"

His nostrils flare the tiniest bit and I know I'm starting to break through this inexplicable facade of his. Is he showing off for this other guy or trying to ruffle my feathers on purpose? He's so much more acceptable when I've got him alone and half naked. He huffs. "Not that it concerns you, but I'm giving Hampton here a tour of the space as he's one of the key investors in this new concept."

"Oh, christ, here we go again with the concept. Baked goods with no sugar or grains."

Wally opens his mouth to respond but his phone rings.

I kick at the gravel on the eroding sidewalk. "What's your timeline for the concrete repair? Have you coordinated the plumbing install with our crew?" I'm starting to get the sense that he either has no idea what's going on with this project or else he's acting like this because I'm a woman. Either way, I'm insulted and pissed off. His phone rings. Again.

He reaches into his pocket to silence it as I cross my arms and tap my work boot, noticing how dirty it looks next to Wally's well-shined dress shoe. He still hasn't stepped back out of my personal space.

Wally's phone keeps ringing incessantly and the Hampton guy keeps staring back and forth between us until Wally finally pulls the phone to his year. "What?" He barks, and then I hear a series of shrieks spurting from his cell.

He sticks a finger in one ear and backs away to take the call, leaving me and Hampton to stare at one another.

"I don't suppose *you* have the plans from the architect?" I raise a brow at him and keep my arms crossed, tapping my tablet against my forearm. He shakes his head. I give it another minute as I watch Wally pace frantically along the sidewalk, gesturing wildly before I watch him take off at a jog.

"I guess we're done here," I say.

The Hampton guy stares as I toss my notes on the ground and walk the opposite direction to drive back to Beltane H-Q.

CHAPTER FIVE
WALT

"Mom!" I have never raised my voice to my mother. Not once in my life. But I'm pretty sure she just said that my father is dead and she's panicking and I can barely hear myself think. "Mom, you have to breathe!"

"Trippy!" She shrieks into the phone, inhales raggedly. "He. Is. DEAD!"

"Okay, where are you right now? Where is Dad?"

I hear her breathing rapidly again, then I hear the rattling sound of pills being shaken from a bottle—her "rescue meds" that I've noticed her using more and more in recent years. I sigh. At least if she medicates I'll be able to understand what she's saying. "I'm at Mercy hospital. Your father is here, too. In the morgue!"

I doubt my mother has ever set foot inside Mercy hospital, the trauma center downtown where Pittsburgh's gunshot and burn victims are taken. Why would my father be there? She continues wailing into the phone as I walk toward my car, climbing in and trying to enter the hospital into my gps app without hanging up on her.

I have just enough time to get the directions on screen before Mom starts babbling again. "He wasn't even supposed to be in the office this morning, Trippy. You know he has a standing tee time at the Heights on Mondays."

I grunt in response as I make my way onto Boulevard of the Allies. I tune out my mother's ranting until I find a parking spot on the street and make my way into the lobby of the emergency department. My mother is there, dressed impeccably, still wailing into her phone as she shakes her handbag. "Mom," I say, touching her on the shoulder. "What happened?"

"Oh," she says, as if confused to see me in person. She lowers the phone and while her face doesn't move, tears begin to fall from her eyes. "He just died."

I should hug her. I know this is a time when normal people would embrace and lean against one another. But the Sheffield family doesn't hug. Dad has been known to slap a few backs at the tail end of a handshake. My sister does the whole cheek kiss thing. But hugs?

I stand awkwardly with my hands in my pockets, not knowing what comes next. I've never been allowed to determine next steps for anything. Eventually, it's clear Mom is also awaiting guidance. She stares up at me, her face unmoving. When did I get so much taller than her?

"Is there someone you should call?"

She blinks again.

I sigh. "Like...a funeral home?"

Mom just starts screaming then. She screams like a woman in an Alfred Hitchcock movie, almost comedically. A woman with short box knots and a lab coat approaches us, telling my mother she needs to calm down. Which of course drives my mother further into hysteria.

"Is there a room where we could sit or something?" I rake my fingers through my hair. "My father apparently died here."

WE ARE USHERED into a barren office with a hospital social worker, who says my mother needs to go identify my father's body, since he came in on an ambulance, already deceased. Mom slips into another fit of hysteria and pops another Ativan into her mouth, after which she just sort of slumps in the chair, her eyes unseeing through tiny pinpoint pupils.

"Can I go instead of my mother? I'm his son," I tell the social worker. "I'm Walton Sheffield the third." She nods and rings for an orderly, who escorts me along my very first trip to a morgue. I learn that my father collapsed at his office and his admin called 911, but nobody attempted CPR or rode with him in the ambulance.

I envision a scene where he simply fell to the ground and his employees quietly observed this occurrence before stepping over his body to carry on with their work. "Did he have high blood pressure or anything like that?"

I realize the hospital staff member is asking me about my father's health. I shake my head. I have no earthly idea. All I know about my father is how he likes his liquor, that he can't tolerate the thought of failure, and that he finds most things about me unacceptable. I guess I should be thinking in the past tense. He's dead. He no longer does any of these things.

"Sometimes heart attacks are like that, man," the guy continues. He gestures for me to step into the morgue ahead of him and he shouts over my shoulder. "This guy's here about the fatal M-I."

"Which one?" The morgue worker looks up over his glasses. I realize he's waiting for me to respond. This entire morning I've felt like a total idiot, unable to respond properly to anything that's been asked of me, from delivering building plans, to Orla-fucking-Brady, to identifying my father's corpse.

"Sheffield," I say, hoping that will suffice. He nods and beckons me toward a table, where a figure lies draped in a sheet. He pulls back the edge of the sheet, and there's my father. I wait for a reaction, for a feeling. For some sort of response from my body, but nothing comes. "That's my father," I say. "It's him."

The employee nods and covers him back up again. "Where we sending him?"

Once again, I realize I'm being expected to provide information, to make a decision. I try to remember where our family held my grandfather's funeral, and of course come up blank. "Sewickley," I tell them. The guy gestures for me to be more specific. I pull out my phone and do a search for funeral homes near my parents' house. Of course there are two funeral places in the wealthy suburb. I see that one is close to the post office, which feels familiar to me, so I blurt out the name.

And then I'm being ushered back to collect my mother, expected to know what to do from here. It would seem that finally, I am viewed as the adult in a situation, but I've had absolutely no preparation for this in my previous 25 years of existence. Was it really just two days ago I took my mother's place as my father's plus-one to his buddy's son's wedding? Just two days since Orla's pussy somehow stabbed me in the dick?

If you'd asked me this morning, I would have said searing penis pain was the most uncomfortable I'd ever be in my life. I guess there's always a lower bar for everything.

I drive Mom home in her car and get her on the sofa before calling an Uber to take me back to the hospital to retrieve her car from the lot. Once that's done and I'm back in the formal living room of my childhood home, I realize nobody has called my sister, so I pour myself a drink from my father's bar and send her a text message to come to the house immediately.

She doesn't respond. I don't have it in me to call her at the moment.

I try to sit and relax, but everything feels unfinished. I look around at the house, out the window at the driveway. There's probably paperwork, I decide. When someone dies there should be paperwork. Life insurance?

"Hey, Mom, is there a lawyer I should call?" I crane my neck to where she's still sitting on the couch. She has a framed family photo in her lap, mindlessly tapping each of our four faces. She turns to look at me.

"What's that, dear?"

I roll my eyes and decide I'm going to have to raid my father's office. Everything since I found out feels simultaneously sped up and slowed down. I'm not sure if it's still the same day. I head upstairs and open the door to Dad's office, the hunter green wallpaper and dark wood furniture greeting me. I step into the room and feel the constant fear of my youth. A summons to this room was the precursor to a stern reminder of my failures. I've never been in here alone before.

I feel like an imposter as I sink into my father's chair, looking around his desk for any information that might guide me toward a responsible adult who knows what to do in situations like this. I set my drink on my father's coaster and catch myself looking over my shoulder, waiting for him to scold me for taking liberties. I remind myself I saw his dead body at the morgue. He isn't going to speak to me, unkindly or otherwise, ever again.

There's a brass box on the corner of the desk and I open it to discover a good, old-fashioned file of address cards. I flip to L, and feel immediately foolish to realize the lawyer would be listed by last name, not occupation. I down the rest of my whiskey and dump the cards on the desk, quickly flipping through until I've pulled out three with "esq" typed after the name.

Relief washes over me when I recognize the name Hampton on one of the cards. I remember a barrel-chested man with red cheeks who shook hands with me and with Dad when I signed papers for my trust fund when I turned 21. I dial the number, and am surprised when a familiar gruff voice answers the call.

"Oh," I mutter. "Hello. I thought maybe I'd reach a secretary."

"Who's calling me at this number?" He sounds irritated. Of course my father would have the inside track to some private line for his lawyer.

"Um, this is Trip Sheffield," I say, hating the feel of that name in my mouth. I think of Orla, refusing to call me by that name. She's maybe the only person who has ever agreed with me that it's terrible.

"Trip!" Watson's voice shifts from unease to jovial. "What can I do ya for, son?"

"Oh," I tell him. "Well. My father died today."

B

It's dark by the time Watson finishes talking at me and we hang up. I stumble downstairs, knowing I should probably eat something but making my way instead toward the bar. I left my tumbler upstairs on my father's coaster, so I just take a swig directly from the bottle before approaching my mother.

She stares at me, her eyes glassy.

"Mom," I say, putting my hand on hers. She looks down at the contact and then meets my eye. "Did you know the money was gone?"

"Oh, Trippy." She pulls her hand out from under mine and then pats my head. "Of course I knew there were some hiccups. Your father sold the boat last year. It's nothing to worry about I'm sure."

"Mom, it's not a hiccup." Watson spent an hour telling me what we needed to liquidate immediately to pay off debts. He described years of failed investments, shady business dealings, negotiations with the IRS. "It's all gone, Mom," I tell her. The empire. The great Sheffield name. All of it, gone. The ski chalet, the business. The cars. All of the cars have to go.

I own my townhouse outright, and my trust fund wasn't impacted, and Mom can keep the house, barely.

But everything else I've ever known, including my father's reputation... his precious *brand*...it's all gone.

Rosemary bustles in the door looking irritated. "This better be important," she snarls. She doesn't look at or acknowledge our mother. I don't blame her. But I do start laughing. For all my yearning about a different life, about a relief from the pressure of being a Sheffield, I would have thought this day would feel lighter somehow. A relief, perhaps.

Instead I laugh, manically. "Dad's dead," I tell my sister, who squints at me. "And we're bankrupt."

CHAPTER SIX
ORLA
JULY

I'm still enraged at the loss of the stupid bakery project I was supposed to manage for stupid Wally and his stupid family business. I should feel empathy for him that his father dropped over dead of a heart attack, but everything that came to light since that day has done nothing to improve my opinion of that family.

Pa Sheffield was apparently a lousy crook with unpaid invoices all over the city. Engineering, construction, consulting...you name it, he left them high and dry in recent years.

The Sheffield business was swimming in debt. Dad says we should feel thankful we only lost some planning-stage work for them. The contractors working on their other projects on entire block are just up shit's creek. No payment. Nothing. Wally's whole family were all living some puffed up, pretend life.

Uncle Mick keeps assuring us that Walton the second was an all-right guy back in the day. Uncle Mick says that about all his gross friends. He and Dad don't even seem all that upset about the bakery deal falling through.

I still haven't gotten a replacement project to round out my final year of supervision, so I still can't start my prep work for the professional exams.

I carry an unhealthy level of anger about it, which is probably tied into inexplicable irritation that I haven't been able to locate Wally since that day we were supposed to be meeting at his business. It's like the other

Sheffields fell off into one of the sinkholes downtown, along with a city bus. Which brings me right back to the purpose of this team meeting I'm not able to stomach today.

Dad stands at the head of the conference table with a laser pointer, fully in his element as he walks us through images of a broken street. "You can see, the episode has severed wires, pipes for both water and gas, and impacted the stability of the foundations of nearby buildings. This is, as they say, pay dirt for our civil and geotechnical crew. Orla, I'm bringing you in to consult for electrical repairs."

My eyebrow shoots up. "Allegheny Power isn't bringing in their own people for that?"

Dad shakes his head. "The incident is due to a city road failure and the city has hired Beltane." He winks at me. "You're getting a redo after the bakery fiasco."

I open my mouth to speak or smile or something, but a wave of nausea crashes over me. I leap from my seat and, right there in the conference room, in front of all my cousins and peers, I puke into the trash can.

Nobody says a thing for a long time. Zack grabs a napkin from the coffee cart and holds it out to me gingerly, and I dab at my mouth. "Sorry, guys," I mutter, feeling a flush creep up my cheeks. "I'm ready, Dad. Tell me more."

My dad's face falls and he starts shaking his head. Liam slaps the conference table. "Out," he barks, pointing toward the door. "We just got Arlan back into daycare after a week home with a fever. I'm not having you contaminate me with your germs."

I have no idea what just happened here, but I doubt I'm contagious. I wonder if I can tell them all I'm just overwhelmed at the responsibility from Dad. "Guys, I was just thinking about someone gross and lost my breakfast. This is not a big deal. Liam. Don't look at me that way." He continues to look at me like I have the plague. "I'm not sick, I swear."

People around the table start to murmur and cringe. "Best to take a sick day, shortcake." Uncle Mick leans against the wall in the back of the room. He hates sitting still and always winds up standing and pacing during meetings. It occurs to me that he might be scared of the smell of my little interruption here, as he and everyone else seem to be leaning far away from me.

"Right," I say, picking up the trash can. "I'll be on email. Let me know the plan for project sink hole."

"Sick day, Orla," my dad says, pointing his laser at the door. I roll my eyes and head out. The nausea has totally passed, almost like it didn't happen. I sigh, staring at the bucket of evidence that it had, in fact, happened. I never get sick. I'm not sick now, actually. But I don't mind spending the day working from my couch, if I'm honest. I haven't been sleeping well this month. Probably because I'm irritated with Wally's family.

I hate that my thoughts of him are so complicated. Hot sex swirled together with douchey behavior and a scummy family. And mixed in there is anger at myself that I thought I had him figured out. I thought I knew he was just pretending to be a windbag. I've spent weeks now pissed off that I thought I saw some sort of connection with him. I carry the puke can to the dumpster outside and text our admin that we need to order a new trash can for the conference room.

When I get to my car, I pull up the Foof group chat and decide to vent a bit.

> Got huge opportunity to lead sinkhole project at work. But got sent home because I yakked in the meeting.

Almost immediately, my phone pings with a response from Maddie.

> You didn't breathe near Liam did you? We just got Arlan back into daycare.

> No worries. I really think it's fine. I feel totally fine now. I think it was nerves.

Sam sends a GIF of a woman recoiling in disgust.

> Orla, girl, you never get nervous. Do not come to FOOF tonight. No parties for pukers.

JUNIPER:

> Amen to that!

> Since when is everyone so concerned with vomit?

NICOLE:

> Since always. Why are you NOT concerned with vomit?

MADDIE:

> Even when I was pregnant and I knew it was just morning sickness, I was concerned with vomit.

EMMA:

Actually, you sort of weren't Maddie.

MADDIE:

Fair. But mostly I just liked to puke and carry on because it bothered Liam so much.

JUNIPER:

I'm so glad I never puked when I was pregnant. I only knew I was preggo because my nipples hurt like hell.

This last text hits me like a sledge hammer. I am sitting in my car pulling my bra away from my chest because my nipples are so sensitive. In the middle of doing this, reading Juniper's text, I realize my nips have been this way for a few days at least.

I look down at them, afraid to exhale because the sensation will feel like razors slicing my skin.

I frown at my phone and start to drive toward my apartment. I start willing myself to feel nauseous again, hoping for food poisoning or maybe a virus, even if it means I get Liam sick. Women get sore nipples, surely. Doesn't everyone go through phases like that? Besides, I can't be pregnant because I have an IUD. It's been settled in there comfortably for years.

I drive and fret and think about Wally. He's the only one I had sex with in…really I can't remember the last time I had sex before that. But Wally didn't even finish inside me. He sprang off the bed when my IUD strings apparently stabbed him through the condom. I start to sweat. My friends all encouraged me to go see my gynecologist after that. Penis-stabbing is not part of the normal IUD experience.

But I got so wrapped up in hate-stalking the Sheffield family after we got shafted on that bakery project, I just let it slip. At least I took care of the STD screening. That counts for something, right?

"Shit." I pull a fast right turn into a parking spot outside a drug store and I stalk through the store like a shifty character, darting around trying to find the pregnancy tests. I locate them along the back wall, under the careful scrutiny of the pharmacy staff. "Great," I mutter, realizing that like the condoms, these must be hot ticket items for desperate people to steal.

Of course there are 30 different kinds of pregnancy tests. Do I need early notification? Do I need something electronic? Digital? Jesus, I have no idea and there's no way I'm asking. I grab the box with the least pink on it, because fuck that marketing.

The heavens shine on me via the existence of a self-checkout station, so

I quickly pay and get the hell out of there. When I get to my apartment, I stare at the box on the counter for a long time. I'm still not nauseous. My nipples still ache. I grab a glass of water and pound it down, and head into the bathroom with the tests. Two agonizing minutes later, I stare at twin purple lines, clear as day.

Pregnant.

CHAPTER SEVEN
WALT

I ALMOST DON'T HEAR THE KNOCK ON MY DOOR, WHICH IS NUTS BECAUSE I'VE BEEN thinking for a week that the silence in my house was deafening. I haven't even been watching the TV. I'm just...existing.

At first, there was so much to do. I had to make thousands of decisions about the funeral because Rosemary just helped herself to Mom's Ativan and the pair of them sat comatose in our living room.

My aunts and uncles always have a lot to say about every element of our lives, but none of them showed up to help me pick out embalming options or write an obituary.

Watson at least barked out orders until we dealt with all the paperwork: Sign this. And this. And this. By the time I was done with him, we'd settled Dad's debts and sold almost everything familiar about my life.

So now Dad's in the ground, Mom's set up with an allowance, and I have nothing to do. I don't have a job. I don't know how to get one or what it would be. I don't have a career and all those frat brothers who vowed to stick together like family? They're not taking my calls.

None of them even came to the funeral. Some outstanding citizen my father turned out to be.

Those thoughts are loud and persistent, but eventually, I do hear the knock. I stagger to the door and open it before I remember to check if I'm dressed. I glance down. Apparently sweatpants count as acceptable, because the guy at the door doesn't flinch.

"Sign?" It's the mailman, holding out a digital signature pad and a large envelope.

"What is it?" I stare as the mailman uses one hand to massage his lower back while he waits for me to sign his form.

"Certified mail, dude." He leans against the wall as I move in slow motion. It feels like I'm swimming through molasses. I wonder how long it's been since I stepped outside. The mailman grunts. "Jesus, I'm beat. I'm on day 13 with no time off coming any time soon."

I stare at him. He stares at me. I say, "I guess that's better than not working at all."

He snorts. "You looking for a job? We need help, bad. You ever take the civil service test?"

"What's that?" I sign the machine and hand it back to him, stuffing the envelope under my arm.

"You know, the civil service test. You pass that and we can get you on a mail route. Take some of the load off my shoulders, man. Think you could pass a drug test?"

"Do those test for liquor?"

He shakes his head at me. "You're a trip, dude. But think about it. The pay's good!" He backs down off my porch and takes a few unsteady steps toward my neighbor's house before picking up his pace. I watch him adjust his headphones and bop his head along to whatever music he's listening to as he works.

"I'm a Trip." I snort. Another reason to hate that awful nickname. But I'm intrigued by his mention of the civil service test. Who knew there was a test to be a mailman?

I try to remember the last time I took an exam. Probably high school, but my mother always insisted I had anxiety in high school and I had a lot of accommodations for tests. I don't recall giving a shit about any of it, and most kids in private school have anxiety.

The liberal arts school I attended for college didn't have exams. We had discussions. And look where that got me. Half naked, staring at my wall. Listless. I head back inside and try to decide if being nothing is better or worse than inheriting generational wealth and fucking it all up like my father did.

I locate my laptop under a heap of takeout containers. It occurs to me that I'm going to have to stop blindly putting things on my credit card. I don't even know how much I have coming in each month. God, I don't even know who pays my internet bill.

Someone must be doing it, because the browser still works when I type in "what is the civil service test." I frown as each site I click seems to be a den of advertisements. By the time I find the actual exam site and realize I can take the test online, right this minute, I click BEGIN before I think about what I'm doing.

I start squinting at addresses on the screen, figuring out whether two listings are the same or different. I find the questions are easy for me, and the questions fly by. I memorize zip codes and street names, clicking my way through until I get to a section that asks about my work history. Work. Have I ever done anything a mailman would consider real work?

Let's see. My internship in college was, of course, at my father's company. I mostly sat in the break room watching as the real interns made copies and took notes at meetings, eager to glean information relevant to their actual ambitions.

I graduated from college and was hired by my father's company as a "manager," and started wearing expensive suits while I went about my days pretending I understood property development. Oh, and then I went with my father to his client's son's wedding and fucked one of the brides-maids and pierced my dick in the process.

I strike that last bit from the answer block. It put me over my character limit anyway. I try not to let myself think about Orla-fucking-Brady.

I save thoughts of her for when I'm alone at night and feeling particu-larly down. I summon her in my mind, all fierce words and long muscles and molten heat. When I'm alone, I relive the experience of pleasuring her, hearing her moan my name.

Here, in the daylight, I silence those thoughts. I fill out the rest of the questions and click submit, and then I take a breath.

Since high school, I've done exactly two things without first consid-ering the impact on my family or our business dealings: I fucked Orla at that wedding, and I took that exam just now.

I sit on the stool, my hands tapping against my legs, and I look around my townhouse. I didn't pick it. It was given to me. It came decorated and furnished. I feel no attachment toward it or anything inside. I feel no ownership. I did nothing to earn any of this.

I did nothing to earn that night with Orla, either. That was a gift, I decide, and the sting at the end was to make sure I knew it was a fantasy. Nothing that could ever continue.

I purse my lips and pick up my phone, opening a checklist app I've never used before. I make a list: Bills to Figure Out, and I add internet to the list. Then, with a laugh, I add "cell phone."

CHAPTER EIGHT
ORLA

My hands shake as I look up the number for my gynecologist. The whole fucking point of getting an IUD is to avoid pregnancy. They're more than 99% effective. Those are statistics that really spoke to my mathematical mind. Who has time to worry about getting pregnant?

The receptionist answers and I robotically spit out the statement I practiced a dozen times before I made the call. "Hello. This is Orla Brady. I'm pregnant and I'm not sure if I want to be."

"Okay, sweetie. Give me just a minute here." Her voice is kind. She must hear this a dozen times a day. "Do you know how far along you are?"

"I don't know how to answer that..."

She clears her throat. "When did you get your last period, sweetie?"

"Well, I don't get them. I have an IUD."

I hear her set something on the table. "You're pregnant with an IUD? You took a test?"

"Yes. I took like three of them."

"Orla, that's a little bit of an urgent situation, sweetie. Can you come into the office right now? Dr. Andrews had a cancelation."

ℬ

All of my limbs twitch as I sit in the waiting room. My mother died of cervical cancer in her thirties, so really anything to do with the entire fields of obstetrics and gynecology is a lot for me to handle. I feel out of place here in my jeans and flannel. I'm still dressed for work, though it feels like a year has passed since my dad sent me home for puking during a meeting. I try to remember if I ate anything since then, and realize I have not. *Great, now my stomach is growling.*

When they finally call my name, I practically sprint through the door and down the hall. "We have to get your weight, dear," says the nurse, grabbing my elbow.

"Oh." I look down at my heavy boots and sigh. It takes me a long time to unlace them enough to slip my feet out and climb onto the scale, and I can't shake the sense that they're waiting for me, urging me to go faster. Of course there's nothing about the nurse's actual behavior to suggest this. It's just my messed up, anxious associations with this office.

Just when I'm starting to calm down a little bit after the weigh-in, they ask for a urine sample. I have to explain that I vomited up my breakfast and haven't had anything else since.

The nurse pats my arms and brings me a carton of orange juice and a packet of pretzels, which I inhale before Dr. Andrews taps on the door.

I feel better just seeing her. I had no idea OB-GYN was a type of doctor I would need until my pediatrician gently explained to my mortified father that women need specialized care once they get their periods. Who knows if Dad was just avoiding this whole field after Mom died, or if he really hadn't thought about me getting periods. Dad looked like he wanted to die of shame that day, but the pediatrician happily referred us to his wife.

Dr. Jessica Andrews is frank and sarcastic, and I love it. I mean, as much as you can love seeing someone once a year who fishes around inside your body.

"All righty," she says, sitting on her stool and crossing her legs. "Tell me exactly what happened." I like that we usually start out appointments fully clothed, just chatting. This feels familiar and I'm not sure if it's her bedside manner or the pretzels, but I definitely feel better about the whole thing already.

I explain about the hotel sex, and she doesn't flinch when I tell her my vagina apparently bit Wally in the dick.

"Yes," she says. "The poor, fragile penis can sometimes get poked by the strings." She reaches for a plastic model of the pelvis and sticks a sample IUD in it. "My suspicion is that your IUD slipped into your cervix. Hence the dick poking."

I stare as she shows me the model. "The slipped IUD would also explain how you could have become pregnant. That, and I suspect the string tore the condom." She sets the plastic pelvis down on the counter and it tips over ominously while she clicks around in the computer. "Looks like you were due to have your device replaced this year at your annual exam which…" She clicks a few more times and sighs. "You're about six months past due for your annual, unfortunately. So there's that mystery solved."

"So this is my fault?" My throat feels dry, and I clutch the edges of the exam bed until my nails dig into the padding.

She shakes her head. "It takes two to conceive, Orla. And I didn't mean to sound like I was assigning 'blame' here." She pats my leg. "Let's focus on what comes next."

Dr. Andrews explains that there is an increased risk of miscarriage because of the IUD still being inside me. "I can try to remove the IUD today, or we can leave it in there. Same risk of miscarriage. If you go that route, it would fall out during delivery."

"But what if I'm not sure I want to be pregnant."

Dr. Andrews nods. "We don't perform termination procedures here. But given your case specifics, if you opted to go that route I could perform something called a D and C to remove both the IUD and the embryo."

"How long do I have to decide?"

She advises we do an ultrasound right now to make sure the pregnancy isn't ectopic, which she explains would mean the embryo is hanging out up in my Fallopian tube. "*That* can be really dangerous for you, Orla. But I also know an ultrasound can be very difficult for women who are opting to terminate."

"I mean, we should make sure my ovaries aren't going to explode," I tell her.

Dr. Andrews nods. "Now. I'm going to have to do a transvaginal ultrasound to be sure." I blink at her, not understanding. She slides open a drawer and pulls out what looks like an electric toothbrush. "So the way this works is you're going to undress from the waist down and then I'm going to use lubricant to—"

"Lubricant? Vaginal? Are you putting that inside me?" My eyes bulge and I squeeze my thighs together.

She blows out a breath through her nose. "Honestly? It's less invasive than the speculum. I know it seems unusual, but we really do need to get a careful look at your uterus and find the location of the embryo."

She steps out of the office so I can disrobe and I try not to focus on the potential time bomb in my womb. Basically, no matter what we see on this thing, it's going to be a lot to process. I fold my jeans and undies and lie back on the table. Before I know it, Dr. Andrews is muttering to herself as she squirts lube on the ice-cold vagina-wand and slides it inside me.

I close my eyes and try not to think about it, which is generally my strategy in dealing with complicated things. I realize that's going to have to change. And clearly fucking strangers to avoid dealing with my relatives is another tactic I should ditch.

"Aha," Doc says. "Excellent positioning for the embryo." She smiles. "No ectopic pregnancy. And I can see your IUD sort of dangling there at the bottom. I could yank that sucker out right now if you'd like."

Five minutes later, I'm sitting in my car with no idea what to do. I've got some sort of miracle fetus determined to exist, despite an IUD and a condom. I've got a physically demanding job. I've got no idea how to find Wally. I should find Wally, right? I look vaguely upward and give two middle fingers to the universe that took my mom away when she wasn't too much older than I am now.

I know exactly why I was late with my annual exam. It's the same reason I'm late with every annual exam. I don't want the doctor to discover I'm wasting away from the same cervical cancer that took my mom. Nevermind the fact that finding it early could help save me. I remember what my mom looked like going through all those treatments. I remember how she writhed in pain, so skinny she said it hurt her bones to lie down.

What right do I have to make a baby if I'm just going to die before I can watch her grow up? And who the hell would take care of her? I don't know the first thing about babies and my dad doesn't need me saddling him with another kid to raise on his own. Although, I guess he's not on his own anymore. He's been pretty serious with Elizabeth for a few years.

I grind the heels of my hands into my eyeballs. I have to find Wally. That's the first step. I pull up my phone and call Dakota.

"Hey, Orla. You feeling better? I heard about the meeting." She cuts right to the point, which I appreciate.

"Worlds better. It wasn't anything contagious. But don't tell Liam. I want him to squirm about it a little longer."

"You're all so mean to each other," she says. "I love it. Makes me feel right at home here." She pauses. "So what can I do for you?"

I take a breath. "Something about the Sheffield project just isn't sitting right with me. I want some closure or something."

"Ugh, join the club." Dakota tells me how all the developers who tried to partner with Sheffield are out millions. "He was taking all their money and investing it in some Ponzi scheme," she says. "You know, like that famous one on TV where people lost everything? It's one of those situations."

"What about the company? Wouldn't that be separate from his personal investments?"

"That's just it." She sounds exasperated. "He was taking money from everywhere. Personal, company. The whole situation is messed up, Orla. Anyway, the company's bankrupt. Totally dissolved. All contracts and payments canceled. We're just lucky we never got past the assessment stage."

"Didn't Uncle Mick know that guy? He's usually not fooled by bull-shitters."

"Dunno. That's more a question for him or your dad, probably."

"Yeah." I take a swig from my water bottle. The more I hydrate, the more I remember that I'm starving. "I'll ask him I guess. You got any contact info for the Sheffield son?"

"Hmm." I can hear her clicking around, searching her computer. "Sorry. Bunch of dead ends even our collections firm couldn't unearth."

"Stupid Wally," I mutter. "Who builds a keto bakery anyway?"

I hang up with Dakota more confused than ever. How can I get involved with a man whose family is under scrutiny for being thieving crooks? I work for a family business. It's pretty obvious Wally would have known what his father was up to. Who knows—the bakery project could have been planned as a front for their swindles.

I don't think I want anyone like that involved in my life. I mean, what kind of father would he turn out to be? Whatever I do, I can do it alone.

Check that. I'm never alone. Not really. Team Brady sticks together. I think about how my dad and uncle moved in together to join forces when their lives fell apart. How I grew up with three cousins that are more like brothers, and how each of them now has a stable relationship.

I sigh. I recall how I helped intervene when my cousins were having problems with their girlfriends. I'm no different from them—all up in each other's armpits. I wouldn't be saddling anyone with anything. If anything happens, there will be at least six Bradys waiting in the wings to get involved.

I think back to something Dr. Andrews said the first time we met. She was explaining the female reproductive system to me properly, filling in the giant gaps left by public school health class and a house full of brothers. "All the eggs in your ovaries have been in there since you were in your mother's womb," she said. "That means if you decide to have children, the egg that grows into your baby will have been inside your mother, too. She's part of you and you are part of her, Orla. Your bodies know each other."

I start to cry, clutching at my stomach. Half this bundle of cells is a clump of DNA that my mother grew. A part of her, in me. I've spent years afraid she passed her cancer on to me, but all signs and tests indicate that she did not. What she did give me was a tiny egg that, despite all odds and without anyone's permission, has fertilized.

I drive home, resolved. I'm going to do this thing. I'm going to have a baby.

CHAPTER NINE
WALT
AUGUST

"Jesus Christ, Sheffield. Again?" My training partner has no pity on me when I swoon along the route. I've been on the job one week and passed all the way out twice, plus a few stumbles.

"There's a heat wave," I tell him, guzzling the water he holds in front of my face.

"What'd I tell you? Small sips at first, man. Are you not hydrating in the evenings?"

August in Pittsburgh means temperatures hovering near 100 degrees, and just about 80 percent humidity most mornings. "I feel like a sous vide fillet." I lean my head back against the side of the van, reveling in the shade as Mark radios to let the boss know we're running behind. They actually keep trackers on our bags these days and yell at us over the radio if we take longer than expected at any point on the route.

Partners isn't quite the right word for me and Mark. It's more like I'm a barnacle he's trying to scrape off so he can get his shit done and go home. I know he has to stay late on the days I'm shadowing him, because a mail carrier can't leave until the route is done. The route is the route.

"I don't know what the fuck Sue Veed did to your steak, but people are waiting for their checks, man. We've got meds to deliver. Can you stand?"

Mark instructs me to grab another water from the cooler in the van. He has a six-pack of 24-ounce bottles for himself and insists I stop at the next gas station and buy myself a gallon of water. Despite my surly, grizzled mentor, I love this job so far. I start every morning with a specific set of tasks. I carry them out, mostly, and then I go home when I'm done. I feel and see the impact of my work immediately. A physical heap gradually disappears as I hand people their mail.

"All right. You ready for Reynolds Street? Yesterday you had a damn temper tantrum about the dogs." I nod and fall in step behind him. Mark makes me carry the mail bag to get used to it. He marches in front of me, setting an impossible pace in this heat. I know he could maintain it with the bag, too, so I say nothing and try to keep up as a pair of poodles sniffs my crotch.

"Yes, who's the best boy?" Mark scratches the dogs. They lick his hands. "Yes, I'm happy to see you, too. Morning, Linda!" Mark gives a salute as I cram a pack of grocery store flyers into the poodle-house's mailbox.

The dogs have probably been the biggest surprise this past week. I had no idea so many people in the city have such big dogs. We see St. Bernards, Newfoundlands, dogs the size of horses. I see dogs in purses and dogs with brightly-dyed hair. Fur? I don't know anything about dogs.

In this heat, they've been licking the salty sweat from my legs. We make our way along Reynolds and Mark drives the van a block back to Edgarton. The houses on this street have more stairs, and Mark decides to lean back against the side of the van with his dark arms crossed, veins bulging, as he watches me.

My first day on the job, when Mark made me slather on sunscreen, I made the mistake of muttering that he didn't have to suffer it stinging his eyes in the heat. "Sheffield, you think Black folks don't die of skin cancer? You know why my eyes aren't stinging? Because I buy water-proof, asshole. Now spray on your fancy paraben-free and try not to pass out."

Mark does not coddle. He isn't kind to me. But I don't need someone to be kind to me, I realized since I started this job. I need someone who has clear, quantifiable expectations. And Mark's expectations are simple: don't say dumb shit, drink my water, keep up. I get the sense that it is someday possible for me to meet his approval. "Don't pass out" is a more concrete to-do list than "Never bring shame upon this family."

℔

It's twilight by the time we finish. Mark slams the sliding door of the van shut and turns toward me. "You drink at least two Gatorades tonight,

Sheffield, and show up tomorrow ready to pick up the pace. I am not missing *Jeopardy* two nights in a row."

"Yes, sir," I tell him, tipping the sports drink into my mouth with one hand and giving him a thumbs up. I strip off my shirt and drape a towel over the seat of my car before I head home. I learned a few days ago that my sweat leaves white rings on my leather interior, and I haven't gotten around yet to figuring out where to go for regular detailing. I finished up my list of bills and got them all in my name, but I've been so exhausted from work I haven't had time to branch out to other basic maintenance stuff.

I found out my dad's assistant at work had been taking care of everything for our family. Literally everything. When there was no money left to offer her a severance when we dissolved the company, I had to ask her how to cut herself a check from my trust fund. The face she made when I asked that—I'd like to never cause someone to make that sort of face ever again.

I'm working on being less useless.

When I get out of the car, I see a flash of something tan in my front yard, which reminds me to figure out who deals with my yard. As I'm adding YARD to my checklist app, I see the flash again. Limping a bit since my muscles seized during the drive home, I make my way toward the thing. It's an animal, obviously struggling.

I crouch down beside it, my leg muscles screaming. It's some sort of furry mammal and it seems to be panting. It's super hot—I'm practically panting and I had the air conditioner on.

"You thirsty, little guy?" This is something I relate to. I take the cap off my water jug and pour a few drops in the small disc. The critter sticks out its tongue a few times, but starts sneezing. And then it sort of sags back into panting mode.

This animal—I'm pretty sure it's a rabbit—is suffering. I feel panic rising inside my chest again as I watch it struggle. I remember the feeling immediately after my father died, of total inadequacy. Much more acute than my lifelong feeling of general inadequacy. When Dad died, there were important things to be done and I had no ability to do them.

"Right," I say. I'm not going to be useless again. I can figure this out.

The rabbit turns its head again toward the little disc of water. I take three long, deep breaths as I stroke its head, and think. I know the phrase "animal control" only because I run into those guys out on the job. Mostly in neighborhoods with vacant lots. I find them trapping feral dogs or groundhogs. Based on my conversations with them, I figure animal control would euthanize this critter.

Back on one of the routes I did a few days ago, there was a house where I delivered three huge boxes of hay. Before that, I didn't even know hay came in boxes or why anyone would mail it, but as I was heaving the last one onto the porch, a woman came out to thank me.

"What's up with all this, anyway," I'd asked.

"I foster animals," she said. "They eat the hay." At the time, I remember thinking I wish she would drive her ass to a hay barn instead of making me deal with the boxes. But now I figure she's my best shot at knowing what to do. I just have to remember which house was hers.

I scoop up the rabbit and wrap it in the towel I had been using to mop up my sweat. I stick him on the floor of the passenger seat and make my way back to Lawrenceville. When I get to the lady's street, I start driving slowly, and then laugh at myself because her house is obvious. The porch is full of bags of dog food and pet carriers. "She'll know what to do," I repeat to my furry friend. "She can help."

I pick him up and nuzzle him against my chest, only then realizing that I'm not wearing a shirt, but I'm still wearing my work shorts and ridiculous black non-slip shoes. Whatever. I inhale, hold my breath, and rap the bunny-shaped door knocker.

The woman with the graying hair and the bright smile answers the door. "Yes?"

I instinctively pet the rabbit a few times before I stutter out, "I found this. And it's sick. And I didn't know what else to do…"

Her face changes and she reaches for the rabbit. "Oh, baby," she says to the bunny. Then she looks at me. "You were smart to bring him here. Come inside."

Feeling good about my choices, I follow her in through a series of rooms where, instead of furniture, she's got large pens full of rabbits and dogs and… "Is that a pig?"

"Mm hmm." She doesn't look up from the rabbit as she sits at her table. She massages his belly and looks into his eyes. "I'm going to take his temperature."

"Are you a vet?"

She shakes her head. "I've been doing this a long time. I can do all the basic first aid. You're lucky today's Tuesday, though." She sighs. "I think this little guy needs the vet and this is one of the days he is open late."

She makes a hurried phone call and writes down an address. And then she looks at me strangely. "Do you have a shirt?" I'm taken aback by the question.

"Uh, well, a dirty one. But sure."

"Okay, good. You're going to drive to this address right now. They're expecting you." She walks out to the porch and grabs a pet carrier and eases in my furry, tan friend with a kiss to his head. She taps the roof of the carrier. "This is the information for our rescue. If you call this number, I'll answer. Any time."

"Uh...you're not going to take the rabbit?"

"Can you not take care of the rabbit?"

I shake my head. "I found him," I remind her. "In the yard outside. He looked sick so I just picked him up..."

"I see." She taps her chin and looks around the house. I think she's assessing whether there's space for another pen here. It looks pretty crowded. Plus this little guy seems like he really might be pretty sick.

"I mean, I guess I could take care of him for a little..."

I can tell that's the right thing to say because she beams. "Where are you parked? I'll carry the rabbit, and you can carry supplies. You'll need some basics after you leave the vet."

Ten minutes later, I'm racing toward the vet my new friend Susan calls the rabbit whisperer. My sleek little car is full of hay and pellets and litter. Because apparently rabbits use litter boxes.

I feel a little euphoric knowing I did something right in taking this animal to see Susan. My little friend is still sneezing in the carrier beside me, although Susan got him to eat a little bit of mushed up lettuce. "Don't worry, dude," I tell him. "We're gonna figure this out."

CHAPTER TEN
ORLA

I NEED TO FIGURE MY LIFE OUT. STAT. FINANCIALLY, I'M FINE. WORK IS GREAT. I'VE got my sinkhole project. I don't think my exams will be hard. But...I have no idea how to be someone's mom. I barely have an idea about how to be a woman in this world.

What I need is a mom or a sister right now, but I don't have those things. I need the next best thing: Foof.

I decide to go Esther's bar, even though I can't drink anything there. Getting unexpectedly knocked up is stressful. I could really use a nice whiskey buzz about now.

Avoiding alcohol has been harder than I thought it would be, simply because I realized I'm used to holding my beer bottle and fussing with the label when I'm out talking with people. Or, more often than not, scowling at people who don't let me talk.

I've been to four industry events this month for electrical engineers and at all four, I was one of the only women in the room. It was like a whole world full of Wallys, men so inflated I fantasized about popping them all with a pin. I briefly worry that my baby will come out holding a dry martini and wearing boat shoes, saying stuff like, "*Well, actually.*"

I find parking near Bridges and Bitters, Esther's bar. She gives Foof use of her event space on Mondays. I make my way to the bar, empty so far. "Be right with you," she yells from the back. I shake my head, wondering how fast she'd get out here if I tried helping myself to a soda or something.

"Orla Brady," she purrs, coming around the corner with a stack of clean glasses. She starts putting them away under the bar as I climb up onto the stool. "You're early."

"I came right from my office." I tap my fingers on the bar nervously. "Didn't feel like lingering there."

"I feel you. Get ya a drink?"

I make a face. "I can't drink anything."

"Since when?"

I bite my lip. "I'm laying off the booze while I study for my exams," I lie, but I'm not sure why. I am not yet studying for my exams. I'm not doing much of anything apart from puking my guts out. I came here for advice, and here I am waffling about asking for it.

Esther snorts. "What do you think I do for a living? I'll make you something that'll put hair on your chest."

I wince. "Please don't."

She laughs, pulling out some different bottles and pouring things together. "Don't worry. It'll taste good enough you won't miss the buzz." She starts arranging a garnish on the glass and looks up at me. "Hey, you ever get paid for that bakery thing that fell through?"

She slides the glass toward me, dark pink liquid shimmering under a little sprig of rosemary. I eye it skeptically. "That's a lost fucking cause. Dad and Uncle Mick have moved on to sink holes," I tell her, leaning in to give the drink a sniff. "What are these eyeballs floating in it?"

"They're pomegranate seeds, fool! Don't you follow the news?" Esther cackles. "That's a super food. Lots of antioxidants and such. Like I said. It'll put hair on your chest. I think..."

The drink is delicious. Tart and refreshing, it hits all the same spots as an alcoholic drink would, without the buzz. I can even fidget with the rosemary stem as our friends start trickling in and making small talk. Foof small talk isn't like regular small talk.

These ladies fill the time before the meeting asking questions about menstrual cups and where to get their will notarized. With them it's more like...big talk that passes the time. I bite into a pomegranate seed, and realize the hard center isn't for eating. I'm working on spitting it all into a napkin when Sam and Maddie start tugging me into the back room so we can get started.

Once a month or so, we all meet here to talk about our goals, brainstorm, and smash the patriarchy. Juniper Jones leaned on Foof to get through two elections for judge. My cousin Cal's girlfriend, Logan, transformed her career when she met Foof. Logan works for Sam now and the two of them are pretty much taking over the tech world *and* venture capitalism, whatever that means.

I usually don't have much to say here, other than last month grumbling about getting stiffed on that consult payment. I feel nervous about telling them I'm pregnant. We don't usually talk about domestic stuff here. We're friends and definitely talk to each other about dating and stuff, but these meetings are usually about our life goals.

It feels somehow inappropriate to bring up this little detour I'm taking, but I remind myself that this is why I came here. To seek their advice.

"Who wants to get us started today," Sam asks, gesturing a manicured hand around the room. Nobody moves. I feel myself getting hot, my breath coming faster. If I don't spill my guts now, I'll either puke on the couch or chicken out.

"Me! I'll go." I slam my drink down on Esther's antique table and adjust my posture on the velvet fainting couch she's got set up in here. The whole place has a speakeasy feel, and I love that Foof meets in here with the echoes of that era where women throughout America started cutting off their hair and stepping up into the work force.

Sam smiles and sits down, shaking out her hair. I pick the drink back up and finish it, and then I remember that it doesn't have any alcohol in it. Oh well. "So," I start, and then I stare down at the pomegranate seeds. My doctor suggested an app that messages me each week to say how big the baby is, comparing it to fruits and vegetables as it grows.

My six-week surprise is currently the size of one of these. I blow out a breath.

"I've decided to have a baby," I tell them. "On my own."

Chloe, a romance writer and hopeless romantic, claps her hands. "Ooh! Are you going to a sperm bank? Can we help pick your donor?"

Esther raises a brow at her and she puts her hands in her lap.

"So I'm already past that part," I explain. I reach into my glass and pick up a seed. I stare at it in my hand. "This is about how far I am into the process."

Maddie and Nicole and Logan look like they're going to explode. None of them has said a word yet. I look them in the eye as I continue. "I haven't told my family yet. Right now, my big thing is panicking because I have no idea how to be someone's mother." Still, nobody says a word. I have managed to shock Foof into silence, which is really saying something, especially from Nicole.

"Orla Brady." Nicole walks over to me and grips my thigh with a firm hand. "You will be an amazing mother. You're an amazing woman and you have an amazing group of friends."

"Yep," Maddie nods and sips at her own drink. As the others murmur agreement around me, I fall to pieces. They know my mother died when I was young and that I was raised by wolves. "Orla, I want you to look at me." Maddie puts her hands on my shoulders. "I came to this family when I was a total mess. Remember? I was unemployed and homeless, and Team Brady took me in. You've got a lot of support here."

"Yeah, but my cousin also impregnated you and made your life even messier than it was." I dab at my face with the napkin.

"What I'm saying is your family did a terrific job with you, and I see no reason why you won't be the most amazing Mom to this little pomegranate seed. And I'll get to be Aunt Maddie! I'm going to be an amazing aunt."

"Oooh, shit, yes, I'm going to be Aunty Nik." Nicole makes a face like a cartoon villain. She always knows how to make me laugh.

"You all really think I can be decent at this? It's not quantifiable and there aren't clear objectives. I do better with clear objectives..."

Sam and Esther laugh. "Orla. You can dismantle your naysayers with a glance. You ran the Boston Marathon twice."

"Three times," I interrupt her.

"See? This baby will have no choice but to worship you." The other women nod.

Juniper leans forward and points a finger at me. "Motherhood is hard as hell. You can always call us to help correct you when you're doubting yourself."

"Yup." Maddie and Emma nod aggressively.

I moan a little bit and suck in a breath. "I don't want to be here talking about personal crap when you're all here for career support." I cry a little harder now and Samantha makes a surprised face.

"Oh, Orla. I'm sorry if we gave you the impression that your personal goals are somehow less valid than your professional goals." She clutches at her chest. "Fresh out of fucks is about letting go of the pressures that keep us back from reaching our dreams. Whatever those dreams are! If you're struggling with how to be a mom, then we're here to help you overcome your blockage." She looks over to Juniper and Emma and Maddie, our resident moms. "Can I say blockage in this context?"

Maddie holds up an index finger. "If you're constipated already, you can have some of my Colace."

"I've also got some Mirilax," Emma adds. "It's good to have options."

"You assholes are offering laxatives?" I sniff, crying a little, and Chloe hands me a napkin. Somehow, that offer sends me over the edge into full-out sobs. Everyone gets up and hugs me until we're a huge octopus of strong arms, squeezing.

"Listen," Juniper bangs an imaginary gavel on the table. "I know you think this is less important than your other concerns. But you need to give fucks about your bowel management tools for pregnancy. Trust me. This is helpful advice."

The ice broken, I reveal my deepest fears to them, that I'll struggle with guiding a child toward adulthood when I barely know what I'm doing outside of work. "What if the kid doesn't know how to make friends? I don't know how to make friends. Don't look at me like that, Nicole. I only met you because you started banging my cousin."

I take one of those shuddering, post-cry breaths. I actually do feel better just saying all that stuff out loud.

Nicole just shrugs. "Well, if your kid can't make friends, they'll just be friends with Maddie's kid."

Emma nods. "And you're connected enough to my family. You can just drop your kid at Stag functions and they'll blend right in. We might not even notice another one hanging around." Juniper laughs at that. The two of them are married to Nicole's boss's brothers. We do sometimes have Brady-Stag combination family dinners, and it's true that there's always a million kids at those.

"But shouldn't I know how to teach these things? On my own?"

Maddie and Emma exchange a glance and then look at me. Maddie tilts her head to the side. "Why would you have to do anything on your own, Orla? You have us!"

I feel something snap inside. Maybe it's my sanity. I start crying again at her words. "I don't want to be a burden on anyone," I whimper.

"Oh my god, Orla!" Foof converges on me in another giant hug. "You are not a burden. We all rely on each other." I'm not even sure whose voice is offering reassurance or if they're taking turns. All I know is that they start ordering me to rely on them, and the thought is terrifying.

CHAPTER ELEVEN
WALT

THE WAITING ROOM IS CROWDED WHEN I ARRIVE AT THE VET. I PLUNK MYSELF DOWN
on the bench next to a woman who has a rabbit carrier on her lap. I tilt my
chin at her in acknowledgment, looking down at my cuddly friend, who has
rapid breathing and is still sneezing.

"Who you got there?" The woman has short gray hair and looks,
concerned, into the carrier on my own lap.

"Not sure," I tell her. "I just found him and took him to...well you probably don't know her."

"Ha!" She barks out a laugh. "I bet it was Susan. She told me to be on
the lookout for a young mailman coming in with a lionhead."

I blink at her, not sure what to say. "Um, lion head?"

She nods at my lap. "That's this guy's breed. You said he was in your
front yard?" I nod. She sighs. "It's that time of year. All the shelters are full
to the brim right now. This is about when people start realizing the Easter
bunny they bought their kids is actually a whole lot of work." She strokes
the bunny in her lap lovingly. "Susan and I find rabbits alongside the road,
just dumped and set loose like they can somehow survive out there in the
wild. In the city!" She snorts.

The other people in the waiting room grumble a little.

I stare at my lap. "People just let them go? Is that legal?"

A woman across the room stamps her foot at that question. "Who's got the funds to enforce it? These are *domestic* rabbits. They ain't meant to live on their own in the wild."

A vet tech comes out and calls a few names, and several of the women disappear into the back at once. The tech looks at me quizzically. "Are you one of Susan's?"

"I guess so?" I look around the room and nobody seems to question this. "I found this guy in my yard. Susan said she called?" The tech nods and gestures at me with her clip board. I ask, "Does everyone know Susan?"

Everyone within ear shot murmurs, "Yes." Apparently I stumbled across THE rabbit lady of the greater Pittsburgh area. Or else all rabbit owners know each other.

I follow the tech into the back, holding my breath when she frowns as she listens to my new friend with her stethoscope. She massages the rabbit and mutters, "fluid in the belly. Rapid breathing." Looking up at me, she says, "I'm pretty sure we've got fluid in the lungs here. We're going to need to do a procedure right away."

I look around, and see about five exam tables where the waiting room folks all stand now, stroking their pets. An older man in scrubs rushes over and pulls out his own stethoscope, talking quietly to the vet tech, whose name tag reads Stacey.

I step back and try to keep out of the way as I hear the words "fluid in the lungs" and "congestive heart failure." I start sweating, remembering the day my father died, how the social worker at the hospital said many of these same words to me while trying to get my mother to calm down. I don't feel capable of going through another cardiac death so soon. I did not sign up for this. I'm just trying to keep a job and figure out how to be an actual adult.

I clutch the stainless steel counter behind me until my knuckles turn white and I startle when I feel an arm drape around my shoulders.

"It'll be okay," says a kind voice. It's the woman from the waiting room who sat next to me. "My name is Rita," she says. "What's yours?"

I stammer. I remember that I don't have to tell her my name is Trip. She doesn't know me from the country club and she's not going to alter her opinion of my family based on what I'm wearing. I'm not going to read a sly dig about this in the program of a fundraiser later. At work everyone refers to me by my last name, but here I can just tell her my name. "Walt," I tell her. "I'm Walt."

Rita nods and gives me a hug and it feels so warm and safe. She doesn't cringe at the smell of me, which I think must be some herculean sign of strength. I came here right from my shift. I can't imagine how much I must be stinking up the clinic.

"I know it's scary when the little ones are sick," Rita says. "Do you know where you're taking him next? Which foster family?"

I shake my head rapidly. I hadn't considered giving him to someone else, especially now that I know he's having a heart attack. "I don't know anything," I tell her. I start breathing rapidly through my nose, feeling like the room is suddenly hot and getting smaller. "Susan gave me a pen and hay and things."

"Hey," she tells me, patting my shoulder soothingly. It's an unfamiliar feeling for me and I snap my head to the side, staring at her. "We'll figure this out, okay? Do you want the bun?"

I nod before I can think twice about it.

I feel a gut reaction, like it's necessary to care for this little rabbit, even if I barely know how to care for myself. I feel like I have to prevent some other creature from dying of a heart attack, which doesn't make any sense because I still can't summon any strong feelings about my father dying. I mostly feel like I have to take responsibility for *something* and have it work out okay.

Rita pats my arm again. "Okay, well then it's your bun. Simple as that."

"But I don't know anything about taking care of him!" The panic starts to seep in again and I whip my head over to the exam table, where the vet is bent over the rabbit, muttering softly to Stacey.

Rita waves a hand. "We'll help you with all that. What's your email? I can send you our handbook. And you've got Susan's phone number? You just call her any time and she'll talk you down from the ledge."

In a few minutes, Rita manages to not only distract me from whatever is going on with the rabbit, but she's also got me in an online group for rabbit volunteers and she typed a bunch of rabbit lady phone numbers into my cell. "It's like you've got five new moms, Walt," she tells me, smiling more warmly than my mother ever has.

Stacey and Dr. Roberts beckon for me to approach, and they explain that the rabbit is in congestive heart failure. "You're going to give him a diuretic and another heart medication twice a day," Stacey says as Dr. Robert pats my rabbit and moves on to another patient. "We just had to clear a lot of fluid from this little guy's lungs, poor thing." She strokes him gently between the ears and his little nose moves up and down a few times.

"How do I...give medicine to a rabbit?"

She smiles. "Total beginner, huh? Well the good news is you can mix it all into some food for him." She hands me a sack of green powder and tells me to mix a little bit with water twice a day and sprinkle the meds on top. "You're going to use a pill cutter."

"Like for old people?" I remember watching my grandfather's house-keeper slice his blood thinners.

"Yep. Like for old people." She shakes open a shopping bag and starts loading in the powder and pills and a pill cutter stamped with the veterinary practice logo. We work together to slide the bunny back into his carrier and she tells me to make sure he has a few bowls of water available in his pen overnight. "And you want to take a cardboard box and cut two holes in it. He'll want to go in there and hide a lot of the time," she tells me.

I slide my credit card to the receptionist and wave to Rita, who shouts for me to call her in the morning with an update. And then I'm in my car, alone with my new pet rabbit. I run a shaking hand through my hair, staring. I've never held anything so fragile, never been needed like this. I realize I've spent most of my life feeling like a hindrance.

Even at my new job, I'm a pain in Mark's ass.

But right now, I'm all this little guy has. I carry him inside my air conditioned townhouse and set him down before I run back out to the car for his gear. I get everything set up in the living room where I can keep an eye on him easily, and then I lie down on the floor next to him inside the opening to the pen. I spread out the hay like Rita suggested.

And then I wait. I breathe slowly and wait, wondering if I've done enough, if I got myself in over my head. If I'm hurting this rabbit by not knowing more about how to care for him. I wait and I pet him gently, and wait some more.

After an eternity, the little dude opens his eyes, hops toward me, and starts licking my hand.

CHAPTER TWELVE
ORLA
SEPTEMBER

I PUKE EVERY DAY NOW. SOMETIMES TWICE. LIKE MADDIE, I KEEP A STASH OF snacks on my person at all times. I consider asking her to borrow some of her fanny packs, but I feel bad since she gave me all her maternity clothes and stool softeners already.

Dad keeps sending me home from work if he catches me puking, which is super annoying because I'm starting to chew through all my sick time and I need to save that for when the baby arrives. I still haven't told my dad, which means the Foof ladies can't tell my cousins, so then I feel even worse for making everyone cling to this huge secret. Yet I keep stalling. Foof have not asked about the paternity of this wee bundle, but my dad will. And I don't know yet what I'll say to him.

Every few days, I look up the Sheffield family again and immediately regret it. Sometimes I find a Yelp review of one of their businesses, where former employees lambast them for failing to pay contracts. Sometimes I find gross pictures of Wally's dad with his arm around politicians who have since been revealed as sexual harassers. I decide to stop looking them up. This baby will be all Brady.

As soon as I tell everyone.

Dr. Andrews says everything looks right as rain in my body. She hooked me up with some classes I can take online to learn about delivery and she sent me a binder of information about breastfeeding. I'll read it all eventually. As soon as I tell my dad I'm pregnant.

I'm almost out of the first trimester, when Dr. Andrews promises I will stop puking and start feeling like myself again...except with a lichen attached.

Today I can't seem to keep down any breakfast, but I really don't want to be late for work, so I just ignore the competing sensations of hunger and nausea.

It's warmer than usual for September, and I tie my flannel around my waist as I survey the progress on the sinkhole project downtown. I found a kick-ass team of female electrical engineering student interns for this semester and brought them with me to the job site to check out the repaired wiring as it integrates with the repaired plumbing and gas lines.

My whole team stands down in the pit taking notes while I snap some photos for our project file. "Who knew all this was right below the surface of the street," I say. We're just about ready for the next phase, when crews are going to fill the sinkhole. My cousin Zack is geeking out over the plastic balls they're using as filler to increase strength and stability around the area of the sink hole.

"Did you know these little guys are made from leftover plastic from kayak production?" He tosses a few spheres in the air. My interns shake their heads. Zack grins, "Not only will this save money, but we're using way less concrete."

I roll my eyes at him. "That's all well and good, bro, but these scholars are here to learn about amps and ohms." I beckon them over to the deepest part of the sinkhole and we review the connections and casings until my Dad pokes his head over the pit and tells us it's time for lunch.

Something about the combination of smells from road tar and sewer gas has my stomach in turmoil, so I skip the sub sandwiches and spend the hour fantasizing about acing my professional exams. If I can take them this winter, I should be able to get everything done before the baby is born. I'm still a little bit shy of my required supervised hours, but I can start studying for the test awhile. I absorb the material more easily while I'm actively working on those projects anyway.

I love the thrill of working on complex electrical engineering projects. I love the mathematical formulas that just click in my mind, the ways I can apply them to make lights turn on and motors spark to life without over-heating their wires. It seems like I should feel timid or tamp down my joy and comfort at this, but engineering just comes naturally to me.

And engineering is bad ass. I just reconstructed the power grid inside a giant hole that nearly swallowed a bus in Pittsburgh. I did it while mentoring student engineers. So why the hell am I having such a hard time telling my dad about what's going on in my womb?

After lunch, the interns hop a bus back to their campus and I huddle with Zack and Liam to coordinate across our disciplines. Another great aspect of Zack's bubble-filled concrete plan is that it makes it easier to drill down to the pipes and wires if we encounter a problem in the future. The sun comes out in force and I feel sweat gathering in my elbow pits while we look over the plans.

"We're not starting a pour today, are we?" I look up at the sky, noting that the light has shifted. "It's got to be near quitting time for the concrete crews."

"Nah," Liam says, waving his hand. "They like an early start anyhow. I think we can wrap up here today and plan for tomorrow to be pour day." We start to climb the ladder out of the sinkhole, and my sweaty hand slips a little on the metal rung. "Easy there, cuz," Liam says, placing his palm on my back to steady me.

His hand feels uncomfortably warm, and I try to swat him away as I resume climbing, but I can't seem to get a grip on the ladder. I reach up to grasp the lip of the sinkhole to pull myself up, but my legs are unsteady.

"Hey, Kel, a little help?" I hear my cousins shouting for my Dad, which pisses me off.

"I am perfectly capable of climbing out of a sinkhole," I shout at them. Only my mouth doesn't seem to be working properly and I hear my words coming out all blurred together. "Aw, hell," I say as my Dad grips me by the upper arm and hoists me to my feet. My knees immediately buckle, and when I open my eyes, I'm sitting in the back of an ambulance, which is parked by the sinkhole.

"Jesus, Dad, an ambulance?"

He frowns at me. "This is protocol, Orla. You think I wouldn't follow protocol if any Beltane employee suffered a medical episode on a job site?"

The paramedic shines a light in my eye and I instinctively swat at him. "Sorry," I tell him when my dad frowns at me. "But really, I'm fine."

"Did you eat today, Ms. Brady?" A second paramedic appears with a clipboard and a pen while the first guy hooks up a blood pressure cuff to my arm. "Are you taking any medication?"

I sigh. "Yes I ate. No pills apart from vitamins. It's just hot out here."

"Actually, she didn't eat lunch." My cousin Liam's head appears over my dad's shoulder. "I saw you spending your lunch break studying and Uncle Kel said I could eat your sub." He shrugs. I roll my eyes.

"Okay, fine. I skipped lunch." The paramedic jots down notes on the clipboard. "Can we have any privacy at all? Just this once? This is embarrassing enough." I glare at my cousins, relieved that at least my interns have gone home for the day. If I'm going to faint climbing out of a pit, at least it's just my family members here to witness it.

"Ms. Brady, is there any chance you might be pregnant?" The first paramedic shouts a blood pressure reading to the clipboard-guy and looks into my eyes. And there it is.

There was the moment before this, and then there's now, when I have to admit in front of my father that I'm knocked up.

Sure, I could send him away before I answer. But if the answer is that I'm not pregnant, I'd just say so with him standing here, and he knows it. An eternity passes while both paramedics poke and prod me with their blue-gloved hands. "It's a standard question. Ms. Brady?"

I sigh. Dad's eyes bulge. I tug at the neck line of my tank top. "Can I have some water?" Clipboard-guy nods and uncaps a plastic bottle of water, handing it to me. It's ice cold and feels so good, I start to gulp it down involuntarily. I thought I at least drank water during lunch, but apparently not. I can feel my pores opening up in relief as the water works its way through my body.

Almost as soon as I gulp down the bottle, I lean forward and puke it all back up on the street behind the ambulance. I reach for my shirt to dab at my mouth as the paramedic clicks his pen open and closed, waiting for me to answer.

"Yes," I say, not looking up. "Yes, I'm pregnant."

Everyone zooms into action. The first paramedic grabs his radio and says, "This is unit 36. We're bringing in a pregnant female, dehydrated. We will administer IV fluids in the rig. Over."

"No," I say. "I'm not going to the hospital. I just fainted. I've been puking. I'm fine."

The clip board paramedic starts buckling me into the gurney in the back of the truck. "This is protocol, ma'am."

"Please don't call me ma'am," I mutter as he reaches for my arm and sticks a needle in it so deftly I barely feel it. He hooks up a bag of saline and I can immediately feel the liquid coursing through my parched body. I must have been really dehydrated. Which makes sense. I sigh again, and notice that my dad looks like it's his turn to faint.

He climbs into the back of the ambulance just as the first paramedic closes the doors.

I'm spared having to talk to him because the driver turns on the siren and it's so loud I sit with my hands over my ears as we rock along the bumpy streets toward the hospital. We pull up to the emergency department and both paramedics haul the gurney out of the ambulance with surprising skill. "I felt that less than the potholes," I tell them as they start wheeling me through the door.

I don't bother telling them I can walk, and I don't bother suggesting that my dad stay in the waiting room. He clings to the rail on the side of the gurney until his knuckles are white, clenching his jaw and staring at me without blinking. Even his beard looks worried.

Once I'm parked in an exam room waiting for the doctor, alone with my dad, he clears his throat. "When were you going to tell me?"

"I was going to get there eventually, Dad. I just...haven't figured out what to say yet."

"Why don't you try something now?" I can't tell if he's angry at me or scared or both.

I lick my lips and look up at the saline bag. I really do feel worlds better now that that thing is almost empty. I wonder briefly why I'm not puking up the fluids from the bag, but then I remember that these bypassed my stomach. I briefly consider asking for a take-home IV bag for days when I'm particularly pukey.

"Orla?" Dad's voice hitches and I worry he might start to cry.

"So," I tell him, reaching for his hand. He squeezes mine. His palms feel cold, which actually feels nice. "I'm pregnant, and I'm going to do this thing. And the guy isn't in the picture... and I don't want him to be." I add this last bit emphatically, squeezing my dad's hand.

"All right," he says, swallowing. "You're in charge, Orla-bear. Tell me how to respond here. If you're worried, I want to reassure you. If you're excited, I'm going to be over the moon with you. Tell me what you need."

I look away from him like I always do when I feel something big and huge, because of course he had to go and say the right thing and turn my insides to mush. I feel a giant ball in my throat as I work to choke down all the emotions I practice shoving aside every day. I consider the vomiting and turmoil of the past few weeks, but then I look at my dad's eyes, glittering with moisture and love and utmost support. "I'm terrified," I tell him. "And super uncomfortable? But...I'm leaning toward excited, I guess."

He climbs onto the gurney and wraps me in his arms, kissing the top of my head and laugh-crying until I start crying. Eventually, we pull apart and he sits back in the chair, still holding my hand. "My baby is having a baby!"

"I know, Dad." And then I start crying in earnest, giant heaving sobs I've been holding in. I'm not sure how long I cry, but I feel my dad's strong arms around me, hear his voice whispering that he's here, that he supports me, that I can do anything I want to do.

Eventually I look up at him, and he says, "Can I make a suggestion? Obviously it's your call."

"Sure, Dad. As long as it's not finding another line of work."

He frowns. "I would never say that and you know it." I nod. "No, what I was thinking was...I've been spending most of my nights at Elizabeth's house."

"Dad, I don't want to hear about that."

He cracks a smile. "That's not what I mean. What I mean is that she's not going to move again, not until Jake starts college. She wants her son to have stability. And my house isn't really big enough for both of them to move in. We both need access to office space."

"Are you telling me you want to shack up with your girlfriend? Maybe build a bridge across the street between your two houses?"

He ruffles my hair like I'm still a small kid with a bowl cut. "Well, yes I want to shack up with Beth, as you say. But what if...what if you moved into my house?" He ducks his head so it's level with mine and meets my gaze. "It's paid for. I wouldn't charge you rent."

"I'm not going to freeload off you, Dad."

He waves his hands in the air. "You could pay the property taxes and utilities. What I mostly mean is, with me and Beth across the street, you'd have support. We're literally across the street. But there's no bridge—we wouldn't come over unless you expressly invited us. So you'd have privacy."

"I do like privacy."

He nods. "I know it. And I don't want to sound preachy, darling, but you're going to need help the first few months. Babies just suck all the energy out of their adults." I recall when Arlan was born and Liam told me he and Maddie hadn't slept more than 90 minutes at a time for weeks. I sort of thought he was exaggerating.

Dad keeps talking. "Beth and I were thrilled to help hold Arlan so Maddie could get some rest. Just imagine how delighted I'll be to snuggle a little Brady Bean of yours, Orla?" He claps his hands then and makes a squeaking sound. "My baby with a baby!"

Something about his facial expression and his kindness and the reality of what's about to happen sends me over the edge. I start sobbing again.

"Oh, honey," Dad says. He wraps his long arms around me again, holding me tight. I snot and sob against his shirt. "Just let it out," he says. "I"m right here."

"I have no idea what I'm doing," I wail, making actual boo-hoo sounds as I cry onto my father, all the rash decisions and denial of the past few months catching up to me at once. "I don't know how to be a mom!"

"Hey," he says, lifting up my chin with his hand and resting his forehead against mine. "You had the world's best mom for ten years. You do know how to be a mom, and better still, you contain all the very best parts of your mother." A tear wells up in the corner of his eye and rolls slowly down his cheek. He doesn't brush it away. "That has to count for something, right?"

Before I can nod or respond, the doctor finally comes into the room, complete with clipboard and frown. "What seems to be the trouble here?" He looks at my dad wedged into the bed beside me, stroking my hair.

"No trouble," I tell him, wiping my face on the flannel shirt still tied around my waist. "I was just telling my dad he's going to be a grampy."

CHAPTER THIRTEEN
WALT
OCTOBER

RITA TEXTS OR CALLS EVERY DAY TO TALK ABOUT MY NEW PET. I SMILE, STILL NOT quite believing that I not only have a rabbit, but that I already gave him a nickname. Pudding Sheffield, my butterscotch-colored lionhead rabbit, has changed my entire life.

At the very beginning, he was dehydrated and feeling poorly from the fluid in his lungs. The vet says that was from an infection he caught out there in the wild.

In a few days, though, he totally perked up. Rita and Susan talked me through everything from how to check his ears for signs of infection, to how to trim his nails. Now? He roams free around my townhouse chasing after me whenever I'm home.

I wake up each morning when he leaps up onto my bed and licks my face, signaling that he'd like me to hurry up and get his pellets. I don't even need an alarm anymore to make it to the post office by six. Pud is up before the sun like clockwork. He circles my feet as I stumble around in the dark looking for the little measuring cup I use to pour out his tiny dish of breakfast. He bounds over and starts nudging his food bowl toward me, using his nose at first and then just picking the thing up with his teeth and hurling it.

"I'm coming," I tell him, rubbing the sleep from my eyes with one hand. But I don't really mind. I sit down on the floor next to Pud while he inhales his breakfast. I stroke him between his ears, laughing as tufts of fur blow around.

In the past month, I've learned how to operate a vacuum cleaner for the first time in my life and I learned to enter vet checkups into my calendar app. I'm deeply aware of how pathetic this is, that I'm pushing 30 and wasn't even aware that I didn't know how to do such basic things. Rita and Susan didn't even make me feel bad when I asked them what sort of vacuum I should buy. I actually felt relieved when I learned that pet owners often have conversations about the best vacuums for sucking up fur.

Pud finishes his food and hops over to get his ball, which he rolls toward me. One of the most surprising things about this whole Pudding experience has been learning how smart rabbits are. He nudges the ball impatiently until I toss it across the room for him, and he tears off after it.

I snap a picture and send it to Rita, then toss him the ball a few more times before telling him, "All right, man. I have to head out." I eat my own breakfast as he dives into his stash of hay and I check the weather. Autumn in Pittsburgh can mean snow or heat stroke, and sometimes both in one day. Now that I'm a mailman—I still don't think of myself as a carrier, even though the guys at work are pretty adamant about that title for themselves—I take weather very seriously. I know I haven't even dealt with my first Pittsburgh winter on the route yet, but I did survive a summer and I'm working through the hazing ritual of endless 80-hour work weeks.

Somehow, I didn't get a single stress fracture yet, even if I passed out one more time since adopting Pud.

"Let's check my gear, what do you say, Pudding?" He turns toward me and ignores me as I set out my spray-on sunblock, tick repellent, and two insulated gallon jugs. I fill one with water and one with powdered sports drink mix that's mostly just electrolytes without the sugar content of the name-brand options.

I decide I'll be safe with my short-sleeved shirt, my floppy hat, and shorts today, and as I ease into my official U.S. Postal Service gear, I take stock of how my legs have changed. I always hit up the gym before, but mostly had no idea what I was doing and definitely never worked on my legs. My skin is now deeply tan and my calf muscles pop out like grapefruits on the backs of my legs, carved by all the steps I've climbed like a pack mule on a Peruvian hillside.

The neighborhoods I visit seem planned out by goats. I've seen people mowing lawns that were nearly vertical and I've questioned my life choices a number of times before ascending 30 rickety stairs to deliver a single postcard welcoming the resident to their new dental practice. But people also give me popsicles and lottery tickets, and sometimes hugs, even if I'm dripping in sweat.

I'm happier now than I've ever been in my life, even if (or maybe because) I have no down time.

I check Pudding's water and hay rack and plant a kiss on the top of his furry head as he keeps eating his hay. I know that as soon as I leave he'll scamper into the cardboard taco truck I bought for him, to take his next big nap. And I know this because I bought a camera so I can look at him periodically throughout the day.

At first, I was just nervous about his health. After he perked up from his heart episode, it was time to take him back to get neutered. I was next-level anxious about that procedure. I felt so worried about Pudding's heart condition with the anesthesia, and Rita and Susan suggested the bunny cam might make me feel better, knowing I could look in on Pudding whenever I want. The camera connects to my phone with an app, and I can even talk to him if I feel like it. I don't, because I don't want to confuse him. I buckle my seatbelt and smile when I see him sprawled out with his butt hanging out the side door of the taco truck.

And then I close out of the app and drive to work, trying to keep my head down and my mouth shut. I'm getting a new route today while that neighborhood's carrier is on vacation, leaf peeping in New England. I know things will be easier and more efficient for me when I get a regular route and really learn the houses along it, but for now I've been happy learning about all different parts of the city, meeting all different people.

The Morningside neighborhood I'm visiting this week used to be a hotbed for steel workers. Half the houses there have side doors leading down to "Pittsburgh potties" in the basement. Just a cement basement with a toilet in the middle of the room and a shower head over a drain in the floor. Legend has it the men used to come home from their shift and strip and hose off so they didn't drag filth throughout the house. I find these things absolutely fascinating, and it's worth extending my day a little bit to stop and talk to long-time residents and learn this stuff.

Apart from the deep dive into Pittsburgh history, the thing I really appreciate about this route is that most houses only have about eight steps up to the mailbox from the sidewalk level, and usually one side of the street is totally flat. My thighs are grateful.

I work methodically, listening to a podcast on double speed. I had to work up from regular speed, but now I can listen to at least a dozen episodes a day. I listen to true crime serials, design podcasts, and even a series about Dolly Parton. I never made much time to read, but I've been inhaling all this aural media. I feel like I'm learning more at work than I ever did in school.

I'm in the zone shuffling mail and slinging packages. Until I see a name that stops me in my tracks.

Brady.

I freeze and pull out my ear buds. Orla fucking Brady.

I start to sweat even though I'm standing in the shade. I remember being with her in that hotel room, how she yelled at me each time I started putting on the asshole shell I used to wear for the world. I remember how she looked at me when she turned up at that job site in Garfield, the day my life turned upside down.

That was the last time I ever pretended to be pompous, the last time I had to consciously try to pretend I was better than everyone around me to uphold the Sheffield brand. A brand so ugly I frequently consider changing my name.

Am I going to see Orla Brady today? There isn't a first name on any of the mail. Her whole family must hate me. I know we fucked over their family firm in that job, but they'll have to take a number if they're looking for a pound of my father's flesh.

I don't know what makes me think the word *flesh,* but as soon as I do I remember Orla's thighs again. God, the length of her legs. I never even saw her fully nude, but what I did get to see has been the stuff of all my fantasies since.

I pause at my truck and take a long drink of water. I check in on Pud, who is napping in a beam of sunshine on my living room floor. I stare again at the letter.

Brady.

I close up the truck and head toward the porch steps, startling when someone opens the front door just as I'm reaching for the lid of the mailbox.

"Oh!" A woman shouts. Time stops. It seems like it's Orla, but this woman is pregnant. She has a tiny, round basketball jutting out the front of her body, highlighted by the tight cotton dress she wears with just a pair of flip flops. I can't imagine Orla wearing something like that on a work day. Even though I fucked her in her bridesmaid dress, I always fantasize about her in her jeans and plaid shirt and hard hat. I don't want her to see me, to remember and think about what my family has done to hers.

"Sorry," I mutter, turning to walk back down the steps, onto the neighbor's sidewalk and on back into oblivion.

"Wally?" She grips the porch railing and shouts my name. I stop with my back to her, certain that if I turn around, my life will crackle into flames again.

CHAPTER FOURTEEN
ORLA

He turns around slowly and we make eye contact. I hadn't considered that I'd ever run into him in person. Which I realize is stupid because we live in the same city and Pittsburgh isn't all that big. But why is he dressed like a mailman?

"Is it you? Did you...come here?" I instinctively rub my stomach, which makes me roll my eyes at myself because I feel like a cliche. But I recently started feeling this little bird wriggle around in there and I frequently find myself clutching at my new shape.

He clears his throat. "Just, uh, bringing you the mail." He shrugs and gestures at the truck. I look at the mailbox, open the lid, and see a letter nestled in there. I pull it out and bring the corner to my lip, and then remember that might be germy and tuck it under my arm.

"Did something happen to Peggy? You're not usually the mailman on this street," I tell him, cringing at how bitchy that sounds. I remind myself that he doesn't know he's the father of this child. He has no idea. He's apparently undergone some sort of career shift and is carrying out his business like nothing happened. But then I remember that his father died and I feel like an asshole again.

"I'm still pretty new," he says with a shrug. "I cover people's vacations. Peggy is leaf peeping in New England with another carrier from our station. But nobody's supposed to know they're together."

"I won't tell a soul," I say, leaning back against the closed door to my house. I don't know why I like that he revealed this bit of information, this slice of personal intel that makes Peggy a real person in my mind, rather than just the woman who delivers my mail. Or did.

Now apparently, I've got Wally doing that. He clicks his teeth and looks up the street like he needs to get a move on, but he doesn't budge. "Hey," I say quietly, with all the warmth I can muster. "I'm really sorry you lost your dad."

He nods. "Thank you." He looks off to the side again, like he doesn't want to talk about this, at least not with me. My heart starts racing a little as I realize the enormity of this. I'm talking to my baby's biological father, who doesn't know that he has a half-baked child.

I swallow. "So, um, you know, I know what it's like to lose a parent."

His face changes. "You do?"

I nod. "My mom died of cancer when I was just a kid. My dad lives across the street just there." I point to the house where he and Elizabeth are probably drinking coffee and staring out the window at me chatting up the mailman. I don't know why I told him where my father lives. I clear my throat. "So yeah. Let me know if you ever want to talk about that or anything. Like I said, I've been there and I know it sucks."

"I hated my father," he says, his eyes flashing ice blue. I nod. "I've never said that before, to anyone." He lets out a long breath.

"Parent loss is a huge deal. It's all really complicated," I tell him. "People don't get it at all unless they've been there. Like, even my dad...he lost his wife, sure. But his parents were still around until really recently. He never had to walk around wondering what his mom would do in this or that situation. So. Yeah. I can talk to you about it. If you need to vent." I'm rambling now, so I chew on my lip and try to stop myself.

Wally nods a few times. "I'd really like that, Orla fucking Brady," he says, grinning. His whole face shifts when he smiles. I forgot I told him to call me that. I laugh. He points at my stomach. "I understand if you have obligations, but I'd really like to grab coffee and...talk about dead parents."

That makes me bark out a laugh. "Sounds like a grand time! We can talk about urn pricing while we're at it, and prepaid cremation."

"I'm trying to get my mom to do that now," he says, bringing a hand up to scratch at the back of his neck. His mailman shirt lifts up when he does and my eyes widen when I catch a glimpse of his abs. "Can I give you my number? To set up the coffee?"

I stare at him for a bit and then nod. I watch as he reaches into his shirt pocket and pulls out a pen, scribbling down his number on someone's junk mail and then springing back up the stairs toward me to hand it over. Our fingers touch as does, and I feel a wave of heat move through me.

Everything Dr. Andrews said about the second trimester comes true all at once. I feel horny and nauseous and energetic all at once and I have to cling to the porch railing so I don't leap down the steps into Wally's arms and demand that he take me to his mail truck and fuck me again.

"I hope you call," he says with a small smile, and I can see how vulnerable he is in this moment, how utterly changed he is from the fucker who threw gross pickup lines at me at Nicole and Zack's wedding.

"I will," I tell him, and I watch as he makes his way down the next few houses before circling back to his mail truck to refill his sack. He gives me a salute as he starts whistling along down the block.

"Who was that?" My dad's voice startles me and I look up to see him jogging across the street, carrying his briefcase.

"Oh, the mailman," I tell him. "He's covering for Peggy. She's in New England."

"Nice time of year for it," my dad says. He peers over my shoulder. "You're not unpacking the heavy boxes by yourself are you?"

I shake my head. I am now fully moved out of my apartment and fully moved back into my father's house, only I've been sleeping in his former room and we're setting up a crib in mine. It all feels super strange still, but I definitely agree with Dad that this was a nice plan.

"My friends are coming over tomorrow for an unpackathon. Maddie's even bringing Arlan so we can let him toddle around and show us where I need to baby proof."

Dad beams. "Excellent! That's really terrific, sweetie. You coming in today?"

I shake my head. "Thought I'd study from home if that's all right?"

He laughs. "I'll check with the boss." Dad and Uncle Mick always let their P.E. candidates study for their exams while on the clock at Beltane. They don't usually allow for remote work, and I try not to take advantage, but I really can make more efficient use of my time if I put in all my study hours at home and then schedule my doctor visits in the afternoon.

"You coming across the street for family dinner later?" Dad hooks a thumb over his shoulder toward his new house. "Elizabeth is making ginger meatballs."

"Is that even a thing?"

"Apparently they're very good with pineapple and teriyaki sauce." Dad pulls me in for a hug and kisses me on the cheek. Then he boops me on the nose and I punch him in the shoulder. He pretends it hurts and I punch the other side. "All right, all right. See you at six, though."

"Wouldn't miss it," I tell him. And then I text Wally my number before I head inside.

CHAPTER FIFTEEN
WALT

"You ready for this, Pud?" I lie on the floor on my stomach, scratching him between his ears while he ignores me and eats hay. I need to coax him into his carrier so I can go meet Rita and Susan for a bunny spa night. I had no idea bunnies needed such a thing, but here we are. Plus it's a fundraiser for the rescue.

I only recently learned that none of the volunteers are paid in any capacity. Not even the two women who run the entire rescue and coordinate everything with the vet, keep track of who is fostering which rabbits... it all sounds like more work than I ever did in my life and it's a side project for these folks who mostly have full-time jobs.

In the months since my father died, I'm discovering an entire, wonderful world full of people who actually care about others. The things these women do aren't motivated by a desire to look good. This is actual charity work for the benefit of these beautiful creatures. Nobody is here to line their resume or gain cred with an investor.

The way my new animal-lover friends interact with each other and the world has been jarring for me, in a good way. I think this is what I've always felt was missing: a moral compass. It feels shitty to think about that, to really see the stark ways my family was different, but somehow felt their way was superior.

It makes my head throb if I think about it too long, and most days at work, I've got nothing but hours of time to think about stuff. Like how I ran into Orla today and my head swirled with thoughts of her for hours. She seemed pleasant enough, but I can't let myself think about her too long. It's pretty safe to say I want her more than I've ever lusted after a woman, but it seems like I missed my window. She's having a baby, clearly off limits. Even if she weren't spoken for, I'm no use to anyone right now. My thoughts are too tangled up. I'm glad I have something to do tonight to distract me from my own head. This is a social event with a good cause.

I know the spa night folks are staying open a little late for me, too. I am working six days on for 12 hours a pop, with only one day to recuperate. Usually, I spend my off-days doing two things. I sleep as much as I can, and I deal with paperwork bullshit for my mom.

Tonight, after my route, I had just enough time to shower and change and still give Pud the opportunity to make his own way into the carrier. It becomes clear he's not going to budge just by being asked, so I move on to the second phase of my plan: I bribe him with food. I recently figured out that he will sniff out every leaf of cilantro in my house. I dropped some on the floor when I was putting together a taco the other day, and Pudding came bounding over like he was being chased.

I trot over to the fridge to grab some of the greens, making extra sure to crinkle the bag. He notices. I laugh as he whips his head toward me. His face is so furry I can barely see his eyes behind all the floof, but his little pink nose wiggles up and down.

"You want some of this? Yeah? Come on, then." I toss a handful into his carrier and sigh in relief when he hops right in. I've already got it set up with a towel and some hay in there, so I clip the door shut behind him and head out to the car.

The vet said it's safest to buckle him in the back seat, so I make sure the seat heaters are turned off and get him situated. We drive to the animal shelter hosting the grooming fundraiser and the place is packed. My rabbit-lady friends all squeal when I get there, and it feels simultaneously good and uncomfortable to enter a room where people are outwardly glad to see me.

I work my way through the crowd, getting my hair ruffled and my cheek pinched. I'm glad they agreed to stop pinching my ass cheeks. I know my body has firmed up since I got my mail carrier job, but it was kind of weird to be felt up by women twice my age.

"Thanks for staying a little later for me." I set Pudding's carrier on the check-in table.

"Are you kidding? We'd do anything for you two." Rita sticks a finger through the grate on Pud's carrier, greeting him. "You want a snack while we get him situated?"

"Well," I happily reach toward the snack tray. "I always want food. You know that about me, Rita. But I'd also really like to come and see, just so I know what to do if I ever have to do the grooming stuff myself."

"Is this guy for real?" A woman starts fanning herself. "What an amazing Bun Dad."

I shrug. "I try." It feels like a line. A few months ago, it would have been the start of a series of lines. But today it's true. I am trying. I want to take care of this guy. I want to be amazing for someone else, to help them thrive. Even if that someone else is a furry little rabbit.

A woman in a green apron, named Cheryl, shouts that Pudding is next as soon as she finishes with Archie, a little lop on her lap. I start to feel anxious, like I always do when Pudding needs medical care. Not that grooming counts as medical care. I'm just always afraid I'm messing up and not giving him the things he needs.

I inhale most of the snacks left on the tray until Cheryl says she's ready for Pudding. "You can go and socialize if you want," she says, kissing the top of his head. "We've got this."

"Oh, I don't want to leave him," I tell her.

She arches a brow. "Go on and gossip," she says. "Let me cuddle this guy and clean him up for you."

I eventually shrug and pick up the snacks. I spot Susan combing a rabbit and wander over toward her. "Hey!" I say, trying to check the enthusiasm in my voice when I realize I sound like a kid in line for a roller coaster.

"Walt!" Her whole face smiles when she sees me and she picks up the rabbit's front foot to wave at me, like they're both saying hello. I crouch down and greet them both. Susan has some parsley in her pocket and we both smile when the bunny discovers it and pulls it out with his teeth as she resumes trimming his nails. "Haven't seen you in action for awhile."

"Oh, they've been moving me to different neighborhoods." I lean in close as she parts the fur on the rabbit's front paw, revealing a tiny little nail in the back. "Do they all have a nail there?"

She nods. "Lots of people forget that one." I watch as she quickly snips the rest of his nails and looks in his ears. "Rita says you're helping out at Bingo night?"

I grin. "I never did anything like that before, but it sounds fun."

Susan raises her eyebrows. "You should bring a friend. Double up the number of young people who attend."

"Ha. I'm sure you're all young at heart." I don't know why I brush off her comment like that, replace it with a line. That's something Trip would do, but I want to be Walt now. I lick my lips and absentmindedly pet the rabbit on Susan's lap. "There is someone I'd love to bring."

She turns her head, giving me a knowing look. "Tell me more!"

I wave a hand. "I don't think...well, I'm fairly positive there's no hope there."

"You'll never know if you don't ask." Susan gently places the rabbit into a carrier and stands up, brushing off her lap. I offer her the snack platter and then we both chuckle because I've eaten everything on it. "It's for a good cause. People can't resist a good cause."

"That's true enough," I agree. "Who wouldn't want to support Pudding and his pals?" Cheryl waves at us from across the room, pointing to Pudding's carrier. "I guess he's all done with his spa treatment."

Susan squeezes my arm. "I hope you'll invite your friend to join us." I flush, trying to imagine myself inviting Orla to hang out with me, much less spend an evening playing Bingo at an animal rescue fundraiser. But maybe Orla's the kind of person who thinks that sounds like a good time. I make my way through all the remaining rabbit ladies, promising I'll add more pictures to the Facebook group.

"Where did you come from?" Cheryl shakes her head and smiles, patting my shoulder as I make my way toward the door. I shrug. "Well, we sure are glad you found us."

I drive home, feeling unsettled by the warmth and kindness we just experienced. After a few decades of posturing and one-up-manship, I'm still unaccustomed to people who say what they mean.

"I think I like these people," I say to Pud, who doesn't respond.

CHAPTER SIXTEEN
ORLA

WALLY NEVER RESPONDS TO MY TEXT AND I SPEND WAY TOO MUCH TIME PISSED OFF about it. He's the one who asked me for coffee. Wasn't he? Am I making that up? Anyway, he definitely gave me his number. He should respond when a woman texts him. This is why I don't pursue men. I can't handle this kind of emotional purgatory.

I remember how he acted when we first met and decide his mailman situation was just a reprieve. Heat stroke must make him act nice or something.

By the time I wrap things up at work, I'm so sick of staring at my phone that I turn it off and stomp out to my car. I drive straight home, where I'm supposed to be making an appetizer for family dinner tonight.

I pull out my mom's recipe box and smile at her handwriting on the little index cards. Last year, Elizabeth suggested we laminate them to help preserve them, and I'm grateful as I feel a tear drop and watch it splash down on the card at the sight of her neat writing in all caps. Even her spinach dip recipe seems to be shouting at me.

But what is she shouting about? What would Mom have said if she were here? Would I have gone and gotten knocked up by a stranger at Zack's wedding if Mom were alive? I doubt I would have felt the urge to storm off and avoid everyone if I wasn't a motherless tomboy. I pull the cream cheese out of the fridge to soften and grab some spinach from the freezer, trying to think about something else.

That just makes me remember that I'm pissed off at Wally. I grab my phone again and check the message. Still no reply.

> Hello? Wally? What gives?

Almost immediately, I see the little dots indicating he's typing something. Huh.

WALLY:

> So sorry about that, Orla. Work was hectic today. I'd love to get together and talk if you're still open to that.

He's so formal. At least he's not trying to be slimy I guess.

> When do you take lunch? I can meet up with you wherever.

WALLY:

> Sigh. I don't get lunch breaks. They literally have a tracking device on my mail bag.

> So you really are a mailman, then? That wasn't like a costume or something?

I LOCATE a small pan to put the dip into the oven to heat up, checking my watch. Everyone is going to start pouring into Elizabeth's house soon and I'll need to get over there with the dip before they eat her house plants or something.

Wally writes back.

> Definitely not a costume. Just call me Mr. McFeely.

> Are you being gross?

WALLY:

> No way! Mr. McFeely. From Mr. Rogers? Speedy delivery?

I laugh, reading his latest message. I had forgotten about the mailman character on that show. Dad used to put the reruns on for me and my cousins. He loved pointing out the different landmarks around Pittsburgh featured in the episodes. Dad used to buy us all our shoes at the shoe store Fred Rogers visited on the show. I type back to Wally.

> My bad. I loved that show! Okay, so no lunch break. When's your next day off? No mail on Sundays, right?

I decide the dip is warm enough, so I pull it from the oven, tuck the bag of bread under my arm, and walk across the street to meet up with my family. Cal opens the door and makes a big show of taking everything out of my hands. "You all right? Should I carry you up the steps or something?"

"Jesus Christ, Cal, if you offer to carry me again I'm going to kick you in the nuts. I'm pregnant, not arthritic."

He holds his hands up in surrender. "Sorry, cuz. I don't know how to be, you know?"

"Just be regular. How were you with Maddie?"

He shrugs. "Regular I guess."

I huff past him with the food, heading toward Elizabeth's kitchen. I roll my eyes when I walk in there to find Dad kissing her as he stirs whatever's cooking on her stove top. She looks up and smiles. "Orla! What've you got there?"

"Spinach dip," I say. "Pan's hot." Without a word, she grabs a hot pad and sets it on the counter. I plunk down the dip and bite my lip, trying to decide if I should run my oven mitts back home or just leave them on the counter. They're really Dad's oven mitts, anyway. I'm working on getting over feeling like a mooch about this living situation.

Elizabeth hustles around, taking the bread from me and setting it out in a basket. Prior to Dad getting with her, we'd probably have just dumped the bread onto a paper plate and all dug in. She definitely has brought a layer of class to our rowdy family dinners. She doesn't even say anything to me about spinach dip not going with teriyaki meatballs.

With nothing else to help get ready in the kitchen and no ability to drink alcohol with my cousins, I decide I'm safe pulling my phone out again to check my messages.

WALLY:

> Actually, I have to deliver packages Sunday. My work schedule is a real bear.

> Well…why did you ask to get coffee if you can't?

I try not to acknowledge how hurt I'm feeling to be rejected by him. I wasn't even trying to go on a date with him. I literally offered to hang out with him and talk about having a dead parent. I shouldn't be surprised that he's being weird; he's a slimeball. God, that's the last time I reach out to him. The last time. He's a sperm donor. That's it. And he's not even aware that he lent me his demon spawn.

I set my phone on top of the oven mitts so I remember to take them home later and look up just as Maddie and Liam arrive with Arlan.

"Hey!" Maddie grins as she shuffles in the door. She's got a million bags dangling from her and Arlan wriggles around as she tries to hold him with one arm. Liam comes in behind, holding the door with his foot and juggling a gallon of juice and what seems to be the entire snack aisle of the grocery store.

"Let me take something," I say, rushing over to them. I was thinking they'd hand me a bag, but Maddie flops Arlan onto my shoulder without another word and bustles past me into the kitchen. She washes her hands and hangs up all her bags while nobody seems to notice I'm holding a toddler.

Arlan also doesn't seem to notice that he has been plopped onto an inexperienced baby-holder. Eventually, he lifts his head and looks at me, realizes I'm not his mother, and starts to shriek. I whip my head toward the kitchen, where my extended family seems not to hear the air horn blasting out of Arlan's windpipe.

Cal and Zack are once again fighting over the guacamole my dad set out, and Uncle Mick just skidded in through the garage door. I feel like Arlan is going to burst my ear drums.

"Hey, buddy," I shout to him, wriggling one of my hands up to cup his cheek. "Hey, man, it's me. Aunt Orla."

At my touch, he stops screaming abruptly and looks at me. His cheeks are all wet from his tears. "La la?"

I chuckle. "Yeah, man. La la. What's got you upset?"

He looks around at the chaos. I expect him to start screaming for his mom or dad, but instead he focuses on my cousins. Cal is now running around the kitchen with the guacamole bowl, huddled low so Zack can't dip his chip.

"Gwock," Arlan says, pointing his fat hand toward my cousins.

"Yeah? You want some guac? Good plan." I shift his weight so he's on my hip and I'm surprised to feel how comfortable it is to hold him that way, like my hip bone is a little seat for his puffy diaper butt.

"Guac!" He shouts again. I nod. I step in Callum's path as he tries to evade Zack and I duck down just as Cal does. I jut out my hand and grab the guac dish, spinning quickly out of the way as Cal and Zack let out a massive groan.

Arlan squeals and slaps his hand directly into the bowl, splashing guacamole onto my face. Both of us laugh as I sink down onto the linoleum. When I look up, the room has gone silent and everyone stares as Arlan smears avocado paste in my hair.

Cal squints. "We can probably still eat it, right?"

"Only if you can pry it away from Arlan here," I counter. I'm interrupted when Arlan sticks a fat finger full of guac into my mouth.

"Try dis," he says, screwing up his face until he looks just like Liam. "Eat!"

ℬ

Eventually, Arlan's parents pluck him away from me to wash up. I dab myself as clean as I can and settle in around the dining room table. I'm relieved by how much better I feel surrounded by my family. I spent the entire day so stressed out. It's nice to be reminded that I have this gregarious place where everything is all right, even for a little while. That is, if you consider food fights and loud arguments about paint color to be "all right."

After dinner, my cousins insist I am off the hook for helping with cleanup for at least a year, so I stay seated at the table, eating a brownie and staring at my phone. Literally everyone else is deeply engaged in conversation about fall baseball, so I don't feel bad checking my messages.

Instead of a text, I see I have a voicemail from Wally.

ℬ

Hey, Orla. I'm so sorry about that confusion. This is Walt. Wally. Anyway, I wanted to explain myself a little better. Now I'm doing it over voicemail and I feel dumb. I do get a day off this week, but I can't grab coffee with you because I already volunteered to help at a charity bingo thing for the animal rescue. Would you want to go? I didn't want to assume anything. Maybe you could come play bingo and we could talk after? I'm happy to pay for your ticket, of course. Also it's a costumed event, and I was told to wear my mail carrier uniform. But that's not usually a costume for me. I'm a real mailman. God, this is so lame. Please call me back and tell me to get lost.

🅱

I STARE AT MY PHONE, stunned by that message. It was so...real. Wally is never what I expect, which is really unsettling for me. I like knowing what I'm getting into. And a costume bingo event benefitting an animal rescue?

"What's got you making that face, sweetie bug?"

Dad leans his chin on the top of my head and tries to look at my phone. I shove it quickly in my lap.

"Oh, just a weird voicemail," I tell him.

He nods. "Wouldn't have anything to do with that mailman I saw you flirting with earlier, would it?"

"I was not flirting with him!" Was I flirting with Wally earlier?

"He was definitely easy on the eyes," Elizabeth chimes in.

Dad flicks her with a dish towel. "Since when do we objectify people, Beth?"

Beth's son, Jake, nods his head. "I saw the new mail carrier. He is an objectively attractive male human."

"Told you," Beth shouts.

Nicole pokes her head back in from the deck, where I'm pretty sure she's smoking a joint with my cousins. "You have a hot mailman?"

Elizabeth nods. "He's new, though. Not sure if he's sticking around."

"I want a picture," she says. "Those shorts really do it for me. Take a picture before it gets too cold and he puts on pants."

I roll my eyes at my family and stand up to gather my stuff together. There's no dip or bread left and the bowl is still soaking in Elizabeth's sink, so all that remains is to hug my dad and ruffle Arlan's hair before I head out.

I walk back across the street to my house wondering what the hell costume animal rescue bingo is all about. I'm tucked into bed and half asleep before I realize I forgot the damn pot holders.

CHAPTER SEVENTEEN
ÒRLA

> What do I wear to costume bingo?

I SPEND THE ENTIRE NEXT DAY FRETTING ABOUT MY OUTFIT AND THEN DECIDE TO reach out to my Brady Ladies group text. I usually keep the conversation muted because they tend to say things about my family members' sex lives and it makes me want to barf when my dad's girlfriend chimes in.

But, you know, sometimes they're useful.

Nicole is, of course, the first to respond.

> Is it drag queen bingo or regular people bingo?

I send a shrug emoji.

> The bingo caller is a hot mailman…

BETH:

> The one from our street?

> Yeah, but don't get any ideas. We're just hanging out to talk about having dead parents.

LOGAN:

> You're going on a date with a hot mailman to talk about dead parents?

It's not a date.

MADDIE:

But there will be costumes? And his is a mailman one? With shorts?

I can see this is going nowhere, and feel frustrated with myself for having such a strong emotional response to hanging out with Wally. Then I remember that I'm carrying a baby he catalyzed into existence...that I haven't told him about. Everything was so different when he was just some asshole I was never going to see again.

I set my phone down on my desk and pull up my exam practice notes instead. I wade through a few hours of practice questions before weighing my costume options. My stomach is too big for my tool belt, so I can't really go as "lady engineer."

Dad never sent me to Catholic school or anything so I don't have school uniforms lying around, and I was never a Girl Scout. "God, all my ideas are terrible." I say the last bit out loud, causing Dakota to stop in her tracks in the hall.

She leans her dark head in my door. "Everything okay in here?"

I roll my eyes. "I'm just being weird. I have this costume thing and I have no idea what to even wear."

Dakota rolls her lips in, considering. "You aiming for sexy or funny or just...not trying to stand out?"

I shrug. "Funny I guess."

She grins.

A FEW HOURS LATER, I'm hauling my pregnant self to charity bingo, and I'm still not sure why. Dakota did my hair in two braided pigtails and had me tie my flannel shirt up under my boobs, letting my little round belly out in the breeze. Then she painted the whole thing orange and drew a face on it using stuff from the supply closet.

I'm very careful not to smear anything with the seatbelt as I drive to the address Wally sent me. When I walk into the fire hall, I am once again halted in my tracks. Nothing about this man is what I expect. The man I met at Nicole and Zack's wedding doesn't match the type of man who invites a woman to something like this. The room is lined with pens of rabbits munching on hay or just lounging around. A few long tables are set up with silent auction prizes, and nearly every seat in the house is occupied by gray-haired women double-fisting bingo dabbers.

I close the door behind me and lean against the wall, trying to get my bearings.

"Oh my gosh, aren't you the cutest thing? Can I help you get situated?" At first, I think the woman is talking to one of the rabbits, but eventually, I realize she's leaning in close, talking to me. Nobody has ever called me cute before. She blinks her eyes, waiting for a response. "You're a farmer with a pumpkin, right?" She claps her hands. "Just the cutest thing. Cheryl, come see!"

The women working the door are wearing rabbit-print sweatshirts and rolls of raffle tickets around each arm. "You here to play, sugar?" I can tell they're the type who would be reaching out and touching my stomach if it weren't covered in paint. I also suspect I wouldn't hate it, which just adds to my feeling of being unsettled.

I clear my throat and adjust my straw hat. I am indeed supposed to be a farmer with a pumpkin. "I'm meeting my friend here. Wally? I mean Trip?"

"Oh!" One of the women claps her hands. "This must be the friend Walt was telling us about. Remember, Peg? He said his friend might come by and to save a seat? Are you the friend? We thought it might be another one of his post office friends." She waggles her eyebrows at this last suggestion, and I laugh.

"Sadly, I do not have a mail bag. But I met...Walt...we're friends. Yes. That's me." I fiddle with the end of one of my braids uncomfortably.

One of the women, Cheryl I think, escorts me to a seat and hands me a sheet of bingo cards. "Girls," she says to the table. "This is Walt's friend. Anyone got a spare dabber for her?"

"Depends whether she's gonna make us stop staring at his backside." The woman to the left of me has a deep, raspy voice and eyes me skeptically.

I shake my head. "I would never dream of depriving you." Everyone laughs and someone slides me a spare dabber. "You'll have to talk me through the ropes, though."

Soon, I'm immersed in bingo lingo, learning about postage stamps and four-corners, and I don't even notice the hush fall over the room as someone takes the stage. I look up as a woman takes the mic, introduces herself as Susan, and thanks everyone for coming. She starts talking about the importance of their rabbit rescue. I listen as she and a few other volunteers express their appreciation for their furry companions, but soon my eyes drift to the man hanging back behind the main table.

It's Wally. He's dressed in a mailman uniform about three sizes too small, and it shows off a body I do not remember him having when I had my hands on it a few months ago. Is my mind totally addled by pregnancy or has he hulked up since I fucked him?

"He's quite the dish, right?" Karen, the husky-voiced woman at my side, leans in conspiratorially. All I can do is nod, because there don't seem to be words for what those little blue shorts are doing to Wally's thigh muscles. I can see all the parts of his quad, flexing and releasing as he fidgets behind Susan, waiting his turn to come forward.

And then he sees me staring at him. I expect to flush and look away, but he holds my gaze and his face breaks into the widest grin. He's stupidly good looking, so much so that I have to fan myself with my hat.

"Is it warm in here?" I break eye contact and look over at Karen, who shrugs.

"We've all got hot flashes, honey. We're always warm."

Susan leads the room in a round of applause, interrupting my train of thought. She smiles. "I'm sure you're all sick of hearing from me up here," she says. "I'll just hand things off to our guest caller for the evening, shall I?" The room erupts into whistles and applause. "Let's hear a big round of applause for our newest and most enthusiastic bun-dad, Walt Sheffield!"

I almost need to cover my ears at the wall of sound erupting around the room. Chairs scrape as people rise to their feet to applaud. "Aw, come on, guys, enough of that." Wally has the mic now and waves his hand around, trying to get everyone to settle. "I'm just here because I'm grateful for the work you all do every day. So who's ready to kick back and have some fun?"

I jump as Karen presses her two index fingers together and whistles, as loud as if we were at an outdoor baseball game. "What?" She whisper yells in response to my expression. "There's good prizes. I'm here to win."

Wally waves his hands again until the room settles back down. He's hilarious up there, hamming it up for this crowd of bunny-loving grand-mas. "Okay, okay. Susan said that usually, you guys call numbers from one of those boring old wire bingo balls. But I thought we'd shake things up a little tonight." He shimmies his hips as he swivels his mail bag around to his front. The crowd is lapping it up. I don't even recognize this man, who is so...at ease here.

He starts pulling bingo numbers from his mail bag, circling the room enthusiastically, even bouncing the little ping-pong balls with the numbers on them off the tables as he makes his rounds. I lose myself in the energy, trying to keep up. We're evidently playing "postage stamp bingo" in homage to Wally, but all I get are sporadic numbers until intermission.

Karen helps me up out of my seat as I look around for the bathroom. "Thanks," I tell her. "I'm still not used to my center of gravity being off."

"I remember that," she says, following me. "Now of course my equilibrium is all whacked out due to the change of life." She pats my arm. "But you don't need good balance to sit and pet a bunny, know what I mean?"

I shake my head. "I don't, actually. I don't have any pets."

She looks stunned, like I just told her she did indeed have to stop staring at Wally's thighs. "Are you here to adopt one tonight?" Of course there's a line for the bathroom, so Karen and I lean on the wall to wait our turn. I shake my head again.

"It's not the right time for me," I tell her. I point at my pumpkin stomach. "I need to get ready to take care of this little bunny. It's just me, you know." And then I bite my lip. I still get overwhelmed talking about this adventure.

Karen pats my hand. "You're going to do just fine," she says, her smile as warm as her voice is husky. Something about her kindness gets me emotional again and I have no explanation for why I blurt out, "My mom died. When I was young. I have no idea what I'm doing."

"Oh, honey!" Karen wraps her arms around me in a tight hug from the side, careful not to smear the paint on my belly. Someone else from our table comes out from the bathroom and, seeing the scene I'm making, joins in the hug before she knows what's wrong.

"You're all being so nice," I say into Karen's hair.

"Oh, baby," Karen says. "We're all here because we've been rescued. You'll soon see. These creatures, they give us so much. We're happy to pass that love right back onto you."

"But why me? You guys don't even know me."

Karen laughs. "Well you're here, aren't you? And you said you're a friend of Walt's. I never met a man who loves his pet like Walt loves his little Pudding Pie."

Even though it's hard for me to imagine Wally as a doting pet parent, I decide these old lady hugs are better than any of the therapy sessions my dad sent me to in the years after Mom died. It occurs to me I should maybe look into getting back into therapy as I listen to the gang from my table telling me stories of loss and loneliness.

Cheryl explains that rabbits thump their back legs on the ground when they're angry. "Well one night I fell asleep on the couch. Woke up to my foster bunny thumping like crazy. Wouldn't stop! Eventually, I walked over to his pen and saw black smoke billowing out of the kitchen. I had left a pizza box in the oven!" She starts to cry. "That little booger saved my life."

There's a murmur of agreement amidst the bingo dabbing, the women agreeing that their pets have saved the humans instead of the other way around.

Wally finishes up calling, ignoring rogue shouts for him to take off his shirt. In the end, I don't win any games, but I pull out my phone to scan the QR code on the table to make a donation to the rabbit rescue.

Karen looks impressed. "You know how to use that bar code thing?" I nod. "Huh. That was Walt's idea. I guess he knew what he was doing after all."

I look over to where he's squatting on the ground, visiting with one of the rabbits. I watch as he pulls a treat from his pocket and breaks it in half, splitting it between the rabbits in the pens on either side of him, and then he scratches them each between their ears.

I stand up. "It was so lovely to meet all of you," I tell them. "Will you excuse me so I can go thank Wally for inviting me?"

"You better thank him." A woman named Carol nods enthusiastically. "Do it for all of us, honey."

I shake my head and wave, promising I'll come visit them all again at their rabbit-Grinch photo event in December. I wade through the crowd over to Wally, who sees me coming and stands, hands in the pockets of those ridiculous shorts. "You came," he says with a shy smile.

"That's what she said," I counter, punching him in the shoulder.

<h1 style="text-align:center">CHAPTER EIGHTEEN
WALT</h1>

ORLA FOLLOWS ME TO THE PARKING LOT AND WE STAND AWKWARDLY BY MY CAR. "Do you want me to drive? I can bring you back here for your car after. I'm not sure what's easiest?"

She shrugs. "Sure, that sounds good." She's halfway into the car before I can say anything else, and I want to say so much. I want to tell her what it means that she spent her evening here with this organization that's become important to me, with no questions asked and no real time spent with me during the event.

I want to tell her how damn sexy she looks with her little belly hanging out of that shirt and those fucking braids. But I also have to remember that the belly is obvious proof that she is not mine to lust after. Not anymore. Probably not ever.

She makes a face at me and I realize I've been staring at her. I clear my throat. "So we look kind of interesting…for going in public." I gesture between us, me dressed as a mailman, her as a farmer. She laughs.

"Oh, yeah. I guess I forgot we were in costume." She bites her lip and buckles her seatbelt carefully so that it doesn't touch her stomach paint. I run a hand through my hair, feeling self conscious. "I guess I should at least untie my shirt." She fumbles a bit with the buttons and then sighs, realizing it won't fasten around her stomach.

"I have coffee," I say. "If that's not too weird? We could go to my place? Nothing inappropriate. I swear."

She curls her lips to the side, considering, then shrugs. "Sure, why not."

I start to sweat at the thought of having her in my house. I can't imagine why I'm inviting her over, knowing I'm sitting here lusting after her and she's just here to be a friend—another person with a dead parent offering solidarity.

I scan through my house, trying to remember how trashed it is. I know the upstairs is a wreck, but there's zero chance she'd go up there, so I decide not to worry about it. The downstairs is Pudding's realm, but that probably won't be off-putting to her based on her experience tonight at the fundraiser.

"So how about those rabbit ladies?" There's a smile in her voice as she asks, turning her body so she can look at me while I'm driving.

"Yeah." I grin. "It's like having a whole bunch of aunts. They're so nice."

"And they pinch your butt," she teases.

"Well, I've asked them to stop that."

I drive in silence for awhile, the radio playing softly. Orla taps her fingers on the leg of her jeans. I find myself wondering if they're special pregnancy jeans or if she just has them pulled down low. Then I'm thinking about her ass again and that's off limits. Shit.

I sigh. Thankfully, she asks a question I'm more than happy to talk about. "When did you become a bun dad? Is that the phrase they used at bingo?"

"Ha! Yes. I'm a bun dad. They want me to grow my hair long so I can be a man-bun-dad."

"They have a lot of opinions about what you should look like, Wally."

I wave a hand. "They're mostly teasing. Anyway, I found Pudding back in August. So it's just been a few months. But it's been...well he's really changed my life."

I pull into the driveway and Orla looks surprised to see we've arrived. My townhouse in Shadyside is nice. There's no euphemism to use about that. I live in a swanky place on an expensive street. My neighbors probably would blow all their botox if they saw all the rabbit stuff I've got inside these days. I put down carpet runners over the glossy hardwood floors so he won't slip and cleared off the bottom shelves of all my built-in book cases so he can perch in there if he feels like it. The great thing is I don't care what they think. It's so freeing, not caring about people's opinions and instead caring about being helpful and nice.

"Come on," I say, hurrying around the car to offer Orla a hand. I'm surprised that she lets me help her out of the car, but I guess it's harder to move around when she's got a protrusion like that. I unlock the door and pause. "We have to hurry inside the storm door so he doesn't get out."

"He's not in a pen?" Her blue eyes are wide, like we're about to enter a haunted house or something.

I shake my head. "No. Pudding roams all around my house. Like a cat. I mean, it's basically his house now."

I pull the door open and hear the click of Pudding's nails on the floor as he makes his way over to greet me. I sneak in behind Orla, trying not to shove her but needing to close the door quickly so he doesn't make a run for it. As a result, I have to squeeze up against her back and the smell of her fills my nostrils. She smells like coconut and something minty. My already-tight shorts become uncomfortable as I catch my breath, and I realize I should probably gate off the front entrance next time.

Stop it. There's not going to be a next time.

I flick on the overhead light and squat down to greet Pudding. Orla stands and stares. I see her take in the tunnel and the wooden castle I just recently got. Pudding also has a wooden doll bed near the couch. He lounges on it while I ice my knees and watch TV after work.

"Wow," she says, her voice trailing off. "You're really...you're very different from when we first met, Wally. Very different."

I don't say anything, but I drop my mail bag and walk into the kitchen, pulling two glasses from the cupboard and filling them with water from the filtered canister on my counter. I slide one glass across to her, since she followed me into the kitchen.

I can still smell her, and I'm not supposed to be lusting after her, so I just dive right into our agreed topic for when we set up this meeting.

"I told you I hated my dad. Hate my dad," I correct quickly, gulping down some water. She hoists herself onto one of the stools. "He...I didn't like myself before." I can't decide how much to lay on her. I mean, she offered to talk about dead parents, but I guess this is going outside the boundaries of that. She draws her brows together, looking concerned.

"Well," she says, spinning her glass on the counter. "You were kind of a douche."

I roll my eyes. "I know it. When he died, everything turned upside down." I wince. "Your business was probably impacted by his shady dealings. I'm really sorry about that."

"It's not that big a deal," she says, in a way that suggests it was actually a big deal.

"Well, again, I'm very sorry. It took weeks to deal with all the paperwork from everything. My mom is left with…I don't want to say she's left with nothing. There are people who actually have nothing. My mom is left with her house and her own trust fund from before she married my father. She has no idea how much money she had before or how much she has now." I shrug. "She's never really done too much on her own. I help her a lot."

"Don't you have a sister?" I couldn't remember telling Orla about my sister, but I guess she probably looked us up on the Internet. I would have, if my business got screwed.

I groan. "She's not a ton of help. Honestly, my parents really hurt her, too. She stopped coming around. But, like I said, I wasn't a great person before. I was…I was useless."

"You weren't *useless.*" Orla arches one brow, suggesting that she's referring to our night together. I swallow.

"I didn't even know how to use a can opener. It's pathetic. Now I'm pounding entire cases of tuna just because it's the fastest way to get protein in me." I chuckle. She seems confused. "I burn like 8,000 calories a day at work. I can barely get enough food into myself."

I refill my water glass and walk around the counter, crouching down to the floor, where Pudding is sniffing around, no doubt hoping I'll get him some food. "I've been…sort of resentful of how much my mom is relying on me after so many years of just relying on my father and his money."

I glance up, expecting Orla to look horrified as I'm spilling my guts here. But she's just studying me intently. I pet Pudding and he rests his chin on my foot until I sink all the way to the ground and he hops into my lap. "Pud was really, really sick when I found him. He relied on me completely. Like, for everything." I look up from stroking his fur and am surprised to see she's joined me, groaning a little as she lowers herself to the floor.

"But." I hesitate. I feel like I'm dumping everything on her. Just slicing open my veins to a woman my family has screwed over. To a woman who yelled at me to fuck her and then her vagina actually stabbed me in the dick. I sigh. "It's been really amazing to experience pure affection from him, with no strings attached." Pud nuzzles against my leg, eyes closed, blissed out as I pet him.

We're both quiet for a while until she says, "I feel like maybe it wasn't fair of me to offer myself as an expert for you, or whatever." She tosses her braids back over her shoulders. "I don't have any experience with that, with what you described." She bites her lip. "But I'm so sorry you never felt affection without strings, Wally."

I swallow and we're quiet again for a bit until Pudding pops off my lap and starts sniffing Orla. She groans a little and adjusts her posture. "Oh, shit," I say, hopping to my feet. "You should be on a couch or something. God, I'm an asshole."

Orla waves a hand. "It's fine. I can sit on the floor, Wally, relax." She reaches out a hand for Pudding, but he backs away from her and hides under the stool. "What am I doing wrong?" She looks up at me with her big blue eyes and the fact that she wants my rabbit to like her is doing things to me. Very uncomfortable things, especially since I'm still wearing the too-small work shorts I borrowed for tonight.

I cough and head for the fridge. "He just doesn't know you yet. I'll get you his favorite treat to give him." I grab a handful of basil and parsley from the bowl I keep in the fridge for his snacks. I start to worry that she's going to think I'm pathetic, turning my house into a rabbit haven and dedicating half the fridge to his special foods.

But Orla's face lights up and she holds out a hand. I give her the greens, and Pudding starts circling her, sniffing wildly. He stands up on his hind legs, wiggling his nose and his whiskers, and she laughs in delight. "You are so damn cute," she says, holding out her palm. Pud wastes no time snatching the entire bunch from her, shoving it into a heap with his paws as he starts trucking it in, chewing loudly.

"You're just the most adorable thing, aren't you," she says, stroking his fur as he eats. He looks up at her occasionally before diving his face back into the greens. I thought Orla was sexy as hell when I met her, but now as she coos and babbles to my pet rabbit, I can barely contain myself I want her so badly.

She sighs and leans back on one forearm. The other drops lazily to her belly, where she starts rubbing. I remember that even though she hasn't talked about the baby's father with me, she's not mine to want.

I clear my throat. "So, you know, am I totally doomed?"

"How so?" She arches a brow at me. I love that she can do that. Her hair is the same butterscotch color as Pudding's fur and I long to run my fingers through it.

I shrug. "How long would you say you were a huge mess after your mom died?"

She laughs bitterly. "Wally, I'll let you know if my mess ever gets cleaned up."

CHAPTER NINETEEN
ORLA
NOVEMBER

"I'd like to offer a special congratulations to Orla today for completing her required supervised hours as a baby engineer." Dad smiles at the head of the table in the conference room. Uncle Mick stops pacing at the back of the room to whoop as everyone else applauds politely. Normally I yell at my dad for putting me on the spot, but damn it, this has been a long time coming.

I smile as my colleagues celebrate. And then, of course, they immediately delve into the horror stories about the professional exams. "You have to prepare to prepare, Orla. I don't think I slept for six months," Liam says, talking about when he sat for his.

"Yeah, but you made color-coded flashcards," Cal jokes. He and Liam are such opposites. Cal is easygoing where Liam is more reserved, and their temperaments led both of them to some really exciting professional opportunities. Liam is working to take over from my dad one day, overseeing all the engineering projects, and Cal is leading a new program developing and engineering unmanned camera devices like pipe-crawling robots and drones.

I listen to them bicker about the exams, and smile. I don't bother to tell them I've already aced a bunch of practice exams. I know this puppy is a pair of eight-hour intense exams, but I can honestly say I feel ready. The next round of registrations is in December, and if I sign up for both parts in the winter, I could be totally done before this nugget arrives.

819

I pat my stomach, remembering my night with Wally the other week. I haven't reached out to him since he dropped me off at my car. I feel really conflicted about the whole thing. He was such a different person than the man who catalyzed this baby. He's an entirely different person from the jerk who talked down to me at the job site.

I wish I could say I understood how the loss of his dad would cause such a dramatic shift, but the truth is I still don't know which Wally was the mask and which is real.

I look up again to see Dad has moved on in the meeting agenda. We need to plan some farewell activities for our interns now that we've wrapped up the sinkhole situation. I volunteer to lead them on a tour of some of our other job sites, along with Dakota. We've got a few interesting things in the works from my perspective, even if Dad and Uncle Mick are more excited about their regional projects updating power lines in a few different states.

As it turns out, updating the lines and transistors is more of a mechanical and civil engineering project and I'm not really involved with all that.

After the meeting, Dakota and I round up the interns from their cubicles and we all squeeze into one of the company trucks to take a tour of Beltane's works in progress. Dakota turns around in the passenger seat to face the interns. "Do y'all know what happened for Orla with the conclusion of the sinkhole?"

"Oh, come on, Dakota. They don't need to hear about that." It's one thing for my colleagues, who are mostly related to me, to make a big deal about this. These kids are still in college and are supposed to be reporting to me. Dakota sets a bronze hand on my shoulder and grins.

"Orla finished up her supervised work. You know what happens after graduation? You have to work three years as a baby engineer, with someone supervising you. Then you sit for heinous exams and basically double your salary once you pass them."

One of the interns nods, and says, "Well that'll be good timing, what with the baby and all. Having more money."

I somehow hadn't considered this aspect of getting my license, but hearing Iris mention it so casually makes me feel like an idiot for not thinking of it.

"Well," I say. "Enough about me. Let's go look at some pipes and wires." I drive to the hockey arena quietly, considering. Beltane is doing a bunch of inspection work for the arena since they updated all their plumbing codes to include more all-gender restrooms.

"You would't necessarily think engineers would be involved in a bathroom remodel," Iris says, totally nonplussed that we're walking around a building where professional athlete superstars are practicing.

Dakota laughs. "Um, it's definitely a major engineering feat. This is a retrofit project, so we had to move walls and move around the things INSIDE the walls. Your girl here was doing math for hours on this." Dakota points her thumb at me.

I pat one of the walls. "Dakota is forgetting to emphasize the work she's been doing for her project management certification. Literally nothing happens at Beltane without Dakota giving us a road map of what to do and when."

The two of us spend the rest of the tour hyping each other up while the interns ask questions and look at some of our plans for the project. By the time we drop them back off, I'm feeling pretty accomplished.

"You doing anything special to celebrate finishing your hours?" Dakota gestures around the city, as if I have so many options to hit the club or something.

"I thought I'd go for a run before my Foof meeting," I tell her. "You really should come sometime."

Dakota ignores this suggestion. "You're still going on runs?"

"Yeah. My doctor said it's fine to as long as I'm not getting winded or having weird pains." I smile. "I was thinking of doing a 10k later this month when everyone else is doing a Thanksgiving half marathon."

She laughs. "I don't know where you all get the energy. Bunch of wiry, running fools."

I head into my office to change, pausing to smile at the sticky note my dad left on my office door: *I'm so proud of you.*

My family usually hits up wooded trails early in the morning to run before work. Dad especially needs the softer terrain for his "old man feet" as he calls them. The hills have gotten to be a bit much for me, though, so I tend to stick to the flat paved trail along the river.

I do two easy miles and grab my car to head to Bridges and Bitters to meet up with everyone, and halt in my tracks when I arrive in the back room. Sam and Nicole stand directing a group of staffers as they arrange power cords and... "Are those arm chairs?"

Sam turns at the sound of my voice. She claps her hands. "Oh yay! You're here! Gals, she's here!" I see more of my friends poke their heads up from an array of boxes. They all wave and make their way over to me.

Piper the personal trainer, Chloe the romance writer, Logan, Maddie... everyone. "What is all this?"

"Well," Sam takes a swig of her drink. "You mentioned you were hitting a career milestone and normally we'd celebrate that with too many martinis. But." She circles her hand in the direction of my stomach. "So Foof pregamed on the vodka and set up a little mini-spa experience instead. Take your shoes off. You're getting a foot rub."

Within minutes, I've got my leggings rolled up to my knees and my feet immersed in wonderful warm water. Esther passes out some amazing non-alcoholic drinks, and everyone carries on the meeting as if it were a regular Monday in the Bridges and Bitters event room.

"What made you think of this," I ask Sam, who has her head back and cucumber slices on her eyes as a nail tech paints her toenails flaming red.

Sam points at Emma Stag and Maddie, who are both blissed out as another pair of techs massages their calves. "Those two said foot rubs are the secret to surviving pregnancy. I'm actually thinking of replicating this at the office for my staff. Hey, Logan!" She shouts across the room to where Logan is sipping her drink through a straw, trying not to crack the mud mask on her face.

"Not now, boss. I'm finding my zen." I forgot that Logan is a spa-night aficionado.

Sam leans back toward me. "I'm sure she'll say yes to doing this at work. Oooh, we should do this for your baby shower, too."

"Baby shower?"

Nicole pipes up. "Yes, Orla. You have to have a baby shower. We're going to give you gifts for your little Brady nugget and in return, you will let us feed you good cake. Sam, we should definitely do this spa thing again for that."

The Foof women who have had children start sharing stories of their pregnancies and baby showers and I find myself feeling overwhelmed yet again. I'm much more comfortable here when we're talking about career strategy or financial planning. I feel like I have no context for talking about pregnancy and I've tried my hardest to avoid baby showers. I don't really have a ton of friends outside my family, so this avoidance was pretty easy until my cousins started *having* babies.

Esther stops by to check on my drink and asks if I'm nervous about the exam.

"Honestly? I'm not. Engineering is the easiest thing in my life right now.

It's all the adulting stuff that makes me squirm." I chug down a huge gulp of her latest refreshing concoction.

"I feel that," she says. "I'd much rather balance the books for my bar than navigate relationships with other humans."

Esther breezes back out of the room and I stare down at my legs as my assigned technician massages them. It feels so good I can't even hold back a groan. I think back on Esther's use of the word relationship and, for the millionth time, I ponder Wally.

Mailman, rabbit Wally is such a different person than suited, smarmy Wally. More like a person I'd want a relationship with. Just admitting that sets my heart racing. I don't do relationships. I've never had a romantic relationship. I do hookups and stick guys in the friend zone.

But then I had to go and re-meet Wally and listen to him bare his soul about his rabbit giving him the first affection of his whole life. All I can think about is growing his baby, who would probably love him unconditionally, and what kind of monster it makes me to keep that opportunity from both of them.

"What do you think?" The woman working on my feet startles me back to awareness of the room.

"Think?" And then I realize she's asking me to endorse her work on my toenails. She painted them a deep purple, and they look lovely, like a fancy woman's feet. "Oh," I say. "They're perfect." Lost to my own thoughts again, I decide I'll spend one more day with Wally to see if he turns back into a troll. "Then I'll tell him," I whisper.

CHAPTER TWENTY
WALT

Hey.

I STARE AT THE TEXT FROM ORLA SO LONG, I'M SURE IT'S COSTING ME TIME ON MY route. I haven't heard from her since the bingo night and now she's sent a vague, one-word greeting. I deliver the mail to five houses and take my phone out again and reply.

Hey!

I pondered the exclamation point for three of the houses. I hit up another dozen houses and my phone pings again. My heart races as I fish the phone out of my shirt pocket. I can't let myself get worked up over Orla Brady. I decide I need to ask her about her boyfriend. Husband? I need to find out so I can more easily stop myself from lusting after her.

I look at my phone.

I feel bad I didn't follow up after you told me about your dad. You doing ok? How's Pud?

Fuck. What do I do with that? She's asking how I'm doing AND she's asking about my rabbit. I send her a selfie I took this morning while Pud licked my banana peel. Then I check my camera app to see what he's up to.

Sleeping in a square of sunshine in the living room. "Nice to be you, Pudding."

And then my phone rings in my hand, startling me. Thinking it might be Orla, I answer right away, but I groan when I hear my mother's voice. "Trippy!" She wails. I switch the call to my ear buds so I can keep working.

"Hey, Mom. What's up?"

"Oh, Trippy, can't you come over and talk to me?"

I sigh, fishing for my keys to unlock the lobby door of an apartment building. "I told you, Mom. I'm working crazy hours. I also can't really talk while I'm at work because I have to concentrate." It's not entirely true once I'm out delivering. Much to Mark's chagrin, I've started getting things down to a science. I have all my mail sorted and rubber banded in neat bundles. I'm finding my groove and I kind of love it, even if they do stick me on entirely new routes every few weeks as people come in and out of various leaves of absence.

The last guy was out with a dog bite, and now I'm covering a lot of apartment buildings after Peggy got a stress fracture in her shin.

"Honestly, Trip, I'm distraught! Have I told you about Thanksgiving?"

"Yes. Several times." My sister is joining her sorority alumnae for their annual tropical pilgrimage. My mother was in the same sorority, but is not attending. It makes my mother sick to her stomach to say something as basic as "I can't afford the airfare" but she also doesn't want to admit that she doesn't want to fly alone. Or find lodging on the island since we had to sell my parents' timeshare.

"I just don't know what you expect me to *do* for the holiday. Do you really want me to be alone?"

"I told you, Mom. We can spend the day together. We can get takeout."

"Takeout!"

I double check that I hit all the mail boxes in the lobby of this apartment building before I make my way back out to the sidewalk. "I didn't say fast food and burgers, Mom. We can order out a nice meal."

"Can't you just check the portfolio again and see if I can swing a first-class flight and a nice villa on the beach?"

I'm not going to check anything again. I'm having to manage Mom's investments and Dad's life insurance pay outs, even knowing I won't get a cent of it. She has no idea how any of this works and despite still working 60-hour weeks with only one day off, I have to make time to meet with the probate lawyer and the investment firm.

I rub my temples. "Mom, I really can't talk right now. I told you, you could sell the house for something smaller and then you'd be able to do those sorts of trips."

"This type of talk is so...primitive, Trippy. You know I don't like it."

"Yes, Mother. I know you don't like anything." I roll open the door to the mail van to refill my bag for the next block. I decide to add a few extra stacks in there to try and make up the time I've lost.

"What a way to talk to your mother. I'm grieving and you're scolding me!"

I'm also grieving, I think. *You're scolding me, too, and you're the parent.*

But I don't say those things. People in my family don't say those things. Except to me, I guess. I sigh. "I have to go, Mom. We'll talk soon." And I hang up before she has the chance to say anything else. I can't handle her shitting on me right now.

I look down at the phone and see I got a message from Orla.

Cute bun! When are you off again? We should hang.

"Hang" with Orla-fucking-Brady. What would that include? Telling her more about my shitty family? Dragging her along to another rabbit event with my circle of bun-moms? Lusting after her so hard my balls ache, despite the fact that she's carrying another man's child? She's the one reaching out to me, though. Because we both have a dead parent, I remind myself. Not because she wants me to fuck her again. I wonder if her vagina would still stab me with a baby inside. I wonder if I'd still mind.

I must be a glutton for punishment. I type back.

Off tomorrow, actually. Coffee near you?

Yes, please! I actually haven't tried that place since I moved in. See you there at 9?

I take off my ball cap and run a hand through my sweaty hair. I don't know why I do these things to myself. I'm trading helping my mother understand her financial limitations for an opportunity to talk about cremation with a woman who makes me burn with lust.

I'll be there!

And then I finish the rest of my route in record time.

CHAPTER TWENTY-ONE
ORLA

Why am I nervous? I've already slept with him. I've hung out with him to talk about dead parents. I shouldn't be nervous to get coffee with a man whose family is a pack of assholes. I repeat this series of mantras as I walk the few blocks down to the coffee shop. The space near my dad's house has gone through a few different iterations since he bought the place.

A few owners ago, it was a gnome-themed coffee shop, which was super cute. Right now it's painted really dark, but I figure that matches my mood and personality. I don't see Wally, so I linger outside until he gets here. It's weird to go inside and get my own drink when I said we'd meet here, right? Or does waiting for him make it seem like a date?

Why is this hard? I'm about to go inside and order, when I spot him walking toward me in all his Ken-doll glory. His blond hair is tousled and damp, like he just recently got out of the shower, and he's wearing jeans. I had no idea Wally could look good in something other than a suit or a mailman outfit, but here he is looking fantastic in a t-shirt and jeans slung low on his hips.

Maddie was right. After the puking stops, pregnancy is basically just one giant battle with horniness. I can practically feel my pussy clenching around him as I watch him walk toward me. I reach up to make sure I'm not drooling.

"Hey," he says, smiling. Why couldn't he have opened with this genuine smile and greeting when we first met at the wedding? Probably because I would have dismissed him and never thought about him again.

"Hey," I say, nodding my head toward the door. "Ready for caffeine?"

I ask about his rabbit. He asks how I'm settling in to the neighborhood.

"So you said your dad lives across the street? That will be nice when the baby comes."

I nod. "That's the idea. I didn't love having to move, but it's working out. Plus the house has more space than my apartment." I feel like I'm justifying my living situation to myself as much as to Wally.

"Is that the house where you grew up?" He points up the hill toward where I live.

I shake my head. "Oh. No. Dad sold that house after Mom died. Too many memories there. His brother had just gotten divorced, so we moved in with Uncle Mick and his boys. That's whose wedding I met you at. One of Mick's son's." I laugh and take a sip of my coffee. "We all grew up together. One big, dysfunctional family."

Wally seems to ponder this. "It seems pretty functional to me. Helping each other out like that." He spins his coffee mug in a circle on the table. "I wish my mom would sell my parents' house, but I really don't want her to move in with me." He pauses. I nod, indicating I feel his dilemma.

And then we sit with nothing to say. I think about wee Wally, growing up in a family that withheld love and also casually fucked over the business community for their own gain. When he talks to me, really talks to me, one hundred per cent of the things he says are kind and empathetic. And I'm sitting here keeping secrets from him.

The dark walls feel a little like they're closing in on me and the smell of the coffee in here is suddenly overwhelming. I spring to my feet.

"Can we go? I can't be in here anymore." I start walking toward the door and Wally hurries to follow.

"Are you all right? Is it the baby?" He looks so concerned. "Should I call...your boyfriend?"

When I step outside I lean against the wall of the building, breathing deeply. "Boyfriend?" I arch a brow at him.

He makes a face and points at my stomach. "Yeah, you know...I guess I just thought...your baby-daddy? What term do you use?"

I laugh. "I don't have one of those," I say, and then I open my mouth to tell him that he's the baby-daddy. I wince. He's definitely not acting like a douche today. But he does look confused, especially when I say, "I'm doing this on my own. My choice."

He nods, and then leans against the wall next to me. "Huh. Well that's... I don't know what the right thing is to say. Good for you? High five? Down with men?"

"Ha! It's an adventure for sure." I take a swig of my drink. "It just got really hot in there. And the smell overwhelmed me all of a sudden. I'm sorry if I scared you."

Wally nods. We're quiet for a few minutes, and I say, "We're sort of exposed here on the sidewalk. Want to go to my place and talk about dead dads? You know, light conversation?"

Now it's his turn to laugh. "Lead the way, Orla-fucking-Brady."

I roll my eyes. "You don't have to keep calling me that."

"Ah," he says, "But you told me to. I wouldn't dream of disobeying a hellcat like you."

"Hellcat?"

He shrugs. "You're pretty fierce. And you've got claws." I wince.

"Is that a reference to my IUD stabbing your dick?"

"Yes," he says immediately. "Yes, it is."

I unlock my front door and plunk down on the couch, kicking off my shoes. Wally does the same, sitting as far away from me as possible on the sofa. I realize I'm disappointed that he's not moving closer, not making a move on me now that I told him there's no other man in the picture. I can smell his expensive shower gel from where I'm sitting, and all my thoughts are drowned out by lust for him. I decide I can take care of all this horny tension and make my own moves, and I start to crawl toward him, but he holds a hand out and makes a stuttering sound.

"Can I..." I freeze.

Is he asking to kiss me? Does he want this as much as I do right now? "Can you what?"

I watch his Adam's apple move in his throat as he swallows. "Can I feel...your belly? I thought I saw it move."

"Oh." Embarrassment tingles up my spine, spreading through my body. He wants to touch my stomach. Of course he does. He has no interest in making out with a pregnant woman who has, in the past, jabbed his penis painfully in a way that tore the condom. "Sure." I roll my shirt up and grab his hand, pressing his warm palm to my stomach. We sit in quiet together as his fingers rest upon my skin.

And then the baby gives a big kick and his face transforms with wonder. "Was that the baby?"

I laugh. "Yeah. I think that was a foot." He stares, transfixed.

"There's a person in there," he whispers. "An actual human being. Wow." We sit close together, him touching me, me inhaling his scent and trying not to jump his bones.

"What, uh...how big...what age baby is that?" He winces. "I don't even know how to ask about babies."

"It's okay," I say, adjusting my position and avoiding the question. I wind up sitting even closer to him and I can feel the heat radiating off his chest. He pulled his hand away while I was adjusting, but I reach for it and bring it back. We both stare at his hand on my skin. "I don't know anything about babies, either. I didn't even pick anything up from when Maddie had Arlan—wait. Do you even know Maddie and Liam?" He shakes his head. "Right. You were just at the wedding because your dad knew my dad and uncle."

Wally seems uncomfortable at my mention of his dad and of his prior life. "Anyway! Because I know nothing at all, my doctor recommended this app. Every week it tells me what the baby is up to in there."

"Really? They can tell all that?"

I shrug. "I guess they know generally what happens each week." I wriggle around and pull up my phone, glad that he doesn't retract his hand. He's stroking my stomach gently now, as if he's caressing the baby, and it feels amazing. "Look." I show him the screen, where together we read about how the baby is the size of an ear of corn and this week, it's growing nostrils.

"Practice breathing," he says. "Huh. I guess they really do start from scratch if they have to practice breathing." I just nod. We're sitting so close and he smells so good. Not like cologne or anything added on. Just soap and Wally. My nostrils are still super sensitive from pregnancy, so I'm being invaded by Wally smells.

I breathe in and out through my nose a few times, my own sort of practice breathing, and say, "I guess we should talk about our parents."

He makes a face. "It feels weird to do that right after we talked about your baby's new skills."

"I don't know," I say. "I try to think about my mom a lot when I think about the baby. My doctor pointed out to me that the egg that became this baby, was inside me when I was inside my mom. It's a small thing, but I really like it. I like that cellularly at least, she knows this baby."

"That is really nice," he says. I might be imagining things, or he might be drifting closer. I place my hand on top of his hand, preventing him from pulling it back. I realize we've never kissed. That night of Nicole's wedding, we didn't kiss at all. We just fucked. I never even saw him naked. I've also never thought this long or this much about kissing someone. Wally's a sure thing, right? Maybe not, now that I'm someone with baggage. I feel the baby move again.

"What was she like? Your mom?" He seems to be breathing heavy as he stretches out a hand to brush my hair back. His fingers skirt along my cheek, leaving trails of sparks along my skin.

"She was really kind," I tell him, licking my lips, trying not to stare at his. "She and my dad were crazy in love with each other. Mom studied psychology and Dad is an engineer, of course. He says she always knew what he was thinking and it worked since he wasn't ever good at communication."

"I have no idea what my parents saw in one another." A darkness passes over his face as he reveals this and I think again of this man craving affection. I feel guilty for how mean I was to him when we hooked up. And then I remember that I'm being cruel to him right now. Right this minute. *Tell him,* a small voice inside me whispers.

I open my mouth to reveal my lie of omission, but he leans in and presses his lips to mine. Wally's kiss is warmth and gentleness. He holds the back of my neck with his free hand, his thumb rubbing the space where my hair meets the skin. He groans softly into my mouth and I open for him, moaning when his tongue slips between my lips.

His mouth is yearning and oh, so sweet. I dig my fingers into his hair, feeling the blond waves beneath my fingers. I want to inhale him, jump into his lap. My blood surges, until he pulls back suddenly. "I'm so sorry," he says, raking his hands through his hair. "I shouldn't have done that."

"No," I say. "I mean yes. You should. I liked it." I lean in to pick up where we left off, but he places a hand on my chest.

"Orla, it's...I'm not okay. And you need someone...you need someone okay."

I want to scream at him that I'm a mess, actually, and I need someone to clean up life alongside me, not someone who has it all figured out to lord over me. I want to blurt that of course I need him because we're having a baby. But I don't say it.

"I, uh." Wally stands and reaches down for his shoes, moving to the arm chair to put them on his feet.

"You're leaving?"

He looks tortured. "I need to figure out Thanksgiving with my mom and it's a total shit show, to be honest."

I nod, collecting my dignity. "I remember the holidays right after Mom died. Everything's different." That's an understatement, but Wally knows that. I can see it in his face. I'm not sure what possesses me to say what I do next, instead of tell him the truth about my burgeoning belly. I begin with a deep breath, and blurt, "You should come eat with my family. Your dad knew my dad and uncle, anyway, so it's not like you're strangers. We're all eating at Nicole's because she has room for everyone. She's the one whose wedding you were at. There will be babies and yelling, and probably crying. Lots of distractions for you if you need to escape feeling depressed about the holidays."

Wally blinks a few times before saying, "That's really nice of you. Truly. Not many of my parents' friends have kept in touch after...everything." He puts on one shoe. "I wish I could say yes. I have my mom and all."

"Bring her!" My voice is high pitched now and I sound like someone on the verge of mania. "There will be corn pudding! Corn! Like the baby is an ear of corn. That's kind of weird how they do food comparisons, now that I think about it. And there's always whiskey at a Brady function."

Wally barks out a laugh as he ties his other shoe. "Mom only drinks gin."

"Perfect," I tell him, standing and wrapping my arms around him in a hug. Is this our first hug? Does he even want me to touch him? I sigh when he embraces me right back and rests his chin on top of my head. We stand there for a long time, until the baby kicks and he jumps back.

I swallow down my feelings and gather my composure. "So you'll come? To Thanksgiving?"

"Orla." He drags a hand through his hair and shakes his head. "Didn't my Dad fuck over your family? With work stuff?"

"Oh." I actually forgot about that, between the pregnancy and the sink hole project. "My Dad and uncle said that wasn't actually a big deal."I shrug. "I'll talk to them and you talk to your mom and you should join us." I feel myself babbling and worry that I sound desperate.

He nods his head just a little.

"Bring some gin," I tell him as he heads toward the door. "It'll be terrific."

CHAPTER TWENTY-TWO
WALT

"Mom, you look great. Really." She keeps fidgeting with her hair and her skirt, looking at herself in the mirror in my car over and over as I navigate over the 31st Street Bridge to go to Nicole Brady's house for Thanksgiving dinner. Mom is almost sick with nerves.

I can see that my mom is anxious about talking with strangers. She's anxious about her first holiday without her husband and how to be in public as Celeste Sheffield, rather than being out as Walton Sheffield's wife.

Me? I'm nervous because the last time I saw Orla I kissed her. I don't know what came over me. As soon as she mentioned that she doesn't have a boyfriend, that was all I could think about. Orla Brady is single. Orla Brady might not be off limits. And now I'm about to hang out with her entire extended family. Again.

This time, though, I don't have to bring my slimy Trip facade. I can be myself, and I'm getting better and better at doing that.

"Are you sure she said just to bring gin? I feel like we should bring more. It seems impolite."

"She said just bring gin, Mom. And I wouldn't dream of not following Orla's instructions to a tee. She probably won't yell at you, but she'll definitely slice me apart if she thinks I'm not listening to her."

Mom looks at me, confused. "And you like this woman?"

When I explained to my mother that we were having Thanksgiving dinner with the family whose wedding she skipped, I assumed that would be enough of a guilt trip to get her to say yes without pressing. But she had an endless stream of questions until I revealed to her that I'd like to get to know Orla better.

"Yes," I tell her, nodding as I put on my turn signal to parallel park near Nicole's place. "I like her very much. She's smart and honest. And beautiful." I walk around and open my mother's car door, leaning behind her to grab the bottle of gin from the floor of the back seat.

She hesitates and I tug her hand, pulling her toward the house a bit like a reluctant toddler. I'm not used to this side of my mother. Honestly, I'm used to her over-medicating herself when she feels strong feelings. The sight of her so vulnerable is difficult to take in. Her anxiety is contagious, but I feel almost immediate relief when I knock on the door and Orla's dad answers.

"Ah, Walt! We're glad you could make it." His smile is warm and inviting and he shakes my hand, gesturing inside with his other. "Come on in out of the cold. But I guess you're used to the cold in your line of work?"

"I'm getting there!" We both step inside and I put an arm around Mom's back. "Kellen, this is my mother, Celeste."

"We're so grateful you welcomed us to your meal," Mom says quietly, tugging her coat lapels.

Kellen's smile softens and he places a hand on her shoulder. "I know what it's like to lose a spouse, Celeste. I'm glad we could be here for you today. Please make yourselves at home."

He heads back toward the kitchen, where a dull roar creeps out along with the savory smell of traditional Thanksgiving foods. My mouth waters as I help my mom out of her coat. I usher her down the hall, past a beautiful wooden table, and into the vast kitchen and living room where Orla's family is...everywhere.

I immediately relax when I recognize the couple from the wedding running around with a toddler. A pair of dark-haired men who both resemble Kellen are smacking each other's hands away from a platter of cheese and crackers. Mom's eyes go wide as she takes in two women dancing along with Kidz Bop on the television.

And then I see Orla. She has her hair braided in a regal crown again and she's smiling as she talks to her uncle, who gestures enthusiastically. They both break out in laughter and I could watch and listen to her this way for hours, admiring the look of her in a royal blue turtleneck and dark jeans. The small bulge of her belly isn't even noticeable from the back, and only when Orla turns to the side can I see the baby I felt moving the other day.

She sees us standing near the counter and makes her way over. "You came!" Her expression is both surprised and happy and I relax even more. Seeing her intoxicates me.

"Yep, and I brought gin as instructed." I hand her the bottle and she laughs. Mom looks like she is trying not to explode, and I realize I neglected to mention that Orla is pregnant.

Orla sticks her hand out toward my mother. "I'm Orla Brady. You must be Celeste." Mom seems unprepared for Orla's firm handshake. Or maybe she's still reeling that the woman I'm interested in is about to have a child. It takes her a few beats before she remembers her hammered-in manners.

"Thank you for including Trip and me in your plans for today, Orla. That was so kind."

"Well, it's our pleasure to have you." I realize that Orla, too, has a persona she puts on for people. I can sense that she'd rather be learning a line dance with the others than making small talk over here. "Oh, you know my Uncle Mick, right?" She grabs the man's arm as he walks past en route to the bar setup. "Mick, this is Celeste Sheffield. And Wally."

"Walt," I say, shaking his hand. Mom looks perplexed. I don't know that she actually remembered my name isn't Trip.

Mick nods at me. Then he turns to Mom. "I knew your husband a long time. Heck of a thing for you all to go through." I notice that he doesn't say my father was a good guy, or indicate that he's sorry for our loss. I admire the artful way he sidesteps those sentiments while still finding something nice to say to my mother.

"You were at the funeral," she says in a whisper. And that shocks me, because I thought Mom was stoned off her gourd for the entire event. Mom refused to come out of her room or contribute any information to the obituary. I had to plan the entire service and deal with all my relatives asking super uncomfortable questions.

Mick nods and reaches to pour himself a whiskey. "Felt like the right thing to do," he says. Orla sets the bottle of gin alongside the array of whiskey. Her uncle grins. "Can I fix you two a drink?"

Mom places a hand on her chest and fluffs her hair with the other. "Gin and tonic would be lovely, Mick. Thank you."

CHAPTER TWENTY-THREE
ORLA

I can't get over how good Wally looks. His flat front slacks and shiny brown shoes are so classy. I expected his mother to show up dressed like Jackie Kennedy, but I am stunned by Wally's good looks every time I see him. I love watching him take care of his mother, even though I know he says he resents how very much he's having to do for her lately.

I'm shaken out of staring at him by Nicole, who hip checks me. "Hey!" She and Logan sidle up to me to grab fresh drinks. Nicole looks at Wally, considering. "I recognize you. Why is that?"

He clears his throat. "I was at your wedding," he says nervously. "My mother wasn't feeling well that day and I came with my dad..." He drifts off as Nicole reaches past him to pour herself a drink.

"And now you're Orla's hot mailman?"

His mom looks mortified. Wally clears his throat again as Celeste excuses herself to use the powder room. "I'm a mail carrier, yes. And I will be in Orla and Kellen's neighborhood for the next while, yes."

I frown. "What happened to Peggy this time?"

He shrugs. "Stress fracture. It happens a lot. They really have us working a lot of hours, and we're starting to get a ton of holiday packages..." Throughout all of this, I notice Logan furrowing her brow. She leans in to whisper something to Nicole. Wally trails off as Nicole screws up her face and tilts her head to the side.

"So, you're dick-stab Wally from my wedding AND you're a hot mailman?"

I turn beet red and Wally nearly falls over.

Logan shrugs. "I saw you leaving with him when Callum and I went to raid the cookie table."

Nicole's mouth forms an O. "You left to bang him in the middle of my wedding? And you stabbed him right in the dick and then...came back to eat cake?"

He whips his head toward me. "You told people?"

I bite my lip. "It was concerning!"

Nicole cackles. "Her pussy bites. It's so perfect. Better watch out for your willy, Wally." Nicole takes a sip of her whiskey. "Man, I am hilarious today." She wanders off toward the kitchen to check on things. Wally leans closer to me, his breath hot near my ear.

"You told your friends we slept together?" I can only nod, my pulse racing as I inhale the close scent of him, feel the heat from his tall, firm body. He grins a wicked smile. "Did you tell them you could feel my cock in your rib cage and that it felt amazing?"

My eyes widen and my jaw drops at his filthy reminders of that night together. I'm drenched with arousal. Wally has thrown down. He wants to be the beautifully tortured guy who rescues animals *and* he wants me to remember how he took charge of my body until it splintered into bliss. "Did you tell them that, Orla?" He stays in my space and sips his drink slowly, appreciatively, like my dad says a man should. Wally licks his lips and his eyes are wicked enough that I start mentally cataloguing the spaces in Nicole and Zack's house where I might drag him.

"Dinner's ready!" My dad beams as he hoists the golden turkey into the air and carries it to the end of Nicole's counter, and it breaks the spell Wally just put on me. Elizabeth follows close behind with the gravy boat and cranberry sauce. "Let's review how this is going to go," Dad says, picking up the carving knife and using it to point at people.

My cousins immediately start shouting out their favorite cuts of meat and their partners swat at them. I see Uncle Mick lean close and whisper something that makes Wally's mom blush. Dad clangs his knife against the carving fork. "Listen up! We've got guests. I'm going to review the rules. Arlan eats first. The rest of you will form a line. No cutting. No asking your girlfriend to trade places with you. No throwing rolls. And for God's sake, do not splash cranberry sauce on Liam's shirt just to irritate him." This last dig is pointed directly at Cal.

"I am insulted," he jokes. "What will our guests think?"

Dad laughs and starts carving the bird while Liam walks Arlan along the buffet. My little nephew turns his nose at every single choice as Maddie laughs from across the room. Uncle Mick ushers Celeste to the end of the counter so she can get her meal first, and I don't miss the wolfish grin he gives her. I can't tell if he's trying to get in her pants or just wants a good shot at grabbing the wishbone.

Eventually everyone jockeys for space, fills up their plate, and crowds around the table. Zack built a few more leaves for the table so it actually accommodates all 14 of us. I notice how Cal swats Zack when he tries to sit next to me and I swallow down a lump when Wally slides into the vacated seat. He puts his hand on my thigh and leans close. "Your family is great. I'm really glad you invited me." I smile and tuck a fallen strand of hair behind my ear. Wally leans in closer. "I'd like to thank you later if you're interested."

And then he sits back in his chair, forking a huge bite of meat into his mouth. He's somehow managing to chew sexily at me. I sit there, wide eyed, not eating, staring at him. I stare and he sexy-chews until Cal's voice rings above the general din.

"So, Walt, what's the wildest thing about being a mailman? The guy who delivers to the office at Beltane said he got chased by a snake once."

Wally dabs at his mouth with his napkin and nods. "Yeah, I've been chased by a lot of different animals." My family all shuts up and leans forward, like this is the most fascinating thing they've ever heard. "But that's not the wildest thing."

"Well, don't keep us hanging, man." Zack rubs his palms together like he's about to hear fantastic gossip.

"Honestly?" Wally looks at his mother, whose face is twisted like she wants to be interested but can't bring herself to show it. He continues. "Senior citizens are the wildest thing. I have one lady who waits for me every day because she needs me to open her bottle of iced tea. Every day. We had to do a training because for a lot of seniors, the mail carrier is the only person who comes to their house with any regularity. A lot of times, it's the mailman who calls 911 if someone has a fall or worse."

There's resounding silence around the table. Nobody was expecting that, least of all me. I stare at Wally, this man who contains so many multitudes. This gorgeous man who now rescues bunnies and opens jars for old ladies.

Wally nods. "So yeah. That's the wildest thing." His mom starts to cry and Wally jumps up.

She waves her hands and dabs at her face with her napkin. "I'm so sorry," she says. "I just...I'm alone now. And when you said that I realized the mailman is the usually the only person I see now."

Celeste stands abruptly and runs toward the powder room. Wally moves to go after her, but Uncle Mick stands up. "Let me talk to her, son. I know what it's like to be alone."

The table is silent, a first for a Brady gathering. Even Arlan looks around from his high chair, studying the adults. Eventually he slams his juice cup on his high chair tray and Maddie leans in to shush him.

Wally taps his fingers on the table and looks around, seeming uncomfortable, until his mother emerges from the powder room with Uncle Mick at her side. "Hey, folks," he says. "I'm going to drive Celeste home. Save me some pie, huh?"

Wally stands. "Mom, I'll take you home. But are you sure? You barely ate."

She waves a hand. "You're having a nice time. Stay with your friends. Michael has business up near the house anyway."

I'm one thousand per cent sure that's a lie, but Uncle Mick gives us a salute and helps Wally's mom into her coat. They walk out the front door and Nicole crosses her arms over her chest. "Well that was fucking weird," she says. Maddie clamps her hands over Arlan's ears but Nicole flips her the bird. "What? It's weird. I for one plan to grill Mick about it later. Wally, you better find a funny mailman story this time to lighten the mood."

Zack pats her on the shoulder, and Wally grins, telling us about delivering a box of sex toys that started vibrating in his mail bag.

"Ha!" Nicole gestures at Zack with her fork. "Remember when you had to sign for delivery for my purple lady rocket?"

Liam and Cal and Dad all groan and start protesting loudly, but the mood has shifted back to normal and I'm able to sit back and watch as Wally joins into the chaos. I realize I like having him here, laughing with my cousins and telling raunchy stories. I like everything about Wally. And that scares me more than the feel of his child wriggling in my stomach. I have to tell him. I should have told him when he was at my house, but it didn't feel right when he started talking about his family's holiday plans.

Tonight, I decide. I'm telling him tonight. Settling on that plan of action, I'm finally able to eat my meal.

CHAPTER TWENTY-FOUR
WALT

I feel a little guilty that Mom left in the middle of dinner with Orla's uncle, but the truth is that once they were gone, my mood lightened. I was already feeling pretty good being here. Then to find out Orla was talking about me to her friends? It's like the final string dropped off the net holding me back from pursuing her.

I eat pumpkin pie with whipped cream, trying to think of the most tactful way to get her out of here, when Orla's dad and his girlfriend make faces at each other like they're plotting a coup. "You know," Elizabeth says in an unnaturally loud voice. "It would be so nice to take Jake to that new action movie that's out right now."

Her teenaged son looks up from his phone, perplexed. "Action movie? That's very vague language. There are several franchises with new releases."

Kellen nods, conspiratorially. "It would be fun to go to the movies," he says. And then he slaps his thigh dramatically. "Shoot, we rode here with Orla. I don't want to exclude you, pumpkin, but pregnant women usually don't like sitting through long movies."

Orla furrows her brow and looks quizzically at her parental figures. Elizabeth gestures across the table at me. "What if Walt gave her a ride? Walt, it's not too far out of your way to take Orla home, is it? Especially since Mick took your mother?"

I grin, catching on to their ploy to get us alone together. Her family is making things easy on me, and I love it. I love it even more because I can tell that Orla is irritated by their interference. She looks torn between wanting to yell at them and wanting to rush out the door.

I rub her thigh with my pinky finger and she whips her head toward me. "It would be my pleasure to give Orla a ride," I say. "I haven't even had any alcohol for hours."

Nicole coughs out a phrase that could either be "bullshit" or "Boy Scout." I dance my hand closer to Orla's leg. "Whenever you're ready to go, Orla."

Cal and Logan leap to their feet and start clearing away Orla's plate. She swats at them. "What the hell are you doing? Who takes pie from a pregnant woman? Give me that!"

Maddie appears with a plastic container and a huge grin. "I bought an entire extra pumpkin pie for you because I know it's your favorite and you eat it for breakfast," she says. "We think you should leave now. With Walt. Alone. Together."

"You are all a bunch of meddlers," Orla mutters when Zack thrusts her coat at her. One of the buttons snags on her crown of braids and I reach to unstick it. Her hair, all bound up, is cool to the touch and silky smooth. I decide I can't wait to unravel it, wrap it around my fist, press my face into it.

"It was great to meet you, Wall-Ball," Cal says, offering me a high five as the Brady clan ushers Orla to the door.

"Don't mind him," Logan says. "He gives everyone nicknames." I smile at it, loving how much better it suits me than "Trip." I hate how families like mine keep recycling the same name for generations and then sticking the third unfortunate namesake with something like that. It's a synonym for falling down, for fuck's sake. No wonder I've always felt set up to fail.

"Thank you all again for having me," I say, before they slam the door in my face.

Orla sighs. "They're not subtle," she says.

I shrug and open the car door for her. "I told you I wanted to thank you later," I tell her. "It's later."

She struggles to get the seatbelt around her stomach, which I've noticed seems a lot larger each time I see her. "A ride home doesn't feel like much of a favor," she mutters. "Not when they set it up this way."

I drape an arm around the back of Orla's car seat as I back up to get out of the parking space. Before I shift into drive I look toward her in the moonlight. "What did you have in mind?" I intend for her to read a sexual innuendo in my voice, and I can tell she receives it. I see her cheeks turn pink in the dim light, her eyes sparkling at me.

She takes a few deep breaths and swallows before saying, "I want your cock again, Wally. So bad."

I drive like I'm being chased, screeching around corners with my hand clenched on Orla's leg. She periodically turns to look at me and licks her lips and my hard-on throbs inside my pants uncomfortably. I screech to a halt in her driveway and race out of the car as Orla fiddles with her keys.

We barely get inside the front door before I back her up against it, fusing my mouth to hers. She makes a small, desperate sound and I swallow it as I work to get her out of her coat while shrugging out of my own.

Our frenzied kiss is interrupted by fumbling limbs as we both work at each other's buttons. I feel the firm sphere of her belly pressed against me and I groan when she slithers out of her jeans and turtleneck. Her nipples jut out like marbles, erect through the material of her bra. I drop to my knees and suck one into my mouth as I thumb the other, and I feel my cock weeping pre-cum when Orla starts moaning in pleasure.

"Fuck, Wally, that feels so god-damned good." She arches her back to bring her nipples closer to my mouth and she reaches behind her back to shed her bra. Pulling my hands from her nipples, I yank down her panties and gasp when I see her fully nude at last.

"Christ, you're gorgeous," I mutter, sinking back onto my heels to stare at her in the dim hall light she must have left on for herself. Her skin is creamy peach in color, and her belly is ringed by silvery marks where her skin stretched to accommodate that life within her.

I reach out to stroke the marks, and then dot kisses along them, feeling how the skin there is different from the more supple skin of her thighs, and the puckered pink around her nipples. "Wally, I'm so horny all the time," she whimpers. "I feel like I'm going to come just from what you're doing to my boobs."

I bite one of her nipples gently and keep it in between my teeth as I mutter, "That's just fine if you do, Orla." Alternating sides, I suck each breast into my mouth long and hard, and I let my hand travel lower, to the apex of her thighs.

When I reach between her legs, parting her open, Orla gasps and starts sliding to the ground. I toss her coat on the tile and maneuver her so she's at least lying on the wool before she grabs my ears and presses my face to her pussy.

I almost forgot what this tasted like. Almost, but not quite. The aroma of her, salty and fresh, washes over me as I rub and lick and suck at Orla while she screams and pulls my hair. It's rough and messy and frantic. Her knees jerk and she starts coming. Deep sounds roll from her throat as I feel her spasm around my fingers.

I have to reach between my legs and unfasten my pants, just to give my dick some relief from the pressure of being so hard. There's so much blood rushing to my crotch, I'm afraid my cock might explode.

Orla squirms on the ground, flailing her arms and moaning my name. She calls me "Walt" for the first time—not Wally—like she finally takes me seriously, and the sound of it does something primal to me. I feel savagely aroused and I climb up her body, feeling those hard nipples against my chest as I kiss my way back up to her mouth.

"Take off your fucking pants, sir," she says between kisses. She bites my lower lip, a move that almost made me come prematurely last time we were together like this. Orla reaches for my fly and yanks my throbbing dick out of my pants.

"Oh, god, yes, please," I groan as she starts to stroke me. She has a firm, confident grip and starts tracing a thumb around the head until I drop my forehead onto hers, unable to concentrate on anything else.

"I need you to fuck me, Walt," she breathes. "I need it."

"Okay," I pant, and roll off her, kicking out of my pants and reaching for my wallet. Orla makes her way up to her hands and knees and wags her ass toward me, making me lose my concentration again so I drop my pants back to the floor.

"We have to do it this way," she says. "I can't lie on my back."

Her braids have come undone and strands of blond hair drape over her shoulders as she moans in front of me on all fours. I stop what I'm doing to wrap one hand in those silken waves, kissing her shoulders and rubbing my palm over the rest of her. I squeeze her ass and slide a thumb back in between her legs to where she's still soaking wet from my mouth and her own orgasm.

"Please, Walt," she breathes. "Please, now." She bucks her hips back toward me and I pull away, looking again for my wallet. "Walt, what are you doing? Come on!"

"Easy now," I tease. "Just looking for a condom."

"I haven't been with anyone since you," she says, crawling back toward me again, crowding me. "And it's not like you could get me pregnant again."

"Ha, true." I abandon the wallet and kiss her lower back, palming her ass. It's such a fantastic, round ass. I could kneel here all night just studying it. "I haven't been with anyone else, either, and I had a physical before I started my job..."

"Great. Cock. Pussy. Now." She arches again and I tug on her hair, positioning her so I can line myself up at her entrance.

But then something occurs to me. Something that should have been obvious to me for weeks, something that's maybe been simmering just below my consciousness since Orla told me she doesn't have a partner.

I swallow and place my palm on her back. "Hey, sorry. Um. What do you mean pregnant *again?*"

Orla sinks down to her forearms and rests her cheek on the floor. "Fuck," she yells. "Fuck!"

I lean back against the wall, my hard-on quickly deflating. "Orla. You have to tell me what's going on here." She shakes her head and groans and rolls onto her side with a forearm draped over her eyes. "Orla. Is that my baby?"

CHAPTER TWENTY-FIVE
ORLA

WALT STARES AT ME AS I TRY TO COVER MY NAKEDNESS. I DON'T SAY ANYTHING, AND eventually he helps me get my shirt up and over my head. Then I sit up and try to wrap my arms around my knees, but I can't reach, so I just sprawl out on the floor inside my front door.

"You are the baby's father," I whisper. The muscles in his face shift and twist as he tries to figure out what to say next. I watch as he cycles through a number of emotions all at once.

I take a deep breath and say, "When I found out I was pregnant, it was right after the incident at the keto bakery. The news had just surfaced that your family had swindled dozens of Pittsburgh business owners. And you were such a douchebag."

I groan as I start to get a cramp in my lower back and I start to roll to hands and knees so I can stand up. It's a whole process these days and before I can get fully erect, Wally is there helping to lift me at the elbow. It's such a fucking contradiction. "I don't know what to do about you," I tell him. "It's like there's Wally before and...Walt now. You went from some smarmy prick I didn't want anything to do with ever again to being a guy who helps old ladies walk down the stairs and rescues dying animals."

"Were you ever going to tell me? Ever?" I waddle across the room and sink into the sofa with my legs splayed open. And then I remember that I'm not wearing any underwear and I'm flashing my crotch at him. I sigh again

845

and tuck my legs under me, grabbing a throw blanket and letting my head fall back against the wall. It's good that it's mostly dark in here. I can't bear to look at his face right now.

"I looked for you a few times, right after I found out. All we could find was information about your family's lawyer, and the office was pretty clear that a lot of fucking people were trying to find Walton Sheffield. They didn't know I wasn't calling you about money."

Walt barks out a pained laugh and settles into the other end of the sofa, letting his own head flop back against the wall. "This is unbelievable," he mutters. And then says it a few more times. I stay silent, resting my hands on my stomach, then feeling like shit because my stomach is a secret I kept from him, on purpose, for months now. Finally, he pulls his head up and leans toward me. "When I saw you again this fall...you didn't say anything. We kissed. I told you about my dead father. You didn't fucking say anything about us creating a life together, Orla!"

"How was I supposed to know which Wally was real? Maybe I didn't want the stinking Sheffield family getting their dirty hands and shitty morals on my kid! This is *my* baby, Walton. Mine!"

He springs to his feet. I'm not sure when he fastened his pants and tucked his dick back inside, but as he stands there in the dim light, with no shirt, towering over me, he looks like Thor, glowing and fierce with his blond hair glinting in the low light. He raises a hand and clenches it into a fist and roars. I want to hug him. I want to hit him. I want to fuck him, but I'm sure I lost my chance at that.

"Well apparently it's *my* baby, too, Orla. I have a right to be in my child's life, god damn it! You can't keep me from being a father."

He spins on his heel and stoops to grab his shirt and coat from the ground and opens the front door. I spring to my feet. "Walt, wait. Don't leave like this."

"I'm going home to feed my fucking rabbit and calm down. Do not call me." He looks over his shoulder on the steps. "When I'm ready to talk to you, I'll find you."

He backs out of the driveway and squeals off into the night.

I sink to my knees in the doorway and sob. I cry harder than when I thought about becoming a mother with no mother. I cry from shame and regret, because he's right. I should have told him weeks ago. I knew at bingo night that Walt is a transformed person. He's right that he deserves to be in his child's life. And he's right that I'm horrible for keeping that from him.

I fumble around in the dark for my phone and try to text the Foof group chat, but my fingers are slippery with my tears and I accidentally start a group video call. Nicole and Sam and Esther answer first, and Nicole squints into the camera.

"Didn't you just leave my house with the sexy mailman? Girl, *why* are you not naked right now?"

"What's this about a sexy mailman?" Esther is in sweats in her living room. Her bar is only closed a few days of the year and I feel bad bothering her on one of her rare evenings at home.

I wipe my nose on the back of my hand and blurt out, "I did something really shitty and I'm a horrible person."

Maddie has joined the call. "Oh, sweetie, did your vagina stab his penis again?"

Sam's face brightens into a grin. "Oh, the mailman is the dick stab guy? Hey, whatever happened with that? Did the doc say your IUD was fucked? I guess it's moot anyway now that you're preggo."

There's a pause for a minute while I continue to sniffle and the other women seem to be considering. Esther finally stands up with her phone and I watch as she moves through her house to her kitchen. "Wait. Nicole got married in June, the night your IUD stabbed a man in the penis. And you're six months pregnant."

"Ho-lee shit." Nicole starts smacking at Zack next to her on their sofa. "Wally with the willy is your baby-daddy?"

Maddie nods. "And you didn't tell him. But today he did some math?"

I just start sobbing again.

Sam sighs. "Oh, honey. Do not move. I'm coming over."

"Me, too," Esther says, snapping off lights and grabbing her keys from a hook.

"No, guys, it's a holiday. I can't keep you from your family."

"Um, hello? You're in my family." Nicole keeps the video on as she stoops to kiss Zack, who has fallen asleep on the couch. "I'm going to Orla's. Don't wait up." He just grunts.

"I feel bad," Maddie says. "I can't come. I have to lay here with Arlan or he'll wake up..."

"We've got this, Mad-dog," Esther says. "How about you fill in Piper and Chloe."

Before I can interject, my friends have ended the video portion of the call and are texting logistics back and forth, instructing me not to move because we're going to have a giant slumber party.

I've never actually had a slumber party before, and I try not to let myself feel excited about it because I'm supposed to be wallowing in shame right now. Before I can settle on an emotion, the doorbell rings and Esther bursts in the door with an arm full of chips.

CHAPTER TWENTY-SIX
WALT

I don't even remember the drive from Orla's house to mine. I think my body drove on instinct. By the time I unlock the door and get Pudding his heart pills, I notice my hands are shaking. It occurs to me that this is the sort of situation where a person would call a parent or a best friend for advice.

I don't even know how to name the feelings that are choking me right now. I certainly can't burden my mother with this information and the "friends" I had before were all the sons of my father's friends from the country club.

I play fetch with Pudding for a bit, trying to slow my heart rate, but my head isn't in the game and he can tell. He hops over and rubs his chin all over my feet, and ordinarily that would lighten my mood. But not today.

I try to go to bed, but my interactions with Orla just cycle through my mind as I toss and turn. I remember seeing her in early October, and just assuming she was having a baby with someone else.

I remember mentioning a partner and her telling me she was going it alone. I just assumed then that she got pregnant from a similar situation to ours. I don't know why I didn't pause to wonder if the baby was mine. Maybe I did wonder, but I was so overcome with learning not to feel useless that I couldn't allow myself to go there.

I spend a few more hours wondering if I'm the asshole before I decide to give up on sleep. I pull on my cold-weather postal gear and drive in to the mail depot. It's Black Friday, which means the start of a brutal month. I shouldn't voluntarily offer more hours, but what the hell else am I supposed to do with myself.

Might as well put some of my frantic energy to good use. By the time I clock in, Mark is already directing traffic as the conveyor belts are cranking packages to various bins. I nod at him, he nods at me, and I fall into pace alongside everyone else. Some of the guys are joking around, but most people look bleary-eyed or hungover. I briefly wonder how many of them have fathered babies they weren't aware of, but I can't dwell on that drama or I'll collapse.

For hours, I sort packages and load trucks and once the sun is up, I head out with Mark for the first route of the day. We don't talk, which is fine. He sits in the drivers seat and double parks in front of each house as I scurry to and from the porches with the packages. We go about this for a few more hours before I realize that Mark hasn't criticized me once today.

The fact that I'm obviously doing things well enough to meet his approval sends me right over the sleepless, emotional edge. Halfway back down a set of icy wooden steps, on a steep street, I lose my concentration and slip. I land on my ass on the steps and instead of getting up, I just lean forward and put my head in my hands.

Some time later, I feel a hand on my shoulder and notice a growling, moaning noise. And then I realize I am making the noise, and I stop. I look up at Mark, whose gloved hand is extended with a disposable cup of steaming coffee.

I eye it warily, but he sits down on the step next to me. "The wife made it," he says. "I've got a whole thermos of it. This ain't gas station coffee."

I nod and take it from him. I don't drink coffee black, but I also don't usually sit down at work and practically cry, either. The first bitter sip slithers down my throat as Mark sighs. "I know you didn't hurt your ass on that fall. And I know that's not a face someone makes about this job."

I shake my head and take another sip. By the third sip, I've gotten used to the bitterness of the coffee and can drink it without wincing.

Mark swats at my shoulder. "You gonna tell me what's eating at you so we can get back to work? We're eating daylight here, Sheffield."

I take another swig of the coffee and then look at him. "I got someone pregnant."

Mark scowls. "Well that's not so bad. I've done that myself. It works out okay."

I shake my head. "It happened months ago. She didn't say anything. She just...wasn't ever going to tell me."

"Hm," he says, pouring himself a cup of coffee and smacking his lips as he drinks it. "Why'd she tell you now then? She looking for a check?"

"I don't think so. I don't think she meant to tell me at all. She..." It's one thing to think terrible thoughts about myself for years and listen to my parents spew mean things about me. It's another to say them out loud to a coworker I look up to. "My family did some pretty awful things. Stole money from people." Mark's eyes widen. "She thought I was involved." I crush the empty cup in my fist. "She didn't want anyone like that involved in the kid's life."

Mark scratches his chin with the back of his glove and stands up, pacing on the sidewalk. "Your family stole money from her family?"

I nod. "I mean, my father's business stole from her family's business. Not personal theft. Not that it makes much difference. But I wasn't involved. I swear."

He offers a hand and pulls me to my feet. "Sounds to me like she did what she thought she had to do."

"Yeah, but now I have a child. Well, almost. I want to be involved. I can't just let my kid grow up with no father. Or...it's *my* kid. Even if I have no idea how to be a father at all."

I realize I'm rambling now, pacing up and down and banging on the side of the mail van for emphasis. I also realize Mark must have pulled over and parked when I didn't get up from my fall. I look at Mark and feel something break inside, whatever was holding all my emotions in a tidy column before now. "I cannot abandon my child. Not physically, not emotionally, not financially. I have a responsibility here."

He nods and puts the thermos inside the van before setting both his hands on my shoulders to look me in the eye at arm's length. "Here's what we're gonna do. We're going to deliver the rest of this shit and then you're going to go home and get some rest, because you look like you haven't slept in a few days. Then you're gonna go find your baby-mama and tell her what you just told me."

"I don't think I can do that."

He scoffs. "Man, you put your dick inside her. You can talk to her about the child you created. Being a father is about showing up. So you go over there and you show up. But first you show up here at work, because I ain't finishing this route alone."

He shoves me toward the passenger seat of the van and I climb inside. Mark floors the gas pedal before I can respond and we dive back into our silent rhythm, working together in the cold.

CHAPTER TWENTY-SEVEN
ORLA

MY ENTIRE HOUSE IS COVERED IN BLANKETS AND PILLOWS AND SLEEPING WOMEN. I wake up in my bed alone with all my pregnancy pillows, and there are women on the floor of my bedroom, plus a few on the floor in the living room and Nicole spread eagle on the couch.

In the bathroom mirror, I notice that my eyes are puffy from crying. When Foof got to my house, I just let it all rip to them, how I've been keeping the baby's father a secret not only from them and my family, but from him as well.

They pretty much just let me cry until I fell asleep.

I tiptoe to the coffee maker and get a full pot going just as Sam and Logan emerge and stagger toward the kitchen. Logan squeezes my arm and says, "It was my turn to bring the feel-better-brunch."

I furrow my brow at her. "What do you mean?" She laughs and reminds me that Foof swarmed her apartment when she was going through a rough patch with Cal. Logan leans into my fridge and miraculously procures two giant boxes of mini quiche while Sam flings open a pastry box on the counter.

"Where the hell did you guys get all this on Thanksgiving?" My mouth waters as Sam hands me a croissant.

She winks at me and says, "I know people. Now sit and tell us where your head is."

Nicole comes into the room just as the coffeemaker beeps that it's ready. Soon, we're all gathered around my table apart from Esther, who kissed the top of my head and said she had to go get ready for Black Friday drinkers.

I look at the clock and realize it's nearly noon. I must have slept for hours, although I feel exhausted and drained.

"It was so much easier when he was just an asshole, lost to the paperwork of foreclosure," I mutter around bites of pastry.

Nicole pats my hand. "His family did very, very shitty things," she says. "I actually felt bad for his mom yesterday. She seemed like she's not holding her shit together very well."

Logan considers this. "Some people feel trapped by societal expectations," she says and shrugs. "It can be really scary to think you're going to be kicked out of your perceived safe space."

I sigh. "From what Walt has said, he's always felt on the brink of being ejected from his family's good graces."

Sam groans. "I love you, Orla, and I support you. But you have to talk to him, honey. You need to be having this conversation with him. Both of you are hurting."

Logan nods. Even Nicole is silent apart from her fingernails tapping on her coffee mug. She finally says, "You've been hanging out with him for two months. You owe him a heart to heart."

I bury my fingers in my hair, trying not to scream. "I don't think he wants anything to do with me." I can't look up at them.

"Well," I hear Sam's voice. "Honey, even if that's true, you need to have a conversation about the baby. You can't put this back in the vault."

I'm about to answer her when there's a knock at the door. I raise my head and look to my friends. They all shrug. Logan says, "Maybe it's Elizabeth checking in?"

She pads to the front door and I hear a small gasp before she runs back into the kitchen. I feel the cold air of the door being opened and hear someone hustle inside, boots on the tile in the entry. "It's him," Logan whispers. "He's here."

I stand up and try to smooth down my shirt as if that will help me look more presentable. I make my way around the corner to the door, where Walt is leaning in his full U.S. postal winter gear, complete with fur hat.

"Hi," he says. "I'm Walt Sheffield." He holds out his hand and I furrow my brow but return the shake, wondering what the hell he's doing. "I thought maybe we could start fresh since I think it's fair we both made some missteps early on."

As I stare at him in the doorway, I hear a clatter behind me. I turn over my shoulder to see Nicole has just upended the plastic table cloth into a giant bundle and is trying to shove the whole thing in the trash. "I was eating that," I moan, but she holds up a finger.

"Nope. We're leaving. Wally can make you replacement waffles later. You two have shit to hash out." Sam and Logan flit around the living room gathering up shoes and folding my blankets.

Walt clears his throat. "Actually," he scratches at the back of his neck making a pained face. "I was hoping I could persuade you to ride with me to my house to talk? I came here straight from work and—"

"Oh, babe, we can tell." Sam pats him on the shoulder as she squeezes past him. "You wouldn't think those pants would do it for me but they definitely do..."

"Are you guys objectifying my baby-daddy?" I feel suddenly possessive. It was one thing when the gray-haired ladies teased him about how good he looks, but *these* women are supposed to be on my side.

"Only a tiny bit," Logan says, folding her coat over her arm. "Hey, boss, can you drop me at my house?"

Sam and Logan hustle away, and Nicole backs out with a wave so that Walt and I are alone inside my doorway. He raises his eyebrows, his face hopeful. "So anyway, I came right from work and I have to give Pudding his pills. But I didn't want to let this go another night..."

I nod and follow him to his car. He smiles as he backs up and does a three-point turn. I rest my hands on my belly as he drives us toward his house and I chew on my lip while he greets his rabbit. "He just doesn't seem like he's sick," I tell him, attempting to squat down and pet the bunny, but giving up when my belly gets in the way.

"Well, that's because I make sure he gets his meds." Walt grins again as he scoops a bit of pumpkin into a silver bowl and sprinkles cut up pills on top. The rabbit comes bounding over, circling his legs until he sets the bowl on the ground. He and I both laugh at the sound of the little tongue lapping up the food.

Walt stands and leans back on his counter. "So," he says. I swallow.

"Can we sit on the sofa while we do this? I don't think I could get off and on your stools at this point."

He gestures toward the living room and I settle into his couch, noticing that it smells like his hair and then feeling awful all over again. I take a deep breath. "I slept with you because I was pissed at my family," I blurt. "They were pressuring me about work, about relationships. I was feeling down about my mom being dead and you were there and hot."

"I slept with you because you told me to," he tells me, grinning as he unbuttons some of his mailman layers. Jesus, I'm fucked if he turns this into a strip tease.

"Okay, so by the time I found out I was pregnant, your father had already been revealed as an uber-douche." I wince, but Walt gives a "go on" gesture. "Even deciding to have the baby at all, that was more about me than you. I just felt like...it was a freaking miracle. The IUD just happened to slip and rupture the condom? It seemed like fate really wanted this baby to exist. And I think I told you about how much it meant to me about the cellular connection with my mom."

"You did. Thank you for sharing that with me."

"When the hell did you learn the right things to say to people?" I snap at him, taken aback by how he's handling this conversation. "Sorry. But see? I'm shit at emotions and communicating. I was raised by emotionally unavailable men. Well, my dad is good at emotions, but he was a grieving mess for most of my formative years. Anyway this whole thing was about me and maybe learning how to be a whole person by becoming a mother. I didn't factor you in."

Walt stares at me unblinking, but I can see his throat working as he swallows and he's practically vibrating. "I acknowledge all of that. And you know I'm still working through a lot of emotional baggage with my own family." I nod. "But you and I have been connecting, Orla. I'm not imagining it. We've shared things the past two months."

I close my eyes. "I was going to tell you. A few different times I wanted to tell you, but then either you kissed me and I got distracted or..." I drift off and press my palms over my eyes, and take a deep breath. "I apologize, Walt. You have a right to know your child, at every stage, and it was fucked up of me not to tell you sooner."

"Thank you," he says, and he scoots closer to me on the couch. He stretches out a hand. "Can I?" He looks so vulnerable, like he might cry.

"God, yes, of course." I grab his hand and press it to my side, where the baby is kicking windmills while we've been talking. When I look up at Walt again, there are tears in his eyes.

"Will you tell me about him? Her? I don't even know what sort of child I have."

I shake my head. "I haven't found out! I sort of wanted a surprise. And you know, the sex doesn't necessarily mean a whole ton." He nods, and keeps his hand still. His smile grows with each movement of the baby.

"Oh, I can show you something. Hang on." I arch up to extract my phone from the pocket of my leggings and search for the video I saved of the ultrasound. "This is the anatomy scan," I tell him, starting the video. "That's what they call it when they look over the whole baby to check everything. Organs. Toes. Bones. All of that."

He clutches the phone like it's made of fragile ice, and stares at the video. "This is my baby? Our baby?" I nod.

"And everything looks good, by the way. The doctor says everything is perfect."

"Christ, Orla, look at that." I smile and watch as the baby rolls over. I remember sharing a laugh with the tech when that happened because we had to wait for a better position to keep scanning.

"So, like I said, I have no idea what I'm doing. I don't know how to be a mom, and I don't know how to be a partner. I've never had any examples of functional adult relationships in my life, and my mom died so long ago I can't tell if my memories of her or real, or just fairy tales at this point."

Walt sets the phone down and places a warm palm on my leg. "Maybe your memories of her are both." He moves his thumb in small circles and I just sit with the affection in that. "Maybe...maybe we can figure everything out together," he says, his eyes dancing as he looks back and forth between mine, hopeful.

"I'd like that," I whisper. "I'd like to try." Walt pulls me into his arms and, with my belly between us, we sit that way, breathing, forgiving. Eventually I must fall asleep because I wake to a swaying sensation. I yelp as Wally sets me in the middle of his bed and starts to tuck me in to the covers. "Hey," I whisper as he starts to back out of the room.

"Oh. I'm sorry I woke you." He puts a hand on my leg. "I'm too tired to drive you home, but I can sleep on the couch."

"No," I say, trying to sit up. Suddenly the thought of sleeping alone is overwhelming, too much. I need his scent here and his arms to reassure me that things can be okay.

He freezes. "I could call your dad or one of your cousins if you'd—"

"I mean no, like don't sleep on the couch. Come and hold me." I toss the covers back and lie back down on my side, looking up at him. He nods and unfastens his pants, which drop to the floor in a clatter of belt buckles and keys. It should be sexy, but I'm so exhausted that I just sigh as he climbs in behind me and pulls me against his chest. I fall asleep in his arms, his hand splayed across my stomach, across the child we've created together.

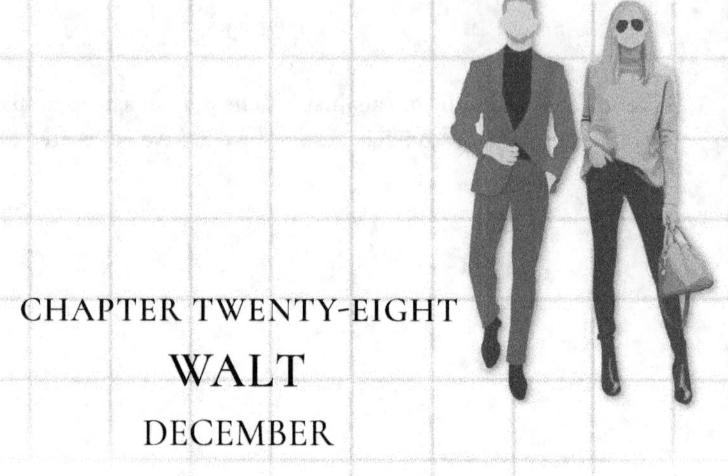

CHAPTER TWENTY-EIGHT
WALT
DECEMBER

"Come on, come on!" I resist the urge to honk the horn of the mail van while I wait impatiently for the car in front of me to finish turning right. I'm late to meet Orla at her doctor's appointment. After we talked, I said I want to be here for all of it. I survived an awkward dinner with her dad when she told him I fathered her baby, and he said absolutely nothing for seven straight minutes before nodding and shaking my hand.

Then Orla sent me a truly shocking schedule of appointments. I don't know how people manage to get enough time to attend them all.

It's going to mean I get home even later tonight, but it'll be worth it to hold her hand while we listen to the heart beat.

The Buick finally gets out of my way and I tear into the hospital parking lot. I know it's a shifty thing to do, but I park the mail van in the taxi lane with the blinkers on and rush inside. If I took the time to find parking in the garage I'd miss the entire appointment.

I hustle through the lobby with my head down, not wanting to make eye contact with receptionists who'd want to chat. I'm not actually here to pick up the mail, after all. Marla is on this route today. I pull my hat a little lower, not wanting to run into her, either. She'd definitely give me shit about leaving the van like that.

I finally weave through the maze to the office where I find Orla biting her lip and looking around just as she's about to follow the nurse through a

858

door. "Wait, he's here," she says, and I feel the warmth of her smile right through to my frozen bones.

"Sorry," I mutter, wondering if it's okay to lean in and kiss her, and then deciding I don't care what other people think. I drop a gentle kiss on her cheek and rub her belly, feeling the baby wriggle beneath her shirt.

I never get tired of feeling that. I delight in it, in the mystery of it, the promise. The baby is a chance to go our own way. We haven't really talked about us as a couple, but I see her almost every day to make baby plans.

Orla hands me her boots before getting on the scale, and the nurse gives her a thumbs up. "Excellent weight gain, Ms. Brady. This little one is plumping up."

I follow Orla into the exam room and cringe as the nurse hands her a cup for a urine sample. I relax a bit when I figure out there's a side door to a private restroom for that process, and then I laugh as Orla narrates what she's doing in there, complete with swear words when she can't reach around her stomach to hold the cup.

"I have faith in you," I say through the door.

"Fuck you, Walt. Come help me."

"Are you sure? What if you reach around via the back? Instead of trying the front?" I bite my lip and shirk out of my heavy coat, warming up at last. I hear a groan from inside the bathroom.

"Ugh. I hate that that worked. Everything is uncomfortable."

"Next time, I'll help," I promise, grinning when she emerges shaking her hands, flicking water at me from washing them.

Dr. Andrews knocks as she opens the door and lifts her eyebrows when she sees me helping to hoist Orla up onto the exam table. "Special delivery?" She laughs at her own joke and I decide I like her. I feel a swell of pride when Orla tells her I'm the baby's father, until the doctor says, "This is the guy you stabbed in the peen with your expired IUD?" She looks at me. "How's that going for you? Any lasting damage?"

I freeze with my mouth hanging open, but Orla and Dr. Andrews both laugh. "Sorry. So sorry. I shouldn't mess with you. I've known Orla a long time. And this does happen sometimes. The poking...it really is just a scratch, although I'm sure with all those nerve endings it was uncomfortable." She thrusts out a hand. "Dr. Andrews, baby catcher."

I laugh awkwardly. "Walt Sheffield. Baby...maker?"

Dr. Andrews nods as she pulls on rubber gloves. "That'll do. Let's take a listen, shall we?" She helps Orla lie back on the table and pull up her shirt. She pokes her belly and measures it with one of those measuring tapes that tailors use. I listen, awed, as she mutters things about the baby's position—excellent—and growth—right on track. Then she squirts goo on Orla's stomach and touches a little wand to it, and the room fills with a swirling, churning sound.

It's the heartbeat. Steady and present and so real, I can't bear it. I sink into a chair and lean close, not wanting to miss a single note of this most beautiful melody. Dr. Andrews smiles at me over the swell of the baby. "Everything seems perfect." She hands Orla a towel and cuts off the power to the magic wand. "What's going on with you, Orla? Still going running?"

"Mmm hmm," Orla groans as she tries to sit back up. I help lift at her shoulders. "It's more like waddles these days. Slow jaunts."

Dr. Andrews raises one eyebrow and turns her attention to me. "You going along on these adventures?"

I shake my head. I start to explain that I don't have the time, but Orla interjects. "I try to go with my dad or one of my cousins, but they all complain about me holding them back."

"Ha. Sounds like the Brady family I know. I'm fine with you keeping those up, but prefer if you stick to routes near civilization and not isolated park trails way into the woods." Orla nods. Dr. Andrews looks up at the wall calendar. "We're getting pretty close to fully baked, and you just never know what will happen with a first labor."

I swallow and stare at the wall. "I thought Orla said February? It's only mid December."

Dr. Andrews rolls her eyes. "Only the baby really knows when the baby is going to show up. Could happen safely any time between mid-January and Valentine's Day."

ß

As I walk Orla to her car, I debate how best to convey the concern that bubbled up for me listening to the doctor talk about the baby's timeline. "Orla, when's your second exam? I know you have the first one coming up soon."

She waves a hand at me as she lowers herself into the drivers seat. "It's January 15, but the baby isn't going to come before then. A Brady would never do such a thing to another Brady."

"Okay, but...that baby is half Sheffield."

"Are you saying your demon sperm are going to make the baby come early just to fuck up my career? Those exams are a real bitch to reschedule and there's certification timing and it's a whole thing, Walt."

I take a deep breath. "I'm just concerned based on what the doctor was saying. That's all. I definitely don't want you to miss this professional opportunity." I take her hand and kiss her knuckles. "The world needs you and your brain to be out there making electricity safe."

She laughs. "That's not really what I do."

I shrug and close her door, waving as she pulls away and then jogging back to the mail van before people figure out I used my work vehicle to wheedle easy parking.

It's late when I finish up my route, too late to call Orla. She's been studying almost around the clock for her exam next week, but she told me she's been falling asleep around nine. By the time I shower and take care of Pudding, I'm too tired to hold the phone to my own head anyway. I send her a text asking if there's anything she needs the rest of this week, and then I drift off to sleep remembering the sound of the baby's heartbeat.

In the morning, Orla messages me that all she needs is a catheter bag so she can at least complete one practice test without having to pee 14 times. I can't tell whether she's serious, and spend too long looking up accommodations for pregnant people during professional examinations. I consider asking her dad whether she can get some sort of variance, but she finally types back that she's on it.

Of course she is. Of course she would have dealt with every potential problem prior to going into the exam. She's the most competent person I know. Apart from the rest of her family. They're all grotesquely competent. It drips off of them. But they're not even assholes about it. I allow myself a small smile, a moment to feel proud that I've managed to sneak into their good graces. I can't dwell on it for long, though, before I have to dive in and focus on my own, seemingly endless work.

CHAPTER TWENTY-NINE
ORLA

"Oh thank god that's done." I throw down my pencil and march up to hand in the last part of the exam. My tailbone hurts from sitting on a wooden chair all day. I shouldn't say all day, because I spent at least as much time in the bathroom as I did taking the test.

I smile at the proctor and gather up my things. I fire off a text to Walt, grinning.

> Only took eight hours and 24 million bathroom breaks, but I finished that fucker.

And then I panic a little because it scares me that I texted him first and not my family or the Foof group chat.

I can't think of a single other piece of news that I didn't first want to share with my family. I send them all the same message as I get situated in my car, cramming pretzels in my mouth as my stomach gurgles. My phone pings with a thousand responses offering congratulations and assurances that everyone knows I did great. I do know I did great. I can feel it.

But again, I'm taken by surprise when I feel a flutter in my chest seeing the response from Walt.

> Never doubted you for a second. How do you want to celebrate?

How do I want to mark this occasion? A vastly pregnant person who has done nothing but study and practice for weeks? How do I want to celebrate when I'm repeatedly distracted by memories of Walt fucking me with his face, on the floor inside my front door?

We've kissed on the cheek a few times since Thanksgiving, and done plenty of chaste cuddling. But I really need more from him and I'm hoping he's on the same wavelength. I send him an eggplant emoji, a peach emoji, a hot dog emoji, and a taco emoji.

My phone begins to ring almost immediately. "Hey," he says. I can hear the beep of his mail truck and know he must be out delivering packages somewhere with his four-ways blinking. His voice is breathy. I like it.

"Hey yourself." I turn on the car, but I find I don't need the heater. Between thinking about celebrating and this damn baby turning me into a furnace, I'm already sweating.

"I want to make sure I don't misinterpret your text message..."

"Walt, I need you to fuck me tonight. What time do you get done with work?"

"Oh, fuck, Orla." His voice sounds strangled and I think he nearly dropped whatever he's carrying.

"Yes, Walt. Exactly that. What time?"

"Jesus. Um, shit. It's five now? I can do six. I can make this happen."

"I'll meet you at your place." I don't want him slithering away midway through to go take care of Pudding. I haven't had a dick inside me since the night we made this baby. I just took the most intense exam of my life. I'm going to need him at least three times.

I stop for takeout and run home to grab an overnight bag and get to Walt's house just as he's screeching into his driveway. He leaps out of his car looking crazed. I grin. "I take it you're excited about my celebration plans?"

"Orla. Fuck." I meet him on the step into his front door and he grabs my hand, pressing it to his crotch where I feel how very enthused he is about this party. I love how he gets when he's horny. Walt becomes assertive and confident and uses his fingernails and tongue like tiny, magic pleasure sparks.

His lips on mine are possessive, hungry. He fumbles with his keys and we burst into the house. He seems to snap out of his sex haze, remembering his rabbit. He grabs my hand and drags me into the kitchen. "Do you need some water or anything?" He looks over his shoulder as he hurries to toss lettuce in a dish for Pudding, who is trying to climb his pant leg.

"I'm good. Can I help this go faster?"

"Meet me upstairs," he barks. He looks down at his pet. "I'm giving you your pill and saying goodnight. Sorry."

I chuckle as I climb up his steps, shedding my clothes along the way. I find his bedroom in the semidarkness and switch on the lamp on his night stand and then...oh god, he's got baby books by his bed.

I swoon onto the covers and sprawl out, just as Walt bounds up the stairs. "I'm here for celebratory orgasms," he says, and then he blushes. "That sounded sexier in my head."

"Come here," I say, patting the pillow beside me. He doesn't waste an invitation. In an instant, I'm pressed against his naked chest, my nipples pebbling against his, Walt's tongue circling the shell of my ear.

"I want to lick every inch of you," he moans, thrusting his hips and hooking one of my legs up over his to press his cock against my center.

"Mm, maybe later," I tell him. I bite his lip, and nibble my way around his jaw and down to his collar bone. "It's been seven months since I've had a dick inside me. I need it."

He groans. "I'm not going to deny a beautiful woman." Walt tugs my ponytail until my throat is bare to him and he licks the entire length of my neck while he reaches between my legs. "Shit, Orla. You're soaked." I moan in response as he dips a finger inside me. "You're ready for me already, aren't you?"

I try to nod but my head is immobilized. He strokes and pets as he tugs my hair and kisses everywhere but my mouth. I start to writhe on the bed, my hands clawing at Walt, needing to hold on to him so I don't float away off the bed.

He slides a second finger inside me and I feel my orgasm starting in my knees, twisting its way up my spine and bursting through my body as Walt gently kisses my nipples. Our limbs are tangled like wires as we lay on our sides and I hear myself grunting, feel myself pulsing around his hand as Walt pulls out my orgasm, extending it.

He rolls onto his back, pulling me on top of him so my legs straddle his waist and my belly presses between us. I rise up on my knees and he puts his hands behind his head, lacing his fingers. "I could look at this sight forever, Orla. Jesus, you're phenomenal."

His dick is flat against his abdomen, squashed beneath the swell of my stomach. I readjust until I can grip it and I stare down as the tip weeps pre-cum. "I'm going to sit on this," I tell him.

"Please do," he growls, and then releases a torrent of curse words as I sink down onto him. "Oh fuck, oh hell. Orla. Christ you feel good." I think he keeps talking to me but I can't concentrate. I brace my hands on his shoulders and circle my hips, grinding my clit against his pelvis.

Soon, we are both gasping, hissing as we join together, grunting as I rise up and down, impaling myself again and again on his hot length. "Your cock feels so good," I shout. I tug on Walt's chest hair and toss my head back, feeling the approach of another orgasm.

Walt reaches out to stroke my skin, his palms skirting along my breasts and my thighs. "Look at you. You're a goddess. It's never been like this, Orla. Oh god, are you close?" He's gasping now, his hips lifting up to meet mine as we collide like electrons jumping between atoms. There's a current flowing from him to me and from me right back.

I meet his eyes and feel like he sees through me, inside me. I feel like the time before him has been a holding place, like my whole life has been guiding me right here. Tears swell in my eyes as I tumble over the edge again. "Yes, yes, yes now. Walt, now. Oh god, I'm coming so hard right now." I collapse on his chest as he pulls me tight and I feel him swell inside me. I feel the hot pulse as he groans into my hair.

An eternity passes before I finally roll to my side and start searching for a tissue. "What do you need," he asks, his chest still moving rapidly as he tries to calm down.

"Something to wipe up the mess you made." I prop my head up on my hand and just enjoy the look of him, disheveled and exhausted and...mine. I think. Maybe.

He arches a brow and gazes down. "Me? Make a mess?" I nod, and then laugh when he lifts up my thigh.

"What the hell are you doing?" I tip over onto my back as he examines my crotch.

"I want to see." He bites his lip and reaches out a finger, tracing it around. "Hmm. I really did do a number on you."

"You're such a weirdo." He plants a kiss on my hip and springs out of bed. I watch his cock bob as he hurries out of the room.

When he comes back with a damp washcloth to clean me up, he makes good on his promise to lick every inch of me. By the time he's finished, I wish I could take the P.E. exam every day to come home and celebrate like this.

CHAPTER THIRTY
WALT

"I can't sleep without you anymore, Walt." I don't even try to hide the giant grin on my face when Orla calls me at work. "Can you come over tonight?"

I sigh. "You know I want to. But by the time I get done working and give Pudding his pills, you'll already be sound asleep." I grunt a little as I hoist a new bin of mail forward in the van, tossing the empty one in the stack behind the passenger seat.

"This is dumb," she says, and I hear her moving around the house in the background. "I'm just going to stay at your house."

I feel a rush of warmth bloom in my chest at the thought of Orla in my bed. Not even because I want her sexually, although I definitely do. But I crave all of her. Her wit and her temper, her vulnerability that I might just be the only one to witness. "I'd really like that," I tell her, hustling a bit. Maybe I can shave a few minutes off my day.

"Where are you in 20 minutes? I'll come meet you and get your house key."

⅌

She finds me a half hour later and greets me with a steaming cup of hot chocolate and a grin. She looks like some sort of Celtic goddess in a white, puffy maternity coat and her hair tumbling around her beneath a white beanie. I halt in my tracks at the sight of her, and then am overcome with an urge to let the world know this woman is spoken for.

I rush into her arms and kiss the hell out of her, loving the little moan she offers in response. Can it be real that this woman is interested in me for me, is responding to my affection? It still feels foreign, to want to give affection and then receive it in return. I'm drunk with the experience of something as simple as a cup of cocoa from my girlfriend. I'm pretty sure she's my girlfriend. It occurs to me that we didn't really discuss that. We just sort of slid from discussing the baby to celebrating her exam to me giving her all the sex she can handle whenever I'm not at work.

I fish in my pocket for my key ring and hand her the key to my condo. "You should go make yourself a copy." I kiss the tip of her nose.

"I'll definitely do that. Oh, hey, before I forget. Maddie and Liam are hosting Christmas. They're asking about a head count. We do it Christmas Eve in the Brady family…"

"Christmas?"

She rolls her eyes. "Yeah, you know, dumb party games, another turkey, the guys competing in a gingerbread structure competition…it's fun. You'll come with me, right?"

It seems to have just occurred to her that I might not come, and I can't think of anything better than another holiday in a house full of people who actually enjoy each other. "I—" I haven't talked to my mom about any of this. My parents usually went to stiff, fancy holiday gatherings at their club. There were tuxedos involved, and special silverware. Not that those things in and of themselves are bad, it's just that I always spent the entire night sweating and trying not to talk lest I embarrass my father. Or else putting on my Trip costume to ward off any women at the start before they could reject me.

She holds up a finger. "Your mom is invited. Obviously. Maddie just needs a head count for this one game she's planning."

"Hmm." I also still haven't told my mother about the baby being mine. I haven't told my mother much of anything in the past few weeks, and I feel a little bad that it's been pretty great. Stuff with my father's estate seems pretty wrapped up. The life insurance payments are all situated for my mother. And I've just been focused on Orla and making plans for the baby. Plans that I haven't wanted to include my mother. "So," I tell her, scratching the back of my neck uncomfortably. "The thing about my mom is—"

"Oh my god, you haven't told her yet."

I shake my head.

"Well are you planning to ever tell her? Invite her to the kid's high school graduation with a surprise note?" Orla has her hands on her hips now, looking fierce.

I lick my lips and then have to reach for my lip balm. I go through my whole process of preventing chappage while Orla stares at me. "I promise I will tell her before Christmas," I mutter, stuffing the tube back in my jacket pocket. "I have to figure out the best way to tell her. But put us both down for the Brady party."

ℬ

Every day when I come home from work, there are more of Orla's things scattered throughout my house. I look at her annotated textbooks, unable to even comprehend some of the equations I see on the open pages she leaves piled on my table. I find leggings draped over the shower curtain rod and plaid button-down shirts on the hooks in my bathroom.

I showed her how to take care of Pudding and he's started responding to her, approaching her in the kitchen and circling her ankles when she walks to the fridge to get herself a snack. She told me she read about Christmas trees being potentially dangerous for rabbits since they get treated with pesticides, and so she suggested we decorate with fir boughs on higher surfaces and battery-operated candles with no cords that Pud might chew.

Never in my wildest fantasies did I imagine holiday decorating with a partner like this. I find it hard to breathe when I realize that she is making room in her heart for me and for my pet, that she's considering his wants and his needs and making adjustments to the ways she celebrates this season. For us.

I walk around corners and spy her long legs crossed on my couch as she props a notebook on her belly to study as she eats her cereal in the mornings. And when she hears me enter a room, she looks up at me and smiles, happy to see me.

Terrified of losing this, I avoid telling my mother. I start to appreciate why Orla withheld the truth about the baby. I know that this news will trigger in my mother a deep-seated response. Thoughts of a baby will activate words like "heir" for her and she'll begin talking about prep schools and nannies and finding the proper personal trainers for golf and tennis.

My mother knows I'm dating Orla and she knows Orla is pregnant. By the time I leave to get her for the Christmas Eve party, I rationalize that it's probably going to be fine if she doesn't know yet. I'll offer her lots of gin and hope she sticks close to me and avoids small talk.

I slide open the door to Maddie and Liam's loft and hear Mom gasp at the sight inside. There's a Christmas tree set up behind a bright-colored plastic fence. It's chaotic in a delightful, welcoming way. Every corner on every surface has a padded cushion attached and there are labeled bins everywhere that seem meant to contain toys, but the floor is scattered with all the "people" and "wooden animals" and "miniature motor vehicles" instead.

Cal looks up from pouring himself a drink and sees us at the door. "Hey, everyone, the Sheffields are here. We can start the ball game."

The chatter at the party stops and people turn to look at us. I wave as Maddie comes over to greet us. "Hey, Walt." She stretches up to kiss me on the cheek, a move that takes me by surprise and I forget to greet her.

"Mrs. Sheffield." Maddie grins. "Merry Christmas! Can I take your coat? We're tossing them on the bed. Everyone's itching to see what's in the foil ball this year, so why don't you two grab a drink. Try not to sit near Zack. He throws elbows."

I look around, dazed at the frantic, excited energy. I spy Orla perched on a bench and make my way over to her with my mom in close pursuit. I stoop to kiss Orla's cheek and she moves to stand up when she sees my mother. "Don't get up," I tell her, shaking my head.

"I'm just skooching over to make room for Celeste," she says, patting the bench. My mom smiles politely and sits.

"So...what do I need to know about what's going to happen?" I nod my head in thanks to Cal, who hands me a beer and then starts passing out oven mitts.

Orla smacks her lips. "Okay, so this is a very important piece of Brady family tradition. Most families do this with a ball of plastic wrap, but Liam can't handle the environmental implications of that so we use aluminum foil, which we obviously recycle afterward." Orla places a hand on my mom's shoulder to reassure her, as if recycling were in some way important to her. I laugh, seeing my mom nod. "The host fills a ball of foil with random little gifts. Chapstick. Bath bombs. Gum. But there are also lottery scratch tickets in there and, because it's the Brady family, the center of the ball is always a gift certificate for a Pittsburgh marathon registration. Pretty sure Uncle Mick foots the bill for that grand prize. It's hard to say whether people are more excited for the scratch tickets or the marathon entry.

Maybe the scratchers, since all of us are obligated to enter the marathon regardless."

Mom furrows her brow. "You all run marathons?"

Orla nods and looks a little insulted. "Yes. Multiple times a year. We've even got Nicole working up to a full and Maddie has started doing some 10k races." Orla looks me up and down, considering. "Walt, you probably walk 20 miles on a work day, right? You'll have to start at least doing the corporate relay with us. We get really competitive about our time."

"You're kidding!" I feign surprise and laugh into my beer as Mom asks Orla why on earth people are wearing oven mitts. We learn that the game is played by someone in oven mitts unwrapping as much of the ball as they can, and they get to keep whatever falls out during their turn. The person after them in the circle rolls a pair of dice and when they get doubles, they get the ball and oven mitts.

All the Bradys squat on the floor in a long-limbed circle. Arlan toddles around staring, clutching a ring-pop Logan gave him to keep him occupied during the game. "Everyone ready? Celeste, Walt, you know the rules?" Maddie arches a brow at me, keeping one hand on Liam's back as he sits poised to open. Cal stares intently at the dice in his palm, ready to drop.

"We're good," I say, but Mom looks mortified. I know she's terrified she'll make an error, violate a social rule. I wish I could convince her that that seems to be part of the fun for this particular game, but Maddie screams "GO!" And pandemonium ensues.

Liam, decked out in Santa-patterend oven mitts, growls at the foil ball, using his teeth to help him while his brother swears at the dice. Small bottles of liquor roll out of the foil before everyone shouts as Cal rolls double 4's.

Everything gets passed around. Even mild-mannered Kellen shakes his fist with enthusiasm as Elizabeth unrolls the first set of lottery tickets.

Before I know it, Zack is stuffing oven mitts on my hands while Nicole starts rapidly dropping the dice to the polished concrete floor. I laugh at the awkward foil ball in my hands, at my utter inability to grip it and start unraveling. "Use your teeth, Walt," Orla shouts, slapping at my shoulder as I kneel on the floor beside her. I can't bring myself to put foil in my mouth, but I finally catch an edge and start peeling, giggling with glee as a few lottery tickets and chocolate bars fall by my knees.

Suddenly, Orla yanks the ball from me and starts stuffing the mitts on my mother's hands. Mom seems frozen with anxiety, but Orla is already rolling the dice and cackling. "Come on, Mom, you can do it," I prod. She sits there, staring, as if she can't believe her life has come to this. But then she turns and looks at me and there's an expression on her face I haven't seen before. Maybe lightness? Acceptance? She starts pressing the ball into her knees for leverage and digging in with the thumbs of the oven mitt.

"Aha!" She shouts as a pair of lottery tickets falls on her lap. "I did it!" She doesn't seem to notice when Orla snatches the mitts and the ball for her own turn. "Trippy, I won!" Mom holds the tickets against her chest, forgetting herself for a moment, sitting in the frenetic energy of the game, and I want to cry because I've never seen her so content.

It passes just as briefly and she's smoothing out her skirt again, patting her hair and looking on as Nicole screams at Zack to win her all the liquor. "None of those stupid candy canes, husband. We want the Jose Cuervo!"

Eventually, the foil is all unwrapped, Elizabeth's son Jake has won his first marathon registration, and everyone lucky enough to get lottery tickets is happily scratching to see if they won. Everyone but Mom, who keeps staring at hers until Nicole comes over, holding out a penny.

"Here you go, Grandma! Gotta see if you win that bambino some college tuition." Nicole's smile slowly sags as my mom blinks at her, unmoving. Orla whips her head to look up at me. I close my eyes and groan. Nicole presses the penny into Mom's hand and looks to Orla, silently pleading for guidance.

CHAPTER THIRTY-ONE
WALT

ORLA CLENCHES HER TEETH AND SAYS, "HEY, WALT, SEEMS LIKE MAYBE YOU STILL have some things to discuss with Celeste?" Nicole backs slowly away and I swallow. Orla jumps to her feet, hands on her hips. "Yeah, so I'm going to go get myself some food, and when I come back over here, we'll all be caught up, right?"

I nod and she stomps across the room to join Nicole, who I see apologizing as Orla shakes her head and gestures with her hands. I take Orla's seat on the bench next to my mom, who is still sitting with the penny in her palm and scratch tickets on her lap. "Grandma?" She looks like she might cry. Or run away. Maybe both, although I've never seen her run before.

I blow out a breath. "So, Mom, before Dad died I had a—I had an affair with Orla. And got her pregnant."

"An affair? Trip, how could you be so careless? What will people *think?*" She looks aghast.

I tug at my collar. "People think it's great," I tell her. "Look around this room." I wave a hand. "Everyone here is excited about it. Look." I point at Orla, who rolls her eyes as her father places both hands on her stomach and beams at her.

Mom stands abruptly, the tickets falling to the ground. "I'd like to leave," she says. She starts walking toward the bedroom where Maddie took our coats. I rush to follow her.

"Mom, you can't run away like this. Look, I know this is a big deal. I should have told you before the party. I'm sorry, okay?"

She whips her head around and hisses at me. "You're sorry? You hid a love child from me for months. And now you caused me to be embarrassed at a party."

"There's nothing to be embarrassed about, Mom."

She makes a disgusted sound. "You don't think it's embarrassing to be the only person who doesn't know a secret? What does that tell them about our relationship?" She starts to rummage through the coats. "What on earth do you expect to happen here, Trip? You have told me repeatedly there is no money for frivolity. I can't fly first class with your sister to Turks and Caicos and you expect me to fund a college trust for a love child? If your father were here, he'd—" She claps a hand over her mouth, like she's just remembered that dad is in fact not here and won't ever be again.

Her nostrils flare as she leans against the wall, her eyes glittering with tears.

"Mom." I reach for her and she winces. My mother winces at my touch. I lick my lips. "Mom, listen, the baby will be fine. I have a nice job. Orla has a terrific career. We're not worried about all of that."

Her eyes glitter with tears that haven't yet fallen through the makeup on her cheeks. She shakes her head. "None of this is...this isn't the life I planned for you, Trip. This wasn't how things were meant to be!"

I want to hug her. No, I want her to want me to hug her. I reach for her hand instead and squeeze. "It's going to be okay," I tell her. "My life right now is better than it's ever, ever been."

"How can you say such a thing when your father is barely cold in the ground?" She starts to cry then and begins dabbing at her eyes with the side of her index finger.

"Mom, I know you're grieving. I am, too, but I'd like you to be happy for me that I found someone. I found someone, Mom, and she looks at me like I make the room light up. And I have a job that you don't approve of, but I like it. I like what I'm doing." I grab her hand again and press it to my chest. "Can you try to understand all that? For me? And the baby—your grandchild?"

She takes a shuddering breath and shakes her head a few times, and then puts her party face back on, the wooden smile that doesn't quite reach her eyes. "Of course I can, Trippy. Now, I have had a bit of a long night and I would like to go home."

I look down the hall, toward my pregnant girlfriend, toward the room full of people I really want to join. Mom sees me looking and pats my forearm. "Call me a ride, darling. You stay and enjoy the...festivities."

I nod and pull out my phone, ordering the black car service my parents used to hire to take them to and from the airport. I bend to kiss her cheek as she makes her way toward the door. "Merry Christmas," she tells me, waving and hurrying down the hall.

"Merry Christmas, Mom," I mutter at the back of her head as she disappears from sight.

ℬ

I WALK BACK to the party with my hands in my pockets and Maddie greets me with a pair of lottery tickets. "I rescued these from the floor," she says, gesturing for me to take them.

"Thanks for doing that," I tell her, sighing as Orla wanders toward me, looking irritated. Maddie smiles and pats my shoulder as Orla leans on the wall, her arms crossed over her chest. "I didn't tell her," I say, running a hand through my hair until I feel it standing up.

"Yeah, that was obvious. Walt, that wasn't fair to her."

"I know," I tell her. I lean against the wall next to her and close my eyes. "But I was right that everything seemed better without including her in it."

Orla runs her hand along my arm and I look down, meeting her eye. "She seemed like she was trying tonight," Orla says.

I nod. "I'm going to call her tomorrow. And I mean it this time."

We're quiet for a beat and Orla looks at the lottery tickets in my pants pocket. "You gonna scratch them and see if she won?"

"Orla!" I feign shock. "That would be cruel. I'm going to mail them to her."

She laughs and swats me on the arm. "Come on, sir. Kiss me under the mistletoe."

874

CHAPTER THIRTY-TWO

ORLA

JANUARY

BRADY LADIES GROUP CHAT
NICOLE:

So do you live with Wally now or what? I need to know where to send the spa chairs for your shower.

> I really don't want a shower.

MADDIE:

Think of it more like you get another professional foot rub and there will be cake!

ELIZABETH:

I got a little confused when I saw shower and chairs in the same sentence. We're talking about a baby shower, right? Kellen says I need to ask where you're registered.

NICOLE:

This bish hasn't registered! She is infuriating. I don't know how those things work so someone else needs to step up and be forceful here.

> I don't need people to buy me things. Honest, it'll be good.

LOGAN:

Oh, I love making registries! I make pretend wedding registries all the time and then delete them…

MADDIE:

Okay, Logan, we're going to need to address that news separately. But if you're volunteering to make Orla a registry, I'll email you the list of baby Arlan things I already gave her.

LOGAN:

Orla, do you have a theme for the nursery? I'm seeing that lemons are really in right now as far as patterns for bedding and accessories.

A theme? It's a bedroom, right? Shouldn't the theme be sleeping?

NICOLE:

Don't listen to her, Logan. But no to lemons.

ELIZABETH:

She should get a jogging stroller, don't you ladies think? How cute will she look out there running with the baby?

I'm not cute. Please don't make me cute.

LOGAN:

She'll be super cute. And fierce and imposing, too. Don't worry, Orla. You will always be our Lagertha.

ELIZABETH:

Was that one of those auto corrects? Lagertha?

MADDIE:

Ooh, she's from that show Vikings. She's a bad-ass warrior mama. You're totes right, Logan. Orla is our Lagertha.

NICOLE:

I'm fierce, too!

LOGAN:

Nicole, you could totally slaughter your enemies with an axe OR an arrow.

MADDIE:

Ooh the theme could be stars and arrows!

LOGAN:

[screen shot of forest pattern] Look! There's arrows AND foxes AND pine trees. This is so great.

I'm putting this thread on mute. No shower before my exam, okay? I can't focus on two things at once.

I TOSS MY PHONE ACROSS THE ROOM SO IT LANDS ON THE ARM CHAIR. MY EXAM IS tomorrow and, apart from editing inspection reports and double checking my peers' work before they submit to Dad, I've been focused full time on studying since Christmas.

I have a crib set up in the baby's room and a bunch of diapers, plus an entire plastic bin full of clothing from Maddie. My dad assured me that's fine to get started with. This exam is the most important thing in my life right now.

Walt is working basically around the clock still, despite the snow and Polar Vortex temperatures. It's a good thing he has me staying here at the house to make sure the pipes don't burst. I don't tell him I also am glad I'm staying here because I actually get to see him a little bit each day. I miss my guy when he's not here, and I'm getting a little more comfortable admitting it. I thought things would slow down for him after Christmas, but he says now people are spending their Christmas money and ordering shit in the mail, so he's still racking up obscene amounts of overtime.

Since I can't have Walt here, I really like spending the day with Pudding while I'm studying. Walt is really good at back rubs...and rubbing other things...but Pudding has been hopping up on the couch with me while I'm studying and he just nuzzles up against my leg and falls asleep. It's the sweetest thing. I definitely see how Walt got so smitten with this critter.

And after spending a little bit of time with his mom on Christmas Eve, I also see how he'd be craving affection. Walt says when he talked to her, she wouldn't stop obsessing about the baby's financial future. He tried a few times, but she wasn't ready to talk to him about anything beyond that. "Maybe he shouldn't have blind-sided her at a party," I mutter to Pudding.

My back starts hurting so I decide I need to move around a bit. I fix lunch for myself and grab some parsley for Pudding so we can eat together. "I'd sit with you on the floor if I thought I could ever get up again," I tell him. He doesn't seem to notice as he slurps the parsley in like spaghetti. I wince as a cramp tightens up my back muscles.

Dr. Andrews did say I'd start having practice contractions as my body gets ready for labor. "All right, baby," I say to my stomach. "I see what you're saying. Training is important and all that." I feel another quick squeeze on the under-side of my belly. "Okay, I think we're going to try a bath."

I soak in Walt's tub until the water gets cold, and then I drain the tub to fill it again, loving how the pressure is eased from my joints when I'm floating on my side. I'm not sure what time it is when he pokes his head in the bathroom, but I'm on my third refill, so I must have been up here a long time.

"What's going on in here?" He squats down next to the tub, his nose pink from being outdoors. He always smells sweaty when he gets home from work and it's probably gross, but I kind of like it. "Everything okay?" He runs a hand along my wet head, his eyes filled with concern.

"I just wanted a bath. It feels amazing not to be supporting my own weight right now." I grin at him like an idiot, but he's so damn cute in his polo shirt over black thermals. I like messy, disheveled Walt way more than Fancy Suit Walton Henry Sheffield. Probably because I now know I'm seeing the real him when his guard—and society manners—are down.

"How about I make us dinner and you start to de-prune? Your toes look as wrinkled as peach pits, babe."

"How about you strip and join me instead?"

He arches a brow and splashes water on me. "As tempting as that sounds, I truly need to eat or I'm going to pass out."

I sigh and climb out of the water, dripping on the bath mat for a bit and staring at my stomach. I wonder what my mother thought about when she was this far along with me. Dad has some pictures that I've been staring at obsessively the past month or so. He tells me she had an easy labor, because I was always an agreeable child. I'm not sure where he got that idea. All my memories of myself include me snapping at my cousins, yelling at them just so I'd feel heard. I sigh, because of course Mom didn't know me when I was a girl thrust into living with three boys. She got me as an only child in a house where I learned to behave because my mother was often sick from chemo, and resting.

I make my way downstairs as I start to smell garlic and onions from the kitchen. My mouth waters when I see Walt sautéing chicken, dancing along to pop music on the radio and tossing veggies to Pudding as he works.

"Hey," I say, trying to hug him from behind, but finding I can't reach. But just as I do, he spins in my arms and wraps his around me so we're pressed close together. His kiss is sweet and familiar by now, salty and warm. I feel his smile as he pulls back. "I like this," I tell him.

He frowns. "What's that happening there? In your belly?"

"You can feel that?" I drop my hands to where my muscles are tightening again, same as earlier. It stopped when I was in the bath, but it seems like my body is gearing up for another practice session.

Walt nods. "I can totally feel that. Is that...that's not kicking?"

I shake my head. "Dr. Andrews said there would be practice contractions. Hiccups or something."

"Braxton Hicks?"

"Yes. That! Why do you know that word?"

He shrugs. "You know I've been reading."

"I love that," is what I say, but in my head, I think *I love you.* I swallow as he serves me a plate of aromatic food.

Just like that, I think I love Walt. Or maybe it's not "just like that." I sit next to him at his table, in his house where he gave me a key, and think of the past few months. He's been honest with me, and real. He hasn't wanted to change me, has only been supportive of my goals. He works all the fucking time, but when he's here, he's present and thoughtful. God, I really do love him.

"This is delicious," I tell him, but what I'm really thinking is that he understands me. He...completes me. The hugeness of it overwhelms me. Or maybe it's another Braxton Hicks. Or maybe the baby just kicks me in the ribs, but I don't say it to him.

"I want to run through my notes one more time," I tell him. "And then I'm going to try and sleep." Walt jumps up and grabs the plates. His is wiped totally clean, because he always inhales his food after work. He takes a few bites of mine as he walks to the sink and rinses both plates. And then he joins me on the couch, rubbing my feet while I review equations I could identify in my sleep. Through contractions, if I needed to.

I WAKE up to Walt bringing me coffee in bed. It's not yet light out, but that doesn't mean much in January. I don't usually have to be up as early as him, but he agreed to be my alarm clock today. "Hey," I say, brushing the hair out of my eyes. "Oh my god. This smells so good. Doesn't this smell so good?" My sensitive nose sends the hot coffee aroma buzzing through my body before I even take a sip. I don't know that there's anything more decadent than hot coffee in bed, and I sip it as I watch him get dressed.

"I could get used to this," I tell him, grinning above my mug.

"I sure hope so, Orla." He crawls across the bed once he's dressed and pries the cup from my hands. "I'll give it back," he promises. "I just want to kiss you properly." He gives me a peck. "For luck." He slides his tongue into my mouth and I forget to worry about anything. I know he has to leave, and that I won't see him until late, so I dig my fingers into his collar and try to keep him here with me, knowing it's wrong to wish him away from his job, but past caring.

"I'll try to get home early tonight," he whispers against my lips. And then he's gone.

ℬ

I SHOULD BE nervous about my exam as I drive to the testing center. My future at work depends on this. The next few years of my life depend on this. But I know I'm ready. I'm as confident in that as I am about my next breath reaching all the way in to my lungs. Instead, I think about Walt, and how I don't want my life to disentangle from his. About how thoroughly I've switched from a mindset of raising this baby on my own, to not being able to imagine embarking on this journey without him.

My phone rings and I grin, seeing my dad's face on the screen. "Hey, Dad."

"Are you there yet?" I can hear the excitement in his voice.

"You know I'm here ten minutes early."

"On time is too late," we say in unison, and I laugh, finding comfort in the routine predictability of his advice.

"Well I'll let you go, but I just wanted to say I'm proud of you."

I feel warmth spread through me, even though he says this at least a dozen times a week. "Thanks, Dad. I love you."

"I love you, too, sweetie. But also, Orla, I hope you know..." His draws a shaky breath. "Your mother would be so proud today." I squeeze the steering wheel as he takes a pause. "I can just imagine her calling me every few hours today, asking me how I think you're doing."

"Aw, Dad, come on." A surge of emotion powers through me and I close my eyes, trying to see if I can feel my mother out there in the universe somewhere, somehow.

"Call me when you're done?"

"Of course, Dad. Sure thing." We hang up and I sit in the car for another minute, pressing my hands against my belly, feeling grateful.

As I'm checking in to the exam, the practice contractions start up again. "Of course," I mutter. But I ignore them and get to work. I stand periodically, swaying back and forth at my work station when a particularly stubborn wave rolls through my lower back.

By lunch time I'm sweating and using my marathon breathing techniques to concentrate on the problems each time my body decides to cramp up without my permission. In through the nose I breathe. I solve an equation. I hiss my breath out through my mouth as I squeeze the pencil and turn the page in my exam book.

During one of my bathroom breaks, I sneak out my phone and power it on to text Maddie.

> These practice contractions are super inconvenient!

MADDIE:

> Oh no! Are you having a big one during your exam? How's it going?

> One? Try one hundred. Test is great. I was having these ctx last night, too. So annoying.

MADDIE:

> Hm. I only had like a handful of those before it was real labor. You really had 100? You okay?

> Totally fine. I've got this. Just gotta breathe through and keep doing that math, right?

I power my phone down and waddle back to my work station. I think I'm ahead of schedule for the problems and I decide to work through my afternoon break to get ahead. I groan a little as the next wave seems to be squeezing my spinal column. I decide I'll finish the test standing up and I'm just about to get started on the last problem when the door to the room bursts open and Walt rushes in.

"What the hell?" I drop my pencil and clutch the edge of the desk. I want to yell at Walt, but I groan instead, deep and low. This is a really big one.

"My girlfriend is in labor," Walt announces. The exam proctor looks at me, and then I groan again and he looks like he's going to pass out. The proctor stares at the floor as if I leaked amniotic fluid all over it.

"I think that's an exaggeration, Walt," I say. Only I don't say that. I hear myself bellow like a lowing cow and it occurs to me that Walt is right. This isn't practice labor at all.

I scrabble for the test paper and scratch out the final details for the high voltage problem I was working on. "I AM DOOOOOOOOOooonnnneeeeee," I start wailing. Walt scoops up my notes and hands them to the proctor as I clutch the edge of the desk and breathe.

"Come on, Orla," he says, tugging at my hand. I take a few steps and bend over, putting my hands on my thighs. I shake my head. "Come on, babe. You've got this. The car is the finish line."

"Not," I huff and take a few steps. "True." I take a few more. My entire body seems to be squeezing and rendering me unable to walk. Walt scoops me up and carries me, bridal style, out to the parking lot.

He tries to buckle me into the seatbelt but I growl at him and turn around so I'm draped over the head rest, panting, with my ass toward the windshield. He starts to drive and I'm aware that he's very calm. I feel like a god damned disaster. How can he be calm?

"How are you here?" I hiss, resting my head on the seat during a blessed break in between contractions.

"Maddie called me," he says, keeping his eyes forward as he speeds along the highway toward Oakland and the hospital where I'm delivering.

And then I enter my own space inside my head, where there is nothing but me humming with my mouth hanging open, and the squeezing of my back and front muscles all at the same time. At some point, I hear Walt asking me if I can get out of the car, but I can't pay attention to him right now. There is nothing but my body and this tiny circle of black leather on the headrest, where I am focusing my vision as I huff.

I think I hear Dr. Andrews's voice muttering something about a gurney, and then I feel arms on my arms, tugging me out of the car. I squeeze on to the head rest, roaring and panting. Finally, someone pulls my pants down and I feel them around my knees. "Get it off, get it off, get it off," I chant in rhythm with the pulsing of my body. The pants are peeled off my body by unknown hands. I close my eyes and breathe.

There's a moment in between contractions and I sag against someone's chest. Walt. I smell him and sink my head back against him, inhaling deeply. I think he's lowering me to the ground and I briefly feel the icy wind on my ass before I drop forward, with my hands on concrete. My body starts to squeeze. No. It's pushing. "I'm pushing!"

I close my eyes and I recall my mother's face as she pushed me on a swing. I looked back over my shoulder at her in the sunshine and she smiled. "Harder," I yelled to her. "Push harder!" But the fantasy shifts and it's not me yelling. Or maybe it is, but there's another voice here, too, telling me to push, telling me that I am beautiful.

And then I feel burning pressure, so much pressure, followed by immediate relief. I collapse, not onto the sidewalk. Onto Walt. "You caught me," I pant, and then I realize.

"Our baby! Where's our baby?"

"She's right here," he says, turning my face toward the screaming, slimy bundle that Dr. Andrews is hoisting into the air. She thrusts the bundle at me and I pull her close.

"She?" I look up at Walt, who has tears running down his face as he smiles.

"She, Orla. We have a girl!"

I look down at the baby in my arms. My baby. Our baby. "She's here," I say, and I lie against my Wally as my ass goes numb on the frozen sidewalk outside the hospital.

CHAPTER THIRTY-THREE
WALT

"I'D SAY YOU'RE JUST ABOUT EVEN NOW," DR. ANDREWS SAYS AS SHE LOOKS UP FROM working on Orla. I haven't let go of Orla's shoulder as she works on feeding our brand new baby. We got Orla wheeled into a room to get checked out and apparently she needs a few stitches.

"Even?" I look down the bed and see a bunch of blood and wish I hadn't. Dr. Andrews cackles.

"Oh, you know, her vagina poked your willy and now I'm having to stitch her perineum. Seems like you two are on equal footing now, is all I'm saying." She snaps her gloves as she peels them off and tosses them into the trash. She walks up to the top of the bed and Orla beams at her. Dr. Andrews places a reassuring hand on Orla. "We'll get some nurses in here, get you cleaned up. You did great, mama."

She leaves the room and we're alone together in the warm, low light, and Orla starts crying. "Hey," I say, climbing into the bed with her and our daughter. "Hey, Orla, I...I love you." Her jaw opens and her eyes widen. "I love you so god damned much, and you were so amazing today. Do you see what you did? I mean, look at this baby!" We both laugh/cry and look down as our girl latches on to Orla's nipple like she was born doing it.

"And I love you, too," I tell our babe, kissing her head as she sucks with her eyes closed. I want to do everything to keep them both safe and warm. I feel fiercely possessive, and totally terrified. Orla rests her head against my chest and continues crying. I stroke her cheek as I hold them both in my arms and we stay that way even when the nurse comes to try and get things clean.

When we're alone again, Orla turns up to me. "I think I love you, too, Walt. I...I know I do. I wanted to tell you yesterday. When I was in the bath, is when I realized it."

I kiss her forehead. "We have every day to say it," I tell her, and help the nurse lift her up a bit to slide fresh sheets onto the bed.

"I'm so tired," she says, and I nod. "You did quite a lot today, between the exam and, you know, birthing a baby in the parking lot."

She laughs. "I had a parking lot baby. Oh god, we have a parking lot baby!" Her eyes go wide. "Holy shit, I finished all my exams and then I had a parking lot baby."

"Damn right you did, Orla." I adjust my weight, but I know I won't be able to stay with them in this bed for long. The baby pops off Orla's breast and sighs and Orla and I both sigh in response as we stare down at her. "Did you have any ideas about a name?"

She shakes her head. "I was going to really buckle down and consider that after my exam."

"Hm," I say. "Well your test is done, so there's that." We laugh again. I love this, laughing with her. Staring at our daughter. It's like there's nothing else in the world at this moment except my small family in my arms, in this bed.

Orla slides the baby off her chest and into the crook of my arm, and Orla twists her body so she can stare at both of us. Orla is sweaty and gleaming, her eyes sparkling in the lights. "I was reading a name book," I tell her.

She nods her head. "Of course you were."

I shrug. "Anyway, I know Irish names are important to your family. So, I thought, what about Nora?"

"Nora," Orla says, reaching for our baby, stroking the fat little cheek that's visible as I cradle her against my chest. "I really like that. It's an Irish name?"

I nod. "Yep. And it pays homage to the sounds of your name. Orla. Nora. Like mother, like daughter."

She smiles. I love when she smiles. "What's it mean?"

I kiss Orla's head and then bend my neck to kiss our girl. I inhale, and am distracted by the magical scent of her tiny head with wisps of white-gold hair. "It means light," I murmur. "And yours means golden princess, so it's a nice combo, I think."

Orla closes her eyes and sighs. "Nora. Let's do it."

B

ORLA FALLS ASLEEP EVENTUALLY and I pace around the room, holding Nora, talking to her, promising that I will always do my best to love her. "And I want to love *you*," I tell her. "I don't want you to ever have to pretend with me. Okay? You tell me who you are and I'm always proud of you." When she, too, falls asleep, I set her in the bassinet by Orla's head and work on activating the family phone tree.

My phone is practically ruined, scratched to hell from dropping it in the parking lot, but I can just barely manage to use voice commands to call Maddie. "Hey," I whisper when she picks up. "Orla is asleep so please DO NOT screech."

"Just gimme the update, Walt. Gimme, gimme! Oh my gosh, I'm so excited you're calling me first. Am I first? LIAM! We're first to find out."

"Are you there?"

"Yes. Sorry. Update?"

"Miss Nora Helen Sheffield was born in the parking lot outside the hospital a few hours ago—" I'm interrupted by a loud squeal that sounds like it's coming from Liam. I hear Maddie slapping and scolding him and telling him to shush. "Orla's terrific. Had a few stitches. She's sleeping. Nora's sleeping."

"When can we come?" Liam must have wrestled the phone away, because his deep voice exudes joy.

"I'm getting my purse," Maddie yells in the background. I laugh. I make them promise to let everyone know, and ask if they'd please call my mother for me since my phone is messed up. An hour later, the room is full of Bradys clucking and shaking their heads.

Kellen hugs everyone multiple times, and does nothing to wipe away the tears of joy streaming down his face. Mick slaps me on the back and hugs me, as if I did anything, and he must note my confused look, because he says, "She really trusts you, son. I can tell." And I think about that, how few people I myself have trusted and how the number of people who trust me must be much smaller than that.

But actually, recently, maybe that number is growing a bit. I stand amidst the back pats and hair ruffles and consider that the people in this room all trust me with their beloved Orla, and the realization isn't scary or overwhelming at all. I feel a sense of pride in this relationship.

When a nurse comes to kick them all out at the end of visiting hours, I make arrangements with Logan to take care of Pudding. Once she has my key ring, she and Cal tell me they'll come back to the hospital with a car seat, and I'm grateful this big, nosy band of relatives is thinking of these sorts of details since my exhausted brain had not considered that.

We spend a sleepless night figuring out diaper changes and keeping track of which breast Nora eats from and when, getting checked and poked until somehow the hospital staff determines that we are qualified to go home with this baby.

"Are you ready for this?" I ask Orla as I walk slowly beside her to the front door. As long as I agreed to carry Nora, the hospital staff agreed that Orla didn't have to use a wheelchair, perhaps because she gave them a look that suggested she would burn them to a crisp if they didn't.

"I'm definitely not ready for this," she says, clutching my arm and wincing a little as she walks.

"Aw, come on, now, any woman who can complete an engineering exam in active labor can surely handle one little newborn!"

Orla gives my arm a squeeze. "She weighs nine pounds," Orla says. "That's not even newborn size diapers." I situate Nora in the car seat, awkwardly tugging on the straps while Orla climbs in the back to ride with the baby. We decided we're going to stay at Orla's house in Morningside at least for now, because having Kellen and Elizabeth across the street seems a lot more important now that Nora is actually here and seeming so fragile.

When I pull in the driveway, we laugh because our lawn is filled with bright decorations and IT'S A GIRL signs. I hurry up the steps to the front door with the car seat and jog back down to support Orla as she makes her way up to the porch. "What's that?" Orla points at a piece of paper taped to the front door.

I pluck it down and hold it up so we can both read:

You're welcome for the lack of pink decorations. We all broke into your house last night to set up all the crap we would have given you at the shower. You're not getting out of the spa event, though. And we're going to serve booze now!

~FOOF

ORLA SMILES and looks like she's holding back tears when I open the front door to reveal a house transformed. A glider rocker has been set up in the living room with a diaper changing table and stacks of creams and wipes. I see a machine I assume is a little radio, but when we look closer, we discover it's a breast pump with a note from Maddie about how to use it.

The walls are covered in banners and congratulatory decorations. Nora's bedroom is decked out with a crib, the dresser drawers are full of washed and folded clothing, and the master bedroom is now home to a bassinet, white noise machine, and another case of diapers.

Orla clutches Nora to her chest and hums, turning in circles. "This is... it's all just a lot," she says.

I just nod. I feel teary myself, thinking about how much folks care to band together like that at the last minute, like it was nothing. "This is everything," I say to my girls. "This means everything to me, that people would do this for you."

Orla squeezes my arm. "For us, Walt," she says. "They did it for *us*."

CHAPTER THIRTY-FOUR
ORLA
FEBRUARY

 time of day. I've taken to just lying in bed with my tits out, sleeping in two-hour chunks. Periodically, someone brings me the baby. It seems to be a different Brady Lady each time—my cousins are all too squeamish about seeing my boobs to enter the bedroom.

My family is here because Walt works all the time. He was supposed to be able to get a few weeks off, but his supervisor wouldn't approve the leave. I definitely mind it a lot more when I'm not neck deep in exam preparations. If my dad and Elizabeth weren't bringing over portions of their dinner every day, I'm not sure I'd ever eat a meal. I feel like it's all I can do to keep Nora fed and dry.

Things felt so magical with him at the hospital and when we first got home here. It was just the three of us, cuddled up. He told me I'd be responsible for Nora's input and he'd handle the output, but now he's so exhausted from work I've just been tackling night detail alone.

He has to literally haul packages uphill in the snow all day, and I've got relatives dropping by all the time, letting me rest during the day. Logan and Cal even went to Walt's house to fetch Pudding and some of his gear so he'd be here with us and Walt wouldn't have to worry about Pud's medication.

I love setting Nora down in her bouncy chair and watching Pudding give her a few sniffs. Sometimes the three of us sit on the floor together, staring at each other. I guess if Walt can't be here more often, he at least left me with two really cute companions.

Today, Walt has promised to be home by six because his mom is finally coming to meet Nora. Celeste was being weird about driving in the snow, but agreed that the roads should be pretty safe for her to journey down here from the suburban hinterlands. She told Walt she didn't want to intrude, so that's why she hasn't come any sooner to meet her grandchild.

"I shouldn't be a bitch," I say to Pudding as I stroke the fur between his ears. Eventually, Nora seems soundly enough asleep that I decide to risk a shower. It seems so decadent, such a simple thing. I leave the door open so I'll hear if Nora starts to cry, and I stand under the water until my skin feels like it'll melt.

When I get out and changed, Nora is still asleep and Pudding is sprawled out next to her, also asleep, so I snap a picture and text it to my hot mailman. Celeste is supposed to be bringing dinner for us, but our fridge is stocked up from my family running errands for us, so I decide to whip up some spinach dip while Nora finishes her nap.

I'm feeling pretty damn high on life when the oven timer bings just as Nora starts stirring. I've got my hair combed, my teeth brushed, and I'm wearing an outfit that counts as real clothes, even if they're still maternity clothes. I unlock the front door and settle into the glider rocker to feed my daughter.

A few minutes later, I hear a knock, and I shout "come on in!" I'm sure it's Celeste, and when nothing happens, I holler, "Come in, Celeste. It's open! I'm feeding the baby."

The door creaks open slowly and she pokes her head in timidly. She gives a little gasp when she sees me. "Oh I just...I can come back."

"Please come in! Sit with us."

She looks around, maybe searching for Walt, but he hasn't gotten home yet. "I didn't know...is Trippy here?"

I shake my head and move to switch Nora to my other boob. I'm not super adept at working my nursing bra, which means Walt's mom is getting an eyeful. But she's the grandma, and these cans are cranking out the milk that's chunking up her first grandchild. I don't have time to care if Celeste is uncomfortable. I smile again, squeezing Nora's thigh. "She's gaining almost two ounces a day," I say and look over at Celeste.

Her eyes widen. "That sounds like an awful lot."

"I mean, we want her to chunk up! She's getting primo liquid gold right now, too." I start blabbing nervously about all the food people have been bringing over, because I don't know what else to say to Walt's mom. "Not only is my dad letting us stay in his spare house, but he and his girlfriend have been making us dinner every day! And Elizabeth knows all the different foods that help milk production, so everything has oats or fennel. And so much protein. I've never eaten so much meat in my life."

I feel myself rambling and decide to just take a pause. Nora's just finishing up, so I say, "Would you like to hold her?" I offer the baby out like Rafiki in the Lion King and bite back an urge to make a joke about everything the milk touches.

Celeste swallows and takes Nora from me and I put my boobs back inside my shirt. I smooth out my clothes and move over next to Celeste on the couch. She is speechless, just keeps shaking her head and saying "oh" at the baby. "Oh, my."

"She looks like Walt, don't you think?" I tickle Nora's foot as Celeste holds her kind of awkwardly.

Celeste turns to look at me. "She is absolutely breathtaking."

I bite the inside of my cheek and look up at the clock. It's 5:55. "Come on, Wally," I mutter under my breath. I sigh in relief when I hear his car door close and his footsteps on the stairs out front. He bursts in the door and I waggle my eyebrows at him. He looks fine in his winter gear, what with the blue trousers and the fur-lined hat and that jacket that shouldn't turn me on but does.

He beams when he sees us. "All the best women in the world, right here on the couch," he says. And I feel smug when he kisses me on the cheek first before greeting his mother.

"I made spinach dip," I tell him, gesturing toward the kitchen.

"Oh, you're a goddess," he says. I follow him in there and laugh as he crams an entire ladle-full into his mouth without bothering to dip in chunks of bread. As he chews, he pulls me in for a proper hug and then gives me one of those old Hollywood kisses, where he dips me backwards a little.

He sets me back upright and tugs my ponytail. "I'm going to grab a shower. Then I'll be back to eat the rest of that dip."

I watch him jog up the stairs, admiring the view, and I sink back onto the couch. "I could get used to this," I say, grinning. But Celeste looks at me strangely. I know she doesn't really approve of Walt working as a mail carrier, so I just chalk her attitude up to that. I don't love his job so much myself right now, but I don't want to talk with her about how much he's been gone. I am not about to create a situation where he feels ganged up on again.

ℬ

A FEW DAYS LATER, I'm having another great day where I shower, get dressed, and even manage to check my email.

Pudding hops over to nuzzle my feet as I sit at the table with my laptop. "No news about your daddy," I tell him, and click the lid shut. It's getting dark and I haven't heard from Walt at all today, so I decide to take advantage of Nora's nap and eat my dinner without him.

It's definitely starting to get a little ridiculous how many hours he's working. I mean, sure, he gets paid overtime, but what good does that do him if he has no opportunity to ever spend it? I'm in bed feeding Nora by the time he gets home and crawls in beside us.

"I missed you," he whispers, and his lips are cold against my skin.

"We missed you, too," I say. I try to roll over so I'm facing him. It takes a few minutes and he finally scoops Nora up and starts covering her with kisses. "I hate how much you're gone."

"I know," he says. "I put in for my parental leave again. I'm waiting to hear from my union rep when that will be approved."

"Listen to you talking about union reps." I kiss his scratchy cheek. He doesn't grow much of a beard but he does tend to get stubbly by night time. I rub against him like a cat as Nora drifts off to sleep between us. "Do you have any other work lingo?"

"Mmm," he hums. "COA. Hot case." His thumb traces circles on my shoulder blades as he talks and I want to be turned on, but I'm too tired and sore, so instead I fall asleep in his arms, vaguely aware of him scooping up Nora and talking to her softly as he changes her diaper.

Walt kisses us both goodbye in the morning and spends time romping around on the floor with Pudding before he sighs and starts layering on his outdoor gear. I tug his hat on his head and try not to pout as I wave goodbye to him from behind the storm door.

I'm halfway to the kitchen when I hear a knock on the door, and I grin, assuming it's Walt back for one last kiss. "Did you forget something?" The words die on my mouth as I open the door and realize it's not Walt, but a stranger.

"Orla Brady?"

I furrow my brow at the man, who is wearing a suit and looks like an evangelist. I'm definitely not ready for unsolicited company. "Yes?" I cross my arms over my chest, worried I'll start leaking milk before I can get rid of this person. He hands out an envelope, which I accept and stare down at it.

"You've been served," he says, and turns to rush down the stairs before I can ask questions.

Served? I close and lock the front door and sit down on the couch, pulling Nora up onto my lap as I open the envelope. Inside is a thick packet of papers with lots of legal jargon. I haven't had coffee yet and only slept in small increments last night, so I'm not entirely sure what this is.

I see the words "DNA verification" and "paternity" and "financial responsibility" and I start to panic. What is this? I set the papers down and take a few deep breaths. I'm not thinking clearly and this isn't my forte.

I pick up the phone to call my dad, who answers immediately. "Is something wrong? Does Nora need her Grampy?"

I smile. "Nora always needs her Grampy, Dad. But, actually...something weird happened this morning. Can you stop over on your way to work and take a look at something for me?"

He's bounding out the front door within seconds and I shake my head as I watch him dash across the street. I let him in and wait patiently while he cuddles Nora, greets Pudding, and then asks me what's going on.

He studies the documents carefully, saying nothing. His face gives nothing away until he gets to the last page for the second time, and I see him press his lips tightly together.

"What is it, Dad? Something about Nora and Walt?"

Dad shakes his head and inhales sharply through his nose. "This is a subpoena for you to submit Nora for a DNA test, Orla. The documents call for establishing paternity and creating a custody and support agreement."

I hear him saying those words, and they make no sense to me. "Why would Nora need a DNA test?" What has Walt been up to all this time he hasn't been here at home with us?

Dad squeezes my leg. "It looks like the Sheffield family is concerned about their assets, sweetie. These papers...they make it seem like you are trying to go after their money."

I snap my head back. "What money? Walt said there is no money. His stupid dad squandered it all away." I stand up and clutch Nora against my chest. "Don't answer that. It's undignified and against the point. Me? A gold digger?"

"Orla, let's talk about—"

I'm pacing in tight circles now. I can't begin to verbalize how angry I'm feeling right now. "I didn't even want him to be involved. I didn't want anything to do with the fucking Sheffield family after I learned the truth about their business dealings." I think about how rarely he's here. I think about how loving he seems when he is here, and how strange it is for him to be arranging to send legal paperwork to the house without discussing it with me. My eyes flare wide and I feel my heart racing. "I knew his whole Good Samaritan mailman persona was a long con. God, he had me fooled."

"Where is Walt, Orla? Let's ask him why he would have these sent to the house."

I burst out with a high pitched sound. "He's at work, obviously. He's always at work! I'm surprised he could get a day off to bring me and Nora home from the hospital."

Dad nods and I can tell he's trying to consider this whole thing rationally. But there is nothing to rationalize. Is there? Dad sighs. "I have a hypothesis here, and I know it's going to be upsetting."

I halt and stare at my father. He blinks. "God, Dad, don't leave me hanging here. What? Your hypotheses are never wrong..."

Dad licks his lips and sighs again. "This really seems like something Celeste would have set in motion. Have you spoken with her since she came over to meet Nora?"

As soon as he says the words, I know he's right. I set my teeth and pull my daughter close, kissing the top of her head and pausing for a long sniff because I can't help it. "You're right," I tell him. "And no. I haven't spoken to her. I've barely even seen Walt. He works all the damn time."

Dad nods. "He has a challenging job."

I'm pacing tight circles now, my heart racing. "Is he trying to get out of being with us? Because I can make that happen for him really quick."

I snarl and rant and Dad stands up, walking toward me. "I'm sure that's not what's happening here, sweetie."

"Yeah? Between the long hours and this bullshit legal crap?" I thrust Nora out toward my dad and I go into the bathroom to splash cold water on my face. I stare at my reflection, at the dark circles under my eyes from not sleeping, at the puffy chin I still have from the weight I gained carrying Nora.

I let myself rely on him. I let myself believe we could be a family together. Custody and support agreement? "Fuck him," I shout at myself in the mirror.

I storm out of the bathroom and stomp over to the couch, where Dad is still sitting, looking concerned. I grab my cell phone and look up the number for the locksmith.

This shit ends right now.

CHAPTER THIRTY-FIVE
WALT

They have me in Bloomfield again this week, which means a lot of visits with senior citizens waiting for meds or simply company. I smile as I jog up the steps to greet Mrs. Natali, who wraps her short arms around me in a hug.

"Walt! Oh I'm glad it's you again. I've been waiting."

"Well who was here last week, Mrs. N? Wouldn't they help you out?"

She waves a hand. "One of those grumpy gals. Said she doesn't have time." Mrs. Natali points inside the door to a flat of tins of cat food. I sigh. Mrs. Natali's fingers aren't strong enough to pry open the pull tabs anymore, but I can't let myself worry about how the cats were getting fed during the time I wasn't on this route.

I crouch and start to open the tins of food. "You want me to just open them a crack or all the way?"

"Take 'em off," she says. Her two cats come to the door and start circling her feet. I smile and reach out my hand to pet them, but they back away.

"It's okay, guys. I probably smell like rabbit." I open the last lid and stand up, brushing rock salt off my knees. "You have foil or something to put over the tops?"

She nods. "I've got all that sorted out. Thank you so much, Walt. You're really a life saver."

"Don't worry about it, Mrs. Natali. I'd want someone to help me feed Pudding!"

She grins. "Can I see another picture of that bunny? Such a sweetheart."

I pull up a picture Orla sent me, of Pudding guarding Nora in her bouncy chair, and flash it toward Mrs. N. "Oh my stars and garters," she cries, snatching the phone from me. "Is that your baby? What a sweet thing! What's her name?"

I can't control the giant grin on my face when I tell her about Nora. And when Mrs. Natali pulls me in for a hug and congratulates me, I carry the warmth of her embrace back out into the frigid streets.

When I pick up the outgoing mail from the corner store, I show the owner my picture of Nora, too, and they give me a tray of ravioli to take home. I'm intoxicated by the well wishes and smiles from all the people along my route. I'm not bragging about her because I want free stuff. Nonetheless, by the end of the day, the passenger seat of my mail van is weighed down with lotion and scones and roses for Orla and my baby girl.

I drive home and skip up the front steps with my arms full of the well-wishes from all my postal customers, but I find the storm door locked. I peek in the front curtains, but the living room is dark, so I assume Orla and Nora are napping. I grumble a bit as I set down my bundle to fish for my keys, but then I can't get my key to fit in the lock.

I try futilely for a few minutes until I hear someone clear their throat behind me on the stoop. I turn and see Kellen standing with his hands in his pockets, looking very serious. "Kellen, hi. I'm having trouble with the door, but you want to come in once I get it open?"

Kellen grimaces, his mouth a thin line behind his white beard. He reaches out for my arm. "I think you'd better find somewhere else to stay tonight, son."

"What?"

He sighs. "Orla received a subpoena this morning. Have you touched base with your mother recently?" My stomach drops and I jiggle the door-knob again. Then I get angry and pound on the glass.

Kellen touches my shoulder. "Orla's pretty upset. I tried to talk her out of changing the locks, but she hasn't slept in a long time."

I swallow, feeling like I'm going to choke on the lump in my throat as I realize what Kellen is saying. "What should I do?" I plead with him, like he's my own father here to offer advice, but of course he's Orla's father. He's always going to be on her side and I'll never have that kind of support in my life. "What did my mother do?"

Kellen smiles briefly at me. "Talk to your mother. Find out what's going on with the papers. And son?"

My mouth is dry at his endearment. It feels so overwhelming to hear another man call me that, a man who has never been anything but nice to me. He shakes his head. "Talk to Orla about those long hours at work. You've got a newborn."

Kellen extends an arm back down toward the driveway and doesn't say another word. I stare at him for a few minutes before I clear my throat and point to the pile of things on the porch. "My customers sent all these things for Orla and Nora," I tell him. "Can you please see that they get them?"

His nod is barely perceptible, and I back down the stairs and climb into my car. Kellen stands on the porch with his arms crossed, so I back out of the driveway and down the block before pulling over to think.

I haven't even seen my daughter since this morning. Orla received some sort of court summons in the mail and I wasn't even available to help her navigate that.

I groan and pull up our lawyer in my contacts. "Watson, hey, it's Walt Sheffield. I was wondering if you knew—"

"Trip, hey. No worries. I got the notification that Ms. Brady was served this morning. I thought your mother would have told you."

"My mother?"

He laughs. "Yeah. She said she was setting all this in motion for you."

Jesus Christ, my family. "You have to know I was not involved in setting this in motion. How in the hell can you serve my family a subpoena without my permission? I got home today and I think my girlfriend changed the locks on me."

He makes a sympathetic sound. "Yeah, that'll happen in these cases."

"What cases? Watson, you're helping my mother fuck me over. Now, talk to me like I'm five here. What did my mother have you do?"

I DRIVE to my childhood home in a blind rage and barge in the front door without knocking. I find my mother in the dining room, clutching a wine glass to her chest and looking alarmed. "Trippy! What on earth are you doing here?"

"Cut the crap, Mom."

She sputters. "Is this about the paperwork? I can assure you Mr. Watson said it's all very standard. You're not married. A DNA test is standard in these cases, sweetheart." She sets her wine glass down and folds her hands on the table.

I throw one of the dining chairs and walk closer to her. "DNA test? For what? You need to tell me exactly why you had Watson serve my family with court papers."

"Please sit down, Trippy, you're upset..." Her face has gone paler than usual and she pushes her plate of food away from her.

"Do NOT call me that anymore. I hate that name. Call me Walt, Mother. And you're damned right I'm upset. You, for some reason, took it upon yourself to meddle into my family and make my girlfriend think that I think she's a gold digger. Or, God, what if she thinks I'm trying to get out of my responsibility to Nora?"

"The way she was talking the other day...relying on charity to provide food...squatting in a house she can't pay for! What kind of message does that send? I'm just looking after our assets, sweetheart. "

I throw another chair. "Mother. There. Are. No. Assets. What in the actual fuck is wrong with you?" Her eyes widen. I squat on the ground in front of her. "Listen to me. Your husband, my father, left us with nothing. You are barely hanging on to the house. You are clinging to a lifestyle you can no longer afford, even with the life insurance. There is nothing for Orla or anyone to come after."

She starts shaking her head and I stand up and stomp my foot. "How dare you accuse her of that. Do you know what she was doing when she went into labor? She was seven hours into one of the most comprehensive engineering exams around. Do you know how few people can even attempt to take that, let alone do it? Orla Brady is an absolute rock star and I don't deserve her and now, thanks to your meddling, I've most likely lost her."

I put my hands on my mother's shoulders and force her to look me in the eye. "You might have just cost me my daughter, Mother. My child." Mom starts crying, but I don't have time for her emotions right now. "You're going to fix this. You're going to tell my family that this is your doing, and you're not going to meddle into my affairs ever again. If you ever want to see me or your granddaughter, ever again, you are going to make this right."

I storm out of the house without waiting for her response.

CHAPTER THIRTY-SIX
ORLA

I don't feel like having a spa night with my friends. I don't feel like doing anything at all. I've been walking around in a haze. Elizabeth and Maddie come over periodically to make sure I'm drinking enough water.

My own father stood on the stoop and tried to be good cop talking to Walt, like it's okay for his family to meddle while he's out working every single hour of the day. Fuck that. I didn't invite him into this whole situation just to raise the kid on my own anyway.

Today, when Nicole burst in the front door to collect me, I just assumed it was another hydration intervention, but she hauled me and Nora into the car. "I know you already got the presents. That's the best part, Orla. Now we can stick you in a chair and rub your feet and sniff your baby while Esther plies us with drinks!"

I snort and try to comb my fingers through my hair. I'm not sure when I last showered. I actually don't know how much time has passed since the subpoena, but I haven't been good at keeping track of time since Nora arrived. Nicole parks outside Bridges and Bitters and scoops Nora out of her car seat, and I follow behind with the diaper bag.

The back room is full when we walk in, and everyone cheers. Nicole is immediately swarmed with Foof ladies wanting to meet Nora, and Esther escorts me to one of the pedicure chairs. I slump into the chair, only briefly caring that I haven't shaved my legs and the nail technician is going to be rubbing her hands through stubble.

Emma Stag hands Nora to me to nurse and when she's done, Maddie scoops her back away. I don't even have the energy to put my boob away, and so I'm sitting there with a Moscow Mule, tits out, getting my toes painted, when Juniper Jones shouts at me.

"Hey!" She taps her foot and I startle, nearly dropping my drink. "First of all, you have to put your boobs back in your bra, Orla. I know we're friends here and I myself breastfed giant Stag babies, but you, my friend, are a mess."

The nail tech blushes. I sigh and set my drink down so I can fasten my nursing bra with both hands. Juniper smiles and helps me up out of the spa chair, guiding me over to a station where another vendor is threading eyebrows. This is actually a pretty great event Nicole put together. I feel bad that I'm not able to be more present.

"Now," Juniper says, taking a seat across from me and putting on a sweat band to hold her short hair back from her forehead so she can get her brows done. "Once I'm done here, I'm going to look at the papers your family tells me you were served. Sound good?"

I nod and watch as she doesn't even wince as her dark brow hairs are yanked out of her face. I'm not nearly as stoic when it's my turn, yelping and squirming, but I share in Juniper's observation that the results are pretty great. "I look like...more me," I tell her, turning my face a bit to stare in the handheld mirror.

"Damn right," Juniper says. "Now give me the papers. Nicole said she was going to slip them into the diaper bag when she went to get you."

I raise my newly-shaped brows and rummage in the bag to discover she is correct. I slide the folder over to Juniper, who scoots her chair closer to mine and mutters to herself as she traces along with her finger. "Okay," she says. "This is really standard paperwork for families of financial means, even sometimes if the couple *is* married." She flips through the final few pages. "But the fact that Walt didn't mention anything to you is very odd, not gonna lie."

"Well," I snort. "In order to mention it to me he'd have to come home sometimes during waking hours. Which, in case you don't remember, are all the hours because WE HAVE A NEWBORN."

Juniper pats my arm. "We're going to figure this out, okay?"

Just then a hush falls over the room and I look up when Nicole says, pointedly, "This is a private engagement."

"Oh, hell no," I say, when I see who she's talking to. I stand up and say, "That's Wally's fucking mom. I don't want to see her."

Foof forms a human wall around me, all standing with their hands on their hips, regardless of what stage they are at in their spa treatments. Esther comes in the door holding what appears to be a polished chrome pipe, smacking it against her hand menacingly. She says, "If you've got more papers to serve you can just leave them and be on your way."

Celeste wrings her hands and seems to tremble. She opens her mouth to say something but no sound comes out. I'm standing behind my wall of friends, holding Nora against my chest, but I'm way taller than Emma and Chloe in front of me and I can see Celeste wobbling, like she's going to fall over. "Please," she begs, her voice cracking. "I need to tell you something."

Nicole looks like she wants to drive a spike through Celeste's heart, but she says, "You have exactly two minutes and then I'll drag you out of here myself if we don't like what you have to say."

Celeste looks around the room, and the rows of angry eyes fixed on her. Logan taps one fingernail on her watch and Celeste draws a shaky breath. "I had the papers sent to you, Orla. I was the one who called the lawyer after I came to meet the baby."

She fishes in her pocket for a tissue and tugs on it with both hands. "Trippy—Walt—is furious with me. He's refusing my calls." She closes her eyes and a tear slips out. "Do you know what it's like for your own son to refuse your phone calls?"

Nobody says anything and Celeste keeps talking. "He says I have to make this right, that I have to make you understand. Well...I suppose after I left your home I imagined that you were rather desperate for money, because you were talking about receiving meals and free rent."

Maddie snorts. "Oh, come on! Seriously?" But Logan elbows her and she closes her lips.

Celeste looks just at me now. "I assumed that because I would have been, in your shoes. Desperate that is. The way I was raised...there was never any question that I'd stay home in support of my husband and his career. I...I want to tell you something not as an excuse for my behavior." She sniffs. "But perhaps you'd accept an explanation from me?"

I don't encourage her, but I don't tell her to kick rocks, either, so she continues. "College was for meeting sorority sisters from good families, building connections. Finding a husband. You have to understand, Orla, that that is all I've known."

Nicole is frowning now and staring at Celeste intently, but Nik no longer looks irate so I let myself relax my posture a little as Celeste continues. "I barely knew Walton when we married. My father owed his a favor, if you can believe that, and encouraged me to spend time with...it was practically arranged."

Piper walks over and offers Celeste a chair, and gradually the Foof ladies return to their seats as Celeste keeps talking about how she's been groomed her entire life to be a model housewife. "Walt came to my home and told me about your exams and your career, Orla, and he talked about you so passionately. With so much pride. I saw in his face that he was in love with you and your drive and your *goals!*" She dabs at her face. "I've never had goals other than the ones my family set for me, to marry up and raise respectable children. And the men deemed acceptable for me, well, they would never take pride in a woman doing such things as that."

Sam murmurs, "Fucking patriarchy," and everyone around me groans in agreement.

Celeste turns to face her. "I was a teen in the 70s," she says. "Feminism was a bad word at our country club, a word for crass women who couldn't land a proper husband." She shudders. "My husband's love was always conditional," she says. "I always knew my looks mattered more than anything I had to say about him or his work or his ideas. I was just supposed to look good and be pleasant." She shrugs. "And if I didn't feel pleasant, I drank gin or took pills until I could pretend." Celeste shudders. "My husband never once looked at me the way I saw my son look at you when he came home from work the other day, when I was at your home."

She swallows and closes her eyes and she's silent for a long time. Nobody says a word until she opens her eyes. "I'm so sorry, Orla. I don't know how to be a supportive mother to Walt. I don't know how to be a mother-in-law to an ambitious woman. I don't even know how to be among society anymore. Not after the humiliation of my husband's final years..."

She drifts off and starts crying until eventually, Chloe walks over to sit next to her and pulls her in for a hug. I watch as my friends gather around her and offer her drinks of water and tissues. Celeste cries harder in the face of their kindness. "How can you possibly forgive me?" She shakes her head. "What matters is that you forgive my son. This was not his fault. He says he's been trying to escape me for years. My son. I drove my own son away from me."

As Celeste breaks down I sigh and walk toward her with Nora. Chloe gets up from the seat next to Celeste and I sink into it. "Look," I say, turning Nora to face her grandmother. "I'm terrible with feelings, mine and other people's. Yes, it's fucking awful the pressures you and your husband placed on Walt growing up. Nobody needs that bullshit." She starts crying again. I hold out my hand. "But it sounds like you suffered through the same bullshit for your whole life, too, and you were just...I don't know. I don't know what I'm saying here. But I promise I'm not after your money."

She clutches at her chest. "Oh, god, I know that now. I apologize for setting those papers in motion. I've called Mr. Watson and told him to shred everything."

I feel the urge to say thank you, but I know that's not the right emotion to convey in this situation. "I'm glad you did that," I say, finally. I bounce Nora on my lap and stare at this wounded woman who has inflicted so much pain, and has been harmed as well.

Then, like she's reading my mind, Chloe stands up and says, "Hurt people, hurt people." She squeezes Celeste's shoulder. "It's good that you came here to say all that today, Mrs. Sheffield. It's a good first step."

Celeste swallows. "I don't know what comes next." She looks around the room. I think this is the quietest a Foof meeting has ever been.

"Well," Sam says, tapping on the table. "This group here, we call ourselves Fresh Out Of Fucks. We gather together to help each other overcome these kinds of problems." Celeste's eyes widen at Sam's flagrant use of profanity. "Feminism isn't a bad word. It's not about destroying men. Feminism, and Foof, is about empowering women to make their own damn choices. Pursue their own goals. Hell, just having a goal is a radical act for a woman, apparently."

There's a chorus of agreement. Celeste nods, slightly.

Sam grins and looks around the room. "Well, ladies, we have a new member whose goal is to atone for shitty meddling." She raises her brows at Celeste, whose jaw drops open. Sam continues. "And! I think Celeste is going to work on identifying some personal goals now that she's newly single and currently not employed."

"Oh, I've never been employed," Celeste says.

Sam waves a hand. "Doesn't matter." She steps toward Celeste and sets a hand on her shoulder. "We're going to help you, Celeste, but you have to let go of your fucks. Can you do that?"

Celeste's eyes are wide and her lip trembles. She whispers, "I have no earthly idea!" She looks around the room, and she looks at me and finally at Nora.

Nicole nods and says, "We can work with that."

CHAPTER THIRTY-SEVEN
WALT

I feel a huge sense of deja vu as I sit in my living room, just staring at the wall. I have no girlfriend, no parents. At least I have a job ... a job that denied my request for parental leave and is impacting my relationship with my girlfriend. And my baby.

My Nora. I ache to hold her, to see her. I don't know how I'll ever forgive my mother for what she did, for jeopardizing the family I started to build for myself, on my own terms.

Nora is supposed to be my chance to show someone all the love and warmth I never felt. And, damn it, Orla, too. I need her. I need her to understand that I would never do something like this to shake her trust in me. I cannot bear to think she thinks of me as the same sort of person my father was.

A lifetime of anger throbs through my veins until I feel helpless. I've tried calling Orla hundreds of times, but she clearly has my number blocked, or else her phone really has been turned off for days. I understand the urge. After I drove up and screamed at my mother, I blocked her number, too. I just am not ready to listen to anything she has to say about the situation. Not yet.

I have to figure out something I can do to at least talk to them. Half of me wants to run to the police station and demand that they make sure I can spend time with my daughter.

It's killing me not knowing how her face has changed, or if she has a rash or all those thousand things I got to learn about her every day, even if I had to be at work.

I hear a knock at the door and I ignore it, assuming it's a political canvasser or the mail carrier with more certified mail for me. I scoff at the absurdity, but the knocking persists. When I look outside, I see Orla on my stoop looking irritated and I open the door so fast, she topples inside with the baby carrier.

I catch them both before we all hit the floor.

"Orla!"

"Hey." She looks at me, and doesn't say anything further. I feel like I can't breathe. I want to hide, and squeeze them. I want to scream and laugh.

"Oh, god, my baby girl!" I reach for Nora, who is awake in her seat and staring at me from beneath her knitted, replica mailman hat that Orla found online. I scoop her out of the seat and pull her close, inhaling her, peppering her with kisses. She brings her tiny hand up to grab at my nose.

I hear a click and look up to see Logan grinning from the stoop, taking a picture with her phone. "You're so cute with her, Walt," she says, smiling. She looks at Orla. "Okay, well you're here. I'm going to give you privacy now."

Orla looks at her. "What if I hurt him and you're not here to protect him?"

Logan pats Orla on the head as she helps her to her feet. "Nobody is getting a smackdown. I trust you with your baby daddy."

Orla glares at me as Logan waves and walks toward her car.

I squat on the ground holding Nora, frozen in place and afraid to move. I want to spring up and wrap Orla in my arms. I want to just blurt out all my apologies for ever bringing my stupid parents into her world. But I've also spent decades being told to keep my trap shut, so I lean into that training and wait for Orla to talk.

She turns toward me, blowing her hair out of her face with a puff. "Your mom came to my baby shower," she says.

I groan. "Oh, god, I'm so sorry, Orla. Please let me explain that—"

She holds her hand up. "Celeste told me that all the paperwork was her idea. And then she talked about how she's always been a prisoner of her privilege."

I raise my brow, surprised to learn my mother would say anything of this nature to Orla. She continues. "I'm still really fucking mad at her, Walt.

I just don't downshift that fast, especially knowing how much you have been hurt by her and your dad over, well, over your whole life."

I nod, swallowing down a lump. Is it possible to choke on emotions? To actually suffocate? Orla takes a deep breath. "I'm really sorry I was so fast to lock you out and I'm sorry I kept you from Nora, Walt. That won't ever happen again."

"I understand why you did it," I say. I want to hug her. My arms burn to be holding both of them. I don't want crippling indecision to stand in my way, so I just say, "I really want to hug you, Orla. Can I hold you?"

She holds up a palm. "Not so fast. I'm not done." I swallow and nod my head toward the couch. She doesn't sit, though. She stands in front of me with her arms crossed, frowning down at me. "You work too much."

I slump against the couch. "I know I do, but what can I do? I don't have my own route yet. I keep getting shuffled around and it's taking me 10 hours to do something that Mark can do in six."

"Well then fucking have Mark do it, Walt. You took one day off when your baby was born. One day!"

"Yeah," I snap. "And I caught a lot of shit for it."

Her eyes flash. "Do you really want to work in a place that gives you crap for taking one day to get your baby home from the hospital? The hospital, Walt."

I scrub my palm down my cheek, noticing that I haven't shaved. I think about what she's saying and I know she's right, but I also need her to understand how this job is the first thing I've ever had on my own terms. The first thing I ever was able to take pride in. I take a deep breath. "I'll talk to them again about my hours, but I need you to appreciate that I'm committed to this job."

Her nostrils flare and I watch as she takes a deep breath, considering. Finally, she nods and sits next to me on the couch. "I want to work on shit with you, Walt. I love you. I suck at trust and communicating and I'm stubborn, but I love you and I need you."

"Oh, god, Orla I need you, too. I need you and Nora so much!" I pounce, pulling her close with one arm while Nora is cradled between us. I inhale the scent of the top of her head, never wanting to be apart from her long enough to forget how this feels. Ever again.

I'm not sure how long we sit there, hugging in the living room. Eventually, I feel something wet and sticky on my arm and we realize Nora has blown out her diaper. This leads us both to further realize we don't have any baby stuff here apart from what's in the diaper bag.

Orla washes Nora's butt in my kitchen sink with the dish sprayer and it feels so good to laugh with her about the mess, about the chaotic reality of life with babies. Slowly, my body begins to unclench from the past few days. We can work on this. She wants to work on this.

Nothing about our evening is elegant or refined, and yet I'm more comfortable in the middle of a literal shit storm than I've ever been, because I'm not alone. Orla packs Nora into my car and we drive back to the house in Morningside. And I breathe easy because I'm back where I belong. For now.

CHAPTER THIRTY-EIGHT
WALT
APRIL

"Did you pack her giraffe?" Orla shouts from the kitchen where she's packing lunches for all of us. Bottled breastmilk for Nora, a regular lunch for herself, and an entire cooler full of fat and protein for me.

"I got the giraffe *and* the crinkle thing." We're so lucky that we don't have to take Nora very far for childcare. Elizabeth watches her two days a week across the street and my mom has been sitting with her at our house the other three days.

It's been a challenge. Orla wasn't thrilled with the idea, but we didn't want Nora to start at a daycare center before she had all her vaccinations. We argued a lot about relying on grandparents instead of me being able to take parental leave. We argue about my job a lot, actually.

Orla pokes her head around the kitchen wall. "Today's an Elizabeth day, right? It's Friday right now?"

"Yep. Totally Friday."

"Okay, then I'm not going to worry about the dishes until later." She's down the hall before I can remind her that she doesn't need to worry about the dishes while my mom is here, either. Mom has been working really hard on herself. She's probably never going to be best friends with Orla, but I really think Mom has come a long way.

"You know," I shout. "I caught my mom cuddling with Pudding the other day."

Orla freezes in her tracks and comes into the living room, where I'm squatting as I stuff diapers into Nora's bag. "She was cuddling? Like on the ground?"

"Yep." I pop my P as I point to the guy in question, currently chewing on one of Nora's little moccasins. "Gimme that, you rascal." I pry the shoe away from him and grin at Orla. "I've caught Mom nuzzling with Pudding enough that I am trying to get her to come with me to the next bingo fundraiser."

Orla's jaw hangs open in surprise. "You're trying to get your mother into a fire hall to play bingo with other ladies?"

I nod. "Give me three months and I think Susan will have her signed up to foster." Orla raises a brow at me and grabs her bag.

"Well, keep me posted on that. You okay to drop her off over there?" I nod and she kisses us both and rushes out the door to ride into the office with her father.

They wave at me from across the street as I finally start walking down the porch steps. Elizabeth greets me with her usual friendly kiss on the cheek. It feels really good to be a part of a big family like this, even if Orla's cousins do get annoying when they argue about the structural stability of my messenger bag or show up here unannounced.

Not that I'm home much for the unannounced visits. I sigh, as I drive to the station. My work hours are probably at least half the reason Orla's cousins show up as often as they do. She went back to Beltane without missing a beat, starting up a new fire detection project and even bringing in Cal to partner on autonomous fire protection something-something.

I sometimes come home to find the two of them on the couch with Nora, asking the baby her opinions about fire safety along power lines in remote locations. It's sweet, and I remind myself it's good that she has the support, even as the thought eats at me that it should be me there asking my daughter questions, not Nora's uncle.

The Bluetooth in my car picks up an incoming call from Orla just as I'm pulling into the lot. "Hey," she says, sounding frenzied. "Do you think your mom would come with me to Kentucky?"

"What? Why would you ask that?"

She sighs. "Cal and Liam and I are presenting our proposal to the utilities managers in Lexington. I don't want to deal with the milk pumping to leave Nora at home."

"Okay, first of all, that's amazing. And second, why wouldn't I be the one to come with you?"

She pauses. "Walt, when could you go to Kentucky? Are you saying you could get time off to go on a multi-day trip?"

My heart sinks as I realize she's right. But what's worse, she's accepted this as the truth. She can't rely on me when she has to take a business trip, and she seems resigned to looking elsewhere for support. "I don't know what to say," I tell her.

"Okay, well take a few hours and think about it because I need to start making arrangements. Elizabeth can't come because Jake has finals and she can't leave him home alone, obviously."

"Sure, sure. I just...can't believe my mom is the option here."

"Hey, babe, Dad is here to brief me on our strategy for this. We just found out they liked our proposal so this is all unfolding really fast."

We hang up and I stare at the parking lot, where my colleagues are bustling around already. Some of them have been here for hours. I see Mark and give him a wave, smiling when he grins back at me. I do enjoy my work, and this job really saved me when my entire life was fraying at the seams.

I chew on the inside of my cheek. My life is fraying at the seams now. Orla and I have had a very chaste, businesslike arrangement ever since the incident with my mom and the paperwork. I know we have a newborn, and I know that's rough on all relationships. I also know she resents how much I'm gone. I just didn't know she had mentally recast me as a side character in her life.

I look at my picture of Nora on my phone lock-screen. Mark circles over to my car and raps his knuckles on the window, pointing at his watch. I wave him off. I stare at my daughter's picture and think about the reality that my partner cannot rely on me for physical support. We've established that we love each other and I know she relies on me emotionally. And that alone is deeply meaningful to me, but this stings. It makes me feel useless again, powerless.

I scoff, shaking my head. I know that my hours at work will theoretically ease once I earn my own route. But my family needs me right *now*, and the one thing that's more important to me than anything else is to be present as a father.

"Christ, it's not like we need the money," I mutter, climbing out of the car. We're sitting on the sale of my townhouse until we figure out where we want to live permanently, and Orla gets paid a bad-ass salary for bad-ass work.

I've also worked, plus overtime, nearly every day of the past ten months, and with that one phone call from Orla I realize that it's not something I can continue to do. Being a mail carrier helped me stop being Trip and learn how to be Walt, but now the job is keeping me from being a dad.

Panicking and sweating, I climb out of the car and swerve past my colleagues, into the main offices. I need to talk with my manager.

CHAPTER THIRTY-NINE
WALT

When Orla walks in the door, I greet her with flowers. I also got some apple blossoms for Pudding to eat, since I didn't want him to feel left out, so there's a convenient trail of pink petals all through the house as my Celtic queen walks in through the garage with her eyebrow arched.

"What's all this?"

"Well," I lean against the counter. "First of all, our daughter is still across the street, so any reactions you have can be as loud as you'd like."

"Reactions to what? Why are you here? During daylight?"

"I want to go to Kentucky with you," I tell her. "I want to go everywhere with you." I beckon for her to step closer, and as soon as I can reach her, I tug on the belt loop of her jeans. She's got a tool belt in one hand and her hard hat in the other and it's taking all my self control not to yank the leather gloves from her back pocket and beg her to put them on.

"I'm super glad you want that, Walt. Is that even possible?"

"I quit my job today," I tell her, and I smile when she holds a hand over her mouth in surprise.

"But you love your job."

I shake my head. "Not as much as I love you and Nora," I tell her, holding up a hand. "But that's not the end of the story."

I take the hard hat and tool belt from her and set them on the counter behind me. Pudding hops around the counter and starts eating the petals he spilled on the floor earlier as I squeeze Orla's ass and pull her close.

"As you know," I say, running my fingers through her ponytail. "They're very short-staffed at the post office." She nods. "After we hung up today I felt like shit. I sat in my car until Mark started kicking it, and then I went inside to quit my job."

I tell Orla how much I hated doing that, how I've been a kept man my entire life and it made me feel like trash. I tell her how much I enjoy being a bright light in people's day, about opening cat food cans for Mrs. Natali. "But," I add. "I also know that I can't be the type of man whose partner doesn't even consider him among the short list of adults she can rely on."

Orla's shoulders sag. She opens her mouth to say something, but I stop her. "I know you want to rely on me, Orla. But you're right that you can't. Not with how things are going at work. I mean, what's the point of having a union if I can't even get a few days off when my baby is born?"

Orla stares at me and picks at a piece of fuzz on my shirt.

I sniff. "So, anyway, I tried to quit, and I was walking back to my car when my boss actually chased me down and begged me not to." She raises a brow at me. "He told me I've got great aptitude for this work and they have me on a short list to get my own route. Don't roll your eyes! I'm getting to the good part. I told him I need a month off."

She squints and tilts her head to the side. "A month? An entire month?"

I nod. "I explained how my very important girlfriend had very important work out of state and I need to be available to care for my newborn. And then I reminded him that he had declined my request for parental leave when Nora was born and I really got going. I threatened to have Watson call him about violating labor laws."

Orla grins at me. "Would you do something like that?"

I shrug. "Probably not. But you need me here."

She exhales. "I do need you, Walt. That's very true."

"I like hearing you say that," I tell her. I know it's a big deal for Orla to be vulnerable like that and admit that she needs someone. "I want to be here to hear you say that, and anything else you need to say to me."

"They can't just work you all the time like that," she says. "I don't understand how they can stay in business when they treat people like that."

I kiss her on the temple and feel her sink into me a little more. I like this, holding her. Listening to her be mad on my behalf. "I'm off for a month, and then I'm being promoted to regular."

Orla makes a face. "Regular? What the hell are you now?"

"I'll have you know I've been a city carrier assistant."

"Hm," she says, reaching up to rub my face. "I don't like how they treat their assistants."

"I promise I'll never treat my assistant that way if I get one."

She grins and calls me a doofus, but then she lets me hug her, and eventually she lets me carry her to the couch, where I hold her for a long, long time.

CHAPTER FORTY
ORLA
MAY

It's ironic to me that I live with a mailman and I'm pacing around waiting for the mail. I should officially receive my license certificate any minute. I try to go about my morning, feeding Nora, showering, putting on pants that zip. But I'm too distracted by anticipation.

I negotiated working from home one day a week when I came back from maternity leave. It was my dad's idea. Sometimes I hate that he suggests these things to me, since I already work for the family business and feel a little bit like a schmuck getting a leg up. But damn it, I'm doing cool stuff and I'm bringing in a ton of new business for Beltane. Studying for my test, I learned about all these cool systems to place smoke and fire detectors throughout forests, linking them to electronic alert systems. I've become obsessed with it, reading up while Nora's nursing and grilling dad hardcore about the project he and Liam are working on with power lines throughout Appalachia.

I just need the damn paperwork about my professional license. I even have the frame all ready to go.

I watch a few episodes of *Vikings* at Logan's suggestion, but watching Queen Lagertha engineer defensive walls around her realm just makes me even more anxious to find out if I met the mark in my own engineering work.

I spend most of my afternoon standing in the picture window, staring at the street, looking for that damn mail truck to park. It's late when I finally see it, and I can't identify the mail carrier when they start at the other end of my street.

I debate getting dressed and bundling up Nora to rush out and storm the truck, but I remind myself that the mail will get here faster than I can get a newborn out the door. She's *just* about asleep when the truck moves up a few houses. I bite my lip, but the guy is doing the far side of the street first.

That mother fucker is doing our house last. Why, today of all days?

I set Nora down in her bassinet and listen for the metal clang as the mail guy lifts the lid outside, but it doesn't come. Instead, I hear the front door open and I pad down the hall to see Walt standing in the doorway with a big grin on his handsome face.

"Special delivery," he says, waving an envelope in the air.

"You beautiful asshole! You covered our street today?"

He nods. "I wanted to be the one to bring you the good news."

I gasp. "Did you open my mail? That's a crime, sir."

He shakes his hand and holds my letter up high while he drops his mail bag on the ground and shrugs out of his coat. "I don't have to open it. I know what it says." I resist the urge to jump at the letter he's holding up high. I put my hands on my hips and glare at him until he laughs and hands me the envelope.

He spins me around and pulls me against his chest, looking over my shoulder as I peel open the corner of the envelop and slide out the letter. "Don't read out loud," I tell him as I feel him gearing up.

Dear Ms. Brady:

ℬ

We are delighted to inform you that

ℬ

I stop reading and clamp my hand over my mouth to squeal. "Nora's asleep," I whisper-yell to Walt, who is squeezing me and pulsing his arms around me almost like he's doing the Heimlich. I jump up and down as best I can in his hug and then I sigh, sinking back against him. "That's such a weight off," I tell him.

He sucks on my neck. "I didn't know you'd been carrying it," he murmurs. "I would have told you that any woman who can blast a baby out in a parking lot can pass a silly old test." I swat him with the letter.

This feels like an opportunity where I should be mature and open about my feelings. This is what my therapist tells me. I started seeing a counselor after Walt moved back in. She herself lost her mom at a young age, and I can bring Nora with me to my appointments. I've only had a few so far, but I like that she gives me specific homework. Such as telling Walt my feelings.

I spin around to face him, glad he doesn't let go of his hug. "I wasn't anxious that I'd fail," I tell him. "But I needed that hurdle so much. I needed to prove that I could do it, and I need that qualification to do the next project I want to work on."

He nods. "I want to hear all about your project." He starts kissing my neck. "Do you want to tell me first or do you want to celebrate?"

I laugh. "How do you know how I want to celebrate?"

"Hmmm." His voice is low and deep and I love how his chest rumbles against me. "Last time you finished a goal I believe there were euphemism emojis."

He thrusts his hips against me and I feel exactly how excited he is about celebrating. And then I realize how strange it is for him to be home like this. "What are you doing here, really?"

He bites my neck. "This is my route now."

I pull back to look him in the eye. "Seriously? You got a route?" He nods and honks one of my boobs. "What does it mean?"

"It means." He kisses my throat. "I deliver the mail in Morningside every day." He kisses my ear lobe. "And then I come home to make dinner for my hot goddess girlfriend."

Pleasure zings through my body as he nuzzles against me. "You'll really be here every evening?"

"Every one you'll have me." Walt reaches for my crotch and I draw back. I don't know if I'm ready for this. We've had a few makeout sessions here and there since Nora arrived, but I've mostly been too tired to take it any farther. "Hey," he soothes, putting some space between us but not letting me go. "Tell me what you're thinking."

I bite my lip and shake my head. "Tell me, Orla. I'm right here."

"I'm afraid Nora broke my vagina. It's a mess." I clap a hand over my mouth after I blurt it out. I've been holding that suspicion on for a long time, but between fighting about Walt's job and learning to be a parent and getting stitches I just haven't wanted his monster cock in there at. All.

"Your vagina is perfect," he says as he licks my ear lobe. When did my ear lobe become such a sensitive body part? This feels amazing. "It looks exactly like it should look after a human being passes through it."

"When have you been looking?" My instinct is always to tease him when he says something nice, something emotional. I need to tell him how I feel. "I'm afraid you won't think I'm sexy right now."

He stiffens. "Is that really what you think?" He looks aghast.

I chew on my cheek. "You get hotter every day, with your mailman butt and your forearm veins. And I'm not even able to go running right now and I think my crotch looks like chopped ham."

Walt sinks to his knees and rests his cheek on my stomach. He looks up at me and his blue eyes are glistening. "Orla fucking Brady, you are the most beautiful woman in the entire world. From the moment I saw you, I've been obsessed, not just with how you look but with all the parts of you." He starts squeezing my thighs and tracing fingers along my belly, making me shiver. "You are fierce and brilliant and I'd be honored if you let me make you come in celebration of passing your big, impressive milestone."

"God, Walt, you can't just say things like that." I start crying.

"Why?" He stands back up and dabs at my cheek with his thumb.

"Because you're making me feel things." He kisses me. "Big, loving things, like I can't imagine life without you when you say shit like that." He kisses me again. "You make me feel...cherished."

I squeak as he scoops me up and carries me down the hall toward our room. "I do cherish you, Orla. Let me show you how much."

"Mmm, yes, please." He sets me on the bed and starts taking off his work clothes. I slither out of my nursing shirt and jeans and before I know it, I'm sighing under the weight of a naked Walt, pressing me into the mattress while he kisses me all over.

He moves to put his mouth on my breast, but I put up a hand to stop him before he gets to my nipple. "Please no," I groan. "It's too weird for me with nursing."

He kisses my sternum and smiles. "You got it." He settles his weigh on one forearm and stares into my eyes as I feel his hand slide lower and lower. Finally, his fingers reach my hip.

"Your hands are cold," I breathe. "But I like it." And it's true. I like everything he's doing right now, the way he's so gentle. The feel of his hard length pressed against me. The way he's making everything about me today. "Mmmm," I moan as he traces his fingers above my clit. He kisses my mouth, sliding his tongue inside mine just as he slides a finger along my wetness. I wince, not because I'm uncomfortable, but because I'm afraid it will hurt.

"Tell me if it feels good," he says.

I nod, and then I gasp, because it suddenly feels very, very good. "Holy shit," I say as he presses the pad of his finger to my body. "Oh my god it's been so long. Ah! Walt, yes. Please keep doing that." I babble and roll my hips as he circles and flicks.

"Oh, Orla, you're so hot." His voice rasps and I feel him jerking and thrusting against me. "I'm going to lose my mind." I feel his weight shift as he pulls his hand to his cock, tugging at himself wildly as he continues to rub my clit. I realize he's so turned on by making me feel good that he is chasing his own orgasm, too.

"Are you touching yourself because of...me?"

He nods, his hand moving faster. It's so sexy, watching him come apart like this. I watch and relax as his fingers gently, perfectly knead at my clit. And then I lose all ability to concentrate. There is nothing other than his hand and my nerve endings. I start to scream, and Walt presses his mouth against mine and bites my lip until I quiet.

"I'm going to come," I pant and his grin lights up the room. The orgasm makes me shudder. It rockets through my stomach. I feel like I'm flying off the bed, even though I know I'm held in place by a warm, tall man who can't stop smiling.

As I'm panting and clawing at his chest I feel him still, apart from his wrist moving frantically up and down his shaft. "Come with me, Walt," I tell him, staring in wonder as he does. I feel his release, hot against my skin like a brand. Like he's etching his joy into my body.

"I love you," I whisper into his ear as he catches his breath. "I love you so much."

Later, we get dressed and walk across the street for Brady Family Dinner, where Walt sits with pink cheeks and tousled hair, batting his eyes at me from across the table.

His mom even joins us today, surprising me when she takes a seat in between Elizabeth and Mick.

"Hey, everyone," I say, reaching for a chip. "Walt got his own route today."

"Old news," Zack says, swiping the bowl of chips out of her reach and grabbing a handful. "Elizabeth told us when we got here."

"What? How did she know?" I look around at my family, irritated that they all know everything about all of us. Is nothing secret?

Everyone laughs, including Celeste, who leans across the table to squeeze his hand. "He told us earlier when he delivered the mail." I look at Walt, who seems like he's going to float away with joy at the notion that his mother is accepting his career choice and celebrating with him. Feeling my jaw start to drop, I focus on eating the chips instead.

Kellen clears his throat to announce that Beltane is moving ahead with power line inspections throughout Appalachia, along with some side projects along the high-voltage lines.

"More old news," Cal barks, as everyone nods. Word spreads fast in the Brady family. Even Nora nods, and the room erupts in excited conversations. It's an energetic, chaotic room and I marvel at how right it feels for me to be here, with my daughter and my Wally.

"I love you," Walt mouths, as Uncle Mick passes around shots of whiskey so we can all celebrate. Because we have a lot to celebrate.

"I love you, too," I whisper.

EPILOGUE: WALT
NEXT YEAR

"Mama?" Nora keeps shouting for Orla from her perch up on my shoulders. She pats me on the head with her chubby hands as I look through the crowd of runners for Orla.

"Not quite yet," I tell her, watching as the stream of athletes streaks past. Orla's family let me have the final leg of the marathon relay, which means I get to run through Bloomfield and downtown, to see my old stomping grounds and wave at my old customers.

Of course, since I was taking Orla's place on the Brady marathon relay team, she argued that she should be allowed to run the full. I like that she has a running partner on the whole course. The relay event breaks the course into six-mile chunks and is run at the same time as the regular marathon, so Orla should be running alongside Cal as they come down the hill from Highland Park.

"There she is, Nora-bear," I say, shaking Nora's foot at her uncle and her mother, gliding along in the sunshine looking fresh even after 19 miles. How many humans could do this six months pregnant? I feel so proud I might burst when Orla spots us and starts waving.

"Is that my baby? Hey, baby!" Orla blows kisses to Nora as I hand her off to Cal so I can start my leg of the race alongside my love. Some people use a baton at relay race exchanges. The Brady family uses toddlers. Orla can't slow her pace to wait for me, so I kiss Nora's leg while Cal scoops her up and I hurry to catch Orla's swishing ponytail.

"Hey, pretty lady," I say, falling into step beside her. She turns her head to grin as we make our way down Liberty Ave.

"Nice legs," Orla says, winking at me. We run together past a band on the corner, past the cheer squads and people offering beer to the runners. I see a group of older women handing out sports drinks and I wave.

"Walt! Oh, yoo-hoo! It is you!" Mrs. Natali found out I was running the relay and signed up to help at the hydration station, passing out cups from the tray of her walker. I pause to drop a kiss on her cheek as I grab a cup from her. "Is that your lady?" She cups her hands around her mouth to shout after us and I give a thumbs up after I toss my drink in the trash can.

And then we approach the post office and Orla starts laughing when she sees a hundred mail carriers banging empty mail bins together and hollering as we approach. We swerve to the left side of the street, running through the gauntlet of high-fives. Mark even sprays us with a hose, which feels terrific even though I'm barely a mile into my section of the race.

Plus, Orla's shirt clings to her boobs once it's wet and I'm glad I get to look at that while we run these last few miles together.

"Well," she says, brushing her hair out of her face, "That was unexpected. They didn't get the papers wet, did they?"

I shake my head and pull a plastic baggy from the pocket of my running shorts. "I thought ahead." I grin at her. "I assumed I would spill Gatorade on it or something, but it covers a lot of contingencies."

Orla and I decided to get married once we found out she was pregnant with our second baby, but neither of us wanted a big wedding. Her family always has a huge cookout feast after the marathon, complete with cake, so we both agreed it might be fun to crash the party with surprise wedding news.

She and Nora met me at the City County Building this week to get a marriage license when we picked up our race bibs. "We are the king and queen of multitasking," Orla says, puffing a little.

"You doing okay?" I promised her I'd only ask once along the course, and she promised she'd tell me if she wasn't. Each of the Bradys who ran a chunk of the course with her was responsible for making sure she stuck to a nine-minute mile and didn't try to go faster. Dr. Andrews said it's fine as long as she doesn't feel winded.

Orla gives me two thumbs up and I shake open the marriage license. I pull the pen out of the baggy and she and I start looking around to see who we will ask to witness our self-uniting ceremony on the go. "That guy," Orla says, pointing to a dude walking the course in full firefighter gear.

I nod and trot over to him. "Hey, man, my girl and I are doing a self-uniting wedding mid-race here."

"You serious?" He adjusts the oxygen tank on his back, looking a little like he should be using it at this point. "That's so cool."

"Yeah." I can't help but grin again, still not quite believing that this woman, this life is mine. "Will you sign here to witness for us?"

The guy's eyes widen as I shuffle alongside him and Orla swerves closer, grinning and grabbing my arm while she holds her pace steady. "I promise myself to you, Walt," she says. "Are those the official words?"

I shrug. "I think so. Anyway, dude, you just need to sign and print your name." He shakes his head and laughs at us, beckoning to lean on my back as he signs the marriage license.

"You guys are nuts!" He yells as we keep on running.

"You're one to talk, Mr. Full Gear 24 miles in." Orla blows him a kiss and I look around for another witness.

A woman in a tutu trots up to me. "I heard the whole thing," she says, panting a little. "I think it's terrific. Pick me for your second witness?"

"Sure!" I grin at her and point to the second space on the license. "I swear, we're serious about it."

"Oh, I can tell," she says, using her forearm to scribble her name. "I think that's it!"

"That's totally it," Orla says. "Whew." I feel her pull back her pace a little, but she smiles at me. "I'm good. So good!"

The tutu-witness whistles and shouts. "These two just got hitched! In the middle of the marathon!" People from the crowd start cheering and waving their noisemakers at us. I tuck the license back in the baggy and squeeze Orla's hand.

I reach in my other pocket and pull out the little cardboard box of rings I bought to surprise her. I bring our clasped hands to my lips and kiss her knuckles, and slide one of the blue silicone bands on her finger. "What's this?"

I hold the other one out for her. "Those lightweight bands. I keep getting ads for them. What do you think?"

She holds her hand out, staring at the ring. "I can wear this to work," she says. "It won't catch on anything. I can barely feel it!"

"Put mine on me. I want to see." I hold my hand toward her and she stumbles on a manhole cover, but rights herself as she rolls the ring onto my hand. "This is awesome."

And there's no other word for it, really. We round the final turn downtown and we can see the finish line. "Ready, husband?" Orla grins at me, clasping my hand as we approach the chute. I nod as we pick up the pace to finish the last few yards, listening for the beep that signals we have officially crossed the finish line.

I pull her to the side and scoop her into my arms, kissing her until I can't breathe. She leans her forehead against mine and I feel our baby kicking between us. "That was some bridal kiss," she says. "I love you, my husband."

"I love *you*, my wife." I lean in to steal another kiss from her just as her family locates us.

Kellen looks like he's been fretting since he parted ways with her at mile six, but his face relaxes when he hears Orla laughing as I slide her back to the ground. Cal and Nora must have taken the shuttle bus to the finish party because I see my baby girl toddling toward us.

Orla scoops her up and twirls her around. "Mama run race?" Nora pats Orla's cheeks and Orla nuzzles against her nose, cooing. "Daddy ran, too," says my bride, and it's probably the best sentence I've ever heard. I drape a sweaty arm around both of them and we stand there, letting the chaos blend into the background.

Until the Brady guys start slapping us on the back. "Well, Orla just set the unbreakable record," Liam says, sounding a little forlorn. "None of us can ever compete with running a full marathon while pregnant."

"Speak for yourself," Maddie says, elbowing him. He whips his head around to look at her, and she rolls her eyes. "Relax. I just mean it's not outside the realm of possibility. For me." Orla hands Nora to Maddie and turns back into me, like she can't stop hugging me. I'm not about to complain.

Mick trots over with a pair of finisher medals dangling off his arm. "Figured you two would forget about the hardware," he says, handing us each the correct medal for our distance. I do a double take when I see my mom at the finish along with the rest of the Brady crew.

"Hey," I say, walking over to hug her. We've been hugging more since Nora was born. It was awkward at first, but we're getting better at it. Even in public. "I thought you said you had plans today."

She smiles. "These are my plans. Surprise!" Mom wraps her arms around me briefly, but then pulls back when she feels how wet and sticky I am, between the sweat and the hose. I'm pretty gross, I'll give her that. We all make our way toward the park where there's more room. Plus Orla keeps insisting she needs two bananas since she ran the race for two. Nobody is about to argue with her.

We find a place to sit down under a tree, chugging down water and cuddling. I start massaging Orla's shoulders and kissing her neck until I notice her father standing above us, his brow furrowed.

He points at my hand as I work out a knot in Orla's neck. "Walt," he says, putting his hands on his hips. "Want to tell me about the bling you picked up since I saw you last?"

I grin at him. "Oh, this? My wife gave it to me."

Orla bursts out laughing and rests her head back on my shoulder, snorting. "How long have you been planning that line?"

I kiss her ear. "At least a week."

"Wife?" Kellen looks more shocked than when Orla first told him I was Nora's father, more surprised than when she told him we were having a second baby. "Orla, what on earth is going on?"

Orla springs to her feet and shows her dad the blue wedding band on her left hand, beaming. "Walt and I decided to do a thing," she says, waving her hand around like I gave her a giant diamond instead of a stretchy blue band. But to Orla, the practical band means more. I'd buy her a hundred diamonds if she wanted them, but I know that what she wants most in the world is to be herself, to traipse off into the woods checking the electrical grid and helping to supervise her former interns before their engineering exams.

I know that Orla wants a man she can rely on, who supports her and loves her for all that she is. And I know that becoming that man has meant more to me than I can say. I spin my own ring around my hand, excited for the promise it brings, for tomorrow and the day after that.

Kellen looks back and forth between us. "Can you get married in the middle of a race like that? Is that a thing?"

Orla pecks him on the cheek. "Let's go home." She pats her stomach. "I'm hungry and I'll tell you over barbecue."

RESTORATION
A SILVER FOX REDEMPTION ROMANCE

CHAPTER ONE
MICK

TODAY IS NOT TURNING OUT HOW I THOUGHT IT WOULD. I'M ALMOST A HALF HOUR late to meet my own kid. I don't tolerate lateness from other people—my schedule is all that helps me get through each day. I have no explanation for my own tardiness today. But here I am.

I climb out of the car, check for my phone and my wallet, squeeze the car keys to make sure I have them, and then lock up. I need these routines, or I'll lock the keys in the car, drop my wallet in the sewer, or worse.

And here's my son, smiling at me like I haven't just kept him waiting. Maybe I didn't? I'm relieved that Cal takes charge of the moment, draping an arm around my shoulders and dropping into conversation.

"Been here long, kiddo?" I'm about to tack on an apology when I see him furrow his brow.

"We're early, Dad. But I knew you would be. No worries." He shakes it off and heads inside, but I'm rattled. I got the time wrong. I start patting my pockets, looking for my notebook as Cal drags me inside the diner. I write everything in that notebook, except sometimes all my reminders to myself get in the way of the schedule for each day. Did I get it wrong?

The diner smells like grease. Cal can always be relied upon to know where to find unhealthy food, but I decide not to ride him about his diet at the moment.

I sink into a booth while he sets about getting us a basket of fries and a pair of deli sandwiches from the counter of a diner I didn't realize was so close to our office.

"I know you prefer juicing mid-day to this sort of thing," he says, popping a fry in his mouth. "But you look like you need something greasy, Dad."

Maybe he's right. Maybe I need more protein. I swallow and reach for the fry, spinning it in my hands a few times before going ahead and eating it. I like the crunch on the outside, and decide to eat another one. "So why the late lunch invite, son? I thought you're deep into that fire detection project with Orla."

He nods, chewing and swallowing. "Today I wanted to talk about something personal. You sure you don't want to talk about you first? You seem pretty...off."

"I need a minute to gather my thoughts," I tell him, tentatively reaching for the sandwich and realizing he's right. "You go on ahead and talk." The food is helping to settle me down. I'm ready to listen.

Cal takes a breath. "Well," he says. "It's Logan."

"I like her," I tell him, putting a fry inside the sandwich and taking a bite, enjoying the mix of textures. Cal's been living with his lady for a few years now and she's been really good for him. She complements him, slows him down a little. The whole family is just waiting for them to inevitably announce I have another wedding to fund. I've got money set aside for it already.

"Well, I love her. I do. But..." He stares out the window for a few beats and for once, I don't feel the urge to tell him to just spit out whatever is bothering him. "She's really pressing me to get married."

I purse my lips, considering. "Well, it's been years, son. It's a reasonable expectation that she'd want to lock that down."

Cal belches into his hand and then looks me straight in the eye. "If I'm being honest, Dad, I've never had an example of a strong marriage in my life."

I stare at him for a beat. "I'll concede that point halfway," I tell him. "Your uncle and Helen were solid. They were a huge part of your life."

He rolls his eyes. "Okay, sure, but...come on. I was a kid when Aunt Helen passed. And look at me, Dad. I'm impulsive and reckless just like my old man. I just..."

He drifts off and now I do grow impatient with him. "Out with it, kiddo. Come on."

"I just worry I'll be like you if we get married. That I'll...stray."

His words hit me hard, perhaps harder than they would otherwise since I'm already tender about mixing up our meeting time today. Something isn't right. "Cal," I start, and then I swallow another bite of sandwich, but it feels like sand in my mouth. "Cal, I know I messed up with your mother."

He raises an eyebrow.

I nod. "You know I live with that regret every day, the way I behaved in my marriage...marriages. Hey, between you and me, Zack's mom doesn't really count."

I mean it as a joke, but it falls flat and he looks upset. "This is exactly what I'm talking about, Dad." *Shit. Why do I always blurt these things out?*

"Cal," I continue. "I know we've talked about this. You're not like me. Not in that way. Son, you're thoughtful and kind and so present with Logan. Hell, anyone in the room can tell you think she hung the moon." I reach for his hand and give him a squeeze. "You're already more patient with her, and make more time for her than I did with either of my wives."

I watch him relax, watch some tension slip from him that he's obviously been clinging to. I watch his relief as I assure him he's nothing like me. He takes a swig of his water and eats another fry. "I appreciate you saying that, Dad."

"Of course, son."

He can't bear the thought of being like me. My lifetime of bad choices, impulsive wrong steps.

We don't say much more as we finish our snack and he heads back to the office soon after. I decide to stick around a bit, just staring out the window. Our conversation sticks with me, hard. What sort of model did I show my kids? My son just pretty much told me I ruined his life.

I sigh and wipe up the ring of water my glass left on the table. I shake my hand, trying to free the wet napkin from my palm. I don't want to make excuses for how I've behaved, but these mistakes cling to me like the soggy recycled paper. I can't change what I've done.

When I do finally walk back to Beltane, I don't even stand in the lobby to give thanks for the business my brother and I were able to create. I don't look around at the building we own and remember our beginnings sitting on milk crates above the machine shop on Smallman Street. Instead, I think of Logan, a woman I already consider my daughter-in-law, and how she's missing out on the wedding I know she dreams of because my own son doesn't want to end up like his old man.

CHAPTER TWO
CELESTE

I DON'T KNOW WHY I THOUGHT I COULD DO THIS. DRIVE INTO THE CITY DURING rush hour? What was I thinking? I should never have canceled my car service. Does this meeting really need to start at 5:30 and not seven, once the roads have calmed down? My son's partner—he keeps reminding me I'm supposed to say partner—Orla, attends meetings with brash women and, well, they invited me to join them.

It felt like such a pity invite when they first told me to come, but I couldn't decline because I've behaved so terribly. I need every chance I can get to show Orla how sorry I am. How much I want to be part of her and Walt's lives, and their children's lives. My grandchildren. Thinking of Nora and the unborn new baby helps me calm down a bit. I can do this.

I remind myself these women all work, and the meetings begin at 5:30 because they come straight from their various offices. Another reminder of how very different I am from all of them. When have I ever worked in my life? I've been a kept woman and spent my entire life up until recently trying to fit in with society.

Orla is the absolute opposite of that, and my son adores her. I hate that I tried to break them up.

I showed up uninvited to one of these meetings when Nora was a newborn, and I confessed to Orla what I'd done to drive a wedge between her and Walt. And then I found myself just spilling all my secrets. A lifetime of bottled-up anger at the way I'd been groomed to live a particular sort of life, and I just blurted it all out to a room full of women. And then the strangest thing happened. They told me to stay, and to come back, and to tell them more.

Foof, they call themselves. I can hardly bring myself to say what it stands for. But then, they told me I have to work on it if I want to be welcome. Another driver cuts me off, sliding into my lane with inches to spare, and I scream "Fuck!" And then I look around, as if someone might be standing nearby to rap my knuckles with a ruler.

Fresh Out Of Fucks is the name of the group. Foof. I, Celeste Sheffield, am driving into downtown Pittsburgh at rush hour to go to a fancy new bar and learn to let my fucks fly with Foof.

It's not actually rush hour. Not yet. I get anxious about finding parking and I left my house in the suburbs at three. I decided to find the closest garage, pay whatever fee is asked, and then I'll find somewhere to read until the meeting. Maybe sip some tea. No more alcohol.

I stopped drinking gin at my husband's funeral, when I realized how heavily I'd been relying on it to get me through the agony of living that sort of life. How strange, that stopping all the Ativan and liquor-for-lunch feels...carefree.

My head has never been clearer, even if my conscience aches with all I've done and said.

And here I go, shouting out fuck when someone cuts me off in traffic. But I didn't call for a car service to bring me in today. Instead, I spent the morning researching parking garages and drove to the bank for cash in small bills so I could tip a valet if it really came down to it. How pathetic is it that driving into the city feels like a victory? What on earth have I let my life become that I get a thrill coaxing my sedan through a parking garage?

This isn't exactly something meaningful I can contribute to the conversation tonight. Most likely, I'll wind up just listening again while the others, twenty years my junior, share details of publishing contracts and elections they've won. Clients they've landed. The sort of talk I always associated with my husband.

I slide out of the car, careful not to nick the door against the car parked to my left. I make sure to put the garage ticket in my purse and find the elevator down to street level. Esther's bar is open already, but I don't feel right going in two hours early. I looked up cafes nearby when I was researching my trip.

Researching my trip—as if this were an international vacation that required planning rather than a 20-minute drive to meet with acquaintances. As I wait for the elevator I decide to finally click send on the message I've been not sending my daughter. Rosemary has been telling me for years how my words and behaviors have hurt her. How she felt I was putting my friends' opinions ahead of her needs.

In the past few months, I've been trying to tell her that I hear her now. Acknowledging that I am at fault for our strained relationship. This is something the Foof group has helped me with, something I have felt all right sharing with them. Rosemary is the same age as all those young women. I often find I wish she were with me at the bar, holding my hand while we both express our hurts and our hopes. Not that we've ever actually done such a thing before.

ROSEMARY DOESN'T RESPOND to my text, but I hadn't expected her to. I ride the elevator down to the street level and turn right, reciting the steps I memorized to find the cafe without having to look at a map like some sort of tourist. A few minutes later, I find myself outside the door, and I actually clap my hands in excitement at having navigated there on my own. I check quickly to see whether anyone saw this little outburst of joy, and then I feel guilt at this instinct. Why can't I just let myself take pride in doing something new? "I can celebrate, even small things," I say, pushing open the door and looking around for an empty table.

I'm never sure if I should sit or wait to be seated by the host, but this seems like the kind of place where I can tuck into a corner table and read the magazine I brought with me. Then I hear the last thing I expected to hear today.

"Celeste? You hoo! Over here!" Michael Brady has his hands cupped around his mouth, hollering across the cafe to me. I freeze, not sure how to respond. Every time my son brings me to a Brady family function, I'm flustered by Michael.

When Walt first brought me to Orla's family Thanksgiving, the year my husband died, I thought it was just my grief that gave me strange, tingly feelings about Michael. But then I remembered how he came to the funeral, when my all the rest of my husband's former friends stayed away. That Thanksgiving, when I was overwhelmed, Michael offered me comfort, and even gave me a ride home. *"I know what it's like to be alone,"* he'd said.

I've always thought he was ruggedly handsome, but I don't think I ever realized how very kind he is, too. And now he's waving at me across a restaurant like he's delighted to see me.

"Join us!" Is he...beaming? I flush.

His companions don't even look put out by his behavior. I see his son Liam is sitting there, along with an older gentleman I can't place, but vaguely recognize. Probably someone my husband impacted with his unsavory business dealings.

Finishing school training takes over and I raise my hand in a timid wave. I make my way to the table and before I can think twice, I'm being tucked into the chair by Michael's side. Should it surprise me that he rose to pull out my chair? Should I feel this flutter in my stomach that he did so?

"Clayton," Michael is saying, gesturing toward me. Why does he always seem to shout? "This is Celeste! Another grandparent to a Brady kid."

The man's face brightens. "Maddie's mom?"

Michael shakes his had. "Nah. Walt's mother. Lives with Orla? Say, you probably knew Walt's father. Sheffield..." He drifts off, and we all seem to wait to see how Clayton will remember that name.

Clayton tilts his head to the side, considering. I see the recognition pan across his face, followed quickly by sympathy. He clears his throat and offers a hand. "Clayton Monroe," he says. "Pleased to meet you, Celeste."

"Likewise." I plaster on my public smile, choking down the simmering anger at my deceased husband for violating all the trust we had from our community. For plunging me into this awkward space where I have to relearn to be a person in a world where I don't understand the rules. I wonder how Clayton Monroe can stand to be in a room with me. I'm sure he thinks I was complicit in my husband's behavior.

"You hungry, Celeste?" Michael leans close and offers me a small bag of nuts from his shirt pocket.

Flustered, I shake my head. "You brought your own food to a cafe?"

He shrugs. "I get hungry all the time." He starts cracking pistachios, his long fingers working the nuts open as I watch. He forms tidy piles, stacking the shells, and I hear Clayton mention that Maddie, too, always has snacks on hand.

"You'd think she was born a Brady," Clayton says, and Michael and Liam both laugh.

Michael furrows his brow and points a shell at Clayton, asking "How do you know our Maddie again?"

I'm curious about this as well, since I know Liam's partner works in healthcare communications and is an unlikely companion for any client of Beltane Engineering. "I owe her my life," Clayton says, patting Liam's hand warmly. Seeing that Michael and Liam appear just as clueless as me,

Clayton explains that he and Maddie are both Type 1 diabetics, and that Maddie convinced him to try some sort of insulin pump and monitor system.

Liam's eyes widen. "She talked to you about all that? While I was busy trying to get your business?"

Clayton beams. "I'm free from pricking my finger and injecting multiple shots into my thigh every single day of my life," he says, dabbing at his eyes with a napkin. "She gave me the courage to take back control of my time. Of my wife's peace of mind."

Liam seems so proud he might burst, chiming in that his partner takes her own health very seriously. I marvel at the personal touches happening here at a business meeting I seem to have crashed...Michael and Liam genuinely care about Clayton as a person in addition to whatever they have going on together professionally. No wonder my son loves the Brady family.

Michael squints and leans back, crossing his arms over his chest. "I didn't think old dogs like us could learn new tricks, Clay."

Clayton turns very serious and leans forward. "I used to think that way, too. But we can. Even old barnacles like us can make a big change. You just need the right motivation."

Michael raises his glass to that and I think about my son. Walt always seemed to be following along in his father's footsteps and then...he told me the pressure of that was killing him on the inside. He changed his entire life. I think about how Walt is so happy now, with his strange-to-me job and his beautiful daughter. And his own son on the way.

I think about Rosemary, how I never knew what to do with a child who wanted nothing to do with the world I inhabited. And I think about how I've been kicked out of that world for all intents and purposes. Why should the people from our club want to spend time with the family of the man who swindled them?

But I think I have made some changes. Small ones, like driving into town on my own. Is Clayton Monroe right? Can I find purpose and meaning? Or will I continue to drift along at the outskirts of my family, dragging the heavy weight of my mistakes? I suppose that's why I'm downtown, making myself uncomfortable and meeting up with women who frighten me with their drive and confidence.

The problem is I don't know what I want. Just that I want it all to be different.

CHAPTER THREE
CELESTE

I TRY TO STOP FOCUSING ON THE FIT OF MICHAEL BRADY'S SUIT PANTS AS HE WALKS out of the cafe. His smile and parting wave are just friendly, nothing more, surely. I shouldn't be having these sorts of thoughts at my age, and not about my son's in-laws. I'm not here for that.

I finish my tea slowly and wander over to Bridges and Bitters, Esther's bar, where the Foof ladies gather. I've been to a dozen meetings by now but still bite my lip as I push open the door, feeling inexplicably self-conscious.

From behind the gleaming bar, Esther greets me with a wave and a smile that seems genuine. That first time I came here in a desperate attempt to find Orla and apologize, Esther came after me with a chrome pipe. She never swung it, but she held it the entire time I was speaking and I remember thinking I doubted anyone would ever protect me so fiercely.

"The gals are in the back," Esther trills, mixing up a tray of something fruity. Maybe strawberry, since those are in season right now. I make my way up to her.

"Can I do anything to help?" As the words leave my mouth, I realize I don't think I've ever uttered them before. Yet I didn't even think about it, and they just popped out.

It feels warm and wonderful when Esther slides me a tray with six wide glasses on it. "Sure—you want to take this first round back for me while I mix up some more? I'm doing strawberry basil shag today."

"I thought that was strawberry!" I watch as she muddles the fruit and the fresh herbs before shaking in enough vodka for two more glasses. "The fresh berries are so delicious right now."

"Mm hmm." She grins. "Got these at the market this morning along with the basil. There's a woman-owned farm nearby. I like to buy their herbs and stuff."

"That's so lovely that you support other small businesses." Esther shrugs, and I can tell I've said something uncool, as Rosemary would call it. I probably should have *assumed* Esther would support other small businesses, just because it's the right thing to do. I take a deep breath and smile, trying not to tip the tray as I walk toward the back room.

Esther's banquet room is done up to look like a speakeasy. The entire establishment is very polished, very gilded age, but this back room has velvet settees and an ornately carved table in the center of the room. I half expect to see flappers with long cigarette holders, but it's just a group of modern women in business attire.

I teeter over to the table and set the tray on the edge, beaming when I don't splash a single drop of the beautiful cocktails.

"Holy shit, Celeste brought booze." One of Orla's friends notices me arrive and soon, I'm crowded in by a band of smart, professional women who cuss like sailors.

"Esther says they're strawberry shag," I say and, seeing my pregnant daughter-in-law on the settee, I add, "I believe she's bringing in a round without the vodka, too." I find a seat and just listen while Foof gets going, giving each other high fives and releasing loud, genuine peals of laughter at each other's jokes.

I don't even need the vodka to feel intoxicated by this group. I know I'm decades too old to be hanging around them, but I can't seem to stop coming and trying to absorb their confidence. I like being here one week when someone mentions a goal, and then hearing a few weeks later that she's achieved it.

When I was in a sorority at college, we had regular meetings like this, but I always got the sense that the sisters were secretly banding together to undermine one another. They talked in coded language about how to throw elections for organizations or cheat on difficult exams.

"Ugh. I wish I could have a do-over." Samantha Vine slips into the seat next to me.

"What's that?" I startle, realizing she's talking to me, that she came over to talk to me.

Samantha rolls her eyes and sips her drink. "I put my foot in my mouth at a meeting at work today," she says. "Stick me in a board room with fundraising guys, and I take off running. But when I'm talking to nonprofits about ways Vinea can give back to the community? Ugh." She slumps into the seat. "I'm lousy."

I open my mouth to say that I'm sure she wasn't lousy, just as Orla says, "Tell us what happened." I listen as Samantha explains that she told a middle school teacher she didn't think young students would gain much from touring Vinea, that Sam felt the technology was beyond them.

"This guy thinks I feel that way because the students are poor. I really meant that I actually thought young tweens aren't ready to talk about advanced algorithms. But either way, it was utterly stupid of me to say that because duh! The kids can benefit from the same presentation." She groans and shakes the ice around in her empty glass.

I pat her leg and say, "What if you called and explained? Said you realized your mistake and invite them to bring the students after all?"

Samantha cringes. "Ugh. Apologies are the worst, though. Like, now this guy is going to know I say dumb things when I go off book. Can I make Logan call?"

Logan throws her hands in the air. She lives with one of Orla's brothers. Or cousins. Anyway, one of the Bradys. "I'm just the finance gal," she says. "You're the one with your name on the building."

I clear my throat and take a small sip of my non-vodka drink. "You all are the ones who have taught me the value of apology. And of the growth that can come from it."

Orla smiles at me, and I carry the warmth of that gesture until Sam pats my leg and asks if I have anything to share with the group. I think of the unanswered message I sent to Rosemary, of the gaping hole our relationship...or lack of...leaves in my heart these days. "I want to mend fences with my daughter but she's still too angry to take my calls."

"Want me to invite her over to see Nora and then you 'drop by'?" Orla offers, but I shake my head.

"That would seem like an ambush. I'll just keep reaching out. But that's my thing that I'm working on. You know, apart from accepting that everything I thought was true in the world was all a big, hurtful lie."

Esther slides me another drink as she makes her way over with a fresh tray. "You're doing great, Celeste," she says. "I can feel your fucks gradually slipping away each time you come in."

But I don't feel like they are, not as I sit and listen to the other women whose challenges feel real and monumental compared to mine.

"I think I need to get laid," Sam says, definitively. I'm about to pat her arm and tell her I don't really think that will solve anything, when the other women raise a glass to her and support this idea wholeheartedly.

I hear them telling her it'll relieve some stress, make her feel powerful. Is all that true? Can casual sex really and truly have that sort of impact? I wouldn't know, but as they talk about it, the only person who comes to mind is absolutely off limits anyway. Why is it my thoughts drift immediately to Michael Brady and his trim waist? And the scent of him as he leaned in to help me to my seat in the cafe?

No. That is not the solution to the problems I'm having. Michael Brady is the boisterous head of the family my son has joined. He's not for me to fantasize about. After all, most of the women in Foof are fighting against problems caused by society and inappropriate expectations. My issues, I brought on myself.

CHAPTER FOUR
MICK

Marathon Sunday is a Brady Family tradition. We each run one leg of the corporate relay, meet up at the race finish line after our portion, and then we feast at my brother's house afterward. That's just the way things are done. Only...my brother quit running on roads a few years ago when his feet got bad.

That worked out okay in the end since Nicole takes his spot now, but Orla has gone rogue. She insisted on running the full marathon instead of her usual five-mile leg through Oakland. All the dominos began to fall after that.

Instead of my usual pre-race routine, I felt anxious on the verge of panic thinking about shifting our roster around. I said if she insists on running a marathon six months pregnant, that's her hill to climb. But of course the family felt differently. It is Pittsburgh, after all, so there are plenty of hills along the marathon course. Maddie and Logan made complicated plans to show up along the course with signs and snacks if she needed them.

All my kids wanted to stick by Orla the whole race, so we lost the competitive edge that made it all so special for me. We're not running for time this year...oh, no. The Brady family is running for fun! The kids are all gung-ho about this, as if they haven't been killing each other to beat their own personal records since they were old enough to register for the race. And damn it, this is my last year to clock a seven-minute mile in the 50-plus age group.

Everyone else seemed to take all the adjustments in stride. "What's the big deal?" they kept asking me. "Walt is running Orla's leg, and we're all running a little bit slower in support of her," they kept insisting. They're probably right.

I sigh and look over at her, and she beams at me as we huff along the 10th Street Bridge. Well, she huffs. I'm pouting. I admit it.

But routine is all I have these days. Detours don't seem to derail normal people, but I've never been normal. It's going to be a long time before I feel like I'm getting the steps right for the "new" Brady Marathon Sunday.

I hear a familiar voice shouting, "Wooo! You look fantastic!" Orla waves over at the sidewalk and I see Maddie and Logan waving their signs. Orla starts blowing kisses. I must be frowning because Maddie yells, "Wipe that sour puss off your face, Mickey! It's a beautiful day for a run!"

I do chuckle at that. I've said the same thing to Maddie when she started tagging along on some of our family runs. She does okay for someone who claims she's not a runner. I remind myself that it's a good thing that my kids have meaningful relationships. That they've adapted and rather than using running as a way to get away from their partners, my boys and Orla keep bringing their partners along on our adventures.

We push on for another few miles and someone sticks a medal in my hand at the relay exchange. Liam surprises me with a hug before he trots off after Orla, and he wraps an arm around her shoulders in greeting, too. I pause in the lane to look at them, realizing for the first time how amazing it is that she's doing this. Of course she didn't register for the full marathon just to irk me. She wanted to achieve something amazing before giving birth again.

I wasted an entire marathon leg pouting beside her when I could have been encouraging her. Even stoic Liam is excited for her. No wonder people think I'm an asshole.

I hop on the shuttle bus to the finish line and find Kellen, Elizabeth and Celeste holding signs, waiting for all the kids to come in. Kellen shoots finger guns at me and I wave him off, trying not to stare at Celeste in her nice white pants and polka dot shirt. She looks like sunshine and happiness, and I have to remind myself I'm all sweaty so I don't pull her in for a hug along with the others.

"You look refreshed for having run so far," she says, seeming impressed.

I wave a hand. "I do this distance every day. It is refreshing for me." Celeste hands me a cup of water and I take it gratefully.

"How's my girl doing?" Kellen asks, offering me a granola bar.

"Kel. I'm not eating that. It's full of sugar." He looks down at the package, frowning. "Orla's great. She really liked seeing Maddie and Logan on the bridge."

I look around my brother's shoulder for the refreshment tables, spying a banana. I wish I had thought to ask one of them to bring me pistachios or something without preservatives. When I look up, the three of them are staring at me, wide-eyed.

"What's that?"

Celeste places a hand on my arm and I stare down at her fingers on my sweaty skin. I feel the heat from her palm radiating inside my arm. "Kellen asked if you saw Liam," she says, and her voice sort of hypnotizes me.

I bite into the banana and nod. "Yeah," I say. "He was my exchange partner. He's great. I'm sure they're all great."

Everyone keeps staring at me and I'll be damned if I can figure out why. "What?" I say, crankier than I intend. I finish the banana as my brother scratches his chin.

"I just got the sense that the kids are up to something," he says. He takes a breath. "I'm sure it's nothing."

"It's not *nothing* to change our tradition," I say. "This was a very big deal."

Elizabeth sort of squints at me but Celeste translates again, putting that hand back on my arm. It's like she activates some sort of pause switch in my brain when she does that. It's unnerving, how good it feels just to have her touch me and then look at me kindly.

"It seems like maybe Orla is trying to cram in some adventures before the baby comes," Celeste says. "Running the full race, maybe some other things." She shrugs.

Kellen takes to pacing and checking his phone obsessively and I remember again that being six months pregnant is hard on the human body. I drag a hand through my hair, wondering what's wrong with me that I'm not more worried about Orla.

Celeste leans in close so I can hear her above the pep band at the finish line party. "He's worried, I'm sure, but Orla is so tough," she says. I look at her. She nods. "Orla wouldn't want anyone to be anxious. If anyone can do this sort of thing, I think it's her."

"You're absolutely right," I tell her. "It didn't even occur to me to worry."

Celeste grins. "I'm more worried they'll lose track of Nora when Cal and Walt swap out." Her worry is quickly abated, though, because I see Cal spring off the shuttle bus with Nora on his hip.

"Dude," he says, jogging over to us. "I'm pretty sure Orla and Walt are eloping in the middle of the race."

CHAPTER FIVE
MICK

I CAN'T HELP BUT LAUGH. ORLA BRADY PULLED SUCH A MICK MOVE. MY NIECE finagled a way to get married on the run, literally while running. She and Walt got some sort of self-uniting marriage license and asked witnesses to sign it while they ran the last leg of the marathon. She said it was a formality so she could get on Walt's health insurance, but the wink she gave me suggests she mainly wanted to avoid the hassle of planning her own party after.

I pop up to my condo to shower and change before driving to Kellen's for the after-party-turned-wedding-reception. And then I forget that Kellen moved across the street to live with his girlfriend, but I decide it's fine to leave my car in my niece's driveway, since she and her new husband moved in to Kellen's place.

What in the hell were they thinking, eloping during the marathon? I shake my head, laughing. It's something I probably would have done at their age.

Shit. I'm going to have to get Orla and Walt a wedding present. I pat at my pockets, looking for my little notebook. Their "wedding" was just today, so I probably have a little time before they notice. I write GIFT $$ in big letters so I don't forget. I should just give them a wad of cash right now, but even I know you're supposed to put it in a card at minimum.

If I handed them a fist full of cash, it wouldn't be the first time. People expect that kind of thing from me and think it's me just being weird. But the truth is I often do that because I know I will never, ever remember to pay someone back if I wait until I have an envelope or my check book. *Maybe I should keep a bunch of envelopes in my glove box...*

I HEAR the ruckus of the whole Brady crew and make my way around back. I pause for a moment under Elizabeth's dogwood tree, just watching everyone. I still marvel that they all turned out so great. All three of my boys have found someone, even if Cal is feeling a certain kind of way about his prospects as a husband. My brother found love again. Despite a lifetime of me making shit decisions, this family has stuck together.

I hear a high-pitched laugh that startles me, pulling my attention toward the deck. There, I see Celeste laughing with little Nora. Celeste seems transfixed by something the little gal is saying, her face utterly transformed by joy. She's just radiant. Not that she doesn't always look stunning. I've been lusting after Celeste Sheffield since way before it was appropriate.

I puff out a breath, relieved again that Celeste never showed up with her husband when we used to golf together. It never bodes well to be thinking those kind of thoughts about your buddy's wife. I know all too well the trouble those thoughts can cause if you act on them. And so, apparently, do my kids. I've been doing okay in my old age, though. It's been years since I made a rash decision in the female department.

It's a shame Walt Jr. kicked the bucket so young. I would never have said I enjoyed his company, per se. But he was always good for a laugh. I've been thinking a lot more about my old friends. Orla calls them gross. Maybe she's right. It's not like I'm still going out drinking and chasing tail with those guys, though. I've kept my head down, focused on work. And it's been good. The family business is better than ever, especially now that we've got Liam teed up to take over for Kellen running the engineering side of things.

And between Cal and Zack, my other boys are getting better at landing new clients and selling the *idea* of engineering possibilities. We've done great professionally. I know we have. But I think I've also done okay raising these boys into successful men in their personal lives. Cal will work through his hesitation with Logan and it will all be all right. It has to.

Celeste laughs again and I realize I can't keep hiding here behind a tree. And then I pause to wonder if anyone thought to get a cake. This isn't just a marathon party. It's a post-elopement party. I jog back across the street to my car, thinking I can probably grab a ready-made cake at the grocery store bakery.

Sure enough, there's a generic ice cream cake in the cooler. Chocolate Oreo sounds pretty decadent for a family of committed runners, but how often do you celebrate a wedding and a marathon on the same day? I slip the teenager at the counter a tenner to pipe "Congratulations Orla and Walt" in fancy cursive on top.

These little touches matter. I've always said that at work and it's true with family, too. I've always known this. So why's it so hard for me to keep all these little things in line in my life? I gave up counting the number of times my wives screamed at me for forgetting to take out the trash or stop at the pharmacy on my way home. It's like I always, always, always am forgetting something important. Case in point: by the time I get back to the car with the cake, I realize I left my wallet sitting on top of the cake counter. Story of my life.

Back to my brother's house I go, eventually, blasting the air conditioning in the car in hopes the cake stays salvageable. This time I park in Orla's driveway on purpose, since I'm less likely to forget my keys in the car if I'm doing things in my routine. Cake. Phone. Keys. Wallet? Yes.

This time, I announce my presence as I head out back. "Hey you rascals! Listen up. I'm coming in hot with wedding cake!"

Orla's face lights up when she sees me. Everyone else in the family is tipsy by now. "Uncle Mick! Thank you for bringing something I can actually consume at my own wedding party." She pats her pregnant belly and elbows her new husband, who looks like he's been toasting pretty heavily with Kellen's whiskey.

"Anything for you, pumpkin." I set the cake on the table and grin when Elizabeth heads my way, knife in hand.

I'm about to cut into it when Elizabeth shrieks at me. "Mick, no! The bride and groom are supposed to cut their cake."

I freeze and stare down at my hand. Of course she's right. This is what happens when I act without thinking. Thankfully, I didn't make it to the cake and I step back as Orla and Walt press the knife through the crisp fudgey icing. I cheer along with everyone else when she and Walt cram cake in each other's faces, and then I drop my arm around my brother's shoulders when he looks all teary.

"My baby girl got married," he says, leaning his head against mine.

I squeeze him tighter. "I know she did, Kel. She grew up to be a real fine woman."

I feel him tense up and he says, "Her mother would have been overjoyed today." My brother's wife died of cancer when Orla was small. Right around the time of my second divorce. I moved him and Orla into my house. It was impulsive, but in the end it was the right move. Neither of us was fit to be raising kids alone, but together, somehow, we made it work.

"Helen would have been overjoyed today," I tell him, giving his arm another squeeze. I feel like I should say more, but there's a cacophony as Liam's kid starts grabbing at the cake and shoving it in his mouth before his mother can stop him.

I let out a laugh, watching my son and Maddie chase Arlan through the back yard. My grandson has a piece of ice cream cake in each fist and judging by his speed and agility ducking around obstacles, he's going to be a heck of a cross country athlete. I pull out my notebook and write myself a note to see about youth running clubs. Maybe three is too young for that. I still think this kid should look into it.

Celeste comes by with two plates of cake, and my brother wipes his eyes and takes his piece. "Thank you," I say, making sure not to let my fingers brush against hers as I reach for the plate. This woman might technically be available, but I can't start any funny business with my niece's mother-in-law, much as I'd like to.

Celeste flushes and smiles, gazing over to the deck, where the four Brady kids sit arm-in-arm with their lovers. She's gorgeous with a blush, all rosy and happy. But then her face tightens a little and she bites her lip. "I'm trying not to think about how it wasn't a proper wedding."

"Proper?" I arch a brow at her, even though I know damn well what she means. I'm not sure why I'm forcing her to say that she'd have felt more comfortable if the kids had a quarter million dollar reception up at the country club. Lord knows I just paid for one of those for Zack and Nicole a few years ago.

Celeste waves a hand. "You know. At a church." She sighs and doesn't say anything further, still gazing over at the deck.

I shrug. "You know, I had two of those. Church weddings. I think Orla and Walt have already been together longer than my second one lasted."

Kellen snorts and slaps me on the back. He shakes his head at me, but turns to Celeste. "Orla was never going to do anything conventional," he tells her. I nod.

Celeste fiddles with her necklace. "I know. She's such a confident person." She sighs again and Kellen, finished with his cake, gestures toward the deck.

"Come on," he says to her. "Let's go send these young folks off to celebrate properly. You can hang out with Nora and Elizabeth and I can try to wrangle Arlan."

"I can take him with me," I say, knowing nobody will ever agree to that but feeling like I need to at least offer to take my own grandson for a sleepover.

Kellen furrows his brow. "Why don't you help Beth clean up," he tells me. "We've got a room here all set up for the kids anyway. Plus you'd have to move a car seat if he went to your house."

He and Celeste send all the adult kids off with Orla as the designated driver at her own wedding reception. I'm sure she'll make up for it after the baby is born and she calls in babysitting favors.

I sigh. She won't be calling in babysitting favors to me. Liam and Maddie don't, either. Why would they? I can't even keep track of my wallet. I wander around the back yard with a trash bag, trying to shake off that dejected feeling as I scoop up paper plates and leftover pasta salad.

CHAPTER SIX
CELESTE

"I really appreciate you staying with Nora." My son smells like too much whiskey as he bends over to hug me yet again. Hugging is still new for us.

For far too long, we've had a stiff, formal relationship. It was what I had with my parents. It was what I thought was expected for him to fit in with our friends. I wish I hadn't subjected him to all of that, especially since the "friends" who meant so much to me have been nowhere to be found since my husband died.

I can't dwell on all the years of missed affection, though. I can only hug him now, and hold my granddaughter tight. It took a lot for Orla to forgive me enough to trust me watching Nora. I also know the two of them prefer having her with family to taking her to daycare, and I've worked hard to build and keep their trust in me.

"I've got a second chance," I mutter, inhaling the sunshine smell of Nora's toddler head. She's still going strong despite a whole day with no nap. Between the excitement of watching the race and her parents getting married, she hasn't wanted to miss anything.

I have too much time to think about all the ways I did things differently with my kids. I look at how Orla and Walt are raising Nora to ask questions and get dirty and belch and I try to squash down my snap reaction that those things are improper. Says who? Who exactly made all those rules? I'm thankful that spending time with Orla has taught me to ask those questions.

Because the truth is, nothing all that great came out of me being proper. What have I got to show for myself? A fraught relationship with my daughter and...well, things are going better with my son. That's entirely because he has a kind heart.

I hate that I meddled with his relationship when Nora was first born. I still burn with the shame of it, how I set paperwork in motion to ensure Orla couldn't get Walt's trust fund. I'll never forget the look in his eye when he told me I almost cost him the most important things in his world.

I've never had anyone feel that strongly about me before, fight for me in that way.

ALL THE KIDS have piled into Elizabeth's minivan to go out bar hopping. Elizabeth's teenaged son has retreated to his room to play video games, and I find myself alone on the deck. Michael already cleaned up out here. Apart from the bar cart.

Nora and her cousin are content playing in the yard, and I decide to let them tire themselves out a bit before bed. There's no harm in me finally taking that celebration shot of whiskey. There's a difference between abusing alcohol and being dependent on it. I don't crave it. Toward the end of my marriage, I relied on it to numb my feelings.

But I haven't felt the need to do that anymore. And this seems festive.

I've never been a big bourbon fan, but Kellen and Michael Brady have joked repeatedly about the fire water of their people playing an important role in all things Brady family. I haven't had the heart to point out that I'm not actually in the Brady family. I'm just the tag-along mother of one of their inductees.

I sigh and shake those thoughts away, pouring myself a splash of the whiskey. I lean on the porch rail, watching Nora and Arlan chase a butterfly across the yard. The forsythia and rose of Sharon serve as enough of a hedge to keep the kiddos contained if I'm this close.

Is it wrong to rejoice in this moment? If my husband were still alive, I would most assuredly not be here, witnessing two precious children delight in the bobbing path of such a delicate insect. But Walton's death catalyzed a long series of events that did bring me here, right now. And I feel a little bit like a butterfly myself. Well. Maybe a moth.

I spent 55 years crawling around slowly, taking in small specks of affection and nourishment. Never feeling like I was woman enough. Never feeling like my body was small enough. My son seemed to shed all of that with such ease, but I feel worried I'll never be able to shake that mantle.

Seeing Nora and Arlan bend close, watching the butterfly sipping nectar from one of Elizabeth's daisies, I raise my glass to them. "Thank you," I whisper, and I slowly sip the warm liquid. I feel it hit my belly, tingly and hot. I remember again why they call it firewater.

Draining the last sip, I lean inside the sliding door to set the glass on the counter, keeping one eye on the back yard where the children are toddling around. "Elizabeth?" I hope she and Kellen are close by. I need to start wrestling Nora to bed but can't leave Arlan unattended or he'll climb the trellis and jump from the rooftop. That boy has more energy than his grandfather, and nobody has more zest than Mick Brady.

Mick. It feels like such a strange name. I always call him Michael. To me, it always sounded more refined, although that never seemed important to him. That's me, with the hangup on proper and refined.

Mick. I've enjoyed spending time with him this past year. His brother, Kellen, is kind and welcoming but if I'm truly honest, I've always felt a spark of attraction to Michael.

Not that there was ever anything to do about that. By the time I met him, I was already betrothed to Walton. I hear it now, the way it sounds to use words like "betrothed." But that's what it was. Our fathers made arrangements. I shudder and lean back out the screen door, seeing Nora and Arlan right where I left them. "Elizab—oh. There you are."

She and Kellen emerge down the hall, looking a bit like I might have interrupted them as Kellen hurries to tuck his shirt into his jeans. I hastily clear my throat and point at the glass I set on the counter. "I'm just going to grab Nora and get started on bedtime," I tell them. "I'm sure you have a routine with Arlan and I'll let you get to it."

Elizabeth opens her mouth to say something—maybe to protest or try to say they weren't off down the hall getting fresh. But I'm off the porch before she can get the words out.

"Nora!" I force my voice to sound cheerful as I stoop to gather her up. "Mimi is going to put you to bed now. How does that sound?"

"Shitty," she says, pushing back on my shoulder as my jaw drops.

"Young lady! Where did you learn such language?" I start walking her across the street, noticing that Michael's car is still in the driveway. He must still be around somewhere.

"Mama," Nora shouts, and I can't tell if she's saying her mother taught her to curse or if she's looking around for Orla.

I take another deep breath. None of this is natural for me. Another example of my granddaughter being raised to be free of the unspoken rules for how I had to inhabit the world. Nora isn't limited to saying certain things, or doing certain things. And now my life is intertwined with this family, where the women are outspoken and athletic and financially secure in their own right as they dive into careers they find fulfilling.

Where do I fit in here? I wonder for the thousandth time.

"Nora, what book would you like to read?" That I can do. After all, I'm well trained at following a script. It just so happens that these books are a rather different set of morals than the ones I'm used to. She wriggles out of my arms and down the hall to her bookshelf, where she slides *The Paperbag Princess* from the shelf.

I read it to her, doing the voices as she instructs, and read it to her a second time, because she asked nicely, and I'm rewarded with a kiss on the cheek as I lower her into her crib. Nora rolls over and is asleep before I hit the lights, leaving me alone to ponder the ending of the story—where the girl overcomes the monster but still winds up alone.

I don't want to be alone. That's the crux of it all. I know now that what I had before was unfulfilling and harmful. But at least I had someone. My husband has been dead for three years now and despite gaining a large family via my son's in-laws, I feel the deep loneliness of having been with someone...but not really with them...for decades.

I've never really gotten to be me, to see who I am and learn what I like. And I've certainly never found someone like Elizabeth has, who sneaks away with her for secret touches and kisses that make her glow.

With all these thoughts swirling in my head, I step into my son's kitchen to find Michael shoving pans of pasta salad into the fridge. "Oh, hey, Celeste," he says, bent over, rearranging the juice boxes on the bottom shelf to make room.

Feeling vulnerable and emotional, I walk up behind him, wondering what on earth has gotten into me. "Michael," I say, my voice husky as I tap my fingernails on the counter.

Mick. It feels too sinful to me. The word is so close to...fuck. I blush as I even think it.

My husband and I had decades of perfunctory sex. He was my first, and it was always just fine. Sometimes it was good. But Mick seems like a man who doesn't have perfunctory sex. Even as a silver-haired man nearing 60, I bet he *fucks*.

I think I've forced myself to call him Michael to keep these thoughts at bay. This will never do. This is not the answer to being alone. *But what would it be like to have him?*

He stands and turns, startled to see me standing so close to him. What would it be like, to let loose and succumb to passion? For once—just one night.

I am overcome with the scent of him. He smells like trouble. A little bit like whiskey, a little bit like whatever cologne he's wearing. The grassy, earthy notes of it make me feel woozy.

I watch as he swallows and wedges himself away from me, still standing too close. "I'll, uh, let you be," he says, closing the refrigerator door. "Let Orla and Walt know the extra cake is in there." He nods his head toward the refrigerator. And with the snick of a door latch, he's gone.

I grip the edge of the counter and fight back tears, ashamed of what I almost did. Of where I allowed my thoughts to drift. I make my way to the sofa and sit in the growing darkness until Orla and Walt stumble home.

CHAPTER SEVEN
MICK

And I absolutely cannot act on this impulse. I have to be a better man, a better role model for my boys. The thought pounded through my brain as I ran this morning, so much so that I set a faster pace than usual and Liam couldn't even keep up with me.

I'm not really going to make good on my threat to make him cover the tab for this afternoon's off-site meeting, because Liam seemed really upset that he couldn't keep up with his old man.

I'm my usual level of distracted during the meeting, cracking pistachios to keep my fingers occupied while Liam talks to the client about civil engineering options. If I don't have something to fidget with, my mind wanders right on out of the room. I wipe my hands on a napkin before we all shake to our ongoing business together. Once the client leaves, I toss a bunch of bills on the table.

"I thought you said this one was on me," Liam says, patting his leg for his wallet.

I wave him off. "You save your money and work on your mile pace."

Liam shakes his head and sighs. "Maddie and I have hardly been sleeping, Dad. I'm just...I'm more exhausted now than I was when Arlan was a newborn."

He tells me how Arlan is up every few hours, wanting to talk about clouds, wanting a drink of water, wanting to wander around the house.

957

"Sounds like me when I was a kid," I tell him. I drape an arm around my oldest son's shoulders, noticing that he's got a few strands of gray hair around his temples. "Why don't you let Arlan stay with me this weekend? You and Maddie can get some rest."

I see Liam consider this. He pauses, and that pause is so telling. He doesn't quite trust me to remember to feed Arlan. But he must be desperate because he nods. "Liam," I tell him, "It's not like I'm going to leave him unattended while I go out clubbing. Your boy will be in good hands. I promise." We walk back to the Beltane office together and he starts making verbal lists of all the things I'll need to do if Arlan sleeps over. I tune him out, because if I've learned anything, it's that young boys can thrive with a lot less gear than their parents think they need.

But it's true that I haven't had anyone in my home for months. Usually it's just my housekeeper inside my condo downtown, and I don't ever actually see her. Just the notes she leaves about what supplies she's going to order and put on my card. She used to ask me to go buy the things she needs, but between the small print on the bottles and remembering to actually get the supplies in time...it was just better for me to give her a credit card for expenses and for her services.

I think about the old Brady homestead, when Kellen and Orla lived with me and the boys. You'd think with five men living there, we'd have taken care of the yard at least, but the whole place was an overgrown weed patch and the inside may as well have been a jungle gym.

What was the point of buying a sofa, I asked Kellen at the time. The kids were just climbing the rafters anyway and nobody but Kellen ever sat still for more than a second. He bought himself a recliner and we set up the TV across from my treadmill.

Those were the best days of my life. Now it's just me alone in the barren condo in a trendy building that looks like...well, it looks like an old man lives there alone.

"Hey, Em." I lean on the receptionist desk after Liam swipes his ID so we can get in the building. I lost my ID ages ago. But when you own the place, chances are high you'll get buzzed in quickly regardless.

"Mick!" Em looks up from a spreadsheet where she'd been typing away. "What can I do for you?"

"You've got kiddos at home." She nods. "What sort of things would I need to get to have my grandson sleep over this weekend?"

Her face lights up. "Ooh," she coos. "Is Arlan sleeping over with Grandpop?"

I nod, and I remember Maddie saying that his only foods right now are yogurt and strawberries. Lord knows why I can remember that but leave my wallet sitting on counters. "Can you help me order some food and...does he need a special bed? I've got a queen in the guest room."

Em suggests I buy bed rails for the existing bed and a waterproof mattress cover. We order a case of yogurt with cartoon dogs on the containers and she even finds a way to have fruit delivered later in the week.

"I'm not an engineer," I start to tell her.

"Oh, I know that, sir," she says, patting my hand like she's offering condolences.

"What I mean is even though I'm not, I know everyone else with my blood running through them likes those building toys. The logs and those bricks that snap together. Can three year olds play with those?"

Em spins her computer monitor around and shows me a bigger version of the building blocks that Arlan can't choke on. We order enough for us to build an entire city inside my condo. And then she makes a face like she wants to say something but is worried about how I'll react. I can always read people, even if I can't remember my keys.

"Spill it, Em." I rap my knuckles on the counter above her desk. "You know I can take it, whatever it is."

She looks over both shoulders at the artwork I've brought to Beltane from my trips. I know none of it matches anything else, but each thing reminds me of the places I've seen, the people I've met. The problems our business has helped solve. Em sighs. "I wasn't sure if you have ... artifacts at your house. Like you do at the office." I purse my lips, considering. "It's just that a three-year-old might break things. I'd be worried about your treasures." Em shrugs.

"You're absolutely right," I tell her. Some of the carvings I bought from Inuit elders or clay bowls from Peruvian potters are irreplaceable. "I definitely don't want Arlan to smash my mementos." I only started really going on trips once my boys were a little bit older so I never had to worry about them smashing stuff. Plus when we all lived in the bigger house, all my stuff was in my office or my room.

I do a mental review of my living room and guest room. I've got my treadmill in the living room...Arlan could hurt himself on that. I make my way up to my office worried that my entire home is a death trap. Why didn't I do something about this sooner so my grandson could come over?

I'm sure Kellen has knickknacks sitting around, and all the kids are at his house every week. I write myself a note to ask him about it later, how he decides what to leave out and where to put it all. I head into another meeting, hoping I don't forget to read my reminder.

THE NEXT DAY, I meet my brother for a run in the park *after* work, which means it's more than 24 hours since I last cleared my head. I prefer to go in the mornings, but Kellen said he had something to show me. My whole day has been off, but at least I remembered to throw my running stuff in my car before I drove to the office. I know I'm supposed to ask him about something, but my notebook is back in my car at the trailhead and it's just me and Kel running along the dusty rocks in Frick Park.

"I'm doing a sleepover with Arlan this weekend," I tell him, hoping to spark whatever is on the outskirts of my memory.

"Better rest up. That kid's like an eel in olive oil when he's running away from you."

"Why would he run away?" I might not ever babysit him, but Arlan has spent plenty of time with Grand-Pop. He knows I have snacks in my pocket.

Kellen laughs softly and asks if I'm ready to see what he's got cooking up.

"Hit me."

"You know that fancy new housing development? Somerset in the Frick or something like that?"

"The mansions on the old slag heap?"

Kellen nods. "That's the one. Wait til you hear what's going on up behind there."

The whole neighborhood butts up against Frick Park, but sits above the Monongahela River, behind where the steel mills used to dump the byproducts from their raw materials. The architects and planners of that place have been working on it for 25 years and only recently started actually building the houses.

I don't know why I'm able to focus and listen as Kellen tells me about a group of hipsters gone rogue on the hill above the Somerset properties. "So there's a row of what? Five houses off Beechwood Boulevard," he tells me. "And the folks on the end are trying to make some sort of hillside farm back there. They had chickens, tried to get some beehives. Anyway! What do you think they went and did so they'd have better access to their tiered property?"

I shrug. This is a hilly area of the city. There's a reason the guidebooks say some neighborhoods look like they were designed by mountain goats. These aren't the kind of details I'm usually involved in, and Beltane has only done the one residential project—for Nicole when she had a landslide —so I'm not sure where this is headed. Kellen slaps my arm. "They started digging out an access road! No permit."

I realize Kellen has taken us running through the section of Frick Park adjacent to the housing development in question. He starts heading up a dirt path that's pretty steep, but we're both fit enough that we can keep talking even while we climb the Pittsburgh hills. "No permit? This is getting interesting."

Kel nods. "Next thing you know, the hill slides away. Whoosh! One of the row house owners is friends with my plumber. Guy had two decks off the back of his house, and they're both just dangling off the back of the brick. Whole row of houses is condemned. There!"

Kellen stops and points up at a little crop of old farm houses nestled in the hill and...a giant heap of broken swimming pools and garage roofs, swing sets and pieces of evergreen trees. The land just vanishes right at the edge of the foundations of the row of houses, a steep and jagged cliff where the earth just fell away. I imagine the heap is full of kids toys and lawn-mowers, too. Entire backyards, just slid down and away. "What a mess!"

Kellen nods, pointing at the house with the dangling decks. "So the other homeowners, their insurance wants to know who caused the land-slide. In other words, who should have to pay out the policies."

I shrug. "Road carving hipsters, right?"

Kellen shakes his head. "Their insurance is blaming the Somerset archi-tects for eroding the hillside. Something about improper stormwater management."

I scratch my neck, squinting at what's left of the dilapidated houses. Five families' entire lives uprooted, either because someone didn't do their job or someone else acted impulsively without considering the conse-quences. "You said this is a Beltane project?"

Kellen grins. "Insurance agency wants to bring in a geotechnical engi-neer as an expert witness. I thought Zack might want to do some research, given his recent expertise in landslides and property reinforcement."

I grin right back at my brother. "I love it, Kel. Where do I come in? Sounds like this is a done deal already?"

He shakes his head. "No, this is all second hand from the plumber. I need you to plant a seed with the insurance company."

Suddenly the day has purpose.

I head back to the office and my energy feels laser-focused. I realize what it was I forgot to ask Kellen, but it'll have to wait. This project is hot and present and I'm feeling ready to jump in, even though it's very nearly close of business for the Texas-based insurance agency. It doesn't take me an hour to set up a call with the homeowners insurance company representing 3 of the impacted homes.

I even manage to email them spec sheets and project narratives that Zack had typed up after he figured out the landslide situation in Nicole's back yard. All while I was on the phone! With the attachment, thank you very much.

I hang up the phone and sit back in my chair, feeling conflicted. Half of me is elated at this new triumph. We brought in new business today for work we've essentially already done. My kid just has to go poke around back there and offer his professional opinion on what caused this landslide. And how did he get that expertise? I sent him to Nicole. I sent him to South America to work on landslide remediation. Was I a little brusque with him while all the pieces of those projects came together? Sure.

But damn it, this work matters for people and when an idea is hot for me, it throbs like a sore tooth. How can I be so great at one thing in my life and still manage to forget to feed myself half the time?

I can't dwell on that. I need to loop Zack in so he doesn't feel in the dark this time around. Before the idea slides away like all the others, I pick up the phone and call my youngest son.

CHAPTER EIGHT
MICK

I skip my run Saturday morning because I have big plans to take Arlan out with me. I'm not sure why my Liam doesn't take his boy out for runs with him if he's having trouble sleeping. That's what always worked for me with all the boys. They were pounding out 5k distances by the time they were out of diapers.

Hm. I wonder if Arlan is out of diapers. That should have been something I asked before now. I don't have to wonder long, though, because there's a buzz at the intercom, the doorman asking if a Liam Brady can come up.

"Sure, sure," I say. And then I pause. "Hey, Leon, you can always send up my kids without asking first."

There's a long pause, during which I realize Leon hasn't met my kids. "Yes, sir," he says into the buzzer. I make a note to show him pictures of my boys. Orla, too. Does Leon even know what Kellen looks like? I'm pacing the room, pondering all this when there's a tap at the door, which then flies open and Arlan explodes into my house.

"Grand-pop!" He shouts, only it comes out sounding like "gwand pop" since the kiddo hasn't got his R sound yet. I scoop him up and toss him over my shoulder.

"Who said that? I don't see anyone?"

"It's me." He giggles into my back as I spin around.

"Who's *me*? There's nobody there?" I keep this up for a few beats, spinning around until Liam makes his way in from the elevator carrying enough luggage for a week-long trip.

"You moving in?" I ask, setting Arlan on the ground.

Liam rolls his eyes. "We didn't know what you'd have, and Maddie... hey, Dad, please don't call us this weekend? Please?" My son looks so tired. He's got heavy bags under his eyes.

"I've got this," I assure him. "You go get some sleep. Arlan can come every weekend if you want."

Liam puffs out his cheeks and sets some of the luggage down. "Okay, well here's his pull-ups for night time and his potty. And this is so he doesn't slip in your tub. It's a sticky mat thing. You have to watch him the whole time or he'll jump out all wet and then slip on the tile. And we've got some warm clothes in case it gets chilly—"

"Liam." I put my arm on my son's shoulder as Arlan runs around opening every cupboard in my kitchen. I sure am glad I remembered to move all my breakable stuff. "We'll be okay." He opens his mouth to protest and I shake my head. "I'll call Kellen and Elizabeth if something goes wrong, okay? And they'll tell me if I need to disturb you."

Liam takes a deep breath and sighs, then squats down. "Hey, Arlan? Arlan? Can you stop for a minute? Hey, buddy? I'm going to leave now."

"Bye, Daddy." Arlan doesn't look up from the cupboard where he's pulled out a metal sieve and put it over his head like a helmet. Finding a rolling pin in there, he starts banging it on the cupboard as I walk Liam to the door. This kid is indeed a firecracker.

I sit next to him for a few minutes as he tests the sound the rolling pin makes on different surfaces in my kitchen before I grab one end of the pin. "Want to go for a run with me by the river?"

"River!" Arlan drops his end of the heavy wood and runs to the door. He almost has it open as I jog to catch up, trying to remember if any of my boys had quite *this* much energy. I know I definitely always heard people say it seemed like I was run by a motor. I scoop Arlan up again and we head out the side door of my building, across the street from the entrance to the Jail Trail, or whatever it's really called.

The paved path goes along the Monongahela River. If we make it far enough, we can grab something to eat at the shopping plaza that now stands where the steel mills used to be.

Arlan tries to wriggle out of my arms, but I shake my head. "No way, pal. I'll set you down when we're away from the cars." But as I get to the path, I see that the bicyclists speeding along in between the roller skaters aren't going to be much safer for him. Maybe this wasn't my best idea after all. Liam didn't leave me a carseat, though, so I don't think I can drive Arlan anywhere that would have a path in the woods.

"We're heading east today, young man," I say, starting to run, hoping he'll follow along behind me. At first, he sprints way ahead and I rush to catch up, only to stumble when he stops abruptly and bends over to look at a pile of gravel. "No stopping yet, son," I say. "We've got to put in some miles."

He looks up at me and then down again at the gravel, like he's surprised to find himself stopped there. "I can relate. Want to hold my hand?" He nods and reaches up, and we run that way for a bit, me leaning uncomfortably to get my hand low enough to clasp his, but despite a few times tugging me to the side, he keeps pace with me for an entire mile in his little light up sneakers. I don't even mind running slower for him.

"See? This is nice, right?" I look down at him, but Arlan is staring straight ahead, like he's focused on keeping pace. I like it. Seems the kid is a natural runner.

I decide I don't want to push my luck on our first run together, so we turn to head back. I'm feeling pretty smug when we get back to my building, neither of us out of breath or sweating too much. I give Leon a wave as Arlan pushes the elevator button 600 times. "What should we drink for our recovery session?" I've been reading more and more about chocolate milk being good after a workout and, men my age can always use more calcium.

I pull out one of the sippy cups Em told me to get and a pint glass for myself. I hear Arlan digging in his bags as I search the fridge for the chocolate milk and then I hear him crinkling a wrapper as I carefully pour out two glasses.

"Here you go, my boy." I slide Arlan his glass and raise mine to toast. I'm about to say something about drinking to our cardiovascular health when Arlan looks up, a mouthful of crayons dangling from his lips. He's got multi-colored wax all over his teeth and starts spitting out bits of wrappers.

"Well, hell, kid. What on earth did you eat those for?" Arlan shrugs as I drag my hand down my cheek, wondering what to do next.

CHAPTER NINE
CELESTE

I'm surprised to see Michael Brady's name come up on my cell phone this early on a Saturday. Before I answer, I rack my brains to see whether I've forgotten about a family function or a babysitting responsibility. Coming up empty, I hesitantly answer. "Hello?"

"Celeste, I need your help." He sounds a bit panicked. "I'm baby-sitting Arlan this weekend and he, well the kid ate most of a box of crayons while I was pouring him a glass of chocolate milk."

I can't help the puff of exasperated laughter that slips out of my mouth. "He did what?"

"Celeste, what should I do? Who do I call? Do I have to take him to the hospital?"

I sink into my couch, trying to recall if any of my children ever ate a crayon, trying to remember what they're even made of. Then I glance at the cabinet by the sink, where the bright green Mr. Yuck sticker assaults my decor. Walt said I had to put one there if Nora was ever going to come play at the house, so I made a concession.

I walk over to the sticker. "Okay," I tell Michael. "Okay, I'm pretty sure you need to call poison control and ask them what to do."

"Poison control? That sounds serious."

"Well, I've never called. But Walt and Orla seem to know all about it. Should I text you the number?"

966

"Oh," he sounds relieved. "I was so worried I'd have to try and find a pen. Ha. I guess I could use the stubby end of a half-eaten crayon!"

"I'll text you the number and you call, then call me back and let me know what they say."

"Right," he says, and I can hear a ruckus at his house. I'm not sure if it's him pacing and slamming doors or if Arlan is still on the loose. Michael hangs up the phone and I text him the number from the sticker.

And then I wait. Foolishly, I go up to my vanity and check my hair and powder my nose, as if he's going to see me when he calls back. An hour passes, way more time than it should take to call poison control. I open my laptop and search for what to do if a child eats a crayon, and breathe a sigh of relief when I read that they're considered non-toxic.

Michael seemed so upset, though. I remember that he doesn't really get to babysit Arlan on his own very often. Maybe never. I check my phone again to make sure the volume is turned on. Seeing no calls, I try his number, but it rings until his voicemail picks up.

I hang up without leaving a message and bite my lip, worried. I make a decision to get in my car and drive downtown.

I know Michael lives in the fancy new condo building near a parking garage. I remember him talking about it before and filing away the name of the garage if I ever needed to find parking downtown. I get there with relative ease and marvel at how few people are out on the streets compared to weekday afternoons. This feels manageable, even.

Tucking the garage ticket into my purse, I make my way into the lobby of Michael's building. "May I help you, ma'am?" A friendly-looking doorman stops me and I experience a small wave of panic, not anticipating security in the building.

"Uh, well, I'm here to see Mr. Brady," I tell him. He reaches for the phone to presumably call up, but there's no answer. I lean close to the podium. "He's watching his grandson today and called me for reinforcement."

The doorman nods. Then he shakes his head and grins. "I saw those two go in and out earlier, going for a run I think. That boy is a ball of energy."

"Isn't he, though? I'm worried Michael would be too distracted to answer the intercom. Would it be all right if I just went up?"

Leon—he wears a shining name tag that he taps as he considers—sighs. "Just today he did tell me I should let his kids come up. Only, I don't know that I've met his kids!"

I nod. "My son is married to Orla. Kellen's daughter?" Leon shakes his head. I wonder if he's new or if it can possibly be true that the Brady family has not imprinted themselves on Leon's memory yet.

"Here," I say, pulling out my phone. I open a photo Walt texted me from a few weeks ago, when he and Orla eloped. Cal had used a selfie stick to capture the entire crew in Kellen's back yard after Michael had shown up with a cake. I hadn't really studied the photo much, but now, as I show it to the doorman, I see how very happy everyone looks.

I stand to the side of the photo cradling Nora, and Cal must have snapped the picture just so, because I don't really remember allowing myself to feel happy that day, and yet there I am with a smile on my face.

"That's a real nice family," Leon says, grinning at the picture.

"Isn't it, though?" Leon presses the button for me in the elevator, letting me pass with a wave, and I suddenly feel sheepish, sneaking up to Michael's apartment uninvited. What am I even doing here? Accosting the man I tried to kiss when he's trying to spend time with his grandson.

Before I can worry too hard about that, I reach the proper floor and make my way toward the door that simply has to belong to Michael Brady. In a hall of white doors and white walls, one door is adorned with a gilded, Celtic cross.

I tap on it lightly and wait. Inside, I hear a series of curses and a clatter, so I take a chance and push the door open.

Michael whips his head around and visibly relaxes. "Celeste, thank god." He throws his hands up in the air. "Now Arlan is puking everywhere and I don't know what to do."

CHAPTER TEN
MICK

At least I don't have carpet. That thought keeps cycling through my head as I ransack my kitchen for a bowl or something to put near my grandson. The poison control woman warned me he might get an upset stomach from eating crayons, but I wasn't expecting neon blue barf in such quantities.

I probably won't admit it to Liam, but I went into this sleepover a little smug. I'm clearly a little rusty when it comes to keeping up with toddlers. As soon as I get this under control I'm going to bring my A-game. Bradys do not give up. No, sir. No more incidents.

I push a hand through my hair, forgetting that I probably have blue gunk on my hands, and stare at Celeste. I forgot to call her back after I finally hung up with poison control. Did poison control exist when my kids were young? I don't think any of mine ever ate something they shouldn't.

"Shit," I say, as Arlan lets loose another round, and then sort of flops onto the floor exhausted.

"Shit," he echoes. Celeste looks like she's going to bust out laughing.

"I know this isn't funny," she says, covering her nose with one hand as she sets her bag down inside the door. "It's just...a little bit funny."

She comes to stand beside me and the two of us survey the room. I hazard a guess that it's been a few decades since either of us have cleaned our own houses. Professional household help has been an important part of my life since the second I could afford it. Something tells me Celeste could always afford it.

She takes a deep breath and taps her nails on the counter. "Right," she says, looking down at Arlan. "One of us should give him a bath and change his clothes. The other should find your mop and floor cleaner."

My eyes shoot wider as I stare at her. "You're going to help with one of those?" She's dressed to kill as always, wearing slacks that hug her slim hips and a shirt that looks expensive and buttery soft. She nods. "Well," I ask her, "which one of those would you want to do?" *Please say bath. Please say bath.*

"I think I'd like to give young sir a bath, if that's all right with you." I nod furiously as she slips off her shoes and squats down next to Arlan. Relief rolls over me along with an unfamiliar feeling as I watch her talk softly to my grandson, taking his hand and asking him where to find the bathroom.

I hear the water turn on in the guest bath and snap out of my funk, tossing open all the cabinets until I find a mop and a bucket and a bottle of bleach. Probably not the best choice for my hardwood, but I don't entirely care. I dump a capful in the bucket as it fills with water and get to work.

I do my best not to get anything on my clothes as I wring out the mop after every pass. It only takes a few minutes and the floor is gleaming. Despite the bleach odor the room smells a lot better, too. I rinse everything off, throw away anything it seemed like Arlan splattered, and turn on all the ceiling fans before heading down the hall to check in.

I swallow down a momentary bolt of lust when I come upon Celeste on her knees talking to Arlan. I absolutely should not be staring at the heart-shaped ass of Orla's mother-in-law. I shake my head and look around the room, noticing Arlan's clothes and a few towels heaped on the floor already. "I'll stick these in the wash," I say, and then pause when I notice his sneakers. "What do I even do about those?"

Celeste turns to smile at me, one hand remaining on Arlan's shoulder. "Orla and Walt toss Nora's shoes in the wash all the time," she says. "I think kid shoes, you can do that with."

"Hmm," I mutter, bundling it all up in yet another towel. "That's quite a concept. Would that translate into engineering somehow? I wonder if any of the kids can do anything with that idea."

"You mean Nora and Arlan?"

I let out a laugh. "Nah." I keep the messy bundle in one arm and open the linen closet to get her some more towels. "My kids. Zack and Liam and Cal. They're always kids to me."

Celeste nods slightly. "I used to think that about mine," she says, and a cloud moves across her face. "Walt is definitely a man now, and, well, maybe it is childish that Rosemary won't even talk to me these days."

Crap. Her kid still isn't in touch after all this time. I remember when Celeste's husband first died, she mentioned that Rosemary and she weren't on the best of terms. I relate to this when I think of Zack's mother, totally absent since the day our divorce was final. But if it were one of my own kids? Treating me like that? Hell, I barely go eight hours overnight without seeing my boys. "I'll be right back," I tell her. "I want to hear more about this."

I quickly get the wash started and find one of the suitcases Liam brought for Arlan, thinking I could find some toys or something for the bath. I quickly give up and just grab a few clean cups from the dishwasher instead.

And then I sit next to Celeste on the floor by the tub, watching Arlan make waterfalls. I thought she'd open up more about her situation with Rosemary, but instead she looks at me quizzically. "What made you call me? When Arlan ate the crayons?"

"Oh." I scratch my hair where it meets my shirt collar. "Well, I didn't want to disturb any of the kids. My kids. And, well, I'm not quite ready to have Kellen know I let my grandson eat something hazardous an hour into our sleepover." I shrug slowly. "I thought you'd be nice about it. And know what to do."

Her lower jaw drops, just a little, and I can see her pulse tick in her throat, like she's breathing heavy at that revelation. "And you did," I say. "Know what to do, that is." I grin and lean back against the wall, bending my knees to my chest and looping my arms around them as Arlan lies on his back, declaring that he's a beluga.

I INVITE Celeste to stay for lunch, and then we play Legos with Arlan for a few hours, using every brick I bought to make tall towers and long roads. It's great watching him come up with new ideas for the bricks. When my own kids were this age, I gave them these things to occupy them while I got other stuff done. I suspect Celeste is also pretty new to playing alongside a kid like this, because she has a look of wonder on her face as Arlan instructs her to build a stack taller than him. She slowly and fastidiously obliges him until I declare we should order pizza.

The mention of dinner excites Arlan so much he kicks over his tower, and the sound of the bricks tinkling to the floor mingles with Celeste's laughter. By the time she heads out at Arlan's bedtime, I can't decide if I'm still just lusting after her or whether I'm enamored by her willingness to just roll with the punches today. She was so relaxed and at ease, and amazing with Arlan. He clung to her and peppered her with kisses as she tucked him in to bed in my guest room.

For a brief moment, I have a vision of what it could be like to tackle every day with her like that. Partners. I blow out a breath, remembering I forgot to call her back and she only drove over here to begin with because she was worried something terrible had happened. It's better if I let these thoughts slip away, just like all the important details seem to disappear. How does that song go? Dust in the wind.

That's pretty much all my promises were worth to my ex-wives. I'm not cut out to be anyone's partner. I know that. Only, recently, I'm starting to feel upset about it in a way I never did before.

CHAPTER ELEVEN
CELESTE

I MESSAGE ROSEMARY FROM THE PARKING GARAGE BEFORE I DRIVE HOME TO MY empty house, full of echoes and ghosts. Rosemary's room, for instance, is still filled with neatly labeled bins of her childhood things. Top of the line sports equipment that never got used. Walton always insisted she play tennis, and she loathed the sport.

I think it made her anxious to compete, especially in singles. Usually I stood back and yielded to him when he forced her to go to practices and matches. He pointed out that it was good for her to try difficult things, and important for her to be skilled at tennis and golf.

But I saw how she hated it. I sit on her bed when I get back to the house, looking in the closet at her old school and sports uniforms hanging there. I can't remember if she was competing for school or just at the club, but there was one match where she was just beside herself. She was sick to her stomach with nerves and begged me not to make her go.

So I stood up to my husband, told him she felt feverish, that I believed her illness was real. He growled and stormed off with Trip—Walt—in tow, leaving Rosemary and I behind. We sat in my bed and watched movies that day. It felt so nice to be close to her, to have done a small thing to help her when she was so visibly upset.

I set my glass of water on her night stand and reach for my phone again. She hasn't responded yet.

I wish I had done more to support you,

I add, and then gasp when I see the dots at the bottom of the phone screen, indicating that she's replying to me.

Then the dots stop, and I gasp again as my phone rings in my hand. "Rosemary?" My voice is a whisper. I try not to cry.

"Hey, Mom," she says, her voice flat and uncertain. "What happened with the sick kid?"

I smile and tell her the story. I don't mention that it's Michael Brady, and I'm not sure why. Rosemary has met him before. She is, I'm sure, aware of the family ties with her brother's wife. It feels dishonest to hold back this piece of the story, but I'm so excited to be talking to my daughter about anything, that I decide to just leave it vague.

She laughs about the blue spit-up, and then there's a silence. I can't tell if it's a loaded silence for her as well as for me.

"I thought I'd hear ice rattling in your gin glass," she says, her voice flat.

I could get defensive. I could yell at her to watch how she speaks to me. But those responses got us here, to this strained silence. I brace myself, clenching, and say, "All those years of gin-haze left me feeling like a shell of a person. I don't want to live life in a fog. I've been making changes."

She's silent for a long time and I can hear her breathing. "I wasn't expecting a real answer," she tells me.

I take a breath, wanting Rosemary to make the next move, but not sure if I should extend a hand again. I want to prove to her that I'm working on being less uptight, that I want to mend fences. I bite my lip, and finally she says, "I called you because I have to tell you something. Something about myself."

I nod, but she can't see that. I can barely form words even though I've been preparing for this moment. I told myself repeatedly that no matter what Rosemary says, the next time we speak I'm going to respond with "I love you." And then I'm going to apologize and we will go from there. *I love you. I love you.* I repeat it silently as I listen to her click her teeth together.

"I've missed you, Rosemary. I'm so glad you are ready to share something with me."

"Mom, I'm gay," she says.
"Oh," I respond. "Oh. That fits," I say, and then she starts to cry.

CHAPTER TWELVE
CELESTE

"Hm?"

"You said 'that fits.' What do you mean by that?"

"Oh." I hate that I didn't first tell her I love her like I planned. Like I was practicing up until that very second. And now I've missed my window. "It just…fits. Now that you've told me, I see it." Memories race to the surface, of Rosemary telling me she doesn't fit in, of her refusing to attend various events simply because it was expected of her. I imagine now that Rosemary was well aware of the pinched lips and whispers from the women in our sphere about people who "adopt that lifestyle."

"I'm so very glad you told me," I tell her, wishing I could reach through the phone. I want to say so much, to tell her I've been suspended between worlds for so long, unable to figure out how to stand on steady feet. I want to tell her about the cloud of wrongdoing hovering over me, that I need to atone. "I love you," I say, finally, as a tear rolls down my face.

"My whole life, I've been made to feel terrible about everything about myself." Her words are harsh but not unexpected. Her brother said many of these same things to me a few years ago.

"I'm not proud of how I lived my life until your father died." I remind myself that telling these things to my daughter is me giving fucks about the right things. Her breath anchors me to the moment. "I apologize for my role in perpetuating that … atmosphere, Rosemary."

She snorts. "Atmosphere." I can practically hear her rolling her eyes. "I thought you were going to ask me if I poisoned the minds of my sorority sisters or something." I slowly run my palm along her childhood bedspread, feeling the smooth material as I let my daughter express her hurts.

"You're not even a little concerned about how this will make you look in front of all your posh friends?"

As her words sink in, I feel the weight of our separation these past few years. She has no idea how isolated I've been. How utterly rejected I was from my entire world once word got out of her father's misdeeds. "Rose-mary, I..." I don't even know how to begin to explain any of this to her. I've hardly seen her since her father's funeral.

"I have been banished from that life." The word doesn't quite fit in, because while I was brutally kicked out of the only network I've ever known, I now don't really want to go back. Doesn't banishment imply a mourning, a sense of loss?

"What do you mean? You were freaking out that I wasn't bringing you along on that trip last Thanksgiving."

"That was two Thanksgivings ago, actually." Do I launch into a long explanation of how I hadn't yet accepted that Rosemary's sorority sisters and their mothers wouldn't welcome my presence? That I was still pretending I wasn't the topic of gossip and pity?

Not today, I decide. I reach for the pearls I can't seem to stop wearing, rolling them between my fingers. "I want to hear more about you," I tell her. "Are you seeing someone?"

I hear her inhale slowly. "I am," she says, and it sounds like she's tapping her nails on the table just like I do. "She's Black."

"Okayyy." That seems like an odd piece of information to lead off with before Rosemary even reveals her name, but my daughter charges onward.

"I'm telling you that now so that if you ever meet her, you don't say something awful about her looking ethnic or some shit."

I reach for the water, swallowing the cold liquid down along with the hurt that my daughter thinks I would do such a thing. Because truthfully, the last time Rosemary knew me, I might have. In this conversation, I see how very far I've come since I began spending time with the Brady family. How my first instinct is to think about a person's character traits rather than surface level nonsense. *My fucks really are flying away.*

I try to hide my smile at that thought and get back to business. "I'd be honored to meet your partner. Do I say partner?"

"Yeah. Partner. I'll text you a picture." I jump as I feel the phone vibrate and pull it away from my head to see an incoming message. A photo of Rosemary with her arms around a woman with short, natural hair and huge, wide eyes. The two of them are smiling brightly with a sunset sky in the background. "You both look so happy," I say. "What's her name?"

"Bisi," she tells me. "She's Nigerian. Well, she's American. But her *family* is Nigerian."

"I'd love to learn more about her."

A dog starts barking outside, shrill and persistent and I stand to look out the window. "Everything okay over there?" my daughter asks, but it's like a spell has broken. By the time I'm able to respond to Rosemary, I can feel her protective walls are back up. She's still so very hurt and worried I will continue to hurt her. I try to change the subject.

"Did your brother tell you what he and Orla did?"

Rosemary snorts. "Eloped! In the middle of a race. What a weirdo."

I grin. "It still feels odd to me, too."

We sit in silence for a bit until Rosemary asks, "What about you? Walt's married and I'm with Bisi. Are you seeing anyone?" Taken aback, I drop the glass to the carpet, splashing my legs with cold water. Rosemary must hear the commotion, because she quickly says, "This friend with the sick grand-kid...you said it was a man, so I'm sort of jumping to conclusions here."

"Oh." I wave a hand in the air. "I'm not ready for that. Not yet. He really is just a friend." A friend I practically mauled in his kitchen who later had the grace to pretend that did not happen. A friend who always smells like fresh outdoors and coffee, but not coffee breath. I often wonder if Michael walks around with fresh coffee beans in his pocket. I laugh quietly, imagining him doing that very thing.

"Mom!" Rosemary's voice carries laughter. "You're blushing. I can hear you blushing."

I raise a hand to my cheek, which does indeed feel warm. "I'm just embarrassed," I counter. Desperate to change the subject yet again, I ask Rosemary if she knows when I might meet Bisi.

"Does Walt know?" I ask, imagining a Sheffield get-together like the Bradys have, with both my children and their partners bringing warmth into my home. I get lost in the fantasy of it until Rosemary sighs.

"Not yet," she says.

"Oh. Well I will go with your timeline." I remember hearing Samantha use that phrase at one of our Foof meetings when she was talking another one of the women through a problem.

Rosemary promises to think about letting me meet Bisi and we hang up with a plan to talk soon. Even that feels like a gift to me. I practically float as I clean up the spilled water. I've hurt my daughter for a long time. My instincts and urges are still to first think or say harmful things. But we've broken the seal. I've made headway.

Suddenly, all I want to do is share this news with the man who called me in his hour of need.

CHAPTER THIRTEEN

MICK

In a stroke of mercy, Arlan sleeps through the night. When he springs out of bed at five, I'm already up in the kitchen brewing my first pot of coffee for the day. "Hello, sir," I say, offering a salute. He toddles over to me and hugs my leg, and I catch a whiff of his full overnight diaper.

"You need to throw that thing in the trash," I tell him, and he looks at me incredulously as I measure out a scoop of beans, enough to brew three strong cups. "You just pull it down and then toss it in the trash," I say again, adding the beans to the machine.

"You do it." He folds his arms across his chest.

"No." This is not a game I'm going to lose. "You do it, and I'll let you share my coffee." Placated, Arlan deals with his garbage and somehow manages to climb one of my kitchen stools. He scoots across the counter island until he's sitting bare-assed by my coffeemaker.

"No balls near my beans, kid." I scoop him up with one arm and push the start button, which makes Arlan scream as the grinder begins pulsing my caffeine. "Sorry," I tell him, trying to help him cover his ears. "I should have warned you." Why didn't it occur to me to let him know I would be making a loud sound? Hell, it's a good thing he woke up before the sun or that would have done the trick.

I help him get dressed and pour him a few drops of coffee into a mug full of milk. We're sitting at the island with our drinks and the newspaper

980

when Liam and Maddie burst in the front door. "You're up early," I say as Maddie rushes to scoop up her son and smother him with kisses.

"We're not used to sleeping in anymore," Liam says, stifling a yawn.

"Grand-pop gave me coffee," Arlan says by way of greeting, trying to slurp his drink around his parents' affection.

"Jesus Christ, Dad. We told you he hasn't been sleeping." Liam looks like he wants to strangle me despite 24 hours of kid-free time.

I wave a hand in the air. "It was a few drops in his milk. Nothing I didn't offer you kids when you were younger."

"I'll go gather up Arlan's things," Maddie says, heading down the hall as Liam leans against the wall, his arms crossed on his chest like he's about to reveal something serious.

"Our pediatrician thinks he might have ADHD," Liam tells me, and then sighs like he just revealed the kid has a fatal disease.

"He's three years old," I counter. "Of course he has no attention span. Say, I took him for a run yesterday, like I used to with you kids, and he slept through the night just fine."

Liam is about to snap back at me when Maddie comes stomping back down the hall. "Did our son seriously eat crayons, Mick? And vomit on your floor?"

I wave a hand again. "This is nothing I can't handle. They're non-toxic." Liam starts rubbing her back and talking about how Arlan never, ever sits still. As he tells me this Arlan drags the tub of Lego bricks into the hall and dumps them on the floor with a clatter.

Maddie and Liam jump. "I've never sat still, either," I counter.

My son glares at me and then takes a deep breath. "I'd like you to hear what we're saying, Dad. We're telling you something that concerns us and we'd really appreciate if you listened."

I want to interject that my boys all turned out fine and they started out juiced up like electrons, too. But then I remember how Arlan ran down the path, tugging me with him. How quickly he stuffed those damn crayons in his mouth while I was getting the chocolate milk.

I look at Maddie's face and see the hurt in her eyes. "You're right," I tell them, shifting my weight from foot to foot, suddenly feeling antsy. It's about time for my run now that my first coffee is hitting my veins. "I do know what it's like to raise high-energy boys. I want to help," I tell them. "I am more than happy to have Arlan over any time you two need a break."

Maddie starts to cry then and flings her arms around my neck, thanking me. It feels so strange that I don't return her embrace at first. I'm not used to saying the right things, especially to women. I don't quite know what to do next, so I ask her to let me know what the pediatrician says. This just sets her to crying again.

"We were so worried you'd be a dick about this," Maddie says, wiping her eyes and reaching into her fanny pack for a tissue.

I look at my son, who stares up at the ceiling. "Well, I love you. You know that, right? I love you all and I don't quite understand the issue, but I can see that it's really got you upset."

"It's just that he puts himself in danger so frequently," Maddie explains, as Liam scoops Arlan from the countertop. I laugh, unsure how he got up there so fast.

"Well," I say, reaching for Arlan and putting him up on my shoulders. This conversation has my mind whirling, so I start marching in place as Arlan slaps out a rhythm on the top of my head. Liam reaches for his son, but I shake my head and keep on marching. "Like I said, I remember how exhausting it is to be a parent. It always helped when other Bradys could lighten the load."

Arlan slaps out a finale while his parents hug me and promise they'll take me up on my offer to have Arlan overnight again.

Eventually everyone calms down and I get them all out the door so I can go for my long run. My mind races for the first mile, as per usual. My thoughts flit back and forth between work, potential projects I'm exploring, inspiring things I see along the trail. But then I hit a rhythm and I wait for my mind to settle on a topic I can ponder for the duration of my run.

Celeste. Her name pops up along with the vision of her helping me yesterday. How she came over without judgement and stayed calm, even through hours of building blocks. Celeste who, I recall, has been occupying my thoughts a lot lately.

I raise my arm to check how many miles I've run and realize I never put my watch on in all the confusion this morning. I look at my surroundings but can't decide if this has quite been three miles from home, so I push onward, wondering if there will ever come a time when I get myself together.

Maybe I have ADHD. The thought shows up uninvited and I freeze, hearing a muttered curse as a bicyclist behind me has to swerve around me like a speed bump. I don't think ADHD existed when I was young. But as I recap everything my son was saying about my grandson, I hear how much of myself was echoed in his words.

I spin around and hurry toward my apartment, eager to get my hands on some research before I drive myself insane wondering what-if.

CHAPTER FOURTEEN
CELESTE

On Tuesdays, I get to babysit Nora. At first, I bristled at being asked. I felt equal parts overwhelmed to be responsible for an infant and worried I'd do something wrong. And I sensed how much Orla worried about me being alone with her baby. Now, I cherish these days. Nora is nearly two and able to actually do things.

After my time with Arlan, I decided Nora should also have some of those bigger Lego bricks and spent nearly an hour with her on the floor, just marveling as she built things. Unlike her cousin, she didn't want me to build giant towers for her to crash to the ground.

Instead, she created tunnels and hid things inside them, including Pudding, their pet rabbit.

I never got to really just enjoy my own children in this way. I know many grandparents feel this way. By the time Walt was this age, I was pregnant with Rosemary and exhausted all the time. By the time Rosemary was this age, I was already running ragged getting my son to and from preschool and tennis lessons and swim practice.

I really enjoy the stillness that Orla and Walt create for Nora, even if it doesn't necessarily seem still as my granddaughter buzzes around me creating a zoo for her mermaids. What a beautiful thing that a small child can look at a green plastic block and imagine it is a mythical sea creature. When have I ever been encouraged to look past an object, to see its *potential* and not just what it is on the surface?

Eventually, Nora grows bored of the blocks and she and I head out for a walk around the neighborhood, where we see Elizabeth outside her and Kellen's house.

Motherhood and grand-motherhood seems so effortless for Elizabeth, who I recently found out had a similar sort of marriage to my own. Unlike me, turning to gin and Ativan to numb my senses to the hurt of it all, Elizabeth tried and tried to fight those pressures for her son's sake, until she eventually just left her husband behind.

She squats in her garden now, trimming some wildflowers, and Nora tugs on my arm, wanting to go and say hello. We walk over and Elizabeth tucks her snippers into an apron pocket, scooping up Nora and twirling her around. "Just the helper I was looking for," she says, setting Nora down and gathering the daisies and hyssop she already trimmed. "Can you help me hold these?"

Elizabeth smiles up at me and winks as Nora clutches the bouquet. I stand in the shade, not knowing what to do with myself, and finally say, "Your garden is just beautiful."

Elizabeth stands again, wiping off her knees and arranging the flowers into a tidy bouquet. "Thank you. I just love all these native perennials. I barely have to do anything!" She admires the purple and yellow bouquet and asks if Nora and I would like to come inside while she puts the flowers in water.

Nora is halfway up the porch steps before I have a chance to say we shouldn't impose, and she's soon helping to fill a blue glass jar with water. I watch as Elizabeth opens a bottle of soda and pours some into the glass. "This will help to keep the flowers fresh," she tells Nora, who is then offered a small sip of the remaining soda before Elizabeth takes a big swig.

"Where did you learn all this about gardening?" I know the neighborhood where Elizabeth used to live with her former husband. It's not the sort of place where people tend their own landscaping. I almost don't know what to expect when I go outside these days, since our gardener handles all of it. I sigh, thinking again how right Walt is that things would be much easier for me if I just sold the house and moved somewhere cozier.

Someplace perhaps like this house.

Elizabeth shrugs. "I took some classes at Phipps. You know, the conservatory?"

"They offer classes?" Walt and Orla have a membership to the beautiful greenhouse in Schenley Park. I often take Nora to tour the gardens, inside and out, just spending our day amidst the beautiful blooms.

As Nora helps herself to a snack from the cupboard, Elizabeth fishes around on the counter, looking for something. "They have tons of classes," she says. "Aha. Found it." She folds open a brochure. "They do native plant landscapes, rain gardens. Ooh, look—they're doing cooking classes now, too." She beckons for me to come closer, and I do, admiring the colorful images advertising seminars on the history of different garden styles, as well as hands-on classes.

"Those all sound really lovely," I say, but I hesitate. "I don't know if I could just go on my own to something like that. You really went as a beginner?"

Elizabeth grins and nods. "Total newb, as Jake would say." Her teenage son uses video game lingo a lot, but I've gotten used to hearing these terms. We laugh together at the reference and she tells me to keep the class list. "Getting Jake ready for college applications, I won't have time for any classes this quarter," she says.

I'm about to tell her I remember those days and see if I can't offer advice, but I suspect her approach to college will be more about her son's interests than about forming networking opportunities and ensuring legacy Greek life membership. I don't have to worry about it for long, however, when Kellen pops in the side door with his brother in tow.

Elizabeth brightens and greets Kellen with a kiss as I smile shyly at Michael. "What are you two doing here?" Elizabeth pats Michael on the shoulder and offers Kellen the bottle of soda.

He waves it away. "We're going to do a walking lunch to discuss a new venture," Kellen says.

Elizabeth laughs. "Giving up on jumping rope while you air your ideas to your brother?" She and Kellen laugh and I realize they're talking about Michael.

They must see my confusion because Kellen says, "My brother says he thinks best in motion. For years, he used to jump rope in my office while we talked. Never even breaks a sweat."

Michael waves a hand. "That's because I'm in top cardiovascular health."

"More like it's because you drink a pot and a half of coffee every day."

"Brother, you know I replaced most of that with my Yerba mate. I'm down to only a pot of Joe." I like listening to their easy teasing. I'm reminded again at how comfortable the Brady family is speaking their mind. These personality quirks aren't shunned or shamed away, but acknowledged as odd and just accepted.

Michael looks around the room then, seeing Nora munching on graham crackers and not really paying attention to us. "I've, uh, actually been doing some thinking," he tells us. "About my energy levels." He seems like he wants to reveal something serious, but his brother launches into stories about him roller skating in the office so he could spend less time walking to and from peoples' desks when he had ideas.

I meet Michael's eye and I can tell there was something else he wanted to say, but the moment is lost. The brothers leave for their active lunch break and I gather Nora up to get her across the street for our less-active lunch.

"Think about the class," Elizabeth says as we depart. But I know I'll never draw up the courage to attend one alone.

CHAPTER FIFTEEN
MICK

MY BROTHER IS MY BEST FRIEND. THIS HAS ALWAYS BEEN TRUE. BUT AS I TROT alongside him during our active lunch, I realize he might be my only friend. I guess that's not entirely right. Celeste is my friend. She said as much when she came to help me with Arlan.

Sure, I have hundreds of business acquaintances. I have maxed out the contacts in my phone. If there's a person in Pittsburgh doing something interesting, I know them and I probably visited them at least once.

But...my brother and my kids are the only people who have been at my side through everything I've done. Nearly sixty years of detention and putting my foot in my mouth and realizing it's not normal to keep pistachios in my shirt pocket, and my brother has stood by my side for all of it. He's been the most meaningful relationship of my life.

"So." I want to get back to the conversation I started in the kitchen. "For real, Kel. I want to talk. About my excess energy." He ducks under a branch on the park trail before answering.

When I want to run with Kellen, I have to do it in the damn woods because his old man feet can't handle the pavement anymore. I've told him he needs to be using a foam roller. I've been foam rolling since before it was hip. But he's got... "What's it called with your feet again?"

"Plantar fasciitis." He answers right away.

"That's right." The trail widens and I pull up alongside him, marveling again that he doesn't care that I flit between conversation topics. We were going to talk about me and my brain.

Kellen runs in silence a bit longer. Finally, he says, "You know how I watch those historical documentaries?"

"Of course I do. It's your only hobby."

He shakes his head. "Not true. You know Beth and I are gardening. And camping. And I'm teaching Jake how to take care of the car."

"Okay, okay. You watch the documentaries even though they're boring as all get-out."

He frowns. "There was one a few years ago about Teddy Roosevelt. As I watched, I remember thinking the narrator could have been talking about you." My brother outlines the former president's habit of drinking copious amounts of strong coffee, of pacing, of cranking out more correspondence than any president before or since.

"I'm flattered that you'd compare me to the leader of the Rough Riders, baby brother."

He bobs his head along in step with our movement. "I guess I'm just saying...you're eccentric, and you know that. But look at what we've built together! How could we have done that without your unbelievable energy? You've got that same eccentric spirit and look at all Teddy accomplished. You're a very successful man, Mick. What could be wrong with that?"

I'm not sure what to say to him, so we just run along in silence for a spell. "I can't help but think about Sheila," I say, referencing Liam and Cal's mother. "I regret that I was unfaithful to her."

Kellen sighs long and hard at that. "Well, who's to say whether you two would have stayed together regardless? I'm not condoning that choice, Mick, but..." He shrugs. "She owns her own business, has a nice house. She's loving being a grandmother. I think it's all okay."

I nod and fall into step behind him as the trail narrows again. We run a bit more as I try to make sense of the fact that my ex-wife might be okay, despite all the shit I did to her.

By the following week, I decide to call one of the doctors listed on the website for an adult ADHD study in Pittsburgh. One of the docs says he has a special interest in patients who are over 50 and were never diagnosed. "These aren't just senior moments," he writes on his website.

Of course, by the time I work up the nerve to call him, it's after hours and I get their voicemail, which encourages me to register online. I print out a load of questionnaires I'm supposed to fill out before our appointment, and I know I'm never going to remember if I don't take care of it immediately. Usually, I would just disregard this sort of paperwork, but I see at the top of one of the sheets that this sort of attitude is one of the symptoms and, well, I get sucked in.

As I run through the questionnaire, it seems like a map of my life. I start sweating as I read the questions. *Do you tend to make decisions and act on them impulsively—like spending money, getting sexually involved with someone, diving into new activities...*

The words "sexually involved" jump out from the page as if the survey heard me talking about my first ex-wife with my brother. I loosen my tie and keep reading. *Do you get so wrapped up in things that you can hardly stop to take a break or switch to doing something else?*

Do you tend to do or say things without thinking and sometimes feel that gets you in trouble?

Do you often find yourself tapping a pencil, swinging your leg, or doing something else to work off nervous energy?

I read that question and realize I'm standing up with the questionnaire, pacing my office, where my jump rope is slung over the back of a chair in case I need to work off the ants in my skin. I swallow thickly, recalling how many nights I lost track of time, to answer the phone when a sobbing wife begged me to come home and help with the boys.

I drag a hand down my cheek. I always thought these traits were me being terrible. Unreliable.

I put the papers on my desk and stand in the middle of the room, shaking. I don't know how to name all the things I'm feeling right now, although regret and shame seem to top the list as I think about all the years I've done wrong by my boys. My boys! If I'd known about this sooner, maybe I could have done something. Improved something. Been better for them.

I start to feel like I can't breathe, like the room is closing in. I step in the hallway, thinking I'll walk up and down the stairs a few times, but I notice that everyone's gone for the day and I walk to my car instead. By the time I pull into Orla and Walt's driveway, I realize I've driven to a house my brother no longer lives in.

Desperate to find some sort of comfort, I let myself in and walk inside.

CHAPTER SIXTEEN
CELESTE

ORLA AND WALT WENT ON A DINNER DATE WITH KELLEN AND ELIZABETH AND ASKED me to stay with Nora. Is it normal to feel this giddy about being asked to babysit my granddaughter?

I bought child-safe nail polish so the two of us could do our toes together while we watched *Raya and the Last Dragon*. Kids' movies today are so interesting and moving. No more princesses being saved by princes. Now it's all young girls saving the world and working together with other young girls to overcome challenges.

I tear up as the movie ends and Nora pats my arm with her blue fingers. "It's okay, Mimi," she says.

I wipe my eye and kiss her cheek. "It sure is okay," I tell her. "I'm always okay with you." She smiles and yawns, and I'm glad I don't have to say anything more in-depth about the importance of trust in the movie and in real life.

I get Nora down to sleep and hesitantly pick up the garden center brochure Elizabeth gave me last week, still on the coffee table beneath a stack of kid books. Why on earth does it feel like such a big deal to even look at the class list? What does it say about me that I can't bear the idea of taking a group class? I know what it's about. I'm certain I'd be terrible and everyone would see and they'd pity me.

I'm sick of being pitied.

I notice there's a class called The Bartender's Garden. I smile and think of Esther, visiting farmer's markets to source local herbs and fruits and garnishes. This seems like the sort of class she'd enjoy. No. That's not true. This seems like the sort of class she could teach, for heaven's sake. Esther already knows all of this information.

I file away the idea for later, deciding I'll suggest it to her as something she could offer at her bar. She hosts those paint nights sometimes, where people come in and paint while she serves them drinks. Esther is so clever, pairing up the drinks to match the theme of whatever art they're working on.

I look more closely at the class. You'd think with all the alcohol I consumed, I'd know more about mixing drinks, but I only added ice to my gin and Walton liked all his liquor neat. Muddling fresh herbs with fruit and simple syrup sounds thrilling somehow. Soothing, at least.

I'm on the verge of signing up when Orla's garage door opens. I look up, startled to see Michael standing there. He looks distraught.

"Shit," he mutters. He drags a hand through his hair. "Kellen doesn't even fucking live here anymore."

I hold a finger to my lips, indicating that Nora is sleeping, but I gesture my head toward the living room. We can talk in there with less risk of waking the babe. "What's wrong?"

Michael shakes his head, but shuffles after me, yanking his tie loose and shrugging out of his suit coat. I've never seen him so disheveled. Michael Brady might keep snacks in his pocket, but he's always got crisp creases and polished shoes.

He sinks into the couch, dropping his head back, and I sit hesitantly beside him on the couch. For once, I relish the small piece of furniture, even if I shouldn't delight in this forced proximity. I wonder if I should reach out a hand to comfort him. "Do you want to talk about it?"

He shakes his head and then sits up. "I don't feel like I thanked you properly," he says. "For helping me with Arlan. It was rude of me not to call you back after I found out he was okay."

"Oh, don't worry about that." I hesitate before adding, "I enjoyed myself." His eyes widen and I continue, hurriedly. "I mean not that I enjoyed that he had a crisis. It was fun playing together. Spending time with you both. That's all."

He nods slowly. "I enjoyed spending time with you, too."

I swallow, feeling my heart begin to race at the nearness of him. Wanting to shift the energy, I tell him, "I had a conversation with my daughter. With Rosemary!"

His face brightens. "That's really great, Celeste. What's she been up to?"

I fill him in on her relationship with Bisi and he tells me about a trip he took to Nigeria, how the culture there is so entrepreneurial. "Hmm." I tap my fingers on my leg. "I'm not sure what Bisi's profession is. Rosemary didn't say."

Michael slings an arm across the back of the sofa and my pulse surges. "I'm sure she does something fantastic," he says, "if your daughter chose her."

"Well, I wouldn't know," I spit out. "I don't get to meet her yet." I shouldn't feel this way. I know I haven't yet earned the chance to be back in Rosemary's life or to know the people who are important to her. But I'm allowed to voice my impatience to my friend, right?

His hand moves to my thigh, squeezing a few times, and I gasp at the contact. "You'll get there, Celeste," he says.

I'm sure I'm imagining the look in his eye, the look that says he's maybe thinking about me the way I've been thinking of him with growing frequency. The way I find his scent intoxicating. The way I see his vulnerability when others, even in his family, perhaps just think he's being eccentric.

I have to change the subject. If he keeps that hand there I might melt in a puddle of my own desire. "Michael, what happened? Why were you searching for your brother?"

He shakes his head again. "You're the only one who calls me Michael," he says. "Why is that?"

I shrug. "Mick is...I don't know if it suits you."

He snorts. "It's my name!"

I shake my head. "No," I insist. "It's your nickname. An abbreviation, like nobody has time to say the whole thing or something. And Michael is such an interesting name! Michael was the leader of heaven's armies, right?"

He rolls his eyes at me. "I didn't last long in the army, Celeste."

I sit up straighter. "You enlisted? It seems so unlike you!"

Michael shrugs. "Everyone enlisted before Desert Storm."

I pick at the seam in the couch cushion to ground myself, trying not to remind him that *everyone* most certainly did not include my husband. Walton was not what anyone would call valiant. "But your boys must have been tiny babies."

"Oh, they definitely were." He shrugs. "Sheila was irate when I went to enlist. Threw a jar of baby food at my head." He points to a small scar above his eyebrow. "Who knows why I really went down there? Maybe I thought I'd get more sleep in the military." Michael sighs and sags deeper into the couch.

"Doesn't matter anyway, because I couldn't pass the exam."

I recoil into the arm of the couch. "You? Surely you know all that material. What do they ask about?" I lean back in to listen to his response.

He shrugs. "I'm sure I do know it." He turns to face me, resting his elbow on the back of the couch and his cheek against his fist. "I'm lousy at tests, Celeste. I'm lousy at a lot of things."

I can feel heat radiating from his body and I'm overcome by the nearness of him. But I also sense how intensely he's seeking something right now. Comfort. Reassurance. I can give him that. "I know that's not true," I whisper, thinking about how easy it would be to move my head just a few inches and take what I've been fantasizing about.

I could pull his face to mine and taste those plump lips, just once. I could let go of caring about the consequences and just do it.

Michael swallows and rests his head against mine. In a small voice I have to strain to hear, he says, "Well, I'm a lousy father anyway. Cal thinks I ruined his life."

I pull my head back, eyes wide. "That sounds so unlike him, Michael. Did he say that?"

He closes his eyes, leans his head back against mine and tells me how Cal is afraid to get married, afraid he's not cut out for it. "He said he's so much like me. He said he thinks he'll stray."

I wrap my arms around Michael without thinking, holding him close. I wish I knew how to tell him his children are wonderful people, that all of them have grown up fine under his care. But I don't know what to say, so I just sit with my arms around him, feeling him.

"At least he's talking to you about it," I say into his hair. His hair that's just as soft as I imagined, but I can't focus on that right now because he's here for comfort. Comfort.

"I guess that's true," he says. We breathe together for a few minutes. Finally, he huffs. "What the fuck did we do to our kids?"

He settles against my chest, resting his cheek on my shoulder. We stay this way for a long time.

CHAPTER SEVENTEEN
MICK

I PLOD THROUGH THE WEEK MORE DISTRACTED THAN USUAL WITHOUT MY NORMALLY-bottomless energy to keep my spirits up. It seems the secret to getting the insects in my blood to lie still is to just expose the raw and painful truths I've ignored for decades.

I'm so busy feeling like shit about being a shitty parent and a shitty spouse that I damn near forget about the team leads morning meeting. We're facing a new fiscal year and Kellen says we need to summarize our predicted spending, map out which projects we've contracted and which ones we're still shooting for.

I slip into the meeting late and nobody bats an eyelash. I lean against the counter in the back of the room as my Zack talks about the conclusion of his international geo-technical partnerships. "We've secured hillsides throughout South America," he says, fighting back a grin for some reason. "We've also studied landslides here in Pittsburgh. You guys all heard about the townhouse lawsuit. Beltane has proposals out to county agencies in neighboring areas to help shore up problem areas along their highways. Data shows that strong rains are increasing..."

I zone out as he presents the work he's led for the past four years. Instead of listening, I recall the feel of Celeste's body pressed against mine. This wasn't like one of the women I used to take home for a quick romp. I can remember everything about how she felt, how she smelled. Soft and kind and nothing I ever sought out before.

I cannot allow myself to think sexual thoughts about Orla's mother-in-law. This whole situation I'm in, this whole identity crisis is because I've always been so bad at that.

I shake my hands and adjust my weight. I see that Cal and Orla are talking now, flashing diagrams of the different applications they've found for unmanned robotic devices. They're building drones *and* robotic snakes that can explore pipes underwater. Liam chimes in and the three of them beam as they click through some numbers for their collective projects. Liam closed the deal to inspect the power grid in most of the central United States and Cal and his team will be devising and building the custom drones needed to inspect power lines in rural places, while Orla has landed a partnership with the forestry service to engineer, build and install devices that detect fires.

I catch my brother's eye and see that he's on the verge of tears, and I allow myself a moment to feel proud of the children we've raised to be such innovative engineers. This is our legacy right here. These kids are going to make the world a safer and more efficient place, despite any influence I might have had on them.

Eventually, the meeting wraps up and Kellen announces that we will most certainly keep the lights on for another year. Everyone files out of the room and Kellen pauses where I'm shifting my weight from foot to foot. "It's pretty remarkable, isn't it?"

I nod and reach into my pocket for a packet of nuts, only to realize that I forgot to stock up on my snacks today. Damn it.

Kellen squeezes my shoulder. "You were pretty insightful to call this company Beltane," he says. As if sensing my distress, he leans behind me and grabs a pack of crackers from the basket in the conference room. I raise a brow at him. He knows I try not to eat grains. Kellen waves a hand and continues. "Beltane. You know, how it's a holiday that's about beginnings. We were just the beginning, Mick."

He dabs at his eyes with a handkerchief. "Say," he says, nudging me with his shoulder. "You have a pretty important birthday coming up. We should do a big fire, celebrate our Gaelic heritage."

I wave a hand. "I don't want all that fanfare."

"Mickey." Kellen stands with his hands on his hips. "We're not *not* having a party for your 60th birthday. It's been a big year for the family."

"Make it a Beltane party, then," I tell him. "Keep the focus on the work. You're right, brother. We were just the beginning. Look at those kids of ours."

We do. We admire them, heads bent together, mapping out plans excitedly. Laughing at the ways their differing interests are coming together like different rays of the same sun. "Beltane was a good name, Kel. It's true."

"And Mick Brady is a fine man," he counters. He punches me in the shoulder lightly. "We'll keep it small. Just the family."

I snort. "*Just the family* is 15 people."

"Is it that many?" Kellen moves his lips and counts on his fingers, and I smile, because it's good that our family has grown like this. Not everyone needs three hands to count their loved ones, and even if I did set a shitty example for marriage for my boys, I made damn sure they all understood the importance of being there for their family. However we define family.

Just as Kellen is finishing up his Brady count, Cal comes jogging over toward us. "Hey, Dad, Uncle Kel--you got a minute?" He doesn't wait for us to answer, because he knows that we do. That we always make time for family. Even when I'm mad as a kicked hornet's nest I have time for my boys. I just might not always be the best at communicating it in the moment.

"Listen," Cal charges on, interrupting my train of thought. "Can we switch up family dinner to tonight?"

Kellen scratches his head. "I'd have to check in with Beth before I say yes to that—"

Cal waves a hand. "Logan and I are hosting. We already talked to Elizabeth and Mom is going to come since it's usually our night to hang with her."

"You're bringing Sheila to family dinner?" I feel like checking over my shoulder to see if I'm being filmed. "Does she know you're inviting me?"

Cal rolls his eyes. "Dad. Of course Mom knows you'll be there. Please say yes."

"What's so important about family dinner tonight?" I reach in my pocket for my notebook. I need to make sure I'm not double-booking myself.

Cal flashes a crooked grin, reminding me so much of myself when I was his age. "I'll tell you tonight," he says. His phone starts buzzing in his shirt pocket and he pulls it out. "I gotta update Logan. See you all at six!"

As he darts out of the room, Kellen furrows his brow, considering. "Pregnant or engaged," he asks, scratching his chin.

I lick my teeth and think about our conversations recently. "Maybe both?" We both laugh and I ask my brother to remind me about the change in plans before he heads home for the day. The last thing I want to do is miss whatever my son has cooked up for tonight.

CHAPTER EIGHTEEN
CELESTE

I'm surprised to see Orla's name on my caller ID. Worried something is wrong, I rush to answer, dropping the phone on the ground. "Celeste?" Orla's voice comes through over speaker, which I must have bumped in my haste.

"Yes! I'm here! Is the baby all right?"

"What? He's fine. I was just calling about dinner tonight."

"Oh." I finally pick the phone up and get it situated by my ear like a normal person. "Dinner?"

"Mm hmm." It sounds like Orla is eating something while she talks. I'm glad she's remembering to eat. I remind myself that it's more important for her to eat than it is for her to have good phone manners. She audibly swallows. "Cal and Logan are having everyone over. I told Walt I'd call you since he is on a complicated route today."

"Cal and Logan?"

"Can you believe they switched Walt around? He's supposed to be the permanent mail carrier in our neighborhood and they've got him hoofing up and down stairs on the South Side Slopes. He's probably going to eat at least three portions of dinner. I wonder if Logan knows about his appetite..."

"Orla?"

"Yeah?"

"I'm a little confused about what's happening tonight."

She sighs. "Well, we all have a pool going to see whether Logan is going to announce that she's preggo or engaged. They're hosting family dinner and they wanted to do it tonight so Cal's mom can come since they usually eat with her—" She cuts off. "I'm babbling. Can you be at their place at six? Do you need someone to come get you?"

I think about driving in to the east end of the city in rush hour and shudder, and then I think about Michael driving me home later, just the two of us alone with his leather interior. Maybe he'd rest his head on my shoulder again. I shake my head. He'll want to be involved in whatever they're celebrating tonight.

"I can make it," I tell her. "Are you sure they want me there, though? I'm not even in the family."

"Of course you're in the family," Orla says, matter of factly. "You're my mother-in-law. And Nora's grandmother!" My heart swells at Orla's insistence that I'm part of her family. I know what it means for her to say such a thing and I'm touched by her acceptance and insistence. I'm nearly overcome.

"Well," I stutter. "What should I bring?"

"TBD," Orla says, chewing again. "I have no idea if Logan's getting catering or what. For now, maybe just bring comfortable pants. Anything could happen, Celeste." Orla laughs and we hang up.

I change into jeans. I've been wearing jeans sometimes now, especially on the days I'm with Nora. I regret all the years I spent avoiding jeans in favor of high-waisted dress slacks. These stretchy denim pants are so comfortable. I wouldn't ordinarily wear jeans to a nice family dinner, but Orla specified comfort. I'm learning that with the Brady family, I'm just as likely to wind up climbing a tree to fetch down a child as I am to pivot to a trendy bistro at the last minute.

I'd be lying if I didn't admit I find the unpredictability a bit thrilling. I decide if I leave now, I can avoid busy traffic and maybe even stop by Esther's bar to tell her about that gardening class. I opt against doing that, though, because I don't want to just be that woman who drops by and tells Esther how to run her business. Lord knows she's doing a beautiful job with her bar. It's always so full and such a welcoming space.

I drive directly to Logan and Cal's neighborhood instead, parking on the street and wandering over to the restaurants across from their building. I'm delighted to see a pop-up stand where I can buy to-go bottles of fizzy drinks. I buy several bottles of mojitos and pink lemonade and by the time I get myself back across Penn Avenue to the condo complex, I run into Maddie and Liam chasing Arlan down the sidewalk.

"Hey now," I say, getting in the little guy's way. "Where are you off to?"

He halts in his progress, giving Maddie a chance to catch up. "What's that," Arlan asks, pointing at the brown glass bottles I've got under my arm.

"Why don't we go upstairs and I'll show you?" Maddie mouths a silent thank you as Liam gets the door open, hustling us all inside and sagging against the elevator door.

"He's going to give me a stroke, I swear," he says. I want to offer up another weekend with Michael, but remember that it's not my place to do that. I wonder if they'd ever agree to have him up to my house. I have so much land that never gets used. Arlan could run around more safely without risking running into traffic.

That thought will have to simmer, because the sounds of the Brady family echo down the hall from Cal and Logan's apartment already. "We must be the last ones here," I say as Maddie hoists her son up over her shoulder.

"Hey!" Logan grins and rushes over to greet us at the door. I'm surprised when she wraps me into an embrace. "I'm so glad you're here with us, Celeste."

"Well," I say, truthfully, "I'm so glad to be included." Logan hustles Liam and Maddie inside and I find a plastic cup to pour Arlan a fizzy lemonade as promised. "Now, you have to stay sitting in the stool while you drink it," I tell him. "You can't get your aunt and uncle's house all sticky."

I help him climb up into a stool at the counter and pour him two inches of the bubbly pink liquid. I decide to pour a glass for myself as well, and we clink cups in a toast. His eyes go wide as he tastes and I'm charmed by how much he's enjoying himself.

"I can't believe you got him to sit still." I turn my head to see Maddie at my side, making faces at her son.

"It's the lemonade," I tell her, taking another sip. "Would you like a glass?"

"Nah," she says. "I can't do the sugar right now." She holds up a bottle of water, though, and laughs as we all clink glasses. Then she sighs and leans on her elbows. "Do you think wedding or baby?"

I laugh incredulously. "It could be anything," I tell her.

She nods. "That's true. Shit. I hope they're not moving!"

Just then, Nicole bursts in the door carrying two giant bags. They must contain food because the aroma of garlic takes over the room. Maddie squeezes my arm and we both look at Arlan, sitting like a perfect gentleman. I can't help but draw her into a hug. Where has this urge come from? I'm hugging people left and right today. But she seems comforted by the gesture and leans her head on my shoulder. "He's a terrific kid," I tell her. And then he slams his empty cup down and belches.

Maddie steps back and picks up Arlan, making room at the counter for the bags that Nicole hoists up. "I hope everyone came hungry," she shouts. "I bought the entire menu. Seriously." Someone comes and grabs the bottles of drinks I brought and starts passing them out, leaving Nicole more counter space and nobody to help unpack the dishes of food.

I step in to assist and she gasps. "Oh lord," she says. "It's happening."

"What?" I look around, expecting to see something broken or someone bleeding.

Nicole points to a woman about my age, looking sharp with bright glasses and a short, gray bob haircut. "Sheila and Mick in the same room."

I swallow a lump in my throat and watch as Sheila hugs Cal and Logan. I recall that this is Liam and Cal's mother, Michael's first wife. Liam and Maddie make their way over to her and she brushes right past them to scoop up Arlan, which makes all of them laugh.

And then I see Sheila catch Michael's eye from across the room.

CHAPTER NINETEEN
MICK

"Screw hot girl summer," Nicole says, passing out paper plates. "This is Hot Brady Summer." The room erupts in laughter but she shakes her head. "I'm serious! We've got Mickey Boy turning 60. Don't look at me like that, Mick. You don't like being called 'boy'? Stop calling me *honey*." She winks and I know she means well, but given all the discussions I've been having with my family lately, her comment stings.

I shouldn't be calling her any of those names. The thing is I feel for her, Maddie and Logan the way I do about Orla. They are all my kids and my sweethearts and my honeys, just like Cal, Liam and Zack. I blow out a breath, trying to focus while she continues. "From what I hear, all you geeky, grumpy engineers have been doing some exciting math all over the country."

Zack interjects. "We don't just do math. It's much more complex—"

Nicole places a finger over her husband's lips. "I'm working toward a point, babe. Jake graduates high school. Orla's popping out another kid. We're celebrating whatever it is Cal and Logan are going to plunk on us today. It's Hot Brady Summer. We need a bonfire."

My brother's face lights up. "I've been saying we need a bonfire!"

"Oh, lord, here we go." Elizabeth reaches for the bottle of mojitos that Celeste brought and laughs as Nicole and Kellen begin conspiring. I feel a little better about the whole thing given the diminished emphasis on my birthday. It could be nice to just have a family party. If Nicole and Kellen are co-planning it, I know it will be one for the ages.

I return my focus to my main task of the evening: avoiding looking at my ex-wife. I was feeling pretty good about remembering this change in plans from when Cal approached me this morning. I didn't even need the reminder from Kellen before he left work. I had not remembered that Sheila would be here.

I've seen her a few times, mostly since Arlan was born. But she's spent the better part of 30 years avoiding me, and who could blame her? Needless to say, I'm caught off guard when she approaches me with a tray of food.

"Mick Brady." Sheila looks terrific. She always does. She holds out the platter of shrimp. "Take a tempura. Nicole says we have to eat them all."

"Sheila." My throat is dry. I grab a toothpick from the tray and spear one of the appetizers and hold it up to her in toast. "Thank you." I worry I'll have to dig for something to say, to fill the silence or slice the uncomfortable atmosphere, but she winks at me and slides over to where Celeste is talking to Nicole.

I exhale a breath I didn't realize I was holding and lean against the wall, munching the snack, until Cal stands up on his couch and clangs two serving forks together. Logan starts tugging on his arm. What on earth goes through that boy's head, standing on his white couch in his shoes?

But I look at him gazing at Logan and I remember that he's not a boy at all. He's a man. All my sons are men. Cal bangs the forks together again and tips his head toward Logan.

"Hey, everyone. Thanks for changing your schedules so you could all be here today." Nicole opens her mouth to add a witty retort, but Cal points a fork at her. "And thank you to those of you who went across the street and bought the entire menu from the galley restaurants so we'd have 75 different things to eat."

He tosses the forks on the coffee table with a clank and wraps his arm around Logan's shoulder, pulling her in close. She beams and holds a hand up to his chest, and it's then that I notice the glint of a gemstone on her finger. *I'll be damned.*

"So I know all you assholes had a poll going about what our announcement would be today."

"Callum, please don't say swear words while we share our news." Logan bites her bottom lip and grimaces and he kisses her on the forehead.

"All right, all right. Brady family, I want you to know that I asked Logan to join us officially, as my wife, and she said yes."

The room bursts out in cheers and wolf whistles and Logan jumps up and down as Nicole and Maddie swoop in to get a look at her ring. Elizabeth even starts making out with my brother, and in an attempt to pull my gaze away from that, I wind up staring at Sheila again.

She dabs at her eye with a napkin, smiling, and I realize I need to go talk to her. Our kid is getting married, after all. "Hey," I say, making my way toward her amid the din of Arlan and Nora jumping on the couch like Uncle Cal.

"Oh, Mick." She sighs and squeezes the napkin. "Isn't it wonderful? Both our boys, settled down."

My instinct is to make a joke about Liam being anything but settled as he now struggles to keep his son off the balcony, but I hold on to the serious tone Sheila is sending out. "It's great," I tell her. And we smile at each other, and it's not awkward. It just feels still, which is strange since the energy in this room is anything but.

"I wasn't sure Cal was ever going to leap," Sheila says. "Logan has been wanting this for so, so long. Did you know she has a wedding binder?"

I scratch at my stubble. I guess I forgot to shave this morning. "I wouldn't have taken her for one of those brides." I raise my eyebrows at Sheila. "I'd have thought she'd be more sensible about it. Like you were."

"Our wedding was very classy," she says with a nod. And she's right. A church ceremony, nice meal at the country club, tasteful jazz band.

"You planned a beautiful day," I tell her, raising my water bottle at her. She smiles into her mojito. I feel the pressing weight of Cal's confession to me a few weeks ago, that his greatest fear is that he'd do what I did to his mother. And I know I need to talk about it with my ex-wife.

I know this probably isn't the right place for such a conversation, but once the idea enters my head, it starts circling there until I feel again like I have ants under my skin. I have to either blurt my feelings or jump rope, and I don't think Cal has a rope handy.

"Sheila," I say, reaching for her arm. She looks up at me, still smiling. "I...I wasn't a good husband to you."

She shakes her head. "You were not, dear. That's true." She pats my arm. "But you know what? You've been a wonderful father to our sons."

I snort out a laugh, because she's either drunk or delusional. But Sheila grips my arm tighter. "Mick. You are. It's true. I should know, right? They're my sons, too. Look at them!" She gestures around the room. "Look at this whole thing. Logan told me how you set up a trust for Arlan as soon as Maddie found out she was pregnant. And you've pushed the kids to reach their full potential at work. Jesus, Mick. They've got love and prosperity and family."

I'm not quite ready to accept that what she is saying is at all attributable to me. I shake my head. "Well, I came over here to apologize," I say. "I owe you an apology. For how I treated you and our family."

I freeze as Sheila wraps her arms around me, pulling me in for the same sort of hug I've seen her give our children. "I accept your apology." She releases me and starts smoothing out my shirt, laughing. "I think things turned out just as they were supposed to."

"You mean that?" All I can remember is the look in her eyes when I would come home hours later than I said I would, how I broke my word to her again and again, half the time not even on purpose but because I genuinely forgot which day it was.

Sheila puffs out a breath. "I mean it, Mick. I've got a great career. I've got amazing sons. I've got a grandson who reminds me of his grandfather." She nudges me with her shoulder. "I do okay in the romance department."

My eyes widen at that revelation and she rolls her own behind her funky glasses. "Don't act like that, Mick. Be happy for me. I'm happy for me." She stretches up to plant a kiss on my cheek and walks off toward Logan, arms wide. By the time she's squeezing our future daughter-in-law, I'm slumped back against the wall, uncertain what to do with my emotions.

CHAPTER TWENTY
CELESTE

NICOLE:

So. We need a plan for Hot Brady Summer.

ORLA:

Dad seemed all about that at Calogan's the other night…

MADDIE:

I really don't think Calogan is the portmanteau winner. Sorry.

ORLA:

Portmanteau? Is that a real word?

ORLA:

Shit! Learned something new. Maddie, you really are the best writer anywhere.

MADDIE:

Thanks, sis.

ORLA:

What about Logum? Logan plus Callum? Anyone?

ELIZABETH:

I'm not sure Logum works either, but Kellen is here and says he wants to help plan the bonfire.

NICOLE:

Elizabeth. You can't invite men into the Brady Ladies chat!

I think maybe you added me here by accident.

NICOLE:

Nope. I don't do anything by accident, Celeste. Hear me out. Huge ass bonfire at the Sheffield Estate.

ORLA:

Ooh fantastic idea! Walt's house has an actual pond out back. We can just scoop up the pond if anything gets out of control.

NICOLE:

We're not going to kill the koi and nothing will be out of control, because Liam and Kellen will make sure of it.

You want to throw a party at my house?

NICOLE:

Hot Brady Summer is happening, Celeste. We have to do it before Orla squirts out the baby. And isn't Mick's birthday soon? Ooh! Can we do fireworks?

MADDIE:

No fireworks!

ELIZABETH:

I say no to fireworks.

LOGAN:

Oh my gosh! I was in a meeting and I missed so much! Bonfire party at Celeste's house! That sounds terrific!!

ORLA:

Logan has used up all the exclamation points. There are no more exclamation points.

NICOLE:

Okay, rager at Celeste's; no fireworks. Also, Logan —no eloping and trying to have the bonfire double as your wedding reception. Orla already fucked up marathon Sunday and Mick is Not Over It.

MADDIE:

As if Logan would elope! That was such an Orla move.

RESTORATION

MY PHONE FINALLY SETTLES AS THE MESSAGES STOP FLYING IN AT ME. I DON'T EVEN know what to say. Me, hosting a party? I haven't had anyone to the house in years. Since well before Walton died. But it didn't seem like I had the opportunity to say no. Is it a birthday party for Mick? Or a celebration of life for the Brady family? I'm not entirely sure.

I look out the back window. Walt has been urging me to sell this house. And, if I'm honest, I've been considering it more seriously lately. My life is increasingly taking me in to the city. My son is in the city, my grandchildren are in the city. What a shift my life has taken.

I tap my nails on the dining room table where I sit, realizing that I'm going into the city to get my nails done these days, since it's been easier to combine that outing with my days babysitting Nora. I just stop at the cute little nail place down the hill from Walt and Orla when he gets home from work. There's no spa music and the linoleum on the floor is a little shabby, but Nancy the nail tech does as fine a job as anyone from a more expensive spa experience.

I even drove to the East End at rush hour for a family dinner where we ate takeout from paper plates. And I had a delightful time...apart from the churning I felt in my guts when Michael and his first wife hugged. I'm still trying to figure out what was going on there, why I felt like I had a dragon in my chest when she kissed him on the cheek.

I'm overcome with an urge to phone Rosemary and tell her about the series of events that just unfolded. We haven't talked on the phone since the last time, but we've texted and I know she will be interested to know that there's going to be a party at the house.

I dial her number, and she answers with a question. "Mom?"

"Rosemary! You'll never guess what just happened."

"Umm, that's probably true."

I laugh and fill her in on the party idea and I hear the surprise in her voice. "Back up. Did you say you used paper napkins?"

"I've been doing a lot of things. I keep wanting to tell you about them all. Do you think we have enough parking here? For the bonfire party?"

"I...don't know where to start with that question. When's the last time you had anyone out to the house?"

"Do you know? I think it might have been your high school graduation? I can't remember having anyone by after that point."

"Yeah, probably because Dad was already scamming everyone by then." We are silent for a few beats as the truth of that sinks in. I turned a blind eye to so much, and a critical eye toward so much more in a desperate attempt to stay in the good graces of people who haven't ever called to check on me.

"Well," I say, and take a deep breath. "Would you want to come to the bonfire? Of course Bisi would be welcome, too." I close my eyes and count to five, waiting for her to say anything. When she doesn't, I add quickly, "Forget I mentioned it. A large crowd like that would be overwhelming when you...well, when we haven't seen each other in a long time."

Rosemary's voice wavers and she says, "I think I'd like to come. It..." She drifts off as my heart races. "It'll be good to see you and Walt. And Orla and Nora."

"Oh, Rosemary, that makes me so happy!" I think about the emails Esther sends around sometimes before the Foof meetings, about all the ways the events she hosts feel so welcoming. "Will you let me know if you or Bisi have any dietary restrictions before the bonfire?"

Rosemary makes a choking sound and I hear her set down a glass. "Wow, Mom. Um, I don't think you've ever asked anyone that question before."

I sigh. "I know. I'd really love to see you, though. I'm learning so much from my new—" I almost claim the Bradys and the Foof ladies as my friends. Almost. But it doesn't feel quite earned. Although Michael did say he thought of me as a friend. As someone he can rely on to be kind to him in a time of need. "My friends are teaching me so much, Rosemary, and I just really want you to feel comfortable."

"I'll message you after I talk to Bisi, okay?"

"Yes. More than okay. I'll touch base soon."

We hang up and I feel an energy I haven't felt in years. I cannot wait to begin preparations for the Hot Brady Summer Bonfire. I recognize an urge to make the party perfect, not because it will look good or raise my esteem in some way, but because I want the people coming to feel at ease. I want my home to be a place where people feel welcomed.

I freeze, walking through my dining room, because I realize I do not know how to set that sort of atmosphere. I have no idea how to help people have fun, apart from toddlers. But I also realize I know a group of women who know exactly how to do it.

CHAPTER TWENTY-ONE
CELESTE

For the first time, I burst into Bridges and Bitters without hesitation. I need this Foof meeting. I need the input and opinions of all these women and I take a moment to appreciate how it feels to walk confidently into a space and feel excited about the reception I'll receive. "Esther!" I rush up to the bar as she's lifting the tray of drinks she's about to carry to the back. "Let me help."

"I got this one, Celeste. You seem a little jumpy." She winks and gestures for me to walk alongside her as she makes her way to the back.

"I am jumpy, now that you mention it." I am bouncing out of my pumps as I make my way to the banquet room, which is already filled with the Brady Ladies. "Oh, good, you're all here already." I slide into a chair next to Nicole, who is reaching excitedly for the tray of drinks Esther sets on the wooden table. "I've been thinking about Hot Brady Summer," I tell her.

Nicole claps her hands. "Yes. Excellent. Let's compare notes."

"That's just it," I tell her. "I don't have notes. I haven't hosted a party at the house for years. Years! And I used to hire people to plan all those details."

"Can we play Stump?" Orla pats her stomach and raises an eyebrow at me.

"Stump?"

"Oh, I'm not sure that's a good idea." Maddie frowns. "Arlan would get hit with the hammer and smash a finger."

"Hammer?" I feel like these women are speaking a foreign language and I take a deep breath, hoping party traditions have not changed so drastically since I was last in the scene.

Nicole rolls her eyes. "Stump is a game where there's a literal stump of wood and some nails half hammered into it and people stand around it in a circle and *throw* a hammer at the stump. That's more of a 'Nicole and Zack backyard event for Brady siblings' than a Hot Brady Summer item."

"Throwing a hammer? Oh, please, no." I clutch at my shirt, thinking of Nora and Arlan running around while their energetic aunts and uncles get competitive the more they drink.

"Honestly, I don't think we need activities," Nicole continues, sipping at her drink again. "Bonfire, chairs, food, booze. Hot Brady Summer."

"About the chairs," I begin, but Logan arrives and makes her way over to us.

"I heard you talking about the party! Sam has a new catering company she's been using at Vinea. It's full service—chairs, food, all of that. Should we get a tent, too?"

I sigh in relief. I like the idea of outsourcing all the decisions. "I think we can always bring everyone inside if it rains," I tell them. But the girls are already talking about LED twinkle lights and asking me questions I have no idea how to answer about my sound system.

"I'm just going to ask Walt," Orla says, pulling out her phone and tapping on the screen. Our house was never really set up for that level of entertaining. We don't have outdoor speakers, I'm sure. But before I can interject about that Logan announces that Cal will set up a sound system outside and curate a playlist for the party.

"All that's left is deciding a menu," Nicole says, tapping her nails on the table.

"That's what I wanted to talk to you about," I burst in, leaning toward them. "I need your help. Rosemary has agreed to come to the party!"

Nicole, Maddie, Logan and Orla gasp, clutching at each other. "You talked to your daughter?" Logan beams. "That's so great, Celeste!"

I sigh. "It feels really huge. And I need to make sure they feel welcome. Rosemary is going to bring her girlfriend." I add the second bit before I remember that my daughter hasn't told her brother this information yet. Orla doesn't seem to flinch or react strongly, though, thankfully.

"We'll make sure they feel welcome," she says, and she actually squeezes my hand. I look down at the gesture, touched.

I draw a shaky breath and tell them, "Rosemary and Bisi are vegetarian.

We need to make sure there's something for them. Options for them. And some non-alcoholic drinks, too," I add, thinking of my own preferences even as I gesture at Orla. "Logan, can your catering company sell alcohol or do we have to buy that separate? Because I'd really like to use that Goodlander business across from where you and Cal live."

Logan furrows her brow. "I don't know that one," she says. "Is it directly across the street?"

I shake my head. "Around the corner. They did those fizzy mojitos and that wonderful lemonade! So summery. I know your family likes whiskey, but minty lime drinks just feel so festive to me..."

Logan has procured a pad and pen and has begun taking notes as we talk. "I love that idea, Celeste. Cal and I can pick up the drinks on our way up to the party and the caterer can do the pails of ice." She nods. "I'm sure this company can do cozy chairs and a spread we can all enjoy. Want me to call them?"

I feel delighted that the others like my suggestion. Esther winks at me as she takes a swig of her own drink. Encouraged, I nod and start telling the group about how Rosemary responded to me asking about their dietary restrictions. "She was so stunned by me considering her needs," I say, my voice wobbling. "I know this is just a party, but I really want to make it an experience where everyone can have fun being themselves. I want to show my daughter that I'm ready to know her as she is! I've done so much damage to my kids, expecting them to bend to inappropriate and, frankly, unobtainable standards set by the people I grew up around. I'm learning so much from all of you." I tear up, looking around the room at all their strong, confident and caring faces. I shake my head. "I think it might be too late to repair my relationship with Rosemary."

Sam pats the table from where she sits on a velvet high back chair. "It's really, really huge that you've admitted your mistakes to her. Validated what she's been trying to say for so long. I think it's great that she's agreeing to come to the party, Celeste. Small steps, right?"

"I hope you're right."

Sam clicks her tongue and reports that she is working on mending fences with the school teacher she inadvertently insulted at Vinea. Soon I'm lost in the din of the other women discussing their challenges. Piper is full of spit and vinegar that a group of men tried to kick her fitness class off a city field even though she had gotten a permit to be there. Maddie is having to fight with insurance to cover Arlan's evaluation for ADHD. Everyone is going through so much and I see how they all trust each other with their problems, and work to find answers.

Sam looks stern when Chloe suggests she doesn't want to share today because her problem isn't as important as Maddie's. "Listen," Sam says, gesturing with the swizzle stick from her drink. "Just because a broken leg is more serious than a sprained ankle doesn't mean either injured person should walk around like that."

Chloe bites her lip and Sam charges on. "All of us are here because we are fresh out of fucks, and that includes mentally ranking our problems against one another. We are all here for all of each other. Now, tell us what your husband did this time."

Chloe laughs a little bit and begins to share some of the ways she's working on her relationship. This group really is a gift, giving me so many nuggets of wisdom to savor as I work on myself. More than once, I wish Rosemary could be here with me, soaking it all in.

As the meeting wraps up, I help carry some glasses to the bar area to be washed. Esther beckons me around behind the bar to set the tray near where she's washing glasses. "Thanks, Celeste. You seem way more grounded than when you first got here."

"I definitely am!" I watch as she cleans glasses upside-down over a nozzle of cleaning solution. "I was thinking of you the other day," I tell her.

"Oh yeah?"

I nod. "I was looking through the course catalogue at the botanical gardens and they're offering a class called 'The Bartender's Garden.' I thought, you could totally be the teacher for that."

She laughs. "I probably could. But they probably also want someone with some sort of advanced degree for teaching in their space."

I bite my lip, hesitating, but decide to just tell her my idea. "I was thinking you could do something like that here, though. Like how you pair the special cocktails for the paint night."

Esther pauses midway through rinsing a glass and tilts her head to the side, considering. "That's kind of a great idea, Celeste. It's July already, though...if I offered something like that in August is there enough time now to market it?"

I shrug. "I don't know much about how those things work. But you have a Facebook page for the bar, right? I think I left you a review."

"You sure did." She stops to fill a pint glass from the tap for a customer and dries her hands on the towel tucked into her jeans pocket. "You've really got me thinking. I could totally do a little workshop muddling herbs, making the strawberry shag. People like learning to do that stuff. They see how hard it is and they just buy more drinks here from me." She laughs again and I'm glad I brought the idea up to her after all.

"I'd sign up," I tell her.

"Thank you," she says. She runs off to wait on another customer while I make my way out the door, eager to get planning for Hot Brady Summer.

CHAPTER TWENTY-TWO
MICK

I WAKE UP ON MY 60TH BIRTHDAY AND STARE AT MY HANDS. I'M NOT SURE WHAT I expected to see differently. They're still tan. Relatively smooth. I use expensive moisturizer I picked up on one of my trips. I remember the woman working at our construction site had flawless skin and she said she was pushing 70.

We were over there so Kellen could design plans for a sewage system for a village that didn't have one. That's something to be thankful for. I've had a really blessed life, just looking at sanitation opportunities alone. The woman...why can't I remember her name? She seemed so touched that I asked about her skincare.

I did my part brokering the deal between Beltane and their government leadership. Kellen was doing all the hard work. What did I have to do at that point other than talk to the people on site about their experiences?

I do a quick overview of the rest of my parts—still accounted for. I suppose that means I have no excuse to miss the bonfire tonight. I really hate being the center of attention at these things. Nicole said the party is called Hot Brady Summer. It should be about all of us. Yes, today happens to be my birthday.

I roll my eyes and get dressed as the coffeemaker does its magic. I decide it's still early enough that I won't get run over by tourists if I run up to the Strip District to get more coffee beans from the Italian market. I love running through there. I can still remember it in its heyday, my brother and

I going with our parents to see the wholesale produce vendors operating alongside the river.

Kellen loved watching the foundries and mills crank out their goods to the shipping lanes. Hell, the Strip District is probably why he became a civil engineer and why I decided to help sell engineering services. I have no idea how to make any of that happen, but I saw how it all functioned together, and lord knows why, but I started thinking about the future of all those machines.

Now, the neighborhood is full of fancy coffee shops and souvenirs. So much of the industry we started with has moved elsewhere in the world. I try not to focus on that on my run. I think about what the kids are doing, how they're breathing new life into the work Beltane does. I think again of that sanitation work we did in foreign countries and I wonder how Zack would feel about checking up on that when he meets with people about his landslide prevention ideas.

All in all, it's a pretty good run for me, with a coffee bag in each hand for balance on the jog back home.

I clean myself up and get ready to go to Celeste's house. Only I don't like to think of it that way. It doesn't seem to suit her, all isolated up there in the woods in the suburbs. I think she feels out of place there now, too. It's like she was a different person when she lived there with her husband. I don't like thinking of him, either. Or of her life with him in it.

"Nope. Focus on the party," I tell myself. I run a razor up and down my face and splash on some witch hazel, slip into some dark jeans and a nice shirt and brace myself to have my family pick on me for the next few hours.

When I get to Celeste's I have to laugh at the sign someone put at the bottom of the driveway. It's a massive banner with all our faces on it, probably photos taken the last time we played the foil ball game at Christmas. We all look like we're going to kill each other. And it says HOT BRADY SUMMER with the letters painted in a flame pattern.

I park along the drive and note how someone has cleaned up the landscaping, making a flagstone path around the side of the house. Rows of fairy lights line the path and I can see the little solar panels on them, telling me they'll probably flick on as soon as twilight settles.

I don't know that I've ever been in Celeste's yard, but right now it looks idyllic, with blue hydrangeas and a hedge of Rose of Sharon in bloom along the perimeter. The party is furnished like a poolside resort, with cushioned lounge chairs, cushioned arm chairs, and tables of food everywhere. I snort out a laugh seeing my sons working on getting the fire started.

Kellen is close by leaning against a tree, supervising. Everyone back there seems to be doing what they like best. I sigh. I should be excited about that. I hear a car door close behind me and I turn around to see two women walking hand-in-hand toward the path.

"This is where you grew up?" The taller woman's eyes are wide at the sight. I don't blame her. But the shorter woman also looks surprised by the party scene.

"It didn't always look like this," she says in a low voice.

I realize this must be Rosemary Sheffield. "Ah, you're the daughter, then?"

Both women recoil. Shit. I didn't phrase that well. I stick out a hand. "Sorry. Mick Brady. Pleasure to finally meet the youngest Sheffield."

She furrows a brow at me, sizing me up. "You look familiar."

I shrug. "Well, I did meet you at your father's funeral. I don't think you were feeling your best that day." She takes my hand, pumping it a few times with a firm grip. I approve and extend my hand toward her companion.

"This is my girlfriend, Bisi," Rosemary says, with heavy emphasis on girlfriend, like she's waiting for me to judge her. I'm sorry about the things she must have experienced to lead off with that defensive instinct.

I tip my head. "After you, ladies. I hear tell there's good food and a carefully-constructed bonfire." They walk hesitantly down the path toward the party and I watch as Celeste leaps up from a chair, rushing forward to greet them. I love seeing her happy like that, glowing. I linger back a bit more, but eventually Arlan and Nora spy me and they come running, sloshing lemonade out of paper cups.

"Grand Pop is here!" Arlan announces my arrival and I'm not going to lie. It's nice to hear a cheer go up at the sound of my name. Sure, I'm walking into my own birthday party with my family. But it's still nice to be greeted with a smile.

Maddie comes to get Arlan and pecks me on the cheek. "Now we can get started," she says, ushering me toward the food table. Celeste really pulled out all the stops with the catering. Charcuterie plates, with all my favorite things, are placed on tables around the fire, where everyone sitting can easily grab bites of cheese and prosciutto and dried apricots. "And of course, pistachios," Maddie says, handing me a bowl with a laugh. "You can throw your shells in the bonfire. I already asked Liam."

"Thank you, Maddie," I say, pulling her in for a hug. I get a little choked up when I see there's a present table. I don't want them to spend their money on me. I have enough things. They should put it all toward diapers and soccer camp. Who am I kidding? Private track coaches. I pull out my notebook to write that one down. In a few years, I bet these kids will all have enough kids to make it worthwhile to hire a private coach. The Brady cross country dynasty can continue.

"Mick!" I look up and Kellen is snapping his fingers in front of my face. "Where'd you go? Mentally I mean?"

I look around and everyone is staring at me. How long was I making notes? "Just thinking about something," I tell him, sliding the notebook in my pocket. "What did I do now?"

"Now, brother, we force you to listen while we all say nice things about you." He pushes me down into a chair and stuffs a package into my hands. I try to shove it back, but he glares at me, so I slowly unwrap the paper.

"This one's from me," Sheila says. Christ, when did my ex-wife show up at my birthday party? I peel back the wrapping and see that it's a Lego set to build a tiny, yellow Fiat.

My jaw drops. "Is that mine?"

She grins. "For those of you who don't know, Mick used to drive one of these when the boys were tiny."

"Back when we had that office in the Strip District. Remember that, Kel? We didn't have furniture. Used to sit on crates I nicked from the produce terminal."

He nods and Sheila continues. "One evening, Mick showed up at our house in a taxi because he'd sold our only vehicle earlier that day." She squeezes my shoulder and I stare down at the Lego kit. "We had a horrible fight about it, and he failed to tell me that he had done that because Beltane couldn't make payroll. A client hadn't paid on time and Mick wanted to make sure his employees got a paycheck, even if he didn't. Even if it meant selling the family car and putting his own kids on city buses for a few weeks until he dealt with the cash flow problem."

For once, all my kids are silent as Sheila tells that story. The shame of it stings a little less now. At the time, I couldn't figure anything else out. I even went to that client's house at five in the morning to ask where our money was. He tried to sic his dog on me, but I had beef jerky in my pockets in those days.

"I never told you how much I admired that move, Mick." Sheila grins. "I just wish you'd given me a heads up first."

I swallow a lump in my throat at her kind words and I stare more intently at the Lego set in my lap.

"Well, Dad, do mine next." Cal holds out a shoe box that isn't wrapped.

I make a face. "Liam said we all had to use eco-friendly wrappings." He shrugs. I roll my eyes a little and pull out a pair of truly hideous sneakers.

"Who are these for?"

Cal grins. "They're special walking sneakers. See how the soles are so thick, back at the heel?"

"You must have meant to give these to your uncle," I tell him, trying to push the box toward my brother. "My feet are just fine, thank you."

Cal clears his throat. "I got you these because I remember another time you put someone else's needs ahead of yours. You and I went to breakfast one day, just us. We took the train into Station Square and rode the incline up Mt. Washington for an adventure. I guess Zack and Liam were somewhere else." Cal shrugs. "You gave every dollar in your pocket to a pan handler, and we had to walk home. Down those crazy steps in the South Side Slopes. I kept asking you why you'd do that and you told me to be thankful we have healthy bodies."

"Well, look at you," I say. "All of you. Top shape of your lives."

Cal nods. "It's true. But you also taught us to be thankful for what we have, and kind to people who don't have as much. Some of your teaching methods are unorthodox, but what I want to say here, at Hot Brady Summer—" Nicole interrupts with a loud whoop, repeating the name of the party. Zack glares at his wife, and she snaps her red lips shut. "What I want to say is that we're all very grateful you're the head of this strange group of grouchy geeks. You mean a lot to us, Dad."

"Aw, come on." I try to shove him away, but suddenly he and Nicole are both wrapping their arms around me and her wild, curly hair is getting in my mouth. And all of it makes me feel like I'm going to choke. This kid who, a few weeks ago, was afraid he'd wind up like me in some ways is apparently glad to be like me in others. I start breathing fast and shallow. "I need a minute," I tell them. And I make a mad dash for Celeste's screen door before I cry in front of my family.

CHAPTER TWENTY-THREE
CELESTE

Is it odd to feel so proud of how the party turned out? Because I do. I am beside myself with happiness right now, seeing my yard aglow with fairy lights and a crackling fire. The flowers are in full bloom, too, and Walt brought some sort of special bug deterrent he heard about at work, and it's really keeping unwanted pests away.

I shimmy a little every time someone groans with pleasure at the taste of the food. I suggested a bunch of different charcuterie plates for Michael's birthday because, well, the man loves snacks. I even have a variety of herbal teas I ordered from South America for later, when we serve his cake. I know how much he loves getting foods from the places he's visited.

And then I see my daughter and I absolutely lose all sense of decorum. "Rosemary!" I rush over to her, and have to physically grab my own wrists so I don't wrap my arms around her. I don't want to overwhelm her.

She smiles a thin smile, but then the woman at her side gives her hand a squeeze and Rosemary looks up at her, beaming. "Mom," she says. "This is Bisi."

"I'm so very glad to meet you," I say, holding out my hand and then squeezing hers with my other hand. "You and Rosemary look so happy together." Bisi makes a strange face at Rosemary and then smiles at me.

"Thank you for having us."

I gesture around the yard. "You are always welcome! I wanted to let you know the platters of food over there..." I point to a cluster of chairs on one side of the fire. "Those are all vegetarian. Lots of hummus and grape leaves and even falafel and—"

I'm interrupted by a loud chorus of cheers as Michael arrives at the party. I tuck my hair behind my ears nervously as he tries to silence his family and I feel the heat rise in my cheeks when he catches my gaze. I really need to get myself under control.

Rosemary raises an eyebrow at me and I reach for her hand, absent-mindedly squeezing it a few times. Once the din dies down, I say, "Last thing. There's a keg of mojito over there and another of just pink lemonade by the picnic table. I ordered them from that wonderful place near Bakery Square. Goodlander. Have you heard of it?"

Bisi nods. "I love that place. Have you tried their Moscow Mules?"

Rosemary, eyes wide, starts shaking her head. "I'm sorry," she says. "What is going on here?"

"At the party?"

She shakes her head harder and throws her hands in the air. "No, Mom. With you. What is going on with you? You're wearing *shorts* for fuck's sake. No pearls. You're squeezing my hand? You're not even saying shitty things about anyone's outfit."

My nostrils flare as I feel shame rise in my throat. I swallow and nearly choke. "I just wanted to make sure everyone had a nice time and felt comfortable at the party."

Bisi smiles at me. "It is a really nice party."

Rosemary wags her index finger at her girlfriend. "No. You don't do that. Do not defend her. This is the woman who questioned every dessert I ever touched in my entire life because *was I sure I wanted to risk the bulk on my hips.* I'm sorry, Mother, but I do not downshift this fast. I am just not prepared for you to be some sort of woke ally."

"Rosie—" Bisi puts an arm on Rosemary's shoulder, but Rosemary shakes her head and steps out of her grasp.

"I can't. This is too much. I'm not ready." She rushes across the yard to her brother, who frowns at her as she quickly stoops to hug Nora. And then Rosemary and Bisi are gone.

I can hear my heartbeat in my ears, thudding out a rhythm of "not forgiven. Not forgiven." Hot and dizzy, I make my way inside, where I sit at the table and stare across my empty dining room.

. . .

I'm not sure how long I'm sitting there when the screen door bursts open and Michael Brady trips into my house. "Oh," he says, dragging a hand through his hair. I hardly even stop to think about how soft his hair must be or wonder what brand of shampoo he uses to maintain that much volume. "You're in here too?"

I nod, swallowing again. I take a deep breath, then another as he pulls out the chair nearest to me. "I ruined my daughter's life," I say.

He nods. "I ruined a lot of my kids' lives, too."

We sit in silence for a few minutes while I think about his statement. He's said that to me before. I would think the gathering outside would add evidence to it not being true. "Did one of your boys bring that up again?"

He places his palms flat on the table and shakes his head. "I don't know? They're out there bringing up stories about me, but it all sounds different the way they're telling it today."

"What are they saying?"

He shrugs. "Just remembering things that I did. Things that stuck with them."

I nod. I stare into his dark eyes for a few beats, watching as he blinks. "Everyone has a little something prepared," I tell him. "It was Maddie's idea for people to put together some stories about you. She...well, I don't want to ruin her gift. But you know she's a writer." I shrug.

He stares at me for a few minutes. "What was your story going to be?"

I smile at him. "I was going to talk about how you came to Walton's funeral even though he had done your family harm. It's always stood out to me, because I think it was the right thing for you to do. And I believe you always do the right thing, even in a crummy situation. Especially where people have to make decisions very quickly." I place my hand on top of his. "You always know what to do in a crisis."

He closes his eyes and I think I might see a tear in the corner of one lid, but soon he sighs and looks down at the ground. "I've been thinking lately... Liam got me thinking that I might have ADHD. That maybe that's why I ruin everything."

"Hm," I tell him, thinking about the people I knew whose children have ADHD. Kids who were never welcome to eat in the dining room at the country club or who always needed a sitter even at outdoor events. I used to feel pretty smug about my own children knowing how to behave better, but then I met Arlan Brady and realized you just can't change someone's temperament. I think about all the family jokes about Michael's impulsivity and how he mentioned his energy levels in the past. "I can see how you might have ADHD. But, Michael."

I squeeze his hands in both of mine, leaning closer to him. "We just talked about how you have *not* actually ruined anyone's lives. Your kids just shared stories about wonderful things you've done. Is it possible that ADHD helped you solve problems you couldn't otherwise?"

I smell the clean scent of his cologne as he sits near me in the kitchen. I can hear the muffled sounds of laughter and singing from outside and I start to wonder a bit what the Brady family is getting up to out there. But the guest of honor is in here, with me. Upset.

"I...haven't considered that angle," he says, coughing.

"There have to be positives and negatives. Have you called a doctor or anything to find out more?" Michael shakes his head. "Well, I'd be happy to go along with you. If you need a friend. At the appointment, I mean."

"You'd do that?"

I feel like I want to melt. "Of course I would," I tell him. "I know Maddie has said it's really helpful having someone go with her to take notes when she sees a new doctor." I shrug. "I would happily do that for you, so you can concentrate on what the doctor says."

"Celeste." His voice is low and there's heat behind it. "That would really mean a lot to me."

"Well," I start to tell him that he means a lot to me. But I stop, remembering why I'm in here to start with. I'm not a person who says such things to other people—honest things, vulnerable things. Much as I want to change, I still carry around the shadows of my past mistakes. I think about the first thing that came to mind when Maddie asked us to think of "Mick Memories."

My cheeks heat and I bite my lip, leaning closer to him.

"Did you know there are other things I remember about you," I say to him, my voice huskier than I intend. "I could never share this in front of everyone...but I have another memory. About you."

One side of his mouth hooks up in a grin. "What else, then?"

I slide closer still. "I saw you in a hall once, at the country club, with a date." My blood heats at the memory of Michael watching his date, his hands busy inside the fabric of her skirt, both of them shrouded in shadows.

He swallows. "A hallway?" He shakes his head, his smile slipping. "I never did have any sense."

My heart races as I remember the look on his face that night, wolfish. He was pleased to be giving her pleasure, whoever she was.

My voice barely a whisper, I say, "I've always wondered, Michael, what it would be like. With you."

He blinks a few times, licks his lips. I stare at his mouth and wait for him to say something, but he doesn't. I can smell the faint scent of whiskey on his breath, and then I lean in and press my mouth against his. Michael's lips are cool at first and so soft. His mouth yields to mine and soon he is kissing me back, a small groan in the back of his throat.

Oh, to hear a groan from a man, and know it's for me. I never thought I would experience this again. I sigh into him, placing my hands on his shoulders, my nails squeezing into the fabric of his shirt as I practically pull myself into his lap.

He makes another small sound as he moves his lips against mine and I close my eyes, reveling in the smooth feel of his skin against my cheek, of the scent of him everywhere. And then just as suddenly, he jumps to his feet. "The kids," he says. His eyes are wild as he looks over my shoulder, trying to see if people are watching us. He shakes his head rapidly. "We can't let that happen, Celeste. I...I'm sorry I let that happen."

"It was a birthday kiss, that's all," I lie, climbing to my feet and rushing over to him. I feel pathetic as I try to pull him closer to me again, but now that I've kissed him I want more. I want to feel his body against mine. I want to unleash everything I've held back.

And then I realize what I've done. I've made it about me. This man came inside seeking comfort and I mauled him, brought up his past. I shake my head, wondering how to salvage this moment, certain I'm on the verge of ruining everything yet again. "It doesn't have to mean anything," I say, gesturing around the kitchen.

But Michael recoils and his face crumples. That's the only way to describe what happens as he slinks away from my touch and backs toward the door. "Doesn't mean anything? Like a quickie in the hall between golf rounds? That's what I'm good for, huh?"

"Michael, no," I start, but he shakes his head again.

He quickly moves out the screen door to the party, slamming it so hard behind him that it bounces back open.

I hurry over to close it, wanting to follow and tell him he's misunderstood my meaning. That what I meant is we don't need to tell the kids. Not that I think of him as... *That's what I'm good for.*

I don't even know how to explain to him that making me feel alive, sexually, is life altering. I had no idea widows thought about such things, and when he's around, it's almost all I can focus on, and ... it's not meaningless at all. It feels special and electric and I went and messed it up instead of cherishing him for helping me relearn something about my body.

I sink to the floor, sobbing as I realize he's left his own party. Once again, I drove someone away.

CHAPTER TWENTY-FOUR
CELESTE

I EVENTUALLY WALK BACK OUTSIDE, CERTAIN I'LL BE BOMBARDED WITH BRADY Ladies wondering what happened. But when I start circling the outskirts of the bonfire picking up plates and empty cups, nobody seems to notice. They don't seem to notice that Michael has left his party, either.

Zack and Nicole are cuddling, her sitting on his lap at the fire despite the heat. Liam is in a rocking chair with a sleeping Arlan on his chest while Maddie dances with Sheila by one of the speakers Walt installed. I see my son cradling his wife, his big hands rubbing her pregnant belly, which twitches periodically as my grandson moves around inside his mother.

Logan and Cal seem to have disappeared as well and Nora sits with Elizabeth and Kellen, holding what appears to be a dead insect. I can hear Kellen explaining the engineering of the exoskeleton to Nora as she looks on, riveted. I'm surrounded by contentment, as if the scenes with Rosemary and then with Michael just hadn't happened.

But they did. My daughter ran away from our reconciliation and I acted inappropriately with my friend. Bradys begin to leave the party, waving at me sleepily as they make their way down the fairy-light pathways. I continue to wander around picking up garbage, but eventually a black-clad caterer taps my arm and reminds me we paid for them to come back and clean up. So there's nothing for me to do but slink inside.

I walk up to my room, thinking how easy it would be to curl up in bed with a Valium and let the world drift away, and my guilt and shame along with it. I actually stand in the master bathroom where I know I still have prescription bottles standing like suits of armor in the medicine cabinet. Only, I don't need that sort of protection anymore.

No, I decide. I'm capable of feeling these feelings now. I wasn't in years past, but I am now. I think about all the things I've done recently that would have sent me into a tailspin of panic in the past. I spend every Tuesday with a toddler. I figured out poison control. I can figure out what to do next once I've made a mistake.

I open the cabinet and collect all the remaining prescription bottles, stuffing them into the waste bin. With a satisfied huff I slam the door closed and climb into bed for what I'm sure will be a fitful night of sleep.

In the morning, I feel groggy but determined. I lay awake most of the night thinking about Rosemary. I should have encouraged her to meet with me before coming to the big party. I knew it would be overwhelming to jump into something like that without having seen one another or talked much in so long.

I should have shouted after Michael, begged him to come back inside and finish talking to me about what happened so I could understand how he really felt, and tell him what I meant more clearly.

It's evident I need to speak to both of them. If months of Foof meetings have taught me anything, it's also clear I need advice before I do. I find myself wishing that Foof had a bat signal. Samantha seems like she would be the one most likely to design something like that. She runs a tech company. Surely she could figure out a summoning method for emergencies like this.

I roll my eyes at my own foolishness when I remember that group texts serve this very function. Only I'm not in a group text with Foof. Orla tips me off when there's changes to the meeting schedule. I'm in a group text with the Brady Ladies, though. "Gah," I say, tugging at my hair and marching downstairs in search of coffee.

The Brady Ladies can't be involved in this until I've had an opportunity to speak with Michael. The walk from my room to the kitchen feels interminable, but I eventually make my way to the little espresso machine and wrangle a pod into the top. I remember the coffee grinder in Michael's kitchen, the way he explained that he makes his coffee so fresh each morning.

I remember my ex-husband used to mock people who made fresh coffee that way, talking about how long it all took, calling it a waste of time. Seems to me, it takes about as long for my packaged pods of inferior coffee. I stare at the machine, and past it, at the empty rooms I don't even use. This whole house is just big and empty and lacking purpose.

Michael does all those eccentric things with intention. His gaudy knickknacks remind him of his trips and things he learned. These stupid paintings I hung just remind me that I spent too long trying to blend in with everyone else. Why do I have all these rooms and hallways when it's just me here?

When the machine beeps its readiness, I grab it and take the first sip. Then another. My head clearer already at the first hit of caffeine, I sit down to think. I can't fix my entire life in one morning. I have to choose a plan of attack, and Rosemary comes first. I need advice from Samantha. *Think.* Logan connected me with the caterer based on a tip from work. So I have an email she forwarded me from Samantha.

Samantha puts her cell number in her email signature and Samantha is in Foof. "Ha!" I shout into the empty house, delighted to have figured out someone I can call for guidance with this pickle. I decide to text first.

> Samantha, it's Celeste Sheffield. Thank you so much for the caterer recommendation. They were delightful. I wondered if I could ask your advice for a more personal matter? I understand if your schedule is tight.

A few moments later, my phone rings in my hand, and as soon as I press the button to connect, I hear her voice. "Oh my god, please tell me you boned Mick Brady."

"What? No...not exactly. That's not what I—"

"NOT EXACTLY! Hold on." I hear a commotion in the background, the obvious sound of high heels clacking down a hallway, the clatter of a door being slammed shut. "Did you impulse-bang the silver fox? Tell me everything, you glorious hero."

"No, I...well I kissed him. That's an entirely separate personal issue I need advice about."

She cackles. "This is so great. I mean, it's probably awful right now. But it will be great."

"Samantha, it's about Rosemary...And Michael. But mostly Rosemary is why I was calling."

"Okay. Right. Did she and her girlfriend come to the party?"

I fill her in on our argument, how Rosemary was so taken aback to see me being kind that it made her deeply upset and she left. "What do I even do about this? Where do I go from here?"

"God, I wish I could talk to my mom about this kind of shit."

I recall that Samantha lost her mother some time ago and had to step into a parental role with her siblings. "Oh, I wish you could talk with her, too," I offer.

She sniffs. "I was thinking about you and Rosemary earlier, though," she tells me. "Even before you said she was coming to Bradyfest. Did I ever tell you my sister doesn't talk to me?"

"You didn't. Oh, I know how hurtful that is. Even if I felt like I deserved the distance, it hurt me a great deal."

"Yeah, I don't deserve the distance. My sister isn't well. But that's sort of what got me thinking. I'm not saying this is what's going on with Rosemary at all. But what I think my sister wants is for me to run after her and beg her to love me. I think she really wants our mom to still be around parenting her, but she's convinced herself she wants me to chase her down." She takes a deep breath. "Anyway, it seems like...you actually *are* Rosemary's mom. And she's probably always wanted you to dote on her like you were probably rocking that hostess role. And maybe she got jealous?"

I nod, and then remember again that people on the phone can't see physical gestures. "Hm. That could be."

"I think you should fight for her. Show up at her house with a tray of party leftovers."

"You think so?"

"Yes. In fact, hang up with me right now and go to her house before she leaves for softball practice, or whatever. Do you realize you texted me at seven in the morning?"

"Is it that early? Oh dear! I'm so sorry. I didn't sleep well and had just had my coffee."

"I don't ever sleep! I was already at work. But I bet Rosemary isn't!"

SHE HANGS up with me abruptly and, upon opening my refrigerator, I notice stacks of neatly wrapped and labeled leftovers from the party. I grab a few with the vegetarian options and climb in the car.

As I crawl along the highway, anxious to get to my daughter, I wonder why people live this way. Why move so far outside the city to build a huge house full of rooms I don't use, only to have to fight traffic to get to my family?

Both my extended family and Walton's grew up in the same suburb where we built our home. But none of them speak to me anymore. Why stay there? By the time I'm merging onto the road to Rosemary's apartment I've decided the party was the last hurrah for that house. I can pack up and move knowing it held good memories. Sort of.

I knock on the door of Rosemary's townhouse and Bisi answers, looking confused. "Celeste?" She seems like she was expecting the newspaper delivery and not her girlfriend's mother.

"Good morning, Bisi. Lovely to see you again. Is Rosemary in?" I feel the familiar speech patterns slipping back in as I present a cheerful face to Bisi, when both of us know I'm walking into an angry hornet situation.

Bisi looks over her shoulder, looks back at me, and gives me a conspiratorial look. She beckons for me to come inside as I hear Rosemary shouting, "Who was at the door, babe? Did we forget to renew the paper?"

She walks into the front room in her robe, a towel on her hair fresh from the shower, and she shrieks when she sees me. And I know it's because I'm seeing her disheveled, and my heart aches for that.

"Rosemary," I begin. "Sweetheart. I came to apologize." I shuffle the containers of food in my arms and look around for somewhere to set them down. Eventually, Bisi skitters over and takes them from me. "Thank you," I mouth to her as she waves a hand and disappears into the kitchen.

My daughter stands with her arms crossed over her chest, leaning against the wall. I take a deep breath. "I know I wasn't there for you or your brother in a nurturing capacity. Not the way you needed me to be, and I cannot change that. I could talk to you about how I did the best with the skills I was given, but I also knew that the things I was grooming you to do and think and say...I knew those things were..."

"Shitty." Rosemary interjects. "It was a shitty way to live."

I nod. "You're right. And I'm so deeply sorry. And I will work every day for the rest of my life to show you how very sorry I am. I'm thankful every day that your brother has given me another chance, that he lets me be part of his children's lives and I will do my damndest for another chance with you, Rosemary."

She doesn't say anything. I don't say anything. We stand staring at each other as she drips a bit in her hallway. Finally she groans and says, "Well, what now? What do you want from me?"

I throw my hands in the air, about to burst out that I want her to just spend time with me, to let me know her. Instead I say, "I want you to come with me to this Bartender's Garden workshop at the Bridges and Bitters bar."

Rosemary's eyes widen and after a beat, she says, "Well, that actually sounds really interesting."

I nod. "Okay, well, I'll text you the details and see you there."

"Okay."

"Okay." I brave a smile at her, and she returns it. Bisi, who had come back into the hall at some point, rolls her eyes, and shoves Rosemary toward me.

I catch her with open arms and squeeze her tight. I hold her for a long time. And she hugs me back, tentative but fierce, both of us relaying our hope and need for each other in this first, conciliatory hug.

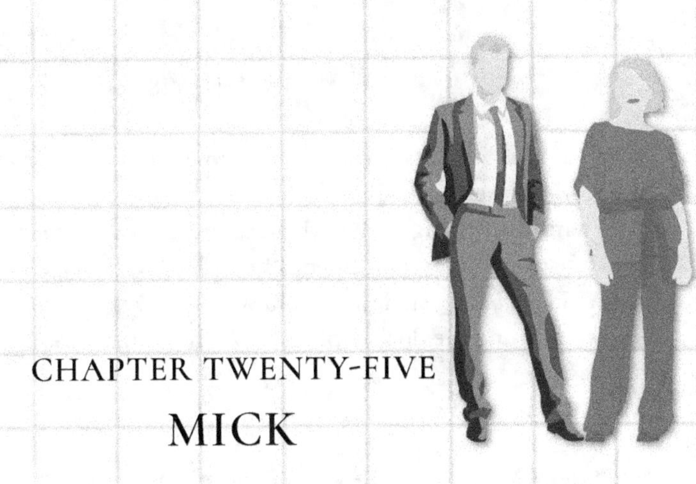

CHAPTER TWENTY-FIVE
MICK

Something has to give.

I never really stopped to appreciate all the medical experts in this city. I hardly ever see any of them. But now that I've got this bug in my brain about ADHD, I can't get past the fact that we've got researchers studying ADHD in guys my age. Specific research into guys like me? There's more of me? I don't know how to explain what's holding me back from doing something about this, so I just decide to rip off the bandage.

I call the number again and they're eager to get me in to the office, so I just wander up town from my office to theirs. I'm the only one in the waiting room, and the receptionist doesn't even look at me strange when I start tapping my knee. My legs are usually pretty jumpy if I have to sit, and this is especially bad today. I'm probably shaking her entire desk.

"We've got some more forms," she says, sliding a clip board to the edge of her table. "Want to get started on those?"

I nod and take a look. It's similar questions to what I found online, and as I look at the questions about "how often do you have problems remembering appointments" and "how often do you misplace things," I just draw a straight black line down the "very often" column.

She hands me another stack of tests and I don't even know how long I spend answering questions. I've just about worn a hole in the carpet pacing as I work on them, though.

I hand everything back to the receptionist and a few minutes later I get called back for my appointment. Instead of a medical exam room, I'm just sitting in a wooden chair in a room with a desk. Left alone, I pace the small space, counting the doc's diploma's on the wall before he pops in the door smiling at me.

"Michael Brady?"

"Call me Mick. Pleased to meet you."

"Glad you came in today, Mick. I'm Dr. Offutt. Based on your responses on this paperwork, I'm guessing you've been thinking about ADHD lately. Tell me a little bit about what brought you in here today."

"For starters, I'm sick of being the person people go to when they're looking for a good time." I think of that kiss with Celeste, how much I wanted it, how hard it was to stop for the sake of our kids. And how she was just looking to get her rocks off with the guy who is known for doing that sort of thing. I reach for a little pile of magnets on the doctor's desk. They click together in my hand, smooth and cool, as I tell him what Liam and Maddie are experiencing with Arlan. "The more I kept saying the kid reminded me of me, and my son kept saying they thought something was wrong...the more I realized I might have something wrong, too."

The doctor leans back in his seat. "Well, Attention Deficit and Hyperactivity Disorder does have some negative connotations, and the word deficit is in the name. But many people also find there are aspects of the condition that give them a leg up in certain respects. You said you own your own business?"

I nod. "My brother's a brilliant engineer. Back when he got his degree, I started realizing a lot of people probably needed his services but didn't know they did."

"And what were you doing at the time?"

"Me? Selling cars. I can sell anything to anyone. I'm not good at much, but I can read people."

He takes notes and keeps nodding. "You notice small things?"

"I notice your office is spotless and your trash can is empty. Tells me you probably pay your staff well enough that they work hard for you. That tells me you probably have everything in place so you can do your best work diagnosing hopeless cases like me."

He smiles and puts down his pen. "Nobody is hopeless, Mick." He spins a computer monitor toward me. "You signed releases for your medical records and I can see you are in excellent physical health." He holds out his hands.

"You're thinking I've got it, then?"

"Your questionnaire and personal anecdotes would suggest that you do. In fact, I'd say you meet every one of the clinical criteria."

"Never got a perfect score on a test before now," I joke.

He grins. "You've indicated this is a lifelong condition and not something that sprang up in your senior years. I don't see any evidence of mental decline. I feel comfortable diagnosing you with ADHD. I think you'd be a terrific addition to my study if you're interested."

"You really want to study me?" I arch a brow at him and lean back in my chair.

He nods. "Very much so. Right now, a lot of patients like you are getting misdiagnosed with Mild Cognitive Decline. I'm working on building screening tools for clinicians. You could really be part of a life-changing solution for a lot of people."

I have to take some deep breaths at the notion of me being helpful for others, in a meaningful way like he describes. The doc goes on about taking my data, writing down my response to medication, having me talk to him about my life.

"I don't think my life should be a guidebook for anyone..."

He leans forward, his face reflecting empathy. "You told me all about how you notice things. Well, let me tell you what I notice from talking to you and from your chart. You've spent decades building coping tools. Some of these, like running, have had tremendous positive impact for you. I also hear you describing avoidance. You avoid carbs and sex because you can't moderate your intake, so you just don't engage at all."

My jaw hangs open as this guy just lays my life out for me, like he can see right through me. He pats my hand. "Mick, I believe I can help you make big changes. And I believe you can help me help others. What do you say?"

I nod, silently, not sure about what comes next.

Doc pulls up some charts and says, "I have no concerns at all about blood pressure. I'm sure you've read that a common treatment for ADHD is a stimulant medication. The right molecule and the right dosage shouldn't impact your blood pressure at all. You're 60 now, so I will bring you in two weeks from now to check again, and again two weeks after that. My recommendation would be to start with a quick-release medication."

I swallow a thick lump in my throat. "These pills—are they going to make me a zombie?"

"I'm sure you've heard myths like that, but really the right medication is going to help you focus. It won't change your personality. Other patients have told me they just feel more like themselves, like the best version of themselves."

I think about how I feel at the end of a long run or when I've got a new client excited about what we can do for them at Beltane. "I could stand to feel like that more often," I admit.

I leave the office with a prescription and a schedule of return visits, and I head home to stare at the pills for a long time, afraid of what will happen if I take one. Afraid of continuing on if I don't.

THE BUZZER above my door rings and I walk over to it, confused. My whole family is at work right now and I doubt anyone sent me anything here at the condo. I squint through the peep hole to see Celeste standing in the hall.

"Hey," I say, cracking the door just a bit. "Is everything okay with the kids?"

She nods. "Everything is fine with all of them. I came here to make amends with you, Michael."

Michael again. I can't decide if I like it that she calls me that. Maybe it means I'm special to her. I open the door and she steps inside. "I'd like to explain what I meant the other night. After we kissed."

I sigh. "I guess we're talking about that, huh?" She nods. "You want a drink?"

"Water would be lovely. Thank you."

She sits down at my counter and I see her notice the prescription bottle and the pile of paperwork. I slide a glass of water over to her and sit in the stool next to hers. "I haven't worked up the courage to take it yet," I say, gesturing at the pill bottle.

"You went to the doctor already? I would have gone with you." She sets her hand on mine. "I wanted to be there for you with that."

"I didn't want to spend another day being the person everyone remembers for bad behavior."

Celeste squeezes her hands together. "Michael, I don't think of you that way. I never intended to imply that, and I apologize because obviously that is how you took my meaning." She closes her eyes. "I've been thinking about kissing you for a long time. I've also been feeling like a terrible person for a long time. Like no matter what I did it was never quite enough. Until I met your family! And all of you act like all you want from anyone else is for them to just be themselves."

"Well, yeah. Who else are you going to be?"

She presses her palms flat against the counter. "That's just it. I have no idea who I am or what I want or what it even means to be myself. I spent so long trying to conform. Then, thanks to my son, I stumbled into this wide net of people who just...you're all so comfortable being imperfect!"

"Ha!" My laugh spits out dramatically. "We certainly are that. Maybe not Kellen."

One side of her mouth hooks up into a grin. "Maybe not him."

Celeste takes my hand again, and I like it. She squeezes and I squeeze back. She says, "I keep thinking about what your friend Clayton said at the cafe. How it's never too late to make a change."

"He did say that, didn't he." I pick up the pill bottle with my free hand. "I'm terrified that if I take this and it's amazing, I'll die of the regret of not doing it sooner."

"How could you have known sooner?"

I shrug. "How could I not have known? It's not normal to live like I have."

"Michael Brady, do you need another pep talk? Because you're not normal one bit. You're extraordinary."

"Ah, come on."

She slides off the stool and stands in front of me, putting her hands on my shoulders. "I mean it. You're unfailingly kind, especially to me and even when I didn't necessarily deserve it."

"Everyone deserves kindness and respect," I tell her, trying hard to focus as the scent of her overwhelms me. Her nearness. It's too much.

"Not everyone feels that way," she says. "How about if you just take my word for it that your worldview makes you special?"

I give her a small shrug. She keeps talking. "Your family has really made me examine myself, make changes. I think you've all made me a better person and I'm starting to finally feel comfortable saying that. I've gotten better!"

"You're like a fine wine, Celeste." I can't control my impulse to reach up and stroke her cheek with my thumb, but then I remember what happened the last time I let myself touch her and I lean back.

She squeezes my shoulders. "Thank you, Michael. Thank you for being my friend. It means so much to me."

I take a deep breath and open the pill bottle. I put one of the pale yellow tabs on my tongue and reach for Celeste's water, swallowing it down. She stares at me, a question in her eyes.

"I don't feel different yet," I whisper.

"Maybe we should get some lunch or something? Wait for it to kick in?"

"I'd like that," I tell her, truthfully. "Okay if we eat here? I don't want to be out in case it gets weird or something."

"Here is great," she says, following me into the kitchen. I walk over to the fridge and fling it open. Lately, I've been buying a lot of prepared meals from a local chef because I can just heat them up when I remember I'm hungry, and I don't have to worry about preservatives or unnecessary chemicals.

"You want salmon with edamame and carrots or...flank steak with edamame and carrots?"

"Someone's on a protein kick," she jokes, pointing toward the salmon.

"Protein is very important. Especially for our old brains."

"You're older than me," she says with a laugh as I slide the containers in the microwave.

"Is that right? How long do we have until your Hot Sheffield Summer?"

She opens her mouth to answer, but the microwave bings, cutting her off. We eat together at the counter until I realize that I feel different. I pause with my fork midway to my mouth.

"What's wrong?" Celeste jumps to her feet and places a hand on my forehead, as if I'm sick.

"It's still," I tell her. "Inside my head. It's calm and quiet in there." Usually I'm distracted by swirling thoughts at all times. I hear everything at the same volume, the fridge motor and the HVAC system and the clock three rooms away. "It's just still," I repeat, feeling the noise sift to a dull murmur.

Celeste beams. "That's great," she says. "Sounds like the medication is working?"

I nod and shove the plate away from me. I feel like everything is whittled down, like I can focus. And what I'm focused on is her. I see her hands and her smile and the fine lines around her eyes that tell me she's been smiling a lot lately. I want to make her smile more. At me. I turn and face her. "I'm not feeling impulsive or reckless," I tell her.

I stand and crowd her space, watch her breath quicken.

"No?"

I shake my head. "Not a bit. And you know what I want to do?" She shakes her head back at me. "I want to kiss you again, Celeste. And I don't want to stop there."

"I think that's a good idea, Michael."

CHAPTER TWENTY-SIX
CELESTE

Michael tugs me off the stool and pulls me against his body, kissing me hard. I feel his heart racing against my chest and I know mine is doing the same as I lean into him, drowning in sensation. He moans softly into my mouth and then backs up, taking my hand.

He kisses my knuckles and nods his head toward his bedroom. "I want to be able to take my time," he says. I nod and follow him, feeling terrified and elated all at once. How many times have I imagined what this would be like? To spend a passionate afternoon with this man?

Except... "I don't want this to be a one-time thing," I tell him. I fling myself into his arms again as we cross the threshold into his room.

He grins at me, looking very much like a gray wolf as he loosens his tie. "Good," he says, and he drops back against the bed, pulling me into his lap so that I'm straddling him.

I squeak as he bunches up the sides of my skirt, running his hands along my bare thighs. I moan as I realize he's grown hard beneath me and I gasp as I feel his length pressed against me. "Oh, Michael," I breathe, leaning against his shoulders.

Every move feels tingly, electric. I almost want to cry as I realize my body can still experience arousal like this.

He traces his hands everywhere, feeling the curves of my body with seeming equal fascination to the material of my clothing. "Everything feels amazing," he says. "I can just focus on you. Only you, Celeste."

I love knowing he's sharing a monumental experience, too, his first time taking a medication that could change his outlook on everything. "I'm right here," I tell him, placing the palm of my hand flat against his chest, right over his pounding heart.

"I want to be so tender and kind with you," he murmurs, rubbing my back and pulling me closer, closer against his body. I hear a crackling sound as the seams of my skirt begin to give way.

I pull myself back just enough that I can unfasten it, wriggling it down and tossing it on the ground. "Tender and kind sounds nice," I say, settling back where I was. I don't even have time to feel self conscious about him seeing my body. The feel of him against me lights me up with an energy I've forgotten I love so much.

"But?"

I bite my lip, exploring his body with my hands as he tilts my chin up so I'm looking him in the eye. "But I've never had wild and rough and…"

I drift off, and he grins again. "And you want to be ravaged?" I nod as he places his hands on my breasts, giving them a squeeze.

He bites my lower lip. "Celeste, I'm going to figure out a way to give you both, damn it."

He rolls us so I'm lying on the bed beneath him, legs splayed around his trim hips. What a gift, to be here, getting naked with a man. With this man. He presses light kisses to my stomach as he starts to unbutton my blouse, and I realize the skin there is sensitive to touch. I've barely paid attention to my stomach since the children were born, and now, as he licks his way along the stretch marks on my sides, I shudder, realizing they can be a source of pleasure.

"Oh my, that feels so good," I say.

"You're so soft, Celeste." He rubs a cheek against my belly and I delight in the feel of his rough cheeks. I moan softly as he peels open the blouse and lifts my camisole, sliding it all off me until I lie there in just a bra and panties. I hadn't been expecting this today. I would have worn something more attractive and less…shapewear.

But he doesn't seem to notice the control top panties as he thumbs across my nipples. We both stare as they harden into stiff points inside my bra. "What if," he says, pausing to peel down the cups and then blow on my tingling nipples, "What if I tenderly caress these and then bite them?"

He doesn't wait for a response, but does as he says he will and it draws groans from deep inside my chest. Pleasure shoots through my skin until my hips buck up against him. "Michael!" I bite down on his shoulder as he crawls back up my body, grinning.

He rocks up on his knees and starts to remove his shirt, but I sit up, shaking my head. "Let me," I beg. "Please?"

"Oh, sweetheart, yes." He seems to delight in my touch, and I hurry to strip him down until he's kneeling in front of me in sexy black boxer briefs as I kneel in front of him in my high-waist granny panties. I start to lose my nerve as I stare down at the lean muscles he's obviously carried his entire adult life.

I move to curl an arm across my chest, but Michael shakes his head. "I want to look at you, Celeste. God, you're amazing." He dips his silver head again, lapping at my nipples, alternating sides and leaving the exposed skin wet and cool as my skin feels hotter and hotter.

His erection juts out in a bulge of black cotton, twitching as Michael works on my chest. Between his groans and his words, I'm feeling more and more comfortable, succumbing to the energy that's rolling through my body in waves.

"Oh, Christ," he says, reaching inside my panties. I gasp as he touches me, his long fingers parting my folds. "You like that?"

I nod as Michael lowers me to the sheets, and then I stiffen as he starts to crawl down my body, licking at my stomach and kissing my thighs when he begins to tug down my remaining piece of clothing. "Oh, I don't know," I start, placing a hand on his head.

He leans an elbow on the bed and rests his head on his hand, while the other continues its exploration of my most private places. "Celeste, there's something you need to know."

"Oh, god, what?" I can barely contain myself as he touches me, my hips jerking as I squirm in mounting ecstasy.

He rocks back and sits on his heels as he tugs my panties off my body and shoves my thighs apart. "Mick Brady is a man who eats pussy."

I laugh incredulously, until he dives back between my legs and makes good on his word, lapping at my body like an ice cream cone. It's not tender and it's definitely not slow. No, this is just as I imagined it would be. Wild and unruly, and I am just as savage as I grunt in pleasure while he pets and presses on my body with his fingers as his tongue delves into my depths.

"Oh god," I moan. "Oh god, oh god, oh yes. Oh!" The orgasm takes me by surprise, slamming into me with force and causing me to kick my legs out until I'm splayed like a starfish on his bed. "Oh, it's so sensitive. Oh my god, I came. Michael. Mick!"

At this last word, he sits up again, wiping his mouth with the back of his hand. His hair is wild and his boxer briefs seem strained as his erection throbs against the material. "I like it when you call me that," he whispers.

Feeling too limp to move, I extend a tired hand to stroke at the fabric of his boxer briefs. "Mick," I say again, smiling as he grins back at me. "Please fuck me now."

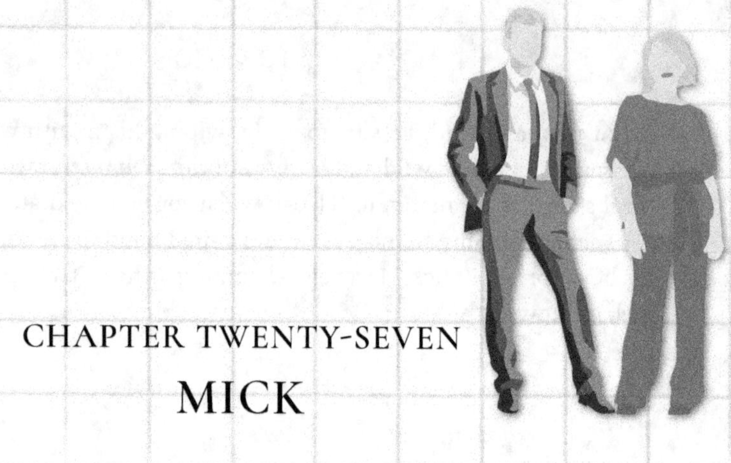

CHAPTER TWENTY-SEVEN
MICK

I THOUGHT 'MICK' WOULD BE THE HOTTEST SOUND TO COME OUT OF CELESTE'S mouth, but hearing the word 'fuck' pass her lips has me harder than I've been in decades.

"You got it," I tell her, wiggling out of my underwear and sighing in relief as my cock springs free. "Couple things first." I lean back over her, kissing her cheek and loving the feel of her naked skin spread beneath me.

"Hm?"

"So, I haven't done this for a long time. It's been years. I've had physicals and I'm healthy."

"I...only ever was with one person," she says, blushing. I stroke her cheek, knowing it means a lot for her to trust me with that information. "I'm healthy, too. And, well, I can't get pregnant." Her cheeks flush all pink and perfect. "I trust you," she whispers.

"This is going to be amazing," I tell her. It's been years since I've been inside a woman bare. And the way my head feels right now with this medication, like I can do anything and focus on that one thing entirely... "You're amazing."

Celeste's entire body is glowing. She's so damn sexy, post-orgasm, limp but wanting more. She looks gorgeous in the low light and I love watching her skin pebble as I trace a finger along it, learning the contours of her body. "I have lube in the night stand," I tell her. I lean across and fish it out, placing it nearby for when we need it.

"I've never just been myself like this before," she says. "I...I moaned for you."

"Damn right you did." I press a thumb to her clit again, loving the way she shudders when I do. "It was sexy as hell."

"It was?"

"You kidding me? Look at this." I gesture at my hard-on, practically straight up against my stomach.

Celeste seems pretty pleased, and reaches out to wrap her hand around it. I make sure to return the favor and moan right back, diving in for another kiss as she starts to stroke me. She continues to do it, with her palm wrapped around my length until I'm worried we won't be able to finish the way I intended.

"That feels too good," I tell her, reaching for the bottle. "I want to be inside you when I come."

"Oh," she says. "Oh, yes. That sounds good." She nods and writhes on the sheets as I dribble some of the lube on her folds. I slide a finger inside Celeste and we both moan together at the feel of it.

She's tight and I don't want to hurt her, but she yells, "More, Mick. More!" And so I add another finger. My hips rock against her as she thrusts into my hand. It's amazing to watch her come unraveled for me. I'm making her feel this way. I almost can't handle it.

"I'm just so honored to be here with you," I tell her. "God, Celeste, this is so good."

"It's sooo good," she says, and she grabs my cock. "Please, Mick, please fuck me now."

"God, I love hearing you call me Mick," I say, lining myself up at her entrance.

"Mick," she says again, and I slide inside.

"Oh," we moan together. It feels so good to have chosen this, to have put thought into being here with her, together, like this. We've come so far from me calling her in a panic. I knew she'd know what to do then, just as she knows I know what to do now.

Celeste wraps her legs around my waist, and I feel every inch of her skin. She breathes quietly against me, arching her back to find the pressure she needs. "Yes," I groan. "It feels amazing." I press my forehead against hers, moving slowly inside her, cherishing her, and then I remember that she wanted it wild.

So I pull out and flip her over as she yelps. "Ass in the air," I tell her, biting her shoulder as I press inside her again. I rest my hands on her shoulders, sinking deep inside as Celeste groans and thrusts back against me. She's incredibly into this, and that makes it so much hotter for me as I ram into her.

"Mick! Oh my god! You're so deep." I reach around her hip and circle her clit as she wiggles beneath me, and then she's coming again, screaming and bucking into me until I can't hold back anymore and I spurt inside her.

"I can feel you coming," she breathes. "I feel it. I feel it."

"Celeste!" I pant her name and collapse diagonally across her. We both lie on the bed, our chests heaving with exertion, until she starts laughing. "Something funny going on?"

She groans as I pull out, but seems content when I tuck her against my side. "It's just that it was so perfect," she tells me, kissing my chest and tracing her fingers through the hair there.

"Yeah? Perfect?"

"Are you kidding! We were like teenagers or something. I feel like I could conquer the world now." Her smile is so bright it lights up my entire condo.

"You can do anything," I tell her. "I'll help you."

"I like that," she says, burrowing her head into my shoulder like she's settling in for a nap.

I lie beside her, trying to make sense of my thoughts. I was worried I'd feel the familiar sense of dread sneak over me after having sex, but it's not there. I feel nervous about telling the kids that I'm going to be with Walt's mother, but the churning ache of regret is totally absent.

"This was a good move," I say out loud.

Celeste startles, like she was maybe on her way to falling asleep. "I'm sorry," I whisper. "Go back to sleep."

She shakes her head. "No," she says. "Tell me more about us being good."

"Actually, I think we were very naughty." I flick one of her nipples, feeling satisfied when it firms up right away at my touch.

"Michael Brady, you are incorrigible." Celeste grins and flicks my nipple this time. I'm surprised to realize I like it. I wonder what other things I'll notice now that I can pay attention to things for more than one second at a time.

"Am I Michael again? I thought I finally convinced you to call me Mick."

"Hm." She rolls on her side and rests her head on her fist. "Only in bed."

"What do you call this?" I gesture around the room and she grins, leaning forward for another kiss. I remember the feel of her lips from a few moments before, and I revel in the sensation of that familiarity. And then my stomach growls, reminding me that we didn't finish our lunch.

I lean back again, rooting in my night stand and coming up with a plastic packet. "How about we eat a snack before round two?" She starts laughing and I look around the room, trying to figure out what I did now. "What's funny?"

"I'm sorry," she says, reaching into the bag and helping herself to a nut. "It's just a little bit silly that you even keep pistachios in your night stand."

CHAPTER TWENTY-EIGHT
CELESTE

I keep looking around as if other people can tell what I did with Michael yesterday. And then I catch myself because maybe I want them to know, and that all feels very confusing. I've never thought of myself as sexy, or as someone who enjoys sex. Yet here I am, reliving every blissful moment again and again. Physically and emotionally, it feels very, very good. Tiny muscles I didn't remember have been activated, and every step I take carries a gentle reminder of our escapades.

That man! I flush, remembering how he worshiped my body...and I'm sitting alone in my own kitchen. I can't even imagine what I would do right now if I were in the same room as him.

I shake my head happily and sip my coffee, remembering that I decided to spend the day learning more about ADHD so I could better support Michael. It turns out, there's quite a lot to learn. For starters, this isn't just about being a naughty kid who can't sit still. The brain is a very complex organ.

I scroll through a huge number of click-bait articles, as Samantha would call them, but do manage to find a few that have substance. Soon, I'm engrossed, leaning close to my laptop screen as I read. I even enlarge the text so I can read it more easily.

I know Walt says I shouldn't print out copies of all the interesting articles I find online, but I can't help myself. The more I click around, the more I read that just reverberates inside me somehow. I print until I run out of toner on the laser printer.

Then, I gather up the whole stack of articles I skimmed, and I take the whole thing out back. I keep expecting the yard to draw up strong feelings for me, but I just feel peace back here now. I pause to appreciate that this house and yard isn't necessarily a cage where I'm stuck with all my mistakes. It's just a house, and I can leave it any time I want to go and talk to the people I love.

For now, though, I very much appreciate the privacy as I sink into a comfortable chair on the patio to read. I gingerly cross my legs, and realize my post-sex body isn't quite ready for that position. Not only am I a little tender, but I have red marks from Michael's stubble. On my thighs. I have sex marks. Me!

"Fuck it," I say, and just spread my legs out wider until the skin no longer chafes. I sink in to the loveseat and pore over first-hand stories of older adults who realize they have ADHD when they can't manage the lack of structure in retirement life.

I don't know if it's my posture or thoughts of my lover—I've decided to use that word and Mick agrees it suits us—I don't know what forces combine in that moment but as the papers flutter in my hands, caught in the gentle breeze ... I start to see myself in these pages as well.

One of the articles interviews a woman who struggles to make decisions and doesn't really know herself, and can't read people easily. I gasp, reading her description of sensory overload while driving on busy roads. It's like a mirror into my own life.

But how could this be about me? I'm not like Michael at all, not in that way. Then I read this woman's history of self-medicating with alcohol when she got overwhelmed, and I drop the papers on the patio, reaching for my phone.

"Michael," I gasp his name as soon as he answers.

"Good morning to you, my lovely."

"Michael, what if I have it, too?" I blurt the question without context, realizing too late that this probably makes me sound insane. *Or maybe it just proves you have ADHD.*

"Have what, now?"

"ADHD," I tell him. I stoop to pick up the papers before they blow away. "I've been reading about it."

"Celeste, honey, I don't want you to take this the wrong way, but you don't exactly act like you have Swiss cheese for brains."

I shake my head, knowing he can't see, but needing to verbalize what I'm reading. "This article says it looks different in women. That we do different things, but it's the same condition."

"Like what?"

He sounds interested, curious, not critical, and I take a deep breath before reading from the interview article. "What if…what if saying impulsive, hurtful things to my family and cleaning when I'm nervous…what if there's an explanation for all that?"

Michael is quiet for a bit. Then I hear him inhale. "Well, I can tell you, knowing the explanation doesn't erase what I've done, Celeste. But having that explanation, it means something. You know as well as me that it's still a lot of work to make amends. That doesn't go away." He's quiet a moment and I feel my heart racing. "But knowing I have it—that's been a powerful thing to realize."

I tap my fingers on my leg, letting his words sink in.

"Did you call me first? When you had this notion?"

I smile at his tone, liking that he's pleased I turned to him for support. "I did. I thought of you immediately."

"I like being the guy you call first," he tells me. I know he's not anywhere close by, but I swear I can feel his breath on my skin, like he's really there whispering into my ear.

"Well, I like having you there to answer when I call."

I hear him rummaging around in the background, maybe opening some drawers in his desk. Then, he says, "Aha! Found it. Honey, I'm going to send you the info for this doc I'm seeing. Remember how I told you, he specializes in working with folks our age. With ADHD."

"Do you think it's okay? If we see the same doctor?"

He laughs. "I don't think it's like divorce lawyers, Celeste. Plus he's a specialist. You should have the best there is, sweetheart. You don't have to tell him you know me."

I bite my lip, but then decide to go ahead with the remark on the tip of my tongue. "What if he asks me why I'm smiling so much?"

Michael laughs, a low rumble that reminds me what it felt like when his bare chest pressed against mine. "If he asks that, you tell him Mick Brady knows how to put a smile on a woman's face. Every time."

CHAPTER TWENTY-NINE
MICK

"Michael?"

"Nora go down for her nap already?" I try to keep my voice at a reasonable volume, but I know I'm lousy at that. It's interesting, though. With the medication, I seem more able to manage an "inside voice" as Maddie and Liam would call it. Interesting.

"I'm just backing away slowly from her bedroom," Celeste says and I hear the roar of Nora's sound machine in the background. "Whew," Celeste sighs into the phone.

"Honey, you can't talk about bedrooms and then sigh like that while I'm at work."

"Oh," she says, and I laugh.

"You're probably blushing. Wish I could see it."

"Stop it, you wicked man."

"I won't. That's why I'm calling. Stay with me tonight."

"Tonight?"

"Yeah. What's stopping you? I'll make it worth your while, I promise."

"Hmm." I hear her tapping her nails. "I didn't pack a bag or anything."

"Celeste, I happen to know you always pack 'play clothes' when you babysit Nora on Tuesdays. And today is Tuesday."

She gasps. "How do you know about play clothes?"

"I hear things," I tell her. "And now that I'm taking control of my ADHD,

I actually remember things. Like the fact that my lady has a bag of spare clothes with her right this very moment."

"You're something else," she says. I hear her rummaging around in the background, and I hope it means I'm wearing her down. We've talked every day since she blew my mind in the bedroom, but I haven't gotten a chance to see her in person. And damn it, I miss her.

"I just can't stop thinking about you and I want a repeat of last week." I can tell I've said the right thing because she agrees to meet me at my house when Walt gets home from work.

The rest of the day seems to crawl by, despite signing some new contracts for expert witness gigs. This is a whole new line of business that's proving to be quite lucrative for us. Who knew half of Pittsburgh was going to be caught up in landslide lawsuits? Between the sink holes and the storm water mismanagement, our geotechnical engineers are in geek heaven.

I cut out of work a bit early to make sure I meet Celeste, and when she finally taps on my front door I pull her inside, laughing when she squeaks in my arms. "I like that I can just kiss you if I want," I say, and do so.

"I like it, too," she responds in kind. I back her up against the door and reach for the tote bag she's carrying, tossing it across the room.

"You don't need any of that right now," I growl into her neck. She smells like fruit punch and I love that she probably shared a glass of it with Nora while she was babysitting. Dipping my tongue in Celeste's mouth, I confirm that she tastes like fruit punch and I moan appreciatively.

I stroke her hair and nibble on her ear lobe and remember one last thing I wanted to discuss before I give in to my lust. "Do you ever cook?"

"Never," she whispers, her voice shuddering a bit as I rub a thumb over her nipples and slide my other hand down to her waist.

"I never do, either," I tell her.

"Probably a good thing." Her head falls back against the door with a thunk as I reach inside the waist of her pants.

"Okay, so we'll order in later. That's settled." I take a half step back and unbutton her pants, dropping to my knees on the mat and nudging her legs apart as she steps out of her clothes.

"Oh, Michael. Oh god."

I nip at her thighs with my teeth as her hands flutter into my hair. "Thought you agreed to call me Mick in bed?" I tease her with my thumb and she gasps and tries to clench her thighs together, but I stop her as I look up at her face.

"We...not...bed...Mick, please!"

My lady said please, and I'm happy to oblige.

If someone told me thirty years ago that ADHD medication would make sex better for me, I would have led a different life. I can't believe how well I can focus on Celeste, how I notice the ripples in her body and the changes in her breathing when I'm doing something she likes. I change the pace of my tongue or adjust my fingers gliding through her silky folds as she pulls my hair and bangs the back of her head against my front door.

When she comes, with my name on her lips, I don't just hear it. I feel her pulsing around me, notice when she starts sinking down the door, weak with pleasure that I delivered. I feel like a million bucks.

And then my eyes fly open when Celeste shoves me on my back, yanking my own pants down with a wicked gleam in her eyes. "Your turn, Mick," she says, emphasizing my name with a click on the K sound. She licks her lips and then wraps them around my cock, her silvery hair falling all around her head and tickling my stomach and thighs.

I love this sight of her, disheveled, her shirt still on but her ass bare as she bends over my body. Her tongue glides along my shaft and I love how much I can focus on the sensation, how I'm so totally in the moment. And then, I can't hold back. "Celeste, honey, I'm going to come," I manage to choke out. I feel my body stiffen and I hiss, but she doesn't pull back. "Oh, god," I moan, as I fire off into her mouth, her cheeks hollowed out as she sucks down my release.

I drop my head to the floor, a sweaty heaving mess, and she crawls up my torso, nestling into my armpit. "I've always wanted to do that," she says, and my eyes fly to her face in shock.

"Celeste. You never sucked a man off before?"

She shakes her head, sighing contentedly, running her nails along my chest. It feels nice through my shirt. I think my skin would be too sensitive for her to touch it bare like this. Everything is too much right now, and yet just right. "Well, if I forget to tell you later, you're great at it." She laughs and I feel her chest vibrate with the joy of it.

"I love trying new things with you. I feel..." She rests her chin on my chest to look up into my face. "What's the opposite of lonesome?"

I shrug. "Together, I guess?"

"Yeah."

"I feel like that, too."

. . .

IN THE MORNING, my eyes fly open at five as per usual, but for once I don't spring immediately out of bed. I'm wrapped around a naked woman, and I want to savor it. But I haven't taken my meds yet, so my typical restlessness sets in pretty quickly and I know I need to get up and go for a run to center myself. I have a plan for this, too. "Thank you, medicated-Mick of yesterday," I mutter as I start to shake Celeste awake.

"Hungh?"

"We're going for a run, honey."

She sits up and pulls the sheets up to her chin. "Michael. I don't do that. I don't run."

I grin at her as I tug on my shorts and a black tank. "Put your play clothes on," I tell her. "I'll meet you in the lobby."

Five minutes later, she's frowning at me in front of my building as I program a bright orange electric scooter. "Cal has been telling me about these." I beckon for her to climb on, and she stands hesitantly with one foot on the scooter. "They're all over the city. It's like five bucks for a half hour or something." I shrug. "Thought you could keep pace with me, keep me company."

She raises an eyebrow at me, shakes her head, and then laughs nervously. "What if I fall?"

"Then I'll help you up!" I start jogging backwards down the sidewalk, beckoning for her to join me. "Come on! You like trying new things, right?"

"Michael Brady, you're the worst." Celeste bites her lip and presses the "go" button, fumbling a bit as she gets her feet situated. In just a few minutes, she's ahead of me, laughing as she cruises down the street. Soon, I match her pace.

She tells me about calling Dr. Offutt, how she has an appointment to meet with him soon.

"Having a terrible time?" I nudge her with my elbow and she swerves a little, so I put my hands on her waist to steady her, both of us laughing.

"Thank you for pushing me to do this," she says. I know her "this" refers to a few things, and I'm glad she feels good about her choices lately.

"Now keep it at 8.5 miles per hour and help me get my race pace."

She nods and then raises a fist in the air as she sails through a green light.

We turn onto the paved trail and I run at her side for miles as the sun comes up along the river.

CHAPTER THIRTY
CELESTE

I'M HOSTING BRADY FAMILY DINNER AS A LAST HURRAH AT MY HOUSE. ALMOST everything is gone already, apart from the outdoor furniture since we'll eat outside, and I've been staying with Michael for the past week until my condo is ready. Walt is delighted that I'm downsizing. He insists I will be much more comfortable financially without the expense and upkeep on the huge house.

I'm just ready to start fresh in my own space, even if that space is one floor below my boyfriend's condo. Boyfriend isn't the right word, but he's more than just my secret lover... and it's what we've got. And we're telling the family tonight, just as soon as I finish building up my nerve.

The last month with Michael has been thrilling. We have dinner together nearly every evening, and nobody seems to notice that we show up together for family dinner night. The only night we missed, in fact, was when I went to Esther's herb workshop with Rosemary. She and I had a great time grinding up actual rosemary and blending it with different fruits in seltzer. She added wine and even rum to some of her concoctions. I stuck with grenadine.

I've never felt so focused, so vulnerable, or so strong. I've been meeting with Dr. Offutt for his study and am learning about ADHD in women. I talk to my daughter every day, and we have had some challenging conversations. But I asked her to come to dinner tonight so she'd be here when I tell everyone about Michael. It wasn't easy sitting through a Foof meeting, knowing I had huge information to share but having to keep it close until Michael and I spoke with Walt and the Bradys. The ladies were of course ecstatic to meet Rosemary at the workshop, so I rode that wave of emotion right through our last meeting and spoke truthfully about how difficult and rewarding and amazing it's been to finally begin to repair my relationship with both of my children.

The doorbell rings and I greet the food delivery excitedly, glad for their help as I set everything up out back. I know Elizabeth and Kellen cook from scratch when they host, but that's just not who I am and that's okay. It's also okay to order from a restaurant instead of a fancy caterer. I affirm that out loud for myself one more time, "It's okay to serve takeout to guests," when the entire family converges on the back yard at once.

They come in one cacophonous wave, with Arlan rushing in the lead and Bisi bringing up the rear as she chats up Logan about her wedding plans. I grin as they all make themselves at home, diving into the chips and guac and pouring lemonade without waiting for a formal invitation. This, I realize, is my family now. Loud and comfortable and present. And I love them. Most of all, I love knowing that they love me back.

Nora rushes up to me waving a piece of paper. "I drew you today, Mimi," she says, beaming as she holds up a drawing of what looks like a raisin with hair.

"I'll treasure it, Nora," I tell her, truthfully. I kiss her on the cheek and rise as Michael makes his way over to me. He tugs me behind a juniper bush and kisses me feverishly. "Not yet," I say, but there's not a lot of fight in my voice. It's hard to resist his kisses now that I've gotten to experience them regularly. It turns out regular sex puts me in a much better mood to mend fences with my kids.

Michael smooths my hair with one hand and kisses me on the forehead. "You ready to face the jury?"

I shrug and peek out from behind the bush. Nobody seems to have noticed we snuck away. "Let's do it," I tell him.

I make my way to the head of the group of tables and clear my throat, but nobody stops talking and Cal looks like he's about to punch Liam to get at the guacamole. I look up at Michael, not sure how to proceed.

He bangs his fist on the table and shouts, "Listen up, Brady Family! We've got news." Everyone freezes and looks at us and I blush as Michael drops an arm around my shoulder. They all seem to be waiting for a big headline. "Celeste and I are together," Michael says.

Nobody reacts. "Romantically," he adds.

Nicole grimaces. "Isn't that old news?"

"What! No. It's very recent," I gesture to emphasize my point, so that Walt knows I haven't been hiding anything from him.

My son waves a hand. "Honestly we thought you guys were doing it for at least a year now."

"Seriously?" Michael leans forward on the table toward Walt. "You thought I seduced your mother?"

Walt hands Nora a plate of rice and vegetables and looks up at us. "Didn't you just say that you did?"

Michael is very rarely speechless and even more rarely does he stand still. But right now he is frozen at my side just staring at the family, who quickly forgets us and goes back to fighting over the shredded cheese. Michael turns to me eventually. "They just don't even care."

I bite my lip. "I think they care," I tell him. "I think it just seems so natural to them that they're fine with it."

He nods. "Well, I'm more than fine with it."

"Me, too," I tell him.

And he leans in to kiss me, pressing his hand into my back to pull me close until Kellen yells, "Get a room!" Everyone laughs and I pat my hair back into place, sinking into a chair and squeezing Walt's hand.

"You're really okay with this? With me seeing Micheal?"

He smiles at me. "I'm glad you have someone, Mom. It's good to see you happy."

"I am happy," I tell him as Michael kisses my cheek again. "So happy."

Rosemary smiles at me and then she clears her throat like she wants to say something. Once again, the Brady family doesn't quiet down. Noticing the situation, Bisi puts two fingers into her mouth and whistles loudly, causing everyone to freeze.

"Oh, I like her," Nicole says. "You need to teach me that."

Bisi winks at her. "We have an announcement, too."

Rosemary smiles and looks like she's going to float away. "We're getting married," she says, and everyone bursts into applause. I sit back in my seat, casually chewing my meal, watching as the people around me celebrate in my family's joy. There is light and laughter in this house and it feels good to move on to another chapter with this energy as our legacy here.

"Can I officiate?" I look up at Michael, stunned by his question. He shrugs. "I'm great with a crowd. I'll stick to a script, promise."

Rosemary laughs and gives him a thumbs up. "Sure, Mick."

"Excellent." He takes a swig of his beer and grins. "I'll start working on my online ordination tomorrow."

I shake my head and laugh. "You always surprise me," I tell him. "You blurt things, but they're always the most interesting things."

"That's why you love me," he says, winking just for me.

"You know, I think you're right."

"Wait, seriously? I was just kidding around."

I reach for his hand under the table and take it inside both of mine. "I'm serious. I love you, Michael Brady. I want to go through life with you at my side."

"You've got me, Celeste, as long as you'll have me." His eyes gleam as he beams at me, and then he pulls me close. He kisses me long and hard, and this time, the Brady family doesn't interrupt.

EPILOGUE: MICK

"Hey, Celeste! Your phone is blowing up." My lady is in my guest bathroom with Arlan, who did not eat crayons this time, but did manage to dump an entire bottle of shampoo in the tub while I turned to get him a towel, so Celeste took over the rinse process.

"Go ahead and read it to me," she hollers. I pick up the phone, still vibrating like mad.

BRADY LADIES GROUP CHAT
MADDIE:

I'm just so glad Mick and Celeste have Arlan tonight. I'm going to think thoughts all by myself!

LOGAN:

Are you sure you don't want to hop in the car and come glamping with Foof? We've got spare room in the yurt.

MADDIE:

I'm good. Celeste, you guys doing okay with the Arlanator?

NICOLE:

You assholes are all out doing amazing things and I'm stuck with snobby professional athletes, managing contracts at Stag Law.

ELIZABETH:

I'm just over here sobbing as I pack my baby up for college. Don't mind me.

NICOLE:

Aw, so proud of Jake, though! Full ride for engineering!

ELIZABETH:

[blush face emoji]

MADDIE:

Liam did let me know the conference is going well. All the Bradys are presenting their best practices for some sort of something.

NICOLE:

I can see why you're a professional communicator.

ORLA:

Hey, so I think this baby is about to fall out of me. Can anyone come get Nora?

"Oh shit!" I sprint down the hall. "Orla's in labor."

Celeste stares at me. She's got half of Arlan de-bubbled, but at least three quarters of her own body is soaked in suds. She blinks a few times and scoops Arlan up in her arms. "Well, we have to get to their house. Text her that we're on our way. She moves fast when she's got a baby coming."

I nod. "Should I ... does Arlan need clothes?"

"Just grab something quickly," she yells, shoving her feet in her shoes and walking quickly toward the door. "I've got a car seat in my car. Arlan can fit in it. Let's go."

"I'm nakey bum!" My grandson hollers in the hall as Celeste charges toward the elevator.

"Push the button, sweetheart," she tells him, angling his towel-clad body toward the panel. He pushes the button rapidly until I huff up behind them, dragging what I hope is Arlan's clothing bag. Once again, his parents sent enough luggage for a European summer tour. Knowing my luck I grabbed the bag of toy vehicles.

I've still got Celeste's phone in one of my hands and I realize I don't have mine. Or my keys. She must notice me patting myself frantically, because she says, "It's okay. I have my purse with my car keys and we'll just stay at Walt and Orla's overnight. Or one of us can run back here. It'll be just fine."

"I love that you think so," I tell her, shifting the phone into a pocket of the duffel and reaching for Arlan. I hold a hand over his exposed ear and whisper, "I can see your nipples through that wet shirt."

She grins and swats at my shoulder. The elevator bings and we emerge into my building's parking garage. "Want me to drive?" I know Celeste gets nervous driving in the city, but I also know she's working hard on tackling her fears. So I add, "It'll help me keep my hands still if I do." She tosses me the keys and leans across to get Arlan situated in Nora's seat. I watch, because I can see down her wet blouse.

Once he's buckled, she and I climb into the front seat and after I back out of the parking spot, she clutches my hand while I drive to Morningside. Her phone starts ringing again and she manages to wrestle it away from Arlan. "We're six minutes away," Celeste shouts, and then the phone picks up the bluetooth in the car, somehow hanging up the call but starting up some music.

"Nice jams," I say, reaching for her hand again. In the back, Arlan sings Beyonce's Halo, and I join in despite my surprise that he knows that song. I squeeze Celeste's hand tighter as I croon, "You're the only one that I want; Think I'm addicted to your liiiight!"

I squeal the tires pulling onto Walt and Orla's street. "Keep the driveway open so they can leave," Celeste says, gathering her purse like she's ready to leap out before I stop the car.

I skid to a halt at the curb and I see Walt half carrying Orla down the steps. I unbuckle and rush over to help him, but she swats both of us away. "I can walk myself!" She takes a few steps and then doubles over, making a mooing sound, which Arlan imitates as he stands at my side, buck naked.

"We're here to help," I tell Walt with a wink. He rolls his eyes.

Celeste pecks him on the cheek. "Don't worry about a thing," she says. "We can feed the rabbit, feed the kids, all of it. Take your time."

Orla stands back up and waddles into the car. "Let's go, Wally," she bellows. "This kid is coming out."

"Don't forget Pudding's heart pills," Walt yells out the window as he backs out the drive. I give him a thumbs up. I reach for my notebook and write RABBIT PILLS on a fresh page. I took my meds today, so I know I'll remember to check it despite the chaos. I hop inside their house and am pleased to discover we do indeed have clothing for Arlan. He and Nora sit playing with the pet rabbit on the floor for a few hours while Celeste's phone continues to vibrate like mad on the coffee table.

"I'm going to order a pizza and then turn this thing off," I tell her, but she shakes her head.

"We have to leave it on at least until the baby arrives." She flits around the house tidying things up behind the children, who leave clouds of Lego and bunny hay in their wake. I look at the phone one last time and pump my fist in the air.

"He's here," I say. "I'm serious!" I flash the phone for her to see the picture of Walt grinning over a flushed-looking Orla and a very round baby. And then I start crying when I see the name they chose.

"Kellen Michael Sheffield! Oh, how lovely," Celeste coos. "Nora, come look at your brother."

I'm so overcome that my niece would name her son after me that I sink into the couch, pulling Arlan into my lap. I kiss his tiny head as he wriggles away, taking his big energy over to the phone to see what all the fuss is about.

I'm still overcome later, when Celeste and I tuck the kids into bed with their white noise machine blasting cicada sounds inside Nora's room. I sit in the dark living room marveling that I'm here right now, surrounded by people who respect me so much. "They named the baby after me," I say to Celeste, who pauses to pat the rabbit on the head before she joins me on the couch.

She tucks her feet up under her as she leans her head on my shoulder. "They sure did," she says, her fingers tracing along my chest. "An excellent choice, I think."

"I remembered Pudding's pills," I say, wrapping my arm tight around Celeste.

"I know you did. He's doing great."

I run my fingers through her hair, the silver strands catching the street light through the front window. "I'm still not used to remembering to do things." I shift my posture so I can pull her fully into my lap and press a kiss to her forehead. "I'm not used to having someone around to tell when something small feels big."

Celeste kisses me softly and burrows in deeper against my chest. "I want to make a joke about something else that feels big," she says, pinching my side in the ticklish place she discovered a few weeks ago. We were both delighted to learn about it. It's been great discovering things with her.

"Please mention it," I tease, pressing my hand over hers as she moves it toward my crotch. "Seriously, though, can we do this here?"

Celeste nods, nipping at my ear lobe and reaching one arm for Arlan's discarded bath towel on the carpet. "We'll just lay this on the couch."

I laugh. "No, I mean won't the kids wake up? Is anyone coming over?"

She presses back on my shoulders and straddles me, her knees bunching up the terrycloth. "Everyone is either at work, glamping, or at the hospital." Celeste yanks open my fly and I hiss as she reaches inside. "Let's celebrate and then we can go to bed."

I arch a brow and squeeze her rear end. "Where we can celebrate a second time?"

"Michael Brady, you are insatiable." She peppers kisses along my jaw.

"You love it," I tease. And she nods.

"I love you," she says, smiling in the sliver of light.

"I love you, too."

ℬ

Want to check in on Mick and Celeste?

My newsletter subscribers get a bonus epilogue! Visit LaineyDavis.com to snag it.